PRAISE FOR *SHADOW COUNTRY*

"*Shadow Country* is altogether gripping, shocking, and brilliantly told, not just a tour de force in its stylistic range, but a great American novel, as powerful a reading experience as nearly any in our literature. . . . In every way, *Shadow Country* is a bravura performance, at once history, fiction, and myth—as well as the capstone to the career of one of the most admired and admirable writers of our time."
—MICHAEL DIRDA, *The New York Review of Books*

"The book took my sleeve and like the ancient mariner would not let go." —*Los Angeles Times*

"Watson's story is essentially the story of the American frontier, of the conquering of wild lands and people, and of what such empires cost. . . . Even among a body of work as magnificent as Matthiessen's, this is his great book." —*St. Petersburg Times*

"The language is wonderful . . . very different from the descriptions of pioneering we have become accustomed to—a great advance on Walt Whitman. Or even Robert Frost."
—SAUL BELLOW

"A masterpiece of world literature. I would give it every prize and award on earth." —ANNIE DILLARD

"Peter Matthiessen's work, in both fiction and nonfiction, is a unique achievement in American literature. Everything that he has written has been conveyed in his own clear, deeply informed, elegant, and powerful prose." —W. S. MERWIN

ALSO BY PETER MATTHIESSEN

FICTION

Race Rock
Partisans
Raditzer
At Play in the Fields of the Lord
Far Tortuga
On the River Styx and Other Stories
Killing Mister Watson
Lost Man's River
Bone by Bone

NONFICTION

Wildlife in America
The Cloud Forest
Under the Mountain Wall
Sal Si Puedes
The Wind Birds
Blue Meridian
The Trees Where Man Was Born
The Snow Leopard
Sand Rivers
In the Spirit of Crazy Horse
Indian Country
Nine-Headed Dragon River
Men's Lives
African Silences
East of Lo Monthang
African Shadows
Tigers in the Snow
The Birds of Heaven
End of the Earth

PETER MATTHIESSEN

SHADOW COUNTRY

✦

A NEW RENDERING OF THE WATSON LEGEND

THE MODERN LIBRARY
NEW YORK

Published in the United States by Modern Library,
an imprint of The Random House Publishing Group,
a division of Random House, Inc., New York.

MODERN LIBRARY and the TORCHBEARER Design are
registered trademarks of Random House, Inc.

Originally published in hardcover in the United States by Modern Library,
an imprint of The Random House Publishing Group,
a division of Random House, Inc., in 2008.

This is an abridgment and revision of three novels by Peter Matthiessen
published separately by Random House, an imprint of The Random House
Publishing Group, a division of Random House, Inc., as follows:
Killing Mister Watson (copyright © 1990 by Peter Matthiessen),
Lost Man's River (copyright © 1997 by Peter Matthiessen), and
Bone by Bone (copyright © 1999 by Peter Matthiessen).

ISBN 978-0-8129-8062-2

Printed in the United States of America

www.modernlibrary.com

2 4 6 8 9 7 5 3 1

Book design by Simon M. Sullivan

With love to my brother Carey
and
my ever dear Maria

ACKNOWLEDGMENTS

✦

Over its long history, in its various manifestations, this book has been much benefited by a number of helpful readers, beginning as ever with my kindly, keen-eyed, and mercifully candid wife, Maria, and by Neil Olson, an ever patient, thoughtful reader who is also my longtime agent. As a neighbor in the book's cretaceous days when the whole was still inchoate, crude, and formless, John Irving was uncommonly generous with his time and strong clear comment. Jason Epstein, its first editor at Random House, was a strong advocate of the first of what became the so-called trilogy and so was his assistant Becky Saletan—already a fine editor when she took over the project but eventually snatched away by another publisher. Several others would preside who would also vanish elsewhere, perhaps in dismay over Watson's length; one of these was Scott Moyers, the excellent young editor who was instrumental in placing the present volume with the Modern Library. Subsequently, I am pleased to say, the book found its way into the sure hands of the exceptionally intelligent and insightful Judy Sternlight, its present and (I trust) ultimate editor; in recent years, it has also been blessed by the discerning eye of my gifted assistant, Laurel Berger.

For the encouragement of all of these friends in the long throes of what can only be called a thirty-year obsession I am very grateful.

—*Peter Matthiessen*

AUTHOR'S NOTE

✦

"The Watson Trilogy," as the original has been called, came into being as a single immense novel which in its first draft manuscript must have been more than 1,500 pages long. Not surprisingly, my publisher balked at the enormity of what I had wrought and so, like a loaf of bread, this elemental thing was pulled into three pieces corresponding to its distinct time frames and points of view. The first part was then cut free and finished as Killing Mister Watson (the original title for the whole), and the second and third parts were given new titles as each was completed and published—Lost Man's River (after a wild river in Watson's region of the remote southwestern Everglades) and Bone by Bone (from a beautiful strange poem by Emily Dickinson).

Although the three books were generously received, the "trilogy" solution never fulfilled my original idea of this book's true nature. While the first book and the third stood on their own, the middle section, which had served originally as a kind of connecting tissue, yet contained much of the heart and brain of the whole organism, lacked its own armature or bony skeleton; cut away from the others, it became amorphous, reminding me not agreeably of the long belly of a dachshund, slung woefully between its upright sturdy legs. In short, the work felt unfinished and its wretched author, after twenty years of toil (the early notes, as I discovered to my horror, dated all the way back to 1978), somehow frustrated and dissatisfied. The only acceptable solution was to break it apart and re-create it, to ensure that it existed somewhere (if only in a closet) in its proper form.

In a Paris Review interview (TPR #157, Spring 1999), I confessed my intention to devote a year to its remaking, though I had no serious expectation that whatever came of it would find a respectable publisher. However, the year set aside for the re-creation of this work has grown to six or seven. This was because

Mister Watson and the desperate people who shared his desperate life came alive again in the new pages and utterly reabsorbed me, and also because—in the necessary cutting and distilling that reduced the whole by almost 400 pages—their story has inevitably deepened and intensified.

In my original concept, the three books of the novel were interwoven variations in the evolution of a legend. In this new manifestation, the novel's first book would be analogous to a first movement, since the whole feels symphonic in its rhythms, rising and falling, ever returning to one man's obsessive self-destruction set against the historic background of slavery and civil war, imperialism, and the rape of land and life under the banner of industrial "progress." Indirectly but perhaps most importantly, it concerns the tragic racism that still darkens the integrity of a great land like a cloud shadow.

Retained as prelude more or less intact and recurring variously throughout is the myth of Watson's violent and controversial death. By design, this "ending" is given away at once, to get the plot out of the way of the deeper suspense of the underlying mystery. A powerful, charismatic man is shot to pieces by his neighbors—why? It is the why? that matters. How could such a frightening event take place in a peaceful community of fishermen and farmers? Was it really self-defense, as claimed by the participants, or was it a calculated lynching? How will Watson's sons deal with the killing? And the lone black man in that crowd of armed whites—what was he doing there? Set against the horror of the Jim Crow era, Henry Short's strange story has endless reverberations. In Shadow Country, this enigmatic figure is given his own voice as an observer and also his own final accounting.

The present book draws together in one work the themes that have absorbed me all my life—the pollution of land and air and water that is inevitable in the blind obliteration of the wilderness and its wild creatures and also the injustice to the poor of our own species, especially the indigenous peoples and the inheritors of slavery left behind by the cruel hypocrisy of what those in power represent as progress and democracy.

E. J. Watson was an inspired and exceptionally able frontier entrepreneur in the greatest era of invention and advance in American history. He was also a man severely conditioned by loss, reversal, and ill fortune who became so obsessed with taking part in the new century's prosperity that he finally descended into lawlessness, excusing his ever more reckless actions by citing as precedent the corporate ruthlessness and murderous labor practices on the railroads, in the mines, and elsewhere—cold outrages common and flagrant in turn-of-the-century America that were indulged and even encouraged by a newly imperial U.S. government.

In the third book, we have Mister Watson's own version of events, from early boyhood to the moment of his death—the final word, since surely he knows better than anyone else who he has become, this "shadow cousin" whom no relative will mention. The reader must be Watson's final judge.

Though the book has no message, it might be argued that the metaphor of the Watson legend represents our tragic history of unbridled enterprise and racism and the ongoing erosion of our human habitat as these affect the lives of those living too close to the bone and way out on the edge, with no voice in the economic and environmental attrition that erode the foundation of their hopes and nothing with which to confront their own irrelevance but grit and rage. The ills of our great republic as perceived through the eyes of backcountry Americans might seem inconsequential, yet people who must deal with real hardship in the pursuit of happiness, not mere neurosis, can be bitterly eloquent and darkly funny, which is why I have always enjoyed their voices and enjoyed writing about them. In the end, however outlandish such characters may seem, their stories, too, are born of the human heart—in this case, the wild heart of a shadow cousin and so-called desperado.

In regard to Watson, reviewers of the original three books have cited D. H. Lawrence's idea that "the essential American soul is hard, isolate, stoic, and a killer." To a degree, this may be true of Watson, but he is more mysterious than that. As best I understand him after all these years, he was neither a "natural-born killer" nor a man of stunted criminal mentality—such men aren't interesting. On the other hand, he was obsessed, and obsession that isn't crazed or criminal is enthralling; in thirty years, I have learned a lot about obsession from too much time spent in the mind of E. J. Watson.

—Peter Matthiessen
Spring 2008

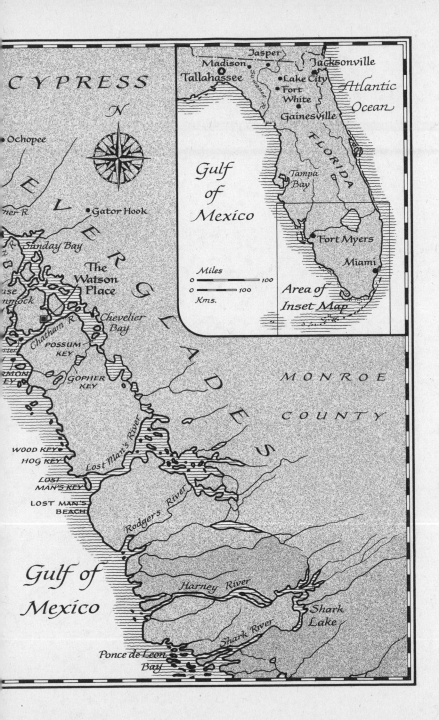

E. J. WATSON

✦

His ancestors:
    John and William, sons of Lucius Watson of Virginia, moved to
Edgefield District, South Carolina, in the middle of the eighteenth
century. John's son Michael, who became a renowned Indian fighter
and hero of the Revolutionary War, married William's daughter
Martha, his first cousin. Their only son was Elijah Julian (1775–1850),
who consolidated the large family holdings and left a plantation at
Clouds Creek at Ridge, north of Edgefield Court House, to every one
of his eleven children, including Artemas.

His paternal grandparents:
    Artemas Watson (1800–1841) and Mary Lucretia (Daniel) Watson
(1807–1838)

His parents:
    Elijah Daniel Watson ("Ring-Eye Lige")
        b. Clouds Creek, S.C., 1834
        d. Columbia, S.C., 1895
    Ellen Catherine (Addison) Watson
        b. Edgefield Court House, S.C., 1832
        d. Fort White, Fla., 1910

Edgar Artemas* Watson:
        b. Clouds Creek, S.C., November 11, 1855
        d. Chokoloskee, Fla., October 24, 1910

*Changed his second initial to J in later life.

1st wife (1878): Ann Mary "Charlie" (Collins) Watson, 1862–1879
    Robert Briggs "Rob" Watson, b. Fort White, Fla., 1879–?
2nd wife (1884): Jane S. "Mandy" (Dyal) Watson, 1864–1901
    Carrie Watson Langford, b. Fort White, Fla., 1885–?
    Edward Elijah "Eddie" Watson, b. Fort White, Fla., 1887–?
    Lucius Hampton Watson, b. Oklahoma Territory, 1889–?
3rd wife (1904): Catherine Edna "Kate" (Bethea) Watson, 1889–?
    Ruth Ellen Watson, b. Fort White, Fla., 1905–?
    Addison Tilghman Watson, b. Fort White, Fla., 1907–?
    Amy May Watson, b. Key West, Fla., 1910–?
Common-law wife: Henrietta "Netta" Daniels, ca. 1875–?
    Minnie Daniels, ca. 1895–?
Common-law wife: Mary Josephine "Josie" Jenkins, ca. 1879–?
    Pearl Watson, ca. 1900–?
    Infant male, b. May 1910: perished in Great Hurricane of October 1910

EJW'S SISTER:

Mary Lucretia "Minnie" Watson, b. Clouds Creek, S.C., 1857, d. Ft. White, Fla., 1912
    Married William "Billy" Collins of Fort White, Fla., ca. 1880
    Billy Collins died in 1907 at Fort White
The Collins children:
    Julian Edgar, 1880–?
    William Henry "Willie," 1886–?
    Maria Antoinett "May," 1892–?

ALSO:

EJW's great-aunt Tabitha (Wyches) Watson (1813–1905), 3rd wife and widow of Artemas Watson's brother Michael: instrumental in marriage of Elijah D. Watson and Ellen Addison, d. Fort White, Fla. 1905
Her daughter Laura (1830–1894), childhood friend of Ellen Addison.
    Married William Myers ca. 1867
    Married Samuel Tolen ca. 1890

BOOK ONE

Look at a stone cutter hammering away at his rock, perhaps a hundred times without so much a crack showing in it. Yet at the hundred-and-first blow it will split in two, and I know it was not the last blow that did it, but all that had gone before.

—Jacob Riis

PROLOGUE: OCTOBER 24, 1910

✦

Sea birds are aloft again, a tattered few. The white terns look dirtied in the somber light and they fly stiffly, feeling out an element they no longer trust. Unable to locate the storm-lost minnows, they wander the thick waters with sad muted cries, hunting seamarks that might return them to the order of the world.

In the wake of hurricane, the coast lies broken, stunned. Day after day, a brooding wind nags at the mangroves, hurrying the unruly tides that hunt through the flooded islands and dark labyrinthine creeks of the Ten Thousand Islands. Brown spume and matted salt grass, driftwood; a far gray sun picks up dead glints from the windrows of rotted mullet at high-water line.

From the small settlement on the Indian shell mound called Chokoloskee, a baleful sky out toward the Gulf looks ragged as a ghost, unsettled, wandering. The sky is low, withholding rain. Vultures on black-fingered wings tilt back and forth over the broken trees. At the channel edge, where docks and pilings, stove-in boats, uprooted shacks litter the shore, odd pieces torn away from their old places hang askew, strained from the flood by mangrove limbs twisted down into the tide. Thatched roofs are spun onto their poles like old straw brooms; sheds and cabins sag. In the dank air, a sharp fish stink is infused with the corruption of dead animals and over-flowed pits from which the privy shacks have washed away. Pots, kettles, crockery, a butter churn, tin tubs, buckets, blackened vegetables, salt-slimed boots, soaked horsehair mattresses, a ravished doll are strewn across bare salt-killed ground.

A lone gull picks at reddened mullet cast on shore, a dog barks without heart at so much silence.

A figure in mud-fringed calico stoops to retrieve a Bible. Wiping grime from its caked cover with dulled fingers, she straightens, turns, and stares toward the south. The fingers pause. From the black mangrove forest down the Bay, a boat motor, softened by distance, comes and goes and comes again, bound east through Rabbit Key Pass from the Gulf of Mexico.

"Oh Lord no," she whispers, half-aloud. "Oh please no, Mister Watson."

Along toward twilight, Postmaster Smallwood, on his knees under his store, is raking out the last of his drowned chickens. Hearing the oncoming boat, he groans in the putrid heat. Soon one pair of bare feet, then another, pass in silence on their way down to the landing. More men follow. He knows his neighbors by their gait and britches.

Over low voices comes the *pot-pot* of the motor. Three days before, when that boat had headed south, every last man on the island watched it go, but the postmaster had been the only man to wave. He, too, had prayed that this would be the end of it, that the broad figure at the helm, sinking below the tree line into darkness at the far end of the Bay, would disappear forever from the Islands. Said D. D. House that day, "He will be back."

That old man's Sunday boots descend the Indian mound, then the bare feet of his three sandy, slow-eyed sons. The oldest, Bill House, climbs the steps and enters the store and post office, calling to Smallwood's wife, his sister Mamie. Bill House's feet creak on the pine floor overhead.

In the steaming heat, in an onset of malaria, Smallwood feels sickly weak. When his rump emerges from beneath his house and he attempts to stand, he staggers and bangs heavily against the outside wall, causing Mamie to cry out in the room above. He thinks, This dark day has been coming down forever.

"Lookit what come crawlin out! Ain't that our postmaster?"

"Keep that spade handy, Uncle Ted! Might gone to need it!"

Wincing, Smallwood arches his back, takes a dreadful breath, gags, hawks, expels the sweet taste of chicken rot in his mouth and nostrils. "Got four rifles there, I see," he says. "Think that's enough?"

The old man pauses to appraise his son-in-law. Daniel David House is silver-bearded. He wears no collar but is otherwise dressed formally, in white shirt, shiny black frock coat, black pants hauled high by galluses. He is crippled. He says, "Where's his missus?"

"Inside with her young'uns. With your daughter and your grand-children, Mr. House." When the elder grunts and turns away, Smallwood's voice pursues him. "Them women and children gone to have 'em a good view. That what you want?"

Henry Short has stopped behind the House men, holding his rifle down along his leg. "You, too, Henry? You're making a mistake."

"Leave Henry be," says Bill House from the door. House is thirty, a strong, florid man creased hard by sun. He is followed outside by his sister, who is weeping. Mamie Smallwood cries, "Shame on you, William House! Shame on you, Papa!" The old man turns his back upon his daughter. Lloyd House and Young Dan at his heels, he hobbles down the slope toward the water.

In a shift of wind, the *pot-pot-pot* of the oncoming boat comes hard as a pulse. A frantic young woman runs out of the store—"Oh dear God!" She hurries down the steps, calling her little boy.

Near the shore, Henry Short leans his old lever-action .30-30 into the split in the big fish-fuddle tree that the hurricane has felled across the clearing. The rifle is hidden when he turns, arms folded tight in sign that he is here against his will, that none of this is any of his doing.

The men are gathering. Charlie T. Boggess, ankle twisted in the hurricane, limps past the store. He turns and shouts back at a woman calling, "All right, all *right*!" To Smallwood he complains nervously, "Ain't you the one said he was gone for good?"

"Not me! I *knowed* he would be back!" Isaac Yeomans, fiery with drink, acts cheered by what the others dread. "His kind don't like to be run off. You recall Sam Lewis, Ted? At Lemon City?"

Smallwood nods. "They lynched Sam Lewis, too."

"This ain't no lynching," Bill House calls.

"Don't think so, Bill? What if he's just coming to pick up his family, keep on going?"

The men stare away toward the south as the oncoming boat comes into view, a dark burr on the pewter water. Most have worn the same clothes since the hurricane, they are rank as dogs and scared and cranky, they are anxious to enlist Ted Smallwood because the participation of the postmaster might afford some dim official sanction.

If nobody is innocent, who can be guilty?

"No hanging back!" shouts Old Dan House, glaring at Smallwood.

Isaac Yeomans breaks his shotgun and sights down the barrels, pops a shell in, sets his felt hat. "Best throw in with us, Ted," he urges his old friend. "We don't care for this no more'n you do."

"He always pays his bills, plays fair with me. I ain't got no fight with him and you fellers don't neither."

"Hell, Ted, this fight ain't nothin to be scared of! Not with his one against more'n a dozen."

"Maybe I ain't scared the way you think. Maybe I'm scared of murder in cold blood."

"*He* ain't scared of cold blood, Ted. Colder the better."

The twilight gathers. Hurricane refugees from the Lost Man's coast have gathered by the store, fifty yards back of the men down by the water. "You fellers fixin to gun him down?" one hollers. "Thought you was aimin to *arrest* him."

"Arrest Watson? They tried that the other day."

The postmaster can no longer make out faces under the old and broken hats. Too tense to slap at the mosquitoes, the figures wait, anonymous as outlaws. Behind the men skulk ragged boys with slingshots and singleshot .22s. Shouted at, they retreat and circle back, stealthy as coons.

In his old leaf-colored clothes, in cryptic shadow, Henry Short sifts in against the tree bark like a chuck-will's-widow, shuffling soft wings. Dead still, he is all but invisible.

Not slowing, the oncoming boat winds in among the oyster bars. Her white bow wave glimmers where the dark hull parts the surface, her rifle-fire *pot-pot-pot* too loud and louder. The boatman's broad hat rises in slow silhouette above the line of black horizon to the south.

The wind-stripped trees are hushed, the last birds mute. A razorback grunts abruptly, once. Mosquitoes keen, drawing the silence tight. Behind the rusted screen of Smallwood's door, pale figures loom. Surely, the postmaster thinks, the boatman feels so much suspense, so much hard pounding of so many hearts. The day is late. A life runs swiftly to its end.

In the last light Ted Smallwood sees the missing child crouched in the sea grape, spying on all the grown-up men with guns. In urgent undertones he calls; the amorphous body of armed men turns toward him. He does not call again. He runs and grabs the little boy.

Hurrying the child indoors, he bangs his lantern. His wife raises a finger to her lips as if the man coming might hear. Does she fear denunciation of her husband for attempting to alert the boat? Hadn't they learned that, warned or not, this man would come in anyway? Mamie whispers, "Is Daddy the one behind this, Ted? Bill and Young Dan, too?" He squeezes a mosquito, lifts his fingertips, winces at the blood. "Light that smudge," he tells his little girl, pointing at the mangrove charcoal in the bucket.

He says, "They're all behind it." He cannot stop yawning. "They want an end to it."

The motor dies in a long wash of silence. His daughter whimpers. The postmaster, queerly out of breath, sends her to her mother. He joins the young woman on the porch. "Please, Edna," he entreats her, "go back inside."

In the onshore wind out of the south, the boat glides toward a point just west of where the store landing had been lost to storm. Like a shadow, Henry Short crosses behind the men and positions himself off the right hand of Bill House, who waves him farther forward, into knee-deep shallows.

Smallwood's heart kicks as the bow wave slaps ashore: a wash and suck as the wood stem strikes with a violent *crunch!* of dead shell bottom. Bearing his shotgun, the boatman runs forward and leaps. A moan rises with the rising guns.

The earth turns. Time resumes. The reckoning has been deferred but the postmaster's relief is without elation. An exchange of voices as a few men drift forward. Starting down the slope toward the water, Mamie Smallwood and her friend are overtaken by the little boy, who runs to meet his father.

The shift toward death is hard and sudden. Rising voices are scattered by the whip crack of a shot, two shots together. There is time for an echo, time for a shriek, before the last evening of the old days in the Islands flies apart in a volley of staccato fire and dogs barking.

The young woman stands formally as for a picture, brown dress darkened by the dusk, face pale as salt. Though Mamie Smallwood drags her back, it was Mamie who shrieked and the young woman who takes the sobbing Mamie to her bosom; she regards the postmaster over his wife's shoulder without the mercy of a single blink. He stumbles toward them, stunned and weak, but his wife twists away from him, mouth ugly. In a low, shuddering voice she says, "I am going, Mr. Smallwood. I am leaving this godforsaken place."

The young woman goes to her little boy, who has tripped and fallen in his wailing flight. Patches of hurricane mud daub his small knees. She pulls the child away from the churning men, who in the dusk are milling on the shore like one great shapeless animal. In a moment, she will crawl under the house, dragging her brood into the chicken slime and darkness.

"No, Lord," she whispers as the terror overtakes her.

"No, please, no," she moans.

"Oh Lord God," she cries. "They are killing Mister Watson!"

ERSKINE THOMPSON

✦

We never had no trouble from Mister Watson, and from what we seen, he never caused none, not amongst his neighbors. All his trouble come to him from the outside.

E. J. Watson turned up at Half Way Creek back in 1892, worked on the produce farms awhile, worked in the cane. Hard worker, too, but it don't seem like he hoed cane for the money, it was more like he wanted a feel for our community. Strong, good-looking feller in his thirties, dark red hair, well made, thick through the shoulders but no fat on him, not in them days. Close to six foot and carried himself well, folks noticed him straight off and no one fooled with him. First time you seen the man you wanted him to like you—he was that kind. Wore a broad black hat and a black frock coat with big pockets, made him look bulky. Times we was cutting buttonwood with ax and hand saw, two-three cords a day—that's hot, hard, humid work, case you ain't done it—Ed Watson never changed that outfit. Kept that coat on over his denim coveralls, he said, cause he never knew when he might expect some company from up north. Might smile a little when he said that but never give no explanation.

Folks didn't know where this stranger come from and nobody asked. You didn't ask a man hard questions, not in the Ten Thousand Islands, not in them days. Folks will tell you different today, but back then there weren't too many in our section that wasn't on the run from someplace else. Who would come to these rain-rotted islands with not hardly enough high ground to build a outhouse, and so many miskeeters plaguing you in the bad summers you thought you'd took the wrong turn straight to Hell?

Old Man William Brown was cutting cane, and he listened to them men opining how this Watson feller was so able and so friendly. Old Man William took him a slow drink of water, give a sigh. Willie Brown said, "Well, now, Papa, is that sigh a warnin?" And his daddy said, "I *feel* somethin, is all. Same way I feel the damp." They all respected Old Man William, but there weren't one man in the cane that day that took him serious.

All the same, we noticed quick, you drawed too close to E. J. Watson, he eased out sideways like a crab, gave himself room. One time, my half-uncle Tant Jenkins come up on him letting his water, and Mister Watson come around so fast Tant Jenkins thought this feller aimed to piss on him. By the time Tant seen it weren't his pecker he had in his hand, that gun was halfway back into them coveralls, but not so fast he could not be sure of what he seen.

Being brash as well as nervous, Tant says, "Well, now, Mister Watson! Still es-pectin company from the North?" And Watson says, very agreeable, "Any company that shows up unexpected will find me ready with a nice warm welcome."

Ed Watson had money in his pocket when he come to Half Way Creek, which ain't none of my business, but in all the years I knew him, right up till near the end, he always come up with money when he had to. We never knew till later he was on the dodge, but Half Way Creek was too handy to the lawmen for his liking. Ain't nothing much out there today but a few old cisterns, but Half Way Creek had near a dozen families then, more than Everglade or Chokoloskee. Course back in them days there weren't hardly a hundred souls in that whole hundred mile of coast south to Cape Sable.

Mister Watson weren't at Half Way Creek but a few days when he paid cash money for William Brown's old schooner. Ain't many would buy a sixty-foot schooner that didn't know nothing about boats. Time he was done, Ed Watson was one of the best boatmen on this coast.

Mister Watson and me cut buttonwood all around Bay Sunday, run it over to Key West, three dollars a cord. I seen straight off that Ed J. Watson meant to go someplace, I seen my chance, so I signed on to guide him down around the Islands. I was just back from a year down there, plume hunting for Chevelier; I turned that Frenchman over to Bill House. We was just young fellers then, a scant fourteen. No school on Chokoloskee so you went to work.

Folks ask, "Would you have worked for Watson if you knowed about him what you know today?" Well, hell, I don't *know* what I know today and they don't neither. With so many stories growed up around that feller, who is to say which ones was true? What I seen were a able-bodied man, mostly quiet, easy in his ways, who acted according to our ideas of a gentleman. And that was all we had, ideas, cause we had never seen one in this section, unless you would count Preacher Gatewood, who brought the Lord to Everglade back in 1888 and took Him away again when he departed, the men said. Some kind of a joke, wouldn't surprise me.

Most of our old Glades pioneers was drifters and deserters from the War Between the States who never got the word that we was licked. Moonshiners and plume hunters, the most of 'em. Thatch lean-tos and a skiff and pot and rifle, maybe a jug of homemade lightning for fighting off the skeeters in the evening. Had earth in a tub, made their fire in the skiff, had coffee going morning, noon, and night.

Man on the run who used the name Will Raymond was camped with a woman and her daughter in a palmetta shack on that big bend in Chatham River, living along on grits and mullet, taking some gator hides and egret plumes, selling bad moonshine to the Injuns. We seen plenty like Will Raymond in the Islands, knife-mouthed piney-woods crackers, hollow-eyed under wool hats, and them bony-cheeked tall women with lank black hair like horse mane. Go crazy every little while, shoot some feller through the heart. Will done that more'n once in other parts, we heard, and got that habit. Seems the law wanted him bad—dead or alive, as you might say. When deputies come a-hunting him out of Key West, Will said nosir, he'd be damned if he'd go peaceable, and he whistled a bullet past their heads to prove it, but he was peaceable as the law allows by the time the smoke cleared. The law invited the Widder Raymond to accompany his mangy carcass on a free boat ride to Key West, and she said, "Thankee, boys, I don't mind if I do."

Old Man Richard Harden, then the Frenchman, was on Chatham Bend before him, and the Injuns before that; biggest Injun mound south of Chokoloskee Island. Most of the Bend was overgrowed cause none of 'em weren't farmers, and Mister Watson would cuss Will Raymond every time we went downriver, saying how pitiful it was to see that good ground going to waste. One day Mister Watson went ashore, made an offer for the quit-claim, and Raymond come out with a old musket, run him off. Fortnight later, a posse come a hundred mile north from Key West and killed that pesky feller, and next thing you know, Ed Watson tracked the widder down and bought the quit-claim, two hundred fifty dollars. That was a pile of cash in them days, but what he got was forty acres of good soil, protected on three sides by mangrove tangle: anybody who come huntin E. J. Watson would have to come straight at him, off the river.

E. J. Watson had grand plans, about the only feller down there as ever did. Used to talk about dredging out the mouth of Chatham River, make a harbor for that wild southwest coast. Meantime, he sunk buttonwood posts to frame up a new cabin, had wood shutters and canvas flaps on the front windows, brought in a woodstove and a kerosene lamp and a galvanized tub for anyone might care to bath. We ate good, too, fish and wild meat, sowbelly and grits, had a big iron skillet and made johnnycakes: put some lard to his good flour, cooked 'em up dry. I remembered them big johnny-cakes all my whole life.

Will Raymond's shack weren't fit for hogs, Mister Watson said, had to patch it up before he put his hogs in it. We had two cows, and chickens, too, but that man had a real feel for hogs. He loved hogs and hogs loved him, come to his call from all over the Bend, I can hear him calling down them river evenings to this day. Brought 'em in at night cause of the panthers, fed 'em garden trash and table slops and such so they wouldn't get no fishy taste like them old razorbacks at Hardens that fed on crabs and lowlife when the tide was out. Kept a old roan horse to pull his plow, break that hard shell ground, and sometimes he'd ride around his farm like it was his old family plantation back in South Carolina.

Mister Watson experimented with all kinds of vegetables and tobacco. Only victuals we traded for was salt and coffee: bought hard green coffee beans, wrapped 'em in burlap. hammered 'em to powder with a mallet. Made our own grits and sugar and cane spirits—what we called white lightning. Seasons when vegetables done poor, we'd pole inland up the creeks and out across the Glades to the piney ridges, get Injun greens and coontie root for starch and flour, cut some cabbage-palm tops in the ham-mocks. Worked his crew like niggers and worked like a nigger alongside of us. Brung in regular niggers from Fort Myers, and *they* worked hard, too—that man knew how to get work from his help! Them boys was scared to death of him, he could be rough. But they sure liked to listen to his stories, least when he weren't drinking. Told 'em nigger jokes that set 'em giggling for hours—nerves, maybe. I never did get them fool jokes. Me'n niggers just don't think the same.

Ed Watson was the first man since the Injuns to hack down all that thorn on Chatham Bend. Dug out palmetta roots thick as his leg, raked the shell out of that black soil and made a farm. Grew all kinds of vegetables, grew cane for syrup, and tomatoes and then alligator pears. Chok folks hooted when he tried seed potatoes, but Mister Watson shipped them things for three-four years and almost made 'em pay, and never failed to raise a few for our own table.

We got good money for our produce but too much spoiled before it reached Key West, so pretty quick, we give up on common vegetables and stuck to sugarcane. Next he figured that making cane syrup right there on the Bend made a lot more sense than shipping heavy stalks, because syrup could be stored till he got his price. First planter in south Florida to let his cane tassel before harvest so the syrup would boil down stronger without sugaring. Burned off his field before harvest, too, figuring the work would go much faster once the leaves and cane tops was burned away: nothing but clean stalks to deal with, not much sugar lost, and a smaller crew. And he learned not to wait too long: he's the one discovered that cane sugar don't extract good from the stalks even a few days after the burn.

Locally we sold every jar of syrup we produced so we invested in a bigger schooner that he called the *Gladiator,* packed our syrup in screw-top gallon cans, six to the case, shipped 'em to Port Tampa and Key West. *Island Pride!* Our brand grew to be famous. Them fellers at Half Way Creek and Turner River made good syrup but our Island Pride had left 'em in the dust.

All this while we shot gators and egrets when they was handy. Up them inland creeks past Alligator Bay, white egrets was thick, pink curlew, too, and we never failed to take a deer for venison, sometimes a turkey. Trapped coons and otters, shot a bear or panther every little while. Mister Watson was a deadeye shot. I could shoot pretty good, too, but the only man in southwest Florida could shoot as quick and clean as E. J. Watson was Nigger Short.

When D. D. House moved his cane plantation from Half Way Creek down to a big hammock north of Chatham Bend, he took Short with him. Sundays, that boy might visit with Bill House at Possum Key or go to Hardens. Henry and me got on all right, I never held nothin against him, but them damn Hardens let that nigger eat right at their table.

Besides me and Mister Watson, the only man hunting plume birds in our section was the Frenchman. One day we seen Chevelier's skiff come out Sim's Creek that's back of Gopher Key. Sometimes that old man had Injuns with him, and this day I seen a dugout slide out of sight into the greenery.

Mister Watson never paid them Injuns no attention, only the skiff; he made me a sign to ship my oars, drift quiet. When Chevelier lifted his straw hat to mop his head, he shot it right out of his hand, just spun it away into the water. That old man yelped and grabbed his oars and skedaddled like a duck into the mangroves. "Stay off my territory!" shouts Watson. Picking up the floating hat with that new hole in it, he was grinning, kind of sheepish. Never a whisper from the mangroves and nothing to be seen but them red stilt roots, water glitter, and green air. "You'll find your hat at Chatham Bend!" he yells.

I told Mister Watson how Chevelier was collecting rare birds for museums, used small-gauge bird shot so as not to spoil the skins. The Frenchman had all kinds of books, knew all about Injuns, spoke some of their lingo; he had wild men visiting at Possum Key that would never go nowhere near Chokoloskee Bay. Traded their hides and furs through Richard Harden, who claimed to be Choctaw or some such, though nobody never paid that no attention. The Frenchman was always close to Hardens, and probably it was Old Man Richard who brought them Injuns to him in the first place.

All the while I was talking, Mister Watson watched me. That feller would look at you dead on for a long minute, then blink just once, real slow, like a chewing turtle, keeping his eyes closed for a moment as if resting 'em up from such a dretful sight. That's how I first noticed his fire color, that dark red hair the color of old embers or dried blood, and the ruddy skin and sunburned whiskers with a little gold to 'em, like he glowed inside. Then them blue eyes fixed me again, out of the shadow of that black felt hat. Only hat in the Ten Thousand Islands, I imagine, that had a label into it from Fort Smith, Arkansas. I took to whistling.

"What's he up to over yonder, then?" Mister Watson interrupts me. I told him about that Injun mound hid away on Gopher Key and the white shell lining the canal that come in there from the Gulf. My opinion, Chevelier was hunting Calusa treasure.

On the way home, he was quiet. Finally he said he wouldn't mind having him a chat with a educated man like Jean Chevelier—*Che-vell-yay*, he called him, stead of *Shovel-leer*, the way us local fellers said it—and he reckoned he'd picked a piss-poor way to get acquainted. He was right. That old Frenchman had some sand or he wouldn't have made it all alone here in the Islands. This hat business weren't over by a long shot.

We hung that hat on a peg when we got home but the Frenchman never come for it. After that day, we had them plume birds to ourselves.

RICHARD HARDEN

✦

I done a lot, lived a long time, and seen more than I cared to. I mostly recollect what I have seen and sometimes learn from it, but I was born on the run like a young fawn and never had no time for improvement. What little I knew I owed to this Frenchified old feller who was Mister Watson's closest neighbor next to me.

First time I met that mean old man I tried to run him off this river. That was the winter of '88, when we was living at the Bend which is the Watson place today. Forty good acres on that mound, they say, but we planted just a half one for our table. Salted fish, cut buttonwood, took egret plumes in breeding season, gator hides, some otter, traded with the Indins, just eased on by.

One morning I'm mending net when I feel something coming. On the riverbank I see my old woman hollering across the wind, her mouth like a black hole, but in a queer shift of light off the river, what I see is not my Mary but a tall bony prophet woman pointing toward the Gulf like she seen a vision in that glaring sky, her scowl half hid under her sunbonnet that looks more like a cowl. Mary Weeks don't bother to come hunting you, just hollers what she wants from where she's at. Sometimes I play deaf, pay her no mind, but this day I set down my net needle and went.

A skinny old man has rowed upriver from the Gulf, three miles and more. He is wearing knickers, had a jacket laid across the thwart, looked like a city feller off one of them big steam yachts that been showing up along the Gulf Coast in the winter. Has to row hard against the current, quick jerky little strokes. He rowed strong, too, but by the time he hits the bank, he's looking pale and peaked. He has thick spectacles that bottle up his wild round eyes, and cheeks so bony that they catch the light, and wet red lips and a thin mustache like a ring around his mouth, and pointy ears the Devil would be proud of.

"How do you are!" he calls, lifting his hat.

"Git off my propitty," say I, hitching the gun.

"Commaung?" His voice is very sharp and cross, like it's me who don't belong on my own land. Takes out a neckerchief and dabs his face, then reaches around for the fancy shotgun he's got leaning in the bows. He's only moving it because it's pointing at my knees, but I never knowed that at the time and couldn't take no chances, not in them days. "Git the hell back where you come from, Mister." I hoist my rifle so he's looking down the barrel to let him know not to try no city tricks.

When he pulls his hand back from his gun, I see he ain't got all his fingers. "Do not self-excite," he says. He hops out of his boat, pushes my gun barrel out of his way, and climbs the bank. Seeing my hair and dusty hide, he has mistook me for some kind of half-breed help. "You are vair uppity, my good man," he says. Hands on hips, he looks around like he's inspecting his new property, then puts on glasses so's to study the breed of riffraff he is dealing with—me and the big woman in the doorway of the shack and the boy watching from behind her skirts.

I jab my gun barrel into his back, then wave the barrel toward his boat, and damn if he don't whip around and wrench that gun away, that's how quick and strong he is, and crazy. Backs me up, then breaks my gun, picks out my cartridge, tosses it into the river.

Any man would try that trick when the home man has the drop on him has *got* to be crazy, and this is a feller getting on in years who looks plain puny. Even my Mary ain't snickering no more and she don't overlook too many chances. Bein Catholic, she knows a devil when she sees one.

Around about now, young John Owen comes out of the shack lugging my old musket from the War. At six years of age, our youngest boy already knew his business. Not a word, just brings the shooting iron somewhat closer so's he don't waste powder, then hoists her up, set to haul back on the trigger. I believe his plan was to shoot this feller, get the story later.

The stranger seen this, too. He forks over my gun in a hurry while Mary runs and grabs her little boy. She don't care much about me no more, but John Owen is her hope and consolation.

"Infant shoot *visiteur* in thees fokink *Amerique?"* the stranger yells, point-

ing at my son. "For *why?*" He has come from France to collect bird specimens, he's hunting egret plumes to make ends meet. Looked like some old
specimen hisself, damn if he didn't—black beady eyes, quills sticking up
out of his head, stiff gawky gait—the dry look of a man who has lived too
long without a woman, Big Mary said. Looked all set to shit and no mistake.
Spent too much time with his feathered friends, I reckon, cause when he
got riled, his crest shot up in back, and he screeched as good as them Carolina parrots he was hunting, being very upset to find squatters on a wild
river bend that was overgrowed and empty when he passed by here a few
years ago. Only last week, he complains, folks at Everglade had told him he
could camp at Chatham Bend. "For why nobody knows it you pipple here?"

"They know we're here."

He sinks down on a log. *"Sacray-doo,"* he says. *"Holy sheet."*

Because Msyoo Chevelier, as he calls himself, was taking it so hard, I told
him he could stay awhile, get to know the place. Never says thanks, just lifts
his shoulders, sighs like he wants to die. All the same, we go fetch his gear
off a Key West schooner anchored off the river mouth. He is aboard,
packed up, and debarked again in about six minutes. The skipper hollers,
"When shall we come pick you up?" That rude old man don't even turn
around, that's how hard he's pestering me with questions. Don't wait for
answers, neither, just answers himself according to his own ideas all the
way upriver.

First time he come to Chatham River, the Frenchman shot the first
short-tailed hawk ever collected in North America—something like that.
Weren't much of a claim cause it weren't much of a hawk—tail too short,
I guess. Why he thought that scraggy thing would make him famous I
don't know. He finally seen his Carolina parrots in some freshwater slough
way up inland, bright green with red and yeller on the head, but they was
shy and he never come up with no specimens.

Them parrots used to be as thick as fleas back in the hammocks, I told
him. Us fellers always took a few, out deer hunting. You *eat? Le perroquet?*
He squawked and slapped his brow. Well, that was a long time ago, I told
him, and I ain't seen one since: somebody told me them pretty birds might
of flewed away for good.

"*Sacre Amerique!* Keel ever' foking ting!"

One evening Msyoo Chevelier asks my kids if they would like to help him
collect birds, and wild eggs, too. He spells out all the kinds he wants. When

he says "swaller-tail hawk," I smile and say *"Tonsabe."* At that he flies right at my face—"Where you hear *tonsabe?*" I tell him that is Indin speech for swaller-tail hawk, and he asks real sly, *"Which* Indiang?"

"Choctaw," I says—that's my mother's people. He shakes his head; he is grinning like some bad old kind of coon. *"Tonsabe* is *Calusa,* Ree-chard, it ees not?"

He had took me by surprise and my face showed it. That word ain't Choctaw and it ain't used by Mikasuki nor Muskogees neither, it come straight down from my Calusa granddaddy, Chief Chekaika, who killed off them white settlers on Indian Key. But Chekaika was a dirty word to white men, so I only shrug, try to look stupid.

He sets down careful on a fish box so we're knee to knee. "Vair few Calusa words survive," he says, holding my eye like he wants to read my brain. He'd studied the archives in Seville, Spain, and every big Calusa mound along this coast. Said Calusa warriors in eighteen canoes attacked the first Spaniards, killed Ponce de Leon. Calusas layed low in these rivers to escape the Spanish poxes, which done 'em more harm than all them swords and blunderbusses piled up together. Said Chatham Bend was a Calusa village before Spanish times—that's why he wanted to dig it up so bad. And somewhere not far from the Bend, well hid from the rivers, there had to be a big burial mound full of sacred objects, built up higher than the village mounds, with white sand canals leading out to open water.

The Frenchman gives me that skull smile of his when I do not answer. "You know where ees it? You tekka me?"

"Heck, I ain't nothin but a dumb old Indin," I tell him.

He sits back, knowing he is pushing me too hard, too fast. "Indiang pipple say 'dumb Indin'; white pipple say 'dumb Injun'—for why?" I ponder some. "You reckon dumb Indins are too damn dumb to say 'dumb Injuns'?" He waves me off. He ain't got time for dumb-ass Indin jokes. *"Ay-coot,"* he says. "I am vair inter-est Indiang pipples. Foking crack-aire pipple are know-nothing, are grave robb-aire!" He was a real scientist, born curious, but I seen his crippled hand twitch while he spoke: this man would rob them graves himself, being some way starved by life, bone greedy.

"Well, now," say I, "my oldest boy and me, we was out robbin graves one sunny mornin, had twelve-thirteen nice redskin skulls lined up on a log, y'know, airin 'em out. One had a hole conched into it, but a pink spoonbill plume we stuck into that hole made it look real pretty. Them redskin skulls done up artistic for the tourist trade might bring some nice spot cash down to Key West." I hum a little, taking my time. "Chip the crown off for your ashtray, fill that skull with fine cigars? For a human humidor you just can't beat it."

Kind of weak, he says, "Where this place *was?*"

"Nosir," I says, "I wouldn't let on to my worst enemy about that place! *Indin* power! *Bad* power!" I drop my voice right down to a whisper and I tap his knee. "When we lined up all them skulls, Msyoo? All of a sudden, them ol' woods went silent. *Dead* silent, like after the fall of a giant tree. Seemed like them old woods was waiting, see what we would do." I set there and nod at him a while. "Oh, we was scared, all right. Got away quick and we ain't never been back. Left them skulls settin on that log grinnin good-bye. Know what that ringin silence was? That was the 'vengin spirits of Calusas!" And I show that Frenchman my Indin stone face, refuse to answer no more questions for his own damn good.

Msyoo had to accept that silent teaching out of his respect for the earth ways of the noble redskin. This foreign feller knew more about our old-time Indins than Indins theirselves, let alone white folks. Hell, some of them Bay people are still yellin how they ought to shoot redskins fast as they show their faces, cause redskins is just as ornery and treacherous as your common Spaniard.

Msyoo was hissin over the idea that a Indin man could desecrate Indin graves, but we seen he was determined to do some plain and fancy desecratin on his own. I knowed just the kind of mound he wanted, and after that day, one of my kids was always guidin him up the wrong creek to make him happy. Every slough had some kind of small shell mound at the head of it, he could hack his way into a hundred, never hit the right one.

South and west of Possum Key in them miles and miles of mangrove was a big ol' hidden mound called Gopher Key, had a Calusa-built canal we called Sim's Creek that led out to the Gulf of Mexico: we figured Ol' Sim for a Civil War deserter, hid back in there on that mound huntin gopher tortoise for his dinner, never got word to come out and go on home. The Frenchman got all flustered up when he seen that straight canal lined with white shell—a sure sign, he said, that this mound was a sacred place. Had enough shell on Gopher Key to move around for the whole rest of his life, so that furious old feller was in there diggin every chance he got. No wind back in them swamps and not much air, only wet heat and man-eatin miskeeters that bit up his old carcass somethin pitiful. My boy Webster— that's the dark one—Webster said, "Time them skeeters get done with that old man, his French blood will be all gone and he will speak American as good as we do."

First year he showed up in the Islands, 1888, the Frenchman bought my quit-claim on the Bend. Once we was piled into the boat, ready to go, he told us we could hang around so long as he could run us off any time he damn well wanted. I shook my head. The truth was, I had sign to go. I never liked the feel of Chatham Bend. Dark power there, the Indins told me, somethin unfinished from some bad old history.

Indin people go by sign, they don't need no excuse to leave some place that don't feel right; they just pick up their sorry ass and move it elsewhere. Ownin no more than we could pack into one boat, we traveled light, and where we went was Possum Key, inland and upriver, handy to them big egret rookeries in the Glades creeks. That spring we done some huntin, too, sold our plumes to the Frenchman, traded with the Indins.

Them Mikasukis back up Lost Man's Slough was maybe the last Indins in the U.S.A. that never signed no treaty with no Great White Father. Called 'em Cypress Indins cause they hollowed dugouts out of cypress logs. Never paddled hardly but stood up in the stern, used push poles, followed water paths that in the Seminole Wars was very hard for the white soldiers to see. Standin up like that, peerin through tall sawgrass, they most always seen you first, you were lucky to get a glimpse of 'em at all. Down in the rivers, Indins was watchin us most of the time. Watched us when we come into their country and watched us when we went away. Give you a funny feeling, being watched like that. Made you think the Earth was watching, too.

One dugout that come in to trade at Everglade in the late eighties was the first wild Indins them white folks ever seen, but that band traded with Hardens two-three years before that. Brung bear meat and venison wrapped in palm fans, wild ducks and turkeys, gophers, palm hearts, coontie root and such, took coffee and trade goods for their furs and bird plumes, with a few machetes, maybe an old shotgun, and some cane liquor thrown in.

• • •

Chevelier slept poor at the Bend the same as us, but it took him a whole year to admit it, that's how scientifical he was. And he purely hated giving up all that good ground—that was the greed in him. When I told him that ground was no good to him if he didn't farm it and couldn't get no sleep, he'd shout at me, waving his arms. My kids could imitate him good: "What you tek me for to be? A soo-paire-stee-shee-us domb redda-skin?" As Webster said, most every kid along the coast could speak his lingo pretty near as good as he did, maybe better.

Anyways, Msyoo sold his quit-claim to the first hombre who showed up, a man named Raymond. "Is only for I cannot farm this forty ay-caire, is only for is foking shame to waste!" We took him upriver to Possum Key, built a nice little house to keep his old skeeter-bit bones out of the rain, even tacked up shelves for all them books and bird skins, and never got so much as a *mare-see*. Shooed us out like a flock of hens, glad to see the end of us.

We kept the Frenchman in our family though he didn't know it. To his last breath, he frowned and squabbled like a coon. For a while he had Erskine Thompson helping, and after Erskine left with Mister Watson, he had young Bill House. Yanked those boys by the ear and kept them scared of him, never let 'em in too close for fear they might learn about the treasure that any day now he was sure to find on Gopher Key.

That Frenchman said he never held with no Father Who art in Heaven. "Man ees made in Hees ee-mage? Who say so? Black man? Red man? Which man? White man? Yellow man? God ees *all* thees color? *Say tabsurde!* Man got to sheet, same like any fokink animal: you telling to me your God in Heaven, He got to sheet, too?" And he would glare around at the green forest walls, the white sky and the summer silence. "Maybe you got someting, Ree-chard. Maybe thees fokink Hell on earth is where He done it."

Or he might point at a silver riffle on the river. "Looka queek! You see? *That* ees God, *ness pa*? Birt sheet on your head? *That* ees God *oh-see. La Grande Meestaire!*"

"*Grande Meestaire*, that means 'Big Mister,' case you don't speak French," I told my Mary. As a Catholic, Mary purely hated all that heathen talk about sun and silver riffles. Even a God who moved His bowels was better than one who jumped out at a body from all over the darn place, couldn't be trusted to stay up there in Heaven where He belonged. To keep the peace,

I'd shake my head over Chevelier's terrible French ways, but deep in my bones, I felt God's truth in what he said about sun and silver riffles, yes, and bird shit, too.

After Will Raymond was wiped out at the Bend, his widow sold his quit-claim to a stranger, and that stranger stayed here in the rivers close to twenty years. I got friendly with this man and took some pains to keep it that way, because E. J. Watson was our closest neighbor, never much more than a rifle shot away. Good neighbor, too, but I warned my boys to keep their distance even so. In all them times we was up and down his river, we never tied up to his dock, not even once. We only seen Ed Watson when he come to see us, and we never knew when that was going to be.

Possum Key was well inland where miskeeters plagued the younger children, and their mother couldn't hardly fight 'em off; doin her chores, she had to lug a smudge pot. Some of them gray summers in the Islands when the rain don't never quit and the miskeeters neither, never mind the young'uns all bit up and cryin, and that heavy air wet as a blanket and thick enough to stifle a dang frog—them long empty days of mud and hunger and unholy heat made a man half wonder if Judgment Day weren't just another name for a man's life. So pretty quick I moved my gang to Trout Key off the river mouth where Gulf winds blew them skeeters back into the bushes: that place was named after the sea trout on the eelgrass banks off its north shore. But along about then, someone found out that Richard Harden had a common-law wife and some grown children up around Arcadia, so they called me not only a dang half-breed but a dang Mormon, too. After that, our home got known as Mormon Key, which is on the charts today.

Way back in the 1880 census, them Chok Bay folks put me down as a mulatta not because my skin was dark but because I had took a white man's daughter to my bed. Course Mary Weeks was darker than her husband and still is, but she was daughter to the pioneer John Weeks who passed for white, so nobody paid her color no attention. When we scrap, my wife don't never fail to tell me how she rues the day that a half-breed went and stole a white girl's heart.

Henry Short was here one evening and winced when he heard her say that; I seen the muscle twitch along his jaw. Henry would come visiting Bill

House when Bill worked for Chevelier, and later years he would stop over at Mormon Key. Fine strong young feller, color of light wood, looked more like a Indin than I did. Lighter shade than any of us Hardens except Earl, Annie, and John Owen, and his features weren't so heavy as what Earl's were. All the same, Bay people called him Nigger Henry, Nigger Short.

My oldest, Earl, he hated it that Henry ate with us, said if Hardens had a nigger at their table, folks was bound to say that we was niggers, too. And Webster who was pretty dark would look at Earl until Earl looked away. "I reckon I can eat with Henry," Webster would say, "if Henry can eat with me." Which don't mean Earl was wrong about what folks would say. He weren't.

Course truth don't count for much after all these years cause folks hangs on to what it suits 'em to believe and won't let go of it. So them Bay people can call us mulattas if they want but we are Indin. What color they see comes down from times when runaway slaves and Indins was on the run together all across north Florida, but we weren't nothin but Indins in Mama's heart even after she joined up with the Catholic mission. My wife, Mary Weeks, her mother was full-blood Seminole, supposed to been a granddaughter of Chief Osceola, so if this Harden bunch ain't Indin, they ain't no Indins left in the U.S.A. But white folks are welcome at my table, and nigras or breeds passin through is welcome, too. In Jim Crow days, these lost rivers in south Florida might been the one place a man could get away with that, which don't mean them rednecks on Chok Bay aimed to forgive it.

According to Chevelier's way of thinking, there ought to be a law where any man who got his offsprings on a woman of his own color would be gelded. That way ol' Homo might stop his plain damn stupidhood about this skin business and breed his way back to the mud color of Early Man. Said us Hardens was off to a fine start, we come in almost every human shade, all we was missin was a Chinaman.

Crackers don't know nothin about Indins and most Indins you come across don't know much neither. Back in the First Seminole War when runaway slaves fought side by side with Creeks, them black men lived as Indins, took Indin wives, and their offsprings call theirselves Indins today. Some of them Muskogee got a big swipe of the tarbrush but you'd never know that from the way they act toward colored people.

Our Glades Indins, who are Mikasuki, still know something about Indin way. In the old days, if a Mikasuki woman trafficked with a black man or a white one, her people might take and kill 'em both, leave the child to die out in the Cypress. Made 'em feel better, I suppose, but it won't make a spit of difference in the long run. People move around these days, get all mixed up. Like Old Man Jean Chevelier says, it don't matter what our color is, we're all going back to bein brown boys before this thing is finished.

If you live Indin way, then you are Indin. Skin color don't matter. It's how you respect our mother earth, not where you come from. I go along with Catholic somewhat, and read my Bible, cause I was raised up in a mission, Oklahoma Territory. But in my heart I am stone Indin, which is why I drifted south to Lost Man's River, as far from mean-mouthed cracker whites as I could get. This Lost Man's coast is Harden territory. We mind our own business and take orders from nobody.

HENRY SHORT

✦

Here's what Houses told over the years about their nigger. I learned it mostly from overhearin by mistake whether I wanted to or not.

My natural-born mama was a white man's daughter, born not far from the Georgia farm of this House family. She was still a young girl when she got what they called dishonored by a buffalo soldier on his way home from the Indian Wars out West. When she told him he'd got her in a family way, he marched straight to her daddy, declared he loved her, aimed to marry. From the pale look of him, her daddy thought he must be white; the only trouble was that he denied it. *Nosir, I'm a buffalo soldier from the Injun Wars and proud about it!*

This was still Reconstruction times so by law a buffalo soldier was a free American. Without no experience of bein a slave, this light mulatter boy was one of them smart nigras they called "the New Negro." Never knew his place, they said, so he was bound to turn into a beast and go night-huntin for white women to ravage, same way white men went tom-cattin around after the darkie girls. But according to Mr. D. D. House, this soldier loved his white girl truly and she loved him, too. True love in such a situation was a damn crime if there ever was one, and knowin a dirty trouble-maker when they seen one, they naturally took him out and lynched him. Mr. House could not recall his name except it was Jacob and the last name wasn't Short.

Hearin all this as a boy, I crept away and wept, just crawled off like a dog and got dog sick. But I kept my mouth shut and I done that ever since.

Later I learned from Mrs. Ida House that the mother was thrown down and whipped severely but did not lose the baby as was wanted, so her daddy took his ruined daughter back. Her baby looked white so was tolerated till age four. Then his grandfather got rid of him, sold him off to a farmer bound north for Carolina. About this time along come Mr. Daniel David House who had decided he would pull up stakes and head south for the Florida frontier. That farmer was whipping that little boy along the road when the House family run into 'em, and Mr. House bein who he was, he got riled up, struck the man to the ground after an argument, and pulled that cryin child up behind him on his horse. So the owner hollered, "Hell, that pickaninny's mine! I paid hard cash for him!" And Mist' Dan yelled back, "Ain't you never heard about Emancipation? I'll get the law on you!"

Miz Ida liked to tell their children how her husband was a hero, rescuin that little feller's life, but Mr. House did not mind saying in my hearing that he might never done that in the first place had he knowed I was some pick-aninny child. "Nosir," he said, "I would of rode right by." That come to be kind of a family joke but I smelled truth in it.

That's how come I got raised up by the House family and I will say that they was mostly kind. Miz Ida always told me I was better off bein sold away than stayin in Georgia with my sinful mama. For many years she drilled into my head that the one thing lower'n a nigra is some "po' white" female intercoursin with a nigra. Before she was done, I naturally despised the lovin mama I remembered, despised her for a scarlet woman, as Miz Ida called her. This mixed me up because I missed her bad and was very sad when day by day and year by year I come to forget her kindly face. With Miz Ida seeing to my Christian upbringing, I reckon that was what was wanted.

Oldest boy Billy was my same age so we come up together from age four, done about everything together boys could do, hunted and fished, went swimming and exploring back up in the rivers. Them first years I slept in the boys' room, but around about ten, I was moved into a shed back of the cookhouse, and Miz Ida told me I better get used to calling Billy "Mister Billy." That weren't Billy's idea because first time I tried it, he hollered how next time I "mistered" him, he would punch me bloody or push me off the dock or something worse. But he must of got the hang of it cause after that day everything changed. We wasn't really friends no more and Mister Billy got the habit of that, too. From that day on, I lived in lonelihood out in the shed where I belonged, the only nigger on Chokoloskee Island.

Nobody knew no name for me exceptin Henry but the House kids used to call me "Shortie" on account I was so small. Later years, when I grew up close to six foot, I went by the name "Short." I was very light-colored in my skin but I had them tight little blond curls, what they called "bad hair," so I was "House's nigger" or "Black Henry." There was a white man around there that was somewhat darker'n what I was. Some called him "White Henry" so folks would know which was the black man.

BILL HOUSE

✦

Me'n Henry Short worked for the Frenchman collecting wild birds and their eggs. The Frenchman claimed that except as a collector, he never shot uncommon birds, and he liked to tell how he'd trained up boys like Guy Bradley from Flamingo and myself never to shoot into the flock but single out the one bird we was after.

Plume hunters shoot early in breeding season when egret plumes are coming out real good. When them nestlings get pinfeathered, and squawking loud cause they are always hungry, them parent birds lose the little sense God give 'em. They are going to come in to tend their young no matter what, and a man using one of them Flobert rifles that don't snap no louder than a twig can stand there under the trees in a big rookery and pick them birds off fast as he can reload.

A broke-up rookery, that ain't a picture you want to think about too much. The pile of carcasses left behind when you strip the plumes and move on to the next place is just pitiful, and it's a piss-poor way to harvest, cause there ain't no adults left to feed them young and protect 'em from the sun and rain, let alone the crows and buzzards that come sailing and flopping in, tear 'em to pieces. A real big rookery like that one the Frenchman worked up Tampa Bay had four-five hundred acres of black mangrove, maybe ten nests to a tree. Might take you three-four years to clean it out but after that them birds are gone for good.

It's the dead silence after all the shooting that comes back today, though I never stuck around to hear it; I kind of remember it when I am dreaming. Them ghosty trees on dead white guano ground, the sun and silence and dry stink, the squawking and flopping of their wings, and varmints hurrying in without no sound, coons, rats, and possums, biting and biting, and the ants flowing up all them white trees in their dark ribbons to eat at them raw scrawny things that's backed up to the edge of the nest, gullets pulsing and mouths open wide for the food and water that ain't never going to come. Luckiest ones will perish before something finds 'em, cause they's so many young that the carrion birds just can't keep up. Damn vultures set hunched up on them dead limbs so stuffed and stupid they can't hardly fly.

The Frenchman looked like a wet raccoon—regular coon mask! Bright black eyes with dark pouches, thin little legs and humpy walk, all set to bite. Maybe his heart was in the right place, maybe not. Chevelier generally disapproved of humankind, especially rich Yankee sports that come south on their big yachts in the winter.

Home people never had no use for invaders. Fast as the federals put in channel markers for them yachts, we'd snake 'em out. Us fellers don't need no markers, never wanted none. From what we heard, there weren't a river in north Florida but was all shot out, not by hunters but by tourists. Hunters don't waste powder and shot on what can't be et or sold, but these sports blazed away at everything that moved. Crippled a lot more than they killed, kept right on going, left them dying things to drift away into the reeds. Somewhere up around the Suwannee, we was told, they was shootin out the last of them giant red-crest peckers with white bills—*"ivoire-beel wooda-peckaire,"* the Frenchman called it.

Course our kind of men never had no time for sport, we was too busy livin along, we worked from dawn till dark just to get by. Didn't hardly know what sport might be till we got signed up for sport-fish guides and huntin. This was some years later, o'course, after most of the wild creaturs and big fish was gone for good.

Sometimes the Frenchman's hunting partner, young Guy Bradley from Flamingo, would come prospect in new rookeries along our coast. Guy was quiet but looked at you so straight that you felt like you had better confess real quick whether you done something or not. He was the first hunter to warn that white egrets would be shot out in southwest Florida. "Plain disagrees with me to shoot them things no more," he said. "Ain't got my heart into it." I never did let on to Guy how I was collecting bird eggs for the

Frenchman. Swaller-tail kite, he give us up to fifteen dollars for one clutch, depending on how bright them eggs was marked.

One night the old man come home dog tired from Gopher Key. To cheer him up, I laid out a nice swallow-tail clutch next to his plate, but all he done was grunt something cantankerous about halfwit foking crack-aire kids setting down rare eggs where they was most likely to get broke. When he didn't hardly look 'em over but just cussed me out, waving that shot-up hand of his to shoo me off, I recalled how Erskine Thompson warned me that the old frog croaked at everyone just to hide how lonesome his life was, so I try again, sing out bright and cheery from the stove, "Come and get it, Mister Shoveleer!" He didn't need no more'n that to huff up and start gobbling like a tom turkey.

"For why Monsieur le Baron Anton du Chevalier ees call 'Meester Jeen Shovel-*leer*'? For *why?*" He stabbed at the venison and grits on his tin plate. Next he thought about Watson and jabbed his fork like he aimed to stab my eyes out. "This *Wat*-son! Fokink crazy man! *Satan foo!*" Chevelier held up thumb and forefinger to show how close Ed Watson's bullet clipped his ear that morning. When I wondered aloud if Watson had been joking, he shrieked, "*Choke?* With bullet? That ees *choke?*" The Frenchman purely hated E. J. Watson.

Next day I rowed him downriver to consult with Old Man Harden. Nearing the Bend, I seen Mister Watson far out in his field. I edged the skiff in closer to the bank so's he wouldn't see us, then shipped my oars and drifted past so's our thole pins wouldn't creak. Damn if that man a quarter mile away don't stiffen like a panther caught out in the open. Turned his head real slow and looked straight at us, then dropped to one knee and reached into his shirt. I felt a chill. How did the man know we was there? How come he went armed in his own field? And why was he so quick to draw his weapon?

I found out quick. That old French fool behind me had stood up with his shootin iron and now he's ricketing around, trying to draw a bead on Watson. I yell *Sit down!* and I row that boat right out from under him. He falls back hard, nearly goes overboard. Sheltered by the bank, I row all-out to get down around the Bend, scared Mister Watson might run up to the water's edge and pick us off. Please, sir, I holler, don't go pointing guns at Mister Watson, not with young Bill settin in the boat!

Offshore, I flagged down the *Bertie Lee*, Captain R. B. Storter, who would carry the Frenchman to Key West: the old man told me to work my keep at Hardens till he got back. Trouble was, I weren't real easy in their company. That family never got along good with us Bay people, bein too white to fit with Injuns nor nigras but nowhere near fair-skinned enough to suit most whites. Old Man Richard called hisself Choctaw, had Injun features, sure enough, but one look at his boy Webster told you that Choctaw weren't the whole story by a long shot.

Times we worked for the old Frenchman, Henry Short and me used to visit with the Hardens, and Henry held a high opinion of that family, but I don't believe he thought that they was white or he wouldn't have never felt so much at home. While I was living there, Henry would come visiting, to be sure I was getting along—probably believed that, knowing Henry—but the one he really come to visit was young Liza.

Liza Harden weren't a woman yet and she weren't entirely white, but she was as pretty put together as any critter I ever saw, made me ache to look at her. I would have give up my left ear to see her stepping slow into the river without clothes on, see all that golden honey in the sun. It thickened my blood to think about that, even, and Henry was in the same fix I was, though he'd never dare say it. One look at each other and we'd look away, embarrassed, that's how jittery and fired up that young girl made us from an early age.

Henry's mama was white, his daddy mixed, what some call redbone. High cheekbones, narrow features, looked more white than Injun and more Injun than nigra. One time Old Man Richard was carrying on about his own Injun ancestry, told Henry he looked like he might be Choctaw, too. Henry got more agitated up than I ever seen him, cause being a born stickler for the truth, he would choke telling a lie. Finally he whispered, "I ain't no Choctaw, Mr. Richard. Chock-full o' nigger is more like it." Old Man Richard laughed and laughed. "Well," he said, "best not let on about that to my Mary, son, cause she got you figured for a white boy with a drop of Indin, same as us."

Course Old Man Richard knew as well as I did that Henry might of said chock-full o' nigger just to show Bill House that eating at the Hardens' table hadn't give him no wrong ideas about his place. Or maybe the whole bunch was leading on this white boy, come to think about it. First time in my life I ever felt like the outsider—ever try that? I didn't care for it.

In Chokoloskee, when I told the men what Henry Short said to Richard Harden, they laughed somewhat louder than I wanted, and right away they got it twisted all around: "Nigger Henry told that old mulatter, *Hell, no, you ain't Choctaw, Mister Richard! What you are is chock-full o' nigger, same as me!*" "No, no," I told 'em, "that ain't what he said!" Trouble was, I got tired of explainin, just grinned and went along with it, which is why they are laughin yet today about chock-full o' nigger.

Anyways, when Henry said them words, Earl jumps up so fast he spills his plate. "Well, *we* ain't niggers in *this* family, boy, at least *I* ain't, but it sure looks like we got nigger-lovers around here!" Earl was watching me so I got the idea this was a message that Bill House was supposed to take to Chokoloskee: *Mr. Earl Harden don't care to eat with niggers even if the rest of 'em puts up with it.* "I would run you off, boy," Earl told Henry, "but it ain't my house." Earl grabs his plate and marches out onto the stoop cause he can't look his daddy in the eye.

Richard Harden never liked commotion, and he ain't figured out yet how to handle this. Watching his brother stomping out, Webster just laughs. From outside Earl hollers, "Go to Hell, Webster!" Hearing that language, his mother comes a-running from the cookhouse and whaps Earl's ear a terrific lick with her wood ladle. I catch Webster's eye and wish I hadn't. He tried to smile, but I seen he was very angry and humiliated.

Right from a boy, Earl Harden was out to prove something to Bay people, and I guess you could say he finally become friends with one or two families at Chokoloskee—Lopezes, mostly, who weren't never really trusted, being Spanish. Earl tried to be friendly to me, too, but because he was so ornery with Henry, I could not warm up to him and never did, the whole rest of my life.

Two weeks later Jean Chevelier showed up again with Captain Eben Carey, who aimed to go partners with us in the plume trade. With E. J. Watson not a half mile down the river, Chevelier wanted company, and to make sure he got it, he had promised Captain Carey a share of Calusa treasure. He was getting too old to dig all day in hot white shell mound with them bad snakes, heat, and wasps, but being a miser, he refused my help for fear I might let on at Chokoloskee if he found something.

It was Cap'n Ebe who told us what took place at Key West in Bartlum's produce auction room, how Ed Watson come in somewhat drunk and asked Adolphus Santini of Chokoloskee for advice about filing a land claim on both banks of Chatham River. Surveys would be needed because almost all of southwest Florida was "swamp and overflowed," turned over to the state back in 1850; the state had give most all that territory to the railroad companies. But the Everglades and the Ten Thousand Islands were still wilderness, and nobody really knew what was where nor who owned what.

Dolphus Santini was one of the first settlers on Chokoloskee and its leading landowner and farmer. Along about 1877, Santinis filed a claim to "160 acres more or less on Chokoloskee Island among the Ten Thousand Islands of Florida." That's mostly less, cause there ain't hardly one hundred fifty acres on our whole island. Except for Storters in Everglade, who was somewhat educated, people made do with quit-claim rights—pay me to quit my claim, get the heck off, that's all it was, and maybe a handshake thrown in: Ed Watson wanted a real paper claim like Santinis and Storters. We figured later what he aimed to do was tie up as much high ground as he could from Chatham Bend to Lost Man's River, then file a claim the way Santini done, but bad rumors about E. J. Watson had commenced to wander, so he figured he needed an upstanding citizen to back him up.

Santini had heard a lot more than he cared to about this feller Watson down on Chatham River, how Watson raised the finest hogs, "how Watson could grow tomatoes on a orster bar, grow damn near anything and a lot of it." He also heard rumors that Watson was an outlaw and a fugitive. Santini advised Watson that the State of Florida would never grant a land claim to any man "who has not paid his debt to society," so Watson better tend to his own business.

According to Ebe Carey, both men were drunk. Watson never spoke a word, just kind of nodded, like what the man was saying made good sense. But while he nodded, he was moving toward Santini, and the whole crowd skittered to the side like baby ducklings, that's how fast they made that man some room. And this was before they knew what they know now about Ed Watson.

It was the look on Watson's face that scared 'em, Ebe opined. Mister Watson could cuss him a blue streak when he got aggravated, but the louder he cussed, the easier you felt, knowing he'd end up yelling something so outrageous that he'd bust out laughing. When he was truly angry, his face went tight. That day them blue eyes never blinked but once, Cap'n Carey swore, and that one blink was very, very slow.

The auction room fell still. Watson hadn't touched Santini but he stood too close, having slowly backed him up against a counter. Maybe he hadn't heard too good, he whispered, but it sure sounded like some dirty guinea slander. Would Mr. Santini care to make his meaning plain? Watson's soft voice should of been his warning, but Dolphus was too puffed up to hear the quiet and he probably thought he had this feller buffaloed. He winked at the onlookers and said, "Nosir, our great sovereign State of Florida don't welcome desperaders, Mr. Watson."

Watson's knife was at his throat before he'd hardly finished. Watson told Santini to get down on his knees and beg his pardon. Santini kneeled but was too scared to speak. Hearing no apology, Watson shrugged, then drew that blade along under his jaw just deep enough to spatter blood onto the cucumbers. Looked calm and careful as a man slitting a melon. But when they grabbed his arms, he just about went crazy, and he was so strong it took four or five men to rassle him to the floor. By the time they got his knife away, the man was giggling. "Dammit all, I'm ticklish!" he told 'em.

Somebody run quick and fetched a doctor, and it was known Santini would survive by the time the news got back to Chokoloskee, though he carried that thick purple scar for life. Later on, Dolphus told his boy that Watson reached around him from behind and cut his throat without no warning. Might be true but that ain't the way Ebe Carey told it.

At the hearing Watson raised up his right hand, swore on the Bible that he never meant to kill Mr. Santini because otherwise it stands to reason that he would have done it. Said this so innocent and so sincere, them blue eyes wide, that the crowd had to laugh to see the indignant Dolphus strangling with rage inside them bandages. Mister Watson paid Santini nine hundred dollars in hard cash not to take the case to court and that was that. But the Monroe County sheriff weren't so sure that justice had been done, so he used his new telegraph machine to see if this man had a record. An Edgar A. Watson was the only man taken to court for the murder of Belle Starr, "Queen of the Outlaws," in Oklahoma Territory, back in '89, but Edgar A. was killed a few years later in an escape from Arkansas federal prison. However, an Edgar J. had been suspected in a slaying in Arcadia just a few months before Mr. E. J. Watson first turned up in Monroe County. By the time word come to arrest him, ship him back to the Arkansas penitentiary, he was safe at home in Chatham River.

The man killed in Arcadia was named Quinn Bass. Our House family homesteaded in Arcadia a while before we drifted south to Turner River and my pap had knowed the dead man as a boy. From the point of view of his community, he said, that feller might be better off deceased. De Soto County sheriff must of thought so, too, cause he let Ed Watson pay his way into the clear, same as he done in Key West with Santini. Only difference was, Quinn Bass never sat up to count his money.

That's how word got out on the southwest coast that E. J. Watson was a wanted man, which explained why he come to the Islands in the first place. And even though plenty of other men was known to have come to the Everglades frontier for the same reason, folks begun to worry. We felt more at home with common ol' backcountry killers than with some well-dressed desperader out of the Wild West.

Not that anybody put hard questions to this feller. If lawmen was hunting him across four states, that was not our business. His life was his own responsibility and he took it. If any man could of used a change of name, it was Ed Watson, but except for changing "A" to "J," he was always exactly who he said he was, never denied it and was not ashamed. You had to respect that. He was a hard worker and a generous neighbor, and for many years we done our best to live with him.

Ted Smallwood knowed Ed Watson from their days at Half Way Creek, they was always friendly. Both come here from Columbia County, in the Suwannee River country of north Florida. Ted worked for my dad up Turner River for a while, married our Mamie in '97, bought a small property from Santinis when he went to Chokoloskee that same year. About the only settlers on the island then was Santinis, Browns, Yeomans, and McKinneys. A half dozen families was at Half Way Creek, another half dozen at Everglade, with a few more perched on such high ground as could be found down through the Islands.

C. G. McKinney started out by farming them old Injun mounds back in Turner River. Wonderful black soil but once it was cleared, the full sun killed that land. Burn off another mound, make a fine crop, and the next year it wouldn't grow an onion. McKinney come on to Chokoloskee, built a house and store, got in his supplies from Storters' trading post in Everglade. His billhead said, "No Borrowing, no Loaning, I Must Have Cash to Buy More Hash." Sold extra-stale bread that he called "wasp nest." Set up a sawmill and a gristmill, founded the post office, tried his hand at common doctoring without no license, done some dentistry, delivered babies; the kids all thought he brought them babies in that big black satchel.

Mr. McKinney was a educated man who didn't hold with plume hunting. The Frenchman used to rant and rave about plume bird rivals such as Watson but he hollered *"Eepo-creet!"* about McKinney, who went on just one egret hunt, then give it up for good. C. G. seen all them crows and buzzards picking on the nestlings, figured what they'd went and done was not God's will.

Ted felt the same way about plume hunting but he had a blank spot in his heart when it come to gators. The year after he married our Mamie was the great drought year of '98 when a man could take a ox cart across country. Every alligator in the Glades was piled up in the last water holes, and one day out plume hunting, I come on a whole heap of 'em near the head of Turner River. Got wagons and a load of salt, got a gang together and went after 'em. Me'n Ted and a couple others, we took forty-five hundred gators in three weeks from them three holes that join up to make Roberts Lake in rainy season. They was packed so close we didn't waste no bullets, we used axes. Don't reckon them buzzards got them carcasses cleaned up even today. Skinned off the belly skins, what we call flats, floated our flats down Turner River to George Storter's trading post at Everglade and got good money. That year Cap'n Bembery Storter's *Bertie Lee* carried ten thousand flats up to Fort Myers out of that one hole, and after that, it was war against the gators. Hides was coming from all over, deer and otter, too. Trader Bill Brown from Immokalee, he brung in one hundred eight otter on one trip, got a thousand dollars for 'em, along with gator flats by the oxwagon load. Another trip he hauled twelve hundred seventy flats into Fort Myers after selling eight hundred there not three weeks before. Said he'd brain every last gator in the Glades before he'd see one wasted. Thousands of God's creatures was laying out there skinned and rotting before we seen that even gators can't stand up to massacres. The gator trade was pretty close to finished.

Them wilder Injuns up the southwest rivers was close to finished, too, though they didn't know it. Injuns, now, they never had good guns nor traps, and bein lazy and not greedy, they only took enough to trade for what they needed. They never killed 'em out, not the way we done.

Ted Smallwood never cared to say if all that slaughter was in God's service or not, but he sure had some nice cash set aside, cause pretty soon he bought the whole Santini claim on Chokoloskee. Santinis being one of our pioneer families, some folks was surprised to see 'em pull up stakes. Dolphus's brother's wife's sister was Netta Daniels who had a child by Watson, and maybe that time at Key West, Dolphus said something ugly about Watson's morals that he wished he hadn't. Anyway he sold his place, sailed around to the east coast at the Miami River, about as far from E. J. Watson as he could get.

ERSKINE THOMPSON

✦

Mister Watson had a wife and children but never said too much about 'em in front of my mother, Henrietta Daniels, who come to keep house for us at the Bend the year before. I thought they must be crazy to get into the same bed the way they done first night she got there but she said she loved him and she went ahead and had his child. Also she brought along Tant Jenkins, her half brother, skinny as a fish pole with black curly hair. That day Mister Watson come home so excited, Tant was off hunting in the Glades. He snuck upriver every time Mister Watson went away, left the chores to me.

Henrietta—he called her Netta—was setting there on the front stoop, her little Min hitched to her bosom, and I'm down at the dock helping with the lines. Mister Watson ain't hardly tossed the bow line before he hollers, "Netta honey, you best start thinking about packing up, I have my people coming!" And he laughed out loud about the happy turn his life had taken.

Mister Watson was so overjoyed that he clean forgot about our feelings. I didn't know where to look, that's how shamed I was for me and my mother both. After two years, Chatham Bend was home, the first real family home I ever knew. I seen Mister Watson kind of as my dad and he let me think so, that's how kind he treated me.

My mother was good-hearted, never mind her loose bosom and blowsy ways. When she first come to Chatham Bend, I already been on my own for a few years, so she seemed more like an older sister. With her and Min and Tant and Mister Watson, we made a regular family at the table, we got to feeling we belonged someplace. And here he was fixing to toss her out like some ol' shiftless nigger woman and his own baby daughter along with her. Me'n Tant'd have to start all over with no place to go.

I felt all thick and funny. When he swung that crate of stores up off the boat deck and across to me, I banged it down onto the dock so hard that a slat busted. That *bang* was somewhat louder than I wanted and the noise surprised him cause his hand shot for his pocket. Then he straightened slow, picked up another crate, carried it off the boat hisself, and set it carefully on the dock longside the other.

"Swallowed a frog, boy? Spit it out."

I set my hat forward on my head and spit too close to them Western boots he wore when he went up to town. Scared myself so bad I couldn't talk knowing my voice would come out pinched or all gummed up; I give him a dirty look and stacked the crates, to let him know Erskine R. Thompson was here to do his work and didn't have no time for palaver.

He was waiting. Stone eyes, no expression. Put me in mind of a big ol' bear I seen with Tant one early evening back of Deer Island, raring up out of the salt prairie to stare. It's like Tant says, a bear's face is stiff as wood. He never looks mean or riled, not till his ears go back, he just looks *bear* down to the bone, that's how intent he is on his bear business. Mister Watson had that bear-faced way which let you know he had said his piece and weren't going to repeat it and didn't aim to take no silence for no answer.

I couldn't look him in the eye. "You want me to tote this crate or what?" But my sassy voice come out all squeaky so I cleared my throat and spat again just to show who didn't give a good goddamn. Mister Watson gazes at his boot, nodding his head, like inspecting another feller's spit is common courtesy. Then he's looking me over again, still waiting.

"Well, heck now, Mister Watson, sir, ain't you the daddy of that baby girl up in the house? Ain't *we* your people, too?"

He blinks for the first time, then turns his gaze away like he can't stand the sight, same way that bear done when it give a *woof* and swung down to all fours and moved off into the bushes. He steps back over to the deck and swings me another crate, hard to the chest. "What I'll do," he says, "is train my oldest boy to do your job—"

"I knew it! Gettin rid of us—"

He raised his palm to still me. "And you and Tant can run the boat. I'll need a full-time crew."

He seen the tears jump to my eyes before I could turn away. Know what he done? Mister Watson stepped over to the dock and took me by the shoulders, turned me around, looked at me straight. He seen right through me. "Erskine," he says, "you are not my son but you are my partner and my friend. And Ed Watson needs every friend that he can find." Then he roughed my hair and went off whistling to make his peace with Henrietta Daniels.

I picked up a crate, set it down again, turning away to dab my eyes with my bandanna in case they was laughing at me from the house. At sixteen years of age, a man could not be seen to cry. For a long time I stood there, thumbs looped into my belt, frowning and nodding like I might be planning out ship's work. My first plan was, I would be the captain. Tant might be four years older and a better hunter but he wouldn't never want the responsibility.

That afternoon, to get away from Henrietta, Mister Watson brung his hoe into the cane. Me and the niggers clearing weeds was near sunk by the heat and Mister Watson outworked everybody. Sang all about "the bonnie blue flag that flies the single star," and straightened only long enough to sing the bugle part—*boopety-boopety-poo! tee-boopet, tee-boopet, tee-boopet, tee-poo!*—as he marched around us, hoe over his shoulder like a musket.

Mister Watson usually wore a striped shirt with no collar that Henrietta sewed him from rough mattress ticking. Never took his shirt off, not even when it stuck to them broad shoulders, but no ticking weren't thick enough to hide the shoulder holster that showed through when he got sweated. Even out there in the cane, he had that gun where he could lay his hand on it. Never hid it from the niggers, neither; they hoed harder. "Keeping your shirt on in the field is just good manners," he said. "You never know when you might have a visitor."

Tant spoke up. "From the North?" Mister Watson turned and looked at him then said, "Don't outsmart yourself," which wiped the smile off that boy's face almost till supper.

That was the day that Mister Watson, chopping a tough root with his hoe, swung back hard and struck me up longside the head. Next thing, I was laying on the ground half-blind with blood, and them scared niggers backing off like I'd been murdered. Mister Watson went right ahead, finished off that root with one fierce chop—"*That* got her!"—then stepped over and picked me up, set me on my feet. Blood all over and my head hurt bad. "Got to give a man room, boy, that's the secret." Never said he was sorry, just told me to go get Netta to stick on a plaster.

Henrietta was caterwauling in the kitchen. "I bore his *child*!" she howled, jouncing poor Min, kicking hens, and banging a tin pot of sweet potatoes on the stove. When my mother seen my bloody face, she gasped straight off, "He done that a-purpose!" That scoundrel was out to murder her poor boy, she concluded, having heard tell that he had killed in other parts. She was taking me straight back to Caxambas was what she yelled as he come up on the back porch. "Don't *never* turn your back on that red devil!" Folks might say that Netta Daniels was short on good sense as well as morals but no one ever said she lacked for spirit.

Mister Watson paid her no mind whatsoever. He washed his head at our new hand pump from the cistern—the only pump down in the Islands at that time, we was pretty proud about it. But when he straightened up to mop his face, them blue eyes sparking like flints over the towel, he caught me gawking at the dark place under his arm where the sweat outlined his weapon. He held the towel there under his eyes until Henrietta stopped her sputtering, started to whimper. Then he snapped it down, gleeful cause he'd scared her. He got out his private jug of our cane liquor and sat down to it at a table in the other room, keeping his back into the corner same as always.

For once, she was too scared to nag him for tilting chairs back and weakening the legs—her way of showing what good care she took. *Home Is Where the Heart Is At* was needlework hung on our parlor wall to make things cozy and hint what a good wife she would make a man of taste who could appreciate the fine points.

Mister Watson took him a long pull and sighed like that old manatee when Tant shot her baby calf for sea pork. Finally he whispered, "Mind that loose tongue, Netta. Even a red devil gets hurt feelings."

She pulled me out onto the porch. "I ain't leaving you alone with that man, Erskine!" She was whispering loud in case he might be deaf, and he made a funny bear growl for his answer; he was laughing at us. "You're coming home with me, young man, and that is *that*!"—the very first time since I was born that Henrietta ever planned to take me anyplace. She never even brought me here, it was me brought *her*, and she didn't have no home no more'n I did.

"Home," I scoffed, rolling my eyes. "Where's home at? Where the heart is?" I felt meaner'n piss.

"That nice needlework come down in our own family!"

"*What* family?"

"*Our* family! Your grandma married Mr. Ludis Jenkins that pioneered on Chokoloskee twenty years ago! Jenkinses and Weekses and Santinis!"

Old Man Ludis never come to nothing, I knew that much, Jenkinses neither. Had enough of it one day and blew his brain out. I said, "Tant's daddy weren't no kin to me at all."

Tears come to my young mother's eyes, made me feel wishful. All the same I whispered, "I ain't leavin, Netta." And she said, "Don't you dare to disobey, you are my child!" And I said, "Since when?" That hurt her feelings, too. Anyway—I am still whispering—"I ain't no kid no more, I am the new captain of that schooner." "Since when?" she said, rubbing the blood off my hair too rough, like she was scraping vegetables. "Look out!" I yell, "I ain't no sweet potato!" "Since *when?*" she said. We break out giggling like kids, our nerves, I guess. She hugs me then and cries some more, wondering where her and Little Min would go to starve to death.

I went all soft and lonesome then and hugged her, too. I missed somebody real bad but didn't rightly know who it could be. I ain't so sure I found out to this day but it sure ain't Jesus. Mister Watson was the one cured me of *that*.

"Called her Minnie after his rotten old sister. I hate that name and Min will hate it, too."

When Mister Watson is drinking, his silence comes right through the wall. That talk about his sister Minnie made me nervous and I hushed her.

"Get in here, Captain." Mister Watson's voice was so low and hard that Henrietta clapped her mouth, her big eyes round. Had that man heard us? As Tant says, Mister Ed J. Watson could hear a frog fart in a hurricane. That don't come so much from hunting as from being hunted.

THIS DIARY BELONGS TO MISS C. WATSON

✦

SEPTEMBER 15 1895

The train from Arcadia stayed overnight at the Punta Gorda deepo before hedding north again so the kind conducters let us sleep on the red fuzz seats after brushing off the goober shells and what not. Papa had wired that we were to rest up in the new hotel as soon as we arived but Mama said she has lernd her lesson not to count on any rest in life or anywheres else so we was not to spend good munny on hotels in case something went wrong as it usely did and Mr. E. J. Watson faled to appear and anyway this mite be the wrong Watson. Her husband was Mr. E. *A.* Watson when she knew him. Mama was in a funny mood and no mistake.

Last nite I was so tuckered out I was sleeping and sleeping. Had a dretful nitemare about Florida crocadiles but luckily waked up. At daybrake they shooed us off the train like chikens and left us in a little huddle on the sand. The train gave a grate whissle and hard *bang* and pulled away getting smaller and smaller down to a black smudge. We waved and waved and waved then the train was gone no rumble and no echo only two thin rails like silver arrows thru the sand and scrub. Where the rails came together their shine made a brite point against the sunrise.

The deepo is locked until next week and not one sole to be seen. Here in southern Florida the sky is white as if ashes was falling from the sun. In the hot breze the spiky palmetos stick up like black knifes and the fire in the east sharpens there edges. With the sun up the wind dies and the redbirds and mockers fall still and a parched heat settles in for the long day. Dry dry dry dry!

Well here we are at the end of the line in sunny southern Florida! said
Mama as if all this hot sand and thorn and silence was what we had
pined for all of our hole lives. She did her best to cheare us up but her
smile is sad.

And still no sign of Mister Watson and no word.

I call him Mister Watson just like Mama who is strict about our
maners. (Good maners is about all we have left she says when she is blue.)
But in my heart I think of him as Papa because thats what we called him
when we were small. Oh I remember him I do! Mostly he was so much fun
that he even cheared up our dear Mama. Once he brought toy soljers from
Fort Smith and sat right down on our dirt floor to play with us. I gave
Eddie the dam Yankee bluecotes, him being too young to know the
difrince. Lucius was only a baby then he cant remember Papa hardly just
pretends. Rob was too old to play of corse he was out slopping the hogs.
But Eddie and me have never forgot our dear dear Papa and shurely Rob
being almost grown has never forgot him either.

Plenty of time for you today Dear Diary because poor Mama is nodding
off Rob is serly and I am dog tired of trying to soshalize with little
brothers. Papa gave me this fine idea of my Dear Diary long ago when I
was little. He was riting in his lether book under the trees. It had *Footnotes
to my Life* berned into the cowhide cover and a little lock. I asked him what
his book was about and he took me in his lap and smiled and said Well
honey its a daily jernal. He wouldnt never show it to a sole he said. I
powted and intreated. Never? Perhaps one day Papa said. He warned that
any diary that was not completely privet is no longer a diary because it is
no longer honest and cannot be a trusted frend. Anyway he wouldnt
show it on acount his riting and speling were no good because as a boy in
Carolina he had to take care of his mother and sister with his father gone
off to war and he hardly had no chance to go to school. Taught himself to
read and rite and kept up his jernal from his youth. Mama said she was
plain terified to touch Papas jernal let alone read it.

Rob was near twelve when Papa went away. That was back in the
Indian Nations when Lucius was a baby. Rob stood up to those rough men
that came galoping in. He told em they better look out cause they was
trespissing on Papas propity and might get shot between the eyes. And
one man said In the back more likely like Belle Starr. Rob went after him
and it was terifying that big scared horse and that pale thin boy socking so

fureous at that mans boot. Got his hand cut bad by spurs and got knocked sprawling.

Mama said Papa had bizness in Oregon and might be gone awhile. Oh we were so cold and hungry in those years. But finely our cousins sent some money for our rail tickets back to Fort White Florida. We stayed almost a year with Granny Ellen Watson and Aunt Minnie Collins.

That darn old Rob has acted mean about coming to see Papa. He made Mama admit she wrote to Papa and that Papa never sent for us until she did that. Probably has another woman now is what Rob told her. Its bad enough Rob is rude about our Papa but hes also rude to Mama reminding her every two minnits that shes not his real mother so he doesnt have to mind her less he feels like it. And Mama says clamly I may not be your mother Rob but Im the best youve got. Just goes on about her busyness leaving Rob looking kind of twisted up and funny. One time Rob caught me looking at his tears and raised his fist to me. Scowled something terrible but never said one word.

Rob passes for hansom with his black hair and black brows and fair white skin with round red blushes on his cheekbone that jump out on his skin like dots of blood when hes upset. From Papa he got those blue blue eyes like the highest heaven where blue comes from. Blue eyes with black hair are not comon Mama says. Papa is so weather browned and ruddy that his blush dont hardly show. His blushes arent so comon either Mama says.

Lucius has Papas blue eyes too—what Granny Ellen in Fort White called crazy Watson eyes. He will be the tall one. Eddie takes after Papa more same dark redish chesnut hair that turns gold brown in summer, but his hole demeener Mama says is very diferent. He has Papas fire color she says but his flame needs a good stoking.

I was first to see the sail white as a wing way down toward the mouth of the Peace River. We had never seen a sail before! I wanted to run right over to the landing but Mama said Wait till we know for sure its Mister Watson.

Soon the sail was so near that when the boat turned toward us we heard the canvas rumpus in the breeze. Mama said Just in case thats Mister Watson wed best stand up sos he can see us and not make him go over there to that hotel for nothing. So we stood up in a line outside the deepo all but Rob who was slowched off to one side. Rob wanted to make it plain as plain that he had no part in this hole dumb plan of accepting Papas charity down in south Florida.

It was pretty close to noon there was no shade and we stood in the hot wind watching as two figures walked toward us. In the glare they looked like two black insects a thick one and a thin one kind of shimering on the white sand flat. When I reconized Papa I cried out because I wanted to run to meet him but Mama only shook her head. We just stood there stiff as sticks. Here come our long lost Papa and nobody calling and nobody smiling! I started to cry.

Mister Watson was dressed in a linen suit string tie and black boots glissening and big mustash and sideburns. Stopped a few yards away took off his black Western hat and made a little bow. Nobody made a move nor spoke a word. Im sorry we are late he said after a look at a gold watch on a chain. Rough wether on the gulff. His voice was deep and pleasant kind of gruff but he looked real glad to see this gloomy bunch saying My O My with a big smile for us four frights in our stupid line that dared to call ourselves his family. He kept his hat off but he came no closer so as not to scare us.

I could see Mama yerning to smile back. The new rose bonnet she had scrimped for saying over and over how buying it was a disgraseful waste cause who knows she might never wear it again—that pesky hat had tilted and gone lopsided like it was melting. Poor Mama never even noticed thats how wore out the poor thing was from no sleep and bad nerves. Her red hands she was so ashamed of were clenched white at her waist and her elegant face so pale and peaked broke my heart.

Papa said Well Mrs. Watson thats a fine looking family you have there!

Mama nodded being too upset to speak. The best she could do was give a smile to the strange boy who came with Papa and looked just as shy and scarred as all the rest of us. He was skinny and brown hair near white from the hot sun and very long legs in outgrown pants which came to a stop high above his long bare feet. Probably no underware which I admit is none of my fool bizniss.

I gave this boy a suden smile that scarred the daylites out of him. Went tomato red frowned something terible looked up at the sky serching for birds then faced away from us trying to whissle.

Finely Papa stepped across the space holding both hands out to Mama.

I saw her hands how the poor fingers started up then quit and clutched each other and how Papas hands were closing. All four hands were quitting. Someone had to *do* something. I let out a yip and darted forward threw my arms around our Papa and hung on for dear life. He was hard as any tree. I felt him gazing at Mama over the top of my red ribbon bow. Then he let out a breath and put his arms around me but was too shy to hug his very own daughter.

When I turned around Mama was smiling a beautiful smile kind of crooked but full of hope. I never saw such a deer expresion on that lonesome face. Her smile was a signal to the boys to run and jump on Papa the way fool boys do for the pure heck of it. Mama was covering up her tears by scolding them for rinkling his linen suit but he was happy Papa Bear woofing and rolling around just like he used to. Thretened to run off into the woods with a hole armlode of kids that he wood eat up later in his cave. Eddie was screching due to nervous fright but little Lucius only six was quiet. He let himself be bounced and tossed turning his head sos to watch Mama over his Daddys shoulder and make sure she didnt run away and leve him.

That darn Rob never budged one inch from where he was. Kept his hands in his hip pockets giving Papa his worst serly stare and making the hole family look at his bad maners and his old curled lip. But Rob could not meet Papas eye so he jerked his chin at the strange boy as if to say *You better keep your durn eyes to yourself or Ill punch your nose off.*

Mama warned him. Just a murmur. *Rob?*

Papa put the small ones down then stratened his coat up kind of slow. Well son he said and stepped forward to shake hands. Oh how that scared us knowing Rob was going to refuse! But Papa had gessed what Rob would do and he was reddy. Kept his hand out there maybe half a minute till Rob terned red and that serly stare fell all apart and he shot a despert look over at Mama.

Then Rob came out with that braking voice he had since Arkansas where he first grew that pathetical mustash to go with all his hickeys. *How come you run off? Never left word and never sent for us? Never would of neither if your wife hadn't come crawling!* But that durn fool stopped short rite there because Papas fist flew up and back cocked like a pistol hammer.

Mama cried Mister Watson please hes just upset he means no harm! Those were her first words to her husband in five years.

He brought his arm down and he spoke real quiet. I have some explaining to do that is correct boy and I aim to do that when Im ready. But next time you speak about your mother in that way you better be mighty careful I dont hear you.

Rob had scarred himself. He backed up set to run. She *aint* my mother!

Papa said in fury Sonborn you are dam lucky to have her!

He turned away and jerked his chin toward the lanky boy with the bare feet. This young feller here is Erksin Tomsin. Hes going to make me a fine schooner captain. Erksin I have the honor to present Mrs. Jane Watson. She is a school teacher and I hope she will see to your further education and mine too. This beautiful young lady is Miss Carrie Watson and these fine fellows are Eddie and Lucius.

Lucius is six but Papa picked him up like he was two to gayze into his face. I have not seen this feller since he was in diapers he told Erksin Tomsin setting him back down. Hes turned out fine. Lucius gave Mama a shy look to see if she thought hed turned out fine like Papa said.

Erksin Tomsin shook hands all around. He looked clean and did not smell too bad. His hand was very hard and callised. I hung on an extra second so I could watch him serch the sky again but I let go quick when I saw Papa watching. And this said Papa is my oldest son Master Robert Watson.

Sonborn Rob wispered.

Rob? He was only teasing Mama said.

When Erksin Tomsin put his hand out Rob yanked him off balance but he did not fall. He gripped Robs hand and looked over at his boss. Papa put his arms behind his back and looked toward the gulf and hummed a toon.

The boy yanked Robs arm around behind and twisted it up hard til Rob squeeked. We knew Rob would not squeek again not even if his arm got twisted off like a boyled chicken wing. But this boy did not know that yet so Mama said gently Erksin? Please. Let him go.

Rob jammed his hands into his hip pockets. He looked from Erksin towards our father and then back noding his head like he was ploting his ravenge. I knew what he was thinking and felt sorry for him. If Papa had only sent for us a few years ago his oldest son would be his scooner captain not some skrawny cracker.

ERSKINE THOMPSON

✦

Like most Island families, what we called home weren't nothing but gray ol' storm boards flung together, palmetta thatch for roof and a dirt floor, but when Mister Watson learned his family was coming, he had new lumber for a honest-to-God house shipped down from Tampa Bay. Two carpenters came, too. Used Dade County pine, which is workable when green but cures so hard you'd be better off driving a nail into a railroad track. Best construction wood they is. When the house was finished, he painted her white and that white house stood so high up on that mound you could see her over the mangrove tops, sailing upriver. Except Storters at Everglade, there weren't no home close to her between Fort Myers and Key West, and we got her finished just in time.

Sailing north to Punta Gorda, Mister Watson and me hit rough seas in the Gulf right up to San Carlos Bay. Punta Gorda at that time was the end of the South Florida Railroad, so unless we come for 'em by sea, the family had to go on south by horse and hack, five hours overland on the old cattle trails to the Alva ferry across the Calusa Hatchee. The railroad train was gone back north when we come in. This made me sorrowful. That train was the first I ever would of saw.

Mister Watson and me walked over to the depot. Miss Carrie was real pretty and her smile put me in a haze. Mrs. Watson was kind to me, they was all friendly except Robert, who was a year older than me and didn't look nothin like them others. He was black-haired and pale, like the sun couldn't figure no way to get at him. Mister Watson got mad at him, called him Sonborn or something, made him cry.

We stayed that night at the Henry Plant Hotel. Ordered up our grub right in the restaurant. Set sail at daybreak bound for the Islands with a following wind and put in after dark at Panther Key, named by Old Man Juan Gomez for that time a panther swum across and ate his goat. Johnny Gomez boiled 'em their first Florida lobster. Never took that broke-stemmed old clay pipe he called his nose-warmer from between his teeth and never stopped talking. The Watson kids heard every one of that old man's tales, how Nap Bonaparte bid him godspeed in Madrid, Spain, and how he run off for a pirate. Mister Watson got some liquor into Johnny, got him so het up about them grand old days on the bounding main that he got his centuries mixed up, that's what Mrs. Watson whispered, doin her best not to smile. Bein a schoolteacher she had some education and advised me to take Senor Gomez with a grain of salt.

One thing there ain't much doubt about, that man were old. Claimed he fought under Zach Taylor at Okeechobee, 1837, way back in the First Seminole War. And that could be because one day there at Marco, Bill Collier Senior told the men how he had knew that rascal Johnny Gomez even before the War Between the States, said he was a danged old liar even then.

Old Gomez carried on into the night and Mister Watson done some drinking along with him, slapping his leg and shaking his head over them old stories like he'd waited for years to get this kind of education. He was watching the faces of his children, winking at me every once in a while, I never seen him so happy in my life. He were a stately man for sure, setting there right in the bosom of his family. In fire light under the stars over the Gulf, Miss Carrie's eyes was just a-shine with worship, and mine, too: I couldn't take my eyes off her.

When I went outside the fire light, Mister Watson followed me, we was standing shoulder to shoulder back of a bush. In a whisper he warned that his Carrie weren't but only ten years of age and here I thought she must be going on fourteen which is mostly when girls marry in the Islands. I like to perished out of my embarrassment and slipped my pecker back into my pants as quick as possible. The coony questions I'd been asking about his daughter were maybe not as coony as I thought.

Sailing down the coast next day in a fair breeze and the spray flying, Mister Watson's family all got seasick, and I had to hold Miss Carrie by the belt to keep her from going overboard. Miss Carrie got slapped hard and soaked by a wave that washed up along the hull, but that girl was delighted, she was laughing and her face just sparkled. That was when my heart went out to Carrie Watson and I ain't so sure I ever got it back.

I rigged 'em bait lines. Eddie was eight and Lucius six and them little green-faced brothers had some spunk. They was all puked out but trolled like their lives depended on it, and their sister, too. We was flapping big silver kingfish and Spanish mackerel onto the deck until their red-burnt arms wore out, they couldn't pull no more. Mrs. Watson called 'em forward to see the dolphins play under the bow. I stared, too, wherever that lady pointed. For the first time in my life, I really looked at my own home coast, the green walls broken here and there by a white strip of beach. Back of that beach rose a forest of royal palms and back of them palms the towers of white clouds over the Glades.

Rob was watching very careful how I done my job. I hardly noticed him, I was so busy showing off for that dark-eyed girl. That day at sea was the happiest I ever knew and I never forgot it.

All the way south, Mister Watson told his plans for developing the Islands. Watching him pound his fist and wave his arms, Mrs. Watson said, "He's still waving his arms in that boyish way." She kept her voice low but he heard her all the same. "No, Mandy," he said, "I only wave my arms when I am happy." He spoke real tender, reaching over from the helm to touch her. She smiled a little but she looked worried and wishful.

Mister Watson warned Netta before we left that she better be packed up ready to go by the time we got back. Said already gone would be okay, too.

She had not left. She had not swept up nor even done the dishes. She stood in the front door of the house with her ginger-haired baby, waving Little Min's fat arm at the visitors. Seeing Mister Watson's face, she begun to dither, said her brother Jim never come. He knew she was lying. She had stuck around out of her spite, knowing he would not harm her in front of company.

Mister Watson went up close, put his hand on her collarbone near her neck. We couldn't see his face but hers went white. Then he lifted his hand, turned around, and introduced her as the housekeeper, but his family was staring at Min's hair, which in the sun showed the dark rust color of his own.

Mister Watson gathered himself up and come right out with it. "Children, this is your baby sister. Her name is Minnie, after your aunt Minnie Collins." He made a small bow to Mrs. Watson, who acted unsurprised. She took out a lace handkerchief and dabbed her lips, even smiled at Henrietta just a little. But after my mother scooted back inside, she told her husband, "Too bad the place wasn't swept out before we got here."

I run my mother to Caxambas the next morning.

Mrs. Watson was already poorly when she got to Chatham Bend, and within the year her husband had to carry her outside into the sun. He'd set her down real gentle in her wicker chair under them red poincianas where the breeze come fresh upriver from the Gulf and she'd sit real still in her faded blue cotton dress so's not to stir the heat, her head bent just a little, watching the mullet jump and the tarpon roll and the herons flap across the river. Sometimes she might see big gators hauled out on the far bank that come down out of the Glades with the summer rains. I always wondered what sweet kind of thought was going on behind her smile.

One day when I called her "Mrs. Watson" she beckoned me in close and said, "Since Little Min is your half sister, Erskine, we're family in a way, isn't that true?" And when I nodded, she said, "If you like, then, you may call me Aunt Jane." When she seen the tears come to my eyes, she took me in her arms and give me a quick hug so both of us could pretend she never noticed 'em.

Aunt Jane always had her books beside her, but after a while she looked at them no more. Mister Watson read to her from the Good Book every day and brung God's word to the rest of us on Sundays under the boat shed roof. *Pour out the vials of the wrath of God upon the earth!* Might keep us on our knees for an hour at a time with his preachings of hellfire and damnation. *And the sea became as the blood of a dead man, and every living soul died in the sea!* He'd work himself into red-faced wrath, looming over us booming and spitting, a regular Jehovah—either that or he was making fun of God. That's the way Rob seen it and I reckon Rob was right. For refusing to love the Lord, Rob got the strap; his daddy beat him something pitiful most every Sunday. He never called Rob by his rightful name no more, it was always Sonborn. A joke, I figured, but I could see that Aunt Jane disliked it and Rob hated it.

As for Tant, he carried on somewhat more holy than was wanted, rolling his eyes up to the Lord and warbling the hymns until Mister Watson had to frown to keep his face straight. Pretend to love God same way Tant does, I advised Rob. He only said, If I did what Tant does, Stupid, he'd beat me for that, too.

Tant had a sassy way with Mister Watson, having learned real quick that he ran no risk at all. Just by making that man laugh, he got by in a way I could never even hope for. And the thing of it was—this ate my heart— Tant never cared a hoot about them warm grins I would have given my right eye for and Rob, too. All he seen was another way to get out of his chores and have his fun.

Mister Watson read to us one time from a story called *Two Years Before the Mast.* Captain Thompson is flogging a poor sailor. The sailor shrieks, Oh Jesus Christ, Oh Jesus Christ! And the captain yells, *Call on Captain Thompson, he's the man! Jesus Christ can't help you now!* We was all shocked when that part was read out, not the words so much as the heartfelt way he read it, looking at me.

Aunt Jane did not like him drinking on a Sunday, she told us not to pay him no attention. To her husband she said in a low voice, "You do them harm." But he would only tease Aunt Jane by telling how all the finest hymns was wrote by slavers who never repented till after they got rich. She tried to smile but looked unhappy and ashamed, lowering her eyes when he lifted his strong voice like an offering:

> *Through many dangers, toils, and snares*
> *I have already come.*
> *'Tis grace has brought me safe thus far,*
> *And grace will lead me home.*

Mister Watson never had no interest in such hymns before his family come and he never had none after they was gone. Me neither. One time I asked him, Sir, do you believe in God Almighty? And he said, God Almighty? You think He believes in you? I never found out what he meant. Time he was done with me, I believed in nothing in the world but what I seen in front of my own nose.

• • •

One early morning we was woke by a man hollering. "E. J. Watson, this here is a citizen's arrest!" When I run downstairs, Mister Watson was already at the window with his rifle. Three armed men was in a boat out on the river, and one of 'em was that crazy old Frenchman.

Mrs. Watson was all trembly, in tears. She said, "Oh, please, Edgar!" She didn't want trouble, not with little children in the house. So what he done, he took a bead and clipped the tip of the handlebar mustache off of the ringleader, Tom Brewer, who howled and ducked down quick. In a half minute, that boat was gone. With one bullet. Mister Watson had run them citizens right off his river.

Next day, Bill House come by to tell about the citizens' posse. What excited him was Mister Watson's marksmanship—had he really clipped Brewer's mustache on purpose? Bill told that story all his life. The truth was, Mister Watson skinned him by mistake. All he aimed to do, he said, was pass his bullet so close under Brewer's nose that he could smell it.

I worked for Ed J. Watson for five years in the nineties and run his boats for him from time to time in later years, so if he done all the things laid at his door I would of knowed about it. Plenty of men worked at Chatham Bend at one time or another and plenty more had dealings with him; if you could take and dig 'em up, they'd say the same. He drove him a hard bargain when that mood was on him, but the only one claimed that Mister Watson done him harm was Adolphus Santini, who got his throat slit a little in that scrape down to Key West. There's men will tell you Santini had it coming. I don't know nothin about that cause I wasn't there. I do know Mister Watson got a mule that year and named him Dolphus.

BILL HOUSE

✦

Not long after Captain Eben Carey joined the Frenchman on Possum Key, along come a well-knowed plume hunter and moonshiner from Lemon City on the Miami River. Crossed the Glades, then paddled north from Harney River, brought quite a smell into our cabin. Kept his old straw hat on at the table, never cared about spillin food on his greasy shirt. Claimed beard and grease was all that stood between him and the miskeeters. Had a big chaw of Brown Mule stuck in his face and spat all over our nice clean dirt floor.

Rumor was that this Tom Brewer would spike a barrel of his shine with some Red Devil lye to fire up his heathen clientele so's they couldn't think straight, then trade 'em the dregs for every otter pelt and gator flat he could lay his hands on. Rotgut—what Injuns called *wy-omee*—killed more red-skins than the soldiers ever done, give traders a bad name all across the country. Had him a squaw girl, couldn't been more than nine-ten years of age; lay her down right in his boat and had his way, then rented her out to any man might want her. No harm in that, he said, on account her band had throwed her out for fooling with a white man, namely him.

Tom Brewer were a sleepy and slow-spoken man, thick-set and sluggish as a cottonmouth, but even when his hands lay quiet, them black eyes flickered in a funny way, like he was listening to voices in his head that had more interesting business with Tom Brewer than what was happening around our table. Passed for white but more likely a breed, with bead-black Injun eyes and straight black hair down past the collar. Claimed to be the first and only white man who ever crossed the Glades in both directions so Mister Watson nicknamed him the Double-Crosser. The law on both coasts was after this feller for peddling *wy-omee* to the Injuns, taking away good business from the traders, so he was looking for a place to settle, get some peace of mind.

"From what I heard," Tom Brewer said, handing around his deluxe jug that had no lye in it, "that ol' Injun mound at Chatham Bend might be just the place I'm looking for." Cap'n Carey, a big pinkish feller, took him a snort of Brewer's hospitality that made his eyes pop. He banged down the jug and give a sigh like some old doleful porpoise in the channel. "Whoa!" he says. "Count me out! Man already on there, Tom!"

"I heard," Tom Brewer said. Them other two looked like they expected him to explain hisself. He didn't.

Whilst we was pondering, the Frenchman sniffed his cup of shine, one eyebrow cocked and bony nose a-twitching with disgust. That nose was sayin, *This here shit sure'n hell ain't up to what your quality is served back in the Old World!* But it was plenty good enough for Cap'n Ebe, who grabbed the jug and hoisted it frontier-style on his elbow. Next time he come up for air, he coughed out a Key West rumor: the man who had let on to the sheriff where he could apprehend the late Will Raymond was none other than this selfsame feller Ed J. Watson.

"We heard about that clear across to Lemon City," Brewer said. "Any sumbitch would snitch on a feller human bean ain't got no right to private property if you take my meanin."

"In a manner of speaking, Mr. Brewer, sir, you are correct," says Captain Ebe. "But he paid off the widow for the claim, so he has rights according to the law."

"Law!" the Frenchman scoffed, disgusted. "*Satan foo!* In *la belle Frawnce*, we cut off fokink head! *La geeyo-teen!*" And off he went on one of his tirades, quoting Detockveel and Laffyett and some other Frenchified fellers that could tell us dumb Americans a thing or two about America. (Erskine Thompson told me Mister Watson called Chevelier the Small Frog in the Big Pond. Erskine never did know why I laughed, him not being too much of a help when it come to jokes.)

"*Fokink!*" Brewer repeated, trying out some French. Said the news was out in Lemon City how this skunk Watson were a wanted man in two-three states. Here was our chance to do our duty as good citizens, says he, and a good turn to ourselves while we was at it. So us good citizens sat forward, put our heads together, while Brewer laid his cards upon the table or maybe some of 'em. His plan was that him and Carey and the Frenchman would get the drop on Watson, claim they had a warrant, hogtie that sumbitch, Brewer said, and get his fancy ass sent back to Arkansas, leaving the plume birds to upright citizens such as ourselves. Tom Brewer figured that bringing in a famous desperader would improve his reputation with the sheriff on top of earning the reward.

I tried to warn him there was just no way of coming up on Watson by surprise. His small clearing on the river was the only break in a thick wall of jungle a greased Injun couldn't slip through, and when the water rose in time of storm and flood, the high ground on the Bend was the worst place for rattlers and cottonmouths in all the Islands.

"We'll come downriver in the dark," Brewer decided, "and take him when he comes out in the mornin."

Cap'n Carey's chuckle didn't sound so good. "Mister Watson never goes unarmed and he is a dead shot," Ebe says, his voice real tight. Brewer takes his rifle, steps to the door, and shoots the head clean off a snake bird that's craning down from the top of a dead snag over the creek. He let that bird slap on the water and spin a little upside down, legs kicking. Then he comes in, sets his gun back by the door. "We got three guns to his one," he says.

I sing out, "Make it four!" I ain't got one thing in the world against Mister Watson, I just don't want to miss out. I shoot pretty good for a young youth, better'n most, and I aimed to make sure none of these drunks shot my friend Erskine, who was down in the mouth enough already without that. But the Frenchman called me *whippaire-snappaire*, shooed me away, so I never got to join that Watson posse. Had to wait another fifteen years.

In Cap'n Ebe's opinion, which me and the Frenchman got to hear nightly, we gentlemen was sick and tired of bloodshed in south Florida. What with desperaders hiding out here in our swamps like dregs in the bottom of a jug of moonshine, violence on the Everglades frontiers was worse than out in the Wild West where men was men.

There was no law in the Islands, I reminded 'em (though the Islands was kind of like them Hardens, Isaac Yeomans used to say, they never was as black as they was painted). Of course Key West was trying out some law so Watson paid Santini not to take the case to court. Most folks concluded that Dolphus was right to accept Ed Watson's money but Cap'n Ebe said Ebe P. Carey disagreed and didn't care who knew it, he slapped his hand down on the table, spilling drinks. "Watson had that money on him! Nine hundred dollars in blood money right there in his pocket! And every red cent of it ill-gotten, you may be sure!" A wrong done to a wealthy citizen should never go unpunished, Cap'n Carey told us.

Nine hundred dollars was stiff punishment, it seemed to me: that's what Santini got from Smallwood for his whole darned claim when he cleared out of Chokoloskee. Ebe Carey never knew Santini, never knew how he got to be so rich back in the first place: you show Dolphus nine hundred dollars, his eyes would glaze over like a rattler. But he earned every penny and I guess you could say he earned Ed Watson's money, too.

Anyways, he took it. Maybe he thought the prosecutor might bring a poor attitude to the case just because he drank with Watson at Joe's Bar. More likely, Watson had him scared. Having no choice about the scar, he decided he would take the money. This way, next time they met, there'd be no hard feelings. *How's that ol' throat coming, Dolphus?* And Dolphus says, *Thanks for asking, Ed! Nice little scar and she's coming along fine!*

"Mr. Santini accepted a bare-faced bribe instead of putting that villain behind bars where he belonged," Ebe Carey complained. "I was astonished!"

"Ass-toneesh!" The Frenchman inched a little more of Brewer's lightning into his glass like it was medicine. "I am ass-toneesh from first fokink day I set my foots in fokink Amerique!"

To make a long story somewhat shorter, Tom Brewer could shoot him a blue streak, and by the time they had his moonshine polished off, Chevelier and Carey could shoot pretty good, too, so it sure looked like this deadly bunch would bring Watson to justice. Only trouble was, Ebe Carey had no heart for the job. Maybe he seen that one of his partners was a drunk outlaw with an eye on Watson's property and the other a loco old foreigner so angered up with life he couldn't see straight let alone shoot. Every little while, Ebe described Ed Watson cutting loose down in Key West, shooting out lights in the saloons, never known to miss. Drunk or sober, he said, Mister Watson was no man to fool with. His partners was too liquored up to listen. First light, they fell into the skiff and pushed off for Chatham Bend, figuring to float downriver with the tide, and Cap'n Ebe never had the guts not to go with 'em.

Come Sunday, I snuck off to Chatham Bend, where Erskine and me fished up some snappers while we swapped our stories. I told Erskine how them three deputies was up all night getting their courage up and he told me what happened the next morning. Maybe the posse was bad hung over and nerves wobbly, he said, because all they done was stand off on the river and holler at the house. Chatham River is pretty broad there at the Bend, and being they was way over toward the farther bank, they had to shout their heads off to be heard at all.

Mister Watson got up out of bed and poked his shooting iron through the window. He knowed Tom Brewer from the saloons at Key West, knowed him for a polecat east coast moonshiner, and he also knowed that the Key West sheriff would never appoint no such a man to be his deputy. So when Brewer hollered, Mister Watson fired, and his bullet clipped most of his handlebar mustache on the left side. Brewer yelped and them other citizens near fell out of the skiff, putting their backs into them oars too hard, too quick. What he *should* have done, his boss told Erskine, after he cooled off some and got to laughing, was give them varmints a bullet at the waterline, sink their skiff and let 'em swim for it, cause there weren't nowhere but the Watson place for them to swim to.

When that citizens' posse slunk back to Possum Key, Ed Brewer shaved off what was left of his mustache, cussing real ugly when the razor bit on his burned lip: took it out on that squaw girl of his, knocked her down right on the dock. Before noon he headed east for Lemon City on the Miami River, where he accused E. J. Watson of attempted murder and told all about his shoot-out with the worstest outlaw as ever took a life around south Florida. Cap'n Carey spread his version in Key West—that's how Watson got that name "the Barber." A few years later they were calling him "the Emperor"—the Frenchman said that first—because of his grand ambitions for the Islands. It was only when he was safe under the ground that anyone dared to call him Bloody Watson.

After that morning Mrs. Watson made up her mind to leave the Bend. She didn't want her children risked in a dangerous place where men might come gunning for her husband—Erskine himself heard her say that. A few days later, Mister Watson took his family to Fort Myers, put his kids in school. In Fort Myers, Dr. Langford told him Mrs. Watson was looking too darn old for a woman only in her thirties. Said life in our Islands was too rough for a lady gently reared and he rented her rooms in his own house until she recovered. Miss Carrie stayed there, too, to help take care of her, and the two younger boys were put in school and lodged nearby.

SHERIFF FRANK B. TIPPINS

✦

I was born in Arcadia in De Soto County and went back there on a cattle drive at the time of the range wars in the early nineties, heard all about how a stranger named Watson wiped out a local gunslinger named Quinn Bass. This Quinn was a killer and a fugitive from justice but when the stranger came by the jail to pick up the reward, a mob of rowdies and Bass kinsmen tried to storm the jailhouse, set to lynch him. Rather than see his new jail torched, the sheriff concluded no injustice would be done by unlocking the cell and encouraging the prisoner to get out of town while the getting was good. The prisoner took one look through the window, then went into a cell and lay down on his bunk. "The getting don't look so good to me," he said. "I'll sleep better behind bars." Toward daybreak, with the crowd distracted, the sheriff rode him to the edge of town.

"Yessir. E. Jack Watson. Got it wrote right in my ledger. That darn Jack Watson was the friendliest sonofagun I ever met," the sheriff told me.

At that time, I was working for the Hendrys as a cow hunter, rounding up the long-horned cattle scattered out through the Big Cypress. I did the hunting for the cow camp. I was content with my simple sun-warmed tools of wood and iron, the creak of saddle leather and the stomp and bawl of cattle, the wind whisper in the pines pierced by the woodpecker's wild cry or the dry sizzle of a diamondback, and always the soft blowing of my woods pony, a stumpy roan. Had me a fine cow dog for turning cattle, became a fair hand with the lariat and cracker whip, and packed a rifle in a scabbard for big rattlers and rustlers, too. The Indians, forever watching, would gather when we moved our cow pens and a family would move in and plant new gardens on that manured ground, sweet potatoes the first year, then corn and peanuts.

The lonely day was Saturday when most of the riders yipped and slapped off through the trees to spend their pay in the Fort Myers saloons. Old Doc Langford's boy was also a cow hunter for Hendrys, a hard rider and a hard drinker, too. Walt Langford wanted to be liked as a regular feller, not some rich cattleman's spoiled son, so he led in all the galloping and gunfire that kept nice people shuttered up at home when the riders came to town. Fort Myers was never as uproarious as Arcadia, no cattle wars or hired guns, but that Saturday pandemonium reminded the upset citizens that our new Lee County capital was still a cow town, cut off from the nation's progress by the broad slow Calusa River and falling farther behind, our businessmen complained, with every passing year.

Walt Langford was the one who told me that E. J. Watson, a new planter in the Islands, was supposed to be the Jack Watson who killed Quinn Bass; the lovely young girl boarding at Walt's father's house was Watson's daughter. The first time I saw her, Carrie Watson was skipping rope and laughing with other girls down at Miss Flossie's store. I knew right then that when the time came, I would ask her desperado daddy for her hand, but as life turned out, Walt Langford beat me to it.

Cattlemen had run Fort Myers before it was a town at all, starting way back with Jake Summerlin at Punta Rassa. Old Jake was ruthless, people said, but at least he had cow dung on his boots. This newer breed, Jim Cole especially, worked mostly with paper, brokering stock they had never seen, let alone smelled. (With Doc Langford and the Hendrys, who bought out the Summerlins at Punta Rassa, Cole would make a fortune provisioning the Rough Riders. One July day of 1899, according to the *Press,* these patriotic profiteers shipped three thousand head from Punta Rassa to their Key West slaughterhouse for butchering and delivery to Cuba.)

When I opened my livery stable that same year, I had an idea I might run for sheriff in the next elections. Some way Jim Cole got wind of this, and one day he came and offered help, having already figured what I hadn't understood, that I was pretty sure to win with or without him. Folks resented the cattle kings and their pet sheriff, T. O. Langford, who ignored our town ordinance against cattle in the streets.

One Saturday Walt Langford and some other drunken riders caught a nigra in Doc Winkler's yard and told him he would have to dance or have his toes shot off. This old man must have been close to eighty, white-haired, crippled up, bent over. He cried out, "No, suh, Boss, ah jes' cain't dance, ah is too old!" And they said, "Well, old man, you better dance," then started shooting at the earth around his shoes.

Doc Winkler came running with a rifle. "Now you boys clear out of here," he hollered, "let that old man be!" He ordered the nigra to go behind the house but the cowhands shot into the ground right at his heels. Doc Winkler fired over their heads just as a horse reared and Doc's bullet drilled a cowboy through the head.

At Cole's request, Sheriff T. O. Langford called the episode an accident. Walt Langford and his friends were not arrested and there was no inquest; Doc Winkler was left alone with his remorse. But the flying bullets and the senseless death brought new resentment of the cattlemen as well as a new temperance campaign to make Lee County dry. Because Cole was making another fortune on the Cuban rum he smuggled in as a return cargo on his cattle schooner, he led the fight against liquor prohibition, knowing the "drys" had only won thanks to that shooting death in Doc Winkler's yard.

The Langfords took Jim Cole's advice to marry off young Walter, get him simmered down. Of the town's eligible young women, the only one Walt really liked was a pretty Miss Hendry whose parents forbade her to associate with "that young hellion." This caused the stiff feelings in both families that led to the bust-up of the Langford & Hendry store which was the biggest business in our town.

Because she lived under his own roof, Walt couldn't help but notice Watson's daughter. Her mother was a lady by Fort Myers standards, but the husband of the refined and delicate Mrs. Jane Watson was the man identified in a book passed around town as the slayer of the outlaw queen, Belle Starr. The lucky few who had met Mr. Watson had been thrilled to find that this "dangerous" man was handsome and presentable, a devout churchgoer when in Fort Myers, and a prospering planter whose credit was excellent among the merchants. In regard to Carrie, it was said he had met privately with Cole in the hotel salon at Hendry House, though what those two discussed was only rumor.

Knowing Walt Langford, I feared the marriage was inevitable. Her father's dark past made Carrie Watson all the more attractive to rambunctious Walt. When her engagement was suddenly announced, a rumor spread that "the desperado's daughter" was in a family way. Hearing loose talk about a shotgun wedding, I spoke up, furious, although I'd hardly met her, defending her chastity so passionately that folks began to look at me in a queer way.

Walt and Carrie were married in July. At the wedding, stricken by her big deer eyes, I mourned for my lost bride, this creature so different from the horse-haired women of the backcountry. When the minister asked if anybody present knew why Carrie and Walter should not be united in holy matrimony, my heart cried, *Yes! Because she is too young!* But what I meant was, *Yes! Because I love her!*

Love, love, love. Who knows a thing about it? Not me, not me. I never got over Carrie Watson skipping rope at age thirteen, that's all I know. I only put myself through the ordeal of her wedding for the chance to see what her father might look like, but the notorious Mr. E. J. Watson never appeared.

RICHARD HARDEN

✦

What took the fight out of the Frenchman was the news that come from Marco Key in the spring of '95. Bill Collier was digging swamp muck for his tomato vines when his spade hit what turned out to be Calusa war clubs, cordage, and a conch-shell dipper, also some kind of wood carving. Cap'n Bill just had the luck to stumble on what Old Jean had searched for all his life.

Collier weren't much interested in old Calusa stuff but he showed his find to some tarpon-fishing Yankees. Next thing you know, them sports was in there shoveling for fun and what they didn't bust they took for souvenirs. Folks up in Philadelphia heard about it, and a famous bone digger Frank H. Cushing made two expeditions paid for by that Mr. Disston whose money paid for dredging the Calusa Hatchee. Collected bone jewelry and shell cups, wood masks and ladles, a deer head, a carved fish with bits of turtle shell stuck into it for scales, then lugged all this stuff north to Pennsylvania. Them Yankees had went and stole the Frenchman's glory.

What really twisted Jean Chevelier was a wood carving of a cat kneeled like a man. A drawing of that cat made the front page of the Fort Myers paper. When Eben Carey brought that paper to Possum Key, Msyoo give it one look and begun to weep. He never went back to Gopher Key, he just give up on life. He didn't last the year.

I always liked that cantankerous old devil. He spoke too sharp but he knew some things and give me a education. Jean Chevelier was the first to see that E. J. Watson would mean trouble and begged us to shoot him like a dog first chance we got.

Bill House had been gone awhile from Possum Key and Eben Carey only came and went. Toward the end, as lonely as he was, the old man got tired of Cap'n Carey. "I am alone," he would complain, "no matter he speak or not. Silence is better."

Ebe Carey was a man who needed talk, he couldn't put up with no damn solitude. He was getting so crazy back in the scrub jungle that he could hear the sun roar in the day and the trees moan in the night, is what he told us. He was listening to his Creator as any redskin could have told him and what he heard put a bad scare in him. Besides that he was always scared that Watson might recall him from that Brewer posse and come put a stop to him.

When Chevelier never answered him, only glared up at the sun, Ebe Carey gave fine speeches to the wild men hid in those green walls. Red devils was spying on him night and day, they was up to no good, in the captain's estimation. Got so he'd *feel* 'em, whip around, and see 'em standing there. Tried to laugh real loud and friendly like they'd played a joke to fool him, but they never give him back so much as a blink. Swapped their plumes and pelts for his cheap trade trash and some moonshine, went away as deaf as ghosts.

When he got desperate, Cap'n Ebe would call on Hardens, still hurt because that mean old foreign feller wouldn't talk to him. We didn't have nothing to say to that, and anyway nobody spoke much in the Islands. Nothing to talk about. That river silence closed over empty words like rain filling a fresh coon print in the mud. We simmered him down with fish or grits but he would not go home. He'd want to stay up talking half the night even though he was uneasy in our company.

One morning he heaved up from the table and kept right on going, headed south. Left some money but not much, waved good-bye like his life depended on it, that's how afeared he was we might think poorly of him, which I guess we did, knowing this was the last old Jean would see of Eben Carey. His big cabin on Possum Key, that's all thorned over now and windows broke. Varmints slinking in and stinkin up the corners, vines pushin through the chinks.

Msyoo was old and poorly, rotting in his death bed, with just my boy John Owen and our young Liza to tend him. They would set him outside while they cleaned the cabin. "I am home sick," he would tell my children, to explain his tears. "How you say it? Sick of home?" Called 'em his godchildren, kind of let on how he would leave 'em his property to repay their kindness. And my boy Owen was happy about that, cause Possum Key was our old home. But toward the end the old man never noticed 'em, showed no interest in his feed, just set there staring deep into the sun till it struck him blind. "Earth star," he sighed. Never let them bath him any more, just waved 'em off so's not to be interrupted while communing with that burning star in his own head.

One day Owen took his brother Earl to Possum because Liza was putting up preserves with my old woman. Owen was maybe nine years at the time, Earl two years older. Going upriver with the tide, the boys passed the Watson place and never seen a soul but when they got to Possum Key, first thing they see was Mister Watson. Earl was all for turning tail and heading home but his brother said, Nosir, not till we give Msyoo Jean his fish and vegetables.

Watson watched them beach the skiff. He never moved. They was kind of sidewinding to walk past him before he said, "Good morning, boys. You want something?" When Owen told him they had vittles for the Frenchman, Watson said, "He won't be needin 'em. He has died off of old age."

My boys was speechless. One day old Jean was snapping like a mean old turtle and the next day he was gone! Finally Owen gets up his nerve. "Msyoo Jean never left no paper? About me'n Liza?" Watson shakes his head. Tells 'em he owns the quit-claim now and that is all he knows about it, period. Owen blurts out, "Msyoo Jean was lookin pretty good, day before yesterday!" Hearing his suspicion, Watson points at the fresh mound of earth where he has buried him. "Well, Msyoo don't look so good today," he said. Earl give a moan and lit out for the boat, his brother close behind.

Not wanting to scare 'em, I had never told my kids too much about our neighbor. Owen knew that heartbroke old man would probably die sometime that week without no help from Mister Watson, and they admitted Ed never said nothing to fright 'em. Must of been shock that the old man was dead or maybe the mystery of how Watson come to be there. Anyways, they took off for home as fast as they could row.

Naturally the Frenchman's death was laid on the man from the West who was known to have his eye on Possum Key. Ed Watson was riled by the bad stories but we noticed he never quite denied them. His reputation as a fast gun and willing to use it kept invaders out of his territory and helped him lay claim to abandoned cabins, which was pretty common on the rivers by the time he finished.

. . .

When I seen E. J. Watson next, in McKinney's trading post at Chokoloskee, I never asked that man a single question. Never asked how a dying man planned to spend the money Watson said he paid him for the quit-claim nor what become of that money after old Jean died. Nobody asked Watson questions such as that. Them men in the store trying to stay out of his way probably told themselves they never knew Chevelier, never liked him: he was some kind of a dirty foreigner who hated God and hobnobbed with the Devil and never cared who knowed it, so maybe it was the Devil come and took him. Maybe them Hardens done him in or maybe his Key Wester crony Eben Carey, who's to say? Never trust a conch Key Wester, ain't that right? Nobody suspected Watson, not out loud, that's how scared they was that he might hear about it.

I seen as quick as I come into the store that Watson was set for trouble. If I spoke up and he drew his knife never mind his pistol, none of these Chokoloskee men would jump in on the side of no damn brown man asking hard questions of a white man—that's what they'd say before they would admit how much they feared him. The only one who would jump in was my boy John Owen, and I'd never risk Owen even if I felt like going up against Ed Watson, which I didn't. I told my boy, Go back outside and stay there.

Watson had on the frock coat he wore when he went anywhere on business. Seeing who was in the doorway, he took out his big watch and looked at it, which is as close as he ever come to a nervous habit. As I moved forward, he shifted his feet and set his canned goods back onto the counter to free his hands and give me warning, both. I could feel him coiling. His expression had no give to it at all, he was just waiting on me.

"Morning, Ed," I said.

"Mm-hm." His dead tone warned that there weren't no way to ask my questions without insinuating that he knew more than he should, so Mr. Harden better back off while he had time. I did. I sure ain't proud about it, not after my long friendship with Chevelier.

To save my pride, he offered his hand first and a grin with it. "What news from the Choctaw Nation, Richard?" I was raised not far from where he'd lived in the Oklahoma Territory so this teasing was his way of letting me know bygones was bygones. But them men in the store took what he said as a joke on that darned mulatter and laughed real loud to flatter their friend Ed. I grinned, too. "Indins ain't never got no news, you know that, Ed." I taught myself long, long ago to slip right past and pay no mind to the mangy ways of white people.

Trouble was, my oldest, Earl, just couldn't let it go, kept telling folks he was a witness and how it sure looked like Watson killed the Frenchman. Earl was scared to death of Watson, claimed he hated him, but the rest of us had growed somewhat accustomed to a neighbor who had never failed to help when times was hard. In later years, Owen got friendly with him and Owen's lively Sarah even more so. They knew who Ed was and liked him anyway. He's who he is, who he appears to be, and that ain't all bad by no means, they would say.

Nothing wrong with him that a bullet wouldn't cure, Earl would chime in. I reckon he'd heard that said in Chokoloskee, where some liked Earl because he was ashamed of his own blood.

My opinion? Ed Watson never killed my friend and he never paid a penny for his quit-claim. He was the one who found Jean dead, that's all. He wanted Possum for the high ground and good soil and that freshwater spring just off the shore so he just took it, and with only them Harden kids complaining, folks was content to let him get away with it. No one else would ever squat on Possum Key, not even when he disappeared at the turn of the century. Not till they believed he was never coming back did some say aloud it was Watson done away with that old foreigner and stole his claim along with his hoarded-up money.

In a way that's what Ed wanted people to believe, knowing we'd never do nothing about it. A lot less trouble to scare us off the last pieces of high ground than it was to shoot us, and for a time, he seemed to enjoy the stir he made every place he went. He never learned that cracker people was dangerous enough without scaring 'em, too.

There's a sad ending to that Jean Chevelier story. When the Indins learned what Bill Collier dug up at Marco, they didn't like it. An old Indin burial place had been disturbed and angry spirits set loose because land and life was bleeding bad from the white man's greed and general destruction. So the chief medicine man, Doctor Tommie, tracked a trader from Fort Shackleford hauling his wagonload of gator flats into Fort Myers and climbed up on that wagon bed and give white people fair warning that something bad was bound to happen if them sacred masks dug up on

Marco Island were not returned to the mother earth where they belonged. Only thing, none of his listeners spoke Mikasuki.

That was 1898 when they were cranking up the Spanish War and nobody had time to listen to no loco old savage in queer headgear and long skirt. Weren't two weeks after that Indin come to town that Bill Collier's schooner capsized in a squall in the Marquesas. Two of his young sons drowned in the cabin along with a family of his passengers, and Captain Bill, who hardly got away with his own life, would be cursed forever by the sight of them little hands clawing the porthole glass as his ship slid under—Bill Collier, who never had nothing but good fortune all his life!

That ain't all. Mr. Hamilton Disston killed himself who paid for that whole Marco expedition and his archaeologist Frank Cushing died at less than fifty years of age, before he could enjoy his fame from his great discovery. Soon after his death, his house burned down and most everything he took from that sacred ground was returned into the earth by way of fire.

Not bein Indin, you will say this is all funny coincidence. Indins don't know nothing about coincidence. That's just white-man talk.

Toward the turn of the century, every creek and river was crawling with plume hunters and gator skinners, never mind the sports off them big yachts in the winter and gill netters all summer and moonshiners the whole damn year round. You'd see some stranger once a month where before you never seen a man but once every other year, and you'd be leery of that stranger, too. Never wave, just watch him out of sight so he don't follow when you go your way.

Anyways, wild creatures grew so wary that most hunters and trappers from the Bay went over to fishing. But fish was scarce, too, so some of 'em come south and set their trout nets right there on our grassy bank north of Mormon Key. Next, they was wanting our key for their camp. Anchor in too close, shout ashore at night: *You mulatters got no damn claim!* Took to crowding us so much we was fixing to wing one, give the rest something to think about, but Ed Watson warned they was just trying to provoke us, they *wanted* us to shoot. "Give 'em their excuse," he said, "to run you off or worse."

Finally I sold my claim to Watson and moved another ten miles south to the Lost Man's River country, as far away to Hell and gone as a man could get. Settled on Wood Key north of the river mouth, raised up board cabins, built a small dock, dried and salted fish for the Havana trade.

Bay folks will tell you that Hardens cleared off from Mormon Key because we was scared to live so close to Mister Watson. Well, Hardens was always friends with Mister Watson, for the first thing, and even if we wasn't, we was on this coast to stay and Watson knew it. All three boys, Earl, Webster, and John Owen, could shoot as good as me, and their mama and their sisters weren't no slouches neither.

OWEN HARDEN

✦

Daddy Richard Harden moved south to Wood Key because he'd lost his taste for local company, said his own family was as much human society as a man could handle. But squatters was roosted on every bump between Marco and Chokoloskee, and some was already pushin south toward Lost Man's. Beyond Chatham River, the only settlers besides ourselves was the James Hamiltons at Lost Man's Beach and Sheldon Atwells back up Rodgers River. Then Daddy let Gilbert Johnson perch on the far end of Wood Key because them two enjoyed squabblin, and us Harden boys was very happy because Mr. Gilbert brung along two pretty daughters.

Sarah Johnson was a slim little thing without no secrets: skipped and laughed and danced and said most anything she wanted. One day—we was out running my coon traps—I walked a log and jumped to cross a swampy place, landed barefoot on a half-hid cottonmouth, a big one: I sprang away quick but felt the strike. When I looked down and seen that deathly white mouth waving, I turned so weak I had to lean against a tree.

"What's the matter?" Sarah hollers.

"Think I'm snake-bit!"

"*Think?* You snake-bit or ain't you?"

She comes across the creek, hikes up my britches. There ain't a sign of nothing on my leg, only dried dirt.

"Well," I said, "I think I'm feelin somewhat better."

"Too much thinkin, boy." She pokes that snake till it raises up its head and whacks it dead with one cut of her stick.

Sarah was calm but looked as pale as how I felt. Not until later did my deathly snakebite strike her as comical: *Think I'm snake-bit!* She was sitting on the sand, arms around her knees, and she whooped and laughed so hard rememberin my expression that she rolled straight over backwards, kicking them small brown feet up in the air in the pure joy of it. Bein strict brought up, she kept her skirt wrapped tight, and I weren't lookin: even so, I seen the full round of her bottom, and it looked to me like a heart turned upside down. I loved that Sarah for the joy in her, and all that a young girl was, but I was drawn hard to her body, too. It weren't only the wanting her. Her body was like some lost part of my own I had to fit back into place or I would die. That heart turned upside down was my heart, too.

This frisky gal had a way with E. J. Watson, knew how to smooth him down. It kind of surprised me how shy he seemed around her, almost like he needed her approval. She was blunt! Aimed to winkle out the truth about his life and made no bones about it. He was happy that such a pretty girl cared to hear his sad life story, and it got so he confided in her, told her things he would never say to no one else. Maybe what he told was truth, maybe it wasn't.

DIARY OF MISS C. WATSON

✦

MARCH 2, 1898

What a glorious year, and scarcely started!

On January 1, electric light came on for the first time at the new Fort Myers hotel and also in several business establishments, Langford & Hendry for one. Last year when Mr. Edison lit up his Seminole Lodge, that glorious blaze was the first electric lighting in the nation! (He had already offered street lights but the men refused them, claiming night light might disturb their cattle!)

On February 16, the international telegraph station at Punta Rassa got America's first word of the explosion of the battleship *Maine* while lying at anchor in Havana Harbor. 260 young Americans, killed in their sleep! The "dastardly Spaniards," as our paper calls them, claim the ship's own magazines blew up, but nobody believes this sinful lie.

And here is the third piece of historic news! On 8 July, Miss Carrie Watson will marry Mr. Walter G. Langford of this city!

But but but—yes, I respect Walter and admire him, truly, but no one can say any thought of this marriage was mine. I was simply informed how lucky I would be to make such a good match "under the circumstances" (Papa's shadowed reputation); I was not to be silly about it because "grown-ups know best." I'm not a grown-up, I suppose, just a child bride.

Naturally the child is scared she'll be found wanting. Thanks to dear Mama, I am educated by our local standards and can cook and sew. I have taken care of little brothers since the age of five so I might manage a household if I have good darkie help—is that enough? Am I a child? (I think about my tomboy days and snoopy Erskine, and how Papa promised he'd tie net weights to my skirt hems if I didn't quit climbing trees.)

In the evenings after school these days, Mama tutors me and my squirming little brothers. We are reading *Romeo and Juliet*. Juliet was just my age when Romeo "came to her," as Mama puts it (once the boys are gone). She is trying to teach me about life while there is time, but the poor thing goes rose red at her own words, and as for me, I screech "Oh *Mama!*" pretending more embarrassment than I really feel. Is it sinful to be curious when a grown man nearly twice my age (and twice my weight) will clamber into my bed, climb right on top of me?

Mama feels sure he is a decent young man. "What can be decent," I protest, "about lying down on top of a young girl without his clothes on!" Saying this, I have a fit of giggles, because really, it's so *comical*! Mama smiles, too, but feels obliged to say, "Well, Papa will talk to him." And I cry out, "But what can Papa say? *Don't touch a hair on my daughter's . . . head, young man, if you know what's good for you?*"

I know, I know. It's not funny in the least and yet I giggle idiotically. The whole town must be snickering.

One day on a buggy ride with Walter, we saw a stallion covering a mare in a corral. Walter got flustered, wrenched the buggy reins and turned us right around. I won't deny it, I wanted to look back: it was *exciting*! This body I drag around is so inquisitive! Cantering along the river, a queer feeling in my "private parts" makes me wonder if that "fate worse than death" might not be bearable.

Reverend Whidden has upsetting breath and no good answers to such questions: I know that much without even asking. "I daresay," (he dares say) "things will work out in the end." What *I* don't dare say, least of all to him, is anything about this earthly flesh, this female vessel that yearns and fidgets and perspires in his face, pretending that her sweet virginal inquiries arise from some pure source.

If anybody finds this diary, I will throw myself into the river.

Walter is gentle and he tries to tell me that he will not hurt me, but he can't find a way to say this that doesn't embarrass both of us to death. He supposes I have no idea what he is getting at, and I can't show I understand lest he think me wanton and so we nod and smile like ninnies, blushing with confusion and distress. He is so boyish, for all his reputation as a hell-and-high-water cowboy! His embarrassed moments are when I trust him most and love him best.

After church, he courts me on the old wood bench beneath the banyan tree where our good shepherd, Mr. Whidden, can spy on the young lovers through his narrow window. Is this why Walter doesn't kiss me?

In the evening my shy beau walks me down to the hotel to see the new electric lights in the royal palms that line the street or attend the weekly concerts of the Fort Myers brass band at the new bandstand. The whole town turns out to hear patriotic marches in honor of "our brave boys in Cuba." We're shipping our cattle to Cuba again, not for those cruel Spanish anymore but for Col. Roosevelt's Rough Riders. Who would have thought the Union banner would ever be cheered here in a southern town? The Stars and Stripes are everywhere! *Remember the* Maine! our cowboys yell, galloping through the streets, raising the dust.

Walter says he would like to "go bag me a Spaniard," but he cannot abandon his mother when his father is not well, so will stay home and run their cattle business. Dr. Langford is an excellent doctor, he takes good care of Mama, but in recent years—here's Papa again—his side interest in business makes him pay more mind to profits than to people. "Doc" Langford and Captain Cole are grazing stock on Raulerson Prairie at Cape Sable, where Papa says the horseflies and mosquitoes will show them what damn fools they are if saline coast grass doesn't starve their cattle first. (If Papa's two cows at Chatham Bend had no screened shed between sunset and sun-up, he says, they'd be sucked dry of blood let alone milk.)

Sometimes I think that Mama is getting better. When we first came, she had a queer shine to her skin like a coon pelt scraped so thin the sun shines through. With rest, she has some color back and her old curiosity, too, and even dares to question Papa's views about the War. Being an invalid with time to read, she keeps herself so well informed that even Papa pays attention to her comments. In her quiet way, Mama despises the cattlemen's "tin patriotism," all this flag-waving and fine speechifying. Our brave young men, who have no say about it, are sent off to be killed, while our rich businessmen wave the flag and rake in the fat profits from what the Secretary of State has called this "splendid little war." Mama asks, "How 'splendid' is it for scared homesick boys who must do all the screaming and the dying?"

Although the words "brave Yankee boys" still set his teeth on edge, Papa is fiercely patriotic, but hearing the Langfords and Captain Cole gloat over their war profits has made him cynical. (Captain Jim Cole chortles unabashed that war "is the best d— business there is.") "*Captain* Cole!" he growls, disgusted. Says this so-called captain has no give to him and people see that so he takes Walter along to grease his way. Walter admits that Mr. Cole is a "rough diamond," but like Mama I find no diamond in the man, a hard dull money glint is all I see. Papa suspects these public patriots of selling cattle to the Spanish on the sly.

Dear Papa says he will never salute the Stars and Stripes. The war with Spain is very like "the War of Yankee Aggression," as he still calls the Civil War: the South, he says, was the first conquest of the Yankee Empire, and Cuba and the Spanish colonies will be next. Yet he also denounces Mr. Twain for writing that Old Glory deserves to be replaced with a pirate flag, with black stripes instead of blue and every star a skull and crossbones. Mama nods, swift needles flying. She quotes an editorial: "The taste of Empire is in the mouth of the people, even as the taste of blood—"

"Mrs. Watson." Papa snaps his paper. "Kindly permit me to read in peace."

Mama hums a little to soothe Papa, whose newspaper is lifted high to block her from his sight. I watch her bosom rise and fall in her emotion. "This is the Good Lord's war on Spain, they say, and we are but His servants. Don't you agree, dear?"

"Mrs. Watson, be still!"

"With all this money being made, it's so appropriate that we inscribe Him on our coins—*In God We Trust!* I believe the Germans share our feeling: *Gott mit uns,* they say." Speaking more and more softly, Mama knits faster and faster. "So even when our women have no voice—and our poor darkies are tormented, burned, and hung—we can take comfort in our faith that God is on our side."

Papa's paper falls still as he turns his gaze to her in dreadful warning; she raises pale innocent eyebrows and resumes her knitting. "A brave lady"—she pretends to address her daughter, as if only females could make sense of the ways of men—"has recently petitioned President McKinley about the lynching of ten thousand Negroes in the past twenty years alone, almost all of them innocent of any crime." She is upset that the Supreme Court has upheld segregation on the railroads. " 'What can more certainly arouse race hate,' " she reads aloud, quoting the dissent of Justice Harlan, " 'than state enactments which in fact proceed on the ground that colored citizens are so inferior and degraded that they cannot be allowed to sit in public coaches occupied by white citizens?' "

Papa slaps his paper down and leaves the house. Lucius and Eddie beg permission to run after him to Ireland's Dock, knowing he will buy them sweets at Dancy's Stand before he sails. The two boys twist like eels upon their chairs, and Eddie pretends he is suffering a call of nature, but Mama doesn't let them go so easily: in her quiet way, she is determined to advance her "liberated" ideas, about women's suffrage especially.

Mama says that Indians, too, would suffer "Jim Crow" laws if we hadn't wiped most of them out with bullets and diseases. In south Florida today, there are few left, but Papa says they have started to come in to trade at Everglade with dugouts full of deer hides, plumes, and pelts. The women like calico in yellow, red, and black—coral snake colors, says Lucius, who knows everything there is to know about Indians and the natural world of the Glades country. Probably the coral snake has sacred meaning, our little boy explains, until Eddie scoffs at his opinions, reminding him that he is only nine. Eddie is happy here in town but Lucius badly misses Chatham Bend.

The Indians are still afraid that the few families left in the Big Cypress and the Glades will be captured and removed to Oklahoma. They call themselves Mikasuki, denying they are Seminole, but nobody listens to them, least of all Captain Cole, who declares he would gladly round up the whole bunch and ship 'em as far as New Orleans in his cattle schooner at no charge to the government—"just to be rid of 'em," he says, "cause they won't never be civilized, no more'n wolves nor panthers, and sooner or later they will get in the way of progress." Papa says this was the first d—d thing he ever heard Cole say that he agreed with. Said the man sounded sincere for once, all but that part about not charging for the shipping.

MAY 6, 1898

Captain Cole, looking too serious, has brought Mama a book. In a hushed voice, he asks her to read a brief marked section; he would come back for his book a little later. "Always first with the news," Mama said warily, turning the book over. "Bad news especially." She held it on her lap for a long time before she opened it.

The book was called *Hell on the Border*, and the marked pages told about Belle Starr, the Outlaw Queen, and her life of reckless daring, and how that life had ended on her birthday, February 3 of 1889. Mama closed the book again, got up to leave the room but paused in the doorway when I read aloud from the marked passage. *About fourteen months earlier, a neighbor, one Edgar Watson, had removed from Florida. Mrs. Watson was a woman of unlimited education, highly cultured and possessed of a natural refinement. Set down in the wilderness, surrounded by uneducated people, she was attracted to Belle, who was unlike the others, and the two women soon became fast friends. In a moment of confidence, she had entrusted Belle with her husband's secret: he had fled from Florida to avoid arrest for murder.*

After Belle was slain, the book continued, *suspicion could point to none other than Watson, who was released for want of evidence but was later imprisoned in Arkansas for horse stealing and killed while attempting to escape from an Arkansas prison.*

"Well, there you are!" I cried to Mama. "That last part proves that this darn know-it-all has the wrong Edgar Watson entirely!"

Mama sat down and resumed her knitting. Soon her needles stopped. "No, Carrie, dear." She put her work down. My heart leapt so that I had to press it back in place with my fingertips. Papa was never indicted in the Belle Starr case, she whispered, and that murder in Florida was committed by Uncle Billy Collins's brother. One day Papa came home to their Fort White farm and told her to pack everything into the wagon, they were going to Oklahoma. He said a shooting had occurred which was being blamed on him, said they'd be coming for him. He never accused Lemuel Collins, and never said another word about it.

She held me tight. Though I could not see her face, I could feel her stiffness. Finally she let me go and we sat quiet. My heart was still pounding so I knew it wasn't broken but an awful dread came over me all the same.

Mama said that Maybelle Starr was a generous woman in some ways, by no means stupid, yet very foolish in her hankering after a romantic Wild West that never was. Her father was Judge Shirley of Missouri, so Belle had a little education, played the piano fair to middling, and paid Mama to tutor her in this and that. She wanted above all to be a lady even though she consorted with outlaws and bad Indians.

The Oklahoma Territory Mama knew all too well was a wild border country, a primitive and violent place where life was rough and cheap; its inhabitants were mostly fugitives and savages and the most barbaric savages were white. Negroes had come early as Indian slaves, and after the war, many black folks drifted west into the Indian Nations, where the worst elements of all three races—Mama spoke with fervor—were mixed together in an accursed hinterland of mud and loneliness, race prejudice, rotgut liquor, blood, and terrible tornadoes where the civilization left behind was a dream of the far past, all but forgotten. There was little worship and no law, no culture, morals, nor good manners, and nothing the least bit romantic about any of it.

"Mama," I said after a while, "did Papa kill Belle Starr or not?"

Taking me in her arms, the poor thing clung for dear life so as not to meet my gaze. In my ear, she murmured, "The case was dismissed because of insufficient evidence. Your father never went to trial."

In the old days, Mama reflected, a man's whole honor might depend on his willingness to fight a duel over almost *anything.* I knew she was thinking about Papa, our fierce Scots Highlands hothead who sometimes drinks too much and gets in trouble, all the more so when he imagines that his Edgefield County honor has been slighted. Grandfather Elijah back in South Carolina whom Papa never mentions had also been too quick to take offense, as were many other Edgefield men, well-born or otherwise. When I asked if Papa was well-born, she said, "Yes, I believe so. Your granny Ellen in Fort White is an educated person of good family and the Watsons are still prosperous Carolina planters. Your father was taught manners but his education was woefully neglected."

At the start of the Civil War, Papa's father had gone off as a soldier, and Papa had Granny Ellen and his sister to take care of when only a young boy. Though he'd never complained, she'd learned from Granny Ellen that his childhood had been hard and dark indeed. "You children have to be begged to do your lessons, and here is Papa, already in his forties, still

trying to learn a little about Ancient Greece." She points at Papa's
battered schoolbook, *The History of Greece,* which resides on the table by
his chair; it had traveled all the way to Oklahoma and she'd brought it
back.

It is one thing to hear rumors about Papa's past and quite another to see
them printed in a book. Captain Cole believes that *Hell on the Border* will
cause a public scandal. "They's people snooping through this thing that
couldn't read their own damn name, last time I heard," he told Walter on
the veranda. "Begging your pardon, miss!" He had glimpsed me inside and
knew I was near enough to hear him cuss. A man like this is a born
politician, always on the lookout for an audience; as Mama says, he never
wastes his gaseous windbaggery by confining it to the person he is
talking to.

Since that famous article appeared a few years ago about our refined
and cultured life here in Fort Myers, all our gentry try hard to live up to it,
and dime adventure novels from New York about the Wild West and the
Outlaw Queen are a popular diversion among our *literati* (an Italian term,
our paper tells us, for "people who can read"). Everybody in America
today knows everything there is to know about Belle Starr, who is already
immortalized in a book about eminent American females. "Women are on
the march!" says Mama, waving a knitting needle like a baton. She smiles
at me when Papa steps outside to spit, neglecting to come back to join the
ladies.

Though Walter has not mentioned it, Captain Cole assures us that the
Langfords know all about *Hell on the Border* and are "much perturbed."
(An unfailing sign of vulgar pretension is the choice of a long word or
elaborate phrase when a short, clear, simple one will do, Mama fumed
later, and anyway, who was it who perturbed them first by showing them
that dratted book?) Captain Cole hints that it might be best if "Ed" did not
attend the wedding—here Mama cuts him off. Our family will not be
requiring your counsel in this matter, she informs him, bidding him a very
cool good day.

But Mama knew Jim Cole was right and I did, too. Alone upstairs, I
cried. I'd imagined a beautiful church service and dear Papa giving me
away. How handsome and elegant he would look in black frock coat and

silk shirt and cravat, how much more genteel than these "upper-crust crackers," as Mama calls the cattlemen. And how ashamed I am for giving in to everybody's wishes, being terrified Papa might drink too much, insult our guests, or provoke some violent quarrel (as he does regularly in Port Tampa and Key West, Walter confirms). Heaven knows what might happen as a consequence. Walter might withdraw from our marriage—or be withdrawn, perhaps, for nobody knows how much choice the poor dear had about his own betrothal. Papa suspects that Captain Cole, "who can't keep his damned fat fingers out of *anything*," had manipulated our peculiar match from the very start.

Dr. Langford has been ill, he hasn't long to live (we just hope he will be strong enough to attend the wedding), and Walter wonders if Mr. Hendry will give him a fair chance in the business after his father's death or just write him off as a young hellion. If that should happen, he will quit the partnership and start out on his own. Since the terrible freeze in '95, Walter has had his eye out for good land farther south, and Mr. John Roach, the Chicago railroad man who has taken such a liking to him, is excited by what Walter tells him about prospects for citrus farming out at Deep Lake Hammock, where the war chief Billy Bowlegs had his gardens in the Indian Wars.

There are still Indians out there but Papa says they are too few to stand in the way of planters who mean business. Walter rode that wild country a lot in his cow hunter days, and he claims those old Indian gardens have the richest soil south of the Calusa Hatchee. The main problem will be getting the produce to market. From Deep Lake it is a long hard distance west across the Cypress to Fort Myers but only thirteen miles south to the Storter docks at Everglade, so a small-gauge Deep Lake–Everglade rail line might be just the answer. And who does John Roach credit for this idea? Mr. E. J. Watson! The man who told Walter about Deep Lake in the first place!

Poor Papa has these sure-fire ideas that other men cash in on. He has earned a fine reputation as a planter and his "Island Pride" syrup is already famous, but he lacks the capital, Walter says, for a big agricultural development like Deep Lake. That's why he has confided in others who might be his partners.

Mr. Roach thinks it a great pity that E. J. Watson is confined to forty hard-won acres in the Islands, considering what such a progressive farmer could do with two hundred acres of black loam. But when I asked if there might not be some way Papa could join the Deep Lake Corporation, Walter shook his head. "The partners believe that Mr. Watson had better stay in Monroe County." That was all he'd say. The Langfords and Papa used to get along just fine, but these days my in-laws have withdrawn from him. Everyone seems to know something that I do not.

Friday last, Papa stopped over on his way to Tampa with a consignment of his "Island Pride." Picked up Mama and took her up the coast to a concert at the Tampa Theater. Mama did not really wish to go— she is feeling weak, with a yellow-gray cast to her skin—but she knew she would have him alone. In Tampa she finally murmured something about the difficulties that might be caused by his presence at the wedding.

"He refuses to be banished from his daughter's wedding," Mama sighed when she came home. "He won't bow down to these people. And of course he is angered by his family's lack of confidence in his behavior." She was very tense and upset and so was I; we hated to have Papa feel humiliated. For such a self-confident, strong man, says Mama, his feelings are easily hurt, although he hides that.

Before heading south, Papa took me for a promenade down Riverside Avenue, nodding in his courtly way to passersby. Such a vigorous mettlesome man, folks must have thought, with his adoring daughter on his arm; he is groomed as well as any man in town. If Papa has a past to be ashamed about, he doesn't show it. He looks the world right in the eye with that ironic smile, knowing just what our busybodies must be thinking.

I got up my nerve and finally asked if he knew about *Hell on the Border.* He twitched as if he had been spurred but walked along a little ways before he said, "The author imagines, I suppose, that having been reported dead, E. J. Watson will take these insults lying down." When he makes such jokes, there is a bareness in his eyes, one has no idea at all what he is feeling, and my laugh came like a little shriek because that strange expression so unnerved me. He watched me laugh until, desperate to stop, I got the hiccups. We never spoke about that book again.

In silence, we walked downriver toward Whiskey Creek. Turning back,

Papa confessed that, at the start, he'd been dead set against the wedding, not because he disapproved of Walter (he likes Walter well enough), but because he disliked all this meddling in our life by this damnable Jim Cole who had appointed himself spokesman for the Langfords (Papa made me giggle with his deadly imitation of that mud-thick drawl) and seemed to regard Ed Watson's daughter as negotiable property like some slave wench. Enraged, he stopped short on the sidewalk. "Is my lovely Carrie to be led to the altar like some sacrificial virgin in order to restore our family name?" And he set off on one of his tirades about how our forebears had been landed gentry even before the Revolution and how Rob's namesake, Colonel Robert Briggs Watson, was a decorated hero of the Confederacy, wounded at Gettysburg. The Watsons were planters in South Carolina when these crackers were still ridge runners!" he shouted, as I glanced up and down, afraid some passerby might overhear. "One day I'll grab that gut-sprung cracker by the seat of his pants and march him down this avenue and horsewhip him in front of this whole mealy-mouthed town!"

Not long before, a cattle rustler in Hendry County had stung up Captain Cole with a few shotgun pellets. "Too bad that hombre didn't know his business," Papa said, with a very hard expression. That made him laugh and he calmed down then and apologized for all his cussing: it was too long, said he, since his knees had suffered the chastisement of a hard church floor.

A moment later he removed my arm from his and turned me around to face him. In a tone cold and formal he said he'd consented to this marriage because it would be beneficial to our family. "I accepted their conditions only because I'm not in a position to dictate my own. Even so, I intend to protect my loved ones from the mistakes I have committed in this life." He brooded a few moments. His expression hushed me when I tried to speak. He took my hands in his. "Your marriage has my blessing if you want it. You needn't beg me to stay away; that won't be necessary." He squeezed my fingers urgently in his hard hands. "Please assure your mother I won't shame the family with my presence."

"Papa, I'm the one who was disloyal! It was my weakness, too!"

"Your mother is not weak." He rebuked me sharply. "A weak woman would not stand by me as she has nor confront me as she did."

I wept. I was mourning his decision to stay away but my sudden tears only revived his hopes. For just a moment his eyes went wide, inquiring.

But I said nothing so he simply nodded as if everything was for the best. How that stoic dignity twisted my heart!

"And Rob?" I sniffled. "Will Rob come to my wedding, Papa?"

"Sonborn? I'll need him."

He released my hands and we walked back to his ship without a word.

The old schooner drifted off, then swung downriver. I ran along the quayside, calling good-bye to my father and my brother, waving both arms trying to summon enough love to banish so much bewilderment and hurt.

Rob was aloft clearing the boom, which had somehow got hung up. Being Rob, he probably assumed I waved only to Papa, not to him. I did not stop until, still hesitant, he raised his hand at last. Though they were a little distant now, I could hear Papa bellow from the helm. Rob stopped waving and returned to coiling up the lines.

ERSKINE THOMPSON

✦

Aunt Jane and the family left, went to Fort Myers, and with them younger voices missing, the place fell quiet. Our house grew smelly, seemed to mope like a old dog off its feed. Me'n Rob was close to the same age but Rob was plain unsociable. When I asked him why he had not stayed in Fort Myers with Aunt Jane and his family, he spoke sarcastical. "That's *not* my family. She's not my mother and she's not your 'aunt Jane' neither."

Round about 1899, his stepmother persuaded Rob to join them and attend Fort Myers school. He was older than any kid in class but done poor and give everybody trouble. Give his stepmother some trouble, too, from what the Boss let slip. Though she was kind and done her best, Rob stayed only one school season, so rude to everyone that his daddy took him back.

Mister Watson had went sour, set inside a lot. Him and his son hardly spoke a word, they was like strangers come in off the river just to camp here, make a mess. It was real lonesome. After Bill House quit the Frenchman and the Frenchman died and them Hardens went to spend a year down to Flamingo, we scarcely seen a livin soul from one month to the next unless you'd count the drunks and niggers rounded up for the fall harvest.

Miss Carrie was soon spoken for by Walter Langford who was kin to the Lee County sheriff, so her daddy knew he'd get no trouble in Fort Myers that he didn't ask for. Mister Watson's rowdy ways got him throwed in jail a time or two in Tampa and Key West but he always ducked bad trouble in Fort Myers. Sail up the Calusa Hatchee in the evening, tie up after dark. Never stayed long, never went to no saloons: we done our business first thing in the morning, went on home. In Fort Myers, Mister Watson dressed nice and talked quiet, never wore a gun where you could see it, but he always had a weapon on him and he kept his eye peeled.

Aunt Jane begun to waste away but stayed real cheerful, so her husband told me. She was sick of her illness and did not want to keep Death waiting too much longer. When he said, "You're not afraid of death, I see," she smiled and said, "I guess I had it coming," Telling me this, he smiled himself, though I never knew if he was smiling at her joke or smiling because she could joke about such things or smiling because this Island boy didn't get poor Aunt Jane's joke and don't today.

Once in a while, we'd visit Netta and our little Min, who was living these days at George Roe's boardinghouse at Caxambas: Netta aimed to marry Mr. Roe and later done so. At Roe's, the Boss made the acquaintance of Josephine Jenkins, my mother's half sister. One day he invited my aunt Josie home to stay but not before asking Netta if she minded. Netta had some rum in her that evening and was feeling sassy. "Mister Ed," said she, "I don't mind a bit so long's you keep that durn thing in the family." Everybody laughed to beat the band and I did, too, cause it felt so good just to belong.

Josie was small and flirty as a bird, switching her tail and tossing her black curls. Said she only come to Chatham to make sure the boys—her brother Tant and me and Rob—was treated decent by that old repperbait, but as Rob said, what she was there for was to look after Old Repperbait under the covers. At supper she just danced away when he reached out for her, but them two didn't waste no time getting together after dark, and next day us boys was told to sleep down in the shed. "This place ain't built for secrets!" Josie said.

Josie had a baby while she lived there called Pearl Watson. What with Rob and Tant and Baby Pearl, along with Netta and Minnie at Caxambas, Mister Watson and me had us a real family like before.

Tant was only a young feller then, not much older than me. His mother was my grandmother Mary Ann Daniels. There was Danielses all along this coast and big litters of their kin. The men was mostly straight black-haired and black-eyed, breed Injun in their appearance, and they moved around from one island to another. By the time they got finished—and they ain't done yet—everybody in the Islands had some kind of a Daniels in the family.

Tant was more Irish in his looks. Black hair but curly, had a little mustache and Josie's small sharp nose. He was tall and scrawny. Never farmed nor fished if he could help it, had no truck with common labor. Times Mister Watson went away, he fooled around making moonshine from the cane or went out hunting, you never knew where Tant would be from one day to the next. Never married, never lived a day under his own roof, but he was a sprightly kind of feller who made people feel good and was always welcome. Played hell with the plume birds while they lasted, brought wildfowl, venison, and shine from one hearth to another all his life. "I'm livin off the land," Tant liked to say, "and drinking off it, too." He were mostly drunk even when working, nearly passed out into his dinner plate. One time he leaned over and mumbled into the Boss's ear so all could hear him, "Planter Watson? Ain't none of my damn business, Planter Watson, it sure ain't, but it sure looks like some worthless rascal been drinking up all your profits." How the Boss could grin at that I just don't know.

We hardly seen hide nor hair of Tant, come time for cutting cane. Tant hated stooping all day long amongst the bugs and snakes, muscles burning and brain half-cooked and the earth whirling. Nobody who ain't done it knows how frazzled a man gets with weariness and thirst, whacking away in the wet heat at that sharp cane with them hard leaf tips that could poke your eye out. On top of half-killing you, the work was risky; them big damn cane knives, sharp as razors, could glance off any whichy-way when a man was tired. One swing from the man next to you could hack your arm or take your ear off, or your own blade might glance off stalks and slash an artery. So what he done, he persuaded the Boss how he'd save him money supplying fresh wild victuals for the harvest workers, venison and ducks and gator tail or gophers, whatever was wanted. A hunter as good as Stephen S. Jenkins would be plumb wasted in the cane field, is what he said. "That's right, boy," Mister Watson would agree, "because you are bone lazy to start with and too weakened by cane spirits for a good day's work." And Tant would moan real doleful, saying, "Oh, sweet Jesus, if that ain't the God's truth!" Mister Watson would curse and threaten him, but in the end, he always laughed and let him go.

· · ·

Mister Watson scraped his help at Port Tampa and Key West, lodged 'em in a bunkhouse in the back end of the boat shed. Told 'em the roof and corn-shuck mattresses was free of charge but a half day's pay would be deducted for their grub. Them field hands worked all that hot cane in bad old broken shoes, no boots, no gloves, nor leggins, not unless they rented 'em from Mister Watson.

Like I say, most of our cutters was drinkers or drifters, wanted men, run-away niggers, maybe all them things at once. Anyplace else that sorry kind of help was here today and gone tomorrow but on Chatham Bend there weren't nowhere to go to, nothin but mangrove tangle and deep-water rivers swarmin with sharks and gators. Them men was prisoners, couldn't get away, and the Boss's talk of Injuns and cottonmouths and giant crocodiles kept 'em too scared to try. Knowing how hard it was to train new help, Mister Watson made sure them men was always owin. He never let 'em off his plan-tation except they was dead sick or too loony to work or just beggin to give up all their back pay for a boat ride to most anywhere, county jail included.

Aunt Jane was hearin rumors in Fort Myers, the Boss told me. Laughed about it but I seen that he was bothered. She said, "Do unto others, Edgar Watson, as you would have them do unto you." And he asked her, "You think them scum wouldn't do the same unto Ed Watson the first chance they got? That's human nature." "You've grown hard-hearted," she would say, shaking her head. And he said, "No, Mandy, I am not hard-hearted but I am hard-headed, as a man must be who aims to run a business in this country and support his family." He'd talk about that big hotel we seen at Punta Gorda and the Yankee railroad men who was investing in frontier Florida on both coasts. Them capitalists and tycoons and such used up whole gangs of niggers and immigrants, treated 'em any way they wanted and no interference from the law, having paid off all the bureaucrats and politicians—he'd go off on a regular tirade.

As time went on, something changed there at the Bend. Mister Watson grew heavy and stayed dirty. The crew took to drinking up Tant's moon-shine, having got the idea they were free to let things go. When he shouted, they would all jump up, rattle things around, go right back to their drink-ing. Finally he went on a rampage, cleared that whole bunch out. Told 'em they had drunk up all their pay along with all his profits. He picked a day when Tant were gone, not wanting to fire Tant, who drank more than the rest of 'em put together.

That day I come in from Key West, I hardly had the boat tied up when Josie and them others come quacking down the path like a line of ducks, with Mister Watson right behind kicking their bundles. Ought to be kicking their fat *bee*-hinds, he roared. Hollered at me to haul them whores and riffraff off his river before he blowed their brains out, them's that had any. Take 'em out into the Gulf and feed 'em to the sharks. His own little thin Pearl looked scared to death.

Nosir, they weren't sassing him *that* afternoon! They had played with fire and they knowed it. Only after they was safe downriver did they start in bitchin and moanin about unpaid wages.

CARRIE

✦

Frank Tippins thinks he loves the girl who married his friend Walter Langford!

Mr. Tippins, who might run for sheriff, is in his early thirties, tall and lanky, black handlebar mustache. His black and bag-kneed Sunday suit, white shirt, string tie and waistcoat, cowboy hat and boots, remind the ladies of *Wyatt Earp of the Wild West,* a book much admired by our reading circle.

Like his colleague, Mr. Earp, Frank Tippins seems calm, courteous, soft-spoken, though much more at ease with horses than with me. He confided that his broad Western hat, which provided shelter from the sun and rain in his cow hunter days, had also served as a water vessel for his bathing. (He might still bathe in it, for all I know.)

From Mr. Jim Cole's point of view, says Walter, Frank Tippins would make a mighty fine sheriff mainly because, as a onetime cow hunter for the Hendrys, he was bound to sympathize with the cattlemen in regard to disorderly conduct by the cowhands and undue enforcement of cattle-roaming ordinances. Those men also like Frank Tippins because he is so amiable with Yankee visitors, making a virtue of the flies and cow dung and dirt streets that decent citizens perceive as the greatest of our fair city's afflictions. (Walter says that honor falls to the disgraceful lack of a river bridge and a road north, far less a railroad, that might permit our isolated town to enter the Twentieth Century.)

After his cow hunter days, Mr. Tippins worked at the newspaper. Being somewhat educated, he no doubt supposes that his education is the way to show a former schoolteacher how serious he is, how deserving of her daughter, never mind that this young flibberty-jibbet is already married. And so he speaks carefully, wishing to display his knowledge of local history (and good grammar) in a modest way.

When he arrived here from Arcadia in the early eighties, the last Florida wolves still howled back in the pinelands and panthers killed stock at the very edge of town. Fort Myers had no newspaper, its school was poor, its churches unattended, and shipping was limited to small coastal schooners. "Even so, Mr. Tippins," Mama assured him, "your city seems quite splendid to someone from the Ten Thousand Islands, not to mention the Indian Territory or even Columbia County in north Florida where Mr. Watson's family is located—" She stopped right there. We both sensed this man's craving to know anything we might reveal about her husband, and knowing he'd been found out, he became uneasy. "Yessir, ladies, this was a cattle town right from the start, the leading cow town in the second-largest cattle state in our great nation. The only state that has us beat is Texas. Course cowboys are pretty much the same wherever you find 'em. Called us cow hunters around these parts because we had to hunt so many mavericks that would not stick with the others. Some of the older riders called 'em 'hairy dicks'—"

"Hairy dicks?" inquired the child bride.

"*Heretics,* I believe Mr. Tippins said." A rose-petal flush livened Mama's pallid cheeks. Mr. Tippins glared down at his boots as if he had half a mind to chop his feet off. "Yes, ma'am! Hairy-ticks! Hid back in the hammocks. And some folks called us cracker cowboys because we cracked long hickory-handled whips to run the herd. Besides his whip, each man carried a rifle and pistol to take care of any two-legged or four-legged varmints he might have to deal with. A good cow hunter can whip-snap the head clean off a rattler and cut the fat out of a steak."

I watched him, eyes wide, biting my lip. He knew we were amused but could not stop talking, like a show-off boy bicycling downhill who gets going too fast and scares himself by risking an accident.

"Between the wolf howl and the panthers screaming and the bull gators chugging in the spring, the nights were pretty noisy in the backcountry, and weekends here in town were even noisier. Saturdays the boys would ride in drunk and make a racket, but we didn't have houses of ill fame like Arcadia."

At Mama's little *hymph!* I giggled, and Mr. Tippins glared down at his boots again, convinced he had scandalized these genteel Watson ladies. He was probably reminding us of Walter's youthful scrapes but Mama gave him the benefit of the doubt. "I pray you, please continue, Mr. Tippins."

"Well, the churches were pretty strong here. Which means good strong women," he emphasized, to recapture some lost ground. "Maybe that's why some of our boys had to let off steam. One time they rode their horses right into a restaurant, shot up the crockery. Course the fact that the new owner was a Yankee might had something to do with it. That restaurant closed down right then and there. The owner had to take work as a yard hand. A *white* man!"

"Wasn't your friend Walter one of those wild boys, Mr. Tippins?" He took quick cover by inquiring about Mama's maiden name, only to blush over his own loose talk of maidens.

"Jane Susan Dyal." Mama offered a sweet smile, spreading her fingers demurely on her shawl. "As a young girl in Deland I was known as Mandy but there is no one now who calls me that."

"Except for Papa."

"Except for Mr. Watson."

When Mr. Tippins suggested that a visit home to see her family might do her good, she shook her head. "I'd already escaped Deland when Mr. Watson found me teaching in the Fort White school."

"Before his association with Belle Starr?" His innocent expression didn't fool us. Mama's long pause was a rebuke.

"Before we emigrated to the Oklahoma Territory, Mr. Tippins." She looked up from her knitting to consider his expression. "You appear to be very interested in Carrie's father, Mr. Tippins. He takes care of his family, helps his neighbors, pays his bills. Can all of our upright citizens who gossip and trade rumors say the same?"

This feisty side of Jane S. Dyal of Deland always astonished me. I'd only seen it rise in defense of Papa. Ignoring the man's stammered answer, she held out a tiny sleeve of pale blue knitting. "I'm starting this for your first boy, sweetheart. Papa's first grandson." I recall that little pale blue sleeve because his grandson was never to arrive.

BILL HOUSE

✦

Isaac Yeomans liked to take a risk, see how far he could stretch his luck.
One day at Everglade, Mister Watson was tyin up his boat when Isaac sings
out, "Any truth to that there readin book about a feller name of Watson
and the Outlaw Queen?" And Isaac's friends grinned kind of nervous,
makin it worse.

Mister Watson finished off his hitch before turning around to look us
over. "That same book says this Watson feller died breaking out of prison,"
he said then. "Nobody asking nosy questions better count on that."

Isaac give a scared wild yip, threw his hands up high as if the man had
pulled a gun; the rest of us done our best to laugh, pretend it was all a joke.
Watson grinned a little, but Isaac, bein drunk, couldn't let it go. "Ed? What
I mean to say, how come such a friendly feller as yourself is always gettin
into so much trouble?"

Storters' bluetick hound was laying on the dock. That was the lovinest
dog I ever come across: just so you touched her, she would pick the place
most underfoot so she might get stepped on. Darned if that bitch don't
jump up and run off sideways, tail tucked under like she just been caught
with the church supper. By the time Watson's eyes come back to him,
Isaac's tail was pretty well tucked under, too. Told us later he knew how a
treed panther must feel, snarling and spitting at the hounds, and the
hunter taking his sweet time, walking in across the clearing, set to shoot
him.

You never knew how anything was going to strike Ed Watson: another
day, he might have played it as a joke. But this day them blue eyes of his
went gray and dead. He cocked his head to see behind Isaac's question,

then hunted down the eyes of every man in case anyone else might have something smart he'd like to add. You could of heard a spider sip a breath. Then he turned back to Isaac, wouldn't let him go. He never blinked. Isaac done his best to stay right with him, make no sudden moves, but his grin looked stuck onto his teeth. "I don't go hunting trouble, boy," Ed Watson whispered finally, "but when trouble comes to me, why, I take care of it." And he looked up and down the dock, making sure that no man there had missed that message.

What I think today, the man was mocking our idea of desperado speech, but fun or no fun, the way he said "take care of it" was scary. In later years, my sister Mamie liked to recollect how E. J. Watson said them words to her but it was Isaac.

Life weren't the same down in the Islands after all them stories started up. On our coast it was a long long way to the nearest neighbor, too far to hear a rifle shot, let alone a cry for help. Men knew this but would not admit it, lest they scared their families. I do believe most of 'em liked Ed Watson— you couldn't *help* but like such a lively feller! Some called him E. J. same as Ted Smallwood and was proud to let on what good friends they was with the Man Who Killed Belle Starr, but in their hearts, they was afraid. And though most of our women couldn't never forgive him for murderin a woman, others flat refused to believe he done that: his mannerly ways was fatal to women all the time we knew him.

Ed Watson was humorous, told a good story, and most folks claimed they was always glad to see him. But after his wife and kids moved to Fort Myers, his riffraff crew made a mess of Chatham Bend. He went back to hard drinking and got heavy, kind of mean, and didn't waste no time at all hunting up trouble.

OWEN HARDEN

✦

It weren't Tucker and his nephew, the way Bay people tell it. Wally Tucker run away with his young Bet, come north from Key West in a little sloop. Took work on the Watson place to get some farm experience, save some cash, then start out someplace on their own. Like most young people, Bet and Wally thought the world of Mister Watson.

One day that couple upped and quit without no reason, asked for their back pay. Mister Watson needed every hand to finish up his harvest, which went from autumn right into the winter, so naturally he was furious. Hollered that they broke their contract, never give notice, called 'em ungrateful after all he taught 'em, run 'em off and never paid a penny.

Headed south, the Tuckers stopped over at Wood Key for water and a bite to eat. Wally was still raging about their pay, so when he muttered that him and Bet left Watson's place because they was scared to stay, we never paid too much attention. They wasn't accusing nobody of nothing, they said, all they wanted was what they had coming.

The Tuckers had learned enough at Chatham Bend to farm, fish, and get by. When they asked our advice on a place to settle, we suggested Lost Man's Key, which had some high ground in the mouth of Lost Man's River: across the south channel, at the north end of Lost Man's Beach, was a freshwater spring and good soil for a home garden. The Atwells back in Rodgers River had never used their quit-claim on this key so they was glad to let Wally knock down the scrub jungle, build a shack and dock in payment. We give 'em a gill net and some tools and seed to get 'em started.

Still, we worried. Us Lost Man's people had big families for support in time of trouble. Without that, few would last long in the heat and insects, all that rain and rainy season mold and always that green mangrove stillness all around. The men had ways to fight the silence—work like mules, drink moonshine, curse and yell—but the women, half bit to death in the same old muddy yard, faced the same toilsome chores every day for years with nothing to look forward to. It was mostly women who went crazy in the Islands.

Tuckers was different said my sweetheart Sarah when she got to know 'em. Said Bet had the real pioneer spirit. The husband seemed a bright enough young feller but Sarah found out he was on the run from bad debts in Key West and also from Bet's daddy, having never took the time to marry. Sarah figured he might lack the backbone to hack him out a life here in the Islands. His Bet could take the hardship and the loneliness but Wally Tucker would not last the year.

Turned out that Wally had a lot less brains and a lot more grit than Sarah give him credit for. He was ready to stand up to Watson, which few did, because Ed could shoot and Ed *would* shoot, that was the story. Us Hardens could shoot as good as most but we wouldn't trade shots with no desperader less we had to, and by the time we knew we had to, we'd be dead, said Earl, who knew everything bad there was to know about Ed Watson.

Storters in Everglade and Smallwoods at Chokoloskee held registered land claims, and both them Bay families are well-to-do today, but Hardens didn't want no part of surveys. All we knew was, no good could come from letting no surveyor anywheres near to Lost Man's River. What filing a land claim meant to us was claiming land we was already entitled to, having cleared it off and hacked and hoed for years. Pay taxes with nothing to show for it— no school, no law, no nothing. And it weren't only just the payment we was dodging but the whole damn government, county, state, or federal, don't make no difference, because any folks who would think to live on a coast as lonesome as Ten Thousand Islands don't want no part of the law, we never cared if the whole world passed us by. Never got it through our heads that without that claim we'd wind up losing everything to some damn stranger that aimed to steal all our hard work right out from under us. Show up waving a paper giving him title to our land that we had cleared before this feller ever heard of such a place. Got a couple of fat-ass deputies along to make sure these squatters clear off quick, don't try no tricks on this slick city sonofabitch that calls himself the rightful owner.

Watson was smarter. Watson knew that whoever had title to the few pieces of high ground on the mangrove coast would control development of the whole Ten Thousand Islands. Watson knew that, he was first to see it. He had filed claims on Possum and Mormon Keys as well as Chatham Bend, but the linchpin of his plan was that small key in the mouth of Lost Man's River.

Mister Watson's grand idea was to salvage the huge river dredge that the Disston Company had abandoned up the Calusa Hatchee, ship it on barges south to Lost Man's, dig a ship channel upriver through the orster bars and dredge out First Lost Man's Bay for a protected harbor. Docks, trading post, and hunting lodge, bird shot, bullets, fishing tackle, wild meat, fresh fish, homegrown garden produce, fine quality cane syrup, maybe cane moonshine of his own manufacture. Yankee yacht trade in the winter, hunters, trappers, mullet netters, and maybe a few Mikasuki all year round. That long mile of Lost Man's Beach with its royal palms and pure white coral sand would beat any touristical resort on the east coast.

Maybe six months after Tuckers got there, E. J. Watson spread the word that he aimed to buy up Lost Man's Key just as soon as them conchs up Rodgers River seen the light. Not rightly knowing what he meant by that, the Atwells felt uneasy. Wanting to be neighborly to Mister Watson, they let him know they was considering his offer, then laid low back in Rodgers River, never went nowheres near to Chatham Bend.

It weren't that Atwells didn't like Ed Watson, they sure did. The year their field got salt-watered by storm tide, Old Man Shelton and his boy Winky went to Watson to buy seed cane for replanting. Ed put 'em up for three days at the Bend, sent 'em home with seed cane, hams and venison, anything they wanted and no charge.

Atwells was twenty-five years in the Islands, had two good gardens, fruit trees, melons, all kinds of vegetables, but before that year was out, they moved back to Key West. Old Mrs. Atwell said she was going home to the place where she was born to die in peace and any offsprings who wanted to tag along was welcome. Turned out the whole bunch was raring to go but they needed some quick cash to make the move. So Winky and his brother sailed up to the Bend to pay a call on Mister Watson, have a look at his fine hogs while waiting for his generous offer for that key. Never let on how bad they needed money to move the family to Key West till after Winky pocketed the cash.

Watson was so excited his grand plan was working out that he offered shots of his good bourbon and a toast to Progress, declaring that the U.S.A. was bringing light to the benighted, spreading capitalism, democracy, and God across the world. Said, "You boys ever stop to think about them Filipino millions? Just a-setting in the jungle thirsting for Made-in-America manufacture and Christ Jesus both?" Ed was overflowing with high spirits, Winky told us, and hard spirits, too.

When Josie Jenkins served 'em up a fine ol' feed of ham and peas, E. J. got boisterous, hugged her round the hips, sat that dandy little woman on his lap, introduced their daughter Pearl. (His oldest boy Rob, he come in, too, but soon as he seen his daddy drinkin, he headed back outside without his meal.) Ed gave them Atwells lots more whiskey, told comical stories about black folk back in Edgefield County, South Carolina: *No call to go arrestin dis heah darkie fo' no Miz Demeanuh, Mistuh Shurf! Ah ain't nevuh touched no lady by dat name!*

One time at our Harden table, Ed told that same old story. When we didn't laugh much, he opined, "Well, I don't guess Choctaws care too much for darkie jokes." We knew he was baiting us and didn't like it but Daddy Richard never seemed to mind. Said something like, "That's us dumb Indins for you, Ed." And those two men would grin and nod like they knowed a thing or two, which I reckon they did.

Indins was one thing but nigras was another. Most of the settlers in southwest Florida came south in the old century to get away from Yankee Reconstruction, and they brought hard feelings about nigras to our section: just wouldn't tolerate 'em and still don't to this day. Ed Watson, now, he joked with nigras, talked with 'em like they was people. Got mad at 'em, sure, like anybody, but he was one of the few men on this coast who didn't seem to have it in for 'em on general principles—one reason why us Hardens had to like him.

When our guest departed, Webster said, "You notice how he mostly uses that word 'darkie'?" I reckon we all noticed that, which don't mean anybody understood why it was so. And naturally Earl told his dark brother, "Don't matter what you call 'em, boy, a nigger is a nigger." And Webster said, "Takes one to know one, don't it." Webster's tongue could whip Earl back into his corner, and if Earl went for him, ol' Web could handle that part pretty good, too.

That day, Watson told them Atwells how he didn't need no damn Corsican like Dolphus Santini to instruct him about land surveys, not no more, because his daughter had married her a banker and his son-in-law's friends the cattle kings had such good connections in the capital that any bureaucrat who messed with E. J. Watson over deeds and titles might be hearing about that from Ed's good friend Nap Broward, the next governor of Florida. Yessir, Ed said, he was on his way and didn't care who knowed it.

So they all drank to Ed's great future and their own safe journey to Key West, and after that he stepped out into the sun in his black hat and spread his boots and stuck his thumbs in that big belt of his and stood in front of the only house white-painted on this coast. Yessir, says Ed, I'll be down that way tomorrow, have a look at my new property. That's when Winky finally got around to notifying the new owner that those young Tuckers were still camped on Lost Man's Key.

Before saying that, Winky let go his bow line—let the bow swing clear of the dock and turn downstream with the current. But hearing that news, Watson put his boot down on the stern line that was slipping off the dock, and the sloop swung back hard against the pilings. Still had his whiskey in his hand and still looked calm, but that calm was only just his way of getting set for the next move, same as a rattler gathering its coils, and his face warned 'em that good news better be next and damn quick, too.

Winky's words come out all in a ball. He assured Ed that Wally Tucker had no claim on Lost Man's Key, no rights at all. It was just that Atwells never used the place so they never seen no cause to run him off.

Watson nodded for a while, with Atwells setting in the boat saying nothing that might turn him ugly: they was nodding right along with Ed like a pair of doves. "I'll tell you what you people do," Ed said in a thick voice. He cleared his throat and spat the contents clear across their bow into the river. "What you do," he said, "you notify that conch sonofabitch that E. J. Watson bought that quit-claim fair and square. And you tell him to get his hind end off that property just as fast as he can dump his drag-ass female aboard his boat and haul up that old chunk of wormrock that he calls an anchor. That clear enough?"

Watson's fury was so raw that Winky got a scare: he had clean forgot Watson's quarrel with the Tuckers. But what with all the whiskey he had drunk, he got his courage up and tried again: Only thing about it, Ed, young Tucker has built him a thatch-roof cabin and small dock, cleared a piece of land across the channel, got his crops in; also, his wife is about to bust with her first baby. Knowing how generous Ed could be, his neighbors hoped that maybe he could let them young folks finish out their season, have their child in peace. Reminded him that as the rightful squatter, he would get to inherit Tucker's cabin and any and all improvements—

"No!" yelled Watson. Why in hell should he ride herd on them damned people? Atwells let Tucker on there, dammit, so it was up to them to get him off. And Winky said that sure was right, Ed, it was only that Tucker was a proud kind of young feller and it seemed too bad to tell him to clear off with all that labor wasted and nothing laid by for his family to eat and not one cent to show for his hard work—

"That's enough!"

Watson's boot was still pinning the stern line. The only sound in that slow heat was the current licking down along the bank. Waiting out that silence, Winky said, they felt like screeching. Finally Watson said, "I sure do hate to hear that kind of talk. Pride don't give him no damn right to dispute the man that has paid cash for the title. Law's the law."

Winky couldn't believe that a man so generous to his neighbors could turn cold-hearted so quick but he knowed Atwells was in the wrong. They should of got it straight with Tucker first, they would have to return the money. Being so nervous, Winky stuck his hand into his pocket kind of sudden, and the next thing he knowed he was eye to eye with a .38 revolver.

Very very *very* slow, Winky come up with Ed's money, stood up in the boat, and held it out. Watson had put that gun away and he paid no attention to the money; he let Winky's arm just hang there, never looked at him. He was red-eyed and wheezing, staring down into the current like he was planning what to do with these boys' bodies.

Winky's nerve broke and his voice, too. All he meant was, Winky squeaked—he was squeaking just describing it!—Atwells would be happy to return Mister Watson's money until they got this Tucker business straightened out. Watson shook his head. "That's your money," he said, "You can stick that money up your skinny damn conch ass for all I care. That island's mine. So get your squatters off my property by Monday next."

Winky said, "Why, sure thing, Ed, just write it on a paper what you want and we'll take that paper straight to Wally Tucker."

Ed Watson reared back and throwed his whiskey glass over the water as far as he could throw it, then stomped inside and scratched a note and brought it back. Never said good-bye, just headed straight into his field.

At Lost Man's Key, Tucker read that note, read it again. He looked up at the Atwell boys, who could not read. Winky said, Well, what's it say? And Tucker read it out:

> *Squatters and trespassers are hereby advised to remove themselves and all their trash human and otherwise from my property upon receipt of this notice or face severe penalty.*

> *E. J. Watson.*

Wally Tucker was a fair-haired feller of a common size, took the sun too hard, went around with a boiled face. Reading them words out loud made him redder still. He turned to look toward his little cabin, where his young woman stood watching from the door. In a queer voice, he told 'em how Ed Watson, drunk, took to patting Bet's backside and how Bet had to slap him. "That's why he calls her 'trash,' " he whispered, dazed. "Bet's fixing to have our baby any day now. She sure don't need this kind of aggravation."

Him and Atwells hunkered down and talked it over. "You fellers have sold our home right out from under us," Wally told 'em, making angry X marks in the sand, "and you sold what you never even owned. This is state land, swamp-and-overflowed, think I don't know that? You ain't even got quit-claim rights no more cause you never squatted here and never made improvements." He waved at his dock and cabin. "It should have been Bet and me was paid, not you."

Winky glanced over at his brother, then fished out Watson's envelope. "That ain't the way we figure it here in the Islands," he advised Tucker, "but we aim to be fair so we will split it with you." Tucker snatched the wad and peeled off a few bills before handing it back. "Tell him he now owes you what he used to owe us in back pay." He was writing his own note. "Tell him Bet and me ain't getting off here till she has her baby."

Alarmed, they warned him about Watson's temper. Wally looked scared but bravely said, "Long as I don't turn my back, I'll be all right. Anyways, we got nowheres to go."

The Atwells took his note to Watson the next day. Watson never told 'em what was in it, just tossed it on the table and went away into the field without a word. They never asked him for the money owed them. They set sail for Key West, left it all behind them.

A fisherman, Mac Sweeney, showed up on New Year's Day. Mac was a drifter, lived on an old boat with a thatch shelter. Didn't belong nowhere, took his living where he found it. Just at daybreak, headed north from Hamilton's on Lost Man's Beach, he had heard shots on Lost Man's Key—one shot and in a little while another.

"Varmints, most likely," Sarah said, gone pale as lard. That girl weren't but twelve that year, another year went by before we married, but she was already the saucy kind that gets into the thick of the men's business. Sarah said, "We better go right now." "No," Daddy Richard said, "the day is late. The boys will go there first thing in the morning."

That same evening Henry Short come in. He was looking for Liza but was too shy to go to her straight off, though he could hear her singing by the cook shack. Henry knew that he was always welcome but Earl made sure he also knew how Earl Harden felt about a brown boy sniffing around our little sister, never mind that the sister was somewhat browner than what he was.

So Henry hunted hard for an excuse for having rowed all the way south from House Hammock, though it was true he'd forgot his pocketknife or some fool thing. We helped him off his hook as best we could but Earl was nervous, finding trouble every place he looked. Earl said, "Your knife ain't waitin on you here, boy, and our sister neither." Daddy Richard asked had Henry noticed anything at Watson's on his way downriver? Henry said he seen no boat, no sign of anyone: the Bend was silent as he drifted by. Mac Sweeney moaned, "Oh Jesus, boys! It's like I told you!"

We crossed to Lost Man's first thing in the morning. We come too late. Winding in around the orster bars, Henry pointed at something laying over in the shallows.

"Oh Christ, what's that?" Earl yelped.

"Shut up, Earl," I said. I felt sick. I didn't want to look.

Wally's hair was lifting and his eyes ringed black with tiny mud snails were sunken back into his head. Scared of his touch, Webster reached deep for a boot, aiming to draw him alongside, but the boot leather was slick as grease from the salt water and it slipped away. I jumped over the side, took a deep breath, and seized him up under the arms. Walking backwards, hauling him out onto the sand, I seen the shadow of a shark move off the bar into the channel.

Dead blood was still leaking from a hole blowed in his chest. "Oh Christ!" Earl said again and begun coughing. Webster looked peculiar for a dark-skinned feller, kind of a bad gray. Henry's light skin had went a little green and I was fighting hard to keep my grits down. We hollered and swore to keep from crying, all but Henry, who was not free to join in, not with Earl watching.

Near the cabin was a silver driftwood tree and near the tree Wally's net needle lay in the gill net we had lent him and blackish blood was caked thick in the mesh. His sloop rode peaceful on her mooring. No sign of Bet. We hoped she had run off and hid but no voice answered when we hollered, only the whistle of black orster birds out on the bar.

We rolled Wally in sail canvas, hoisted him into the boat. Hunting for Bet, we crisscrossed the island back and forth, even searched the end of Lost Man's Beach, across the Channel. The long day passed. We called and called. Once a hoot owl answered, way back in the trees. Dusk was coming and dark overtook us before we reached Wood Key.

Sarah stared at the boots that stuck out from the canvas.

"How come you brought him back?"

"Didn't want to leave him there alone, I reckon."

"You left Bet alone." First time I ever seen her cry.

It was Sarah's idea we should take Wally back, bury him close to his little shack; that's why he was still with us in the boat next morning. Crossing the flats, I seen a keel track in the marl. My heart give a skip just as Henry said, "Mist' Watson." Most Island men had learned that keel mark. Never knew when they might need to know he was around someplace.

I felt Bet near and pretty quick I seen her. Over the night she had surfaced in a backwater behind the point. Face down and all silted up ain't no damned way to find a good young woman big with child whose smile you won't never forget from the last time you seen it. Using an oar, Webster drew her toward the boat, but she got loose, rolled over very slow. Them little snails was pretty close to finished with Bet's face. Without no lips, her white buck teeth made her look starved as a dead pony. Only mercy was, no eyes was left to stare.

This time we all jumped into the shallows, very angry. Earl grabbed an ankle, taking no time to get a proper hold under the arms. Earl is always in a rush, that's the life itch in him. Not wanting a scrap with him that day, I took the other ankle, but when we hauled, her head went under and her shift hitched high on the oarlock coming in, laying bare her blue-white thighs and hair and swollen belly. The careless way we handled her made me ashamed. When I yanked that old rag of a shift back down, it tore half off her hips. "Show some respect!" Earl hollered. We almost capsized the damn boat, dragging her in.

Much too rough, Earl rolled Tucker out of his canvas, flung the canvas across to me, firing orders as usual. "Make her decent!" he yells. But what was indecent mostly come from his own hurry. To Henry, he says, "Don't go lookin up her shift, you hear me, boy?"

Henry squints past him like he's studyin the weather in the summer distance. No more expression on his face than on the dead man layin in the bilges. But Webster who is generally real quiet said to Earl, "We all hear you and we seen you lookin, too. White boys only, right?"

"This ain't no time for this," I said.

We hunted around till we come up with Wally's shovel, dug two pits in the sea grape above tide line, stuck two stick crosses in the sand. We lowered Bet first, unborn babe and all. Earl hesitated to throw fill onto her face, he looked real shaky. When Webster cut the back out of his shirt, laid it across the head, Earl grumped, "Smelly damn ol' shirt. That ain't no good." And Webster snapped, "Just shovel."

Back at the boat, I took a deep breath, took the dead man underneath the arms. Webster and Henry took his ankles. His clothes had dried and warmed a little, but under that warmth he was cold, stiff, smelly meat, like a dead porpoise on the tide line after a storm.

A dead man totes a whole lot heavier than a live one, who knows why. I hoisted the shoulders so's to clear the gunwales; his dank hair flopped over his face, his body sighed. I held a breath against the sudden heavy stink.

We laid him on the ground beside the hole. His eyes looked bruised and the lids sagged open like he didn't trust us. I felt ashamed of humankind, myself included. I said, "We come too late, Wally. I sure am sorry." Them words twisted right out of me, tears right behind 'em; I was ready to fight Earl if he noticed, but he was busy hawking up the taste of the dead man's smell and spitting it away. Couldn't hurt Wally's feelings none but that hawking turned my stomach. I grabbed the shovel back from him and covered Wally as fast as I could swing it, covered that puffed face staring at the sky. With one shovelful, I closed them eyes, filled that dry mouth with sand, which shook me so bad that I let loose a groan. The next load I shot straight at Earl's belly to wipe away his smirk and he knew better than to say one word.

I have buried men since and buried children, but that young couple with their unborn child was the saddest sight I ever care to see. When the graves was banked, I jammed the shovel blade into the sand with all my might.

Webster growled a Webster kind of prayer: "God Almighty, here is two more meek that has inherited Your earth." Webster spoke in his own peculiar way; we never did learn how to hear him. Sudden and loud, Earl hee-hawed at his brother's prayer, shaking his head over something or other as Webster watched him.

Richard Harden always claimed that Watson could not help himself, being doomed by accursed fate. In later years that give Sarah her excuse for forgiving him a little bit for what he done here. Ain't doom the same as fate? I ain't sure what Daddy Richard meant, unless God put a curse on E. J. Watson. But if God done that, then who was we to blame for them dreadful murders?

One funny thing: along the shore we came across two sets of fresh prints. Who did them other prints belong to? Cause we knew Rob Watson was a friend to Tuckers, he even come here once to see how they was getting on, also to warn 'em.

Mac Sweeney had left for Key West and two deputies showed up a few days later with orders to deputize them Wood Key boys who found the bodies. Earl Harden advised the deputies that foul deeds had been done and that E. J. Watson was the only man suspected. He never told about the second set of tracks we found crossing the Key.

Webster went out the back door as the law come in the front, that was *his* answer. To me, they said, "How about you? Two dollars just to show us

where he's at?" I said, "Nosir, I sure won't." I felt sick angry at Ed Watson
but I didn't want no part of it. Daddy Richard told 'em nothing one way or
the other. Cornerin Pap was like tryin to nail a orster to the floor. He give a
kind of muddy groan, mumbling and carrying on about deputizin boys too
young to die and such as that, but I believe what worried him the most was
Hardens takin the law's side against a neighbor.

Pap said, "You fellers might could deputize that female settin over there
fixin them snap beans. She can shoot a knot out of wet rope and won't settle for no ifs, ands, nor buts." Mama banged her pot down, went outside,
and the two deputies, who was scared of Watson and sufferin from ragged
nerves, advised Pap that they was here to solve a case of cold-blood murder
and had no time for no damn mulatta jokes.

I said, "Better look out who you go calling mulatta," but Pap hushed me.
"Now don't you fellers get us wrong," he said. "This family don't hold with
cold-blood murder of no race, color, nor creed." Said young folks was
bloody murdered, yep, they sure had that part right, but he ain't seen no
evidence it was Ed Watson. "Hell, Pap," Earl yelled, "we seen his keel track!
Ain't that proof?" And Daddy said, "Might been proof, but like I say, I never
seen it."

Scoffing, Earl stepped forward and got deputized. Once he had his badge
pinned on, he told his feller deputies, "Looks like my brothers might be
scared of Watson."

Pap grabbed my wrist before I went for him. "You said a mouthful that
time, Earl," Pap told him in a dead voice. "You might be correct, who is to
know? But the law here ain't got nothin on Ed Watson, and you will have to
live with him after these fellers are gone."

Come time to leave for Chatham River, their new deputy had already
begun to sweat. Looked back over his shoulder, hoping his daddy would for-
bid his boy to go. Pap took no notice, just set there in the sun, whittling him
a new net needle out of red mangrove. Rest of his life, Pap was civil to Earl
but he was finished with him. That's the way our daddy was. Never got
angry, just dropped bad stuff behind him like he'd took a crap. Life was too
short to waste time looking back, he said, or too far forward either.

When the law dropped him off on their way back south, Earl was raring
to tell every last thing he seen. Evidence in the case was confidential,
Deputy Earl advised us, but quick as a goose squirt, it come out: Watson
and his son was gone, his house was empty. On the floor they found Wally

Tucker's crumped-up message, but not wishing to admit they could not read even big letters printed out with pencil, the deputies never bothered with it. "Handwrit note don't count for nothin in no court of law"—that's what they told Earl. Even so, Earl had the sense to save it.

Sarah read it out loud and got furious before she finished. "Might mean nothing to deputies but it sure is proof that Wally Tucker was the fool who got Bet murdered!"

> MISTER WATSON WE WILL STAY
> ON THIS HERE CAY TILL OUR CHILD IS BORN
> COME HELL OR HIGH WATER

Hell showed up quicker than poor Wally expected, and high water, too.

ERSKINE THOMPSON

◆

First day of January, 1901, sailin north from Lost Man's Beach, I seen the black smoke of a cane fire from way out in the Gulf, smelled that burned sweetness in the air like roasting corn. That fire was still going strong when I passed Mormon Key and tacked into the river.

At the Bend, the trees was just a-shimmering in that heat, and the hawks and buzzards comin in from as far away as cane smoke can be seen to feed on small varmints killed or flushed from cover.

What was burning was our thirty-acre field. This year we was too broke to hire outside labor for the harvest season, so there was only the Boss and me and Rob, and maybe Tant if we were lucky. *The Boss must of gone crazy—* that's the way I figured. He was firing a cane field we could never harvest.

Tying up, I seen no sign of Rob, let alone Tant. All I seen was Mister Watson on the half run in his field setting fires like he'd heard a shout from Hell; he was drifting over the black ground in a ring of fire like a giant wind-swirled cinder. Had his shotgun in his other hand, and that made no sense neither, cause he hadn't lit fires on three sides the way we done when we wanted a shot at any critters that might run before the flames. Something was on the prowl here in the hellish air and spooky light where the sun pierced the smoke shadow. I never hollered or went near the house, just waited on the dock.

Toward nightfall, with his fires dying down, he come in from the field, eyes darting everywhere. "Who's aboard that boat?" He was coughing hard, fighting for breath. He went on past, then swung that gun around quick as a cottonmouth, like he meant to wipe me out. I yell out, "Hold on, Mister Ed! I come alone!" but he don't lower the muzzle. Don't like turnin his back to me but minds his back turned to the schooner even more. And damned if he don't go aboard, checking on me over his shoulder, and poke that shotgun into every cranny on that boat, from stem to stern.

Coming out, he growls, "No harvest, boy. I'm broke." He explains the fire: if the cane is left unharvested, with no burn-off, next year's crop would be choked out. We walked up to the house, me in the front.

Tant and Josie were gone. Rob never come to supper. Me and Mister Watson ate Tant's cold venison, left on the hearth. No bread baked, no greens. No life in that house, just us two men chewing old cold meat not smoked through proper because Tant never banked the cooking fire, just let it die, as usual; damned meat had a purply look and a rank smell to it. I never get none down, that's how dry my mouth was. Mister Watson threw it to the dogs and we et grits. He gets the bottle out, then forgets about it, just sits there panting, staring out over the river. And right then I begun to know that our good old days at Chatham Bend was over and I'd better be thinking about moving on. I was near to twenty and had my eye on young Gert Hamilton at Lost Man's Beach who was boarding at Roe's up to Caxambas while she went to school.

Mister Watson coughs and hacks. He says, I am sorry for the way I acted, Erskine. You are my partner, are you not? Yessir, say I, very serious and proud. Then he tells me he is leaving in the morning and all about what he wants done in his absence. He nods his head awhile, and after that, starts in confiding about his bygone life.

As a young feller in Columbia County, Mister Watson had a good farm leased, made a fine crop, but lost his first wife that was Rob's mama in childbirth, broke his knees in a bad fall, was bedridden while his land went all to hell, drank himself senseless, got in bad trouble. Never said what the trouble was and I never asked him. "Matter of honor," Mister Watson said. So him and his new wife head west with the kids. Left by night and lit out northward for the Georgia border.

The next spring—this was 1887—they sharecropped a farm in Franklin County, Arkansas. Got his crop in and went on west into the Injun Nations, Oklahoma Territory—the first place he felt real safe, he said, because Injuns figured that any white in trouble with other whites must have some good in him. Plenty of renegade Injuns, too, and the worst of 'em, Mister

Watson said, was Old Tom Starr, head of a Cherokee clan on the South Canadian River where the Creek, Choctaw, and Cherokee Nations come together.

"Tom Starr was a huge man and he killed too many. Got a taste for it, know what I mean, boy?" Mister Watson nodded, kind of sarcastic, when I piped up real eager, "I sure do!" In one feud Tom Starr and his boys set fire to a cabin and a little boy five years old run out and Tom Starr picked him up and tossed him back into the flames. "I don't know that I could do a deed like that, how about you, Erskine?" Mister Watson was frowning like he'd thought hard on this question before deciding.

"Nosir," I said.

" 'Nosir,' he says."

So Old Tom Starr asked a white Christian acquaintance if the white man's God would ever forgive him for that black deed he done, and this Christian said, "Nosir, Chief, I don't reckon He would." Mister Watson's queer laugh come all the way up from his boots, and that laugh taught me once and for all this man's hard lesson, that our human free-for-all on God's sweet earth never meant no more'n a hatch of insects in the thin smoke of their millions rising and falling in the river twilight.

Right away he was looking grim again. "I'm not so sure I'd want to give that answer to a black-hearted devil like Tom Starr. What's your opinion on that question, Erskine?"

"Nosir," I said.

"Nosir is right." He was peering into my face, shaking his head. "Looks like I will have to do the laughing for us both," he muttered.

A woman named Myra Maybelle Reed lived with Tom Starr's son. Mister Watson was there only a year when somebody put a load of buckshot into Maybelle, shot her out of the saddle on a raw cold day of February '89 and give her another charge of turkey shot in the face and neck right where she was laying in the muddy road.

At her funeral, Jim Starr accused Mister Watson of murdering his woman. They tied his hands and rode him over to federal court in Arkansas but after two weeks he was released for want of evidence. Went on home, got framed by friends of Belle, jailed for a horse thief but escaped from prison, headed back east. That's how he wound up in southwest Florida, which was about the last place left where a man could farm in peace and quiet, and no questions asked. Only thing, going through Arcadia, a killer named Quinn Bass pulled a knife in a saloon. "Gave me no choice. I had to stop him."

Mister Watson cocked his head to see how I was taking his life story. He never said who killed Belle Starr nor what "stopped" meant for Bass.

"Any questions, boy?" Them blue eyes dared me.

"I was only wonderin if that Quinn Bass feller died."

"Well, death was the coroner's conclusion."

Mister Watson never talked no more that evening. For a long while, he sat leaning forward with his hands on his knees like he aimed to jump right up and leave only couldn't remember where he had to go. But what he'd told gave me plenty to think about while me n' him set at his table in the lamplight, waiting for Rob to come and get his supper. He never come.

I went outside for a moonlight leak, feeling small and lost under cold stars like I had awoke in that night country where I will go alone like Mister Watson, knowin him and me won't get no help from God.

I stared again. The schooner was gone, drifted away, like I had forgot to tie her up. I backed away, wanting to run, but there was nowhere but them blackened fields to run to. The earth was ringing in a silver light, the stars gone wild.

FRANK B. TIPPINS

✦

In the first days of 1901, a young feller from the telegraph came by my office with a request from the Monroe County sheriff that Lee County detain an E. A. or E. J. Watson as the leading suspect in the murder of two Key West runaways at Lost Man's River.

In order to locate Mr. Watson, the first place I would have to go was his own house. To console myself after Carrie's marriage—to pick the scab, said sly Jim Cole, who saw right through me—I'd continued paying calls on Mrs. Watson after she and the boys moved to Anderson Avenue because Carrie came to visit every day. Ashamed of myself, I observed young Mrs. Langford for signs of discontent with Walter while listening carefully for any stray word that might feed my nagging curiosity about her father. At that time, I had glimpsed that man just once and from behind, a broad-backed figure in a black Western hat and well-cut suit, walking down First Street to the dock one early morning.

Ordinarily I walked unarmed around Fort Myers. That day I strapped a pistol underneath my coat. With Miss Carrie's mother failing fast, it seemed wrong to intrude on that sad family, and halfway there, I decided it made more sense to find Walt Langford and see what information he could give me, accepting the risk that he might warn his father-in-law. Circling back toward Langford & Hendry, I wondered if I was afraid, then caught myself brooding yet again about how a bad drinker like Walt Langford might abuse a girl—a woman—who was no more than a child. This rumination made me shift my wad and spit my old regret into the dust, making old Mrs. Summerlin—*Good morning, ma'am!*—hop sideways on the boardwalk, pretending I was out to soil her shoe.

Like all of our town's small emporiums, Langford & Hendry down on First Street was a frame building, slapped up quick on a mud street in a weedy line of ramshackle storefronts, livery stables, and blacksmith sheds—downtown in a cow town, as Cole said. Outside the door which led to the upstairs offices hunched Billie Conapatchie, a Mikasuki Creek raised up and educated by the Hendry family. Billie wore a bowler hat instead of the traditional bright turban; his puff-sleeve calico Injun shirt with bright red and yellow ribbons had been stuffed into old britches which stopped well short of his scarred ankles and scuffed feet. Squatting at favored lookout points, he spied on white-man life while awaiting the next public meeting or church service, or funeral or theatrical or wedding. Despite faithful attendance at these functions, he understood scarcely a word—or so he pretended, having come close to execution by his people for learning his mite of English at Fort Myers School. What passed through Billie Conapatchie's head was a great mystery, but I suspected that, even as an outcast, he served his people as sentinel crow, alert for some dangerous shift in course these white men might be making. At the same time, he had never lost his deep indifference to our ways and so he only grunted at my greeting, keeping an eye on the thickset curly man now crossing the mud street who was fixing us in place with a pointed finger.

"Nailing down the Injun vote there, Sheriff?" In his dread of silence, hurrying from one encounter to another, this man would shout some jovial insult to get attention to himself, taking over every conversation even before he waddled in to join it. When I pretended not to notice the big pink hand already thrust in my direction, it fell to yanking at the crotch of his big trousers. Undaunted, Jim Cole yelled at Billie, "Who gets to vote first? Injuns or women?" Cole jeered his silence. "How'd that go, Chief? Don't go talking our ear off, Chief!" He coughed up a short laugh at his own wit and followed me into the building, heaving himself up the narrow stair behind me.

Like all our cattlemen, Cole had invested his war profits in a big new house, but unlike the Summerlins and Hendrys, and the Langfords, too, this man had no love for the land nor any feel for cattle. Despite all his coarse cowboy talk, as old Jake Summerlin used to say, Cole sat a horse with all the style of a big sack of horse shit.

Banging open Langford's door, he boomed, "Well, lookee who's settin in his daddy's seat, and poor ol' Doc not cold yet!" He shouted his raucous laugh to the whole thin building. Grinning, Walt waved his guest into the one comfortable chair, where Cole sprawled back like an old whore and slapped his hands down on the leather arms. "How's the child-wife, you damn cradle robber? How come we ain't seen no sign of kiddies?"

I ignored Cole's wink, ashamed because I'd wondered the same thing, and sorry that poor Walt felt obliged to snicker. No longer ruddy from his years out in the pinelands, Langford was red-streaked near the nose from the whiskey he sipped to kill long hours in his father's office.

"Got some business with you, Walt," I said. Cole grumped, "Well, spit it out then, we ain't got all day," and Langford said, "No use trying to keep a secret from Cap'n Jim, ain't that right, Jim?"

"*Isn't*," Cole said, mopping his neck. "Ain't Carrie told you about *isn't*? You ain't out hunting cows no more, young feller, you're a damn cattle king! If I'm putting you up for county commissioner, you got to talk good American, same as the rest of us iggerant sumbitches."

There was something shrewd and humorous about Jim Cole, something honest in his cynicism and lack of tact. All the same, I found it hard to smile. To Walt, I said, "I heard your father-in-law might be in town."

Langford moved behind his desk and waved me to a chair. "That so?" he said.

I took my hat off but remained standing, gazing out the narrow window at the storefront gallery across the street where on election day a Tippins crowd had been scattered by gunfire and the whine of bullets from the general direction of the saloon owned by Taff O. Langford, the incumbent's cousin. I stayed where I was until a few regathered, then spoke the lines that won me the election: *They have the Winchesters, gentlemen. You have the votes.* Sheriff Tom Langford was turned out of office the next day.

"Goddammit, Frank, don't stand there looming just cause you're so tall." Cole's smile looked pinned onto his jowls. The eyes in his soft face were hard—the opposite of Langford, whose eyes were gentle in a face still more or less lean. Cole had a long curlicue mouth and nostrils cocked a little high like pink and hairy holes, snuffling and yearning for ripe odors. "First you take ol' T. W.'s job and now you're doggin Carrie's daddy who ain't even in your jurisdiction. And here Walt's daddy ain't been dead a year and Carrie's mama fadin down right before our eyes. That's what Walt here has to tend to every morning, noon, and night. And even so, you come banging in here—"

"Easy, Jim." Langford was smiling, holding both hands high. "Frank and me rode together in the Cypress, we're good friends. He's always welcome."

Jim Cole had been hollering so loud that folks had stopped out on the street under the window. What Cole was really angriest about was my refusal to support his alibi when, three months earlier, a revenue cutter impounded his ship at Punta Rassa. On her regular run, the *Lily White* had delivered cattle to the Key West slaughterhouse, and rather than make the return run with her holds empty, she had met a Cuban vessel off the Marquesas to take on a rum cargo on which no duty had been paid. Cole testified that his rascally captain had taken on that contraband without his knowledge. No one believed this and some wondered at the greed that drove prosperous businessmen to skirt the laws of the democracy they claimed to be so proud of, steal from their own government by overcharging for their beef while paying their lawyers to cheat it of its taxes.

I said to Langford, "Trouble in the Islands."

"I know that, Frank."

"He's in town, then?"

"No." Walt raised his hands as if I'd said, *This is a stickup.* "I never saw him and I don't know where he's headed so don't ask me."

"Dammit, Walt, he's got no *right* to ask you!" Cole exploded. "Got no jurisdiction!"

Langford accompanied me onto the landing. "He's the only suspect, then?"

"So far." I shrugged. "No known witnesses, no good evidence, and not much doubt." I started down the stairs.

"Don't upset Carrie, all right, Frank? She never saw him. He stopped only long enough to say his last good-byes to Mrs. Watson. Admitted there'd been trouble. She told Carrie." Langford awaited me. "That's the truth. He's gone. Which don't mean I will let you know if he comes back."

Jim Cole boomed out, "If he comes back, I'm running that man for sheriff!" Langford guffawed briefly. "Ol' Jim," Walt sighed, pumping out another laugh, as if unable to get over such a comical person. I shook my head over ol' Jim, too, to help Walt out. That old Indian watched us.

SARAH HARDEN

♦

Mister Watson snuck back from north Florida a few years later, and after that he was seen twice each year. Stayed just long enough to see to his plantation, disappear again. He got away with behaving like nothing happened because that's the way his neighbors behaved, too. Never so much as a scowl or a cold word, not even from folks such as us who was friends with those poor young people and had to bury them. Nobody accused, far less arrested. Them Tuckers were just runaways, just conchs, Key Westers— those were the excuses. But the real reason—and Owen was the only one who would admit it—was our fear. Knowing how bold the killer was, we knew he might be back. And when he came and seen he'd got away with it, he showed up more often, until finally he came back for good.

Not that Hardens were real warm to Mister Watson, the way we were before. But we weren't as cold as I thought we should be neither, and he made it harder to be cold each time we seen him. He had eased up on his drinking and lost weight, he was cheerful and lively, and he got his plantation up and running in no time at all.

By now, me'n Owen was married up, but times was hard. Plume birds gone, the fishing poor—it was all we could do to get enough to eat. Mister Watson brought canned goods, extra supplies to tide us over, always protesting how he couldn't use it; having been so poor himself, he said, he never liked to see stuff go to waste. He done the same for the whole Harden clan, even two-faced Earl who had tried so hard to get him arrested.

Me'n Owen done our best to repay him. Gave him fresh fish or turtle when we had some, manatee for stew, maybe palm hearts or wild limes, but we was always more beholden than a proud man like Owen knew how to live with, and his brother Webster felt the same. Only the older brother took advantage. Earl grabbed everything he could lay his hands on, then sniped at the man's back as soon as his boat was out of sight. Jeered at Owen for not taking more while the taking was good, claimed Mister Watson was just paying in advance for Harden guns to back him up if it come to trouble over Tuckers. I hated Earl for saying that—hated him anyway for how mean he was to Henry Short, not to mention his own wife who was my sister Becky—but I couldn't be so sure it wasn't true. Earl's ideas ate at Owen, too, until finally my man ordered me not to accept so much as a quart of syrup from Ed Watson.

BILL HOUSE

✦

From the Frenchman I'd learned the names of his plume buyers and done my best to supply 'em. I even had neighbors helping out while the egrets lasted, cause people was dirt poor at Chokoloskee, all but Smallwoods. Storters still grew cane at Half Way Creek, Will Wiggins, too, but nobody lived there anymore. Mr. D. D. House had moved his cane field from Half Way Creek to the black soil of a shot-out rookery northeast of Chatham Bend that we called House Hammock. C. G. McKinney raised his garden produce on Injun mounds up Turner River and Charlie T. Boggess had a plot at Sandfly Key. Ted Smallwood had two hundred and fifty alligator pear trees on the old Santini claim, shipped pears by the barrel to Punta Gorda and on north by rail, five cents apiece. But most of 'em on Chokoloskee had give up their gardens. Too much rain or not enough for shell mound soil, which has no minerals to speak of: that soil got tuckered out in a few years, same as the women.

Course the tame Injuns, Seminoles and such, was taking the last plume birds same as us, and them rookeries over by Lake Okeechobee was shot out first. By the turn of the century the east coast birds was gone and the west coast birds was going and the white plumes was bringing twice their weight in gold. Men would fight over egrets and shoot to kill. At Flamingo, the Roberts boys went partners with the Bradleys and for a few years they done all right back in Cuthbert Lake, but elsewhere them birds growed so scarce that hunters would set up at night guarding what small rookeries was left. Them Audibones was agitating harder'n ever, and in 1901, plume hunting was forbidden: our native state of Florida had passed a law against our good old native way of living.

Most of us thought that law was meant to simmer down them bird-lovers but all it ever done was put the price up. Only man who give a good goddamn about enforcement was Guy Bradley who got hisself hired the first Audibone warden in south Florida and took his job too serious for his own good.

When Guy was shot dead off Flamingo, July 19-0-5, rumors blamed Watson. Then another warden got axed to death near Punta Gorda and that one was laid on Watson, too. Course every man at Flamingo and Punta Gorda knew the names of the real killers but no one turned 'em in. I ain't saying that's good, I got my doubts, but any local judge knows better than to mess with an old-time clan that is only taking the wild creaturs that is theirs by God-given right.

When a third warden got wiped out in Carolina, somebody hollered, Well, E. J. Watson *come* from Carolina! Made no sense, but all the same, the man's bad reputation come in handy for anybody in south Florida who was out to cover up a killing. And all this while, not one word said about those Tuckers.

Before my daddy crippled hisself up with his own ax and I moved south to House Hammock to help out, I worked as guide for a Yankee sportsman, Mr. Dimock. Like most sports, Mr. A. W. Dimock shot at anything in sight, deer, birds, and gators, crocs, and even manatees. We harpooned big saw-fish from Chatham River all the way south to Cape Sable, hacked off the saw to sell for tourist souvenirs, left the rest to rot. Them big ol' fish from long ago is very scarce today.

Mr. Dimock wrote up his adventures in a famous book called *Florida En-chantments.* Had his son along snapping pictures for his book that spent most of the day with his head in a black bag. The photo of his guide was kind of murky but it might been me, cause the man from the east coast who took my place got pulled overboard by a sawfish, split his guts out. Weren't familiar with the way we done things in the Islands.

A. W. Dimock was very curious about Ed Watson, who was mostly what us local people talked about in them days. Mr. Dimock put our tales into his book. I couldn't read but I was told about it good. Mr. Dimock called E. J. Watson "J. E. Wilson" cause his book claimed Wilson had killed seven in these parts and he didn't want Ed to take him into court for heartburn.

Sure, the men suspected Ed of maybe two or three, but I'm damned if I know who them seven might of been, unless they was black cane cutters on his plantation. And if his own neighbors never knowed about them seven, how did that old Yankee find it out? If Ed was killing all them people, seems funny their own families never mentioned it.

Anyways, he weren't the only feller in this section who had took a life, not by no means. Among plume hunters especially, there was murdering aplenty: rob the plumes, then slip away like otters through the creeks, hide out far back into the Glades. Sheriff never cared much who hid out back in the rivers. If a few went missing, the law seen it as good riddance and was probably right.

ERSKINE THOMPSON

✦

In the early days, Mister Ed Watson was touchy about people tellin slander, but he always enjoyed the attention he got for knowing famous outlaws in the Territories and he made the most of them bad stories about himself. Didn't encourage 'em so much as not quite deny 'em, cause his reputation as a fast gun and willing to use it kept other men from staking claims anywhere near him.

Good dry ground was running out along the southwest coast but very few tried to settle what was left. People came and then they went: they never stayed long. After Tuckers, that country emptied out all the way south to Rodgers River. Used to be three plantations up that river, royal palms, date palms, too, and tamarinds. Well, quit-claims to all of 'em was up for sale and had no buyers. After all the hard years Atwells put in, their gardens was long gone, cabins sagging, cisterns lined with slime and rot from animals that fell in trying to get their water. Later years when the Storter boys went up in there seining for mullet, they seen crude-painted skull-and-crossbone signs stuck into the bank. Might of been a warning or it might of been a certain feller's idea of joke, most likely both.

Around Lost Man's there was two strong families left. Hardens lived on Hog Key and Wood Key, just north of Lost Man's River, that was one clan; the other was Old Man James Hamilton and family and their Daniels kin south of the river mouth. That was the long white coral beach Mister Watson had his eye on, and all them people knew that, too, because when I married young Gert Hamilton I told 'em. I was helpin Hamiltons construct a shell road through the jungle to a big Injun mound we called Royal Palm Hammock but along with that I ran his ship for Mister Watson.

Headed south to Flamingo or Key West, Mister Watson and me used to enjoy the view of all them royal palms back of Lost Man's Beach. One of them cattle kings, Mr. Cole, claimed them palms was goin to waste out in the wilderness so he had 'em all grubbed out, using our dead-broke Island men for the hard labor; he was out to prettify the city streets to bring more tourists to Fort Myers. Tropical paradise, y'know. Course most of them street palms died in the first dry spell because nobody thought to water 'em, so they might's well have stood where they belonged. Like the Boss said, Cole should of ordered up some gumbo-limbos—what us local folks call the tourist tree for just a joke on account of that red skin bark that's always peeling, get it?

After the wild things was all gone, there weren't much left but donkey work digging clams and ricking buttonwood for charcoal, so our whole gang went over to Pavilion Key for the clam fishery that supplied the new Yankee cannery built at Caxambas. My uncle Jim Daniels was the captain of the dredge and my mother and George Roe set up a store and post office. Aunt Josie was there, too, with her latest husband. Josie took seven by the time the smoke cleared, counting the man that she took twice, and she seen every last damned one of 'em into his grave.

In later years them two ladies who had kept house at the Bend would relate wild stories about Mister Watson to get attention to theirselves, claim some credit out of a hard life. Netta and Josie was hooked hard on that man and always would be, so it seems kind of funny it was them two women started up a rumor that Ed Watson was killing off his harvest help on what folks took to calling "Watson Payday." Naturally his business competition was happy to pass along a story which explained why Mister Watson done so much better with his cane than they did.

That puts me in mind of his old joke down in Key West. Feller might ask him, "What you up to these days, Mister Watson?" And he'd wave his bottle, maybe shoot a light out, yelling, *"Raising cane!"* I would laugh like crazy every time I heard that story, tell it every time I had the chance. Warmin up them ones that might of missed the joke, I always laughed a little more while I explained it: "Raisin *Cain—C-a-i-n!* You get it?" And one or two might laugh along with me a little, but in a way that made me feel bad, kind of left out. When folks finally told me I might as well forget it, I'd sing out, "Well, nobody can't say that Erskine Thompson got no sense of humor!"

MAMIE SMALLWOOD

✦

Mr. C. G. McKinney made the bad mistake of losing track of his post office cash: when the federal inspectors showed up, he didn't have it. I'm not saying it was stolen, only loaned out or mislaid, but by law he had to have it handy. Mr. Smallwood lent him the money to keep him out of jail and got appointed postmaster instead. By now my Ted was the biggest farmer and biggest trader and owned most of Chokoloskee, so I guess you could say that Smallwoods had replaced Santinis as our leading family.

Nobody forgot that day in 1906 when E. J. Watson brought his new young wife to Chokoloskee. Paid a call on Storters over in Everglade, opened a new account, then done the same with us. Not only that but he showed up in his new motor launch, *pop-pop-popping* down the Pass from Sandfly Key. (Called her the *Warrior* but the men called her the *May-Pop* because she didn't always start when he cranked her flywheel.) Though not all of us knew it, we were way behind the times and hungry for a look at something new, so folks left their tomato patch and hustled along after the children who came flying and hollering down to our landing.

Even a quarter mile away out in the channel, we recognized the helmsman, the strong bulk of him and that broad hat. My heart skipped like a flying fish—*he dared come back*! When he saw the crowd, he lifted his hat and the sun fired that head of dark red hair—the color of dried blood, said my mama, Mrs. Ida House. A quiet fell like our community had caught its breath, like we were waiting for lightning to break from those dark clouds that in deep summer build in mighty towers over the Glades: a great split of thunder, then that cold breath of coming wind and rain.

"Speak of the Devil," Mama sniffed, though nobody besides herself had spoken. Ida B. House was looking straight at Satan and she knew it. Some of our fool women moaned and gasped, raised fingertips up to their collarbones and rolled their eyes, *O Lord-a-mercy,* staring wall-eyed like a flock of haunts. Then all together they dared look again, with a grisly moan of woe like Revelation. Wouldn't surprise me if I moaned right along with 'em. Regular Doomsday! Nobody tore their hair far as I know, but a few God-fearing bodies went squawking and scattering like fowl, hurrying their off-springs home, not because they really thought E. J. Watson might do them harm but only to show the other biddies how decent Baptist women should behave when faced with a Methodist murderer.

As Mister Watson came into our dock, a young woman with a babe in arms stood up beside him. The females fleeing, hearing a babble from the other women, turned right around, picked up their skirts, tripped down the hill again. Might have been scared of Mister Watson, but they were a lot more scared of missing out on something. By the time he helped the new young wife step out onto the dock, it was a barnyard around here, pushing and squeaking and flapping off home to find a bonnet or a pair of shoes for such a high-society occasion.

Say what you like about Ed Watson, he looked and acted like our idea of a hero. Stood there shining in the sun in a white linen suit and her on his arm in a wheat-brown linen dress and button boots. When she picked up her sweet baby girl in sunbonnet and pink bow frock, that handsome little family stood facing the crowd like they were posing for a nice holiday photo. That's the picture I see every time I recall how that man died on that very spot on a dark October evening only four years later, with that young woman huddled in my house staring out at the coming dark, and that little girl like a caught rabbit, squeaking in the corner in the wild crash of men and their steel weapons.

Since that bad business at Lost Man's Key, we'd heard plenty of talk that if Ed Watson dared to show his face around these parts again the men would arrest him, turn him over to the Monroe County sheriff, or string him up if he offered the least resistance. I guess Mister Watson knew that, too, because when he came back the first few times, he steered clear of Chokoloskee; he stopped off quick at Chatham Bend and was gone quicker, after burning off his cane field. Though we never heard he'd been there till after he was gone, we got used to the idea that he'd be back.

I will say I admired the man's nerve. He took all the steam out of them that said he would never dare return, that he'd have to sell his house and claim and his cane syrup works. Turned out he'd been back every year, tending to business all along; he'd even seen the Lee County surveyor about getting full title to his land. Brought in a carpenter to build him a front porch, gave the house a new coat of white paint—not whitewash, mind, but real oil paint. But some way that carpenter died there on the Watson place, and bad rumors started to fly again, and next thing we knew Watson was gone.

When he didn't show up for another year, it looked like we'd seen the last of him for sure. The men concluded he was on the run, having killed that carpenter along with the Frenchman and the Tuckers and probably Guy Bradley, that young warden. Lynch talk started up again, and Charlie Johnson, that boy Earl Harden—some of these fellers got just plain ferocious.

Well, here was their chance: the villain had walked into their clutches, but no one seemed to recollect about that lynching. Those same fools jostled for a look when Ed Watson stepped ashore, that's how bad they wanted to step up and shake his hand. Not a man hung back when his turn came to show how much he thought of Mister Watson, and joke and carry on with our long-lost neighbor. Charlie T. Boggess wanted to know what kind of motor Mister Watson had in that there motorboat, and the man said, "Why, that's a Palmer one-cylinder, Charlie T., and she's a beauty!" And all the rest of 'em winking and nodding as if any man but Charlie would have known that motor was a Palmer soon's he heard it pop-pop-popping up the Pass. Charlie and Ethel Boggess, they're our dear old friends, they were married back in '97, same year we were, but that man was a pure fool around Ed Watson, and he wasn't near as bad as some of the others. Probably told their wives later, "Well, them Tuckers was just conchs, y'know, goldurn Key Westers. Might have had it coming for all we know."

Young Earl Harden was here who was all for lynching E. J. some years back. A young Daniels had some drink that day and told that Harden boy, "It ain't your place to go talkin about lynchin no damn white man!" And Earl said, "You sayin I ain't white?" Oh, those two had one heck of a fight behind our store! Well, here was Earl Harden gawking with the rest and smiling like his life depended on it, too.

The only man who stood back a little was my oldest brother, who would puzzle over E. J. Watson his whole life. Bill never stopped working long enough to get any kind of education but he had more sense than most when it came to people. He had often talked with Henry Short, who helped those young mulatta men with that Tucker burial, and though Henry would never accuse a white man in so many words, Bill had to conclude that E. J. Watson was the killer.

Bill had grown up broiled beef-red by the sun, broad-shouldered and steady as a tree. I reckon Mister Watson felt his eye. He turned around and eyed him just a little bit too long, then said real quiet, "Hello, Bill." And Bill said, calm and easy, "Mister Watson," tipping his straw hat to the young woman. "Glad to see you again," Ed Watson said, like he was testing him.

Bill House hated all his life to seem unfriendly but he hated false friendliness even worse; he could not go that far with E. J. Watson so he didn't. *Looked* amiable enough, I guess, but all he did was nod and put his hat back on by way of answer. Mister Watson considered that before he nodded back. But maybe because Bill was a well-respected feller he wanted on his side, my brother was the first man Ed Watson introduced to Mrs. Watson and his baby girl, who had the same auburn red hair as her bad daddy.

Kate Edna Watson was a handsome taffy-haired young woman, serious, not solemn, with a sudden shy beguiling girlish smile. Mister Watson said, "This fine young lady is a preacher's daughter so you boys watch your language, hear?" He was just teasing along, just being sociable, but my mama Ida Borders House was determined not to take it like he meant it. Nearly knocked herself cold, that's how hard she sniffed; she dearly liked to make a point with that big sniff of hers. Then she said loudly, "Praise to goodness, there's no call to instruct First Florida Baptists about *blasphemies!*" But Mama could not meet Ed Watson's eye, even when his expression was as pleasant as it was now, and she was glaring someplace else by the time she finished.

All this while, young Mrs. Watson soothed her infant. She had nice manners by our local standard, smiled politely, but she was tuckered out from travel, with a babe in arms and another on the way. I watched her face to see how much she knew. She cast her eyes down when she caught me looking, from which I saw that she'd heard plenty but did not know what to think. Then she looked up again and smiled as if she'd spotted me as a new friend of her own age. I went forward to welcome her and the women followed.

Ed Watson acted more tickled to be home than the Prodigal Son.

Declared how homesick he had been for fresh palm heart and his canemash-flavored pork at Chatham Bend, and how fine it felt to be back here in the Islands. Never raised his voice, just toed the ground with his tooled boots, waiting for these folks to inspect the Watsons and be done with it. But even while he smiled and nodded, he was looking our men over one by one, as if he might see from some shift in their faces who had spoken out in favor of his lynching.

Ed Watson broke that uneasy silence by looking at the ground, looking up again, then declaring he'd be proud to have a look at our new store. Leading the way, he took his hat off as he climbed the steps and crossed the porch, and most of the others, pushing in behind him, snatched off their hats, too—the first customers I could recall who ever came in bare-headed.

Looking around, our guest smote his brow in wonder, unable to believe his eyes. He was just brimming over with congratulations to Ted and his "Miss Mamie," said no place of business had Smallwoods beat this side of Tampa. He reminded Ted of the good old days when they first met at Half Way Creek, back in the nineties, and how far both had come in the decade since.

Well, E. J. Watson built him a fine house and plantation in the Islands beyond any that was seen down there before or since, but he never did near as well as Ted, who never had to kill to get ahead. My man worked hard for everything he had: getting him to *stop* work was the problem! Lord knows where Watson's money came from or how much innocent blood might have been spilled to pay for those fancy boots and a linen suit, not to mention that new motorboat.

Our man of God (who would last no longer than the others) came hurrying down to meet the newcomers, tell them how welcome they sure were to worship with us on a Sunday, when the Good Lord hung His hat in Chokoloskee. This young man was small-headed with droopy ears, looked more like a sheep than like our shepherd: he raised his eyes to Heaven and said "Amen!" in a little bleat when E. J. Watson told him that while Chatham Bend was a long distance from a house of God, he aimed to continue his lifelong custom of reading aloud from the Good Book on the Lord's Day whether his people needed it or not.

When everybody laughed, C. G. McKinney frowned. He pulled his long beard and coughed real loud and sudden to warn folks not to joke about Sunday worship. Being our local humorist, Mr. McKinney was never one to encourage jokes from other people: if any jokes were to be cracked, it was C. G. McKinney who would crack 'em or know the reason why. So C. G. told his trusty story of the first man of God to reach the shores of Chokoloskee Bay. When Reverend Gatewood arrived at Everglade back in '88, his first sacred duty was to preach last rites over the body of a man slain in a dispute with the skipper during the voyage.

I reckon E. J. Watson knew the Gatewood story but he had the manners to pretend he didn't. Said he sure hoped that darned boat captain paid dearly for that sin cause what was needed in the Islands was some law and order. Hearing those words from a desperado, Isaac Yeomans whooped and hooted until he heard his own voice in the quiet and fell still.

While Mister Watson was away, a story spread that after he had killed Belle Starr, he "throwed in" with the James and Younger boys who rode with Quantrill in the Border Wars and later became outlaws. Our men could talk of nothing else for weeks. You would have thought those bloody renegades were the greatest Americans since General Nathan Bedford Forrest and Robert E. Lee. And some way, just for knowing outlaws and getting the credit for killing that outlaw queen, Ed Watson became some kind of a hero, too. If he'd showed up here a few years back with a jug of moonshine and a bugle, yelling, "Come on boys, we're headed for them Philly-peens to kill us some dirty Spaniards, are you red-blooded Americans or ain't you?" why, half the fool men on the island would have marched off after him, tears of glory in their eyes, without once asking where or why they might be going, or what was wrong or right in the eyes of God.

E. J. was talking very fierce, pounding his palm. "If the Ten Thousand Islands have a future," he declared, "then those who place themselves above the law have no place in our peace-loving community!" Everyone stared and he stared back with a great frown like Jehovah. "A-*men*!" he shouted. Except for Isaac, who would laugh at the Devil Himself, my Ted was about the only one who dared to smile. Then Charlie T. smiled because Ted had smiled, and Isaac whooped again and slapped his thigh, and everybody got to laughing but C. G. McKinney. Naturally our more pious females started hissing about sacrilege but they couldn't keep it up. Heck, they were thrilled! And the silliest just tittered happily, *tee-hee-hee-hee.*

I wasn't smiling, not because of sacrilege but because this man was treating us like ninnies. He saw that I saw this—saw that Mamie House Smallwood and her brother Bill were not folks liable to forget about those

Tuckers or forgive either. Knowing what he was up against with our House family, he did not scowl to scare or threaten, he did something worse: he disarmed me with a wink, a reckless confidential wink that made my right-eous indignation feel downright foolish, made everything he'd told this crowd a joke, made all our hopes and struggles in this world simply ridicu-lous for the fundamental reason that our precious human life, for all its joys, was blood-soaked, cruel, and empty, with only sorrow, fear, disease at its dark end, fading to nothingness. Staring back at him, I thought, Was this a society of human beings or some purgatory where folks was con-demned to live their lives with a laughing killer loose amongst them like a wolf?

Ted leaned and whispered it was only fitting to put 'em up in our house for the night. A murderer? That was my first reaction, I admit. No, I didn't want to do it. *No?* I *had* to! After all, I told myself, no one else had a spare room. The real truth was, I didn't want some other household claiming our famous visitor. Hadn't my Ted called this man his friend before most of these other folks had even met him?

Aunt Lovie Lopez—Penelope Daniels she was, married Gregorio—Aunt Lovie was jealous, and she could not hide it. "You'd shelter a desperado under the same roof as your little children? You ain't scared?" I was uneasy, yes, I whispered, but my man's wish was good enough for me. "Wouldn't be near good enough for me," Aunt Lovie humphed. Course her Gregorio "come with the bark on," as the men said, he was *rough.* A Spaniard with any kind of pride had to act crusty in those patriotic days when we ran 'em out of Cuba and the Philippines. Right from Injun times, the Spaniards been disliked here in south Florida and that won't change.

That evening E. J. gave Ted news of Columbia County where the Small-woods came from. In the kitchen, young wide-eyed Mrs. Watson described the new house her husband had built north of Fort White and how his hard work got that land producing after years of erosion and ruin. Yes, she confided, she knew all about the blame laid on her Edgar in his youth due to his hellfire temper, as she called it, but if she'd heard anything of his reputation in the Islands, she did not let on. She was out to redeem him, it was plain to see, she'd made that her holy mission in this life, she got all breathless just whispering about it. Mister Watson called her Kate but all the rest of us who came to love her called her Edna.

"E. J.'s got a bad feud brewing in Columbia County," Ted whispered when he came to bed.

"That why he's suddenly so homesick for Lee County?"

Ted reached across and put his hand over my mouth, lest our guests hear me from the other side of a slat wall. I was irked that my husband seemed so proud of having a killer for a friend. Saying nothing, I just lay there in the dark. I felt an intrusion in my heart, like a poison tendril twitching through the wall from the spare room. Ted was puffing, he was dreading my sharp tongue, yet just as eager as the rest of 'em to be first with his Watson news. Finally he muttered, "Family trouble over land. He come back south till things cool off. Didn't care to shoot nobody in self-defense."

There was something hungry in his voice I didn't want to hear, something I picked up every time he told his tales of the bloody mayhem he had witnessed up around Arcadia or over on the east coast, Lemon City. Being a peaceable good man who hated fighting, he was bewitched by men of violence, of which we had more than we could use down around south Florida. Most of our Chok neighbors were just as bad, yet under their patched shirts and scraggy beards, they were gentle fellers, same as he was. For all their big talk, they were boys and pretty childish.

I kept after him. "That man Quinn Bass that Daddy knew up in Arcadia— didn't your 'friend' call that self-defense, too? If your friend is such a peaceable feller, how come all these men try to attack him?"

"Mamie, his wife believes in him, you seen that for yourself, and she was up there with him in Columbia and knows his family a lot better'n we do. Heck, she's a preacher's daughter. If she believes in him, we got no reason not to."

"Maybe those kinfolk are in his way like those poor Tucker people. One day your family might get in his way, too, ever think of that?"

My husband said, "It just ain't fair to talk like that. We know he cut Santini but that's all we know for sure. All the rest is rumors. There ain't no proof he ever killed a single soul."

My Ted has a fine head of hair, big black mustache, and a big deep voice he only has to raise to clear the drunks and drifters from the store. Generally "his wish is my command," as Grandma Ida likes to say about her feisty husband, Mr. D. D. House. This was different. E. J. Watson had Ted Smallwood in his pocket, others, too, and no good could come of it. Ted fought off my questions, getting angry, but our little kids were right under this roof with Mister Watson. I would see this through.

"How come he dusted out of here so fast after that Tucker business? And again two years ago when his carpenter just happened to die, too?"

"Weren't his fault that feller's heart quit! E. J. knew the blame would be laid on him, and by golly, it was. When Guy Bradley got murdered a hundred miles away, who was the first man they laid it on? He might of been lynched! He's scared of men taking the law in their own hands and you can't blame him."

"I don't believe he was *ever* scared our men might lynch him. He's too hardened by his sins to be scared of anything." Thinking about that wink of his, I got upset all over. "Does what he pleases, then laughs at us, dares us to stop him."

Ted's big hand covered my mouth again; he pointed toward the wall. And suddenly I was so frightened that I wept and trembled. He took me in his arms. "E. J. is a fine farmer," he murmured, starting in on the little speech that most all the women got to hear that night in every shack on our scared little island. "A real hard worker with a good head for business, always ready to help his neighbors. They ain't a family in the Islands won't say the same."

But this time the old refrain of his same old song left him still restless. "All right, sweetheart," he whispered. "But maybe this new family will steady him down. He opened an account this evening, paid down two hundred dollars in advance. I got no choice but to give that man a chance."

"It's your friendship he has paid for, Mr. Smallwood. Paid in advance. He thinks if he's got the postmaster on his side and the House clan, too, Chokoloskee won't give him any trouble. Well, he hasn't got the House clan. He hasn't got Daddy nor my brother Bill, nor young Dan neither, only Mr. Smallwood."

"And Smallwood's wife? You always liked him, Mamie."

Ted rolled over with his back to me when I didn't answer. We lay awake for quite a while. I wanted to holler in his ear. "Where does his money come from? You said yourself, If E. J. had no money, he'd be on the chain gang to this day for the attempted murder of Adolphus Santini." But Ted would assume that E. J. had made money on his farm crop in north Florida and tell me to hush up and go to sleep.

Ted's esteem for E. J. was sincere, of course. Even Daddy House admired the man's enterprise and plain hard work. And because folks liked him, our local families were all set to give him the benefit of any doubt. "E. J.Watson ain't the only one who makes his own law in south Florida," Ted always said. "Those plume hunters and moonshiners will take and shoot at anyone who messes near their territory! Look what they done to young Bradley!"

It was Gene Roberts visiting from Flamingo who notified our community all about that murder. The Florida frontier is far behind the nation's progress, Mr. Roberts said, because men continue to settle their accounts with knives and pistols. But when I asked Ted if that included his friend Watson, who was suspected in the Bradley case, Ted rolled away again with that big sigh that said, *There's no sense talking* no *sense to a woman.*

With Ed Watson's return, folks would be waiting to see what my menfolk would do. Ted and Daddy were leaders in our community and my brother Bill was thought to have good sense. If these three men made up their minds to give Ed Watson a fresh start, the rest would go along. Charlie Boggess, Wigginses, and Willie Browns were already on E. J.'s side, and that was close to half the Island families.

I gave in to Ted after a while. I had to admit that once they got used to the idea, most folks were content to have Ed Watson back: he took some interest in our common lives, which we had thought so dreary. He was full of curiosity, he kept things lively, and his great plans for the Islands gave us hope that the Twentieth Century progress we had heard about might come our way. Maybe we weren't so backward as we thought if a man as able and ambitious as Ed Watson chose to live here.

CARRIE LANGFORD'S DIARY

✦

Christmas, 1908

When Walter and Eddie and Captain Cole came back from Papa's trial in Madison County, Jim Cole was the only one who even mentioned it. Was your daddy innocent, Mis Carrie? Well, we got him acquitted, didn't we? If I frowned, I knew, he'd guffaw even louder, thinking I'm charmed by him. The man's so stuck on himself and so insensitive! "That old piney-woods rooter," that's what Mama called him.

Papa will sell his Fort White farm to pay his lawyers and return to southwest Florida for good, so Walter says. This evening I asked Mr. John Roach in front of Walter if a position could be found for Papa at Deep Lake. Mr. Roach's tactful answer was, "Well, your dad has some excellent qualifications, we all agree." But my own husband, interrupting, burst out, "Absolutely not!"

Walter *never* speaks to me so sharply. "It's not as if my father were a *criminal*," I protested later. "He was acquitted!"

That may be, Walter insisted, in that measured voice that warns me he is digging in his heels, but if Captain Jim had not pulled a lot of strings, it might have been a very different story. "Was he guilty, then? Is that what you were trying to say in front of Yankee strangers?" "If John Roach was a stranger," Walter reproved me, "why did we name our little boy for him?" At the mention of our lost little John, I wept. Walter took me in his arms, patting my shoulder blade, that brisk little pat-pat-pat that has no warmth in it and precious little patience. "I don't claim to know about your daddy's guilt or innocence. All I know is, you are very cold with Captain Jim, considering all he done for Mr. Watson."

"*Did*," I said, picking the wrong moment to correct his grammar. Walter took a deep breath and let me go. For the first time in our married life, I cannot sway him. He says, "I perjured myself for your sake, Carrie. That don't mean he's welcome in my house." Walter wants nothing more to do with Papa. And though I flew at him, said hurtful things—"You're just scared your bank partners won't like it!"—he would not relent. He went off to the bank as miserable as I was.

DECEMBER 30, 1908

Papa showed up on a Tuesday with Edna and her two little ones. Faith and Betsy shrilled *Grandpapa!* from an upstairs window; I heard them come thumping down the stairs. I cut them off as they rushed toward the front door and made them cry by shooing them back upstairs to their uncle Eddie, who is living here until the boardinghouse has a free room. Eddie had testified for the defense that one of the slain men had tried to ambush Papa at Fort White, but now he only parrots Walter, saying perjury was as far as he aimed to go. He did not come out to greet his father and Lucius, of course, was away at Chatham Bend.

Through the curtains I watched Papa give the knocker a sharp rap. The others hung back, out in the street. His darkie was a sullen-looking man in dirty overalls. In a cart behind them, dragged from the railroad station, was their sad heap of worldly goods, right down to the bedsteads and the burlap sacks of tools; I thought of those desperate homesteaders we felt so sorry for during the land rush into Oklahoma Territory.

Papa was unshaven and pasty-white from months in jail, his teeth were bad. His Edna looked hollow-eyed, drained of her color, and their sallow children too worn out to whine. It's hard to think of these forlorn creatures as my brother and sister when they're even younger than my little daughters.

The girl asked if she should show them in. I shook my head. Just bring some milk, I whispered, and a plate of cookies. I went to the door and opened it and we all faced each other. I was trying not to witness my father's humiliation. Then I realized that humiliation was not what he was feeling; was it only my imagination or was there something haunted in his gaze? "Oh, Papa," I said, taking his hands, "I'm so relieved about that awful trial!"

My voice sounded false and faraway. He saw right through me. Though he mustered a smile, there was no spark in his eyes, and the smile turned sardonic as he waited to see if I would ask them in. He made no attempt to hug me, which was most unusual; was he afraid I might not hug him back?

"Happy New Year, Carrie," Papa said. "Where are the children? Are those sweet things hiding from their bad old grandpa?" Because they adore him and have fun with him and always fly to the sound of his growly voice, he was stung that Faith and Betsy had not even called out. How shameful to make my father feel unwelcome just when he needs his family most!

A dreadful pause—where oh where were the milk and cookies? Because Papa was trying to be cheerful, I tried not to weep.

Then his face closed. He said abruptly that they would not come in, having only stopped by to say hello on their way to the dock to catch Captain Bill Collier and the *Falcon*. As he spoke, the girl appeared with milk and cookies. She set the tray down too quickly on the steps, everything sliding and askew. The silly thing was deathly scared of Papa, all the darkies are, though how they hear those dreadful rumors I don't know.

I came forward and hugged his gloomy kids and pecked the wan cheek of my stepmother. After days of hard travel, they all smelled like poor people. I said good morning to the black man, who did not respond or even lift his hat. Mama taught us that what people call sullenness or stupidity in darkies is often no more than fear and shyness; they have learned that it is much more dangerous to act decisively and make mistakes than to be passive and slow, despite the abuse and contempt they will surely suffer. Nonetheless I was surprised by the man's rudeness and astonished by Papa's patience. When Papa spoke to him in a low murmur, the man gave a violent start like a dog in a nightmare and removed his hat. As if unaware I had already said good morning, he muttered, "Yes'm, thank you." Papa said, "He went to trial with me up north. Maybe he's not quite over our close call." He drew his finger under his chin and popped his eyes out like a hanged man, but he was very angry now and those eyes had no relation to his smile.

That black man never heard me, I now think, because he was sunk in dreadful melancholia. Later I asked Walter if Negroes suffer melancholy the same way we do and Walter said that he supposed so, though he hadn't thought about it. Overhearing, Eddie burst out, "That's ridiculous!" Eddie is most vehement when most uncertain.

I encouraged the children to take a cookie. "They're not pets," said Papa, pointing at the plate, which still sat on the step. Mortified, I snatched it up and offered it. "Of *course* they're not, Papa!" I burst into tears for he had turned, saying, "Good-bye, then, Daughter." He stalked away. Watching him lead his little group toward the river, I could not know that we would never speak again.

BILL HOUSE

◆

All Watson had for help at Chatham while he was in north Florida getting in trouble was a man wanted for hog theft in Fort Myers. Green Waller had a way with hogs same as his boss, who kept hogs as a boy back in Carolina. Drunk or sober, them two could talk hogs all day and night. But one evening when Watson was away, Waller got drunk, went to the hog pen, and give his hogs a speech and their freedom, too. Them animals went straight to the damned syrup mash, tottered around, keeled over drunk, and one full sow that was sleeping it off got half et by a panther. Waller left the Bend before his boss got back, but the next year he showed up again and presented Watson with a fine young sow, said he had seen the error of his ways. Mister Watson admired that young sow so much that he forgot that she was probably stolen property. He named her Topsy, trained her to do tricks.

Watson was in Storters' trading post one day when Green Waller come in with a lady three times the common size. Miss Hannah Smith from the Okefenokee Swamp had cleared and farmed for C. G. McKinney up in Turner River, then drifted down to Everglade where Waller come across her. He introduced her to his boss as a prime female who could outwork four men ricking buttonwood and show a horse a trick or two about spring plowing. Watson said, "You aim to put the traces to her, Green?" When she busted out laughing, he bowed real courtly and informed her that his mule Dolphus was getting on in years and if Miss Smith would care to come on home with him, he could yoke her up alongside Dolphus when time come to plow. Or maybe—he whispered this loudly behind his hand—him and her could get yoked up together while this old drunk of a hog thief here was snorin away under the table.

Well, we all had a good laugh over that except Green Waller, who had fell deeply in love with that big female. Hannah was handsome the way a man is handsome—looked like a man wearing a long-hair wig—while Green was horse-faced with bad skin and a gimp, all bones and patches. Watson told her that the sorry help at Chatham Bend these days couldn't pour piss out of a boot that had the instructions written on the heel. When the men laughed again, he tipped his hat to Waller—this was the bully that come out when he was drinking. Hannah looked worried about what Green might do but all he done was belch.

Hannah Smith related how her sister Sadie was camped in the south Glades over east near Homestead when she got word from their folks in the Okefenokee who wanted to know where her Little Sis was at. Asked Sadie would she hunt her up, see how she was getting on. Sadie learned that Hannah was working all the way across to the west coast with a hundred miles of Everglades between, so she bided her time until the dry season, then hitched two oxen to a cart and yee-hawed and wallowed and hacked her way clean across the state. First time *that* was ever done, and most likely the last; she weren't called the Ox Woman for nothing. Come north along Shark River Slough and west through the Big Cypress, dug her wheels out of the muck, chopped her way across them strands and jungle hammocks. Parked her oxen near Immokalee and made her way south to Chokoloskee Bay. Just showed up one day in her black sunbonnet, smelled like a she-bear.

Up to that time Hannah Smith, called Big Squaw by the Injuns, was the largest female ever seen around south Florida, but Sadie went a whole hand taller, six foot four, built like a cistern, with a smile that opened her whole face like a split watermelon. Said she was hunting Little Sis, aimed to come up with Little Sis or know the reason why. "You boys think us girls're big? We got two more that's bigger yet back home." Sadie's husband got hisself hung at Folkston, Georgia, so she took work hauling limestone, cutting crossties for the railroad. Ran a barbershop in Waycross for a while, claimed she could handle a razor so good she could shave a beard that was still three days under the skin.

The Ox Woman, and Hannah, too, could work a ax good as any man we ever saw, made that ax sing. Them two was that old style of pioneer womenfolk that come roarin up out of the swamps and down out of the mountains. Allowed as how their sister Lydia liked to set in a rocker on the porch with her husband in her arms, singin him lullabies. Ed Watson said, "It's a damn good thing they don't make women of that kind no more or they'd run the country."

Hannah had her a sweet voice to go with her feats of strength and winsome ways. Evenings she hauled on her other dress and set out on the dock singing "Barbry Allen" to the Injuns that come in to trade. Remembering that heap of womanhood singing so pure under the moon over the mangroves, and them Injuns by their fire gazing past her so polite while keeping a sharp eye on this big wild thing that might turn dangerous any minute still gives me the shivers just to think about it.

Tant Jenkins was an expert in the hunting line and always claimed that common labor disagreed with him. I told Tant that if he was smarter'n what people said he was, he'd send away to the Okefenokee for one of them big lonesome sisters to do his chores for him, keep him in whiskey, and rock him to sleep when he come home at night drunk and disgusting.

Them two giant girls celebrated their reunion, drunk Tant and Isaac and two-three Daniels boys to a dead halt. Sadie said that while they lasted, them nice fellers made a body feel at home, but in a day or two, she hitched up her oxen, yee-hawed north, found a big hammock with good soil east of Immokalee. She lived on there quite a while, died on there, too, likely from heartbreak over the bad news that was comin her way about her Little Sis.

Not long after Sadie took her leave and Waller went back to Chatham Bend, Big Hannah got sick and fidgety on McKinney's Needhelp Farm, pining away for her hog-loving admirer and fighting off the skeeters for a year alone with no man to help her with the crops except a dirty old Injun called Charlie Tommie, who chased her even harder than the skeeters, till finally she had to slap him away, too. Not till April 1910 did Green and Watson pick her up at Smallwood's store as they had promised. Watson warned her that her man had stole hogs all his life, so the first time a hog went missing at the Bend, a well-knowed hog thief might come up missing, too. Waller could hoot over coming up missing but he never laughed none when it come to Hannah because he was deeply in love—them were his words—and women in his life was very few and very far between. When his sweetheart went off to fetch her stuff, he confided to the men how he'd promised his mama at her deathbed that her virgin boy would go to his grave as pure in the Lord as the first day she wiped his bottom. "Them holy words made my old mama die happy. But Satan sent me this big Smith girl that is stronger'n what I am," Waller moaned, "and next thing I knowed about it, boys, she had me down and was doin somethin dirty!"

Hannah brung her ax and gun and a spare dress in a burlap sack she slung across her shoulder. Follered her boyfriend to the boat and headed south for Chatham River and that was the last time we ever seen her. From what we heard, that big bashful lady and her dog-eared boyfriend got along like rum and butter; they done their sinning in that little shack downriver from the boat sheds. Hannah chopped wood for the syrup boiler, helped the young missus with the chores, ate a whole lot, washed up good under the arms, and lugged her hog thief home, took him to bed. Ed Watson claimed they yelped all night like a pair of foxes.

MAMIE SMALLWOOD

✦

In early 1909, when Ed Watson got acquitted in north Florida and came south after nine months in jail, he announced that he was home for good and darned glad of it. The whole coast was leery now, including them few who was too scared not to greet him, but even folks who dreaded him finally cheered up and relaxed, cause it sure looked like Edna had changed his ways. For over a year they had no trouble down on Chatham Bend or we'd have heard about it from Miss Hannah, who kept in touch with her many friends around the Bay.

The first person to hint something was wrong was Erskine Thompson. Course Erskine was always the first to hint something was wrong, but he had worked for Mister Watson since a boy and knew his ins and outs as well as anybody. One day in Fort Myers an old nigger woman came up to Erskine and asked if her son was still cutting cane for Mister Watson. Said she'd had no word for more than a year, said another field hand who had lived awhile with the colored there on Safety Hill had never come home either. "Ain't never seen him since," the woman said.

"Took his pay and run off to Key West, I reckon," Erskine told her. "Prob'ly heard about them Yankee nigger-lovers down that way." (Erskine never bothered his head about nigger feelings and my brother Bill tells me I'm darned near as bad. Says, "How come you're so nice to Injuns, Mamie, then turn around and be so mean to coloreds?" "Well, Bill," I told him, "you just go ask Daddy. Know what he'll tell you? *A nigger is a nigger, boy, and that is that.*")

One day Erskine told me how two white men showed up at the Bend in a small sloop, claimed they were just out gallivanting from Key West. E. J.

Watson took to brooding, thinking this pair might be deputies out to make their mark at his expense or maybe thieves that had stolen this nice sloop. However, the cane was ready so he put 'em right to work, kept a close eye. Well, one day after harvest when Erskine arrived back from Port Tampa, their little sloop was still tied to the dock but the men were gone. Mr. Watson said he had bought the sloop and paid 'em off, then run 'em up the coast as far as Marco. Erskine never thought a thing about it till he cleaned out that sloop's little cabin and came across a photo of a woman and small kids in an envelope slipped into a dry slot in the cabin ceiling. He was so surprised something like that would be left behind that he put it away in case they sent for it. They never did. Mr Watson finally sold that sloop, made some good money, too.

This sun-baked feller was E. J.'s old friend and had taken pains to keep it that way so I was surprised to hear any such tale out of his mouth. I asked him what was he really saying—was Mister Watson killing off his help to avoid paying them? Because if Erskine had no such suspicions, how come he was spreading these darned stories—not spreading 'em exactly, just letting 'em drop here and there for folks to sniff at? He backed up fast, got mean-mouthed on me, saying it just goes to show how rumors get their start: *gossiping women!* Said he never believed any such thing about Mister Watson! Why, that man was like a father to him, always had been! Ask Tant Jenkins, Tant would say the same! When I reminded him that Tant left Chatham Bend after that Tucker business and never went back, he said he had no time for gossip and walked away.

I had known this feller for too many years for him to fool me. (Erskine was mostly loyal to his old boss until later in his life when he needed drinking money, which was all he got for that fool interview about his dangerous youth with "Bloody Watson.") I wondered if he was spreading stories as a way to ease his worry. And if Ed Watson's ship captain was worried, so was I.

Henry Short was with the Harden boys that day at Lost Man's Key. One morning in a funny mood, I asked Henry straight out if he thought Mister E. J. Watson killed those Tuckers.

Henry never said a word, just kept on sorting gator pears in the hot sun. In 1910, cruel punishment would come to any upstart nigger who dared hold dangerous opinions about white folks, and anyway, a careful man like Henry Short would never be caught talking alone with a white female, even chubby me whom he had known since a small baby. I ordered him to give me a hand packing tomatoes and he followed me over toward the produce shed where the men could see us talking but not hear us. "Yes or no, Henry?" I said. "I'll never tell."

Henry was looking straight at the tomatoes. Finally he turned his head away. I heard him mutter, "Mist' Watson always been real good to me, Mis Mamie." Not denying. That was Henry's sign.

For a nigger, our Henry was a real good Christian who read his Bible every evening, also a strong hardworking man who could farm, fish, run a boat, mend net, set traps, go hunting deer and never come back without one. Knowing this, Ed Watson was always after him to work at Chatham Bend. Afraid to refuse, he got Daddy to notify Watson that we could not spare him.

One time when Mister Watson was away, Henry made the mistake of sailing Watson's produce to Key West for Erskine Thompson, who said he was too busy at Lost Man's but more likely was just feeling lazy. As a ship captain, Henry was not experienced and Erskine knew this: he counted on Henry's natural ability and good sense and sent him off, persuading him that he would have no difficulties in such fine weather. Henry Short sank E. J. Watson's ship and cargo in a squall down off Cape Sable and was picked up by a sponge boat headed north. Went straight to Watson and took full responsibility, which is more than most white fellers would have done. As Old Man Gregorio Lopez said, "That nigger must been too damned scared to think if he took news as bad as that to E. J. Watson!"

Mister Watson and those Hardens chased off Key West scavengers, raised his ship, but he never raised his voice to Henry Short, just told him he would take him home. They went alone, camped overnight at Possum Key. Something happened there but neither of 'em would ever talk about it. Anyway, Henry was grateful but never forgot what was done at Lost Man's Key. Sometimes he seined mullet with the Storter boys, set gill nets down around the mouth of Chatham River. Claude Storter told my brother Bill that whenever they came upriver past the Bend, Henry loaded that old rifle Daddy gave him and kept it handy in the bow, "in case he seen a deer or something," he would say.

• • •

In that last long summer of 1910, most everybody knew that something bad was brewing on the Watson place, and Edna and her kids mostly stayed with us. One morning she broke down and told us that a chain gang fugitive was working there, a desperado who had killed a lawman in Key West; another man tending the hogs and that hard-faced nigger who came south with them in early 1909 were jailbirds, too. Except for his son Lucius, his only law-abiding help was Hannah Smith.

What brought this whole stew to a boil was a stranger who showed up on Chokoloskee around the time of the Great Comet in the spring. Said he was looking for an E. J. Watson, hawked and spat out the door when he was told that Mister Watson was away in Key West, with his wife expecting. This stranger was a husky young man, scar on his cheekbone but handsome in a hard-set way, with dark brown hair grown long, down to the shoulders, and green eyes set too close under thick brows that met in one heavy line. Had an old-fashioned kind of black frock coat that he wore over his farm clothes, made him look halfway between a gambler and a preacher.

Mr. Smallwood was leery of this stranger from the first minute he came into the store. When he asked "John Smith," as he called himself, if he might be kin to Miss Hannah Smith at Chatham River, the man shook his head, surly and uninterested. He sat out on our porch while we hunted up someone to run him down to Chatham River. "E. J. may be tickled pink to see this hombre, but I doubt it," Mr. Smallwood fretted, watching him leave on Isaac Yeomans's boat. "That frock coat might be hiding a whole arsenal." And I teased him, saying, "Same style of coat your friend E. J. wears, you notice?"

Ted did not feel like being teased. He reminded me that it was this day in the month before, on April 22nd, that the white wake of the Great Comet was first seen in the east, thirty degrees above the horizon, with its scorpion tail that curled across the heavens like an almighty question mark. That question mark set our preacher a-howling about the eternal War between Good and Evil, and how that scorpion tail was the first sign of Armageddon. The Good Lord had imparted to Brother H. P. Jones His intention to wipe out us poor sinners, leave only the few pure-in-hearts such as Mrs. Ida

House still breathing easy. Pure-in-hearts were never plentiful around the Bay, and once the sinners had been packed off to Hell, it might get pretty lonesome around here, I warned her, crying in the wilderness and such as that.

E. J. Watson kept bad company but doted on his family and anyone who knew him said the same. In 1907, he had took dear Edna home to Columbia County for the birth of little Addison, and her Amy May, born in May of 1910, was delivered at Key West because he would not stand for having his young wife pawed over in her labor by that barefoot mulatta man at Lost Man's River who would probably use his oyster knife to shuck her out. Ted didn't like it when his wife talked rough like that. Said E. J. was good friends with Richard Harden but insisted on more up-to-date care for his young Edna, and anyway, he added, getting cross, there was quite a few was shucked by Old Man Richard that were still alive today to tell the tale.

Maybe Ted defended that old man because he let Hardens sneak into our store, not wanting to lose customers to Storters. Any Harden with a few pennies in his hand could knock on our door late of a Sunday evening and Ted Smallwood would go right down in his nightshirt, though he didn't care for that mixed-breed bunch any more than I did: never knew their place or paid it no attention, I don't know which is worse, and probably stole.

On their way home from Key West, E. J. and Edna and little Amy May passed through on their way to Chatham River. Told about the man awaiting him, E. J. stopped short and said, "That man look Injun?"

"Dark straight hair. Could be a breed."

"Look like some shiftless kind of preacher?"

"No." Ted would not grant any resemblance between that stranger and a man of God. I didn't contradict my husband but Mister Watson glimpsed my doubt. Making that little bow, he asked "Miss Mamie" if he might impose on our hospitality once again? Would we look after Edna and the children while he saw to his visitor at Chatham Bend?

In two days he came back for the family. The Watsons had a quarrel up in our spare room before Edna came down teary-eyed to get the children ready. Plainly this stranger's presence on the Bend was a dreadful blow to that young woman. Not that she ever spoke of him, that day or later.

All that hot summer, Edna and her children spent more time at Chokoloskee than at Chatham Bend. Stayed under our roof most of the time but also with Alice McKinney and Marie Lopez, who was newly wed to Wilson Alderman under that dilly tree at Lopez River. Wilson had worked on E. J. Watson's farm in Columbia County, knew a lot about his murder trials in north Florida but would not speak about it. All the same, I reckon it was Wilson who let slip this John Smith's real name.

OWEN HARDEN

✦

With the wild things scarce and fishin poor, me'n Webster went to digging clams off Pavilion Key. We was glad to find Tant Jenkins there that we
hadn't hardly seen since he left Mister Watson, he was stilll lank as a dog
and lots of fun. One day Watson showed up, and he hardly got ashore before ol' Tant was riding him. "Lookee here what's come to call! Damn if it
ain't that dretful desperader!" Us onlookers was hunting for a place to hide,
but Watson was so tickled to see Tant, he just smiled and waved. Seeing
that, Tant started showin off. "Well, men, I'm tellin you right here and now
that Mr. S. S. Jenkins don't aim to take no shit off this here dretful desperader just on account he's some kind of a *Emp*-erer!"

Mister Watson dearly loved that bony feller, he'd take about anything off
Tant where he might of took his knife to someone else. But after the Tuckers, it seemed like Tant's teasing had grew an edge to it, and this day he
strutted around cocking his head back like a turkey gobbler, looking Mister
Watson up and down. "Nosir, boys, I ain't a-scaird of no damn desperader
just on account he's packing so much hardware under that coat he cain't
hardly *walk*!"

Mister Watson laughed till he had to wipe his eyes. Tant purely made
him feel good, you could see it. Only thing, feeling that edge, he made Tant
finish what he started.

Tant seemed to know that if he dared grin, dared let the air out of his
own joke, he would lose the game. And this day he went too far, went to
bobbin and weavin in and out, fists up like a boxer. His little mustache was
just a-bristling. "Step up and take your punishment lest you ain't man

enough!" Watson grinned some more but that grin was a trap. He enjoyed letting this mouse run. Tant knew that, too, but couldn't help himself, he bust out laughing, and Watson's grin closed down tighter'n a orster.

Ed Watson fished his watch out, looked it over, as if figuring how many minutes of life this man had left. The men all knew Ed must be foolin, but they couldn't be dead sure so they edged away. Very sudden, Watson barked into Tant's face, "You never heard about that feller who died laughing?" And them words purely terrified ol' Tant, had him strugglin to pull some shape back to his face.

Knowin Ed Watson as he did, Tant guessed quick that the man wanted him to put up some kind of fight, so he come right back as best he dared: he turned to us onlookers and swore in a tight voice that S. S. Jenkins had just seen the light and would never again make fun of this here Emperor, not even if we was to pay him fourteen dollars.

With no money left when he came home and more work to be done than his home crew could handle, Ed Watson took any harvest labor he could find. Chatham Bend already had a reputation for hiring escaped convicts and got a worse one when rumors went around that field hands were disappearing. Course nobody knew who was down there in the first place, but people were hinting that Watson must be killing off his help when the time come to pay 'em. He had killed before, they said, he had that habit.

Us Hardens never put no stock in what folks took to calling "Watson Payday." But knowing what we knew about the Tuckers, we couldn't quite forget about it either.

The foreman at the Watson place was Dutchy Melville, a Key West hoodlum who got caught looting after the Hurricane of 1909, then burned down a cigar factory on account them Cubans wouldn't pay him not to. Killed a lawman who tried to interfere but escaped the noose due to his youth and winning ways. Escaped from the chain gang, too, while he was at it, and stowed away on the *Gladiator*, it being well-knowed around Key West that Planter Watson weren't particular about his help. Dutchy told his friends, I'll go to Hell before I go back on no chain gang, and I ain't goin neither place without I take a couple lawmen along with me. Probably meant that, too, Florida chain gangs being as close to Hell on earth as a man could get.

Dutchy Melville was a common-sized man, kind of a dirty complexion. Folks knew his people in Key West, good people, too, but if you didn't know how much they hated Spaniards, you might of seen a hair of Spanish in 'em. In one way Dutchy was like Mister Watson, very soft-spoke, nice to meet, and everybody liked him, but some way wild and crazy all the same. Wore big matched revolvers on a holster belt for all to see. One day there on Watson's dock, young Dexter Hamilton from Lost Man's Beach got to hold his gun belts while he did a real front flip, landed on his feet soft as a cat like a regular acrobat out of a circus.

First year Dutchy come, Mister Watson made him foreman, cause those six-guns scared the crew so bad they was glad to work any way the foreman told 'em. Dutchy made fast workers out of slow ones by letting 'em think he had nothing left to lose; if he got the idea to blow their heads off, he might just do that for the target practice. But after him and Mister Watson quarreled over money, Dutchy spoiled a whole year's worth of syrup while Watson was away, took off on some boat and wound up in New York City. From there he wrote his boss a sassy postcard. *Mister Ed, Hope you enjoyed yourself spending up my pay at Tampa Bay.* Watson stood on the porch and read that card he got from Dutchy Melville and just laughed, Erskine Thompson told us. Said, "That young feller knew enough to go a thousand miles away before he wrote me *that!*" Then he swore he would kill him the first chance he got.

Spring of 1910, a stranger come. "John Smith." Turned out later that his rightful name was Leslie Cox. Some said Cox was Watson's cousin and some said he saved Watson's hide one time up north, and later we learned he was a killer that run off from the chain gang, same as Dutchy. Cox had a voice deep as a alligator and a sly mean mouth, said Isaac Yeomans, who run him down from Chokoloskee to the Bend, but he weren't around here long enough for folks to picture him. Some said his black hair was long like a Injun, some said it was cropped short, looked more like fur. Maybe that was their imagination. I seen him myself a time or two but don't recall what his hair looked like, only that I didn't like his looks.

Tant Jenkins, out hunting in Lost Man's Slough, come downriver in late spring with a young Mikasuki squaw and dropped her at the Bend. Injuns wouldn't work for whites, wouldn't work for nobody, but this girl was a drunk whose people had turned their back on her for laying with Tom Brewer to settle what she owed for Brewer's moonshine; she was huddled on the bank dead sick, and if Tant hadn't of come along, she might of died. Nobody at Chatham Bend spoke enough Injun to tell that girl where she should sleep at; probably figured that redskins mostly curled up on the ground out in the woods. Watson ordered her to help his wife with the chores because Big Hannah had men's work to attend to. Girl never understood a word he said but with Ed Watson, people generally got the drift of what was wanted.

Leslie Cox didn't hold with no cajolery. He took and raped that girl, done that regular and got her with child, is what we heard. And knowing her people would never take her back, knowing she had no place to go, the poor critter got so lonesome and pathetic that she hung herself to death out in the boat shed.

That was a story that never did get out until long after, cause by the time the posse went to Chatham Bend, her body was gone. But I got friendly with them Injuns in later years and they all knowed about it. How they took care of it they would not say.

With Dutchy gone and Green Waller mostly drunk, Mister Watson made Cox his foreman, but in the late summer of 1910, Dutchy popped up again with a friendly word for everybody, told 'em he was real glad to be home. Only thing, he didn't care for the new foreman, flat refused to take his orders, said he aimed to take back his old job. "I'm fixing to run this somber sonofabitch right off the property," he told his boss with Cox standing right there. Said he made his ma a solemn swear never to consort with common criminals, which was why he had felt honor-bound to run off from the chain gang.

Common criminals and honor-bound, coming from the mouth of this young killer, purely tickled Mister Watson, and him and Dutchy had a good laugh over that. Dutchy was so cocky he actually thought the Boss was smiling on him like a son; that boy thought a heap of "Mister Ed," thought Mister Ed was sure to let bygones be bygones over that spoiled syrup. Might of been true that Watson liked him but "like" don't always mean forgive, not when it comes to a year's worth of hard-earned money.

When a bear rummaging around too close raises up when he gets your scent, you load quick but you load real easy, with no extra motions that could startle him, and you don't ever look him in the eye cause a bear can't handle that and he might charge. Dutchy Melville was not the kind that took precautions, he was only excited to see what the bear might do; he was like a pup barking and jumping around that bad ol' bear, scaring the onlookers by trying to play, cause the bear don't know the pup is playing and don't care.

Weeks Daniels likes to tell about the day when Melville tagged along with Mister Watson when he went to Pavilion to see his little daughters and while away the afternoon with Josie Jenkins. Hearing Josie's brother holler insults by way of telling his old boss hello, Dutchy figured, well, if that fool Tant can ride him, I can, too. Wanted to show them clam diggers and riffraff that Dutchy Melville had no fear of man nor beast nor E. J. Watson neither. So what he done, he follered his boss and teetered him off the plank walkway across the tide flats, hooting like hell to see him slog ashore. Nobody else who seen this laughed because Watson got his good boots ruined by saltwater mud.

Watson never looked back. Waded ashore, kept right on going over to Josie's shack. But Tant seen his face as he passed by, claimed he knowed right then that Dutchy's days was numbered.

TANT JENKINS

✦

That last summer of living in the Islands, the hunting was so poor that me and my cousin Harvey Daniels and my sort-of cousin Crockett tried setting set gill nets on them sea trout flats northwest of Mormon Key. One early morning before light—we was still anchored, half asleep—we was woke by the motor of a boat coming out from Chatham River. Not many motorboats back then so every man knew any boat from a long ways off. Sure enough, Watson's black *Warrior* come sliding into view. The coast was empty, then there she was, clear of the last mangrove clumps, popped up like she come downriver underwater. Thirty-foot long and nine-foot beam, with a trunk cabin forward, canvas curtains aft, and that black hull.

Next thing we knew, she swung off course headed straight in our direction. Never hailed us, only circled us where we lay anchored, with nobody out on deck, no sign of life. Round and round she went, two-three-four times, slow and steady as a shark. All our guns was loaded, set to shoot, that's how spooked we was, though we was fellers who liked Ed most of the time, him being so friendly with our Daniels family. If he wanted us off them fishing grounds, all he had to do was wave us off and we'd go someplace else.

Not knowing what he was fixing to do next, we could only whisper and sit tight and wait for him to recognize us, leave us alone. I'd worked for him right up until that Tucker business and was still friendly with Lucius. Harvey's dad was his old friend Jim Daniels, Aunt Netta's brother and captain of the clam dredge, and Harvey was the engineer on Bill Collier's *Falcon*, which carried the clams north to the factory. On his day off, Harvey worked on other boats as a mechanic: just recently he'd done motor repair for Mister Watson and was owed eighty-five dollars, which could buy you a rebuilt motor back in them days. Two-three Sundays at Pavilion, Harvey had worked on Mister Watson's boat right alongside him. What I always recall, when you seen Ed Watson from behind, them ginger whiskers under that black hat would be sticking out from both sides of his head.

Mister Watson was generally a fair man to do business with, but this day was along toward the end when he was broke from his troubles in north Florida and behind on all his debts and slow from booze. His black boat circled us four times, then come ahead from dead abeam like she aimed to cut our little boat in two. Crockett and me jumped up, waving our guns, but Harvey had more sense, being the oldest; said he had no wish to trade shots with E. J. Watson, especially when we couldn't even see him. Told us to lay them guns down quick, making sure Watson seen us do it, and then get set to dive over the side and swim underwater far as we could, come up for a quick breath and down again, cause we might not make it to the shore if we was full of lead. But at the last second—we was yelling at each other to get set—the black boat sheared off and headed north. Was that all he wanted? Scaring us, I mean?

Speck—that's what Watson called Crockett, I can't rightly recall why— Speck were now close to sixteen and pretty reckless, so being bad spooked was hard for him to handle. He promised Harvey, "If he don't pay you what he owes real quick, we'll slip upriver on a night tide, set in the reeds across from his damn house, and first time he steps outside, I'll pick him off for you." He meant that, too. Never killed nobody far as I heard but you knew this boy could do that if he had to. It was something you seen in certain fellers: Crockett Daniels was that kind. And he was a boy who could pick up his rifle and nail the small head of a floatin terrapin spang to the water.

Harvey was the other kind, thoughtful and steady—sooner lose his pay than see a man shot dead on his account. Also, he knew that bein so hot-headed, Crockett might not have such a cunning plan as what he thought. Harvey said, "Maybe you ain't doing this to settle up my debt. Maybe you're doing this just to prove that you ain't scared of him."

Speck got somewhat hot, of course, but he don't really deny it. "One of these damn days," he swore, "I'll take and fix that sonofabitch to where he don't scare *nobody* no more!"

BILL HOUSE

✦

Hurricane of October 1909 tore away half of Key West, blew the cigar trade all the way north to Tampa Bay. Who could have known that a storm much worse would strike in 1910? Maybe the Great Comet in our night sky in April-May was our first warning.

Ed Watson's house at Chatham Bend was strong constructed, and she sat up on a Injun mound as high above the water as any place south of Chokoloskee, probably as safe a place as you could find on this low coast. So you have to ask why, a few days before the hurricane, Watson run his family back to Chokoloskee unless he knew what might happen at the Bend and wanted his people safe out of harm's way. Watson told Smallwood he had brung his wife and kids because his crazy foreman was out to kill somebody. And all this time he called him "Smith," as if hiding his identity, which seemed suspicious at the time and does today. Edna confided in my sister and Alice McKinney that she could not abide Chatham Bend with "John Smith" there. Never let on what she knew but only said that wherever that man went, trouble would follow.

Somewhere around October 10, Watson come here visiting his family, bringing one of his outlaws along with him. Folks was leery of this feller Dutchy Melville but allowed as how he was always full of fun. That October day at Chokoloskee, Dutchy got foul-mouthed, sneered at Watson to his face in front of everybody. Called him Ed. Said, "Ed? How about let's you and me just settle this fucking goddamn thing right here and now?"

Watson told him calmly that no man could draw as fast out of his pocket as a feller drawing from a holster. "You want me dead as bad as that," he said, "you better shoot me in the back." And Dutchy said, "Back-shooting,

Ed? I always heard that was *your* damned specialty." Mister Watson cocked his head, eyes just a-shivering. Told Dutchy, "You ain't careful enough for a feller who talks to me as smart as that." Then he turned his back on him, kind of contemptuous.

There come a gasp but Watson knew his man. Dutchy was no back-shooter and never would be. "What this young feller needs is another drink," Ed Watson said. They drank together, took the jug along for the trip home to Chatham Bend. That was the last we ever seen of Dutchy Melville.

OWEN HARDEN

✦

All that long summer of 1910, crops withered in the worst drought Daddy Richard could remember. With fishing so poor and the last clam beds off Pavilion staked out by Bay crackers, all we had left was ricking buttonwood for charcoal.

For ricking, a man has got to cut ten cords a day. Tote 'em and stack 'em, cover the rick with grass and sand to make it airtight, all but a vent on top and a few holes at the bottom to fire it. Get twenty bags of charcoal at the most for all that donkey work and still don't make a living. Man winds up with a sooty face and a crook-back, is about all.

For fishermen used to open water and Gulf breeze, ricking is killing work in the wet heat. Up at first light, work till dusk, lay down stinking cause you're too tired to wash. Get up bone stiff, sore, half bit to death, still stinking, do the same damned thing all over again, day after day, year after year. See any sense to it? Daddy Richard weren't up to the chopping and stacking, not no more, not ten cords in a day. No feller that age is going to last long ricking but our stubborn old man aimed to die in the attempt. Down at Shark River, they was cutting out the last of them giant mangrove trees for fuel for tanning, but that work was too heavy for him, too. So it looked like Hardens might have to leave all our hard years behind—clearings, cabins, fish docks, all our gear. Say good-bye to Lost Man's and our old free life, go to Caxambas to work in the clam cannery because Daddy Richard had worn out his heart down in the rivers and it was too late in life to start again.

Up till very near the end, my folks never bothered their heads about all them Watson stories. Hadn't Ed been our good neighbor? (But maybe they were forgetting certain stuff, cause when I was little, my ma used our neighbor as the Bogeyman: *You don't jump into that bed real quick, John Owen Harden, Mister Watson'll gitcha!*) Only now in his despair did Richard Harden listen to Earl's gossip about "Watson Payday." He came to fear that his friend Ed Watson would take over Wood Key as soon as our family left to find work elsewhere. "Well, that's better than *before* we leave, like Tuckers!"—that was Earl and for once nobody hushed him. Dread was growing in the Islands, dread was always in the air, like haze from Glades wildfires over eastward, and finally Hardens got infected, too. In my nightmares—I never mentioned 'em to Sarah—Mister Watson loomed up in the night window, the moonlight glinting on his gun and whiskers.

HOAD STORTER

✦

Early October, with my brother Claude and Henry Short, I was fishing the bayous up inside the Chatham delta (what's called Storter Bay on the marine charts of today), and selling the catch to the clam diggers on Pavilion Key. My good old friend from boyhood, Lucius Watson, usually came down-river to fish with us, but Lucius had left the Bend after some trouble, he was in Flamingo.

One evening we were at Pavilion selling mullet when Jim Cannon from Marco and his boy came in and caused a uproar. The Cannons were farming vegetables on Mr. Chevelier's old place on Possum Key. Some said they were prospecting for the Frenchman's treasure (or maybe the miser money folks claim Ed Watson killed him for) but Jim was just provisioning the clam crews, same as we were. Bananas and guavas were still thick on Possum in the years bears didn't clean 'em out, also the gator pears and Key limes put in by the Frenchman. His garden was kept cleared and his cistern fresh by Indians who camped there on their way north from Shark River.

After Watson came back to Chatham Bend in early 1909, the Cannons never cared to stay the night at Possum Key. Camped with the clam crews on Pavilion, went upriver each day on the tide. On that dark squally morning, Jim's boy saw a pale small thing breaking the surface. "Pap," he calls, "I seen something queer stick up, right over there!" And Jim Cannon says, "No, you ain't never! Must been some ol' snag or somethin." The boy hollered, "Nosir! It was white!" Well, Cannon paid him no more mind, and they went on upriver. But that boy worried all day about what he'd seen, and coming back that afternoon, he was on the lookout, and pretty quick he's hollering and pointing.

Know that eddy just below the Watson place, off the north bank? Jim Cannon swung the boat in there, saw something white and puffy sticking up that turned out to be a woman's foot. The current curling past it was so strong that they had to take a hitch around the ankle just to stay put, but there was nothing to be done, they could not come up with her. That corpse seemed moored to something deep down in the river and they pretty near capsized trying to boat her.

The boy was scared and getting scareder: he figured that the giant croc reported from this stretch of river must have a hold of her. Staring at that ghosty face mooning deep in the dark current and the hair streaming like gray weed, he burst into tears of fright, he was shivering in some kind of a fit. So Cannon cut her loose, said, "Never mind, son, we'll just go ashore, report this here calamity to Mister Watson." Having more sense than the father, the boy screeched, "Nosir, I ain't going!" He had heard those stories about Watson, he was scared stiff.

Jim told him to hush up so he could think. He concluded that whoever committed this foul deed had nothing to lose by getting rid of witnesses and he'd better go back to Pavilion, find some help.

Next morning, a party went upriver. Henry Short was very much afraid but he went with us. Kept his old rifle handy and nobody objected, the body being just below the Watson place. That giant woman had been gutted out like you'd gut a bear, then anchored off with sacks of bricks left over from the syrup works and some pig iron. When she bloated up and floated all that iron off the bottom, that one foot broke the surface and wigwagged the first boat that came along. Every man was boiling mad to see a woman as good-hearted as Hannah Smith treated so brutally. Some of 'em were talking big about going up to Watson's house, but except for Henry we weren't armed so we never went, and nobody came out of that house to see what we were up to.

Hannah's hog-thief boyfriend was still with her. Somebody looked down and there he was! He had been weighted separately but their lines tangled, he rose with her, and that spooked us, too.

Those bodies had been there a few days and nobody wanted to look at 'em, let alone smell 'em—made our eyes water. We dug a pit on the south bank down the river, maybe thirty feet in from the point where Watson had been clearing off another cane field. Henry Short helped dig the hole but he knew better than to lay a hand on her. Maybe someone mumbled a few words and maybe not.

Returning downriver, someone spotted a third body wedged into the mangrove roots, all torn by gators. We rigged a hitch to Dutchy Melville and towed him back and buried what was left of him beside the others. One feller threw up and I came pretty close.

A man can go there yet today and see that lonely grave. Big and square, maybe sunk about a foot, and nothing growing, even some years later, as if someone had lifted a barn door stuck in the marl. Those three lost souls are laying in there right this minute. You open that pit, you'll have a look at Hell.

We hardly got back from the burial when in came this big nigra from the Watson place, dark husky feller in torn coveralls. He had taken a skiff and got away from Chatham Bend—a desperate act because he was no boat-man, his palms were raw from pulling on old splintery oars. One minute he was moaning and blubbering so much you could hardly make him out, the next he was quiet and his eyes were steady. Captain Thad Williams, who came in that day to pick up any people who wanted to go north before the storm, gave that man a hard cuff to make him talk straight, and finally he hollered that three white folks had been bloody-murdered on the Bend.

"Jesus, boy, we *know* that!" a man yelled. "Tell us who done it!"

"Yassuh! Mist' Watson—"

"Y'all hear that? Watson!"

But before we could pin him down, he cried, "Nosuh, I mistook myself! Mist' Watson's *fo'man*!"

The ugly silence in that crowd was partly outrage against any nigra who would dare to get his white boss into trouble. Captain Thad talked rough with him, told him to be careful who he went accusing; Thad told me later he had been afraid this excited crowd might lynch him. The nigra was moaning and carrying on but back of all that noise and fear I sensed some-thing cunning.

Watson's back-door family—that whole Daniels-Jenkins bunch that lived off and on at Chatham Bend—that bunch wanted to shut this black man up right then and there. And seeing the way the wind was blowing, the man insisted, "Nosuh, ah sho' mistook mahself! Mist' Watson nevuh knowed nothin about *nothin*! Mist' Watson *gone*!" But not until he got Watson suspected had he switched his story.

Watching him work his story back and forth, I realized this feller knew what he was doing from the start. Cox might have killed him at Chatham Bend and he had no place to run, so he risked coming to Pavilion Key to warn the nearest white men about a dangerous killer. If he'd left it at that, he might have been all right. But as we could see, he was in a rage, maybe mule-headed by nature: he put out that stink of suspicion rather than let his white man boss get off unpunished, then backed off from a flat-out accusation. Didn't want to die, but if he had to die, he would not go before he risked the truth. As Henry Short found out and told us later, this man was determined to see justice done, even if his idea of justice was an act of revenge that could very well get him killed. He had dug himself a deep dark hole of trouble, probably too deep to climb out.

When this nigra was told how the woman's body had surfaced in the river, he let out a yell, "Oh Lawd Miz Hannah! Lawdamercy!" They slapped him again, to shut up all his racket. Everyone was trying to think what we should do. When Thad demanded, "Who gutted out those bodies?" he blubbered how Mist' Les Cox tole him he was done fo' if he didn't shoot into the bodies and help "in the guttin and haulin," said Mist' Cox tole him if anybody asked, just blame it on Mist' Watson. This was the first time most of us learned that the foreman's name was not John Smith but Leslie Cox.

That black man was plain crazy to confess he had shot and manhandled a white woman. When someone yelled that this damn nigger had been in on it from start to finish, there rose a kind of ugly groan and a man whapped his face. "You shot a white woman, that what you said? Laid your black hands all over her? What else you do?" If there'd been one tree limb on that key that had not been chopped for fuel, they would have strung him up.

But if he was mixed up in it, why had he come here? Why had he talked himself into so much trouble? Those watchful yellow eyes gave me the feeling that this man had done just what he aimed to do. When he saw I'd seen that, he cast his eyes down. Bone reckless, maybe, but no fool.

At the fire, the clammers were drinking shine, angry and frustrated; most agreed that shooting this man could do no harm. But Cap'n Thad declared that his vessel was the only one that could carry them all home from

Pavilion Key to escape the coming storm, and anyone who harmed this crucial witness to the crime would get left behind. He marched the nigra over to his schooner for safekeeping, and once the man was out of sight, the crowd calmed down some, deciding to see justice done in court.

Tant's sister Josie was still spitting mad that a white man had been slandered by "a dirty nigger." She'd had some drink and they let her rant and rave. Swore she'd never board that rotten ship with such a bunch of yellerbellies, not if it was her last day on this earth, and neither would her man Jack Watson's baby boy. "Spittin image!" one drunk yelled when she lifted him above her head for all to see.

HENRY SHORT

◆

Friday evening October the 14th the Marco man brought word about dead bodies in Chatham River. First light Saturday morning a party went up there, hauled them poor souls out, and buried them on that point down from the Watson place. Put all three in the same hole because they wanted to get back with a storm coming. Being the nigger, I done most of the digging. Heard a man inquire if that albino nigger in the hole was the same one who buried them young Tucker folks on Lost Man's Key.

Black feller from Mist' Watson's showed up Saturday evening with the story. He had escaped, he was near starved, he talked too much out of his fear. Not wanting to pay for his mistakes, I eased away into the dusk and Mist' Hoad follered me. Said I best sleep aboard Captain Williams's ship in case there was trouble. That black man was brought on board right after me, they locked the two coloreds in the same cabin for safekeeping. One man said to Mist' Hoad, "That's all right, ain't it? Both bein niggers?" Mist' Hoad looked across at me, see how I took that. Him and me and Mist' Claude Storter been fishing partners for some years, he knew me pretty good. I shrugged to show I understood. There weren't nothing to be done about it.

When the white men were gone, this feller said, "What they fixin to do with me?" I said, "All I know is, you best calm down and get your story straight." He jeered real ugly, "Who you, boy, the pet nigger around here? That cause you so white?"

"This ain't no time to go picking fights," I warned him.

"Nosir, Mr. Nigger, it sure ain't," he said, his voice gone quiet. He lay down on the floor, turning his back to me.

Raised up and living all my life in a frontier settlement where black folks were not tolerated, I have only talked to few but I can say I never met a black man hard as this one. Course a lot of his anger likely come from nerves. He was scared, all right—he'd be a crazy man not to be scared—but he weren't panicky.

I couldn't sleep and I knew this man weren't sleeping so when he rolled over next, I asked his name. He said that "Ed"—he used that name!—always called him Little Joe, which worked as good as any. From this I knew he was a wanted man same as them others. Said he'd knew Ed for some years but could not recall where they first met. This was a lie and he never tried to hide that: this feller knew plenty about Mist' Watson and his foreman, too. He shrugged me off, saying this fool conversation weren't none of his idea and anyway it weren't my business so leave him alone. But in a while he muttered, "Name ain't Joe. It's Frank, okay?" He rolled back toward me. "Mights well get my real name just in case they got a nigger guestbook down in Hell showin who passed through."

With no way to know what might be coming down on him in the next hours, he must have needed somebody to hear him out, even if only just another nigger, cause when I didn't ask him no more questions, he started talking on his own—not to me, not to nobody in particular, he just wanted to get it off his chest once and for all. Talked along in a dead voice about the awful deeds done at the Watson place and why he reckoned he weren't slaughtered like them others. All the while he spoke, he kept his face hid and his voice low like this was a secret God Himself should never hear.

Mist' Ed Watson took Dutchy along to Chokoloskee, leaving Cox and the others behind. The restless weather all that week before the storm had riled up everybody's nerves, they were all drinking. From out in the kitchen, this black man listened to everything, including Cox's nigger jokes told specially for him to overhear.

The trouble started when Green Waller went to the boat shed for another jug, came back in howling that the Injun girl was over there hung by her neck. Big Mis Hannah took to blaming Cox because he raped that girl and made her pregnant so the least he could do was go take her down and close her eyes, lay her out decent. Cox said, "What she done to herself, that ain't my business." Said if Big Hannah wanted her took down so bad, she better go take care of that herself "or let the nigger do it," meaning him.

So then Mis Smith come out with something rough about the foreman's manlihood, and he called her back by a filthy name this man Frank would not repeat out of his respect for Big Mis Hannah. Green Waller yelled, "That ain't no damn way to go talking to a lady!" And Cox said, "I ain't talking to no lady, Pigshit, unless you mean this here big freak out of the circus." And Waller comes back, "White trash like you wouldn't know a lady if she come from church to help your mama off the whorehouse floor!"

Cox said, "That done it." He pulled out a pistol. Mis Hannah screeched at Green to shut his mouth, didn't he know that white trash loves their mothers good as anybody? Waller was scared to death but wouldn't quit. The man was plain crazy in love, showing off for his sweetheart so she could see her man weren't just some drunken hog thief the way Mister Watson said. He pointed at his own chest, said to Cox, "How about it, kid? You yeller enough to shoot a man in his cold blood that is twice your age?"

Maybe Mist' Green Waller had Cox figured for another Dutchy Melville, Frank said, dangerous talker but not all bad at heart. Mis Hannah Smith did not make that mistake. She was struggling up out of her chair trying to get between them, telling Cox, "Don't pay no attention to that idjit!" Frank claimed he called in from the kitchen, "Nemmine, Mist' Les, Mist' Green was only foolin." But like Frank said, Cox had more excuse already than his kind ever needs. Bein drunk, arm wobbling, he said, the foreman had trouble getting Waller in his sights. "Sit still, you sonofabitch," he yelled, "don't make me go wastin these here bullets!"

Mist' Green Waller finally understood the fun was over. He brought his hands up slow and careful so as not to flare the man behind that pistol. Cox lowered his weapon into his lap, then fired anyway underneath the table. Ever hear a gun go off in a small room? Their ears exploded with that noise. Even Cox looked stunned. "That was a accident," he muttered. But this nigra swore that Cox done that on purpose, shot him in the belly cause that hurts the worst.

Mist' Green was still setting at the table clutching his belly. Looked kind of sheepish, Frank said. "Well, Hell," he whispered. Them were his last words. Scowling, he leaned into the table, then toppled over soft onto the floor.

Mis Hannah had barged out of her chair. She flew and shook him, moaning, "Christamighty, Green, ain't you never going to learn? Oh, Christ-amighty, sweetheart!" Howled with woe and headed for the kitchen. Cox jumped up with his pistol, took off after her and she darned near beheaded him, splitting that door frame with the big two-blader ax which she kept leaned in the corner behind the kitchen door. Cox went down but sat up and fired before she could try him again. She took a bullet in the shoulder, dropped the ax, crashed off the wall, threw a pan at Cox with her good arm, then headed for the stair.

Cox picked himself up, very bad scared by his close call. He was furious Frank never warned him. Pointing his gun, he said, "Stay right there, nig-ger. I got business with you."

Miss Hannah was cumbersome climbing the stair and Cox overtook her before she reached the landing. Knowing how strong she was, he gave her room, stood a step below while they got their breath. Miss Hannah weren't the kind to beg for mercy and she knew she'd never get none if she did. She screeched, "Run, Little Joe! We're done for! Run! He'll kill you, too!"

Time he heard that, he was already outside, out past the cistern. Two shots came, then another. From the wood edge he could hear a *thump, thump, thump* of someone falling, then a queer high laugh like a horse nick-ering. Being drunk, Cox had shot so poorly that he had to sneak around be-hind, give her a brain shot, he told Frank later. Only she weren't done yet cause her big leg kicked, knocked him off balance: he slipped on the blood, fell down the stair, but never hurt himself, being so drunk. That nickering noise weren't nothing but his nerves. When he seen Frank was gone, he commenced to holler, told him to come give him a hand with this here manatee before she bled all over, nastied up the place for Mis Edna. The dead woman went a good three hundred pound and he could not work the body down the stair. Couldn't stop hollering out of his excitement. "Ah *Jesus*, will you look at that damn mess!" he moaned. "Know who will catch hell for this? Les Cox, that's who!"

Mister Watson's old skiff was some ways down the bank, overturned with the old oars underneath, all growed over by bushes. Frank doubted Cox ever knew about that skiff, probably forgot about it if he had. Trouble was, he couldn't make a run for it without crossing open ground. Before he could make up his mind, Cox came reeling out, threatened to shoot him in the belly same as he done Green, leave him for the bears or panthers or the crocodiles, whichever ones got to him first. Next, he tried to talk reasonable. He was sounding scared again. *Hell, I was only foolin, Joe!* Promised not to shoot him and the nigra reckoned he meant it, at least until they finished cleaning up.

Right about then, they heard the *pot-pot-pot* of Watson's boat rounding the Bend. Cox screeched *Shit!* in frustration, which told him Cox was probably scared that "Little Joe" would get to the Boss first with the true story. Cursing real disgusting, Cox ran inside and came right out with Waller's shotgun. Waving the gun at Frank in warning to keep his mouth shut, he crossed the yard and ducked inside the boat shed door and screamed again because he had bumped into that hanging body.

Frank was relieved when the boat drew near, knowing that once the Boss was back, he would be all right. All the same he remained hidden, scared that with Watson coming, Cox might try to kill off the last witness. But when he saw Cox disappear into the shed armed with a shotgun instead of going down to meet the boat, he realized the foreman was planning on an ambush. The intended victim could only be Cox's sworn enemy Dutchy Melville, who was this nigra's friend.

Dutchy was already on the dock but the boat was drifting off into the current. Frank heard Dutchy sing out, "Where you going, Mister Ed?" By the time Frank ran out yelling a warning, Dutchy had smelled the trap and lit out zigzag for the nearest cover. That was the boat shed. Cox poked the shotgun through a loose slat in the door and Dutchy Melville took a charge of buckshot in the throat, died kicking like a chicken with the head cut off.

Cox had heard the nigra's yell and swung around in time to catch him in the open. Frank put his hands up, sure he was a goner. Instead Cox marched him to the dormitory behind the boat shed and locked him in with the four field hands he locked up every night so's they wouldn't steal nothing or eat a chicken or run off on him—though where them poor fellers would have went to in them miles and miles of salt marl mangrove only God would know. Anyways, they were too scared to try anything. They cringed like mutts when the foreman came around, which was how Cox wanted it. Those colored boys had heard the shooting so when they saw Cox they could only moan.

· · ·

Afraid to go back into that bloody house, Cox spent what was left of that night drinking shine out on the porch. At sunup he came and let Frank out but not those field hands; probably imagined he still might get away with what he'd done and didn't want four more witnesses to see those bodies. Walked him at gunpoint to where Dutchy was laying, ordered him to pick up one of those six-guns, shoot into the body without turning around, then go inside, put bullets in the others, and drop the six-shooter on the ground.

I asked Frank did it cross his mind to swing and put his bullet into Cox instead. He said he thought about it only Cox was too nerved up and had him too close covered the whole time. Anyway, it didn't matter what he did. He was still a nigger and a fugitive from justice and nobody was going to listen to him, let alone believe him, and besides, he said, real bitter and sarcastic, I weren't doing them dead people no harm. Said he would hang no matter what for the murder of three whites—make that four if he shot Cox. But as he said, a nigra could never dream of no such thing, let alone do it.

Full of fear, Frank helped drag Miss Hannah down the stairs. That started her leaking all over the place but finally they got her hauled across the porch and down into the yard. Cox planned to sink her in the river, but first we got to gut her out, he said, so she don't gas up and come back on us. Said he hated to see black hands on a white body, then handed Frank the kitchen knife and held his gun on him while the nigra done this terrible sacrilege on a human woman and the same for the two men, gagging all the way. Next they weighted Hannah and her man with pig iron and bricks and pushed 'em off the dock into the current.

By then there were no weights left for Dutchy, who was buzzing with green flies in the thick heat. Cox said, "To hell with him, let them gators have him." Cox stripped off Melville's fancy holster belt and they rolled him in, too. He made no mention of that Injun girl in the shed behind him, acted like she weren't even there and never had been.

Since the night before they had never ate a bite but they weren't hungry. Cox ordered Frank to mop that blood that nastied up the floor, "get everything tidied up real nice for Edna." Cox laughed when he said that. He was putting down a lot more shine, and pretty quick he forgot about the blood. Made the nigra sit down in Mist' Green's chair, pushed Green's glass across the table, said, Let's don't go wasting this good likker, boy. Go ahead, drink, maybe try out some of your nigger conversation, cause we're in this thing together, ain't that right? Just like old times, right? Telling this, Frank glanced at me to see if I had noticed that him and Cox must of knowed each other good from someplace else.

Cox made him promise he'd back up his story, tell Mister Ed how his foreman weren't at fault. Tell him how them two drunken fools was abusing him for no damn reason. How Green had his shotgun hid under the table (a lie, Frank said) and Hannah had her big ax ready so his foreman had to shoot in self-defense.

After that, Cox didn't hardly talk no more. Frank was very nervous, sitting across that table from a dead drunk killer with a revolver by his hand who might take and blow his head off any moment. He kept quiet, kept his eyes down so as not to trigger him. He recalled staring at a file of ants, crossing the table to the late Green Waller's spilled pea soup.

Early afternoon, Cox finally dozed but his hand was still on the revolver, and he caught the black man when he tried to slip outside. This time Frank was sure the man would kill him. Instead he locked him in with the four hands again and went back to his drinking and ranting. Went on for three days and all that while those men in the shed had no food nor water.

Cox scarcely went back into the house, just darted in to grab something, came right back out again. Cox seemed to have no plan, no need for sleep. Reese thought the man must have gone crazy.

Nights passed and days. The prisoners, starved, thirsty, and half bit to death, were crying out for mercy. All this while Frank was chiseling out the hinge screws with a broke-blade clasp knife. He finally got the door loose enough to pull it back and slip on through, then waited until dark. He just whispered good luck and went. He did not tell the hands about the skiff, knowing the old boat was unseaworthy and anyway too small to carry all five. Too terrified of Cox to follow, they just watched him go, thinking he meant to escape inland through the scrub, Frank ran down past Hannah's cabin to the growed-over boat and got away downriver, bailing all the way. Passing through the mangrove delta into the open Gulf, he thought he heard distant shots but could not be sure.

· · ·

When he finished his awful story we lay quiet. The night passed very slow and very fast. Toward dawn he got up, glancing out the porthole like he might die and go to Hell at the first light. "You reckon they'll believe me?" he said suddenly. "Sheriff and them?"

"Might ask how come you never mentioned them four field hands when you told your story over on the shore."

He looked surprised. "Never thought about it," he confessed. "You really think them white people would of cared about them fellers?"

"No, I don't," I said, "but they might try to test your story."

"Maybe them boys come out okay," he said. "Go fuck yourself," he said, resentful. "How do I know what happened to them poor damn bastards? All I know is, I couldn't take 'em with me." I believed that and was sorry— sorry for Frank, too. Those four young men would always be his lonely secret.

Next morning when they let me out, I turned in the cabin doorway to tell him something but I found no words. He come forward and said quietly, "I didn't kill nobody, Henry. You believe that?" When I nodded, he nodded, too. Said, "Tell them white people my story, then. Remind 'em how this nigger come here on his own and never had no reason to tell lies."

"I'll do my best," I promised.

He said calmly, "Nothing you can tell 'em gone to save my black hide, I understand that good as you do, Henry. But knowin that the real truth has been heard, that makes it better. Not okay, just better."

He stuck his hand out, cracked a little grin. "So long, nigger," he said. I could not find a smile to give him back. I said, "Good luck, then, Frank," and went away very sad and angry. Might have been wanted, like I say, but he weren't all bad and he weren't sorry for himself. It was me was sorry. Sorry a brave man had to die so bitter.

HOAD STORTER

✦

The men were troubled by the wind shifts and nobody liked the looks of that hard sky. Folks took those murders at the Watson place for an evil sign like that white swath of light across the heavens in the spring, so far away in deepest night, beyond all knowing.

Saturday morning a report came in over Cap'n Thad's ship radio that the strong offshore storm coming up the Gulf had sheered off westward. Thad didn't trust that and by midafternoon had everyone aboard that hadn't already taken off in their own boats. The only person who refused to leave was Mrs. Josie Jenkins. She came down to the shore, put her young daughter on board, and stayed to call good-bye, waving her baby son's fat little arm. Mother and babe would brave the storm alone, she cried, because even her own brother had forsaken them. That was more guilt than poor old Tant could handle, so he left Pearl in the care of Josie's latest husband and returned ashore to reason with her. Got nowhere because both of 'em were drunk. When Tant's friends went to moderate and failed to return, Cap'n Thad got fed up. It was too damned late to sail today, he would sail without fail at daybreak Sunday, and any fools that weren't on board would be left behind.

Sunday dawned with light winds and fair weather, all but that cold purple off to westward like a deep bruise in a pale sky.

I and Claude and Henry Short went north in our own boat. I told Henry I was sorry about locking him up the night before with that black prisoner. He said the man's real name was Frank and reminded us that Frank was the one witness to what really happened, because even if Leslie Cox was caught, he would surely lie. Then he told the story. Claude asked Henry if he believed that story and Henry said yessir, he did. That man had took too big a risk to go making up lies for just another nigger, Henry added.

I had never heard Henry speak in that hard way. Henry knew how he had sounded, too, and tried to smooth it over. Said he believed this man had implicated Mister Watson because Watson had betrayed Melville to Cox.

Henry caught our quick exchange of looks. "Frank and Dutchy were friends some way," Henry explained. "Feller fugitives," he said, ironical again.

Claude ignored this new Henry, being worried about what would become of that tough black man. "Think they'll hang him?" he asked me. When I nodded, Claude looked kind of sorry.

SARAH HARDEN

◆

Soon after word come about them murders at the Bend—this was mid-October—Mister Watson turned up out of nowhere. We heard that motor from a long ways off, come across the wind like muffled rifle shots but steady. Then that popping stopped, leaving a hollow in the silence, and the *Warrior* came drifting down around the point. He poled her over to our dock, took his coat off, and begun to tinker with his engine. Hardens had no quarrel with him, nothing to be afraid of, but I had to wonder why his boat just happened to break down so close to our place.

Owen was back in Lost Man's River seining mullet with his brothers. My mother-in-law said, "I sure do hope them boys heard his darned motor." They heard it all right and came quick as they could but that weren't quick enough.

We always went down to the shore to welcome visitors or run 'em off, that was the custom amongst Island neighbors. But this day Daddy Richard stayed back in the cabin, sore as a darned beetle blister cause what he called his arthur-ritis had flared up on him. What with the life pains he was feeling, he was very quick to cock his rifle and draw a bead on Mister Watson's heart as soon as that man shut his motor down and straightened. When me'n Ma Mary started outside to go to meet him, Daddy Richard growled, "Mind you women stay well clear of my line of fire." His wife was disgusted, told him to stop scaring his own womenfolk for nothing. He snapped back that he knew what he knew, and I reckon he still did, most of the time.

Ed Watson seen straight off he was unwelcome. Never left his boat, just tinkered, closed the hatch again. The onshore wind held her snug against the dock, though with that chop, she lifted and thumped against the pilings. "Good day, Mister Watson!" Mary Harden's work-red hands was white, that's how hard she clenched 'em, but I believe she was more upset about not offering our neighbor a bite to eat than fearful that this man might do us harm.

Though he doffed his hat, Mister Watson did not answer. He was hollow-eyed and grizzle-chinned, his clothes looked slept in. Seeing Daddy Richard's boat moored off the dock, he must of wondered if his old friend was in the cabin and why he never came out nor even called hello. He studied all around a while, the better to listen to the silence in that clearing, which any moment was going to explode. Out of the corner of his eye, he kept the cabin window covered, never lost sight of it, as if he knew that though that hole in them gray boards looked black and empty, our old man was crouching down behind it, fingering his trigger. When Mary Harden moved a step, put her big body between him and the window, he pretended he never noticed, but now he knew for sure. "And a good day to you, Mis Mary," he said finally. "Richard around?"

As he watched Ma Mary struggle with her lie, his smile was quizzical. Told us he was on his way north from Key West where he'd spent some days on business, told us he was calling in to see if there was anything we needed in Fort Myers, where he would be headed in the next few days. I thanked him, said we lacked for nothing.

Ma Mary blurted, "The men's just over yonder!"—a bad mistake, because hearing they were nearby might make him stay. To get his mind off that, I squawked, "How's Topsy? She still doing tricks?" Mister Watson shook his head. Topsy had et up all her shoats so he had a mind to slit her bristled throat, eat *her:* might teach her not to try that trick again. When he winked, I giggled out of nerves.

(Later, Ma Mary exclaimed, "A man who could joke about his sow eating her shoats had killing on his mind, for sure!" Daddy Richard said, "A female who could say such a fool thing as that don't know the first thing about killers!" He never talked to her so sharp before; his nerves was wound tight, too.)

Mary Harden stood twisting her hands, never offered our neighbor so much as a cup of water, and still he acted like he never noticed. And all the while she was shifting to stay in Daddy Richard's line of fire, in case our visitor went for his pocket handkerchief, thinking to blow his nose, and our jumpy old man hauled back on the trigger. Mister Watson watched her peculiar movements and he watched her eyes. I believe he knew his old friend had a bead on him.

A restless wind out of the northeast was racketing the sea grape and palmettas. The wind had held in that quarter for two days, with squalls and rain. This was Saturday, October the fifteenth, when the radio was already reporting that a strong offshore storm was sheering off toward the west, through the Yucatan Passage, but we never had no radio back then, we went by the winds and sky; the men was troubled by that wind and didn't like the look of the horizon.

Mister Watson said kind of matter-of-fact that he believed a hurricane was coming. Said he'd like nothing better than to set awhile but had to get back to take care of his people. When he stooped half out of sight to spin his flywheel, Ma Mary screened him, spreading the wings of her big brown dress like a broody hen. He saw this, too, because when he straightened—knowing she'd never hear his thanks over the motor—he put one hand behind his back and made that kind of fancy bow men do for queens and such; that bow startled my mother-in-law so bad that she tried to bow back in a kind of a gawky curtsy. Smiling, he tipped his hat toward the empty window and shouted out over the motor, "My respects to Mr. Harden and the boys!"

We watched him head his boat offshore and turn toward the north. His outline at the helm was hunched and black against a narrow band of light out to the west where that wall of weather was slowly moving in off the Gulf of Mexico.

MAMIE SMALLWOOD

✦

In early October when E. J. Watson brought his family, he told us all signs pointed to a hurricane. "Something bad is coming down on us"—those were his very words. I don't know how he knew about the hurricane but he sure did, though it held off for another fortnight. You reckon that man felt it in his bones? Inkling of his own dark fate or something? Said he trusted his house on Chatham Bend to stay put in any storm, but with Baby Amy only five months old, he was taking no chances on a flooded cistern and bad water, and Chokoloskee was the highest ground south of Caxambas. Later he told Sheriff Tippins he'd brought his family here to Chok because "John Smith" was a killer, but he never said anything like that to us. By this time it was well known that John Smith's real name was Leslie Cox.

E. J. Watson came back here alone on October 16th, a Sunday. Late that same day, young Claude Storter came in from Pavilion Key with word of dreadful murders. Claude's news caused a hubbub of excited talk about arresting E. J. Watson, talk that was still going on when Watson came into the store and took a seat with its back into the corner. When no one could look him in the eye, he eased onto his feet again and straightened his coat, gazing around the room. Maybe he didn't growl the way Charlie Boggess told it, but he sure smelled trouble, and he picked out the Storter boy right away. "Something the matter, Claude?" Seeing E. J.'s burning face, the poor boy whispered as soft as he knew how what some nigger said Cox had perpetrated at the Bend.

"By God," Watson swore, "that skunk will pay for this!" He was off to Fort Myers to fetch the sheriff before "that murdering sonofabitch—if you'll forgive me, Miss Mamie—can make his getaway!" Well, it was E. J.

Watson made the getaway, right from under the men's noses. His determination to seek justice was so darn sincere that it put 'em off the scent, or so they told each other after he was gone.

Was I the only one suspected that E. J.'s outrage was put on to fool us? You never saw an upset man with eyes so calm and clear. Runs upstairs, hugs his wife and children, comes down again with that double-barrel shotgun, shouting out how he had to rush to catch Captain Thad at Marco and question that black man. He was out the door before anybody thought to stop him, they were falling all over themselves to clear his way.

Our men weren't cowards—well, not most of 'em. My brothers were all strong young fellers who enjoyed a scrap and most folks would speak up for a few others. But that day the men were upset and confused and they had no leader. Mr. Smallwood was across the island on some business with Mr. McKinney and my dad and Bill were harvesting down at House Hammock. E. J. Watson took our island by surprise.

HOAD STORTER

✦

Sunday evening in strong southeast wind with the barometer falling fast, Mister Watson crossed over to Everglade. His *Warrior* was low on fuel and anyhow too small to weather a bad storm on the open Gulf. It was urgent that he confer with the sheriff, he said, and he offered good money to my dad to carry him as far as Marco first thing next morning.

Captain Bembery said he sure was sorry but even for his friend, he would not risk his ship and crew in such black weather. His crew was his two boys. Mister Watson kept after him, he was a hard man to say no to. Mother was frightened for her men but also for her house in rising waters, because Everglade was little more than a mudbank on a tide creek, with no high Indian mounds like Chokoloskee. Also, we had brought the news of the murders at the Bend, so she feared that Dad's old friend might do away with him, being a desperate man who might try anything.

By daybreak the wind had backed around to the northeast. It was gusting to forty knots and more by the time we came out through Fakahatchee Pass into the Gulf; our little schooner was banging hard and shipping water. We didn't like the strange cast of the dawn light nor the ugly way those purple clouds off to the west were churning up the sky. Off Caxambas at the south end of Marco Island, the wind veered back to the southeast, then around to the southwest in a whole gale, sixty knots or better. Worried about home, my dad notified Mister Watson that we could not take him as far as the Marco settlement but would drop him at Caxambas before heading back.

Mister Watson went all wooden in the face, knowing he'd have to walk across the island to Bill Collier's store at the north end, then find someone else to carry him to the mainland. When he jammed his hand into his pocket, I was scared he would pull a weapon and force us to keep going, or maybe shoot us, dump us overboard, and take the helm. Cussed a blue streak but gave that up when he saw it would do no good; he must have figured he had trouble enough without killing his old friend. When we set him ashore in the lee of the clam factory dock, he thanked us warmly, got all wet shoving us off—that man was strong!—and wished us a safe voyage home before striding off toward the north, rain slicker flying.

MAMIE SMALLWOOD

✦

That Sunday night in our Smallwood store, our menfolk got real busy spreading blame. No sooner was E. J. Watson gone than some started arguing how he should have been arrested; others said it must have been Cox who made that nigger put the blame on E. J. Watson. Well, now, I said, no nigger with the brains to get away to Pavilion Key would be fool enough to accuse a white man and implicate himself while he was at it.

Ted returned in time to hear me say that, and his frown told me he didn't care for strong opinions from his woman in men's company. But after all, I had only spoke the truth, I told him later; to risk his life that way, that nigger had to have a reason. *"Nigra,"* Ted complained.

Anyways, it was too late. Watson was long gone, headed for Everglade, where he sweet-talked Bembery Storter into running him as far as Marco Island even though the hurricane was on its way. (Had to pay Bembery pretty dear, I shouldn't wonder; those Storters never give you much for nothing.)

First time the wind gusts quaked our house came after dark on Monday evening. Santinis had built this house above the drift line of the '73 hurricane, plenty high enough for the '96 storm and also 1909. But it weren't nearly high enough for the Great Hurricane of 1910, which came roaring in with wind and seas all jumbled up together. Chokoloskee Bay is three miles inland from the Gulf, but big waves broke through the outer islands to come pound our shore, and our island shrank smaller and smaller as the water swirled around us. When we finally lost sight of the mainland, it seemed like our little tuft of land had been uprooted and was drifting out to sea, and that was when we fled uphill to the schoolhouse, which was ten

foot above sea level. Edna Watson and her kids were staying with the Aldermans: Wilson Alderman lugged little Addison while Edna toted Baby Amy
and led Ruth Ellen by the hand.

The storm flood rose till four that morning, left a line on the wall ten
inches above the schoolhouse floor. According to C. G. McKinney, who
passed for somewhat educated, nine tenths of Chokoloskee Island and ten
tenths of Everglade went underwater. Finally the men knocked our schoolhouse down, made rafts out of the walls; their hammers were all that could
be heard over the wind.

Coming from an inland county, Edna Watson had never imagined such
a fearful storm. She had promised her kids safety in the schoolhouse only to
see that last shelter destroyed. The men dragged their rafts to the top of the
highest mound we call Injun Hill, and all nine families were up there in
that weather without cover, every last soul huddled together, teeth chattering, turning blue, and staring out blind into the storm, scared to death
those rafts might break apart. The kids were crying and Edna was close to
hysterics but she kept her head. Finally the Good Lord heard our prayers
and the roar eased a little. The seas weren't climbing anymore but slowly
falling, leaving behind dark dripping silence, mud and ruin.

No real dawn. We trooped downhill in the half-dark to see what we had
left. Goods from our store that weren't washed into the Bay were carried
back into the scrub; I lost my whole new set of china. I broke down then,
just shook my head and cried, but in a little while I got the nervous giggles.
My mama shrilled, "How can you giggle, girl, with everything you possess
lost in the mud?" Oh, Grandma Ida was real disappointed in the Lord. And
I said, "Well, Mama, I am very thankful we are all still here and still alive, so
this ol' mud don't look so bad to me."

Only person hurt was Charlie Boggess, who dislocated his ankle jumping off a boat onto our dock when it weren't there no more. My Ted took
him up under the arms, leaned back, and let him holler when C. G. pulled
his heel straight, let the ankle bone snap back into her socket. Ted carried
him on his back across the island, told him to stay put at home and not
cause any more trouble. But being a feller who hated to miss out, Charlie T.
was right back at our landing when E. J. Watson showed up again a few
days later.

OWEN HARDEN

◆

Sunday had thin sun and a light wind, but by ten that evening, the barometer commenced to fall too fast, with gusts to thirty, forty, fifty miles, and rising. By noon next day she'd shifted, coming out of the southeast, then around out of the south. That afternoon of Monday, October 17th, is when the sky turned black and the storm blew hardest, rolling all the way across the Gulf from the Yucatan Channel.

That's when the walls budged. Our thatch roof shifted, even lifted once as the wind moaned, trying to pry the lid. At high tide, the seas washed over the shell ridge into the cabins. We floated the skiff right to the door and threw some stuff in. Something banged and something tore and the roof was gone and the storm exploded amongst the walls and the door frame was suddenly empty. Rain slashed straight across in sheets, whipping our faces. The sky caved in and the Gulf of Mexico crashed on our coast, so wild and heavy that the waves was lost, there was only roil and thunder. We took to the boats before they disappeared, they was jumping on their moorings like wild horses.

Wood Key was flooded over when we chopped the lines, let the storm carry the boats away inland. Where they finally snagged, we lashed 'em tight into the jungle trees. Hour after hour, our folks prayed to the Lord Almighty for deliverance; in the next tree, a family of possums, white faces staring out, seemed to pray, too. My Sarah cried, "Are we in Hell?" And Daddy Richard yelled into her ear, "No, girl! We are still here on God's earth!" Ma Mary screeched, "Well, then, God's earth is Hell enough for me!"

Them winds of the Great Hurricane of 1910 lasted thirty hours, seemed

like the world was coming to an end. When the barometer blew away at
Sand Key Light, down by Key West, it already registered 28.4, the lowest
pressure ever recorded in the U.S.A. until that day.

When the storm eased some toward morning, a great emptiness came in
behind it although there was still considerable wind. We were very thirsty
but at least could catch a breath. All agreed that the Great Hurricane was
foretold by that silver light across the heavens in the spring. Such a terrible
storm, just seven days and seven nights after so much bloody murder, could
only be sign of the Lord's Wrath, but Mister Watson's infant boy, drowned
at Pavilion Key, was the only life He took on this whole coast.

ERSKINE THOMPSON

✦

Our sloop drifted us way back into the woods. Gert set her washtub over our smallest, trying to keep him dry. By daybreak, the worst of it was past, the wind was down, but the sloop's hull got stove in, all busted up. She never made it back to the salt water.

All the world looked heavy dead lead-gray, like all life and color had been bled away. The river was thick with mud and broken branches; gray marl crusted the banks and trees like a disease. With Lost Man's Key awash from end to end, the river mouth looked a half mile across, with tide and current jumbled in thick roil and tree trunks passing. Some trees had varmints clinging tight, looking back where they come from as they was rode far out to sea. After that long night, the women and kids was all wrung out exhausted, and seein them wild things starin back as they passed away forever is what finally gave our kids their excuse to cry.

The shore was empty, all our cabins gone. Hamiltons lost about everything except their lives. Seeing what had befell him in that one black night, Mr. James Hamilton looked all around him like a little child woken up. Everything that old feller had put together in twenty years' hard work was twisted down or washed away. Never cursed nor wept nor acted jagged, only stared around him hour after hour. After that day, talk didn't interest him, he hardly spoke again, just took to murmuring his memories of lost hopes in times gone by.

Having no regular family, then marrying young Gert, I become kind of a Hamilton, and like the Hamiltons was not so proud about our Harden kin, but when Owen come over from Wood Key to see how we was farin, I was glad to see him—took that storm to make us talk like neighbors. Him and me sailed his skiff north to the Watson place to see who might be left. That white house was still there but she looked stranded, up on her bare mound, and the outbuildings was all smashed flat: boat shed and bunkhouse swept away and the cabin, too. Called and called but got no answer, only silence. Neither of us made a move to go ashore. We never spoke about it. It weren't we were ashamed so much as havin no words to explain what we was feeling.

Some way the *Gladiator* had rode it out lashed tight to them big poincianas and the busted dock. With my sloop gone, I reckoned Mister Watson would not mind if I used his ship to carry our Lost Man's folks to Chokoloskee. Owen told me Hardens would stay put, start rebuilding right away, but Thompsons and Hamiltons sailed north next day, taking Andrew Wiggins along with wife and baby. Having lost their boat, that family abandoned the Atwell place and had picked their way along the shore to Lost Man's Beach from the mouth of Rodgers River. We was anchored off Smallwood's by early evening and got our first word about the Chatham massacre an hour later. Hearing that news, and recalling that silence on the Bend the day before, give me the creeps all over again, cause me'n Owen never knew about them dead, never imagined this man Cox might of been watching through some broken pane. Maybe he never answered because he had drew a bead on us, to kill us, too. That night I had a ugly dream about Cox laying in wait, mouth set in the way a snake's mouth sets, little fixed smile.

By the time the hurricane struck in, Cox was all alone on Chatham Bend, if you don't count that dead squaw in the boat shed or the corpses across the river or Mister Watson's old horse running wild, shrieking and crashing through the cane. Maybe Cox never believed in God, no more'n me and Mister Watson, but if he did, he must of figured God had come to blast him straight to Hell for his black sins. We was down there in the rivers and we seen it: the roaring of the Hurricane of 1910 would of scared the marrow out of anybody, let alone a killer that has slaughtered feller human beings and gutted out their carcasses like they was hogs. Cox would of spent that storm night on his knees wild-howling for forgiveness, never knowing there weren't nobody to forgive him.

At Pavilion Key, Tant hoisted Aunt Josie into the mangroves, but waves broke all across the island and tore her babe out of her arms. Found him by miracle at low tide next morning, little hands sticking up out of the sand— like he was cryin for his mama to come pick him up, Tant said. Maybe folks made too much of it that Mister Watson's offspring was the one soul lost but it makes you wonder, don't it? Even if you don't believe in God.

After all them years, the time had come to say good-bye to Lost Man's River. Thompsons come out all right, far as our health, but that hurricane blowed what fight was left out of our families. Lost our boats, our homes, had to take charity from kinfolk that didn't have nothing neither. We moved Grandpap James Hamilton to Fakahatchee but he never found his way back from that storm and died soon after.

Them Hardens swept off of Wood Key settled again near our old ground back of Lost Man's Beach. The dark one, Webster, built a cabin a good ways up into the river like he wanted to hide from hurricanes (or maybe his own niggerness, as I told Gert). All them people ever wanted was, Let us alone. Course mulattas never had no right to that proud attitude, never mind all the good fishing ground they claimed, but say what you like about that family, them Hardens was the only ones that never left. I'm talking about real pioneers trying to make a life down in the Islands, not moonshiners nor fly-by-nights that came and went.

FRANK B. TIPPINS

✦

When that black prisoner was delivered to Fort Myers, I telegraphed the Monroe County sheriff that he could find his witness in my jail. That same day, I traveled south as far as Marco, which was an unholy mess after the storm. Collier's Mercantile Store, built of burnt oyster shell, had a wall crack three inches across from roof to ground and was still draining the eighteen inches of floodwater inside. The homes were worse, and having no place to roost, nearly every man in the small settlement was in there drinking hard to ease his nerves. Left their women and kids sloshing around back in the shacks, waiting in darkness for a scrap of food or maybe another beating if the husband was a drunkard, which many were on the Florida frontier.

"You boys know Sheriff Tippins," Bill Collier said when I came in. Worn by the hurricane to a nervous edge, the unwashed men looked snarly, set to bait me. These people complain that they have no law so they have to make their own, but when the law shows up, there's not much of a welcome. One man belched and another rasped, "Finally turns up when he ain't needed." Another wiped a stubbled chin with the back of his hand, got me in focus. "Them bankers and cattle kings gone to cover up for him again, ain't that right, Sheriff? Got you in their pocket, too, from what we heard."

Collier put down the ax blade he was filing and hoisted this small feller off the floor and set him down again, facing the other way. Teeter Weeks turned, drawing his fist for a roundhouse punch while letting himself stagger back to a safe distance. There he spat on his hands and commenced bobbing and weaving. "Cap'n Bill? You lookin for a scrap? You found the right man this time, Cap'n Bill!"

Bill Collier was storekeeper and postmaster, trader and ship's master, shipbuilder and keeper of the inn, also the owner of the dredge that worked the clam flats at Pavilion Key. Had a copra plantation of five thousand palms and a citrus grove on the mainland at Henderson Creek with fifteen hundred orange-bearing trees. So naturally it was this lucky feller's spade that struck into those Calusa treasures back in '95 while getting out muck for his tomatoes. Having done much and seen more in life, he had no time for the likes of Teeter Weeks; he banged his ax head on the counter to command attention for the sheriff and resumed filing.

I asked what anyone could tell me about the whereabouts of E. J. Watson or his foreman. So far as they knew, Cox was still at Chatham Bend. As for Watson, he had come through yesterday on his way north to Fort Myers, looking for me.

"If I'da knowed what I know now, boys, I'd of never saved his life." The men half-listened as Dick Sawyer told his story of that day he'd hailed the *Gladiator* at Key West and had gone aboard and found his friend Ed down sick with typhoid fever: he had run to fetch a doctor. "Not a word of thanks for saving the man's life," Sawyer complained, "and that is funny, cause Ed's manners is so excellent."

Jim Daniels grinned. "Friend Ed is a mannerly man, for sure, especially when he has you where he wants you."

"Had a couple of your sisters, Jim, right where he wanted 'em. Netta, and then Josie—"

Jim Daniels cut him off just by sitting up straight, but Sawyer, drunk, refused to let it go. "Them Hardens now, they's kin to you, ain't that right, Jim?"

Bill Collier intervened smoothly. "I bet Dick ain't forgot that time E. J. needed a boat ride back to Chatham River because Hiram Newell setting over there who was Watson's captain at that time had Watson's boat up on the ways. So them two went over to Sawyer's, that right, Hiram? And Hiram hollered through the winder that Mister Watson was outside, wanted to know if Dick would take him home to Chatham River. Thinking Hiram was joking, Dick sings out, 'Why don't you and your damned Watson go to Hell?' But when he seen who was standing at his door, ol' Dick turned nice as rice. Said, 'Howdy, Ed! You needin a ride home?' "

Hiram Newell cleared his throat. "Well, I ain't ashamed to be in friendship with Ed Watson. If Cap'n Bembery or Willie Brown was here tonight, he'd say the same. Under that rough bark, Ed got him a big heart—"

"Jesus, Hiram!" Jim Daniels wheeled around. "Too bad them Tuckers ain't here tonight to tell us about that big heart of his! Jesus Sweet Christ!"

"One time in Tampa, what I heard, he knocked some Spaniard down, hauled out his Bowie knife. Says, 'Maybe I'll fillet this greaser here cause I never got to ride up San Juan Hill!' "

The door banged open in the wind, banged closed again. The Marco men heaved back, groaning like cattle. Back to the door, Ed Watson stood observing me; probably had me spotted through the window before he came in, and he didn't miss the shift I made to free my holster. I heard a voice whine, "Oh my God!" Not till I hoisted my boot onto a nail keg and clasped both hands on my knee where he could see 'em did he withdraw his hand from the right pocket of his coat.

Ed Watson looked exhausted, waterlogged, his ruddy face packed with dark blood, his breathing hoarse, but the man could have been dead drunk and buck naked and still had this bunch buffaloed. One feller that made a half move toward the back door froze like a dog on point when Watson turned, and his tin mug clattered to the floor. Scared faces were watching me to see what the law would do, knowing this man would resist arrest and somebody was going to get hurt.

Keeping his hands loose at his sides, Watson spread his feet a little. "I didn't do it, boys."

"Ed? Ain't none of us never *said* you done it, Ed."

That was Dick Sawyer. Watson never glanced at him, never took his eyes off mine. "Looking for me, Sheriff?" When I said, "Yep," he yanked open the door. "Let's go," he said.

"You men stay put." My voice was pinched and reedy. When I crossed the room, Watson swung the door wide to the wind, followed me out. But not until the door was closed did he show his revolver, waving my hands up before he took my weapon. Even at this galling moment, prodded toward the dock, I had to appreciate his tact in not disarming me inside.

"That gun necessary?" I said. "We'll see," he said.

Swift black clouds across the moon, a pale light on the sand: we boarded Collier's schooner. At her mess table, by lantern light, I had finally met Ed Watson face-to-face. He was slouched into the corner of the bulkhead where he could not be shot at through the cabin window. "You'd be safer in my jail," I remarked sourly, my heart not calm yet.

He shook his head. "Ever hear Smallwood's story about Lemon City? Mob goes right into the jail to lynch this feller, shoots the nigra jailer, too, while they are at it." He emptied my revolver, dumping the cartridges onto the table. "Don't try telling me they won't hang Watson the first chance they get."

"Not in Fort Myers."

"You can't promise that. And if a mob gets to me first, I'll get no chance to clear my name." He hauled a small flask from his pocket, found two blue tin cups. "Deputize me, Sheriff. I'll go get the man you want."

"He's still there?"

"No way to get off. John Smith can't run a boat, can't even swim, and he's dead scared of the water. Doesn't know where the nigra went, doesn't know anything went wrong. I can come right up on him because he won't suspect me."

"Something went wrong, then?"

"If you were John Smith and the only witness to your crimes got away to Pavilion Key and shot his mouth off, I reckon you might conclude something went wrong."

"If I was Ed Watson, I might feel the same." I paused. "Mr. Watson, you are under arrest."

Grimly he considered me. "Am I a suspect, then? I wasn't even there."

"Your nigger said you were behind it."

" *'Nigger said.'* That good enough for a Lee County jury?"

"Why don't you use John Smith's real name, Mr. Watson?"

"Because he don't."

"What was his motive?"

"That boy don't need a motive. Not to kill."

"Yet you kept him at Chatham Bend with your wife and children."

"They stayed away." He shrugged. "Owed him a favor."

"You still owe him? Why should you be trusted as a deputy?"

He picked up my weapon, making a face as if to say, *You're asking too many stupid questions for a man at the wrong end of this revolver.* He sipped a little. "Tastes like some lawless sonofabitch been distilling my good syrup."

I spoke carefully. "You're resisting arrest. You have disarmed and abducted the Lee County sheriff. You want a fair hearing, Mr. Watson, you better stop breaking the law." I was talking too much and too fast because he made me nervous.

"Look," he said, suddenly impatient. "I traveled to Fort Myers in a hurricane to report a dreadful crime. I wanted to tell you my side of the story before a damn mob put a rope around my neck. If I was guilty, would I chase after the law?"

"In Fort Myers, I have no jurisdiction, as you know. And you have family and friends—"

"My daughter's friends. They'll do their best to get me off to avoid a family scandal, yes, but it's a gamble." Watson offered the flask. I shook my head. "I thought about running. Very simple. Railroad north or a ship out of Key West." He looked up. "Where would I go this time?" He shook his head. "I'm tired of running. Anyway, I'm innocent."

We sat silent for a time, listening to the schooner creak against the pilings, the clack and rustle of her rigging. Over by the store, torn metal banged on metal.

"I never told Cox to kill those people. You ask about his motive—how about mine? I have the best plantation in the Islands. Most every household, Tampa to Key West, uses my syrup. One day you'll find it on every table in the country." He paused. "I have grown children, pretty grandchildren, a fine young woman for my wife and three new kids. I have a land claim pending and a great plan for developing this coast. Emperor Watson! Ever heard of him?" He grinned briefly. "Why would Emperor Watson ruin his imperial prospects?"

The ship lifted and banged.

"It's no dream, Frank. I get things done and I know powerful people. I know Governor Broward. Hell, I knew Nap Broward at Key West back in the days he was running guns on the *Three Brothers.* He came to my rescue in north Florida and he'll help again."

"Mr. Watson?" I cleared my throat. "The governor is dead."

Shocked despite himself, he raised his gaze, making sure I had told the truth. "That's too bad," he said then, seemingly indifferent. "You met the Chicago railroad man, John Roach? Bought Deep Lake with Walt Langford for growing citrus?" Watson sat back, eyes alive and shining. "Those men have as much as promised that if I stay out of trouble, I'll take over there as manager, because Deep Lake has serious labor problems, transport problems, and I have ideas. As John Roach told my son-in-law, any planter who can prosper on forty acres of hard shell mound way to Hell and gone down in the mangrove rivers, there's no limit to what such a man could do with three hundred acres of black loam at Deep Lake!" He was nodding to himself. "No limit," he repeated. "With new canals draining Okeechobee and the Glades, you're going to see modern agriculture across this state and I'll be in on it. Why would I risk such a great future by doing something stupid at the Bend?"

He sounded reasonable, sincere, yet something was very wrong. Did he really think cold-blooded murder was merely "stupid"?

"I want my children proud instead of nervous and ashamed. I want my Carrie proud." He eyed me carefully, nodding a little, and I saw he had always known I loved his daughter. "If I was the killer some folks say, do you think my family would be loyal? The only man against me is the biggest crook in southwest Florida. Uses the law to break the law." Holding my eye, he nodded. "I bet you don't like him any more than I do, Sheriff."

"Weren't for Jim Cole, you might have been hung up north, from what I hear."

"Rigged the jury, that what you heard? Probably did. Spared Langfords a big scandal and got damned well paid for it." He continued drunkenly, as if suddenly determined to make things worse. "Pays you, too, I hear." He cocked his eye. "Slave labor at Deep Lake?"

Sending county road-gang labor to Deep Lake to help our friend Walt Langford had been Cole's suggestion. But the original idea, Cole told me once, came directly from this man across the table.

"I can't wait for Deep Lake," he was saying. "Know what Glades drainage means? A big road across the state and development of both coasts in your lifetime." Wind-whipped sand from the bare yard scoured the schooner cabin. His gaze searched my eyes. "But not in Ed Watson's lifetime—that what you're thinking?" He drank off his cup.

"We're wasting time. Why would I *want* those people dead? Hell, they were friends of mine. Miss Hannah? Green? Some days I even liked young Dutchy!" His voice was rising. "Think I don't know the rumors? Sure I have debts. Those lawyers ruined me. But killing off hands on payday—*that's* not going to help! I'm a *businessman*, dammit. I pay my goddamned bills. Ask Storters. Smallwoods." In his despair, he seemed to lose his thread. "Just deputize me. I'll take care of Cox."

"Deputize a man pointing a gun at me?"

Watson opened his hand, let my cartridges roll across the table, then extended my revolver. He extended it barrel first, pointed straight at me. I pocketed the cartridges, then I took hold of the barrel. For a moment he did not let go. "All right, Frank? Yes or no?"

"If Cox is taken alive," I said, "it becomes your word against his, and his word might get you hung even if you're innocent. If I deputize you, you can go kill him legally or help him escape."

Disgusted, he released the revolver. "Don't try reloading." He took up his own weapon. I rose carefully to my feet. "Mr. Watson, you are under arrest." I stuck my hand out to receive his gun. "Your clean record in Lee County will help, of course—"

"Just shut your stupid mouth, all right?"

Waving me ahead of him onto the deck, Watson turned his back as he closed the door behind him. Was he inviting me to jump him, try to overpower him? To the back of his head, I said, "If you go down there and shoot Cox, you'll be making a bad mistake. You'll be suspected of those murders and charged with a new one."

Watson said, "You're a fucking idiot." Seeing his expression, I was suddenly so scared I had to piss. "Just trot over to the store," he said, contemptuous, "and don't look back."

In a stew of bad emotions, I crossed the moonlit sand. Before going inside to brave the questions, I reloaded my gun, peering about into the night. My nerve had unraveled, I was exhausted. I had no idea where he had gone and no stomach for pursuit. I should go back to Fort Myers, wait for the Monroe sheriff, find some deputies. Whatever I did, Ed Watson would reach Chatham Bend with a three-day head start.

In the heavy wash of seas in the night channel, I pissed my fear and my defeat into the roaring dark.

MAMIE SMALLWOOD

✦

When E. J. Watson came back south on October 21st, he was red-eyed with hard travel, looked half crazy with exhaustion; his eyes were dull and his teeth mossy, and that shiny auburn hair looked dank and dead. While Ted fueled his boat, he stretched out on our long counter with his revolver on his chest, breathing heavy, one eye on the door. Told us Sheriff Tippins had refused to deputize the only man who could come up on John Smith unsuspected so he had no choice but to deputize himself. We advised him to shoot Smith down same as a panther or a wolf, and he said he needed a few buckshot loads to put a stop to that mean varmint. (By this time, of course, we knew from Wilson Alderman that John Smith's real name was Leslie Cox.)

Back then, most shotgun shells were paper-wrapped so all we had were storm-soaked loads, all swollen. "These ain't the shells you want when you go *man*-hunting!" Ted told him. And E. J. said, "If these are the best you've got, they will do fine." Which my brother Bill would take to mean he weren't too serious about shooting Leslie Cox.

That day Bill was working at House Hammock. When Daddy House and Charley Johnson, a few others, showed up with a plan to arrest him, he had his double-barrel out where the men could see it, said he'd come too far to tolerate interference. He called to Edna, "I'll be back for your birthday, sweetheart!" as if to warn them not to try to stop him. Picked up the gun, walked down to the shore kind of sideways, pushed off in his boat.

Daddy House, who had some dander, called out, "If you are aiming to come back, you better bring Cox with you." Ed Watson said, "Is that a warning, Mr. House?" And Daddy said, "Take it any way you want to, Mr. Watson." E. J. didn't like that, not one bit. "Dead or alive?" he said, and

Daddy said, "I reckon dead will do." And Watson said, "If I don't bring him, I will bring his head. That good enough?" Gunned his motor loud to drown out Daddy's answer.

If that feller had one bit of sense, we'd seen the last of him, those men promised one another, same as they did earlier that week. Maybe we were finished with him but he weren't finished with us, I thought, not with his family left behind for hostage.

E. J. was hardly out of sight when Edna felt a shift in the air like a cold draft through the door crack. Folks moved out of her way, wouldn't meet her eye. It got so bad she couldn't let her kids out of her sight for fear they might be harmed. The silence that followed that poor body all around our ruined island was nothing but pure fear turning to hate—fear of her husband and his murdering outlaws, and more fear yet because her being here with his three children might draw that devil back. All of a sudden they resented this fool girl who had never learned what bloody breed of man fathered her children—that's what Mama and some other biddies took to muttering. And coldest of all, poor Edna told me after it was over, were those fair-weather Watson friends where she and her kids were lodged.

HENRY SHORT

✦

On that first Black Monday come three murders at the Bend. Second Monday, that was the Great Hurricane. Third was Monday October 24th of 1910, goin on toward evening.

House men was ready. Hearing that boat, Old Mist' Dan and his three boys loaded their guns and headed over to the shore. Mis Ida waved me to the cookhouse, told me to go with 'em. Look after Mist' Dan, she said, on account he was all agitated, fired up, might take and do some foolishness, get her boys killed. But it was her was agitated, not Mist' Dan. Mr. D. D. House always knew just what he wanted, he had set like glue.

I stood there looking straight ahead like I was hit by lightning. No nigger had no business over there, she knew that, but being so frightened for her men, she never cared what fool thing she told a colored man to do.

When I started to foller 'em, Mis Ida called after me, "Where is your rifle, Henry? You take that rifle, hear?" I was so scared I sagged down to my knees, went to rolling my eyes back like some gospel nigger.

"No ma'am, no please no, Mis Ida, Mist' Dan ain't told me come! Ain't no place for no nigger with no shootin iron, no, ma'am!"

Miz Ida got all flustered up and angry. Commenced to hollering how I owed my life to Houses on account Mist' Dan done saved this colored child back up the Georgia road and raised him up in a fine Christian family. Was this the gratitude they got? Those was the words I was most afraid of—how these kin'ly white folks saved this pickaninny's life so the very least that he could do was give it back.

Miz Ida sunk down a-weeping and a-praying, got the Good Lord on her side for sure. I known right then that Henry Short was done for. I mumbled,

"Yes'm," went to fetch my old Winchester .30-30, which I kept oiled and polished up like new. "See there!" she yelled. " 'Member how Mr. House give you that rifle, Henry? How he done spoiled you? So mind you load it good! You never know!"

Oh I knew, I knew.

As I passed the store, Mist' Smallwood warned me I was making a mistake, but being a nigger, I never had no choice. I was praying, praying, praying for some sign. All I wanted was some place I could hide out from life till I was safe again. In them days, his safety was all a black man could ask for.

BILL HOUSE

✦

When I got back from House Hammock, Mamie told me that Watson came through and some men collected and our dad told Watson he must wait there for the sheriff. Watson declared he'd seen him just the day before at Marco, said unless they stood aside, the killer Cox was going to escape. Claimed it was his bounden duty to them good friends that perished on his property to straighten out that blood-splattered sonofabitch once and for all. They never realized his shotgun was empty all the while he was bluffing them to let him go. My dad still wanted to arrest him, put a stop to Ed J. Watson once and for all, but none of them others had the stomach for it. Not till his boat was under way and disappearing out of sight did the men start in about how they would of grabbed him but for this and that and how they aimed to take care of him the very next time he tried his tricks around these parts. That sheepish bunch that was aiming to detain Ed Watson lined up instead to wave good-bye. He had talked his way into the clear again, just like he done so many times before. That feller was a borned politician, could of got to be president if he stayed sober and didn't shoot nobody on the train to Washington, D.C.

Daddy House was hopping mad. Naturally he blamed his stupid son for staying at House Hammock to clean up after the storm the way he told me to. Said his fool neighbors was "bamboozled" by Ed Watson, as if he weren't nothing but some bystander. Already—because they wanted it so bad—those neighbors had convinced themselves that if Ed did not kill Cox, Cox would kill Ed, and either way this coast had seen the last of 'em. Never occurred to 'em that Watson might of went straight to the Bend to help his partner make his getaway. When two days went by and he never come back, a story spread that he'd carried Cox down to Florida Bay and across to the Key West railroad, which laid rail that year as far south as Long Key: heading north up the east coast was their best chance of escape. So long as Watson lit out with Cox, maybe we could just forget about them murders, that was their thinking, though they never owned up to that out loud. It wasn't justice folks was after but a good night's sleep.

We was just ordinary people that didn't care to go up against no desperader; we was grateful to be buffaloed out of a showdown if E. J. Watson would just go away and keep on going.

Our house was not far east of Smallwood's store. When that *pop-pop-pop* come on the south wind toward the dusk, Daddy straightened up to listen, set his chisel down. "That's him," he said.

With no sign of the damned sheriff, we was obliged to arrest the man ourselves. We had talked it out. Daddy and me and Dan Junior and Lloyd loaded our rifles and went on down to Smallwood's landing. My father-in-law, Jim Howell, who lost his house in the hurricane, come along soon after. By the end of it, eighteen to twenty was there, almost all the Island men and a few others visiting. Some might of only carried guns so's not to be thought cowards by the rest; others, I ain't saying who, was declaring for the past three days that if Watson dared show up again, we should lay for him and shoot him down, ask questions after. Better to finish him for sure and get some justice, them men said, because otherwise, what with all his son-in-law's connections, he was bound to wriggle free like he done before. Claimed to be worried about justice but I believe they was a lot more worried that Ed Watson, left alive, would settle up his business quick with any man who had dared stand up against him. Ed always aimed to clean up his accounts, like Smallwood said.

Ted would not join the posse. Said E. J. was his best customer, all paid up fair and square, said he had nothing against him, never did. Anyway, he was down with his malaria, he said, though on that very afternoon, as we all seen, he felt strong enough to crawl under his house after them drowned leghorns. The more Ted talked, the harder it was to tell what he really hoped would happen, and I doubt he knew.

According to my sister, her husband was the only man with enough guts to speak out against the murder of a neighbor. Well, he wasn't. Willie

Brown done that and he done it louder, and Bembery Storter, too, but those men being from Everglade, they were not present. As for them neighbors that straggled in from the Lost Man's country after the hurricane, them men stayed back by the store, they only watched. Even Erskine Thompson, who was kind of backdoor family to Ed Watson, never raised no sand. In their hearts, I believe, them Lost Man's fellers was as anxious as the rest to see this business finished. Wanted the suspense over and done with.

The men was bunched up on the shore. Near dusk but plenty light enough for him to see that body of armed men before he come in range. Why did he keep coming? Stood straight as a statue at the helm, never hesitated, never even slowed, just peered around kind of quizzical, pretending like he never noticed all his neighbors till that moment; then he waved and smiled, tickled to see such a fine welcome. Never paid no attention to them hefted weapons.

The hurricane had took away Ted's dock so the *Warrior* come in just east of the boatway. Cut his motor maybe twenty yards out, let her wake come up under the stern and ride her high onto the shore.

Grounding her fast and hard like that, with that loud *crunch,* Watson took the whole crowd by surprise. The fellers behind us give a grunt and snort as they backed up, jostling like steers at the chute, and somebody shit his pants cause we could smell it.

Some has said he never left his boat. Well, our House gang was right up front and seen it. Timed his move forward as she went aground and jumped as the bow struck, holding his shotgun up across his chest and twisting in the air so's to land where he could cover the whole crowd. Must of knowed he risked getting hisself shot by the most nervous one out of buck fever, cause right away he dropped his barrels down along his leg, no threat to nobody but where he could still swing 'em up fast if he had to.

E. J. Watson knew his neighbors, knew we lacked experience at pointing guns at feller men, never mind pulling the trigger. All of us stood stock still and staring, feeling stupid, as if we'd come outside at evening to have us a bat shoot or something. On that twilight shore on October 24 of 1910, the only man who appeared easy—the only man who "leev in his own skeen," as the old Frenchman used to say—was E. J. Watson, but I believe that underneath he was as scared as we was.

Knowing how quick and wily Watson was, we had no doubt he had calculated his chances pretty close long before his bow struck ashore. Probably figured if he made it into court, he'd beat the charge, because only his nigra had him implicated, and even that man had backed off his own story, put it all on Cox. As usual, there really weren't no good evidence against him. But being so smart, he would also figure that some of us might be smart enough to know that, too, and might just lynch him.

"Evening!" he said, his smile friendly as ever. "Anybody seen Mrs. Watson and the children?"—his way of reminding us that Ed J. Watson was a family man and not no common killer. The man knew from start to finish just what he was doing. Having bluffed us twice in the last fortnight, he was pretty sure he could pull it off again. Them double barrels down along his leg reminded us how fast us ones up front could be laying there stone dead, whilst his friendly grin took the last fight out of those fellers that wasn't scared half sick to death already.

The soft water sound of the *Warrior*'s wake, still follering in, riffled and washed along the muddied shore. Dusk had come and the miskeeters. We was too tense to pay 'em any mind.

D. D. House was the man nearest to Watson. I stood alongside him on his right hand, young Dan and Lloyd on his left. The rest were kind of bunched on that left side.

D. D. House was an impatient man, never liked to wait. He said, "You got a body in that boat? Where's his head?"

Boys, Watson said, he sure was sorry to disappoint 'em. He'd shot Cox as planned when that skunk come down to meet him at the dock but damned if the body didn't roll right off into the current. Worked for two days with gator hooks in that storm flood, never come up with him. Nosir, all he had to show was the bullet hole in Cox's hat. And he dragged a crumped-up brown felt hat out of his coat pocket and held it out to Daddy with a rueful smile.

Daddy shook his head, he wouldn't take it. "That hat ain't good enough."

"Sir? Not good enough for what?" Watson's voice turned cold.

Someone leaned and whispered in my ear, "Cox never wore no hat, the times I seen him." Watson with his wolf ears snapped, "How'd that go, Wilson?" and I thought, Lordamighty! What's he doing here? Alderman had worked for Watson in north Florida and still passed for his friend; the Watson family was lodging in his cabin.

When my dad would not accept the hat, Ed Watson poked a finger through the bullet hole and beckoned comically like he might do with little kids or dogs or idiots. Angry that Pap refused to take his word, maybe outraged that Alderman stood there with us, he was rubbing our noses in that hat, defying us. (Erskine Thompson seen it later, claimed it were the same hat Watson shot off the old French man's head back in the nineties that had hung on a peg in his kitchen ever since.)

Watson lifted the hat with his finger through the hole and twirled it. Nobody spoke. Some feller broke wind. Nobody laughed. This weren't no kind of joke but a damn insult. Watson waited, gazing from face to face. Eyes flinched when he yanked his hand out of his coat to slap a skeeter on his neck. Didn't slap it exactly, just reached up slow and pinched it dead, then studied the blood between his thumb and finger like that blood was a sign of something he should know about.

A breeze came racketing through the storm-torn palms, died away too quick. Isaac Yeomans spat, maybe more loud and disgusted than us other fellers might of wanted. "You use your revolver, Ed? That shotgun never made that hole in that damn hat."

Watson smiled a disappointed smile, shaking his head. At the Bend, he had left his shotgun in the boat to make sure Cox let him come close enough to talk, after which he had taken care of him with his revolver. "See for yourself." He pointed at his boat. "Got his damn blood all over my stern."

Pap said, "You told us he fell off your dock."

"That's correct. Fell headfirst onto the transom, bleeding like hell, thrashed off the stern into the current before I could grab hold of him."

Isaac waded out to inspect the cockpit. "There's blood all right," he said. He put his finger to the blood, then sniffed it. "Smells like fresh fish," he said. "It sure ain't three days old."

That's when Pap said quietly, "Might be a good idea to hand over your weapons, Watson."

Slow and growly, Watson said, "Nosir, Mr. House. That ain't a good idea at all." When he hitched his gun onto his arm, there come a gasp and shuffle, and I never had to look behind to know which ones was getting set to scatter. Why was his neighbors acting so suspicious, Watson inquired kind of grieved. He could not figure for the life of him why his friends and neighbors would treat him like some kind of a criminal when they knew Cox was the guilty man and Cox was dead.

But he wasn't really arguing no more, he was gathering himself for his next move. Pap must of seen it that same way cause he warned him hoarse and urgent, "Better drop that gun." But Watson only gazed over his head toward the store where Mrs. Watson had come outside with my sister and was starting down to meet him. Maybe he seen her. Maybe he seen his Lost Man's friends, just watching. Maybe he wondered why none of them friends such as Erskine ever tried to warn him, wave him away from shore, never even hollered at him now to drop his weapons. Not one man came down to meet him. They were keeping a safe distance, out of shotgun range.

He looked lost—the only time I ever seen Ed Watson seem unsure what to do next. For one second there, I might have felt a little sorry for him. That feeling passed quick. In the shift of an eye, he had a ears-back look, real hard and mean, like he would take your life and not think twice about it. Of course that look might of been put on to bluff and scare us.

"Mister Watson, you are under arrest," I warned, to back Pap up. "Citizen's arrest," said Isaac Yeomans.

"Citizen's arrest?" Watson spat out his contempt and ground the spit into the ground, hard, with his boot toe. "You boys are full of shit," he grated, shifting his feet a little, shifting his weapon. "You have a warrant?"

Hearing that anger, so sudden and so cold, beyond all reach, the line of men went wobbly, and some of 'em, I ain't saying which ones, begun to whine: *If there ain't no warrant, it ain't legal, ain't that right, boys? Ed ain't all wrong on that, y'know. . . . Well, I mean, to heck with it, we best go on home till we think this over.* But D. D. House had to finish what he started, sons or no sons, he never really knew no other way. When he growled, "Watson, lay that gun down by the count of three," his sons stiffened, set to fire at the first wrong move.

We was all bad scared, which makes men skittish, very dangerous. We was tense and all bunched up; he could do some heavy damage with a shotgun. But after so many close calls on so many frontiers, the man might have seen in them stiff weary faces that this time his neighbors meant business, that maybe his luck was running out, that the day had come when he might not talk his way into the clear.

When D. D. House stepped forward to take his gun, Ed Watson raised his palm up high like some kind of old-time prophet in the Bible. At first I thought he was about to say, *Okay, I quit. You win.* Later I realized he had stopped us at good shotgun range if killing and crippling more than two was what was wanted. Maybe that were not his plan but that's the way it looked. Two charges of buckshot would knock down the leaders, scatter the rest, and he might keep 'em ducking with his revolver while he pushed his boat back off the beach, crouched to reload, shot his way out of there. At that range, with a panicked crowd, he might have got away with it; the trouble was—so's to keep his gun handy when he jumped instead of fooling with a bow line—he'd run his boat aground on a falling tide to where he'd never push her off without some help.

A bad mistake, some said. I don't think so. I don't think Watson made mistakes like that. I doubt if he ever considered shooting his way out. His chances were poor and anyway, a man so proud would not leave his family behind.

When Watson swung that shotgun up, my guts clenched tight to meet the burning lead. I knew we was done for, Pap did, too, because we was looking down both barrels and we seen them jump, that's how hard Watson pulled his triggers. To fit storm-swollen shells into the breech, he'd peeled 'em down too much, the paper didn't hold, that was the theory: when them barrels tipped, the buckshot rolled right out the muzzles. I ain't saying I seen them pellets but some claim they did.

I don't recall swinging my rifle up or squeezing the trigger but I do know I fired. After that, all them guns let go together.

Ed Watson was spun half around but didn't fall. I reckon he died before his shotgun hit the ground, but his legs kicked back some way and drove his body on, pitching him forward against that roar and fire. His coat and shirt jumped, whacked by lead, the sound of his hard life being whacked out of him. Some say they seen his gun stock splinter, seen his revolver spin away. Me, I seen his mouth yank, seen blood jump where his left eye burst. Christ. And still he came.

Hell, we all seen it, ain't one man won't say the same: with all that lead in him, Ed Watson kept on coming, that's how headstrong that man was even in death—that was the demon in him, Mama Ida House would say for long years after, cause only a demon could scare folks as bad as that after they exercised him. He never crumpled but fell slow as a felled tree.

Seeing him come ahead that way, the men yelled and crowded backward. Then the evening broke apart, the line surged forward, near to knocked me down. It was purely uproar, hollering and cussing. They were a damn mob now for sure, with young boys running up and down snapping their slingshots at the body, yapping like dogs, and every dog on that dark island howling.

Our neighbor lay face down on the bloody ground like he wanted to peer into the darkness all the way down to the center of the earth. The broad back in the black coat had no breath to swell it. Never jerked nor spasmed, never groaned nor gargled. Them fire-colored curls on his sun-creased neck was all that twitched even a little in the evening wind.

Fallen angel, Mama Ida said, and it was true. Laying so still at our feet, Mister Watson looked like he had fell all the way from Heaven. You never seen a man so dead in all your life.

HOAD STORTER

◆

In Everglade the cisterns were four-five feet below the ground, two above, and the water generally stayed cool and clear, but after the Great Hurricane they were flooded out with brine and mud and after that we had more'n a month of wind and a hard drought. The heavens were gray as old torn rags wrung dry.

On October 24, late afternoon, my brother and I had rowed across to Chokoloskee, hunting fresh water. We were rounding the point west of Smallwood's store when a loud racketing of guns broke out; it was just dark enough to see the muzzle fire. For a few moments, silence fell over that island like a blow, and out of that silence for just one brief moment rose the voice of a night bird, over and over, so loud and clear I had to wonder if that bird had sung right through the shooting and continued on through the dog and human outcry we heard next.

Mister Watson had run his *Warrior* right up on shore. His body lay on the bank just off her bow, circled by sniffing dogs. No man stood near him. We went ashore with our water jugs, trying to keep out of the way. Watching from a little distance we could see that while some men were yelling angrily, others were crowing in relief, passing a jug. Some seemed to wander around shocked, avoiding talk with anyone at all; other ones could not stop talking—not listening, you know, just talking, the way crazy people do— and these ones swore it was nobody's fault, the dead man tried to attack the crowd, kept coming after he was shot to death three or four times over. And all this while, over the excited voices, that night bird came and went, over and over and over, *wip, wip, WEE-too*!

BILL HOUSE

✦

What I never forgot was the shock of silence after the shock of noise. First thing I heard out of that silence was a woman's high clear voice—*Oh God! Oh God! They are killing Mister Watson!* By the time Edna Watson realized what had happened, her husband was dead and on his way to Hell.

Watson's young family was sunk down on the store steps in a sobbing heap. Poor Edna was plain terrified, my sister said, that this "mob," having tasted blood, might turn on the dead man's widow and his little children. I hate to admit this but she weren't all wrong. Their fear made these men vengeful, and the most dangerous was the very ones who had looked the other way for all them years—the ones claimed Watson never killed a soul, only one-two riffraff on his place that had it coming. Same ones who was so angry he had scared 'em all them years that they pumped bullets into the dead body. These same brave fellers scared his widow so bad that she grabbed her kids and crawled on hands and knees under the store, even cheered and jeered the fine round of her hip when her frock tore as she crawled into the dark, then dirty-joked about Old Man Watson mounting his young mare. If that man laying there had could of heard how them men terrified his wife and little children, he'd of flew straight back from Hell like an avenging angel.

I hollered, tried to shame 'em off like I'd caught 'em peeping at some lady in the bushes, then quit because I weren't no better. I peeped, too.

Mortified, I called under the store, "Come on out, Mis Edna! Ain't nothing to be feared of!" (To say something that stupid with my rifle barrel still warm and her dead husband, too? That poor widow must of thought I lost my mind!) All that come back was little squeaks and whimpering. Poor things was huddled in there amongst them putrefied chickens for damn near an hour, laying still as rabbits, though the skeeters was whining something terrible and that stink was sickening, just awful.

My sister done her best to soothe 'em, murmuring down between her storm-warped floorboards like she might talk to a scaredy-cat or something. When finally the last men was gone and she could coax 'em out, them poor souls stunk so bad that the family·where they was lodging wouldn't take 'em back. That stink was only the excuse for what them people was aiming to do anyway. They had a new baby and was scared Cox might come prowling after Edna like he done up in north Florida, was the excuse. Told that little family they weren't welcome because they had the stench of Hell on 'em. Pushed her stuff at Edna through the door crack. Didn't want no truck with outcasts, not with armed drunks wandering around, not with Cox still on the loose. And here Wilson Alderman who was supposed to be Ed Watson's friend was right there alongside of us down at the landing, though of course he would claim he never pulled his trigger. Didn't want either side to think the less of him, I reckon.

So here it was black moonless night and the mother crazed by her own fear and them broken kids bewailing that queer mound down by the water that had been their daddy.

Mamie took Edna and her kids into her tore-up house. My sister has ugly ideas when it comes to nigras, but she has grit and a big heart. Lots of our Chokoloskee folks are that same way. Mule-head ignorant, suspicious of everyone except their own, but good, tough, honest, God-fearing Americans that lives out a hard poor life and don't complain.

HOAD STORTER

✦

We never got home to Everglade till bedtime. We told our family all we'd
seen and heard, and still they pestered us with questions, trying to figure
out what they should feel as their dead friend's friends. I told 'em what we
had been told (the official story, as Dad called it, kind of bitter), how Mr.
Watson tried to murder Mr. D. D. House but his damp shells misfired, by
which time the posse was already shooting.

"The *posse?*" Dad shook his head, disgusted. "If his shells misfired, what
makes 'em so darned sure he pulled his triggers?"

"One man claimed he saw his barrels yank when he tried to shoot. Saw
pellets rolling out the barrels."

"What man?"

"You sound like you doubt Hoad's word," my mother chided him. "It's
not Hoad's word I doubt," Dad said. "It's the whole story. Something's missing." But I got the feeling that in the end, they felt some way relieved.
Didn't *want* to feel relieved, just couldn't help it.

Some would say in later years that folks just had enough of Mister Watson, they got tired of him. Said the lynching had been planned by Houses,
who wanted to make sure his 150-gallon boilers and new machinery didn't
put their own small sugar operation out of business. Others in the crowd
protested, said if they'd known this was supposed to be a lynching they
would have never taken part. His neighbors were split bad over Ed Watson
and they are today.

Altogether, we saw close to twenty men, mostly Chok fellers, with two or
three who were there that day from Marco and Fakahatchee, and a few
fishermen passing through. Isaac Yeomans, Andrew Wiggins, Saint De-

mere, Henry Smith—all those men were in on it. Harry McGill, who would marry my sister Maggie Eva, was among the few who fired and never denied it; Charley Johnson was another, and Mr. House and his three older boys would never be ashamed that they took part. Hard to say who else for sure because over the years too many changed their stories. I do know that some who later claimed to be among the men who killed Ed Watson were not even present on the island. Others like Wilson Alderman decided they only went there to arrest him, not to shoot him, so they never fired. A lot of 'em have poor memories, I guess.

Just lately, a young lady told me that her dad was among the shooters. Well, he wasn't. He was with me in my skiff. We saw the finish.

Folks had hung on in the Islands after bad hurricanes in '73 and '94 and 1909, but the Great Hurricane of 1910 cleaned 'em right out. Their boats and cabins were all wrecked and their gardens spoiled by four feet of salt water, leaving almost nothing they could work with. The green emptiness of the Everglades for a hundred miles to eastward and the gray emptiness of the Gulf out to the west—the dead silence and the loneliness, along with the knowing that all a man had cleared off, hoed, and built, all the hard labor and discouragement of years and years, could be washed away overnight—that knowledge broke their spirit, that and the scent of human blood back in the rivers. By the time Lucius's father was shot down a week later, all but the Hardens had cleared out, and not one of those Island clans ever came back, because any stranger glimpsed around some point of river could be Leslie Cox, who might kill you in cold blood. That fear that was always lurking there plain wore 'em out.

After those murders came that hurricane, then the death of E. J. Watson—all on Mondays, one after the other. And after those three black Mondays came the drought. People forget about the drought. Here we were deep into the rainy season and no rain for weeks and weeks, into December. It was spooky! Such little water as we had turned green and poisonous and cisterns all around the Bay went dry. Had to row way up beyond the tides in Turner River.

Folks saw all these calamities as signs of the Lord's wrath. All folks could talk about was Revelation and Apocalypse, bowl of wrath and burning bush. Those first Pentecostals who came to save us were shocked to learn that the doomed sinners on this accursed Bay had no house of God. That called for an emergency Revival. Forty souls were baptized in the Bay, right out there in front of McKinney's store. And Charley Johnson who was in the Watson posse and never did mind being first and foremost, Charley stepped up and hollered loud and clear how he was a rum-runner doing the Devil's work. When it came to sinners, nobody came close to Charley G. Johnson, Charley swore. Yessir, he was burning to repent, ol' Charley was, he aimed to get saved or know the reason why. To prove it, he took his rum boat all the way north to Fort Myers and brought back a cargo of lumber for the new church. When it came to saving souls on Chokoloskee Bay, Mr. McKinney said, the Lord got a helping hand from E. J. Watson and the demon rum.

Willie Brown likes to recall how he tried to find my uncle George to get a warrant for Ed Watson's arrest, head off the showdown. Justice of the Peace George Storter was the closest thing to law we had back at the time, but that week Uncle George was away on jury duty in Fort Myers, and C. G. McKinney, too—those two men were right there in the courthouse when the Chokoloskee witnesses were brought in. Sheriff Tippins took some depositions and the court clerk wrote 'em down and that court clerk, so help me God, was Eddie Watson, the dead man's son, Uncle George told us.

After leaving the Bend in late September, Lucius had gone gill-netting with me and Claude, provisioning the clam crew at Pavilion Key; in early October, he was fishing with the Roberts boys out of Flamingo. That's where he was in mid-October when the word came of bloody murders at the Bend, along with the first warnings of the Great Hurricane. He departed next day but was turned back at Cape Sable by the storm. Because his boat got damaged and needed repairs, it was late in the week before he started out again, rounding Cape Sable and camping that night at Shark River. Next morning at Lost Man's, the Hardens informed him that his father had stopped by two days before the storm, behaving strangely; they could not quite make out why he had come and seemed uneasy.

Lucius rushed north. Finding nobody at Chatham Bend, he came to our house in Everglade, where we broke the awful news. He went out on the dock and watched the river for a while; Lucius was always beloved in our family, and as Mother said, it was a blessing that he was with good friends at such a time. We talked all night and he left for Fort Myers at dawn. Because he had refueled at our dock, he did not stop at Marco, where he might have learned that his father had crossed paths with the sheriff before heading south to deal with Cox at Chatham Bend. What actually happened there will always be disputed and it seems unlikely we will ever know.

BILL HOUSE

✦

If Watson's gun had not misfired, Daddy House would of been dead—
Daddy knew that, too. He turned his back on all the racket and just walked
away looking real old and rickety because some way he had busted his one
gallus and was holding his pants up with a forearm across his belly. Walked
stiff and slow like he had a bad gut.

His sons was pretty twisted up about how it ended. All the blood and
them damned dogs and kids running around. Young Lloyd, follering his
daddy home, was so mad he was in tears but never could figure out what he
was mad at. For days us boys tried to talk it out, but our dad would never
join in. What happened there at Smallwood's had went bad in him and
turned him sour. I reckon that was his first day as an old man.

When the crowd drifted off into the dark and the dogs forgot why they was
barking, Charlie Boggess fetched a lantern, helped Ted turn him over. Ted
tried to fold the arms across the chest, but on account of rigger mortis,
them arms opened out again like the claws on a blue crab speared through
the back. Or that's how Charlie Boggess told it, because Charlie T. made up
for his short size with his tall stories. He was spooked by them slow arms
much worse than by that one bloody blue eye—that's what he related to
visitors in later years after everyone had put away the truth, Charlie T. included. Seems Ted had tried to close that eye but come too late. The lid was
stiff, it just peeled back off the eyeball. Hunting around amongst the hurricane scraps spread through the bushes, them two come up with a toy flag
from the Fourth of July, spread that over the eyes. (D. D. House had rode for

a soldier in the War Between the States and never had no use for the stars and stripes, but he concluded that a Yankee flag was good enough for the man that tried to kill him.)

Even his friends knew Watson's time had come, that's why them Lost Man's fellers stood back there by the store and watched him killed. From the way he brought his boat ashore in the face of all them guns, I got to believe Ed Watson knew it, too.

The men agreed there would be no burial on Chokoloskee. Even dead, that body scared the women. At sun-up, we would take him out to Rabbit Key. But leaving a man I knew most of my life lay out all night alone by the cold water, that bothered me. I couldn't sleep. Toward dawn I went back over there to pay respect or something. Dogs had snatched that bloody flag and one-eyed Ed lay staring at the stars, arms wide. One boot was stripped off, the other shot away, and those dead feet with cracked old toenails looked like lumps of dough.

I never sucked up to Watson and I never had no regrets, that day or later. We done what we had to do. But I will admit I was ashamed of how some kept shooting after he was dead, like they was trying to wipe him off the face of the good earth and their own guilt with him. Some shot until their guns was empty, and more'n one reloaded, shot some more. One wild boy Crockett Daniels run in afterwards, put his .22 to the back of the dead man's head. I believe it was them boys robbed the corpse for souvenirs, cause his tooled big-buckled cowhide belt was missing, also his black felt hat from Arkansas. Watson weren't often caught out in the sun without that hat on, and now that white skin under his hairline made him look naked.

In the lantern shine, the one bald eye glared out through the black tracks of dry blood down across his forehead, but the dust-caked bloodied mouth in them stiff whiskers was the worst of it: front teeth all busted out, lips tore and stretched, but still a little twist to 'em, a little grin. He sure looked like he could use a glass of water. Well, Mister Ed, I whispered, hoarse, I come to say good-bye. It ain't that I'm sorry about what was done but only that your neighbors had to do it, men like me that weren't never cut out to be killers.

· · ·

By the time we went for him at sunrise, to run him out to Rabbit Key in his own boat, Watson had lost his good eye to some night varmint, maybe a poked stick. His clothes was mostly rags, black-caked with blood. Shirt ripped, hairy belly button. Them mean red spots was pellets deep under the skin. In the hard light of day it was plain he was shot to pieces, mostly buckshot rash but plenty of bullet holes, too, and flies already humming. A few men scared themselves all over again, telling how Watson, grinning like a skull, come after the posse through that hail of fire. (They was calling theirselves a "posse"; nobody cared to be a member of no "mob.") I warned Mamie what the dead man looked like and she headed off his widow before she went down to visit with the deceased. "Give us a hand," I told the men, and Tant Jenkins who had took no part was first to step forward and grab the ankles. Straining to hoist, Tant puffed out the opinion that dead men are unnatural heavy cause their bodies pull down like dowsing sticks, yearning for eternal rest under in the ground. "Well, that could be," I told him, "but being full of lead might make a difference."

"It ain't no joking proposition, Bill," sighed Tant, who most days would joke his way right through a funeral. Tant was tearful, might of had some drink, but there ain't no doubt that except for Tuckers he truly loved Ed Watson. Later he told me my remark upset him because it was just what Watson might have said with a straight face about his own damn death. Watson loved them sour kind of jokes, which I enjoyed myself. I mean, ain't life some kind of a sour joke? Might's well laugh, that's the way him and me seen it, whether nice folks seen the joke or not. One time when Watson caught me grinning along with him, he give a wink and lifted up his hat.

A angry moan come from the burial party when we swung that bloody carcass onto the transom. A couple of men flat refused to help us lay him in the cockpit, nor even touch him, as if even one drop of this devil's blood was curtains. We had to listen to this horseshit right while we was struggling to heft him, and sure enough he got away from us, slid off the transom, flopped into the shallers. I was outraged and I spoke too rough and later some would use that anger to show how Houses always hated E. J. Watson.

"Come on!" I yelled. "Stop screwing around! Let's get it over with!" I grabbed some line, bound up his ankles, run a hitch under the arms and worked it snug, then rigged a bridle off the stern cleats. Went aboard, cranked up his motor while them others clambered in, and snaked him off that shore like a dead gator, as yelling kids run out into the shallows, kicking water splashes after the body. Might been Billy Brown or Raleigh Wiggins who was wearing Watson's hat, or maybe that tough Caxambas kid he nicknamed "Speck."

"Get away!" My own voice sounded cracked, half kind of crazy. Where were their families, who claimed to be Watson's friends? How come they let their kids behave no better than camp dogs? Were they too scared of us ones who done the shooting? But when I calmed down, I was angry at myself for hauling him off the shore as rough as that, which only encouraged the other men to act rough, too.

We towed him all the way to Rabbit Key. Sometimes he come twisting to the surface, causing a yell of fear; other times that grisly head was thumping on the bottom, I could feel the thrumming when I took in on the bridle—*damn!* It turned my guts. In the main channel, he towed pretty good, but a boat motor in them days had more pop than power, and his dead weight dragged as bad as a sea anchor. In one place he got drawed across a orster bar, got tore up worse, and by the time we pulled him out on Rabbit Key, his clothes was all but gone, ears and nose, too. With limbs bound tight and no face to speak of, he looked less like a human man than some deep ocean monster thrown up by that storm.

They buried him face down—"Give that red devil a good look at Hell!" yelled Isaac—then toppled two big coral slabs on top, one across the legs and the other across the back, to make sure he would not rise at dusk and come hunting in the night for thems that slew him. One feller hitched a noose around the neck, run the bitter end to a big old wind-twist mangrove on the point, the only tree left standing by the storm.

By the water, Tant Jenkins was weepin about how good he was treated all them years by Mister Ed but even when he seen 'em lead that hanging rope out of the grave he just stayed out of it. That's Tant. I stomped over there, got hot about it, told 'em to take that noose off his damn neck cause he were as dead as the law allowed already.

"Ain't no sense gettin lathered, Bill. We rigged that rope so's them cattle kings can find the body case they send for it."

"Around the *neck*?" I said.

Them others backed that feller, feeling ugly, they was spoiling for a fight. Mister Watson didn't scare 'em, not no more. They felt free to punish that sorry red carcass for all the fear they felt when this thing was alive. I walked away. I was relieved that he was dead, the same as they were, but I have buried my share of men that had a lot less spine than Ed J. Watson.

Sheriff Tippins was there with the Monroe County law when we got back to Smallwood's about noon. The men had agreed not to mention Henry Short because around Frank Tippins, things went hard with nigras. We never did learn what become of Watson's black man that Tippins handed over to this Monroe sheriff. Can't even recall his name if they ever give him one.

The men notified the law that nobody lynched nor murdered E. J. Watson, it was self-defense. "This death don't smell like self-defense," Tippins advised. "Smells more like lynching." Right from the start, the sheriff seemed crisscrossed about this case, he couldn't stand still for a minute, he was fuming. "You men *all* claiming he shot first?" he says, rough and suspicious. They scratched their heads, looking around for somebody who might recall something.

"Well, he sure tried," I said.

Tippins turned toward me slow, looked kind of ironical—that's a lawman's habit—to let me know he aimed to keep his eye on me. "He sure *tried?*" Him and his sidekick exchanged that lawman look that's supposed to mean something but don't, cause they don't know nothing. "Your name House? I heard you was the ringleader."

"We never had no ringleader. No leader, neither."

"How come you're so het up, Mr. House? Ashamed of something?"

"You're the one looks het up, Sheriff. I ain't got one damned thing to be ashamed about."

"I reckon we'll see about that, won't we?" said the other lawman. They were trying to make me mad so I'd bust out with something. I was mad already because even my own sister had announced how we ought to be ashamed. Said she knew Ed Watson for what he was and never said no different but hated "the way you men licked his boots, then turned on him and shot him like a dog."

We wasn't bootlickers, not by no means. We was just ordinary fellers that never knew how to handle this wild hombre till we had him laying face down in the dirt. If ever a man brought perdition on himself, it was Ed Watson, but some way we was blamed for doing exactly what those blamers wanted done. Now that we had him good and dead, some that took part was growing nervous about wiping out a neighbor. Trouble was, he never fit their idea of a outlaw—shifty, dirty, knife scars or pocked skin, maybe an eye patch or a missing ear. Ed Watson never looked much like a criminal. Men might speak of them ice-blue eyes in their dark ring that could fix a feller in his tracks, but them blue eyes was part of his good looks, the women said. Them ones that was suddenly upset by how he died, they got to saying that all the trouble come from rumor and misunderstanding, that the killings at the Watson place only started when Cox come, that it was Cox who give Watson his bad name. That just ain't true. His troubles started back in the old century.

One thing for sure, folks was very nervous that Leslie Cox might be somewhere on this coast. Chatham Bend is on a big swamp island between rivers and Cox couldn't swim. And there was no one left to come by and take Cox off because the hurricane had cleaned them islands out. So unless Watson killed him, which nobody believed, Cox was still there. Only thing was, to believe *that*, you had to believe he set there on the Bend for a good ten days, all through that storm, until Watson finally showed up. And you had to explain what happened then.

A few of us guided the lawmen down to Chatham, found no sign of him. That started a new argument: was Cox watching us from hiding? Or had the man we killed the day before told us the truth?

Canefield, sugar works, boathouse and sheds, good dock, big cistern, strong white-painted house up on its mound—nothing anywhere in the Ten Thousand Islands come close to the Watson place before that storm. His fine plantation was what Ed Watson had to show at the end of his hard road. But now all them outbuildins was gone and his fine house stunk, black blood and flies.

We wasted half an afternoon trying to catch his old roan horse, which wore no halter. That wild-eyed critter might be running down there yet.

Before leaving, the *Falcon* took aboard four thousand gallons of cane syrup. Four thousand gallons! Lord! The hot hard hours that man must of worked, raking the shell out of forty acres of hard mound in the meanest kind of snake-crawling scrub jungle. *Forty acres!*

Tippins informed us we were going to Fort Myers for a court hearing. The *Falcon* picked up the other men at Chok before heading north. Edna Watson would not travel with us. My sister glared at us like we was convicted felons, boarding that ship in chains.

MAMIE SMALLWOOD

◆

No one ever forgot the Great Hurricane of October 1910, not around here. Everything not torn away was salt-soaked and rotted, trees down everywhere and marly muck. It seemed like our world would never come clean again, nor our souls either. Ted removed most of our drowned chickens but that reek of death came up through the floor a month or more before we could get the store put back together and he had time to crawl back under there, rake out the last of 'em. Mama Ida called it the sulphur stench of Satan coming up from everlasting Hell where you-know-who was suffering the torments of the damned this very minute, her expression said.

Because he had stayed out of it, my Ted was one of the few men with no cause to feel ashamed. Course Daddy and the boys felt no shame either, which explains the hard feelings in our families that's still festering today.

On October 25th, Frank Tippins finally showed up with the Monroe sheriff. The men informed 'em that the law had come too late. *Where they ain't no law, you got to make your own*—I'll bet those sheriffs heard *that* one a few times! But Tippins chose to see that as a confession and issued a summons to Lee County Court for the whole darned bunch, Daddy included.

I'd heard a whisper that the feller who shot first was the same man whose bullet killed Ed Watson. I was frightened it was Bill or Daddy. When I asked my brother about this, he just shook his head. "Well, Bill," I said, "what does that darned headshake tell me, yes or no?" And he said, "Mamie, there ain't no way to explain. It ain't a matter of yes or no so just forget about it."

FRANK B. TIPPINS

✦

While those men told how E. J. Watson died, I only grunted, shifting my chaw. Something was missing in their story, I informed them after I had spat; we would have to take them all to court, procure some depositions under oath for a grand jury hearing. Their faces closed. They had agreed on their story, I saw that, and the law could take it or leave it.

Sheriff Clem Jaycox from Key West, taking the hint, whistled in disgust and sucked his teeth. Never mind if Watson had it coming or he didn't, there was murder perpetated on the shores of Monroe County, Jaycox advised 'em, so someone had to pay. Mr. C. Boggess explained in a big hurry that while he himself had took no part, he could not find it in his heart to blame his neighbors for what they had to perpetate in self-defense. All the men nodded, all but Smallwood, who only shook his head and turned away.

At Chatham Bend we found no sign of Cox nor the dead squaw that nigger had reported. The men suggested that her people must have come and cut her down and taken her away. But how did those Injuns learn that she was dead? Had that nigger lied about that squaw, and if so, why? And if he lied about the squaw, what about Cox? All we had there was that nigger's story.

On the way back north, we took the witnesses aboard. Though Ted Smallwood disapproved of what they did, these men wanted the postmaster to come to court to testify to their God-fearing characters, him being the closest thing they had to a federal officer. Smallwood had an awful mess to clean out under his store but agreed to go. "All right, Bill?" he asked his brother-in-law, kind of sardonic. The man shrugged. "Up to you," he said. I had my eye on this House feller, who was short-spoken that day with almost everybody.

House's daddy, Mr. D. D. House, stood arms folded on his chest, close to the boiling point. The men had made Bill House their spokesman, and House announced he would refuse to testify if the law dragged an old man away like a damn criminal that throughout his life had been too honest for his own good. If his dad was left out of it and his young brothers, too, why, he would give all the testimony we needed. When I agreed, his brothers squawked—they were all slicked up, with shoes on, set to go—but the old man turned and marched 'em home, never looked back.

The Widow Watson and her children were all packed and ready, but when she came down to the shore, she saw that dark stain, like a shadow, where they let her husband lay all the night before. This upset her badly. Seeing the suspects watching from the *Falcon*'s deck, she started to tremble, then fled back to the store. Mrs. Smallwood advised me she would tend to Mrs. Watson and the children and put them on the mail boat in a few days' time. She was furious. She flew down to the boat and hollered, "Which one of you brave fellers stole his watch?" Nobody answered. Those men were angry, too. Whole coast was angry.

I said quick and hard, to startle them, "I heard there was a gang of boys around the body." For a second there, nobody said a word. Then one said, "Might could been that Daniels kid took his gold watch. Crockett. One they call 'Speck.' " And another snapped, "Takes a damn fool to say a name when he got no proof."

Rabbit Key was four miles west of Chokoloskee, on the Gulf, and the Monroe County line passed through it, west and east. Captain Collier sailed out Rabbit Key Pass so I could see just where the grave was. Man named Yeomans sang out, "We run that devil clean out of Lee County, planted him over on the Monroe side!" Charley Johnson crowed, "Wrapped him nice and tight, ready to box and ship!" They gazed away when I asked why they hog-tied a corpse. Then some man muttered that with bound limbs, the body towed better. "Superstitious, that's why," Smallwood commented. "Scared that otherwise he might rise up in the night, walk on water back to Chokoloskee." And why, I asked, had they towed the body in the first place instead of wrapping it in canvas and laying it in the stern? "Treating him like a dead animal," Smallwood said, "made E. J. seem more guilty and them less."

Bill House kept his mouth shut till he'd thought that over. Then he said, "Ted? How come you claim to know how we was feeling when you don't hardly know how you felt yourself?" And Smallwood said, "You and me ain't going to settle that one, Bill. Not today and not tomorrow. Maybe never."

Smallwood took his hat off as the *Falcon* passed the grave, but the others only stared away till that lone mangrove fell astern, and even then, they stayed quiet a good while, looking out to sea.

On the voyage north, one man drawed near while I pissed over the rail, tried to whisper away his own role in the killing. Pled self-defense asking a lawman to believe that Mr. Watson had made a felonious assault on twenty or more armed men. (Turned out all twenty had fired at the exact same instant, making it impossible to say who fired first.) Anyway, this feller recollected that he had missed the victim on purpose, out of his great respect for human life.

By now, the rest had learned what he was up to and were crowding around to make their own excuses. Bill House was the only man who did not try to explain and the only one, as I had already guessed, who would give me trouble.

These men weren't killers. They were honest settlers, fishermen and farmers, most had wives and children; they had built a schoolhouse (lost in the storm) and sent away for a teacher and they held prayer meetings whenever they could find a circuit preacher. Yet when twenty men slay one, some responsibility must be taken. Were they protecting somebody? Maybe House's tough old daddy? Even if they'd been telling us the truth, it wasn't the whole-truth-and-nothing-but-the-truth a court of justice would demand. That truth would have to be scared out of them when they were under oath at a court hearing.

Thinking about that night at Marco when the victim sat across from me at this very same table, I was already impatient with their story. I can't say I made friends with Mr. Watson but I had to respect him. I had wanted to believe him. Maybe that's why I tended to believe he had killed Cox after all, just as he'd said.

• • •

Bill House kept himself apart, in heavy humor. When I told him all he had to do was give his best recollection of the shooting, give an affidavit, he said he disliked being arrested like a criminal when no crime had been committed. Like these men said, they all fired in self-defense. Was I questioning their word?

"Just doing my job," I said. "Did Mr. Watson inflict injury on any man before you killed him?"

The men swapped quick uneasy glances. Jaycox pretended to make a note. House glared straight past me.

The *Falcon* sailed north, putting in for water at Caxambas. But Caxambas had no water to spare: not a drop of rain, folks told us, in the fortnight since the storm, and no sun either. In this dead gray weather, that settlement looked like broken pieces of some godforsaken outpost that the hurricane had flung onto this coast, ripping off the clam factory roof, smashing in the store; kids were diving for canned food in the channel. These refugee families huddled every night in Mrs. Barfield's lodging house, known as the Barfield Heights Hotel because it sat high on the big Indian mound here at south Marco.

A small wild woman from Pavilion Key led a young girl down to the dock to screech, "Lookit these here yeller dogs that massacreed your daddy! Took this whole pack to pull one good man down!" She wore her hair loose like she'd just come from bed, though this was considered trashy and her child seemed to know it. Maybe ten years old and skinny, the child had fair thin hair and a scared face that looked worried about what might become of her, while the woman tossed that hair around and cussed out my witnesses so vilely that I had to warn her against causing a drunken disturbance. "A lady has prescribed herself a draft of spirits for a broken heart," she wailed. "Is that a sin?"

All the men knew that Tant Jenkins's sister had lost her infant son at Pavilion Key during the storm. The woman hollered that her baby had been taken by the hand of the Almighty so Charley Johnson hollered back (as most of the men laughed) that she sure was right because her baby was the spawn of that bloody-handed devil who had brought the Almighty's wrath down on this coast back in the first place. "The child of deviltry and mortal sin"—that's what Mr. Johnson called that little perished boy.

· · ·

At Fort Myers, I led the men straight to the courthouse, where Eddie Watson, dropping papers at the sight of his father's slayers, claimed he'd stayed late to finish up some work. One man knew him by sight and the rest learned in a hurry who he was. Bill House exclaimed, "For Chrissake, Sheriff, how about giving *that* young feller the day off?" I didn't like his tone but he was right. I told Eddie he could go, I'd find someone else to record the depositions. Nosir, Eddie answered loudly, he weren't brought up to cut and run from a gang of lynchers: this was his job as deputy court clerk of Lee County and he aimed to do it. He took up his pad and sat himself stiff as a stick in the clerk's chair as I struggled to control my aggravation.

In his reddish looks, Eddie took after his daddy, with the same kind of husky mulishness about him; what was missing was the fire in his color. He put me in mind of a strong tree dead at the heart.

Bill House nodded at Eddie before beginning his account, which would turn out to be the official Chokoloskee version of the Death of Watson; having little to add, the others mainly testified that they agreed. Being uneasy around Watson's son, some frowned real fierce to justify what they had done while others only looked a little sad, as if to hint that their experience of shedding blood might have wounded them somewhat worse than it had his father. One or two tried a friendly smile, to show that all that unpleasantness was in the past or anyway nothing personal. Eddie ignored them. That young feller took it all down in his notebook, he could have been reporting the church supper. When the men were finished, he rapped the notebook down and slapped it shut, to show his contempt for the false witness of a lynch mob.

Well, it weren't that simple. Eddie Watson had kept strictly to himself whatever he knew or thought or felt about his daddy's trial in north Florida two years before, including his true opinion of his guilt or innocence. Since returning to Fort Myers, however, he had missed no chance to state or otherwise establish that he was E. E. Watson, not E. J. Watson Jr. so it seemed to me that this show of filial loyalty came somewhat late.

Ted Smallwood testified that he had not witnessed the shooting, only heard it, so he could not say that Bill House's account was not true "far as it went." House looked disgusted but remained silent. Smallwood and a couple of others signed their names and House and the rest took pains drawing their Xs, to make sure that X would not be mistaken for somebody else's. I told 'em they were free to go on home and wait for the grand jury to decide whether or when they were going to be indicted.

"Decide if we are criminals?" Bill House asked. "That what you mean?"

Walter Langford and Jim Cole had arrived in time to hear me mention the grand jury, and Cole was bitching even before I finished. How could a grand jury indict when the only eyewitnesses were the defendants? By law, these men could not be compelled to incriminate themselves so it made no *sense* to summon a grand jury—!

Langford raised both palms to slow Cole down. The new president of the Florida First National had a stiff collar and cravat to go with his new million-dollar smile, served up these days with everything he said. Ol' Walt had the jowls of a drinker and banker both; the days were gone when those honest cowboy bones showed through the lard. His honey hair was slick and tight as a wild duck's wing and his nails were pink and he reeked like a barbershop, but all that lotion couldn't cover up the whiskey.

Langford spoke in a hushed voice "on behalf of the victim's family," glancing at Cole for approval every few seconds while forgetting the victim's son a few feet away. He urged the sheriff to understand that the most merciful solution was to shelve the whole tragedy as soon as possible rather than "waste our public money dragging these men through the courts when there was no way justice could be done."

The suspects were already upset by Eddie's presence and Langford gave them the excuse they needed to get mad. House jumped to his feet. "*His* death weren't no tragedy! The tragedy was all them deaths at Chatham Bend!" Isaac Yeomans hollered out. "Justice *was* done, you stupid bastard, and I'm proud we done it!"

"Lordy!" Walt went red as beef. "Look, I'm only trying to *help* you people—"

"Go on home, then," Charley Johnson said.

I advised the banker that by law, a violent death could never be ignored and that due process had to follow an indictment.

Taking me by the elbow in that way he has, Jim Cole eased me out into the corridor as if we were up to something sneaky. "Walt's right, you know." He was wheezing as he pleaded, and his breath smelled of old liver and onions. "Why not just drop it, Frank? Forget it."

"Lee County can't 'just forget' a murder."

"It ain't murder if you deputize 'em as a posse."

"Little late," I'd say, "to form a posse."

"Is it? State's attorney owes me a favor, and he won't pester you for no damn dates. You got my word."

"Your word." I felt worn out. "How about justice?"

"How about it, Frank?" Cole snorted that fat laugh of his, slapping my biceps with the back of his thick hand to remind me I was in his debt because young Frank B. Tippins came into this office with Jim Cole's support and had made a few mistakes that Jim Cole knew about.

Well, I came in honest. I never asked for his support, never understood at first why he was so eager to befriend me. Had to learn that the cowmen and their cronies owned this town and ran it any old way they wanted, laws be damned. To do my job, I had to work around that, learn to give and take. So, yes, I took a little finally, cut a few corners.

My worst mistake was leasing out buck niggers off my road gangs for labor at Deep Lake. Cole fixed it with Langford. They paid nine dollars per week per head, plus one dollar per week for the Injuns I had to hire to hunt those boys down when they ran away. Paying convicts directly for their labor was against the law but I always aimed to turn over that pay when their time was done. However, very few showed up to pester me, they just disappeared. Same old story: the cash box sat there month after month, and one day I borrowed out of it, forgot to put it back.

Cole got wind of this some way; he would wink and nudge each time he brought the money. "Don't let me catch you giving one red cent to them bad niggers, Frank. Don't want my sheriff doing nothing that ain't legal." *My* sheriff! And he'd slap my arm with the backs of his fat fingers in that same loose way he did it now, to remind me how deep he had me in his dirty pocket, along with all the crumbs and sticky nickels.

I went back into the courtroom in a fury and deputized every man but Smallwood. A mob of murder suspects got appointed as a posse to arrest the man they'd killed, a man already stone-cold dead under the sand. And nothing was done that day or later to establish responsibility because deputizing the shooters made the shooting legal. As a sheriff's posse my new deputies went home feeling much better about what they did that day at Chokoloskee, not as a mob but in the line of duty.

The only angry feller besides me was William House, who refused to be sworn in. He punched the wall, then came forward and denounced the sneaky way he and his neighbors had been implicated and then let off although no crime had been committed in the first place. Said he'd damn well go to trial by himself if that was the only way he could clear his name.

"Well? What do I do now, goddammit?" he demanded when I ignored him.

"Do anything you damn well want. None of my business any more."

He nodded. "That nigra who risked his neck, broke the case open for you. What happens to him ain't none of your business neither, ain't that correct? You'll turn him over to Monroe County and then you're clear of it, correct?"

"Correct," I said, not looking up from the court clerk's desk where I pretended to sort through some papers. When he didn't move, simply waited there, I cocked an eye in warning. "That nigger's gonna see some justice, Bill. Same justice you gave Mr. Watson," I added, "according to your Chokoloskee story."

For a florid feller, House went a dangerous red. I expected a fight and an arrest and I was spoiling for it. I gave him a last warning.

"No loitering in the courthouse, Bill, unless you aim to loiter behind bars."

He swore and wheeled and followed the rest outside into the sun.

Sheriff Jaycox said that whoever he was, Leslie Cox had closed the book on Dutchy Melville, the fugitive most wanted in Key West. Green Waller, if that was his real name, had been wanted in Fort Myers as a hog thief; I scratched that name off the books, too. As for Cox, most people believed he was still at large down in the Islands, and nobody could say when or if or where he might show up.

Trying to piece it all together, I came up with more questions than good answers. The only witness to those murders had fooled the men at Pavilion Key by acting the part of a scared coon after doing his best to implicate Ed Watson. No matter how much I cuffed him in the jailhouse, that hard nigger stuck to his doctored story like stink on a dog. *Nosuh, nosuh, Mist' Edguh nevuh knowed nuthin about it! Ah jes 'cused him cause Mist' Les done promise he gone kill me if ah don't!*

But if Watson was innocent, why did his nigger make up that first story, which could only get both of them in trouble? Was he really so scared of

Cox he couldn't think straight? Or had he concluded that his boss had wanted him killed along with all the others, and seeing no hope anyway, took his revenge?

I had to conclude he told the truth the first time, risking his life to tell it, God knows why. If he hadn't—if Cannon and his boy had not passed by or if sharks and gators had beat us to the evidence, no one would have ever known the fate of those three people. All we would have had were some more rumors about E. J. Watson.

Those deaths having occurred in Monroe County, I signed my prisoner over to Sheriff Jaycox for transport to Key West. On the dock, with his suspect standing there in front of him, Clem Jaycox summed up his understanding of the situation: "Yep! Confessed to abettin in the butchery of a white woman. Probable rape and left for nude," he said, putting his X to the release. "No Monroe jury going to stand for that, not from *no* damn nigger. Don't hardly seem fair to ask my voters to waste tax money on no trial when we know the verdict 'fore it starts, ain't that right, Frank?"

"The prisoner is now officially in Monroe custody," I said. "I reckon you'll do what Monroe thinks is right." Clem Jaycox winked at me to show he understood, which I don't believe he did.

"It's been a pleasure working with Lee County, Frank," he said, and darned if he don't wink at me again!

Hands cuffed behind, the prisoner stood straight, observing us. He refused to sit down on the cargo crates where I had pointed. Jaycox spoke to him real soft and low, hiking his belt: "What *you* lookin at, nigger boy?" Risking a blow, the man ignored him. I said, "Your last chance, boy. Did Mr. Watson order Cox to kill those folks or didn't he?"

He regarded me like I was dead or like we all were. A very, very dangerous breed of nigger. I weren't surprised when news came from Key West that he fell overboard and drowned on the way south. Tried to make a getaway on the high seas, I reckon.

Learning from Eddie that their father's "gruesome carcass"—Eddie's words—had been towed out to a sand spit on the Gulf and thrown into a pit without a box, Carrie Langford came over to the courthouse to inquire.

When she busted out in tears about her Papa's lonesome fate, I took her by her nice soft shoulders, gave her a quick family kind of hug—first time I ever even touched her. I told her I'd have his remains recovered and brought to Fort Myers for reburial, if she wished, and go along to make sure all was done with respect.

I took the coroner along. Jim Cole wanted to know why, since nobody had asked for an autopsy. "That's a sleeping dog we might as well let lie," Cole said. Everyone wanted to let him lay, even the coroner. There were too many rotted corpses in his line of work, Doc Henderson complained. Doc finally admitted he was leery of the dead Ed Watson glaring up at him out of a hole.

"They laid him in face down," I assured him.

When I told Lucius, "You're not going, son, and that is that," he followed us to Ireland's Dock, came up behind as silent as my shadow. This quiet in Ed Watson's boy was unsettling to certain people, and so was his determination, which was not what you expected from the look of him. Lucius favored his late mother, very gentle in his ways. That slim young feller could do handsprings in the courtroom and you'd hardly notice while Eddie could peek through the back window and you'd feel his weight all over the damn building. "You're not going," I repeated. "One day you'll thank me." Lucius doffed his hat politely as he stepped aboard.

At the courthouse the day before, Lucius had arrived too late to protest the family decision not to prosecute, which his brother and sister had approved. He demanded an explanation: was it true that his father's confessed killers had been let off? Still angry about the so-called "posse," I said, "Better take it up with your family, son." Eddie was defensive and aggressive, refusing to show him Bill House's deposition or even the witness list on the grounds that it was "confidential evidence."

Since their participation in his father's death had not been contested by the perpetrators, Lucius insisted that these men go to trial. Though he was furious, intense, he never raised his voice. And he was right, of course. House and the others might have told the truth but it wasn't the whole truth and I knew it.

· · ·

Planter Watson lay beneath two crossways slabs of coral that the hurricane had broken from some reef and heaved ashore. The sight and stench brought a great gasp and moan from Doc's two diggers, who backed away. Sure enough, he lay face down, ankles bound tight. The gray flesh around the bindings was so swollen that it almost covered over the rough hemp.

I shivered the hard shiver of a horse, took a deep breath, then kneeled by the pit with a short length of rope and hitched it to those bindings; the raw thing was hoisted from the hole and swung onto a canvas tarp brought by the coroner. Within moments, flies mysteriously appeared and small sand fleas hopped all over the body. Doc Henderson, a trim and silver man, stepped forward, saying to Lucius, "Sure you're ready for this, son?" His voice was muffled by the gauze over his face.

Doc cut the last rags off the body, which was crusted with blood-black sand. He paused to rig a sort of loincloth—very professional, I thought, since there was no way this thing could ever be made decent. His small knife flashed in the white sun and the first lead slug thumped into his coffee can.

When the body was rolled over on its back, Lucius looked away, nose in his neckerchief. I stared at the black-and-blue face. The tanned neck and arms were savagely mutilated, the dead-white farmer's body already blue-gray. Doc's hands jittered and he coughed. "Oh Lordy! Lordy!"

Lucius pitched toward the water, puked, and returned very pale. I moved up close behind in case he fainted. I said sharply, "Had enough, boy? Seen what you came to see?"

He began to shake. I took him by the shoulders, spun him, and slapped him three times hard across the face, shouting with each slap, *Forget it!* Then I turned him again and pushed him back toward the boat. On that still shore, emerald reflections shimmered on the white paint of the hull and gulls yawped mournfully in the smoky autumn sunlight of the last day in that long doomed October. Another Monday.

An hour passed, its silence broken only by those small dull thumps as thirty-three slugs, one by one, clunked into the coffee can. Doc never bothered about buckshot.

Lucius was back. He cleared his throat. "He's been cut enough," he said. Doc's ears turned red and his hands stopped but he did not look up. "I ain't done," he said. "They's more there yet."

"Your coffee can is full," said Lucius. "That's enough."

I advised the coroner that Lee County was satisfied that the proximate cause of death had been determined. Doc snickered, then reproved himself with a doleful cough like a dog sicking up a piece of bone. "I kind of think of this," he said, reluctant to say good-bye, "as my own patient."

"This!" Lucius mourned.

"Doc," I said. "It's time to quit." We all backed off a ways to get a breath. The coroner wiped his thin knives on his cloth. "I heard they fill 'em full of lead out West but I never thought I'd see that in south Florida," he said.

The diggers wrapped rags around their hands before touching the cadaver, and no amount of threats and shouting stopped their moans and prayers and yelps and nigger racket while they rassled the carcass into Doc's pine box. Well, you couldn't blame 'em.

Lucius knelt. He touched the forehead with his finger. He said, "God be with you, Papa." He laid the lid, took up the hammer, and did his best to nail that stink in tight, but any man going ashore on Rabbit Key can get a whiff of Mr. Watson yet today.

CARRIE WATSON

✦

OCTOBER 26, 1910

It's over now. I am sunk down with exhaustion, as if I had fled this day for twenty years.

This leaden ache of loss and sorrow, made much worse by shame: *His daughter turned her father from her door.* Shame that is never to relent, that is the awful knowing.

Oh Mama, our Lord seems far away. I open my torn heart to you, knowing you know how much I loved him, praying that wherever you have gone, you might hear me and forgive me.

It's for the best—that's all Walter can offer me in solace. *It's for the best*, says Eddie, who sounds as pompous when he copies Walter as Walter sounds when he copies Mr. Cole.

Mama, I need you to hug me! Because I'm *glad* it's over. Do you forgive me, Mama? I grieve with all my heart yet I am glad. I repent but I am glad. May God forgive me, I am glad. I'm *glad*! And yet I am ashamed.

OCTOBER 27, 1910

I can't imagine what goes through Eddie's head. I love my brother dearly and it hurts to see his nature so congested, yet I long to kick him. As a boy he was still open to life, but when he returned here after Papa's trials in north Florida, something had thickened, he had lost all curiosity. He talks too much, he drones, he blusters, he is conceited about his clerk's job at the courthouse though everyone knows it was invented for him by Frank Tippins. He flaunts his small official post like a loud necktie.

When I commiserated with him about how terrible it must have felt to commit to paper the lies told at the hearing by those awful men, he sighed, shrugging philosophically. "They are not *awful* men, dear sister, they are merely men." Good grief! But that's the kind of wearisome stale thing he says these days. He affects a brier pipe, which doesn't suit him, only encourages him to weigh his words (which have no real weight so far as I can tell!).

Eddie goes deaf when Papa's name comes up. He was living with Papa at Fort White when all that trouble came, but he won't discuss it with Lucius or me, just frowns and mutters about some "family code of silence" with our Collins cousins. We're your brother and sister, I cried, we're his children, too! And Papa was found innocent, isn't that true? Wasn't he found innocent? And finally he grumped, "The defendant was acquitted, which is not the same." The *defendant*!

Because of this unspeakable hurt we share, we are estranged. Is it possible to love your brother but detest him?

Lucius seems less bitter about the slayers than about Papa's so-called friends, men like Erskine Thompson who looked on but failed to intervene. Lucius went straight to Eddie for the list of men brought to the courthouse but Eddie told him it would be improper for the deputy court clerk to reveal the names of prospective witnesses. Lucius retorted that the deputy court clerk seemed less concerned about his father's murder than his own official title, which wasn't nearly as important as he imagined. They had this ugly argument in public, nearly came to blows. Oh, what can folks think of our poor ruined family!

To lose his head and shout that way is so unlike our Lucius, who is taking Papa's death harder than anyone: he can't seem to deal with it without great anger (though I'm not sure he knows what makes him angry unless it's the fact that Papa died for Cox's crimes). Lucius lived mostly at Chatham Bend and was friends with those poor wretches who were murdered—that's part of it, of course. He refuses to believe that his jolly generous Papa was the killer people talk about now that he's dead.

When Lucius demanded a copy of the W. House deposition from Sheriff Tippins, Frank was sympathetic but refused him, saying his investigation of Mr. Watson's death was not yet over. Meanwhile, Lucius has talked to someone who claims to have witnessed the whole terrible business; he has actually started a list of those involved! He is *too* intense about this; I am really worried. Even Eddie says he is concerned about his "little brother's" safety. Yesterday evening Eddie warned him to "leave bad enough alone." Eddie's words showed disrespect for Papa, according to Lucius, who jumped up and demanded that Eddie take them back or step outside.

Leave *well* enough alone, then, said Eddie, winking at Walter, who just rattled his paper unhappily, trying not to notice. And Lucius said bitterly, "What's well enough for you may not be well enough for me." I saw Eddie's fists clench but he controlled himself and merely sneered, as if nothing his younger brother might say should be taken seriously. His attitude enraged Lucius all the more, and Walter had to walk him out of doors.

When Walter came back inside, he said, "That list of names is just his way of making sense of all his grief. He won't *hurt* anybody." I snapped, "Of course not, Walter! Can you imagine Lucius *hurting* somebody?" Walter sat down and picked at his paper, saying, "Eddie's right. He'd better not go questioning those men."

"Stop him, then!" I cried. But Walter doesn't care to interfere in Watson family matters, never has and never will. He hid behind his paper. "That boy is stubborn," his voice said. "If he has his mind made up, there ain't *nobody* can stop him."

"*Isn't!*" I cried, jumping up and snatching his paper away to make him face me. "*Isn't* nobody can stop him," Walter said, taking his paper back. "If I know Lucius, he'll be asking himself hard questions all his life."

OCTOBER 30, 1910

My stepmother is four years my junior. I paid a call on her at Hendry House (where they are kind Walter's guests). She has a glazed look, a dull morbid manner. How changed is poor young Widow Watson from the girl Papa brought south only four years ago! Miss Kate Edna Bethea, as I still think of her, lacked our mama's elegance and education. Papa truly admired those qualities in Mama, but I suspect that Kate Edna's girlish spirit, her high bust and full haunches, her prattle about farmyard doings back in Fort White, suited his coarser tastes and needs better than Mama's indoor virtues ever had.

Oh, she was his young mare, all right! I don't care to think about it! Papa walked and spoke like a young man again, he fairly strutted, and this only four years ago. He had stopped drinking—well, not quite, but he had regained control—and he was full to bursting with great plans for the Islands, full of *life*!

At the hotel, Kate Edna tried her best to be polite but she can scarcely bring herself to talk. Isn't it peculiar? The matronly daughter wept and sniffled while the young widow never shed a tear, just sat there stunned and scared, breaking her biscuit without eating it, scarcely sipping her tea. Edna won't go to her people in Fort White but to her sister in west Florida where no one knows her. She wants to get clean away, says she, so she can *think*. What her simple brain wishes to think about I cannot imagine.

Edna's clothes are nice (Papa saw to that) but she was wearing them all wrong, as usual, and of course they looked like she had slept in them, which no doubt she had. I urged my darling girls to play with their little "aunt" Ruth Ellen, but Papa's second batch of kids are muted desperate creatures and no fun at all. The boy Addison pulls and nags at Edna— *When is Daddy coming? Where is Daddy?*—and Amy's big eyes stare out in alarm even when she's nursing. Five months into human life, poor little thing, and scared already.

But Edna scarcely notices, she cannot hear them, just soothes her brood gently as if tending them in dream. In normal times she must be a doting mother, since she is so easy with them even now when she is homeless, with no idea of what awaits them and no money to tide them over. Papa had only a quit-claim on Chatham Bend because his legal claim had not yet been approved: technically, he never owned his own fine house, Walter has learned. It's so unfair!

Edna has given Walter power of attorney to sell the last shipment of cane syrup—she would have given it to anyone who asked. Walter tried to explain to her that Papa's huge legal expenses of two years ago had put him deep in debt but she scarcely listened, didn't seem to care. Nor did she find words to thank him when he advanced her money for her journey, promising to send after her whatever might be salvaged from "the estate"—Papa's boats and livestock, farm equipment, odds and ends.

When I told her we would rescue Papa from that lonesome sand spit on the Gulf and give him a decent burial here in Fort Myers, she said simply, "Next to Mrs. Watson?" She meant dear Mama! And she didn't say that with the least resentment but only to be polite, in the tone in which she might have said, "How nice!" After six years of marriage, three young children, and her shocking widowhood, she has never really seen herself as his honest-to-God wife.

Like Walter and Eddie, my stepmother believes that the less we speak of the whole tragedy the better. The important thing is to protect the children from malicious tongues, which will of course be much much easier for her than it is for us. We cannot flee as she can to north Florida, leaving everything behind. She won't even stay long enough to see her husband buried, having convinced herself that her little family is in danger. For that I will never quite forgive Edna Bethea.

Well, that's not true, I hope you know that, Mama. I forgive her with all my heart. To think what the poor soul has been through! Her voice is numb and her gaze faraway, and her stunned manner shows how terrified she was, how frantic she is to put all that behind her. Even my girls noticed the way she steals glances back over her shoulder as if that lynch mob, as Lucius calls it, might still catch her!

We took them to the train in the new Ford—their first auto ride. (Little Addison, at least, cheered up a bit.) Edna hurried them aboard to avoid any more awkward talk or prolonged good-byes, preferring to sit huddled in that stuffy car, clutching her infants and her few poor scraps until the train could blow its whistle and bear them far away to somewhere safe.

Through the window, I said I dearly hoped we would meet again one day. She looked past me, then blurted, "No, I don't think so." She meant no harm by it and yet she hurt my feelings. Am I being silly, Mama? Have I always been so silly?

The train whistle startled us. The train jolted. I trailed along the platform a little way, my fingertips on the lowered window, seeking her touch. I wanted so to hug her—hug anyone who might share this awful pain. Edna seemed aware of my yearning hand, but not until the final moment did she lay cool fingers shyly upon mine. "Please say our farewells," she whispered, in tears for the first time, as if those tears had been yanked out of her by that hard jerk of the train.

"Farewell?" I sniffled, walking faster now, too upset to realize she referred to the reburial.

"To Mr. Watson," Edna said in a hushed voice, still in tears. Yet that lorn face at the window never once looked back nor did she wave. A moment later she passed out of our lives.

NELL DYER

✦

A few days after we heard the awful news, I was picking up Mother's medicine at Doc Winkler's drugstore when Carrie Langford came in with her little daughters. Doc Winkler was the only doctor in Lee County and what is more, his shop sold ice cream sodas. Poor Miss Carrie had gone all dark around those big dark eyes, and her glorious thick hair, pinned up too tight in mourning, had lost its shine. Her little Faith came over to me and whispered, kind of scared, "Our Mama's been just crying and crying and we don't know why."

Darn it all if I don't bust out with: "She's crying cause some bad men shot your grandpa!" Those terrible words flew out like bats the moment I opened my mouth. Her grandpa had been real good to me at Chatham, so naturally I was upset, too, but at my age of almost twelve, I should have known better!

Hearing those words, Faith became hysterical, *Grandpa, Grandpa!* She would not stop wailing. Then Betsy started, *Grandpa, Grandpa!* because five-year-olds need attention even worse. They would not stop until their mother warned them to get their grief under control if they still wanted ice cream sodas. And just that moment—would you believe it?—the doorbell tinkled and in walked the first real live Indian we ever saw. Came right through the door in a high silk hat with an egret plume and a Seminole men's frock with red, gold, and black stripes. This Indian walked straight out of the Glades into Doc Winkler's Drug and Soda!

Betsy switched from *Grandpa! Grandpa!* to *Mama! Mama!*, never missed a breath, and Faith cried, "Mama? Is he going to scalp us?" Because back in those days, folks still talked about the Seminole Wars and the last redskins lurking in the Cypress and Shark River. Later I learned that Old Ice Cream Eater at Doc Winkler's had been threatened with death by his own tribe for hanging around palefaces and gobbling paleface ice cream, too, for all I know.

Miss Carrie said, "No, child, that is Mr. Billie, he's not here to kill little girls but only to enjoy a bowl of ice cream." And we watched Mr. Billie hike that skirt way up to seat himself more comfortably upon his stool, and lo and behold, he didn't have a stitch on underneath! Plopped his bare old brown behind right down and dropped that skirt over the stool and borrowed a toothpick off the counter to dig into his ear while he was waiting!

My mother made clothes for Mrs. Langford and her friends and was deathly afraid of losing her modest livelihood. When she found out what I'd said to those Langford girls, she burst into tears. Only a month before she'd had to send me over to apologize to Miss Carrie for having picked a beautiful big yellow rose that escaped out through her pickets and bloomed over the sidewalk. I picked that rose for my dear mother's birthday present because she was sick and I didn't have a penny, but not knowing that, my poor ma wept, saying, *This child will be the death of me.* I remembered those words on the day she died only a few years later.

When I went over to apologize, Miss Carrie invited me in for milk and pie. Neither she nor her brother Mr. Eddie visited Chatham while my family lived there so all I really knew about her was that Lucius Watson adored her instead of me.

Well, no wonder! Miss Carrie was beautiful, with a bountiful bosom and long soft brown hair and a complexion clear as a cowry shell and a faint scent of wildflowers—just an amazing person altogether and a good, good woman. And here was poor Nell with her home haircut close-cropped high above the ears so my ma could wash my neck. On top it shot up crazily like a hair fountain and fell down any old way over my spotty face. As Lucius teased in later years, I looked kind of odd and spiky—"like a wind-borne seed hunting some place to attach," those were his words—but in my ma's mirror I looked like some insane girl poking her head out of a bush.

Maybe because I was so uncouth, Miss Carrie insisted that I join her and her girls in their weekly tutoring in the ladylike speech and genteel deportment expected of a bank president's family. Because I remembered her daddy very kindly and we both loved Lucius, we were soon fast friends.

• • •

I first met Mr. Lucius Hampton Watson around 1903 or 1904 at Chatham Bend, where my father Fred Dyer had been hired as the foreman and my mother was the seamstress and my older brother Watt showed up on school vacations to pester and bully his little sister. What I loved about Lucius was the way he protected me from Wattie and also his gentle way with all young animals, including a certain bucktoothed little fool who imagined him to be some sort of knight.

Lucius paid me no more mind than my ma's knee patch on his britches but he only spoke sharply to me once, to shoo me out from underfoot. The addled child had strayed too close to the cane syrup boiler and the fire he was tending. Too young to understand that he was more frightened than furious, I ran off weeping. From that day on, utterly crushed, I gave him a little room, but my dirt-streaked face was poking around corners everywhere he went. All I could think about was this lean graceful boy—he was sixteen that year—whom I loved with all my heart.

In the late summer of 1905, my father packed his family onto the mail boat in a great hurry while his boss was absent in Key West. Wattie was glad to go back to Fort Myers but I was inconsolable, and fondly hoped that our sudden departure upset Lucius, too. Though I imagined I must be the cause, I realize now that his concern was for my parents, whose contracts read that if they quit their jobs before the harvest, they would forfeit every cent of that year's pay. Having no idea why my father was so frightened, Lucius was urging him to reconsider. I urged, too, in my shrill silly way— not that I cared a hoot about their pay. Staying close where he couldn't miss me, I wailed over the tragedy of our parting but could not get his attention; he was too busy scribbling a note to be given to his sister Carrie, recommending Mrs. Sybil Dyer as a seamstress. Thanks to this kind act, my mother would become established as a dressmaker to Fort Myers ladies, not only Miss Carrie and her friends but the Summerlins and Hendrys and in the winter season Mrs. Edison, upon whose bust she would make finery to be sent north in the summer to New Jersey.

I never saw my hero again until the day of Mr. Watson's burial five years later. My mother wanted to attend but my father forbade it. I disobeyed him because I knew how awful it all was for the Watson children, not only the horror of their father's death but as Mama said—she was grieving wildly, too, which was why my father got so angry—the dreadful scandal in our small provincial town.

On that cold sad November day, hoping to glimpse Lucius, I went to the cemetery by myself, looking as respectable as I knew how by hiding my horrible Sunday dress under my green sweater. Lucius spotted me and raised his hand, though not quite sure he recognized me. Once the grave was filled, however, he drifted away from the departing mourners and came toward me. He looked exhausted. "Nell?" When his pale face broke in a warm smile, I lost my head and ran and jumped and threw my arms around his neck, crying, "I'm so sorry, I'm so sorry!" He had to detach me like a big green tick and set me down. While the mourners paused to wonder who that rude child might be, he answered gently. "I know you are, Nell, I know that. Thank you." Courteous as ever, he asked after my family while making me feel he was glad to see an old friend from Chatham days even if that friend was only twelve.

CARRIE LANGFORD

✦

NOVEMBER 3, 1910

A norther blew on the day we buried Papa, and a cold hard winter light glanced off the river. The mourners gathered under the great banyan tree inside the gate. The Langfords turned up not to mourn but to be mannerly, that is, not so much courteous as proper: they wished to appear steadfast, correct, and faintly disapproving.

The old cemetery had sunk under hard brush and thorn since Mama's burial ten years before, but Lucius had worked like a madman for days to clear off enough ground for Papa to be laid in there beside her (Walter had paid darkies to do this hot, mean job but Lucius was so desperate to do something that he sent them away). It's comforting to think that Papa—though "somewhat the worse for wear," as he might say—is reunited with dear Mama. When I whispered this to Eddie, he retorted too loudly, "Nonsense, Sister! How can they be united? Our father is in Hell!"

The gravediggers stepped back, doffing their hats. Perhaps the two who went to the Islands with Lucius and Frank Tippins had passed the word, for these men knew all about the frightful corpse inside that casket. I'm not being oversensitive. They *knew* something!

The sheriff ordered them to finish quickly, his voice rough and loud: he seems to dislike nigras. Looking severe in his black suit, he stood guard over Papa's casket as if to defend him from a vengeful Lord. It was kind of Frank to come, and goodness knows, our dreary little party needed all the support that it could get. When I thanked him, he exclaimed, "Mr. Watson had my respect, Miss Carrie, ma'am, no matter what!" He was very embarrassed, as if he'd said something crude and tactless rather than kind; his mustache, overlong and droopy, gives him a hangdog air. I wonder if he still imagines that he loves me.

After Papa's trial in north Florida, Walter and Eddie hinted that he would not have been acquitted without political connections. A month later, a drifter at the jail had been condemned to hang for slaying some local lout in self-defense, and Walter remarked that if the defendant had had local friends or influence, he would surely have gone free: for the crime of being a stranger, he would hang. I asked Frank Tippins if this was just. The sheriff said, "He was found guilty by a jury of his peers and condemned to death. That may not be just but it sure is justice. Justice under the law."

At Papa's burial I whispered, "Was justice done here, too?" Knowing what I referred to, Frank said, "No, ma'am! No due process! This was murder!" He had spoken loudly; turning red, he stood gulping like a turkey. Then he whispered, "This was murder, Miss Carrie. But some would say that this was justice, too."

Four of Papa's friends came from the Islands. Stiff and shy, they stood apart in threadbare Sunday suits and white shirts without collars buttoned up tight. Lucius introduced them to Eddie and me: Captain Bembery Storter and his son Hoad, Mr. Gene Roberts from Flamingo, Mr. Willie Brown. The men paid their respects and offered a few words of formal regret. Where, I wondered, was Postmaster Smallwood? Or Erskine Thompson or Tant Jenkins, who had known us since childhood?

When Lucius moved away, the Island men, very uncomfortable and nervous, urged us to prevail on our younger brother not to return to Chokoloskee Bay asking hard questions; for Ed Watson's son, it would simply be too dangerous. "He won't listen," Eddie grumped and moved away.

A little woman stood with Lucius, very bright dark eyes and long black hair—cheaply dressed but pretty, I suppose, in a common way. She had a girl with her, a ten-year-old or thereabouts, eyes hollowed out by weeping, rather plain. When the child caught me staring, she smiled a small shy smile, then dropped her eyes.

Lucius had embraced these females a bit freely, so it seemed to me. When I asked him who they were, he said, "Tant's sister from Caxambas and her daughter Pearl."

"The one who kept house for Papa? Lost her baby in the hurricane?" Lucius nodded. "Is that the one that he called Netta?" He shook his head. "Aunt Netta's half sister." I kept after him, jealous because he knew an intimate side of Papa's life that I did not. I said meanly, "And did this female betray Mama with Papa, too, like your 'aunt Netta'? Why is she sniffling so hard? She have a cold?" Lucius gazed at me, not sure how much I knew. "She loved him, I think." His mild tone chastised me.

By now Sheriff Tippins had overheard us. Trying to smooth things after Lucius moved away, Frank Tippins said, "Lucius is taking this real hard, Miss Carrie. At Rabbit Key—" I cut him off, indicating that Caxambas delegation. "He's not the only one, it seems."

Poor Frank was embarrassed. "Well no, ma'am. I mean—" "My father was no saint," I murmured, to let him off the hook. "No, ma'am," he said. "That pale child is my half sister, isn't she?" I said after a pause. "I reckon so, Miss Carrie." I thanked him for his candor and he tipped his hat. "That the same old hat you bathed in?" I said, hating my own mood. He took it off and looked at it. "Yes, ma'am. Same old hat." Like Lucius, he soon moved away and who could blame him?

Sun came, sun went. The clay earth of the grave was yellow-orange, dead, unwelcoming. Who could rest in peace in such poor soil? But I was glad of this cold norther because even in the wind, the odor of that box was shocking, truly. Driven back, the circle of Baptist faces looked stuffed tight, sipping their breaths, and women coughed, resorting to their hankies. I was grateful to those brave few who still pretended that they noticed nothing, but surely, they, too, were horrified by that frightful stench and the very thought of the putrefying corpse inside.

The only one who dragged out his big kerchief and held it to his nose, the only one who hawked and spat, was Mr. Cole, who drove up late in his new red Reo, scared he might miss some mean little moment he could chortle over later. Jim Cole hated Papa for not hiding his contempt: he had no business here among the mourners. Unable to hide my resentment, I turned away from him.

Knowing how shallow and vain I was, I prayed that all these Baptist folks considered such a ghastly stench some sort of satanic emanation, not the remains of Carrie Langford's parent, the source of her own flesh and blood. Oh, Lord, I thought, when my time comes, please hurry me into the ground before anyone can even imagine worms or the dank gray hair and spidery fingernails that are said to grow like fungus in the grave. Pray they remember that rose-scented young virgin, Carrie Watson.

My good Walter supposed that I was grieving and put his arm around my shoulders. Eddie stood off to one side, stiff as a wooden Indian, as if trying to remember how to breathe. Lucius, unable to stand still, had wandered away from our stricken party to rejoin Papa's woman and the frail half sister I had never set eyes upon before today, then crossed the cemetery to greet Sybil Dyer's adolescent daughter—all by herself at a burial, imagine!

In the first days of 1901, when Papa came north through Fort Myers, poor dying Mama guessed that he was on the run. Knowing this meeting would likely be their last, she asked him what might have become of that poor Rob. "What has become of him?" Papa said coldly. "If God knows, He has said nothing to me." Relating this, Mama looked unhappy and bewildered, as if wondering if she'd known her husband after all.

In her last hours of consciousness, Mama lay with her hands flat on the coverlet, those fine hands with their long sensitive fingers that would have the same cool ivory hue in death as in her life. She was mustering up strength, I think, for composing a final message to her children.

> *There is a great wound in your poor father I could never heal, and may the Good Lord who gave him life have mercy and forgive him at the last, and give him rest. Because Papa, too, is made in our Lord's image. He is a man, a human being, whose violence is the dark side of him never redeemed. Yes, he is accursed when in his drink, hard, cynical, and tragically self-destructive, and I fear for his immortal soul. But as you well know, having seen it, he can be kind and generous, too, and does not stint, and he is manly. That side of him is loving, humorous, courageous, aflame with energy and enterprise. That is the side I loved and you must cherish, knowing that, for all his grievous faults, your unfortunate father loves you children very dearly.*

Though the family had decided there would be no eulogy, I had copied that passage from Mama's scrawled ungainly note. I summoned up nerve and read it out aloud at Papa's graveside, in the hope that his true mourners might take comfort. Lucius wept silently, tears glistening. As for Eddie, I prayed that Mama's words would ease his anger and permit him grief, but how could her words affect a son who was striving to pretend his heart was absent, somewhere else entirely?

I suppose Eddie was lucky to be sure of how he felt. Here was the grieving daughter at the grave, still torn about her father's guilt or innocence and hopelessly confused about what her own feelings should be. What seems simplest is to go along with Eddie and Walter and never speak his name after today; I would tell my children not to mention Grandpa because it upset Mommie.

Lucius feels no such obligation. In a way I am touched by his loyalty to his father, but refusal to abide by our family decision is a lot easier for a young footloose brother who can always escape than for me and Eddie, both married with small children, who are stuck in Fort Myers probably for life and must suffer all the stares and whispers.

Mama and Papa lie just near the Langford plot, which shelters my own little John Roach Langford, 1906–1906, and Infant Langford, stillborn in 1907. Two little stones. Whichever family I am put in with at the end, I will be near them.

For Papa, Lucius had ordered a simple small white headstone with no epitaph, just the bare name and dates. At the sight of it, my tears came quietly, at last, at last.

EDGAR J. WATSON

NOVEMBER 11, 1855–OCTOBER 24, 1910

When my Faith asked in her sweet clear voice what the J. stood for, the mourners looked startled. Nobody knew. All these years he had been E. J. Watson; it took a child to ask about that *J*! Mama once told us that his given name was E. *A.* Watson: why he changed the *A* to *J* she did not know.

Papa's woman from Caxambas turned when she heard Faith's question. In a whiskey voice, more like a croak, she called out "Jack!" Lucius hurried her along, but she tottered sideways, seeking my eye, and called again: "E. Jack Watson!" Lucius would confirm that she had called him "Jack," though why he could not say. "What does it matter?" Lucius said.

Leaving the cemetery, Walter's aunt Poke, the deaf one with all the rings, asked Walter loud enough for all to hear if Eddie Watson had considered using his middle name—*if he actually intends to remain here,* is what she meant. Calling himself "Elijah" might spare the poor boy (as she called him) future embarrassment.

I suppose we'd all thought about "Ed Watson Junior" but no one before Aunt Poke had said a word. And we all knew she was speaking for the Langfords. Eddie restrained himself from bursting out with anything unseemly in a cemetery but Lucius stopped and turned. "Are you afraid your family will be shamed if he doesn't change his name? Because our family will be shamed if he *does.*" And he gave that old lady a fierce look that challenged not only Aunt Poke but all the Langfords.

That ringed hand flew towards her throat but she made no sound. It was only afterwards, as we filed through the gate, that she whispered to Walter, "That boy has something of the father in him, don't you agree?"

HOAD STORTER

✦

In early November, I went north with Captain Bembery to pay our respects at the burial of his friend E. J. Watson. But all I could think about was Lucius, who had boarded with my family in Everglade when we were ten or eleven, gone to school with me and got some tutoring from Mama, who adored him. I bet he read every darned book we had. He was my best friend and I thanked the Lord he had not been a witness on that shore at Chokoloskee. He would have done his utmost to protect his father and might have gotten himself killed right along with him.

After the burial, Lucius took me aside and asked me to look after his dad's boat until he came back to reclaim the Watson place and "get to the bottom of this ugly business." I warned him right there at the cemetery that he must *not* return, not now and maybe never. Those men were afraid of him, it would be too dangerous. Cap'n Bembery told him the same thing and so did Willie Brown and Tant: he nodded politely, but I don't guess he paid us much attention. For such a quiet modest feller, Lucius Watson can be very very stubborn, and watching his eyes, I was pretty sure that sooner or later he was going to be back.

BOOK TWO

Good and evil we know in the field of this world grow up together almost inseparably.

—JOHN MILTON, *Areopagitica*

A man's life of any worth is a continual allegory—and very few eyes can see [its] mystery.

—JOHN KEATS

If we had a keen vision and feeling of all ordinary human life, it would be like hearing the grass grow and the squirrel's heart beat, and we should die of that roar which is the other side of silence.

—GEORGE ELIOT, *Middlemarch*

WINTER

That ruined winter of 1910–1911, Lucius Watson worked as a fishing and hunting guide out of Fort Myers, serving Yankee sportsmen and business associates of Walter Langford. As a skilled boatman, fisherman, and hunter, he was well qualified, but he was so quiet as he went about his work that his brother-in-law received complaints about his daunting silence. Try as he would to be "one of the boys," he remained hobbled by melancholy and introspection. Even his humor, once so cheerful, had turned cryptic and laconic, to the point where he was thought unsociable—the worst of defects in a sportsmen's guide.

In the end, Lucius had heeded his family's pleas and his friend Hoad's solemn warnings at the burial to stay away from Chokoloskee Bay, where local emotions were a volatile bad mix of guilt and fear and where the appearance of a Watson son with a reputation as an expert shot would be asking for serious trouble. Though Lucius understood this well enough, he felt, in addition to his grief, unbearably ashamed that Papa's murderers had never been held accountable by his grown sons.

Alienated from his brother Eddie, Lucius longed for Rob's advice in deciding how to deal with their father's killers. Unlike Eddie and Carrie, Lucius had lived with Rob at Chatham Bend, and having been closer to his hair-trigger half brother than anyone in the family, he was desperate to know why he had run away after the Tucker deaths in 1901—had he participated, then?—and what had ever become of him. Yet over the years, on the few occasions he had dared inquire, his father had met him not with anger or evasion but something worse, something strange and scary, a hard obdurate silence, as if Rob's name had never been mentioned at all.

In early spring, unable to rest, Lucius set off on a vain search for his brother, traveling north to Columbia County in the hope that Rob might have been in touch with Granny Ellen Watson and their Collins cousins. As it turned out, Granny Ellen had died a few months before her son, and Aunt Minnie Collins, afflicted by a morbid condition known as "American nervousness," had been sheltered from the family scandal and sequestered from her own life by morphine addiction and premature senescence: she could scarcely recall who this young man was, far less what he might want of her. Like one rudely awakened, on the point of tears, the Widow Collins could not deal with an intense intruder who brought only confusion to her household in what would turn out to be the last year of her life.

As for her children, they scarcely recalled this Cousin Lucius who had lived among them briefly long ago when all were little. Sympathetic at first, they became uncomfortable when queried about his father's life here in Fort White. Disgraced in their rural community by Uncle Edgar, they reminded Lucius of the family code of silence agreed upon with Cousin Ed before he returned to Fort Myers.

"But he was acquitted!" Lucius protested. "He was found innocent!"

The Collins brothers had loved lively Uncle Edgar, they acknowledged, but they would never be persuaded he was innocent. Willie Collins called from the train platform, "Y'all come back and see us, Cousin Lucius!" Though this farewell invitation was meant kindly, he knew it was not really meant at all.

While in Fort White, Lucius had learned the whereabouts of his father's widow, who had gone to live near her sister Lola in the Panhandle. Edna Watson was close to Lucius's age, they had been dear friends at Chatham, and he looked forward to a visit with his little half sisters Ruth Ellen and Amy and their roly-poly brother, christened Addison Watson after Granny Ellen's family in South Carolina. But Ruth Ellen was still terrified by the din and violence of that October dusk, which Little Ad, unluckily, had witnessed, and even Amy, only five months old when her father died, struck Lucius as pensive and withdrawn.

As for his young stepmother, she was friendly and very nervous; he had dragged unwelcome memories to her door. "Mr. Watson is a closed chapter in that poor girl's life," her sister warned him, gently pressing him to leave. At the railroad station, Lola informed him that Kate Edna would soon marry Herkimer Burdett, her childhood sweetheart, who had offered to give his name to her three little ones.

THE UNDISCOVERED COUNTRY

In the dull white summer of 1912, Lucius enlisted in the Merchant Marine, taking along a duffel full of books. Since his arrival there at the age of seven, Lucius had been fascinated by southwest Florida history, all the way back to the first aborigines and early Spaniards, and his interest had widened like a circle in a pond to encompass the natural history and archaeology of this low flat limestone peninsula lately risen from the sea, whose only hills were the astonishing shell mound accumulations of the seagoing Calusa which the Indians had climbed in time of hurricane. Ever since, he had explored every corner of its history, from its subtropical flora to its coastal fisheries, ancient and modern, also its pirates, pioneers, plume hunters, and gator poachers, its rum-runners, smugglers, and fugitives, from the Calusa Hatchee River south to Cayo Hueso or Bone Key, now called Key West.

On his return to Fort Myers he was prevailed upon by Carrie and Walter to attend state university and study for a degree in Florida history. The topic he proposed for his senior thesis was an objective study of the Everglades pioneer sugarcane planter Edgar J. Watson that might challenge the lurid legend propagated in the press about the man now commonly referred to as "Bloody" Watson.

Lucius Watson's proposal was rejected as "inappropriate," by which was meant that its subject's identity as the author's parent must surely compromise his objectivity. However, the faculty was much impressed by the applicant's wide knowledge of remote southwestern Florida and invited him to prepare instead a history of that all but unknown region called the Everglades Frontier, which in 1916 was still a wilderness of swamp and raining river, lacking a written history more recent than the U.S. Army accounts of the Seminole Wars of the mid-nineteenth century.

Discomfited (though not honestly surprised) by the rejection of his first proposal, Lucius was nonetheless intrigued by the proposed history of "the undiscovered country," as his father had called the Everglades, invoking its immensity and mystery with that metaphor for death from Mama's cherished *Hamlet*. In his father's honor, he chose "The Undiscovered Country" as a working title, and with so little new research to be done, commenced at once. Proceeding too rapidly, perhaps, he was nearing completion when his inspiration faltered: he lost faith in his thesis structure and kept wandering off course to work on the aborted biography of E. J. Watson at the many points where the two books overlapped. He drank too much. Debilitated and depressed, he "forced" his prose, doing it such damage with his fitful scribblings that finally, trying to patch all this poor stuff, he came to hate it. Late one evening, reeling drunk, he uttered a despairing howl and swept the whole unpaged scrawled manuscript off his table, notes and all. A fortnight later, after an alcoholic odyssey that ended disreputably in jail, he was suspended from the university a few months short of receiving his degree.

Returning to Fort Myers weak and ill, in a deep pit of melancholy, Lucius went directly to the Langford household to accept responsibility and blame for his disgrace. His sister gasped at his haggard demeanor. "Oh, it's such a waste!" she mourned: she was not referring to the lost tuition fees, though Lucius heard it that way. Lucius's morbid clinging to the past, his refusal to grow up, his brother Eddie informed him, were what caused him to drink too much and fail to finish everything he tried.

A minor officer at Walter Langford's bank, Eddie Watson was already well settled as a married man with children, a churchman and sober citizen who shared most if not all of his brother-in-law's conservative opinions. Sprawled in an armchair, one leg over the arm, he shook his head over his brother's chronic folly while deploring his ingratitude to their generous host, whose vision and hard work had paid for that wasted tuition. Embarrassed, Walter frowned judiciously, rapping out his pipe. Whether he frowned over the waste of money or the waste of Lucius's education or in simple deference to the onset of his evening haze, brought on by whiskey, was not clear, but that frown intensified Lucius's regret that he had accepted family assistance in the first place.

Because he'd never lived in Fort Myers long enough to make good friends and had not felt much like making any after his father's death, Lucius became a loner. Absurd as it seemed even to him, a young girl, Nell

Dyer, had become his only confidante, hearing him out on those rare occasions when he felt like ranting and encouraging him to eat something when he felt well enough.

NELL DYER

Lucius had first laid eyes on Nell in early 1903, not long after his father, passing through Fort Myers on his flight north, hired her parents to manage Chatham in his absence. Fred Dyer was handsome, black curly locks and wiry, with too much energy for his own good. Though acting as foreman, he worked mostly as a carpenter, building a new cistern and the boat shed and the small cabin for his family a hundred yards downriver that a few years later would be occupied by Miss Hannah Smith and the hog fancier Green Waller. Fred's wife was Sybil and they had two children, a secretive, sullen ten-year-old named Watt, or "Wattie," who lived with relatives in Fort Myers, disliked Chatham and only visited on school holidays, and a sprightly five-year-old named Nell whose bowl haircut, trimmed high over the ears to deter fleas, was permitted to fountain on top, then fall over her face, half blinding her. Nell wore odd garments sewn by Sybil from checkered flour sacks and toddled around on tubular small legs lacking visible knees.

The occasional clear day with wind was what Sybil called "the Mosquito Sabbath," when those demons rested and she walked out in the sun and played along the river with her little daughter. Those bugs were God's Own Malediction, sighed Mis Sybil. Her little girl's nostrils were black with oily smoke from the kerosene rags burned in the smudge pots, and she had to rig netting to Nell's bonnet and wrap old newsprint around her legs every time the child went outdoors to the privy: in wet weather, the ink came off the paper and turned her legs a dark bruised blue. Day in, day out, they remained shut up indoors, which in those dark months was damp and stifling, with air so heavy that the lungs grew weary hauling it in. No child was allowed out of doors at night because of bugs or for fear of bears or panthers, not to mention the cottonmouth moccasins that collected on the mound in time of flood. Everyone used chamber pots—"chambers," the child called them.

In those first years of the new century when his boss was mostly in Columbia County, the new foreman often accompanied Erskine Thompson on the Watson schooner, trading cane syrup, gator hides, and plumes for dry goods, hardware, and materials. According to Erskine, Dyer prowled the cathouses everywhere he went, drinking more than he could handle and running up debts that harmed the Island Syrup Corporation's reputation. He persisted in these reckless habits even after his employer had returned from northern Florida.

Sybil Dyer made most of their clothes. She was fair-haired, rather delicate, and in E. J. Watson's fond opinion, "pretty as a primrose." As a widower, he had been lonely, and around Sybil, this hard-minded man, chuckling and blushing, would turn warm and soft as buttered hominy. In quest of her good opinion, the heretofore godless Papa held Bible readings every Sunday morning, leading his makeshift and indifferent congregation in spirited renditions of "Jesus Loves Me," "The Old Rugged Cross," and "The Little Brown Church in the Dell."

As time went on, especially when drinking, Papa would confide in the foreman's wife the saga of his shadowed childhood and the loss of the family plantation in Clouds Creek, South Carolina. Inevitably his unsophisticated seamstress would conclude that she alone was privy to the heart of Planter Watson, so generous and kind despite his ill repute; doubtless she imagined, like so many, that the love of a good woman could heal his soul and redeem his sinful ways.

Years later, it occurred to Lucius that while Papa might shout disgustedly when his foreman passed out or turned up late on the job, he actually encouraged Dyer's absences and lapses, the better to remove him from the path of conquest. Even when Fred was present, Papa acted possessive about Sybil and enjoyed teasing her husband, and Dyer had laughed along too loudly because, for all his lip and strut, he was afraid. In his coast travels, the foreman had heard tales concerning the young Key Westers killed at Lost Man's Key, and in the summer of 1905, when the Audubon warden was murdered at Flamingo, his nerve succumbed to the false rumor that Ed Watson had killed Guy Bradley in a plume dispute. The Dyer family had departed on the next mail boat, and the only one Lucius truly missed was the child Nell.

Except for a brief encounter at his father's burial, Lucius did not see Nell again for years: she was fourteen by the time he came across her next in a Sunday crowd on the Fort Myers pier. Feeling compelled to turn around, he found her watching him. The girl was still dressed artlessly, almost randomly, with only a slight modification of that haircut (it no longer looked clownish, merely quirky), yet her appearance startled him, like a figure emerged from a dream upon awaking and beheld in sunlight and fresh air for the first time.

Though the day was cloudy, the girl's face shone like a wild lily in a sunshine between rains. He saw in the first instant that this face had been dear to him forever, she had always touched him, stirring happiness. In that instant, for want of words, he longed to kiss the freshness of her teeth and lips, but since this was unthinkable in public, he teased her about how peculiarly pretty she'd become—" 'Peculiar' is right!" she laughed. Then they fell quiet, searching each other's gaze, smiling and smiling, until simultaneously they looked down, putting away their delightful secret without a word. At Dancy's Candy Stand, Mr. Lucius H. Watson treated Miss N. Dyer to the chocolate ice cream that she'd been about to pay for out of her clutched cigar box of old pennies.

They perched together on the pier end, swinging their shoes over the current, recalling Chatham. The tar and rope smells of the splintery dock timbers brought back fine memories of the sailing schooners and the southward voyage on the *Gladiator*. She offered a turn at licking her ice cream cone. She said, "I have missed you." In that moment, chocolate mouth and all, the girl struck him as delightful in her Nell-ness, perfect and complete just as she was. In his inexperience, undone by strange emotions, he had not yet recognized first love. The following day when they met again and wandered along the river holding hands, Nell swung their arms up toward the sun as a way of working off her happy tumult and high spirits, summoning up a disgraceful twitch in her companion's trousers.

By her own account, Nell had wept for weeks after her family left Chatham, so heartsick had she been for her lost Lucius. A year later, after her mother died, she would confide that Sybil Dyer had sobbed without restraint when the news reached Fort Myers of his father's death. It seemed that Mr. Edgar Watson had declared his love for his sweet seamstress, and yes! she, Sybil, had loved him in return! Mr. Edgar Watson had the most glorious blue eyes she ever saw! Recounting this, Nell laughed affectionately at her simple-hearted parent. And there was more. Increasingly over the years, despite his black hair and pasty skin, her brother Watt had reminded Fred Dyer of E. J. Watson, until finally he'd confronted his wife on the evidence of her unseemly grief at the time of Watson's death. Accusing him of being drunk, she expressed hurt and astonishment that her husband dared abuse her after all his well-known infidelities.

Nonetheless, his suspicions rose from day to day, and his voice, too, and in the end, driven to distraction by his hounding, her mother abruptly conceded, out of her outrage and exhaustion, that in the early nineties, a stranger named Watson, arriving in Fort Myers after a journey on horseback to southern Florida from Arkansas by way of South Carolina, might have taken advantage of an unwary young woman kneeling before him while painstakingly engaged in taking pant leg measurements for his new suit.

Nell parodied the parental exchange to make it less embarrassing to relate: her ear for her parents' accents was so good that he had to struggle not to laugh aloud at this distressing tale—

"Weren't that right before you signed me up to marry, woman? *My lands, Frederick, Mr. Dyer dear, I suppose it was!* And weren't that why you was in such a rush after tellin me no for close onto a year? *Well, I don't think*— Never mind thinkin! Answer me! Weren't that damned kid already in the oven when we wed? *I wish you wouldn't put it that way, Frederick—* Jesus Christ! You got the guts to stand there and admit this? *My lands, Mr. Dyer! No need to raise your fist and scare these children*—Answer me!"

It was finally agreed that E. J. Watson might have been Watt's parent and furthermore that he and Sybil had renewed acquaintance, so to speak, after Mr. Watson, hearing that her husband was out of work, offered employment at Chatham Bend a few years later. Was it her fault that one afternoon when Frederick was absent as usual and her children off in the skiff somewhere with Lucius, Mr. Watson had forced his way into Mr. Dyer's cabin—

"Forced his way into Dyer's wife, ain't that it?" Dyer raged. "How come you never told your own damn husband you was raped?!" And she cried out, "For the same reason you didn't want to know! You would have had to act and he might have killed you! "

In the end, unconsoled by moonshine, her father had collapsed across the table, weeping in shame and rage, unable to decide whether his wife had confessed the truth or was exacting some perverse revenge for all his gadding. With no strong brain but keen instincts for survival, Sybil had emerged as the injured party: indeed, she had transcended the entire matter, saying, "Mr. Dyer, let us never speak of this again."

"My God," Lucius said in awe.

For some months, Nell's parents chewed on their hard situation. But one day her father grew so incensed at the sight of surly Watt that he drove him barefoot from the cabin, throwing his boots after him. Discovering this too late to call Walt back, her mother, whose dressmaking paid the rent, ordered her husband to pack up and be gone. He departed penniless, fatally bitter, and was not invited to return. In the years since, Nell's unfortunate father would swallow his pride down with his liquor and rant about his wife's affair in the saloons: "No, no, boys, weren't no damn rape about it! If it were rape like the way she claimed, how come she never used the gun he give her to run him off when he was drinkin? How come that bitch give her bastrid kid that name? Nosir, boys, I would of kilt that sonofabitch if them Chuckerluskee fellers hadn't beat me to it!"

It was true that in his all-embracing way, Papa had been courtly with the ladies, unusually attentive and considerate, and that he had bought Sybil that small, silver revolver as a protection against his drunken self, though of course this gesture had been drunken, too. But in a man so wrong-headed when rampant, love alone might not have deterred him from a tender rape. When Ed Watson drank, the whole coast agreed, he was a buccaneer and an unholy terror. At the palm-thatch whore shack on Black Betsy Key, south of Flamingo, he'd once declaimed in festive spirit, "When *I* fuck 'em, they *stay* fucked!" Their "Jack" took all he wanted when he wanted and the way he wanted, too, his Caxambas ladies would attest, with shy smiles that looked oddly askew.

Lucius's river walk with the Dyer girl had been observed, Eddie complained that evening, creating gossip that their family could ill afford at such a time. "Oh Lord, Eddie! She's a schoolgirl! Scarcely fourteen!" Lucius was offended, knowing that Eddie was snobbish about Nell because her mother was the seamstress and the father a disintegrating drunk and the brother Watt a runaway to God knows where. Carrie would agree, he knew, that Eddie was exaggerating, but she only snapped crossly with a glance at Walter, "At fourteen I'd been married for a year."

. . .

One day in 1917, Lucius vanished without warning. Fifteen months would pass before his family learned that he had enlisted in the Army and gone off to the Great War in Europe. He wrote to no one, not his sister, not his lovelorn Nell.

Carrie Langford invited Nell to tea at the Royal Palm Yacht Club. "He was always our best hope for this family," Carrie mourned, "and now we've lost him." Very upset, she commanded Nell to banish any notion of a future with a man who could only be counted on to hurt the ones who loved him most. "You've lost him, too, so accept that, girl, and get on with your life. Because if that fool doesn't get himself shot over in France, he'll find some way to get the job done here at home, even if he has to shoot himself to do it." She took Nell in her arms. "I don't mean that, sweetheart. I say those hard things to shield myself, in case."

Only Lucius despised Lucius, Nell observed: the contempt he saw in the eyes of others was only the reflection of his poor opinion of himself.

IN NO MAN'S LAND

As a practiced hunter and a dead-eye shot, Private L. H. Watson had been proud at first to be made a sniper, only to discover once in combat that he detested what he had to do. In growing alarm, he observed himself moving like a wind-up toy through the mechanical routine of checking his weapon and its ammunition, selecting vantage points, aligning sights, and firing at some distant figure or more often just the head—a pop-up soldier silhouette, never seen up close as a human being. It became routine, a target practice, so long as he closed down thought, grew numb, so long as he shut off all discussion of it with other soldiers; he hid his mind behind an iron wall of cold and mechanical inhumanity, accepting his assignment as his patriotic duty. In the grinding attrition of trench warfare, executing anonymous "enemies" became a job as mundane as any other, and that illusion, for a time, sheltered his sanity.

One early morning close to the front lines, Private Watson became separated from his patrol when the small group fanned out under fire and was overtaken by a heavy winter fog. In this no man's land, moving in any direction might be fatal: he crouched down in a gully, in hopes that the drifting fog might lift enough to reveal the whereabouts of friend or foe and better determine his position.

Before long, from somewhere not far away, came little sounds that betrayed the movement of another man; he raised and pointed his weapon, trying to still his pounding heart. Then the murk lifted just enough to reveal a crouched form with the spiked German helmet, the pallid face with small spaced teeth peering from beneath it. He had murdered that young soldier as the face turned toward him, its eyes and mouth wide open, too frightened to cry for mercy; he extinguished that life even though, in the suspended instant before squeezing off his trigger, he had seen that the Enemy was not crouched but squatting, pants down, his only weapon a clenched handful of dead grass. He had watched that soldier topple over and lie still, mud-splashed white buttocks quivering, his life relinquished for the rare blessing of privacy in the thick fog. For taking a crap, he had died bereft of dignity, as the silent fog slowly enshrouded him again and the American soldier backed away in shock.

When Private Watson's brain stopped whirling, the questions he dreaded surfaced one by one. Had his reaction been automatic, too committed to stop? Or had there been time enough to hold his fire? Had he been cold-blooded or merely cowardly? Or had instinct told him what was evident upon reflection, that in those circumstances of proximity and drifting mist, he could not have taken the boy prisoner *(Put your hands up when you're finished, Fritz)* without revealing his own location to that soldier's comrades?

None of this mattered. Private Watson turned in his sniper scope, reporting to headquarters that they could shoot or discipline him as they liked but his days of executing men were over. Angry in his desolation, the near-legendary sniper from the Everglades notified his superiors that war was monstrous, the greatest of all sins against Creation. After due consideration of the commendable number of the enemy this soldier had destroyed, he was sent to the rear echelons to rest his brain and receive another decoration to reinvigorate his American red blood. His refusal to take part in the ceremony brought mutterings of courts martial, execution for cowardice, rank dereliction of duty in time of war, but in the end, the political problem posed by Private Watson was eliminated with a dishonorable discharge. In 1918, he returned home stunned by so much criminally insane behavior and a little ashamed because he had survived it. His medals were discovered in the bottom of his soldier pack after he'd left for Chatham River.

"Useless Lucius," he commented sourly. "Couldn't even die for his own country."

"Oh that poor creature!" Carrie had protested when Lucius acknowledged he had not written to Nell nor even called on her since his return. "For God's sake, marry the girl and settle down to something!" cried his older brother, who forsook his wife and small children almost every evening for the tranquil atmosphere and superior cuisine of a banker's hearth. Lucius snapped, "Mind your own damned business, Eddie," and took his leave before his brother could hold forth on domestic mores.

The first time Lucius saw Nell in the street, his caught breath closed his throat. Although an encounter was inevitable, he had not expected to be stricken by a pounding of his heart that threatened to bring him to his knees. It was already too late, he told himself, he must pretend he hadn't seen her. She was already hastening, handkerchief to her mouth as if sickened by the sight of him. He would have cried, *Nell, Nell, please wait for me* had he not known how weak and destructive that would be in the light of his behavior. Nell must be twenty, almost an old maid; he could not ask her to wait for him one day longer.

Confronted later by his sister, he had lied, saying he had not seen her, although he knew that Nell knew better, having seen him switch his eyes away like a guilty dog. But an exchange of fixed smiles and desperate greetings—how much worse! He simply could not bear to face her before he had dealt with the greater shame about his father. Until then, anything he said, however honest, would ring false.

Lucius was drinking so relentlessly again that the Langfords shut their door. Eight years after his father's death, his life had wandered away from him, he knew that. Subsisting on his one-third share from the sale of his mother's house, he had no prospects, no direction or ambition, nothing to show for life but two book projects long abandoned. He nursed thoughts of suicide. Yet all along he had known what he must do to salvage his self-respect: whatever the consequences, he must overcome his dread and reclaim the Watson place at Chatham Bend. Subsisting as a fisherman, he might sniff out the true circumstances of his father's death and the identities and motives of the men who lynched him. What action should be taken after that could be decided later.

Papa's old launch *Warrior,* refitted with a new engine, would be ready the next week. More and more excited to be leaving for the Islands, he packed rough clothes and a rifle, bought a new shotgun, gill net, and other gear as well as a supply of dry stores and canned provisions.

On the eve of departure, Lucius submitted himself to a final broken evening at the Langfords', who had lately removed to a new brick house on First Street, at the foot of the Edison Bridge over the river. Joining them for coffee, Eddie declared that Lucius's "morbid obsession" with his father's death was merely an attempt to lend significance to a feckless existence. "You're nearly thirty! Sober up, go find a job, get on with life!" said Eddie, reminding his brother of those stern warnings against returning to the Islands "at your father's burial"—"*your* father," not "our father," not "Papa," Lucius noted.

"That was eight years ago. I'm sure it's all died down."

"Then you're a fool!" Eddie exclaimed. His conviction that his brother must come to harm brought tears to Carrie's eyes and deep furrows to the ever-ascending brow of her balding Walter, who rose at once and stepped into the pantry to fortify himself with another noble whiskey. Knowing better, Lucius joined him, and whiskey would fire a final dispute over Lucius's vow to find out what evidence there was, if any, that Papa had ever killed a single soul.

"Name one person who can claim he ever saw Papa shoot at *anyone.*"

"That's ridiculous," Eddie said, even as his upset sister begged her brothers not to talk about their father anymore. "You promised, Lucius."

"*You* people promised. I never promised a damned thing." Clearly his upright siblings lived in dread, he said, not merely of scandal but of what their ancestry might signify if even one of those terrible stories about "Bloody Watson" proved to be true. If Papa deserved his monstrous reputation, then what did it mean to be the get of such a man, the blood inheritor? "That seed might sprout in one of his descendants, ever think of that? That doesn't scare you?"

"You're talking crazy," Eddie said.

"Maybe I *am* crazy. Maybe you are, too, ever think of that?"

Going out the door, he heard his sister reprimanding Eddie. "He's *not* crazy! He's just idealistic and impractical!"

Lucius knew he had been unreasonable and also that Carrie did not disagree with Eddie, not entirely. He no longer cared. After eight years of wandering in his own head, he felt anarchic, in no mood to mend things. He was so relieved to be *acting* on a brave new life that he actually exulted over his break with his Fort Myers family. Scared, he suppressed a longing to seek out Nell for the blessing and encouragement he did not deserve.

TO LOST MAN'S RIVER

Lucius headed south at dawn next day. At Caxambas, he was disappointed to discover that his father's "backdoor family" had mostly moved north to find work in the new coastal resorts at Naples and Fort Myers Beach. Caxambas itself had all but disappeared since the Great Hurricane, lacking even a store, and its high dunes were for sale to Yankee developers, who were planning a new winter community. Knowing the long history of this place as an Indian site, he found this saddening.

In Everglade, where he refueled the boat, the Storters told him that their trading post on the tide creek known as Storter River would be sold and rebuilt as a hotel for Yankee anglers. Hoad still thought that his friend's return to the Islands was a bad idea, and Lucius left early next morning in sunken spirits, going straight west to the Gulf through Indian Key Pass to avoid Chokoloskee. Off Rabbit Key, he passed a stone crab boat whose crewmen recognized Ed Watson's *Warrior* and straightened from their work to stare. Neither man returned his wave.

At Chatham Bend he found a boat tied to the dock and Willie Brown and family camped in the house. An old friend of his father, Willie seemed unable to imagine why Lucius would come back to the Islands, even when he explained. Kicking dirt, Brown said, "I spoke out agin it and I took no part and I don't aim to tell you who did. For your own damn good, boy! Any man gits the idea the son is huntin him might feel obliged to git that damn fool first, you take my meanin?"

Willie said his family would move out as soon as Lucius was ready to come in (by "ready to come in" he meant "prepared to live alone"). Staring at his childhood house where all those folks had died, he was overtaken by loneliness; he invited the Browns to stay. They seemed uneasy about this. A few days later, when he returned from Everglade with fresh supplies, their boat was gone.

In river twilight, Lucius wandered the overgrown plantation. Long swords of untended cane struggled up through thorn and vine. Back of the cistern—it must have smelled fresh water—lay the long toothy skull of Papa's ancient roan, run wild and finally abandoned. Deep in rank weeds not far away was the rust-red skeleton of the Model S Ford brought into this roadless wilderness by Papa. The children had admired its big single headlight and the lantern and hand grips on the rear wall of the "cabriolet" half-roof where Sip Linsey had perched on the toolbox as the only auto ever to arrive in the Ten Thousand Islands bounced and back-fired around the cane field. "Looky dis nigger ridin shotgun," Sip was heard to say to nobody in particular, as he suffered this ass-busting indignity.

He fetched his whiskey from the boat and sat on the ragged porch all that long evening, until finally he stumbled off the steps and fell, wrenching his shoulder; a despairing howl rose from his cry of pain. He dreaded the house, the broken glass in its black empty windows: he could not sleep there. Lying down on the *Warrior*'s cabin roof, he stared across to the far bank where the huge crocodile of boyhood had hauled out "to keep watch on my house," Papa had said. One day it furiously attacked and killed a large alligator that had strayed into its territory, and Papa said, "I reckon that's not much of a gator anymore, not after *that*." Papa's baleful understatement seemed mostly uttered for his own grim amusement. He used the incident to reinforce his strict instructions to the children, who were never allowed to splash in the shallows unless that croc across the river lay out like a drift log in plain view.

In dream, Lucius rowed across the water. Very slowly, the brute opened its long jaws in warning before raising itself on its short legs and rushing at him with horrid speed, jaws wide, before thrashing away in a thick roil into the current. In terror that the crocodile was just beneath the skiff and must surely rise to capsize, seize, and drag him down, he was awakened by his own cry and gasped for breath. He sat up on deck in the cold mist and dew, peering fearfully into the river deeps.

Yes, he was full of dread and could not hide this from himself. He went at dawn to Lost Man's River, where Owen Harden and his Sarah had always been his friends and made him welcome. That same day, on impulse, he offered them the Watson place: he could rebuild the Dyer cabin. Troubled by his distress, they refused to take the offer seriously. There was no sense wasting Chatham's forty acres of black soil on fishermen. Anyway some development company had recently acquired rights to the Watson property. Bill House, who was working not far upriver on the high ground at House Hammock, would take over as caretaker early next year.

"The leader of the lynch mob! Living in your daddy's house!" Sarah exclaimed.

"Acquired rights from *whom?*" Lucius demanded. These damned developers were usurping Papa's land claim and perhaps his vision for the future of this coast. But Lucius had no heart for a legal battle which he probably could not win.

Owen Harden kindly invited his friend to build a driftwood cabin here on Lost Man's Beach and use the Harden dock and icehouse. And as Sarah pointed out, this cabin project would allow a little time for his father's executioners to adjust to Lucius's sudden reappearance in the Islands.

He began his inquiries gradually, trying to remain objective and avoid recriminations. From early on, he kept a secret list with notes. The Island men had liked "Ed's boy" back in the old days, and at first some put their wariness aside, even volunteered information about Ed's early years on Chatham Bend, his farming innovations, his quickly acquired seamanship, uncanny marksmanship (which he never minded showing off), his humor and good humor, and the colorful tales, not all of them apocryphal, of his riotous behavior in Tampa and Key West—everything, in short, but the background and events of that black autumn evening in October of 1910. Keeping Lucius at a distance, they nicknamed him "Colonel," less in amicable teasing than in recognition of his educated speech and manners—for even at their most obliging, they mistrusted him, so fearful were they that those quiet manners might be hiding schemes of bloody retribution. The situation worsened as his inquiries became more specific, touching on the identities of posse members: he always said "posse" though he wanted to say "mob."

Rumor spread quickly. The Islanders grew taciturn, then cold; he braved cold-eyed silences everywhere he went. The men might head their boats off course as his approached; their women might simply back indoors and let him knock repeatedly without response. Knowing that if he touched that latch, some frightened body behind the door might blow his head off, he went away. That this soft-spoken man would take such risks, that he kept coming, only served as further evidence that Lucius Watson must be crazy, maybe just as dangerous as his daddy. From the start, Bill House and his brothers—the patriarch D. D. House had died—refused to deal with Watson's son at all.

To Lucius's surprise, friends such as the Browns who at the time had denounced the Watson execution as a lynching were as reticent about the lynchers' identities as those who had been involved. Even Erskine Thompson, his father's ship captain, seemed to avoid him—very curious, since Erskine had no reason to be nervous. Or did he? Lucius often wondered what had happened to the schooner, which at Papa's burial he had asked Hoad Storter to see to: Hoad later reported that the ship was missing. Had someone sold her and pocketed the money?

Lucius caught up with the lank, sun-baked Thompson on the dock at Everglade. After some stiff conversation, he asked this old friend from Chatham days if he still believed that E. J. Watson's death had been planned in advance. Erskine nodded in assent, but when asked who the planners might have been, he said, "Damned if I know." Asked whom he had noticed at the scene, the only man he could come up with was Mr. D. D. House, four years deceased.

"Nobody else? You sure? You were right there, Erskine."

Over the years, Thompson had soured in the way of lazy men, and Lucius's incredulity turned him peevish. He was soon insinuating that no son of Ed Watson should go around Chokoloskee Bay asking nosy questions: that whole business was better left alone, less said the better. Instead of asking his fool questions, Thompson called back, starting away, the son should settle up all those back wages that the father had never paid his schooner captain.

"Speaking of schooners," Lucius shot back, "whatever happened to the *Gladiator*? Isn't her captain the man who should know best?" Thompson cupped his ear, feigning deafness, before waving Lucius away with disgust and finality and walking on.

NIGGER SHORT

Though even his father's friends concealed the identities of the posse members, these families made sure that Watson's son heard rumors that "Nigger Short" had participated in the shooting. Lucius dismissed these stories as absurd until Hoad Storter told him that he, too, had heard this. Hoad said unhappily, "Well, he might have been there, Lucius. People say they saw him. That doesn't mean that he participated: don't let 'em tell you that. Henry's *colored* and he's not suicidal. He's got very good sense."

He asked the Hardens. After a long pause, Owen said flatly, "Sure. He might of been there. Houses' orders, probably." He shrugged it off as insignificant but it was clear that, for Henry's sake, he didn't want to talk about it.

In the interests of objectivity, Lucius felt obliged to seek Short out, hear him deny any participation in his own words, but Short had not been easy to track down. He no longer visited the Hardens, who had no idea (they said) where he might be found. Probably this was more or less true, but it was also true, as Owen and Sarah admitted, that though they trusted Lucius, they could not count on what he might do as Watson's son. Did they doubt his sanity or his intentions? Lucius wondered. And why were they so protective of Henry if he had not been involved?

It was Henry Short, as it turned out, who had dismantled the Frenchman's shack on Possum Key (an act that for years had been attributed to Leslie Cox). In his sailing skiff he had moved it piece by piece all the way south to West Cape Sable and lugged the boards three miles or more inland to a desolate area of scrub and brackish water where nobody would come looking for him, let alone find him. "That whole cabin traveled on that one man's shoulders," Sarah marveled.

"Henry Short come straight to Lost Man's after your daddy was killed. 'Wait and see,' Henry said. 'They'll try to hang it on the nigger.' But Daddy Richard had taught that man the Bible. Henry was a fine strong Christian, swore by the First Commandment so we knew he could never line a man up in his rifle sights and pull the trigger."

"And anyway, he had nothing against my father," said Lucius.

"I ain't so sure. Remember Jane? Light mulatta gal that come down from Fort White to cook for your daddy at the Bend?"

Lucius smiled. "Jane Straughter? Sure. I thought I was kind of in love with her."

"Me, too. That's how I learned I could love two girls at once." Owen glanced at his young wife in comic fear. "Well, Henry confided he had loved Jane dearly and believed she loved him, too, but your daddy found out and sent Henry away. When she went back to Fort White, that poor feller was heart-broke. Took him years to get over her. Finally married my sister Liza, got tore up again.

"Course Hardens had nothing against mixed blood, so when Henry started courtin Liza, nobody objected 'ceptin Earl, although Liza was coffee and Henry the pale color of new wheat."

"Henry has a lot more white than most of those po' whites who call him 'Nigger,' " Sarah said.

"I guess Henry never talked enough to suit my sister. As the only colored in a cracker community, he never had much practice. Liza complained that Henry *never* talked, never gave her more than the bare facts even when he talked about the weather. Our Liza dearly loved a conversation, and she couldn't bear that. So pretty soon that girl run off with a white man who told her he had money which he didn't."

Sarah said, "Liza announced her marriage to Henry was annulled because it was performed outside the Church and therefore didn't count in the Pope's eyes, but she never could remember who annulled it. Being strong-minded like her mother, she most likely annulled it herself.

"Our ma admired Henry Short, no matter what," he reflected after a while. "She never had much use for her daughter after she run off with that cracker, who had a bad habit of pickin up anything loose he could lay his hands on, my sister included. Liza bein Henry's consolation for a lonely life, he never got over it. Followed our family to Flamingo, fished around Cape Sable, but when he returned to Lost Man's River, who should he find living there but Liza and her man; they were not real friendly but made him drink with them to let bygones be bygones. That was Henry's first liquor and he couldn't handle it, and that night he was heard to mutter how somebody might take and shoot that thievin redneck. We knew he was just easin his torment but that kind of wild talk could of got him killed."

"Even before Liza took up with Henry," Sarah said, "some of them Bay women called her 'white trash,' not because she done wrong but only because their menfolk—every man along that coast—would have sold his soul for what Henry had and those ladies knew it. So they were happy thinking she'd humiliated her family by marrying 'Nigger Short' and over-joyed when she run out on him: it did their hearts good to see God Almighty humble that mulatta who dared to marry that supposed-to-be-white woman after raising up his gun to a white man."

"Ma said Henry was a high type of man who had a low opinion of him-self. White people had robbed him of his chance for a home and family and now they had took his self-respect as well. But I believe that losing Liza might have saved his life. The young fellers let off steam crackin mean jokes and shootin off their mouths instead of gettin drunk and comin after him. Because when there's too much lynch talk in the air, it's bound to happen."

One day Owen Harden said, "Henry's at the Bend."

To avoid scaring Henry Short back into the scrub, Lucius slipped up Chatham River on a night tide and was at the dock at daybreak. Calling out softly to calm the dogs and announce his presence, he walked unarmed toward the house.

Bill House, already outside in the porch shadows, stood in his nightshirt like a ghost. Perhaps to warn Henry, he sang out, "That a Watson? You lookin for me?"

"Looking for Henry. Heard you might know where to find him."

"We ain't seen him. What you want with him? Next time—oh Christ-amighty!"

To House's annoyance, Short had appeared at the corner of the boat shed. When Lucius said good morning, Henry lifted his hat politely but did not come forward. Instead he retreated behind the shed, possibly to escape the cool breeze off the river but more likely, Lucius guessed, to make sure they were out of earshot from the porch. Was this precaution for his visi-tor's sake or for his own?

"We heard some man been huntin him," House said. "That you?"

"Nosir," Lucius said, "it's not."

Short awaited him, standing not stiffly but very straight, as if to accept any punishment his hard life had in store including its own immediate re-linquishment. His ancient Winchester, leaned against the shed, had been left or placed well out of his reach, though Short must have heard the *War-*

rior coming upriver and could have kept the weapon handy if he'd wished. If I were to put a revolver to his head, Lucius supposed, this man might flinch but he would remain silent, less out of fortitude than a profound fatalism and possibly relief that all his trials, Lord, would soon be over.

Henry bent to brush raccoon scat off a fish box, providing his visitor a seat. He was a strong, good-looking man with blue-gray eyes, composed and very clear in his appearance. Like most men in the Islands, he went barefoot, but unlike most, he kept himself clean-shaven and his blue denims were well patched and clean.

Lucius opened the conversation with civilities, then rather abruptly came right out with it, keeping his voice low. He'd heard rumors, he said, keeping his voice amiable, that Henry Short was present at the Watson killing.

Yessir, Henry agreed after a pause. He had gone down to Smallwood's landing on that day. Why? Because Ol' Mis Ida House, she told him go keep an eye on Ol' Mist' Dan. And he had taken his rifle along? He was told to bring it. And why should he be believed?

Near expressionless, Henry raised his gaze and looked his inquisitor straight in the eye. "I don' know that, suh."

"You were only following orders, Henry. I believe that. But some say you took part. They say they saw you raise your rifle."

"Nosuh, nosuh!" Shaking his head over and over, Henry retreated into negritude. "White folks roun' de Bay was allus good to me, Mist' Lucius. Must of mistaked dereselfs, dass it. Dey was all lookin at Mist' Watson, see what he might do. Nobody nevuh paid no min' to no darn nigguh."

Lucius groaned in frustration. As a man who had lived his whole life among whites, Short usually spoke like one; he must have known that his visitor would not be taken in by this performance. Lucius sensed carefully controlled anger. What Short was really saying was, *Is a minstrel show what I must offer before you will let me be?*

"Some even say you fired." He tried to startle him, pointing at the rifle. "Is that the weapon you pointed at my father, Henry? Yes or no?"

Henry met his glare, less defiant than stoic, resolute. Slowly he shook his head. "No cullud wouldn' *nevuh* raise no gun to Mist' Edguh Watson!" Then he said strangely, "Mist' Edguh knowed dat."

Lucius searched his face for sign of ambiguity. Short's expression was impassive. For one more moment, they held that gaze before the colored man deferred to him and looked away.

The previous evening, at his camp under the moon at Mormon Key, his purpose had seemed clear, but standing here in the bright sun of morning, he was no longer quite sure why he had come. Now that he had finally caught up with Henry Short, his whole inquiry seemed unreasonable, ridiculous—what could this man tell him? And how could he act on anything he confessed, since even if Short had raised his rifle to a white man, that reckless act would not have changed the outcome in the smallest way. A confession would signify nothing.

At a loss, he muttered, "So the rumors are untrue?"

The nod was a mere twitch, as if Henry were bone tired of telling an old truth that would never be believed—tired of running, tired of hiding, tired of lifelong loneliness and fear. His apathy seemed to signal that the white men could believe whatever suited them and their black man would go along out of his helpless resignation.

"Thank you. I'm sorry if I troubled you."

"Your daddy always treated me real good, Mist' Lucius," Henry said, not to ingratiate himself but to ease the absurd situation in which his visitor had put them; he had reverted to his normal voice. And Lucius told him, "You have nothing to fear, Henry. Not from me." And Henry nodded, understanding very well what had passed unspoken. He murmured softly, "Okay then, Mist' Lucius."

Henry, like a polite host, followed him out from behind the shelter of the shed. Lucius had always known that he and Henry Short were natural allies, as the Hardens had suggested to them both from the beginning, and saying good-bye, he had an impulse to offer his hand; under House's sharp eye, he could not bring himself to do that. The gesture would be seen as weakness and might compromise Henry, too. But in years to come, when their boat courses happened to cross, the white man would respond in kind when the brown one touched his hat. Rarely, one or the other made a vague half wave and once, nearly colliding on a narrow bend, both men smiled, though they looked away quickly and kept going. As outcasts befriended by the outcast Harden family, their condition might have disposed them to a common trust, yet they shared an instinct not to seek the other out. In mute respect, they felt no need to speak. And though neither thought of it in terms of "friendship," a silent bond was what it had become.

As the visitor walked past the porch, Bill House said, "Well, that was quick." Lucius raised his hand without stopping and the little boy at House's elbow waved back shyly. "How's that ol' list comin?" House called after him. "I sure hope you got my name spelled right." When Watson did not turn but kept on going, he yelled angrily, "Don't slip up on us so quiet next time, hear?"

Lucius Watson's visit to the Bend served only to fire up a rumor that Watson might be gunning for Nigger Short.

THE LIST

One by one, from varied sources—cryptic gossip and sly woman talk, drunk blurtings—Lucius learned the names of every armed man present in that October dusk at Smallwood's landing and in most cases the extent of his participation. New information gave him reason to eliminate a name or add another or simply refine the annotations that kept his list scrupulous and up-to-date. With its revisions and deletions, comments and qualifications, ever more intricate and complex, the thing took on a whole different significance, as what had begun as a kind of morbid game evolved into a kind of obsession.

Eventually the folded packet of lined yellow paper, damp from the salt air and humid climate, had gone so transparent at the creases from sweat and coffee spills and cooking grease and fish oil, so specked by rust, so flecked with bread crumbs and tobacco, that his neat small script all but disappeared and the list had to be replaced. The painstaking writing-out of a fresh copy was no chore; on the contrary, he welcomed it as a ceremony of renewal and a source of inspiration. As vital research for the suspended biography that might redeem his father's name, the creation of the list somehow justified his return to the Islands; at the very least, it helped compensate for a wasted decade of inaction. So long as it continued to evolve, he saw no reason to give it up; so long as critical details were missing, so long as minor corrections might be made, it would never be finished. Not until much later would he face the fact that he had dreaded finishing the list because he questioned his ability to act on it, although he had known almost from the start that this was so. Any capacity he might have had for taking human life had ended in those days of mud and carnage on the Western Front.

And so, once again, he was overtaken by the dread that he had failed his father in some way, that he had betrayed the hickory breed of old-time Carolina Watsons who, according to Papa, would have risen in the very teeth of Christian morality and consequences to avenge their Celtic blood. His own vague alternative was confrontation—a succinct damnation (as he imagined it) uttered while staring deep into the eyes of each listed man, a stare long enough and cold enough to dispel the smallest doubt that Watson's son knew the precise degree of his involvement. Each man would have to deal with the enigma of what this son might do in retribution; each man's suspense and fear would be his punishment.

Though Lucius kept his list concealed, the time would come when he was shunned on Chokoloskee Bay. Toward the end of his first year in the Islands, rough warnings changed to threats. One twilight up in Lost Man's River he heard the echo of a rifle shot that followed a bullet's hornet whine across his bow. A stupid joke? Harassment? Something else? Glimpsing a skiff's worn blue paint through the mangrove branches on the point, he had suspected Crockett Daniels, known as Speck, a poacher and moonshiner who as a youth had been present in the dusk at Chokoloskee and was already a suspect on his list.

Lucius received word of Walter Langford's death too late to reach Fort Myers for the funeral. When he turned up next day at his sister's house, Carrie assured him she had understood his absence but it was plain she could not quite forgive him. "Nobody seriously expected you," Eddie said sourly. With customary spite, he informed his younger brother that the president of the First National Bank had died of drink and liver failure, having neglected to provide properly for their sister.

Nell Dyer was present. They greeted and chatted painfully, hurried apart.

While Lucius was absent in Fort Myers, the *Warrior* was rammed and sunk at Everglade, where she had been tied up at the fish dock. Though shaken, he would not retreat, dreading the lurking danger less than what he saw as a crippled life of cowardice or weakness. The Storter trading post had been enlarged as a new lodge for sportsmen, and Hoad had moved to Naples; it was the Hardens—the last friends he could trust—who finally prevailed on him to leave the Islands; he headed south around Cape Sable to fish out of Flamingo until things cooled down.

Returning to Lost Man's some months later, Lucius learned that in his absence, a stranger had come looking for him in a rented skiff, having rowed south twenty miles from Everglade. "Feller with straight black hair and a thin beard, spoke short and crusty," Owen said. "Knew what he was doin in a boat and seemed to know this coast. Got too much sun and his hands was raw, all blistered up, but he was tough, never complained. I said, 'You off a ship someplace?' and he said, 'No, I rowed from Everglade.' I reckon that was far enough for a man whose hands ain't callused up from pullin oars. 'What can we do for ye?' I said. From the start, we thought he looked some way familiar.

"This feller told us his name was John Tucker. Claimed to be Wally Tucker's nephew, said he wanted to pay respects where his kinfolks was buried. I took him over to the Key, showed him where we buried 'em that day in 1901. He went all pale and sweaty, could not hide it. When he asked the whereabouts of Lucius Watson, we guessed he had a feud to settle, so I told him that the last we heard, Lucius Watson had left for parts unknown. That stranger give me a hard eye, very dissatisfied and cross. He said, 'That's what they told me in Chokoloskee, too.' And I said, 'Well, for once they told some truth.' "

"From his questions we figured he knew more than he should about the Tuckers, considering there weren't no witnesses that could have told him," Sarah said. "Finally it come to us why he looked familiar, beard or no beard. 'John Tucker' weren't nobody else but E. J. Watson's oldest, that wild Rob that run off to Key West, taking his schooner."

Owen said, "He never believed our story that you went away. He seemed convinced that Island people, maybe us, might of killed his brother, hid the body in the mangroves. That's why he left here angry and dissatisfied."

"I wrapped his blisters in greasy rags before he rowed away, headed back north," Sarah told Lucius. "Didn't hardly say thanks."

While in Flamingo, Lucius had decided to rid himself of his incriminating list. He cursed the hours had he wasted revising and refining it, down to the smallest detail, in his hunger to get closer to some "truth" that might free him from the past. Far from easing the old pain in his heart, its existence had become a burden and reproach, reminding him of the great folly of years wasted in self-exile—years that might have been spent in the company of Nell, raising pretty children, finishing his education and his books.

Though he knew the thing by heart and was sick of looking at it, he could not bring himself to burn so many years of work in a few moments—work that might eventually be used in the biography. To eliminate the risk of loss or discovery, he sent the list to Nell Dyer for safekeeping; in the same packet he included a note for Rob in the hope that his brother might turn up again. But in the course of changing households, Nell would misplace the packet, as she confessed in the same letter that brought word of her impending marriage to the senior Mr. Summerlin. So stunned was Lucius by her abandonment that he scarcely reacted to the news of the lost list.

At Lost Man's, he resumed a hard sparse life as a commercial fisherman, and over time, the Island men got used to him, as talk died down and the list that nobody had ever seen reverted to vague rumor. Without hope of Nell, however, he had lost heart for Island life, yet had no other. Only an idiot would have assumed, he mourned, that despite his years of folly and neglect, his first love would wait in limbo while he solved his life so that they could travel on together into a golden future, having never aged.

OWEN AND SARAH

Despite his sorrow over the loss of Nell, Lucius was plagued in this time of loneliness—plagued disgracefully, in his opinion—by a desperate attraction to Owen Harden's wife. Sarah loved her husband, he felt sure: she was mainly upset because Owen had been eking out poor fishing seasons by working part-time with Crockett Daniels, who had now acquired a local reputation as "the last of the plume hunters"; Speck Daniels shot egrets wherever he could find the scarce and scattered birds and smuggled the plumes to foreign markets by way of Cuba.

Because Lucius had prevailed on Owen to give up plume hunting, Sarah made him her confidante in her campaign to return her husband to a lawful life. Almost daily, she sought his counsel, wandering barefoot down the beach to his bachelor's shack with fresh fish or spare greens and once a week a small basket of his laundry. She also provided endless anecdotal information on the Island families, all the more useful now that he had re-sumed bad-weather work on his two books.

By her own account, Sarah had married Owen in rebellion against the prejudice in her own family, in particular those kinsmen on Chokoloskee Bay who made life disagreeable for the Hardens. Sarah's outspoken disdain of redneck ignorance—"They ain't just *red*neck, they are *no-neck*!"—had stirred a lot of old-time meanness back to the surface, until finally his own family chided Owen for not bridling his wife's sharp tongue. This had led to quarrels with her husband, confessed Sarah, unrepentant, even gleeful.

Though Sarah made no secret of her admiration for Owen's educated friend—and certainly no effort to hide her visits—the fact that she turned up mostly in the daytime when her husband was off somewhere in his boat made Lucius uncomfortable: Lucius, not Sarah, was the guilty one because he, not she, hid an impure heart that leapt every time he saw her coming, this slim small-breasted girlish woman, in her thirties now, flaxen hair bound up in braids with deerhide thongs, small brown feet skipping light as fishes in the tide shine at the water's edge.

Sarah Harden was inquisitive and indiscreet, thin-skinned, scrappy, blunt, yet easily hurt or angered. Her unhappiness about Owen's associates led her to nag her quiet husband, comparing his prospects as an "outlaw" with those of his educated neighbor down the beach. Owen's resentment had already seeded vague suspicions and having foreseen this, Lucius tried hard to avoid those moments when through door or window of their cabin he'd glimpse Sarah naked or half-dressed—a crisis that was ever pending, since the unself-conscious Sarah wore little in the humid heat except soft faded overalls gone slack in the front or light cotton smocks with nothing underneath, at least so far as he was able to determine from his unwilling and unstinting study of her curves and shadows. In Sarah's mind, she had no neighbors, therefore no peepers, only the harmless bachelor a hundred yards away, who in fact had longed to peep on her from the first day she had leaned into his window to ask how his work was going and he saw nestled between the loose blue straps of her overalls those untethered and confiding small brown breasts as warm as fresh-laid eggs.

One day coming and going they collided clumsily in his doorway, and his hand, bearing a paper, brushed an erect nipple. Like a demon's wand, the touch unleashed them; they embraced and kissed with a common moan of joy and consternation. Sarah gasped, "Oh my God!" and fled. Without thought, he rushed after her, calling her name not once but twice before seeing Owen, who was just docking his boat. Lucius halted abruptly and abruptly waved; Owen paused a moment, staring after the disappearing Sarah before waving back.

Called Owen, "She forget her drawers? Or ain't she wearin any?"

He was joking, of course. Owen enjoyed wryly outrageous jokes. But also he was not joking, and Lucius's laugh, to his own ears, rang hollow and deceitful. It was time to leave Lost Man's Beach. His disloyalty to Owen was no longer to be borne and his Island life was no longer enough and he missed his studies and library research. Excited by fresh ideas about how to shape the unfinished history and the roughed-out biography, he had already started a new set of notes.

CAXAMBAS

Months before, his common-law kinfolk of the Daniels-Jenkins clan had offered him the use of a small shack built on the deck of an old cane barge run aground at high water in a tidal creek under the high dunes of Marco Island. Rising behind the prehistoric site known to the old-time Indians as Caxambas, "Place of Wells," these elevations overlooked the white ribbons of surf where the Gulf Coast curved back toward the southeast at Cape Romaine. The great dunes seemed to him a monument, mysterious and moving, to those seagoing Calusa fatally dispersed by the *conquistadores*. The Spaniards, too, had come and gone away, and the smugglers and pirates and runaway African slaves, and finally the ancestral farmer-fishermen, the pioneers—precisely the atmosphere he wanted for his work.

Like Everglade, eight miles to the southeast through winding island channels, the small settlement on Caxambas Creek was isolated at the far end of a rough track only suitable for large-wheeled oxcarts and all but unnavigable in most seasons by the tin-can autos honking south like geese in the great Florida Land Boom of the Twenties. Acquiring most of Marco Island, developers had moved or destroyed the small cabins at Caxambas and burned down the clam cannery while they were at it, leaving the concrete floor to crack in the hot sun, sprouting hard weeds. Even the old store had been boarded up, the better to speed the last inhabitants on their way. The master plan—to level the dunes and clear the scrubby sabal palm and gumbo-limbo to make way for hotels, winter homes, and artificial lawns—would be shelved for decades by the Great Depression, already on the wind.

Lucius struggled to support himself as a fishing and hunting guide for sportsmen lodged in a new resort at Marco, working on his manuscripts in stormy weather. The following year, dead broke and in debt, he sold his boat and accepted an assistant teacher's post in the history department at the university. There he resumed his graduate studies and completed his doctoral thesis, *A History of Southwest Florida and the Everglades Frontier.* To his surprise, it was very well received and the university press selected it for publication. For the time being, he kept secret his greater ambition to complete and publish *The Undiscovered Country,* his objective biography of the pioneer sugarcane planter E. J. Watson.

Between terms at the university, Lucius returned to his barge shack at Caxambas. His friend Hoad Storter, who now lived not far away at Naples and had turned up in Caxambas on a visit, had been delighted by his friend's decision to leave Lost Man's and return to his unfinished books, including the Watson biography, which Hoad thought would fulfill his responsibilities to his father and set his heart at rest in a way that darned old posse list could never do. Hoad also thought that E. J. Watson was destined to become famous. Some ten years earlier, he'd been seining mullet with his brother-in-law in the little bays inside the mouth of Chatham River. One day, short of water, they went upriver to the Bend. "The cane fields were all overgrown, looked rough and shaggy, but new sprouts were volunteering through the tangle. We grubbed 'em out, stacked 'em on deck, ran 'em north to the Calusa Hatchee and on up east to Lake Okeechobee at Moore Haven, the only camp on Okeechobee at that time. Those cuttings were the start of this whole new sugar industry, did you know that, Lucius?" Hoad shook his head. "After all his hard years, your dad's fine cane will make fortunes for other men. 'Great waste and a pity' as Cap'n Bembery used to say."

Lucius nodded. Oh, God, how he wished poor Papa could have stood on those high dikes and enjoyed that view.

.   .   .

On the wings of his published history, Lucius submitted his biography proposal to the university press; his vantage point as Mr. Watson's son, he said, would not blind him to the true nature of his subject's character.

This bold energetic man of rare intelligence and enterprise must also be understood as a man undone by his own deep flaws. He was known to drink to grievous excess, for example, which often turned him volatile and violent. On the other hand, his evil repute has been wildly exaggerated by careless journalists and their local informants, who seek to embellish their limited acquaintance with a "desperado"; with the result that the real man has been virtually entombed by tale and legend which since his death has petrified as myth.

The most lurid view of Mr. Watson is the one perpetuated by the Islanders themselves, for as Dickens observed after his visit to this country, "These Americans do love a scoundrel." Because his informants tend to imagine that the darkest interpretation is the one the writer wishes to hear, the popular accounts (until now, there have been no others) are invariably sensational as well as speculative: the hard facts, not to speak of "truth," are missing. Also, this "Bloody Watson" material relates only to his final years in southwest Florida; one rarely encounters any reference to South Carolina, where Edgar Artemas Watson passed his boyhood, nor to the years in the Indian Country (always excepting his alleged role in the slaying of Belle Starr), nor even to the Fort White district of Columbia County in north Florida where he farmed in early manhood, married all three of his wives, and spent almost half of the fifty-five years of his life.

In Watson's youth, the Piedmont hinterlands of South Carolina were little more than frontier wilderness, and to judge from my limited correspondence with the last Watsons in that region, our subject's branch of a strong Carolina clan is all but forgotten now in Edgefield County. As for Fort White, his sister's family maintains a stern vow of silence about "Uncle Edgar," and locating the scattered elders who might relinquish scraps of problematic information would probably not repay the journey. Even here in southwest Florida, much local lore has disappeared under the earth of cemeteries.

The biographer's difficulties are inevitably compounded by the

*immense false record—"the Watson myth"—as well as by the failure to
correct that record on the part of Mr. Watson's family, whose reluctance
to come to his defense by testifying to the positive aspects of his character
is surely one reason why a dangerous reputation has expanded so
grotesquely since his death. In the absence of family affirmation of that
humor and generosity for which Edgar Watson was noted even among
those who killed him, he has become a kind of mythic monster. The
biographer's aim is to discover the hard truths and reconstitute E. J.
Watson and restore him to humankind as a paleontologist might
reconstruct some primordial being known only from a few scattered
shards of bone. As his second wife, the former Jane Susan Dyal of Deland,
observed to her son Lucius not long before her death in 1901, "Your father
frightens them not because he is a monster but because he is a man."*

*To honor her wisdom and redeem my subject's essential humanity is
the task before me.*

THE INDIAN

Lucius Watson rose onto one elbow, ransacking torn dreams for the hard
noise that had awakened him—that rattling *bang* of an old auto striking a
pothole in the sandy track through the slash pine wood north of the salt
creek. Who could that be? He had no neighbor on Caxambas Creek nor
even a mailbox on the old road to Marco, a half mile away, that might betray his whereabouts.

A dry mouth and stiff brain punished him for last night's whiskey. Licking his lips and squinching his nose to bring life back to his numb skin, he
rose softly and peered out through the screen, certain that some vehicle
had come in from the paved road and eased to a stop inside the wood edge
where the track emerged onto the marsh—the point from where the black
hulk of his old cane barge, locked in the shining mud of the ebbed tide,
would first loom into the view of whoever had come down along the creek
on midnight business.

For a time he saw nothing, heard nothing, only the small cries of earth
that formed within the ringing of the great night silence. Tree frogs shrilled
from the freshwater slough on the far side of the road, in counterpoint to

the relentless nightsong—*wip-wip-WEE-too*—from the whiskery gape of the gray-brown mothlike bird half hidden by lichens on a dead limb at the swamp edge, cryptic and still as something decomposing.

The Gulf moon carved the pale track and black trees. An intruder would make the last part of his approach on foot—*there!* A shape had detached itself from the tree shadows. An Indian. How he knew this he could not have said. The figure paused to look and listen then came on again, walking the sand track's mane of grass in order to leave no sign.

Lucius yanked pants and shirt onto his bony frame. Lifting the shotgun from its rack, he cracked the cabin door, wondering briefly (as he often did) why he would isolate himself way to hell and gone out on this salt creek without neighbor or telephone, or plumbing or electricity, for that matter. Yet simplicity contented him, simplicity was what he needed, as another might crave salt. A cracked cistern and a leaning outhouse near the burned-down shack on shore, a small woodstove and a storm lantern with asbestos filament. Once in a fortnight, he retrieved his negligible mail at Collier's Marco Store, bought a few stores, then took a meal with a few speakeasy whiskeys at Rusty's Roadhouse.

Approaching the sheds, the intruder's silhouette had stopped and turned in a slow half circle, sifting night sounds like an owl before passing behind the outhouse and old boat hull and pausing again at the foot of the spindly walkway over the salt grass. Then he came along the walkway, gliding out over the bog, in silhouette on the cold shine of moonlit mud. Whatever he carried on one arm was glinting.

Breaking the shotgun, Lucius dropped two buckshot loads into the chambers, snapped it to. Though the click of steel was perhaps thirty yards away, the Indian stopped short, his free hand rising in slow supplication. He stared at the black crack of the opened door. Very slowly then, he bent his knees and set his burden down on the split slats with a certain ceremony, as if it were fragile or sacred. When he straightened, his hands were held out to the side, pocked face expressionless. "Rural free delivery," he told the door crack, trying a smile.

Under the moon, the canister appeared to pulse. Widening the doorway with his shotgun barrels, Lucius stepped outside. He pointed toward the shore. "Move," he said. "Take that thing with you."

"It ain't a bomb or nothin," the Indian murmured. He was a big man, round-shouldered and short-legged and small-buttocked, long black hair bound in a braid by a red wind band: he wore a candy-striped Seminole blouse, old pants and sandals, with a beaded belt slung below the curve of a hard belly. When the white man only motioned with the gun, he bent and retrieved the canister in one smooth motion and, as Lucius followed, returned over the walkway to dry land. There he squatted on his hunkers on the track, arms loose across his knees. Asked if he had come alone, he nodded. He identified himself as Tommie Jimmie, spiritual leader of the Shark River Mikasuki.

Where the track entered the woods, in the night shadow of the trees, Lucius could barely make out an ancient truck. "You came halfway across the Glades in that old junker to deliver this—"

"Burial urn. White feller sent it. Seen your notice in the paper about Bloody Watson."

"Mr. E. J. Watson? Planter Watson? That what you meant to say?"

"Okay by me." The big man shrugged. "Indin people down around Shark River, they always thought a lot of Mister Ed. Give 'em coffee, y'know, somethin to eat, when they come up along the rivers. Good moonshine, too. Killed some white folks and some black ones, what we heard, but he never killed no red ones, not so's you'd notice."

Lucius had to laugh, which hurt his head. Feeling stupid clutching the gun, he pointed its barrels at the ground. "This white feller," he said. "What's his name?"

"Went by the name of Collins when he first showed up couple years back. Course that don't mean nothin. Them people out at Gator Hook don't hold so much with rightful names. They call him Chicken on account of he's so scrawny."

"So Chicken said, 'See that Lucius Watson gets this burial urn on the stroke of midnight.' "

The Indian nodded. "Stroke of midnight," he assented slyly. "Them was his very words."

The urn was a cheap one, ornamented with rude brassy angels. When Lucius stooped to pick it up, the sudden motion smote his temples. "Dammit! You come sneaking in here in the middle of the night—"

"Long way from Shark River." Tommie Jimmie yawned. "Guess I'll be gettin along." Black eyes fastened on the gun, he made a move to rise, thought better of it. "Oh Lord," Lucius said. He broke the gun and ejected the shells, which he stuffed into his pocket. "Who's *in* that thing? How come this Collins didn't bring it here himself?"

"Down sick. Feller name of Mud come by my camp, told me Chicken wanted to see me cause I had a truck. Claimed Chicken been rottin in his bedroll goin on three days. So I went over there and Chicken told me where you was livin at. Said, 'This here urn belongs to Lucius Watson, cause they's bones in there that used to be his brother.' "

Lucius sank to his knees in the white sand, laying the shotgun on the grass. He lifted the urn and turned it carefully in both hands as the tears came. To clear his head, he took deep breaths of the night air with its heavy bog smell of low tide. He set the urn down again and used his sleeve to wipe his eyes. Whoever he was, this Chicken Collins must know what had happened to Rob Watson, being custodian of his remains before his siblings even knew that Rob was dead.

Tommie Jimmie rose, easy as smoke. "Gator Hook," he said, and went away down the white road. At the wood edge, he looked back but did not wave. Then he vanished into the dark wall, leaving the white man alone with the brass urn under the dying moon.

IN THE BACKCOUNTRY

Perhaps a month after Tommie Jimmie's visit, Lucius drove his Model T onto the new Tampa-Miami Trail, which forged east across empty savanna and the strands of giant cypress to the vast shallow marshes that the Indians knew as Pa-hay-okee, Grassy Waters. In the Seminole Wars, the Mikasuki had crossed these marshes to isolated hardwood hammocks where tropical forest hid their palm-thatch villages and gardens from the soldiers. Only in this last decade had the sparkling expanses been torn and muddied by steam shovels and drag lines, until wild human inhabitants, like its bears and panthers, could scarcely be imagined anymore. Yet the hidden dangers that had sapped the will of the U.S. Army were still present, Lucius thought with satisfaction, the tall scythes of toothed sawgrass, the quicksand and muck pools and solution holes in the jagged limestone of the ancient sea floor concealed beneath the silt that had torn the soldier boots to pieces: the biting swarms, the leeches and squat moccasins, opening white mouths like deathly blossoms, the coral snakes, the Florida diamondbacks, greatest of all rattlesnakes, whispering across the dry leaves on the hammocks.

Though the new road was rough, the stately pace of his old "T" putt-

putting along permitted a calm appreciation of the morning. In the fiery sunrise, strings of white ibis flapped and sailed toward hidden destinations. In hawking course over the savanna flew a swallow-tailed kite that in recent days had descended from the towering Gulf skies at the north end of its migration from the Amazon. In time the Trail crossed the shady headwaters of Turner River, where in boyhood Lucius and the Storter boys came hunting, working upstream in a canoe from the salt mangrove coast of Chokoloskee Bay to the freshwater grasslands.

Beyond the trees at Turner River, the glittering expanse spread away forever. In the distance, isolated hardwood hammocks, shaped like tears by the remorseless southward flow, sailed ever north against the sky like a green armada. The hammocks parted the broad watershed that the Indians knew as River Long or Hatchee Chok-ti, transcribed by early white men as "Shark River," which in other days had betrayed no sign of man except dim shadow paths in the floating vegetation made by narrow dugouts. Only in recent years had the Shark River Mikasuki, drifting north, erected thatched *chekes* on the spoil banks of the black canal that ran along this new "Tamiami Trail." In this past year, with the near completion of the road, it seemed certain that the last Indians would be driven from Shark River to make way for a huge wilderness park.

At the Monroe Station rescue post for pioneer motorists, Lucius turned south then east again on an abandoned byway pocked by limestone potholes and marl pools; the road was all but hidden in hot crowding brush that raked and screeched at the old Ford's sides as it lurched along. Farther on, the track was flooded by clear water, and sprinklings of sun-tipped minnows shot back and forth between the silvers of pond cypress swamp to northward and the warm gold of the marshlands to the south. This track had been cut by the Chevelier Development Corporation, so named because its destination, never to be reached, was Chevelier Bay in the Lost Man's River region in the intoxicated days of the Florida land boom; Lost Man's Beach had been envisioned as the new "Gulf Coast Miami." The Depression had deflated the boom utterly, and the Chevelier Road, still ten miles short of its destination, was abandoned to this wooded swampland.

On a pine ridge along this road was Gator Hook, a shack community where the vacated sheds and decrepit dwellings of the road construction crews had been usurped by fugitives and drifters, also gator poachers, moonshiners, and retired whores, in a raffish society often drunk on its own moonshine before noon. Cut off from the rest of Monroe County by hundreds of square miles of roadless Glades, the Hook lay beyond all sane administration, to judge from the fact that the Monroe County sheriff had never set boot in this isolated and unregenerate outpost of his jurisdiction.

Lucius Watson had heard stories of a drifter at the Hook so obsessed with the tale of Leslie Cox and E. J. Watson as to stir speculation that he might be Cox himself. Many still believed that dreaded killer had made his way to the wild Mikasuki, who would shelter a white fugitive as in the past they had absorbed runaway slaves. With his high cheekbones and straight black hair, Cox might have passed for a breed Indian, remaining unrecognized year after year, before drifting to this backwater at Gator Hook. However, the whole story seemed so unlikely that Lucius Watson had never been inspired to go find out.

By mid-morning the sun had clouded over, casting a pall of gloom over the swamp. His sunrise mood evaporated with the dew, giving way to restlessness, disquiet. All his life, Lucius's moods had been prey to shifts of light, and now a leaden melancholy dragged at his spirits. In forcing his way into this lawless country, he seemed to push at a mighty spring which would hurl him backwards at the first faltering of his resolve.

Gradually the clear water withdrew and the track ascended onto a low rise where blurred paths wandered into thornbush and palmetto. The red rust of a tin roof showed through the shrouds of graybeard lichen; in the roadside ditch, bald tires languished. Strewn through the catclaw and liana lay rain-rotted cartons, bedsprings, gimcrack objects in bad chemical colors, bottles and tin cans. At a road bend, in an informal dump, four men playing cards at a sawhorse table turned to watch him pass, but no hand rose to return the stranger's wave. None of the four reminded him of Cox, though of course he might not have recognized the man, having last laid eyes on him in September of 1910, more than fifteen years before. He retained only a dim memory of that husky, sullen figure on the bank at Chatham Bend, standing apart from the small knot of waving folks whom he was to murder scarcely a fortnight later. However, Cox would not have lost those small ears set tight to his head, as in minks and otters, nor the dim shadow of the mule hoof on the left cheekbone, nor the dull, thudding voice, as heavy as the grunt of a bull gator.

"Gator Hook Bar"—the name was slapped crudely in black paint on the outside wall of a sway-backed cabin of greened wood set high on posts as a precaution against flood and patched with tarpaper and rusted tin against the rains. In the rank growth alongside was a rust-spotted white refrigerator, some rust-rotted oil drums, a charred stove of that marbled blue so ubiquitous in rubbish heaps throughout backcountry America. Near the blue stove sat a big pink touring auto with mud flaps and bent chrome. The auto's rear axle had been hoisted on a jack and its right rear wheel had been missing for some time, to judge from the heavy growth around the hub.

By reputation, Gator Hook served the rudimentary social needs of the swamp's male inhabitants and their raggy squalling females—backwoods crazies of both sexes, he had heard, apt to poke a weapon through a screen and open fire just for fun on any unfamiliar auto wending its slow way amongst the potholes, blowing out headlights as it neared or taillights as it fled and sometimes both. On this morning of late spring, a few dilapidated pickups and scabbed autos had emerged from the woods well before noon. Through the door screen came hoots and hee-haws rolled into one screech by a gramophone blare that escaped outside to die away in the pond cypress swamp north of the road.

The makeshift roadhouse was entered and departed through a loose screen door on the small landing of a steep ladder-stair down which drunk clients were at risk of tumbling at any hour of the day or night. A scraggy man in brown cap and soiled shirt whacked the screen door wide and reeled onto the stoop: "State yer damn business, mister!" When Lucius said he was looking for Mr. Collins, the drunk cocked his head, trying to focus, then waved him off, disgusted: "Never heard of'm!" The man had long hard-muscled arms, tattoos, machete sideburns, a small tight beer belly. "Don't I know you, mister? Ain't you some kind of a damn Watson?"

"Tommie Jimmie around?"

"No redskins ain't allowed. You Colonel Watson? You sure come to the wrong place." The man jerked his thumb back over his shoulder. "Don't go no further, Colonel, lest you want trouble." He nodded over and over. "Name is Mud." He grinned when that name was bellowed by a rough voice from inside. Turning, Mud lost his balance, almost falling. He clutched the rail and sagged down onto the steps in a pule of oaths and spittle.

The man's cap had fallen off: Lucius retrieved it from the stair. By now he had recognized this no-account Braman from Marco, prematurely drink-blotched and near bald. Confronted by Mud's scalp up close as he ascended, the eruptions and scratched chigger bites, the weak hair and the ingrained grime in the pale skin, Lucius perched the brown cap gently on his head, stepping around his stale rank smell and continuing up the steps.

With the appearance of a stranger's silhouette in the torn screen, the voices within went silent in sudden hush, like marsh frogs stilled by a water snake winding its way through flooded grasses. Two men on the point of leaving sank back into their places, and two squawking women with hard helmet hair stopped their raucous dance.

Inside the door Lucius found himself blocked by a husky barefoot man whose sun-baked back and neck and shoulders were matted with black hair. From hard green coveralls—his only garment—rose an aroma of fried foods and sweat, spilled beer and cigarettes, crankcase oil and something else, a smear of rancid mayonnaise, perhaps, or gator blood, or semen. The man crowded him without expression and without a word, as if intent on bumping chests and backing him out through the screen door onto the landing. But now the harsh voice that had bellowed "Mud!" yelled "Dummy!" and the barefoot man, dead-eyed, indifferent, turned away.

The yell had come from a man waving him across the room to the makeshift bar who merely sneered in sardonic response to the newcomer's wince of distaste at the sight of him. Raven-haired, with a hide as dark and hard-grained as mahogany and a dirty grizzle all around a wry and heavy mouth, Crockett Daniels had thickened but not softened since Lucius had last seen him in the Islands. Filling two cracked coffee cups with spirits from a jug, he shoved one at Lucius, who acknowledged it with a bare nod.

The two leaned back against the bar, sipping for a while before they spoke. Daniels's green eyes were restless, scanning the room but always returning to a big bearded man, shirtless in dirty jeans and a black leather vest and missing his left arm; the big man leaned on the far wall, fixing the stranger with a baleful glare. A hard brush of coarse black hair jutted from his crown like a worn broom; on his upper right arm was a discolored tattoo—the American flag with fasces and an eagle rampant, talons fastened on a skull and crossbones. The red and white of the stars and stripes were dirtied and the blue was purpled, all one ugly bruise.

Intent on Lucius, the big man resumed a story interrupted by his entry. "Like I was sayin, you go to huntin gators in the backcountry, you gone to earn ever' damn red cent you make! And that's okay, that's our way of life, takin the rough nights with the smooth. But these days when you go out there and go to doin what your daddy done and your grandpap, too, you might could find yourself flat up against some feller in a green frog outfit sneakin around for the federal fuckin government. Know what he wants? Hell, *you* know what he wants! He wants our huntin country for a fuckin *park*! Wants to confuscate your gator flats, clap your cracker ass in jail!"

The big man turned, pointing a thick finger at Lucius Watson. "Or maybe that fed slunk through the door there, tryin to look like ever'body else!"

"That big boy you are lookin at calls hisself Crockett Junior," Daniels informed Lucius, not sounding pleased. "Wants to know what you're doin out here, Colonel. That's what your friends call you, ain't it?"

"You my friend now, Speck?" Lucius drank his glass off to the bottom and came up with a gasp and a warm glow in the face. The moonshine was colorless, so purely raw that it numbed his mouth and sinuses and made his eyes water.

The big man's self-stoked rage was building.

"Damn fed might belly right up to that bar, pertend to be your friend, then turn around and stop a man from supportin his own family!" Crockett Junior bawled. "And you out there in that dark swamp night after night, way back in some godforsook damn place you can't even pole to in a boat, half bled to death by no-see-ums and miskeeters, worn out, wet, and froze with cold, and damn if one them stupid shits don't have you spotted! Maybe just waitin to step out of a bush where you left your truck back at the landin!"

Here Crockett Junior paused in tragic wonderment. Softly he said, "Speakin fair now, what's a man to do if that feller tries to haul him off to jail?" He gazed about him, shaking his head over such injustice. "Now I ain't sayin he's a real bad feller. Might could be a *likable* young feller just tryin to get by the same as me. Might got him a lovin little wife waitin on him at home. Couple real nice *little* fellers, or maybe just the sweetest baby girl—same as what *I* got!" Crockett Junior looked around him wide-eyed, making sure his listeners understood how remarkable it was that gator hunter and game warden might both have wives and kiddies, and also the depth of his concern for the warden's family. *"But!"* He looked around some more, and the soft voice grew more and more confiding. "But if that ol' boy tries to take away my gators? I got my duty to my family, ain't that right? Got to take care of my sweet baby girl at home, ain't that only nacherl?"

"We heard this same ol' shit in here a thousand times," Speck said, disgusted.

"You folks recall that plume bird warden that Bloody Watson killed down around Flamingo?" Junior nodded with the drinkers. "Now I ain't sayin what ol' Bloody done was right. All I'm sayin is—and it would be real pathetical, break my damn heart—all I'm sayin, if any such a feller tries to keep me from my livin?" Here he fixed his gaze on Lucius once again, raising his good arm to point southward toward some point of destiny in a far slough. "Well, you folks know that Crockett Junior Daniels would be heartbroke, all tore up, but that feller ain't left me no damn choice." He dropped his voice to a hoarse hard whisper. "I reckon I'd just have to leave that sumbitch *out* there!"

The clientele turned its slack gaze upon the stranger. "Tragical, ain't it?" Speck Daniels snickered. "Leave that sumbitch *out* there. That's about the size of it. Invaders got to watch their step in *this* neck of the woods and that's a fact.

"Course Junior there, he's crazier'n hell, and them other morons he keeps with him might be worse. Mud Braman been a drunk since the day his balls dropped, don't know where his ass is at from one minute to the next, and that other one with all the personality"—he tossed his chin toward Dummy—"he might bust loose any minute, shoot this place to pieces, and you'd never know why in the hell he done that, and him neither."

Waiting for Daniels to make his point, Lucius said nothing.

"Leave him *out* there! Yessir!" Speck Daniels sighed. "Some days I think ol' Junior might be better off if I was to leave *him* out there. Run his dumb ass into the swamp back here and put a bullet in his head for his own damn good, 'fore he gets us in trouble shooting some stranger who just wandered in here off that road."

"You threatening me, Speck?"

For the first time, the poacher turned and contemplated Lucius Watson, sucking his teeth with distaste. "What you huntin for out this way, Colonel? Ain't me, I hope."

Lucius shook his head. "I never knew you lived here."

"Well, I don't. When I ain't livin on my boat, I got me a huntin camp back in the Cypress, big army stove and a regular commode, nice fat Guatemala girl that come by mail order. But these days," he whispered—and he cocked his head the better to enjoy Lucius's reaction—"I'm caretakin in your daddy's house, down Chatham River."

A couple of months earlier, Daniels explained, he had been contacted by a Miami attorney who was seeking to reinstate E. J. Watson's land claim on Chatham Bend; the attorney wanted somebody camped on the Bend to keep an eye on the place until the claim was settled. "Man heard that Crockett Senior Daniels knew the Watson place real good and might be just the feller he was lookin for." He gave Lucius a sly glance.

The attorney was trying to reach the Watson heirs. "He was complainin how he couldn't catch up with the Watson boys. I told him, 'Well, the oldest run off from a killin at the turn of the century and the next one is a upright citizen around Fort Myers, don't want nothin to do with swamps and such. Course Loo-shush might be interested,' I says, 'but you might have trouble findin Loo-shush cause he makes hisself scarce and always did.' "

Affecting indifference, Lucius shrugged. "So who is he? What's his name?"

Mr. Watson Dyer, Speck continued, had big connections in this state; he was a crony of politicians and a fixer. "Wants a nice ronday-voo for all them fat boys, wouldn't surprise me—booze 'n girlie club, y'know. I been thinkin I might join up to be a member." But there was no mirth in Daniels's wink, he was watching Lucius closely, and Lucius maintained his flat expression, not wishing to show his astonishment—*Watt Dyer!*—nor how much he resented the idea of Crockett Daniels infesting Chatham Bend. After Bill House left, Papa's remote house on its wild river had been looted and hard used by squatters, hunters, moonshiners, and smugglers, and Daniels was all of these and more—the Bend just suited him. From offshore, no stranger to that empty coast could find the channel in the broken mangrove estuary where Chatham River worked its way through to the Gulf—one reason why Papa chose that river in the first place—and even boatmen with a chart might ream out their boat bottom on the oyster bars. But these days, with the new canals draining the Glades headwaters for more sugarcane plantations, the rivers to the south ran shallow, with snags and shifting sandbars, and smugglers such as Daniels and his gang had to rig chains to the few channel markers and drag them out.

"Loo-shus." Speck considered him a moment. "Course if this big Glades park goes through, they'll likely burn your daddy's house down to the ground. Raggedy ol' place three-four miles back up a mangrove river, windows busted and doors all choked by thorn and vines? Not to mention bats and snakes, wasp nests and spiders and raccoon shit—smell like a bat cave in there. That house ain't had a nail or a lick of paint in years. Them damn Chok people that was in there, they just let her go. Screen porch is rickety, might put your foot through, and the jungle is invadin into the ground floor. Hurricanes has stripped off shingles, took the dock and the outbuildins, too."

"Why do you care? It's not your place."

"Not my place?" Speck cocked a bloodshot eye. "You sayin the Bend don't belong to us home people? And the whole Glades backcountry along with it?" Hearing Speck's voice rise in a spurt of anger, Junior Daniels turned their way. "Why, Godamighty, they's been Danielses usin this backcountry for half a hundred years! I hunted here all my damn life! You tellin me them fuckin feds and their fuckin park has got more rights than *I* do?"

But Lucius noticed that much of his outrage was feigned and the rest inflated. In fact, Speck laughed, pleased by his own performance. "Know the truth? Them squatters has stole everything that weren't nailed down and quite a lot that was but they never done your daddy's place real harm. Storms tore the outside, which is all them greenhorns look at, but inside she's as solid as she ever was, cause your daddy used bald cypress and hard pine. That man liked ever'thing done right. His house might look gray and peaked as a corpse but she could stand up there on her mound for another century."

"Mind telling me what you're up to on the Bend? When you're not caretaking, I mean?"

Daniels lit a cigarette and squinted through the smoke. "That ain't your business." Reaching to refill Lucius's glass, he winked to show he was only kidding, which he wasn't.

Lucius sniffed at the white lightning. "You make this stuff down there?"

Daniels measured him. "You sure ain't obliged to drink it, Loo-shus. You ain't obliged to drink with me at all." Asked if he owned Gator Hook and if this bar was an outlet for his shine, Speck took a hard swallow and banged his glass down. "Still askin stupid questions, I see. You ain't changed much, bud, and I ain't neither, as you are goin to find out if you keep tryin me." In a gravelly voice, he growled, "I asked you extra polite just now what you was up to out this way. All these folks in here want to know that. So we ain't feelin so polite no more about not gettin no answer."

Lucius pushed his glass away, trying to focus. He was sick of baiting Daniels, sick of being baited. "I'm not a fed. I'm looking for a man named Collins."

"No you ain't. You're a damn liar." Speck announced this to the room. "Here I ain't seen you in dog's years and all of a sudden you show up way to hell and gone out in this swamp. Think I'm a idjit? Think I don't know why?" When Speck raised his voice, Junior pushed himself clear of the wall and started across the room, and the one called Dummy followed. "All these years you been snoopin and skulkin, makin up your damfool list! You know how close you come to gettin shot?"

Lucius tried to keep his voice calm. "You the one who winged that bullet past my ear, down Lost Man's River?"

In the quiet the customers awaited them. Crockett Daniels told the room, "Mr. Gene Roberts at Flamingo thought the world of E. J. Watson, said he was as nice a man as ever lynched a nigger. So in later years, when Watson's boy here was layin low down there, Mr. Gene told them Flamingo fellers not to run him off or sink his boat but let him work that coast. Told 'em he'd fished with E. J.'s boy and drank his whiskey with him, cause Loo-shus here liked his whiskey and a lot of it, same way his daddy done. Gene would say how E. J.'s boy had the sweetest nature he ever come across and all like that"—Speck turned to him—"not knowin that his sweetness weren't but weakness."

"Course it's possible," Speck said, holding his eye, "that Loo-shus here would do you hurt if you pushed him hard enough. But I believe this feller is weak-hearted. He just wants to live along, get on with ever'body, ain't that right, Loo-shus?" He paused again, then added meanly, "Makin a list of them ones that killed his daddy but afraid to use it."

Speck cocked his head, looking curiously at Lucius as if to see how far he'd have to go to make him mad. "I always heard you was a alky-holic," he said softly. "Any truth to that?"

Lucius turned away from him. "The man I'm looking for calls himself Collins," he told the onlookers. "Has a nickname—Chicken."

"Chicken Collins?" a woman called. "He ain't but four damn feet from where your elbow's at. He's comin off his drunk under the bar."

Annoyed, Speck followed Lucius around behind the bar. The man lay on a soft bed of swept-up cigarette butts, wrapped in a dirty olive blanket black-poxed with burn holes. Daniels toed the body with a hard-creased boot, eliciting an ugly hacking cough. "When this feller first washed up here, Colonel, we made him janitor, paid him off in trade. All he could put away and then some and he's still hard at it. Come to likker, the man don't *never* quit! Don't know the *meanin* of the word." Speck toed the body harder. "Come on, Chicken. Say how-do to your visitor cause he's just leavin."

Greasy tufts emerged from the olive blanket, then reddened eyes in a soiled, unshaven face. This wasn't Cox. The ears were wrong and the mule hoof scar was missing.

From beneath the blanket rose a stale waft of dead cigarettes, spilled booze, old urine. At the sight of Lucius, the eyes started into focus. A scrawny claw crept forth to grasp the tin cup of mixed spirits from abandoned drinks which Dummy ladled for him out of a tin tub; he knocked the cup back with one great cough and shudder. Then the head withdrew. "Go home," he muttered from beneath the blanket.

Lucius went down on one knee and shook his shoulder gently. "Mr. Collins? It's Lucius Watson. You sent for me."

From beneath the blanket came more coughing. "Hell, no. Get on home, boy."

"Come with me, then. We have to talk."

With his big hand jammed under his armpit, Crockett Junior hoisted Lucius to his feet. "That man's sick!" Lucius protested. "I'll take him with me!" But Junior impelled him toward the screen door where Braman, entering, got in the way. Placing his palm against Mud's face with fingers on both sides of his nose, Dummy shoved hard with one thrust like a punch, sending the man out through the loose screen door and down the outside stair. A scaring *whump* rose from the bottom of the steps. Stepping outside onto the landing, looking down, Speck shook his head. "That fool has flew down them damn steps so many times you'd think he'd get the hang of it but he just don't."

On hands and knees, panting with shock, Mud wiped the blood from his gashed brow with the back of a grimy hand. "See how they done?" he complained to Lucius, who had jumped down the stair to help him. Braman waved him off, crawling away through the weeds to the pink auto and dragging himself into the backseat. He tried to shut the door behind him but the rusted hinges and rank weeds kept it from closing. "Any man," Mud hollered from within, "thinks Mud R. Braman gone to take any more shit off them dirty skunks better think again!"

Lucius walked toward his old Ford as Speck called from the landing. "*Loo-shus* Watson! Ain't nowhere near the man his daddy was."

Speck stood rocking on his heels, hands in hip pockets, grinning. "Don't aim to tell us how that ol' list of yours is comin?" Getting no answer, he rasped angrily, "What I hear, Nigger Short ain't on your list, and he ain't never died off that I heard about. Or don't a nigger count, the way you look at it?"

Lucius turned his old car around and cranked the window down so he could hear better. Over the roof peak, a turkey vulture circled, the red skin of its naked head like a blood spot on the blue.

Speck said in a low voice, "You and me ain't the same breed, I am proud to say. If I believed a man helped kill *my* daddy, I sure wouldn't go to drinkin with that feller like you done this mornin and I sure wouldn't need no damn ol' list to tell me what to do about it, neither. That man would of come up missin a long time ago."

"Crockett Daniels." Lucius pronounced the name slowly, as if to lock it in his memory. "I do believe that is the last name on the list."

Wobbling the clutch into gear, he exulted at the flicker in Speck's grin, but as he drew away, his heart was pounding. A man as wary as Crockett Daniels would hear those words as a threat, and a threatened man, as Papa used to say, was not a man to turn your back on in the backcountry.

WATT DYER

One day at the Marco store where he picked up his mail, Lucius received a formal letter from Attorney Watson Dyer, in Miami. Attorney Dyer urged the family to refile the late Mr. Watson's claim on Chatham Bend before the U.S. government condemned the property, which lay within the boundaries of the proposed Everglades park. In closing, he offered his own services and a phone number. Oddly, the letter made no mention of the fact that he was Nell's brother, or that Lucius might remember him from years ago.

Lucius went straight to the pay telephone. When Dyer answered, they barely exchanged greetings, far less spoke of Nell, before Watt got busy explaining that should the new park go through, any property under pending claim would revert to the federal government. Furthermore—pursuant to federal policy that a new park be returned to its natural condition as a wilderness—the last signs of man's presence would be eradicated, not only the ramshackle habitations but docks, rain cisterns, crops, and trees. Even the well-built Watson house would not be spared unless it was established that a claim had been pending in advance of the first park proposals, in which case it might be approved as an in-holding within the park for which life tenure, at least, might be negotiated—

"What do they mean by 'natural condition'?" Lucius inquired. "Before Indian settlement or after? Because if they want Chatham Bend the way it was, they will have to shovel the whole forty acres into the river. It's nothing but shell mound, don't they realize that? One huge Indian midden. To eradicate all the shell mounds and Calusa canals in the western Everglades would cost millions, and anyway, it couldn't be done without gouging out far more man-made scars than they were eliminating."

Like an unseen presence in the dark, the lawyer's silence commanded him to be still. Then Dyer said, "Indians don't count." His tone was less cynical than flat, indifferent. He went on to say that his specialty was real estate law and large-scale land development and that in this field, his extensive political contacts would prove useful. Would the family authorize him to pursue this matter?

Lucius suggested that the Watson family might waive its claim if the new park would restore the house and take good care of it—perhaps make it a historic monument to pioneer days? Dyer sighed. An offer of waiver before the claim had been reinstated could only undermine its legal standing.

"I'm afraid I can't afford a lawyer—"

"Pro bono. Sentimental reasons, you might say." The lawyer forced a snort of mirthless laughter. He finally reminded Lucius that Fred Dyer was caretaker at Chatham Bend just after the turn of the century and that he himself had visited in summers as a schoolboy. "You don't recall Wattie Dyer?" Another disconcerting snort. Lucius tried to picture the boy Wattie, wondering what the man at the far end of this phone line might look like. He hesitated. His sister had mentioned that Nell and her brother had never been in touch, not even after their mother died during the War. Small wonder, he thought, recalling now how Watt had bullied her as a little girl.

Parting Nell's hair to crack his hard-boiled egg upon her pate then exhaling his hated egg breath into her squinched face was a favorite diversion. Occasionally, Lucius had felt obliged to intervene. For this the boy had hated him as much as he loathed everyone else. From an early age, Watt Dyer had made himself disliked by everybody on the Bend. He was especially unlucky, Lucius reflected, because he had always known this without really knowing what he knew.

All he required for the moment, Dyer was saying, was power of attorney in order to file for a court injunction against any attempt by park proponents to burn down the house before approval of the park charter became final. In Dyer's opinion, the Watson claim could not be summarily vacated or dismissed if E. J. Watson's heirs renewed the claim in time. Well, said Lucius, Rob was unavailable and Carrie and Eddie would want no part of any action that might stir up old scandal. As for the children of the second family, they had been given their new stepfather's name and might not even know that they were Watsons.

"Looks like it's up to you, then," Dyer interrupted. "You'll be hearing from me." He hung up abruptly before anything had been decided, leaving Lucius frustrated and annoyed.

AFFIDAVIT OF BILL W. HOUSE

Completing his research for the biography of E. J. Watson, Lucius had placed notices in local newspapers requesting information. These notices attracted the anticipated motley of old Watson anecdotes, but astonishingly, they also produced a copy of the affadavit given by Bill House in the Lee County Courthouse after his father's death—the document that his brother Eddie had refused to show him.

> *My name is Mr. William House residing at Chokoloskee Island, Ten Thousand Islands, Florida.*
>
> *Mr. Ed J. Watson was at Chokoloskee when the story come about the Chatham murders. He swore that Leslie Cox had done him wrong and not only him but the three people he murdered. Watson left to fetch the Sheriff and the men thought they'd seen the last of him. This was Sunday evening, October 16, the eve of the Great Hurricane.*

Three days after the storm, Ed Watson come back through. Mr. D. D. House advised he better stay right there until the Sheriff come and Watson said he didn't need no Sheriff, said he knew his business and would take care of it himself. Aimed to go home to Chatham River "and straighten that skunk out before he got away"—them were his own words. He promised to return with Cox or Cox's head.

Watson was red-eyed in his appearance, very wild, and nobody didn't care to interfere with him. The men there at Smallwood's landing figured he'd keep right on going, head for the east coast railroad or Key West. This time they'd seen the last of him for sure. But last Monday October 24 toward evening, his motor was heard coming from the south'ard and a bunch of fellers went to the landing to arrest him. Watson seen that crowd of armed men waiting but he come on anyway, he was that kind.

The hurricane had tore the dock away, weren't nothing left of her but pilings, so he run his launch aground west of the boat way. He jumped ashore with his shotgun quick and bold, got himself set before one word was spoken. Had his weapon pointed down but hitched, ready to swing. He told the men he had killed Cox but the body fell off his dock into the river and was lost. He drawed a old hat out of his coat, showed the bullet hole from his revolver. Then he shoved his middle finger through that hole and twirled the hat on it and laughed. Some of us seen he was laughing at us. Nobody felt like laughing along with him.

Mr. D. D. House was not the ringleader, never mind what some has said, but no other man stepped forward so my dad done the talking. I and my next two brothers, Dan Junior and Lloyd, stood alongside him. Mr. D. D. House reminded Watson that a head was promised and a hat weren't good enough so the men would have to go to Chatham Bend, look for the body. And he notified Mr. Watson he must hand over his weapons in the meantime. That brought hard words. After a short argument, Watson swung his shotgun up at point-blank range. Some has said the man just meant to bluff the crowd back while he escaped: I believe he aimed at us with intent to kill, only his shells misfired. We opened up on him all in a roar and he fell down dead.

Some has been trying to point fingers, claiming we was laying for him, fixing to gun him down no matter what. Might of been true of some of 'em. Houses never knew nothing about no such thing.

Others give hints that one man lost his head and fired first and that this man was the only one responsible. I don't rightly know who fired first and they don't neither on account of the whole bunch fired together. We took the life of E. J. Watson to defend our own and all present was in on it from start to finish.

X

[William W. House: his mark]

Transcribed and attested: (signed) E. E. Watson, Dep. Court Clerk
Lee County Courthouse, Fort Myers, Florida, October 27, 1910

Oddly, this document had been sent anonymously, without a note, in a coffee-stained envelope mailed from Ochopee, a construction camp post office out along the Trail. What startled Lucius was his brother's signature as deputy court clerk: he had almost forgotten that Eddie had transcribed the testimony of those men. In his biography-in-progress, Lucius sought the historian's objective tone:

While this affidavit is critical as the one firsthand account of E. J. Watson's death that has come to light, it raises more questions than it answers: its main interest lies in what can be inferred between the lines. House's statement makes clear that E. J. Watson was killed despite the Negro's testimony at Pavilion Key that the brutal slayings at Chatham Bend had been committed not by Mr. Watson but by his foreman, Leslie Cox, a convicted killer and fugitive from justice who had turned up at the Watson place a few months earlier.

As for the murder at Chokoloskee on October 24th, Bill House asserts that killing Mr. Watson was an act of self-defense while conceding that Watson did not open fire on the crowd or otherwise assault or harm any man there. It has been argued that no malice aforethought was involved—that the horrifying murders at Chatham Bend followed so swiftly by the calamity of the Great Hurricane had driven this isolated community to a breaking point of terror and exhaustion which caused those men to meet Watson's bluff with that fatal barrage. However, widespread rumors in the community suggest that at least a few of the participants had planned the shooting in advance, justifying what amounted to a lynching with the argument that otherwise Watson might have evaded justice "as he had done so often in the past."

The House account leaves open another urgent question: did one man execute him with the first shot and the others fire reflexively in the confusion? Though House denies this, the evident need to deny it gives substance to a rumor that the undersigned had dismissed as highly improbable. If there is truth in it, then who was House so anxious to protect?

In appraising Mr. Watson's degree of responsibility, one must first determine whether or not Cox killed his three victims on Watson's orders and whether or not Watson killed Cox when he returned to Chatham Bend after the hurricane. If he did, was he enforcing his own code of retribution, or—as Sheriff Tippins believed—was he eliminating the one witness whose testimony could do him damage in a murder trial, on the not unreasonable assumption that even if the Negro had not retracted his unsupported account of Mr. Watson's involvement, a black man's testimony might well have been discounted by a white jury?

In the climate of fear in the community, almost nobody believed that Leslie Cox had been eliminated by E. J. Watson; to this day, a local dread persists that Cox survived. If so, what became of him? Is he still alive back in the Glades? With the passage of years, it seems ever less likely that we shall learn the fate of that cold-blooded killer who appeared so randomly and wreaked such havoc, only to vanish. Somewhere in the backcountry of America, an old man known in other days as Leslie Cox might still squint in the sun, and spit, and revile his fate.

In preparing his case for the reinstatement of E. J. Watson's claim on Chatham Bend, Attorney Dyer had asked to see Lucius's early draft of his Watson biography. What drew his attention immediately was Hoad Storter's account of transporting new cane from Chatham River to Moore Haven on Lake Okeechobee, which seemed to establish that Planter Watson's hardy strain had provided the seed cane for the huge new agriculture in central Florida. Ever scrupulous, Lucius felt obliged to append a footnote: when the bad hurricane of 1926 broke down the Okeechobee dikes and drowned more than a hundred souls around Moore Haven, the devastation was blamed locally on "Emperor" Watson, whose "bad seed," as one news-paper called it, was "steeped in human blood."

Excising that fool reminder of those hurricane mortalities, Attorney Dyer had shown the story of E. J. Watson's cane to United Sugar Associates ("U.S.A. SPELLS AMERICA!") for whom he served as legal counsel in its on-going appropriation of huge swaths of public marshland in that region. U.S.A., Dyer predicted, would endorse any worthwhile literature about pio-neer sugar plantations and the early prominence of sugarcane in south Florida agriculture and might well subsidize its publication; the published biography, he felt sure, would also lend strength to the Watson land claim.

Because of the favorable reception of his *History*, Lucius had been of-fered a small advance on the Watson biography by the university press. At the last minute, however, the press had stipulated the use of a pen name for the biography lest the author appear less than objective. Refusing to hide behind a pseudonym, Lucius threatened to withdraw the book, whereupon Attorney Dyer fired off a furious letter, reminding him of his responsibili-ties: without the enhancement of E. J. Watson's reputation in "our book". said Dyer, there was little hope that the Chatham land claim would survive on its merits in court.

SARAH HARDEN

The person who persuaded Lucius to cooperate was Sarah Harden, who came by one day to inspect his "houseboat," walking all the way from the county road. The twin braids of long cornsilk hair were gone and the worn overalls but she looked wonderful in a red blouse and gray skirt. Told of his dilemma, Sarah reminded him of how important it had always been to mend his father's reputation: a pen name was certainly preferable to wast-ing so much work. Having fun, they devised a composite "family" name, "L. Watson Collins." Smiling happily, delighted to see him again, she cele-brated his new name with a hug and a kiss on the cheek.

Before he could ask after Owen, Sarah told him what he'd already suspected, that she'd left her husband. Despite all her warnings, threats, and pleas, he had given up fishing to work with Crockett Daniels. "Rum-running, moonshine, poaching gators, any ol' darn thing to make a buck!

And hemp—you ever smoked a reefer? Anywhere there's smuggling involved, you'll find Speck Daniels, and he never gets caught. Owen says he pays off Sheriff Tippins.

"Owen couldn't feed us—no fish, no work, no money. He's too proud to live like that. Owen is a good kind man who works with redneck criminals. He's not one of them and if it comes to trouble, it's Owen who'll wind up in the state pen. He kind of knows that but he's stuck in his old code, some old Island way of thinking. Except for the money, he has no use for those men, and no respect, because they're dead ignorant and lazy. Too bad you don't know that well enough to quit, I said, cause you don't respect Owen Harden, neither, or you wouldn't work with 'em. And he thought a minute and then he said that he reckoned he respected himself well enough, it was his wife who disrespected him. That wasn't true—he only said that because he got jealous of you at Lost Man's—but I thought it might be good for him to think that way, at least for a while, so I shut up. Then Speck branched out into running guns south to the Spanish countries, and Owen started to feel guilty, but even then, he didn't give it up, just went to drinking—well, that finished it. I didn't aim to live with a damned drunk who made his money peddling deadly weapons. I warned him I would leave and I finally did."

When Lucius said he was truly sorry and hoped things would work out, she only shrugged. "I'm sorry, too, I reckon. I sure tried." Though she said nothing more, she raised her eyes and returned his gaze for one dangerous second too long. Both nodded then, smiling a little as they cast their eyes down. Not sure what all this meant—or if it meant anything at all—he was careful not to touch her. As Nell had said, Lucius Watson knew little about women's ways, and since he tended to agree, he was afraid that if he took this high-strung Sarah in his arms at the wrong moment, she might fly to pieces.

She stood up, straightened her dress, brushed off her bottom. He said, "Miss? May I help with that?" and laughed out of jangled joy and nerves. "Not today, thank you," she answered flatly, without the flirtatious inflection he'd expected. Love-besmirched, he dusted off his own inconsequential ass before taking her home to her cousin's house in Naples.

Weeks later, having thought about little else, he went to find her. Forgetting what he'd come to say—and knowing how feeble this must sound—he cried, "How are you?" She led him into the front room and sat down beside him on the thin settee before answering sadly, "I don't think I know."

To comfort her, he took her hand and she took his in both her own and settled the three hands in her lap. Her impulse seemed innocent enough, yet feeling her warm lap through the light cotton—God have mercy! His hand was a mere inch from what his father, in affectionate reference to Josie Jenkins, had once referred to as "milady's honeypot." His fevered brain must have sent these rude vibrations, for Sarah abruptly tossed his hand into the air as if freeing a wild bird. She lifted her arms to pin her hair, releasing a light captivating scent of perspiration. Edgy, she said, "Let's go somewhere." They had not mentioned Owen.

In a booth at Rusty's, his spilled-beer-and-sawdust roadhouse on the Marco road, Lucius repeated his staid hope that his old friends might find their way back together. Sarah looked away when she raised her glass to acknowledge his kind wishes. Unspoken was the shameful knowing on both sides that he coveted that old friend's wife, and that she, too, was confused by mixed emotions, confessing now that she and Owen were negotiating her return; he understood that she was not yet ready for another man. Saddened but perhaps also relieved, they consoled themselves with Sarah's flask and the unhappy rewards of love virtuously relinquished.

"Here's something you white-boy historians don't generally put in books," she teased him, wisely detouring their thoughts onto a safer path. "Learned this from Owen, whose grandma was descended. Chief Osceola was a breed named Billy Powell ashamed of his own blood, only he was ashamed of the white blood, not the other—not like some! Most of his warriors were black Seminoles, what they called maroons, and later on, he took black wives along with a few red ones, had offsprings on every dog-gone one, which accounts for the mixed-up bunch that's running around south Florida today. Some of our so-called Injuns got a nap so thick you couldn't put a *bullet* through it!" Her hoarse smoker's laugh had a deep rue in it, and he laughed with her, she delighted him. Her barefoot toes, seeking his foot under the table, shot small honeyed arrows into his groin.

"It's mighty fine to see ol' Lucius *laugh* this way!" Sarah cried happily. But pointing out laughter put it to death, and she looked cross. "Course folks weren't too particular in frontier days. Some of my kin at Chokoloskee who are so mean about nigras better not go poking around too much in their own woodpiles. Might be some red boys in there at the very least." Her bare foot kicked his calf under the table. "Don't laugh. I know what I'm talking about. Better'n you."

In the car again, she smoked one of her "funny smokes." When she proffered a second, raising it to his lips—"Come *with* me!" she breathed, comically mysterious—he held on to her warm fingers and drew on his first reefer. At her whispered instruction, he held the smoke a long time in his lungs, then swallowed on it, suffusing it all the way up to his temples. When he exhaled at last, the smoke seemed to drift out through his ears. His brain swam and his mouth slid toward a grin. "Reefer madness," she laughed, her mouth so close to his that he longed to fall into it and close it after him.

Right beside him sat the lovely Sarah Harden of Lost Man's River—how had this happened? Why was Sarah sitting so close to Lucius in his old Model T, smiling at him in this soft, beguiling way? He cleared his throat, determined to counsel Owen's sweetheart against leaving a fine man: was she really so sure it was all over? Couldn't they patch it up? However, no voice came.

He was feeling at rest in the present, neither here nor there. "Where to?" his voice said, though he'd already turned toward home. Did this wild creature want him to make love to her? She laid her hand upon his arm and leaned to blow smoke into his ear. "Can I lay low on your old barge if I stay out of your way and don't cause trouble?"

"Lay low," he heard his voice agree. And now this strangely languid and unbridled person draped herself across his arm and shoulder. Cocking her head, she peered close around his chin in comic awe until her lips brushed the corner of his own.

"Better back off." He kissed her hard without slowing the car, stirred by the sweet smell of her hair.

"Just a-hangin on my darlin's every word, is all it is."

"Stay away from bad girls, Mama tole me—"

She hushed his mouth with another fulsome kiss. "Oh, I ain't so bad," she murmured huskily, surfacing again. "Under my glitterin ve-neer, a plain ol' cracker gal is what I am. First Florida Baptist bad-ass cracker, that is me." She lay her head back and went pealing off into some private laughter.

"And how do your Baptist forebears feel about your sinful tendencies?"

"Sickens 'em. Just purely sickens 'em. They feel like pukin." Suddenly her smile was gone, her scowl was real, she looked as if she might well puke on purpose. Something anarchic surfaced in her eye which he tried to deflect before she blurted something they might both regret, and in his distraction, on a curve, he rolled two wheels onto the shoulder, coming too close to running the car into the roadside canal.

Sarah took this near-disaster calmly, ignoring his apology. In guilt, her mood had turned bitter and morose. Brooding, she peered out the window. Then she said in a peculiar voice, "Stay on the gray stuff, all right? You're getting your balls in a uproar."

He felt the heat rush to his face. "Hey, come on now."

"Go stick it in the mud. You stick it into *me*, by Jesus, you will goddamn well regret it! I'll tell Owen."

"Oh Lord—"

"And another thing"—she was yelling now—"stop lookin me over like some mutt dog eyin meat! You *always* done that, since the first day you showed up at Lost Man's! Think I never noticed? Go find your own damn woman! Find that widder you was mopin about 'stead of trickin young women that's already spoken for into your tin tooter!" She banged the outside of the car door. "What are you anyway, some kind of a fanatic? That why she give up on you? Cause your daddy's death is all you care about? The past?"

She fell back, spent, gasping for breath.

He held his tongue, drove on in silence; how could he have considered an affair with a friend's wife, this drug-crazed cracker, when what he really needed was a wise and gentle person such as Nell—but here good sense quit him and he turned to the fray.

"Miss?"

" 'Mrs.' Mrs. John Owen Harden to you. Your ol' buddy's everlovin little wife, case you forgot."

"Wasn't it my ol' buddy's wife who came slipping around to Caxambas to renew acquaintance? Who's been flirting for the last three hours—"

"You want me to get out and walk? *That* what you're saying? Slow down, Buster!" But moments later, weeping, she subsided. "I'm a mess. I drink too much, Prof. So do you. In fact, come to think of it, this fight is all your fault." Though she fished out a hankie and blew sniffles, she could not hide her smile. Soon she laid her head against his shoulder and languorously touched his leg, trailed her fingertips along his inner thigh. When she sat back, sighing, the backs of her fingers rested in his lap, light as a kiss.

In awe of their wordless decision, they drove in silence to Caxambas and made their way in half-embrace out the walkway to the barge, where they drank up the last of his whiskey and made urgent love on the narrow cot, in an intoxicating mix of body smells, grain alcohol breath, and needy lust. By turns shy, rapt, omnipotent, he felt like a man lost and then returned among the living. He heard himself cry out that he loved her, which in that moment was true.

In the morning, yawning, she rolled languidly away from his attempt to take her in his arms, saying she must first go brush her teeth; she left him to doze, never to return. When he awakened, she was dressed and restless, making coffee. He must take her to Naples right away, she said, to meet with Owen and the lawyer.

"Today, you mean?" He could not accept the idea of losing her just when he'd found her. Yet he knew his panic was not reasonable and his shock not entirely honest; lying there before desire overtook him, he'd even wondered if an early parting with his old friend's estranged wife might not be best.

"Are you sorry, Sarah? You regret what happened?"

"I'll never regret it, sweetheart. It was always in our future and I always knew it. But I also know it's all we're going to get." She touched his cheek. "I have to let you go while I still can." To disguise her real upset, she parodied a country lyric: *"Darlin', ah swore ah wouldn' . . . nevuh be . . . tore up bah yoo."*

"Please, listen—"

She put her hand over his mouth. "Gonna miss me, sweetheart?" Her eyes misted. She said fiercely, "You're a good man, don't you know that? Think it's easy to give you up, a man like you?"

"Can't I come see you? We have to talk—" He was routed by her expression. His heart felt open and exposed as a shucked oyster on the half-shell, mantle curling at the first squirt of the lemon.

ARBIE COLLINS

Returning home one afternoon of spring, Lucius was met halfway along the walkway by the molasses reek of a cheap stogie. In the tattered hammock on the deck, a thin man in tractor cap and discolored army overcoat lay sifting pages, the bent cigar a-glower between his teeth. On the floor beside him sat a dog-eared satchel and a sagging carton of old papers. Removing the cigar, the man spat bits of tobacco, the better to recite from Lucius's notes on Leslie Cox.

" '. . . *an old man known by some other name may still squint in the sun, and sniff, and revile his fate.'* Not bad! Same way *I* write," Chicken Collins said, his very tone renouncing the Gator Hook derelict in favor of this jaunty new identity. He rested the notes on his belly. "Yep," he said. "I heard Cox was seen down at Key West and another time in the river park there at Fort Myers. Then this Injun friend of mine who used to be a drunk up around Orlando told me that a feller of Cox's description had been holed up for years out at the Hook. I was curious so I went out there to look, never made it back." He resumed reading.

Lucius took the worn blue canvas chair. "And if you'd found him?"

Collins lowered the manuscript again. "I'd probably pretend I hadn't. Make a list or something," he added meanly.

"You've seen my list?"

"Rob Watson gave it to me."

"I was told Rob never received it. Anyway, it was supposed to be a secret."

"Only one who thought it was a secret was the damn fool who wrote those names down in the first place." He winked at Lucius, blowing smoke.

"And you're the one who showed it to Speck Daniels. That's how he learned about it."

Collins shrugged. One evening out at Gator Hook, noticing the name Crockett Daniels on the list, he'd called it to Speck's attention. "Just for fun, y'know."

"Speck think it was funny?"

"Nosir, he did not. Said you were lucky you never got your head blown off."

"I'd like that list back, Mr. Collins."

"It's not yours. Property of the late Robert B. Watson, who left it to yours truly." Rob Watson, he explained, had died the year before in the Young Men's Christian Association in Orlando. He had left instructions for cremation, and the YMCA had shipped the remains, together with a few clothes and some papers, to his cousin Arbie. He pointed at himself.

"Cousin Arbie, at your service." Asked how the YMCA had known where to send it, Collins scowled at the pointlessness of such a question, and Lucius let it go. "Rob never married?" he inquired. "Never had children?"

"Nope," said Collins, adding sourly, "Only mistake that feller never made."

For his arrival in Caxambas, the erstwhile Chicken had perked up his worn amorphous clothes with a bright red rag around his throat; Lucius had to admire this flare of color, this small gallantry. Despite his long hair and scraggy beard, Arbie Collins reminded him of his Collins cousins— black hair, fair skin, slight, wiry, and volatile. "Look," he said, "are we related in some way?"

"By marriage, I reckon. I'm kin to Rob on his Collins side." Raising the manuscript, he resumed his careless reading, dropping pages, creasing them, flicking ash on them, until finally Lucius stood up and crossed the deck and snapped his notes off the man's stomach, exposing the navel hair that sprouted between slack button holes of a soiled thin shirt of discolored plaid.

"I'm fussy about strangers rooting through my notes without permission—"

"Found 'em inside," Arbie explained cheerfully. "Look to me like notes for a damn whitewash. *Notes on the Family Skeleton!*—how's that for a title?" He sat up with a grunt, swung his broken boots onto the deck, and dragged his big loose weary carton within Lucius's reach. "Official Robert Watson archive," he announced. "Better read it, son. Might learn something."

Expecting no surprises, finding none, Lucius leafed politely through the carton. Dog-eared folders full of yellowed clippings mixed with scrawled notes copied from magazines and books—sensational exposés, inventions, lies, and brimstone editorials from the tabloids, dating all the way back to newspaper reports from October 1910—the usual "Bloody Watson" trash, of far less interest than the provenance of this collection.

Anticipating questions, Collins related how he'd helped Cousin Rob Watson sell his father's schooner and escape on a freighter out of Key West after Watson's murders back in 1901; he was the only relative, he said, with whom the grateful Rob had stayed in touch throughout his life.

"*Alleged* murders. Nobody was ever charged, far less convicted."

"*Never charged?!*" Collins winged his cigar butt at a swallow coursing the salt grass for mosquitoes. "Is that all that matters to L. Watson Fucking Collins, Ph.D.?!" The man's dark eyes glowed in repressed fury.

Lucius persisted. "Did Rob tell you what actually happened that day?"

"Of course. I know the whole damned story."

"Tell me," Lucius said, after a moment's hesitation which the other noticed.

"Maybe. I'll think about it." Arbie shifted, irritable. "That was kind of long ago."

Lucius set the urn on a white cloth on the small table inside, placing beside it a small pot of red geraniums grown on his cabin roof. He poured two whiskeys and they drank in silence, considering the writhings of the urn in the play of light and water from the creek. That this garish canister enclosed all that was left of handsome Rob filled Lucius with sadness. The family would have to be notified about his death but who would care?

"Rob came to find me a few years ago but I never saw him," he muttered finally. "I haven't laid eyes on my own brother since I was eleven."

Collins picked up the urn and turned it in his hands. "Well, you might not care to lay eyes on him now 'cause he don't look like much." He shifted his hands to the top and bottom of the canister and shook it. "Hear him rattling in there? People talk about ashes but it's mostly bits and pieces of brown bone, like busted dog biscuits." To prove it, he shook the urn again.

"Don't do that, dammit!" When Lucius took it and returned it to the table, Arbie Collins cackled. "He won't mind," he said. And Lucius said, "*I* mind. It's disrespectful."

In the next days, Arbie sorted his yellowed scraps. "I been updating Rob's archives, Professor," he might say, picking up one of Lucius's pipes and pointing the pipestem at its owner before clearing his throat and quoting from his clips. " 'Bad Man of the Islands.' 'Red-bearded Knife Artist.' How's *that* for data?" Slyly he would frown and harrumph, weighing his words in what he supposed was an academic manner. "Speaking strictly as an archivist, L. Watson, that man's beard was not what a real scholar would call red. It was more auburn, sir, more the color of dried blood."

"Color of dried blood, yes, indeed." The archivist's colleague frowned judiciously in turn. "Doubtless a consequence of his well-known habit of dipping his beard in the lifeblood of his victims, don't you agree, sir?"

"Precisely, sir. Point well taken, sir."

It was soon clear (though they had not spoken of it) that Arbie Collins had quit Gator Hook for good and made the barge his home. For the moment, this was agreeable to his host, who enjoyed his company and was waiting to be told Rob's account of the Tucker story.

Arbie Collins was infuriated by any perceived defense of Edgar Watson. In an attempt to soften his savage prejudice (based largely, it seemed, on what Rob must have told him at Key West), Lucius read him a passage from his biography describing the violent circumstances of young Edgar's upbringing in South Carolina.

> *According to his mother, Ellen Addison Watson, the boy had scavenged the family's food throughout the Civil War while receiving only rudimentary schooling. Even after the War, jobs had been scarce, child labor cheap, and the family poor and desperate. Her son had toiled from dawn to dark at the mercy of a dirt farmer's stick, an ordeal worsened by the return from the Civil War of his drunken distempered father.*

Lucius raised his gaze to see how his colleague was receiving this. Arbie glowered, silent as a coal, but for once he held his tongue. " 'Surely the dark temper of Edgefield District,' " the Professor resumed, " 'blighted the spirit of an unfortunate boy who had been but six when the War began and reached young manhood in the famine-haunted days of Reconstruction.' "

"Dammit, these are just excuses!" Bristle-browed, hoarse from cigarettes, beset by strangled coughs, Arbie rummaged up a letter clipped from the Florida History page of the *Miami Herald*: its author, D. M. Herlong, "a pioneer physician in this state, "had known Edgar Watson as a boy in Edgefield County, South Carolina, and had later become a Watson neighbor in Fort White, Florida. After some strenuous throat hydraulics topped off with a salutary spit, Collins launched forth on a dramatic reading, which he shortly abandoned, turning the clip over to Lucius.

> *He inherited his savage nature from his father, Elijah Watson, who was widely known as a fighter. In one of these fights he was given a knife wound that almost encircled one eye, and was known thereafter as "Ring-Eye Lige." At one time Elijah Watson was a warden at the state penitentiary. He married and two children were born to them, Edgar and*

*Minnie. The woman had to leave Watson on account of his brutality
and dissolute habits. She moved to Columbia County, Florida, where
she had relatives.*

Lucius read this to himself as Arbie, gleeful, watched his face. "Old stuff
like that probably won't interest serious historians like L. Watson Collins,
Ph.D., correct?"

"You think Herlong has these details right? I mean, 'Ring-Eye Lige'?"
Just saying his grandfather's name aloud made Lucius chuckle in astonishment: here was the first document of worth in Rob's ragtag "archive," the
first real clue to those early years which Papa had scarcely mentioned.
From the rest of Herlong's letter he was able to deduce that Granny Ellen
Watson and her two childen must have fled South Carolina not long after
the 1870 census, when Edgar was fifteen; if his drunken father had abused
his wife, it seemed reasonable to suppose that he'd beaten his son, too. The
Florida relative who took them in had been Great-Aunt Tabitha Watson,
who had accompanied her married daughter and her son-in-law to the
Fort White region a few years earlier. By the mid-eighties, when Herlong's
father left Edgefield and moved south to that Fort White community, Elijah
Watson back in South Carolina was already notorious as Ring-Eye Lige.
The Herlong reminiscence was wonderfully complementary to an account
of Watson's later life by Papa's friend Ted Smallwood which had turned up
in a recent history of Chokoloskee Bay. These two narratives from different
periods and regions were nowhere contradictory, therefore more dependable than any biographical material he had found to date.

Arbie reached for his clipping, grinning foxily when Lucius appeared
loath to give it up. "This Herlong feller knew all about Edgar Watson's
checkered past," Arbie assured him, "because Herlongs lived less than a
mile from Watsons in both Edgefield and Fort White. Got some Herlongs
in those Fort White woods even today." Arbie was transcendent with self-
satisfaction, all the more so when Lucius referred to him slyly as "a historian of record" and promised to acknowledge "the Arbie Collins Archive"
in his bibliography and notes.

Intrigued by the Herlong clipping, Lucius wondered if he should not return to Fort White for further research. His chances of finding significant
new material by poking through old county records seemed remote, but
after all these years of family silence, a kinsman ready to talk about Uncle

Edgar might be located, and even perhaps a few old-timers who knew something about the fate of Leslie Cox.

Unfortunately the university press would underwrite no further research: his teaching salary was negligible, he was nearly broke. However, Watt Dyer soon phoned to say that his client United Sugar Associates stood ready to underwrite the author's travel and would also sponsor a series of paid lectures to educate the public about Planter E. J. Watson, sugarcane pioneer, controversial frontier figure, and confidant to the late Governor Broward. And because U.S.A. had a powerful lobby in the statehouse, the attorney's politician clients could be prevailed upon to endorse the Watson land claim and perhaps the preservation of the Watson house as a state monument.

Although delighted, Lucius was aware of a recent news report that the U.S.A. corporation was notorious for the dreadful living conditions and near-slavery of its field workers and also that its massive use of chemical fertilizers was a serious threat to the future of the Everglades. Even so, as a reward to their "Big Sugar" campaign donors, another writer claimed, the federal government was abetting the state in its wasteful draining of the Glades for agriculture and development, including the construction of huge concrete canals to shunt away into the sea the pristine water flowing gradually south from Lake Okeechobee as the Shark River watershed.

"Oh for God's sake!" Dyer's derisive mirth had a hard edge of anger. "Can't we leave all that negative stuff to those left-wing whiners in the papers?" Things were moving! he said. Court hearings on the Watson claim were scheduled for the following week at Homestead, and the first of several public events designed to organize local support would be sponsored by the Historical Society at Naples, which would offer an evening with the distinguished historian Professor L. Watson Collins.

"That name won't work in Naples. Sorry," Lucius said. "Too many people know me on this coast."

Emitting that curious hard bark, Dyer simply hung up, leaving the question unresolved.

MURDER IN THE INDIAN COUNTRY

Rob Watson's carton contained notes on his long-ago wanderings to Arkansas and Oklahoma to investigate what lay behind the legend of his father's career in the Indian Nations. From these, Lucius put together a brief survey of that obscure period in his subject's life.

Edgar Watson fled Fort White in north Florida in late 1886 or early 1887 under circumstances still disputed in that community. Although there is no clear record of his movements, it appears that in the spring and summer of 1887, he sharecropped in Franklin County, Arkansas, continuing westward after the crop was in and settling near Whitefield, in the Indian Territory, in early January of 1888.

The period in Mr. Watson's life between January 1888 and March 1889 is relatively well documented, due to the part he was alleged to have played in the death (on February 3, 1889) of Mrs. Maybelle Shirley Reed, whose multicolored legend as Belle Starr, Queen of the Outlaws, has generated endless articles and books, poems, plays, and films, to the present day.

Hell on the Border, a grim compendium of Indian Country malfeasance published in 1895, was the first book to suggest that Belle Starr's slayer was a man named Watson; this name appears in the closing pages of most of her numerous biographies, despite widespread dispute as to her real slayer's identity. Was the culprit one of those shadowy assassins who intervene in famous destinies only to vanish in the long echo of history? Or would the same man reappear as the notorious desperado shot down by his neighbors on the coast of southwest Florida in 1910?

In the federal archives at Fort Worth, Texas, is a lengthy transcript of the hearings held in U.S. Court at Fort Smith, Arkansas, in late February and early March of 1889, to determine if evidence of his guilt was sufficient to bring one "Edgar A. Watson" before a grand jury on a murder charge. From this transcript, together with reports from the local newspapers and some speculative testimony winnowed from the literature on the life and death of Maybelle Shirley Reed, one may assume that the "E. A. Watson" accused in Oklahoma was none other than the "E. J. Watson" gunned down in Florida two decades later. Whether or not he was guilty of Belle Starr's death may never be known, but it should be noted that many if not most of her acquaintances disliked the victim and that almost as many were suspected of her death by her various authors.

What can we conclude about his years on the frontier apart from the widespread allegation that Watson was "the Man Who Killed Belle Starr"? At least three of Mrs. Starr's biographers declare that after his departure from Oklahoma, Watson was convicted of horse theft in Arkansas and sentenced to fifteen years in the penitentiary and that he was killed while resisting capture after an escape. (Here as elsewhere they follow the lead of Hell on the Border, *published within six years of Belle Starr's death and considerably more accurate than many of the subsequent accounts, despite its premature report of Watson's end.)*

Watson's destination after his escape from the Arkansas penitentiary remains unknown, though he later related that he headed west to Oregon, where he was set upon by enemies in a night raid on his cabin. Obliged to take a life, possibly two, he fled back east. Another account states that on his way to Oklahoma, Ed Watson passed through Georgia, where he killed three men in a fracas. Like the many false rumors from South Carolina and Florida, these seem to be "tall tales" unsupported by separate testimony or even anecdotes within the family.

Ed Watson reappears in Florida in the early nineties, in a shooting at Arcadia in DeSoto County in which, by his own account, he slew a "bad actor" named Quinn Bass. In the rough frontier justice of that region, our subject was permitted to pay his way out of his difficulties, according to one of Belle Starr's hagiographers, who asserts that "a mob stormed the jail, determined to have Watson, but the sheriff beat them off." In a different account, outlaws Watson and Bass disputed the spoils of a marauding expedition whereupon Bass was shot dead through the neck.

Though E. J. Watson (as a fugitive, he appears to have changed his middle initial) is rarely identified as an outlaw, it should be noted that in the nineties, range wars, cattle rustling, and general mayhem were rife in De Soto County, and gunmen and bushwhackers from the West found steady work. It is also true that Watson turned up at Chokoloskee Bay not long thereafter with enough cash to buy a schooner, despite his reported recompense to the Bass family for the loss of Quinn. Considering that he was penniless when sent to the penitentiary and without known income or employment after his escape, one can only speculate where that cash might have come from.

In his first years in southwest Florida, Mr. Watson assaulted Adolphus Santini of Chokoloskee in an altercation in a Key West auction house; this knife attack, which did not prove fatal, was also taken care of

with a money settlement considered very substantial for that period.
Again, our subject's source of funds after long years as a fugitive remains
mysterious. One cannot dismiss the possibility that from the time of his
prison escape in Arkansas until he took refuge in the Ten Thousand
Islands, E. J. Watson made his living as an outlaw.

BLACK MOON MIRRORS

In the next days, inviting his guest along on research visits to Fort White,
Fort Myers, perhaps Chatham Bend, Lucius was taken aback by the vehemence of Arbie's refusal. "To hell with that damned place!" he yelled in regard to Chatham Bend. "Burn it to the ground, burn that damned stain
out!" When Lucius stared at him, he yelled some more. "Don't look at *me*!
Rob told me about that bloodstain on the floor—*black* blood, he told me!
Said the only way to get it out was *burn* it out!"

Arbie had tried to dissuade Lucius from making these research expeditions, but in the end, he decided to go along. Was this curiosity about his
Collins kinsmen in Fort White or real interest in his new role as researcher?
Unwillingness to be left behind on a remote salt creek or—conceivably—
the fun of his host's company? For even their bickering and hard teasing was
good fun. Lucius concluded it was all of these. "Free food," grumped Arbie.

Driving north to Lake City, where Columbia County records might be
found, Arbie picked through Lucius's research notes, fuming crossly over
phrases. Flicking the pages with nicotined fingers, he rolled his eyes and
whistled in derision—to no avail, since Lucius ignored his provocations,
scanning the citrus orchards and broad cattle country that replaced the
subtropical growth of the lower peninsula at the Peace River.

" 'E. J. Watson was known from Tampa to Key West as the most ambitious
and innovative farmer who ever lived in the Ten Thousand Islands'—*that's* what
he's known for?" Arbie slapped the notes down on his knees. His eyes glittered and his tongue flew, hell-bent on outrage. His long black hair and
rakish sideburns with their dangerous swerve toward the corners of his
mouth gave this taut, irascible man the wild aspect of a peregrine, Lucius
noticed. At the same time, he was aware of something brittle, something
fractured; he was careful not to feed the instability that flickered like heat
lightning in Collins's eyes.

Perversely then—unwillingly amused by his own indignation—Arbie let a boyish smile suffuse his face, but when Lucius smiled with him, he scowled at once, as if his privacy had been invaded. "L. Watson Collins, P-H-D!" he jeered, fending off any sign of his host's affection. Behind his abrasiveness, Lucius guessed, was self-dislike, or even detestation of a man who, by his own description, was nothing but "a damn-fool drunk and life-long drifter." From the deep pallor, wary eyes, and side-of-the-mouth speech, Lucius was coming to suspect that a good part of Arbie's life had been spent in prison, which might explain why he had holed up for so long at Gator Hook.

"If this new Everglades park comes through," Lucius mused, "our attorney Watt Dyer—"

"Watson Dyer? What's that guy want with you?"

"You know him?"

"Speck caretakes for him at Chatham Bend. Speck can tell you all about that skunk. Big real estate lawyer, made a killing on the land boom. Represents the bunch that's trying to stop that park."

"Can't be. Not if he's trying to help the Watson claim."

"Probably working both sides of the street like all the rest of 'em."

"Don't you trust *anybody*? Dyer thinks we might even petition for maintenance of the Watson place as a historic monument."

Arbie stiffened like a dog on point, and his burnsides fairly bristled. "Historic monument? How about a *murder* monument? First monument to bloody murder in the whole U.S. and A.! Massacre museum! Gobbet bar! Nice ketchup specialties! Red rubber skeletons!" Unable to maintain the huff and pomp of indignation, Arbie hooted, but within moments he was scowling again. "You really hope to make that house a monument to Pioneer Ed? That's already a monument to dark and bloody deeds? Dammit, I'm not joking!" He was pointing his finger into Lucius's face. "Have you ever *seen* somebody murdered? And *heard* it, oh my God, and *smelled* it? It's terrible and scary. I know what I'm talking about. You don't. That's why you can write about a killer as some kind of hero."

That German soldier with his pants down. Yes, I have seen somebody murdered. Yes. I murdered him.

Arbie had tossed the notes onto the dashboard. Lucius swerved the old car onto the shoulder as a loose page wafted out the window. He jumped out and chased his paper down as Arbie poked his head out. "You're twisting the evidence to make it look like your father never hurt a fly! I know how much you loved him, Lucius, and I'm sorry, but there's no way you can write your way around a murderer!"

Out of breath, Lucius got back behind the wheel. "Don't toss my work around like that, all right?"

That Arbie had witnessed violent death was plain, yet Lucius did not feel he could question him about his past, not yet. Already this tightly wound man had turned away from him, taking refuge in a few loose notes on Lucius's discussions with the attorney. "By the time you boys get done with Planter Ed," he said, "folks'll roll their eyes to the high heavens thanking their Merciful Redeemer for that kindly farmer whose magical seed cane put our sovereign state of Florida where she's at today! Yessir, old-timers all over the state, reading this stuff, will repent all their mean tales about Bloody Ed. *So maybe Ed was a little rough around the edges, but so was Ol' Hickory Andy Jackson, right? First U.S. president to hail from the backcountry! First of our good ol' redneck breed that made this country great!*"

They spent that evening at a tourist camp on the Withlacoochee. While Arbie slept off his long day, Lucius drank his bourbon in the shadow of the porch, contemplating the reflections of the giant cypress in the still moon water of the swamp. The gallinule's eerie whistling, the ancient hootings of barred owls in duet, the horn notes of limpkins and far sandhill cranes from beyond the moss-draped walls, were primordial rumorings as quintessentially in place as the lichens and shelf fungi fastened to the hoary bark of the great trees. And he considered how the Watson children, and especially the sons, had been bent by the great weight of the dead father—pale saplings yearning for the light twisting up and around the fallen tree, drawing last minerals from the punky wood and straining toward the sun even as the huge log crumbles in a feast for beetles.

From bare spring twilight came the ringing call of a Carolina wren, and the urgency of its existence on the earth filled him with restlessness. He could not dispel, or not entirely, Arbie's denunciations of his father nor his dread that if those charges were correct, he had wandered far from his own life in a useless search for vindication of a man whose reputation was beyond redemption.

"Morbidly obsessive"—that's what Eddie called him. Was it obsession because his father's life enthralled him far more than his own? The ongoing search for the "truth" of E. J. Watson that provided a dim purpose to his days—was that to be his recompense for a life of solitude and slow diminishment? With the death last year of Mr. Summerlin, he had thought with longing about young Widow Nell: would she ever be open to him again? Would he always be too late?

The scent of charcoal in his whiskey evoked the warm and woody smells of Papa's fine cigars. Rueful, he toasted the great emptiness and silence all around. *Papa? I miss you,*

Startled by those words spoken aloud, feeling himself observed, Lucius turned to confront the scowling visage in the cabin window. Arbie Collins had watched him talking to himself, watched him raise his empty glass to the black moon mirrors.

IN COLUMBIA COUNTY

In the early days of the Florida frontier, what was now Lake City was a piney-woods outpost known as Alligator Town, after the "Alligator Chieftain," Halpatter Tustenuggee, Lucius told Arbie, and Tustenuggee was the name of the old Methodist community founded by their Collins kin, who had fought the Indians as pioneers. "And?" Arbie said. After a long road journey of three days, Arbie had grown so irritable that Lucius was sorry he'd encouraged him to come. They took a room at a traveler's inn at the edge of town.

Over the telephone, a wary Julian Collins welcomed "Cousin Lucius" back to Columbia County, but when Lucius mentioned the purpose of his visit, his kinsman informed him that Uncle Edgar remained a forbidden topic in the family. Trying to soften his own stiffness with a nervous laugh, Julian added, "I guess he's what the old folks call a 'shadow cousin.' "

"A shadow cousin? Julian, I'm his son—"

"So's Cousin Ed. You've never discussed this with your brother?"

"Eddie was living here back then. Went along with your family on that vow of silence. Wouldn't talk about Papa even to me or to my sister."

"Best for everybody."

"But there's so much I need to know. My father lived and farmed here, met all three of his wives and had four of his six children in this county.

Can't we discuss his domestic life, at least? His farm? I want his biography to be accurate—"

"Our family can't help you, I'm afraid."

"Can't or won't?" Lucius said, exasperated.

"Good day, Cousin Lucius. Enjoy your stay."

"Wait, Julian. Listen   " But Julian Collins had hung up.

Arriving early at the library next morning, they peered into the empty rooms through bare windows that skewed their reflection: a lanky figure in the worn green corduroy jacket of the old-fashioned academic and a bearded drifter in faded red baseball cap and olive army coat much too heavy for this warming day.

Inside, they waited at a shiny maple table while the librarian fetched the documents requested. Mr. A. Collins, archivist, impatient at the delay, reared around like an inchworm every few moments to stare after her, such was his zeal to begin a rigorous inspection of the material. As it turned out, the librarian had tarried to ring up her friend the features editor at the newspaper, who came speedily to meet the southwest Florida historian, Professor Collins. Together, these ladies managed to persuade him that a newspaper interview might unearth one or two informants. Still irked by Julian Collins's attitude (and ignoring the eye-rolling of his colleague), Lucius emphasized that Planter Watson had been a pioneer entrepreneur and beloved family man—"I beg your pardon? *No*, ma'am! He was acquitted! He was not some common criminal!"—upon which Arbie snorted, kicked his chair back, rose, and left.

Lucius spent that soft spring morning ransacking the census records for the names mentioned by Herlong. Edgar Watson was missing from the 1900 census for Columbia County, having returned here from south Florida in early 1901: the rest of the Watson-Collins clan were present as were two households of Tolens, the clan detested by his father. However, the several Cox households listed no Leslie, or not under that name—very disappointing, since the solution of the mystery around this man was critical to the biography. If Cox was alive, had he ever returned to this county? Was he a shadow cousin, too?

In the afternoon, at the librarian's suggestion, he wandered down old grass-grown sidewalks to the ends of narrow lanes where the giant oaks had not been cleared nor the street paved, where the last of the old houses greened and sagged beneath sad Southern trees, arriving at last at Oak Lawn Cemetery. Here on thin and weary grass amidst black-lichened stones tended by somnolent gravediggers and faded robins stood a memorial to those brave boys of the Confederacy who died at Olustee, to the east, in a long-forgotten victory over Union troops.

Near the war memorial, an iron fence enclosed three tombstones tilted by the oak roots:

TABITHA WATSON, 1813–1905

LAURA WATSON TOLEN, 1830–1894

SAMUEL TOLEN, 1858–1907

The Watson headstones were tall, narrow, and austere, as Lucius imagined these Episcopalian women might have been. Great-Aunt Tabitha had survived her daughter by a decade, tussling along into her nineties: her haughty monument held no cautionary message for those left behind. Her daughter's stone bore the terse inscription *We Have Parted*, while Tolen's marker, squatted low in attendance on the ladies, read *Gone But Not Forgotten*—not forgotten by whom, Lucius wondered, since to judge from the 1900 census, his wife had been barren and both women had preceded him into this earth. Samuel Tolen had been born almost thirty years after his bride, and Lucius wondered if this discrepancy in age had not been a catalyst in the fatal family feud: had Greedy Sam infuriated Dangerous Edgar by marrying Aging Laura for her Watson property? Had the Tolens ordered Sam's inscription as a warning to his killer that this business wasn't finished? In this silent place, he could envision Sam Tolen's embittered brothers in stiff ill-fitting black suits: did they already suspect blue-eyed Edgar Watson, standing there expressionless among the mourners?

At the newspaper, his classified notice requesting information on E. J. Watson had failed to smoke out a response from the Collins family. However, there was a small note in smudged pencil:

Sir: I suppose I am one of the few people still living in this area that knew
Edgar Watson, having been raised in the same community near Fort
White. I was too small to play on the old Tolen Team our country baseball
club. I thought Leslie Cox was the greatest pitcher in the world. My
brother Brooks was the catcher. They played such teams as Fort White
and High Springs and most always won if Leslie was pitching. The Coxs
were our friends until the trouble started.

Grover Kinard

Leslie Cox! At last! Not Leslie Cox, Cold-blooded Killer, but Leslie Cox, Greatest Pitcher in the World, whiffling fastballs past thunderstruck yokels on bygone summer afternoons in those distant days before World War I when every town across the country had a sandlot ball club, when Honus Wagner, Cy Young, Ty Cobb, Smoky Joe Wood were the nation's heroes— Leslie Cox, grimy pockets stuffed with chewing gum, jackknife, and one-penny nails, scaring more batters than Iron Man Joe McGinnity himself. The broken-voiced hoarse yells of boys and shrills of girls at each crack of the bat, all oblivious of the workings of the brain behind this young pitcher's squinted eyes, in the shadow of the small-brimmed cap that was all most country teams afforded in the way of uniform.

Lucius telephoned Mr. Kinard at once, arranging a visit for two days hence.

The Columbia County Courthouse, where he went next morning, was a fat pink building overlooking the town pond, called Lake De Soto in commemoration of the great conquistador who had clanked and swatted through these woods on the hard way of empire. In the county clerk's office he inquired about arrest records and court transcripts pertaining to an E. J. Watson, accused of murdering one Samuel Tolen about 1907. Though he mentioned quickly that this was a historic case that had involved Governor Broward, their sighs protested that official staff had more important matters to attend to than digging out old dusty ledgers and disintegrating dockets.

The county clerk, flushed from an inner office, was a quick little man, thin-haired and squeaky. "Yessir? What can I do you for today?" Told what the gentleman was seeking, he titillated his staff by winking when he said, "Excuse me, girls, while I go peruse them terrible murders we got stored up for our perusal outside the gentleman's toilet in the basement." When eventually he reappeared, he whisked from behind his back a thick file packet stuffed with yellowed papers, presenting it with a small bow and flourish. "We got us a E. J., all right, but the victim was Mr. *D. M.* Tolen, and it ain't nineteen ought seven, it's ought eight. That close enough?"

On a public bench out in the hall, Lucius entered the old pages with dread and elation. Though the neighbor cited in that Herlong clipping had specified Sam Tolen, the file concerned the murder less than a year later of Sam's younger brother Mike. Furthermore, E. J. Watson had a codefendant, a black man named Frank Reese.

He scribbled notes. In the year previous, the circuit court had indicted Reese for the murder of S. Tolen on the basis of a D. M. Tolen affidavit. Why had Mike Tolen accused Reese, not Cox or Watson? Why had he never heard about this man indicted in both Tolen killings? Were black men so bereft of status in those Jim Crow days that even Negro murder suspects went unmentioned?

Another mystery: on April 10 of 1908, based on the coroner's inquest in late March, Julian and Willie Collins had been arrested as "accessories after the fact in the murder of D. M. Tolen." Had his cousins provided testimony that led to the indictment of his father?

All courtroom testimony had apparently been sealed, but a few scraps from a grand jury hearing in Lake City on April 27 accompanied the court documents. Most intriguing was a cross-examination of one Jasper Cox, who testified on behalf of the defendants. In helping the defense attorney establish the fact that no fair trial could be held in Columbia County, this witness declared that on March 26, three days after the murder of Mike Tolen, he had been approached at the courthouse by a jury member who told him he "was helping to get up a mob to get these men and asked if I didn't want to assist them, and I told him it was out of my line of business."

Q. These defendants here are under indictment for killing Mike Tolen, are they not?
A. Yes.

Q. And your nephew is under indictment for killing the other one, the brother of Mike Tolen?

A. Yes.

Q. There was no charge against Leslie Cox at that time—

A. No, sir.

This exchange—the only mention of Jasper's nephew in the thick packet—established that Leslie Cox, not Watson, had been arrested for Sam Tolen's murder, and Watson, not Cox, for the murder of Mike Tolen the following year.

Included in the sprawling file were contemporary clippings.

MIKE TOLEN MURDERED ON FARM

> LAKE CITY, MARCH 23. Mike Tolen, a prominent farmer residing between Lake City and Fort White, was murdered by unknown parties on his farm about 8 o'clock this morning.
>
> News of the murder was immediately brought to the city and a posse, headed by bloodhounds, were soon off to the scene. The authorities suspect certain parties of the murder and it is believed that arrests will be made tonight and the prisoners brought to this city. Sam Tolen, a brother of the dead man, was murdered by unknown parties last summer. The trouble is the outcome of a family feud.
>
> —*Jacksonville Times-Union*, March 24, 1908

> The special term of the Circuit Court called for Madison County convened Monday for the trial of a murder case on change of venue from Columbia County, the defendant being E. J. Watson, a white man, and Frank Reese, a negro, indicted for the murder of one Tolen, white, in Columbia County. The case is one which excited the people of Columbia greatly, all the parties concerned being prominent.

> The defendant Watson is a man of fine appearance
> and his face betokens intelligence in an unusual degree.
> That a determined fight will be made to establish the in-
> nocence of the defendants is evidenced by the imposing
> array of lawyers employed in their behalf. At this writing
> a jury is being chosen.
>
> —*Madison Enterprise-Recorder,* December 12, 1908

On December 19, the jury found the defendants not guilty and they were discharged.

Lucius telephoned Watson Dyer, who was in the state capital on official business but had asked to be kept posted. He was not in the least curious about Frank Reese. "All that matters is, E. J. Watson was found innocent. 'Innocent until proven guilty'—that's the American way."

"I suppose so. At least when the accused is the right color."

Ignoring this quibble, Dyer said, "And if he was proved innocent of killing Samuel Tolen, he may well be innocent of other allegations. In our book we can say—"

Irritated by that "our book" even before he'd figured out what was objectionable, Lucius interrupted sharply, "Let me repeat. My father was charged with killing D. M. Tolen. Mike. The man indicted for the murder of Sam Tolen was Leslie Cox."

"Is that a fact?" Surprise rose slowly in Dyer's voice like the first thick bubble in a pot of boiling grits.

"It's possible, of course, that both were involved in both those murders."

"Or that neither killed either. There's always that nigger, right?" Dyer said he could not talk now, being late for an appointment at the governor's office. He would be driving south tomorrow and would stop by Lake City for consultation and an early supper.

The interview with L. Watson Collins, Ph.D., in the newspaper next morning attributed to Professor Collins precisely what he had denied—in effect, the reporter's notion that E. J. Watson, "formerly of this county," had been the mass murderer of his era.

Lucius rushed to the newspaper office to demand a retraction, knowing it would do no good. Any hope of cooperation from his cousins had been blighted. But wonderfully, feckless reportage had pierced Collins defenses where earnest entreaty had failed. A note hand-delivered to the newspaper stiffly disputed the visitor's observations and opinions.

> *Sir: It is very doubtful that you spoke to the Collins family because those who knew of Uncle Edgar are of an older era when family business was just that and was not told to strangers. I am writing to tell you that I greatly resent Uncle Edgar being compared to a mass murderer. If you've done any research at all, you would know that my uncle could be a very considerate and courteous neighbor. . . .*

Indignant that old family detritus had been stirred into view like leaf rot from the bottom of a well, a Collins had broken all those years of silence. What's more, Miss Ellen Collins did not hang up on him when he telephoned to apologize, so determined was she to chastise him. "Is Collins your real name? Or are you passing yourself off as kin just to snoop out scurrilous information?"

Taken aback, he felt a start of panic. "I *am* a relative," he said. Still gun-shy from Julian's rejection, desperate not to lose this precious chance, he withheld his real name, awaiting a better moment. "And I've been talking to another relative," he added hastily, lest the conversation lapse. "Mr. Arbie Collins."

The anticipated outcry—*Cousin Arbie!?*—was not forthcoming. "R. B., you say?" If this R. B. was a bona fide Collins, he was a distant one indeed, her tone implied. "I don't suppose you mean R. B. *Watson*? Whose *mother* was a Collins?"

"Oh Lord, I'd forgotten that! Do you recall her name?"

His eagerness kept his flapping kite aloft: Ellen Collins was still there.

"Oh heck, let me think back." She'd been shown the gravestone as a child. As a second cousin, Rob Watson's mother had been buried in New Bethel churchyard, south of Lake City, not in the family cemetery at Tustenuggee near Fort White. "There's still a few of us back in those woods," she sighed, "on our old land grant or what's left of it. Uncle Edgar lived there, too." Then she snapped, "I've talked too much already," and hung up. Shortly she rang back: if he was really a history professor, she had decided, he should know the truth. If he promised that Julian Collins in Lake City and Cousin Ed Watson in Fort Myers would never hear about it— and on the condition that he made no mention of "that Tolen business"— the family in Fort White would meet with him the following day. "I'll be there, too," she warned.

At the billiards emporium and pool hall, Lucius found Arbie showing off for a lacquered female of uncertain age who sat with one hip cocked on the corner of the table, her cerise bootie dangling and twitching like a fish lure—the only whore in town, Lucius suspected. The archivist turned pool shark, giving Lucius a cool nod, racked his balls and broke the rack with a ferocious shot that left him square behind the eight ball. "Damn fool shot his own dog," he muttered, walking around the table to inspect the catastrophe from another angle. "Story of my life."

WATSON DYER

Watson Dyer, seated squarely in the hotel lobby, was a heavyset man but not a fat one, clad in the big suit and damp white shirt favored by politicians. Lucius had only a dim memory of the sullen dark-haired boy at Chatham Bend, yet the adult manifestation was unmistakable. His wellgreased hair was slicked back from the high forehead of a moonish face, and white crescents beneath the pupils made his pale blue eyes seem to protrude, though they did not: lacking depth, they appeared to be inset into the skin like stones in hide. Strong brows were hooked down at the corners, hooding those eyes, and the left eyebrow but not the right was lifted quizzically as if in expectation that whoever stood in his way must now get out of it.

"Mr. Dyer? Lucius Watson. And Mr. Arbie Collins."

Creasing his newspaper, Dyer considered this information, as if how such people were to be addressed was for W. Dyer to decide. His eyes seemed to be closing slowly, as in turtles, and when they opened once again, Lucius noticed a rim of darker blue on the pale pupils, and also a delicate shiver on the skin surface around the mouth, as if this man were fairly trembling with inner rage. When Dyer grinned, which he did rarely and as if by accident, those delicate shivers played like mad under his nose.

"So you're still calling yourself Watson." Mustering the meaty good-guy grin of the corporate executive, Watt Dyer pushed himself onto his feet in a waft of shaving lotion, extending a well-manicured hard hand.

"That's his name," Arbie said sharply. Though Arbie had more or less shaved for the occasion, Dyer's hairline was so crisp that the other, by contrast, appeared disheveled; his red neckerchief, lacking its usual flair, made him look raffish, even seedy.

Dyer appraised him. "R. B. Collins, you say?" He took Lucius's elbow and guided him toward the dining room, letting the disgruntled Arbie fall in behind. "Let's get things straight," said Dyer. "The noted historian I'm sponsoring at Naples—the *objective authority* my sugar folks wish to sponsor—is Professor L. Watson Collins, author of *A History of Southwest Florida*." He strode a ways while that sank in, then summoned Arbie alongside. "Now, boys, I ask you," he complained, "if a lecture on a controversial figure by a published Florida historian wouldn't be more . . . *credible?* Than a lecture by his own son? Avoid any suspicion that our author might be . . . *prejudiced?*"

"Our author?" Arbie sneered. "You don't even know him."

"I know all about him," Dyer said in a soft voice, leaning in close for a long moment to peer through Arbie's eyes into his brain, "and all about you, too, sir. Routine background check," he added, raising both palms to quell Arbie's protest. "Standard business practice. Before underwriting a project, you first investigate the background of all participating individuals."

As for the land claim, Dyer explained that what he required were affidavits from "the Watson boys," endorsing their father's title claim to the Chatham property. Meanwhile, the newspaper would cover the Naples meeting where Professor Collins would point out the complete absence of hard evidence that E. J. Watson had ever committed murder. "Next, we encourage petitions to save the historic frontier home of the man who brought the sugarcane industry to Florida—"

"Oh, Lord." Lucius shook his head. "I never claimed that."

"He won't be a party to some con game!" Arbie spat this impudence into Dyer's face. Those eyes that considered Arbie reminded Lucius of a bear hunt with his father as a boy—the morose animal biding its time until the sudden swipe of long curved claws gutted the dog and left it whimpering, confused by the waning of its life.

Dyer said in an intense cold voice, "Tell me, sir, what is it that you call yourself? *R. B.?*"

"None of your damned business."

"Incorrect, sir. It is very much my business." Controlling his anger, Dyer frowned at his watch and whacked his leg hard with his newspaper, startling the hostess; she beckoned them inside. Tossing the paper onto the spittoon for someone else to deal with, Dyer strode ahead.

At the table, Lucius produced his synopsis of Arbie's notes on the Belle Starr case. Dyer skimmed the entire document while the waitress stood there awaiting their order with poised pencil; he sat hunched forward over the table, mantling the papers like a raptor. "A hearing in Arkansas federal court. No indictment. Won't hurt us a bit." He slipped the document into his briefcase. "All the same, we have to scrutinize any material in our book that might cast a bad light on our subject."

Arbie sat arms folded on his chest as if trying to clamp down on chronic twitches. In a silence, he demanded, "What's in this thing for you?"

"I mean, it must be a lot of work," Lucius added tactfully. Though annoyed again by that "our book," he was more annoyed that Arbie was asking questions he should have asked himself.

"Not a blessed thing." Dyer sat back in his chair to beckon the waitress. "Call it nostalgia for the old family place, call it my sense of fair play." He spiked the next question before Arbie could ask it. "No fee, no commission. The family won't owe me one red cent."

"Well, thank you! That calls for a drink." Lucius waved the waitress to the table.

"No liquor served here," Dyer said with satisfaction. "Fine old-fashioned fundamentalist family. *'God is our Senior Partner'*—got that right there on the menu." He smiled at the bill of fare. "The cheapest dinners are the best. Deep-fried chicken, deep-fried catfish, crispy and golden—they do it up real nice."

"Crispy and golden it is," Lucius muttered, cross about his drink. But just as the waitress fluttered in, Arbie stood up. When Dyer said equably, "Might's well get your order in," he stopped short, cocking his head. "You talking to me?" The attorney nodded. That Watt Dyer was so calm in the teeth of the other's unreasonable hostility was impressive, Lucius thought, and a little scary. "Make mine the Cheap Golden Dinner," Arbie told the waitress. He moved away among the diners, shoulders strangely high and stiff as if set to ward off a blow.

Lighting a cigar, Dyer shuffled through more pages. "You establish here that Cox was responsible for those last murders. Unlike Cox, E. J. Watson was a solid citizen. . . ."

"Yes, in his way—"

"You doubt that? You don't mean what you say here?" He snapped open a page and read aloud: 'The great majority of these Watson tales are rumors unsupported by real evidence.' In all your interviews, all your research, you never learned of a single witness to even one of his alleged murders, isn't that correct?"

"All true. But it's not so simple—" Lucius stopped because Arbie had come back. "Hell *yes*, there was a witness," he told Dyer. "His own son."

Dyer watched Arbie produce a pint bottle and dose two water glasses under the table. "I understand from the Professor's notes," he began quietly, "that you claim to have encountered Robert B. Watson at Key West when Robert B. Watson turned up there with his father's schooner?" He paused until Arbie assented. "And you now assert that Robert Watson told you some wild story about how his father murdered somebody named Tucker?"

"Wild story? Hell, no—"

"And you further assert that you aided and abetted Robert B. Watson in the illegal sale of his father's stolen ship and his flight from Key West on a steamer?" Dyer fired his questions at increasing speed, maintaining a dangerous, neutral tone. "Is *that* your story, sir?"

Lucius protested, "Hold on, Dyer—"

"Is that or is that not your story? Yes or no?"

"You calling me a liar, mister?"

"Not yet." Dyer wrote some notes. "And after Robert B. Watson had escaped, you spread his wild tale about the alleged murder of these Tucker people. Is *that* correct?"

Arbie stood up in disgust and left the room.

"Why all this lawyerly bullying?" Lucius demanded. "What reason do you have to doubt his story?"

"None." Dyer squashed out his cigar. "I have no reason to accept it, either. Anyway, hearsay evidence is worthless. So if, as you say, there were no known witnesses to the other alleged killings, then it's plausible that E. J. Watson never killed *any*body, isn't that true?"

Though Lucius had made this argument himself, hearing it from this man's mouth seemed to cast doubt on it. "It's conceivable, I guess."

"It's conceivable, you guess. Well, that is how we shall argue if the Park Service maintains that E. J. Watson's land claim should be forfeit or invalid because of a criminal record or whatever. And I hope that no Watson nor any Watson relative"—he peered at the door through which Arbie had gone—"will contest our argument. Should that occur," he warned after a pause, cementing his points as neatly and firmly as bricks, "then the Watson house which was to stand as a monument to your father's pioneering achievement will receive no further protection from the courts and will almost certainly be condemned and destroyed."

Dyer spread his napkin as his food arrived. "I have a caretaker watching the place. I'll file for an injunction against its destruction first thing next week," he said, over a raised forkful of golden chicken. He spoke no more until he had finished eating, after which he locked his briefcase and stood up, leaving Lucius to pay the bill. He was still "on the road," he said, "taking care of business," but in two days he'd be headed home.

"Where the heart is," Lucius said, unable to imagine a Mrs. Dyer and the kiddies.

"Most good Americans have faith in that," the attorney warned him. However, it was true that he had no wife or children. He didn't lead that sort of life, he said.

Lucius found Arbie hunched near comatose in the car, in his lap his small flask of corn whiskey: Okefenokee Moon 100 Proof. Guaranteed Less Than Thirty Days of Age. A rivulet of saliva, descending from a cleft in his grizzled chin, darkened his neckerchief. Lucius helped himself to a jolt of Arbie's rotgut, then urged him erect and guided him to their room. " 'Routine background check!' " Arbie bitched as he fell back on the bed. " 'Participating individuals!' " When Lucius suggested that Dyer might be bluffing, Arbie squinted at him. "You think that sonofabitch is bluffing?" And Lucius said, "No, I don't."

"He's bad news," said Arbie. "Stay away from him."

Next morning, Arbie lay so still in bed that Lucius was afraid to awaken him in case he couldn't: he was loath to touch him. His neck was arched and the parched mouth stretched too wide; his bloodless lips were dry on dry small teeth. With his dry hair, he looked as flat and scanty as a run-over rabbit on a summer highway.

The cadaver sucked up breath and coughed. One eye sagged open, contemplating Lucius, as a spavined hand went palpitating toward the cigarette pack on the bedside table. Lighting up, he growled in phlegmy tones that he had better things to do than waste a day with some gabby old-timer.

ANN MARY COLLINS WATSON

New Bethel Church, just off the main road on the way south, had been "built of heart pine back in 1854 and was solid as ever," said the old sexton in the churchyard gate, shielding his eyes to admire this house of God in the fresh morning light. "Watson? Was she a Collins? Come in here back in the eighties?" He pointed. "You'll find her over yonder."

Lucius hunted the old rows until a flit of sparrows drew his eye to a lone juniper; half hidden by that tree was a tilted headstone with eroded lettering crusted by black lichens. He knelt on the sparse grass to piece it out.

ANN MARY WATSON
WIFE OF E. A. WATSON
AND DAUGHTER OF
W. C. AND SARAH COLLINS
BORN APRIL 16, 1862
DIED AT HER HOME IN
COLUMBIA CO. FLORIDA
SEPTEMBER 13, 1879

Ann Mary, dead at seventeen on that unlucky thirteenth of September. Her headstone was a precious record, all the more so because particulars engraved in stone could be depended on. This one provided not only the name and dates of Papa's first wife but the earliest record of his original initials Lucius had come across. That middle *A* was still appearing ten years later on Arbie's court transcripts relating to Papa's stay in the Indian Nations; subsequently he had changed it to J, presumably to obscure his identity as a fugitive.

THE DEACON

Turning off the old Fort White road, Lucius followed Grover Kinard's directions into low dust-filmed woods ("alive with redskins," according to an 1838 report). At the specified address, he was shown inside by a bespectacled man attired in black trousers, cream-colored jacket, and open-collared shirt. Deacon Grover G. Kinard bade him no welcome and scarcely troubled to introduce him to his wife, a pretty-pink person sitting primly on the front room sofa in a bower of artificial flowers and silver-framed photos of smiling offspring seated with their own smiling offspring; she was listening to a sermon on her radio. "That there's Oriole," said the Deacon, passing by without a glance, and Oriole Kinard fluttered timid fingers at the visitor as her husband marched him into her shining kitchen. The churchman offered him no coffee, just sat him at the kitchen table while he hammered out on its linoleum just what was what.

"Yessir, I knew all them folks," the Deacon said, drumming his fingers. "I'll show you where Edgar Watson lived, tell you all about Coxes and Tolens and all the killing down in them old woods." Kinard jerked his thumb in the direction of the little person on the other side of the pasteboard wall. "She ain't a Cox exactly but she's related," her husband said. Over the churchly exhortations on her radio, Oriole protested, "No, I ain't never! Leslie's grandmother's daddy was my granddaddy's cousin, but I wouldn't know that murdering devil if I bumped into him in church!"

The sight of Lucius's notebook made the old man suck his teeth. "My information must be worth a lot to you," he suggested. When Lucius cheerfully agreed, the Deacon coughed, then got it over with. "How much?" he said. "Forty dollars?"

"Well, to be honest," said Lucius, taken aback, "most folks *like* to talk about old times. I guess you're the first I've come across who wanted payment."

The Deacon squinted, not shamefaced in the least but ready to dicker. "Thirty, then," he said. When his visitor forked over the money, he counted the bills twice before getting up and going out back to squirrel them away. Returning, he said, "Guess we can go then, lest you want coffee," but he never slowed on his way toward the front door.

"Back later," he informed his wife. "Next year, maybe." Outside, he climbed into Lucius's car. "That old rattler of mine don't run too good," he said, once he was settled. The Deacon had a certain grim mean humor, Lucius decided, but a painful hacking was as close as he would come that day to honest mirth.

The narrow county road shot south across farmland and woodlots, straight as a bullet. Sixteen miles out of Lake City, near a pasture pond on the east side of the road, Kinard tapped Lucius's arm. "Where you see that grove, that was Burdetts. Old cabin might be in there yet. Many's the time I been there Sunday visiting, the way us country people done back at that time. And these woods on this side, this was Betheas. Ain't no cabin there no more. Betheas rented from Sam Tolen, they were sharecroppers, same as Burdetts. Young Herkie Burdett was courting a Bethea daughter, we thought Herkie and Edna would get hitched, but Preacher Bethea was dead set against it. Burdetts was dirt poor, even poorer than Betheas, so he wanted his pretty Edna to marry better.

"By the time Ed Watson come back to this community, the whole county had heard that Mrs. Billy Collins's brother was a desperader out of the Wild West, so folks was surprised that Edna's daddy encouraged her to go to him instead of Herkie. According to gossip, Preacher Bethea figured any outlaw must be rich and he did not intend to let that rich man get away, no matter if he broke his daughter's heart. Folks mean-mouthed Ed Watson and the Preacher both."

The Deacon coughed awhile. "Our house was down yonder where them woods are now—still there, far as I know, grown up in trees. The baseball diamond was right out back of it—that's gone, too. Herkie Burdett played a pretty good third base but he was shook apart when Edgar Watson took his girl away to them Thousand Islands. Just moped around, he never married, couldn't hardly play third base no more. And two-three years after that, all hell broke loose."

A white clay lane left the county road to enter the forest shade. "Turn there," his guide commanded. "Herlong Lane. Runs west a few miles to the railroad. We still got Herlongs back in here, you know. Old Man Dan Herlong was the first to come south from Carolina, and he always said the Carolina Watsons was good people, prosperous farmers, all but Edgar's daddy. Still got Collinses here, too. Live in the old schoolhouse over yonder, far side of the woods." He pointed south. "Edmunds's store was over that way, too, but they didn't have no post office or nothing." He shifted in his seat. "All along this north side, that's Myers's plantation, the old Ichetuck-nee Plantation from before the Civil War. Twelve hundred acres, one of the biggest around. Once Sam Tolen got hold of it—he married the Widow Myers—he called it Tolen Plantation, and when our post office come in, he got that called Tolen, Florida. But Sam sold off a lot of land, drove Watsons crazy, on account they were kin and seen it as family property."

The car ran silent on the soft white track under the trees. Spanish moss swayed listless in the air. "It's kind of spooky how these woods ain't changed, when most places are growed over so much I can't hardly recognize where I grew up. Them black-and-white cattle you see in there back of them trees is the same stock Tolen raised, turn of the century, and these white clay tracks ain't never changed since Watson came along here on his horse. Course there weren't so much scrub oak back then, we had open woods and great big virgin pines, but all of them big trees got timbered out."

He signaled Lucius to pull over. "See where that track is blocked by that deadfall tree? That's Old Sam's road. Runs a quarter mile through the woods up to his house. I never seen that road closed off before." He peered about him. "You want to walk in there, have a look, you go ahead. I don't want no part of that old place."

THE EMPTY MANOR

The carriageway was still dimly defined by a woodland aisle through the tall trees. Burled oaks and hickories were interspersed with vine-shrouded magnolias and tupelos, rising through long shafts of morning light to fragments of blue sky. In the forest, the old road was innocent of wheel tracks, nicked only by neat heart prints of deer, the flutter marks of dusting quail, rat tail of possum and thin hand of coon, the wispy tracings of white-footed mice. Cardinal song, sweet plaint of titmice, the spring bell note of a jay in the fresh forest air.

In misty sunlight where the deepwood opened rose a white-columned facade with broad veranda, strangely out of scale with the frame house and the small kitchen wing stuck on behind. Its twin brick chimneys looked too thin, and an upstairs room under the eaves had a pinched small window. Chinked sheds and a dying barn sagged down amongst the live oaks; the worn pasture beyond had given way to ragged woodlots.

How odd that in this abandoned place, the ground-floor windows were unboarded and the grass all around the house appeared rough-mowed. No junked vehicle or rusted harrow, no litter of neglect, only the bareness of worn paint, only the silence. Everything looked tidied and in place as if the house awaited guests. Strangest of all, the kitchen door stood open. Had the inhabitants fled, hearing him coming?

He was startled by the shriek of a red-tailed hawk, poised for flight from its nest limb in an oak by the house corner. The nest's location so close to the building was sign that the house was uninhabited and yet he felt a childish dread of arousing unknown denizens, quick or dead. Something—this heartbreaking spring wind—had swept the intervening years from the veranda where on such a morning Great-Aunt Tabitha Watson might have creaked in her high-backed rocker, gazing without forgiveness at the forest wall from which old friends from Carolina had never arrived for a long visit, hailing her gaily from among the trees.

After her death, the rich widower Sam Tolen had lived here all alone. In the years since, Kinard had said, others had come but quickly gone away again. All had shunned this high queer manse at the end of its dark path through the forest, this dwelling where the mold of dread could never be aired out.

Lucius stood still and simply listened. Though drawn toward the door ajar on the back steps, he hesitated to approach, but neither could he turn his back on it, lest the shade of Tolen loom into the opening, threatening to set his hounds on a damned Watson.

Returning down the shadow drive, he glanced back more than once at the lost house until finally it withdrew behind the trees. In the midmorning heat, birdsong had stilled. The crack of a dead limb, the rush and earth thump of its tearing fall. The doleful groan of cows from the feed barn on the far side of the county road came as relief.

THE FASTEST FASTBALL IN THE U.S.A.

"Sam Tolen growed him a big stomach," the Deacon resumed of his own accord once they were under way. Grover Kinard was busy earning his thirty dollars and any questions would be interruptions. "Besides whiskey and cattle, the only thing Sam cared about was baseball. Sent all the way to St. Louis for *The Sporting News.* Never played himself, y'know, just got het up over it, mowed off some pasture for a baseball diamond. Might been the one time in his life that feller gave something for nothing.

"Tolen and the Cox boy was friendly for a while because Sam had the diamond and Les was his star pitcher. America was crazy about baseball then. Every boy aimed to be a professional ballplayer and every community that could scrape up nine young men had 'em a ball club. The Tolen Team would go from place to place and teams came here to play, had games every Saturday all spring and summer. Find some horn players, have a parade out to the field before the game. Played some grand old Confederate marches and some new tunes, too.

"My brother Brooks was catcher for Les Cox and when them two played we wasn't beat too often. Les could throw the hardest ball I ever heard of and he never minded throwing at your head. Batters was scared to stand close to the plate: just poked at the pitch as it flew by, got no real cut at it, he'd strike 'em out as fast as they come up. We figured Leslie had the fastest fastball in the U.S.A. and I guess Les thought so, too. Sam Tolen said them Major League scouts was bound to hear about this boy, come get him, pay him a hundred dollars every month just to play baseball. Might of went to his head cause he grew kind of overbearing, and he had him a hard and raspy tongue would scrape the warts off you. Made some noise, he jeered a lot, but he never had too much of a sense of humor. Local hero when we won and when we lost, he blamed his team. Took razzing all wrong, wanted to fight, same as Ty Cobb on the Pirates. No matter what, Les always figured he weren't getting a fair deal and that give him a real ugly disposition. Folks pretended to like him because he was a baseball star but in their hearts nobody liked him much. I imagine Les was kind of lonely but maybe he wasn't—very hard to tell.

"As I remember Les at age nineteen, he was five foot and eleven, maybe six, not extra tall but husky for his age and looked much older. They say he had some Injun from his mother's side, dark straight hair and them high cheekbones, and maybe his revengeful streak come from the breed in him. My sister's best friend, May Collins, was crazy about Les but her daddy thought Coxes was po' white, wouldn't allow him in the house. Pretty soon Billy Collins died—this was before all the bad trouble started—and with May's mama sick most of the time, Les hung around the Collins place, which is probably how he got to know Ed Watson.

"Sam Tolen drank heavy, and when that man was drinking, he had no friends. One day Sam cussed out Les's daddy. Will Cox was one of his share-croppers, had a log house right there at the southwest corner of this crossing where I'm pointing at. Hearing Tolen talk rough to his dad, Leslie went inside and got Will's rifle, come back out on the stoop without a word: he was fixing to shoot Sam Tolen dead and might of done it if Will hadn't knocked away the barrel. Seeing that rifle, Sam wheeled his horse, he just departed. But he hated being run off by a boy because folks heard about it and they laughed, and after that, Sam was spoiling for a showdown, never mind that this young feller was star pitcher on his team.

"Freight train came south from Lake City in the morning, went back north in the afternoon: see that old railbed shadow through them trees where these two lanes meet? There was crossties piled there. Les was setting on them ties a few days later when Tolen rode up drunk, threatened to kill him, which ain't a good idea around backcountry people.

"Sam never lived long after that. He was waylaid along the road—growed over now—that used to cut back through these woods to Ichetuck-nee Springs. Rumor was that Edgar Watson might of been involved but there weren't no evidence and no one looked for none. These old woods kept their secret," the Deacon said, peering about him.

"That was the finish of Sam Tolen and our Tolen Team. Sam loved base-ball more'n he loved people. His brother Mike had trouble with him, too, but in those days, with our kind of folks, you might not like your brother but you stood behind your family all the same. At Sam's funeral up in Lake City, Mike declared over the grave that he knew who killed his brother and he would take care of it—very bad mistake! Course the killers couldn't act too quick without drawing suspicion so they laid low till March of the next year. Mike was ambushed right here at this crossing.

"Down here on the west side of the lane is a big old log cabin in a oak grove—see there yonder? That was Mike's place. Kinards took it over from Mike's widow. When our family moved here, there was nothing left inside but some old broke cane chairs, cedar buckets, a bent pot. Dead silence. Bat chitterin and cheep of crickets and the snap of rats' teeth in old mattresses stuffed with graybeard moss right off these oaks. Our dad burned them mattresses and us kids was glad, cause with so much blood on 'em, they drawed the ghosts. There's stains on the wall in there right now from the day they brought Mike home, that's how much blood there was. Rat musk everywhere, I can still smell it. A house can have bloody rape and murder or shelter folks who live good churchly lives—either way don't mean nothing to them rats. Gnaw a hole in your body or your Bible, just depending.

"So these ol' woods was buzzing like a hornet swarm, and the men gathered, all riled up and ready to go. When the sheriff showed up from Lake City, his deputy come across hoof prints in the woods and followed that track south a mile to Watson's place. Folks suspected Leslie was in on it but he run off someplace. Anyway, they didn't have nothing on him.

"Ed Watson stood boldly in his door though he surely knew what that crowd of men was there for. Come time to step forward and arrest him, there weren't no volunteers, nobody weren't as riled as what they thought they was. So Josiah Burdett—that's Herkie's daddy—Joe said, "Well, I will go." Just upped and done it. Dogged little fella, y'know, soft-spoken, he seemed to hide behind his scraggy horse-tail beard that come down like a bib right to his belt buckle, but when he said that he would go get Watson, they knew he meant it. My brother Brooks was so impressed that when another volunteer was called for, Brooks raised his hand and said, 'Well, I'll go with him.'

"Them two went up the hill to Watson's gate. Watson had gone back inside, so Joe called, 'Edgar, you better come on out!' When he came out, they had their guns on him but didn't have no warrant, so Watson said, 'I'm sorry, Joe, but if you have no warrant then I can't come with you.' And Joe Burdett said, 'Well I reckon you better come.'" Probably didn't care to shoot him down in front of his boy Herkie's childhood sweetheart.'

"Watson took that very calm, never protested. 'If you boys aim to arrest an innocent man,' he said, 'let's get it over with.' Seeing Herkie's dad, Edna busted right out crying, and her babies, too. 'Uncle Joe, Mr. Watson ain't done nothing wrong! He's been home here right along!' But Joe Burdett only shook his head, so Watson said, 'Well, then, I'll just step inside, change to my Sunday best, cause I don't want to give our community a bad name by going up to town in these soiled overalls.' Burdett says, 'Nosir, Edgar. You ain't going back inside.' So Edna brought him his clean clothes and Watson says, 'I'll just step into my shed to change, be with you fellers in a minute.' Joe Burdett was too smart for that one, too. Told Brooks, 'Go take a look, make sure there ain't no weapon hid in there.' And sure enough, Brooks found an old six-gun, loaded, back of a loose slat on the crib wall.

"Ed Watson changed his clothes outside on a cold March day, stripped right down to his long johns. Joe told him he better instruct Edna what he wanted done around his farm, and Edgar said, 'Nosir, that will not be necessary, cause bein innocent, I will not be gone for long.' Said he would sure appreciate it if he could just step inside while he give his dear wife a kiss good-bye. Joe Burdett shook his head. Let Watson get a foothold, see, there wouldn't a-been no Josiah Burdett and no Brooks Kinard neither. Watson, he knew how to shoot, he didn't miss.

"Edgar told his wife to calm herself, he'd be home soon, on account he was innocent and had a alibi. Never turned to wave, never looked back. That man walked down to where the crowd was waiting, looked 'em in the eye, and strode off down the road like they'd made him their leader. They had to hurry to keep up.

"For years after, all them fellers spoke about Ed Watson's inner strength that saw him through. If he was afraid he never showed it, and that scary calm got poor Brooks worrying that Mr. Watson might be innocent just like he said; Brooks prayed for guidance from the Lord when he went to bed. But our older brother Luther told him, 'Boy, a guiltier man than Edgar Watson ain't never drawed breath in this county so don't you go pestering the Almighty. The Good Lord got plenty to take care of without that.'

"Watson hired fancy lawyers, got his trial moved after a lynch mob went to get him in Lake City. Luther Kinard was in that mob. These were the men most outraged against Watson. But when Watson ducked the noose, and Les Cox, too, they were the ones most frightened, knowing that them killers knew who had wanted to see 'em lynched and was honor bound to seek revenge. Might show up after dark, y'know, drill a feller coming from the barn or through the winder while he ate his supper. All that winter, the whole countryside was on the lookout. So when Edna's family passed the news that Edgar had took her away to Thousand Islands, folks was overjoyed. Then came that January dusk when someone seen Cox walking down the road.

"That spring there weren't no Tolen Team so Leslie tried to pitch for Columbia City. It was so pitiful that I felt bad for him because his nerves was gone. Lost his control, he was just dead wild, and the worse he pitched, the harder he threw, till the other team become afraid to go to bat. The crowd sat quiet, watched him fall to pieces. I can see him yet today, slamming his glove down on the mound, raising the dust. Finally his own team wouldn't take the field behind him, he was out there on the pitcher's mound alone. So naturally Les picked a fight, punched some feller bloody till they hauled him off. Went stomping off the field in a bad silence because nobody dared razz him. Far as I know, he never pitched again.

"Les finally seen there was no place for him, not around here. He wanted to go to Watson's in the Islands but he needed money and he knew just where to get it. I reckon he felt humiliated, and when that feller felt humiliated, someone would pay."

THE BANKS FAMILY

"Beyond that line of pecan trees is where the Banks family had their cabin. Two rooms with a kitchen shed out back, same as the rest of us. Calvin Banks had him a farm, run eighty head of cattle, worked hard cutting railroad ties, and done odd jobs. That nigra aimed to get ahead and had sense enough to save some money but not enough to take it to the bank. Calvin was taught that Jesus loved him so he trusted people. Carried his dollars in a little old satchel over his shoulder, and when he bought something, he'd take that satchel out and pay, so people seen he had money in there, twenty-dollar gold pieces and silver dollars and some greenbacks, too. My dad would say, 'If he don't look out, somebody's liable to take and rob that nigra.' Well, somebody done that, robbed and killed Calvin and his wife and another nigra along with 'em, and that somebody was William Leslie Cox.

"We figured Les tried to scare Calvin into telling where his money was hid, then shot him when he wouldn't do that. Calvin Banks was maybe sixty and Aunt Celia well up into her seventies, near blind and she had rheumatism, couldn't run no more: might been setting on the stoop warming her bones. Looked like Les shot her right out of her rocker but some has said she slipped down off the stoop, tried to crawl under the cabin. Don't know how folks knew so doggone much unless Les bragged on it, which knowing Les, I reckon he sure did. Killed the old man inside, Aunt Celia on the stoop, then the son-in-law out here on the road. Didn't want no witnesses, I reckon.

"Story was that Leslie got thirteen thousand dollars but our dad said it weren't no more than maybe three hundred at the most. Back in them days a field hand got paid twelve to fifteen dollars a month, so even three hundred was a lot of money. One thing for sure, Les tore through that little cabin. I seen the mess next day. They said it was him took that metal box that two years later turned up empty in the woods, said it contained all silver dollars, so his mule had a tough time, had to walk lopsided. Les borrowed that mule from his cousin Oscar Sanford who told my brother Luther all about it.

"Our family field was directly west across the Fort White Road. On that late autumn afternoon us Kinards was picking cotton when Oscar Sanford come along, headed toward the Banks place on his mule. We heard one shot across the fields and then another, then in a little while another. Stood up to listen but finally decided someone was out hunting. Not till next day did we learn it was them poor coloreds getting killed.

"At the sound of those shots, Oscar turned that mule around and headed back home in a hurry. My brother Luther was putting in a well for Sanfords that same day, stayed over so he could finish work early next morning. In the evening Cox come by all pale and out of breath. Made my brother nervous, cause Luther had joined the Watson lynch mob and Les knew it. But Les paid no attention to him, just jerked his head toward the door, and him and Oscar went outside to talk. Might have wanted the borrow of that mule to go fetch that metal box.

"Because Bankses was nigras, Les might of got away with it, except folks knew that this young feller was mixed up in the Tolen business and most likely the guilty one; them killed nigras give 'em a second chance to see some justice. Luther Kinard was his teammate on our baseball club but even Luther turned state's evidence against him. Folks wanted that mean sonofagun out of the way.

"Will Cox was good friends with the sheriff but his boy was convicted all the same. Les spoke up in court, 'You're giving that life sentence to a young feller that can't tolerate no cooped-up life! I weren't cut out to make it on no chain gang!' Maybe the judge winked, as some has claimed, maybe he didn't, but everybody heard him say, 'You'll be all right, boy.' That judge knew what he was talking about, too.

"Les was sent to prison for the rest of his natural life and stayed three months. He was on the road gang out of Silver Springs. One day his daddy was out there talking to the guard and a railroad car got loose some way while Les was on it. Rolled down the grade to where he jumped off and run. Never been seen since, not by the law. Supposed to be dead but there's plenty who will tell you he came back in later years hunting revenge. Nobody around this county could believe Les Cox was dead and they don't today."

FORT WHITE

At the paved highway they turned south toward Fort White, then west again on the Old Bellamy Road. Where wisteria and a few old pecan trees recalled to him a long-gone homestead, Mr. Kinard said, "As a young feller, Edgar lived a while in an old cropper's shack used to be right over yonder, shade of them oaks. Later years, he bought some Collins land just down the road here, built his own house and farmed several hundred acres. Good farmer, too, cause if he'd of been a poor one, we'd of knowed about it."

On a hilltop on the north side of the road stood a sallow house with a dark-shaded porch and a rust-streaked tin roof shrouded by the Spanish moss on an immense red oak. "That's the place. That's where Brooks Kinard and Joe Burdett served him that warrant. I was up there one day with my dad, we was driving him a well, fixing his pump, so I remember Edgar. He was thick through the shoulders and uncommon strong, my daddy told me."

Across the Fort White Road was Elim Baptist Church which Grover Kinard wished to visit. Though the church had been replaced, his parents awaited him in the old churchyard, also his sister and his brother Brooks. "See his dates? May 1910, same month we seen the Great White Fire in the sky. Some thought poor Brooks had took sick from that comet but I reckon he died of his consumption." The lettering on the Kinard headstones was blurred by moss and lichens and the stones had shaggy grass around the base. "My folks ain't hardly had a visit since the day they come here," mourned the Deacon, scraping the lichens uselessly with a weak penknife.

Not far from the Kinards lay D. M. Tolen, 1872–1908. His gravestone read, "How Desolate Our Home Bereft of Thee"—a graveyard irony, Lucius thought, since according to Kinard, Mike Tolen's widow had fled that bloodied cabin and gone straight back to her Myers family in South Carolina.

Nearing Fort White, the county road narrowed to a shady village street of gaunt frame houses in old weedy yards. At a counter in the grocery store, they bought barbecue ribs with soft rolls and soda pop, then carried their lunch outside to a wood picnic table where three old black men hitched along to the far end of the bench, ceding most of their space to the white men.

Working his toothpick, the Deacon frowned and muttered, patting the pockets of memory for something lost. "Born right here in this ol' town and I ain't been back in years," he sighed, "and it ain't like I live so far away. Eleven miles! Just goes to show how life leaks away when you ain't paying attention. One day you look up, look around, and the world is empty. Not empty exactly but something is wrong, there ain't no color left to life." Outraged, he glared at Lucius. "Watsons long gone and Coxes moved away, Burdetts and Betheas, too. Ain't none of them good old families left. Died out or gone off to the cities, gone away like they was never here at all."

CRAZY WATSON EYES

Following Kinard's directions to the Collins house, Lucius traveled south through the old woods on a clay track as white as bonemeal, with dust so fine that the tires made no sound. He passed no cabin, heard no dog. Then the wood opened and the old schoolhouse rose on a knoll under great oaks.

Already in the door was Ellen Collins, a rather thickset person who looked cross. Over her shoulder, gazing at him from the wall across the room, were three figures in a large old-fashioned photo in an oval frame. A young girl in a white dress, full-mouthed, not quite pouting, stood behind a pert, quizzical old lady in a black dress with white scarf and brooch who was seated beside an imposing man in a dark suit, white embroidered shirt, and black bow tie. The man's gaze was forthright and his brow clear. His hair was plastered to his head after the fashion of the time, and a heavy mustache flowed down into bushy sideburns that extended to the corners of his jaw.

"Great-Uncle Edgar, about 1904." Ellen Collins swept her arm in introduction, having missed his start of consternation at this unexpected confrontation: why was a portrait of unmentionable Uncle Edgar hanging on the wall of a Collins house? "With Great-Grandmother Ellen Watson and my aunt May Collins as a girl," Ellen Collins was saying. She introduced Cousin Hettie Collins and her daughter April before pointing him to a chair.

When pretty Hettie welcomed him with a warm peck on the cheek, her daughter teased her. "Mama? Are we 'kissin' cousins'?" April Collins, not yet twenty, had taffy hair hacked short—by herself, from the look of it—and the same bald gaze as the great-uncle on the wall, the same white crescent underneath the pupil. "Yep," she laughed. "I got 'em, too. 'Crazy Watson Eyes.' "

Lucius saw nothing crazy in his father's eyes, only that fixed gaze, as if he had never blinked in all his life. But as he watched, Papa's likeness seemed to shift and resettle into a visage swollen with intransigence—a change effected by that crescent, white and hard as boiled albumen, as if a trapped madman were glaring out through the eye slits of a mask.

From their hard settee, the silent ladies watched him, mystified by his intense absorption in the portrait. He took a deep breath and let the vision go. On the wall, a serene Papa resumed his place between his mother and his niece.

"That's the first photograph I've ever seen," he explained, finding his voice.

"That's the *only* photograph: how could you have seen it?" Cousin Ellen sat stiffly, arms folded on her chest, ready to bar his admission to this household. "If I hadn't told you, how would you even know that that was him?"

"He's kin, Aunt Ellie! L. Watson Collins? *Got* to be kin!"

"For all we know, that's an alias," said her aunt severely. Plainly she was having second thoughts about permitting this self-styled Collins to cross their sill. "If Julian ever got wind of this, or Cousin Ed—"

Lucius cut her off by asking boldly if, in the opinion of this Collins family, Great-Uncle Edgar had really been a cold-blooded killer. Startled, his cousins deflected the question. April jumped in. "When that man smiled, watch out! Uncle Edgar—"

Ellen Collins cut her off. "Uncle Edgar could be ever so pleasant and considerate, but nobody dared cross him. Oh, just a *violent* temper! My brother has that explosive temper, too. He'd pick a quarrel with a fence post. More than once, I've heard him say, 'If I had lived in Uncle Edgar's day, I'd have killed those Tolens, too.' "

"Uncle Edgar was acquitted, Ellie," Hettie reproved her. "But he never learned to control his temper, that is true. We know something dreadful happened in his youth in Carolina. That story arrived with the Herlongs, who came south from Edgefield County after Granny Ellen, but the grown-ups would never repeat it."

Ellie inquired, "I suppose you know about Belle Starr? That was a story he never quite denied. He always said he'd had no choice because she'd ride around his place, shooting her pearl-handled six-guns, spooking his horses, so one day, he just stepped out and took care of it."

"Probably fooling," Hettie said. "Everybody said he liked to tease."

"Granddad Billy Collins was very offended by that Belle Starr story. He told his boys it was dishonorable to shoot a woman, even an outlaw queen. Granddad died young, before the Tolen trouble, but he'd made up his mind about his brother-in-law before he went."

"One thing we heard, Uncle Edgar sang 'The Streets of Laredo' with real feeling. Claimed it came from an old Celtic lament which had tingled up the iron blood of his Highlands ancestors, but we think he brought that song from Oklahoma along with his black hat. You never caught him out without that hat on."

"Probably going bald," April suggested. "Wore black hats and sang sad songs because he knew he would die before his time and was remorseful for his misspent life."

"Oh, what nonsense, girl!" The ladies tittered.

Lucius liked these new cousins very much, especially Hettie, who was pretty in her old-fashioned brown dress, though slight and fragile as if ill. He knew he should confess right now that he was Cousin Lucius but this would make them instantly suspicious—*Why are you masquerading as a Collins?* Once they mistrusted him, they would tell him nothing. On the other hand, the telephone could ring at any moment—strait-laced Julian warning them that nosy Cousin Lucius was in town.

His kin awaited him in a stiff row like frontier women squinting over the hammers of long muskets. Mind racing, he frowned intently at the picture.

"I'm named for Granny Ellen," Ellie Collins said. "And that's Aunt May at about fourteen. Her brothers are my daddy, known as Willie, and my uncle Julian, who won't so much as mention their late uncle."

April grinned. "Hold everything they know so tight that nobody knows if they know anything at all!" Hettie and her daughter laughed with that affectionate malice reserved for family folly. They seemed quite willing to air out old closed rooms, since the Collins clan had nothing to be ashamed of, but for the moment, Ellie's presence kept them in line. "Collins honor," she reproved them, trying not to smile.

"*Watson* honor!" April cried. "If it weren't for darned old Cousin Ed, this family might have loosened up a little after all this time!"

RAKING LEAVES BY MOONLIGHT

The ladies recalled that Uncle Edgar's four children had returned with their mother from Oklahoma to live in this community while their father was finishing his new house in the Everglades. When these cousins departed, all tears and smiles, they promised to come visit, but the only one who ever did was Eddie.

"Cousin Ed must have been fifteen when he came back here to help out on his father's new farm. Like Rob and Carrie, he was born in that old cabin near the Junction but the place he called home was Uncle Edgar's new house on the hill.

"Over the years, Cousin Ed never tired of talking about Carrie Langford and her banker and her fine riverside house. He rarely mentioned his brothers, so the Collins memory of Rob and Lucius more or less died out. Ed said he knew little about Robert and Lucius because he only heard from those two when they wanted money. As for Edna's children, they weren't Watsons anymore. His stepmother—Ed always said 'my stepmother,' although he was older than she was—had changed her name and cut off communication with the family."

Hettie sighed. "Ed's saying that doesn't make it so, because much as we loved our dear cousin, he mostly saw things in a way that suited his idea of himself. We told him where to get in touch with Edna but he wasn't really interested and never tried.

"When Ed got his first auto, he would come through on vacations twice a year and bring his children. They'd stop here coming and they'd stop here going, and every visit without fail, he would tell us about yesteryear, how he went to Fort White school and got beaten with peach switches when he failed his lessons, and all about the meat and biscuits in thick syrup that the kids brought to class in their big lunch pails, and the three brass cuspidors lined up for tobacco-spitting contests at the general store, and the town marshal with a club lashed to his wrist and a big pistol, and the saloon where passersby might see some poor fellow pitched through the swinging doors. There wasn't one detail of the old days in Fort White that Ed forgot."

April laughed. "Year after year, we hoped he would forget. He never did."

"Well, Ed had a sincere attachment to these woods," her mother reflected. "He'd drive into the yard and get out and look around at the oaks and hickories, hands on his hips, y'know, then heave a great big sigh and say, 'I sure feel like I've come home when I come back here.' We never could figure why these old woods meant so much to him, cause when he got here he hardly took a step outdoors."

"After his first wife died, Ed thought nothing of bringing a female friend, might be a week," Ellie said with disapproval. "One was the weirdest woman we ever saw. Before she sat down to her supper she would take her belt off, put it around her *neck*!"

"Didn't want to constrict her stomach till she et up all our food. And Gussie! Tell about the one he married, Mama."

"Augusta was too lady-like to sweat, you know, didn't even *perspire*. All us poor country women were worn out and soaking wet from the damp summer heat, hair gone slack and *beads* of sweat on brow and lip. And here was Augusta perched on the edge of her chair, cool as a daffodil, even though she was buttoned up right to the chin. Him, too. Buttoned up tight.

"We never saw him without white shirt and tie even when cooking. Oh yes, Ed dearly loved to cook! Before Edna Bethea came into their life, Ed cooked for his daddy in the new house on the hill—Uncle Edgar wouldn't pay a cook just for the two of them. Ed never tired of telling how hard his daddy worked him, how he raked the yard by moonlight after doing chores all day. And without fail his Gussie would pretend she'd never heard that story. 'Raked the yard at *night*?' She'd turn real slow, hand to her mouth, and stare at him round-eyed, just a-marveling. And Cousin Ed chuckling along to let us know something pretty good was coming our way. Then he'd bust right out with it—'Well, *heck*! We never had free time during the day!'

"Then those two would hee-haw and carry on, just enjoy the heck out of that story right through supper. Couldn't get over it, y'know. *'Never had free time during the day!'* Year after year."

The women whooped and gasped for breath, falling all over one another with the exploits of Cousin Ed. *"Raking leaves by moonlight!"* April cried. "They never let that grand old story die!"

Hettie smiled at her guest to assure him that this family irreverence was all in fun and was not meant unkindly. And though Lucius was laughing, too, he felt disloyal, knowing such stories would never have been told had his cousins known that he was Eddie's brother. Sensing his discomfort, the ladies had stopped laughing. "As for his father," Hettie sighed, "Cousin Ed approved the vow of silence, saying his sister Carrie felt the same: only Lucius was still living in the past, Ed used to say."

A loud bang on the door announced Paul Edmunds, whose family had owned the local store. Mr. Edmunds wore a blue serge Sunday suit, white socks, and high black shoes; his denim shirt, buttoned to the top, pinched his jumpy gullet. Behind him, his long-limbed Letitia in dust-colored woolens much too hot for such warm weather crept in out of the sunlight like a large timorous moth.

"Your store's still standing out there in the woods," April Collins called by way of greeting. "I bet I could still find it for you, Mr. Edmunds."

Sent word last evening that a real historian was coming to research Edgar Watson's years here in Fort White, Mr. Edmunds was eager to get down to business, which signified men only. "Well, now, mister," he began, "me'n Hettie here has talked for years with every last soul in these parts that might remember anything, and we think we've got the history down as good as you are going to get it." Bending a bushy eyebrow on the interloper in sign that he would brook no opposition, he cleared his throat at exhaustive length to ensure himself ample speaking room.

"Colonel William Myers, who married Edgar's cousin, came here with his slaves during the War for fear he might lose 'em to the Yankees. He left his bride and her mother in Athens, Georgia, because this Suwannee country was still wild and life uncertain. Sure enough, Myers was killed by lightning in 1869 and his widow and her mother came to see to the estate."

"Colonel Myers willed that huge plantation to his *mother-in-law*," Ellie Collins informed Lucius, still indignant.

"Well," Hettie said mildly, "Cousin Laura was very kind and generous but perhaps a bit simple-hearted, apt to give too much away—"

"Simple-minded, you mean. Probably retarded."

"There's no reason to assume that, April dear. That's just your idea."

"You have a better explanation, Mama? Why else would Colonel Myers leave the whole thing to her mother with instructions to pass it straight along to his Myers nephews?"

When Lucius said he understood that those Myers nephews were Watsons on their mother's side, Ellie's expression made it clear she resented the idea that an outsider should be privy to such information.

Paul Edmunds stuck his hand up as he must have done in this same room as a boy scholar in knee britches, kicking clay off high black shoes of the same country style he wore today. "I don't know about all that," he harrumphed in impatience. "Herlongs claimed that before Edgar left Carolina, some nigger threatened to let on to his daddy that Edgar was planting peas in a crooked row. Well, somebody went and killed that doggone nigger."

He scowled at his wife, who was fluttering for his attention: "Church folks say 'nigra' these days, dear."

"*Nigger*-a?" Old Paul glared about, suspicious.

"Perhaps that Herlong story was mistaken," Lucius said shortly. "I've always heard that Edgar Watson got on fine with black folks, much better than most men of that period."

"Well, darkies were never treated cruelly around here." Hettie's pained gaze begged the Professor to believe that this community was no longer mired in crude bigotry. "Oh, there's a social difference, yes, but as far as mistreatment, or not taking care of a black neighbor—no, no. Folks in Fort White aren't like that."

"Not all of 'em, anyway," scoffed Paul Edmunds, for whom all this darn folderol was pure irrelevance.

"Granny Ellen used to confide that his daddy whapped Uncle Edgar once too often, knocked his brain askew." April tapped her temple.

"Nobody thought Uncle Edgar was crazy, miss. Hotheaded, yes. Violent, yes. But *crazy*? No! He was exceptionally intelligent and able—"

"Aunt Ellie? He went crazy when he drank, we sure know *that*!"

"There were plenty of bad drinkers back in those days," Mr. Edmunds said. "Nothing else for the men to do once the sun went down."

"Well, in frontier days, not all men who resorted to violence were crazy or unscrupulous," said Hettie. "No, far from it. But because of his bad reputation, Uncle Edgar was thought guilty of many things he didn't do, which made him bitter. Granny Ellen would say her son started out fine but his father came home from war a brutal drunkard who beat his son unmercifully. You keep whipping a good dog, he will turn bad."

SHINING ON UNSEEN BENEATH THE PINES

When Edgar Watson returned here from the West in the early nineties, he was a fugitive on horseback, passing through at night, Mr. Edmunds said. After his wife died at the turn of the century, he came back, stayed several years. "Leased a good piece of this Collins tract. Nothing but bramble and poverty grass when he took over but he brought these oldfields back. Built his own house, too—I seen him buildin it. Used to hear him target-practice up there on his hill. Doc Straughter did odd jobs for Watson, and the rest of his life, that old nigger-a would talk about how his boss man worked a revolver. Set out on his back porch, pick acorns off that big red oak that's up there yet today. Most every man back then could work a rifle pretty good but they couldn't hit their own barn with a handgun. Ed Watson could beat your rifle with his damn revolver."

"Do you remember what he looked like, Paul?" Letitia inquired dutifully.

"A-course I do! That silver glint in them blue eyes made a man go quaky in the belly."

"Did he ever look at *you* like that?" she whispered, awed by any man scary enough to have such an effect on Paul T. Edmunds. But her husband only snorted and stamped as if she were some sort of pesky fly.

"When Billy Collins died in February 1907, Uncle Edgar and Edna came back north to be with the family. That was when the whole Collins clan moved in with him."

"Which means they were all living in his house when Sam Tolen was killed a few months later," Lucius said. "Would Julian and Laura have stayed under his roof if they thought he was a killer?"

"I do know they worried," Hettie murmured, looking worried, too. "There was *so* much talk up and down the county even before the Tolen trouble. But they could hardly turn against this generous uncle who took care of the whole family after Granddad Billy died."

"Well, Calvin Banks must of knowed something," Mr. Edmunds said, "cause they had that old nigger-a up there to Edgar's trial."

"Do you recall the other black man in the case? Frank Reese? I found his name in the court records as a defendant in both Tolen murders."

All turned toward the visitor in disbelief. "Nobody in our family recalls any such name," said Ellie in a tone of warning.

" 'Pin it on the nigger,' that's all that was," April said. "Nigra, I mean." The women deplored her cynical view of Southern justice but Paul Edmunds nodded; her time-honored remedy needed no defense.

"Calvin Banks was Colonel Myers's coachman," Edmunds resumed. "Knew the location of his buried gold. Kept the secret from the Watson women for fear the Tolens might get wind of it. That secret was lost with Calvin so that gold is out there right this minute." Mr. Edmunds jerked his thumb toward the window.

"Shining on unseen beneath the pines," Letitia said. April opened her eyes wide and the ladies giggled.

"Mr. Edmunds? Do you think that story's true?" Lucius tried not to sound skeptical.

The indignant old man blew his nose. "Take it or leave it, mister. Don't make a goddamn bit of difference to us home people."

"Now, now, Paul," Letitia murmured, patting his old knee, which twitched in fury.

"When Watson was in jail, he got word to Cox that a thousand dollars was waiting for him if he killed that witness. If Les found Calvin's gold, why, they would split it," Edmunds cackled. "Cox come back here all his life hunting that money, having gone and killed the only man who could tell him where it was!"

Lucius held his tongue, resigned. Just when he thought he was getting things sorted out, local rumor had turned things murky yet again. But the legend of the buried gold rang with a mythic truth and would prevail.

"Course that is hearsays," Mr. Edmunds snarled. "Can't put no trust in us local folks that has lived in these woods all their lives and talked with every last living soul who might of knowed something."

But even the ladies were protesting. "Where would Uncle Edgar get a thousand dollars, Paul? After all his legal expenses, he was *poor*. The whole family was poor. We were burying our dead with little wooden crosses."

"None of my damn business where he got it. But he always come up with money, we know that much."

There was no good evidence for any of this stuff, Lucius thought, disheartened.

WITCHED APPLES

Hettie tactfully changed the subject. "I think Leslie must have been some kind of hero worshipper. Here was this handsome, well-dressed man from the Wild West, supposed to be a desperado who had shot it out with famous outlaws in the Indian Nations—"

"And what Uncle Edgar saw was a dull, vicious boy sent straight from Heaven to do his dirty work," Ellie Collins interrupted, in sudden resentment of Uncle Edgar. "He was smart and Leslie wasn't—it's as simple as that."

"No, Leslie was not well thought of around here," Hettie agreed wistfully, as if still open to the possibility that the Cox boy might have been held in high esteem in other parts. "He was a sort of rough-and-ready person, you might say." In her wide-eyed light irony, she smiled innocently at Lucius, who smiled back, happy to be included in the family teasing and even happier that this lovely Hettie seemed to like him.

"Trashy, that's what my daddy called 'em," Ellie said grimly. "We always wondered how Great-Aunt Tabitha could permit her daughter to marry a white trash Tolen. But *Leslie*! Now there was a *real* son-of-a-bitch, my daddy said."

"Most of those Coxes were good people and still are," Hettie reminded her, pale eyebrows raised in mock alarm at Ellie's sporty language. "Well connected, too."

"Well connected with the sheriff! Got that skunk turned loose off of the chain gang." Edmunds's knobby knee jumped about in agitation. "Everybody in this section knew that Leslie was dead mean, but Watson could be likable from what I seen, tending our store. I talked to the old-timers all about it and never met a one who got crossed up with him."

April laughed. "Know why? The ones that got crossed up with him were dead."

"Leslie and I, we were just *children*! Looking out through these same windows!" Hand at her mouth, Letitia stared out of the windows, marveling that she had actually survived her attendance at this school with a cold-blooded killer. "He had the shadow of a beard at the age of twelve!"

Stilling his wife with a fearful frown, her husband usurped her modest contribution to Cox lore. William Leslie Cox, he informed them, was full-grown by the time he was sixteen and when unshaven, he looked close to thirty. "Come here to the school on muleback, whistled up May Collins through them winders, and eloped with her."

"May Collins ran off with Cox?" Lucius vaguely recalled having heard this from his father in the summer Leslie lived at Chatham Bend.

Hettie nodded. "After Granddad Billy died, her mother paid her less and less attention. Granny Ellen was getting feeble and Aunt Cindy was half blind so young Miss May talked to any boy she wanted."

According to Lucius's notes, the murder of the Banks family occurred on a Monday of early October, 1909: the bodies were discovered Tuesday morning and Leslie Cox was arrested the next day while applying for a marriage license at the Lake City courthouse. Perhaps swayed by his friendship with Leslie's father, the sheriff thereupon released on bond the only suspect in the "foul and brutal murders of three hardworking peaceable negroes," as the victims were called in the paper that same morning. However, the groom agreed to turn himself in after his wedding.

Since Leslie could have fled after the killings instead of going to Lake City for that license, then passed up a second chance to flee when granted permission to go get married the next morning, he must have thought the whole thing would blow over. "Figured there wouldn't be no problem over killing nigger-as," Paul Edmunds said, "and it looks like the sheriff thought the same. Not only let him out on bail but let him cross the county line to marry."

"Somebody was sent to invite the bride's family to a friend's house in Suwannee County, so May's brothers knew right where to find 'em," Ellie recalled. "Uncle Julian decided to stay home, but my daddy rode straight over and warned Leslie that if he tried to make off with his sister, he would kill him."

"Willie might have had his hands full, Ellie," Mr. Edmunds reminded her, not unkindly. "Les was a husky six-foot feller and the Collins boys was always pretty skimpy."

"Justice of the Peace Jim Hodges married 'em." April recited her fact proudly. "I talked to Justice Jim many's the time. He said, 'Miss May, are you aware that on your wedding night, this young man will lay his head down on an iron bunk in the county jail?' And May Collins answered smartly, 'No sir, Judge, I ain't aware of no such of a thing. All I know is I aim to marry up with this here feller so let's get a move on.' But when she was told she could not sleep with him in jail, she headed home."

"Miss May Collins did what she darn pleased no matter what!" Ellie exclaimed.

"The train back to Lake City was flagged down at Herlong Junction and Leslie was arrested," Hettie told Lucius. "So in the Lord's eyes—and our Collins eyes, too—that unholy wedlock was never consummated. As the years went by, even Aunt May came to believe she was a virgin."

"Don't smile, Hettie Collins! That is the Lord's truth! When Daddy got there, they were already married, yes, but her brother would not let her board that train. And Leslie didn't try to fight or Daddy would have killed him!"

In Columbia County Court on December 11, 1909, William Leslie Cox was found guilty of first-degree murder, but the jury begged the mercy of the court in order to spare this fine-looking young man the death sentence. Reading between the lines of these accounts—the release on negligible bond so that he might marry, the jury's plea for compassion—Lucius doubted that Cox would have been indicted for those negro killings had he not been previously implicated in the death of whites.

"After Leslie was sent away, May went to live with Coxes because this family was so scandalized they wouldn't have her." Censorious, Ellie shook her head. "Even after she came home, one of those Coxes would show up once in a while, take her away, and after a few days, she would come home again. This was after he escaped and before he left to go join Uncle Edgar in the Islands. Aunt May would never say she had seen Leslie but we suspected it."

"When she wasn't claiming that Uncle Edgar had led her young husband astray," Hettie told Lucius with delight, "Aunt May would declare that she couldn't be blamed for running off with Leslie because Leslie had given her a bewitched apple. Once she had eaten that terrible witched apple, she was obliged to obey his least command." She and Lucius laughed together, enjoying each other very much.

Ellen laughed, too. "Now where d'you suppose that boy found that darned apple? At the Edmunds store?"

Paul Edmunds hooted. "Not unless he paid down most of that Banks gold. We sold witched apples pretty dear, them bony-fidey ones."

Unnerved by the tension in the room, Letitia Edmunds, frantic to depart, had risen from her chair. Her husband ignored her. Not until his wife had hugged the Collins women and peeped good-bye to the Professor did he get slowly to his feet. "Murdering fool, that Cox boy was," Paul Edmunds grumbled. "Within six months, he killed three more down in them islands. Counting nigger-as, he killed eight head, and here he was, only nineteen years of age." From the doorway, he told Lucius, "If Leslie's dead, he ain't been dead too many years." He turned and went outside into the sunlight. "Rotting in some hole out in these woods, wouldn't surprise me," his voice came back. "Best place for a mean varmint such as that."

A FAILURE OF THE SPIRIT

While his kin said good-bye to their guests, Lucius inspected the framed photos of Billy Collins and his sons. Like their father, Julian and Willie had been slight, with curly black hair, fair skins, and refined faces, and a pensive quality in their dark eyes like a foreboding. Anxious to pursue his questions before a phone call from Lake City ended the interview, he asked how the family had reacted when Julian and Willie were arrested as accessories after the fact in the Mike Tolen case and jailed on one thousand dollars bail. He assumed the family knew of this since it was on the record at the courthouse.

Agitation entered the room like a wild bird through the window, thumping and fluttering behind the curtain. The ladies stared at him.

"*Jailed?*" Ellie Collins drew herself up to stare him down: her baked expression seemed to say, *Is this how you repay me?* The family knew no such thing, she told him in a tone suggesting it could not be true and that, in grubbing through court documents, this self-styled "Professor" had indulged in unprofessional and dishonorable behavior.

"Detained, perhaps?" Hettie ventured carefully.

"Detained, I mean." Lucius hastened to say there had been no question of Collins complicity or guilt; he spoke formally and a bit pompously, hoping that an officious tone might dignify his indiscretion. But of course he knew—and knew that they knew, too—that if the brothers had testified against an uncle of their blood, they had transgressed the oldest code of those Celtic ancestors who, despising all authority, loyal only to the clan, had borne their tattered pennant of archaic honor across the seas into the New World.

"When they were detained as witnesses, Julian and Willie refused to take the stand and tell lies under oath—that was their upbringing as honorable young Christian men," murmured poor Hettie. "And Julian's Laura had no choice but to support her husband, though it broke her heart. She had always adored kind Uncle Edgar."

"But what was their testimony?" Lucius said.

"We were never told," Ellie said shortly.

In the stillness of the old schoolhouse, he suffered with them the weight of shame inflicted on this family by Papa. In the end it mattered little what those young men had said. Through no fault of their own, his cousins had found themselves in an intractable dilemma. No wonder they had clung so fiercely to that vow never to discuss or mention Edgar Watson. But these years of silence, so dignified in the family legend, had only embedded that painful splinter of ambiguity and guilt, that ineradicable black line under clear skin.

In her black bombazine and Sunday bonnet, chin held high, Granny Ellen had made a fine impression at the trial, smiling in proud witness to the innocence of her distinguished son as well as to the honor of her handsome grandsons, there to attest to her son's guilt. In the court recess, she bestowed thin smiles without discrimination, handing around nice mincemeat sandwiches in a napkined basket.

Minnie Collins had not attended her brother's trial. Even before her Billy's death, they told him, she had sunk away into a long slow dying, passing the remainder of her days all but unnoticed. By all accounts, she had always been a colorless person, with faint life in her, and her likeness was utterly absent from the family record. As if her countenance had been too tentative to be caught on film, no known photograph existed, nor was there a family memory of what she had looked like, thought, or said. Minnie's one known attribute was her rare beauty, but what form her beauty might have taken, none could recall.

"Minnie Collins *hated* the idea of her own likeness, no one knows why," said Ellie. She had died in 1912, two years after her brother, and even her children had only a vague memory of what she looked like.

"In later life, she had this malady that doctors used to call 'American nervousness,' " Hettie added. "Paregoric was prescribed which contains opium and it seems she was susceptible." Hettie supposed it was her drug addiction that caused her family to turn its back on the poor soul. It seemed more merciful to help her pretend she wasn't there than to struggle to include her in her household life. After a time, they scarcely saw the spectral figure creeping past, still gently tended by her mother's former slave. Only Aunt Cindy had been present when Minnie Collins, still in her fifties, died of pure failure of the spirit on a cold March day. She sat unnoticed in her corner until the tall black woman tried to rouse her for her evening gruel.

"Aunt Cindy saw to everything," Hettie said. "Cinderella Myers was born a slave, an old-fashioned slave of good strong character who stood by her young mistress after she was freed. She even left her own new family to go south with her Miss Ellen, knowing how unfit she was to manage on her own."

Lucius suggested the young slave girl might have come from the Myers Plantation in Columbia, South Carolina, perhaps as a wedding present to Ellen Addison, since according to the census, they were approximately the same age. But of course such facts told nothing about who Cindy really was, a young woman with her own desires who had endured her long travail on earth so far from home and family. "How lonely the poor thing must have been," he said.

That an outsider should be so concerned about their servant's feelings struck his cousins as perverse. Chagrined by how little they knew of her themselves, they could not answer his upsetting questions. No, there was no known picture of Aunt Cindy, either. After Granny Ellen and her daughter died, the old woman had persevered without complaint in her shack behind the house, tottering about her chores and chickens even after she started to go blind, until finally, in reward for her half century of faithful service, she was sent home. Her little satchel had been packed for weeks when a "Miss L. Watson," her "baby daughter" of long, long ago, came to fetch her back to those Carolina uplands her old eyes would never see and her mind could scarcely imagine anymore.

"Nobody was home the day Aunt Cindy left, that's what my daddy told me," Cousin Ellie said. "Isn't that awful? Daddy never forgave himself. Not a sign of her, not even a note, because in all those years no one took the time to teach her how to read and write."

"The poor old thing just vanished," Hettie agreed. "Aunt Cindy gave this family her life, and no one was home to thank her for her life or even say good-bye."

TWO GREEN ONE-CENT STAMPS

Hettie rummaged from her box a letter postmarked Somerville, Massachusetts, January 14, 1910. It carried two green one-cent stamps bearing the profile of Ben Franklin and was addressed to Mr. Julian Edgar Collins, R.D. #2, Fort White, Florida.

> *Dear Julian,*
>
> *Your very nice and interesting letter reached me yesterday and as usual I was delighted to hear from you. Glad to hear that all the folks are well. As to May, I have not heard from her. I am very sorry that she blames me for my opinion of Leslie, but I am sure that I have not wronged him and that he himself is to blame for the opinion held of him by all good people. . . . If I understand his case correctly, robbery was his motive, therefore making it a most dastardly crime. I doubt very much if Leslie cares for May as such people are not capable of true affection.*
>
> *Hope that eventually I will be able to come back and settle down and marry some fair southern maid. I have no time to bother with the girls now as I have to work Sundays and holidays. Hoping that you will grow more prosperous as you grow older and with my very best wishes to Laura and babies I remain,*
>
> *Sincerely, Rob*

"We think that can only be Rob Watson. But he never came back or Julian would have said something about it."

The last time Lucius had seen him, Rob was a tense dark-eyed young man of "poetic" appearance, with straight black hair worn nearly to his shoulders. What did he look like now? *I have no time to bother with the girls.* Had he had time in the years since? Rob's lonely moralizing letter made him sad.

"That's the last letter?"

"That's the *only* letter. Rob makes it sound like a regular correspondence but it wasn't. We can't even imagine how he found out what he seems to know. Clearly he needed to feel closer to the family, being homesick and lonely but afraid of coming home." Hettie looked distressed. "Long ago, you see, Rob took his father's ship and sold it at Key West with the help of a young Collins, at least that's what Uncle Edgar told this family."

Lucius nodded. "That was Arbie Collins," he reminded Ellie. "The cousin I told you about."

The women glanced at one another. Ellie spoke sharply, "Sir, we can't imagine who this cousin of yours might be."

"Well," Lucius said, "he almost came with me today," as if this explained things. He resisted the intuition now fighting its way to the forefront of his brain.

"You see, Professor"—Hettie was almost whispering in her distress—"our cousin Lee told us years ago that *he* was the Collins who helped Rob sell that schooner."

"There's no R. B. Collins in this family," Ellie declared flatly. "I tried to tell you that over the telephone but you didn't want to hear it for some reason." She pointed at Hettie's lineage sheets, spread on the table. "We rechecked every name before you came this morning, just to be sure."

"Now R. B. *Watson*—Robert Briggs Watson—that's Cousin Rob, of course," Hettie said carefully, her eyes pleading with Lucius to absolve himself. "And Rob's mother was Cousin Ann Mary Collins, as you know—"

September 13, 1879. That date had tattered the corner of his mind since the visit to the New Bethel churchyard early this morning. Ann Mary Watson's death date was the birthday never mentioned in Papa's household even when Rob was still a boy. He studied Rob's letter. *Oh God. Of course!* The oddly familiar script, with its looping *y*'s and *g*'s, could have been written by a young, stiff, priggish Arbie, whose hand he knew well from all the margin notes in his "Watson Archive."

"We can't find 'L. Watson Collins,' either," Ellie persisted. "If that's really your name, sir, we have no idea who you might be."

"No, of course not." He set Rob's letter on the table. " 'L. Watson Collins' is a pen name." He stood up and crossed to the window with loud creakings of the old warped pine floor. With his back to them, he said, "I'm your cousin Lucius. I've deceived you. I am truly sorry."

He turned to face them. Having had no luck with Julian, he explained, he had hesitated to identify himself before he'd learned a little more about his father's life here in Fort White; he had feared his cousins might be less than candid had they known that he was Uncle Edgar's son. He had planned, of course, to confess this before leaving—but here he stopped short and raised his hands and dropped them, sickened by his own half-truths and excuses. He moved toward the door.

Speechless, they made no effort to detain him. But he'd seen tears mist in Hettie's eyes and to her he offered a last plea from the doorway. "It seemed so important to establish the truth—" Unable to bear her wondering gaze, he stopped again. "Please forgive me," he said.

Cousin Ellie's unforgiving voice pursued him outside. "The truth seemed so important that you lied!" He closed the door, went to his car. The window was open and Ellie would speak again, and he was not sure that denunciation by these newfound kinswomen he liked so much would be quite bearable.

At the road corner, a woman walking toward the schoolhouse waved him down. "Mist' Lucius? Don't remember Jane the cook? From when you was a boy at Chatham Bend?" The woman, handsome, simply dressed, was indeed familiar, and when she smiled, he recognized Jane Straughter, who had accompanied Julian and Laura Collins on a year's visit to the Bend; he vaguely recalled a crisis over Jane and Henry Short, which Papa had resolved by banishing Henry from the Watson place.

Without preamble, Jane Straughter asked after "Mr. Henry Short," how he was faring. Where was he living? Lucius could not help her since he did not know. Yet she seemed confident he would see Henry again. "When you see him," she said, "kindly give that man the warmest wishes of Miss Jane Straughter. Please say it that way, Mist' Lucius: *Miss* Jane Straughter. Tell Mr. Short that Miss Jane was asking after him. Inviting him to please come visit one day if he wishes."

THE CLARITY OF CHURCHYARDS

At the Collins cemetery in Fort White, the white church at the end of its long lane through the woods was spare and clean in a way that reminded Lucius of Hettie Collins, who was fashioned from the same native heart pine. They had responded to each other and now, already, she was gone. His emotion was so poignant that for the moment he'd forgotten Arbie— *Rob!* He could scarcely believe it. Who could have recognized the prim Rob of that letter in the unshaven and disreputable "Chicken" at Caxambas, stripped by hardship and rough company of all the manners and good grammar taught him by dear Mama in those years of patient tutoring, and disguised further by that cryptic urn said to contain Rob Watson's bones?

In the wistful melancholy of a country churchyard which time and weather and the woodland creatures were gradually taking back, he wandered among the modest headstones that had lately replaced the wood crosses Hettie had referred to. Here was Uncle Billy Collins, gone to his reward in February of 1907, three months before Sam Tolen. Nearby lay Granny Ellen Watson, dead at eighty in June of 1910, just four months before her son. In a narrow grave between mother and husband lay what was left of timid beautiful Aunt Minnie, safe at last.

The clarity of churchyards: everything extra worn away and what remained in order and in place, sequestered from the tumult of the world, in pristine stillness. He tried to sort his feelings. Old cemeteries made him homesick, wasn't that it? In the Collins schoolhouse, he imagined he had sensed long-buried roots here in Fort White, yet these uplands of the north-central peninsula were not his home. Home was that lone house on its great bend of Chatham River, no destination anymore but only the source of a vague sadness he thought of as "homegoing," a returning to the lost paradise of true belonging. Chatham for him was what Clouds Creek in the Carolina Piedmont had been for Papa.

One day when the sun caught it, he had seen a little pool shining in the heart of an old stump on a Glades hammock, a silver black glitter like a black diamond, filled with exquisite light. Here no wind breath feathered the surface, only perhaps a leaf speck or breast feather, a wild bit of color fixed minutely to this reflection containing all—high wind clouds and eternal sky all mirrored, immanent. That was home, too.

He strayed across the sun-worn grass among old lichened monoliths, touching and tracing the inscriptions. The pains taken with the lettering astonished him—the knowing hands of nameless artisans, themselves long buried, incising stone calligraphies in memory of strangers. The age of these granites, hewn from crusts heaved up into the sun by planetary fire from miles beneath the surface of the earth, stirred him and humbled him. In quest of eternity, the upright stones yearned toward the firmament, even as they too were gnawed minutely by the bloodless fungi and blind algae that worked with the wind and rain to obliterate man's scratchings.

The slow stone metamorphoses filled him with longing—longing for what? Simplicity? Was simplicity the true nature of homegoing? The simple harmonies, earth order and abundance. In this churchyard in a woodland meadow at the end of a white road, he missed what he had never known, the peace of living one day then another in communion with others of one's blood and at the end, at the close of one's works and days, to draw that last breath and come to rest in earth where one's bones belonged.

Belonging. His encounter with his kin would not change his fundamental isolation from his family—his "lonelihood," as Henry Short once called it. In a knowing beyond knowing, he knew that lovely Hettie, on a none too distant day, would be left behind here in the silence after the last mourner had departed Tustenuggee. Perhaps her transience, her mortality, explained why, so suddenly and strangely, she had touched his heart.

The sad solace of old cemeteries was a morbid sort of healing, though not to be despised on that account. The country graveyard in the woods was a last sanctuary, inviolable, not to be transgressed—man's last hope of equity, as Papa might have said, with everyone content in their own bones. Yet even here, the car horns could be heard, searching every distance. In the end there was no escape from the bonds of space and time short of release into the void, leaving no more trace of one's swift passage than the minnow's glimmer on the flooded road to Gator Hook or the disintegrating mushrooms become dust in the sunny leaf-bed of this autumn wood or the circles of great raptors gyring high over the Glades in the passing of ancient winds across the sky.

A jay's blue fire crossed the sun from one wall of spring leaves into another. In the stillness, a stray thrush song came in wistful query from the wood. He turned to listen. Nothing. Only the fall of a lone acorn, a small point of sound on the surface of the silence, a point of emptiness in the great roar of the turning earth.

At the hotel, he found an unsigned note. "Fort White was a bad idea. Look for message at Gen. Delivery, Fort Myers." Fear of exposure at Fort White explained Rob's resistance to coming, Lucius decided, but why had he changed his name? Was he a fugitive?

He telegraphed Rob in care of General Delivery and sent him money, assuring him that his brother was neither angry nor upset but only looked forward to finding out who the hell was in that urn.

Before checking out, Lucius rang Hettie to apologize and say good-bye. She seemed relieved to hear from him, saying she quite understood why he might have wished to conceal his identity; she'd worried about him ever since he'd left, realizing how shocked he must have been by the sudden resurrection of his long lost brother. "Please tell Rob how happy we would be to welcome him back into the Collins family. And Lucius, too," she added, her soft smiling voice warming his heart. He asked if one day he might pay another visit and she told him that she dearly hoped he would. "Come soon," she said, by which he knew she shared his premonition. He said, "I will, Hettie, I will," and put the phone down.

Catching his own sappy smile in the lobby mirror, he thought of Nell and reviled his inconstant heart. His despair was sincere and yet he was still smiling.

ALACHUA PRAIRIE

South of Fort White, Lucius followed the old county road across the worn-out cattle range of the Alachua Prairie. The potholed road passed a humble church then a few poor habitations patched into the scrub edge.

Will Cox, winding down his days in a blue shack surrounded by junked autos, stood in his narrow doorway with his hat on. "Next time you might find my grave but you won't find me," he sang out cheerfully, as if this stranger had turned up late on a long-awaited visit. Paying no heed when

Lucius got out and introduced himself, he crossed the yard with bony steps and climbed into the backseat. "Been a while since I seen where I am headed for," Mr. Cox said. "Let's go have us a look."

The little church back up the road had been founded by Will Cox after his family had been "hated out" of the Fort White district. He mentioned the exile without bitterness, far less self-pity.

Lucius helped the failing man out of the car. His Second Adventist church consisted of one white room with a cheap upright piano and small narrow pulpit; the unfenced yard was bare hard clay haired lightly by sparse weeds. No bird call brought the hot scrub wood to life, no color refreshed the petals of the artificial flowers in the rusted wire holders at the graves. "Be here for good before you know it," Will Cox declared, gazing about with satisfaction. "I am just ate up with cancer, so they tell me."

Cox shuffled forward, removing his old felt, and pointed a proud trembling finger at twin stones ten inches high and barely wide enough to carry the small initials. "W. W. C. That's William W. Cox only I ain't in there yet. And C. F. C., that's Cornelia Fralick Cox. She's down there now, bless her heart! Before she knows it, she'll be layin beside her darlin same as she always done." Will Cox contemplated his wife's grave. A toppled jam jar lay behind the stone. "Been aimin to get me and Ma a big ol' tombstone but I been down sick about ten years and never got to it."

Asked if he'd seen Leslie in recent years, Mr. Cox said, "My boy Leslie Cox weren't a-scared of *nobody.*" He glanced behind him in case Les might have turned up at last out on the road. When Lucius pressed him—had his son ever returned?—he shook his head. "If Les ever come back, folks would of knowed him, cause Les had a scar right to his ear where that mule kicked him, laid him out stone cold. We thought that boy would never sit up again. And when he did, his momma seen into his eyes, then whispered, kind of funny, " 'This here ain't the same boy no more as we have knew.' " Out of respect for his loved ones, he took his hat off, put it on again, and stood a while, hands folded simply on his breast. "Had a big picture of Les up on the wall before our neighbors burned us out and we come here. Him and his wife May, they was both on there. Burned down to nothin.

"Les weren't never a bad boy the way they say. Went to church regular and done his lessons, got to be star pitcher on the ball club. Folks thought the world of Les. Never had no trouble before Watson come." Saying this, the old man gave his visitor a hard sharp look. "You're a Watson, I reckon."

When Lucius nodded, he did, too. "Yessir. We been waitin on you." When he did not explain this, Lucius caught a fleeting scent of backwoods menace, like the quick sharp musk of mink on a night road. "Let me know if you get tired, Mr. Cox," he said.

"I *stay* tired," the old man said, holding his eye. But in a moment, his attention wandered. "Now that is a thing I wouldn't hardly know," he muttered, responding to some inquiry in his own head. "That was way back yonder, long, long time ago. Ed Watson warned me. 'Listen, Will, these Tolen skunks raise hell with croppers so you got to go along with 'em somewhat.' And I says, 'Nosir, Ed, I don't got to go along with *nobody* if they don't do right.'

"Along about that time, Sam Tolen showed up at our fence, told me what I could do and could not do, carried on like he founded the damn county. Our rent was settled but Tolen claimed there was more land than he figured so he needed more money. I told him, 'Mister, have it surveyed out, and if I owe more money, I will find it some way.' " Cox shook his head. "Nosir, we wasn't lookin for no trouble but Tolens brought it and my boy Les took care of it.

"Where it started, Jim Tolen done Ma's sister wrong so Ma swore a feud against all Tolens. Knowin I don't hold with blood feuds and the Fralick boys bein all killed off or in the pen, she went and mentioned to her oldest how he had to revenge poor Sister's honor, bein as how she was fresh out of brothers. My boy went to Watson for advice. About that time Jim Tolen slunk off home to Georgia, so maybe Watson advised Les to make do with the next one." He gazed admiringly anew at the small C. F. C. stone in the sand. "Cornelia Fralick had a piece of Hell in her, y'know. When them deputies come to arrest Leslie for Sam Tolen, she reared so high they had to put the cuffs on her till they got him away."

Was Mr. Cox saying that his son dealt with *both* those Tolens? Will Cox lifted his felt hat to scratch his scalp before he nodded. "I reckon. I reckon it might been Les who done 'em both." The direct question had not bothered him, since unlike the Collins clan, so proud and prim, the Coxes were unashamed and unequivocal: whatever Leslie might have done, he was their blood and, for better or worse, had stood up for his family.

Had he never believed Ed Watson was involved?

The old man frowned. "I thought a lot of E. J. Watson, had a very high opinion of that man, but I never heard Les say Watson was in on it." He pulled his ear. "Judge sent my boy to jail for life after that nigger trouble. Had to run off from the rail gang."

"Guards never tried to catch him?"

"Nosir, not so's you'd notice." Will Cox almost smiled. "Our boy come home, worked in our field the same as always. His wife was livin with us, too, on account of her own people didn't want her. Our family thought the world of Miss May Collins! Then some fool seen Leslie in the field, told Will Dick Purvis, 'That boy is up to Coxes, Sheriff, best go git him.' So Les hid up under the roof when Purvis come. Will Dick never tried to hunt him, he just sung out, 'Well, if I was Les, I'd sure head out for other parts, cause if he gets caught in *this* neck of the woods, folks just might hang him.' "

"The judge had no business sending Leslie to prison for killing that black family—that the way the sheriff saw it?"

Cox squinted at him hard. "That's the way *ever*'body seen it, mister." He set his hat straight. "Anyways, Les got sick of hidin, wearin women's clothes out in the field and all like that. Stayed to help with spring plantin, then told us all good-bye for now, take care of May, he'd see us soon. Went on south to Thousand Islands and that was the last he was ever knowed about exceptin hearsays.

"Feller who generly told the truth claimed he run across Les down around the coast, said 'I'm your cousin.' Said Les told him, 'Well, that don't mean that if you ever say you seen me, I won't shoot you.' "

Will Cox squinted. "Some said it was Watson done for Les. I said, 'You talkin about E. J. Watson? Shit, no!' I said. 'E. J. was my good old friend, he never done no such of a thing.' "

Will Cox toed the clay soil with his broken shoe. "We heard it was a nigger man killed Watson. Heard Ed's own boys never raised a hand to set that right." He studied Lucius. "Which boy was you?"

"I'm Lucius, Mr. Cox."

"Times must of changed when I weren't lookin, Lucius." Will Cox spat tobacco juice, turned back toward the road. "Me'n my younger boys, we was fixin to go south to Watson's, find out what they done with Les, hunt up that nigger, too, while we was at it. But like I say, I been down sick and never got to it." He spread his hands in the hot sun and both men watched them shake. "Don't look like I'm ever goin to get there, what do *you* think?"

"Nosir," Lucius murmured gently, "I don't think you are."

Baleful, Cox regarded him. "Don't think so, huh?" Both grinned and Lucius took him home.

Lucius's instinct was to take Will Cox's word that after his son's departure in the spring of 1910, his family never laid eyes on him again. Either Leslie had lived out his bad life in other parts or Papa had shot him dead at Chatham Bend just as he'd claimed.

Lucius remembered Leslie's mule kick scar—"pretty good scar upside his head," Grover Kinard had called it. Coldness and detachment, fits of violence, indifference to the suffering of others—weren't those known symptoms of brain damage?

To judge from Will Cox's pride in him, his family seemed well satisfied that Leslie had killed both Tolens—another argument in Papa's defense. In north Florida as well as south, it was turning out that the murders behind much of the Watson myth had been committed by another. Yet he felt uneasy. Had Papa encouraged hero worship in the unsophisticated Leslie and then exploited him, prying wide a dangerous fissure in his brain?

And what of "Uncle Edgar"'s brain? Yet Papa had never beaten his children nor appeared deranged even in drink, at least at home. For forty years after leaving South Carolina, he had farmed and traded, maintained neighborly relations, and remained beloved of his family, always excepting the one nicknamed Sonborn—the prodigal son, the long-lost brother, Robert Briggs Watson. R. B. Arbie. Rob.

IN THE FALL

After supper on his last evening at Chatham Bend, Lucius had joined his father on the river porch. Papa awaited him in his rocking chair, placed in the darkest corner. He seemed to know that this would be a showdown over Cox.

In his power, Papa's foreman had grown so intimidating that the field hands would fall mute the instant he appeared, shuffling about their work with eyes cast down, reduced in moments to drones of the human animal, stripped of every trait of voice and movement that each man might have shown without Cox present. They moved like penitent dull beasts rather than draw the smallest attention to themselves. Cox's utter indifference to their welfare, their very humanity, had made them indifferent to it, too: he moved them about like checkers on a board he might knock over on a whim at any moment, scattering these lives into the grass. In other years it had pleased Papa to tease the hands, cajole them into acceptance of their hard and dangerous labor. Now he scarcely noticed, and when Lucius protested Cox's cruelties, roughly waved his son away, not wanting to know what the foreman was up to so long as the work got done.

Lucius's outrage and frustration drove him to challenge his father on another matter. Declaring his intention to find Rob, he asked if his father knew what had become of him, and this time he did not back off when Papa sighed, his eyes half shut, sinking heavily into that iron silence. "Papa? He's my brother. I have a right to know."

Through the window, the porch was dimly lit by the kerosene lantern on the supper table inside but he was unable to make out the expression of the figure in the shadows. Lucius said, "If you don't know, please say so. Maybe I can locate that Collins cousin he knew in Key West."

His father sat up in a sudden rage, upbraiding him for resurrecting ugly stories. Lucius heard him out, then protested mildly, "Papa? I'm only asking about Rob."

Papa seemed to sense that this time his son meant business—that he might in fact be on the point of losing the last of his older children from whom he was not estranged and the one, further, whose assistance was critical for that autumn's harvest. He rose and slammed inside. Lucius thought he'd gone for good. Instead he lit a fresh cigar at the table lantern, came back out, and resumed his seat. While he smoked, the tobacco ember glowed. He cleared his throat.

For years, he said, he'd been sad to see the fear behind the feigned warmth in his neighbors' faces. Fairly or unfairly, his reputation was torn beyond repair, and since he was already fifty-five, that situation was unlikely to change. Though he'd never been unduly bothered by public opinion, he explained, he hated the idea that because of rumors, he might be thought a cruel killer in his own family, and in particular by the son who would inherit this plantation and the syrup business. (In the near dark the cigar ember described a sweeping arc to include the boats, outbuildings, house, and fields.) Kate Edna and her kids, he said, would have to be content with the Fort White farm. Not once did he mention his three older children.

Waiting out this preamble, Lucius said nothing. Annoyed by his silence, his father said that Lucius could believe any rumor he wished: the truth was something else. Here he stopped to grind out his cigar, as if to bring this degrading discussion to an end, but in a moment, he said, "There's no evidence. Two sets of tracks reported by some mixed-blood fishermen. Who took them seriously? People would have forgotten the whole business a long time ago if your brother hadn't lost his head and run away."

"Was Rob guilty, Papa?"

"The whole thing was an accident."

"Both deaths."

His father nodded. And because Rob had fled, he added, it had seemed sensible to remove himself, too, to avoid questioning. When he returned a few years later, he was never challenged. Before this evening, in fact, he had never mentioned that day to anyone except Lucius's mother. "You are the first person to confront me, boy."

"If it was an accident, why would he leave so suddenly? Taking your ship?"

His father leaned back into the shadows. "He was afraid, I reckon."

"Of his own father?"

"That, too. Of being arrested and accused . . ." His voice trailed off.

Lucius took a great big breath. "Papa? Are you saying—you seem to be saying—"

"I'm saying I take sole responsibility for what happened at Lost Man's Key. Satisfied? Now leave me the hell alone."

Lucius followed him inside and back out again. "How come we can't ever mention Rob? Why did you call him Sonborn? He *hated* that!"

" 'Son Born' was the only notation in the Columbia County register in Lake City because I turned my back on him from the first hour and never bothered to go there and record a name." Blurting this out, his father was gasping in distress.

"Did you ever love him, Papa?"

"No. Yes. Much too late. I never realized it until that day at Lost Man's. After I'd harmed him."

"Did you let him see it?"

"He was probably too stunned to see it, and he fled before I found a way to reach him. After that, I didn't want to think about him. I couldn't—I still can't—handle it. Not man enough, I guess." Papa had always been caustic about his own weaknesses, the drinking, women, and propensity to violence that had led to his worst missteps; he seemed to take a perverse satisfaction in catching himself out on even the smallest evasions. But this remark bared a weary self-disdain that his son had never thought to see.

"Oh Lord, Papa." They sat a while. "Why didn't you explain to people that the whole thing was an accident?"

"Who would have believed that, for Christ's sake? You don't believe it even now and you're my son."

"I do believe you, Papa." This was true. As far as it went, he trusted his father's account, and for the moment, he was even grateful for its ambiguity. As Papa had probably intuited, he didn't wish to know any details that might oblige him to condemn father or brother, though it was mostly his unwillingness to entwine his father in a lie that had kept him from resuming his inquisition. Two young people had been shot. Somebody had shot them. Was it really possible that both had died in the same "accident"? *The girl, Papa? Why was she killed?*

That evening, he had had no wish to crowd him further. His father had exonerated Rob—that had to be enough. Yet clearing Rob of responsibility fell short of saying that Rob had not taken part. His father had specified that the full responsibility was his alone. **Was** this tantamount to an admission that he'd killed those people? That **accid**entally or otherwise, he had been the shooter?

This much was to his credit: in refusing to discuss the episode with **anyone**, not even to defend his name, he had chosen to live with the local opinion that E. J. Watson had been solitary in that dreadful act. He had done his best to spare Rob any consequences—which was only just, Papa explained, since the plan to run those squatters off his claim had been his alone. However, he had not wished them to die, the way people said. And it tortured him to think that his younger son and his dear Kate Edna might suspect that he had murdered them. . . . Unable to finish, he raised his big hard hands and dropped them on his knees, as if to say, *I shall go to my grave bearing terrible slanders that will never be put to rest.*

Again, his son was silent. What could he say? But in denying his beloved father his filial reassurance, he had wounded him, that much was clear. He had also angered him, set him to brooding, so that when eventually he thanked Papa for easing his mind about Rob's role, remarking in passing that he'd never thought Rob capable of violence, his father had made that unsettling deep grunt, shifting his boots on the porch floor. "You were pretty young back then, still a schoolboy in Fort Myers," he had muttered, as if to suggest that Lucius had not really known his brother.

Lucius disliked this insinuation just when he thought Rob's innocence had been confirmed, and perhaps his quick stare of resentment—*Do you mean what you seem to be implying, Papa?*—had stung his father, who had given him a long appraising look. "You don't remember how wild-tempered he was?" he said. "The crazy way he killed his dog that morning?"

Lucius met his eye. "I remember," Lucius said. But his brother had been wild-hearted, not wild-tempered, and in no way crazy.

It had happened there between the river and the porch at a time when Rob was very dark in spirit, brooding for days over some rough thing Papa had said. On that hot noon, coming from the field, Papa had removed his coat and hung it on a chair before going inside. The revolver butt protruded from the inside pocket. Rob, coming behind him, had taken out the gun and with a queer look on his face placed the muzzle in his mouth to scare his younger brother. It had scared him, of course, not because he imagined Rob might kill himself—Rob had always seemed far more likely to kill Papa—but because Rob might have forgotten that even at Chatham, Papa's gun was always loaded. That's who their father was.

"Watch out with that thing, Rob!"

In a peculiar voice, Rob said, "All right." He kneeled in front of his young bluetick hound, which lay twitching flies in a noon snooze. "Rex? Want to play roulette?" Lucius never forgot the soft thumping of Rex's tail. His brother picked five of the six rounds out of the chamber, spun it a few times, then put the muzzle to the dog's head. Shaky, he whispered, "Good luck, Rex, because I sure would miss you, but I aim to fire, so this may be your last day as a dog." Even as Lucius yelled, Rob pulled the trigger.

That scaring *Bang!*, the spurting neck, the blood-drenched animal in spasm pushing itself in a half circle on the dirt as if to screw itself into the ground, had shocked Rob so that he jumped up with a screech, hurled the revolver after Papa, and lit out around the house. Headed nowhere, he ran only to escape himself. Round and round and round he went, screeching each time he passed the twitching body of this pup that his kind step-mother had given him. He was trying to run right off the earth.

Papa strode out in a red fury. He stooped and took Rex by the tail and cir-cled once as he ran forward toward the bank and whirled the carcass through the air into the river. Next he intercepted Rob at the house corner, hoisted him with his legs still running, and shouted into his face, "God damn you, Sonborn! What the hell's the matter with you!" When his son closed his mouth tight over locked teeth, Papa hurled him to the ground, then grabbed his collar, yanked him back up onto his feet, and knocked him sprawling. He stood there panting, staring down at Rob as he got his breath.

Rob lay quiet, watching Papa. Never wiped his face and never spoke a word. "Damn you anyway," Papa said quietly. Retrieving his revolver, he re-turned inside.

On their last evening in September, 1910, they were civil when they said good night but there was no healing the disease between them. Next morn-ing when Lucius told him he was leaving, Papa said, "Do what you must," and turned his back. Not until Lucius was casting off his skiff did his father appear; he stood apart from the others on the riverbank. He had not waved like Hannah Smith and Green and Dutchy and even the hard black man known as "Little Joe," who offered a grin and a half wave from the kitchen doorway.

Off to one side, a horseshoe toss away from all the rest, slouched the foreman, hands in his pockets. He did not wave, either. The black faces of the four new harvest hands watched from the field. When Cox turned that way, the four dark heads ducked down behind the shining swords of cane. Not until years later, as Lucius resumed Papa's biography, would those four cane cutters, never accounted for, rise from the abyss of dream memory as wild petroleum seeps up from the earth crust to form strange rainbows on black marshland pools.

That September day his father's features were so deep in the deep shadow of his hat that he seemed to be peering out from hiding and his fists were shoved so hard into his black frock coat that his outline bulged. Only at the very last, as the water spread away and his son's skiff was rounding the bend, on the point of disappearance, the bulky figure might or might not have wrested one hand from his pocket and lifted it halfway as if to take an oath, in dim presentiment, perhaps, that this was their final parting.

On the bank, the figures blackened in the glare before dissolving into the white sunlight. A few weeks later, when he learned that most of them were dead, he would recall those shifting silhouettes, those shades.

A MEMORY OF SHADOWS

Before his trip north to visit his Collins cousins, Lucius had written to his father's widow, asking if he might pay a call on the way back from Fort White. In affectionate teasing he signed the letter, "Your loving stepson, Lucius." There had been no answer to that letter nor to a later postcard. To judge from the silence that returned like the echo of a shot across long miles of swamp, red plain, and muddy river, reaching shy Edna was like whistling to an unknown bird hidden in the leaves.

But forwarded to his return address—he had specified General Delivery in Lakeland—was a note scrawled in carpenter's pencil on lined yellow paper. Its formal tone contrasted oddly with the writing. Mrs. Herkimer Burdett wished to inform him that she could not receive him at this time nor assist in his biographical research. The letter was signed not by Edna but by "A. Burdett." He had hardly reread it when the phone rang. In a voice gruff and grudging, Mr. A. Burdett announced that Mrs. Edna Burdett would receive his visit after all. He did not explain why she had changed her mind.

"Mrs. Burdett resides in a town that will go unnamed," the voice added—for the pure love of that phrase, it appeared, since without being privy to her whereabouts, Lucius could not have sent his letter in the first place. Downing his bourbon to calm himself, he said, "So she wants to see me after all?"

"I thought it was *you* who wanted to see *her.*"

"And you've decided to accommodate me. Why?"

Taken aback, the caller protested, "Now hold on a minute, mister! Are you drunk? My mother is shy about the telephone; she asked me to call!" When Lucius was silent, the voice cried, "I think you're drunk!"

"Addison? Is that you? We haven't met since you were four but I'm your brother, remember?" He listened to trapped breathing. "How about tomorrow?" They could meet at his mother's house, Lucius suggested, making the point that he knew the address and could go there with or without Addison's permission. More silence. "I wouldn't want to intrude, of course," he added quickly. "I have no wish to see her unless she wishes to see me." Though said to dispel Addison's wariness, this happened to be true.

"I'll call back." The caller hung up, and Lucius groaned. But within minutes, his gruff brother called back. He would meet Lucius next day at noon at the gasoline station in Neamathla.

A. Burdett, checking his watch, turned out to be a husky young man in an ill-fitting steel gray windbreaker, baggy khakis, and paint-splatted high black shoes. He was built much like their father, Lucius noted, but otherwise looked nothing like him. Thin brown hair was plastered back on a big brow; a downturned mouth clamped a tense and worried face. As in much older men, the ears and knobby workman's hands looked too large for his body; he had the hollow look of a man uncaressed by woman. Without meeting Lucius's eye, he needlessly identified himself, still using the initial. "A. Burdett," he said, already at a loss for what he might say next.

"*A* for Addison, right?" To dispel the clotting atmosphere, Lucius spoke enthusiastically. "Last time I saw you, Ad, you were just a little boy, playing around Papa's dock at Chatham."

Ad Burdett looked wary. "*Papa*," he muttered. "That's what us kids call Mr. Herkie." He stared in gloomy resignation at his paint-splotched shoes. "Might as well get going, then," he said. In his poky auto, he led his older brother into the village.

In sycamore shade of a quiet street of modest houses, Edna Burdett awaited Lucius, standing on her stoop. At the sight of him, she slipped inside and awaited him anew, holding up his *History of Southwest Florida* like a hymnal. "Would you be kind enough to sign your book, Professor Collins?" Only then did she offer a small smile. She was a bit thicker through the waist than he remembered, otherwise much the same—not quite pretty and yet handsome, with long honey-colored hair pinned up behind. Kate Edna Bethea Watson Burdett. Had she dropped the "Watson"? Papa had been the only one who called her Kate.

On the upright piano in the sitting room perched her wedding portrait with Herkimer Burdett and framed photographs of Addison and his sisters at various young ages, also a tinted photograph of a new child, Herkie Junior, who was off at school, she said. Lucius inquired about all of them before taking a seat.

Edna had backed herself into a stuffed chair under a lamp. From this redoubt, having smoothed her feathers, she permitted herself a better look at him. *What do you want with us?* her scared eyes said.

Addison stood awkward in the doorway, hat in hand. "Addison, do please sit down," his mother said, as if he were a pupil standing up at his school desk for no good reason. When Lucius tried to include him in his questions about their family, Ad said gloomily, "How long does he aim to stay? I have to get back to work."

His mother said, "You're not expected back today, you know that, dear." To Lucius, she said, "Addison is a housepainter like Mr. Burdett."

The spring day ticked past on a big loose alarm clock in another room. She showed Lucius an old schoolbook, *The History of Ancient Greece*, that Papa had cherished and read over and over all his life. Lucius was touched that Edna had thought to take it when she fled.

"Your father was always good to me and kind and loving with his children; you do know that, don't you, Lucius? When my sister came to visit in Fort White, she could not get over how much time that busy man would spend with his little children—very unusual for any man back in those days." She passed him a faded photo of dim figures grouped on the porch steps at the Bend, and Lucius recognized the husky man in black suit and black hat whose features were lost in the dark of the hat shadow. "That's all we have—that shadowed face. A memory of shadows!" She took a great deep breath. Edna could not bring herself to use his name, not even "Mr. Watson." When Lucius mentioned him, she tweaked her blue blouse, crisscrossed her ankles. But neither did she betray resentment or shame or regret: his father's actions had nothing to do with her, her manner said, nor alter the truth, that she had been a faithful God-fearing wife.

"Those bad things happened when us kids were small," Ad complained suddenly. "Horrible crimes that none of her neighbors know about. But for her, they are not safely in the past." His voice was rising and his color, too. "*What would folks think of us if they knew?*—that's what scares her."

"Addison? Please, dear." Edna's glance assured Lucius that Ad was voicing his own trepidations and not hers. "Poor Amy was only five months at that time. She never knew her father and was never told what happened. One day, a woman whose uncle was in that mob told her dreadful tales. I suppose this person wished to justify what those men did, but for poor Amy, it was terrifying. To this day, the poor thing cannot bear to hear one word about her father. If anyone asks, she says she knows nothing about him except that he died long ago of a heart attack."

"My mother and her sister can't even mention him," Ad grumbled, "and you intend to *write* about him."

Edna sighed. "Amy was only a babe in arms when that storm struck Chokoloskee. I've been deathly afraid of rough weather ever since. And when your father perished in that very place just a week later, that hellish noise terrified us all over." She put her hand over her heart. "Lucius? That day was my twenty-first birthday. That's why he came back."

"You're still one week older than I am," he said, trying to lighten things; she scarcely heard him. "Before your father left Chokoloskee that last time, I begged him not to risk his life by coming back for us. I knew the evil feeling on that island. He must get away to Key West while he had the chance, I told him, and send for us later if he wished. But he was a bold and willful man, and he just smiled and kissed me, saying, 'A twenty-first birthday is important, Kate, and a promise is a promise.' Your father was killed because he kept his promise, did you know that?"

"She still forbids any celebration of her birthday," Addison complained.

Widow and children had traveled to Neamathla to stay with her sister Lola. "Mr. Burdett came to visit. He stayed on and we married. He gave my children his name."

"We felt lost," Addison muttered, avoiding Lucius's gaze. "I said, 'Well, Mama, who *are* we, then?' We felt like nobody at all. Then kids in school found out our real name."

Lucius nodded. "Someone always finds a way to let you know what you don't need to hear."

"For years after we left Chokoloskee, I exchanged letters with Mamie Smallwood, who took us in that day and was so kind. A few years ago my Ruth Ellen went there for a visit. Wilma Smallwood—she never married—was running the store by then. Wilma showed that poor girl these dreadful clippings—terrible things that had been written about her father. She didn't ask to see them, Wilma just showed them. Ruth Ellen was horrified. When she came home, she asked if it was true that Papa had murdered our dear Hannah and those men, and I said, 'No, honey, it was his foreman.' "

Upset by her own reference to Leslie Cox, Edna rose abruptly, then busied herself at the piano, straightening the photos.

Because "John Smith" was not only a fugitive but a kinsman by marriage to whom he was indebted, his father had instructed Edna to keep his real name secret. Lucius himself had never been told much more about John Smith than he had picked up in the first five minutes. He could have used a friend of his own age to hunt and fish with but Leslie Cox had no idea how to be a friend, let alone have fun. All he cared about was killing more game than anybody else and getting the credit for bringing back more meat. He stayed mostly half drunk, he terrorized the workers, he made mean remarks, poking up trouble.

Edna looked around as if hearing someone slip into the house, then lowered her voice to a near whisper, confessing that Leslie slipped in close every time her husband turned his back. Complaining that "a man needed a woman," he would whisper that her husband was betraying her with those Daniels sisters on Pavilion Key. But after all the trouble at Fort White, she was so scared of more violence that she dared not tell her husband she was being harassed. In those last weeks of that long hot summer, afraid for her children in the deadly atmosphere at Chatham Bend, she had mostly stayed with friends in Chokoloskee.

Lucius nodded. "I left, too. And three weeks later, all hell broke loose, just as you feared." He turned to Addison. "Your mother is right, Ad. Those killings were Cox's doing and so were the killings at Fort White. Your dad was not to blame." But saying this, he felt obliged to add, "As far as I know."

"Or *want* to know, right?" Ad said unpleasantly.

"Lucius? Remember when your father hitched our dog Beans to a little red wagon and trained him to pull Addison? And the wagon tipped over, rolling our little boy down the riverbank, and Little Ad so scared of that awful crocodile that he could not stop crying? I can still hear him, across all these years!" She gazed fondly at her son, who was glaring at the wall. " 'Little Ad' is what Mr. Burdett called him before Ad got so big! And Ad was the first one who went south to seek the truth about what happened to your father."

Lucius smiled at Ad. "*Our* father," he said.

"Time off between jobs, that's all," Ad grumped. "I never really cared about this Watson stuff."

"Addison? You took your whole vacation! Went all the way down there by yourself!"

"That's none of his damned business!" Burdett lurched to his feet, his big face so menacing that Lucius stood up, too. "Don't put that in your book! I'll sue! How do *we* know what you're going to write? Why should we trust you?"

"Please stop shouting. This is *Lucius*."

" 'It's a closed chapter in my life'—that's what you said, Mother! So for God's sake, leave it closed!"

Edna flinched but let his swearing pass. "Lucius is a *historian*, Ad. And he's found out your father was not so bad as people made him out. You're not glad to hear that?"

"What do I care if the man was bad or good, or what was said about him? I care what people say about *our* family." To Lucius he said, "Just leave us out of your damned book, okay?" He was deep dull red in the face, his breathing heavy. "I'm not a Watson, I'm a Burdett. I have a good name and I want to keep it."

"Those dark things happened a long time ago," his mother mourned. "Maybe folks reading Lucius's book will understand your father in a different way and we won't have to be so nervous about who we are."

"It's important to establish the truth," Lucius added quietly, less and less sure of this.

"*The truth!* Ruth Ellen was toddling around with the Smallwood kid back in the store, she never saw it. But I ran down to the landing hollering 'Daddy! Daddy!' " Ad gasped up a few breaths before resuming in a stunned low voice. "I fell down in the mud. That crashing of those guns, oh God, I thought the sky was falling down. And dogs! Those dogs were mean and scary, *they bit children!* They never quit howling and fighting all night long." His lip was trembling. "I was three years old! Know what I saw? I saw my father fall. I saw the blood. *That* the kind of truth you're after here? *Professor?*"

"I'm still your brother, Ad. I'm asking you to trust me."

Burdett shook him off, frantic to go. Lucius followed him toward the door. "Listen," he said. "Since you feel this way, why did you let me come?"

"I was against it. I still am. But she wanted you and I knew from your letter you would find the way sooner or later." He went out.

For a little while they sat in silence, giving the house a chance to get its breath. Finally Edna cleared her throat. Ad had gone south a second time but had never said a word about it; she had learned of it in a Christmas letter from the Smallwoods. "And I never questioned him, that's how scared I was that he'd found out something worse than what we already knew."

This explained a nagging mystery, Lucius told her. A few years before, someone had gone to Chatham Bend and given the wind-weathered house a fresh coat of white paint.

"That's him. I'm so glad you mentioned it. Oh, he's a fine housepainter, Lucius! But even as a little boy, he always seemed . . . *you* know. Troubled." Edna tried to explain that Ad's abrupt and hostile manner stemmed from confused feelings. "He even considered changing his name to Watson—"

"His name *is* Watson." Despite his sympathy, Ad had made him cross.

She shook her head. "Not legally." She hurried on. "Ad grows lovely vegetables, you know. Spends all his spare time out in his garden." She stared at the clenched hands in her lap. "He is very very upset today. He will go and drink. His father was a dangerous drinker, as you know." She looked up. "Lucius? Do you have a good life? Do you have children?" When he shook his head, she flushed and hurried on. "Addison has few friends left: he's become a loner. He won't even come to family gatherings. He can't take a drink but he drinks anyway. He gets aggressive, very very angry. We worry that this violent anger might be dangerous to other people."

When Lucius answered, "I'm sure he'll be all right," his stepmother nodded doubtfully. "Well. We have lots to be thankful for. I mean, everybody has to live with *some*thing, isn't that true?"

Seeing the fear in her face, he took her hand. "I dragged my kids under the store," she murmured, holding his hand tight. "That's how scared I was those men were going to kill us. And I worry that it was my fear that scared Ad worse than anything. He still hears those guns in his sleep, wakes up hysterical. He just can't rid himself of the smell of those drowned chickens." She pinched at the bridge of her nose. "Me, either. How many years?" Her voice had diminished to a whisper. "I'll go to my grave with that stench of death, I'm sure."

She gave him the Greek history. "That's yours now, Lucius." For his sake, Edna had revisited her life as Mrs. E. J. Watson but now she wanted him to go.

"I'm sorry you didn't meet Mr. Burdett and Herkie Junior or see your little sisters." From her doorway, waving a shy hand, she invited him to visit next time he came through, but probably she knew as well as he did that they would not meet again, which was all right, too. When he turned to wave, she only gazed at him, head cocked ever so slightly. *Lucius? Why did you come? What do you want with us?*

SOUTH

On a green and blue day, Lucius headed south to Arcadia on the Peace River. In his father's day, as the new capital of Manatee County, Arcadia had claimed such frontier comforts as hard drink, whores, and gambling, knife fights, shootings, and common brawling: according to a local account, as many as four men had been killed in a single fight and fifty fights might occur in a single day. Untended stock on the county's unfenced range had encouraged a spirit of free enterprise in which cattle were stolen by the herd, and in 1890, four luckless strangers, denying to the end that they were rustlers, were hanged without formalities from the nearest oak. Inevitably the range wars attracted desperadoes from the West, and death by knife and bullet was a commonplace when a fugitive from Arkansas named E. J. Watson turned up in Arcadia and, according to later memoirs by friend Ted Smallwood, slew "a bad actor" named Quinn Bass:

> Watson said Bass had a fellow down whittling on him with his knife and Watson told Bass . . . he had worked on the man enough. And Bass got loose and came towards him and he begin putting the .38 S & W bullets into Bass and shot him down.

The date of Watson's arrival in Arcadia, his livelihood and length of stay—Smallwood set down no such details, only that Watson had paid his way out of his scrape before leaving town.

At the county clerk's office at the courthouse, a stately edifice on the main square, the town's earliest Criminal Docket Book, exhumed from the basement, made no mention of a Watson. However, a LeQuinn Bass had been arrested on September 19, 1890, for carrying concealed weapons, and again on October 23 of the next year, this time for murder. Bass had been acquitted on November 6, 1893—his last appearance in the docket book. Since his surname was otherwise absent from this record of every felony committed in the new county between 1890 and 1905, only LeQuinn could have been the Quinn Bass of Smallwood's account, yet his demise at the hands of E. J. Watson was nowhere recorded.

THE DOMESDAY BOOK

Arriving in Fort Myers the next day, Lucius found a note from Arbie—*Rob!*—at General Delivery saying that Lucius might find him in late afternoon at the bar of the Gasparilla Inn, where Lucius had arranged a supper meeting with Watt Dyer. In the meantime, he would visit the library and newspaper, noting Watson references and dates.

A sketch of Sheriff Frank Tippins in a local history attested that Tippins, "who arrested many desperate criminals during his career and acquired a statewide reputation for fearlessness," had always been frustrated by the "unsolved killing of Ed Watson. Due to the fact that Watson was said to have killed the notorious Belle Starr, his murder attracted national attention and stories about him are still being printed." Lucius was much encouraged by these references to the "unsolved killing" and "murder" of his father and also the mention of the thirty-three bullets removed from the riddled corpse, which reflected the sheriff's skepticism that an armed crowd of twenty or more men shooting a lone man to pieces had acted in self-defense.

At the Lee County sheriff's office, the stiff leaves of old court ledgers long unopened exhaled the breath of desiccation, and the sepia ink was as faint as the blue watermark. In these stained pages, the first name of interest was "Green Waller," jailed in 1896, 1898, and 1901 for "larceny of hog." Subsequently this dogged pig thief had found sanctuary at Chatham Bend, where he could commune with these estimable animals to his heart's content. Waller also appeared in the Monroe County census for May 1910, where he was listed in the E. J. Watson household as servant and farmhand. His mountainous lover Miss Hannah Smith was registered as cook;

field hand "John Smith" was the fugitive Leslie Cox. Last on the census list was "Lucius H. Watson, mullet fisherman." His own name startled him, flying off the faded page like a medieval moth trapped in the Domesday Book.

As in Arcadia, Lucius was mystified by the dearth of information on his father. Sheriff Tippins's records for 1910 made no reference whatever to the triple murder at Chatham Bend on October 10, nor to the murder of Ed Watson at Chokoloskee on the 24th, nor even to the court hearing in regard to that death held by Tippins two days later in Lee County Court: how was this possible? That the records were missing was all the more peculiar since these crimes had been prominently covered by the newspapers in Fort Myers and Tampa and both accounts had specified that the unnamed "negro" being held in connection with the Chatham massacre had spent a fortnight in the Fort Myers jail before being turned over to the Monroe County sheriff. Under the circumstances, it seemed incredible that in this official record (in which the miscreant's race was invariably noted), there was no mention of any black man taken into custody in Lee County in October of 1910, nor any notation in the sheriff's fees book, which recorded disbursements for the transport and feeding of each prisoner.

The most notorious murder case in Tippins's long career had been wiped from the record or it had never been transcribed. Either way, the culprit could only have been the deputy court clerk, Mr. E. E. Watson: was Eddie also responsible for his father's absence from the criminal dockets in Arcadia?

To bulwark his request for old court records, Lucius had laid a copy of his *History* on the counter. The deputy had picked at the thick book as if fingering strange fruit, then closed it in unconcealed relief that he need not read it. "Got a man restin his bad bones back in our cells who might know quite a lot about that case. Him and Tippins loved to swap old yarns about Ed Watson so what he'd tell might have some truth to it if he's feelin truthful." The deputy chuckled as he led the way down the back hall. "The feds asked us to hold this feller but it ain't nothin but harassment. County, state, and federal law knows all about him but none of 'em can nail him, he skitters out from under every time. Can't even jail him on his income tax cause he don't show no income on his books—ain't *got* no books! Got all his money in old feed sacks someplace, wouldn't surprise me. Yesterday he beat the charges same as always, he can walk out any time he wants, but he likes livin off the taxpayers while he's up to town."

The deputy had made no effort to keep his voice down, and approaching the cell door, he pitched it louder for the inmate's benefit. "When this feller was booked, I told him, 'Man, you are in *real* bad trouble this time. You are goin straight to prison to pay for all them felonious activities.' And he says, 'Nosir, I sure ain't, cause they know I'd take half the elected idiots in south Florida to the pen with me.' " The deputy laughed loudly as he fiddled with his keys, shaking his head in admiration. "Ol' Speck! He'll be back out in the Glades in two days' time, moonshinin and bootleggin, shootin the livin shit out of the gators."

Lucius stopped short—"*Speck?*" But it was too late, the deputy had banged open the cell door. "Yessir. How many Specks y'all acquainted with? This Speck you're lookin at is Crockett Daniels, that right, Speck?"

CROCKETT DANIELS

Crockett Daniels, sitting on the bunk edge, had been bent over tying up the laces on his sneakers, in feral instinct to be ready for whatever was coming at him down the hall. When the iron door swung open, he withdrew beneath the upper bunk in a kind of coiling, reminding Lucius of a cottonmouth's sidewinding retreat among the buttress roots of a swamp cypress before coming to rest half hidden in the shadows.

"Goddammit, Depitty, you pat him down good? This crazy sumbitch been threatenin my life!" When the deputy just laughed and slammed the door, Daniels cursed him. Eyes fixed on Lucius, he emerged slowly and perched on the bunk edge in the bad light from the fly-specked bulb high overhead. "That smart-mouth peckerhead is goin on report. Prisoners' rights ain't only just the rules, they're the damn *law*!" He glowered at his visitor, hard face fringed with dirty stubble. "God A-mighty! What do *you* want? Ain't laid eyes on you in years, then all of a sudden you show up way to hell and gone out to the Hook, and next thing I know, you track me right into my cell in the county jail." He raised his voice to shout after the deputy, "Stupid bastard! Locks me in with a damn Watson and don't even frisk him!"

Lucius turned and spread his arms, palms to the wall. "Go ahead," he offered, baiting Speck's nervousness. He regretted this when Daniels sprang and collared him and banged his chest violently against the wall before pat-

ting him down, then gave him a contemptuous hard shove before returning to the bunk, where he stretched out in the shadow, watching his visitor
from beneath the arm flung across his eyes. "I'm waitin on you, boy. If you
ain't here to shoot me, you better remember pretty quick why the fuck you
come."

Lucius said he'd heard that a man back in the holding cells might tell
him something about Sheriff Tippins's final conclusions on the Watson case.

"Tell *you* somethin? Sumbitch who put my name on a damn death list? I
won't tell you fuck-all about *nothin*!" But when Lucius mentioned the queer
absence of any reference to E. J. Watson in the sheriff's records, Daniels
grew curious despite himself. Frowning upward at the old straw and broken springs that thrust down from the bottom slats of the upper bunk, he
rubbed one temple with a scarred brown knuckle to summon up old talks
with Tippins that might hold a clue.

"That day the sheriff brought that bunch here to the courthouse? Them
men hollerin self-defense when every last damn one admitted they had
went to Smallwood's with guns loaded, set to shoot? Malice aforemost, just
like Tippins said. And after he seen how much lead tore up that body, he
could never believe their Chokoloskee story. He'd get to fumin like a big ol'
bear with a stung snoot and no honey to show for it. Ten years later he'd
still holler, 'Dammit, Speck, you was right there, boy, you *seen* it. Them men
must of emptied out every last load. Thirty-three slugs, not countin buckshot! Filled a damn coffee can! If thirty-three struck home, how many
missed? And they're tryin to tell a lawman that was *self-defense?*'

"Sheriff always aimed to summon a grand jury and reopen up the case
but the family was dead set against it and anyway he never could figure
how to prosecute, not with his whole posse confessin they took part. Not
your common prosecution case at all! Still and all, he couldn't let it go
cause by now he'd heard some crazy story how a nigger was first man to
fire at Ed Watson. Now *that* would eat at Frank P. Tippins, I can tell you!
Sheriff got on pretty good with Injuns but niggers was another breed entirely. This snitch told Tippins he had swore a oath he would never reveal
that nigger's name and he never had to, cause there weren't but the one
colored man on Chokoloskee.

"Now Henry Short were known to be a purty good ol' nigger, but Frank

Tippins could not tolerate that *any* colored man would think to raise a gun against a white man, and when the white man in the case was E. J. Watson, who had every coon in southwest Florida scared up a tree, he flat refused to believe it, especially when none of his damn suspects would confirm that story. Said they never needed no damn nigger to take care of their business. And from the hard way they said this, Tippins concluded that some of these fellers if not all of 'em knew what that day's business was before Watson's boat ever come in and struck ashore.

"All of the same, that rumor ate at him. For years Frank was huntin an excuse to take that black boy into custody and work some truth out of him. Only thing, he couldn't come up with him. Short was gun-shy and kept movin cause Tippins weren't the only man was huntin him. Somebody else was gunnin for him, I always heard. Maybe still is.

"When Prohibition come along and me and the sheriff done some business, he was still bothered. Asked me straight out, 'Dammit, Speck, did that darn nigger shoot at Ed or didn't he?' Well, I never seen it if he did, that's what I told him, not carin to admit I was so far in the back I couldn't see nothin at all. By the time I got my chance to fire, your daddy was already down, deader'n dirt."

"But you fired anyway. Snuck in there and fired a .22 into his head, is what I heard."

Speck raised his hand. "Now don't go barkin up all them wrong trees: we're talkin about niggers, ain't we? That other colored in the case? One you was askin about that ain't on the sheriff's books? I always heard he drowned some way on the trip south to Key West but Tippins heard they got him there, then let him off. Give him a new shirt and sent him home, up Columbia County. Sheriff Frank was just a-*boilin* mad. 'That's Key West justice for you, Speck! Nigger-lovin Yankees, all them foreigners! I mean, God a'mighty, Speck! That boy confessed how he had his black hands all *over* that big lady!' " Speck shook his head. "Feller was tellin me the other day how two different niggers in Key West was claimin to be the one escaped off of the Watson place after them killins. And I told him, 'Why, goddammit to hell, we got another one up to Fort Myers claims the same damn thing!'

"Anyways, Tippins believed till the day he left here for Miami that us fellers took and lynched Ed Watson, concluded we was waitin on the shore to gun him down. Said, 'Maybe you held your fire till he raised his gun, maybe you didn't.' Said Bill House was sincere, all right, believed the hell out of his own story, but somethin was missin all the same. Sheriff called your daddy's death an unsolved crime where most wouldn't call it no damn crime at all.

"That was the first time, Frank would say, that he never done his duty. Course it weren't the last time by a long shot, but he didn't know that in his early days. I believe it was the Watson case that made that feller say to hell with it and give up on common justice.

"As for them court records, you might be correct. Eddie Watson was so scared of talk that he might of wiped his daddy's name clean off the books. Might of been his own idea or maybe not. And Tippins comin from Arcadia, he might have got that taken care of, too, as a favor to the Langfords."

Breaking a rust-rotted shoelace—"Shit!"—Daniels kicked his sneaker off before stretching out, hands behind his head. Enjoying his role as an authority on the Watson case, he was annoyed when Lucius rose to leave. Speck said, "Don't aim to thank the man that found Bill House's testimony?" He grinned at Lucius's disbelief. "Found it right in Tippins's own desk. Chicken Collins stole it off me but it was mine by rights." He studied Lucius meanly. "Goddamn Chicken stole my nice souvenir from that historical-type day when us upstandin citizens wiped out Bloody Watson."

"So it was a lynching. You admit that."

Daniels shrugged. "I only joined up in that line of men to see what was goin on: I weren't much more than a boy." Speck considered this a moment. "Well, later I was bothered some and will admit it. Ed Watson had daughters by two Daniels females and treated our whole Caxambas bunch like family, so them ladies are still scoldin me for takin part. Hell, Josie's Pearl ain't spoken to me since." He grimaced at his own attempt to excuse his role. "You Watsons got nothin to be ashamed about, is all I'm sayin. Ed Watson was his own man, done what he thought was right. Like ol' Tant Jenkins always said, Ed never killed a livin soul that didn't need some killin. Which puts me in mind of a nice story for your book—story Tant's sister used to tell about how good she was took care of by her man Jack Watson."

BULLET NECKLACE

"One fine day on the Bend they was settin there eatin their supper. The white cutters on the harvest crew ate with 'em at that big pine table and this one feller was findin fault with Josie's peas. They wasn't salted, wasn't this, that, nor the other. So your daddy was rumblin to warn that cutter not to hurt Miss Josie's feelins. The man shut up but pretty quick he commenced to grumblin again. Knew a bad pea when he et one, this feller did.

"Mister Ed didn't have no more to say about it. Set his fork down, wiped his mouth, pushed his chair back, and got up real quiet. And there come a hush and this cutter stopped his eatin cause he knowed that somethin terrible was comin down on him. But he was too scared to beg or run, he only set there starin bug-eyed out the winder as if that big ol' croc that hunted that broad water at the Bend was clamberin right out on the near bank, comin to get him. Your daddy stepped around behind his chair and drawed his head back by the hair—didn't yank it, Josie said, her Jack wasn't rough with him or nothin. Laid his knife acrost his throat sayin, 'Please excuse us, folks,' then stood this feller on his feet and marched him outside before he slit his throat so's not to mess up Josie's nice clean floor."

Speck frowned hard to show how serious his story was. "Nobody cared much for that cane cutter to start with, that's how Josie explained it. Prob'ly some kind of a criminal is what her Jack told 'em whilst he washed his hands before settin down to her fine lemon-lime pie.

"When he finished his pie and got done wipin his mouth, he told 'em he was well known for a patient man but could not be expected to put up with such a criminal at his own table. Said, 'Darn it all, the world is better off *without* that darn ol' criminal!' As Josie recollected it, he still had lime cream on his handlebar mustache when he hitched around to look out through the door at that carcass that was nastyin up his yard. 'Lookit that barefaced sonofabitch,' he says. 'Layin out there like he owns the place!' "

Unable to maintain his poker face, Daniels guffawed. "Nosir, Josie never did deny that her Jack put that knife to her own throat a time or two when he was in his liquor, get her to shut up her mouth and mind what she was told. She would of been the first to say it: 'When my Jack told you to do somethin, you done it, cause he never was a man to tell you twice.' Hell, them were the days when men was men. Don't make red-blood Americans like *that* no more!" The moonshiner was doubled up with mirth, hacking to ransack his lungs and farting gleefully.

"Whilst they was washin up the dishes, they all agreed it might be best to let bygones be bygones, say nothin more about it," Daniels told him. "So what they done, they took and flung him to that big croc in the river. Maybe somebody give him a prayer, maybe they didn't—they was purty busy in the harvest season. But Aunt Josie always told young Pearl that she never got her Mister Jack out of her heart on account of how sweet he was that day about her peas, how darn considerate about her tender feelins." Speck nodded a little, wiping his eyes. "If that ain't a nice romantical little story for your book, I don't know what."

"I'm not looking for stories. I'm looking for the truth about his death."

"Man wants the truth about Ed Watson," Daniels jeered. "Where you aim to find it? Smallwoods'll tell you their truth, Hardens'll tell you theirs. Fat-ass guard out there, he'll tell you his and I'll give you another. Which one you aim to settle for and make your peace with?"

Mistaking Lucius's silence for acquiescence, he pointed a hard finger at his eyes. "Maybe nobody don't *need* this truth you're lookin for, ever think about that? Us kind of fellers always thought your daddy was all right the way he was." He lay back on the bunk, one leg cocked across the other knee, old sneaker swinging. "Think I ain't truthful, Colonel? Think I'm a liar just makin up stories about peas?" He yanked open the top buttons of his shirt, exposing a necklace of dull-burnished leaden lumps strung on a rawhide thong. He removed it, pushed it forward. "Count 'em. Thirty-three."

Punched in the heart, Lucius made no move to touch them. The last time he had seen those leads they were black with coagulated blood, heaped in a rusty coffee can on Rabbit Key.

"Got 'em off the coroner's man. Still had the blood on 'em. Paid eighteen dollars in hard cash and wouldn't take a million."

One sneaker on, one sneaker off, he sat up on his bunk edge. "It was Tippins showed me that fuckin posse list of yours—almost forgot that." He nodded when the other turned. "He was holdin it for evidence, Lucius. In case you was to go crazy, Lucius, start in shootin people such as myself, Lucius. And you know who give it to Tippins, Lucius? Eddie Watson."

"Eddie had no right to it. I want it back."

"Tell that to Chicken. He stole it off me along with the House testimony. Anyways, that Christly list don't mean nothin no more. Purt' near all dead on there or half dead anyways. Lest you would count that nigger." Daniels lay back, swearing.

"No colored man on that list as I recall."

"Course not!" In fury, Daniels cocked his knee and kicked the bottom of the upper bunk so hard that he split the cross slats under the thin mattress. "Ever think how a man might feel, seein his own name on a *death* list? Ever think what kind of a damn loon would *make* a list like that?"

Crockett Daniels's rage turned low and cold as the blue mineral flame in a wood fire. He wiped spittle from his unshaven mouth with the backs of his fingers and stropped it on his pant leg. "Chok fellers might be interested to see that list, you think so, Colonel? Them men might be mostly gone but they know there ain't nothin to keep a Watson from makin do with a man's son. Unless that Watson was put a stop to first."

"That a threat?"

"Nosir. That is a warnin." Daniels rolled over on the bunk, facing the wall.

Lucius said to his back, "I lived in the Islands long after I made that list and never harmed anyone. Why would I start now?" To his annoyance, his voice had gone tight and froggish.

"Yep." Speck's voice sounded like he was grinning into the mattress. "Men has got to be very leery of this Lucius Watson. You ever come back into our country, you better not turn your back no more'n you have to. And here's another warnin: don't go tellin family secrets on your damn attorney." Speck lowered his voice. "Big-time attorney, y'know, *big*-time attorney. Watt Fuckin Dyer is the fixer for all the fat boys in this state, from Big Sugar and the KKK up to the governor, and he's got his own political future to look out for. Yessir, they's big money involved in this park fight, that's the story. Dyer's the mouthpiece for them east coast developers that has fought that park idea for years; them boys are workin day and night to grab that real estate before all them nature-lovers and such get the Glades nailed down by the federl gov'mint. You ain't seen all that stuff in the papers? Gettin the public fired up against the feds for wastin half of Florida on this big green nothin? Stead of sellin off that land and cuttin taxes?"

"You a taxpayer these days, Speck?"

"Yessir! Mr. Crockett Senior Daniels! First man up to the winder every year!"

But Speck's grin faded quickly. "Taxes is rigged to help the rich, come out of the poor man's hide. And any poor man asks the wrong questions, them bureaucrats'll paper him to death, scatter the blame all over the fuckin gov'mint. Feds can't pour piss out of a boot that has the instructions wrote down on the heel but when it comes to coverin their butts, you just can't beat 'em.

"What I'm sayin is, with so much money on the line, that man won't want no story comin out about how he is Bloody Watson's bastrid boy. He'll get a chokehold on your book in court, then hit you with a lawsuit. If that don't put you out of business, he'll be comin after you, and he is goin to get you, and he don't care how."

"Oh, come on—"

"That's the story. Might get beat up or you might get a bullet. They say he's got spicks over to Miami will do a nice clean job for fifty bucks."

"Threat number three." Lucius went out and this time he kept going.

"Well, here's another, then!" Speck Daniels hollered after him. "Stay the hell out of my territory! And we won't need no fuckin Spaniards neither!"

"Eddie Watson? Lives over here on Second Street." The deputy walked him to the door. "Lately your brother been tryin to sell me your daddy's famous shootin iron. Bolt-action, single-shot, looked like a made-over rifle with a shotgun barrel—hell of a lookin thing!" Seeing Lucius's expression, he laughed. "Eddie swore this was the weapon used by Desperader Watson on the day he died, claimed it was well known to be his daddy's from the black scorin on the stock. Not only that but this selfsame gun wiped out Belle Starr, the Outlaw Queen—no extra charge! Said it was priceless so naturally I give him fourteen dollars for it." He hiked his belt. "Might been priceless but it sure weren't what Eddie said it was cause later I got a chance to handle the real-life weapon your dad was toting on that day."

"That thing still around?"

"Twelve-gauge Remington ridge-barrel, twenty-eight or thirty-inch twin barrels? Short forearm with the old wood split, put back together pretty solid with squarehead screws? Safety busted, welded back, busted again—that sound familiar?" They nodded together. "Course the stock is all raggedy-lookin from bein shot up so bad and the barrels pitted from layin too long in the salt water. Some fool had went and flung her into the bilges of your daddy's boat, never stopped to think that one day that ol' gun might be worth good money. Sheriff Tippins fished her out, kept her for court evidence, but nobody thought to give her a wipe of oil or nothing, from the looks."

"Who's got it now?"

"I reckon Speck still has it. Claims the sheriff give it to him but it wouldn't surprise me if that rascal misplaced it to where he could find it again after Tippins went over to Miami. Speck collects old Watson stuff, y'know."

Lucius thought about the string of lead slugs hanging on Daniels's neck. "I know," he said.

TANT AND PEARL

Walking down to the river, Lucius passed the old red Langford house between Bay and First streets where he had lived with his mother in his early school days. Mama! The thought of her made him sad: he had missed her more and more over the years. And how kind she had been to her difficult stepson—had Rob appreciated this? And how brave she'd been to reprove Papa for the cold way he treated him.

In the riverside park, a gaggle of pubescent girls in new white sneakers, shrilling and giggling, squirting life, were observed without savor by decrepit men fetched up in the corners of the benches like dry piles of wind-whirled leaves. In the river light, the noisy nymph troupe juxtaposed with those silent figures was unreal. One of these men could be Leslie Cox, drink-ravaged, syphilitic.

Queerly, one man removed his toothpick and pointed it straight at him. In the sun's reflection off the river, the wet pick glinted like a needle. "That you, Lucius? Where you been hidin, boy?" The man was not old, simply worn out. He shifted a little to make room on his bench.

Tant Jenkins, whose mustache had gone to seed, seemed unaware that they had not crossed paths for years. They talked at angles for a while, finding their way. When Lucius mentioned he'd just seen Tant's cousin Crockett, Jenkins said unhappily, "One them Cajun Danielses. We ain't hardly related." He looked away over the water, where gulls planed down the wind between the river bridges. "Which is a lie. It's just I ain't so proud about it." Tant tried to laugh. "One them Cajuns scratched his head, said, 'I'll be doggoned if my own dad ain't my son-in-law!'"

Lucius mustered a chuckle at this old joke to shield Tant's dignity. "Is he kin to me, too? He used to think so."

"Well, I have heard that, which don't mean it's true. Speck weren't born a Watson, he were born a liar. Never had no first-hand experience of the God's truth—just flat don't care about it. Course Josie and Netta lived a while at Chatham Bend, had daughters there. . . ." Tant spoke cautiously, not certain how much Lucius might care to acknowledge.

"My half sisters, you mean."

"I reckon that's right," Tant said, relieved. "But back in the nineties, when your dad first showed up, he met a young Daniels girl one night that ran so wild they called her 'Jenny Everybody.' Just the one time, far as I know, but she claimed her kid was his, never mind that Crockett was kind of dark, looked like a wild Injun. Course nobody never knew for sure just who the father was, not even Jenny.

"Netta's Minnie, now, she has her daddy's color, blue eyes, that dark rust hair. Lives in Key West, never signed up as a Watson, but Netta called her 'E. Jack Watson's love child.' Netta liked to recall how E. Jack Watson 'ravished' her, and when Josie was drinkin, she'd get that same idea: 'That darned Jack took me by *storm*!' Them ladies weren't one bit ashamed about Jack Watson, they were proud about him."

Tant reminded Lucius of Pearl Watson's visits in his Lost Man's days, how she'd hitch rides on the runboat that picked up the Hardens' fish just to go warn him about the Chokoloskee men, beg him to leave. "Young Pearl was out to mother you," Tant said, "and here she was half your age."

Sometimes she called herself Pearl Jenkins, sometimes Pearl Watson. She was a pretty girl and kind, but her life had always been a sad one, looking in the window. "I guess a real home was what that poor girl wanted most," said Lucius.

"Well, she wound up in one. Her mind kind of let go on her so they put her in some kind of a home over in Georgia."

"Oh Lord! I never knew what became of her!"

"Pearl was always so proud how you come and hugged her like a sister at your daddy's burial. Which was more than them others done, she said."

Subdued, the old friends stared away across the broad brown reach of the Calusa Hatchee. Westward, toward Pine Island Sound, the lifting gulls caught glints of sun where the current mixed with wind in a riptide. "Mister Ed and me, we had some fun," Tant mused. "Lots of comical times. I ain't never goin to forget my days at Chatham. Never seen so much food in all my life, that day to this."

"Papa had known a lot of hunger so he enjoyed providing food." Happy to share fond memories of his father, Lucius smiled.

"I reckon he was all right before that Tucker business," Jenkins blurted. "That's when I quit. You ain't asked my opinion and likely you don't want it but I better say it anyways just so we're straight about it." Tant cleared his throat again, frowning and worrying, torn between tact and integrity. "Some way your dad was crazy, Lucius, only he was the dangerous kind that never showed it. Act like everybody else, joke and talk and go about his business, and all the while there's a screw loose in his brain."

"No," Lucius said patiently. "No, I don't think he was crazy." He shook his head. But Tant persisted, eyes wide behind round glasses; he wore the dogged look Lucius remembered. "You realize how near your daddy come to bein killed before they killed him? It's terrible to be so deathly scared day after day, folks just can't handle it. And finally they had enough." Tant glanced at Lucius as they walked along, distressed by his friend's silence. "Naturally his own kids never knew that fear nor his friends neither. Captain Jim Daniels flat refused to believe all them bad stories. 'That ain't the Ed Watson I know'—that was all he'd say."

They paused at the foot of the Edison Bridge to gaze at the brick mansion on the corner opposite. Walter Langford had built that house in 1919 and died of cirrhosis of the liver in 1921, leaving Carrie with more debts than assets.

"Them years you lived down in the Islands, your sister had a dog's share of misfortune, but she had some spirit and she had some style. Liked to drink some, have a good time like her daddy. Never talked about the scandal"—Tant shot a glance at Lucius—"but would not act ashamed about him, neither. Nobody spoke bad about Ed Watson around Carrie Langford.

"In Prohibition, she run the Gulf Shore Inn, down Fort Myers Beach. Had a speakeasy in back but Tippins never bothered her. Course Carrie was well up in her thirties, she'd put on a little heft, but a fine-lookin widder woman all the same. And pretty quick, she got hooked up with a fish guide at the Beach, Cap'n Luke Gates on the *Black Flash*.

"One night I was in there when Gates's wife come in—thin scratchy little blonde, she was just a-*stormin*! Run right over and tore into her husband where he was settin at the poker table. Picked up his glass and let his liquor fly into his face. Cap'n Luke never lifted his eyes up off the cards. Never blinked, never reached to wipe his face. Kept right on studyin them cards with the whiskey runnin off his cheeks. 'See you, raise you five,' he told them men.

"Makin no headway at the poker table, the wife let loose an ugly speech about Carrie Langford's morals or the lack of 'em and how Carrie come by her bad character real natural, her daddy bein a cold-blooded killer. Well, darned if this banker's widow don't ring open the cash register, break out a revolver, and fire off a round into the ceilin. Ever hear gunfire in a small room? And in that silence Carrie said, real calm and ladylike, 'Let me tell you something, honey. That kind of mean and lowdown talk is not permitted in my place just because some little fool can't hang on to her man.' And seein a weapon in the hands of Watson's daughter, that little blonde cooled off in a hurry. She run outside where it was dark and yelled some dirty stuff in through the window but nobody paid her no attention after that."

EDDIE

Tant Jenkins peered across the street. "Methodist Church owns that brick house now but Eddie still calls it 'the Langford Mansion,' comes over here most every day to tell the tourists all about it." Shading his eyes, he said, "I reckon that's him back in the corner of the porch."

At the porch steps, they awaited Eddie, who came forward, saying "Good morning!" much too loudly. Despite the heat, he was dressed formally in linen suit, white shirt, green tie, well flecked with souvenirs of repasts long forgotten. He peered nearsightedly at Lucius, looking uncertain, and for the first time Lucius could recall, he felt a start of pity for his brother.

Tant Jenkins smiled. "Mr. Watson? Care to make the acquaintance of Professor Collins? Famous historian?"

Eddie stepped back with a sweeping gesture of welcome. "I am honored, sir! E. E. Watson, at your service, sir!" Grandly he waved them up onto the porch. "My brother, too, is a historian, comes to consult me—"

"Eddie?"

"This was the Langford Mansion, sir. My sister's husband was the president of the First National Bank and Carrie and Walter entertained the Thomas Edisons and their friend Mr. Henry Ford. I believe that Mr. Samuel Clemens—"

"Eddie, wait—"

"What's that?" Eddie looked alarmed; he recoiled when Lucius touched his arm to calm him. "What do *you* want?"

"I just wanted to ask you a few questions. For a biography of Papa—"

"Oh no you don't!" His brother pushed past him down the steps into the sunlight, where he turned and pointed an unsteady finger. "Damn you, it's family business, will you *never* understand? *Family* business." His arms waved wildly. "You never came to see your sister even after she was evicted from this house! You broke her heart!"

Lucius said he had never been notified; he would go see her right away. "I just wanted to ask about a list of names sent years ago to Rob by way of Nell Dyer—"

"Mrs. Summerlin to you!" Eddie yelled crazily. "Oh, I took care of *that* darned thing, don't worry!" Unable to meet his brother's eye, he glowered at Jenkins. "You people are trespassing! This is private property, *church* property! I'll call the law!" Stumbling, he hurried away and disappeared around the corner. The old river street stood gaunt and empty. They sat down on the steps.

"Eddie's always callin in complaints, kind of a hobby. Depitties don't pay no attention. Most days, he's friendly, maybe too friendly. Still tryin to keep up with the Langfords, I reckon."

Lucius nodded, unhappy.

"I reckon he done the best he could," Tant continued, "bein mulish as his daddy but not strong. Lately he begun to call himself Ed Watson Junior. Figured bein the son of a famous man made him somebody, too, and brung in customers. *Ed Watson, Insurance.* Buy a policy, get to shake the hand of Bloody Watson's son. 'You *the* Ed Watson? You fixin to murder me if I don't pay up my premiums?'—teasin, you know. And Eddie come back with the same answer every time—'Betcher life! So watcher step!'—and went right on fillin out the forms. Never occurred to 'em, I guess, that Watson's son might be a feller with real feelins. Said, 'Why hell, if he can't take a joke, he should of left this town or changed his name.' Go back home and tell their friends that this Ed Watson is the spittin image of his daddy, which he sure ain't.

"Folks always thought of Eddie as pretty meek and mild behind his bluster, but lately he took to hinting how he's a chip off the old block, might have a violent streak. Figured your average American might take to an insurance man with a dangerous past and he weren't wrong. Even hauled out a copy of your list, let on as how he went down to the Islands took care of them ringleaders. 'Didn't have no choice,' he told 'em. 'Watson honor.' "

Chortling, Tant wrote down the phone number of Pearl Watson's institution. "She'd be tickled to hear from you," he said.

In parting, Tant clung a moment to his hand. "You could always count on your backdoor family, Lucius, and you still can, what's left of us."

INSULTED PEAS

Pearl Watson had been nine or ten when their father was killed, a self-starved creature, a fugitive from the sun whose thin pale hair with its thin white ribbon let her scalp shine through. At Caxambas that black autumn, Tant had said, the child had been dumbstruck by her father's death and terrified by the outcry of her mother, who had lost her infant son and fled her agony for days with shrieks of woe.

Pearl's frail voice came over the wire after a long wait.

Who are you? Who is calling?

This is Lucius. Your brother Lucius.

Brother Who?

Pearl, this is Lucius. I just called to say hello, see how you were getting along.

Why are you hollering? Did you say Lucius? Oh Good Lord! Oh, Lucius honey, I was so worried, sweetheart! Lucius? Do you look awful, too? Where are you? Why are you calling?

Please, Pearl, don't upset yourself. I just wanted to hear your voice. Pearl honey? I'm so sorry I haven't called before. I never knew you'd gone away.

What's become of you, sweetheart? Why haven't you called?

I—well, I've been so busy doing a book about our father.

Our Father Who Art in Heaven. Those men killed Mr. E. J. Watson, blew him to Kingdom Come—did you know that?

Pearl, listen—

Did you know J. stood for Jack? Did you know my mother married up with

E. Jack Watson? Had a daughter by Mister Jack and that was me so how come you forgot me?

Pearl? Don't cry—

When E. Jack Watson died my mother was still married to him, common-law. My mother loved him, too, all except his temper. He was a drinker but he loved his children dearly.

Pearl? Did your mother ever tell a story about a hired hand at Chatham Bend who insulted her nice peas?

No, I never heard about insulted peas. But if Jack Watson told you he would kill you, he would do it, Mama said, because being a man who kept his word, he expected the same integrity in others. She was weeping. *Who are you anyway? Whoever you are, you must be a liar! Lucius would have called me long ago! I'm his baby sister!*

Pearl, please don't be upset. I don't mean to upset you. I'll call another day, maybe next week.

They won't let me go home! They say I have no home to go to! I'm all alone and they won't let me go home! They say I have no home!

CARRIE LANGFORD

Carrie Langford lived in the shadow of her husband's bank in a small house off First Street. Turning the corner, he caught her in a dressing gown of faded blue with a frayed pink satin collar, fetching her newspaper at the picket gate.

At the sight of him, her hands flew to her hair. "You could have called first, Lucius. Or are you just on your way somewhere else?"

Fussing with her collar when he leaned to peck her cheek, she withdrew through the rose gate into an arbor of trellised wisteria and bougainvillea. He did not venture through the gate. "Carrie, I'm sorry—" She turned away to ward off any bluster. "Well, come in, then, darn it. You want me arrested for soliciting?"

He held the screen door as she preceded him into a small sitting room overfilled with big dark furniture from the house at the Edison Bridge. "From 'the good old days,' " she sniffed with a dismissive wave. In louvered shade, in the hum of fans, the room was dark and silent like a funeral parlor, as if somewhere within Banker Langford lay in state.

In a formal portrait, proud-bosomed Carrie in white evening gown made a handsome subject, and Walter in a suit of houndstooth tweed appeared portly and prosperous. His hairline, slicked back hard, was rapidly receding, but his eager amiability seemed undiminished. He did not look the least bit like a man whose liver would fail for good just three years later.

Lucius took a hard chair near the door in sign that his visit would be brief; to reassure her, he perched forward on the chair edge, poised for flight. On the sofa, hands folded on her lap, Carrie shrugged off his civilities as he struggled to explain what he'd been up to. "I thought you'd like to know that Papa's bad reputation was much exaggerated—"

"So you've always claimed. That why you've come?"

"That's my excuse. I wanted to see you—"

She checked him again.

"I wanted to see you," he insisted when she closed her eyes. "Though I've never been sure how welcome I would be. I thought you and Eddie—"

"We don't consult about you, Lucius." Changing the subject, she asked crossly if he'd had any news of their young stepmother and her children. "I must say I thought less of Edna for running away before the burial, then changing the children's names like that—"

She stopped, anticipating his frown of protest and accepting it; Carrie had no heart for unkindness. Then suddenly her defenses fell away. "You and Edna left. You never had to deal with those dreadful writers who pestered us year after year for yet another lurid article slapped together to make money with no regard for truth. And how often I thought"—here she looked up, close to tears—"if only I could talk with Lucius. I so hoped you'd come. You never did. The baby brother I adored lived only a few miles down the coast and never even came to Walter's funeral, never bothered to inquire how his sister might be getting on."

"Carrie? I came. I arrived late—"

"Of course you did. I hardly saw you." She paused to compose herself. "I got almost no help from Walter's partners and would not accept it from others—not even my own brothers, had they offered it, which they did not. For different reasons, of course. You, at least, were generous when you had anything, which was almost never." She was teasing now, yet unready to be mollified.

With parents and husband dead, with Rob and Lucius vanished from her life and her two girls married, Eddie was all she had left in the way of family. Fortunately, she added with a little smile, Eddie adored her.

"Kindred spirits," Lucius suggested.

Carrie cocked her head, elevating her eyebrows. "Let's just say," she reproved him gently, "that dear Eddie feels a bit more kindred to his sister's spirit than she feels to his.

"Though Eddie can be very courtly, don't forget," she added dutifully when Lucius smiled. "Mama taught him manners and he has his own peculiar charm, at least he used to. But because of Papa, the poor stick is always out to prove something, make a good impression. You suppose that's why he never dared to drink?" She shrugged, not much interested. "You were the opposite, of course—quiet, a bit pensive, but when you grinned, you really grinned, and your eyes sparkled." That memory made her smile herself and he was smiling with her. "See?" she laughed gaily, pointing at his eyes. "As a boy, you were very handsome, Lucius. You still are. And you drank too much. All the Watsons were handsome"—she took a deep hard breath—"and they all drank too much. Myself included. And I married another handsome drunk while I was at it."

"Carrie—"

"Well, I've made my own way and the girls have married well so we came out all right. But last year I was pretty ill, and I thought, Damn it, I'm not going, not before I see my little brother. I wanted you to come for Christmas, a real visit, but Eddie reported that you were drinking and all you wanted was to rot on your old boat. He said you stayed away because you thought your Fort Myers family was ashamed of you. That broke my heart."

Though Lucius had never said any such thing to Eddie, he knew that, in the past, he might have intimated that idea to others; he did not defend himself. He rose, saying, "I'm sorry, Carrie."

"Oh, don't go, sweetheart, please don't go. I won't make you feel guilty anymore, I promise." With a warm smile, she patted the cushion beside her, but when he sat down, both felt so shy that she jumped up and brought him family photographs. "My wild cracker cowboy became so darned *dignified.* Our little girls asked if their daddy's pajamas had starched collars!"

Carrie read aloud from a school report that little Faith had written about her grandpa the year after he died: " '*I remember Grandpa's ginger brows: he*

looked like he was filled with fire. He always had a nice warm smell of wisky . . .'"
Carrie smiled fondly at her brother. "Papa would perch one child on each
knee and tell them about the big old owl who lived on Chatham Bend. Then
he would pop his eyes open like . . . THIS!" She popped her eyes at Lucius
and her clear peal of delight brought childhood back and with it something
of their old affection for their father and each other.

ROB'S VISIT

Lucius asked her to describe Rob's visit of a few years before. Did she recall
just when it was? When she figured out the approximate date, he realized
that Rob's return corresponded closely with the arrival at the Hardens of
the stranger who had called himself "John Tucker."

"One day Eddie turned up with a bearded man in worn-out clothes, a
merchant seaman. Eddie called him 'our half brother Robert,' right in front
of him. Not having laid eyes on Rob in almost thirty years—since before my
wedding—I might not have believed that this was him except for those
feverish red points on his cheeks, remember? The dark hollow eyes? With
that beard, he looked like some poor martyr out of those old paintings.
'Calls himself Collins these days,' Eddie announced, rolling his eyes the
way he does. 'I use my mother's maiden name,' Rob explained for my sake.

"I said, 'Rob? Is that really you behind that beard? Oh, Rob, for goodness
sake!' And I grabbed him and hugged him hard, though he didn't want
that. For a man who supposedly lived at sea, he was so pale that I thought
he must be ill.

" 'He's looking for Lucius,' Eddie said, to hurry us. Eddie was sulky. I
confessed to Rob that I'd scarcely laid eyes on you since your return from
the Great War. I felt ashamed. I told him how much it worried me that you
were living at the mercy of those people. 'He was safer in the War than he
is down there,' Rob said. 'That's why I'm here.' Eddie snapped, 'Sure took
you long enough,' and Rob said he was unable to come sooner. He did not
say why and we did not dare ask him: he was just as prickly as the Rob of
old but had turned a little hard, a little scary. He refused a drink. 'I can't
handle it,' he said.

"Eddie was still sulking so I led Rob outside. I took his arm and we walked a little ways along the river. I said, 'It's your first visit in thirty years, Rob. Can't you stay for supper? Stay the night?' No, he said, he had to catch the ship that was sailing that evening to the Islands. Said good-bye and turned and walked away. I never learned if he had a family or even where he'd lived since I'd last seen him."

"He's back," said Lucius. He told his sister the whole story of Arbie Collins.

"Oh Lord, we have to help him," Carrie said. At a loss, they sat quiet a while. "We'll think of something, won't we, Lucius?" She did not seem hopeful and soon relapsed into resentment. "Have you called on Nell? That girl adored you, Lucius. To go off to war without a word then run away to the Islands after she'd sacrificed her reputation? Did you care? Were you even aware of the guts it took to live on in a small nosy town after you disappeared? Of how much she was willing to give up for you against all advice? Including mine?"

Carrie's indignation on Nell's behalf was tinged by her own hurt. "Knowing how sensitive you are, I'll bet you felt injured when she finally gave up on you and accepted that old man. She's *poor*, you idiot! She has no family worthy of the name and no security. Women *need* security. Are you really so damn blind?"

He sat quiet. Made unhappy by her own remarks, she said, "We did our best to forgive you, Lucius, because after Papa died, you weren't yourself. Where was our old easygoing Lucius? You were *fun*, remember?" She took his hand. "Nell loved talking about you. She still does! Your 'shy bent smile,' she called it—came straight from Mama, by the way—your 'deep-shadowed wistful eyes.' " Mocking Nell gently, Carrie squinted to verify those eyes. "And Chatham Bend. It seems you protected her from her awful brother, she imagined that Lucius Watson was some sort of angel. She told me how quick and merciful you were around your otter traps and even killing chickens for the table—that made a great impression. The pains you took to remove your fish hook gently: *more than he ever did for this poor fish!* Nell can laugh at herself even when she's sad, and she never complains—I love that about her."

Carrie stopped smiling when her brother said, "Is that Nell's joke or yours? About the fish hook?" Although he tried to say this lightly, his lungs were heavy with remorse for his utter failure to protect the eager feelings of sister and lover who had cherished him so much more faithfully than he'd deserved.

Watching his face, his sister grew alarmed. "Lucius? What is it? Are you all right? Listen—it's important that you know—Nell never spoke out against you this way—the way I do, I mean." She was silent a moment before whispering, "I'm truly sorry. I didn't want to do this."

He sat down again. "Don't apologize. I've neglected you both shamefully, and Pearl, too."

Though Carrie resisted the mention of Pearl, she was anxious to mend things before he went away again. Before Nell's marriage, that girl had called on Nell. Nell brought her here. It was Pearl who told them that Lucius lived in a driftwood shack at Lost Man's River: she sought their help in persuading him to leave the Islands before he was harmed. A little miffed, she parodied Pearl's accent: " 'He'll surely lissen to yew, Miz Nell! Ah seen how much he pahns fer yew, Miz Nell!' No mention of Miz Carrie, you notice."

Nell had sent no message back with Pearl. What good would it do to plead with Lucius once he'd learned that his true love and dearest friend had given up on him and was marrying another? Slightly shopworn, a bit "dog-eared," as she described herself to Carrie, Nell had accepted the spavined hand of Mr. Summerlin, an elderly gentleman with a kind heart and a secure place in society and also an indomitable itch to stroke his young bride's person. About all he ever did, Carrie suspected, though Nell was too loyal to confirm this. "Nothing much to be jealous about, anyway," she assured her brother.

Why, he thought, had Carrie mentioned jealousy if not to make him jealous?

"That girl knew you well, you know."

"Too well for her own good," he answered glumly.

"Stop that! What a fool you are! Go call her up!"

He did. He arranged to go meet her. He came back smiling.

At the door, he turned and they hugged at last. "You must never forsake your silly old sister again," she said. "No," Lucius said. She knew he meant this for she went up on tiptoes and kissed him on the cheek. Like the bossy older sister he remembered, she nagged after him, "Don't you *ever* come to town again, Mr. Lucius Watson, without letting us know."

He waved from the rose gate. Carrie sang out, "She's a rich widow, don't forget! Maybe it's not too late!"

NELL SUMMERLIN

The Fort Myers cemetery lay in a fading neighborhood off the river road. By the iron gate, under dark limbs which extended out over the street, she awaited him in a blue roadster. Coming on foot up the sidewalk from behind, he coughed so as not to startle her.

"Good Lord, is that you?" On the telephone, her voice had faltered. "Can you meet me at the cemetery? It's high time I brought Mr. Summerlin fresh flowers." Skillfully, she'd kept him at a distance, reminding him of that other reality that did not include him.

Nell emerged from the blue roadster with a loud creak of the door hinge. "My jalopy and I," she said, feigning exasperation. "We're in this thing to the finish." Not ready to look him full in the face, she went around to the far side and reached in for her flowers. Face half-hidden in blossoms, she paused a moment to regard him. She wore a simple linen dress of pale gray-green and a wheat-colored broad hat of soft Panama straw—all expensive and in good taste, yet all wrong and ruined by the eccentric indifference to her appearance that had led her to wear tennis shoes and cinch up her outfit with her old beaded Indian belt.

Inept and shy, he cleared his throat. "How are you, Nell?"

She laid her flowers on the hood and, still at arm's length, placed her small cool hands in his rough brown ones, her smile dissolving any semblance of restraint, far less enigma.

She picked up her skirt and moved lightly toward the gate. Passing through dark banyan shade, she reappeared in white stone sunlight—a cemetery sunlight, Lucius thought. He had become a frequenter of cemeteries. He passed under the banyan limbs and Nell's voice called, "On the right! Just off the path!"

A plain small white marble headstone with bare name and date:

E. J. WATSON
NOVEMBER 7, 1855–OCTOBER 24, 1910

How final, those small incisions in cut stone. No inscription—what would his siblings have chosen? What would a watchful society have permitted? *Rest in Peace?* Of course not. *Rest in Hell?* A Texas headstone Papa had admired would have suited him, too: *Here lies Bill Williams: He done his damndest.* Beside him lay his Mandy—Jane Dyal Watson, interred in 1901. No inscription either. Mama's request. Her dates brought an odd prickling to his temples. In a quarter century he had visited her just once, in a cold north wind on the November day of Papa's descent into the ground beside her.

With no river breeze to stir its dusty foliage, the burning banyan writhed and shimmered. Its thick leaves were black, the shell paths hot blinding white, no note of color anywhere, only the slim gray-green figure bent to a headstone. In the pitiless shine on the white monoliths, in a hot scent of wild lime and baked limestone, the air was cindered with black midges. He sank down in near vertigo, only dimly aware of the figure turning toward him.

Nell was there when he came clear again. "I'm fine, I'm fine." He waved her away, disgusted. She hooked her arm in his to balance him erect and led him back into the shade and tugged him down onto a horizontal stone. "Won't bother 'em a bit," she smiled, patting the marble. "I'm fine," he repeated. She was taking his pulse at the wrist. "Of course you are," she said.

Nell felt his brow as she sorted out just what she wished to say. "Be honest. Would you have phoned me if Carrie hadn't urged you?"

"I don't know. I think so."

"Why? I mean, why should I believe that?"

Why do you care, Mrs. Summerlin? He took her hand. "Oh, I think you know."

Nell's nod was vague, her hand cool and inert. What did that nod mean? And the dead hand? In a moment she released him and sat straight again and probed into her linen bag. "Enough of that old stuff. I have your *History.* Will you sign it?" He was taken aback by her crisp manner. Yet she sat close as he inscribed her copy. "L. Watson Collins! I'm so proud of you." She marveled at the printed book and his inscription, *For My Dear Miss N.* "I always hoped—" But she cut herself off.

"Hoped what, Nell?"

"Hoped you might return one day, that's all."

"After that old man of yours was gone, you mean?"

She stared at him, sitting up straight again. "That's unworthy of you, Lucius."

"Yes, it is. I hope it is. Unworthy of me, I mean. I'm sorry. But is it true?" She nodded. Disarmed, he reached to touch her cheek.

"Don't." She shook him off. Though her tears had risen, none had fallen. She did not trust him and why should she? He did not trust himself. What if, fecklessly, he led her on, opened her heart again, did her more harm? He feared his own weakness perhaps even more than she did.

Pressed like a leaf in Nell's copy of his *History* was a faded envelope addressed to Rob. Though the list was missing, his note was still inside.

Lost Man's River
22 May, 1923

Dear Rob,
I've entrusted this packet to a friend, to hold for you in case you should return.

Rumors about the enclosed list of members of the Watson "posse" have made the Island people very leery of "Ed Watson's boy," to the point where it might be dangerous to be caught with it. But Ed's boy is actually quite harmless, I've discovered, having neither Papa's hardihood nor his Celtic code of honor, if these are what's required for bloody revenge.

This list is all I have to show for life at present. As the one person it might interest (other than those listed) perhaps you will know what should be done with it. Having wasted years putting this damned thing together, I'm beginning to think I only persevered for the rare experience of actually completing something, however useless.

Please come back. The Hardens at Lost Man's River will know where to find me. Ask for "Colonel" (as I'm mostly called in this neck of the woods—not a friendly nickname, just a jibe at my "fancy" manners). I think of you often, hoping you are safe somewhere and happy. I pray you have more to show for life than I do and that I will see you again before the smoke clears.

With love, sincerely,
Your brother Luke

P.S. I believe this list to be complete and accurate to the last name.

Nell said, "He never received this letter, you know."

"Nor the list. Which you misplaced. In the excitement of getting married, I believe you wrote." Again, his tone was colder than he felt. "You never found it, I suppose."

"I never lost it. You must have guessed that. Please, Lucius. We were all terrified you might be in danger, and that list was all the proof your family needed."

"Oh, come on! I'd already abandoned all that nonsense, as this note makes clear."

Nell shrugged, saying she'd never read it; she had no right. "But when I saw your list, I got frightened so I went to Carrie. Poor Carrie became frightened, too, and turned it over to Eddie, telling him he must go find you at once. But Eddie only said, 'And then what? He won't listen to me. He's *never* listened to me!' Eddie took the list to Sheriff Tippins, who would not return it, claiming he needed it for evidence—can you imagine? In his mind, your father's death was an unsolved crime."

"In my mind, too. Still is."

"Evidently, the sheriff claimed your list had been taken from his desk. We worried so about who might have wanted it." She gazed at him. "Your letter seemed so sad."

"I believe you just told me you had never read this letter."

"That's what I told you, all right. Another shameful lie." Nell's hurt and anger were rising to meet his. "I told a white lie knowing you'd feel embarrassed because I had learned shameful secrets which of course I'd known for years—I was your lover, for goodness sake!—that you missed your long-lost brother and were incapable of killing for honor or revenge."

Yet from a safe distance, as a sniper, he had killed certified enemies, unlucky youths as young and frightened as himself, executed one by one as they popped up and down out of their trenches like bird heads from behind a log at a huge turkey shoot. Sanctioned slaughters century after century in the ultimate lunacy of the only insane animal ever loosed upon Creation. And finally that last weedy kid who brought him to his senses even as he destroyed him, that defenseless boy taking a crap at such close range that he could smell him. . . .

Nell was peering at him. "Listen," she murmured when he only stared, not quite present. "No more secrets, all right? I want to tell you something. A few days ago, I drove down to Caxambas to thank you for your book, get you to sign it—my excuse for seeing where this L.Watson Collins lived. You were gone, which was just as well. But someone was there, struggling to write something he'd promised you—"

"The long-lost brother. He's all right, then."

"No, he's not all right. He seemed very discouraged, way out on that salt creek with no auto and no food to speak of and the place a mess. He looked just dreadful. I felt sorry for him. I told him that until you came back, there was plenty of room at Mr. Summerlin's. He could finish what he was writing there without having to bother about trying to feed himself."

"He accepted?"

"Yes, he did. Why not?"

"You live there alone?"

"There's a house servant who comes in—"

"I see."

"I wonder if you do."

"Enlighten me, then. A few years ago, you were so concerned about appearances that you felt you had to marry that old man—"

"Not one word of that is fair. Be careful, Lucius."

"Sorry. *Mr. Summerlin.* Anyway, I assume it was quite proper—"

"What right have you to assume *anything*? It's none of your darned business. Isn't it a little late for you to worry about my reputation?"

In Fort Myers, she resumed after a silence, Rob had been very uneasy, he would not go out. He finally confided he was wanted by the law. Though he tried to make a joke of that, he had a great fear of what he called "a half-lived life wasted in prison."

They sat awhile. "He's afraid he might be traced here or someone might report him. He has to leave. He's just waiting in Fort Myers to see you before he goes. Wants to turn his paper in," she added, a little meanly. "Wants to talk to you about it."

"What else might he want to talk to me about?"

"You sound jealous. You needn't be. Please listen: your brother's desperate. He made me a little afraid. And he's scared you might think he told you Rob was dead to make a fool of you, when actually he was trying to protect you from getting in trouble for 'harboring a fugitive'—his words, not mine. If I doubted his story, he said, I could find his name on the public enemy notice at the post office." When he looked skeptical, she said, "Yes, I did. I wanted to be sure. He's been on the run for years. Did you suspect that?"

"It crossed my mind." He could not concentrate. He didn't want to look at her.

"He's talking wildly. He didn't sound sorry for himself but he did say he'll shoot himself before he goes back to prison because the punishment for his escape would be added to a life sentence and he would die there. But he has no idea where to run anymore and no place to hide." Irritated by his inattention, she said, "Listen to me! He has a pistol, Lucius. He might harm himself."

"That's just Papa's old revolver," Lucius said, as if that circumstance took care of everything. Then his fear for Rob caught up with him. "Where is he now? At your house?"

"I'll leave him a message that you might be at the hotel bar at five this afternoon, all right? What's the matter?" she asked when Lucius rose abruptly. He needed to get away from her, needed to quell this absurd jealousy before he could trust himself to speak with her any further.

Nell neatened her cuffs. "Running off again?" Never before had he heard disdain in her voice. "I've often wondered if the love of my life ever understood what true love is." He feared—he had always feared—this might be true, that when it came to constancy, he was deficient, crippled.

"I *do* love you, Nell. I always have."

"How do you tell?"

They longed to find each other but could not. They stared at the white stones. She said, "Lucius? Do you ever mourn the happy man you might have been?" Her words cast him back into his dread that he would miss the point of life, all the way down into the caverns of old age.

"Forgive me," she whispered. "You had better go."

He walked toward the gate. Under the banyan tree, he turned to watch her. Very slowly, arms opening and closing like the wings of a gray-green luna moth, she gathered up her things. In the heat shimmer on the stone, his lost love seemed to palpitate as if just alighted.

DESECRATION

At the Gasparilla, Lucius went directly to the Swashbuckler Bar, which overlooked the river. Bony hind end hitched to the farthest stool toward the window, the resurrected Rob had apparently provoked the bartender, who was banging bottles to let off steam while he reorganized the shelf behind him. Other than these two antagonists, the place was empty.

To give his feral brother room, Lucius sat down several stools away, still sorting through the tumult in his breast aroused by Nell, letting the charcoal fume and heat of a stiff bourbon well up through his sinuses into his brain.

"The Watson brothers," Rob muttered finally, shaking his head at the sheer folly of it all. Lucius recognized the pallid sweaty glaze of that late stage of inebriation after which his brother managed to go right on drinking without seeming drunker. Eventually he might sag down for good but he would not stagger.

"Listen, Arb—"

"Robert is the name. Robert B. Watson, at your service." He lifted his glass to the other image in the bar mirror. When Lucius asked Rob why he had changed his name. Rob said he'd taken his mother's name because he no longer wished to be a Watson. Talking out of the side of his mouth, still facing the bar mirror, he had yet to look his brother in the eye. "I've written down that Tucker stuff for your Watson whitewash," he said. "Anything else you want to know?"

"Yes. Who's that in the urn?" He grinned. "Just dog biscuits?"

Rob did not grin back. Turning his glass to the river light, inspecting the gleaming amber in the ice, he said, "Last time I looked, it was Edgar 'Bloody' Watson."

On his way through Fort Myers in the early twenties, heading south to Lost Man's in search of Lucius, Rob had visited the cemetery on a night of drink with a plan to piss upon his father's grave. At the scene, however, this gesture seemed inadequate. With a spade from the caretaker's shed, starting at the head end, he chipped down through the limestone clay and punched through the lid of the rotted coffin. His revised plan was theft of his parent's skull for use or perhaps sale as a souvenir but the grisly effort required in separating the brown bullet-broken skull from the tough spine had sobered and exhausted him and his palms were badly blistered. However, he persevered.

Lucius jolted down his drink. "Is *any* of this true? Your *father?*" He was horrified. He still hoped Rob was joking.

"My ever-loving daddy. Did my heart good."

"You beheaded your father but you didn't piss on him."

Rob shook his head, disappointed in himself.

Filling the hole, mounding the grave, he returned the spade to the caretaker's shed, where he wrapped his prize in a piece of burlap. Later that day, he bribed a funeral parlor handyman to smash it into manageable pieces and install it in that inexpensive Greek-type urn. "As the rightful owner, I thought I got to do the smashing," Rob said slyly, as his brother glared at him in the bar mirror. "Turned out I had to have a smasher's license."

"Your standard license only covered the looting and desecration." Lucius spun toward him on his stool. "Look. This isn't funny."

Rob swiveled instantly to meet him. "*Lad Exhumes Dad.* You don't think that's funny?"

"I don't think it's true. You'd have to be crazy."

"I guess I'm crazy, then," Rob said.

The brothers measured each other.

"You really hated him that much?"

"Who hated first? It wasn't Sonborn."

"He didn't hate you at the end. In fact, he mentioned your nerve and skill, sailing his boat to Key West. Alone. At night. He said, 'That boy is a real seaman, I'll say that for him.' " Lucius watched Rob's face. "Papa made terrible mistakes, I know, but he wanted to be a decent father."

"He didn't make it." Rob threw his whiskey back and signaled rudely for another. The bartender refused him. "You was notified," he growled, "before this other party come." Told by Lucius that the other party would take responsibility, the man shrugged. "Just watch your mouth," he advised Rob, who merely drummed his fingers on the bar, awaiting his new drink. "The Watson brothers," he said again, sardonic. "Anything else you need to know?"

"Tell me where you've been."

"Mostly at your place." He glanced at Lucius, looked away again. "Then here in town. Nell Summerlin's."

"In your life, I mean. After you left Lost Man's. 1901."

"I know what year it was." Rob recounted how he'd left Key West on a freighter and wandered the earth as a merchant seaman for nine years before taking work ashore. "Learned to drive, got good at it, got special jobs." On a night job as a trucker hauling bootleg liquor during Prohibition, he got caught up in a shooting at a warehouse in which a guard was killed. Most of his life since, he said, had been spent in prison.

Lucius had suspected this—the dead hair, pallor, the quick eyes and sideways whispered speech. But seeing his sympathetic wince as just more skepticism, Rob instantly broke off his account. "You wanted my story, bud," he muttered. "That's what you got. Take it or leave it or shove it up your ass."

Those wild sharp eyes had suddenly gone shiny. On impulse, Lucius took him by the shoulders and, as Rob stiffened, gave him a quick brotherly hug. Rob's heart was beating in his scrawny chest like the heart of a stunned bird felled by its own reflection in the window. Lucius took the stool beside him, saying brusquely, "All right. And Gator Hook?"

"Heard about it from a feller in the pen, friend of Crockett Daniels. Made my way out there after I missed you at Lost Man's River. Very good place to lie low if you don't mind low company."

"So you're a fugitive."

"R. B. Watson is the fugitive. I'm R. B. Collins, remember?"

"Why didn't you tell me all this in the first place?"

"Because if you knew and you failed to turn me in, you'd be aiding and abetting a known criminal. You'd wind up in prison. Anything else?"

"The Tuckers. Did he do it? Just tell me yes or no."

Rob pressed his cold glass to the deep furrows parting his brows. "No yes-or-no," he said after a while." It's complicated. You'd better read what I wrote."

"All right. Where is it?"

"It's up in my room," Rob said, sullen again. He was very drunk.

"Who's paying for your room here? Nell?" That was the bourbon talking. His brother ignored him.

THE CARVER

Lucius had arranged with Watson Dyer to meet for supper at the Gasparilla on Dyer's way through town. They awaited the attorney in the lobby. When he failed to appear, they left word at the desk and went into the restaurant without him.

The Buccaneer Grill had a hearty buffet topped off by a blood-swollen roast beef. The meat's custodian, in chef's apron and high hat, was a big roly-poly black man with a swift red knife and a line of chatter that had the whole room smiling.

"Oh yeah! Yes *suh*! Tha's it! Tha's right! How *you* folks this evenin? Y'all havin a good visit to Fo't Myers? Doin okay? Tha's jus' fine, my frien'! Bes' have some o' this fine roast! Oh yeah! Yes suh! Tha's it! Tha's right! Red for the gennleman, pink for the lady? Jus' a li'l bit more, now, jes' a l'il bit—all right? *Aw right!*"

"Don't know when to quit," Rob said too loudly. Reaching for his whiskey, he almost tipped her tray before the waitress could set down his glass. "Man's playing these old tourists like a school of catfish," he said unpleasantly, "snuffling through the mud after a bait."

He was still bitching when Attorney Dyer came up from behind, yanked out a chair, and settled with a heavy grunt, without a greeting. He considered their liquor glasses before noting coldly that they had not waited for him. "You boys in a big rush or what?" His smile looked rigid. "I thought *I* was the busy feller around here." That delicate shiver of the skin around the corners of the mouth, as if the inner man was trembling with hidden rage, reminded Lucius once again of Papa. Under the scrutiny of those bald eyes, there seemed no doubt that Dyer was a Watson, yet it seemed unnatural to think of him as such since they had nothing else in common, brotherly affection least of all.

Dyer was wearing a white windbreaker with "U.S.A." emblazoned over the heart. "United Sugar Association jacket," he said, touching the red letters encircled by blue stars. "Nice way to show our industry's appreciation of Old Glory and this great land of opportunity."

Considering how much federal land Big Sugar is grabbing for next to nothing, Lucius thought, *I would certainly hope so.* But he stifled his protest, knowing it would be wasted.

The year before, climbing the high dike on the south shore of Lake Okeechobee, Lucius had stared in disbelief at the endless vivid greens stretching away to southward and the high stacks of the U.S.A. factory that violated the clear sky of the waterland and the wall of oily smoke downwind that shrouded the horizon like a dark front of oncoming bad weather. The tons of chemicals dumped into the pristine waterlands, the wretched slave camps for the migrant workers—the price of progress, Papa would have called it, celebrating any and all such evidence of the Twentieth Century cavalcade.

Rummaging among his papers, Dyer scarcely noticed his companions. "Lucius H. Watson residing at Chatham Bend shows up on the 1910 census, the last living Watson to reside on the property—that might help obtain life tenure on the place." The attorney cleared his throat, anticipating resistance. "Naples," he said. For tomorrow night's meeting of the Naples Historical Society, Lucius would be listed on the program as L. Watson Collins, Ph.D.

Lucius shook his head, annoyed. "Too many people know me on this coast, I told you that." He would have to notify the audience right from the start—

"The speaker advertised—the speaker whose lecture fee is being paid by U.S.A.—is Professor Collins. The newspaper will cover a lecture by Professor Collins, 'A New Look at the Edgar Watson Story.' " Dyer was straining to be heard over the rollick of the meat carver, his annoyance rising with his voice. "So why do you insist—" Nostrils flared, he yanked his chair around. "What's that godawful racket? Is that nigger poking fun at white folks?"

"Poking fun!" Rob parried and poked his butter knife toward the neighboring table. "Poke, poke!" He made a thrusting gesture, winking dirtily at the diners. "Poke, poke!" But when they turned their backs on him, his grin faded, replaced by a dangerous cast of eye. He lurched to his feet and reeled away in the direction of the buffet, addressing the near tables as he passed, though not loudly enough to override the black man's boisterous patter. "You men aim to let that nigra get away with poking fun at these white ladies and still call yourselves *men? No* sir! Poking fun at *customers* that has paid down our good money to stuff our gullets? *No* sir!"

Rob was well ahead by the time his brother rose and hurried to overtake him. "I surely do appreciate this kind of old-time darkie, full to the brim with Southren hospitality!" Rob sang out in cracker twang, as an old lady ahead of him turned to offer a sweet smile—"Oh that's so true!"—and Rob smiled beamishly. "Yes, ma'am. *God's* truth!" He dropped his voice to a stage whisper, confiding in her from behind his hand, "Long as he knows his place." When the woman hushed him, glancing fearfully to see if the carver might have overheard, Rob leaned toward her, cupping his ear. "Beg pardon, ma'am? *Uppity nigger,* you said?" The woman recoiled from him in shock. "He's drunk!" she told her husband, whose sun-scabbed pate only hunkered lower in the line.

Rob called, "I just purely love to see all us good folks fixin to set right down to a big ol' plate of fatty beef that'll half kill us, with a heapin helpin of our Christian fellowshippin on the side! We'll realize maybe for the first time in our whole lives how much we like these durned ol' neg-ros that's waitin on us hand and foot, and what a grand country we have here in the good ol' U.S. and A where coloreds can talk to white folks just so nice and friendly you'd almost think they was human beins same as us!"

Before the poor woman could chastise him, Rob turned on her with a beatific smile. "Don't y'all love pickaninnies, honey? So much *cuter* than our pasty white ones, ain't that right?" The woman moaned, utterly routed.

The big black man had fallen quiet. Slowly he turned in Rob's direction, poised knife dripping blood, not because, as Lucius feared, he was outraged by this drunken pest but because he had intuited the anarchic spirit behind this man's parody of that safe racism considered suitable for family gatherings and other comfortable occasions in the American home.

The candidates for fine roast beef, not realizing what Lucius was up to, had resisted his attempt to advance himself wrongfully in the line, but when they realized that this line-jumper was trying to overtake the outrageous disturber of the peace, they made way for him gratefully. "Regardless of race, color, or creed!" Rob was crying senselessly as Lucius grasped his arm.

"Race, color, nor *creed*!" the carver hooted. "You tell 'em, man!"

Now Watson Dyer was barging past, and the carver, sensing danger, withdrew behind his jolly patter. "Aw *right,* suh! How *you* feelin this fine evenin? You fixin to try our beautiful roas' beef?" And Dyer snapped in a hard voice, "Never mind the minstrel show. Just carve." In the sudden silence in the room, people stopped eating and turned toward them in alarm.

"Mins'rel show?" The carver's smile congealed and his eyes tightened.

"*Well,* now! Y'all had you a nice day, suh? Look like you needin a big cut of this fine beef."

"Shut up and carve," said Dyer with terrific anger, solid and efficient anger, smooth as polished stone.

The carver's knife was poised over the roast. He stood transfixed like a sculpture called The Carver. Phalanxes of pale faces stared and waitresses clustered in pink-and-white bouquets by the buffet.

The black man squinted at the point of his raised knife. "Hold on, nigguh! You ain' heard that gen'leman tell you, 'Cut that mins'rel shit, jus' carve the roast'?" He honed his knife, *snick-snick, snick-snick,* appraising the patriotic windbreaker, the cerulean hard eyes. *Snick-snick, snick-snick.*

"*Carve,* boy," Dyer growled in his inexplicable fury. "You're not paid to play the fool for these old farts."

"Oh my goodness!" An old fart dropped a radish as her spouse harrumphed in scared protest and the line, milling in panic, clutched its plates. "For Christ's sake, Dyer!" Lucius, who was right behind him, felt hated by his fellow farts for being associated with a cruel villain out to ruin their heartwarming encounter with this delightful negro personality.

"Playin the fool, tha's right. Tha's what you doin, black boy. You ain't heard the man?" The carver's voice was low and hard as grated pebbles. "Tha's all you doin, Mistuh Black Man. Playin the fool."

"*Carve,*" Dyer panted, out of breath in the ecstasy of his all-purifying anger.

Summoning him closer with a big mad grin, the carver leaned forward to whisper in his ear as if to share a secret. But the real secret was the knife, which he slid across the carving board on the flat of its handle, just far enough to pink the other's belly through his shirt. And his pebbly voice grated, "Back off, mothafuck. Get outta my face." When Dyer sprang back, jarring a table, the carver straightened up again, quaking with mirth, as if this customer had told him some hilarious story. "Yassuh, that sho' is *right!*" Using his blade, he was dumping so many slices on Dyer's plate that the attorney had to lift it high to fend off more bloody meat. "Had enough, my frien'? Doan go to spillin good blood gravy on yo' shirt."

Dyer raised his gaze from the big knife and its heaped meat to the bloodshot eyes in the carver's shining face. The room was still but for the thin scrape of a chair. Lucius watched the black man lick his lower lip, watched his fury weaken, watched his glare slide sideways and the slices fall from the knife.

Dyer dumped his heap of meat onto the cutting board. The carver replaced it with a modest helping. Finding his voice, he mumbled, "Doin my job, tha's all it is, suh. Makin folks feel good, way they wants it."

Dyer moved on past. Sending his plate to the table with a waitress, he went straight to the door. A manager was summoned. He displayed his bloodied shirt. Both looked at the carver as they spoke.

Observing this, the black man turned a furious scowl upon Rob Watson, slapping meat down on Rob's plate. "Happy now? Got what you wanted?" He waved him past with the big knife which he pointed at Lucius's eyes. "*Yes,* suh! You know them gen'lemens?"

Lucius nodded. "My brothers."

"The three brothers! Lo'd A'mighty!" The carver detained him by pressing the knife blade down hard on his plate, pinning the china to the butcher board. "How 'bout you? Got somethin smart you want to say?"

"I want to say that I'm extremely sorry."

The black man had been summoned from his post. "*Sorry?*" He stabbed his knife into the carving board, upright and shivering, as the food line yawed and fell away in fright. "I'se the one gets to be sorry! And my woman! And my kids! On account they's hard times comin in this country and you damn *gen'lemans* has los' me my damn *job!*" He stripped off his bloody apron, balled it up, and hurled it across the steam tables of vegetables onto the soups before banging his way out through the pantry doors.

POWER OF ATTORNEY

The waitress wore a gold chain on her rhinestone glasses, and her ears stuck out through lank black hair like a horse mane. With alarm she watched Dyer attacking his red meat, the knife blade and fork tines grating on the porcelain. "How *you* folks doin this evenin?" she ventured. "Ever'-thin all right?" Unnerved by the attorney's glare, she fled.

Watson Dyer stabbed at his roast beef, forked it away. He made no mention of the carver. Lucius felt too roiled to eat. Rob was muttering, "It's all my fault. I'd better go tell his boss."

"Do it, then," snapped Lucius.

"Save your breath." Dyer spoke through a crude mouthful of meat, not looking up. The management, he said, had already expressed gratitude to a valued customer for reporting an outrage by a loudmouth nigger who had never learned his place; their dinner would be complimentary, the culprit fired. He forked another mouthful and chewed swiftly, processing his food while going through his papers.

Dyer briefed them in a rapid-fire manner. Two days hence, a public hearing on the Watson claim would be held in Homestead. He had been assured by colleagues in the judicial system that the claimants might be awarded lifetime use and historical status for the house. Time was short. What he needed at once was full power of attorney, which would give him the authority to make decisions without prior consultation with the family. "It's quite customary in these matters," he assured them, pushing a form toward Lucius for his signature. "Authority to act swiftly might be critical."

Lucius felt rushed. "My signature has to be notarized, isn't that true?"

"I happen to be a notary," Dyer said, impatient, already digging in his briefcase for his seal.

Something seemed wrong or missing here but Lucius, still shaken by the episode with the carver and anxious to be done with the whole business, said to hell with it and scrawled his signature.

Rob whistled in alarm. "Oh boy," he said.

"I want this witnessed by all Watson heirs here present. No exceptions," Dyer added, turning to Rob. "Not even you." Extending his pen, he contemplated Rob's shock with open pleasure.

Rob rose in a lurch of plates, overturning his water glass. He glared at his brother before telling Dyer, "I won't sign a fucking thing." The attorney grasped his upper arm and held him by main force. "Hold your horses, Robert." When Rob stopped struggling, Dyer released him and placed another document beside his plate, rapping it sharply with his knuckle. "Read this first," he said. Rob glanced at the new document, dropped it on the table, rose again, and headed for the door, where he paused briefly to remonstrate about the carver—in vain, it appeared, for after a brief arm-waving dispute he disappeared.

Dyer addressed his baked potato, which he ate in stolid silence. "How much do you know about him?" he asked finally. "Or should I say, how much do you *want* to know?"

"His life is his own business."

"But you suspected something, right?" Dyer put down his fork to make a note. "Why did you never tell me he was Robert Watson?"

"I didn't know that when we last spoke—not that I would have told you anyway without his permission."

"Any idea why he changed his name?"

"Why is that any of your concern?" He shrugged. "He hated his father. Took his mother's name when he ran away."

"He's still running away." Dyer handed him the copy of the prison record, which Lucius glanced at and tossed back. "You knew this, didn't you?"

"I learned today."

Dyer grinned his rare thin grin. "Not interested in how I found out?"

"Now that I know you better, I can guess. Cheap Golden Dinner? You lifted his fingerprints? Swiped his spoon?"

Dyer nodded, a bit cross. "His fork." He returned Rob's record to his briefcase. "The law knows he's somewhere in the area. The federals may be in town already."

"I wonder who tipped 'em off." Disgusted, Lucius rose. Dyer said comfortably, "A licensed attorney and God-fearing American fully cognizant of his civic duty had no choice."

"You pledged allegiance to your flag and to the republic for which it stands, is that correct? One nation indivisible—"

"No need to get snotty just because you're drunk." He looked coldly at Lucius's whiskey. "Fundamentalist Americans are proud to pledge allegiance. Proud to worship the Father and the Son Who is Jesus Christ Our Lord and also abstain from intoxicating spirits." He pointed his forefinger at Lucius's eyes as his face clotted. "I hate to hear a feller American speak sarcastically about our flag. I really *hate* that."

"Same way you hate 'niggers'?" Lucius sat up straight, took a slow breath. "If Rob will witness your power of attorney, you'll set aside your bounden duty to turn him in: is that your offer?"

Dyer scraped his plate. "There may be questions. I'll need to know where I can find him. Out at your place, maybe?" Dyer leaned back in his chair and suppressed a belch. "You're already subject to arrest and prosecution for harboring a fugitive, by the way." He handed his half brother a card. It had no address on it, only a phone number. "If he leaves town, I'll expect a call. Confidential, of course. All you have to do is call and then you're out of it."

"God, what a prick you turned out to be." He tossed his card back at Dyer. "You're fired."

"It's not that easy." Watt Dyer wiped his mouth, drank down his water, and rose to follow him, forgetting the napkin balled tight in his fist. Hearing a frightened "Sir?" behind him, he tossed it back over his shoulder without turning. Overtaking Lucius in the lobby, he took hold of the back of his upper arm. "Better think that over, Professor," he said, propelling Lucius forward ever so slightly as if he meant to run him through the door. "For your brother's sake."

"*Our* brother, you mean? Go sign your own damn papers, Wattie."

Releasing him, Dyer said in a thick voice, "Let me tell you something, *Brother.* You don't want me for an enemy." His moon face looked swollen again, and those skin shivers appeared at the mouth corners. "I'll expect a call," Watt Dyer said and kept on going.

GUNSLINGER STYLE

Lucius was coming down the hall when a small explosion rattled the door of his brother's room. Inside, Rob's satchel lay open on the bed and a revolver cartridge glinted on the floor. The bathroom door was closed. Hearing a second shot, he jumped for the doorknob shouting, "Rob, NO!" before he heard the screech of tires and the rebel yell—*ya-hee!*

Kneeling at the bathroom window, Rob blew smoke from the revolver muzzle, gunslinger-style, to amuse his brother, as startled voices rose from outside and below. Lucius pulled him away in time to see a black car moving down the street, thumpeting on one rear tire. It stopped for a red light. The green came and then the red and then the green again. It did not move and nobody got out. Black as ants, figures crisscrossed beneath the street light, bent to look inside, looked back toward the hotel.

In the parking lot, a shouting man was pointing up at Lucius, who kept his head and leaned farther out the window. "What's going on?" he called. "Thought I heard shooting!" He ducked inside again.

Fallen back onto the bed, Rob was still crowing. "Ran that cold-eyed sonofabitch clean off the property! Had him skedaddling like a damn duck!" Lucius grabbed the gun and emptied it. "You're a damned idiot," he said. He rushed Rob across the corridor to the fire stairs, directing him to a nearby speakeasy where he was to wait until Lucius came to get him. Rob yelled back up the stairwell, "How about my stuff?," but kept on going.

Wrapping the revolver into his brother's dirty sweater, Lucius replaced it in the satchel, noting what constituted Rob's worldly goods. He owned three spare socks, a grayed pair of spare undershorts, a cheap checked spare shirt, a rusted razor, a frayed toothbrush but no paste, also a few loose cartridges, a large envelope, and a stained packet of folded sheets of yellowed paper with soft slits where the dark creases had worn through. Lucius tucked his old posse list into his breast pocket.

The envelope, marked "For Lucius," contained a penciled manuscript. He considered it a moment, put it back. Why read the thing? Even if Rob had his facts straight and his memory was dependable, his testimony might only mean that Papa had been temporarily out of his mind. Should the extraordinary life of a bold frontier entrepreneur be discounted because of the mad acts of a few minutes?

Well, Lucius, should it? Are you scared to read it?

He put the list back, too. Let Rob have the chance to return it if he wished.

Closing the satchel, he took a last look out the window. In soft evening rain, the black car still squatted in the middle of the street and the crowd was larger. Oh Lord, Rob, he thought, you're finished.

The fire stairs resounded with footfalls and the shouts of people bursting into corridors. From the night streets came the howl of sirens. In the rain slick and night glare, he drove the few blocks to the saloon.

"For a wanted man, you made a bad mistake," he said, sliding into the wooden booth. "I just hope you missed him."

"I never shot at him. Just shot one tire out with Papa's old revolver. Nailed the rear wheel on a moving vee-hickle!" He grinned with bitter pride. "Seeing Sonborn work his shootin' iron would have made ol' Bloody proud."

"You think Dyer will believe that you weren't shooting at him?"

"Who cares? It's the damned truth."

Lucius nodded. "His car's still sitting in the street. Looks like nobody got out. That's the damned truth, too." They listened to the sirens. "Even if what you say is true, you gave him more reason than he'll ever need to have you put away for good."

"I never shot at him, I told you! You don't believe me?"

"Who gives a damn what I believe? You think the law is going to accept that story? Slugs ricocheting around right outside the hotel? Suppose he was hit by accident?" He rose abruptly from the booth. "Let's go," he said.

"It was just kind of a joke," Rob whispered.

"We'll see how hard they laugh." Lucius tossed money onto the table. "C'mon, sober up. You're already a fugitive, 'armed and dangerous,' and you fired a lethal weapon in a public place at the car of a man you were seen quarreling with by forty witnesses only a few minutes earlier. If you get caught, they will rack your sorry ass."

Rob followed him into the street. "Where we going, Luke?" His chastened tone made Lucius feel like the older brother. "Home, I guess, till we figure out what to do. They won't find their way out there for a day or two." But Caxambas would be no solution. He saw no solution anywhere.

In the car, Rob was subdued. "Lucius? Listen. I'm not going back."

"To prison? You might have no choice."

The rain came harder. They passed through a wiper-washed phantasmagoria of dissolving shapes and glimmerings of gold-red liquid light, as if they were newcomers to Hell, he thought, coming in on the highway from the airport.

Nearing a roadhouse, Rob yelled *Stop!* into his ear and Lucius pulled off the road. Grabbing his satchel, Rob clambered out and slammed the door. He bent to the window, blinking away the rain. "They'll come hunting me and drag you into this," he said. "Go on home, nail down your alibi." He waved off his brother's protests, finally persuading Lucius that it might be best to separate. "Let's have that gun before you're caught with it," Lucius said.

Rob fished the revolver from his satchel, but after holding it a moment, put it back. "Family heirloom. I'd better hang on to this. As the oldest son, you know."

"Where did you get this damn thing anyway?" Lucius said irritably.

"Long story. Read all about it." Rob tapped the manuscript envelope. "Sure you want this? I wrote it for our archives like you asked but if you're smart, you'll never read it." When his brother took it, Rob straightened up to peer around him before leaning in again. He said, "Luke? I'm no killer.

Remember that, no matter what." Stepping back, he spread his arms to the night rain as if summoning the gods of the night highways of America to come bear him away home.

In the refracted neon light, his wet stubble glistened. "Maybe I'll show up at Naples for your 'New Look at Ed Watson' show, throw rotten eggs.

"That's *really* crazy, Rob! Don't do that!" Lucius yelled after him. "They'll be looking for you!"

Rob's silhouette crossed the gleaming mirrors of the puddles in a reeling run toward the roadhouse. The door opened in a crack of light, venting a wail of country music and a waft of deep-fried food. Then the light closed on the silhouette and Robert Briggs Watson was gone.

PANTHER ACRES

From Caxambas next morning, sleepless, at a loss as to what to do, Lucius drove to the nearest telephone at Rusty's and called Bill House. "Mr. House? This is Lucius Watson."

"*Colonel* Watson?"

"Yessir." He explained that he had never interviewed a House for his Watson biography and would be grateful for his opinions and conclusions in regard to his father's death. He tried to remain calm as Bill House measured his sincerity in silence, as if awaiting a more persuasive reason for this call.

Lucius studied his scarred boot toe among the cigarette butts and soda bottle caps in the phone booth. A shining grackle waddled past in gawky grackle gait, its cruel eye cocked for a likely scrap to pick apart and gobble.

House's voice was there again. "Just so we're clear about this, Mr. Watson: me and my dad and my brothers Dan and Lloyd, we was all in on it and we ain't never denied it." The voice paused a moment to let that settle. "I ain't real proud about the way it finished but I don't aim to tell you I'm sorry cause I ain't. Want to come all the way out here just to hear that news in person? You sure you ain't got nothin else in mind?"

"I hoped you might discuss your deposition in Lee County Court. And Henry Short."

Another pause. "Wife here wants to know if I'm still on your list."

"I imagine so. I haven't looked at it in years."

"Maybe I can help you, maybe I can't," House said. "Depends." Then the voice growled, "Long as you ain't this sonofabitch that's after Henry with a sniper rifle." When Lucius exclaimed, "No! I know nothing about that!" House said shortly, "Come ahead, then." The telephone was fumbled while being hung up and the man's voice continued through the bump and clatter. "It's all right, Betty, all right, sweetheart. No need to be scared just cause he's a Watson."

Bill House lived northeast of Naples at the edge of Big Cypress, in a new development where the stumps and burned snags and scrub jungle had been pushed back in muddy barriers and broken tangle by the steam shovels left behind by road construction on the Trail. Everywhere brush fires smoldered, the smoke rising to a thick whitish sky. In the distance, the tall cypress, shrouded in graybeard lichen, drew back affrighted from the steel machines at rest among the pale clay pools and the litter of mud-stuck pipe and rusting cable. The makeshift outhouse had a monkey stink and a warped door which banged on its loose hinges in the humid wind.

Bill House had said over the phone that his place was the only inhabited "estate" on Panther Acres. Lucius soon spotted the big florid man in khaki shirt and trousers who filled the doorway of his naked house, peering outward at the desolation. "See any panthers?" House inquired as Lucius got out of his car and walked toward him. Neither offered to shake hands. "Chose Panther Acres on account of all the panthers," House continued wryly. "Hoped I might hear one screamin in the night."

House contemplated the battered landscape as if to fathom the mystery of its great ugliness. "They're clearin these 'retirement estates' way out in the swamp-and-overflowed, sellin most of 'em by mail order. Florida boom! Dredge out ditches, call 'em bayous and canals, build up some high ground with the fill, call that prime waterfront property. All you need is some old swamp and you're in business."

He waved vaguely at the wasteland. "I kind of looked forward to them musky smells and swamp cries in the night. Owls, y'know, bull gators roarin in the springtime. I reckon you heard that sound up Chatham River." House turned back into his doorway. "We won't be hearin no bull gators, let alone panthers, cause these developers ain't never goin to stop dredgin and drainin, strippin off cypress to make way for all them Yankees, God-a-mighty! Smashed this forest flat, never put aside no money to clean up. And now the boom is dyin down and hard times startin up so they can't find no more fools to buy more swamp; they run out of money and before I could back out of the whole deal, I run out, too." He rapped the thin wall of his new house. "You ever need a retirement estate, I know where you could buy one pretty cheap."

Indoors, the small house was neat, with all blinds drawn against the desolation. "Here's Lucius Watson, honey." In the kitchen door, a pretty woman wiped her hands on her apron, peeping out fearfully at the guest. "Don't make no false moves, Colonel," House said for her benefit, pointing Lucius to a chair at the table, "cause that little lady you see there is deathly afraid of Watsons. Scared you might of come out here to bump me off."

When Lucius grinned, House smiled guardedly for the first time. "You might recall Miss Betty Howell from your school days," he said when his wife reappeared. "Her dad Jim Howell worked a year at Chatham."

The two waved shyly at each other as Bill House nodded, bemused by his own memories. "E. J.'s son in the house of a dang House. Now ain't that something?" He folded his big fair-haired hands upon the table. "You recollect that day you come to Chatham lookin for Henry? And snuck in so quiet? I still see that blue cedar skiff, how she tacked up-current, lost her headway, kissed that dock light as a butterfly. Never touched an oar nor cranked his motor," he told his wife as she set down the tray. He shook his head in admiration. "Colonel sung out a hello but waited where he was cause that was Island custom. Good thing, too, cause I had my shootin iron leaned inside the door."

House turned serious. "Let's go back a ways. My dad never took to your'n the way Ted Smallwood done. Never pretended to be his friend like some. I weren't no different. I always said straight out and plain that I fired at E. J. Watson, probably hit him, and that was about all I aimed to say about it."

Betty House, who had perched nervously on a chair at his behest, shifted her feet like a bird about to fly.

"Sure, I felt bad about what happened, far as his widow and her kids, but when D. D. House died off, 1917, I was the oldest, I had the responsibility. And in the twenties, here come Watson's son askin his questions. By then I'd heard about that list so I was leery, knowin Houses was bound to be first ones that son might come a-huntin; I also heard how good that son could shoot. So I reckon I weren't so friendly when you showed up at our dock—your daddy's dock, I mean. I spoke rough and you went redder'n a redbird!

"By then, the Watson story was all skewed around: the House men had waylaid Ed Watson cause we was jealous of his cane crop and big syrup boiler. Houses was the masterminds in a lowdown dirty ambush, Houses shot him in the back." Considering Lucius, House set down his glass of lemonade. "I never had nothin personal against you, Colonel. I was leery, yes, but mostly I was worried somethin bad might happen and we'd have us another Watson layin dead and some more ugly stories." Bill House grunted. "I thought you was crazy to come back to the Islands, I admit it, but some way I respected that kind of crazy. Took some guts."

"No guts at all. I made that list just to be *doing* something before I realized I did not have what it took to act on it—go gunning for revenge, I mean, eye for an eye. I'm glad I didn't but I wasn't glad back then. I was ashamed."

"Well, you're honest. That's what I heard, too." House changed the subject. "Ain't like your brother. Couple years ago, I was in Fort Myers so I went in and bought some insurance off of him to show there weren't no hard feelings on our House side. E. E. Watson acted like he felt that same way, he was real polite. But after my insurance was all bought and paid for, he let me know that he was a good Christian who done his best to practice Christian forgiveness but Mr. House should of took his business someplace else. Boy, I come out of there just steamin. That darned Christian forgive me for just long enough to take my money."

Mrs. House gasped and stood up before Lucius could object. House flushed. "Sorry, Colonel. Eddie's all right, I reckon. Never killed nobody as I know of." He blushed deeper still as his wife fled back into her kitchen. "But like I was sayin, with my family on the Bend, I couldn't take no chances—not that I ever thought you was real dangerous. I mean, you weren't nothin like your daddy, you just weren't that kind."

For some reason, this remark made Lucius cross. "But as you say, you couldn't count on that. You could never be quite certain."

"Nosir. You was Ed Watson's boy. I could never be one hundred percent certain, and I ain't today." Irritated in return, House snapped, "That what you're up to after all these years? Trying to scare folks?" His wife's small cry from the kitchen was a plea to soften his harsh tone, but her stolid husband wore a dogged look, unable to refrain from telling the whole truth and nothing but the truth, so help him God. "I'm speakin my mind plain, Betty," he told her, "same way I done last time."

House was watching Lucius as if appraising him. "Might have some grit but you sure ain't got good sense. You keep snoopin around this backcountry askin damfool questions, keepin lists, how's them boys s'posed to know you ain't a fed?"

"The men on that damned list are mostly dead—"

"I ain't dead far as I know and Speck Daniels ain't neither, not lest he went yesterday."

"Oh hell, if I'd wanted revenge—" But still unsure what he'd wanted, he fell silent.

"That a fact? If you was Speck, would you take a Watson's word for that?"

Lucius drank off his lemonade, discouraged. "Anyway, that's why I wanted to see Henry. Wanted to hear his account of it firsthand—"

Bill House interrupted him. "You come after Henry and now you're back; don't look like you're makin too much progress, Colonel." Briefly, ruefully, they both grinned, to ease matters.

The silence returned. House's clear gaze was a question. Lucius knew that the more he insisted on his peaceable intentions, the more sinister his pursuit of Henry might appear. Finally he rose to go. He understood, he said, why his host had to be careful, but if he'd wanted to harm Henry, he'd had plenty of chances in years past to catch him alone down in the rivers and nobody would have said a word about it.

"You might of had trouble from Houses but mainly that's correct. Folks wanted to put that whole business behind 'em, and if a black man had to pay the price, too bad. Some has tried to blame him anyway, as I guess you've heard."

Lucius nodded. "Later that week of October twenty-fourth, you gave that deposition in Lee County Court. Seemed like you were trying to defend somebody against rumors. Was that Henry?"

House measured him. "Yes, it was. Poor feller been hidin out from rumors ever since."

"The story that Henry was present, that was one thing, but the other rumor—that he was the first man to shoot, that he fired the fatal bullet—doesn't make much sense."

"No sense at all. Them Jim Crow years, Pitchfork Ben and all, was the worst of times for any nigra crazy enough to stick his head up out of the mud, and Henry Short weren't the least little bit crazy. All his life, he's been dead wary around white men and for damned good reason."

"No sense at all," Lucius agreed. "Was there any truth to it?"

"Why don't you consult your goddamned list, see if he's on there?" Quite suddenly, House turned a dangerous red, and his angry voice brought his wife to the kitchen doorway. "What are you after? What d'you think I been tryin to tell you here?"

"I'm not quite sure. I only know that in your testimony two days after the shooting, you already sounded defensive about rumors. So I guess I need to know why that was so."

Bill House sat back exasperated, slapping his big hands down on his knees. "*Why* do you need to know? All that happened long ago. High time you lived your own life, Colonel." But when Lucius simply awaited him, he nodded. "Reckon I'd feel the same. Sit down then. You ain't touched your cookies."

Bill House closed his eyes and sat silent a long while. Then he looked hard at Lucius. "All right," he said. "I aim to tell you the true story, Colonel, so don't go pesterin me with questions till I'm done."

WATSON DYING

"Where do I start? At the first argument? Watson seen our men was scared. Probably knew that because we was bunched up, he could do a lot of damage with a shotgun. Two charges of buckshot would knock down the leaders and scatter the rest, and with his revolver he might keep 'em duckin while he pushed back off the beach, reloaded, shot his way out of there. With a panicked crowd, he might of got away with it."

Lucius thought, *But if that was his plan, why had he run his boat so hard aground on a falling tide that not even a man as strong as Papa could push her off? Was that just a bad mistake, as people said? Papa didn't make mistakes like that, not when he had the whole trip north from Chatham Bend to think his plan through.*

"When Mr. D. D. House asked for his weapon, Watson had to move real quick. Up till now, he had played for time, figuring the crowd might falter, and he wasn't wrong. Truth was, if he'd surrendered up his guns, only one of his Island neighbors had the hard nature it would of took to shoot him in cold blood and that feller was away down to Honduras."

"Gregorio Lopez?"

"Names don't matter."

"Sorry. Go ahead."

"Your daddy's nerves was tight. He lost his temper. 'You want my gun so bad, you're going to get it!'

"Watson moved fast before we could take in what was happening—before we realized that a man we'd known near twenty years aimed to fire into a flock of neighbors like so many turkeys. Some of 'em are still tellin strangers how they seen a shine of crazy anger in his eyes. There weren't time nor light enough to see no such a thing. Most of 'em was so darned scared they couldn't see straight anyways. A couple of the biggest talkers wasn't even there.

"When his gun come up, my heart froze and my guts clenched up to block a charge of lead: I thought we was done for, Pap did, too, but I was already squeezin off my trigger. After that, all them guns emptied, a kind of a running explosion like giant firecrackers or maybe munitions set afire." House squinted at his guest. "It's a miracle some poor soul wasn't killed," he said.

"William House!" his wife cried, horrified.

Lucius refused to smile. "And Henry?" he persisted. "Was he there or not?"

"Oh Lord, does it matter anymore? I couldn't say it at the time I give that deposition but Henry Short was with us that day, yes. Bein a nigra, he naturally didn't want no part of it, and Smallwood tried to scare him off, but that good man knowed what he owed our family so he come along. Stood back by that big ol' fig, never spoke to nobody. What must of went through the poor feller's head, God only knows: we never talked about it, not even long after.

"Henry never come forward till your daddy jumped ashore. That's when I glimpsed him in the corner of my eye, wadin out a little ways, elbow hitched to keep his rifle barrel clear of the salt water. Even then, you couldn't hardly say he was in the crowd. Some of 'em said later that they thought they seen him but most of 'em didn't, cause bein a nigra, he just didn't count. Funny, ain't it? He had no business in that line so he weren't there.

"When your daddy spotted him, he reared his head back, anger flickerin all over his face, quick as heat lightning—I seen it.

"With his free hand, Henry lifted his straw hat and set it down again. 'Evenin', Mist' Edguh'—that is all he said. Daddy House beside me bein deaf as dust, I don't think anybody heard him 'ceptin me'n Watson. He growled somethin like, *Get on home, Henry!* I couldn't hardly make it out with all the whisperin and shiftin right behind us. Some was even slappin at miskeeters, thinkin the worst danger was past. Us ones up in the front knew better. We was too afeared we might die in the next second to pay no mind to no miskeeters, never knew till we was scratchin later how bad we was gettin bit. So them twin muzzles comin up looked big as the nostrils on a bull that's right on top of you.

"Now I bet you will tell me that your dad was only bluffin, which he was well knowed for. Speck Daniels claims he seen that shotgun after, said there weren't no shells in the chambers, but that darned feller is a troublemaker and a born liar. Anyways, it don't make a spit of difference. When Watson spoke so furious and behaved in that wild way, swinging that gun up in the face of close to twenty nervous fellers, the man were as good as dead, no matter if he fired or he didn't." Bill House turned to Lucius, worried. "You reckon he knew he was finished when he done that? Aimed to get it over with?"

Lucius nodded. "That could be." He cleared his throat. "And Henry?"

"Henry never raised his gun, let alone fired. Afterwards I talked it over with them Hardens, who asked Henry for the truth about what happened. Never mind what some folks say—and my sister Mamie, darn it all, she's one of 'em—them Hardens are honest people, and from what Henry told 'em, they come to the same conclusion I did."

House gazed regretfully at Watson's son. "I fired at your daddy, Colonel, like I said. I aimed to kill him, too. Maybe I did. When I seen that red hole jump out on his forehead, I knew there weren't no need to shoot again. His barrels was already comin down and he was, too. Then the rest of them guns let go, and a terrible hail of lead in the next second whapped into him very hard and loud before he hit the ground. I reckon most of that gunfire was nerves, and I can't rightly say I blame 'em. My nerves was ragged, too."

"Maybe they were making sure they could brag later about helping to bring down Bloody Watson," Lucius said sourly. House shrugged.

LONELIHOOD

"When Henry slipped away that night, he went south to Lost Man's, continued on to Shark River and Cape Sable the next day. He weren't never seen on the Bay again until after the World War. Had no home no more on Chokoloskee and no place he belonged. One time I asked him, 'Ain't it lonely, Henry? Livin all alone all them hard years?' And he looked at me kind of funny, sayin, 'Well, Mist' Bill, when a nigger has to hide, I reckon lonelihood works best.' "

"Lonelihood. I guess that's right."

"Ironical, ain't it? Every soul who knew him before all the trouble had a very high opinion of that man. Then he was gone for all them years, and the younger ones comin up had never worked with him, never hunted with him; they knew him mainly by bad reputation as That Nigger Who Raised a Gun Against a White Man. So when them boys crossed paths with him down in the rivers, they might yell over the water. *Hey, boy? We'll git you one day, boy!* One year they stole Henry's skiff and his whole harvest of fresh vegetables and bananas, hid it back in the mangroves till it rotted. Just funnin, you know, the way young fellers will. Never really knowed nor cared about Ed Watson, this was only their excuse to have some fun—"

"Fun," Lucius said, appalled.

"—but other ones, well, when they was drinkin, they still liked to talk about a lynchin, maybe settin a bounty on his head. I sure hate to think any such thing, but I know more'n one of 'em might not pass up a chance to shoot that colored man even today.

"Early twenties, Henry would come work sometimes for our family at House Hammock. Dense jungle back in there where nobody couldn't find him. Done some huntin and fishin, worked his own patch, lent a hand sometimes when I was caretakin the Bend—that's when you caught up with him. Year after that he come with us when we moved up Turner River to Ochopee and pioneered a tomato farm off the new Trail.

"When we had no work for him at Turner River, Henry would head downriver to the Gulf, hunt north or south along the coast for buried treasure. That feller was a fool for gold since back when we was boys. Only thing I ever knew he was a fool about. Had this secret bona fide copy of the map made by the pirate Gasparilla so's he wouldn't forget where he buried all his treasure.

"Course Gasparilla weren't nothing but a publicity stunt for Yankee tourists. Read all about pirate treasure on your place mat at the restaurant with a lot of other history thrown in for free. You got that authentical evidence all laid out on your doily where you can look at it while waitin on your shrimps and Key lime pie. Official art picture of Gasparilla in his black pirate hat with skull and crossbones, sword between his teeth, eye patch, big belt buckle, and all. Wipe off the ketchup and that mat will tell you ever'thing you need to know about that famous Spaniard from the bounding main.

"Come the Holy Day, Henry wouldn't never do no labor, he just read his Bible. But after he got that smell of gold, he would break his own commandment and go dig. I doubt he ever give much thought to where he'd spend up all his treasure if he found some, but after so many years alone, I reckon he had the idea that striking gold might make up to him some way for the life that had passed him by."

House gazed at the wall opposite, looking troubled. "Henry ended with us in a ugly way. Couple years ago, I told him he'd be better off goin south with a bunch of men who was headin for Honduras because he was bound to make more money huntin gators than scratchin for pieces-of-eight. Henry had a bad feelin about them Spanish countries and flat didn't want to go, but after so many years, I reckon it felt unnatural not to do what our family advised him.

"When I run him to the bus up to Fort Myers to board ship, he got out with his little burlap bindle and stood a minute lookin down the street. When I wished him luck, stuck out my hand, he never took it, never even looked at me. 'Looks like your family gettin shut of me before I get too old to work,' is all he said. Crossed over to the bus and went down to Honduras and near starved to death: the gators was all hunted out, the same as here. He made it back, but left our family for good; never came to see us even for a visit. And we was hurt, you know, having raised him up: we never took him for that angry kind of nigra.

"Because of them rumors he had shot a white man, Henry always figured some white man would come huntin him sooner or later. When you phoned today, we thought that man might be you. One day at Ochopee, my boy spotted a stranger circlin around back of our field totin a rifle with a huntin scope. I hollered at the man to lay that rifle down and step out where we could see him, state his business, but he just backed off, headin for the Trail. Some way we kind of knew this weren't the end of it.

"Sure enough, it weren't a month before a feller rung up, said he had important business with Henry Short. 'What you want with him?' I says, trying to figure who he might be. He said, 'That's between him and me.' So I told him, 'Okay, give me your name and address in case I hear where he is at.' All he gives me is a phone number—no name, no address, only that number. And he says, 'No names needed, mister. Just you call, say where he's at, and then you're out of it.' "

Disturbed by his own story, House got to his feet in sign Lucius should go. "I don't know where Henry is these days," he said, leading his visitor to the front door, "but for a time he was living over near Immokalee. Maybe we can find him through his church." He turned in the doorway. "Know something, Colonel? I aim to trust you. I'd like to see him, too. Out of respect, you know. Out of respect."

NORTH

On the white limestone road north toward Immokalee, the worried House could not stop talking about Henry Short. "Few years back, when Henry come with us to Ochopee, we was glad to have him, because black or white, he was the most able man in this coast country." He glanced at Lucius. "I was a good boss to nigras, got some work out of 'em, too. 'Treat 'em like fine horses and they'll run for you'—Daddy House taught me that old sayin from way back in slave days." Lucius wondered what Henry might have thought of that old saying. Intuiting his censure, House flushed red.

"Nigras is supposed to be free men, that what you're thinkin? Well, they ain't free and they never was, not in this backcountry, they was claimed by whoever gave 'em work. Some men called Henry 'House's nigger.' That sounds awful, don't it? Like we owned him! But you know something? He was *glad* about it."

Bill House struggled to explain, "All I'm sayin is, any black man in south Florida would be far better off bein a slave than on his own and that's the truth. Any nigra not attached to a white family can get grabbed right off this road, charged with loiterin or vagrancy and sentenced to farm labor or the chain gang: county sells his labor. But a nigra that belongs someplace ain't never bothered, not even for somethin pretty serious. That's because no red-blooded American won't stand for nobody messin with his property. So if you're black with white people behind you, you can murder your wife and if she don't make too much racket, the sheriff will most likely look the other way. He weren't elected to go spendin up taxpayer dollars on no coloreds."

For all the impacted prejudice, Lucius realized, there was decency in this man, too. House's laconic, deadpan humor reminded him of his father except that its irony was rueful, whereas Papa's irony had been sardonic, sometimes cruel.

House was pointing. "Our Ochopee tomato farm just over east of here is where Henry's past caught up with him. One day two white fellers come along in an old flivver, stepped out and said they was cattle ranchers from De Soto County by the name of Graham, said they was looking for a Henry Short. Two white men hunting up a colored was suspicious. We didn't say nothing. They stood in the noon sun, hats in their hands, and nobody so much as offered 'em a drink of water. So then they said, Sir, if your name is House and that man over yonder goes by the name of Henry, we come to pay him a Sunday call because his mother is our mother, too. Never twisted words about it. If they was sheepish or ashamed, it never showed.

"Them Grahams took Henry aside, had a real visit. Left him a letter from their mama. Henry must of read them words a thousand times, eyes shinin like he seen a miracle. Then he refolded it very careful, like there was a gold piece wrapped in there that might slip out. He never showed his letter to our family, never spoke about it, and we knew better than to ask him. Now and again, he might refer to things it said—he had it memorized—and finally we had the story pieced together.

"I reckon you heard that Henry's father was burned and hung and his white mother whipped severely; you might not know that her daddy took his ruined daughter back. Took her baby, too, till the age of four, then sold him to a man on his way south. Henry finally wound up in our family. Him and me was close to the same age so we come up together.

"Well, this white girl's daddy found some older man willin to take her and she give that man two boys before he died. When the boys was growed, she confided to 'em about Henry. Said that little boy had never left her heart, she purely yearned to know what ever become of him. I reckon her two white sons loved her dearly because even after they located Henry, they came south every other year to make sure he was getting on all right. Steady men of average size, polite and quiet. We couldn't get over 'em. Their mother might of been a sinner but she must of been a very good woman, too, if she could raise up two fine sons who took on the responsibility for a mixed-blood half brother they had never seen, a field hand in south Florida who never even knew that they existed.

"Knowing Henry, he most likely thought them half brothers was plain crazy to go up against common prejudice that way. All the same, he was very very grateful. Hummed and whistled, little secret smiles, he glowed for days after they left, couldn't get over it. We never seen him smile that way in his whole life. Course Henry would never tell us what they talked about and we never tried to work it out of him. Probably thought we might tease him, or to speak about it was some way unlucky and might spoil the only experience of his own blood kin he ever had.

"One time before his white brothers came to see him, Henry whispered, 'The onliest thing more no 'count than a dumb nigger mus' be a white woman that traffics with a nigger.' But after his brothers come and claimed him, and told him how his mother had sent after him, we never heard him speak that way no more. I believe he was tore up, just sick at heart, that he had talked so cold and hard about his mama.

"The last time his brothers came to Turner River, we was so glad to see their truck that we waved and hollered, invitin 'em to come on over to the cabin, eat some good hambone stew. But them words hangin in the air sounded all wrong, so we waved at Henry to come ahead, he was invited, too. But a-course we knew he wouldn't never set and eat with us, all we done was make him more uncomfortable, and when his brothers seen that, they smiled real polite and said, 'No, thank you, Mr. House,' and turned right back to Henry's little fire. The sight of them three brothers down on their hunkers, chucklin and swappin stories while they served each other's plates like Henry had ate with white men all his life—well, I never forgot that.

"What them Grahams stood for, so simple and so clear, made me ashamed. It woke me up and turned me right around, changed my whole way of thinkin about nigra people. Yessir, I was mightily impressed, and I am today. I only seen them brothers two-three times over the years and am real sorry I never knew 'em better."

On their way north, Lucius was so quiet that his companion grew uneasy, asking him finally how he felt about traveling with a House, and perhaps Bill House especially. Though Lucius reassured him, he soon fell silent again, being worried about where Rob was now and what might become of him.

Up the road they met a dusty road-gang truck with a plier-faced guard at the wheel; his sunglasses twitched in their direction as they passed like the huge black eyes of a fly. Two black convicts and two white ones stood on the truck bed in pairs. The young whites swayed recklessly in the center of the bed, thumbs hooked in the hip pockets of their jeans, while the two blacks, indifferent, maintained easy balance with one fingertip on the high sideboards. Being unshackled, any of the four could have jumped and run, but apparently they understood that Plier Face was not a man to pass up a free shot at a human target. In the front seat, a hard-eyed white con was wearing the guard's black cowboy hat. As the truck passed, his tattooed hand, raised above the dented roof, erected a finger in contempt of any values other vehicles might represent.

"Road gangs used to be very bad all over Florida, all over the South, I reckon," Bill House said. "Black convict or white never made much difference, not when it come to chains and rawhide whips. Chain gangs was why them outlaws run away to Watson's—Cox, y'know, and them men Cox killed, and plenty of others, too."

In the west, a lonesome turkey vulture tilted down across the wall of a long cypress strand. "Ever seen Deep Lake? Deep small lake over yonder in a two-hundred-acre hammock; that's where Langford and his partners had them citrus groves. In the dry season, a man can *feel* that good fresh water.

"For many years, Frank Tippins sold convict labor to that outfit. That's why he had his prison camp way to hell and gone out here in the Big Cypress. Companies paid next to nothing for his nigras and the sheriff kept every penny them poor devils earned, being as how it was against state law for them terrible criminals to receive payment. Them Deep Lake partners was rich men, never had to think about them human beins that made 'em all their money. Maybe your brother-in-law knew how Tippins worked things, maybe not, but too much blood and tears fell at Deep Lake.

"Sheriff Tippins learned a live-and-let-live attitude: let him live if his skin ain't the wrong color. That time he killed a nigra prisoner in his own jail—saved that darned nigra from committin suicide, I reckon—the sheriff called it an escape attempt. Later claimed this man was the only prisoner he ever killed in the line of duty. Must of forgot all them poor sinners that never went home from his labor camp out here.

"Tippins kept up his polite reputation in Fort Myers but didn't behave right out in this backcountry where nobody weren't watching. Handcuffed his prisoners, then knocked 'em down, to give 'em a taste of what was comin if they didn't work all out in this heat until they dropped. Sooner or later, every last one that could still walk tried to run off. All swamp country out here where it ain't sand and thorn so they never got too far. Miskeeters and the heat took the last fight out of 'em and anyways, he paid Injuns to track 'em. Left sign any Mikasuki could foller blindfolded and walkin backwards. Never had to catch 'em—had to *rescue* 'em! Hauled 'em back to camp more dead than alive, and the ring leader was usually whipped to death or shot, make an example. They buried 'em in the soft fill on the railway spoil bank. Buildin this road, the county dug up so many bones it was embarrassin."

"Think that spoil bank might have been the source of those bad stories about old bones dug up on Chatham Bend? What some called 'Watson Payday?' "

House remained silent a few seconds too long. "Well, we blame too much on your daddy, that is correct," he said at last. "We forget how much competition that man had on the frontiers when it come to common killin. And I ain't talkin only about plume hunters or moonshiners or backwoods varmints such as Killer Cox. I'm talkin about Christian businessmen who work their feller men to death to make more money, I'm talkin about all them miserable lost lives that gets wrote off to overhead. So if Ed Watson killed a few workers like they say, he weren't the only boss who done that, not by a long shot."

Of Tippins's old Copeland prison camp, little sign was left, only a shadow ruin on white sand back off the roads, grown over by liana and rough thorn. A pileated woodpecker's loud solitary call rang in the noonday heat, over the dry scrape of palmetto, in the sunny wind.

The limestone road north from the Trail traversed the marsh and flat palmetto scrub of the Big Cypress. Across the white sky, dark-pointed as a weapon, a swallow-tailed kite coursed the savanna for small prey. "Cattlemen held a big panther hunt out this way a few years ago, tried to shoot 'em out, but there's still more panthers in the Cypress than anywhere in Florida except maybe my backyard on Panther Crescent," House said wryly. Lucius hid his grin, still reluctant to acknowledge how much he enjoyed this man who had raised a gun and fired point-blank at his father.

The sun was high and the road empty, a ghost path of white limestone dust boring ever deeper into swamp and scrub. On the canal bank, a lone alligator lay inert as a log of mud. Long necks of cormorants and snake birds, like water reptiles, parted the black surface, sank away again. A moccasin coiled in a low stump; a bog turtle paused at the road edge, awaiting its next instinct. The white rock road writhed and shimmered in mirage toward its shining point of disappearance miles ahead.

Southeast of Immokalee, a stringy black man walked the shoulder of the road. Though he had not signaled or broken his stride, Lucius slowed the car. "Pretty hot to be out walking the road," he murmured, and House said easily, "Give him a lift, then. I rode with plenty of 'em."

The car drew up on the road shoulder with a rattle of limestone bits under the fenders; the figure sprang sideways as if startled by a snake. Alarmed that these white men had stopped, he was smiling hard, braced for some loud jape and set to run. When Lucius smiled—"Good morning!"—he doffed a dusty cap. "Yassuh," he said. "Mornin." He took out a bandanna and wiped his brow, not quite meeting their gaze.

"Headed for Immokalee?"

"Yassuh, dass right, suh."

"Get in," House told him, reaching back to find the door handle.

Still wary, the man raised a hard-veined gray-brown hand to the bill of his soiled cap. Slow and careful as a lizard, seeking entry without touching anything, he eased into the backseat in a waft of humid heat and hard-earned odors. Closing the door gingerly behind him, he perched on the fore edge of the seat, ready to fly. "You genlemans ain't slavuhs, is you?" he inquired, daring a little smile when the white men laughed.

Asked how he liked Immokalee, the man chuckled, *cuk-cuk-cuk*, like a dusting chicken. " 'Mokalee." He nodded, feeling his way. He would not look at them. "Yassuh, dass right. 'Mokalee, now dat is a fine town. Man dat nevuh been a nigguh on Sat'day night in 'Mokalee, dat man doan know nothin about livin, so de nigguhs say." He chuckled a little more, *cuk-cuk-cuk.*

When the white men grinned, their passenger relaxed a little, sat back a little, hummed a little, peering out at the savannah to evade their white man's curiosity. Over the pinelands, vultures swirled like cinders on the smoky sky. "Yassuh. Gone be fryin hot t'day."

At a corner at the edge of town, the man tapped a gray fingernail on the window, crooning "Thank'ee kin'ly, kin'ly," soft as a lullaby, "kin'ly, kin'ly," until the car stopped and he got out. He was recognized at once and cheered by a pair of celebrants brandishing small flat bottles in brown paper bags; he hesitation-stepped in a kind of greeting dance. All smiles, he turned to wave. "I'se in good hands now as you kin see!" he cried. "I thank'ee kin'ly, white folks!"

"Kin'ly, kin'ly," Bill House said, amused. "Think they're laughing at us?"

"I do, I really do." Lucius's heart cheered the man's mischievous ironies and buoyant spirit, the poignance and dogged love of life that was so moving in people who owned nothing, and also that in-the-bone endurance that in its way was a shaming of the whites and a profound rebuke.

House asked the men if they might know a man named Henry Short.

"*Deacon* Sho't?"

They told him that Deacon Short was in the hospital. Torching cane fields for the Okeechobee harvest, he'd been caught in a back burn when the wind shifted, and burned severely over most of his body; he was not recuperating and was not expected to live.

"I mean, damn it all," Bill House burst out on the way to the hospital. "Henry's very experienced and he ain't a drinker but that don't mean he should work alone around big fires!" Lucius had never thought to see this man so agitated. "Big Sugar don't care nothin about workers' rights or the damn risks so long as they're rakin in big profits. Know who got convicted on a slavery charge just lately? United Sugar! U.S.A.! *Slavery!* In the Twentieth damn Century! That what they call progress?"

They crossed the railroad tracks and headed west on a main street of auto junkyards, body shops, a dealership in bright green farm machinery, a brown whistle-stop saloon: they were nearing the hospital when Lucius said, "Did Henry ever mention finding bones? On Chatham Bend, I mean?"

"You back on that again? Speck Daniels tell you that or was it Hardens? Either way, don't pay no attention, Colonel. If Henry ever run across something like that, our family surely would've heard about it."

THE BURNED MAN

With no staff around on Sunday to direct them, they had to hunt for the old negro ward, a long room parted by narrow shafts of dusty sunlight. Its sepia cast and weary atmosphere, its creaking fans, its leaning cabinets and streaked stained walls, reminded Lucius of the soldiers' wards in old daguerreotypes from the Civil War. The discreet slow figures wandering the ward were patients and their visitors—women who had walked here after church, Lucius supposed, since most wore Sunday habits. Perched on small chairs by the door were two white men of middle age with weathered faces. Recognizing Bill House, they smiled shyly and stood up to shake hands, but so upset was House by the sight of the patient across the room that he brushed blindly past.

On the narrow cot, pinned to the coarse sheets like a plant specimen, the figure lay still as if extinguished by the heat. His worn blue cotton nightshirt was open down the front and his chest was patched with cracked and crusted scabs leaking thin red fluid. From his iron bed rose a peculiar odor of broiled flesh and disinfectant tinged with sweat and urine.

Peering out from beneath head bandages, Henry Short did not see his visitors until they loomed over his bed, one on each side. Dimly aware of a presence in the light, he muttered, "Them ain't angels. Them ain't angels." The voice emerged so cracked and thin, with scarcely a twitch of the scabbed lips, that his visitors did not realize at first that he had spoken.

House was stricken speechless by Short's condition, and in the end it was Lucius who said, "Henry?" He spoke softly so as not to intrude on the hush over the ward. "Can you hear us?" Henry stared out of fiery red eyes. Through broken lips, the burned man whispered, "That you, Mist' Lucius? How *you* been keepin? You, Mist' Bill?"

Henry had first known Lucius as a boy of eight, down in the rivers, yet it astonished Lucius that a man dying had recognized somebody he had not seen in years and could not have imagined he would ever see again. With his forefinger he pressed an unburned patch of skin on the ropy forearm by way of affirmation and encouragement and Henry responded by raising that arm minutely to press his touch.

Seeing this, House reached across the cot to touch the arm where Lucius had touched it but hesitated and withdrew his hand just as Henry lifted his forearm in response—too high to bear, it seemed, for he clenched his jaw not to cry out. The pain turned his gaze murky. He closed his eyes and gasped out, "Lo'd A'mighty!" Hearing those words, an old woman two beds away called on his visitors to witness that Deacon Short was a true man of God; if he had ever sinned, none could recall it. "Praise de Lo'd!" the woman cried. A shy chorus of assent rose from the ward. The ambulatory patients and their visitors walked past like mourners in a slow procession, crooning warm harmonies. "Hear them angels?" Henry whispered. "Think they comin after me?" Henry Short produced a stillborn smile as his visitors tried to smile back, sick at heart.

Bill House looked around the ancient ward. "Well, now, Henry, these folks treatin you okay?" Short's red eyes watched Lucius. "As best black folks knows how, Mist' Bill." As a dying man in dreadful pain, he did not bother to conceal his sarcasm. House stared at him, shocked that this man he'd known so well could speak so bitterly. He tried to jolly him: how could an old hand like Henry get caught in a back burn? Short had no time for this. Urgently, he said, "Mist' Bill? You member when that man come huntin me? Ochopee?" That same man had come for him again, he told them. He'd seen him assembling a weapon on the dike road. Then he came toward him down the rows, in and out of the molasses smoke of burning cane.

Henry dropped his fire rake and ran, dodging in and out amongst the cane. The smoke that obscured him from his pursuer shrouded the ditch, too; peering back over his shoulder, he had pitched right into it and fallen hard, hitting his head. Lying there stunned, he only came to when the burn overtook him and he woke up choking on the smoke, clothes singed by fire. Afraid to holler out for help, he rolled and crawled along the ditch to the mud puddle where he was found toward twilight. Since the local clinic lacked a ward for coloreds, he'd been shipped here.

Lucius said, "Can you tell us what he looked like?"

"Too much smoke. Seen the big bulk of him, is all. Seen how he walk back on his heels, toes out—"

"That's him!" House cried. "That's the same man we saw in Ochopee!"

"Yessuh. Scairt me so bad I never watched where I was runnin."

Leaving House at the bedside, Lucius crossed the floor and introduced himself to the two men sitting by the door. They had come as soon as they were notified, they said. Their name was Graham. A few years ago, their brother Henry had spoken kindly of Lucius Watson and they thanked him for coming. The Grahams were worried that today was Sunday, with nobody on duty to give Henry something for his pain—not that it mattered, since he was refusing his pain medication. As best they could fathom his fierce code, uncomplaining acceptance of his agony signified some sort of penance, though what he should feel penitent about they could not imagine. They had to leave him every little while to recover from the sight of such hard suffering.

At Henry's bedside, told who those men were, House turned to look. "Them fellers knowed me when they seen me?" Overjoyed, he went to meet the Grahams, who rose and sat him down between them.

Through torn screens in the high windows came the caw of crows in the listless stillness of hot summer woods. Small bits of life crawled and flew about the ward on ancient business. Lucius awaited Henry Short's return. Henry's mouth had fixed itself in a grim semblance of a smile but the broken eyes, discolored red and yellow, had gone glassy with withheld tears. "You're a tough old gator, Henry, you are going to make it," Lucius said, taking the rickety chair beside the bed. "Doan go wishin that on me, Mist' Lucius," Henry gritted, as tears escaped onto his caved-in cheeks. "I done with life. I had my fill."

"All right. Just rest."

With the testiness of pain, Short said, "You ain't come all this way to Immokalee to tell this nigger to just rest, Mist' Lucius. I believe you still huntin fo' yo' daddy." Henry was altogether present and intent on his visitor's expression as if to make certain that he wished to hear the truth. "That day you come to see me? Chatham Bend? I lied that day." Short was gasping. "Been tellin lies about that autumn evenin all of my whole life." He sounded more resentful than remorseful. "White folks ever stop to think how they make black men lie? Good Christian nigras? Lie and lie then lie some more, just to get by in life? *Just to get by?*"

Lucius found a cloth to wipe his brow. "Don't exhaust yourself. No need to talk." Out of his agony, Short summoned the will to glare. "If they ain't no need to talk, how come you settin here? They *is* a need!" Henry rasped this with asperity, in fits and starts. "My time comin. I *needs* to finish. Same as you." He closed his eyes and kept them shut as if reading testimony etched in acid on the inside surfaces of his eyelids. "Got a cryin need." When he emitted a sharp cough of pain, the churchwomen drew closer, fearful that his visitor might drain the Deacon's strength.

"These folks love you, Henry."

"Yessuh," the burned man snapped, impatient. "All God's chillun lovin dere poor ol' Deacon." He was struggling to indicate an old book on a little shelf above his head. When Lucius said he'd be happy to take his word, Short closed his eyes and shook his head. Lucius took the Bible from the shelf and slid it beneath the mitt of bandages on his right hand.

A HUMAN MAN

"Mist' Lucius, I was deathly scared of Mist' Watson but I never felt no hate. Because he *seen* me. Seen me as a man, I mean, a somebody with my own look to me and my own way of workin, not just any-old-nigger with no face but only just his two hands for his work. Field niggers, house niggers, make no difference: they all scared niggers. Your daddy scared 'em, too, got rough with 'em, but all the same, he listened like they was people. He was a very uncommon white man in that way, *very* uncommon. I felt beholden all them years I knew him."

And had he "seen" E. J. Watson in return? Lucius wondered. The great waste?

"Course treatin coloreds with respect don't mean he gone to tol'rate no gun-totin nigger standin amongst white men come to judge him. And that's what he seen that evenin, comin ashore." When Lucius looked puzzled, Short said sharply, "What I told you! *Nigger actin to be a man!* A human

man," he added quietly. He lay still to accumulate strength again before continuing.

"Follerin after 'em that evenin, I was so heavy in my heart I couldn't hardly get a breath. I was dead scared of Mist' Watson and dead scared of them scared men passin the jug around. All I could see there on that shore was the mob that killed my soldier daddy back in Georgia.

"Mist' Edgar didn't hardly look at me, just warned in a scrapy voice, 'You get on home.' But knowin this black rascal could shoot, he took no chances. Easy-like, still talking, he hefted up that double-barrel like he was fixin to hand it over to Old Mist' Dan, way he was told, but by the little shiftin of his feet I seen he was gettin set to swing that gun from the hip, blow that fool nigger off the end of that line of men to show 'em he meant business—show 'em that if he was to let go his other barrel, next one to fall would be a white man and more likely two."

For a moment, distracted by his pain, Henry lost his thought. He had confused himself. He frowned. His dry mouth twitched. After Lucius fed him water in thin sips, he shifted minutely and tried again.

"I was still prayin I would not have to shoot but when his gun come up in a snap swing, mine come up with it. I seen his eyes go wide out of his surprise. Happened so fast," he lamented. "That noise crackin my head as if earth exploded. Mist' Watson's face gone redder'n red, looked like a busted tomato.

"*Somebody shot Mist' Edgar Watson!*—that was the first thought come into my head, seein him fallin. All I could think was, Henry Sho't, these men gone lynch you here today. And right about then my hands told me I had raised that rifle." He gazed bleakly at Lucius. "The feel of 'em. Told me I fired." Henry spoke as if sorry that E. J. Watson had not killed him.

"You figured he might shoot you so you fired first—"

The wrapped mitts jerked on the coarse coverlet. "Tha's what some said later. '*The nigger panicked!*' " Henry shook his head. "Weren't no time to panic. No time for nothing. I just done it." His brow was clenched in a deep frown. In its concave shadow, his temple pulsed.

"Bill House?"

"Mist' Bill shot right behind me. All them Houses was good shots, prob'ly hit Mist' Edguh befo' he hit the ground, but he was fallin by the time they fired."

"You *know* you shot first and you *know* you didn't miss." Lucius paused. "Your bullet killed him."

The dying man set his bound hand square on the Bible. "Help me God," he said.

Lucius sat back. That old rumor was true, then, inconceivable and true. In the worst days of Jim Crow, a black man had killed Papa.

As if in terror of his own confession, Short frowned as hard as his scabbed face would permit. A blackish blood spot rose into the corner of his eye. When Lucius put a wet rag to his lips, Henry whispered, "Hell is waitin on me, Mist' Lucius. After all my prayin."

"You had no choice. And my father would have died in the next seconds anyway." He said, "Henry, I'm sorry. You must think I've been hunting you all my life."

"Ain't Henry you been huntin, Mist' Lucius." He closed his eyes and, as if practicing, he lay as still as the corpse of Henry Short. "No mo' secrets, Mist' Lucius," he whispered. "No mo' lyin."

Saying good-bye, Lucius recalled Jane Straughter's message, entrusted to him at Fort White the week before. Hearing it, Henry showed no response—*too late*, his stillness seemed to say. Lucius leaned forward to repeat it softly: *Please tell Mr. Short that Miss Jane Straughter was asking after him. Tell him Miss Jane said to please come visit one day soon.* Henry's eyes flew wide. "*Miss* Jane." Tears glimmered. "Soon," he whispered.

Bill House and the Grahams rushed to Henry's cot when his heart faltered and hard spasms yanked his body. When he fell back, he lay as if transfixed, mouth stretched in a famished yawn. Then, in a twitch, as the room moaned, his heart restored blood to the grayed skin, and the mouth eased, and the glaring eyes, returned from darker realms, softened and dampened.

House lingered at the bedside as if awaiting the burned man's permission to depart with a clear conscience; he seemed unwilling to accept that Henry Short was dying. (In a note from the Grahams a fortnight later, Lucius would learn that Henry never spoke again but sank away and died a few days later.)

HEENIOUS MURDER

On the way south, House said, "You get the truth from Henry you was after, Colonel?"

"Yes, I think so. Which is more than I ever got from you, Bill. You always gave me the impression you shot first."

"Me or Dan Junior, one. Dan always claimed it." Bill House grinned. "I ain't generally a liar, Colonel. But my dad made us promise never to admit that Henry fired.

"See, no two guns sounds just alike, not to a man that has hunted many years with both of 'em. That man was Mr. D. D. House, and that first whipcrack shot came from his old Winchester that he passed along to his colored boy one year when he was too broke to pay him.

"Daddy he never let on what he had heard till he was on his deathbed, 1917. Summoned his three sons that was down there at the landing, made us swear that what he was about to say would never leave that room. Even then, he was extra careful. He did not tell us in so many words that Henry fired, only informed us that he heard the *crack* of his old Winnie *if he weren't mistaken*—said that part twice. But he did add kind of ironical that *if* Henry fired, he must of been aimin at a bat or something. What he meant: from fifty feet, let alone fifteen, Henry Short were not a man well-knowed to miss.

"Course bein a nigra back when lynchin nigras didn't hardly make the papers, Henry would never admit he pulled his trigger, not even to me, who was raised up with him and standin right beside him when he done it. Not one man in the crowd that evenin would of raised his hand to stop him: they was very glad to have that nigra's rifle in the line, because him just bein there was bound to distract Watson and might keep some of 'em from gettin shot. Trouble was, they never let on to their sons how scared they was—so scared they forgot the color of a man because he could outshoot the man who scared 'em. And bein ashamed, they never talked about it or discussed it in the family.

"So it weren't the fathers but the sons who got hard with Henry. Hated to think that a black man might of took care of Watson and their scared daddies only finished off the job. That's why some of 'em went to hollerin about Nigger Henry, Nigger Short; '*Who in hell give that nigger the idea he could get away with that?'* Pretty soon they was sayin that maybe Short's bad attitude come from the way them Houses spoiled him. Next, some liar spread a story, *'That dang nigger bragged on killin a white man'*—say that real sweet and soft, you know, which is the sign amongst that coward kind that some poor nigra is headed for perdition. Pretty soon they was tellin how the whole thing was Henry's doin. *'Why hell, that nigger lost his head, the way they do! Committed heenious murder! We gone to stand for some hare-brain nigger shootin down a white man in cold blood? We just gone to stand here chawin about it? Ain't we men enough to go learn that boy his lesson?'* But Henry Short had our House clan behind him, seven men and boys, so nobody would lay a hand on him that weren't lookin for more feud than they might have wanted. And their daddies kind of nodded along and shrugged and kept their mouths shut. It never come to much and finally died down, because most of them boys was not so much bad fellers as big talkers, and on top of that, in them first years, they couldn't find him.

"Anyways, I believe today that Henry and me fired shots so close that every man but Daddy House heard just the one, and I don't believe no other shots was ever needed. In them days, I passed for a expert with a rifle, some would say I was right up there with your daddy, but from all our years huntin together, I knew our colored man was better and shot faster. So when Daddy said he heard two shots, I was scared at first it was Henry's bullet killed Ed Watson. Well, it weren't. He never aimed at him, y'see. I did."

Lucius said flatly, "Henry killed him, Bill. Killed him first, anyway."

"He tell you that?" House raised his eyebrows. "Well, if Henry told you, Colonel, that is good enough for me." House stared out the window, digesting his mixed feelings. "In the back of my mind, maybe I knew the truth of it. That hole smack in the forehead—that bullet weren't mine. I aimed for the heart and I don't believe I missed. Only thing, he was still on his feet when I fired. Already dead, I reckon."

"To all intents and purposes," Lucius said shortly.

"Henry went home quick because right away them ones that was drinkin wanted to know who brung along that nigger. Course they knew it was Houses and we spoke right up but that didn't stop 'em, nosir, they was huntin trouble.

"Henry didn't need no warnin. By the time we got home, he already had his gear in his old skiff. Pap had left before the crowd started to turn ugly so he said, 'Them men ain't goin to bother you none, Henry. Heck, they *like* you.' And Henry said, ' 'Spect so, Mist' Dan. They liked Mist' Watson, too.' He left that night."

A few minutes later, Bill spoke up again. He could not put the burned man out of his mind. "Whilst you was over talkin with his brothers, Colonel, Henry told me he was through with life but life weren't through with him. I just hated to see him so bad hurt that he would say somethin like that." He looked stricken. "And knowin no words I could say to help when he was dyin, that made me ashamed.

"After all the years that good man give us, after we promised Daddy House we would protect him, how come we never kept track of him? Let him know he weren't forgotten by our family; tell him we was wonderin how he might be gettin on? I never done that, nosir, I did not. Too much pains to take over a nigra—was that my thinkin?

"Funny, ain't it? My cousin-in-law over to Marco, the one helped lynch that colored feller some years back cause they give him a white man's job in the clam cannery? That cousin never missed a meal till the mornin he never come down to eat his breakfast. Died peaceful in his sleep at home after a nice long life. How do you figure that one, Colonel? You reckon God just thundered down, *'All is forgiven, Boy, cause you ain't nothin but a redneck idjit that never knowed no better. It's them ones like your cousin Bill that knowed better and turned away that I am abominatin in My sight.' "* Bill shook his head. "I never did commit a crime against a black man and darn glad of it but I never done nothin for 'em neither, not even when I had the chance. You reckon that's why I feel so bad about Henry? Because I *knew* better?"

House lifted his hand to shield his eyes from the westering sun that fired the windshield.

"Kind of late to help him now. I missed my chance. Sins of omission, they will call it where I'm headed for."

From here and there across the prospect of Golden Years Estates came the grind and bang of earth-moving machinery. At Panther Crescent, finding Bill's wife away at church, they sat outside sorting the day's events.

Bill said, "So Lucius Watson finally learned Henry Short's story and made friends with the House clan, too—that mean you're through with it?"

"Know something, Bill? I might be. But first I have to get to Hell and hear my father's side of it."

"Lordamighty." Bill House laughed. "Where you off to, Colonel, this late in the day? Which ain't none of my darned business," he added hastily when Lucius remained silent. "What I mean, don't wait around here just to keep me company. You got a long drive home." Lucius assured him he'd be happy to wait until Bill's wife came back in case Bill needed a hand with all those panthers.

Hearing a car coming, they got to their feet. Bill House waved with a broad smile of welcome as his wife climbed out with a food basket on her arm. For how many long years, Lucius Watson thought, had there been nowhere he was expected, no dear friend to greet him with warm supper? All that awaited him was that stranded barge on a remote salt creek; he felt invaded by a dread of home.

"He's back safe, Mrs. House!" he called. "I never got a chance to bump him off!" But he had hailed her with a gaiety he did not feel, and Bill House turned to look at him. "Listen," Bill said. "Better stay and eat some supper with us, Colonel. Talk about old schooldays with Miss Betty here."

"Thank you, I have to go," he said, lest they think he'd been awaiting an invitation. Awkward, he thrust out his hand and House, still puzzled, shook it warmly. "So long, Colonel. Hope we ain't seen the last of you," he added, as Betty House said shyly, "Lucius? I sure am happy to meet up with you again. Will you come see us?"

When his car started up, the Houses waved. "You ain't such a bad feller, Colonel," Bill called after him. "Maybe you never was."

By the time he reached Caxambas, there would be a moon. His mind turned and returned to that brass urn. Was that what he'd been dreading? That waiting presence, gathering moon glints in the window? The thing spooked him—not those brown bones but the spirit sealed in with them. He had no wish to be alone with Papa in defenseless sleep.

Making his way along the woods road to the old sheds by the creek, he took pains with the potholes. He shut the car door carefully when he got out and made his way out to the barge over the spindly walkway. Down the still creek, a raccoon fishing mud clams at the tide edge sat up to peer around and watch him pass.

Noisy on purpose to warn away the ghosts, he wrenched open the salt-swollen door. Framed in the window, in silhouette against the mirror of the creek, the urn awaited him. Stopped short on the threshold by unnamable emotions, he was startled when his own voice said, "Papa? I'm home."

In a tumult of unsorted memories and premonitions, he crossed to the window and with both hands lifted the urn, touching it to his forehead to break its spell. "May God forgive you, Papa"—how inappropriate this was, since, like his father, he had lost faith in any deity. What should he do with this damned thing?

He lay down wide-eyed on the moon-swept cot, clasping his hands on his gut to quell his restlessness. In the morning he fetched Rob's envelope from the car, made coffee, sat out on the deck.

NIGHT RIVERS

Luke:

I am writing down as best I can remember the events of New Year's morning, 1901, so you will better understand why I ran away. It takes all the courage I have left to let you read this. I'm taking you at your word that it's the truth you're after.

You and Eddie were still in school, living with Carrie and Walter in Fort Myers, when Wally Tucker fled Key West with his pregnant sweetheart to escape bad debts and scandal, having heard that Mr. Watson at Chatham River would employ them. Some months later, your father's hogs sniffed out two shallow graves beyond the cane fields. Wandering out there calling in the hogs, the Tuckers discovered the remains of two young cane cutters. These men had told Wally that they wished to quit but were owed more than a year's back wages and could not get "Mr. Ed" to pay attention.

The Tuckers fled the Bend without their pay. I found them rushing their stuff down to their little sloop, almost hysterical. He murdered Ted and Zachariah! *"That's impossible," I said. "He paid those boys last month and took them to Fort Myers. I saw them off myself."* Well, we did, too, but it's Ted and Zachariah all the same! *Though they didn't dare say so to his son, they were terrified of what might happen if the Boss found out what they knew. When I got angry, asking Tucker if*

he was accusing Mr. Watson, he did not back down. *Who else?* he
said. He was in tears.

I ran out through the cane fields to that place and I smelled those
bodies long before I got there. The ground was hog-chopped all around. I
went in close enough to look and had to get away on that same breath to
keep from puking. The bodies were all bloated up, half-eaten, but there was
no question it was Ted and Zachariah.

By the time I got back, the Tuckers were gone. Papa lay like a dead
man in the house. He was drinking very heavily that year. According to
Aunt Josie, who came flying out to warn me to stay away from him,
Wally put his Bet aboard their sloop, then took his gun and walked up to
the house and pounded on the wall to wake the Boss, demanding the
wages they had coming. Your father was furious because two workers
were quitting without notice with the cane harvest hardly begun; he was
further incensed when he threatened to strike Wally and Wally raised his
gun. "You point a gun at E. J. Watson, you conch bastard, you better
damn well shoot him. Go on! Shoot!" That drunken bellow terrified Aunt
Josie because it sounded so insane, but as usual, E. J. Watson knew his
man. Wally Tucker was no killer, never would be. Moving to strike him,
Papa reeled and stumbled and fell down and the Tuckers fled.

I was very frightened. I saw his jug of moonshine on the table. I jolted
a big snort to nerve myself, then opened the storm shutters to let in air
and light. Your father lay snoring on his bed with muddy boots on. When
I shook him awake, he opened one eyelid, raw bright red as the slit throat
of a chicken. Then he rolled over, dragging a pillow over his head; he
couldn't take the light or stand the sight of me.

I told him what had happened. His voice growled from beneath the
pillow that he knew nothing about it. Then he said that Mr. Wally Tucker
better be damned careful about spreading slander against E. J. Watson.
This reminded him that they'd left him short-handed; he reared up with a
roar, rolled off the bed, but blacked out again and crashed against the wall.

At these times, "hair of the dog" was all that helped him. By the time
I fetched the jug, he was sitting up holding his head, wheezing for breath.
His skin was blotchy and his breath came out of Hell. He opened his eyes
and glared at me, then looked away. He did not bother to lie. "How could I
pay 'em, Sonborn?" he said quietly. "Nothing to pay 'em with."

Sick as he was, he went with me after dark. This time I puked and so did he: maybe the first thing we ever did together! We heaped and scraped those remains onto some burlap, made a big sack of it, filled the pits and scattered brush, lugged that sack between us to the river downstream from the boat sheds, and let it go into the current. All that while, we never spoke a word. He was sober now and trying to suggest that Ted and Zachariah had been thieves as well as troublemakers and maybe the other hands had killed them. I wanted badly to believe that. Anyhow, he said, there was nothing to be done about it, and for the sake of our plantation's good name, I must forget what I had seen. Being too needy, too eager to please him, I agreed. He was very worried that the Tuckers might spread lies.

With the Tuckers gone and Tant off hunting, there was no one to talk to but the harvest crew and Josie. I was all alone in my awful knowledge. I don't believe Josie ever learned about those hog-chewed cadavers, but even if she'd known, she would have claimed that no matter who did 'em in, they probably had it coming. Her "Mister Jack" paid no attention to what Josie overheard, knowing this little woman was so crazy for him that no secret that might do him harm would pass her lips.

Unpaid and penniless after their long year of hard work, the Tuckers were taken in by Richard Harden at Lost Man's River. Because they risked jail at Key West, he suggested they camp on Lost Man's Key, which was quit-claimed by the Atwell family up in Rodgers River but uninhabited. Lived aboard their sloop and subsisted mostly on palm tops and on shellfish while they built a driftwood shack, having borrowed tools, gill net, and seed corn from the Hardens. They planted a piece of ground across the river mouth, near the spring at the north end of Lost Man's Beach.

Toward the end of 1900, your father bought that quit-claim from the Atwells, who took back his rough note warning Tucker to remove himself in three days' time. With his vegetables still green and his wife near term, Tucker was outraged: he sent word back reminding Watson that "as was well known or soon would be," he and his wife were still owed a year's wages, and until these were paid, they would not leave Lost Man's Key "come Hell or High Water." My heart sank when I saw that message, knowing your father would take it as a usurpation of his quit-claim and a threat.

On the last night of the old century, your father broke out a new jug of

Tant's moonshine and sat down heavily at the table. Aunt Josie came in with Baby Pearl in hopes of New Year's cheer but took one look at his closed face and went right out again. She knew better than to break his mood and she didn't need to warn me to keep my mouth shut. We sat in the dark kitchen in deep gloom.

Josie warmed up beans but we hardly ate. Your father read Tucker's note over and over; he drank and brooded until nearly midnight. Finally he took a last big slug and shoved the jug across the table, commanding me (as he often did) to hide it from him. I put it on that ledge under the cistern cover—you remember, Luke?—where I placed the buckets when I fetched in water.

In a while he staggered out onto the riverbank to check the tide. We knew where he was going. When he came back in, he took his shotgun off the wall but dropped it on the floor. I picked it up for him, astonished to see him drop a weapon, drunk or otherwise.

Praying he might sag down and sleep, I complained that I was weary—"Sleep, then, damn you!" Maybe we should wait till daylight to depart. "We? You're staying here!" In the doorway, Aunt Josie put a finger to her lips. But desperate to save him from some terrible mistake, I slipped ahead of him into the sailing skiff, which he nearly capsized when he crashed aboard. By that time, he'd forgotten that he'd ordered me to stay behind. Glaring balefully at the full moon, he muttered, "Row then."

There was no wind. I rowed upriver on the rising tide. Drunk though he was, he had planned for that tide, staying our departure until after midnight. Leaving Possum Key to starboard, I rowed south down Chevelier Bay, and all that hour, silhouetted on the moonlit water, he sat motionless, jutted up in the stern like an old stump. Sometime later, we went ashore on Onion Key. It was still dark when he woke me. Exhausted, I protested: it was not yet daybreak. His silence warned me not to speak again. He had sobered some by now but his mood was ugly.

We descended Lost Man's River on the falling tide as he had planned. I rowed hard anyway just to keep warm. Soon there was breeze. He pointed at the mast and I raised her small canvas. With the dark bulk of him hunched at the tiller, the old skiff whispered through cold mists across broad discs of current, westward over the gray reach of Lost Man's Bay.

At daybreak, we slid the skiff into the mangroves on the inland shore of Lost Man's Key. Telling me to wait there, he set off at once, rounding

*the point to the Gulf beach. I followed. My teeth chattered in the damp
and my voice shook when I nagged him: Why were we sneaking up in
darkness? Why not just run them off our claim? Distracted by my
pestering, he stepped into a hole and twisted his ankle and cursed
violently in pain.*

*Where Tucker's small sloop on her mooring could be glimpsed through
the big sea grape leaves, he dropped two shells into the chambers of his
double-barrel. On the beach ridge, a small thatch roof had come in view.
One last time, I begged him not to harm them. He fixed me with a look I
could not read. Was it contempt? I don't think so. Then he limped forward.*

*The Tuckers had no lamps; they lay down at dark and rose at daybreak.
Wally was already outside, perched on a big driftwood tree mending his
cast net. His rifle leaned against the silver trunk beside him. It was too
late to warn him: if he laid one finger on that gun he would be killed.*

*Favoring his bad ankle, your father moved out of the sea grape in stiff
short steps like a bristled-up dog. I heard no sound though I was close
behind him but Tucker picked up some tiny pinching of the sand. His hand
dropped the net needle and flew for his rifle, only to stop short in midair
and sink back slowly as he raised his hands.*

*"You people get the hell off of my claim," your father said—
something like that. He tossed his head toward the shack. "Tell your bitch
to clear her trash out before I burn that pigsty to the ground." Wally
Tucker went all pale and blotched like someone slapped, but sensing
perhaps that this man had spoken brutally to provoke an attack he only
blinked back tears of rage and fear.*

"Go get her," Papa ordered me. "Trot her out here."

I shook my head. "Please, Papa, I can't do that—"

*"Oh for Christ's sake. Keep him covered, then," Papa said, disgusted.
He tossed me the shotgun. Hungover and exhausted, he was jumpy, on
the point of rage. He drew his revolver and limped toward the shack.
Wally whispered, "Please, Rob. Don't let him harm Bet." I sensed a
distraction and backed off a step, yelling, "Don't try it, Wally!" but he had
lunged and grasped the barrels. The morning exploded in red haze. In the
same moment that I shrieked, your father shouted with great violence.
"SHIT!" Fucking Sonborn! Hadn't he told me not to come? Now we
were ruined—all that was included in that one furious word.*

Having spun toward Wally, he had not seen Bet rush outside, clutching a pot. At the sight of her man's body twisting on the sand she moaned and staggered, but she kept her head; she did not run to him but dropped her pot and fled for the shore wood. I see her still, round with child in her white shift, sailing away like a child's balloon over the sand.

I believe murder might have been his intention when he left Chatham Bend, but after he'd sobered during the long hours of the river journey— who can say? Perhaps he never knew himself. He looked bewildered, unimaginably weary. He did not rage at my inattention, only said dully, "Damn fool tried to kill us." He eased himself down like an old man on that same limb on which the dying man twitching on the sand had bent to his mending moments earlier, as if considering how we might start over and relive this sunrise scene in a sane way; he sat with his hands square on his knees, boot toes not five feet from the body, which he didn't look at. Only then did he recall Bet Tucker; he turned in time to glimpse her before she disappeared. Realizing I must have seen her flight—seen it and not warned him—he said nothing, simply handed me the revolver. Still in shock, I dropped it. He picked it up, thrust it at me again. Imagining that out of his remorse he was inviting me to kill him, I raised and pointed it at his unblinking eyes. "No, Rob," he said. I lowered the weapon. Would I have shot him? I don't know. In the expression on his face, this man enthroned on the silver tree seemed stranger than any stranger. He had called me Rob.

"He attacked us, you said!"

"Yes, he did. The gun went off by accident. Who will believe that?"

The families on Lost Man's Beach, his voice said urgently, might come to investigate the shot; we could not stay long enough to make a search, we had to catch her quick; if she got too deep into that scrub, we just might lose her. I stared after her, unable to take this in. Then his voice broke through. "You hear me, Rob? We have to finish what we started."

I could not look at Wally's death throes without retching. My agony burst through. "What you started, Papa!"

"I can't catch her," he said calmly, after getting to his feet, testing his ankle. "I'm too fat and too lame. I'm sorry, boy."

Swallowing and shivering, teeth chattering, I protested wildly. To shoot Bet Tucker in cold blood would be terrible and crazy, we would burn in Hell! He folded his arms upon his chest, saying, "Well, boy, that is possible. But meanwhile, she is the only witness and if she gets away, we are going to hang."

All was unbearable, every breath. To run that girl down, put this hard heavy weapon to her head and pull the trigger—I wept helplessly. "Don't make me do that, Papa. I can't do it."

He was losing patience, though still calm. "Why, sure you can, son,"
he told me then, "and you best jump to it. It's her life or ours." That exhausted look returned into his face. "You are innocent in all this, boy, no matter what becomes of us. But will that save you?" He turned away, looking toward the wood edge. "Too late for tears," he said.

I was running, I was wailing. Unless it was only in my heart, my wail could be heard as far off as South Lost Man's.

Bet had not run far. In the thick tangle, she had no place to go. Small footprints, prints where she had fallen to her knees, hand prints—some animal on all fours—then the whiteness of her shift in the cave of vines where she had crawled, trying to hide. She lay panting on her side in tears of shock, her wet cheek stuck with sand.

Somewhere Papa's voice was calling, coming closer. I sank to my knees beside her, fighting for breath. "Please, Bet, don't look." She gasped, "Oh Rob, we never done you harm."

I crept forward. Her eye was fixed on the root and sand inches away, her lips parted by whimper, the soft skin pulsing at the temple, the life blood pink in the transparent ear—the new life in her . . .

At the sound of sand crushed by oncoming steps, that eye flew wider and her whole body trembled. I bent to her, whispering, "Please, Bet. Forgive me." Forcing my will—oh Christ be quick!—I grasped my wrist to steady my hand, touched the muzzle to her temple, sucked a breath deep to lock my nerve in place, and squeezed the trigger.

A crimson spatter in my eyes as all went black.

Round sea grape leaves in a sunrise dance of shadows on the sand. I lay suspended, praying that this dream of bright water might not end. It was too late. Before squeezing my eyes shut again, I'd seen those boot prints where the girl had lain, the darkened sand kicked over that blood shadow, the stained face of earth. Rob Watson was dead from that day forward and forever. What had taken place was drawn over my corpse like a leaden shroud. I could not move.

The boots returned. He leaned and shook my shoulder. "Time to go." I struggled away from him, struggled to stand and run. I could not. I was too weak. Get away from me! *Were those the last words I ever spoke to him?*

He bent then and with one hand under my armpit lifted my weight without effort, stood me on my feet. With the other hand, he used sea grape leaves to scrape the worst of the red bits and vomit from my shirt and pants. Never before had he taken care of me in this way. But his guilt or remorse, if that is what it was, had come too late. I had no heart left for anything but hate.

He had already fetched the sailing skiff and dragged both bodies off the sand into the channel. As he waded me past Bet's shape toward the skiff, I wondered if the baby in her womb might still pulse with no foreboding of its end.

In the boat, he ordered me to curl up on the bilge boards at his feet. His coat lay folded on the stern seat within reach; the revolver butt protruded from its inside pocket. At the oars, facing astern, he had to turn repeatedly to check his bearing; I touched the weapon twice. On the fourth try I slid it free and slipped it under my shirt. In my great hate, I mourned that I had not shot him when he first gave me the gun.

All New Year's Day afternoon, curled like a fetus, I observed the murderous drunkard at the oars, the blue eyes squinted in the sun, the ginger beard and the black hat, the shoulders hurled forward and back, forward and back against the passing treetops—all I could see while lying in the bilges except the far towers of Glades cumulus off to the east.

Chatham Bend was empty. Perhaps Tant had returned from hunting, heard Josie's tale, and taken his sister and Pearl back to Caxambas. Nerved up and overtired, your father could not sleep. He resumed drinking, shouting threats against imagined enemies, then ran out and torched the cane, which made no sense. He was still out there running like a madman when Erskine Thompson came in on the *Gladiator*. When they went indoors to find something to eat, I boarded his ship and slipped her lines, drifted downriver.

*At break of day off Mormon Key, an onshore wind was chipping up
the surface, a fair breeze for a run south. Passing Lost Man's, I stared
dead away to sea. I still had his revolver, knowing he would come after
me: I have it still.*

*My history in the quarter century since is hardly worth the telling.
Too much of it has been spent in prison and the rest mostly in flight—
another sort of prison, I've discovered.*

Luke, I beg you to believe I was not a killer then nor am I now.

THE ONE SURVIVING WITNESS

Soft mist rose off the salt marsh, thinning in the sun.

Was all this true? Perhaps all Papa had ever intended was to run those
people off his claim and burn their shack. As the man who would be vilified
and damned, Edgar Watson, too, had been a victim of Tucker's desperate
lunge, and in his despair might have succumbed to the seeming necessity of
suppressing that girl's witness rather than see his last hope of redemption
on his new plantation end on the gallows, leaving his penniless family to
the mercies of the Islanders. Bet Tucker's life or his family's future: that was
his terrible choice and he had made it, accepting responsibility for both
deaths and unspoken abomination in his community. Hadn't he concealed
his son's participation, even his presence? Wasn't that why he had made
him lie down in the boat, out of sight below the level of the gunwales? Had
Rob realized this? It would not seem so.

Or was he awarding Papa too much benefit of too much doubt? If Papa
was guilty of the Tucker deaths, how could that upright and responsible
historian, L. Watson Collins, proceed with the "whitewash," as Rob called
it? Had he ignored inconvenient facts and disturbing intuitions because of
his love for Papa (and ambitions for his book)? Had he thought he might
skim over the Tucker episode without risk of contradiction since the only
conceivable witness was the missing Rob?

At least Papa had not lied. Rob's own account established that Papa had
not drawn attention to how panicky or inept or careless Rob might have
been as a cause of that first death nor attempted to evade the fundamental
blame. Because he'd wished his younger son to know that there were miti-

gating circumstances (imagining that his oldest son was gone for good, and in any case safe from prosecution) he had hinted that Rob might have shared the guilt.

Look at Papa's first reaction to Tucker's death, as recalled by Rob. Couldn't that "SHIT!" signify tragic dismay? *What have you* DONE *boy*! Yet apparently Papa had stifled his recriminations, for subsequently—Rob's account again—he had actually attempted to comfort his stricken son, assuring him it was self-defense and not his fault. To protect his son's feelings—and right from the start—Papa had acted with a certain stoic grace, wasn't that true? And ever since, he had stoically endured the massive judgment that those deaths had brought upon him.

Though arguing back and forth this way made him feel a little better, he knew he was skirting his father's apparent willingness to send his son to silence that young woman. And how could an honest biographer account for the execution of those two cane cutters which had brought about the Tucker episode in the first place?

So near its finish after all these years, his life's work would be utterly invalidated were he to accept Rob's testimony. "The one surviving witness," Rob had called himself. How different his biography might have been had that sole surviving witness never reappeared—this was the unwelcome thought he had to banish.

BLOODY WATSON

Arriving that evening at the Naples Church Hall, Lucius lingered outside before his talk, prowling the darkness. At noon that day, a radio report had described the attempted shooting of a prominent attorney outside the Gasparilla in Fort Myers. Already in custody was the leading suspect—a "furious negro" who earlier that evening had threatened the victim with a carving knife and terrified other diners in the restaurant. Though relieved for Rob's sake that Dyer had escaped uninjured, Lucius hated the fact that an innocent man had been unjustly charged, yet saw no way to right this wrong without risking life imprisonment for his brother.

Observing Lucius benignly from the side doorway of the hall was a small slight man with round chipmunk cheeks and a delighted smile. His linen trousers and navy blue shirt, new deck shoes, and a lemon-yellow sweater caped over his shoulders looked tacked on to his wind-burned fisherman's hide. "Professor Collins, noted Watson authority, or I miss my guess!"

"None other." Lucius grinned as they shook hands.

"Good thing no Storters got mixed up in that darned shooting," Hoad Storter said. "Of course Uncle George, after all those years of telling visitors the Ed Watson story, concluded he wouldn't know so doggone much unless he had taken part in it himself. Lucky thing that week's newspaper reported that Justice Storter was away on jury duty at Fort Myers or he might have wound up on some old posse list."

Lucius laughed—"Oh Lord!"—as Hoad patted his shoulder to take any sting out of his teasing, saying, "Storters stayed friends with everybody on both sides of the story and we're friends today." Asked what he meant by "both sides of the story," Hoad said, "Ambush versus self-defense."

Before Lucius could respond, the program director of the Historical Society rushed forward to identify her speaker and tug him toward the side entrance nearest the podium. "You're late!" Already offended by his tardy appearance and failure to report at once to the official in charge, namely herself, this female was aghast at his plan to identify himself to her audience as E. J. Watson's son. She could not permit that, she said. His own son's view of the notorious Bloody Watson would scarcely inspire trust, she complained, and indeed, she already mistrusted him, having caught him red-handed with grain spirits. "Surely you know," she hissed, pointing at the glass, "that intoxicants are strictly prohibited in a church hall."

"Mineral water," Lucius advised her.

"Don't you dare bring that inside!" She hurried through the door and up onto the stage, where she introduced "our guest this evening" as Professor Collins. The applause startled him. Before he could compose himself, this awful woman was beckoning him to the podium. Too suddenly, he found himself exposed in public while still clutching the glass he'd neglected to set down. Smiling hard, she tried to snatch it from him as he drew near and they actually tussled for one hate-filled moment before he was sprung free. Turning that murderous smile upon the audience, she rolled her eyes in abdication of any further responsibility for this speaker's behavior.

In hard, flat light, Lucius found himself confronted by an assembly of Baptist elders fanning the worn-out heat. The ladies wore variants of gloomy dark blue dresses with white polka dots and prim white collars; their consorts—mostly smaller, as in hawks and spiders—favored high black shoes and tieless white shirts buttoned to the throat. From the severe lines of the thin mouths, the asceptic glint of lenses and steel spectacles as the old heads leaned and whispered, he suspected that the identification of this so-called "Professor Collins" as that alcoholic fisherman and lifelong loser Lucius Watson was already epidemic in the hall. (He had decided to cooperate and withhold his real name but acknowledge it at once if he were questioned.)

The back rows were mostly empty. Three shag-haired, sunbaked men lounged in the doorway. One whistled and another clapped, urging the speaker to get on with it. With a start of alarm, he recognized Speck Daniels's gang from Gator Hook. Owen Harden was there, too, a few rows closer to the front, and Sarah was with him. Sarah made a small wave of greeting, her expression a warning that he read as a plea for discretion. Unnerved, he drank off his glass and rapped it down smartly on the rostrum: "Evening, folks!" Far from eliciting warm smiles, his forced heartiness caused the oldsters to glance uneasily at one another as if this speaker had turned up in the wrong hall.

"Tonight," he began, "I'd like to tell you what I have discovered in my researches into the colorful but controversial life of Planter E. J. Watson— research based on reliable first-hand accounts by folks who actually knew him." Though his biography of Mr. Watson was nearing completion, he said, he would welcome comments and corrections after his talk.

"Controversial, you said? I don't think so, mister! Folks was pretty much agreed he was bad news!"

"Well, no doubt you've all read that E. J. Watson killed the Outlaw Queen Belle Starr and many others. Certain tales may have elements of truth but none have proof. And how many of these writers ever laid eyes on the real Ed Watson, far less knew Ed Watson, shook his hand or had a drink with him, heard him sing or tell a story? Did you know he was a marvelous storyteller? And that most of his neighbors liked him? Even those who lynched him?"

Another blunder. An arm shot up, another wig-wagged. "Hold on, Mister!"

"Hold it right there! Ain't you his boy?"

This speaker's features were empurpled by long falling years of drink. Holding body and soul together, his arms were folded tight across his chest, and on his head perched a sadly stained Panama hat. Because he wore his hat indoors and looked disreputable, no one sat near him, nor did they pay the least attention to his provocative question.

When no one else challenged him, Lucius hurried on, presenting a synopsis of E. J. Watson's life, from boyhood in South Carolina during the War Between the States to the successful establishment of his hardy strain of sugarcane at Lake Okeechobee a few years after his death—

"WAIT! Darn it, Mister!" The first voice had returned to the fray. "You sayin his neighbors 'lynched' him?! Who are you to come and tell us local folks about local stuff we know a hell of a lot more about than you do?"

"No, no, Ed weren't near so bad as what them writers try to tell you, not when you knowed him personal the way we done. Give ye the shirt off his back with one hand, put a knife in yer back with the other."

As the ladies hissed and shushed, their elderly men scratched thin silvery ears, cracked knobby knuckles. Lucius tried to smile. He had expected that resistance would be doughty. After all, Watson Redeemed was a far less colorful figure than Desperado Watson, who was not to be reduced to the common clay by some scholarly recital of dull virtues.

An old man in red galluses and a green shirt buttoned right to the gullet stood up and removed his hat. "I'm Preston Brown, age ninety-four," he told the hall. "Had me a stroke so I ain't as good as what I was but most days I got some idea what I am talking about. And these old eyes seen Ed J. Watson in the flesh many's the time, and this old hand shook his'n, and they ain't too many in this hall can say the same.

"Now Ed J. Watson and young Tucker had a run-in so Watson went down to Lost Man's Key and killed him. For many years you could see the blood on that old driftwood tree. Tucker's nephew tried to hide back in the mangroves but Watson sent his boy Eddie in to finish him."

Before Lucius could object, Owen Harden scraped his chair back and rose to challenge Brown. "You old-timers been trading that nephew tale for years and it's all wrong."

The old man squared around to glare at Owen. "Wrong?" He seemed to be sucking on his tongue tip. "I bet you're a Harden, aint'cha."

"Wally Tucker and his wife Bet were good friends of my family at Lost Man's," Owen continued. "No nephew weren't involved in it at all."

"One them damn Hardens," a voice said loudly, but when Owen looked around the room, no one met his eye. In a level voice he said, "Any man who cares to tell me to my face why he don't like Hardens can find me right outside after the show." His tone was quiet but it carried nonetheless, like a voice from far away across open water.

In the stir and murmur, Mud Braman spoke up from the doorway, "Hell, *we* know Owen Harden. Ain't one thing wrong with that boy that a bullet wouldn't cure." Everyone laughed including Owen, who sat down, waving his hand in salute to Mud over his shoulder.

Preston Brown was unperturbed. "Been fishin and guidin down around Lost Man's all my life. Knew Ed Watson, fished with his younger boy many's the time. Had him a nice round-stern cedar skiff. Liked his whiskey, too. Still does, I reckon." The old man peered hard at the speaker.

"Killed that plume bird warden right while I was livin at the Bend." snarled the man in the stained Panama hat. Though he would not face Lucius as he spoke, Lucius recognized Nell's father, Fred O. Dyer. "I was foreman on his cane plantation. Ed was over to Flamingo. Word about him murderin Guy Bradley got back before he did so I packed my family aboard the mail boat, got away from there."

"Heck, I knowed Bradley," Old Brown said. "Plume-hunted right alongside us fellers but went over to wardenin. Aimed to clap Watson in the jail and so Ed shot him."

Lucius said sharply, "Mr. Brown? Guy Bradley was murdered by a plume hunter named Walter Smith."

"Cap'n Walt Smith! That is correct! Got turned loose at Key West cause word had got around it was Watson done it."

"That's wrong, too," Lucius snapped, regretting the sharp tone that was casting a pall over the room. "And another correction, sir, if you don't mind. His son Eddie was still a schoolboy in Fort Myers. He was nowhere near Lost Man's when the Tuckers died."

"Yep! Eddie Watson! Sure as I am settin here this evenin!"

Lucius gazed bleakly at the audience, appealing to its good sense. "You see? These tales are passed down from our parents and grandparents and we just repeat them, until finally errors become legend."

"Who the hell is *we?*" a man's voice called. "You come from around here?"

"He sure does!" Fred Dyer hauled himself up straight again and pointed a bent arthritic claw. "That's Watson's younger boy! That's Lucius! Standin right there under them false pretenses!" He glared wildly around, seeking support, and again his neighbors turned away as if deaf to him.

Old Brown brooded. "Yep. Young Ed helped his daddy kill 'em, like I said. Thems that told me had no reason to lie so no dang professor can't just walk in here and call 'em liars." The crowd muttered approval as Brown said accusingly, "He's coverin up for Eddie, looks like, cause it sure weren't Colonel done it. I knowed Colonel all my life, he been on my boat about a thousand times. Liked hard spirits, visited all the bars. I had nothin against spirits, I was in there, too. Nicer feller you would never want to meet. And you know somethin funny?" Preston Brown pointed at the podium. "This man talkin to us here puts me in mind of him."

"Ain't that what *I* said? Jesus!" Querulous, Fred Dyer took his hat off, scratched his scalp, put it back on again.

"It wasn't Eddie and it wasn't Colonel, Mr. Brown," Lucius said gently. He glanced toward the night windows and asked Rob's forgiveness. "If E. J. Watson killed those Tuckers, and if he was not alone, the only conceivable witness was his oldest boy, who disappeared."

"How's that? I ain't never heard about no older boy." Like a helmsman peering through the fog, Preston Brown raised three fingers as a brim over his eyes to study this dang know-it-all up on the podium. "Yep! Got it wrote right here on my program, 'L. *Watson* Collins'—that's the Watson part." The audience fretted and shifted, scratched and coughed.

"L. Watson Collins is a pen name," Lucius said, lifting his gaze to the room as it fell silent. He scanned the audience, taking a deep breath. "Mr. Dyer was correct: I'm Lucius Watson. E. J. Watson was my father."

The silence burst. A woman shrilled, "I knew it! I just *knew* it!" A man's voice hailed him, "Hey there, Colonel. How *you* been doin, Colonel? I been tellin the wife how much you looked like you." At this, Hoad Storter in the front row shared a smile with Lucius. In his bright yellow sweater, Hoad looked like a seated lemon.

A lady near the back held up his history. "If you are Lucius Watson, how come you're ashamed to use your rightful name on your own book?"

The hall hummed with excitement. Old Brown tried to recapture the floor. "He's just makin it up about that older brother! It was *Eddie!*"

"Tell that cock-eyed old idjit to sit down and shut up!"

Rob's shout had come from the doorway behind Crockett Junior and the others, who ran out after him. Excusing himself, Lucius jumped down from the stage, ran up the aisle, but by the time he made his way outside, they were all gone. He returned frustrated, making his way back toward the front.

In his absence, voices had arisen.

"Well, what we heard when we was comin up, Killer Cox snuck back into the Glades, lived with the Injuns, him bein part of a Injun hisself."

"Might be in there yet! No tellin who's skulkin around back in them rivers, and they ain't many has went in there to find out."

"—so Colonel says, 'If you dang feds set fire to this Watson house to clear the way for your dang park, you will have to set fire to a Watson.' We sure don't want ol' Colonel going up in smoke!"

"Nosir, it weren't nobody but Henry Short killed Watson, way I heard it. Put his bullets in so close you could lay a dollar bill acrost the holes—"

"Thing of it is, Short were a colored man. Still is, far as I ever heard about it. Nigger Short—"

"*Henry* Short," called Lucius, reclaiming his place at the podium.

Old Brown was still standing, fingers working the back of the folding chair in front of him, life fluids all aglimmer in his eyes; he would not sit down, as if afraid that his decrepit corpus might never again propel him to his feet. Raising his hand, he cleared his old throat thoroughly by way of commanding audience attention to an oft-told tale about Ed Watson and the sheriff's deputy. This time Lucius cut him off, reminding the audience that, as a historian, he had to discard undocumented anecdotes, however intriguing.

When Old Man Brown, his tale discounted, suddenly sat down, the faces pinched closed like frost-killed buds and chairs creaked loudly in disapproval. By questioning an elder's recollections, the speaker had undermined local tradition, and now his audience made it plain that any diminishment of the Bloody Watson legend, even by his son, would not be tolerated. In twos and threes and then in rows, the audience rose with a loud barging of chairs and moved off toward the exits.

Lucius hailed their backs: "Good night!" His E. J. Watson evening had spun into a shambles. To avoid confrontations, he remained at the podium, pretending to shuffle notes into some sort of order as Hoad came forward to confirm their plan to dine at the new fishing lodge in Everglade in the next day or two.

Last to depart was Nell's father, who limped past in syphilitic shuffle, evading the speaker's eye. When Lucius followed him up the aisle and touched his elbow, he swung around, alarmed, then backed like a crayfish into the space between two rows of chairs.

"I'm surprised you recalled me, Mr. Dyer," Lucius said. "I wasn't much more than fifteen when you left the Bend." Scowling, the man emerged from the row and continued on his way with Lucius in attendance. "Your son's not here?" Lucius inquired. "I kind of expected him."

"He's your damned kin, not mine." Fred Dyer looked him in the eye for the first time. "What's he up to anyways? Cold-hearted sonofabitch! Couple months ago, he tracks me down where I'm drinkin, orders me a round while he sits there suckin on his sarsaparilla. Says you still telling people I'm Ed Watson's son? *Hell, yes!* You willing to make that statement in a affidavit? *Hell, yes!* Next thing I know, there's a legal paper slapped down on the bar. *'It is the opinion and sincere belief of the undersigned Frederick O. Dyer that the infant male christened Watson Dyer, born December 4 of 1894, at Fort Myers Florida, is the natural son of the planter E. J. Watson of Chatham River.'* " He shook his greasy head. "Them words on that legal paper burned into my brain, what I got left of it, although I been saying the same damned thing for years. And now this feller who threatened to sue anybody who even hinted such a thing has turned around, got me to certify he's Watson's bastard. Made it official."

Fred Dyer seemed bewildered, even a little hurt. "I said, 'For Christ's sake, Wattie, what's this all about? Ain't this here a little late in life?' And he puts his arm across my shoulders where I'm settin on my stool, says, 'Fred, I'm tired of living a damn lie and I bet you feel the same.' First time he ever touched me, let alone called me Fred. Looked real lost and pathetical, so I felt sad, too, and signed his paper. When I look up again, my ex-son is grinning like a alligator. Tucked away that paper quick and disappeared. Never paid my whiskey nor said thanks, never give me so much as a wave good-bye."

At the door of the hall, Fred Dyer yanked his bent straw down on a head of yellowed silver hair that straggled over his soiled collar. "You was always a nice young feller, Lucius, but from what I heard, you never done right by my daughter."

Lucius said, "I aim to do right by her from now on, sir, if she'll have me . . ."

"Ever try askin her?" With a sour look, Fred O. Dyer moved away under the streetlights.

ATTORNEY WATSON WATSON

Outside, Crockett Junior loomed at his elbow. "Where's my brother?" Lucius demanded. The big man seized his arm and yanked him toward the street where a black car waited with its motor running. The front passenger door swung open. Crockett pushed him in and, careless of his ankles, slammed the door behind him.

"Your crazy brother tried to kill me," Watson Dyer said, easing his car forward.

"That's nonsense. All he did was shoot out your rear tires."

"We'll see," Dyer said. He drove his black car to the oceanfront, stopping just short of the beach edge and leaving the motor running. Beyond the sparkle of small breakers, a moon-spun silver swath of sea extended westward to the lowest stars above the Gulf horizon. Gazing straight into the earth galaxy for minute after minute, Watt Dyer saw nothing but his windshield, Lucius guessed: he looked sealed off, impervious to wonder, his window rolled tight against the fresh sea air. "Brother Lucius knows all about my shot-out tires. Brother Lucius was a witness." Dyer turned to look at him. In the bad light of an old-fashioned street lamp, his moon face was moon-colored. "Brother Lucius could go to federal prison as an aider and abettor because he knew Robert B. Watson was armed and dangerous and he did not stop him."

"I hadn't realized he was armed and I don't believe he's dangerous. Reckless, maybe. Otherwise quite harmless."

"Escaped convict? Attemped murder? No court will ever call that 'harmless.'" Dyer's bloodless hands clenched the wheel tighter and his eyes closed in that slow tortoise blink. He said, "We have him. If he is delivered to the authorities, he'll be returned to prison and resentenced with due consideration of his prior conviction and escape. He will die in federal custody. Whereas if his brother cooperates, the law might settle for that black lunatic with the carving knife. Teach that kind of smart-mouth nigger a good lesson. Nice tight case. Plenty of witnesses saw him storming out and can testify to his aggressive state of mind." He watched Lucius's face.

Lucius said, "But *another* eyewitness in the parking lot spotted a white man shooting at the victim's car from a hotel window; saw him plenty well enough to testify that it wasn't some big black man in a white cook's outfit who got loose some way on the sixth floor." He turned to meet Dyer's eye.

"Anyway, you don't know Rob. He'll never let that black man go to jail for him. He feels bad enough that we got him fired."

"That your testimony?" Dyer glared in disbelief. "You'd let your long-lost brother get locked up for the rest of his life just to save some black maniac who assaulted a white man with a carving knife? Slit his stomach?" He drew his power-of-attorney form out of his briefcase. "We both know you're not going to sacrifice Robert so why don't you just sign this and shut up."

"What's missing here? Why is it suddenly so important to you to be E. J. Watson's bastard? I'm talking about that affidavit you extracted from your former father."

The attorney was disagreeably surprised and could not hide it. Lucius recalled Speck Daniels's warning but he was on the scent now and it was too late to stop. "Do I smell big money, Wattie? Big land development? Maybe Papa's old scheme to control all the high ground on the southwest coast? West coast Miami?"

Dyer rapped his document. "Sign it," he said.

"You're a real Watson now? Attorney Watson Watson?" But having no choice, he scribbled his signature. "Where's Rob?" he said.

Watson Dyer did not bother to answer. Tucking away his paper, he yanked his car around and headed back toward the church hall. He said slyly as Lucius got out, "You ever find that nigger you've been looking for?"

Christ Almighty. Of course. "You're the sonofabitch with the sniper rifle."

Dyer actually laughed. "Why, Brother Lucius! I always thought that was *you*!" Abruptly he stopped laughing. He regarded Lucius for the length of a held breath. " 'Watson honor'?" he jeered softly as they neared the church hall. "*Somebody* had to take care of it, right? When none of you 'real Watsons' had the guts?" He drove away before Lucius remembered.

"How about Rob?" he yelled. "Where's Rob?"

BELT BUCKLES AND BUTTONS

The hall was locked and the street was empty. Caves of gloom isolated the few streetlights which waned strangely in the rush and clacketing of the Gulf wind.

Across the street, headlights flicked on. Owen Harden rolled down the car window. Owen had joked a little with Speck's crew on the way into the hall, he said, and loose-mouthed Mud Braman had let slip that they were on the lookout for a man they knew as Chicken Collins.

At their insistence, Lucius locked his car and went home with the Hardens, confiding Rob's situation on the way. "I'm scared," he said. Owen nodded. "Who knows where they took him?" he said. "Big swamp out there." Squashed between them in the truck's front seat, Sarah hushed her husband. "He's probably fine," she said, hugging Lucius's arm. Even in Rob's emergency, her scent and warmth stirred a twinge of his old longing: "Probably they just took him back to Gator Hook," she said, to comfort him. However, she removed her arm when he mentioned having gone to visit Henry in the hospital with Bill House.

At their new cottage in north Naples, she sat him at the kitchen table and asked if he'd like coffee. "I bet he'd like whiskey a lot better," her husband said, and Sarah said, "You gave that up along with Speck, remember? We don't keep liquor in this house," she notified their guest. She rose with a bored cold exhausted look. "I bet you two have lots to talk about," she said, and left the room.

Owen Harden's wheaten hair had iron wisps in it and the sun-squinted green eyes had crow's-feet in the corners. He drummed his fingers, glanced at Lucius, looked away again. "Darn it now if my own wife ain't put me in mind of some bush lightnin. Care to join me if I stumbled over some?"

"You know something? I bet I would."

His host came back with blue tin cups and a brown jug. "I reckon Bill House would remember stuff about your daddy, cause he's still goin on about Ed Watson. Never got over it, y'know."

"Know why? Cause he feels guilty." From the doorway, Sarah glared at their tin cups. "How come you would listen to a House about Henry Short? Owen's family knew Henry a whole lot better than those flea-bitten Bay people who still sling it around about Bloody Watson. Always bragging on how they told Watson this and he said that. The little they know that's not hand-me-down from their daddies comes straight out of the magazines and books, mostly made up."

She accosted her husband, "Didn't your daddy call Old Man House 'the leader of the outlaws'?"

Owen said quietly, "The House boys thought what they done that day was right. They did not back away from it or talk around it, not like some."

Disgusted, his wife went to bed. The two men drank awhile. Owen contemplated his guest with affection. "Ever think back on them good old times we had down Lost Man's Beach?" Owen smiled.

Lucius nodded, half distracted by fear and worry. Too much was happening too fast. In his exhaustion, all his defenses had unraveled. On impulse, before going to bed, he asked Owen what the Hardens might have heard about "Watson Payday."

Owen gazed straight ahead. When Lucius cleared his throat, to prod him, he gave a start, as if just awakened. "For a long time, we never paid no attention to them Payday stories."

"But?"

Owen was silent, selecting the right words. "Maybe a year ago," he resumed slowly, "the warden there at Duck Rock rookery had a young helper who treasure-hunted up and down the coast in his spare time. He was tryin out a early-type metal detector not on the market yet, might been the very first model. I seen it once. Hell of a lookin thing—heavy ol' black box with tin earphones, wouldn't hunt down but about two feet."

"Owen—"

"So Henry Short got the loan of that black box to try her out on the Watson place where he reckoned the old-time Calusa or maybe the Frenchman or your daddy might have buried gold. Next day he shows up at Daddy Richard's cabin on Wood Key—first visit in some years so Daddy knew it had to be something important. Henry was all fevered up and agitated, walking all around. Then suddenly he set down and shoved a big ol' wide-top jar acrost the table. That jar was full of rusty belt buckles and metal buttons, a few spent bullets. Near the house and along the river, he said, all that black box could pick up was metal scrap and a few busted tools: this stuff in the jar come from shaller pits in that unfarmed northwest corner off the cane field.

"So Daddy Richard said, 'Find anythin else?' 'Bones,' Henry said. 'Well hell,' said Daddy. 'Ed had cows on there and pigs, even a big old horse, so bones ain't nothin.' 'Skulls,' whispers Henry. 'And three of them four skulls had holes in back that looked like they was made by bullets and all had a lead slug layin in amongst the bones and one had three.'

"Course my folks was still resistin Henry's story. Daddy got stubborn, argued back and forth, kept mentioning them livestock and them old-time Indins until Henry couldn't handle it no more, he was just too fevered. Finally he said, 'Mr. Richard, there ain't no mistakin a human skull for horse or hog. Anyways, your domestic animals don't generally wear belt buckles and buttons and only very few will tote a pocket knife.'

"Richard Harden lit his pipe, took a few puffs to settle down. That was the first time and the only time that Henry Short ever talked back smart to him that way. Henry looked kind of startled, too, but did not back down. One by one, he was droppin them pathetical ol' scraps back in that jar. Then he said, 'Excuse me, Mr. Richard, I spoke out of my turn, but you know where these four fellers come from as good as I do.'

"So Daddy Richard went upriver with him, seen for himself them molderin green bones in the dirt and leaves. Daddy Richard warned Henry that Lucius Watson might not know about them bones and even if he did, he would not want 'em dug up. Said, 'Henry, let's just you'n me fill in these holes, scatter some brush, never speak no more about it.' "

Owen looked up. "Henry went along with that, stuck by it, too. I believe I am the only one my daddy ever told and I never spoke of it except right now and never will." He watched Lucius, concerned. "I sure hope that's the kind of truth you wanted. I'm sure sorry."

"You never saw those graves yourself."

"Hunt through all that thorn that's growed up now? With all them bad snakes that's back in there?"

Lucius emptied his glass. "It's quite a story," he decided, "but without evidence, it's just another story like the rest."

Owen bridled. "Who you lookin to call a liar, Colonel? Me or Henry?" He jumped up and headed toward the back.

"Oh no, sorry, I don't mean that, Owen!" Lucius called after him. "Somebody killed somebody, all right," he concluded stupidly, as despair choked off his voice. Then Owen was back. On the table he placed a shoe box bound in tarred hemp line. He said, "We been keepin this for Henry." Slowly Lucius opened it and removed the jar and forced himself to look at its rusted contents: four tin belt buckles, old buttons, three small one-blader pocket knives rusted solid, a few spent bullets, and three copper pennies.

"See them pennies?" Owen said quietly. "Abe Lincoln pennies, minted in 1909. Kept a new Lincoln penny in their pockets for good luck."

Lucius closed the box and clumsily retied it. Who knows about this?

Hardens. Nobody else? Owen looked impatient: Lucius could take his word or not, it was up to him. Either way, Owen wanted him to take the box away.

"Think it might of been Cox?" Owen said finally when his friend was silent.

"I'd sure like to believe that. Thank you."

They went to bed without finding a way to ease things.

Lucius awoke at the sound of Owen's truck. Through the thin wall, he could hear his friend's wife in her bath. Unrested, restless, he was bedeviled by the rub of her firm buttock on the tub. He got up and dragged his clothes on. In his dark mood, weighed down by dread, he felt disgraced by lust for Sarah and growing exasperation with his brother: what could be done for a fugitive so self-destructive? Lone pursuit of the Daniels gang would be insane as well as useless and he could not notify the law. Even if Rob escaped them, where could he go? What was to become of him? How long would it be before he was in trouble again?

Steamy and fresh as a big pink shrimp in her white towel bathrobe, barefoot Sarah fixed his breakfast. Watching her hips shift at the stove, he cursed himself—here he was with his brother in mortal danger, still a damned hound dog.

Sarah could feel him. Over her shoulder, she murmured, "Please don't look at me that way." She said her life with Owen was going better: she was mainly cross because her husband had come to bed so drunk and was cranky with Lucius all the way to Naples. Still nagging him for seeking out Bill House instead of Hardens, she dropped him at his car, in no mood to understand his reasons. "You're listening to people who raised Henry up to be their slave!" She was very upset. Later it occurred to him that Owen must have told her Henry was dying.

GATOR HOOK

In his wild restlessness and worry, the need to act overcame the last of his good sense. From Naples, he followed the new highway east to Monroe Station and turned off on the spur track south to the Chevelier Road.

At Gator Hook, on the stair landing, warm sun had gathered in the coils of a big yellow rat snake; it whispered away down a rain-rotted split in the old greening boards. He pounded and called. Descending the stairs, he made his way around behind the building, where in mid-piss he sensed movement too late and was punched hard between the shoulder blades by what turned out to be the steel snout of an automatic. "Let's see them hands," said Crockett Senior Daniels.

"Wait, goddammit—" Startled, hurting, he had wet himself a little. He got things straightened out and finished buttoning, goaded by the weapon prodding his bruised back and also by a careless hacking cough that sprayed his neck. "Feeling jumpy, Speck?" He spoke with all the contempt he was able to muster with a hitch in his voice that betrayed his fear.

"Jumpy, yessir, which is why I am still goin pretty good after sixteen years in my same line of business." For the second time in a fortnight, Daniels frisked him. "I have growed a nose for a certain breed of cockeyed sonofabitch that you give 'em any room at all it's goin to cost you."

Grasping Lucius's shoulder, Daniels spun him roughly and slapped his front pockets with the back of his free hand.

"You fuckin Watsons just won't quit! Dyer sent word yesti'day to grab this Robert Watson, said he might be hanging around the church hall. Warned 'em he was crazier 'n hell and dangerous. Turned out this Robert was ol' Chicken so Junior and his morons never searched him. 'Nosir, Speck', they holler when they show up, 'This fuckin Robert ain't nobody in the world but your ol' drinkin buddy!'

"Had a loaded weapon in his satchel, for Christ's sake! You know about that? Had your damn list with my name on it—you know that, too? You put him up to this? And then you got the guts to tell me I am *jumpy*! *Jesus!* I mean, who you Watsons gunnin for if it ain't Speck Daniels? All the way east, them fools of mine had that spoilbank canal, deep black canal a-crawlin with big gators—my 'ol' drinkin buddy' never should of got as far as Gator Hook."

Daniels led him up the stairs and on inside. "Told me Chicken give 'em one hell of a scrap when them big boys grabbed him." Snickering, he leaned back against the bar. "Know somethin? I always liked that feller. After he got done cussin us out, me'n him got along real good, considerin he had your fuckin list and a loaded gun, aimin to shoot me.

"This mornin I went up to town, got your attorney on the telephone.

Said, 'My boys picked up Robert Watson: what you want with him?' And he says, 'Mr. Daniels, that man tried to shoot me.' Told me he's a law-and-order man, respects the hell out of the law and don't believe in coddlin no criminals; he's out for justice without fear nor favor. Said this Robert has to be removed from our law-abidin society, so what do I think would be best for all concerned? And me, I'm thinkin, *This man wants him dead.*

Lucius nodded. "Lord. And you're still working for him?"

"Not for long. The man won't want no more to do with us once his park business is settled. If he's goin into politics the way it looks, his dealins with the Daniels Gang might cost him. Very practical feller. Don't go off half-cocked like some damn Watson."

"And all his talk of preserving the Watson house as a pioneer monument—"

"Oh hell, Colonel, he never cared about that house. He ain't set foot on Chatham Bend since he left there thirty years ago. Man like that, his old home don't mean no more to him than the damn crap he took yesterday, it's that forty acres of high ground that he is after. But while he's dealin with the gov'ment, he don't want to throw away no high card. Parks will be hot to burn that house cause it don't fit in with their idea of wilderness. Dyer knows he could hold 'em up for years with legal diddlin and they know that, too. But it looks like he will step out of their way in some kind of a trade-off for prime real estate in Miami, leave you Watsons high and dry." Speck emitted a low hard sound of derisive mirth. "Anyways, Junior and them bein on their way to Chatham, I told 'em to take Chicken along, let him lay low enjoyin his old home while I figure how to smuggle him out of south Florida."

"And what's in that for you?"

"Well, me'n Chicken, we go back a ways." He spat. "Course my boys was grumbling. Said they're real busy movin cargos out before park rangers come snoopin around so if Chicken give 'em any trouble, they aimed to take care of him in a big hurry."

"What are you saying? That's just crazy!"

"Might not look crazy to wild boys that's riskin a long stretch in the pen for this, that, and the other. Last thing they need is to get caught harborin some despert fugitive."

"They're willing to kill him? Is that what they're talking about?"

"They're through talkin, Colonel. Ain't like you."

Daniels folded his arms upon his chest, observing him. He said, "Life without parole? You think that's better? Chicken sure don't." He searched Lucius's eyes for doubt and nodded when he found it. "While they had him in the auto, he told them boys how he pissed ten years away doin hard time. Said he weren't never goin back. He meant it, too, cause he told me the same thing. I warned him the boys might have to shoot him if he got in the way; he just laughed at me. Said he would take that as a kindness. Said he was scared to death of dying but slow death in a cage without no hope was worse."

"He's better off dead. Is that really what you're saying?"

"That's what *he's* sayin." He held Lucius's eye. "How about you?"

"He's my brother, for God's sake!" He felt sick and dizzy, hating what Speck chose to infer.

Speck was starting to enjoy this. "Be honest, Colonel. You ain't been thinkin death might be the best way out? For *every*body?"

"I never said anything like that."

"Not in words you didn't." Speck poured two drinks. "Speakin about truths, let's see what you make of this one: your daddy's shotgun weren't loaded. They shot him to pieces for nothin."

"Christ, what a liar you are—"

"That's what they say, all right—'*that goddamn Speck ain't nothin but a liar.*' But who fished that shotgun out of the bilges of his boat where Isaac Yeomans flung it? Who cleaned the salt water out the breech and oiled her up? I was first man to see them chambers, Colonel. They was empty."

"Oh, come on. Men saw the pellets rolling out—"

"Weren't no pellets rollin out because there weren't no shells. But when I tried to tell them men, they felt so stupid about fillin him with lead that they shouted me down, real angry, so I just shut up. Must of imagined up them pellets cause they couldn't handle the plain truth."

"That makes no sense. Why would he challenge that crowd with an un-loaded weapon?" Speck shrugged, bored by the question. Lucius said, "Any-way, you have no right to that gun. It belongs to our family."

"Well, you ain't gettin it. One these days, that old shootin iron's bound to bring me hard cash money."

When Speck said his boys might be back later this evening, Lucius said he'd wait. "Not in here you won't," Speck said.

THE TERRIBLE KNOWING AND NOT KNOWING

Lucius walked all day in search of his own feelings. He went east on the narrow swamp road, mile after mile, all the way to the Forty-Mile Bend where the Loop Road met the Trail. By the time he returned, it was near dusk. Old autos had appeared out of the woods and the Gator Hook Bar fairly bulged with raucous sound. He climbed the stairs. A drunken Speck pointed at a big pan of wild hog ribs on the stove but otherwise left him alone. Eventually the regulars went back into the woods and Lucius lay down in Chicken Collins's mildewed blankets under the bar, leaving Speck alone out on the landing shouting his jeering parody of the developers fighting the new park.

"Yessir, friends, ten thousand fuckin islands layin out there *dead*! No use to *no*-body! Don't them dumb-ass taxpayers realize how much coast gone to be wasted in this fuckin park? When we could pump white coral sand out of the Gulf where it don't do one single bit of good, make tourist beaches same as the east coast? Run concrete yacht canals smack through them mis'rable ol' mangroves, throw up deluxe waterfront condoms just like Miam-uh? Sky's no limit, folks! Condoms a-risin in a thrillin silver line, all the way south around Cape Sable! Sunset on the Golden Gulf, just a-glistenin off them condoms, turnin 'em from silver into gold! If that ain't God bless America, I don't know what!"

All night he twisted like an insect on a pin.

Even if Rob survived and were set free, he would still be on the run. Where could he hide? A hopeless drunkard, unemployable, without money, prospects, or profession, he would inevitably be dependent on his brother, who would be obliged to give up his own life in order to hide and feed this derelict human being. Who else in Rob Watson's narrow world would risk federal prison? Who else would look after him? Next week? The week after? For how long? Five years? Ten? The remainder of their lives?

And yet his mind fought Daniels's insinuation that in the end it might be best for everyone if "Chicken" were to disappear. How had that crooked bastard dared imagine, let alone suggest, that Rob's own brother might see it that same way—

Lucius? Why had the man's inferences upset him so unless his shock and indignation weren't quite honest? Would Daniels have implied any such thing without scenting ambivalence? Had a hypocrite named Lucius Watson actually persuaded himself that death would come as a mercy to his brother, setting him free from a badly broken life once and for all? Had L. Watson Collins been warped by the knowledge that Rob's death might spare him the professional obligation to discard the biography and those years of hard work? Was that work dead at the heart anyway because dishonest? Daniels, in his sly insinuations, had forced his nose into unclean seams of his own nature and forced him to acknowledge, to himself at least, a twinge of regret that Daniels's men had failed to deal summarily with "Chicken Collins" when they first caught him with the list and the revolver.

The terrible knowing and not knowing. He observed his mind's struggle to gain a firm foundation from which it might persuade itself of Speck's cold truth that a merciful end was not merely the simplest solution but the best for all concerned. For Rob Watson, any fate would be better than recapture. On the other hand, to accept Rob's death as merciful, far less as a solution, would be unforgivable, even if he could live with himself thereafter.

The misty swampland lay in darkness, its frogs mute. From across the road a night heron gave its strangled *quock* to unknown purpose. The harsh cry started him from ragged sleep and his first breath was an inhalation of cold fear that he had betrayed his brother. He wandered outside to stare sightless at the moon, wandered inside to be tossed and twisted on the cot, pursued by nightmare.

At first light, he heard tin on iron. Hunched over the woodstove in the corner, a barefoot man naked to the waist was making coffee. Cobwebbed and groggy, not sure which limb might work, Lucius lay inert. Finally he rose unsteadily and made his way toward the open door where the clear aura of the coming dawn to eastward might help him remember how things had been left the night before. He dredged his brain for the worst implications of what he'd said to Daniels, and the way he'd said it, down to the last inflection, although none of this mattered anymore. His brother's fate was in the hands of others.

Stirring his coffee, Crockett Daniels followed him outside onto the landing. "The boys come in last night," he said, getting it over with. He pointed at the marsh boat nudging the bank across the road. "Don't look like things worked out so good down there." Scowling, he went back inside, turning suddenly on Lucius, who had pursued him. "Look!" he yelled, pumping up anger. "Your brother was drinking with 'em, got to raging about them old stains on the floor—*only way to get that black blood out is to burn it out!* And damn if he don't try that whilst they was down loadin the boat."

Speck sipped his coffee, watching Lucius over the rim. "Way I heard it, that black blood—"

"Man lost his arm in the cane mill, bled to death up in the house—*never mind that!*" Lucius barely veered away from losing his temper.

"Nigger man? Took him right into the house?"

"Come on, Speck!"

"Damn fool poured some kerosene out of a lamp. Damn near set his daddy's house afire, and we had munitions hid under them gator flats stacked up in there. Boys flung out whole stacks of prime flats so's they could haul them crates before all hell broke loose, and them things was still outside when it heavy-rained. Left to rot," Speck complained. "That's a whole hell of a lot of gators, bud! Just a pitiful waste!"

"I think they murdered him and I think you know it."

"Figure it any fuckin way you want. It ain't my business. All I know is, they had to load that heavy ordnance, ferry those crates off the Bend in a big hurry. Never had time to fool with no crazy Watson."

"Dyer wanted him dead, isn't that it? That's why they took him there."

"Nosir, it sure ain't. Man was on the run, needed a hidey-hole, like I said."

"Answer my damned question then. Where is he now?"

"What it was, they seen him from the dock settin that fire. Hollered a warning but he wouldn't quit." Speck shrugged. "Had to stop him, Colonel."

"They *shot* him?"

"Well, that ain't how they told it. Never exactly said they had to shoot nobody. Shot over his head, maybe. They said he run out, hid in the trees.

They went ahead, got them crates loaded, said they hollered at him before they left. He never answered."

"Where are they now? Let's see if they tell me the same story."

"You heard their story. I just told it. Anyways, they're at their camp—and never mind askin where that is cause I ain't tellin you. For your own damn good. You go accusin boys like that, you'll only get yourself bad hurt or worse."

Lucius went out. He started down the stairs but halted on the steps at a loss as to what to do. Speck came out and handed down his cup of coffee. "C'mon, Colonel. You think fellers wanted by the law are goin to admit to shootin somebody even if they done it, which I ain't sayin they did?" Speck sat down on the top step. "But *if* they did—speakin fair now—"

"It might have been for the best?"

He sank onto the step. They drank their coffee. "I want to know the truth."

"Don't know the truth. Probably wouldn't tell it if I did," Speck stretched and yawned. "Huntin too hard for the truth ain't a good idea, y'know," he added. "By the time you stumble over it, it ain't the truth no more. Unless there's death in it. I reckon death is about as close to truth as a man can come." Slyly he said, "Only question is, did he get that blood out." He cut off his own snicker. "I *am* sorry, you know that? We was purty good old friends. And I believe them boys are sorry, too."

Speck went inside, came back with his brown jug. "Sad day," he said. "Let's you'n me get drunk."

Lucius went on down the stair.

"Fuck it," Daniels said. Dragging the rawhide string of bullets from beneath his shirt, he gathered them into a ball and tossed them down. "I reckon that belongs to Watsons," Daniels said, and went back inside.

WILD HOG JAMBAREE

He had to talk to someone. Carrie? Nell? Hoad was in Everglade at the new lodge. He would talk to Hoad first, they would take Hoad's boat, go look for him. He drove the rough road recklessly.

Across a slat bridge over a ditch was a small clearing where two swamp trucks, beds jacked high on outsized wheels, were parked outside a low decrepit cabin. Loose-fendered junked autos baked in the thick heat. The yard glinted with metal scraps and bottle caps and broken glass, its edges strewn with defunct batteries, lube buckets, bald tires. Gaunt kids and dragged-out women came to the cabin doorways to see who had pulled over and spavined hounds emerged from beneath the trucks. One swamp machine was a dark gurry red, the other dull crankcase black. On the red truck's door was WILD HOG JAMBAREE in daubed black lettering; the black one bore the name BAD CUNTRY in crude jagged red. Lucius was suddenly so frightened that he had to force his unsteady legs to walk the plank across the ditch.

Dummy and Mud lounged like whores against the trucks, lipping cigarettes and gasping beers. Dummy seemed torpid and indifferent, kneading his testes in a languid manner, but scraggy Mud grinned hungrily at the scent of trouble.

Crockett Junior lay sprawled across the black hood of BAD CUNTRY, using a big hunting knife to scrape crisped insects off the windshield. A heavy key chain at his belt scraped scars on the truck paint when he shifted. "Fuckin Mud! Don't go nowhere at all he ain't got a beer can stuck into his face. He don't know fuck-all, that stupid fuck. I ain't lettin him nowhere near this rig. Wouldn't have fuckin nothin left of it, time he got done!" Ignoring the intruder, he wheezed with his exertions, levering his torso with strong hairy shoulders, thrashing on the stump of the lost arm. Behind his knife hand, the crude head of his dog loomed in the windshield.

When Mud and Dummy straightened and came forward, Lucius stopped. In a voice hoarse with nerves, he said, "Where's my brother?"

"Wants to know where his brother's at." Mud glanced at Crockett for approval. "Never heard of him, ain't that right, Junior?"

Crockett scraped. When Lucius warned them that witnesses at Naples had seen them seize Robert Watson, that they would be charged with kidnapping or worse, Mud took a long slow gulp out of his beer can. Pulling it away, foam on his scraggy beard, he came up with an aggressive belch, wiping his hairy mouth with the back of his hand. "That so? How come you ain't called the law? That because the law's after him, too?" He hooted gleefully. " 'Armed and dangerous'! Come on the radio this mornin. Turned out to be a real bad feller, Chicken did."

"Turned out to be one them fuckin Watsons." Crockett Junior's wet snarl opened his beard stubble like a wound. "Oughta had his fuckin neck broke. This one, too." He turned back to his scraping. In the sun-shined air and hot scrub silence, the knife blade squeaked on the dry glass. "Get goin, mister." He spoke in a low voice without turning.

Lucius nerved himself. "Not till I find out what happened." He knew he had to persevere in the full knowledge it was useless.

Crockett Junior laid his knife down on the hood. He hiked himself onto his stump, then took hold of his big belt buckle with his freed hand in order to hike and shift himself. The maneuver took considerable effort, and he gasped and panted as he made it. Retrieving his knife, he slid off the hood. "You don't listen good," he said.

Dummy kept his eye on Crockett's knife, mouth fallen open. Mud's scared voice warned Lucius, "Never heard Junior tellin you, *Get goin?*" Mud stood ready to snarl or jeer according to the one-armed man's first shift in mood, but he seemed concerned for the intruder, too. "You keep pesterin," Mud blustered, "he'll set that dog on you, run your ass right off this road. So just you back up and get goin like the man told you, hear? Cause us dumb-ass redneck boys don't know nothin about no Robert Watson. Only fuckin thing we know to tell you is the fastest fuckin way off this here propitty."

When Crockett Junior yanked open the truck door, the dog sprang to the seat edge, taut for the next command—a knob-headed male dog of a bad tawny color blotched with dark brown. Shivering in loin and tendon, it strained toward Lucius as he yelled in fear, "Hold that damned dog!" Then Crockett whistled and the creature sprang, striking the ground with a hard thud of bone-filled paws.

Stiff-legged, bristle-naped, the dog circled him slowly as if penning him. From its clamped jaws came a low monotone growl. When it pushed its snout into his calf and left it there, awaiting its next command, a rank stink rose from its hide.

Lucius knew better than to move or speak. Feeling the blood drain from his face, he averted his gaze as a dog will, eyes half closed as if sleepy. He could only hope that his own fear smell would not fatally incite this morose animal.

"If Junior tole him to, ol' Buck'd go for a bull gator," Mud said. "Junior can lay a T-bone by his nose and go out to the store and Buck won't touch it lest he's tole to."

Lucius contained his shaking with main strength. "I'm not armed," he told them. "Call him off."

"Think I don't know what your fuckin brother wanted?" Crockett yelled.

"Think I ain't seen Speck's name on that damned list? Should of blowed his head off!" At that shout of anger, the dog snouted his calf harder, pushing with hind legs, shivering.

"Only we didn't," Mud reminded Crockett. Mud looked scared. Even Dummy seemed uneasy, adjusting his genitals through his greased coveralls.

Lucius said, "I made that fool list years ago. Means nothing."

"That a fact?" Mud said. "If you was Speck, would you take a Watson's word for that?"

Crockett whistled the dog into his truck, which Mud took as a sign to march Lucius back to his car, haranguing him all the way. "You got more guts than brains, know that? You don't know who you're foolin with." He jerked his head in the direction of Crockett's truck. "Your brother run off and hid on us. We don't know where he's at. So don't come back no more."

Shoving the dog into the other seat, Crockett had climbed into BAD CUNTRY and slammed the door. Mud joined Dummy in the red truck. "Hold on!" Lucius protested, extending his arms. Gunning his motor, Mud jolted across the ditch as Lucius jumped onto the running board, trying to hang on to the window. Dummy's paw shot out and seized his shirt and yanked him hard against the cab and carried him a good ways down the road before he pushed him away hard and sent him sprawling. The black truck, following close behind, honked its approval,

Jeers drifted back as the big machines headed east toward Gator Hook. Shock and pain. His brain was ringing. He pushed himself up onto all fours, then rested on his knees a moment before staggering to his feet, his scraped forearm packed bloody with limestone road bits, Dummy's musky smell still in his nose. Slapping distractedly at his dirtied pants, he knew he'd accomplished nothing. Yet for all his outrage and frustration, he felt unaccountably relieved, even queerly elated. He felt free.

EVERGLADE

Though the Everglade Lodge had replaced the Storter trading post and the Storters had moved to Naples, Hoad returned here often. Lucius found him in a wicker chair on the lodge porch overlooking the tidal river, expounding on the river scene to a little boy who looked much like him, chipmunk cheeks and all. Hanging back, Lucius listened to his friend explain everything from the net booms on the big shrimp boats to the gold-purple bronzing on the heads of the spring pelicans on their crude nests on the high mangrove walls across the tide.

Hoad hailed him cheerily and waved him to a seat. "Cap'n Lucius Watson, fish guide! Same old khakis and salt-rotted sneakers!" But Lucius was too restless to sit down, and seeing his exhaustion and the silence in it, Storter gave him time to collect himself while he finished describing to his son how he and Cap'n Watson netted pompano off the Gulf beaches, mostly at night, following the schools from Captiva Island south to the middle Keys. "Wasn't that something, Lucius? To have your own boat at your own dock and go to work only when the tide was right?" Hoad whistled in amazement. "Mullet schools two miles across, not a mile out of Caxambas!" he told the boy, who was twisting in his seat.

The boy ran off and Hoad sat back, a little sad. "Way things are going, our children will never see a mullet school as big as that, poor little fellers." He frowned. "Heck, I have nothing to complain about, I know that. It's our own darn fault. Sold away our good old river home under the trees for a new house on a new street in Naples with no trees at all. My wife likes it, I guess, but a backyard don't amount to much compared to riverfront."

Hoad fell still, awaiting him. He jumped up when Lucius told him what had happened. "We'll go look for him." Hoad's boat was hauled out upriver by the bridge, she only needed to be launched and refueled. They could leave for Chatham first thing in the morning.

They walked along under royal palms toward the village circle, then headed north toward the bridge to see to Hoad's boat, then back along the river. At the far end of every street, the encircling green mangrove lay in wait, as if after dark it might infiltrate and smother the small settlement, reclaiming it as jungle. Already insolent hard weeds were pushing through big cracks in the broken sidewalk.

Hoping to cheer him, Hoad told him that according to the radio this morning, the E. J. Watson claim on Chatham Bend had been dismissed by the state court. "Looks like the new park is on the way," Hoad chortled.

At the lodge, they sat outside gazing across the twilight channel where the sun falling to the Gulf out to the west still fired the highest leaves on the green wall. On other days these common miracles were healing, but this evening, the burning mangrove leaves, the dying light's faint flashes in the current—the quiet beauty in that transience—stirred only loneliness. Arranging with Hoad to meet early next morning, he excused himself and, picking up his glass, went inside and crossed the lobby to the telephone.

GONE AND LOST FOREVER

Startled when he reached Nell at once, Lucius was shy and awkward, stammering remorse for the neglectful way he'd treated her over the years and his unhappiness about the happiness he'd thrown away. But since he'd already made this clear at their meeting in the cemetery, she remained silent, awaiting his explanation of why he had chosen this moment to call. Finally, he told her about Rob.

"Oh Lucius, *no!*" she said. "Oh Rob! When I think how much you missed him all those years—oh Lucius, sweetheart, maybe he's all right. Will you let me know?"

Overwhelmed by her warm concern, he said, "Nell? Will you marry me?" Her silence scared him. "Nell?"

"Goodness," she murmured. "What a strange time to propose." She asked coolly if he had been drinking. He set his glass down, then denied this, but another silence made it evident that she knew better. He heard a soft clearing of the throat in preparation for some final rejection that would be unbearable. To head that off, he entreated her all in a rush, "I've always loved you, Nell, you know that. We could be so happy—"

Gently she cut him off. "Listen to me. Thank you. But since your father died, you've never permitted yourself happiness, so how could we be happy? It wouldn't work."

He said, "It's quite impossible, I agree." Then he said, "Come on, Nell. Marry me anyway."

He heard her laugh a little as he'd intended. But after a moment, she said that while she was glad she'd seen him after so long and would always consider him her oldest and best friend, she did not think they should meet again anytime soon.

In panic, he pretended she was testing him although in his heart he knew that she was not. "Please, Nell, listen, don't hang up. I mean it. I'm asking you to marry. Isn't that what you wanted?" She had put the phone down.

Across the lobby, mounted tarpon leapt in painful arcs on the dark wood walls. The ocean pearliness on the Triassic scales of these huge armored herring had faded to a dirtied yellow and the rigid jaws, stretched forever in pursuit of that fatal lure, were shrouded in the ghostly grays of spiderwebs.

At Caxambas, exhausted, he lay awake most of the night. He thought about his clumsy proposal, his slurred voice, the hurtful stupidity of saying, *Isn't that what you wanted?* He would call back and apologize in the morning. But when morning came, his resolve had unraveled. He sat on the cot edge a long while before coming to and dragging on the other sock. He decided that a discreet interval must pass before he courted his true love again. He must be patient, then draw near carefully so as not to spoil their romantic reunion. Sincerely moved by that prospect, he was also inadmissibly relieved, though he would not face this until weeks later when he realized she was truly gone and lost forever.

At daybreak he placed the brass urn in a box together with the humble collection of anonymous belt buckles and buttons. Before leaving, he added the manuscript of the biography. His decision to accept the loss of years of work had its seed in Rob's confession, but only now did he behold it in the light, like a magic toad escaped from his own mouth. He felt no astonishment at his decision nor did he feel overwhelmed by failure—quite the contrary. Like the confrontation with the Daniels gang, it was oddly exhilarating.

HOMEGOING

The *Cracker Belle* was a small fishing boat, formerly white, now driftwood gray. They idled her downcurrent past the rusty fish houses and the leaning bulkhead stacked with sea-greened crab pots. Emerging from the mangrove wall into Chokoloskee Bay, they headed out the north channel to the Gulf and traveled south along the coast, passing Rabbit Key with its lone mangrove clump on the seaward point; it rose ahead, passed on the port side, and fell astern.

Though Lucius was silent, Hoad knew where his mind was. Hoad was the one friend with whom Lucius would discuss that black autumn evening. "Trouble was, nobody could rest easy with Mister Watson laying out there in the moonlight. That's why they towed him way out here. I bet every darn kid on the Bay had bad dreams for a month about that cadaver bumping down Rabbit Key Pass on the flood tide."

Hoad smiled apologetically at Lucius, who could not smile with him. The seeds of legend, he was thinking, sown in his father's blood. It was not like Hoad to talk this way: had he forgotten he was talking about his friend's father and his own father's best friend? Was Papa in the public domain to be pawed over and patronized now that he was the legendary "Bloody Watson"?

Hoad had remembered to put a shovel in the boat. Was he uneasy about what might await them at the Bend? Hoad hated violence just as his father had ("Cap'n Bembo couldn't kill a chicken; his wife had to do it," Papa said).

"Course those Chok fellers ran that rope around his neck so the family could locate the body when they came for it," Hoad was saying.

Lucius said, "Hoad, I saw no noose and I was there, remember? They probably got that tale about the hanging rope out of the magazines."

Hoad apologized. "I'm sorry, Lucius. My point was—"

"I know what your point was. Let's forget it." In the next hour, they did not speak again.

The *Cracker Belle* was the lone boat on the empty coast. Far offshore to westward, a tiny freighter smudged the Gulf horizon.

Traversing the old clam beds east of Pavilion Key, Hoad mentioned that this shallow shelf was now so plagued with sharks that men disliked going overboard to wade for the few clams left, and nobody knew what drew the sharks from the deep water. Some folks said that that plague of sharks foretold that the old ways of Earth were near an end.

DEAD RECKONING

In the southern mist rose Mormon Key off the mouth of Chatham River. Farther on, the cries of oystercatchers purled across the bars, rising and falling. Hoad smiled to hear that sound. "I reckon that wild cry was here when the first Calusa came in the old centuries."

The *Cracker Belle* entered the mangrove delta. "These west coast rivers are so low due to Glades drainage that your dad's schooner would go aground before he ever made it to the Bend," Hoad said. "Got to go by dead reckoning. Got to listen to your propeller." He was talking too much because he was worried about what might await his friend upriver. Lucius nodded but remained silent.

Where storm trees had stranded on a shoal, dead branches dipped and beckoned in the wash of the boat's wake. At Hannah's Point, perhaps a mile below the Bend, was the common grave of Hannah, Green, and Dutchy, never visited and now all but forgotten in the desolate salt scrub as the dark events of that long-ago October passed from local history into myth. "About all us local folks have left is our long memories," Hoad was saying. "Hurricanes roil things up a little now and then but it's bad deaths that carry our remembrances back, sometimes a hundred years."

Still visible back of the mangrove fringe along the bank was a square impression about one foot deep, as if a half-buried barn door had been levered up out of the white paste of the marl. "This place really spooks the few who know about it," Hoad said, "me included. Graves without coffins generally sprout a good strong crop of weeds but nothing grows here."

"Very strange," Lucius agreed politely, anxious to keep moving.

"Those poor folks had no families to come after them like Mister Watson. But they were darned lucky to get into the ground before that bad storm carried 'em out to sea. Course they won't stay."

Hoad pointed to a corner of the grave that was eroding bit by clod into the river.

They listened to the river's *lic-lic-lic* as it curled past. In sun-tossed branches, in the river wind, white-pated black pigeons craned and peered like anxious spirits. From upriver, others called in columbine lament, *woe-woe-wuk-woe*.

"Come on, Hoad, let's go." He spoke abruptly.

In a shift of wind the smell came heavy on the air. Waves fled the bow to crash into the banks in the boat's wake as they rushed upriver. The hard pine in the house had blasted pitch into the sky, casting a sepia pall over the thunderheads. Where the Watson place had stood on its high mound was a strange hollowness, a void, thick shimmerings of heat. Behind the house's shadow presence, what foliage remained on the gaunt trees was gray with ash. All around on the blackened ground lay the belly flats of alligators, curled up in crusts.

They called and called. Circling the dying fire, he clenched his heart against the sight of a charred shape in the crack and shudder of the last collapsing timbers, the whisperings of embers and blue hiss of mineral flame.

Face scorched, Lucius turned from the burning at a call from Hoad. Rob's satchel had been left on the bare ground beyond the gator scraps. Lucius approached and picked it up and finally opened it, extracting the unloaded revolver. The note he dreaded was there, too. Clumsy, he dropped it, picked it up again.

> *Dear Luke,*
> *Thanks for coming. Sorry about the house. I don't ask your forgiveness.*
> *A keepsake—our old family heirloom. I know you wonder why I kept it*
> *all those years. I think I needed it. I think I needed this steel thing and*
> *the cold precision of its parts to hold reality together. In some way I*
> *don't claim to understand, that red day at Lost Man's was the last*
> *reality I ever knew.*
> *So long. No need to wait, no need to worry. Yr ever-lovin brother, R.B.*
> *Watson*

He raised his gaze to the brown river, read the note, passed it to Hoad. Hoad read it and looked up, clearing his throat. "Listen," he began. He stopped. With nothing else to say, they stared away downriver.

Clouds from the Gulf dragged shrouds of ocean rain across the mangrove islands, raising an acrid stream from the brooding fire. He took shelter in the boat cabin with Hoad. In the cramped space, in dense wet heat, among the *Belle*'s rust-rotted life jackets and moldy slickers, Hoad said, "You aim to put all the bad stuff in your book?" This was less a question than a warning. Lucius ignored it.

When the rain stopped, they returned ashore. Lucius buried the box of belt buckles and bullets where the shed had been—the slave quarters, Leslie Cox called it, with that bruising laugh. The urn he took to the leaning poinciana in whose thin shade dear Mama had rested in the long afternoons, watching the passing of the river. Replacing the earth, he remained there on his knees for a few minutes. "Well, Papa," he whispered finally and stood up.

Thin smoke plumes rose like companies of ghosts. Out to the west where the Gulf sky was clearing, an iron sun loomed through the mist and vanished. From upriver came the hollow knocking of that big black woodpecker. In the river silence, it seemed far away and also near.

Hoad was waiting by the boat.

"We're going," Lucius said, fetching his manuscript.

His old friend trailed him back to the fire in alarm. "Wait," Hoad said.

Out of respect for so much work, he lifted the manuscript to the level of his breast before bending and consigning it to the red embers. In silence they watched the top page brown a little at one corner as the fire took hold. A moment before bursting into flame, it lifted on an updraft, danced, planed down again among the gator scraps.

Hoad jumped to retrieve it before it blew away but when his friend only shook his head, he returned it to the fire.

"Okay? Let's go," said Lucius Watson.

Long long ago down the browning decades, in the light of the old century in Carolina, walked a toddling child, a wary boy, a strong young male of muscle, blood, and brain who saw, who laughed and listened, smelled and touched, ate, drank, and bred, occupying time and space with his getting and spending in the world. What his biographer will strive to recover is a true sense of this human being, with all his particularity and hope and promise, in the hope that the reader might understand who the grown man might have become had he not known too much of privation, rage, and loss.*

*From the author's foreword to *The Undiscovered Country: A Life of Edgar Watson* by L. Watson Collins.

BOOK THREE

There is a pain—so utter—
It swallows substance up—
Then covers the Abyss with Trance
So Memory can step
Around—across—upon it
As one within a Swoon—
goes safely—where an open eye—
Would drop Him—Bone by Bone

—Emily Dickinson

Sir, what is it that constitutes character, popularity, and power in the United States? Sir, it is property, and that only!

—Governor John Hammond of South Carolina

For the final consummation, that I might feel less lonely, it was my final wish that as I climbed the scaffold, I would be greeted with cries of execration.

—Albert Camus, *The Stranger*

CHAPTER 1

✦

Oh Mercy, cries the Reader. What? Old Edgefield again?
It must be Pandemonium itself, a very District of Devils!

—PARSON MASON L. WEEMS

DISTRICT OF DEVILS

Edgefield Court House, which gave its name to the settlement that grew from a small crossroads east of the Savannah River, is a white-windowed brick edifice upon a hill approached by highroads from the four directions, drawing the landscape all around to a point of harmony and concord. The building is faced with broad stone steps on which those in pursuit of justice may ascend from Court House Square to its brick terrace. White columns serve as portals to the second-story courtroom, and the sunrise window in the arch over the door, filling the room with austere light, permits the elevated magistrate to freshen his perspective by gazing away over the village to the open countryside and the far hills, blue upon blue.

Early in the War, a boy of six, I was borne lightly up those steps on the strong arm of my father. On the courthouse terrace, I gazed with joy at this tall man in Confederate gray who pointed out to his proud son the fine prospect of the Piedmont, bearing away toward the northwest and the Great Smoky Mountains. In those nearer distances lay the Ridge, where a clear spring appeared out of the earth to commence its peaceful slow descent through woodland and plantation to the Edisto River. This tributary was Clouds Creek, where I was born.

On that sunny day on Court House Square my father, Elijah Daniel Watson, rode away to war and childhood ended. As a "Daughter of Edgefield," his wife Ellen, with me and my little sister, waved prettily from the court-house steps as the First Edgefield Volunteers mustered on the square. Her handsome Lige, wheeling his big roan and flourishing a crimson pennant on his saber, pranced in formation in the cavalry company formed and cap-tained by his uncle Tillman Watson. On the right hand of Edgefield's own Governor Andrew Pickens, who saluted the new volunteers from the ter-race, stood Mama's cousin Selden Tilghman, the first volunteer from Edge-field District and its first casualty. Called forth to inspire his townsmen, the young cavalry officer used one crutch to raise and wave the blue-red criss-cross flag of the Confederacy.

Governor Pickens thundered, "May the brave boys of Edgefield defend to the death the honor and glory of our beloved South Carolina, first sover-eign state to secede from the Yankee Union!" And Cousin Selden, on some mad contrary impulse, dared answer the governor's exhortation by crying out oddly in high tenor voice, "To those brave boys of Edgefield who will sacrifice their lives for our Southern right to enslave the darker members of our species!"

The cheering faltered, then died swiftly in a low hard groan like an ill wind. Elijah Watson wheeled his horse and pointed his saber at Lieutenant Tilghman as voices cat-called rudely in the autumn silence. Most men gave the wounded lieutenant the benefit of the doubt, concluding he was drunk. He had fought bravely and endured a grievous wound, and all was forgiven when he rode off to war again, half-mended.

When the War was nearly at an end, and many slaves were escaping toward the North, a runaway was slain by Overseer Zebediah Claxton on Tillman Watson's plantation at Clouds Creek. Word had passed the day before that Dock and Joseph were missing. At the racketing echo of shots from the creek bottoms, yelping in fear for Joseph, I dropped my hoe and lit out across the furrows toward the wood edge, trailing the moaning of the hounds down into swamp shadows and along wet black mud margins, dragged at by thorns and tentacles of old and evil trees.

I saw Dock first—dull stubborn Dock, lashed to a tree—then the over-seer whipping back his hounds, then two of my great-uncles, tall and raw-boned on rawboned black horses. Behind the boots and milling beasts, the heavy hoof stamp and bit jangle, a lumped thing in earth-colored home-

Book III · 497

spun sprawled awkwardly among the roots and ferns. The broken shoes, the legs hard-twisted in the bloody pants, the queer gray thing sticking out askew from beneath the chest—how could that gray thing be the warm and limber hand that had offered nuts or berries, caught my mistossed balls, set young "Mast' Edguh" on his feet after a fall? All in a bunch, the fingers had contracted like the toes of a stunned bird, closing on nothing.

On long-gone Sabbath mornings of those years before the War, I ran with the black children to our games in the bare-earth yards back of the quarters, scattering dusty pigs and scraggy roosters. In cramped fetid cabins I was hugged with all the rest and fed molasses biscuits, fatback, hominy, wild greens. And always, it seemed, this sweet-voiced Joseph made the white child welcome. Yes, Joseph was guilty and our laws were strict. Alive, he would be cruelly flogged by Overseer Claxton, just as Dock would be tomorrow. Yet in my fear, I wept for poor, gentle Joseph, and pitied myself, too, in this loss greater than I knew.

CLAXTON

At daybreak Mr. Claxton, on the lookout, had seen a small smoke rising from a corner of the swamp and rode on down there with his shotgun and his dogs. The slaves had fled, obliging him to shoot and wound them both— so went his story. He was marching them home when this damned Joseph sagged down like a croker sack and would not get up. "Too bad it weren't this other'n, seein he was the one behind it. I told him, 'Shut up your damn moanin.' Told him, 'Stand that son-bitch on his feet, I ain't got all day.' Done my duty, Major, but it weren't no use."

Major Tillman Watson and his brother sat their big horses, chewing on the overseer's story. The dead boy's homespun was patched dark and stuck with dirt, and a faint piss stink mixed with hound smell and the sweet musk of horses. "Wet hisself," the overseer repeated to no one in particular. He was a small, closed-face man, as hard as wire.

Uncle Elijah Junior complained angrily about "the waste of a perfectly good nigger" but his older brother, home from war, seemed more disturbed by Claxton's viciousness. "Dammit, Z. P., you telling us these boys was aiming to outrun them hounds of yours?" Major Tillman was backing his big horse, reining its head away toward home. "Close his eyes, dammit!" He was utterly fed up. "Well? Lay him across your saddle, then! You can damn well walk him in."

"I reckon he'll keep till mornin," Claxton muttered, sullen.

"You have no business here," I was admonished by Uncle Elijah Junior—not because I was too young to witness bloody death nor because night was coming on but because I was certainly neglecting whichever chore I had abandoned without leave. Major Tillman, half-turned in the saddle, frowned down on me in somber temper. "You're not afraid out here all by yourself?"

"Yessir. I mean, nosir."

"Nosir." The major grunted. "You get on home so you don't go worryin your poor Mama." Trailed by his brother, who would never be a horseman, the old soldier rode away through the dark trees.

" '*Walk* him in!' " the overseer squawked, once the brothers were out of earshot. "They want him that bad, let'm send the niggers with a wagon." Ignoring the dead boy's staring eyes, he stepped across the body to strip his bonds from the wounded Dock, who yelped with every jerk of the rough hemp.

"He's hurt!" I protested. Claxton glared as if seeing me for the first time. "Hurt? What *you* know about it? What you wantin with these niggers anyways?" He climbed gracelessly onto his horse, cracked his hide whip. In single file through the black trees, the two figures moved away along the moon-silvered water into enshrouding dusk, the black man pitched forward, the lumpish rider and lean hounds behind.

In dread of swamps and labyrinths, of dusk, of death—the shadow places—I called after the overseer, my voice gone shrill. "You fixing to leave him out here?" *Out in the dark swamp all night by himself? With the owls and varmints?*—that's what I meant. The man snorted because he dared not curse a Watson, even a Watson as young and poor as me. "Niggers'll come fetch him or they won't," his voice came back.

In the dusk, the forest gathered and drew close. I stood transfixed. In its great loneliness, the body lay in wait. I wanted to go close his eyes, but alone with a corpse at nightfall, I was too frightened. Already that shining face with its stopped blood had thickened like a mask, and bloodied humus crusted its smooth cheek. At last I ran and knelt by Joseph's side, tried to pull him straight, free his gray hand, fold the arms across the chest.

The dead are heavy, as I learned that day, and balky, too. He would not lie the way I wanted. I stared at him frantic, out of breath. The forehead, drained, resembled the cool and heavy skin of a huge toadstool. The brown eyes, wide in the alarm of dying, were dull glazed, dry. Trying to draw the eyelids down, my finger flinched, so startled was it by how delicate these lids were and how naturally they closed, as if he were drifting into sleep, but also by the hardness of the orbs beneath their petals. Who could have imagined that the human eye would be so hard! When one lid rose a little, slowly, in a kind of squint, I jumped and fled.

The overseer saw that I was barefoot and in tears. He did not offer to swing me up behind. He said, "I allus tole 'em they is such a thing as too much nigger spirit." Not knowing what such words might mean, I stared back at the lump that had been Joseph; it was ceding all shape and semblance to the dark, subsiding like humus among roots and ferns. Z. P. Claxton, I knew, would be laid to rest in higher ground, in sunny grasses, in the light of Heaven.

The dead I had seen before but not the killed. Cousin Selden, home from war, had confided that the corpse of a human slain in violence and left staring where it fell looked like some being hurled down wide-eyed out of Heaven—nothing at all like the prim cadaver of the beloved in sedate sleep, plugged, scrubbed, perfumed, and suited up in Sunday best for the great occasion, hands crossed pious on its breast. Those who touched their lips to the cool forehead in farewell held a breath so as not to know that faint odor of cold meat. Or so said Cousin Selden, who composed dark poetry and liked to speak in that peculiar manner. Not that a darkie had been my "beloved," but Joseph had been kind to me, he had been kind, and I had no other friends. How I would miss him! I was still young and could not help my unmanly feelings.

My grandfather Artemas Watson died in 1841 at the age of forty. His second wife Lucretia Daniel had predeceased him at the age of thirty, and his son Elijah Daniel Watson, born in 1834, was thus an orphan at an early age. Grandfather Artemas's properties included sixty-eight slaves, with like numbers distributed to Great-Uncle Tillman and their several brothers. In 1850, my father inherited real estate and property in the amount of $15,000, by no means a negligible sum, but according to Mama he'd squandered most of it on gambling and horses by the time they were married five years later.

The marriage of a Clouds Creek Watson was duly recorded in the Edgefield marriage records: Elijah D. Watson and Ellen C. Addison, daughter of
the late John A. Addison, January 25, 1855. Colonel Addison had commis-
sioned the construction of the courthouse from which the crossroads village took its name (and in which his son-in-law, in years to come, would
appear regularly as a defendant). Ellen's mother had died at age twenty-
five, but Ellen, as a ward in a rich household, was given her own slave girl
and piano lessons until the day she was married off to young Elijah, with
whom her one bond might have been that both had been orphaned when
their fathers died in 1841.

THE CLOUDS CREEK WATSONS

Four years after his bugled glory on Court House Square, Private Lige Watson, having lost his horse, walked home from war. He told his family of the
sack and burning of Columbia by the ruthless General Sherman, describing the capital's lone chimneys, the blackened skeletons of noble oaks.
"You folks at home know nothing of real war," he said, astonished that
Clouds Creek and Edgefield Court House had survived untouched.

His family had known something of real war, of course, having had to
scour bare sustenance from our remnant of the Artemas Plantation. The
rest had been bought or otherwise acquired by Uncle Elijah Junior, who
early in the War had assumed our mortgage, extending but meager help
thereafter to the absent soldier's wife and children. As a precaution against
his nephew's well-known temper, Mama said, he let us remain in the dilapidated house and raise such food and cotton as we might; even so, my
mother, burdened with little Minnie, could not manage alone, not even
with my nine-year-old hard labor. Uncle Elijah Junior sent us the hard-
headed Dock, knowing Dock would run off again at the first chance, which
he did, this time for good. Next, he sent old Tap Watson because Tap, the father of the slain Joseph, no longer worked well under Z. P. Claxton. Ol' Zip
had been too quick on the trigger, sighed Great-Uncle Tillman, but he
scares some work out of 'em, we got to give him that.

A small blue-black man of taciturn, even truculent disposition, Tap had
not forgotten the kindnesses received from the late Master Artemas, that
vague and lenient planter who had owned Tap's parents and who remem-

bered on his deathbed to set this stern man free. Unlike his son, Tap pre-ferred orderly bondage to the unknown dangers of "freedom" and had cashed in his emancipation by selling himself to Elijah Junior for cold coin. "This way, I has my job, somethin to eat." Slave or freedman, Tap had never missed a day of work—that was his pride.

Told that his son lay dead in the swamp, he had set his jaw and turned his back on Claxton. "He's your'n, ain't he? Go get him," Claxton barked. Facing him then, Tap Watson fixed the overseer with a baleful eye, not turning away even when Claxton pointed at the black man's yellowed eyes and lifted his whip by way of warning. Great-Uncle Tillman ordered him to leave that black man be, and Tap finished slopping the hogs before hitching a mule to the wagon to go fetch the body. Never again would he acknowl-edge the overseer's order, voice, or presence, which explained why Elijah Junior had been happy to be rid of him. Also, Tap had fornicated with Mama's slave girl, Cinderella, now the tall young woman whom we called Aunt Cindy, and when he came to us, Mama ordered them to marry.

When I told Papa, home from the War, how Z. P. Claxton had killed Joseph, Papa said roughly, "Runaway? Damn well deserved it." Impoverished, now past thirty, Papa had to start all over as a poor relation of stern prosperous kin who prided themselves on self-sufficiency and independence. A tenant farmer on the Artemas plantation, he was paying a third of all crops raised to his uncle Elijah Junior, and in the lean aftermath of war, struggling to make a cotton crop with his wife and children, he slid into heavy debt to his own clan. As a war veteran, broke and disenfranchised, he would rail against the injustice of his fate, yet he would not tolerate Mama's criti-cisms of Elijah Junior. Indeed he acclaimed his uncle's "Watson thrift" even when this dour trait caused his own household to go hungry. (It was all very well about Watson thrift, Mama would say, but how did such thrift differ from hard-hearted stinginess?) With gallant optimism, my father pledged that one day, with God on his right hand and his strong son on his left, he would reclaim his family land, restoring the line of Artemas Watson to Clouds Creek. Carried away, he roughed my head with vigor. Though my eyes watered, I wished my brave soldier daddy to be proud and did not flinch.

For a time "Elijah D." enjoyed oratorical support from his aunt Sophia

Boatright, a big top-heavy woman with a baying voice whose favorite topic—indeed, her only topic, Mama would whisper—was the Watson clan, all the way back to the English Watsons (or Welsh or Scots or perhaps Ulstermen, sniffed Mama), those staunch landowners and men of means who had sailed in the sixteenth century to New York City, then traveled on to Olde Virginia to claim their tract of free and fertile land. The first New World patriarch was Lucius Watson Esquire of Amelia County in Virginia, whose sons moved on to South Carolina as early as 1735. Their land grants were registered at Charleston, Aunt Sophia assured us, well before the arrival of those Edgefield clans which gave themselves airs today.

A worthy son of those forefathers was Michael Watson, a fabled Indian-fighter who chastised the Cherokees and later led a citizens' militia against highwaymen and outlaws, the foul murderers of his father and a brother. Meanwhile, he acquired a tract of six thousand acres on Clouds Creek, which was consolidated as clan property when he married Martha Watson, his first cousin. (Here Mama dared roll her eyes for her children's benefit, screwing her forefinger into her temple in sign of inbred lunacy and sending our little Min into terrified giggles.)

During the Revolutionary War, Captain Michael Watson had served as a field captain of Pickens's Brigade, a mounted company armed with muskets for the deadly fight against the "King-Lovers" or Tories. At one point, he was captured and imprisoned at Columbia, where according to one reputable account—which Aunt Sophia enjoyed reading aloud at family gatherings—Martha Watson Watson, who was "small and beautiful, with wonderfully thick long hair . . . wound a rope around her body and carried files in her hair for the use of Captain Watson, [who] made his escape." (Here my mother might pretend to struggle desperately with her own hair, risking what she called "the Great Wrath of the Watsons" with whispered parody: *Captain Michael, darlin? Mah handsome hee-ro? Here's a nice li'l ol' file so's you can saw those bars in twain and make good your escape! Just hold your horses, Captain dear, whilst I unsnarl this pesky thing from mah gloe-rious hay-uh!*)

In an early history of South Carolina, our famous ancestor had been described as "a determined and resentful man who consulted too much the counsels which these feelings suggested." Freed from Tory gaol, the choleric Captain rushed straight into battle, only to receive a fatal wound in the forest swamps of the south Edisto. Having turned over his command to Lieutenant Billy Butler, our ancestor composed himself and "died for Liberty."

"Those Edgefield families prate about their 'aristocracy'!" Sophia Boatright scoffed. "How about our Clouds Creek aristocracy? Our Watson forebears held royal grants for two decades before Andrew Pickens came down out of the hills, and they owned more land besides!"

("Even so," Mama might murmur to my flustered father, who could not forcefully suppress her on a family occasion, "it was called Pickens's Brigade, not Watson's Brigade, isn't that true, dear? And that handsome young lieutenant who replaced Captain Watson became General Butler, father of General Matthew Calbraith Butler, who married the exquisite Maria Pickens, whose father, come to think of it, was a general, too. Has there ever been a General Watson, dear?" Such whispers were just loud enough to stiffen the black whiskers of Great-Aunt Sophia.)

Captain Michael's only son, Elijah Julian, would become the landed patriarch of the Watson clan. Through industry and force of character, the "Old Squire" acquired eleven plantations, one for each of his children, among whom "his favorite was always his first little daughter, Sophia," said Aunt Sophia. In the presence of her brothers, Aunt Sophia referred to the late patriarch as "the ramrod of this family"; a shuffle and shift of bombazine and feathers would signal the onset of another anecdote establishing her own ascendancy as the rightful claimant to that title. One day when the Yankees ordered their black militia to drill on her broad lawn, the Ramrod's gallant elder daughter strode forth shouting, "Now you monkeys just stop all that darn foolishness and go on home!" which naturally they did.

We are no Eire-ish nor Sco-atch, nor are we Enga-lish—thus would the Old Squire tease his proud Sophia whenever she put on English airs, according to the recollections of her siblings. With Border folk, he would point out, who could determine who came from where, since none had agreed for seven hundred years where their domains lay? No, the Old Squire had declared, we are proud Borderers, the sons of Watt, and nothing more.

Mama's cousin Selden Tilghman, the young cavalry officer, war hero, and classics scholar, lived alone on his family plantation, known as Deepwood.

Detesting the notorious history of violence in his Tillman clan, attributing their uproar to inbreeding and prideful ignorance, Cousin Selden had reverted to the ancestral spelling in order to separate himself from "those amongst my kinsmen who have grown so contemptuous of learning that they no longer know the correct spelling of their own name."

In Selden's opinion, Mama told us, the early Watsons had probably arrived in the port of Philadelphia in the shiploads of Highland refugees from seven centuries of war and famine in the Border counties. These clannish and unruly Celts, as he portrayed them, had horrified the Quakers with outlandish speech and uncouth disrespect for all authority. Their women were notorious for short-cropped skirts, bare legs, and loose bodices, while the men mixed unabashed poverty and filth with a furious pride that hastened to avenge the smallest denigration or perceived injustice. Worse, they did this in the name of "honor," a virtue which more mannerly colonials would never concede to such rough persons. Inevitably the Borderers were urged westward toward the backcountry of the Pennsylvania Colony, in the fervent hope that indigenous peoples even more primitive than themselves might do away with them.

The Borderers were a suspicious breed of feuders and avengers, cold-eyed and mistrustful of all strangers, or any who interfered with them in the smallest way. They fought their way through Indian territory with fatalistic indifference to hard faring and danger, spreading south like a contagion along the Appalachians into western Virginia and the Carolina uplands. Many were drovers of cattle and hogs, throwing up low cabins of wood or stones packed tight with earth, hunting and gathering the abounding game and fish, trading meat where possible for grain and iron, boozing and bragging and breeding, ever breeding. Scattering homesteads and ragged settlements south and west to the Great Smokies and beyond, massacring the aborigines wherever fortune smiled, they broadcast the seed of their headstrong clans without relinquishing a single dour trait or archaic custom. When times were hard, not a few would resort to traditional Border occupations—reivers and rustlers, highwaymen and common bushwhackers. The Border Watsons were of this stripe, Cousin Selden implied—quarrelsome ruffians disdainful of the law, obstreperous rebels against Church and Crown, as careless of good manners as of hardship and rude weather, not to speak of all the finer sentiments of the human heart. Or so, at least, Celtic ways were represented by Cousin Selden, whose mother had flowered amongst the Cavalier gentry of Maryland, and been chivalrously deflowered, too, her son supposed.

Selden's amused, ironic views, well spiced by Mama, were regularly quoted to her children in their father's presence. Though no match for his tart Ellen, Papa defended the Clouds Creek Watsons with a heartfelt rage. If the Watsons were mere Border rabble, he might bellow, then how would her precious Selden explain their prosperity in the New World? For whether by grant from the South Carolina Colony or Crown patent from King George, enlarged by enterprise, the first Carolina Watsons had acquired sixteen square miles—sixteen square miles!—of the best Clouds Creek country on the north fork of the Edisto River even before the muddy crossroads known as Edgefield Court House came into being. What was more, his late lamented mother Mary Lucretia Daniel for whom our little Minnie had been named was a direct descendant of President Jefferson's great-aunt Martha. "Children, you have a proud heritage to uphold!" he exclaimed with passion, tossing his head dismissively in his wife's direction as he spoke of her "traitorous" Tory antecedents and their "lily-livered longing," as he called it, to be accepted by the Pickenses and Butlers and Brookses at the Court House.

"Spare your poor children these vulgarities, I beseech you," his wife might protest, to hone her point that his credentials as a gentleman were suspect. Ellen Catherine Addison, after all, had been born into aristocratic circumstances, however straitened these might have become. It was scarcely her fault that her feckless husband had sold off all of her inheritance excepting her mother's set of Scott's Waverly novels, which was missing her own favorite, *Ivanhoe*. "How did I ever imagine," she would sigh, "that this rough fellow would be my Ivanhoe!" Gladly would she play the piano for her husband—"to soothe your savage breast, dear," she might add with a girlish peal—could such an instrument be found in a Watson dwelling, or fit into it, for that matter, since for all their prosperity, those Clouds Creek Watsons, eschewing the white-columned mansions of the Edgefield gentry, were content with large two-story versions of the rough-sawed timber cabins of their yeomen forebears.

"Yeomen?"

For his abuse and dismal failure as a father and provider as well as for her own exhaustion and privation, the erstwhile Miss Ellen C. Addison repaid her husband with sly mockery of those "darned old Watsons," as she called them. Any Addison was better born, more educated and refined, and in every way more suited than any Watson to consort with the aristocracy at Edgefield Court House, not to speak of Charleston, far less England— thus would Mama prattle. We scarcely heard her, so frightened were we of the enraged and violent man in the chimney corner.

Mama blamed nothing on cruel providence but kept up her merciless good cheer in the worst of circumstances, as if otherwise our wretched family must go under. A topic that delighted her was the evangelical form of Protestant religion adopted by our country folk such as the Baptist Watsons, so unlike the discreet Episcopal persuasion favored at the Court House. In their "fellowshipping" at summer camp meetings, Mama had heard, the evangelicals lay about together in the grass, and not a few drank ale and wooed their females. Some might even take the time to be "born again," said Mama, shaking her head. "When they've had enough preaching, the whole crowd joins in 'the Great Shout,' as I believe they call it, and something called 'the Feast of the Fat Things.' " Winking at her children, Mama called out toward the porch, "Isn't that what Baptists call it, Mr. Watson? Does our dear aunt Sophia participate in the Feast of the Fat Things?"

"Love Feast," Papa snarled, after a heavy-breathing silence. My sister, close to hysterics over the Feast of the Fat Things, would run away and hide while I, ever more frightened, stood my ground, dreading the oncoming cataclysm.

Mama would be laughing in delight. "The Feast of the Fat Things— imagine! These upcountry weddings, children, you never saw such carryings-on in all your life. The bride is usually with child—she is the Fat Thing, I suppose! They play all sorts of games, dance reels and jigs, and some rush about naked. They sing, 'Up with your heels and down with your head, that is the way we make cockledy bread.' Isn't that quaint? And all the men dead drunk on their Black Betty—"

"Dammit, woman! That's the name for the bottle—"

"—and after all this . . . love feasting? . . . these poor females settle down to their long, hard, dreary lives. To be sure, life is hard and utterly thankless for all women, children. But our backcountry women on dark isolated farms—'too far away to hear the barking of the neighbor's dog,' as the old folks say—toiling like draft animals in the mud, with none of the culture and society of towns, nothing but silence and hostility and worse from brutish husbands—well, pagan or not, those poor creatures need that Feast of the Fat Things to bring a little light into their wretched lives, isn't that so, Mr. Watson?"

"Please, Mama, that's not fair," I whispered, so scared and upset that I scarcely knew what I meant.

"Not fair?" She met my entreaty with a brief cold gaze. "Did you know that your father's peculiar faith celebrates 'Old Christmas'—the Feast of the Epiphany—which actually falls on the twelfth night after our true Christian Christmas? It is not consecrated to hymns and prayer but to hard spirits, horse racing, and chicken fights."

"Cockfights, for God's sake!"

"Cockers and gamesters. Isn't that what you call yourselves, Mr. Watson?"

COUSIN SELDEN

When weary of discounting Papa's family, Mama might praise Cousin Selden's concern for the emancipated Negroes, who could find no work around the towns and villages. In this past year of 1867, under the Reconstruction Act, all our blacks had become wards of the Union government, to be protected henceforth as citizens and voters, and a Yankee detachment had been sent to Edgefield to ensure their rights. In a district where blacks outnumbered whites, and where white soldiers who had fought for the Confederacy had been disenfranchised, our men's hatred of Reconstruction would find its scapegoat in the freedmen, especially those "woods niggers" or "road walkers" who wandered the mud roads between settlements, awaiting fulfillment of the Union's promise of "forty Confederate acres and a mule." The dark-skinned ragged hordes were cursed by seething whites as a menace to white womanhood, and were commonly terrorized and tortured, often worse.

Captain Selden Tilghman, waving a copy of a Freedmen's Bureau report that murdered blacks were being found along our roads and in the woods and swamps, had spoken publicly in favor of federal relocation of all freedmen from our Edgefield District, knowing well that our local planters counted on the exploitation of desperate near-slave labor to survive. The crowd heard him out only because he had "worn the gray" as a war hero with commendable wounds and battlefield promotions, but finally the more bellicose began to shout that Tilghman was a traitor. Wasn't it true that he had freed his slaves before the War in defiance of Carolina laws against manumission, and openly endorsed Damn Yankee Abolition? Was it not Tilghman who had tried to interfere with the lawful execution of black Union soldiers imprisoned at Fort Pillow? Obliging General Nathan Bedford Forrest to ride up and command that the killing resume: *Blood and Honor, sir! In Virginia they take no nigger prisoners, and no more shall we!*

Cousin Selden's relocation proposal never reached a vote. As of that day, the cavalry lieutenant was chastised—"hated out"—with stony silence, hisses, blows, abuse. Next he would suffer thefts, slain animals, the burning barn, bawled death threats intended to drive the hated one to flee the region or destroy himself to expiate his dreadful sin of speaking out in favor of Christian mercy, Mama fretted, distressed that for the sake of her children's safety, she had not dared speak herself (though our safety in her own household seemed not to concern her).

Except to drop off books for me—he had interested himself in my education or the lack of it—the outcast no longer visited our house, but he had the crazy courage of his isolation. Refusing to abandon the family manse, he hung on at Deepwood even after word was passed that no one, white or black, was to enter its lane. The grounds and fields became sadly overgrown even as the old house withdrew like a wounded creature behind the climbing shrouds of vine and creeper.

If only to spite her husband, Mama said that she had always shared Cousin Selden's Abolitionist convictions. Mama's memories were often prejudiced but rarely false, and one of them always rang true: when she asked her cousin why he had risked his life for that great lost cause he had no faith in, why he had not refused to take up arms, he'd said, "I was not brave enough."

Mama told us that despite his gallantry in battle, Cousin Selden's family had repudiated him for turning away from his Anglican upbringing toward the New Light faith, which had always advocated Abolition and had sought—she smiled, pitching her voice toward her husband, seated outside on the stoop—"a more enlightened attitude toward the rights of women. Today our colored men can vote but not white women."

"White men neither!" bawled her husband from the porch. "Not those who fought."

"Addisons being Episcopalians like most of our good families, I had no real acquaintance with the New Light Church, nor with your father's Baptist congregation, for that matter." Eyebrows raised in amusement at the growled warnings from without, Mama invited us to pity those unfortunate women whose husbands were not God-fearing steadfast men who abstained from the grog shops, gambling, and sinful license to which the weak seemed so addicted, to the great suffering and deprivation of their families. Her tone was edged with such disdain that Papa, chivvied to his feet, loomed in the doorway. "And throwing away their wages on mulatta women," she continued. "Harlots, of course, have never been tolerated in Edgefield District. It is the bordellos of Augusta which beckon our local sinners to Damnation."

Mama bent to her knitting with the martyred smile of the good churchwoman whose mission on earth was to purify and save the soul of her crude male lump by shielding him from Satan's blandishments.

"In our church, a man may be excommunicated for wife beating, or even," she added, widening her eyes, "for adultery. With white or black. Or perhaps," she inquired directly of her husband, "you Fat Feasters feel that mulatta girls don't count?"

My heart sank slowly like a stone into wet mud. The son, not the mother, reaped the inevitable thrashing. The father was already exhaling through his mouth like a man with a stuffed-up nose. "Oh please, Mama," I whispered. "Please." And this time, her quiver empty and her arrows all well placed, our mother relented. "Yes, Mr. Watson, we are still your slaves," she sighed, offering a sweet rueful smile. " '*Wives, submit yourselves unto your own husbands as unto the Lord. For the husband is head of the wife, even as Christ is head of the Church.*' " Braving his glare, she added winsomely, "Ephesians, dear."

"Precisely because we soldiers cannot vote," shouted our Papa, "South Carolina remains prostrate, at the mercy of damn Scalawags and their pet niggers! That's Radical Reconstruction for you! *That's* what your precious cousin fought for!" He whirled toward me. "Do you know who forced Reconstruction through the Yankee Senate, Edgar? The leader of the Abolitionists, Charles Sumner of Massachusetts! And do you know why?"

"Oh we do, indeed we do," sighed Mama. "And since we know that story so well, perhaps you will spare us yet another telling—"

"Yes! Because Congressman Preston Brooks of Edgefield caned Sumner on the Senate floor for having insulted Brooks's kinsman Andrew Pickens Butler! And Senator Butler—hear me, boy!—was the son of that same Lieutenant Billy Butler to whom Captain Michael Watson turned over the command of his brigade when fatally wounded by the Tories near Clouds Creek!"

Deftly Mama lured him off the subject of our Watson hero. "Now which Mr. Brooks shot that black legislator the other day, dear? While he knelt in prayer?"

"That was Nat Butler!"

"In any case, children, Congressman Preston Brooks was my father's commanding officer in the Mexican War. Unlike Clouds Creek, the Court House was strongly represented in that war." Before Papa could protest, she cried, "Think of it, children. The Brooks mansion has four acres of flowers! In the front."

But Elijah Watson was not to be deterred. The caning of Senator Sumner had occurred on May 22 of 1856, six months after my birth, and once again Papa invoked that event to imbue his son with the fierce and forthright spirit of the South. He went on to extol John C. Calhoun, grandson of Squire Calhoun of Long Cane Creek, whose family lost twenty-three members to Indian massacres in a single year.

"One day I saw the great Calhoun right here in Edgefield. Same lean leather face and deep hawk eyes as Andy Jackson, Old Hickory himself. Same breed of fearless Carolinian, unrelenting."

"Cruelty and vengeance. Are these the virtues you would inspire in your son?"

Papa, in full cry, paid her no heed. Before the War, said he, our patriots had served in the Patrol, and in these dark days of Yankee Reconstruction, the Patrol's place had been taken by that honorable company of men known as the Regulators amongst whom he was very proud to ride.

"Honorable company!" Mama rolled her eyes over her knitting. Her needle points sped with a clicking noise like feeding beetles. She slapped her knitting down. "Is it considered honorable in this company of yours to harm defenseless darkies?" Braving his glare, she quoted Cousin Selden's opinion that the vigilantes who terrorized the freedmen were mostly "those weak vessels cracked by war." And she dared to cite Papa's "so-called" superior officer, Major William Coulter, who—

"Will Coulter rode with General Nathan Bedford Forrest!"

—who keeps the cropped ears of lynched black men in his saddlebags. "No outrage perpetrated by that man, however barbarous and vile, seems to shake your father's high opinion of him," Mama sighed, implying that her husband, not being warped or cracked like Major Coulter, had been weak to start with. She would even hint that Papa had joined the vigilantes less out of conviction than because he knew no better place for a man with battlefield demotions.

REGULATORS

The Regulators made most of their patrols on nights of the full moon. Major Will Coulter, Captain Lige Watson, Sergeant Z. P. Claxton, and two younger men, Toney and Lott, were the five regulars. Others would come along when needed and a black man on a mule tended the horses.

Lige Watson rode with a rifle in a saddle scabbard, a revolver in his belt, a hidden Bowie knife. From time to time, he would teach his son those arts of which Mama so disapproved: how to race horses, how to shoot, how to wield a knife. Sometimes he let me taste his whiskey, and when he was drinking, he might show me "just for fun" how to cheat at cards. But as I would learn, Papa was barely competent in most of these attainments, which he confused with manhood. Because I was only twelve, I confused them, too.

One happy day, he swung me up behind on his big roan. "Come along, boy, I'll show you something," he promised, grinning. We rode toward Edgefield. At Deepwood, Cousin Selden stepped forth onto the highroad in linen shirtsleeves, stretching his arms wide to bar our progress as the horse danced and whinnied, backing around in its own stomped-up dust.

"Not one word," Papa growled over his shoulder.

Our slender kinsman murmured to the roan, slipping his hand onto the bridle so that Papa could not wheel into him, knock him away. The easy movement was so sure of horse and rider that the muscles stiffened in my father's back. "Stand back, sir," he snarled, shifting his quirt to his right hand as if set to strike Tilghman on the face.

With his long fair hair and shy expression and high tenor voice, Cousin Selden looked less like a brave cavalry officer than a young clergyman. Because he had never married, Papa called him a "sissy" out of Mama's hearing. However, that high voice of his was calm and very cold. "There's three young nigras back up yonder in the branch. Wrists bound, shot like dogs. Since today is the Sabbath, Private Watson, I hoped you might assist me with a Christian burial."

To call a man "Private" who was known as "Captain" to the Regulators was proof enough of Selden Tilghman's madness. "Dumped there last night," he persisted. "These murder gangs ride at night, isn't that true?" He had a fever in his eyes. His quiet fury and contempt seemed just as scary as Papa's red eruptive rage. "Since you claim him as a kinsman, Private Watson, you cannot have forgotten the immortal words of Jefferson of Virginia." Here he shouted, *"I tremble for my country when I reflect that God is just!"*

Papa had raised his quirt but that shout stopped him; he could not bring himself to strike a Confederate officer. "We have no business with traitors, damn you! Stand aside!" Yanking his reins, digging his spurs, he fought violently to ride free, his son clinging like a tree frog to his sweaty back. Tilghman braced against the horse's neck, letting it lift him. Hand clenching the reins under the bit, talking it down, he brought the wheeling roan under control.

Heavy in the saddle, shoulders slumped, Papa, too, appeared subdued. So close to my nose, his smell was bitter, rank. "Damned road walkers," he muttered.

"Road walkers. And how do you know that, Private? How would you happen to know so much about those murdered boys?"

"Because if they were home niggers, sir, a Radical Scalawag and traitor like yourself would know his nigger friends by name! Now stand aside!" Whistling like a pigeon's wing, his quirt struck Tilghman on the temple, knocking him off balance, and still our cousin gripped the reins as the big roan reared and snorted, dancing sideways. A moment later, struck violently again, he fell away. Papa shouted, "Your honorable record in the War is all that stands between you and execution as a traitor!"

Cousin Selden rose unhurriedly, brushed himself off. His pale face was bleeding. "My honorable record. What would Private Watson know about such matters?" he inquired, looking straight at Watson's son.

"Are you challenging my honor?" Papa demanded. "I served four years, Edgefield to Appomattox!" But when I hollered, "Nigger-loving traitor!" at our cousin, my father shot an elbow back, bloodied my nose. "Show respect for an officer of the Confederacy, even this one!" I was astonished by his need to prove to Sissy Selden that Elijah Watson was a guardian of Southern honor.

Cousin Selden and I wiped bloody noses. When Selden noticed our peculiar bond, he grinned; I had to scowl at him lest I grin back. "Send her cousin's fond respects to your dear mother, Edgar," he said quietly, as Papa wheeled, booting his horse into a canter. Hand on the hard-haired dusty rump, I turned for a last look at the figure in the road, and Cousin Selden raised his hand in half salute. "God keep you, Cousin Edgar!"

"Face around, damn you!" Papa shouted, cocking his elbow. "Face around, I say!" I hugged up close, out of harm's way. He galloped homeward.

THE TRAITOR

Desperate to please Papa, I once referred to Cousin Selden as "a sissy." Mama boxed my ears, reminding me that he was a decorated hero and that he had given me those books on ancient Greece to compensate for my woeful lack of schooling. To be so ungrateful to a benefactor was a sin! Hearing how concerned he'd been on my behalf upset and shamed me but I could not admit this. "Who cares about those darned old Greeks?" I said.

"One day, Edgar, you will care," she retorted. "You are still an ignorant boy but you are not stupid."

The day after our ride to Deepwood, the Traitor (as my father now referred to him) appeared at our door in full uniform, hands and face charred like a minstrel's, gray tunic rent by black and ragged holes. Having long since sold his horse, he had come on foot. On the sill he set down a heavy sack containing the rest of his volumes of Greek literature, saved from his burning house. "For your boy," he told Mama, who ignored her husband's edict and implored him to come in. He accepted a cup of water but would not enter the house nor even linger, lest his presence bring trouble down upon us.

In dread, I trailed him down the road toward the square. Already word had circulated that the cast-out hero would defy the Regulators' edict that he leave Edgefield District on pain of death; his apparition on the square ignited a wildfire whispering.

My kinsman hailed the market crowd from the courthouse steps. Off to the east, the black smoke rose from Deepwood. He made no mention of night riders or his half-burned house but simply denounced the murder of three Negro youths on the night before last. The refusal of a lawless few to accept the freedmen as new citizens, he cried, would imperil their own mortal souls and cripple the recovery of South Carolina. "Before the War, our colored folk lived among us and worshipped in our congregations. Most remained loyal during the War and many fought beside us." He paused, seeking out faces. "Yet today there are those who revile these faithful friends, who treat them as dangerous animals and kill them. Every day black men are terrorized, not by outlaws and criminals but by so-called good Christian men, including some who stand here now before our court of justice!"

He glared about him. "Have not these poor souls suffered enough? What fault of theirs that they were enslaved and then turned free? Was it they who imposed the laws that you protest? Friends, it was not!" He raised both arms toward Heaven. "In taking revenge on innocents for the calamity and holy wrath we brought down upon ourselves, we only worsen a dishonorable lie." He paused in the deepening silence. "We lost the War not because we were beaten by a greater force of arms. Yes, the North had more soldiers and more guns, more industry, more railways, that is true. But that was also our excuse, as we who fought knew well." He paused again, lowering his arms slowly in the awful hush. "More than half our eastern armies— and our bravest, too—put down their arms and went home of their own volition. They did that because in their hearts they knew that human bondage could never have the blessing of Him who created man in His different colors."

When yells of "Traitor!" started up and the first rock flew, Selden Tilghman raised his hands and voice, desperate to finish. "Our officers will tell you—those who are honest—that we only fought on so that the lives of our bravest young men should not have been sacrificed in vain. Thousands died for some false notion of our Southern honor and to no good purpose, and now our dear land lies ruined on all sides.

"Where is that honor now? In taking cowardly revenge in acts of terror in the night, do we not dishonor those who lost their lives? Neighbors, hear me, I beseech you! The 'Great Lost Cause' was never 'great,' as we pretended! It had no greatness in it and no honor! It was merely wrong!" He yelled "Wrong!" again into my father's face as the Regulators rushed the steps and seized him.

Dragged down to the square and beaten bloody, our cousin was left in a poor heap in the public dust. I witnessed this. Round and round the crumpled body stalked Will Coulter, hair raked back in black wings beneath his cap, stiff-legged and gawky as a crow. Seeing Claxton leering as he kicked the fallen man, I longed to rush to interfere. Perhaps others did, too, but no one dared invade the emptiness around that thin still form.

When Selden Tilghman regained consciousness, he lay a while before rolling slowly to his knees. Visage ghostly from the dust, he got up painfully, reeled, and fell. Eventually, he pushed himself onto all fours and crawled all the way across the square to the picket fence in front of the veranda of the United States Hotel where Coulter and his jeering men awaited him. Using the fence to haul himself upright, he pointed a trembling finger at the Regulators. "Cowards!" he cried. "Betrayers of the South!" He repeated this over and over. With each "Cowards!" he brought both fists down hard on the sharp points of the white pickets, and with each blow he howled in agony and despair, until the wet meat sounds of his broken hands caused the onlookers to turn away in horror—until at last Captain Lige Watson of the Regulators strode forth at a sign from Coulter and cracked Tilghman's jaw with a legendary blow, leaving him inert in the dust.

Selden Tilghman was slung into a cotton wagon and trundled away on the Augusta Road. In the next fortnight rumors would come that the Traitor was dumped at the gates of the Radical headquarters at Hamburg on the Georgia border, where in 1819, a slave rebellion led by "Coot" or "Coco" had filled Edgefield District with night fears. But nobody really wished to know what had become of him, far less recall what they had witnessed in the Court House Square. When Mama finally confronted him, Papa blustered, "Well, Regulators never killed him, I know that much!"

One day I awoke to recognize that my great pride in my father was shot through with misgiving. Hoping our cousin might somehow reappear—

dreading it, too—I was drawn back to Deepwood over and over. Others in our district avoided it, afraid of "Tilghman's Ghost," which was said to come and go in that charred ruin. Wild rose and poverty grass invaded its fields, the woods edged forward, and wild vines entwined it. When the wind stirred, I imagined I could hear an ethereal wailing and sad whispered warning: *Cousin Edgar!*

RING-EYE LIGE

Late in 1868, "the Bad Elijah" (Papa's nickname at Clouds Creek) sold his share of our Artemas Plantation to "the Good Elijah," my great-uncle Elijah Junior, an uprooting that worsened the tumult of his disposition and hastened the dissolution of our family.

For a few years we lived at Edgefield Court House, in a poor section off the Augusta Road. Our neighbors on both sides were freedmen whom Papa scarcely deigned to greet, not even old Tap, whose people had been black Watsons for a hundred years. Though good for nothing much when not on horseback, he felt humiliated because his wife asked Tap to help him find work as a common laborer, then lost this job in a matter of days for the same drunken insubordination which, according to his uncle Tillman, had gotten him in trouble throughout the War.

Beset by debt, Papa found work at the factory owned by Captain Gregg, whose father, in the first half of the century, had imported Europe's industrial revolution to the Carolinas, constructing textile mills at Vaucluse and Graniteville, southwest of Edgefield. In these dark times when so many needed work, Papa took such pride as he could summon in his new employment, which favored veterans from Captain Gregg's old regiment and was "closed to niggers." At Graniteville he earned nineteen dollars a month, spent mostly in support of his own drinking habit and the brothels of Augusta. Or so his scrimping wife suspected, outraged by the pittance he brought home when he happened to turn up of a Sunday morning.

Papa would remind me how lucky I was to be working out in the fresh air and not in those "dark, Satanic mills" (Mama, quoting Milton) where children as young as eight or nine worked fourteen-hour days beside the adults. He described the pervasive darkness in that deep Horse Creek ravine, the cold, grim aspect that had scarcely changed since the time of the eighteenth-century outlaws and highwaymen who had murdered pioneer Watsons before the Revolution and were finally destroyed by our illustrious ancestor—

"Oh for pity's sake, let us hear no more of Colonel Michael!"

For the fabled Captain Michael of the American Revolution, Mama had perversely substituted that inconsequential colonel whose widow Tabitha had hustled the virginal Ellen Addison into the clumsy embrace of young Lige Watson. In their early days, as a kind of wry flirtation, it had amused my parents to blame their fractious marriage on Aunt Tabitha, and it would be Mama's lifelong view that Auntie Tab with her intolerable meddling had ruined a young girl's life. She would state this grievance as plain fact, not in self-pity, and also as a torment to her husband, whom she pursued with sharp pecks on the head like a redwing harrying a crow. When not bruised blue from his latest drunken beating, I almost pitied him.

As his fortunes diminished and his reputation ebbed, Papa's need for conviviality increased. Wild-eyed and boisterous, he laughed ever more loudly, even as his face betrayed his deepening confusion and anxiety. On Sundays he wandered the still town, invading church meetings and even funerals, in flight from solitude. At the crossroad tavern, he held forth loudly on such topics as fine horseflesh, Scalawags and Carpetbaggers, insolent niggers, weapons, Southern honor, our beautiful Southern ladies, and the Great Lost Cause. Vaingloriously would he extol the warrior society of Edgefield, boasting of those Edgefieldians of yore who fought in the Indian Wars and the American Revolution, not to mention the gallant volunteers, Watsons among them, who rode away to the War of 1812, the Seminole Wars, and the War with Mexico. Modestly might he venture to mention their obedient servant Captain Elijah D. Watson, and also Major Tillman Watson and Colonel Robert Briggs Watson of Clouds Creek, whose gallant service in the War of Northern Aggression had done such honor to the Watson clan and to the great sovereign state of South Carolina.

On occasion, Papa's oratory was challenged by veterans with different memories of his war years—ill-natured men who refused to recall his field commission and sneered at his Regulator captaincy, asserting that Watson was better known for dereliction and courts martial than for deeds of battle. A willing brawler, at least when in his cups, my father dealt forcefully with naysayers until that saloon evening when he was parted from his wits by a well-wielded horseshoe and left groaning in the sawdust, though not before a Bowie knife had carved a ring around his right eye. The raw livid scar made him look bug-eyed, glaring out of a red bull's-eye at impending doom. "Ring-Eye Lige," his sobriquet forever after, became the badge of final disrepute for our forlorn family.

When Papa was absent and then only—for the smallest reflection on his tender honor would propel him into fury—our household was modestly assisted by Mama's brother, who served as an attorney at the courthouse. Uncle John Addison arranged part-time employment for his sister as a clerk and also paid the school fees for her children: for a brief period, I was actually enrolled in Edgefield's Male Academy, from which, however, I was shortly dismissed for backing the frightened pedant into a corner. "Menacing the schoolmaster" was the formal charge. This episode was brought about by the plaintiff's snide reference to "Ring-Eye Lige," which his student, in an "ominous and silent manner," had warned him never to repeat. Far from flogging me, Papa hooted in triumph, having perceived John Addison's assistance with our schooling as a personal insult. "Pity you didn't cane him, boy, like Brooks caned Sumner on the Senate floor!" (He was only deterred by his wife's blighted expression from visiting his favorite story yet again.) Welcoming his son back to the ranks of honest workingmen, Papa ridiculed Mama's despair that I had ruined my best hope of an education. Not until he discovered that the humiliated teacher was a Butler kinsman did he strip off his belt and flog me unmercifully as a young ruffian who had spoiled our family's chance of regaining its place in the society of Edgefield Court House.

When Papa left to go to work in Graniteville, I took his place as a field hand in the cotton, intensifying Mama's bitterness toward her husband. She redoubled her efforts to tutor her young Edgar, whom the school had judged "intelligent and industrious" shortly before pointing at the door. "You were born into this cruel world in the same year that dear Charlotte Brontë was taken from us," she lamented, stuffing my brain with the English literature she so loved as well as the doom-ridden Greek classics left to me by Cousin Selden, the last remnant of his Deepwood library. Much too young to do the chores at dawn and dusk as well as field labor all day, then apply myself to the classics in the evening, I fell asleep in Ancient Greece night after night.

Mama, although not yet forty, was looking pinched and aged from overwork. Even so, she made time to play with my baby sister Mary Lucretia, known as Minnie, in the slave-made wooden toy box in which she herself had rummaged as a little girl. Humming songs of childhood, sorting tops and marbles, she recalled for her daughter her own antebellum memories of village fairs and berry-picking parties, birthdays and spelling bees, of fine silver service and the Addison piano and family china fired from our fine-grained Edgefield clay by an English visitor, Mr. Josiah Wedgwood. On the backrest of her last good chair she had embroidered: *Beauty is truth, truth beauty—that is all ye know on earth, and all ye need to know.* ("Now surely, Mr. Watson, you have no quarrel with John Keats?") She invited "the head of the household" to be first to use the chair, watching his wary seating of himself with that half-hidden hilarity that her uneasy children could not fathom, having no acquaintance with hysteria.

Mama was adept with the floral patterns of embroidery but knew nothing about mending, far less cooking meals or keeping house. For these tasks she depended on Cinderella Myers, the tall Indian-boned black woman in the next cabin, who had been her house slave and was now her neighbor and unrecognized true friend. Aunt Cindy, as we'd come to call her, brought sorghum, boiled potatoes, corn bread, sometimes greens or peas. In summer she made sarsaparilla and in winter parched-corn coffee. In the evenings, when flax was to be had, she wove homespun for both families, linens in summer, linsey-woolsey in the winter. Throughout the War, she had helped her Miss Ellen faithfully, and Tap Watson, in his distempered way, had continued to look out for Marse Artemas's descendants when the War was over. For all his grumbling, he accompanied his wife and little girl when they followed Miss Ellen to Edgefield Court House, where, being handy and dependable, he soon found a job. The daughter, young nut-hued Lulalie, helped out, too.

Though this child was scarcely ten, her innocent touch tingled my skin and a certain provocative aroma made her wholly edible as a baked candied yam. Fortunately she never noticed my adolescent interest in her person, my yearning to caress her. In truth, young Lalie loved another, namely Minnie, whom she strove mightily to bring to life with her own glad spirits, dragging my pale and shrinking sister out into the sun, then racing back inside to fetch the toys. "Gone be back with mo' fun in a minute now, Mis Minnie!" she would promise, already having fun enough for both of them. Blithely Lalie would create fanciful bonnets they might play in, using small thorns to pin bright leaves into their frocks and hair. But out of doors, my sickly dark-haired sister was forever fretting, peering fearfully over her shoulder. Trailing Lalie through the whortleberry patch, Minnie wept woefully over what Aunt Cindy called "brambledy fingers." She soiled her Sunday dress while gathering vegetables and suffered a spurring by our rooster while trying to help her well-wisher feed the chickens. Yet timid Min did well at the Female Academy and soon became what the teachers called "a happy little scholar." "Happy because unpreyed upon," Mama observed, in reference to Papa's habit of baring Minnie's pale behind over his knee and gazing upon it one moment too long before clearing his throat and spanking it rose pink.

After Papa went to Graniteville, Mama joined me in the sharecropped cotton, yanking or whacking down the tough old stalks in the late autumn, digging and manuring the new furrows through the winter, planting in April, thinning in May. In June and July, when the plants blossomed, we cultivated with short hoes and from mid-August late into the fall, we picked the open bolls, hauling the cotton in burlap sacking to the gin, where it was processed and packed for the market. The small fingers that had danced and fluttered light as butterflies over ivory keys of the Addison piano became ever redder and more swollen as her hands turned coarse, but if this dismayed my mother, she refused to show it.

Disrespectful of her lord and master, Mama worshipped her Lord and Maker at Edgefield's Trinity Episcopal, whose severe facade and glinting steeple pointed the sinner's steep ascending way toward the firmament. She looked forward to Heaven. "This World Is Not My Home, I Have No Mansions Here" was her favorite hymn, whereas Aunt Cindy would hum "In My Father's House Are Many Mansions." Like most of the old-time darkies at Silver Bluff Baptist, she preferred the New Testament's Sweet Lord of Love and Mercy on this Earth to her white folks' punishing Old Testament Jehovah, threatening all falterers at Trinity Episcopal with his terrible swift sword out of a cold gray sky.

RABBIT GUM

From the first year of the War, when I was five, until the age of fifteen, when I fled Edgefield District for good, I had very little to show for life besides the calluses and grime of endless seasons of hard labor, lice, mean dirt, and poverty. Every hour of every day not spent hacking a crop, I was trapping and snaring, fishing and gathering, even stealing from other gardens for our hungry family. We subsisted on clabber, that mix of thin milk, curds, and whey which looked like the source of Minnie's pasty complexion.

Black Tap Watson, not my father, taught me how to hunt and gather, how to set fine horsehair snares and sturdy rabbit gums, where to find wild tubers and the gopher tortoise, when to fish the creeks. In the wake of war, the common game—bear, deer, coon, and turkey, dove, quail, and wild duck—had all but vanished from South Carolina. Only young squirrels and blundering possums, with a rare rabbit or robin, fell to my sling. In summer, I gigged frogs and pin-hooked little fish to eke out the clabber and dandelion greens, the hardtack biscuits, dusty beans, and mouse-stained grits in our meager larder.

Occasionally, in winter dusk, returning from my trapline out at Deepwood, I would wrench a few collards and cold muddy turnips from Tap's patch next door. It was no sin to borrow vegetables from people "who had welcomed the Yankee bluecoats, then dared to lord it over their former benefactors," as my father put it. Proudly would Papa have us know that Elijah D. Watson would never "accept charity from niggers," while Mama, for her part, made certain he knew that his needy family was provided daily sustenance by his black neighbors.

One afternoon in the twilight gloom, Tap appeared from behind his cabin. I straightened, putting a bold face on it, bringing from behind my back my stolen greens. Embarrassed, Tap lowered his stave. "You gettin so big, I took you for your daddy." That the irascible old man said nothing else made clear I'd never fooled him; he had ignored my raiding for some time. He disappeared then but his rasp came back out of the dark. "Take what you be needin, White Man, jus' so's you know dat Black Man gots to eat, de same as you." My holler that we aimed to pay him brought a derisive hoot. I shouted, furious, "Think we need charity from niggers?" Hearing nothing, I called, "Tap? I was aiming to bring you folks a rabbit."

"*Rabbit?*" Tap's whoop came from his cabin door. "Some ol' nigger must teached dat white boy purty good, he gwine cotch *rabbits!*"

I tossed those greens onto our table, telling Mama they had come from "the Black Watsons." Though this was true, my sullen way of speaking told her they were stolen, for she banged her heavy pot on the iron stove. "Nigger greens," I teased her. "Just toss 'em out if you don't want 'em, Mama."

In our poverty, waste troubled her far more than theft. "Hush," she said, stoking the fire to boil water. "Our Lord provideth in our hour of need. To despise His bounty would be sinful." Mama would set aside my sin until the greens were eaten; she never refused her share of my ill-gotten gleanings.

Coldly I said, " '*And the thought of eating came to her when she was wearied of her tears.*' " She stared at me. "From Cousin Selden's *Iliad.*" She held my eye a moment, then turned back to the stove. "Good," she murmured, a response to insolence that made me nervous. (Only later did I understand that she was mollified because her son perused the classics.) Told that Tap had dared raise a stick to me, she said "Good" a second time; on Tap's behalf she gave the stove another wallop, scaring weak-eyed Minnie, who was bent deep into her primer as if to inhale her lessons through her nose.

At supper, Mama reminded us that Tap, for all his gall and sour temper, had remained loyal all our lives and was therefore entitled to forget his place in certain minor matters. Old-time darkies, after all, often adopted gruff impertinence for want of a better way to express affection. Being well taken care of by their white folks, they had lost the fear that made most of their people mumble and shuffle and play dumb to get along.

Tap Watson was the old kind of church Negro, Mama said, proud as could be that Silver Bluff Baptist, founded before the Revolutionary War, "was de oldes' nigger church in de whole of de whole country." True, its first minister had been a white man, but back in those days, black and white worshipped together. (Tap had attended "white folks church" without much spiritual reward. "All dat preacher spokin about is niggers strickly mindin Marster and Missus cause dem is de kin'ly-hearted folks dat's feedin you for Christ's sweet sake, Amen.")

Neither Emancipation nor Reconstruction had changed things very much, she said. The evil hostility between the races had begun in the first year of the War when the black faithful were banished to the church balcony. "Since the War, the poor things are not welcome at all, but mercifully they have their own nice church and their own Book of Genesis, too." (Tap Watson preached that Adam and Eve had started out in life as darkies, but after their sin, they turned so pale with fear of the Lord's wrath that they passed for white folks ever after.) These days, alas, the Negro churches were being harassed by the Ku Klux Klan, a mostly nocturnal organization founded by Major Coulter's commanding officer, General Forrest, he who in the last year of the War had approved the slaughter of unarmed black Union prisoners.

Tap was proud of his citizenship, proud of his vote, yet he was still cautious, holding that progress must be nurtured slowly lest it perish. He had been stoic about Z. P. Claxton's execution of his runaway son, and he had not protested the Black Codes, which flouted Reconstruction by discouraging blacks from leaving their plantations, owning land, or even leasing it. Though he understood that for the black man, this was a time of terrible danger as well as hope, he had no interest in emigration to Liberia. Edgefield, where he was born a slave, was where Tap aimed to die as a free man.

White folks pointed to Tap Watson as a fine representative of the Negro race, and because his loyalty was trusted, he was mostly forgiven his acid yellow eye and abrasive tongue. True, he was sour about whites, but he was just as sour about "Negroes." Asked his opinion by the Edgefield *Advertiser*, he would neither repudiate nor approve a black man whose "genteel manner" and "good sense" had won high praise before the War but who was now denounced in the same newspaper for "swagger and bad character" because he had urged new "Negro" citizens to vote. As Tap intoned without a smile, "Them 'Negroes' gone to get us niggers killed."

The Papa I had once revered was drinking so unstintingly that I feared not for his life but for my own. Pleading or protesting, seen as defiance, only fed his drunkard's fury as with hoarse gasps of stinking breath he punched and clouted me about the head or lashed me raw with a green switch across the back and legs. At such times, that rufous face looked demented and misshapen: how could it be that I still prayed this smelly brute might love me?

"Mr. Watson, I beg of you," was all Mama said by way of protest. I learned early to expect no help from my mother. As for Minnie, she wet herself at the first hoarse shout, and her panic when the moment came to flee often caused me to be caught and beaten while trying to save her. Worse, she betrayed me to Papa every time we quarreled, complaining that her brother had been mean. Mama, too, used the threat of Papa's violence to twist me to her will; it was injustice more than burning pain and terror and humiliation which raised tears to my eyes and stoked the rage which made it possible to hide them.

I never let Papa see me weep and never yelped, just set my jaw and bit down hard on pain in the rigid way a dog clamps on another's throat, forging my will like some fanatic in Hell's fire until his demons wore out and his arm, too, all the while swearing secret oaths of vengeance.

"Oh, you poor boy! Are you all right?" Mama's murmured concern always came too late to spare me. When I only gazed at her by way of answer, her eyes got jumpy and veered off. "Please, Edgar," she might beg, "it scares me when your eyes shiver that way." The show of derangement was a poor revenge but I knew no other; my voice would have broken if I'd said one word. Eventually I realized that the "crazy" eyes that scared her were the first manifestation of "Jack Watson," a shadow brother I had conceived out of loneliness after black Joseph's death, having had neither time nor opportunity for friendship. Though Jack came unbidden, I would know that he was there from the sudden uneasiness of others.

The first time Papa beat me to unconsciousness (perhaps I fainted from the pain), Mama fled across the yard to seek comfort on Aunt Cindy's bosom rather than offer comfort to her son, who lay on the dirt floor in a dark realm from which all sun and color and all past and future had been struck away. In a dream, my mother's figure pressed against a wall. Slowly she raised a fingertip to seal her lips, keeping God's secret, bearing witness to His acts, not intervening.

One day Minnie crept out of her cranny to find her brother, his whole body shaking, hauling himself onto his knees, using the bedpost, intent on the father sprawled upon his mattress. I never noticed her until she whimpered. When I turned, that whimper turned to a whine of fear—not at my bloody face but because crazy-eyed Jack Watson peered out through that grimace. The child cringed back as from an apparition.

Though by no means deficient—she was bright—Minnie's speech had become crippled by her fears, but like certain blind folk, she could apprehend what commonly escaped others, and she had been first to recognize an alien presence. "Oh Edgar please, I don't know who you are!" she begged that first time, her voice seeming to call from faraway. Then the black bubble around brow and brain dissolved with a soft pop, and Jack was gone and time and space and sound and colors rushed back in—the thick rufous carcass in its fume of moonshine, the reek of broken dogshit boots, and the little girl shrieking as the body humped up in a great cough and thrash, fell off the bed, rose to all fours and then unsteadily erect.

Elijah D. Watson stared about him like a man emerging from his root cellar after a tornado, wondering if his loved ones have survived. Relieved to see me on my feet, he offered a loose salute and grin. "No man can say Lige Watson's boy don't stand up and take his punishment!"

Incredibly his stupid praise was solace. I could not know that one day soon I would vow to my shadow brother that when the time came, I would take his hidden musket from the rafters and blow that red-faced sweaty head clean off its shoulders.

TURNIPS

The night that old Tap caught me in his truck-patch, Mama said, "I shall have to tell your father"—though not, as usual, until after she et her fill. She had scarcely spoken when her spouse came barging through the door in soiled silk neckerchief and muddy boots and cavalry greatcoat of soiled gray which stank of booze and horses when it rained. Minnie gave a tiny shriek like a rabbit pierced by the quick teeth of a fox. I shouted, waving her outside. Dark eyes round, the little girl was off her chair and scurrying for the door, which the man had left open despite cold blowing rain. When she faltered, whining at the darkness, I shoved her outside into the weather, and she tumbled and blew across the muddy yard toward Aunt Cindy's cabin.

Papa was glaring at the door I had slammed closed. When Mama said coldly, "What is it, Mr. Watson?" he stared at his seditious wife in stupefaction. "Please, Mama," I whispered. But she scarcely saw me, so intent was she upon her quarry.

Mama's vice, too, had worsened with our fortunes: mean teasing had become cruel baiting. She would poke her husband, nip at him, dance back with a delighted cry of fear when he surged suddenly toward rage, then trip forth once more in trembling suspense, prolonging her delight, as if this were the sole ecstasy that her life with him had left her. No longer able to restrain herself, she dared too much, exposing us all to a careening din that would leave the cabin shattered, deathly still. And always she insinuated that the young son was the true head of this accursed family, with responsibility to protect it from the rogue father.

"Have some turnips, Mr. Watson." Mama spooned them up out of the pot and dumped them smartly onto a plate. "All we have to feed your little family, Mr. Watson." In his life defeat, he scarcely heard her. "Nice fresh turnips from your neighbor's garden." she concluded neatly.

Papa lurched to his feet, overturning his chair. "Charity? From niggers?"

She clenched her cotton-pricked hard hands, then folded them beneath her apron—the very picture of sweet Miss Ellen Addison, she of the wasp waist and pretty primrose face and flying fingers. "You see, we are so famished in your household that your son was reduced to theft—" She stopped short. "Run," she told me.

But Papa had caught hold of my arm. I put my other arm around him, trying to slip in under the blows, hugging the thick trunk of him with all my might, but he swung me so violently, hurling me away, that my boots came off the floor. My head struck a log butt in the wall, and the world was obliterated as my brain exploded. People talk about seeing stars. A single star is all I ever saw, bursting forth in blades of fire that flashed through blackness and oblivion.

Ghost voices, apparitions. Had night come? I did not know who or where I was, or why I lay inert. My brain was fixed in an iron vise of agony. I was unable to clear mist from my eyes or move a muscle lest I vomit.

Hiding behind slack eyelids, I half-watched, half-listened; the shadow figures did not know I had returned. The shrouded woman sat holding a hand. My hand? I felt nothing. I wondered if my brain might not be bleeding. The man, in grainy silhouette, was staring out his small window into darkness. He had scared himself. He spoke: "He is too hard-headed. There is no discipline he will submit to." The woman did not bother to remind him that if the son was ungovernable, the father was to blame, having stoked a rebellious nature by these beatings. She said none of that. She said, "I see. It was his fault, then." She put my hand down, having forgotten it. "What a low beast you have become, Elijah Watson. The boy works night and day to support your family, he has never done you harm, no, quite the contrary. It is you who do him harm, time and again."

Hearing her voice speak up for me at last, my eyes welled; surprised, I had to struggle not to weep. "Are you so depraved with all your grog and fornication," her voice continued, "that you would risk his life?"

The man's voice mumbled that it was an accident. He did not know for the life of him why this boy put him in a fury. He was lachrymose, baffled, scared, contrite, but he was also, as I now knew well, quite capable in drink of taking his son's life. I heard a strange voice, dull, slow, and swollen: "If you ever lay hands on me again—on any of us, Papa—I will kill you."

Her voice: "Merciful goodness! Rest, Edgar. You must rest." Had I spoken aloud? Had I imagined it? Either way, my threat made my fingers twitch and my saliva flow, it sent strange ecstatic shivers through my neck and arms that caused a bloodburst in my brain and the return of blackness.

For a fortnight, I suffered fainting spells, unholy headaches. I would force my gut hard against my stomach wall to fire my resolve and keep my head from splitting. When Minnie pled that next time I must beg for mercy, I swore I would never stoop to "that low beast," as Mama had called him, not if he split my noggin like a frozen pumpkin. But of course, by the time I recovered, he was drinking as before, and I was trying to please him as before, being doomed to love him.

When sober enough to sit up in the saddle, Lige Watson rode with the Edge-field Rifle and Sabre Club—a detachment of the Regulators—having earned a reputation as a man who was good with horses and "would do the necessary" to protect the honor of the South and Southern womanhood; he went about his duties with grim fervor. But even Papa, who could be generous and not invariably unkind, had grown disturbed by the fanaticism of his commander. Apparently Sergeant Z. P. Claxton had accused Tap Watson of showing a hostile countenance to a white man. Advised by Captain Watson that this man on Claxton's list was actually "a pretty good ol' nigra," Major Coulter gave him a long look of warning. "Sometimes it gets so us ol' boys might feel like killing us a nigger," Coulter told him in a low dead voice. "At them times it don't matter much if he's a pretty good ol' nigger or he ain't. Whether he done something or didn't, understand me?"

Papa boasted to his family that thanks to his efforts, Tap was spared without ever knowing he had been in danger. Papa hoped his son was proud of his good deed. The trouble was that unlike him, I understood—or at least Jack Watson understood—what Major Coulter meant. Us ol' boys might *feel* like killing—wasn't that the point? Feel like it. Major Coulter's remark gnawed at my heart, less because it sounded so cold-blooded than because it prized out from its seam something unnatural in my own nature—or something worse, a self I feared without knowing who it was, a hidden countenance of profound ire as cold as that chill breath on the wind that is a harbinger of weather change and storm.

Even in Reconstruction days, most men of Edgefield would not tolerate a black who failed to make way for them on the plank sidewalks, and Elijah D. Watson, as his status declined, demanded more respect than most. One day as I trailed him home, his careening gait would not permit an elderly black woman to edge out of his way; she was forced off into the deep mud street just as a man in frock coat, shining boots, and long curved sideburns hooked forward at the lower jaw like a peregrine falcon, came swinging his wood leg around the corner. Blood rushed to my face as he extended a gloved hand and handed the old darkie back onto the boards—hauled her back would be closer to the spirit of it—with a distaste impartially extended to all parties. The man ignored her babble and both Watsons, swinging forward on his wooden leg as the woman hurried off in her muddied dress.

Matthew Calbraith Butler, commanding a cavalry regiment under General J. E. B. Stuart at the battle at Brandy Station in Virginia, had lost a leg leading a charge but returned to his command not long thereafter. When Private Ring-Eye staggered after him, braying that he was not a man to be insulted and further, that Captain Michael Watson had been Butler's grandfather's superior officer in Pickens's Brigade, Calbraith Butler checked the drunkard's onrush by placing the point of his cane against his chest just hard enough to redirect him off the boards. On his knees in the mud, Private Watson was coldly chastised for imposition on a general officer.

Because his son had witnessed his humiliation, Elijah Watson, still on his knees, challenged the young general to a duel. General Butler stated with hauteur that Watson was not privileged to fight a duel since he had never been an officer and was no longer a gentleman. What he was, said

Butler, was a disgrace to a good family as well as to the filthied uniform which he still wore.

Shamed beyond endurance, I cried out, "Duel with his son, then, if you are not a coward!" But my voice broke grotesquely in its adolescent croak, and Calbraith Butler permitted himself a narrow smile. "When it comes to dueling with boys," he told me quietly, "I am indeed faint-hearted, Master Watson." With a slight bow, he turned and kept on going in strong limping stride and shortly disappeared around the corner.

As street idlers hooted gleefully, hailing "Ring-Eye" by that name, my mud-footed father bellowed outrage that an unschooled ragged boy should dare to challenge an Edgefield hero. "Call out General Butler? *You?*" Jeering loudly for his audience, my father swore that this fool boy would be severely flogged for bringing such ignominy upon his family. With that, he seized me roughly by the ear and dragged me homeward, as an infuriating shock of pain tore at my head.

Aunt Cindy, watering her hens, straightened slowly as we crossed our yard. Young Lalie ran to her and peered from behind her skirts at poor ear-twisted Edgar. When Tap came out, they stood as still as oaken figures in that sad spring light as my maddened father roared at them to mind their nigger business. Then the door closed behind and I was slung into the corner, mad with pain. Minnie was bawling. Even Mama cried out in alarm when he seized the heavy hickory behind the door and staggered toward me.

Slowly I stood. My ear and my wrenched arm fired my rage and in a moment Jack was there. Commanded to lean forward, hands spread wide on the log wall, I turned a little in seeming resignation, then whirled and grasped the wood, twisting it free before he could secure his hold.

"Here," he growled, missing my intent. "Give it here."

In the kitchen corner my mother stood, hands clasped, as formal as a mourner. "Edgar?" she said. Her query signified, *Do you realize he may kill you?* The man turned his stare upon his wife as if this unholy insurrection was her doing. I muttered, "Don't you touch her, Papa."

Afraid, I circled out into the center of the room, panting like something cornered. Sensing weakness, he made a sudden rush as Minnie moaned with terror in her cupboard. When I jumped aside, he pitched onto his knees, and I leapt and brought the stick down hard across his shoulders— *whack!* I struck again with all my might, for my life depended on it—*whack!*

Frantic to disable him, knowing his heavy cavalry coat would dull the blows, I went after the head and neck, the kidneys, the limber wood biting into the thick meat of him—*whack!*—and another—*whack!*—another and another. Cursing vilely in pain and disbelief, he dragged his collar up to protect his ears, still on all fours. I was somber, silent, stepping lightly around the yelping hulk, leaping sideways to avoid its lunges, darting in. The beast struggled to flounder to its feet, only to be stunned and struck off balance and crash down again. That hickory whistled as I beat him, beat and beat and beat and beat him, leaning into those blows with every last splinter of old fear and fury. Grunting, teeth grinding, I bent that hard wood with savage cuts—*a-gain, a-gain, a-gain!*—until at last the beast howled in woe and wrapped its arms around its head and hunched bloody-eared, still cursing, in the corner.

The little house was swollen with harsh groans and gasping. The mud-booted mound that was the father lay quaking by the wall. Minnie crept forth but remained crouched behind the chair. Across the yard, Aunt Cindy would have covered Lalie's ears, protecting her from the awful sounds of Mist' Edgar's final moments. And my mother? How was it I felt ashamed to face my mother? How could that be? When I lowered the stick, starting to tremble, she said softly, "Oh, how dare you, Edgar." It was not a question. Quieting her heart, she pressed her fingers to her chest. She was very pale but her eyes fairly glittered. "How dare you," she said.

I felt hatred and I felt like weeping. Lightly, I tapped the tip of the extended stick on the floor between us, marking a boundary she was not to cross. She must have been looking straight into Jack's eyes, and his expression scared her in a way her husband never had, even in violence. "Your own parent," she finished weakly.

" 'How dare you.' " I mimicked her disbelief. "I reckon you think it's me who deserved that beating."

Not once had she tried to intervene. Worse, I had glimpsed her transport, her clenched exultation in my act. I thrust the stick at her. "Your turn," I told her with a harsh contempt I could no longer hide. She stared at the stick, then at the prostrate man, coughing and moaning. The stick fell to the floor between us.

I pushed my few things into a sack, shoved his hickory through the knot of this poor bindle, and departed my parents' house for good. I passed those black folks standing in the yard without a word—instinctively, for their own safety, for I had grown up suddenly in the past hour and knew who my father was. Having heard those blows and cries, they were astonished when I emerged alive, but except for a little cry from Lalie, they kept silent. Only Minnie trailed me, sobbing her plea that I must not forsake her. You always forsook *me,* I thought, but did not say it. I kept on going down the road. As the last houses fell behind me, I was overtaken by a dread of utter solitude in the great turning world.

AMONGST MY DEAD

I walked all night to reach Clouds Creek, where I slept in a corner of Grand-father Artemas's abandoned house. That afternoon, I paid a call on Colonel Robert Briggs Watson, the late Elijah Junior's son and heir. Colonel Robert's large house with its pecans and magnolias, built early in the century on the east side of the Ridge spring by the Old Squire, was set off from the road and its own fields by a wall of crenellated brick which let a listless breeze pass through in summer. The old wood house was quaking with the hound rumpus inside, so eager were his dogs to challenge strangers.

R. B. Watson appeared on his vine-shrouded veranda in his shirtsleeves. A man of a comfortable kind of heft, he was less handsome than steadfast in his appearance, being calm and courtly and well-tempered by the weathers. Unlike most men of Edgefield District, he kept his silvered hair cropped short, and his clothes looked fresh even with dirt on them—just the opposite of his first cousin Elijah D., whose clothes revealed the ingrained grime of unclean habits (not to be ousted from his clothes "wid lye ner dyner-mite," as Aunt Cindy once complained to her Mis Ellen—as close as Cindy ever came to revealing her disapproval of Mis Ellen's husband).

Colonel Robert was a decorated soldier who had ridden home from Appomattox Courthouse to manage the family properties around Clouds Creek. Taciturn, he listened as I asked permission to live in the old Artemas house and sharecrop its fallow land. More intent on me than on my question, he nodded vaguely, inviting me inside for a drink of water, asking politely how my mother might be faring. "You remember Edgar, don't you, Lucy?" he inquired of his wife. "I do," she answered pleasantly enough although not pleased to see me. *What do you want here?* her expression said.

I did not discuss my rupture with my father. I told them about my earnest hope to restore my grandfather's lineage here in Clouds Creek. He said he would think about it and he did. A day later, he put aside the warnings of his kinsmen and gave "Cousin Ellen's boy" permission to sharecrop the Artemas tract and occupy his grandfather's old house, patching it up as best he could.

As a Clouds Creek Presbyterian, Colonel Robert had faith that whatever satisfaction might be found in life was of a man's own making, and that no good would ever come from coddling. On the other hand, he betrayed distress that his father, Elijah Junior, had acquired the Artemas tract through plain hard dealing. While warning me that I would be held to a strict standard, he also looked for small ways to encourage me, bringing old blankets, a new kerosene lantern, basic tools and rough provisions, and a Bible. He invited me to come to Sunday dinner. "After church," Cousin Lucy called, for church attendance was required to receive the blessing of her fine ham and sweet pudding.

And so, most Sundays after church, I dined at Colonel Robert's house, where I enjoyed browsing in the Watson Bible with its list of births and deaths, and also in the Carolina histories and the browned warm-smelling pages of the Shakespeare folios brought into the family by my great-grandmother, the former Chloe Wimberley, daughter of James Wimberley, one of George Washington's generals in the Revolution; the leather volumes, soiled by mold and mice, had turned up in Grandfather Artemas's falling house.

"Those might be yours one day," the Colonel said, filling my heart with the rare joy of heritage and belonging. That I might study in the evenings, he kept me supplied with whale oil for my lamp.

The cold dusk of early Piedmont spring—the naked trees, the urgent ringing of spring peepers—hurt my heart; I was lonely all that April in that empty house. Even so, I was resolute, often content. The return to Clouds Creek had bathed and healed my spirit. These fertile meadows, the clear running water and soft loamy air, filled me with well-being, as if the old roots ruptured and exposed in our family's loss of this plantation had been covered over with good soil and were feeling their way back into the earth.

Soon the woodland twigs came into leaf, with redbud and dogwood and the mountain laurel opening cool blossoms. Then spring birdsong was gone as summer silence descended with the heat, and young redbirds dozed in the thick greens that would shrivel by late summer in the fire colors of the Piedmont autumn. In the old century, the blood red of these swamp maples, the oak russets, the hickory yellows and pale golds had hidden marauding Cherokees. Day after day, working my upland fields, I dwelled in reveries and plans for this home earth, painfully homesick although I had come home.

Somehow I had always imagined that Clouds Creek had been named for its cloud reflections, the soft cumulus passing over on west winds from the Appalachians. Colonel Robert told me that the name came from a trader, Isaac Cloud, whose wife had survived to tell their bloody tale. In May of 1751, she wrote, two Cherokees came to their cabin just at dark. Given supper and tobacco, the Indians engaged the trader in friendly banter until near midnight, when all "dropt into Sleep. And when the Cocks began to Crow, they came to the Bed and shot my Husband through the Head. And a young Man lying upon the Floor was shot in the same Minute. And thinking the Bullet had gone through [my head], one struck me with a Tomahawk. . . . I lying still, they supposed I was dead, and one of them went and killed both my Children; and then they came and took the Blankets from us & plunder'd the House of all that was valuable and went off. And in that bad condition I have lain two days amongst my dead."

Amongst my dead—those words would ever haunt me.

HOGS

Squire Robert B. Watson was a modern farmer who had outgrown the sorceries of our Border ancestors, the potions, charms, and incantations for good crops. He taught me theories and methods of breeding livestock (some of them used formerly in breeding slaves, he commented, without further remark), having succeeded with hogs and cattle, horses, mules—everything, in fact, but sheep, which the Piedmont settlers had detested since old drover days when their immigrant Highlands ancestors moved south along the Appalachians. With the canny brain of the wild sheep long since bred out of them, these dim creatures had fallen prey to wolves and panthers and even to the berry-grubbing bears; suffocating in their dirty wool, they died prodigiously in the damp heat of Carolina summer before their husbandry was finally abandoned.

The merry hogs, on the other hand, took joyfully to the land, rooting through the woodlands as if born to it. Escaped hogs resisted predators, reverting quickly to the razor-backed pugnacity of the wild boar; they grew huge, black, and hard-bristled, with curled tusks. "Some of our 'po' whites' turn feral, too." The Colonel winked, aware of my hard feelings about Z. P. Claxton and the death of Joseph. But unlike feral humans, he continued, wild hogs could be baited in and tamed in pens, rounding off their rangy lines in a few generations and turning pink beneath their bristles, until only the snouts and curly tails and squinty little eyes remained the same.

That first year, when a sow farrowed toward Christmas, I helped the Colonel with the deliveries, tugging each piglet by the shoulders to work it free, and he showed me how to clean off the shining membranes which enclosed the heads, then pump the slimy little legs to get them going. Finally the sow would heave a sigh and push her runt out in a bloody blurt of afterbirth. Since he did not trust this sow not to eat her litter, he promised me a half dozen shoats if I would rear the lot. "For a while you'll have to cook their feed," he said, "raise them by hand."

"If I can catch them!" Idiotically I laughed aloud, startling us both with my new happiness. Seeing my overjoyed face, the Colonel grinned. "First time I've ever seen you smile." The Colonel chuckled kindly along with me. He had almost forgotten, he said, how much he had enjoyed pigs as a boy. "You don't 'catch' a pig, Edgar. You 'fetch' it." As he spoke, Colonel Robert petted the six shoats. Without affection, he explained, they grew poorly and became sluggish, and their curly tails would droop like dying flowers. In a few weeks, if cared for properly, my gang of shoats should be racing around with grunts and squeals, playing tag and mauling one another, much like puppies. "Plenty of water helps 'em gobble up their food so they can grow." He smiled. "No pig under one hundred pounds can call itself a hog, so they're in a hurry." I was in a hurry, too, though for what I did not know. I could hardly wait!

In response to all my earnest questions, Colonel Robert spoke to a young cousin as one farmer to another, evoking great antebellum days when even rich Tidewater planters had been attracted to the short-staple cotton agriculture here in the Piedmont; before the War, Edgefield had shipped more cotton bales than any district in the state. But erosion had leached out the clay soil, and problems had grown with fluctuations in the cotton prices and rising competition from the states along the southern Mississippi. With the onset of the War and the loss of plentiful unpaid labor, "King Cotton" was deposed for good.

These days, despite Reconstruction, said the Colonel, Clouds Creek was stirring back to life. Like his father and grandfather before him, he sold off timber from his wooded lands, grew tobacco, corn, and rice, and was trying grain crops—oats, wheat, rye, and barley. In fact, he said, the Watsons were planting all their former crops except for cotton. He had also made a reputation for fine hogs and cattle, and in this year of my return was putting in small orchards; he hoped to become the first Carolina planter ever to ship peaches outside the state. Listening proudly to my kinsman, I dared hope that my own luck had turned, that the worst of my life was behind me, that there was a future at Clouds Creek for Edgar Artemas Watson.

I started simply with a few chicks and ducklings, borrowing a horse to plow a single meadow in which I planted corn by hand, gold kernel after kernel, row after precious row. Thin fresh green lines, weak and broken at first, came forth mysteriously and rose in a green haze; for a while, I cherished each and every plant among the hundreds, even the weak ones I would later weed away. I felt ingrown in this dark soil, as the Artemas Plantation's heir, putting down soft tendrils like a native plant of our old land. I grew to love the Clouds Creek earth, and in summer I made strange love to it in the soft evenings, lying down upon it naked as the soil gave off the gathered heat of the long day.

Not until I knew the Colonel better did I inquire about my father's career as a soldier. Aware that I needed the truth, the Colonel did not dodge the question but gave me a terse answer, reporting precisely what his uncle Tillman had told him—that Elijah D. had never hesitated to seek privilege or favor from higher-ranking kin and never failed to shun responsibility of every kind, including combat. Early in the War, Uncle Tillman had dismissed him from the Edgefield Volunteers, and within that year, Selden Tilghman had him transferred from the Nineteenth Cavalry to an infantry company of half-trained soldiers, due to general dereliction of his duties. The alternative had been courts martial and imprisonment.

ROGUE'S MARCH

The Honorable Tillman Watson (although illiterate, Mama said) was now a state senator and a vice president of the Edgefield Agricultural Society. Like Andrew Jackson and John C. Calhoun, he was an old Borderer in his appearance, being tall and rangy, with an imposing forehead and fierce deep-set eyes sunk back beneath heavy black brows in a long bony face. Though he had been kind enough during my childhood, Great-Uncle Tillman shunned me now to spare himself the effort of concealing his dislike of my father. As a prosperous man, it pained him, too, to see a ragged boy working his late brother's plantation all alone in the forlorn hope that he might one day earn it back.

As for the other Clouds Creek kin, they were civil but not hospitable, being similarly at pains to separate themselves from "the Bad Elijah." Though I never complained about my solitude, the Colonel worried that living alone in that damp and decrepit house, young Cousin Edgar might sicken or go mad. I was too proud to tell him how much I preferred solitude to the terror of existence under my father's roof.

"I wish you had known your grandfather," Colonel Robert was saying, avoiding my eye so as not to embarrass us both. "A kind and gentle man and well-respected planter until whiskey took him." Though he made no mention of my father, his keen glance was a warning that alcoholic spirits might be the ruin of my lineage. "I shall assist you if you deserve that, Edgar, and not otherwise." He said this harshly. No thanks being expected, I kept still.

Another day, I asked him if he knew what had become of Selden Tilghman. He considered the hands clasped on his knee before muttering what he had heard, that "ruffians without civil authority" had given Colonel Tilghman one hundred strokes of the lash, then tarred and feathered him. In a hoary medieval clamor of tin pots, cat-calls, and chaotic drumming, he'd been ridden backwards on a pole in an old-fashioned "rogue's march," after which he'd been dumped into a hog wallow at Hamburg, the despised Republican settlement on the Savannah River across from Augusta, Georgia. Tilghman had regained consciousness before hogs found him and had crawled away—all that was rumor. Nothing had been heard about him since.

"He is dead, then?"

"I pray that he is dead." Even if the man survived, he would be hunted down and killed should he return to Edgefield District, not because his punishment had been insufficient but because of the bad conscience of his neighbors, to whom he remained a specter of reproach.

Colonel Robert's repudiation of the martyrdom inflicted on a Confederate hero by "that half-mad Coulter and his gang", had been evident since the day he'd fired Claxton. (Again he avoided mention of my father.) "They cannot dignify unlawful violence by calling themselves 'Regulators.' 'Regulation' occurred a century ago when your great-great-grandfather led the citizens' militia. These night riders of today are not patriots but vigilantes, and the cruelties they perpetrate would be villainous even in time of war." He had agreed with Selden Tilghman that renegade violence kept the old wounds open, and that such actions would isolate the South as a polluted backwater of the republic.

While not in sympathy with Tilghman's New Light heresies, Colonel Robert respected the integrity and courage of that God-stunned man. "Your mother's cousin was abominated because he warned the public— publicly—about what had become monstrous in all of us." He flushed. "To enrich ourselves, we Christians sanctioned human bondage, so what can we say now in our own defense? My God! The enslavement of our fellow men even after they were redeemed as our fellow Christians! How did our churchmen defend this for so long?" He shook his head. "My father owned a thousand slaves, Uncle Tillman, too, and Aunt Sophia, Uncle Artemas— all the siblings. We were large slaveholders until the end, saw nothing wrong with it. We went to war for it. And many thousands of our best young men would lose their lives for this great sin and grievous wound to the republic that made a travesty and lie of our Constitution."

I was astonished by these heartbroken words from a Southern officer, wounded at Fraser's Farm and Gettysburg and decorated for gallantry in the Great Lost Cause.

While they were small, my frisky shoats kept me company inside my empty house. I constructed a snug pen in a side room which I bedded with dry straw and mucked out faithfully. Rejoicing in their progress, I hauled slops and mash and gallons of fresh water to this roisterous bunch, talking back to them in their squeal language, with suitable *chuffs* and a few explosive *harfs* of false alarm. I even moved my bedding to a place beside the pen where I could share in their well-fed contentment. They nudged my boots in greeting, seeking treats out of my pocket or a good rub of the bristle tuft between those pale blue eyes. Listening to this gang of mine, in their ear-twitching sleep, I would find myself smiling in the dark, even laughing quietly, drawing forth sweet giggles of pig mirth.

When spring came, I built an outside pen, and on Sunday afternoons, I led my sturdy band across the country. They would hurtle off in all directions, farther and farther in their forays, until they tired and came trotting in, heeding my call and following close behind all the way home. *SooEEEEEEE! Pig, pig, pig!* I sang across the meadows to celebrate my calling as a pig man. Colonel Robert warned me that hearing young Cousin Edgar in the distance and taking his mournful calls for cries of solitude was sorely troubling to certain Watsons on the lands around, and perhaps this good man, despite my reassurances, was the most troubled of all.

A SOMBER HARD-FACED BOY

Sunday dinners at the Colonel's house were gradually reduced to one each month, until finally Aunt Lucy dispensed with my company entirely. So inhospitable did she become that I had to wonder if she was excluding the son out of her bitter disapproval of the father. In wretched loneliness, I longed to whine that my father had hurled me headfirst against a log butt, how I had lain unconscious for hours, how I had suffered headaches ever since. But I refused to solicit sympathy at the cost of such disloyalty, knowing also that betraying weakness before these Clouds Creek Watsons would only convince them that the son was made of the same poor stuff as the father and cause Colonel Robert to lose faith in my resolve.

The final pronouncement on my character was reserved for Great-Aunt Sophia Boatright, who made regular rounds of the Watson households in her buggy. As monitor of the Old Squire's heritage and high standards, Aunt Sophia saw to it that services and prayer meetings were duly attended and family deportment rigorously maintained. One day, careless of the fact that "Elijah D's boy" was reading outside the window in the Indian summer sun (borrowing books having become my poor excuse for hanging around the outskirts of those family Sundays), she held forth to Aunt Lucy on "the fatal weakness" of poor dear Artemas that had led straight to the dissolution of his son. In no uncertain terms she blamed "that spoiled Addison girl" whom Elijah D. had married for the unwashed aspect of that "somber hard-faced boy." As for "that Minnie or whatever they call her," she was dismissed as "rather a pretty thing for a near-halfwit." Aunt Lucy assured Aunt Sophia that poor peaked Minnie was not half-witted, merely scared out of her wits. She confessed, however, that the girl's brother could no longer be tolerated in her house due to his odor, which no doubt emanated from his hogs. Her voice died as she realized that that somber hard-faced boy might be somewhere within earshot.

Young Edgar—the voice of Colonel Robert, who had just come in—had toiled like a wretched slave since early childhood: he had been deprived of education and even decent clothes, as the ladies knew. What did the family expect of him, then? And who had extended a hand since his arrival? How many of his kinsmen knew or cared that Edgar, condemned to spend his evenings all alone, was probably better read already than any Watson in Clouds Creek?

"Well, that's not saying much," Aunt Sophia snorted. "Poor old Tillman can scarcely write his name, let alone read it! Anyway, all this reading is bad for that boy's brain. He talks like a book, which is all the fault of Ellen's cousin, the one who spelled Tillman the old Tory way." Such a pity, she exclaimed, that the boy had not been orphaned; dear old Tillman, with no heirs, might have adopted such a promising young man. Reminded that Tillman had a spry young wife, she nodded grimly. "Yes. A barren wife. Who will inherit everything."

Colonel Robert respectfully rebuked her. "Amelia has been good to him, Aunt." With affection, he quoted my great-uncle, who favored rural accents: "I never had but the one wife and she done me all my life."

Young Edgar was bright, industrious, and very able, the Colonel concluded. With any luck, he would restore the Artemas plantation. "That is doubtless to his credit," the old lady retorted, "but I don't like the look of him and that is that."

"Very likely the boy is aware of your opinion, Aunt Sophia, but you might lower your voice in case he's not." Colonel Robert must have pointed toward the window for there was a stiff silence in that room.

"Oh? An eavesdropper, you mean?" Aunt Sophia's voice flew out into the sunlight as I ducked down to slink away around the house. "Speak up, boy! Are you out there?"

"No, ma'am. I mean, yes, ma'am." The fire of humiliation, the dread of banishment. I hadn't known how I had offended them, nor that my great-aunt disliked my looks, nor that I stunk. The knowing scared me. When they went into the dining room, I slipped through the front door and peered into the hall mirror. What I saw was a common boy, husky for fourteen and roughly dressed, a freckled blue-eyed boy, straight nose, strong chin, hair a dark red auburn. Nothing out of the way except, perhaps, the set cast of the expression, ingrown, solitary—yes, a hard and somber face, just as she'd said, moss-toothed and dirt-streaked. I liked it no better than she did. And I was shocked by my strong smell indoors.

Confronted by Edgar Watson's face, I hated the name Edgar. "Edgar," I whispered. "You stink, boy." But I had no idea how to escape myself.

JACK WATSON

At Christmas, which I spent alone, I was given a real hog-bristle tooth-brush, a bar of brown Octagon soap, and a hand-me-down outfit of spare clothes, including a warm jacket from the Colonel. Winter passed. Imagining unfriendliness in their closed faces, I grew ever more removed from my Clouds Creek kin. In certain weathers, out of loneliness as much as cold, I piled up clean straw and slept in my own corner of my hog pen.

In March, the Colonel hired me for the spring planting so that I might put aside a little cash. The other hands were nigras, all but a newcomer who turned up one day in the next row and kept watching me as we were planting peas. Distracted, I worked sloppily, and finally the other pointed at my "crookedy rows," saying he would not share the blame for such poor work so I'd better do them over. I asked him who he thought he was, giving orders to Colonel Watson's kin, and he just sneered. "That makes two of us," he said.

Rudely I said, "You are no kin to me. I have never seen you around here." "No?" he said. "My daddy is ol' Elijah D. You kin to him?" Angry, I called him a damned liar. "Elijah D. Watson has one son," I said, "and that is me." He laughed at me, having known who I was right from the start.

"Your daddy has two blue-eyed boys," he baited me. "One has a shadow in his blood, that's all." And he pinched the tanned skin of his cheek so hard that it went white. I had noticed his use of crookedy, a darkie word, and now I knew.

"You're a damned mulatta, then? That what you're saying?"

"Yassuh, massuh." He leered into my face. He had blue eyes, all right, but I could see the shadow in the skin.

"Better watch out, telling lies on white men. You best stay clear of me."

"Brother Edgar." He stopped smiling. "Just you plant them fuckin peas straight like I told you, Brother Edgar." He spat those bad words at my eyes like venom.

I threw the hoe aside and went for him. He was ready for me, as furious as I was. In our struggle, rolling in the furrows, he glimpsed Colonel Robert at the field edge and hissed a warning to let go. Drenched in sweat, we went back to our peas.

As it turned out, this angry youth was already in danger from the Regulators, the Colonel said. Jack would have to be sent away for his own safety. "He's too outspoken. Jack knows the Yankees will betray their own Reconstruction Act and the freedmen with it. He is angry and bitter. I have full rights as a citizen, he says, the law is the law. But the law is no longer the law, alas, in Edgefield District."

"*Jack?*" I said. I could scarcely believe it.

"Jacob Watson. From Augusta. Hates the name Jacob because he hates the man who gave it to him."

Stupidly jealous of the Colonel's concern for this mongrel Watson, I felt threatened. "This Jack Watson doesn't know his place, sir. That what you mean?"

"That's what *you* mean, Edgar." The Colonel measured me from beneath his heavy brows. "Sooner or later, they will come for him—those who judge that he does not know his place," he said.

"The Regulators?" I stood up, hot. My heart was pounding. "I didn't mean—"

Jacob's mother, he explained, was a light-skinned slave girl who had worked in this house until she became pregnant. After she was sold away, it was put about by the ladies of the family that she had been raped by some white drifter, but the family knew that a young Watson was the father.

I nodded and got up and went away.

• • •

By 1870, when Elijah D. Watson and his son were listed in the census as "farm laborers," my father had sold off everything he could lay hands on save his horse and rifle. A few bits of hidden jewelry were his wife's last tokens of her family past. Mama was listed no longer as "Mrs." but as plain Ellen Watson, which signified that she was no longer a gentlewoman in our community. For a Daughter of Edgefield, that humiliation confirmed the ruin of her husband's reputation and the loss of our good name.

One Sunday, Tap rode to Clouds Creek on his mule, bringing word that Mama wished to see me. I rode the mule with the colored man up behind, grumbling about his crotch when the mule trotted. At Edgefield, Mama came running out to meet me, scarcely able to contain her happy news.

The previous year, Great-Aunt Tabitha Watson and her daughter Laura, who was Mama's childhood friend, had journeyed to north Florida to see to the plantation of Laura's deceased husband, William Myers. In a letter to Laura, Mama had revealed her unhappy marriage to Elijah Watson, which Aunt Tabitha had famously advocated and supported. Requesting shelter, Laura's old friend mentioned that her strong and willing son was held in high esteem by Colonel R. B. Watson as a very promising farmer: surely this young man would be an asset on her Florida plantation.

Mama told no one what she'd done. A few months later, when her prayers were answered in a return letter sent in care of her brother, she began her preparations for departure. We were to leave in the next days on a cotton cart bound for Augusta, where we would join other pioneers in a wagon train on the old Woodpecker Trail south across Georgia. Asked how she would manage without Cindy, Mama looked surprised. "She will go, too, of course." And Lulalie? And Tap? Mama waved away these complications. Her servant's domestic arrangements were her own affair, Mama said blithely. No doubt Cindy's people would follow when they could.

In her excitement, Mama had never considered my situation either but simply assumed that her son would abandon those dull Watsons to escort his family on this journey. I was silent awhile, not knowing what to say. I felt vaguely homesick for some reason, but whether for Mama's household or Clouds Creek, I was not sure. I had been so excited by my plan to slaughter one of my young pigs and bring my first ham to Edgefield as a Christmas present.

When I told Mama I would not be going, she became exceptionally vexed. "But I promised them! They may not want us there if you don't come!" When I stood unmoved, she pled. "This is a long perilous journey, Edgar. Who will protect us?" Next, she said, "You are my son! And your sister needs you!"

But Mama was ever practical, and seeing my expression, soon gave up. With or without me, she would make good her escape, there was no stopping her. She mustered a sort of smile. "Your heart lies at Clouds Creek, I see," she said in a sincere manner. "I understand. We shall miss you, Edgar, of course we shall," she continued briskly, attention already shifting as the next thing to be taken care of came to mind, "but no doubt we shall get on fine without you."

I could not help wishing that she had entreated me. To stay was my choice and yet, ridiculously, I felt abandoned and even a bit hurt that my family would leave home forever without appreciating Edgar's Christmas ham. I tried to laugh at my bruised feelings but could not. Yet walking home that afternoon and evening, I cheered up a good deal, as my disappointment turned to admiration. "Well, now, Aunt Sophia," I could say to that old blunderbuss, "it looks like 'that spoiled Addison girl' has some grit and spirit!"

At Clouds Creek, Colonel Robert, too tactful to say I had made the right decision, awarded me a rare smile of fond pride: Cousin Edgar knew where Watson duty lay and had the character to make this sacrifice. The good man took me by both shoulders, saying, "I have full confidence in your abilities, Edgar; I have come to cherish the belief that one day you will indeed redeem your family property." And he quoted that notable Edgefieldian, the former governor James Hammond: *Sir, what is it that constitutes character, popularity, and power in the United States? Sir, it is property, and that only!*

All my life, I would be guided by those ringing words.

DEEPWOOD

Still unsettled by my womenfolk's escape to Florida, I needed to reach out some way, make them a parting present, and since I was penniless and my pigs too young to slaughter, I wanted to trap a rabbit or squirrel or possum for a pie. Avoided as a haunt of restless spirits, the old Tilghman place had always been my hunting ground; knowing the wild things' passages through glades and hollows as a nesting bird knows every point throughout its territory, I ran a new trapline through its ancient forest.

One cold morning of late November, I arrived at the greening ring of the old carriage circle and immediately sensed something in the air. The Deepwood manor house, charred and hollowed out by vigilante fire, squatted half-hidden in a copse of oak and juniper. Over the black hole of the doorway, the high dormer was bound in creeper and wild grape, and the shingled roof peak, ragged now, sagged swaybacked in a failing line along the sky. The ruin had the mournful aspect of a harrow left to rust in an oldfield corner or an abandoned stack of dark rain-rotted hay, but on that day as I drew near, its aspect shifted. Though no smoke rose out of its chimney, the gutted habitation hid some form of life.

In those hungry years, any abandoned roof might shelter thieves or desperate black men without means or destination, and this day I sensed that imbalance in the air that is sign of being watched, even awaited. I passed the house, not breaking step, scanning casually for boot prints or fresh horse dung or anything untoward or out of place. I was prepared. Even so, what I now saw snapped my breath away.

I kept my head, let my gaze skip past, walking on a ways before slipping my jackknife from my pocket, letting it fall. Turning and stooping to retrieve it, I scanned that little porch under the peak, scanned further as I straightened and kept going. Beneath the wild bees' nest under the dormer, behind the leafy rail, a dark shape crouched motionless, its eyes burning holes into my back as I walked on. That imbalance in the air was the withheld breath of a living thing too bulky for a human being but not dark enough for a black bear even if a bear would climb up in there. I moaned but seized hold of my panic and did not run and never once looked back, crossing the gullied oldfields over red iron earth where hard brambles and thin poverty grass choked the spent cotton.

When I returned to run my traps a few days later, the same gray weather lay upon the land, yet there was a lightness in the air, and a clear cold emptiness behind the frost-bronzed vine on that high balcony. The dark shape that had crouched there was gone. What had it been? The mystery frightened me.

Probably the thing had fled the region, knowing it was seen. But I had scarcely reassured myself when, at the wood edge, I came across a trail of dirtied feathers, not dove or quail killed by a hawk or bobcat but frayed feathers plucked from some old chicken, beckoning sadly from the thorns and twigs in the browning woodland air.

I stared about me, then moved into the forest, as trees fell in behind, all the while peering through skeins of bare black twigs and branches, in the chill gloom that at this time of year persisted in the deeper woods even in day. Nearing my trap, I sensed some queer vibration, as if a rabbit struggled, and with it, that shift and imbalance in the air. I moved forward in a crouch, then on hands and knees.

In a hickory hollow where low sunlight fired the shagbark, a rough shape mantled my trap like a huge owl, hunched motionless, transfixed in its deep listening. Slowly, then, a tattered head turned in my direction, crest burning in cold rays of autumn light. When the thing rose soundlessly as smoke, clutching my rabbit, I retreated in horror, fell backwards over a log—*Get away!* That screech tore the woodland silence, and when it died, the great owl-thing had vanished. I fled the trees and lit out across the open fields toward the Ridge road before summoning outrage and the courage to hook back toward Deepwood, wanting to make sure that old house was the thief's lair.

Though I had no idea what I would do next, I was desperate to get there first. Rather than leave the cover of the woods, the creature was bound to circle the long way around and approach its den through the west wall of the ruin, which was half-fallen and wide open to the weather. Panting from the run, I crept in through shaggy boxwood to the east wall window. Peering and listening, sick with fright—what did I hope to do without a weapon?—I was on the point of flight when the bulky silhouette loomed up in the jagged opening in the west wall, in failing light. Passing through without sound, it sank into the blackness. The frozen rabbit thumped onto a board. A tinder scratched, a small blaze flickered, jumped to life, casting nervous shadows. The fire glinted in the thing's red eye, lit matted arms and chest and neck and the rough head of stubbled feathers. At the sound of my expelled breath, it rose like a great owl on man's legs and vanished through the wall.

Scrambling backwards, slashed by the hard briar, I screamed to fright the creature that even now was circling the outside of the house, rushing through the shadows of dusk to strike me down. Making its kill, it would hunch upon my body as it had my rabbit, shifting bloody talons, the wintry moonrise glinting on its beak.

When I burst in, Papa jumped up, his ring eye crimson. Gold-red locks matted with sweat, his head loomed huge and wild. "Curse you, boy, don't bang the hinges off my door!" Confused by grog, he would not sit down again to his thin gruel and stale biscuit but swayed beside the table, coughing thickly in the fumes from the oil lamp. He lost his balance, staggered again, bellowed, "What ails you, boy?" into my face. By the stove, Mama made no move to come forward. In her cupboard, Ninny Minnie whined.

Gruff and sullen, I told Papa that I needed the rifle. He stamped the earth floor like a bee-stung horse. "Banging in here demanding my damn rifle? Show some respect!"

"Your father is upset, Edgar. He's been dismissed from Graniteville again."

Not now, Mama, not now! How I hated the excitement in her face. Since leaving home, I had never been sure which parent I resented more, the red-faced violent male or this pale vindictive female who teased her spouse as a child picks at a scab, until it bleeds. But this day, my father was sick with failure, rotten with bad moonshine, and merely groaned at his wife's queer satisfaction in their straits. He sat down hard and blinked and squinched his nose, vented a hacking cough; he drew his knife from his scuffed boot and hacked at the stale bread, gave that up, too. "We ate better on the battlefield." Elijah Watson glowered at his bowl, as if in the bottom of this cracked clay vessel of insipid soup he might descry every last sad gobbet of a hopeless life.

"Papa? Please. I need it."

Lige Watson heaved around, brow furrowed. "What's got you so scared, boy? You never been the scairdy kind."

Indifferent to my fear as well as his fatherly show of concern, Mama got back to business. "Who is to provide for us this time, Mr. Watson? Should this boy come home as head of his father's household?"

"He don't even live in his father's household, last I heard." Papa scowled at the bitter memory of my assault. "I asked a question, boy."

I blurted out what I had seen, a strange man-thing, inhabiting Deepwood. A trap-robber. Mama told me I'd imagined things, but the man said, "Godamighty." He kicked his chair back, lurching to his feet. His illegal musket was dragged down from the beams as its oily sacking fell to the earth floor; he slammed out of the house. The big roan, left saddled, snorted as it wheeled, and the carom of its hooves on frozen clay diminished in the darkness.

"Deepwood?" she inquired, turning from the door. "Is that where—"

"No," I said. "He'll go first to Major Coulter."

"Of course. Where else?" With Papa gone, her eyes had softened and she tried to smile. "How are you, Edgar? How are you getting on?"

Still standing, I was wolfing Papa's soup. She told me to sit down while I was eating. I ignored this. A moment later, she chastised me for wiping my mouth with the back of my hand. I belched loudly just to see her shudder. Because she did not really care, I did not answer when she asked again how I was faring at Clouds Creek. She feared me a little now, I saw, which gave me no satisfaction, only made me feel more lonesome than before.

Mama and Minnie and Aunt Cindy were ready to leave for Florida at the first opportunity. Had I changed my mind? When I said I had not, and wished them well, she took my hands across the table and held my gaze long enough to make quite certain that her son had been full witness to a mother's sorrow. I withdrew my hands. She saw the coldness in my face and straightened up, blew her nose smartly. "Never mind," she said. "We'll do just fine."

Toward midnight, Papa came home long enough to wrap his musket in the sacking and return it to the rafters. He appeared clumsy and shaken, his red brow glistening with sickly sweat, red ring-eye pulsing. At the door, he turned, pointing a finger at Mama's face. "I was home all evening. I slept here. Don't forget that." He lurched into the night and rode away.

THE OWL-MAN

Retrieving the musket, I set off at daylight with the vague idea of driving the Owl-Man off what was left of my precious rabbit. But turning into Deepwood's narrow lane, I was racked by dread of what might have taken place the night before and what I might stumble into.

At the edge of the greening carriage circle, a trail of dark stains led to an old boxwood where something had lain bleeding. Later it had crawled toward the ruin, moving along a shaded wall under an old lilac choked by vines. From the dung and hoof prints, I pieced the rest together. Blowing horses, torches, and wild shots had flushed the surrounded quarry from the ruin. In the dark, they could not track the blood, having rushed here without dogs. When their quarry crawled into the dense boxwood, they had lost him. They had not persisted, being superstitious and afraid.

The blood trail led around the corner toward the hole in the fallen wall. Creeping forward, picking my way through the winter briars, I struggled to keep the musket barrel disentangled.

The wounded creature was alive inside its hole, that much I knew. I checked my load, I cleared my throat, I took a mighty breath. "Come out," I croaked. From behind the wall came the slight scrape of something shifting, followed by a dry ratcheting cough like a raccoon. I forced myself to lean and peer inside.

On a charred board by the dead fire lay my hoarfrost rabbit, stiff as furred wood. Behind it, taking shape in the cold shadows, stretched a man's ragged legs and broken boots. The crusted head, tufts twisted askew, and a swollen black hand more like a talon clutched the heavy bloodstain on the stomach, and there was a sinuous dark stain where blood had probed and found a passage back into burned earth. A road walker, I thought—either that or the skin between patches of crust was black with firesmoke and filth. Black or white, the Owl-Man was surely on the point of death. A broken voice grated something like, "The Coward . . . Watson."

The Owl-Man watched me through raw slits in a mask. A rude scar showed where the head had been half-scalped, then sealed with boiling tar, then crowned with feathers. The mask had no expression. Nostrils and lips scarcely emerged from the leprous stubble. Then the mouth hole opened slowly, stretching dry strings of slime between dry broken teeth. A choked gasp: "Finish it."

The creature's agony was horrifying, it was unbearable—*not bearable!* Eons of human agony in millions of cruel acts over the ages had been distilled here in this being, with no hope of relief but the swift mercy of annihilation. But when I raised the musket, put my finger to the trigger, I could not do it. I was blind with tears and only sagged down weakly, trying not to be sick.

In one thrash, the Owl-Man seized the barrel, twisting it in his black claw with the force of spasm and yanking the muzzle to his throat as I fought to pull away. My wrist was clasped in a hornlike hand, and my yell as I pulled back was obliterated by explosion. Because the gun came free with the recoil, I was thrown backwards through the hole in a roil of smoke. The echo died and the thinning smoke wandered away into the deafened woods.

Muffled footfalls—inside my head?—pursuing me down the lane toward the highroad were my first memory of jumping up and running. *You git away from me! You git away!* I heard my boots ring on the frozen earth, echoing off the rigid trees like rifle shots. *What did you*—I cried, *Why did you*—I never—*never what?* Even years later I did not know what my question might have meant, nor if there had been an answer anywhere. Had I cried out to the Owl-Man or to Cousin Selden? Or to the lost life I would never find again?

Who would come after me? Reloading the musket to defend myself, I stood howling on the county road. To drive the present from my brain, to sink away into the past, into *before,* I howled to highest heaven but, still deafened by my own musket fire, I could not hear myself.

Yesterday Edgar Artemas Watson, a promising young farmer, had turned into that lane and wandered from his life into dark dreaming. Awakened, he must hurry to Clouds Creek to feed his hogs, let his lost life return, fall into place. Whatever had just happened—had it happened?—must be banished. What could hallucination mean to young pigs starved for slops? With grunting and harfing?

Alone on the highroad in the leaden light, I knew my life had lost its purchase. Like a dark bird disappearing over distant woods, the future had flown away into the past. I hurried onward. I longed to run, and run and run and run, all the way home, but burdened with my father's heavy musket, I soon slowed, unable to run further.

TAP

A hard wind searched through roadside trees, cracking cold limbs. Over the rushing of blown leaves, fragments of voice commanded me to halt. When I whirled to defend myself, the rifle's weight swung me off balance. I fell hard on the frozen road.

A hard-veined black hand set down a water bucket and retrieved the fallen musket as I groped for it. When I clambered to my knees, Tap Watson backed away a little, brushing earth off the barrel, checking the load. "What you doin wit yo' daddy's shootin arn? What you runnin from? What's dem tears fo'?" The old man squinted in the direction of the ruin. "You knowin somethin 'bout dat shootin over yonder? Las' evenin, and again dis mornin?"

I shook my head, reaching out to take the gun. "None of your business, Tap."

"Oh Lawd, Mist' Edguh." He took his hat off, bent his head, but would not return the gun. "O Lawdy Lawdy!" Tears shone on his cheekbones, which looked like dark wet wood in the cold sunrise. "Been leavin dese few greens in dat place over yonder. You folks needin any?" He tossed his near-limp croker sack against my chest. Astonished, I made no attempt to catch it. It flopped onto the frozen dust between us.

Tap raised the musket, waving the muzzle in the direction of the ruin. "We's goin back up yonder. Got to look."

"You threatening me, Tap?" I picked up the sack he had dared toss at my chest.

"Nosuh. I b'lieve you is threatin me, Mist' Edguh." He waved the gun again. "Get on now. I gots to tell dem at de Co't House. Gunfire late last evenin, den another shot dis mornin. Gots to tell 'em how I seen dis boy Mist' Edguh Watson runnin off from dere just now totin his daddy's shootin iron, which his daddy ain't allowed to haves back in de firs' place."

I went ahead of him up the red road. "A black man's word won't mean much against mine. Just get you in bad trouble, Tap."

"Barrel still warm, Mist' Edguh. Sposin I telled 'em dat?"

"It won't be warm by the time you get there. Anyway, it's very dangerous, messing into white men's business." No answer came, only a slowing of the scuff of boots on the frozen clay. What would the Regulators do to any nigger who raised a weapon to a white man? I asked next. A nigger who slung greens at that white man's chest like he would toss slops to a hog? And threatened to report him to the bluecoats? If Major Coulter got wind of this, Tap Watson would be a stone dead nigger before nightfall.

But of course Tap's story would be told before the Regulators could shut him up. A loyal nigra, a "good home nigger," a church deacon swearing on the Bible—who would doubt him? Who would believe Ring-Eye's stinky son even if he told the truth, that a traitor long ago given up for dead had been caught stealing from his trapline? That Colonel Robert Briggs Watson's nephew had only gone to get his rabbit back, taking a weapon in case the thief attacked, finding instead the traitor Tilghman, wounded mortally the night before. He had grabbed the gun barrel and the old gun went off. It was an accident.

Wounded mortally? Hold on right there, boy! How you figger it was mortal? You a doctor, boy? Wounded by who? You'd best get your story straight, young feller!

Colonel Robert would deliver a harsh judgment. Was a pilfered rabbit reason enough to kill a starving kinsman? An Edgefieldian, a Confederate officer, a battle hero? Colonel Robert would call it murder.

Oh, I warned you!—I could hear Aunt Sophia now. At Clouds Creek, those "sky-crazed Celts" (Cousin Selden's term) were sure to seize on this excuse to cast out Ring-Eye's lineage for good. In the imminence of such injustice came a pounding ache so violent and a vertigo so sudden that I never even realized I was falling.

A black face inset in the gray heavens, mouth working without sound. Darkness came and darkness went. Jack Watson awakened, in grim humor. Panic had given way to a resolve as clear as that still point when, with the wind's dying, the shattered moonlight on the surface of rough water regathers its shards into one bright gleaming blade. How terrible that blade. How pure and simple.

No one lived near. I rolled up onto my feet so easily and swiftly that the black man stepped back in alarm. Leading the only witness back into Deepwood, I felt strength surge into my step, and every breath renewed me with wild power. I even teased Tap over my shoulder. Hadn't he only wanted me along because black folks were scared to be alone with corpses? With his contempt for darkie superstitions, Tap would normally be caustic in response. Today he remained silent, and when I turned, he stopped short in the road, then relinquished the musket.

"Dis sho'ly ain't no nigguh business, nosuh, it sho ain't." Mumbling, he took out a bandanna, wiping his neck in the frozen air as he might have done in the hot fields of midsummer. "You too young to be mixed up in dis, Mist' Edguh."

"I'm not mixed up in this. Unless you mix me."

"Ain't fixin to mix nobody, Mist' Edguh."

But it was really me who needed company. When I waved him toward the hole in the west wall he went ahead, then slowed. After a few more steps, he went no further. Having glimpsed what lay inside, he placed his hands over his eyes—"Oh Lawdamercy!"—and fell to his knees as I forced myself to look.

I had not tarried long enough to see the Owl-Man's body through the musket smoke. It had no head.

Without a tool to chip a grave in the frozen ground, we piled half-burned timbers on the trunk and legs. Tap mumbled prayers. "You was a good man, Cop'n Selden, suh," he finished, bowing his head. "A very good man. Black folks ain' gwine fo'get you."

Standing behind him, I lifted the musket and sighted down the barrel at the gray-frizzed scalp, the bare skin of the crown, the ears, the twitching skin and throbbing pulse, the humble skull. How fragile and transient the bent human seemed, with death hovering so close. One inadvertent twitch of my forefinger, already half numb with cold on the frozen metal. In leading me to kill by accident, Fate had betrayed me. In tempting me to obliterate the only witness, regaining my lost life, was Fate redeeming me?

At the base of my tongue was a quick metallic taste—not the taste of death but the taste of an unholy power to take life. I held my breath as with great care I lifted that numb finger from the worn and shiny lever of the trigger, but not before Tap Watson jerked his head around and stared into the eye behind the hammer.

FLIGHT

Even as I hurried toward Clouds Creek, my criminal sire, roaring with drink, was driving Major Coulter's cart like a loose chariot, careening around the Court House Square, scaring and scattering old ladies, dogs, and children, whipping his poor roan bloody. When one wheel was struck off by the wood sidewalk and the buggy pitched him headlong into the mud, he was seized and hauled forthwith up the courthouse steps and through the courtroom to the cells behind. Next morning he was charged with disturbing the peace, endangering life and limb, resisting arrest, and public drunkenness—everything the constable could think of that might hold him without bail until the next session of the circuit court.

I knew none of this when on Sunday before church, I went to collect my wage. From the stoop, I called good morning to the Colonel's wife as she crossed the corridor. Aunt Lucy only shook her head and did not answer. Then her husband came. He did not offer his hand, only coldly informed me that someone had reported a charred corpse in the Deepwood ruin and someone else had seen me on the road near Deepwood early yesterday morning. "It seems you were carrying a weapon. And a shot was heard."

He stood in wait, perhaps still hoping that I might explain. I was struck dumb. Who would have gone into that ruin? And just stumbled on a body beneath stacked timbers? Tap had betrayed me.

"You must leave this district." Colonel Robert's voice seemed far away. "You have no future at Clouds Creek."

"Sir? If my work—"

"It has nothing to do with that. You are an exceptional young farmer." Having no son of his own, he looked truly bereaved. He drew forth a money packet. "I've included fair payment for your hogs. Now go at once, you are in danger here."

I searched his face as a shot bird follows the hunter's hand descending to wring its neck. There was no absolution in that gaze. I wanted to howl, *It is not just! It was an accident! And he was already dying!* An inner screaming, a ringing like crazed bells. I must have gone straight over backwards. Later I recalled a faraway *whump* made by my head and shoulders as I struck the ground.

Muffled hog grunts and the croon of chickens. Cold white winter sun.

"Edgar, try to sit up."

"He fainted, did he? Wily as the father!"

A close warm smell of horse tack, burned tobacco. "He has these spells. Look at his color." Less patiently, the man's voice said, "Mrs. Watson, please do as I ask. Fetch him a blanket."

Rummaging, she called, "Does he know his father is in jail?"

I rolled away, sat up—"I'm fine"—fell sideways. Taking me under the arm, Colonel Robert tried to help me up off the cold earth onto the steps. Wrenching away made me dizzy and I sat down hard. I said, "It was not my doing. I never wished him harm."

Cousin Robert nodded, leading me behind the house out of sight of the road. "Yet you know what was done and you know who did it." He paused a moment. "I have come to know you, Edgar. You are prideful and stubborn. You will not betray the guilty. And since, to defend yourself, you must accuse—" He put his big hands on my shoulders, squeezing hard to make sure I understood that he understood. "Pay attention, Edgar. Men are out looking for you. If you're caught, you could be shot or hung." He offered his hand. "You have had a hard bad road for one so young and were set a poor example. I am truly sorry."

"It is not just," I growled in a stony voice, as my kinsman's face began to blur. When I blinked my eyes clear, his hand was still extended. It withdrew at just the moment my own hand started upward to accept it.

"God knows it is not just," he agreed quietly, scanning the countryside. "That is the way of His world." He crossed the yard to the back stoop. With a last warning to stay off the roads till I crossed the Georgia line, he closed the door behind him. On the white wall of his house, in winter shine, the window glass, clear and empty, reflected the black limbs of the trees.

All my life I have recalled the proffered hand of Colonel R. B. Watson, the grained and weathered skin of it, the wrist hairs like finespun golden threads in the cold sunlight.

THE COWARD

I fled across the frozen fields. At Grandfather's house, I flung the hog pen gate clean off its hinge and drove my burly boys to freedom with hard kicks and curses. Their snouts would lead them to the Colonel's troughs. If not, let them run wild, grow black and boarish. I tossed my rags and a few books into some sacking along with cold clabber and a knife and slung this meager bindle from the musket barrel. Leaving the Artemas plantation open to the world for all to pillage as they liked, I headed out across my fields, following Clouds Creek upstream through the home woods to the Ridge spring behind the church. Seeing no sign of riders on the highroad, I headed west toward Edgefield Court House.

Nearing Deepwood, I took to the wood edge at the sound of cantering horses. Armed riders passed. At Edgefield, crossing the back lots, I saw Tap Watson in the distance, gleaning in the field. Climbing the livery stable fence, I paid my father's bill out of my pay, reclaimed the roan. "Heard you had some trouble, boy," the hostler sneered, counting the money. "You and

ol' Ring-Eye both." He knew I was a fugitive, considered seizing me, and sidled up too close, but respectful of the musket and the cold cast of my eye,
he decided against any attempt to take me prisoner.

"Ye're a hard one, ain't ye."

"Try me and find out."

I walked the roan down the dirt lanes between dwellings. In the Sunday
silence, the lanes were empty. At Mama's cabin, a note on the table read
"Dear Son." They had left in haste while "your father" was in jail. She
hoped that one day I might join them at this address in north Florida but if
not, why then, good-bye. Did she mean, God be with you? Not thinking
clearly, I returned the musket to the rafters.

The jail cells were upstairs back of the courtroom. I fiddled the old lock and
slipped in quietly and listened. No deputy, no guard, not a sound. They
were all out on the hunt for the young killer. The lone prisoner, sprawled
upon his bunk, rolled over, squinted, jerked in alarm, yelled for the guard. I
should have realized the whole truth then and there.

He asked me furiously what I wanted. Challenged, I did not know. Had I
come to say I was sorry but I must take his horse? Had I, despite everything,
merely come to bid farewell to my treacherous Papa?

I blurted foolishly, "I am no longer your son."

"You walked all the way here from Clouds Creek to tell me *that*?" Hooting at my pomposity, my father lay back again, boots on the blanket, arm
over his eyes.

"As of today, I am Edgar Addison Watson," I persisted. "Uncle John
Addison—"

"Damn him!" he sat up. "In this family the eldest son shall take the name
of the paternal grandfather or be disowned!" I wanted to jeer—disowned
from what?—but he was already commanding me to go make sure that his
roan was getting the good oats he'd paid for at the stable. I told him that account was settled. Job awaited me outside. "Mama has left home and Minnie, too. I aim to follow 'em."

He shook off this news of wife and daughter as the roan might shiver off
flies. "Don't try taking my horse, you sonofabitch!" he yelled. "I'll get the
law on you!"

"You've already done that, Papa," I said. If he heard, he gave no sign. "Take the musket, then," he begged. "Leave me my horse. I reckon I don't amount to much without that horse," he added, seeking pity.

A shout rose from the square. Someone had recognized the tethered horse. Scared of a mob, Papa was on his feet, his blanket like a hood around his head and shoulders. Having come off the drink the hard way, all alone in his cold cell, he looked puffy and haggard, wheedling piteously, "They aim to hang me, son!"

"Nosir," I said. "It is me they're after."

When he realized what I'd said, he loosed a loud whoop of relief; whatever it was he knew, he'd got away with it. Then he stopped laughing and grew wary. "Don't look at me that bad way, boy. I weren't the one put it on you."

For the second time that day, the blackness swirled so thick before my eyes that I had to grasp the bars. "The Regulators meant to ride out there and take care of that traitor that scared you," he confided. But next morning, returning to finish the job, they had heard a shot, seen Watson's boy run out with a musket. They rode away but somebody must have talked. "Ol' Zip, I reckon."

"I might have gone and murdered that old nigra," I muttered, as the truth fell into place.

"Tap, you mean? Tap knows?" Slowly he rose and came over to the bars.

"You left him dying. You've implicated me." He deserves to die, I thought.

"For the love of Jesus, boy! Don't show that devil face to your own father!" Blaming everything on Coulter, he spat up the rest. Coulter had sent Claxton to the Union garrison with word about a shooting out at the old Tilghman place. As the only person in Edgefield District known to frequent Deepwood, young Edgar Watson was the natural suspect, but just to make sure, Claxton reported that the Watson boy, armed with a musket, had been seen out there early that morning. "Can't hardly believe that skunk'd go and do that to me," my father said. He had lowered his voice, conspiratorial, as if inviting me to help him plot the Terrible Retribution of the Watsons.

Eyes closed, I pressed my forehead to the cold iron of his bars. Until he had confessed it by mistake, I had not even been aware that my life had been put at risk to cover their tracks!

"You're pale, Edgar! Are you all right?" Reaching through the bars, the Coward Watson cupped my nape gently in his big hand. The hand remained too long. I stiffened. Had it occurred to him that I might go fetch his gun and shoot him through the bars? I thought, he aims to break my neck right now while he has his chance.

"You have grown up too fast," Papa said sadly, letting go.

"Yessir." My voice broke with despair. "I have grown up very fast." With all of Edgefield District on my trail—even the jailer was out looking for me—I had risked coming here, not to kill him, not to tell him his family had forsaken him, nor even that I meant to take his horse. After all these years of terror and humiliation, I had come here to see him one last time, hoping to receive his thanks for shouldering the blame for the botched murder of Selden Tilghman.

"You hate me, don't you." He was whining. "First the mother and the girl and now my only son." The victim's eyes glistened in self-pity when I nodded. He whispered, "I am forsaken, then." And I said, "Yes, you are."

I was at the door when he called after me a last time. "Tap knows what happened? That what you come to tell me?" He gave me an awful smile. "Son? You'll take care of that before you leave?" When I was silent, he said meanly, "Never mind, boy, the men will take care of it. Just you run away after your mama, save your own skin." How I hated him for that! "Come back and see your poor old Papa someday, will you do that, son? You promise?"

"Yessir. I will be back, I promise. I aim to kill you, Papa."

Crossing the still courtroom, I heard Lige Watson's howl of woe as the truth of his lost life fell down upon him.

From the courthouse terrace, I stared at my home country—the first time I'd really looked at it since Corporal E. D. Watson of the First Edgefield Volunteers had borne me up these steps in the first year of the War. The terrace was not so high above the square as I remembered, and its noble prospect of blue mountains appeared sadly diminished. The countryside looked commonplace and the world small because my heart and hope had shrunken down to nothing.

The hostler had raised the alarm and people in the square were pointing as I ran down the steps and mounted. Tap was still out in the field. He, too, must have heard I was a fugitive, must imagine now that I was riding out to kill him. Having no place to run, he only straightened as the big horse came down on him. Slowly he laid down his hoe and sack and removed his lumpy hat to await the rider.

"I done jus' like you tole me, Mist' Edguh." His voice was dull and dead. "I ain't spoked to nobody about nothin, nosuh." He was trembling.

Behind me, a shroud of winter dust arose from the hooves of horses. I said, "All the same, you know too much. They will be coming." I told him he must find Lulalie, hide till nightfall, then depart. I handed him all the money left in the Colonel's packet. "Buy a mule," I said. They should slip away at dark, head for Augusta, catch up with the womenfolk on their way to Fort White, Florida.

Tap refused the money. "Nosuh, Mist' Edguh. Dis yere Carolina country is mah home. I ain't done nothin wrong so I ain't goin. Trus' in de Lord! Dass what Preacher Simkins tole 'em at our church when dem riders come for him. Dem white men listened, den dey went on home."

"This kind won't listen, Tap. They won't even ask." But Tap had always known better so he never heard me. He was watching the dust over the town. "I b'lieve dey comin. You bes get goin. Tell dat woman, please, dat Lalie and me be waitin on her when she get ready to come home."

"God help you, Tap," I said, turning the horse.

Avoiding the main roads, I headed south and west and forded the Savannah River near the fall line early next morning. When the roan clambered up the Georgia bank, I turned in the saddle to gaze back. I had left my native Carolina, and everywhere ahead was unknown country.

CHAPTER 2

✦

ON ECHO RIVER

I caught up with the women on the old Woodpecker Trail down west of the Great Okefenokee. Rode up alongside the wagons on a warm afternoon as if joining them had been my plan right from the start. Those poor females looked relieved, Aunt Cindy, too, but seeing that roan horse made them uneasy. Perhaps because I was unsmiling and untalkative, they never asked about Job's ring-eyed owner and I never offered to explain, not then, not later, having no wish to lay open the wound of my lost life at Clouds Creek, and the great waste of it. On that cold afternoon, I hitched the roan to the tailgate of the wagon and crawled inside amongst their bedding and slept straight through until early the next morning.

Seeing my head poke out, Aunt Cindy whooped; she fixed me a big dish of scraps before pressing me about her little family. How was her sweet Lalie getting on? Had that fool Tap sent word?

I could scarcely look her in the eye. The truth would worry the poor woman to distraction, and in the end, a lie—that Tap and Lulalie were on their way to join us—would be still worse. Finally I said that, living at Clouds Creek, I had scarcely seen them. In my gut I knew that Tap was done for, and as for Lalie, who knew what had become of her? Aunt Cindy soon saw that behind my stiff smile and tough manner, my heart was crippled, and she gave me a queer look, but it was not her place to question me too closely so she didn't.

On the twelfth of March of 1871, we crossed over into Florida. With two state lines behind me, I was breathing easier. Only now did I introduce myself to my fellow pioneers—Edgar A. Watson, overseer of the Artemas Plantation at Clouds Creek, South Carolina, at your service, sir. Nobody knew quite what to make of this husky youth who was no boy but not a man yet either. What he was, in truth, was a fugitive from his own land and rightful heritage, angry and dangerous as a gut-shot bear.

The last leg of the journey was by slow barge south to Branford Landing on the Suwannee River, "far, far away, that's where my heart is turning ever, that's where the old folks stay." That old song misted my eyes with up-wellings of loss. Curled in my nest in the warm tar-smelling hemp hawsers on the bow, I wallowed in tender emotions.

Try as I would to find relief in my escape from the cold rain and mud of Piedmont winter with its meager food and numbing drudgery, nothing seemed to ease the ache of longing. The farther I traveled from where I belonged, the more unjust my exile seemed. I reviled my misbegotten father, reveling in fantasies of a dire patricide. From Cousin Selden's *Iliad* I had memorized a passage about the great rage of revenge which "swirls like smoke within our heart, and becomes in our madness a thing more sweet than the dripping of honey." That fury had not abated, nor the will to vengeance, which chewed like a black rat at my lungs. My one consolation was knowing that justice would be done, that one day "in my madness," I would deprive my father of his raw red life.

Before my eyes daily as we sailed way down upon the Suwannee River were visions of spring furrows at Clouds Creek, the warmed earth opened up behind the plow; of wildflowered meadows, cool and verdant, and airy open woods along the shaded creeks, winding southeast to the Edisto. That spring landscape turned forever and away in my mind's eye, changing softly into the gold greens of upland summer in that lost land where I was born, the country of my forefathers, the heart of home. Clouds Creek—my earth—was the wellspring and the source of Edgar Watson, all the Eden he had ever wished or hoped to find.

Then reverie dissolved, leaving cold sweat like a dank swamp mist on my skin. I stared about me at the undiscovered country on both sides of the wild river, a howling waste of dark riverine forest and rank coarse savanna where the eternal seasons passed unchanged. Mourning my sprightly hogs, my sturdy pens, brooding about the weeds and hard sharp briar that all too soon would creep over my farmland, returning it to the oldfield desolation in which I'd found it, I sat stunned by melancholy. When the pain and rage burst from my mouth, my awful squawk silenced every soul on that slow barge.

Deaf to my cry (out of embarrassment), my mother and sister smiled sweetly; they tatted and chattered. Still ignorant of what had taken place at Edgefield, they were afraid of Edgar's darkness, and all the while that stern black woman awaited me, confident I would spit up evil when the time came. Unwilling to meet her suspicious eye, I set my jaw and glared fixedly at the forests of the wild Suwannee (Creek Indian for "Echo River," said the bargeman).

> *All up and down the whole Creation*
> *Sadly I roam*
> *Still longing for the old plantation*
> *And for the old folks at home.*

Once I'd hummed it, that song became epidemic on the barge; everyone hummed, whistled, and sang it, and just when it seemed it might die out, I would start over by mistake, unable to drive its plaint out of my head. Oh how I sickened of that song and self-pity, and of grief-rotted Edgar, too, and of foul nightmares about the Owl-Man, who in my dreams never appeared as Cousin Selden.

Day after day, the strange smells and hidden voices of the passing wilderness, seeking to draw me back into my life, had passed unheeded. And then one day I awoke to find the earth colors returned and "the whole Creation" come alive and clear. As the dark withdrew, the forest stood forth in a light of revelation, and sunrise leaves sparkled and spun, breathing a fresh wind from the west, off the Gulf of Mexico, and I jumped up with a laugh that startled poor Ninny-Minnie. Wasn't I young and able-bodied, able-minded, too? One day I would go home to reclaim Clouds Creek, but meanwhile a virgin land was opening before me. We should reach our destination, the bargeman said, in time for the spring planting.

Here and there, rounding a bend, the barge surprised brown-skinned people on the banks, crouched back like wildcats caught out in the open. The

Cherokees who were chastised by my ancestors were almost gone from upland Carolina, though a few still lurked in remote regions; these Creeks were the first wild men I had ever seen. The women and young would rush into the reeds or flee through the shadows of the great live oaks which spread their heavy limbs over the clearings, but the grown men and older boys, drifting out of gun range, would pause at the forest edge to watch the intruders over their shoulders, in the way of deer; I was awed by the stillness in them even when they moved. They were set to run, they had to be. The bargeman told us that bored, drunken travelers would pass the time blazing away at every furred and feathered bit of life along the river, and would sometimes shoot close to these people's feet "to see them redskins dance," which was why, at the first glint of metal, the wild folk withdrew into the shadows until the intruders were gone around the bend and the forest silences regathered.

I never greeted them, having learned that lesson when even the smallest child among them refused to acknowledge frantic Minnie, though she waved and waved. "Why don't they wave back?" she cried, desperately hurt. I said roughly, "They fear and despise us. Why should they wave?" These wild ones came down from those Muskogee Creeks that Ol' Hickory had chased south out of Georgia, said the bargeman, and most of them were never seen at all, easing down into hiding at the sound of our approach, watching us pass.

These hinterlands, so distant from the settlements, remained uncultivated and unhunted. The bargeman said that in Spanish times, when a road was opened from St. Augustine on the Atlantic coast to Pensacola on the Gulf, there were still buffalo in these savannas, and also the great jaguar, called tigre, and panthers, bears, and red wolves were still common. Sometimes, at night, shrill screams scared Mama and poor Ninny half to death—not white females being violated by naked savages as they imagined but panthers mating, the bargeman assured Mama, who recoiled from this man's vulgar liberty. Bull gators coughed and roared back in the swamps, and once there came a lonely howl that he identified as the red wolf. Flocks of huge black fowl in the glades were bronze-backed turkeys, and everywhere, wild ducks jumped from the bulrushes and reeds, shedding bright water. I shot big drakes and gobblers for provisions and pin-hooked all the fresh fish we could eat. Pairs of great woodpeckers larger than crows, with flashing white bills and crimson crests afire in the sun, crossed the river in deep bounding flight, and hurtling flocks of small long-tailed parrots, bright green as new leaves in the morning light. The wild things were shining with spring colors and new sap and finally I was, too. I would sink my teeth into this morning land like a fresh peach.

The river barge was warped ashore where a tributary, the Santa Fe, joins the Suwannee—the confluence of the Echo and the Holy Faith, I informed the women. (Spanish Catholics! snapped Mama, worn out by her journey and on the lookout for the smallest cause to be indignant.) De Soto and his men, more exhausted and discouraged by the heat and insects than by Indian attacks, had called it the River of Discord, whereas to the Indians, the river was sacred mystery, vanishing quite suddenly into the earth—no suck or swirl, just gone away under the ground. Perhaps because the red-skinned devils had made life Hell for the first settlers, those folks imagined they had found the source of the River Styx, deep in the Underworld, and few had persevered long enough to learn that the current surfaced a few miles downstream as a beautiful blue spring in the forest.

While the barge continued on to Branford Landing, I chose to explore the country before meeting the women at Ichetucknee Plantation. Hollering good-bye to all to insure attention, I rode my big roan off that barge as she touched shore—a staccato clatter sharp as rifle fire as the horse balked, then a mighty gathering of haunches and great leap and splash and upward heave onto the bank. These heroics, alas, were spoiled by the hydraulics of my stallion, which lowered its nozzle to release a stream of piss even while it rid itself of gas, hightailing off in a grand salute of horse farts and manure as the women's cries of admiration turned to giggles, but finally all cheered as grim young Edgar was actually seen to laugh. Minutes later, in my own company at last, I could not stop grinning, feeling near-idiotic with anticipation.

The river trail ran north along the "Santa Fee" (as backcountry Floridians still call it), which descends from a dry sandy land of piney woods and scrub oak to the cypress sink where it is drawn beneath the earth. Farther upriver, the trail turned off along the Ichetucknee, a crystal stream with blue water so clear that streaming underwater weeds like turquoise eels swim endlessly over white sand.

ICHETUCKNEE

The Ichetucknee post office and trading post (also the blacksmith shop and gristmill) was six miles up this woodland stream, on the east bank of the Mill Pond spring and only a few miles from Fort White, in Columbia County. The proprietor, a small quick man named Collins, was eager to relate how Fort White had been built back in '37, during the Second Seminole War, only to be abandoned to the savages a few years later. The first of his name had come as pioneers in '42, twenty years before the Third Seminole War. Soon after came the War Between the States, when this worthy blacksmith-trader-postmaster had rushed over to Lake City— known as Alligator in those days—eager to join the Columbia Rifles and go fight the Yanks. (I did not ask if he'd got his wish, since if he had, I would never have escaped the smallest detail of that wartime saga.)

In a few years, this lively Edgar Collins would become my sister's father-in-law, and because we shared a detestation of our given name, we got on fine. After his wife had packed me some good grub, Mr. Collins pointed me northeast through the woods toward the plantation, but not before warning me to watch my step around the foreman and his boys, a pack of Georgia ridge runners named Tolen.

I remounted and rode on, anxious to reach the plantation before nightfall. Back home in Carolina our roads were iron red, but here in the forests of north Florida the trails were cool white clay, wandering off like ghost paths through the trees. I dismounted and rubbed some of this stuff between my fingers: poor soil for farming. In this spring damp the road clay, beaten hard by wagon wheels and hooves, felt smooth and fine as bonemeal; in summer it would powder to fine dust. Peering about these silent woods with no idea what lay ahead, my high spirits were overtaken and dragged down by a claw of that morbid despair which I thought I'd left behind me.

Aunt Tabitha Watson and her daughter Laura lived in "the plantation house," which was nothing at all like a plantation house in Edgefield. The grand manor that Mama had set her heart on was no more than a big log cabin with two rooms on either side of a center passage. The outside was framed over with rough pine boards with the bark on, and a stoop was tacked onto each end of the dim corridor. Except in size, it scarcely differed from what the old folks called a dog-trot cabin because any hound—or hog, coon, rooster, or inquisitive bear—could travel through from one stoop to the other without so much as a how-d'ye-do to the inhabitants. Yet it was the biggest cabin in the county, well situated on the rich soil of a former cow pen, now a fenced-in grove of bearing pecan trees and black walnut and persimmon.

Great-Aunt Tabitha (for reasons best known to herself, she had decreed that her name was to be spoken as Ta-*bye*-a-tha) was creeping up on sixty years of age. In her appearance, her daughter Laura, though still short of forty, wasn't far behind. Cousin Laura habitually stood one step behind her mother, where both of them (this was clear instantly) thought she belonged. Both were horse-faced females in high collars and white aprons, neither plain nor pretty, but the daughter was only a dim copy of the mother, who had saved for herself every last dab of brains and character. Cousin Laura, Mama had warned us, was kindhearted but not bright. With her large eyes and soft brown hair and creamy skin, she had once passed for pretty, but that wide mouth (as Mama remarked with her customary charity) "lacked the firm jaw needed to control those flying teeth."

"Aunt," I said, holding my hat over my heart in sign of piety and respect, "I am your great-nephew E. A. Watson, at your service."

"A for Artemas." The old lady smiled. "Such a kind good man, for all his foibles. We called him 'Bird' because he sang with such sweet voice."

"If you please, ma'am, it is Addison. Edgar Addison Watson."

"Artemas," she admonished me. "After your grandfather. That is Watson family custom, that is the name assigned you in our family Bible, and that is that." My tart mama and this haughty personage were doomed to tangle, I saw that much, but I held my tongue.

Black Calvin Banks (as old "Cobber" had dubbed himself once he'd become a full-fledged citizen of the republic) told me all there was to know about the plantation, which consisted of four square miles of flat arable land. Originally called Ichetucknee, it had been bought by William Myers of Columbia, South Carolina, who had fled south in the first year of the War to start all over in north Florida, having boarded his ladies in Atlanta until he could provide them a few primitive comforts. Upon arrival, Colonel Myers set his men to girdling the trees to kill the encircling pine forest, and eventually three square miles had been cleared and fenced. By the time I came there, in the spring of '71, five hundred acres had been planted in corn—"twenty-five acres per nigger and mule" was the way they figured, Calvin said—and three hundred and fifty in Sea Island cotton, which had been the cash crop in north Florida since the War.

"What corn we grow, dass mostly for hog and home. Bale up de shucks fo' winter fodder, keep de niggers in cornmeal and hominy. Hog food, corn bread, hominy, sometimes sourins. Folks know about sourins in Carolina? Turn cornmeal sour by sun-cookin it? Pretty good to eat with chicken. Gopher, too. You folks like gopher?" Calvin hummed a little, his mouth working, savoring those tortoise feeds of yore.

Cousin Laura's husband had returned each year to his family home in South Carolina, leaving the management of his plantation to his overseer, one Woodson Tolen. Most of his slaves had stayed on here as freedmen, having neither the wherewithal nor the ambition to find their way back home. Calvin Banks had served as Myers's coachman and remained loyal to the family, knowing freedom was dangerous. During the War, when a Yankee detachment reached Olustee, thirty miles to the northeast, Colonel Myers had buried his gold in a secret place back in the woods. A few months later, just when he was drawing up his plans for the first real manor house in Columbia County, he was struck dead by lightning while standing beneath an oak during a rainstorm. After his employer's death, the former Cobber bought a hundred-acre piece from Cousin Laura, paying $450 in cash. After the War, this land would go for $6 an acre, so he got it cheap, but even so, nobody could figure how that darn nigra had saved up so much money. Naturally the rumors spread that his coachman had been with Myers when the Colonel buried his gold out in the woods and that this black rascal had gone back after his death and dug it up. Aunt Tabitha believed that Calvin was a thief, Cousin Laura did not, which was typical of the differences between them.

Because Laura had no head for business (nor for much else, observed her loyal old friend, my mother) the young widow had been left out of her husband's will. The Colonel had specified that Aunt Tabitha would inherit his plantation, which upon her death would be turned over to his Myers nephews, who were our first cousins on their mother's side. (Aunt Cindy was almost "family," too, since it had been the Myers relatives who had given her to Ellen Addison as a wedding present.) After Cousin William's death in 1869, his ladies had traveled here seeking to break the will, and because wartime conditions were uncertain, Aunt Tabitha decided to stay on in Florida and manage this remote plantation which nobody in Reconstruction times could afford to buy.

Aunt Tabitha had soon discovered that cultivated or even educated people were very uncommon in this frontier county, and she and her daughter came to hate their isolation. Since Mama had been Laura's friend and schoolmate (and since Aunt Tabitha was embarrassed—faintly—by her own role in Mama's failed marriage), her plea for refuge in Florida had been granted. "The family at Clouds Creek informs me that you have done all you could to save the soul of my afflicted nephew," read Aunt Tab's letter, which Mama had shown us on those days on the Suwannee, "and suffered no end of abuse and sorrow for your pains. Forsake him, then, as God is your witness, and take shelter with us in Florida, for your children's sake as well as for your own." And for Aunt Tab's sake, too, Mama was quick to point out. The plantation would need all the help that strong young Edgar could provide, not to speak of Cinderella Myers's contributions in the kitchen.

Calvin Banks fetched our family from the river landing in a wagon. How threadbare the poor things looked when they arrived! I glanced at Aunt Tabitha, who shared this impression and did not trouble to hide it. I was glad of what Mama had confided, that she had hidden her jewelry from her husband from the very first day of her marriage, and had brought along her few small diamonds "to start us out in Florida." She had always worn her hair in a big old rat's nest suitable for hiding diamond rings—two beautiful rings, according to our Ninny, "not just little chips stuck onto something."

WOODSON TOLEN

On my first day, I jumped right in and labored mightily in the spring planting to show I was no mere poor relation but an able farmer, and that just because we had accepted Aunt Tab's hospitality did not mean we sought her charity. Excited by the possibilities of this plantation and eager to understand its economics, I was up early and rode till late, helping out wherever I could learn something. Within months I felt confident that I could run this place as overseer, though it might take a year or so to prove it.

On Sundays, out hunting and exploring, I rode all over the south county. The forests were fairly trembling with deer and turkey, an almost unimaginable abundance after long years in the worn-out woods of home. As for robins, redbirds, orioles—those larger songbirds which I snared for our poor table in the War years—their peaceful choruses arose each morning from the oak trees near the house, intermingled with the ring of axes or the hammers banging on some new construction. Every shack had roosters crowing and hogs grunting and fieldhand families laughing and crooning in the evening, sounds which made Mama homesick for "the good old days," by which she meant the antebellum days of cotton wealth and slavery. All that was lacking here, she whispered, with a wry glance at our benefactors, was amusing company. Oh how she missed her poor lost Selden, Mama sighed, still in hopes that one day her witty, educated cousin might reappear.

As a kinsman of the owners, I was disliked from the start by the overseer, Woodson Tolen, originally hired to keep the place running profitably in those months when Colonel Myers was away; almost certainly this man's designs on the plantation were born on the very day Myers was killed. He knew the old woman could not live forever no matter how hard she might try, and once sharp-eyed Aunt Tabitha was out of the way, Cousin Laura would cheerfully sign almost any piece of paper a conniving skunk like Woodson Tolen might set in front of her. He was already training his oldest boy, thin shifty James, to replace him at the trough when he retired.

A redneck from the Flint River country in the Georgia hills, this man Woodson—a man of the same ingrown breed as Z. P. Claxton—was a wiry small weasel with mean red eyes pinched too close to his nose and traces of ancient grime in every seam. From his vantage point, nose to the ground, this feller spied on my hard work, which he perceived as a sinister attempt to thwart his ambitions for his clan, and he never ever missed a chance to make me look as bad as possible in the eyes of Auntie Tab.

On those windless days in the long Florida summer, the earth slowed to a crawl and the air died, under a sky as thick and white as a boiled egg. On woodland trees along the white clay roads, the dust-shrouded leaves appeared exhausted. On such a day, out hoeing cotton, I stripped off my wet shirt, as all the fieldhands had the sense to do. And on this day the snooping W. Tolen came along on his woods pony with his second son Sam Frank Tolen up behind him.

Seeing my torso shining with sweat, Sammy jeered and stuck his tongue out. I ignored this. Determined to get along at Ichetucknee, I tolerated Fat Sammy's friendship, although he was younger and not much of a friend, having been tutored by his daddy in every little meanness he had not been born with. However, he was the only white boy close to my own age for a mile around, and I must admit that I sometimes enjoyed his comical and very dirty turn of mind. Or was it simply my discovery that I enjoyed laughing?

Woodson squinted across the fence, grinning that dog grin of his that had no fun in it. In his redneck whine he said, "Ah reckon Miz Ta-bye-a-tha won't care to hear how her nephy-yew was workin half-naked longside the niggers." And he pointed his bony finger at my eyes to send me evil luck. (Old-fashioned folk of his mountain breed still wore a little bag around the neck containing a piece of their own shit, to keep evil at bay and decent people, too, but I had no such nostrum to protect me.)

Deep in this backcountry out of sight of Yankee law, our new black citizens were still treated like niggers, never mind what they might call themselves back in their quarters: Calvin Banks was the one nigra in that field who knew his civil rights under Reconstruction. Hearing Woodson's words, he stopped his hoe and the rest copied him. Those boys might not know too much about Reconstruction but they sure knew every last damn way there was to leave off working. When Woodson yelled, "Now y'all get back to work!" I hollered, "Mr. Tolen, sir? Why not send your fat kid over here to help out in the cotton 'stead of riding him around and giving stupid orders?"

That tickled the nigras, set 'em to whimpering, had to turn their backs for fear Woodson would see. I had gone too far and these men knew it and Sam knew it, too. But I will say for Sammy, he tried to help out with a humorous distraction. Shaking his fist at me, he hollered, "Put that shirt on like the overseer told you, Edgar Watson, or I'll come over there and put it on you!"

Laughing, I went back hoeing as if the whole thing was a joke, and

Calvin and the other boys jumped to do the same, but Woodson was wound much too tight to let it go. Sammy was still giggling so hard at his own wit that he nearly shook his pap out of the saddle, so the overseer yanked that pony's head around and rode right out from under his own boy, dumping him onto the road like a sack of feed. He hollered at my back, "Just you do like I told you!" He rode on a ways as if that settled it, leaving his boy moping in the dust.

When his order was ignored, Tolen walked his pony back real slow, reined in, and sat there with one knee propped on the saddle horn. "Jus' sposin," he drawled, after a silence, "I was to let on to Miz Ta-bye-a-tha how her nephy-yew never paid her rightful overseer no mind? Sposin I was to tell about them blast-pheemies you spoke, cussin out that self-same overseer while he was overseein?"

When I paid no attention, went on working, he nodded awhile, then spoke in a hushed voice—the cracker way of letting a man know he's in bad trouble. "Sposin she was to send you back to Carolina?" Since this was the third time he had threatened that, I was pretty sure he'd come by something from Carolina that he would use against me when the time came, to spoil my hopes of a fresh start at Ichetucknee.

My sister would whine about that "horrible Edgar mask" I sometimes wore stuck to my face—"like the real Edgar but dead." At such times Edgar was "beside himself," Mama once commented, more shrewdly than she knew. Had they glimpsed Jack Watson or merely the "somber hard-faced boy" Great-Aunt Sophia at Clouds Creek had disapproved of? These days, Jack only appeared at times of rage, out of that vertigo which sometimes blackened my brain until I fell. I'd never spoken of him, not to anybody, knowing I'd be called crazy. But I was never crazy and neither was Jack Watson. He was always cool, efficient, knowing just when to appear and when to go; since I couldn't summon him, far less control him, I, too, dreaded him a little. Good thing there was fifty yards and a split-rail fence between me and Woodson Tolen or Jack might have run and jumped and hauled that cracker out of the saddle and slit his stringy throat, and maybe his frogmouth son right along with him.

Jack Watson spat his words at Tolen like cold bullets: "You want my shirt on so damn bad, you haul your dirty ass down off that horse and come across that fence and put it on me." Challenged him real clear and loud so there could be no mistake. "Trouble is, you white trash sonofabitch, you are not man enough to do that."

Fat Sam shut off his moaning and picked himself up out of the road, and the fieldhands hurried back to work like bald-eyed demons.

Tolen climbed down off his pony and yanked his rawhide whip out of its holster. Seeing that plaited whip uncoil across his boots like a blue racer, the pony shied and the niggers moaned real low. Jack was gone. I came clear quick. It was much too late to undo such damage, and the overseer did not aim to miss his chance. Expecting me to beg for mercy, he curled that whip back in a coil and climbed the rail. When he jumped down and moved toward me, I called out, "Hold on now, Mr. Tolen!" But fear had rotted out my voice, and hearing that, he kept on coming with stiff, small steps like a mean hound.

"Beg him, Mist' Edguh, beg him!" Calvin whispered.

Scared sick, I drew my knife out of my boot, turning the blade up to the sun so the man could appreciate that quick glint off the tip. I took a good deep slow long breath, then crouched and circled with my left arm out the way my daddy taught me.

Tolen was good with that long whip; he could sit in the saddle and snap the raised-up head off of a rattler. Unless I caught hold of it, yanked him off balance, he would strip me to fish bait before I got in close enough to cut him. But maybe this feller had noticed how handy I was with my old Bowie, playing at mumbledy-peg with Sam, and he never got ten yards from the fence before he wavered. "A man don't knife-fight with no boy," he gasped—the same thing General Calbraith Butler told me on the square at Edgefield Court House except that out of the overseer's rat mouth, it had no truth in it. Tolen backed away across that fence and clambered up onto his horse. "This ain't finished, boy!" he yelled, all out of breath from dragging his fat son up behind him. Sammy looked back at me very upset as they rode away.

For a dirt-floor redneck, that vow of vengeance was an oath more sacred than six swears on the family Bible. A boy had backed him down and his son had witnessed it and the hands, too. No cracker could set aside that kind of insult far less forgive that dog name I had called him. These Tolens might lie low awhile, but revenge was the age-old way of mountain honor and they would never rest until they got it.

I worked my hoe a little while, to ease my breath and simmer down the field hands while I thought things over. Calvin was the driver on this crew when I was absent, and pretty soon he worked his way up alongside, eager to be seen imparting to the white boy the wisdom of his years at Ichetucknee. "Mist' Edguh," he warned, "From dis day on, doan you nevuh turn yo' back no mo' on one dem Tolens!"

Because he had brains and got things done, Calvin had been spoiled by William Myers even before he was a freedman. As Aunt Tab said, "Calvin knows his place but attaches too much importance to it." I didn't want to punish him for disrespect toward the overseeer because his warning showed loyalty to our family and took courage. Even so, he could not be permitted to disparage whites, even miserable po' whites like these.

"Calvin," I growled, "just you mind your business." The others whooped at the boss nigger's expense. I wasn't laughing. I was remembering Clouds Creek and how I'd lost my chance. If I wasn't very careful—if Jack wasn't careful?—I might lose it here.

FORT WHITE

Walking home, I went straight to Great-Aunt Tabitha. Woodson on horseback had arrived there well ahead of me; I caught him slipping off the back stoop like a tomcat, leaving behind him like cat spit-up his twisted tale of how that shirtless boy had cursed him vilely, threatened him with a knife, and called him a dog name for good measure.

When I darkened her doorway, the old lady called out querulously from within, telling me to state my business. I told her I could not work another day with that lowlife cracker and his shiftless sons, who were letting our fine plantation go to rack and ruin.

"*Our* plantation?" Her silence lasted longer than I cared for. When she finally came out onto the stoop, I feigned outrage, requesting her permission to leave Ichetucknee and go work for her friend and neighbor Captain Tom Getzen—a bluff, of course, since she prized my unpaid labor much too much to let me go. Or so I thought until this irascible old woman waved me away toward Getzen's, then sat down in her rocking chair and fanned herself, taking no further notice of me whatsoever.

What a pity, she told Mama later, that such a capable young man should be so hotheaded and insubordinate. "*Like his father* is what she meant," Mama complained, bitterly disappointed that my surly behavior had spoiled all our prospects. Apparently Aunt Tab had mentioned her new plan to make me plantation manager, having heard from Colonel Robert at Clouds Creek that Cousin Edgar was hardworking and resourceful, an exceptional young farmer altogether. The Colonel had said not a single word against me, which put me forever in his debt and reawakened my hope of return. "Ichetucknee is a Watson plantation, Edgar! This could be our plantation and your own great chance!"—that was actually her hope and of course mine, too, until I could reclaim Clouds Creek. Well, said I, if Auntie Tab thinks me so capable, why don't she take that job away from Tolens, give it to her kin? "*Doesn't,*" said Mama, who would never relent in her lifelong ambition to raise her son as a well-spoken young gentleman.

"I'll work hard for Captain Tom, Mama, make a good name for myself. Then I'll come back."

"Is that what you told Colonel Robert, too?" Mama was deathly afraid that Auntie Tab might hear bad stories from "other sources." Plainly she had heard something herself. New tales, she said, had arrived from Edgefield only lately with the Herlongs, those strict, judgmental Methodists who were clearing woodland south of the plantation. It was Herlong darkies, I suspected, who had brought news of Tap Watson's fate along with false rumors of my role in it, for Aunt Cindy had not spoken to me since. She looked right through me.

Mama then said that Cindy's husband had been murdered, and that the Regulators might have had something to do with it; she confessed relief that at the time her spouse had been locked in jail. "Is that true?" I nodded. It was true. However, she persisted, it had been reported that Edgar Watson was the last person seen with Tap in the field where his body was found. "And now there is a rumor that you eliminated him as a witness to some dreadful deed before running away to Florida to escape punishment." When I jumped up, demanding to know who was spreading such vicious rumors, she only hunched over her needlework, shaking her head. "I'm glad to hear you didn't murder Tap," she whispered. "I only hope you haven't murdered someone else."

Tap's killers had taken advantage of my flight to make me the suspect in both deaths, and my own mother begrudged me the benefit of the doubt. Was that because of the scary beating I'd given my father? I don't think so.

I think she begrudged me a mother's faith in her son's innocence for the same perverse reasons she had formerly begrudged me a mother's protection against her drunken husband. Stoked with bile, I disdained to defend myself by telling my side of the story.

I rode four miles south each day to the Getzen plantation, a tract of good land where I worked hard for Captain Tom, and the following spring he leased me my own piece to sharecrop. He took his croppers, black as well as white, to Frazee's in Fort White, told Josh Frazee, "Now these boys each get a hundred dollars' worth of groceries this year." So Old Man Frazee would set up the page: E. A. Watson for One Year—he'd write it down. Bought only coffee and such things because all our vegetables and grain and meat came from the farm and wild meat and berries from the woods around. The plantation supplied fertilizer and common stores and income would be split halfway.

Fort White was the county's second-largest town after Lake City. Phosphate, cotton, and pine timber, and turpentine and resin from the pine sap. The pine gum ran from April to November; after two or three years that tree would be cut for timber. The town had a sawmill, gristmills, cotton gins, and a cottonseed oil mill. Dirt streets and boardwalk, hitching posts and water troughs, kerosene lampposts, well-stocked stores, and a couple of saloons. In the center of town rose three stories' worth of bright yellow hotel, the Sparkman Hotel, where in years to come, I would go to eat my lunch almost every Saturday, swap jokes and stories, and do most of the talking.

THE TOLEN BOYS

Riding home through the woods by different roads, I rode fast with a pistol in my hand, keeping a sharp eye on the trees. Probably those ridge runners were too smart to bushwhack Edgar Watson, since every man in the south county would know who pulled the trigger, but I could not assume they were that smart when drunk. And drunk they were one autumn day when our paths crossed outside the Collins store at Ichetucknee Springs and Old Man Woodson, swaying in the saddle, pointed his bony finger at my eyes like he was sighting down a musket barrel, reminding me how he aimed to take care of me in his own good time.

Sam Tolen was still more or less my friend, we drank shine and rassled, bird-hunted, went fishing. As for his brothers, Shifty Jim was born two-faced but could act real friendly and Mike was an honest, amiable kid who wanted to believe that his daddy's threats against me were just fooling. But that morning I informed those boys that the day I decided their old man was serious about his threats—and I gave 'em a hard squint—that day might be his last on earth, maybe theirs, too.

Jim Tolen had cockeyed ears and a rodent mouth way up under high nostrils, and he had a sniffing manner to go with it, as if he were scenting some nice rotted food. Jim sniffed, then spat. "Pa ain't gone to bother his head about no damn bullshit such as that." Mikey tried spitting, too, and Fat Sam spat extra noisily to mock his brothers. "Your turn, Edgar," he told me with a wink. I winked back, then cleared my throat and hawked the contents very near Jim's boot. He jumped like a mink in slit-eyed fury, pointing at my eyes the way his daddy had; he scowled and left.

Fat Sam said, worried, "This mess ain't none of my doin, Edgar. Got nothin in the world to do with Sam Frank Tolen." Nosir, we were bosom friends so far as Sam Frank Tolen was concerned. But from the day I'd backed his daddy down, we could never be true friends and we both knew it.

Not long after that, Woodson's wife moved out in order to move in with a widower, John Russ, who had four boys of his own. Old Man Woodson slunk on home to Georgia, so the tension around those woods eased up a little. Shifty Jim ran the plantation, making a worse job of it than his old man, and Sammy and I fooled around some as before. I enjoyed teasing him and he enjoyed being teased, that was about it. Never let me forget that the Tolen boys, not Edgar Watson, were running the plantation, and where they were running it, I advised him, was straight into the ground. But mostly I ignored Sam or just played along, convinced it was only a matter of time before Aunt Tab got fed up with these corn rats and begged me to take over. Before that happened, Jim Tolen left for Georgia, scooting out on a shotgun wedding. He left Fat Sammy as the overseer and Sam got drunk, to celebrate. "Too bad you ain't smarter, Ed. Might get you a good job over-seein, same as I got." I grinned right back. "You never know, Sam, I may get there yet." And he said, "Over my dead body!" and we both guffawed.

According to age, experience, and bone ability, not to mention the blood ties of kin, his job should have been mine, but on account of my "checkered reputation," Aunt Tab would not lift her little finger.

UNHOLY WEDLOCK

One evening, Minnie was waiting in the road when I came home. She raised her arms and I swooped her up and sat her astride behind me on old Job; she held my shoulders. As we cantered home, she giggled with the rocking motion in that elation of young girls who don't know what to do with their new juices, disguising her pleasure by simpering her news into my ear.

For some time now, she confided, that darned Sammy Tolen had overlooked no chance to tickle her. I explained that this was his loutish way of reconnoitering a young girl's person. Well, she squeaked, Cousin Laura, though twenty-nine years Sam's senior, had seemed very happy to be tickled, and at one point had become, well, overexcited. "Oh, you horrid boy!" she shrieked, rassling Sammy to the ground and seating herself on what would have been his lap if he'd sat up. Two nights later, Ninny said (daring this topic only because she rode behind me where I couldn't see her face), investigating a racket in the barn, Aunt Tab had caught the Widow Laura seated astride Sammy with her nightshirt up and naked as a lily the rest of the way down, and this morning she had whipped those cringing sinners into the buggy and bounced them eight miles to Lake City, where they were united in "unholy wedlock," as our mama called it.

"Oh, sweet Jesus!" I burst out, incensed. Thrilled, my sister cried, "Edgar, that's blasphemy!" I brooded the rest of the way home. "Shifty Jim's plan," I concluded finally. "Sammy had made a rumpus, got caught screwing that old simpleton, knowing Aunt Tab would act just as she did. Tolens want some kind of claim on our plantation, don't you see that, Ninny?" Shocked by that angry language, the girl protested that Aunt Laura was not a simpleton, she loved dear sweet Aunt Laura very, very much and I was being vile as well as most unkind, and anyway, it wasn't "our" plantation! Minnie had understood nothing, as usual. At the gate, I swung her roughly off the horse and she ran inside in tears.

Sammy had already moved in. He dined with us that evening, sitting beside that sweet coy fool too old to be his mother. His disgusting table manners made our ladies shrivel; they hardly knew where to look or what to say. "Well, nobody can't call me no cradle robber!" he guffawed, spraying food. And damned if this manure-flecked feller didn't wink at me, as if this outrage were the best joke in the world. I'm the Master of Ichetucknee, that wink said. And you? He even offered me a cheap cigar.

When the ladies protested our cigars, we went outside, where Sam let go a self-congratulatory belch. "Looks like you're fucked pretty good now, don't it, Edgar? You and my hot pantaloons old widow." Sam always enjoyed that ugly way of talking.

CHARLIE IS MY DARLING

From the Getzen place, the old Spanish Road led west through Ichetucknee Springs past the Collins trading post. Mr. Collins's gristmill turned so slow that his boy Lem (Lem said) could top its hoppers full of grain and go home and eat dinner and get back to the mill in good time for a smoke before it finished grinding. Lem was my friend and his brother Billy was courting our Miss Minnie. What Billy Collins saw in that crushed girl I will never know. I suppose my sister was beautiful in her way, but this was said by women more than men because she had no spirit. All her life she would speak in a childlike voice, keeping her head flinched over to one side, her pale under-chin pulsing with trepidation; she reminded me of that little tree frog we called "spring peeper" at Clouds Creek.

One April Sunday afternoon behind the store, Lem and I were hard at work on a half jug of moonshine when a girl I had never seen before happened by with Billy and Minnie. From the first, I could not take my eyes off that clear face. Fair skin, smooth and light and pretty as a petal, small nose, and small white teeth in a dancing smile. But what stole my breath were those large black eyes, like the wondering round eyes of some night creature.

Yes, I was pierced clean through the heart, love at first sight. So stricken was I that I reeled backwards, throwing my arms wide, crying out senselessly the name of the old song, "Charlie Is My Darling!" Having read so much, I was articulate enough, but my life had been so solitary, with so much silence, that I had no graces. I used that song to cover my confusion:

all I really wanted to cry out was *Miss, I love you.* The girl went pink and turned haughty and Minnie cried, "Oh Edgar, honestly!"

I flushed but did not falter. I sprang forward on the wings of drink, striking both knees painfully into the dirt, and seized and kissed her hand, which was delicious, cool and warm at the same time. When she snatched it back, I bowed to her little boots, banging my forehead into the dust, astounded by my own oafish behavior. Clearly this Miss Collins thought me crude as well as rude, also swinishly inebriated, which I was. She reproved her cousin Lem for keeping such rough company—though in saying this, she caught my eye and almost smiled. She even tried to assist me off my hook, saying, "You guessed my secret, Mr. Watson, I hate the name Ann Mary. I'm not your darling but by all means call me Charlie if you like." She thought me a bold idiot, she told me later. I was indeed rough company but also such an overjoyed poor fool that she forgave me.

I had known nothing of such exaltation! By some miracle—could it be true?—a dark-eyed angel loved this overjoyed poor fool to the same degree. We sat in the grass, leaning back against the sun-warmed slats of the old mill. I described my fine plantation at Clouds Creek to the sound of flowing water. From that first afternoon, we were delightedly in love, smiling and smiling for no reason, lost in each other's smiling eyes, abiding in the other's smiling heart. Nothing needed to be said, nothing regretted, all was perfect and complete just as it was.

From that day forth, while her life lasted, Ann Mary Collins adopted the name Charlie; she called me plain "Mister," as if that was my given name. This graceful creature had surprised my heart with the first joy it ever knew. I'd been dead and dry as the white clay in the road. My life had been breathed back into me at last.

She heard the bad stories soon enough. Lem Collins's parents got them straight from Herlongs, and Lem warned me. Charlie refused to repeat what she'd been told. There's so much *good* in you, she whispered. She only hoped that her love for me was so pure and so strong that no matter what I'd done, God would redeem me. "Damn!" I swore, startling her. "How do you know that I've done *anything*? Why don't you tell me what they said and I'll tell you the truth."

"You don't need to hear their wicked gossip, Mister, and I don't need to hear your truth. Whoever you are, I believe in you, and that is truth enough for me."

One day that fall I borrowed Aunt Tabitha's buggy and took her to the Ichetucknee, where we'd met. We left the buggy at the store and walked barefoot down along the edge of the blue springs, beneath a canopy of crimson maples, old gold yellow hickories, russet oaks. Charlie picked watercress for our wild lettuce, and a blueberry with reddish stems: she called it sparkleberry. She led my eye to the woodland birds of fall, knew their brown names—hermit thrush, sparrow, winter wren.

Charlie gave me her hand as we walked home. Bravely she presented me to her silent family and bravely I came calling every Sunday and helped with chores whether they spoke to me or not. I burned hickory and boiled ash resin for lye soap, worked flax for linen, parched goobers for coffee, ground homespun dyes from sweetgum and red oak, stuffed Spanish moss and feathers into mattress casings. I even helped with the washing, which I'd always hated. Built a fire in the yard, stirred flour for starch into cold rainwater before heating up the tub, then shaved a soap cake into the water. Barefoot, Charlie sorted the wash into white and colored, dirty britches, rags. We rubbed out spots on a rough board, then boiled them. Never boil the dyed things, Mister Watson, Charlie frowned, wagging her finger under my nose and blushing when I caught it in my mouth. The parents watched.

"Mind you, it's Sunday, miss," warned Mr. Curry Collins.

Fished out with a broom handle, the fresh wash was spread to dry, then the soapy water was applied to the privy bench and floor. I cursed my dirty nature for imagining, God forgive me, my dearly beloved's bottom, neat as an upright pear on that wood seat. I emptied the tin tubs as she slipped indoors and bathed, and of course I pictured that sweet ceremony, too. She came out in a fresh dress, combing the water from her hair, and brewed some tea. Those eyes over her porcelain cup drew me deep into her soul as her mother came and went just out of earshot. We were lost in each other's awe. She pressed my hand. "The greatest blessing ever to befall this foolish girl," she said, "is Mister Watson."

As a middle-aged bachelor, William Curry Collins had married the Widow Robarts, one of whose sons was my friend John Calhoun Robarts, called

"J. C." Ann Mary was their late and only daughter. I offered to accompany Mr. Curry down the Santa Fe and the Suwannee all the way to the Gulf at Cedar Key, where we hired two black men and boiled half the Gulf of Mexico for a few barrels of salt. After that hard expedition, Mr. Curry thought the world of me, informing Ann Mary that her beau was an exceptional young man. "Don't I know it!" cried his happy daughter, that's what J. C. told me.

Mama and Minnie adored Charlie, exclaiming over what this girl had wrought in a few seasons with their abrupt and sullen son and surly brother. These days he reeled off Greek quotations and Romantic poetry, bursting into song and spouting nonsense just to make them smile: "Sappy but happy with no pappy!"—that one made Minnie nervous even now. "I thought you'd never learn to smile," Mama reproved me. I rattled her with a surprise hug just to hug somebody, and Minnie, too. "Our family has never been so happy!" Ninny cried, wailing at the great pity of it all.

THE VIRGINS

Charlie is my Darling. Her sweet tenderness had cracked the ugly crust I'd carried south from Edgefield. From the dull clay of melancholic anger she had fashioned an irreverent fellow who loved to tease and banter, tell outrageous stories. Alone, we could talk seriously, and over time I would confide to her most though not all of what had happened in my boyhood. When finally I blurted out my pain and guilt about the awful way the Owl-Man died in that black ruin, she fell silent for a while and my heart pounded. Then she took my hand. "Our Redeemer always forgives a repentant sinner. We need never speak of this again."

With my scrimped pay, I leased an old cabin on Robarts land just west of the plantation. The front door was gone and the back door, too. The one window was boarded closed and even those boards were half loose and awry. The roof had rotted under heavy moss and fallen deadwood from the live oak and the tin patches were dark copper red with scaling rust, but it would be our house and so I worked on it every spare hour.

One day I was mending roof with cedar shakes when Charlie stepped inside and peered up at the big hole under the peak, her elegant small head turned upward like the head of a slender tree snake paused on a sunlit branch. Seeing me silhouetted on the sun, she sang, "My hero! He Who Patches the Blue Sky!" Next came a cry of delight because just at that moment an oriole had flown in one window, out the other. "Did you see it, Mister? Our good omen!" she called.

I could not bear so much feeling any longer. I climbed down and took both her hands, asked her to marry. Those black eyes widened. Fearing I'd been too abrupt, I implored her to forgive me. "Give it some thought, at least," I begged when tears came to her eyes. She raised a finger to my lips.

"I have given it far too much thought already. I shall marry you," she whispered, kissing my cheek.

We dined in the oak shade out of her napkined basket. Afterward we lay together and we kissed, as we had done on so many desperate occasions, debating old spidery ideas of sin. This day we stopped without a word and turned our backs and clambered out of our cumbersome farm clothes. When I said "One-two-three," we turned, not looking, starting to laugh. I stuck my hands out and when she took them we kneeled naked, facing, on the sun-warmed linen. Excepting the burned copper of our arms and faces, we were milky white. I drew her close and at once felt mysteriously complete.

We were brave virgins, shy and clumsy, but we trusted each other with all our hearts. Trembling, I laid her down and held her tight for a long while before kissing her cheek and her warm throat under her ears and at last her lips. But very soon my monkey hand wandered the small breasts and taut nipples, the silken skin of her inner thigh. When it touched her wetness, she gasped and closed her eyes. Her thigh slid over mine and I eased her over on her back and lay between her legs for near a minute, feeling blessed. When I realized that, awaiting me, the poor thing held her breath, I ran my hands under her hips and raised her gently, and she bent her knees as her legs rose. With a groan of relief, I entered that pearly glisten.

I was awkward and too urgent and I hurt her. Pain was the reason she cried out. A moment later, I cried out, too, as scent, touch, birdsong, Indian summer night were stitched into delirium by a magic insect walking the sun-warmed skin of my bare bottom. Afterward I lay astonished, home at last.

Shyness had returned when we sat up. On a cowardly and idiotic impulse, I took refuge from our silence in one of Sammy's jokes. "You know what Woodson Tolen would have said if his son brought you home and told him you were still a virgin?" A bit puzzled, trying to smile, she searched my eyes. Wary then, she freed her arm, reached for her shift and held it to her chest. I should have stopped right there but did not know how. " '*Vir*-gin?' Ol' Man Tolen would have hollered. '*Hell* no, boy! Don't matter how sweet and purty that gal is! No virgins ain't allowed, not in our Tolen family!' " I grinned, desperate to enlist her. " 'But Daddy—!' the boy said. 'Nope,' says Tolen. "If that li'l gal ain't good enough for her own men, she sure ain't good enough for our'n!"

How could I stoop to such crude mockery of our Christian pieties? How could this innocent creature understand far less forgive such insensitivity at her bravest and most undefended moment? "Turn away, please," she entreated. Covering my bloodied loins—so suddenly my shame—I turned my back on my beloved. We dressed without a word.

I pled for forgiveness, tried to walk her home. "I know the way," she said, looking straight ahead. I stopped then, watched her disappear down the woodland lane. But not long after that, Lem Collins reported, when she overheard some Tolen in the store, she had to stifle laughter and would not say why. I knew why and was delighted, and soon thereafter, she accepted my apology.

She was fifteen then, I twenty-one, but she turned sixteen before we wed. Gaily she sang out "Miss Charlie Collins" when giving her name for the marriage record at Lake City. It is there still: November 24 of 1878. Thanksgiving.

Though raised by Mama an Episcopalian, I attended the Methodist services that the Collins clan had started with the Herlongs in a small house on what was now called Herlong Lane. I prayed hard, frowning, right up front where those tale-bearers from Edgefield could behold me and perhaps bear witness in their letters home that Ring-Eye Lige's son was often to be seen down on his knees seeking redemption. This was not true. I was offering my fervent thanks to the Great Whoever who had blessed my life with such a loving bride.

As the months passed, I would learn Charlie's heart perhaps better than my own. I still hear her little cries as we escaped mortality in each other's arms and fell back awed. *Who are you, Mister?* But I only shook my head, kissing her softly until finally she hushed up and began to touch me.

"Now look what you've gone and done," I'd smile. "Mister is my Darling," Charlie whispered.

GONE AND LOST FOREVER

She was not yet eighteen on the day she died, not ten months after we had wed, on the thirteenth day of a windy cold September. Her family came. Her brother Lee had hatred in his face. Her father stood stoic on the door sill. Her mother sobbed, "The poor child was too young." By this she meant, *She was destroyed by this man's greedy lust.* Thrust at me squalling was the murderous red thing expelled by her dear body, our dear body.

Her lips were parted, her gaze fixed. Where had she gone? The black strands of sweat-bedraggled hair spread on the pillow, the mortal scents and stains of my darling's blood and urine on the coarse moss mattress we had sewn together—our bed of life where this red thing had been created, her bed of death. I would not look at it for fear that cold Jack Watson might seize it up and hurl it to the blood-sniffing dogs outside.

Still on my knees, I took Charlie's cool hand, rested my brow on her cool wrist.

Edgar? Please? For Ann Mary's sake? Give this little boy a name. (Mr. Curry Collins, father of the bride.)

Take it away.

The voices hushed me.

All of you go away. Please. Take it with you.

I lay down in my own corpse beside my murdered wife. They watched from the cabin door. *Son? Get away from there. Now don't go acting crazy!*

Shouting, I drove them all out of our cabin.

Holding cold hands, we stared upward at the cedar roof where I once patched that faraway blue sky. Together we prayed that I might go wherever she might be going. We did not stir. Night fell. I turned cold beside her. *For two days I lay amongst my dead:* the Widow Cloud, Cloud's Creek, South Carolina.

At daybreak, I carved her cross; that same day, I made her coffin. Our own ceremony would be her memorial, and she would lie in our own ground beside our cabin. No. In the end, the families came and shamed me. They whispered at the graying face and melancholy scent. Nobody had closed her eyes nor crossed her arms nor even bathed her. Her stepbrother and minister and my friend J. C. Robarts bent a wayward arm, forcing it to join the rest of her within the coffin. "It's not a chicken wing," I growled. His face went mushy with resentment. *Edgar, don't. We loved her, too. Nobody's trying to hurt Cousin Ann Mary.*

Charlie, I said. Ann Mary Collins was the dead girl who went away nailed up in my pine box, under black crepe, to be bounced and thrown about in a black cart. Every jolt hurt me. I ran after them half naked in the cold, yelling at them to go slow and be more careful. I walked a little ways but being barefoot fell behind and finally did not follow.

In a dream her coffin is lowered into a deep pit in the white clay earth of Bethel churchyard. It is left uncovered. I can see inside. The fair skin which shivered at my touch purples and softens. Shadowed eyes sunk back, grayed small teeth on blue-gray lip, dead hair lank over the skull. She no longer knows me.

Cousin Selden drifts among the mourners, feathers rotting. He is rotting, too. I cry, "Why have you come? What do you want of me?"

Night after night, Charlie returns.

Wandering the woods roads under sleepless stars, I walk and walk, heart dead as the white clay.

Charlie my Darling, gone and lost forever. I swear a terrible revenge but upon whom?

MISS SUEBELLE PARKINS

I moved unseeing through the ache of days. In the evening, I drank rotgut for the pain until I sank to the dirt floor, only to come to in the dark hours and drink more. I reeled into the day in mighty sickness, doing myself harm in violent labor with sharp careless tools, banging and wrenching, boiling off my poisons. But I was cursed with a mule's constitution and by nightfall had regained the will to drink.

On the Sabbaths I rode to the crossroads taverns, slapped shoulders, drew a crowd of men and made 'em laugh. Usually I was still laughing when I picked a fight "just for the fun." Pretty soon, no man would drink with Edgar Watson, and the grog shops drove me out, and I rode too far away from home to return in time for work on Monday morning. All across the northern counties, a man I no longer knew earned a bad name as a crazy-wild mean skunk, quick to pull a knife. When Watson barged into the tavern, the fun was over. More than once, when he refused to leave, he was knocked over the head and dragged into the road and kicked bloody in the public mud.

All the while I was feverish with longing. By early spring, I was visiting Lake City's colored whores with their big soft mouths and round high rumps and candied tongues. Out of respect for my lost bride and common decency, I never took one from the front, only rode her from behind, slamming against that rubbery hind end, forcing her forward till her back bowed and her neck twisted, her head jammed against the wall. At the end, I rammed with all my strength—*a-gain, a-gain, a-gain!*—until she yelped in faked abandon or in fear or honest pain, it made no difference. A fleeting spasm, thin as cloud mist crossing a high sun, before I fell off, dull and dirtied, having failed once more to escape into obliteration.

A shy new wench billed as "Sweet Miss SueBelle Parkins" seemed upset when she was chosen by the grieving widower, in fact insultingly upset: I warned her sharply that I was not so drunk and useless as I might appear, overcoming her reluctance by twisting her arm and pushing her upstairs, where she permitted me to complete my carnal dealings. Passive though she was, inert with terror, she got a hook deep into me, a sick addiction having something to do with the queer contrast between the lacquered whore's mask and the firm young body and clean skin. But when I came there and selected her again, she burst into tears. She was still weeping when, upstairs, she whispered, "Lo'd fo'give me, Mist' Edguh, suh! I has knowed you all my life!" Scarcely discernible beneath her brassy wig and crimson rouge and tear-caked powder lay my childhood neighbor, young Lulalie Watson, the sweet-potato daughter of Tap Watson and Aunt Cindy.

The day Mist' Edguh had left Edgefield, Lalie wailed, her daddy was shot dead in the field by two white men on horseback. When I demanded to know who those riders were, she was too scared to tell me. Finally she confessed that they were known to black folks as Major Will and Overseer Claxton.

Lalie had had sense enough to flee, walking the wood edge all night and the next day to reach the Savannah River. Her mother had left a paper with the address in Florida, but having no kin along the way and finding no work in the winter fields, the girl was reduced to selling herself to pay for a journey hundreds of miles south. Two years passed before she reached Lake City. Being ashamed of what she had become, and fearful of the pain she would cause her churchly mother, she had never dared the last few miles to present herself at the plantation. (It had not occurred to the poor thing that Aunt Cindy's joy at seeing her alive might outweigh her disappointment.) Instead, she took a position, so to speak, at our local cathouse. In tears, Lalie implored me to keep her awful secret. I promised on my honor I would do so, for which I was rewarded with warm tears and a complimentary crack at her sweet person.

I visited Lalie soon again and then again—homesickness, I suppose. And I needed that generous healing nature that had made her companionship so precious to my sister in our childhood. All true, all true, but it was also true that her mortal form did great honor to her Maker. The seed of hunger for Lulalie Watson, dormant since boyhood, needed small encouragement to sprout—not that it helped me to escape my grief. My groan of deliverance would turn in its very utterance to a moan of woe. I reviled the poor creature for knowing that I wept, for knowing that no matter what, I needed her tenderness as much as her brown person—for knowing, worse, that no matter what, her erstwhile young master was now her slave and would be back for more, no matter how often she begged me to forget the lost Lulalie. At the very least, *oh please, sir,* I must deal with her by her professional name and *please, sir,* fuck her under that name, too, is what she meant, as if to avoid additional damnation for some queer kind of incest. I felt slighted but agreed.

Banging through Sweet SueBelle's door stupid with drink, needing to shame her because so ashamed myself, I sometimes hollered, *Sooee-belle, Sooee-belle,* in the voice I used back at Clouds Creek to call my hogs. Pitying me in my coarse grief, she smiled at my tomfoolery. And finally her good simple heart would get me smiling at my own self-pity—before the act, that is, but never after.

As SueBelle became less fearful, even fond of me, she called me "Wild Man." *You bes' come on upstairs with yo' sweet Sooee-belle, cause you my Wil' Man.* Undressed, she lay back like a banquet, breasts smooth and sweet as mangoes, thighs thick and warm and smoky as Virginia hams. But in my soiled grief, I wanted no eyes upon my deed, and would turn her over, hauling her up onto her knees in a surge of anger and taking her like an animal, just as before. She would not join in my abandon, simply endured it.

One night there came hard pounding on the walls. *Shut up that crazy racket in there! Ain't you got no manners?* And another displeased customer across the hall, his door flung wide, hollered downstairs at the boss whore, *Hear that? How come I ain't gettin laid as good as that?* Mirthful, I increased our uproar, rolling off the bed on purpose in a grand finale, dragging the underdog right down on top of me, until finally one plaintiff, provoked beyond endurance, knocked our door down. I jumped up buck naked and launched a surprise attack, as I had been taught to do at my father's knee. Knocked down and kicked hard, still on his knees, the mauled intruder, as naked as myself and mopping dolefully at a bloody nose, agreed to apologize to Miss Parkins, that fine specimen of negritude swathed in pink sheets. "Beggin yer pardon, Miss Parkins," he sniveled. "Doan mine if ah do," said the demure Miss Parkins. I banged the door behind him and went back for more.

Hard drinking and hard fucking were my sole forgetting. For all its rewards, mounting Sooee from behind was a lonely business, and rolling off her, spent and sticky, was worse. Awaking vile-breathed, head pounding from bad rotgut, I felt plain rancorous, soul-poisoned. Dragging my stinking carcass into crumpled clothes and lurching toward the stairs, I was reviled by other lowlifes and their black Jezebels for making such a rumpus at that hour. Outside on a Sunday morning, I was struck sightless by the sun like a bear blundering out of a cave. Occasionally my uproar was assailed by slop jars flung from the upper windows by the religious element among the whorehouse clientele, and always, I was scourged in the street by the cold stares of churchgoers offended by my swinish defilement of the Sabbath morn. Filled with a deep slow-seeping rage, I cursed them vilely to offend them further.

Oh Charlie my Darling, Dearest Charlie, how do you like your filthy Mister now?

SUWANNEE COUNTY

Billy C. Collins married our Mary Lucretia that same year and their first child was dubbed Julian Edgar Collins. The "Edgar" honored Billy's father, but poor Minnie, frantic to please her wayward brother, tried to hint that her sprat was named for me. However, no Methodist Collins would name his firstborn after Edgar Watson, and anyway, her husband much disliked me. Hadn't his vile brother-in-law sent poor Cousin Ann Mary to an early grave? Had he not insulted her memory by refusing to attend her funeral and letting her parents take responsibility for the child?

When Lem and Billy's father died, I paid his estate fifty-five dollars for a beautiful gray filly, long-legged and delicate, with big dark eyes. I named her Charlie. For ten and a half dollars more, I acquired the old man's .12-gauge double-barrel, which in those days was a fancy gun, not used by common farmers. The right barrel threw a broken pattern but I soon learned to compensate for that. I would use that old firearm all my life and without hearing one complaint.

That spring, still shaky, I gave up my night wanderings and made a good crop for Captain Getzen, who had been patient, liking the way I worked. With my debts paid, I tried to heal our family by inviting the Collins boys to celebrate. Entreated by my sister, Billy accepted. And so, one Saturday, we rode to the O'Brien tavern in Suwannee County, the only place for thirty miles around that would still serve me. I had promised Minnie I would pick no fights, even in fun, and that evening things went fine. For such good Methodists, Lem and Billy got uproarious, and Lem toasted me over and over, yelling, "See that, Bill? Ed ain't near so bad as what you thought!" Made me feel so kindly toward my fellow men, even my brother-in-law, that I jumped up on a table to lead all my new friends in a grand old marching song of the Confederacy, to which every man present knew the rousing chorus:

> *Hurrah! Hurrah! For Southern rights, Hurrah!*
> *Hurrah for the Bonnie Blue Flag that flies the single star!*

When I sang out the cornet part (*buppa-ba-buppa-ba-boo, ba-buppa-ba-buppa ba-buppa ba-boo!*), Lem hollered to the crowd that his friend Ed might be the finest kind of farmer but his singing voice was a greav-ious insult to

Southern rights and maybe our blue flag, too. He did his best to haul me off that table, with the whole room cat-calling and laughing, the singer included. But when I caught Lem with a boot swipe to the mouth, he grabbed my heel, and my momentum swung me off the table in a whirl of walls and faces, yells and smoke, and the oak floor struck me so hard that I couldn't place the pain; when I tried to jump up, cursing and laughing, I collapsed and fainted. I was carted home in a wagon, both knees broken.

THE FARRIER

For half a year while my fields went to hell, I lay at the mercy of the women, having gone off alcohol the hard way. When I could concentrate, I read a little in my tattered *History of Greece*, but most of those long days in the cabin I listened to the mice and crickets and suffered the tuneless whistling of Sam Frank Tolen, who never failed to grin in at the door when he happened by.

I had hardly recovered and resumed work at Getzen's when Lem Collins shot the farrier in the blacksmith shop in back of his late daddy's store at Ichetucknee. This man Hayes thought Lem was fooling with his wife and he was right. When the culprit fled out the window, the blacksmith hollered after him that he would tear his head off, and Lem being somewhat slightly built like most Collins men, it stood to reason that a feller twice his size who could rassle any plowhorse to a standstill would fulfill that vow with no trouble at all.

I knew John Hayes. John Hayes meant business. I said, "Lem, you'd better leave this county." "Hell, no!" said Lem. "I *love* her, Ed!" "Well then," said I, "you haven't got much choice." "Gosh," Lem said, "you mean that I should kill him?" "No, no, Lem! I only meant you might start thinking along the lines of self-defense, because John Hayes has sworn he means to kill you so he'd have only himself to blame if you took precautions." I never meant to stoke Lem up, only to cool his passions for his own good: the Lem I knew was not cut out for mayhem.

Unfortunately, the drunken Lem who pulled me off the table at O'Brien, the horny Lem who had fallen so hard for this little Mrs. Hayes—this Lem flat refused to give her up. Anticipating her blessing in his deed, he screwed up his courage with hard drink and swiped my shotgun and went over to

Hayes's place, where he hollered from the yard that he'd come to speak with "the lady of the house." When the man of the house kicked his chair back and came roaring out, he was met as he came off his stoop by a fatal charge of buckshot from Lem Collins—a clear case of self-defense except to those who did not see it quite that way.

Lem's beloved, Mrs. Prudence Hayes, told the grand jury she had no idea why Lemuel P. Collins would wish to murder her dear departed John. If the jurors wanted her opinion, sobbed the little widow, looking the accused straight in the eye, what this man deserved was a good hanging. Repeated those cruel words with her hand on the Bible and her sweet little honeypot keeping its own counsel under her widow's weeds. "I aim to see justice done," she cried, "and who can blame me?" In need of just a little more of that nice limelight, his sweet Prue pointed a trembling finger at poor Lem. *Hadn't this same drunken brute come through her window on previous occasions, bent on God knows what? My goodness, woman! When? Why, sir, only last week, may it please Yer Honor!*

Sweet Prue having overplayed her hand, the grand jury was tempted to indict two lovebirds for the price of one. But even knowing that his darling had betrayed him, Lem remained a stiff and starchy Collins, too well brought up to testify against a tiny widow. The jury being generally agreed that there was understandable emotion behind the death threat made by the deceased, my friend was indicted for murder in the first degree.

As cash poor as most families in our section, the Collinses gave up hundreds of acres of good land plus a large loan from Cousin Laura to make the $20,000 bond for Lem's release. Having no case worthy of the name, Lem jumped bail and lit out for Georgia. Some of the debt was eventually paid off by the sheriff's auction sale of Collins land, but Laura Myers would never recover a penny. Kind Laura forgave this cheerfully enough but her husband and mother did not, and the situation created difficulties in the family which were very hard on the newlyweds, Billy and Minnie.

In short, Lem Collins brought about a fatal downturn in his family's fortunes. Naturally anxious to ease his guilt by transferring responsibility, he wrote a letter to his brother Billy concerning the murder weapon he claimed Edgar had given him, along with some very bad advice. I don't know just what Lem said or what Billy repeated, but pretty soon the death of Hayes was blamed on E. A. Watson. There was even a rumor that Ed Watson went along with Lem and did his shooting for him.

Though my neighbors gave me funny looks, only Fat Sam had the gall to bring it up. "Some fellers been tellin me lately, Ed, how it might been you behind the killin of our farrier. Course I told 'em straight off you was clean as a baby's bottom. 'Why hell, no, boys!' says I. 'There weren't no money in it! Ed never had no damn motive at all!' " Sam gave me that big dirty wink of his but stopped chuckling quick when he saw my expression. "Only jokin, Ed," said Sammy Tolen.

Only joking, Ed. As the saying goes, it's a damned good thing there's enough bad luck to go around because otherwise I'd have had no luck at all. Here I was, still in my twenties, and for the second time in my young life, my reputation was buried deep in mud, and my prospects, too.

I think it must have been about this time that my whole outlook began to change. I was learning the hard way that I had to make my own luck in this life if I aimed to survive. And so, having no choice about it, I grew hard, as a shrub battered by wind grows gnarled and woody.

SONBORN

I was twenty-nine when, in 1884, I married a schoolteacher, Jane Susan Dyal. Jane was a lady even by my mother's standards, well-educated and soft-spoken and pleasant in appearance, though no longer young. If not a creature of passion like my lost Charlie, she was a kind, sensible person, glad of my attentions and not offended by coarse, manly needs, having missed a maiden lady's fate by a cunt whisker.

Goodwife Jane (I called her Mandy) would soon present me with a lovely baby girl. We named her Carrie. Two years later came a boy, named Edward Elijah for good luck after the rich Old Squire at Clouds Creek. As if her own little smellers weren't enough, Mandy worried about Sonborn, as I referred to Charlie's child on those rare occasions when I felt obliged to acknowledge his existence. Since I had refused to ride eight miles to Lake City simply to name him, he remained "Son Born" in the county register and legally, perhaps, did not exist at all; in truth I had not laid eyes on him since the bloody hour of his birth eight years before. I knew, of course, that his mother's parents had taken him, and I also knew because Mandy told me that those folks were old and pretty well worn out. Lately Charlie's mother had been poorly, Mandy added, and Old Man Curry had trouble enough tending his wife and chickens without taking care of a young grandson, too.

My wife meant well but Sonborn was not her business; I notified her she was not to speak of him again. But in the safety of the dark, on our night pillow, she would murmur in my ear, stroking my head and whispering how wonderful it might be, not only for the little boy but for his father. From Minnie she knew something of our family past, and she dared to hint that turning my back on my firstborn might have reopened an old wound inflicted by those long dark years of boyhood. I shouted at her to bluff her back before she said what she said next, that my refusal to acknowledge Charlie's child could only breed guilt and regret. Naturally I became furious, since what she said was true.

When I stopped shouting and fell quiet, Mandy continued, with that gentle resolve that I would come to dread: if the first Mrs. Watson had been the angel I extolled so often to the second Mrs. Watson—I sensed Mandy's fond ironic smile even in the dark—then she surely watched over her loved ones from on high and was grieving that her innocent child had been abandoned. (That idea gave me a start, and not because of Sonborn: if Charlie and the Lord were in cahoots on high, they might have witnessed all my dirty doings with Miss SueBelle Parkins.)

And so on a Sunday I rode over to the house of Mr. Curry Collins, who was whittling a wood toy out on his stoop. As I entered the yard, Ring-Eye's ancient roan, half warhorse and half mule, gave me a walleyed look and stamped and snorted, moving sideways and in circles.

"Been a bear around," Old Man Curry advised me—not much of a greeting. I informed him I had come there for my son, having heard that Mrs. Collins was feeling poorly: no doubt a growing boy could be a burden, and anyway, it was high time he came home.

"Home?" Mr. Collins stood up slowly but did not come down the steps, and he never invited me into his house. "This is the only home he's ever had."

I never even swung down off my horse, which chose this moment to drop a steaming load right in the dooryard. "No sir," said I. "This is not his home and it's not up to him. You tell him to pack up and come out here quick unless you want me to go in there and fetch him." At these words, Charlie's brother Lee came out and looked me over with dislike, hands in hip pockets, then returned inside without a word.

They believed all the bad stories, that was plain. Mr. Curry was concerned for his grandson and never tried to hide it. "We tended little Elton these eight years while you forgot about him. That entitles us to some say in the matter, Edgar."

"Nosir, it does not," I said. "You are entitled to my thanks for your hospitality to your own grandson and you have it. Now let's get a move on."

Already I was talking past him to the small boy in the doorway, who held my eye with a cool and steady gaze. You weedy little shit, I thought, you're not much to show for the unholy joy that went into your creation. In a moment, he ran back inside, but the brief glimpse shook me, for he had his young mama's full black eyes and pale rose-pointed skin. With one look I knew that this child would stir up squalls of that hard grief which I so dearly hoped were at last behind me.

"I am his daddy, after all," I added gruffly.

"First time you acted like it. You never even took the time to go register his name so we named him Elton."

"His name is Robert. After his great-uncle, Colonel Robert B. Watson of Clouds Creek, South Carolina."

A wail rose from the ill woman within. "Elton!" she cried. The boy was already through the door, both arms wrapped around a little bindle.

"Whatever happened to you, Edgar?" Curry Collins said, very sharp and cold. "You were a pretty nice young feller when you first come around these parts, as I recall."

"Say thank you and good-bye," I told the boy.

Robert Briggs Watson stuck his hand out, saying, "Good-bye, Grandpa," but winced and shifted in discomfort, I noticed, when the old man leaned down to peck him on the head—no doubt old breath. "Good-bye, Elton," Collins called after him in muffled voice as the boy ran to my horse. He looked defeated but he kept his dignity and did not call again.

I swung the child up behind me. "Your name is Robert now," I notified him. "You ready, Robert?" "Yessir," he said. As we rode away, Mr. Collins lifted a slow hand which his grandson never saw. The boy had his arms around me, face pressed hard, and I guided his small hands to my belt loops, feeling a coolness where his tears wet my shirt. "I knowed you'd come," came his small muffled voice. And in a moment, he said, "Papa? I been waiting and waiting." Not knowing how to answer that, I said, "Don't set so far back on his withers, boy. Makes the old fool buck."

Even before we arrived home, I knew this boy would bring his mother's ghost into our house—just what I feared most. I glared at Mandy when she came running out with a big smile. "You wanted him so bad so you take care of him." I swung him off and galloped away down the woods roads, headed for nowhere, riding my heart into the ground. In the next days I drank, worse than before. Morning after morning, I woke up sick to death on some sawdust floor or in some shed or ditch, and finally in a stinking Suwannee jail, bruised, bilious, broke, and mean down to the bone.

WILD

That day, riding homeward through Lake City, who should I see but Miss SueBelle Parkins in a rose-decked yellow gown tilting down the sidewalk; plainly she was in that painless state in which she might share her bounteous person with a friend. I eased up behind her. Low and soft, I whispered, "sweet sweet Sooee gal," and a tipsy grin inched all the way back under her ears. Even drunk, she knew better than to display acquaintance with a white man, but she hummed a little as she sashayed her hips back and forth to tease me, blocking my path and murmuring under her breath, "Doan you go to whisperin sweet Sooee, Mistuh Wil' Man, cause SueBelle ain' no white man's li'l shoat." Already those firm smoky hips shifting along under that cloth had fixed me hard as a bird dog up on point, and Sooee knew this, never had to look. She was having such fun lighting the fire in her Wil' Man that she clean forgot to move aside to let a white man through. Folks coming out of church had stopped and some were pointing.

Recalling that day on the square at Edgefield Court House when the neighbors jeered at Ring-Eye Lige for challenging General Butler to a duel, my brain hammered and heat swelled my face. In the next moment, with no warning, Jack Watson banged the hard heel of his hand between her shoulder blades—*Out of my way!* The blow pitched her forward and she almost fell. Finding her balance, she reeled around and squinted at me with a cunning smile, hollering "Wil' Man? Dat you? Ain' you my own big brutha?" What had she meant? Could this be why she had been so full of dread? Did this explain Aunt Cindy's iron coldness toward my father?

Thinking herself safe in the bright sunlight of a Sunday morning, Sue-Belle grinned saucily, waving her perfumed lace whore hankie as she pirouetted. "How come," she cried out loud and clear, "you never come around no mo' to visit?" Only then did she see Jack Watson and squawk and skedaddle in her haste to flutter off that sidewalk, but she was too late. Jack's hand flew from behind and cupped her forehead, pulling her head back against his chest. The other hand held the knife blade to her throat. Her eyes and mouth popped open as he bent her head back onto her shoulder blades so far that her face was almost upside down, eyes staring out from beneath the nose and gasping mouth. That upside-down mask of terror startled Jack and stayed his hand, but not before he feigned a pass across her throat, using the rough nail of his forefinger.

When his hand withdrew, she remained motionless, eyes rolled upward, mouth opening and closing as if struggling to find air. Her eyes entreated but she made no sound. Slowly she sagged, slowly, slowly to her knees, as her fingers wavered up under her chin, dislodging one cheap tinsel earring as her thumbs pressed up to hold her life in. There was only a faint crimson thread, a minute trickle that, seen on her fingertips, she took to be the first freshet of the fatal spurt. At the sight of it, she groaned and coughed, then vomited, soiling her yellow gown.

Church bells. Figures transfixed. The dying bells. No one drew near. When I straightened, the figures backed away.

I left her there. Refusing to make way, a drunken whore had sassed a white man. He had scared her to teach her a lesson. That was that. And I was thankful Jack had done her no real harm. Yet a bad murmur followed me down that street and around the corner. Trouble-making nigras should be taken care of after sundown and somewhere out of sight, and inevitably Edgar Watson would be blamed for an unpleasant offense committed in broad daylight on a Sunday in front of an assembly of decent citizens. *Why, that ruffian came within an inch of spilling nigger blood on our new sidewalk, right down the street from church! He had no call to give God-fearing folks such a bad fright!*

When SueBelle vanished from Lake City, the madam started rumors that Edgar Watson knew more about her disappearance than perhaps he should. Hadn't he killed some nigra back in Carolina? Soon the word was out that this Ed Watson hated blacks, shot 'em left and right. In Lake City, the coloreds shied across the street to get out of my way, causing painful embarrassment to my family, when the truth was, I got on fine with nigras, always had, ever since early childhood with the slaves back at Clouds Creek. Treated 'em as people in those days when most whites hardly knew one from another, couldn't be bothered.

Our Watson ladies at Fort White heard all the gossip thanks to Sam Frank Tolen, who spared 'em no detail, not even those he had made up. However, in my star-crossed mood and ugly disposition, nobody dared ask questions, not even Mandy. Perhaps she didn't care to learn more than she had to. But Great-Aunt Tabitha passed the word to Captain Getzen, who knew no way but to ride straight out and confront me in his field.

Captain Tom was a Confederate war hero, a small, fierce, feisty feller. He did not touch his hat when he rode up but stayed stiff in the saddle, whacking his peg leg smartly with his crop; that crop rapped that hardwood shin like the snap of rifle fire. I rested my hoe, touched my cap, and smiled politely, asking what I could do for him; he cleared his throat and said it might be best if I cleared out of this south county for a while. "Best for whom?" I said. He didn't answer. "Cleared out?" I said. I much disliked the way he'd spoken, as if I were some kind of po' white drifter. I reckon he saw that in my face, for he danced his horse back as I came forward, raising his crop just enough to give me warning. This good old man no longer trusted me not to attack him, and that hurt, too.

"Best for you," he said.

I bowed my head as if to pray and took a few deep breaths. Then I said that Edgar Watson was the man who should determine what was best for Edgar Watson, who had been driven unjustly from his own plantation in South Carolina and did not intend to be driven out a second time, having done no wrong.

"No wrong, you say." Tom Getzen shook his head, extracting a money packet from his coat. He refused to give reasons or name my accusers. I dropped his money in the mud and left at once, before Jack Watson could appear to worsen matters.

Confronted, Billy Collins said that "the family" agreed with Captain Tom: I should leave the county. "Which family do you speak for, Billy?" I demanded. "You weren't a Watson, the last time I heard." He shrugged that off, advising me I could come back when things blew over. "It's not up to you to give me that permission," I told him. "Anyway, don't act like I'm the only one who has brought trouble to this family." At this, Minnie fled the room.

"The reason my brother killed a man—if Lem was the killer—was self-defense." Billy set himself as I swung off my horse, for he was nerved up now or at least felt safer in the proximity of my sister and my little nephews.

"*If?* What are you saying, Billy?"

From the other room, his Minnie screeched, "Tell Edgar you're sorry!"—the boldest thing I ever heard my sister say, which only shows what a terrified creature she was. Billy blurted, "How about Aunt Cindy's man, back in Carolina?" I raised my hand in warning. "Never say that, Collins. It wasn't me."

"And those knife fights over in Suwannee? One of those men nearly died! And that darkie prostitute? Lake City? What became of her?"

I took out my clasp knife and opened it and tested the fine edge with the ball of my thumb. "You aim to insult me every time you open your damned mouth?" When I raised my eyes to his, his nerve ran out. An opened blade will do that to a man. He said, "You'd even murder your own sister's husband? A man half your size?"

Billy was a Collins, he was proud; I was content to let his own shrill voice and shameful plea ring in his ears. I pared my nails. "As for your brother," I resumed after a pause, mostly to reassure my sister, "I only advised him to leave this county because otherwise someone might be killed, most likely him."

It must have been Billy who reported his version of Watson's "confession" to the sheriff, which was all it took to implicate me legally. It wasn't even evidence, it was just hearsay, but the sheriff issued a warrant for the arrest of E. A. Watson as an accessory before the fact in the Hayes murder. Knowing he had no real case, he leaked word of his warrant in the honest hope I might get lynched or flee the county as Collins had done, leave him in peace.

Job, my old strong-hearted roan, was spavined from long months of hard riding. Since it looked like I might need a sound horse in a hurry, I hunted up another roan of the same temperament and gave him that same name.

Sam Tolen came to warn me. "Looks like you might be havin you a necktie party," said pig-eyed Sam, who was all read up on the Wild West, knew all the lingo. "Better light out for the Territory," he added. Sam's little brain was working fast, I could hear it sizzle. He was after my prime hogs and he wanted 'em cheap with my gratitude thrown in.

I said, "Hell, no," to his insulting offer. "Those hogs are the county's best."

"That's why I'm buyin 'em," Sam grinned, hauling out his greasy wad. "You're runnin out of time, Ed. Better take it."

"They say a Tolen will short-change you even when he's cheating you," I said, counting the money. Sammy guffawed and clapped me on the back. I told him not to laugh too hard, he just might hurt himself, but Sam didn't scare as easy as his daddy. He was always a nervy sonofabitch, from lack of imagination or a fatty brain. In his view, fate had nothing disagreeable in store for such a fine fat feller. "Don't forget to write!" he yelled, breaking wind in a loud carefree manner as he departed.

NIGHT ROADS NORTH AND WEST

Anger and rotgut, burning bad holes in my lungs, made each breath hurt. I slung my farm tools into the wagon. Seeing my expression, even Mandy was alarmed. "Mister Watson," she cautioned, raising her hands almost in prayer, "we have each other and we have our children. We will make a clean start somewhere else."

"Clean start!" I turned my back on her. "How many do I have to make?" But remembering how often she'd been patient, and seeing anew the honest goodness in her face, I took my dear wife in my arms. "You don't have to go with me, Mandy," I whispered. "Oh, I do, dearest, I do." She hurried off to pack provisions and our few possessions.

I rode over to my sister's house to settle my account with Billy Collins, who had brought this banishment down upon my head by running to the sheriff. He knew I would be coming, too, because his horse was gone. Minnie ran out, fell to her knees. Clutching little Julian, she begged her good, kind brother to have mercy and not harm a little family which loved him dearly and hoped and prayed for his safe journey and deliverance wherever he might go.

"So long as he goes far enough and never comes back." I pushed past her and sat down on the porch in Billy's rocker to await her husband.

Darkness seeped in from the woods. Hunched in the cold, I suffered a kind of rigor mortis of the spirit. Billy would not be coming home, not with Job hobbled out there by the road. Maybe his wife had begged him to hide and maybe I was relieved I would not have to take revenge—I was too weary. I only knew that I was destitute as ever, still looking for a place where I might prosper.

I rose and went in to Minnie where she was sniveling amongst the crockery; she snatched her baby Julian from the floor as if fearing I might step on him. I told her to tell my friend Will Cox that he could have my cabin, being the one man I could trust to give it back. Knowing we might never meet again and feeling doomed, I took my frightened sister in my arms and gave her a gentle hug, even kissed her brow—the first time ever. Bursting into tears, she hugged me back and kissed me, too, got my face all wet and sticky with the baby's clabber, which she had been eating up for her own poor supper.

Minnie's breath was sour from her frightened hours. "Oh Edgar, please don't harm my Billy. You are a good man, deep in your heart, and we won't forget you."

"Don't," I growled, "because I aim to be back."

I rode on home. Dismounting at a little distance, I circled in through the silent pines, making no sound on the needle ground, eye peeled for any trap. Mandy had the wagon packed and I backed the big roan into the traces, hitching the gray filly to the back of the wagon while she piled the children in under our blankets. Sliding the loaded shotgun under the seat, I climbed up and snapped the reins—*Gid 'yap!*—and Job the Younger kicked the wagon boards a lick that rang off through the trees. I talked him down into a good fast-farting trot.

Pale-faced Sonborn sat up straight, peering back along the ghostly lanes. As if awakened from a bad dream, he cried, "Where are we going?" Mandy hushed him. My wife looked drawn and fearful, which she was. The poor thing thought she was leaving her life behind her, which she was. She thought that armed men might come after us—quite likely, too—and that our children might be harmed. But never once did she complain, nor ease her nerves by fraying mine with foolish questions. "Miss Jane S. Dyal from

Deland," as she had bravely dubbed herself when we first met, was a very good young woman who forgave her husband, though she knew he had named that pretty filly for his own lost love and was dead broke and on the run with no known destination.

Under the moon, the hooves thumped soft as heartbeats on the white clay track, which flowed like a silver creek through the black pines. So quiet was our passing that surely an owl heard little Carrie's pretty sighs or Elijah Edward's greedy suckling at the breast. A solitary light still burned when we passed Herlong's, where the dogs were barking; the silhouette darkening that window was righteous Dan Herlong who had blackened my name with his tales from South Carolina. I'll be back, I promised when the figure vanished and the light was snuffed. Had Herlong heard the wagon wheels? Had he sensed something out there in the dark that frightened him?

At the road I turned the wagon north, taking the night roads north and west under frozen stars which shone on the unknown land where we were going.

CHAPTER 3

✦

IN THE INDIAN NATIONS

Toward dawn, I pulled the wagon off into the woods and picketed the horse beside a little branch. We slept all day, taking turns on watch, and at dusk we ate a small pot of cold hominy. That night we crossed the county line and traveled all night past Live Oak and Suwannee Springs. Beyond the Suwannee River was new country, but taking no chances with my evil luck, I moved through darkness by the light of the half moon until the Georgia border was behind us.

From Valdosta, the way west through chilling rains crossed the Flint River and the Chattahoochee and finally the great Mississippi, crossing from Vicksburg on the ferry to Louisiana, and from there north and west again to the Arkansas Territory, where I had heard that a man plagued by the law might catch his breath.

Already the season had turned cold, numbing our spirits. The Indian Nations was no place to arrive as November was setting in, with its promise of cold and hungry misery for little children, and so I was lucky to find harvest work for a horse and wagon on a late cotton crop in Arkansas. There we wintered. I rented a small farm to make a pea crop before heading westward after summer harvest. In early autumn of '88, I reached Fort Smith and crossed the line into the Indian Nations, Oklahoma Territory.

This hill country of plateaus and river buttes had been assigned to the Cherokees and Creeks, with a few Florida Seminoles thrown in. Some of these Indians still had the slaves they took west with 'em back in the thirties, when Andy Jackson ran these tribes out of the East. Stray blacks had drifted out this way after the War, and a lot more showed up after '76, when Reconstruction was finally put a stop to. Plenty of Southern cracker boys and some hard Yankees, too, because the local government was Northern even if most folks were Southern—Texas, Missouri, Mississippi. In short, all breeds of the human animal were mingled here in various shades of mud, like the watercolors in my sister's little paintbox back at Edgefield Court House, and every last man with a cock between his legs considered himself your equal if not better, since any stranger was likely on the dodge or worse. The buffalo soldiers with Comanche scalps strung on their belts were maybe the most arrogant of all. I kept an eye out for my shadow brother, asked a few questions, and these boys told me that Corporal Jack Watson, having taken care of the local white ladies to the best of his abilities, had been mustered out and gone back east, headed for Georgia.

YOUNGER'S BEND

Under the bluffs out of the prairie winds, the Canadian River country had good alluvial soil down in the bottoms. Neither whites nor blacks could own Indian land, but a woman shacked up with an Indian leased me a good field in the Cherokee territory. This female became Mandy's best friend in the Nations, making a fine show of generosity to our small children when we first arrived and didn't know a soul amongst our neighbors. I will grant she was big-hearted in her way, with her door wide open to strangers and her person, too.

By her own account, Mrs. Myra Maybelle Reed preferred male company to that of the rough women of the Territory. She made an exception of my Mandy, a well-educated lady whose friendship improved Maybelle's repute, fallen low due to her bedtime predilection for bad Indians and breeds.

Maybelle's first husband was Jim Reed, who rode with Quantrill, the James boys, and the Youngers during the bloody Border Wars between Kansas and Missouri. Like a lot of armed riders who passed themselves off as guerrilla fighters, Reed was a killer by inclination and by trade who only joined up with Will Quantrill when those men turned outlaw. After the War, he gambled and raced horses for some years around Fort Smith, joined in armed robberies, shot a bystander while holding up the Austin–San Antonio stage, and generally made a nuisance of himself until the early seventies, when a former partner with an eye to the reward deprived him of his life when he wasn't looking.

The Younger boys were the wild seed of the richest slaveowner in Jackson County, Missouri, who happened to be a family friend of Maybelle's daddy, Judge John Shirley. She was never Cole Younger's lady friend the way she claimed, but later in life, her daughter Rosie Reed took the name Pearl Younger for professional purposes. Her son Eddie remained faithful to his daddy's name and his outlaw profession, too, and even his early end by bullet, as shall be seen.

The Youngers hid out in an old trapper's cabin about six miles west of Briartown, on a rocky bench facing south across the Canadian River. The land was part of a large spread run by Tom Starr, a huge bloodthirsty Cherokee who rustled cattle all the way south to the Red River. Having taken a liking to the Younger boys for no good reason, Tom Starr called this place Younger's Bend. Pretty soon, maybe 1880, the Widow Reed moved in there with Sam Starr, one of Tom's sons, and in no time at all, "boys" on the run were infesting this hideout, including the famous Jesse James, whom she introduced into her social circle as "Mr. Williams from Texas." Pretty soon, the U.S. marshals got wind of this place, too, but Maybelle—or Belle Starr, as she now called herself—told the newspaper that her hospitality to outlaws had been much exaggerated by "the low-down class of shoddy whites who have made the Indian Territory their home to evade paying taxes on their dogs." Belle took pride in her fiery reputation and was often obnoxious whether the situation called for it or not. Man and woman, she was the most shameless liar and noisy show-off I ever came across, bar none.

A few years before our arrival, Maybelle and her Injun Sam had been hauled up for horse theft in the Fort Smith federal court and received short sentences from Isaac Parker, the well-known "Hanging Judge." This was Maybelle's first and last conviction, not because she was hard to apprehend but because she never committed a real crime. Her popular repute as Queen of the Outlaws was born of her own bare-assed lies, since the closest that bitch ever came to the outlaw life was screwing every outlaw she could lay her hands on. When her Sam was shot to death over in Whitefield, Maybelle soon replaced him in her bed with Tom Starr's adopted son, Jim July, tacking Starr onto his name to shore up her claim on Starr property.

Maybelle's haughty airs and gaudy style and even the big pearl-handled .45 shoved pirate-style into her belt did little to distract from her poor appearance. She was a long-nosed thin-mouthed female, hard-pocked and plainer'n stale bread, also wide of waist and slack of buttock from too much time spent on her back with her feet flat to her low ceiling. Her dark skin, leathered by the sun, and the coarse black hair she pinned up under slouch hats when it wasn't down behind like an old horse tail, made her look more halfbreed than her husband. But Mandy decided that this old sack must have some good in her, and needing a woman to confide in, she let it slip to her new friend that her husband had been unjustly accused of murder in the state of Florida and obliged to flee. Since Belle was the widow of two killers and domiciled with a third, the news that I might be a dangerous man only enhanced me in her eyes (despite her devotion to Mandy) and when I ignored her awful wiles and leering blandishments, she became furious. Tearing up my lease and flinging my payment in my face, she claimed she'd been warned by the Indian agent at Muskogee to harbor no more fugitives from justice lest she forfeit her precarious claim on Indian land.

Refusing to pick up the money, I advised her that my lease was duly paid and rode away, leaving her squalling loud and mean as a horny raccoon. A few days later she sent a formal letter stating that her land had been rented to another sharecropper, Joe Tate. That November, I persuaded Tate to have no dealings with this woman, who would only drag him into her own troubles with the law, and once Tate had backed out of his lease, I rode over to Younger's Bend to smooth things over. Before I could even dismount, Belle screeched, "Maybe the U.S. marshals won't come after you but the Florida authorities just might." Hearing that threat, I felt my shadow brother stir deep in my vitals.

CHEROKEE FUNERAL

In January of 1889, I moved my family into a cabin on the land of Jackson Rowe. Another tenant was Belle's son Eddie Reed, who told me his sister Rosie Lee had seen my hard expression from Belle's doorway and had warned her mother to make no more threats against Ed Watson. On February third, on the eve of her forty-third birthday, one of the many worthy citizens who had it in for Mrs. Starr took care of that troublous bitch once and for all, shooting her out of her saddle on the muddy river road south of my cabin. The burial took place at Younger's Bend at noon on Wednesday. Because of that scrape over the lease, it seemed prudent to attend, and poor worried Mandy insisted upon going with me. We crossed on the ferry and rode up the ridge to Belle's place, where Cherokee relatives and a few out-law friends were standing silently before the cabin, squinting hard at every rider who appeared. Sure enough, my arrival caused a stir. No one spoke out but Jim Starr stalked me, flaunting his suspicions.

The casket lay inside the one-room cabin, attended by stone-faced In-dian women sitting in tight rows. There was no service and no chanting, only the suspense of unfinished business.

Armed men carried the coffin from the cabin and set it down near the rough grave. When the lid was removed, the Starr clan and other Chero-kees dropped ceremonial corn bread on Belle's tight-lipped remains, after which the box was lowered into the pit. I stepped forward to help Jim Cates (who had built the coffin) bank the grave, but I had hardly touched the shovel when Starr and his sidekick Charley Acton drew their guns and yelled at me to put my hands up. Starr pointed his weapon at my eyes, ac-cusing me of murdering his woman, as his Indians grunted beady-eyed assent, without expression.

Unsurprised, I remained steady and my wife did, too, despite the likeli-hood that her husband would be gunned down before her eyes. I did not trust Starr, who was very drunk, to keep his head, so instead of raising my hands as ordered, I grabbed hold of Cates and yanked him between me and the guns. Cates implored me to raise my hands or else we'd both be killed, and I finally did so, but not before saying to Jim Starr, "If you kill me, Jim, you will be killing the wrong man." Mandy thought it was my calm de-meanor that persuaded those Indians I deserved a hearing, and eventually Starr, growling, put his gun away.

That evening, however, Starr came to my house with other Indians and put me under citizen's arrest, intending to take me to the U.S. District Court at Fort Smith. He finally agreed to my demand that Jackson Rowe and oth-ers be permitted to accompany our party as witnesses. We left for Fort Smith that very evening, stopping for the night at a farm along the way. Next day, February 8, I was marched before the Commissioner in the U.S. District Court for a preliminary hearing. Starr filed a formal affidavit "that Edgar A. Watson, did in the Indian Country . . . feloniously, willfully, premeditatedly and of his malice aforethought kill and murder Belle Starr, against the peace and dignity of the United States." Deputized, he was given two weeks to assemble witnesses and evidence for a second hearing to determine whether the defendant Watson should go to trial. And so I sat cooling my heels in jail with my lease still unsettled and spring planting near. Crop or no crop, that was fine by me. I felt a lot safer behind bars than waiting for the murderous Tom Starr in the Cherokee Nation.

"I know nothing about the murder and will have no trouble establishing my innocence," I told the publisher of the Van Buren (Arkansas) *Press-Argus*, who quoted me from an interview in the jail. "I know very little of Belle Starr, though she for some reason, I know not what, has been prejudiced against me. I am thirty-three years old and have a wife who is living with me. I have never had trouble with anyone and have no idea who killed her." Quoted in the same edition, Jim Starr said: "I knew enough to satisfy me that Watson was the murderer. We buried Belle at Younger's Bend and I went after Watson and got him. He showed no fight or I would have killed him"—lies, of course.

On the twenty-first, Starr returned to Fort Smith with Belle's two off-spring and ten other witnesses; the hearing commenced on February 22 and ended the next day. Some of my neighbors gave depositions, mentioned a quarrel, said Watson lived close by the murder scene. But Farmer Watson, who had a good reputation with the merchants as a man who paid his bills, made a better impression than Horse Thief Starr. The *Argus* described the accused as a man of "fair complexion, light sunburnt whiskers, and blue eyes" who was "decidedly good-looking and talked well." Furthermore, he appeared to be "the very opposite of a man who would be supposed to commit such a crime."

Jim Starr's so-called evidence being deemed circumstantial, he was granted an extension while he sought more witnesses, but very little new evidence was forthcoming. On March 4, the plaintiff's case was judged too weak to merit the indictment of an honest white American—"a quiet, hard-working man whose local reputation is good," said the Fort Smith *Era* next day. Even so, I had spent two weeks in jail before the Hanging Judge threw out the case.

Furious, Jim Starr rode away to join an outlaw band. He died less than a year later, shot down in the Chickasaw Nation by a sheriff's deputy who reported that the dying Starr confessed to killing his own wife with Watson's gun. By that time, it was widely rumored that Old Tom Starr had killed her to avenge the death of his beloved son Sam, whom she had led into bad company. Pony Starr declared that a white rancher had hired a cowhand to dispose of her and others suspected an outlaw named John Middleton. Ed Watson was the only suspect ever brought to court for the murder of Belle Starr but many others would be nominated for that honor.

With her death, Maybelle was transformed by the newspapers from the ill-favored consort of robbers to the beautiful Civil War spy, border hellion, and Queen of the Outlaws whose lovers were the terror of the West. Her legend got off to a flying start on the day of her funeral in a brief news flash in the *Press-Argus,* which made four errors in its single sentence: *It is reported that the notorious Indian* (sic) *woman Bell* (sic) *Starr was shot dead on Monday* (sic) *at Eufaula* (sic), *Indian Territory.* The "woman" part was accurate but only barely. Next, a Fort Smith editor filed the following dispatch, duly printed on the front page of the New York *Times:*

> *Word has been received from Eufala, Indian Territory, that Belle Starr was killed there Sunday night. Belle was the wife of Cole Younger [and] the most desperate woman that ever figured on the borders. She married Cole Younger directly after the war, but left him and joined a band of outlaws that operated in the Indian Territory. She had been arrested for murder and robbery a score of times, but always managed to escape.*

After the first sentence, this report is inaccurate in every last detail.

Since Belle's son Eddie had sworn publicly that he would "slaughter that old sow," it seemed rather curious that no one wondered if young Reed might not have been the killer, or even if Reed and Mr. Watson, who were neighbors at Jack Rowe's, had not collaborated in the killing, all the more likely since on that fatal Sunday, Reed had left those premises not long before his mother's arrival, just as I had. Called by the prosecution in the hope he would testify against me, Eddie never once mentioned my name.

Dr. Jesse Mooney, who had tended Eddie after a savage beating from his mother, concluded that her son had been her killer, having been told this in so many words by Rosie Lee Reed, alias Pearl Younger, who had covered for her brother by throwing suspicion on me. Rosie Lee related to Dr. Mooney that when she found Belle dying in the road, she lifted her head from the bloody puddle and held her in her arms, at which point Belle opened her eyes and whispered, "Baby, your darned brother done this. I seen him across the fence before he cracked down on me." Mercifully Pearl seemed unaware that her brother climbed the fence and walked over to his mother and fired a second shot into her face. Otherwise, her account was pretty accurate. I know that because I saw him do it. I was there.

A STRING OF PONIES

Unwelcome now in Tom Starr country, I leased a farm in Crawford County, Arkansas. Having lost a month in jail, I got my seed in late and had to watch the weak sprouts wither in that summer's drought. By winter I was in serious debt, with three hungry kids and a new baby. Sonborn was ten now and helped some with the chores, but Carrie and Eddie were still toddlers who helped most when they stayed out of the way.

We called our newborn Lucius Hampton Watson, after the family patriarch Luke Watson of Virginia and General Wade Hampton, our great Carolina hero. In '76, General Hampton was elected governor; later, he became a U.S. senator. People voted for him even though he spoke out against segregation on the railroads. I couldn't go along with that, not altogether, but I had to admire this rare public man who stood up for his principles, which was why I named my youngest after him. I considered "Lucius Selden Watson," but with my lifelong nightmares about Deepwood, I thought that name might curse my little boy with evil luck.

I had not welcomed this little feller, who looked like he had come into this world only to pule and die. Once winter set in, there were times I felt that little Lucius would be far better off dead. He brought no joy to our meager hearth but only plagued us down those cold dark days with his starved fret and yawling. Mandy was shocked when I spoke this way, and reproved me for my "brutal way of talking." I told her that the world was brutal, man's lot, too, so if there really was a God, she had better face God's will. "That is your God's will, not my God's, Mr. Watson," my wife said.

We had no Christmas that year, none, no friends nor relatives nor even neighbors. Huddling with our offspring in a damp and dirty shack, doing our utmost to forget our stomachs and stay warm, we passed that winter in the nightmare sleep that famine brings, a kind of fitful hibernation. The dull cold misery of dark days without end—dark winter days all but inseparable from night—was worse than Edgefield District in the War, as if somehow I had fallen back into that hellish period. I was tormented by the children's hollow eyes, the coughing and mute suffering, as those pinched and staring faces shrank against the bone. In my helplessness, I lay there stunned, breath cold and slow as the toad's breath in winter mud. Poor Mandy did her gallant best to poke up my dead ashes: "Don't lay too long without breathing, Mr. Watson. Wouldn't want rigor mortis to set in." But Mandy's eyes had gone dull, too, and in the dim light from the single bleary pane, her face looked haunted.

Was it Plato who said, Life is terrible, but it isn't serious? Did he mean that man is a hostage to his life while held captive by death, so why take such a life seriously? Fuck it, I thought. Fuck God, fuck everything.

One frozen day three riders with stiff faces brought a string of ponies, offering twenty dollars in advance if I would tend them for the rest of the winter. Two did the talking while the third stayed to one side. If nobody came to claim 'em by the spring, they said, then I could sell 'em. That told me these animals were probably stolen, but I was in no place to ask hard questions.

While those two put their heads together, counting out the coins, the third man, who'd dismounted to piss, eased alongside. He was a halfbreed man in half-uniform, a deserter from the buffalo soldiers from his looks. Says, "Watson? Any kin to a Jacob Watson?" "Reckon so," I said. He had no time to discuss how he knew my name. "These boys are friends of Belle," he warned under his breath. "They won't be back. You better run this string into the Nations, sell 'em quick—either that or chase 'em off your place soon as we're gone." He moved away.

I had no chance to peddle those ponies because the deputies rode in at daybreak the next morning. Pocketed my twenty dollars, lashed my wrists behind my back, and boosted me into the saddle. As we rode out behind the ponies, I heaved around to stare at my huddled family a last time, but with arms bound tight, I could not even wave.

With bitter weather hard behind an iron sky to northward, and no man to help her and no food, Mandy had finally lost heart and sank down weeping. Though I barked at him to stay out of the way, my oldest in his thin torn jacket and split soggy boots came running and hollering amongst their stirrups until he got knocked sprawling in the muddy tracks. Poor

Sonborn thought the world of me and I never did learn why, because my face stiffened at the sight of him and my heart, too. Every time I remember how he ran after me that day, I feel all wrong in my heart but I could not help it.

In the Territories, stealing horses was a crime far worse than murder, which was very common and mostly well-deserved. I could count my lucky stars, the lawmen told me, grinning like coyotes, that they hadn't strung me from the nearest cottonwood. Perhaps these men felt merciful because they were in on the whole frame-up, which they hardly bothered to deny. On January fourth of 1890, in the county court there in Van Buren, I was given fifteen years at hard labor and carted off to Arkansas State Prison.

I will say this for Eddie Reed, he knew what he owed me for my friendly counsel. He moved my family into a good household in Broken Bow, in the Choctaw Nation, where Mandy would earn their room and board as cook and housekeeper. Reed did not live long after that, being even wilder than his father. A drunk at twelve, a moonshiner running likker into the Indian Country by age fourteen, he was a robber, gunslinger, and killer all of his short life. The following year, convicted of horse theft, he was sentenced to five years in prison. The story goes that his sister Rosie Lee pled with Judge Parker before sentencing to give that remorseful orphaned boy another chance, and the Hanging Judge told her it would do no good. Said, "That young feller was born ornery and he won't quit so he's better off right where he is. If I let him out, he'll be dead within the year."

But Rosie Lee wagered the judge he was mistaken, offering her own person as security, so he took the bet. Eddie received a suspended sentence on the condition that he quit drinking and go straight. He took a job as a railway guard, serving when needed as a deputy U.S. marshal. Eddie was always a crack shot, and in a brief gunfight in the line of duty, he killed Luke and Zeke Crittenden, halfbreed Cherokee brothers, who had resisted a routine arrest for shooting up the streets. (The Crittenden boys were also deputy marshals, having never been criminals or drunken troublemakers except in their spare time.) But Reed himself would be slain within the year under similar circumstances and so his little sister lost her bet. In arrears to the Hanging Judge and to her brother's lawyers, the brave girl embarked upon her own career in show business. Under her professional name, Pearl Younger, she showed it all nightly at the Pea Green House in

Fort Smith, a gorgeous whorehouse celebrated far and wide as The Pride and Joy of the Great American Southwest.

BLACK FRANK

I'd been in prison close to a year when a work gang captain at Little Rock told me he'd sure be sorry, Ed, if Florida claimed you before you boys go out in March to bust the sod because for a horse thief you're a good man with a spade and an inspiring example to these other criminals. When no word came from Florida I was rented for hard labor. The leg chains were unshackled and the guards rode up and down with whips and rifles. The farmers worked the gangs like beasts of burden, gave us rotten grub and very little of it. The fields were mostly in the river bottoms, with no bridge nor ferry for many, many miles, so any man who could swim to the far side would have at least one day's head start on the guns and bloodhounds.

Worried about my family, I was desperate to escape. One fine morning I saw my chance and ran off through the cornstalks, along with a bull nigger named Frank and a scrawny halfbreed, Curly. We had a good jump before the first guard yelled and started shooting. At the river I swam underwater, kept ducking as I angled across. Halfway over, Curly took a bullet under the shoulder but his natural-born viciousness gave him a kicking spurt that carried him to where we could run in and haul him out of range.

Curly was goose-bumped blue with cold and bleeding bad, in no shape to go further. "Should of left me drown in peace," he snarled. His eyes darted, following our expressions like a card sharp, knowing we knew he was certain to betray us as fast as they twisted that bad shoulder up behind him. Curly's life luck had run out, with nothing good headed his way—he knew that, too. We would have to silence him, as he would have done to us without hesitation. And so he jeered at what we must be thinking, and cursed us vilely while he still had life. He wanted to provoke us, get it over quick. "Fuckin idiots," he complained bitterly, jerking his chin toward the shouts across the river, but he meant us, too, and all of humankind while he was at it, having the freedom of nothing left to lose. That mean skunk had grit.

Out of respect for Curly's feelings, we went off a ways while we discussed his fate, and Frank said, "Boss, we just ain't got no choice." I said, "All right, go to it." I knew how hard it was sure to be without a knife or club, and I did not have the character required to hold under the river current a man who had risked his life with us only minutes before. Frank looked surprised I would admit that but he felt the same. "In front of company, too," I added, pointing at the knot of men across the river. What we decided was, we would duck this thorny problem—leave him where he was and keep on going. And so we said sorry and so long after trading a lot of jabber about panning for gold in Oregon, which never fooled ol' Curly for a minute.

Our first job was to hunt up two good horses and some common clothing. That afternoon we scouted a big farm, waiting till dusk for our chance to jump the homesteader when he went out back of the barn to feed his hens. That German was real happy to saddle up both of his nags and fork over his fine German revolver and canvas kit for bullet molds and powder, since we all agreed he had no further use for 'em. When Frank frowned evilly, feeling left out, the farmer asked fearfully if "your nigra" might like a packet of smoked ham with some nice cooked grits thrown in. I had to smile at that. Scowling blackly, so to speak, my partner growled, "I ain't nobody's nigra," but after all the horrible grub these tight-fisted farmers had been giving us, his stomach told him to shut up, take the damn packet. "He's his own nigra," I advised the German, who uttered a frantic bray not much like laughter. His nerves let go on him, I reckon.

In days to come we were to learn that while attempting our escape we had been struck by bullets in the head and drowned, according to "the wounded and recaptured convict, an accomplice of Watson and the Negro." Maybe that's what Curly told 'em ("Breeds can't be counted on even to lie," Frank said), but more likely the warden was trying to make us think no one was after us while alerting lawmen all over the West. I regretted Mandy's grief over her husband's demise but could not help it. There was no way to get word to my family.

Having cautioned our benefactor not to leave his farm until next day lest we return in ugly mood, we rode out at nightfall toward the west, having craftily mentioned in the German's hearing that we were off to Oregon. We lost our hoof prints in a stream, then circled out wide and crossed a pinewood before turning back east toward the Tennessee state line.

Mostly Black Frank was silent as a knothole. When I asked him finally why he talked so much, he grinned, a little sheepish, saying he was grieving in advance for the faithless woman whom he meant to murder. He had tracked her "sweet man" to Arkansas—that was how he ended up in federal prison—and now he was headed home to Memphis to finish up the job. "Man got his honor to think about, Mist' Jack," he said. (For a fugitive, a new identity made sense. I had already changed my name to E. Jack Watson.)

"To err is human, to forgive divine," I preached, thinking not to confuse this teaching with the news that I was on my way to South Carolina to kill my father.

"Well, maybe I might forgive that nigguh bitch after I got her good and dead but I ain't promisin." We chuckled a good while over that one.

Scavenging, traveling at night, we rode toward Memphis. But we were fugitives and one of us was white; in Memphis, we would draw too much attention. A nigra in a white man's company was one thing but a white drifter in niggertown was quite another. Not that I didn't trust this man. I did. All the same, my destination and my plans were my own business. If Frank got captured knowing where Watson might be headed, the law was duty bound to whip it out of him.

Frank and I had talked a lot about white men and blacks. If a black man sasses me—well, I won't tolerate it, I told him. But as far as joking, passing the time of day, making sure he gets his feed and some fair treatment, I believe I can say I have done better by the nigras—or coloreds or darkies, or whatever Mandy calls 'em—than most of those damn-Yankee hypocrites who agitated so hard for emancipation, then abandoned 'em after '76 and got so many killed when they turned their backs on their own Reconstruction.

That detachment of Union soldiers quartered at Edgefield in my boyhood—hell, those bluecoats had no feel for nigras, besides being so scared of the hating faces of our home people. They wanted so bad to get along that they cat-called louder than the townfolks at those gussied-up blacks in yeller boots who had the vote and called themselves Americans. The bluecoats never raised a hand to stop the Regulators, not even after a sniper shot a bluecoat, left him kicking in the dust on Court House Square. Their officer never stepped into the square, much less organized his men to hunt the killer, although he probably knew as well as everybody else that it was Will Coulter.

We parted company at the Black River. "Well, Frank, good luck," I said abruptly at the fork, turning my horse off toward the north. I always thought Frank Reese was pretty hard and I still do, but plainly I took him by surprise and hurt his feelings if he had any. He didn't answer and he didn't wave, just sat his horse in the deep shadow of the river woods and watched me go. He wasn't sulking, either. He expected no better out of life. As he once told me, matter-of-fact, "I ain't nothin but a damn ol' nigger. I got nothin comin."

But this man and I had escaped together, we had swum the river. He wasn't just any old nigger, he was my partner. I rode back, stuck my hand out, wished him all the best. First time in my whole damned life I ever offered my hand to a black man. And he didn't take it, not till he looked me over and even then there was an awkward pause. When he finally produced a limp cool hand, he let me do the shaking and that riled me.

I rode away but in a while I turned to see if Reese was still there under the trees. He hadn't moved. His face looked like a block of hard dark wood. I waved but he never twitched, not even to touch his hat brim. I rode back. I warned him how that kind of insolence might draw attention in Memphis, where the law would be on the lookout for a fugitive. If he wanted a fresh start in life, he could ride southeast to Columbia County, Florida, where my friend Will Cox might find him work. I was careful not to say that I might turn up there myself before the year was out.

He nodded but he didn't thank me, didn't even answer. I had nothing more to say, yet I didn't go. We sat our horses by the river in the cool spring wind, watching long strings of brown cranes coming up across the country from the south. I reckon we were awaiting something that might mend our mood. Finally, I said, "Well, so long, Frank," and turned my horse away. I never looked back. Maybe that man lifted his hat, maybe he didn't.

THE SHADOW COUSIN

I rode across the backlands of America, south of the south border of Tennessee. The mountain folk were suspicious of lone riders, and I had to shoot more than one mean hound along the way. Hunting my supper from the saddle, I could not afford to waste my loads, and by the end, I rarely missed with that revolver. I took squirrel, turkey, and one fawn, a red grouse, here and there a rabbit.

Crossing the hinterlands, I took shelter in many a dirt-floor hut on nights of rain, but even where the people weren't half-starved, I gagged down grub that would tumble the guts of an old turkey buzzard, sowbelly and grits slimy with lard, old corn bread dead as seed-bin dust, half-rotten potatoes boiled down to a reeking gruel. And even where these frontier folk weren't too shiftless to step outside and trap or shoot, that wild meat was gulped down shiny purple raw or fried to a hard chip. Few troubled to catch the bream and trout that gleamed in every branch and pond throughout the backcountry.

One day, after twenty years of exile, I rode over the Great Smokies into Carolina. I was torn and filthy and outlandish, I was restless and excited, also unclear and uneasy about what I had come so far to do. However, as a Clouds Creek Watson, I still thought of myself as an honorable man who kept his word, and having promised my father I would take his life, I aimed to do it.

Years ago, arriving in Fort White, Florida, the Herlongs had brought word that Elijah D. Watson was still kicking up trouble around Edgefield Court House. Before tracking him down—probably I was stalling—I was curious to learn what that trouble might have been. Dismounting at the horse trough near the hotel, I crossed the courthouse square to the Archives Library, which kept records of our prominent county families. In these close quarters, in the stuffy air, I was offended by my own badgerish stink and beggar's rags, but the elderly librarian, Miss Mims, quiet and courteous, pretended to take no notice of my condition as she came and went, fetching me documents.

From estate transactions in the county records and miscellaneous information in the Watson family file, I discovered that my father had pissed away far more inheritance than I ever knew. I had scarcely digested this when a very large lady came barging through the door, waving her cane at me even as she entered. From the librarian's resigned expression, it was plain to see that this personage accosted every visitor she chanced to spot as they entered the library.

My great-aunt Sophia Boatright—for it was she—was elderly now, the last holdout of Grandfather Artemas's generation. In pink bonnet and raspberry gown, she looked like a giant peony, and her perfume was no doubt powerful enough to block my scent. "It's always gratifying to see manners, my good man," Aunt Sophia snapped, as I hunched over my documents, "but you needn't stand up on my account." Laying her hand upon my shoulder, she pressed me down like a jack-in-the-box, the better to scan my reading matter. "Aha!" she said. "Since you, sir, no doubt"—she leaned to inspect me closer—"are a stranger in these parts, you might not know all that you should about some of our great Edgefield heroes, the earliest of whom was my forebear." She tapped the page and there he was, the deathless Captain Michael. "Do you know who else was born in Edgefield? William Travis, hero of the Alamo, and Lewis Wigfall, who led South Carolina's secession as 'the flagship of the Confederacy,' and almost every governor this state has had!" She drew from her large reticule a worn copy of an editorial from the Charleston *News and Courier*, which she spread on top of my reading matter on the table.

> *Edgefield had more dashing, brilliant, romantic figures, statesmen, orators, soldiers, adventurers, daredevils than any county of South Carolina, if not any rural county of America.*

"You see? Right there in the Charleston newspaper! And General Martin W. Gary, 'the Bald Eagle of the Confederacy,' came from Edgefield, too: his good friend was my late brother, Major Tillman Watson of Clouds Creek, who sponsored General Gary's wartime company of volunteers as well as his own. General Gary, of course, rallied the Red Shirts from his balcony right up the street at Oakley Park—'The Red Shirt Shrine,' men called it. General Gary and General Calbraith Butler and Miss Douschka Pickens, 'South Carolina's Joan of Arc.' August 12, 1876! Redemption Day! They put on red shirts and marched with fifteen hundred volunteers down here to Court House Square!"

Dutifully I followed her commanding finger, which was pointed at the door onto the square. "Yes, indeed. The Heroes of '76. Centennial of the American Revolution. Put General Hampton in as governor and cleaned the rascals out. So much for so-called Yankee Reconstruction!" She slapped a leaflet down upon my documents. "There," she said. "This nice paper we got up for visitors tells all that history."

In that dark period when South Carolina was prostrate, the honor of womanhood was imperiled, brutal insults forced upon citizens by foulmouthed freedmen were more than flesh and blood could endure and civilization itself hung in the balance.

"See that?" Aunt Sophia tapped the page. "Honor of womanhood." Dutifully I read around that tapping finger.

All over the state, men organized Saber Clubs and Rifle Clubs in utmost secrecy. Even as Paul Revere had ridden for freedom's sake a century before, South Carolina's Red Shirts rode in grim determination, daring all for liberty . . . Danger lurked in ambush, shots rang out from the forests, and a riderless horse might go on its way alone, but the Red Shirts rode on.

"The Red Shirts rode on!" my kinswoman cried with emotion, standing erect and straight as any soldier. Her eyes shone bright and the feather in her cocked hat fairly bristled. No longer a giant peony, she resembled a very fierce old chicken.

Mildly the librarian remarked that Edgefield's Red Shirts had surely been upstanding citizens, but elsewhere red-shirted vigilantes had terrorized black folks and burned the houses of the Radical Republicans who tried to defend them. On the long summer evening of July 8 of that year, in the town of Hamburg on the Georgia border, the birth of the Redemption era on Independence Day had been celebrated four days later by an assault on the black militia by a mob of red-shirted riders led by General Calbraith Butler: five black soldiers were killed and some twenty captured. That same evening, in the presence of their terrified families, according to one witness, these prisoners were hauled into the street and told to run, whereupon they were "shot down in the clear light of a brilliant moon."

" 'Clear light of a brilliant moon!' Isn't that beautiful?" Aunt Sophia, starry-eyed, laid ringed fingers on her breastbone, the better to contain a fond, proud heart.

"So you see, Mrs. Boatright, certain Red Shirts had quite a violent reputation," Miss Mims said, to caution me. Though genteel Miss Mims came from an old Edgefield family of more distinguished antecedents than her own, my great-aunt now inquired if perchance the librarian (whom she'd surely known all her life) had been raised "someplace up north? Otherwise, miss, you would have known that Calbraith Butler was the man who shouted out that the next patriot to shoot a nigger would be shot."

"Some say, madam, that the halt was called because they'd killed every last black man, and shooting into the bodies was just wasting ammunition—"

"Personally, I'm proud of our violent reputation," Aunt Sophia declared, turning her broad raspberry back on this naysayer. "The United States of America, as those Yankees dare to call it, could use a little more of our old Edgefield spirit. This darned country has gone softer than milk toast. Why, all around the world we are accepting any insult, and from any color!"

Perversely I said, "Madam, you appear to be just the person to advise me where to find a man who shared your views; he is the hero Captain Michael Watson's great-great-grandson." She cried, "Of course! Which one?" And I said, "Mr. E. D. Watson." I raised my brows as if puzzled by her consternation. "Otherwise known, so I am told, as 'Ring-Eye Lige.' "

Noticing my stink for the first time, Aunt Sophia recoiled and coughed and put her hand up to her throat. "Sir, this is our archives library, not an almshouse or some low saloon." And firing a last furious glare that fixed all blame for the presence of this lowlife on the unfortunate Miss Mims, she swept out the door in a great waft of funereal perfume.

Still shaken by her own show of courage, Miss Mims ventured that the Watson file contained no recent record of Elijah D.; indeed, his name was absent from the county census after 1870. "Mr. Watson's place in the community, you see . . ." Reassured by my smile of encouragement, she fetched a bound transcript entitled "Trial of the Booth and Toney Homicides," an episode involving Ring-Eye Lige in which four men had died.

On August 12th, 1878, on the two-year anniversary of Redemption Day, with the entire county gathered to hear rousing speeches by Governor Hampton and other dignitaries, a shootout occurred inside and outside Clisby's Store right down the street. Three men were killed, with several others seriously wounded. According to one account at least, Elijah D. Watson had been in the crowd at Clisby's and had probably fired, after which he apparently took to his heels.

Burrell Abney called for the defense, sworn and examined by General Butler.

Q: *Were you at Edgefield Court House on the 12th of August, 1878?*
A: *Yes, sir.*
Q: *Did you see any of the difficulty that occurred there on that day?*
A: *Yes, sir.*
Q: *Will you please state to the court and jury what you saw that day.*
A: *I saw Elijah Watson running toward where I was from Clisby's store with a pistol in his hand.*
Q: *Had the firing stopped when you saw him running off?*
A: *It was just before the firing stopped, for I think there were three or four shots fired afterwards.*

Had my father been fleeing the fray before it ended? Very likely. Was he a coward, then? Despite all his boasting, I had never been certain of my father's courage. In any case, he and Will Coulter were among the four men indicted for murder. My father's attorneys were Gary & Gary and also John L. Addison, my mother's brother. In his summation, General Gary called these homicides "the most desperately fought combat that ever transpired in this dark and bloody region." The Bald Eagle of the Confederacy would discount the testimony that placed Elijah Watson at the scene, whereas Ring-Eye's old nemesis, Calbraith Butler, had passionately argued the reverse. All defendants were acquitted and sent home.

Where home might have been in my father's case was a good question. The transcript established that within a few years after his family had abandoned him, the fallen Lige had wandered into dissolution, sharing a disreputable roof with the Widow Autrey. Being unacquainted with this lady, Miss Mims had no idea what had become of Mr. Watson. When she'd tried to inquire about him from one of the archive's founders—and she nodded toward the door through which Aunt Sophia had made her get-away—she was told that in the eyes of his whole clan, Elijah D. was dead. "They just don't talk about him. They had his name stricken from the census." Miss Mims shook her head in pity. "He's what the old folks used to call a 'shadow cousin.' "

Edgefield's long tradition of violence had actually worsened after 1877, when the new president, a Mr. Hayes, withdrew the Union troops, leaving the "darkies" to the mercies of white vigilantes. Miss Mims produced a contemporary account submitted by a local black attorney to the newspaper. *Colored men are daily being hung, shot, and otherwise murdered and ill-treated because of their complexion and politics. While I write, a colored woman comes and tells me her husband was killed last night in her presence and her children burned to death in the house. Such things as these are common occurrences.* In the same period, it had been established that only half of the two hundred and eighty-five black convicts in this county contracted out for road-gang labor on the Greenwood-Augusta Railroad had survived the job.

Those Herlongs had told Mama that not long before they left, Lige Watson had found work as a state prison guard. Had he also been a road-gang guard during the building of that railroad? An embittered Confederate veteran who had lost his land and reputation and was prone to drunken violence might have struck the authorities as just the man to oversee black convicts.

I caught Miss Mims observing me to see how much I knew. "Mr. E. D. Watson," I said tersely. "Any record of illegitimate children?"

She located a handwritten note, dated 1879, in what looked to me like Colonel Robert's hand.

E. D. Watson: Son Jacob, called "Jack." Mulatto. U.S. soldier. Deceased ca. age 22 in Georgia, date and place unknown. Daughter Lulalie. Mulatto. Whereabouts unknown.

Aching with peculiar feelings, I went outside into Court House Square and gazed about me. The town seemed uninhabited, not one soul to be seen. At the place where the famous homicides had taken place, the name A. A. Clisby was fading on the sign over the door. Standing there, I could envision my red, sweating father, pistol in hand, reeling across these dusty cobbles on a stifling August afternoon. How many times since his family had fled had he been hauled up those courthouse steps and marched into those cells behind the courtroom?

Before riding onward to the Ridge, I made inquiries about my father at the tavern, where the older clients mostly concurred about Elijah D.

"You mean ol' Ring-Eye? Lived with the widder, one we called Ol' Scrap? I heard that feller lost his work gang job a few years back. He was usin up too many niggers buildin track beds for the Greenville railroad. Went through them niggers like goobers, worked 'em straight to death, ol' Ring-Eye did. They told him, 'Ring-Eye, dammit all, maybe them monkeys come down out of the trees, but they don't *grow* on trees, goddammit, and good green money ain't the same as leaves.' And he had him a feud with the Booth boys before that, a real bad fracas right there by the courthouse, three, four men was laying dead by the time them fellers finished.

"Nosir, ol' Ring-Eye could not stay out of trouble, he was givin his family a bad name. So finally them Watsons come to fetch him, put him to work in their boneyard tendin their dead, cause he sure ain't welcome around any that's alive. Ol' Ring-Eye! Yessiree! Now there's a feller could tell you a war story or two and never spoil his tale with the real truth of it."

THE GRAVEDIGGER

I caught up with him over at the Ridge, digging a new grave in our Rock Wall cemetery. He was wheezing in his pit not eighty feet away, spelling himself after every spade of dirt. I sat my horse and watched him for a while to make him nervous. After a few more aimless pokes, he saw me. He leaned the spade into the corner of the grave, put his hands on the brown grass behind, and kicked himself up and back a little so that he was seated on the edge, doffing his soiled hat to the silhouetted horseman on the high-road. "That you, Will? You looking for me, Will? Yessir, you just name it, Will, Lige Watson is your man and proud to help."

Realizing the rider was not Coulter, he became aggressive. "What you after, mister?" For the moment, I ignored him, let him sweat a little. I dismounted and climbed over the wall, affecting to inspect the headstone of our sainted Captain Michael. Seeing my poor clothes, he cried, "What do you want here?" I disdained to answer.

Michael Watson's widow, Martha, had later wed one Jacob Odom, a churlish man of muddy origins who had confirmed the family's poor opinion of him by making her pay room and board for her four small children. On May 21, 1791, General George Washington had honored the hero's widow and her children by lodging with them overnight on his journey from Augusta to Columbia. On this occasion, "the odious Odom," as Aunt Sophia called him, had attempted to charge the first president of the United States for bed and supper. Fittingly, it was young Polly Watson (rather than some Odom offspring) who was taken upon the presidential knee and presented with an enamel snuffbox containing a new twenty-dollar gold piece.

"Private property!" my father bawled in a hoarse whiskey voice. "Family property!"

When Martha died in 1817, her remains, contaminated by Odom's name, were forbidden interment in this cemetery. When one of her two children by Odom was installed here surreptitiously, Aunt Polly—the keeper of the gold piece—had raised an immemorial rumpus. *An Odom has snuck himself inside the Rock Wall. I want him out!* Exhumed forthwith, the half-decayed half brother had passed long dusty days beside the highroad before the disgruntled Odoms came to collect him.

Our Watson stones were of white marble set on brick foundations. Captain Michael's son Elijah (the Old Squire) was present, as well as Elijah Junior (the Young Squire) and his brother Artemas, my grandfather. And here was my father's youngest sister, late wife of Robert Myers of Columbia and my great-aunt Ann Watson Myers, dead at twenty-two:

A MYSTERIOUS PROVIDENCE VERY SUDDENLY REMOVED
THIS WIFE AND MOTHER OF THREE SMALL CHILDREN FROM THE
RESPONSIBILITY OF TIME TO THE AWARDS OF ETERNITY.

Great-Aunt Ann's Robert was the brother of Colonel William Myers who had married Laura Watson, and the "three small children," somewhat older than myself, included the two nephews in William Myers's will who were supposed to inherit Ichetucknee but would only do so over Sam Tolen's dead body.

·   ·   ·

"Hold on, mister! This is Watson property!" Wary of the stranger's silence, my father had clambered up out of his grave; when I turned toward him, he took up his shovel. Behind him, in the corner of the wall, brown leaves swirled like winter sparrows in the cold wind eddies. I let the revolver slide into my hand, hoping he might make my mission easier by using force in an attempt to drive me out. I'm sure he was considering this as he sidled forward but something gave him pause. "E. D. Watson, at your service, sir!" Nervous now, he tried to laugh, indicating the fresh grave. "Looks snug enough to curl right up in, don't it? Got half a mind to have a snooze in there myself."

"Do it," I said.

Disconcerted, my father laughed too loudly and too long, in that drunkard's conviviality that so easily turned nasty. He was already squinting in suspicion, trying to make out the man behind the beard.

Lige Watson had changed, too, not for the better. He was shiny-skinned, unshaven, with a pulpy nose and thinning greasy hair with yellowed gray hanks down to the shoulders. When he saw the revolver in my hand, his eyes narrowed and his nostrils dilated in a kind of snarl and his grip shifted on his spade. The scar circling that popped eye of his was livid.

Ring-Eye straightened kind of slow while he figured his next move. "Old soldier," he blustered, pointing at his eye. "A poor man like yourself." A moment later, his eyes widened and he forced a garish smile, spreading his bony arms for an embrace. "Edgar," he gargled. And he shook his hoary head in awe of that Mysterious Providence which had returned the long-lost prodigal to the pining father. Shortly he abandoned this farce, too, crouching a little, hefting the shovel, undecided whether to charge right now or work his way in closer.

An impatient sideways gesture of the revolver barrel persuaded him to drop the shovel. He looked me over, nodding. "Never come to much, I see, no more'n I did." His old pants snapped in the wind, his wheeze was rapid, his eyes darted. He could not fathom why I remained silent. "Your mother and sister," he pled next. "They're getting by all right?"

I waved the revolver toward the open grave. "Do it," I repeated.

"Come to kill me, Edgar? In cold blood?" Sneering, he lifted his filthy coat, pulled out his empty pockets. The sneer was for his own rags, not just mine. He hiked his pants, exposing begrimed shins and broken boots—he had no stockings—to show me how paltry my revenge would be. Then he dropped his pant legs and stood straight, took a deep breath, and composed himself, looking around the little cemetery at the poor monuments to our departed kin before sinking to his knees at the grave edge. "Still need revenge, boy? After twenty years?" His grin was brief, more like a wince, but it was genuine enough. "Might be the one way I'll get into this damn place." Frowning, he brushed dirt off his dirty knees before climbing in. Looking around him one last time, seeing no hope, he lay down in the fresh grave with a desultory groan, folding big liver-marked hands upon his chest. "Give that sainted bitch, your mother, my respects," he sighed, "and shoot straight like I taught you." His voice was a little shaky. Though he would not beg, he could not stop talking, eyes clenched tight.

Ring-Eye Lige was not a steadfast man and in a moment would be choking on his terror. "Cold-eyed son of a cold-hearted bitch!" he yelled, to keep his nerve up. "Finish it!" But standing there over his grave, I no longer cared whether this man lived or died. My mortal vow of twenty years had blown away like a bad smell. I'd come all the way across America for nothing.

His eyes were still clenched as I backed away. He thought I was still there. From the damp hole his voice rose in despair. "Shoot straight, damn you!" When he dared open his eyes, in two minutes or ten, all he would see was the grave mouth, a rectangular window on the void of the gray firmament, broken only by the clouds out of the north and the dark wind-borne autumn birds, leaving no trace of their passage down the sky.

At the Artemas Plantation, the black ruin, bound in creeper vine, seemed smaller, all drawn in upon itself. My fields, descending to Clouds Creek, had been hacked into ragged plots by transient sharecroppers and gullied in long scars of raw red clay. Disheartened, I did not dismount but rode directly to Colonel Robert's house. What could I hope for after twenty years? I hoped that I hoped for nothing.

At the racket of his dogs, he came outside before I reached the steps, drove the dogs off me. A quiet in the house that drifted out the door behind him told me that his wife had passed away.

Robert Briggs Watson looked heavier and grayer. Unlike my father, he knew me at once despite my heavy beard and begrimed appearance, which told him everything the Watson clan might care to know about how the Bad Elijah's son had fared in the great world. He would even know that my fine horse must be stolen. His expression was unsurprised, neither cold nor warm.

"Sir, I shall always be grateful you had faith in me," I whispered. "I named my firstborn in your honor." Awkwardly, I offered my hand, as one day long ago in this same place he had offered his. He did not refuse it, simply would not see it. Edgar Watson, like his father, was a shadow cousin. Gazing past me toward the road was his way of saying he had never seen this fugitive and that if I left at once and kept on going, he would not betray me. In a moment he would return inside and close the door.

I remounted and rode away, bruised to the heart. Yet Colonel Robert had rekindled a small hope. Without once meeting my gaze, he had uttered two words before turning back inside. "Not yet," he said. Had I imagined this?

THE ROAD TO GEORGIA

On my way west to Edgefield Court House and the road to Georgia, seeking some sort of empty absolution, I rode into the old carriageway at Deepwood. The old house had fallen. All but vanished, it lay beneath a blanket of wisteria and creeper and dark ivy. The ancient sheds leaned away into the weeds, seeking the earth. I sat my horse, not daring to dismount, in dread of spirits. Since the Owl-Man's death, I had dreamt of Deepwood many times, a nightmare involving a buried body sure to be discovered. The grave, too shallow, quaked underfoot, as if the cadaver was on the point of emerging from the earth. Unable to flee, I was often awakened by my own sharp cry.

Riding hard, I arrived toward dark at Hamburg on the Savannah River. A few years after Selden Tilghman's torture in this small, sad, sorry town, half of it had been burned to the ground as a "nest of Radical Republicans" and the rest rechristened North Augusta, Georgia.

An old hostler who shared his bad cold food confirmed the story that Hamburg was the place where a war hero turned traitor had been tarred and feathered as a lesson to the Republican inhabitants and their detachment of black militia. "Them Regulators whipped that feller to *strips*! He was just a-beggin 'em to kill him!" He also related the details of the celebrated massacre, just four days after Independence Day of 1876, when the unarmed black militiamen had been taught their lesson. The old man had seen both events with his own eyes. When I asked if a big rufous man with a red ring around his eye had taken part, the man gave me a queer look. "Damn!" he said. "Know something? He sure did!"

For all their talk, the Northerners never knew black people and never really liked 'em. Our home nigras learned that truth real quick when they were sold out by the Yankees, who turned their backs overnight on their black friends. The quiet ones were living along as best they could but many were treated no better than those smart-mouths who were paid off for their swagger with the rope and bullet. Slavery was gone according to the law, but with the Black Codes and the KKK and then Jim Crow, life hadn't changed much for the black man. A hell of a lot more burning and lynching was still going on than anybody could remember back before the War.

In this great depression year of 1893, Cousin Selden's cousin Ben Tillman and his rabble-rousers would found their own Populist Party, which jeered at other parties (and the press) for their shameful subservience to the industrialists and their bought-and-paid-for politicians. The Populists joined with factory workers and the small black vote to go after the capitalists, who hogged all the profits and bribed the police to pound on any who protested while permitting the poor to starve in the cause of progress. Pitchfork Ben would go on to win election to the U.S. Senate, taking his safe seat away from Calbraith Butler. But very soon, Ben would revert to the know-nothing nigger-baiting of his snag-toothed faithful, who had barely scraped acquaintance with the English language. *Maht not know nuthin but Ah sho' knows whut Ah know!* By that time, he had lost his black supporters. "The negro has been infected with the virus of equality," he complained.

Pitchfork Ben would go far in life with his foaming at the mouth about black rapists out to sully the sacred honor of our Southern womanhood. As my fellow fugitive Frank Reese had once observed, only white rapists could be found in prison because black ones never got that far alive.

Next morning, crossing the Savannah on the ferry, I headed south to Waycross, over east of the Okefenokee. There I hunted in vain for Lemuel Collins, being curious to hear my erstwhile friend explain why he'd shifted the blame for the John Hayes killing onto Edgar Watson. However, I was able to locate that Mr. Smith who had kindly befriended me on my first journey south back in 1870. We went to a tavern for some talk. Remembering my name, he cocked his head to look at me more carefully. Finally he told me that a young feller named Watson had got himself lynched here in this district just a few years back. "Kind of looked like you, is why I mentioned it. Jack Watson. Ever hear of him?"

"Nosir, I never did."

"Ain't nobody forgot Jack Watson, not around here," Mr. Smith was still disturbed. "White as you or me to look at but called himself a nigger. *'Nigger to the bone!'* Had to be crazy as a shithouse rat but he showed plenty of sand there at the last of it." Eager to relate the whole grim story, he was only restrained by my show of indifference. "Lynchings are all pretty much alike," I said, "when you get right down to it."

Mr. Smith invited me home to wash my feet and meet the daughters. There were four if I counted correctly, and every one a head taller than their guest, huge strong young females twice my weight who ate like stallions and drank me right under the table. Once their daddy had turned in with a loud snoring, those giant girls came down there after me and played hell with the clean duds their dad had lent me while mine got a wash. I never saw such love-starved critters in my life. The biggest lugged me over to her corn-shuck mattress to finish up the job and I do believe the others had their way with me before the smoke cleared. I did my best but never got the hang of 'em some way, they just weren't built right. I was glad to make my getaway next morning, clawed and gnawed up pretty good but in one piece.

The daughter known as Little Hannah would loom into my life again years later, by which time, with no sisters around to steal her thunder, she was called Big Hannah. By then we couldn't quite recall just what had taken place under that table, but it made Hannah blush. "You had you a whole heap of young womanhood, for sure," she giggled, "and done pretty good with it, too."

MISS JANE STRAUGHTER

Crossing into Florida, I headed south along the river road on the west bank of the Suwannee. *All the world is sad and dreary everywhere I roam*—that's how that old song really feels to a man way down upon the Suwannee River in swamp forest in dark winter weather, all that Spanish moss like dead gray hair and doleful vultures hunched on the black snags. I sorely missed dear Mandy and the children and worried how they might be getting on. I didn't even know if Baby Lucius had made it through his first hard winter. For his sake, I kind of hoped he hadn't.

Cypress Creek, White Springs on the Suwannee. Next day I crossed the county line into Columbia but waited till night to ride down past Lake City. No one at Fort White was looking for me but I stayed close to the woods, taking no chances. On the books I was a dead man, drowned in the muddy Arkansas, and I meant to keep it that way, because being dead was the only way I'd ever found to stay out of trouble.

Determined to get things straight with Billy Collins, I went to his house first. Little Julian Edgar, close to my Eddie's age, was already a fine young feller, four years old, and we went hand-in-hand to find his mama. A second boy was toddling around the stove and an infant was toiling at my sister's breast, keeping an eye on me over the tit. With the baby fussing, Minnie did not notice our delegation in the cookhouse door, being pleasured in her nursing in a way that is rarely hidden by that innocent air of milky sweet self-satisfaction peculiar to young mothers, who imagine themselves and their yowling stinky bundle on a golden cloud at the heart of all Creation. But standing back to consider my sister after these years away, I had to acknowledge that other men might admire this scared creature. With her alabaster skin and full red lips, Minnie was pretty, even beautiful, but to me her flesh looked spiritless as ever, with no more spring in it than suet.

"Company for supper, Nin," I whispered.

She gasped, backing away. Deathly afraid for her dear Billy, her eyes implored me even as she babbled how overjoyed she was to see her long-lost brother. If she stayed out of the way while I finished up my business with him, everything would probably come out all right, I told her. Not knowing what "probably" might mean, she started crying.

When Collins came, I was sitting on his porch, in the exact same spot I had sat five years before. He stopped short at the gate. Seeing little Julian on my knee, he mustered up some courage, came ahead. "Well, Edgar," he started, kind of gruff, "this sure is a pleasant surprise."

"So I imagine."

Minnie came rushing out to greet her husband before her brother had a chance to do away with him. She told us both how thrilled she was that I was making such good friends with little Julian. I waved her back inside, wishing to query her husband in peace about local attitudes toward Edgar Watson. Was it safe to come back here, send for my family? I demanded an honest answer, granting him a little time to think that over.

A lovely girl with a shadow in her skin brought a pail of milk, waved cheerily, and went away again. "Who's that?" I said. "Depends," said Billy, "but she is called Jane Straughter." Our eavesdropping Minnie giggled from inside, and Billy said, "Her daddy might be your old friend J. C. Robarts." I thought about Jane Straughter all that evening. She had made me very, very restless. I wondered later if I knew right then that I meant to have her.

At supper I told most of my news, how a son Lucius had been born in Arkansas, how I had paid a call on our male parent. Minnie said, "O Lord, Edgar, you didn't—" She could not speak it and I did not explain. Minnie would never believe the truth, not even if I'd shot her father with six bullets and nailed him tight into his coffin, to end her dread that Ring-Eye Lige might one day track her south to Florida. She would be rapturous with relief at first, then flail herself because she hadn't grieved. My poor sister was condemned by her badly broken nature to find torment in every circumstance while seeking in all directions for forgiveness.

Having stolen Cousin Laura's foolish heart, Sam Frank Tolen was hot after her money and had already renamed our place Tolen Plantation. Sam had made such a mess of the family cabin that Auntie Tab had gone ahead with the construction of the two-story plantation house that William Myers had been planning when he died. Meanwhile dear Mama, Minnie said, had been made to feel unwelcome under the Tolen roof and was anxious to come live in this small house, help take care of her grandchildren. "Unless she brings Aunt Cindy, she'll be no help at all," Minnie complained. "We'll be sure to give her your respects," she added nervously as if I were just leaving.

I wasn't figuring on going anyplace, I said, I wanted to come home and settle down. I turned to Billy, who frowned deeply, weighing his words. "If I were you, Edgar, I would not come home just yet," he said, all in a breath. This community still figured that somebody should pay for the Hayes killing. I was sure to be arrested. And even if I escaped conviction I was a wanted man in Arkansas where I would be returned in chains.

"Wanted in Arkansas? And how do you know that?"

Billy was ready. "Sheriff's office in Lake City was notified by telegraph to be on the lookout for an E. A. Watson."

"That was the first news we had that you might be alive!" cried my pale sister, as her babe suckled, watching me sideways out of shining eyes.

"Also," Billy continued, "Will Cox has been taking good care of your cabin so you won't have to worry about that."

I sat silent, thinking my life over. Life was great and life was terrible and life could not be one without the other, that I knew, which don't mean I understood this or approved it. *Doesn't.* I was saddle sore and weary and begrimed by life, and mortally homesick for a home I had never had unless it was across these woods in my old cabin with Charlie. I couldn't go home to Clouds Creek and I couldn't come home to Fort White. I would have to start all over someplace else.

Seeing my grim expression, my kin were sick with dread, looking away like they'd been whipped across the mouth. The Collins clan, not to mention the Watson women at the plantation—the whole damned bunch, in short—would be greatly relieved if Edgar Watson would make himself scarce for a few more years if not the remainder of his life. Billy was too eager to tell me about the Smallwood and McKinney families who had moved south to Fort Ogden and Arcadia. "Man could do a heck of a lot worse than a fresh start down in that new country, that's what they wrote back to their kinfolks." He frowned to show how much honest cogitation he'd put into this matter. "Yessir, Ed, a *hell* of a lot worse!" That was the first time I ever heard a Collins swear in the presence of a woman. I winced and shifted as if mortally offended, to see if Minnie would squeal *"Bill-lee!"* which of course she did.

Sprawled in the old rocker while Nin scurried to find bedding, I told him, "I will head on south, send for my family when I find a place." Ninny fetched me Mandy's address at Broken Bow in the Indian Territory, so relieved I would be gone by daybreak that she promised the family would send to Arkansas for my wife and children and take good care of them until they could rejoin me. They also promised they would tell Will Cox to keep an eye out for a nigra named Frank Reese, give him some work despite his hard appearance.

Those Collinses were greatly relieved to see the dawn. "You haven't seen hide nor hair of me," I reminded Billy, who came outside as I swung up into the saddle. The moon was going down behind the pinelands. "Last you heard, Ed Watson is dead in Arkansas."

"Watson is dead," he nodded earnestly.

ARCADIA

I forded the Santa Fe below Fort White and headed south across the Alachua Prairie where the early Indians and Spaniards ran their cattle. To the east that early morning, strange dashes of red color shone through the blowing tops of prairie sedges where the sun touched the crowns of sand-hill cranes. Their wild horn and hollow rattle drifted back on a fresh wind as the big birds drifted over the savanna. That blood-red glint of life in the brown grasslands, that long calling—why should such fleeting moments pierce the heart? And yet they do. That was what Charlie my Darling made me see. They do.

Bear and panther sign were everywhere in this wild country. Plenty of deer and wild boar, too, and scrub cattle spooked on their dim trails through the palmetto. I tended south and east along what one old bush rat called the Yeehaw Marshes, from the *yee* and *haw* of the wagon harness of the pioneers moving south down the peninsula. In the Peace River country, I met a man planting wild oranges. He had high hopes that citrus would do well here and invited me to throw in with him; I thanked him but said no. I aimed to clear my own piece of the backcountry. Next morning I rode down along the river and on into Arcadia that afternoon.

As far away as the Arkansas prison, the word was out that a close-mouthed man easy with horse and gun could make good money a lot faster in De Soto County, Florida, than anywhere west of the Mississippi. Unlike most prison rumors, this one turned out to be true. For a few years in the early nineties, the range wars around Arcadia beat anything the Wild West had to offer. The ranchers were advertising for more gunslingers as far off as St. Louis and every outfit had its own gang of riders. With so many rough men in the saloons, a man could get his fill of fighting any time he wanted and be lulled to sleep at night by the pop of gunfire. A lot of these brawls might start with fists but every man was quick to use a weapon before the other feller beat him to it. Fifty bloody fights a day were not uncommon, it was claimed; four men were killed in one shootout alone. The year before, a new brick jail had to be built to hold the overflow, and as it turned out, that new jail saved my life.

A rancher with the wherewithal could hire new riders any day at the nearest saloon, but Arcadia House was where you met all the best people, and a stranger could lean back on the bar and wait there like a whore to be looked over. I had hardly started on my second whiskey when a big man, Durrance, bought my third. Will Durrance spoke of the hard feelings over the rangeland on Myakka Prairie and the cattle rustling all across the county—not just one steer shot to eat by some mangy cracker in the piney woods but whole damn herds up to a hundred head. Most of that range was unfenced and choked with dry palmetto thicket. A steer could wander halfway across Florida, get lost for two years before it wandered out again, and never be missed. Plenty of calves were dropped in the deep scrub and went unbranded, so naturally, an enterprising man burned his own brand as fast as he could get a rope on 'em, figuring the next man along would do the same. Local hospitality for any stranger in the bush was to hang him from the nearest oak for peace of mind. "Better safe than sorry" was a popular expression. A lone rider who wanted to arrive some place picked his own route across cattle country, telling no one.

I was here to put a stake together for a new start in life and had vowed to avoid trouble but Arcadia was no place to say any such thing, not if you wanted a good job. I told Durrance Jack Watson was his man.

"Well, now, Jack, I reckon you know how to ride?"

"Well, now, Will, I rode here from Arkansas by way of Carolina and never split my ass in two, not so's you'd notice, so I reckon I'll make it ten miles out to Myakka Prairie." Durrance paid down cash for my drinks, supper, and bed, also the first real bath since I swam the Arkansas, and he threw in a week's pay in advance.

Next morning I bought me a shave and a new blue denim shirt and rode out to the ranch. Will Durrance lived in a cleared-off pinewood lot fenced with barbed wire. His two-story house had windows high up on the outside wall—too high for assassins to shoot through even from horseback, Durrance explained. He set out a tobacco can and gave me and two other hands new Winchester repeating rifles, saying, "All right, boys, let's see how good you can shoot these Winnies." The other two shot well enough when they lined up each shot, and Durrance nodded: they slid their new repeaters into saddle scabbards, grinning. To buy these new-model Winnies would cost 'em two months' pay. Come my turn, I danced that can all the way across the cowpen about as fast as I could pull the trigger, till Durrance hollers, "That's enough, Jack, for Chrissakes! Don't go wastin them good bullets!"

His cow hunters, as they call 'em here in Florida, looked me over sideways, rolling smokes. Two backwoods brothers by the name of Granger, tall bony fellers with single thick black brows over long noses, looked like *T*'s. I knew this breed, knew that easing by in life was their ambition: Durrance must have signed them on to keep 'em from rustling his stray beefs. The frowns on those T faces told me they were worried this man Watson might set a bad example, make 'em earn their keep. This Jack was no sodbuster, not the way he handled that repeater: this feller had gunslinger written all over him, and trouble, too.

Will Durrance confided that his life was threatened by a feller named Quinn Bass, the bad news in a big cattle clan around Kissimmee. Young Quinn liked to play with gun or knife "with any man at any time on any terms and on any provocation"—that was his boast. Quinn had escaped from the new jail where he was held in the killing of a nigra and what he did was go straight over and kill that nigra's friend who'd been arm-twisted to testify against him, and now he was walking around town acting untouchable. Because the citizenry was naturally upset by the expense and failure of their new jail, not to speak of the failure to arrest an escaped criminal charged with two murders, the sheriff had posted a reward of one thousand dollars for the capture of Quinn Bass, dead or alive.

Having lost faith in the law and having seen me shoot, Durrance made me a financial proposition: he'd add $500.00 bounty to the sheriff's reward if for some reason Quinn was brought in dead.

I was a Carolina Watson and a farmer, not a hired gun, but I guess you could say I'd become a desperado, if that word means a man driven to desperation by ill fortune. At thirty-six, after a hard year in prison and a hard escape, I had no prospects—nothing to show for those long years of toil and deprivation but an undeserved criminal record and a forsaken family, pining away in the rough hinterlands beyond the Mississippi. I was determined to make a fresh start in southwest Florida and avoid any more trouble and equally determined to succeed here in Arcadia in what might well be my last chance to seize hold of my life and take it back. If money was what was needed, a man could not be squeamish about the means, and anyway, I would be doing a good deed. Arcadia's citizens were tired of Quinn Bass, who was a menace to society, even this one; the time had come to put a stop to him. Yet no matter how often I told myself this young killer was better off dead, I had no right to deprive him of his life as a business proposition.

Or so I was counseled by that promising young farmer Edgar A. Watson, first cousin to Colonel Robert B. at Clouds Creek in South Carolina and justly proud of that man's good opinion. Plain Ed Watson or E. Jack Watson, accused killer and prison fugitive, was another matter. E. Jack Watson had his heart set on Durrance's bounty and the sheriff's reward both.

Thus my mind went back and forth and forth and back, never admitting until after it was over that I knew all along I would kill Quinn Bass. For a Watson of Clouds Creek, this was dishonor. I had to accept that, and I did, and I do today. I will only say that many a prosperous businessman and proud American honored for his enterprise in his community got his start in unmentionable dealings such as these.

"All right," I told Durrance, "let me think about it." I went over to the jailhouse and got deputized by the sheriff, then went back to Durrance, told him I'd thought about it till my brain hurt and here were my damn terms, take 'em or leave 'em: "You pay me half your bounty in advance and I will do it." He yelped, "Hell, no, I ain't payin no advance! Suppose somethin goes wrong?" However, he shortly came around to my position.

QUINN BASS, DEAD

One evening later that same week, I was standing at a bar with Tommy Granger when the man I awaited came banging through the doors and paused to scan the place. What I saw in the bar mirror was a whiskered runt whose lumpy hat and a big lumpy tobacco chaw made his head look too big for his squat body. To avoid being noticed, Granger turned away too quick—a bad mistake with a mean dog that has a nose for fear. When Bass caught his movement, Granger froze—mistake number two—then nudged his drinking partner with his elbow—number three. "That's him," this idiot informed me.

When Bass strutted up, I took no notice, didn't even turn around. Annoyed, he sought my eyes in the bar mirror, sizing me up in an uncouth curled-lip way that told me the sheriff had wasted no time letting slip that he had deputized a stranger who was after that reward. "Lookit these two stupid turds! You boys signed on with any outfit yet? Will fuckin Durrance, maybe?" He spat on the floor between our boots. "Any sorry sonofabitch would take his orders from that shitty bastard ain't no kind of a man at all."

Not wanting to toss him any bone to gnaw on, I inspected my drink, which of course enraged him. "You some kind of a dummy, mister?" He slapped my upper arm with the back of his hand. "I'm talking to you, shithead. What's your goddamned name?" He had half a mind, he said, to put me out of my fuckin misery right here and now, because I sure looked like some skunk on the run from someplace where folks would take my execution as a favor.

Arcadia in 1893 was no different from any pest hole in the backcountry: not to defend yourself against abuse only invited more violence. I could tell by the show of his dirt-colored teeth that Bass had mistaken my silence for a coward's fear, yet was galled by the fact that my gaze in the mirror was steady. Either this stranger was ignorant of Quinn's reputation or indifferent to it—unforgivable!

He was panting. "Let's me and you two yeller-bellies get acquainted," he said in a curdled voice. When Granger grinned, too eager to oblige, Bass hoisted a tobacco-yellowed forefinger in front of his nose. "Yank this lever, friend," he said, shifting his chaw to the other cheek. "Just for the fun."

Tommy's stiff grin, pasted on his face, might have looked more natural if he were dead. He pretended to grab his pecker through his pants—"How about you yank this one, Quinn?" When Bass ignored this, waiting for him, he yanked Quinn's finger, knowing full well that when he did, the other would open that brown mouth—here comes the joke—and let fly a jawful of tobacco spit into his face. Having permitted this, Granger turned to me with an aggrieved expression, wiping his nose and mouth with the back of his sleeve—a backwoods ruse, because his long frame was already uncoiling. Being drunk, Bass followed Granger's eyes and the roundhouse punch cracked him hard in the black bush of his chin and knocked him sprawling.

Tommy had all the time in the world to put Bass out of commission by kicking him fairly and squarely in the balls. Having failed to do so, he was in fatal trouble. Already Bass was reared up bloody-lipped onto his elbows, his knife upright in his hand. Savoring what was coming, he shook his head to clear it before rolling up onto his feet. "Self-defense," he reminded the onlookers almost amiably, and after that he was not smiling anymore.

Granger threw me a whipped look, backing up against the bar. "We sure ain't lookin for no trouble, Quinn! Hell's fire, Quinn, you wouldn't want no man for a friend who let another feller spit his chaw into his face, now ain't that right, Quinn?" He turned to me because he could not face that knife one moment longer. "Ain't that right, Jack?" He aimed to drag me into this, he was counting on Oklahoma Jack to save his ass.

Quinn had backed off enough to give them fighting room. "Come on," he rasped, holding the knife high.

Granger fumbled his Bowie out and stared at it as if astonished to find a weapon on his person. When Bass shot me a warning look—*Stay out of this*—Tommy's nerves let go and he kicked off from the bar, launching himself with a godawful squawk like a dying goose. In a moment, they were down rolling around, holding each other's wrists. Granger was big, rangy, and strong, and pretty quick he had Bass's arm twisted up behind his back. Dropping his knife, Bass squawked, "Ah fuck! Okay, okay!," growling at Tommy to let go. "Okay by me, Quinn!" that fool cried with a kind of sob and let go his own knife, too.

Bass grabbed his knife and sprang astride Granger before he could get up, holding the weapon to his throat; Tommy stretched his arms wide as the Christ Himself on the sawdust floor. His eyes were darting, trying to find mine; he was coughing pitifully, too scared to talk. Because Granger had struck first, in front of witnesses, Bass could play with him or take his life for free or maybe both. He poked the man's chest with small stabs through his shirt, drawing red blots, then raised the point to the tip of Granger's nose. "Slit nostril, maybe?" Bass panted, very excited and all set for the last panicky thrash of self-defense that would trigger and excuse the fatal thrust.

Never having met a man I disliked so much so quickly, I already had enough of him to last a lifetime. Stretching out my boot, I toed Quinn in the buttock. He twisted around on me quick as a viper. "That your fuckin boot?"

"Looks like it, don't it."

With a hard grunt, he came for me, knife blade to the front, held flat and low; at this moment, his sole aim in life was to carve my guts. He was only checked by the sight of my revolver, aimed point-blank. One more step and I would have shot him dead. But like Tommy Granger, I had hesitated, I had failed to finish it—a common oversight among amateurs who aren't natural-born killers—and now he would feel honor-bound to seek my death another day. I would have no control over those circumstances, whereas in this place I had a dozen witnesses that the fugitive killer Quinn P. Bass had come at me with a knife. All this went through my mind in a split second. But if I aimed to claim self-defense, an instant choice had to be made here, and I made it. He was opening his mouth to jeer when I pulled the trigger.

The knife fell as Bass spun away and down onto his knees. When I came around in front of him, he stared past blindly, grizzled jaw dropped open. "Well, shit," he muttered thickly—his last words, and as sensible as any, I suppose.

THE BOUNTY HUNTER

I followed Granger out the back and rode around to the new jailhouse. I was Tommy's hero now, I had saved his life, so he gladly agreed to tend my horse and keep him ready while I went in to collect my reward.

Bass's body had drawn a crowd to the saloon. Out in the road, they shot their guns into the air as newcomers asked who'd done it. A voice hollered, "Ask that gunslinger who rides for Durrance!"

The sheriff arrived shortly in bad temper, mouth tight as a sprung trap. He wasn't sorry Quinn was dead nor was he happy about what he would have to deal with. "A lot of them ol' boys out there are Bass clan first and Bass clan foremost, Watson. Most of 'em know you done this town a favor but that don't mean that they won't string you up. And all the rest is just a-rarin to help out for the pure fun and the justice." He wouldn't advise me to loiter in this town, he said.

Informed I was only awaiting my reward, he asked me coldly how it felt to be a bounty hunter. When I reminded him I was his deputy, he wrenched my star off my new shirt, leaving a tear. "Not no more you ain't," he said, as Durrance came through the door.

Durrance was anxious to inform me that the sheriff's reward took care of his own obligation as a private citizen, while the sheriff said it sure looked to him like a gunslinging stranger had baited a local man into an altercation with intent to kill him in cold blood. I reminded them I had done just what they wanted so I sure hoped they would not try to back out of their obligation. I held the rancher's eye. "I sure would hate to tell the Bass clan, Will, about your private bounty on Quinn's head."

Howls rose from without and a great banging on the door: the sheriff refused to lock me up for my own protection. "You better get goin while the gettin's good," he said. I went to the window and looked out. "The gettin don't look so good to me," I said. I entered an empty cell and slammed the door. Lying back on my bunk, hands behind my head, I suggested he do his bounden duty and send out for some drink and a bite of supper for his prisoner.

"Get the hell out of my cell! You're trespissin, layin in there like that! I ain't gettin my new jail burned down for no bounty hunter!"

"Arrest me for trespissin, then."

He came up to the bars. "Who the hell are you, anyway? And don't give me no name that you can't prove: we got a telegraph."

I told him my new name and lawful occupation: E. Jack Watson, farmer.

"Pretty handy with weapons for a goddamn farmer." He shook his head while we listened to the yells and banging. "You seen that crowd out there. How come you didn't keep on riding, mister?"

"You fellers pay what I've got coming and I'll ride."

Brooding about justice and injustice, the sheriff grunted low down in his chest like an old boar. "You might not have much use for your dirty money when that crowd catches you." However, he went to fetch me my reward and I waved Durrance over to my bars. "I bet you hoped that crowd would have me hung by the time you got here, Will. Better luck next time."

Durrance reached into his jacket, his brow all beetled up with honest worry over good money lying loose in a lynched man's pocket. "Jack, it ain't like you done this just for me—"

"You offered me blood money, Will. Want them to know?" I nodded toward the window. His fingers had emerged empty from his pockets but now they crept back in. Scowling, he forked over a small bag of gold coins, twenty dollars each.

The sheriff returned with the reward in hundred-dollar bills. He walked me to the jailhouse door, recommending that I leave at once. The Grangers were outside around the corner, tending my horse. They would empty their six-guns in the air when the door opened, to scatter the crowd and give me a head start. "Them citizens ain't lookin to get shot," the sheriff said. "Not for Quinn Bass."

These two seemed cheerful in their confidence that their cash would be retrieved from my remains. Swinging open the jailhouse door, Durrance wished me luck. "Same to you," I said. I yanked him in front of me and poked my weapon hard into his back, trotting him over to the horses. The Grangers were already yipping, shooting into the air, and the groaning crowd was milling, stupid as spooked steers at the slaughterhouse gate. Durrance hollered, "Don't shoot, boys! It's me!" Right then, some fool opened fire and a bullet whined too close past my ear. I mounted quick, dragging Durrance up behind to cover my back.

Taking no chances, I rode Durrance to the river. He fell off, sore-assed and stiff, still belly-aching about his money: he claimed that my new Winchester was not part of the deal. Not wishing to risk my good fortune by being greedy, I tossed him the rifle. He didn't thank me, only whined about wild beasts. I scattered a few cartridges onto the ground and galloped to the ford. The night was dark, just a sliver of new moon, as I crossed over the Peace River into new country.

From the shack cluster at Alva, I crossed the broad Calusa on the cattle barge and rode down the south bank into Fort Myers, where I boarded my lame horse at the livery stable, bought a new set of clothes and boots (there were no stores south of here, only frontier outposts), and asked some questions about life on this far southwest coast. After a few days, one jump ahead of an inquiry from Arcadia, I sailed downriver to the Gulf of Mexico on the schooner *Falcon*, which rolled and pitched south past Cape Romaine to the Ten Thousand Islands.

My first impression of the great might of the sea dismayed me, the vastness of it and the unforgiving emptiness and the rough seas that threatened to engulf this craft and all its puking sinners, myself included. But eventually the wind moderated and I splashed my face and struck up acquaintance with the captain, William Collier, who straightened me out with a tin cupful of dark fiery Jamaica rum. Captain Bill imparted a few fundamentals of coastal piloting and entrusted me for a time with the ship's helm so that I might feel the workings of the deep.

South of Marco Island, the few small settlements lay hidden in the bays behind the barrier islands: the wall of green was as faceless as the sea. Yet the prospect of so much virgin coast awaiting man's dominion filled me with excitement, even hope. I was still a fugitive, ever farther from my family, but for the first time in my life, I had the capital to establish my own enterprise on my own land, which was here for the claiming. I would find good soil, get a first crop under way while I built a cabin, bring in pigs and chickens, send for Mandy and the children—that was all the plan I needed for a year or two, but all the while, I would look around for opportunity. This Everglades frontier was a huge wilderness to be tamed and harnessed. I had the strength and an ambition made more fierce by so much failure. It was up to me.

CHAPTER 4

✦

TEN THOUSAND ISLANDS

Three miles inland from the open Gulf, between the Islands and the mainland, Chokoloskee Bay was a broad shallow flat almost nine miles long and up to two miles wide. At low tide, it was so shallow that herons walked like Jesus on the pewter shine a half mile from shore, and all around looked like the end of nowhere—mudbanks and islets gathered into walls of mangrove jungle, with strange stilt roots growing in salt water and leaves which stayed that leathery hard green all year around. For a man from the North, used to the hardwood seasons and their colors, this tide-flooded and inhospitable tangle that never changed was going to take a lot of getting used to.

That professor at last year's World Fair in Chicago who told the country it had no more frontiers had sure as hell never heard about the Everglades: in all south Florida, there was no road nor even a rough track, only faint Injun water trails across the swamps to the far hammocks. This southwest coast, called the Ten Thousand Islands, was like a giant jigsaw puzzle pulled apart, the pieces separated by wild rivers, lonesome bays, and estuaries where lost creeks and alligator sloughs, tobacco-colored from the tannin, continued westward through the mangrove islands to the Gulf as brackish tidal rivers swollen with rain and mud, carving broad channels.

Early in 1894, the *Falcon* set me on the dock at Everglade, a trading post on a tidal creek called Storter River. George Storter Junior ran the trading post and his brother ran its trading schooner. Captain Bembery Storter, who became my good friend, shipped farm produce, sugarcane and syrup, charcoal, otter furs, and alligator hides, bringing back trade goods and supplies for the three small settlements—Everglade, Half Way Creek, and Chokoloskee Island—that perched along the eastern shore of Chokoloskee Bay.

Smallwoods and McKinneys from Columbia County had joined the few families on Chokoloskee, a high Indian mound of 150 acres at the south end of the Bay. Both men farmed and set up trading posts, and C. G. McKinney was learning from a book how to pull teeth or babies, all depending. Both were smart self-educated men, among the few on this long coast who knew how to read. Smallwood had even poked around in the Greek literature, swapping books with an old French hermit down the coast named Chevelier, who had scraped acquaintance with every field of knowledge, said McKinney, except how to get on with other human beings.

I took some rough work cutting sugarcane for Storters, who had their plantation down the Bay at Half Way Creek (halfway between Everglade and Chokoloskee). Cutting cane was mean hard labor for drifters, drunks, and nigras, but I never was a man afraid of sweat, and any old job suited me fine while I figured out how a man might work this country. I saw straight off that these palmetto shack communities, backed up against dense mangrove, were no place for a wanted man without a boat who never knew when some lawman from the North might come here hunting him.

Mr. William Brown at Half Way Creek liked the way I went about my business. He accepted a down payment on a worn-out schooner, the *Veatlis*, and a Chokoloskee boy named Erskine Thompson signed on to teach me the sea rudiments. As soon as we got our stores aboard, we headed south into the Islands, cutting cordwood to sell down at Key West and shooting a few plume birds where we found them. It was Erskine who showed me the great bend of Chatham River which became my home.

In all of the Ten Thousand Islands, Chatham Bend was the largest Indian mound after Chokoloskee, forty acres of rich black soil disappearing under jungle because the squatter on there with his wife and daughter would not farm it; they were mostly plume bird hunters, living along on grits and mullet. Like more than one Island inhabitant, Will Raymond Esq. was a fugitive and killer, glowering from Wanted posters all the way from Tampa to Key West. He liked the Bend because it was surrounded by a million miles of mangrove, giving the lawmen no way to come at him except off the river.

The boy had heard about this mangy bastard and was scared to death. We drifted down around the Bend, keeping our distance. There was a loose palmetto shack on there, and smoke, but when I hailed, no answer came, only soft mullet slap and the whisper of the current, and a scratchy wisp of birdsong from the clearing. The boy slid the skiff along under the bank, put me ashore. I told him to row out beyond gunshot range but stay in sight as a warning to Will Raymond that there was a witness. Not till the skiff was safe away did I call out once or twice, then stick my head above the bank to have a look. Nothing moving, nothing in sight. I rose up slow, keeping my hands well out to the sides, and nervously wasted my best smile on a raggedy young girl who retreated back inside the rotted shack.

All this while, Will Raymond had me covered. I could feel the iron of his weapon and its hungry muzzle, and my heart felt naked and my chest flimsy and pale beneath my shirt, but I was up there in one piece with my revolver up my sleeve, smiling hard and looking all around to enjoy the view.

Hearing a hard and sudden cough like a choked dog, I turned to confront an ugly galoot who had stepped out from behind his shack. Unshaven, barefoot, in soiled rags and an old broken hat, he stunk like a dead animal on that river wind. Even after I presented my respects, his coon rifle remained trained on my stomach, his finger twitching on the trigger. I'd seen plenty of this scurvy breed in the backcountry, all the way from Oklahoma east and south, knife-mouthed piney-woods crackers, hollow-eyed under black hats, and lean-faced females with lank hair like horses and sour-smelling babes in long hard stringy arms. Men go crazy every little while and shoot somebody. Seems Will had done that more'n once in other parts, got the bad habit of it. With his red puffy eyes like sores, Will Raymond looked rotted out by drink but also steady as a stump—a very unsettling combination in a dangerous man.

The muzzle of a shooting iron at point-blank range looks like a black hole leading straight to Hell but I did my best to keep on smiling. Mr. Raymond, said I, I am here today with an interesting business proposition. Yessir, I said, you are looking at a man ready and willing to pay hard cash for the quit-claim to a likely farm on the high ground—this place, for instance. Two hundred dollars, for instance (a fair offer for squatter's rights in this cash-poor economy, Erskine had told me).

Will Raymond wore a wild unlimbered look and his manners were not good. He never so much as introduced me to his females, who kept popping their heads out of their hole like the prairie dogs back in Oklahoma. In fact he made no response at all except to cough and spit in my direction whatever he dredged up from his racked lungs. However, that mention of cold cash had set him thinking. His squint narrowed. While estimating how much money might be removed from my dead body, he was considering that boy out on the river, who was doing his best to hold his skiff against the current. Will Raymond had reached a place in life where he had very little left to lose.

He coughed again, that same hard bark. "If you are lookin for a farm at the ass end of Hell, seventy mile by sea from the nearest market, and have a likin for the company of man-eatin miskeeters and nine-foot rattlers and river sharks and panthers and crocky-diles and every kind of creepin varmint ever thunk up by the Lord to bedevil His sinners—well then, this looks like your kind of a place."

"That's right, sir!" I sang out cheerily.

"No sir, it sure ain't, cause I am on here first. And next time, sir, you go to trespissin without my say-so, sir, I will blow your fuckin head off. Any questions?"

"Not a one," said I in the same carefree tone. I signaled for my boat. While waiting, I ventured to look around a little more, thinking how much my Mandy might enjoy these two big red-blossomed poincianas. "Yessir, a fine day on the river. Makes a man feel good to be alive."

He spat his phlegm again. "You got maybe ten more seconds to feel alive in, mister. After that you ain't goin to feel nothin."

Under my coat, the .38 lay along my forearm, set to drop into my hand. To drill this polecat in his tracks would have been a mercy to everyone concerned, especially his poor drag-ass females. Instead I climbed into the skiff and headed downriver. What I needed more than anything right now was a reputation as an upright citizen, so I put aside my motto of "good riddance to bad rubbish" in favor of "every dog must have its day." This dog had had his day at Chatham Bend and mine would come next or my name wasn't Jack Watson, which it wasn't.

Will Raymond observed our skiff until we passed behind the trees on the next bend. His figure stood there black and still as a cypress snag out in the swamp, his old Confederate long rifle on his shoulder like the scythe of Death. Out on the coast again, looking back, I noted with approval that the mouth of Chatham River, all broken up by mangrove clumps, would pass unseen by any vessel, even from a quarter mile offshore.

CAYO HUESO OR BONE KEY OR KEY WEST

At the end of that week, sailing to Key West, I had my first look at Lost Man's River, said to be the wild heart of this whole wilderness. In Shark River, farther south, huge dark mangroves rose to eighty and a hundred feet in an unbroken wall: the boy happened to know these were the largest in the world. From Shark River, the mangrove coast continued to Cape Sable, the long white beach where Juan Ponce de León and his conquistadors went ashore in heavy armor and clanked inland in wet and heavy heat to conquer the salt flats and marl scrub and brown brackish reach of a dead bay.

From Cape Sable our course led offshore along the western edge of great pale banks of sand, with turquoise sand channels and emerald keys on the port side and a thousand-mile blue reach of Gulf to starboard. Erskine pointed when he heard the puff of tarpon as one of these mighty silver fishes leapt clear of the sea: farther offshore, giant black manta rays leapt, too, crashing down in explosions of white water.

In late afternoon the spars of an armada of great ships rose slowly from the sunny mists in the southern distance. Cayo Hueso or Bone Key. Early in the nineteenth century, Bone Key, now called Key West, had been built up as a naval base to suppress piracy on the high seas, but these days Key West pirates lived on shore as ship's chandlers, salvagers, and lawyers.

On a southwest wind, the *Veatlis* passed the Northwest Light and tacked into the channel. Who would have imagined such a roadstead as the Key West Bight, so far from the mainland at the end of its long archipelago of small salt keys? Or so many masts, so many small craft, so much shout and bustle? New York merchantmen and Havana schooners mixed with old sailing craft from the Cayman Islands, fetching live green turtle to the water pens near Schooner Wharf for delivery to the turtle-canning factory down the shore, Erskine explained. Tacking and luffing, servicing the ships, were whole flotillas of "smackee" sloops with baggy Bahamian mainsails, dropping their canvas as they slipped up alongside—reef fishermen with live fish in the sloop's well, hawking snappers to the Key West Market and king mackerel to the Havana traders. The sponges drying in open yards ashore were shipped to New York on the Mallory Line, which supplied and victualed this city.

Having unloaded our cordwood cargo into horse-drawn carts backed down into the shallows, we went ashore. Key West is a port city, with eighteen thousand immigrants and refugees of every color—eighteen times as many human beings as could be found on the entire southwest coast, all the way north two hundred miles to Tampa Bay. The island is seven miles by three, and the town itself, adjoining the old fort, is built on natural limestone rock. The white shell streets are potholed, narrow, with broken sidewalks and stagnant rain puddles and small listless mosquitoes. Coco palms lean over the green-shuttered white houses in shady yards of bright flowers and tropical trees. Sweet-blossomed citrus, banyans, date palms, almonds and acacias, tamarind and sapodilla—so an old lady instructed me when I inquired about which trees might do well on a likely plantation farther north in Chatham River.

While in Key West, I paid a call on the Monroe County sheriff, Richard Knight, in regard to a certain notorious fugitive depicted on the Wanted notice in the post office. The murderer Will Raymond, I advised him, could be found right up the coast in Chatham River. The sheriff knew this very well and was sorry to be reminded of it. He sighed as he bit off his cigar. My report would oblige him to send out a posse when, like most lawmen, enjoying the modest graft of elected office, he much preferred to defer these thorny matters.

Taking the chair the sheriff had not offered, I said I sure hated to cause trouble for Mr. Raymond, but as a law-abiding citizen, I knew my duty. Looking up for the first time, Knight said, sardonic, "That mean you won't be needing the reward?"

Sheriff Knight and I understood each other right from the first, and our understanding was this: we did not like each other. But a few days later, a sheriff's posse laid off the river mouth until three in the morning, then drifted upriver with the tide (as I'd advised them), and had four men ashore before they hollered to Will Raymond to come out with his hands up. Will yelled he'd be damned if he'd go peaceable, and whistled a bullet past their heads to prove it, but he was peaceable as he could be by the time the smoke cleared. They flung his carcass in the boat and offered his widow their regrets along with a kind invitation to accompany the deceased on a nice boat ride to Key West, and the widow said, "Why, thankee, boys, I don't mind if I do."

On my next visit, when I went to the sheriff's office to offer my congratulations, I happened to mention the information which brought justice to Will Raymond. Wincing, he slid open a drawer and forked over $250 in hard cash reward without a word.

I never kept a penny of that money. I went straight over to Peg's boardinghouse on White Street and offered it to the Widow Raymond as a consolation in her time of bereavement. By now, the Widow was looking a lot better or at least a good deal cleaner. Perky, she said, "Mr. Stranger, this sure is my lucky day and you sure are my savior, bless your heart!" She offered corn spirits and a simple repast, then took me straight to bed, out of pure gratitude and the milk of human kindness.

Buttoning up, I mentioned the late Mr. Raymond's quit-claim, and she implored me to accept it with her compliments, declaring her sincere and fervent hope that she would never set eyes on that cursed place again. Altogether, a touching story with a happy ending. I strode away to the docks with a lilting heart, confident at last that my path in life had made a turning in the right direction.

On my next voyage to Key West, I encountered Captain N. N. Penny, a fine, fierce fellow with a cigar thrusting from the very center of his mouth who had made his mark hauling freed slaves to Liberia after the Civil War; however, his clipper ship would arrive in port somewhere up the coast only a few days later without its cargo; also missing was the heavy anchor chain he was rumored to replace after each voyage. Even today Cap'n Penny was renowned as a practical man who would march his cargo overboard rather than risk capture by a federal vessel. We exchanged but a few words before he recognized me as another man who meant to get ahead in life and entrusted me with the information that the commerce in human beings which had made our nation great was by no means dead. Chinese coolies and other illegal immigrants would gladly pay enterprising captains to set them ashore in Florida, where most wound up as indentured labor for the new railroad companies, resort hotels, large-scale drainage schemes, and development enterprises seeking to bring both of Florida's wild coasts into the modern world. It made his red blood tingle and his pockets jingle, quoth this jolly patriot, to contribute prime "Chinks" to Florida's exciting future.

Captain Penny and I were especially convivial since we shared a liking for hard drink and dark humor; he suggested that we might "do some business." However, I had already perceived that Penny was only a small cog (a very large small cog) in the great engine of our nation's progress. The very next day, introduced by Penny at the Catherine Street mansion of the cigar tycoon Teodoro Pérez, I made the acquaintance of Napoleon Broward, Esq., who was already preparing for the dashing role in Cuban liberation which would get him elected governor of Florida a few years later. With Mr. Broward was the Cuban revolutionary José Martí, a pale small man, very thin and tense, with more hair in his long sad moustachios than on his pate: José Martí's financial support in the fight for Cuban independence came mostly from these rich cigar manufacturers in Key West and Tampa.

Napoleon Broward was a bold sanguinary man of direct action, in the mold of Gould and Astor, Carnegie and Frick—in short, a man who could be counted on not to be squeamish about how the nation's progress was achieved while never losing sight of his private interests, whether in politics or in industry and business. To the sweet chortling of redbirds, which our cultivated Spanish host displayed in small wicker cages like crimson canaries, Broward spoke admiringly of Hamilton Disston, who had pioneered the shipping canal connecting Lake Okeechobee to the Calusa Hatchee River and the Gulf, and I made bold to mention some of my own ideas about the drainage of the Everglades for large-scale agriculture and also the eventual development of the virgin southwest coast and the Ten Thousand Islands. Here Broward raised his beetled brows: "Hold on there, my friend." Mistaking our host, Señor Pérez, for the butler, he snapped his fingers and commanded him to fetch Mr. Watson and himself another round of brandy and cigars.

Broward remarked that we had common interests and must by all means stay in touch. By the time we met again in the year following, I had studied all the Everglades reports, all the way back to the visionary

schemes of Buckingham Smith, who had written the first drainage rec-
ommendation in the days of the Seminole Wars; I also furnished him the
details of that 1850 Act of Congress which had patented this entire
"swamp-and-overflowed wilderness" to the state of Florida. As early as
the 1860s, a colonel of the Army Engineers had estimated that if Lake
Okeechobee's water level could be lowered by six feet, nine inches—the
approximate fall from the lake to the Atlantic—the vast wetlands from the
Kissimmee River south could be settled and cultivated without fear of an-
nual overflow and flood.

"By God, Watson, you intrigue me!" Flushed and fulsome, Broward
vowed that if he were ever to be elected governor as was his ambition, E. J.
Watson would be summoned to the state capital at once to help set Glades
development in motion. "You're an up-and-coming feller, Ed," Nap said
warmly as we parted. "If I am elected, you can write your own damn
ticket." By God, I thought, it's happening! I'm on my way!

ON CHATHAM BEND

Taking a Key West nigra and a mule, I went straight home to Chatham
Bend. With some half-ass help from Erskine Thompson, who placed little
value on hard labor, I got that high ground in production in a hurry since
there was no real forest to contend with. The Calusa who had a village here
before the Seminole Wars had kept the jungle down, and since then, a fisherman, Richard Harden, then the old plume hunter Jean Chevelier—the
last occupant before the late Will Raymond—had burned it over every year
to discourage jungle scrub. What settlers wanted around any dwelling was
nice bare ground that provided no cover for bad snakes, not to mention the
no-see-ums and mosquitoes. In regard to discomfort and disease, the most
dangerous creature in the Glades by far was the mosquito, which had
driven men cast away or stranded on this coast to madness, even death.

With the rains in spring and fall, the river became a broad and burly
flood, sandy brown and heavy with Glades silt, leaving thick crusts on the
marl behind the mangrove fringes. Because the river was brackish from the
tides, what we drank (before my rain gutters and a cistern were put in) was
dead water from a rain barrel, and very glad to have that, too, in this salt
country. That first year I built a palmetto log house with palm thatch

roof—two big rooms and an outside kitchen. Next came a small dock, then a big shed, then a pasture with limb fenceposts cut from the red gumbolimbo tree, which will take root when stuck into the ground. By the end of the year, my horse Job, a mule, a milk cow, and five hogs cohabited the old Raymond shack—more livestock than any settler south of Chokoloskee. All that was missing now was Mandy and the children.

Clearing off that second growth was hot and wearisome, and turning over the black soil, packed hard with shell, was worse. That shell had to be chipped out with a pickax, though once it was reduced to soil, it was black and fertile. I started out with tomatoes and peppers, then peas, beets, radishes, and turnips. All sprouted fine, but by the time we got our produce to Key West, it looked old and limp, half-spoiled. We grew our kitchen vegetables, of course, and planted fruit trees—bananas, mangoes, guavas, papayas, citrus.

Chatham Bend was the first good ground I ever worked on my own behalf rather than leasing or sharecropping for someone else, but truck farming would never make my fortune in the Islands. The following year we cleared more ground and grew a crop of sugarcane on about ten acres. Cane is a cast-iron plant that can survive flood, fire, and brief freezing and does not spoil in the shipping like fresh produce. As a perennial, it yields four or five crops before new cuttings must be planted: I worked out how to double-crop with cow peas to restore the soil and planned to rest each section every few years, leaving it fallow. Learning quickly that cane stalks were too bulky to ship economically to a market eighty miles away, I increased crop acreage, brought a crew in for the harvest, and switched to the manufacture of cane syrup—the first planter in the Islands ever to try it. (I had already replaced the small *Veatlis* with a sixty-eight-foot schooner called the *Gladiator.*)

The cane harvest extended till late winter, early spring, when I got rid of all my crew except Erskine and my new housekeeper, Henrietta Daniels, Erskine's mother. Though glad to have a roof over her head, Netta was terrified of the wild people, and hid back in the house at the first glimpse of a dugout—very strange, since many of her Daniels kin had Injun blood.

Netta Daniels had led an errant life, working as a tobacco stripper in the Key West cigar factories and marrying often. Despite her trials, she remained a fervent Catholic, never danced nor swore nor slept in the same bed with a man who had been drinking, as I discovered on the night of her arrival.

"Listen," I told her the next day, "it's not seemly for a lady to sleep in the same room with her son. That kind of behavior will not be tolerated on the Bend." After that, she bunked with me, which is pretty much the way I'd planned it in the first place. She was a few years older than myself, with hazel-green eyes and light brown hair and small cupped ears that made her look kind of crestfallen when she was tired. Still, she was a pretty woman and a willing one. She would clean a little but not much, can our preserves and feed the chickens, do simple cooking and her bounden duty by her master, namely me.

Erskine mostly ran the boat and slopped the hogs and did a few odd jobs when we could find him. So did Netta's half brother Stephen, who turned up not long thereafter. Mr. S. S. Jenkins, as he introduced himself, was more commonly called Tant. He was mostly famous for the moonshine or "white lightning" he manufactured from raw sugar and chicken feed (a half sack of corn and a half sack of sugar in a charred oak barrel: that oak barrel, which he lugged everywhere, was his trade secret). Ferment worked quickly in this climate, and the "buck," as he called it, was ready to distill in about ten days, but Tant was tasting it for flavor long before that. "Comin along real nice, Mister Ed!" he'd whoop, to keep my hopes up, but by the time he got that shine distilled, he had drunk most of it and had to start all over. Sometimes all we got out of the deal were the checkered feed sacks from his corn that Netta saved to make our shirts. Although still a young man, Mr. S. S. Jenkins was twitching like the dickens, he had to fold his arms around his chest just to stay put in his chair.

Rarely caught in the cane field, Tant fished and hunted our wild food, harvesting wild duck in the creeks and sloughs and sometimes a few of those black pigeons that hurtled up and down the river in the early morning. He was a tall and lanky feller with a small head and a comical tuft for a mustache, and he made me laugh right from the start, distracting my attention from his natural traits of bone laziness and alcohol addiction. Tant understood long before I did that I would tolerate his flaws of character only so long as he kept me amused.

One day at Chokoloskee, knowing I was watching, this fellow snuck up on Adolphus Santini's cow pen, causing a regular stampede by poking his head over the fence and ducking down, up and down, over and over, until those critters went crazy with suspense, galumphing around colliding with one another. I got laughing so hard I could hardly find my breath, even when Dolphus ran out hollering. Seeing me there, Old Man Dolphus folded his big arms like an old blue heron folding its big wings. Never said one word.

Another day we were out shooting white ibis for our supper, back over toward what is now called Watson Prairie. A big gator maybe twelve foot long was crossing some dry palmetto ground between two sloughs, and S. S. Jenkins, drunk as usual, yells, "Look here, Mister Ed!" Ran across the clearing and jumped onto that reptile piggyback, threw an arm lock around the jaw, crossed his ankles under the belly, all the while whooping like an Injun. That big gator was so scared it hauled Tant all over the palmettos, you never heard such a racket in your life, and that fool never let go till he hit the water. "That's the last time I will ever take a bath," Tant told us when he crawled out on the bank. "Don't see no sense to it."

Tant had always been a bachelor and never so much as considered female companionship except when drunk. One evening he approached his half sister on his hands and knees, said, "Netta, I aim to go get me a bride! All you got to do is recommend me, Netta, and I'll try to live up to it!" Netta just smiled. She loved Tant the way he was, never tried to change him and never tried to find him a wife, either, knowing how hopeless that would be. Like many a lovable, whimsical feller, Tant Jenkins was a very lonesome man.

In the breeding season, in late winter and early spring, we hunted the white egret rookeries, stripping the plumes. These we traded to young Louis and Guy Bradley of Flamingo, who had hunted this coast with the Frenchman back in the '80s. In October, when the long chill nights would knock down the mosquitoes, Tant baited his old traps, using salt mullet, and set a trapline along creek banks for otter, coon, and possum, which all humped along the shoreline at low tide. The rest of the year, forswearing hard liquor, he'd journey up the creeks into the Glades, as far from honest toil as he could go, returning with wild turkey and deer meat and hides from the hammocks and pine islands. The venison and turkey breasts were salted overnight, then smoked for a few days on palmetto platforms over coals.

That smoked meat would keep a good long while before it was soaked to remove the salt, then cooked and eaten. The deer hides were stretched on frames and dried; we sold them for credit at the trading posts, along with his gator hide and coon and otter pelts. Occasionally he brought in a big gopher tortoise or swamp rabbits or other varmints; roasted possum tasted almost like young pig if you tasted hard enough, and the white tail meat of a young gator was fine, too. Tant even ate rattlesnakes he'd skinned out— "Fit for a king!" he'd say. Might have tasted like chicken, as he claimed, but he had that snake meat mostly to himself.

Netta was always disappointed when Stephen, as she called him, failed to bring the small wild key limes and wild grapes. She doted on wild butter beans from the hammock edges and prickly pears dug out for making pie. Occasionally Tant brought palm hearts from the inland hammocks, also coontie root; this sold well in the trading posts as "Florida arrowroot," a starch for cakes and puddings. However he detested the insect swatting and hard grubbing in hot windless woods that went into every barrel, and the washing and grinding of the pulp, the soaking, fermenting, and drying. For seven cents a pound, he said, that was too much common labor, and anyway, "I can't abide the feel of sweat and never could." So Netta mostly baked her dough using salt and boiling water and her bread came out like a loaf of hardtack cracker. Well, we told her, hardtack was better than the gray bread in C. G. McKinney's trading post, which C. G. himself sold as "fresh wasp nest."

Cash being scarce on the frontier, most trade was barter. I'd swap cane syrup for big oranges, two for a penny, or saltwater oysters, sixty cents a barrel. At Key West or Tampa Bay, such treats as coffee beans and olive oil and chocolate were available, and sacks of onions and potatoes from the North. On the Bend, we ate better and a whole lot more than I had ever eaten in my life, which made me worry about Mandy and the children.

In April of 1895, a baby daughter was delivered to Henrietta by Richard Harden. Her mother named her Minnie after my sister. Having wanted a son, I was ready to call her "Ninny" and be done with it but Netta would not hear of such a joke.

For a gentle person, Netta had some courage. One day when my old horse Job the Younger would not pull the plow no matter how hard I switched him, I lost my temper and grabbed up a length of two-by-four to knock some sense into his head. Netta called out through the window,

"Mister Watson! Don't you do that, Mister Watson!" I felt sheepish. "Sometimes I'm a damned fool, Netta," I told her later. I was sorry she had scared herself so bad that she begged forgiveness.

CASTING ASPARAGUS ON A MAN'S HONOR

Netta's mother had made Catholics out of her children and Netta's sister had married Tino Santini, a Corsican from a Catholic family who saw no sin in rum-running but had no tolerance for common-law marriage, never mind bastards. That Santini gossip about Minnie's parentage got started after my scrape with Tino's brother at a produce auction in Key West. I was drunk, they tell me, and Adolphus, too. I meant to leave him a thin scar as a reminder to be more civil to Ed Watson, but unfortunately my knife blade nicked his jugular, splattered Corsican blood across baskets of asparagus, making me look like a bloodthirsty villain. Scurrilous remarks about my past were what had started it. ("Mr. Santini cast asparagus on a man's honor," said Tant Jenkins.) Dolphus wound up in the hospital with a sore throat while I was obliged to fork over what was left of my Arcadia earnings to settle the matter out of court.

Having pocketed my nine hundred dollars, Santini wrote to Governor Mitchell complaining that his assailant had never been brought before the bar of justice. I learned this from my drinking companion the U.S. Attorney at Key West, who kept me well-informed in legal matters. (When Dolphus learned that I knew about his letter, he lost his zeal for justice, sold his Chokoloskee house, and sailed away to the east coast at the Miami River.)

Sheriff Knight wanted to hold me in the Key West jail while he looked into Santini's story that E. J. Watson was a desperado, wanted by the law somewhere out West. With his bald eye and sour nature, Knight had been after me ever since he coughed up the reward in the Will Raymond case. This time he sent away on his new telegraph to find out what he could but I left Key West before word came. The governor's office sent a query to Sheriff Knight who sent a deputy to bring me in for questioning. Because this deputy, Clarence Till, planned to run for sheriff in the next election, he struck Knight as just the man to travel a hundred miles by sea to a wild river to arrest a dangerous fugitive single-handed. I got the drop on Clarence, took his guns away, and put him straight to work out in the cane.

Had more guts than brains but a real nice young feller all the same. After two hard weeks I told him, "Clarence, let that be your lesson." I put him back into his boat and waved good-bye. Deputy Till thought the world of me and waved back with a big grin. Disgusted with the sheriff, who had made no effort to send after him, he returned to Key West singing my praises as the only man of progress in that wilderness. In later years, Clarence did his best to look the other way when I cut up rough while seeking recreation in his city.

According to a comical card sent by Sam Tolen, the Santini episode had made headline news in the Lake City paper, the culprit Watson being locally well known as a dangerous drunk and an alleged accomplice in the killing of John Hayes. My Mandy, who had arrived in Fort White with the children, made no mention of those lies in her affectionate letter, which simply inquired if my family might come join me. After all her poverty and suffering—and five long years in the Indian nations with no word from her wandering husband—this excellent woman held no bitterness. She had always known the dark side of my nature and deplored it—she would not pretend—but for some reason she still had faith in me and I was grateful.

As for the children, I missed my pretty Carrie and young Eddie and was somewhat curious to see how baby Lucius had turned out. "He favors me a little, more's the pity," Mandy had written. I chuckled, imagining her shy smile as she wrote that, but a moment later, that innocent sweet memory was ousted by a vision of the warm pink muffin of her rump, which stirred my dog loins all the way from Columbia County.

Netta smelled trouble. I told her straight she would have to make room for my lawfully wedded wife and legal children. "Make room?" Her tone annoyed me. Come to think of it, I said, she'd better clear out down to the last hairpin and take her little Min right along with her. "Clear out, you said? My little Min?" She stood right up to me. "Mis-ter Desperado Watson! Huh!" First time I ever saw this woman truly angry. She called me a liar for persuading her that common law was binding and for never mentioning my "awful lawful wife," as Tant would call her. Her phony husband having turned out to be some kind of dirty Mormon, she was only too happy to depart forever, never to return, and many other words to that effect.

I was sad for I loved Netta in her way, but my past had overtaken us and that was that. I left the Bend that afternoon so as not to have to listen to her any further. Stopping briefly at Caxambas, I notified Captain Jim Daniels that his sister needed fetching at the Bend. From there I went on to Fort Myers to talk business with Dr. T. E. Langford and a Mr. Cole who wished to invest in Island Pride, my cane syrup operation.

Since the Santini story had arrived ahead of me, I was astonished that two such upright citizens would entrust me with their dollars. Seems they were much less interested in Santini's throat than impressed by what Capt. Bill Collier had told them about how fast that feller Watson got his cane plantation up and running, said Ed had enough brains and ambition to develop the Ten Thousand Islands single-handed. Only thing, Bill warned 'em, that man has a hot temper and never lets too much stand in his way. Jim Cole just grinned. For a good businessman, Cole observed, there were few better recommendations than a nose for opportunity and the nerve to see it through.

Jim Cole was a big man in cattle and shipping who became one of the first county commissioners. He had married into the Summerlin family which owned the cattle yards at Punta Rassa and was engaged in various enterprises with the Hendrys, who owned half the town. Because he had political ambitions, Cole was noisily civic-minded, claimed he aimed to drag Fort Myers into the Twentieth Century whether folks liked it or not. A few years later, he paved over the white seashell streets for his new auto, the first such contraption folks had ever seen. I associate concrete with Jim Cole—he loved that stuff.

To ensure their support, Cole put people in his debt. I took his money to build up my syrup business but instead of feeling grateful, I resented it. I reckon he knew that—I never tried to hide it—but as a politician, he could not tolerate unfriendliness and never understood why I disliked having my back slapped by such a big loud jokey feller when most men got along with him just fine.

Jim Cole was out to win Ed Watson to his side or know the reason why. Hearing that the Key West sheriff was still nagging me about Santini, Cole sent Knight a wire saying, "Friend Watson rode in out of the Wild West, he's one of that freewheeling breed that made this country great." Knight wired back, "Freebooting, you mean? Don't tell a lawman not to do his job." Cole thought this exchange was pretty funny. He looked rattled when I didn't smile.

All the same, it was Jim Cole who lined up the local business interests to capitalize my operation and advance me credit, and Dr. T. E. Langford went along. In financial matters, the Langford family did what Cole told them. Before anything could occur to change their mind, I placed an order with Bill Collier for a cargo of Dade County pine, then hired two carpenters to come to Chatham Bend and help me build a good big house, a better dock, a boat shed and attached dormitory for harvest workers, with down payment in advance and the balance billed to the account of the Watson Syrup Company, Chatham River, c/o Chokoloskee, Florida, U.S.A.

WORKS AND DAYS

The great day came when I sailed north with Erskine Thompson to meet my family at the new railroad terminus at Punta Gorda. For the first time since he was one month old, I gazed upon Lucius Hampton Watson, a fair-haired handsome quiet little boy, aged seven. Squealing, my sweet Carrie ran to jump and hug me—*Papa! Papa!*—while Edward Elijah Watson frowned at his sister and furrowed his brow before stepping up and shaking hands in a stern manly fashion. "Good day, Father," this young fellow said. "I am very happy to renew our acquaintance." And finally Mandy shyly took my hand, bending her forehead to my chest to hide her tears. Only Sonborn—I might have known—stood to one side, spoiling for a showdown. I was struck afresh by his resemblance to his mother, the pallid, almost pretty face with the vivid red spots on the cheeks and what Mandy called a poet's long black lock of hair over his eyes.

I led my poor exhausted troupe to a dinner at the Hotel Punta Gorda, an immense pile of masonry with corner turrets and big central tower, thrown together a few years before when this Gulf fishing camp became the southern terminus of the west coast railroad. The hotel contained over five hundred empty rooms, more than enough to bed every human being on this southwest coast. As Eddie rolled his eyes for his father's benefit, Carrie ran wild down the corridors with Lucius hard behind, although both were near tears with fatigue from their long journey.

At supper, my rambunctious daughter declared for the whole dining room to hear, "I bet they wouldn't never dare to serve us beets!" Then the waiter arrived, and he says, "Folks, if there's one item on our menu you just better try, that's our fresh beets." And Carrie sings out, "Well, Mister Waiter, if I was you, I'd just hold back on them beets. If it looks like a beet or tastes like a beet, let alone stinks like a beet, don't you dare bring it to our Watson table."

The boys seized this excuse to whoop, we were all laughing, even Rob, although Mandy pretended to be shocked by her daughter's "wild deportment, uncouth speech, and frontier grammar." Even Erskine Thompson, who was to sour at an early age, smiled a smile as thin as a hairline crack in glass.

Sailing south next day, we stopped off for the night at Panther Key to let my inland family hear sea stories told by old Juan Gomez, famous ex-pirate and world champion liar who came to an end a few years later when he tangled his foot in his old cast net and threw himself overboard and drowned at his official age of one hundred twenty-three. Next morning we trolled fish lines south, had good fishing all the way to Chatham River. Infected by old Gomez with the ambition to be pirates, the boys shouted in excitement as the schooner came in off the Gulf and negotiated the river's hidden entrance. I pointed out the tropic hardwood forest rising behind the mangrove walls as we tacked upstream, and the red gumbo-limbos found on Indian mounds and in swamp country near high water which were always sign of high ground and good soil. "Gumber-limber," Lucius laughed, enjoying those funny words, as Eddie shook his head in pity.

Once they saw that white house and realized it was ours, the children could not stop hollering. They scarcely listened to my short Indian history of this shell mound nor glanced at my thirty-acre field but leapt off the boat and ran ahead. Walking from the dock toward her house, Mandy dabbed her eyes and sniffled as she smiled; she could scarcely speak.

With shingled roof and walls white-painted inside and out—real oil paint, too, not some old whitewash, I told her—the Watson place was the finest house between Fort Myers and Key West, with hardwood floors and a parlor on the riverfront with a fine view. On the west side were two full bedrooms and a small sewing room that Mandy would be using as a schoolroom; she had a good big indoor kitchen with woodstove in the north side wing. Mounting from the hall was a full staircase with a polished mahogany rail—the only full staircase south of Tampa Bay. On the second story, two bedrooms faced the river, and in back were five small children's rooms and a big linen closet off the stairwell. All the rooms had double beds and the bigger rooms two doubles each.

The white house at Chatham Bend, boasted Planter Watson, was by far the biggest and best built in all the Everglades and the Ten Thousand Islands. Worried by the expense of my staircase, Mandy ran her hand down the shining rail. "I cannot justify it, my dear wife"—I hugged her happily— "but never again need you fear cold and hunger."

To keep out bugs, we tacked a cotton fabric over the windows, made palmetto-frond brooms to sweep mosquitoes off anybody coming through the door. The cow was swept, too, as she entered her shed, and a gunnysack door covered that entrance, for otherwise this beast would weaken and die from loss of blood. Mosquitoes were at their worst from June through September, when kerosene smudge pots and wick lamps filled the house with filthy smoke.

At Chatham Bend, we watched out for bad snakes—rattlers and moccasins, sometimes a coral snake—and occasionally we came across the track of bear or panther. These animals were not dangerous, I promised the scared kids, unless surprised in the hog pen or chicken house. The children reserved their most delicious fear for a fire-brown creature the size of my middle finger which our colored hand Sip Linsey called a "scruncher" due to the noise it made, trod underfoot. Sonborn (*Rob*, Mandy insisted) and young Lucius went to great pains not to step on them. Despite the ten-year difference in their age, these two were the closest among the four children. (Rob's mother still came to me in dreams but never spoke. Had time really stopped that day she died or just rolled on without me?)

Even at seven, Lucius was fascinated by wild creatures. He trailed Tant everywhere, unable to learn enough about wild things and wilderness and fishing, always fishing. Sometimes Tant, using the tides, would row the kids downriver to gather oysters, dip-net blue crabs, trap diamondback terrapin in the bays or gill-net pompano off the barrier island beaches. In the sea turtle nesting season, they followed the broad tracks that led out of the Gulf to a place above the tide line where they gathered buried clutches of warm leathery white eggs. Mandy tinned vegetables and jarred wild fruit preserves for her fresh bread, and sometimes we had cake or pie or cookies.

After those hard years in Oklahoma, it seemed to my dear folks that such bountiful food was not to be found anywhere on earth. I watched their happy faces, happy, too.

My worry was the children's love of playing at the water's edge and paddling in the shallows. Sharks came upriver with the tide, Erskine assured me, and immense alligators, fifteen foot and better, drifted downriver from the Glades in the summer rains. Drawn to commotion, gliding underwater toward the bank, these grim brutes were always on the lookout for unwary creatures along shore. One gigantic specimen of a queer gray-greenish color would haul out on the far bank, where it sometimes lay all day like a dead tree. Often its long jaws would be fixed open, and the boys claimed they could see its teeth glint all the way across our wide bend in the river. Uneasy when that thing was missing, fearing its shadow presence in the current, Mandy kept a close eye on the children and the dogs while reading in her chair beneath the poincianas.

One afternoon over lemonade and cookies, discussing our wilderness with the children, she quoted some opinions of the poets. A Miss Dickinson of New England had concluded that the true nature of Nature was malevolent, whereas the self-infatuated Mr. Whitman of New York found undomesticated Nature merely detestable. What could such people know of Nature, Mandy inquired, pointing at that huge motionless gray-green beast across the river: nature was not malevolent, far less detestable, but simply oblivious, indifferent, and God's indifference as manifested in such creatures was infinitely more terrifying than literary notions of malevolence could ever be. To regard such an engine of predation without awe, or dare to dismiss it as detestable—wasn't that to suggest that the Creator might detest His own Creation?

"How about His mosquitoes?" complained Eddie, ever anxious to return indoors.

Lucius led us to a nest of red-winged blackbirds, parting the tall reeds so we could see. Losing its mate after the eggs had hatched to a snake or hawk or owl, the male bird, flashing his flaming shoulders, had simply resumed his endless song about himself (like Mr. Walter Whitman, said Mandy, smiling), by dint of which he won a second female, and now this pair was busily engaged in constructing its new nest on top of the old one—on top, that is, of the live young, which were squeaking and struggling to push their hungry bills up through the twigs. The horrified children longed to rescue the trapped victims, although this meant that the second clutch would be destroyed. Lucius forbade this and his mother nodded. "Even victims are not innocent," she whispered to no one in particular. "They are simply present. They are simply in the way."

Instinctively I had to agree, though Lucius and I could never explain to each other just what she meant. Her words made me feel odd. One moment a man bathing in the river celebrates his sparkling life and the next he is seized by the unseen and dragged beneath the surface, which moves on downriver as placid as before. God's will, Mandy would say. Man's fate, I agreed. Are they the same? But since long ago I had lost all faith, Mandy knew it was useless to discuss this.

GATOR SLOUGHS

In the winter dry season, when the fresh flow weakened, the gators returned upriver into the Glades; in a real dry year, they would pile up in the few sloughs that still had water in them. Taking a skiffload of coarse salt in 160-pound sacks, I set up camp on a long piney ridge near the head of Lost Man's Slough. Tant and Erskine were with me, also Lucius, who came along as camp cook out of curiosity. Working ever deeper into the swamps, leaving a trail of gator pools turned muddy red, we clubbed and axed for three weeks without cease, then stayed up late slashing the soft flats off the bellies and rolling them in salt by firelight. Around our camps hung that purple smell of heaped raw carcass; when we came back through, that smell had turned to the stink of putrefaction, as if the earth had rolled over and died. Lucius, thoughtful and subdued, lagged behind as the days passed and no longer nagged me to let him shoot the rifle.

One day we came across a big boar gator, fourteen, fifteen foot, in a little slough under a willow head. Having eaten or driven off the other gators, it did its best to scare us, too, emerging slowly from the water swinging its long head to run these two-legged intruders off its territory. By now we were low on ammunition, wasting no bullets: I jumped to one side and fetched the thing a solid ax blow to the nape. The brute thrashed back into the pool and kept on thrashing till it rolled and shuddered and finally lay still.

I got my breath and mopped my brow, getting a whiff of my own acrid stink in the steaming heat. "These big ol' dinosaurs take a lot of killing, don't they?" I said to the son behind me, who protested when I started to move on; I had to explain that the belly flat on a gator of this size was knobbed and horny, not worth stripping. He gazed at me in that open way he had inherited from his mama, then waded into the red water and touched the head of the dying gator. Leaving his hand there, he said, "Well, then, why kill it, Papa?" That turned me in my tracks. "Why kill it? That's a bull gator, boy." And as an afterthought, I said, "That's one big gator less to come downriver, take a dog or child."

This sounded like bluster to my son because bluster is what it was. Still polite, he said, "Papa? We going to stay out in the Glades till we kill 'em all?" We slogged on back to camp, where I told the others we were heading home. We all knew we had killed enough but it took a nine-year-old to put a stop to it. In the loaded boats, the flats stacked up above the gunwales. Any more would have been dumped out to rot.

At Everglade, we laid our loads along the dock to be checked and measured by George Storter. We were tangle-haired, bearded, sun-cracked, filthy, our clothes caked stiff and dark with reptile blood. Folks stepped back when we went into the store. Lucius said they recoiled from all that death on us. He never went on a gator hunt again.

THE FRENCHMAN

That summer my wife was feeling poorly; she spent long hours in that river breeze, in the shifting sun and shade. To provide distraction from our insect-ridden life, I rowed her upriver one fine Sunday for some cultured conversation with Baron Msyoo de Chevelier—"Shoveleer," as the local people knew him. Long ago, I'd shot the Frenchman's felt hat off his head as a warning to keep out of my plume bird territory and I warned Mandy that, seeing my boat, he would rush into his cabin for his weapon. When he did just that, Mandy had to smile, but fortunately that kind smile reassured him: he set down his fowling piece and resigned himself to Watson's imposition.

Jean Chevelier sniffed crossly as he picked his way about. Those hooded eyes of his were a raccoon's eyes, bright black and burning. He had long since lost the last of his good manners, having shrunken in old age and solitude to a peevish little gnome who would bark their orders to a firing squad lined up to shoot him. Ignoring my courtly introduction, he neither greeted Mrs. Watson nor welcomed her to Possum Key. Instead, he thrust under her nose the ugly queer black blisters on his withered forearm, cackling in triumph when her challenged husband could not tell her what had caused them. "Man-chi-neel!" he cried. In a perverse impulse of scientific inquiry so typical of this old man, he had purposely taken shelter from the rain beneath a manchineel or poison tree, a small smooth-barked reddish tree found in the Glades country. To tease him, I claimed I'd seen manchineel on Gopher Key—was that where he got those blisters? Rattled, he cried *Am-po-see-bluh!* To the end, he pretended he knew nothing of Go-phaire, though everyone knew he had dug up that whole mound in a frantic late-life hunt for Calusa treasure.

Mandy was plainly entertained by his prickly scientific stance and could scarcely wait to report back to Lucius that the big "ironhead" or wood ibis was not a true ibis, in Chevelier's view, but a New World stork and that the "shit-quick" was the reed heron or bittern. *"Sheeta-queek!"* he yelled at Mandy, who shifted in her seat. "All birts sheeta-queek, for fly away queek, voo com-prawn, Madame?"

Deftly Mandy changed the subject to that huge greenish gator which frequented the riverbank across from Chatham Bend. Firing snippy questions to display her husband's ignorance, the Frenchman sneered that in the unlikely event that my description could be trusted, my giant "alligator" was no alligator but a saltwater *crock-o-deel*, rare in south Florida. Surely a more observant man, Chevelier insinuated, would have noticed the pointy snout, quite unlike the shovel snout of the brownish, blackish alligator, and that even when its mouth was closed, its teeth protruded along the entire length of its lower jaw.

I might have known that the first naturalist to describe this brute had been a Frenchman. But the crocko-deel, Chevelier complained, had been falsely claimed by a mere French colonial, the rascally Jean-Jacques Audubon, who had dared to belittle Chevelier's old mentor Rafinesque—Constantine Samuel Rafinesque-Schmaltz—after robbing him of his discovery. Chevelier's hatred of "fokink Aud-u-bone" was only exceeded by his oft-expressed disdain for God Almighty. (In the face of sacrilege, Mandy batted her eyes prettily, her smile an entreaty as well as a signal that her honor would remain unsullied if her husband did not rise up in wrath to strike this villain down.)

However, to spare Mandy, I distracted him: "Is it true there are white shell canals at Gopher Key?" The old man hitched forward, a gleam of duplicity lighting his eye. Avoiding all mention of Gopher Key, he proposed that the white shell found in such canals could only have derived from a huge clam bed somewhere along this coast—an obvious conclusion that had not occurred to me. If he were a younger man, he assured Mandy—he had yet to address me directly, far less look me in the eye—he would locate and stake out that area for a canning industry. I pictured the coast charts in my head: that clam bed's location could only be the vast shallow bank off the empty coast north of Chatham River, easily accessible from Pavilion Key.

Seeing me distracted, cracking my knuckles, Mandy guided the conversation to the topic of French poetry, agreeing with Msyoo that Edgar Allan Poe was less esteemed in his own country than in France, where he'd been discovered and translated by the poet Beau Delair, *ness pa, Madame?* But what Msyoo was most anxious to discuss was the inferiority of all aspects of American culture when compared with those of La Belle Frawnce, a paradise to which he hoped to return before death caught him *een thees fokink Amerique.*

Msyoo presently declared that France had conquered Florida back in the 1590s, as proven by such local names as Cape Sable and Cape Romaine: had it not been for the Louisiana Purchase, France's rightful territories would include most if not all of North America. He scurried inside to dig out mildewed books by a pair of clever Frenchies who knew a great deal more about America than we Americans could ever hope to learn.

De Tocqueville, who had visited this country in the 1830s, had been appalled on the one hand by the callous indifference with which most Americans regarded slavery and astonished on the other by the slaves' strange apathy and acceptance of their lot, which not only inured them to wretched servitude but caused them to imitate their oppressors rather than hate them. In my own experience, this was also true of chain gangs, cane crews, and other hard-used men, not merely blacks, but Chevelier dismissed my idiotic quibble by flicking his fingers toward my face in the way he might brush cake crumbs off his lap. "Compared to *lay negres*," the Frenchman said, *"lay poe rooge, lay redda-skeen—"*

Here Mandy neatly intervened, observing that most European writers—the French writer Chateaubriand, for one—seemed to cherish a romantic view of *les peaux rouges*, perhaps to compensate for their prejudice against *les peaux noires.* She politely reminded him that to avoid capture and a bitter return to slavery, black warriors had reinforced and often led Seminole resistance to the whites.

"As was recognized by the U.S. Army and most historians," I chimed in, quoting a general who had told the Congress that the First Seminole War was essentially a "Negro war." Even De Tocqueville had remarked, said Mandy—I was so proud of her!—that escaped slaves who in the early days had turned up among Indian tribes throughout the South had to be men of exceptional courage and fortitude to survive a hostile wilderness and its wild peoples. Therefore they were much admired by the Indians and often married into the head families, producing a mixed-blood progeny of fine physical specimens of high intelligence—

"May ben sewer!" cried Chevelier, who had to recapture control at once or jump out of his skin. Was this not an affirmation of de Crèvecoeur? And he read out a passage that Mandy kindly regurgitatated for my benefit: *What, then, is the American, this new man? He is neither a European nor the descendant of a European; hence that strange mixture of blood you will find in no other country. Here individuals of all nations are melted into a new race of men!* The Frenchman cited "the half-a-breed Hardens," as typical of these new Americans, embodying the tough, enduring qualities of the black, red, and white races. The Hardens, he said, with grudging admiration, represented the essential character of *"thees fokink ray-poo-bleek."* I interrupted as he glared: the Hardens were by no means the only family on this coast with dark genes that had sifted down through generations, and they may or may not have manifested his new race of men, but they were good people and the best of neighbors in the Lost Man's country.

To gall him, I added what Napoleon Broward had remarked, that it was the destiny of E. J. Watson to develop this southwest coast. The old man scoffed rudely, *Lemper Roo-er! Lemper Roo-er Vot-sawn!* And my wife smiled to chide me for my boasting: I had not heard the last of "Emperor Watson."

Chevelier was wildly emboldened by her smile. When Mandy suggested that the Ten Thousand Islands, with their myriad channels, evoked the Labyrinth in Greek mythology, he speedily retorted that if the Islands were the Labyrinth, Madame's own *mari* must be the fokink Mee-no-tore. Squeezing my arm to restrain me, Mandy said that the fearsome Minotaur could also be very gentle. "Minotaur Watson?" she would tease me later. "Emperor Watson? Which do you prefer?" (She had never cared for sentimental stale endearments for her husband; she preferred her own pet names, all of them quirky, slightly disrespectful.)

Msyoo le Baron Jean de Chevelier had the gall to be galled by Mandy's fondness for her husband and did not trouble to hide it: he stared at us half-mad, mouth twisting cruelly. (Elderly indigestion, she suggested later.) Plainly this bachelor gentleman had been smitten by an educated lady and was trying to court her with his hard-earned rare knowledge, and when my wife hinted at his real emotion, overtaking him too late in life in this painful way, it seemed absurd to be angered by his insults. Standing up, I reminded him that his bullet-punctured hat still hung on a kitchen peg, to be returned on his first visit to the Bend. Which would be most welcome, Mandy added.

Leaving Mrs. Watson to accept his fond adoos, I bid him good-bye—we did not care to shake hands—and went back to the boat. Mandy thanked him for his kind hospitality, though this old misery hadn't offered us so much as a cup of rainwater. *"Bun shawnce, share Madame! Bella fortuna!"* he called after her (wishing her good luck in two languages, she would explain, to compensate her for the dark fate of her marriage to a minotaur).

All the way home we talked with animation, though I knew my wife had to quell ascending sadness. At the dock she said, "Wait, Edgar, please," too weak to leave the boat. She was watching the silver mullet down along the bank, leaping skyward as if to escape their natural element, only to fall back with those thin little *smacks* into the darkening water.

"Something's after 'em, that's all. Coming up from underneath."

"Hush," she murmured. "Watch."

Hand on her shoulder, I watched with her, indifferent to this everyday sight but content in our shared sadness. The children, worried, came out on the screened porch. Sensing something, they observed us but they did not call. At last she offered her pale hand and I half lifted her onto the dock. She did not explain her sudden dread and said it was not serious but I knew she'd had some sort of premonition.

Mandy seemed to waste away, perishing from the inside out like a hollow tree. Finally I took her to Fort Myers and put her in the care of Dr. Langford, who lived in a big house near the river between Bay and First Streets. Carrie went along to tend her and the younger boys followed in late summer and stayed on for the school year. The only one left at Chatham Bend was Sonborn.

One gray day, feeling a hollow stillness back in the mangroves, I went ashore at Possum Key to see how that mean old man was getting on. He had not answered when I hailed the cabin and so I was not overly surprised when at the door I was met by the smell of death. Then I saw the long white whiskers in the shadows, the small paws in the air above the chest. The Frenchman lay stiff as a poisoned rat. I removed my hat.

I dug his grave in the soft soil of his garden. Putting rags over my hands, I returned into the cabin and lifted the light bundle in its mildewed blanket and carried him like a smelly little bride over the doorsill and out into the sun. Sinking to my knees, I lowered him into the earth, remaining there a few moments out of respect. As an unbeliever, I had no prayer to give, and anyway, no prayer could bless this ferocious God-hater in the hereafter or anywhere else.

"Le Baron Jean de Chevelier." In that great quiet, with the swamp forest listening, I tried to pronounce his name in French the way Mandy had taught me. I had nothing else to offer by way of earthly witness. I had pitied him a little, yes, toward the end, but I had never liked him much and would not miss him.

Quock! The tearing squawk of a flared heron overhead startled me badly; I never saw the bird, only its shadow. Msyoo had loved birds better than people: his grim crier had come. In the next moment, on a limb, I saw a young owl, all woolly with astounded eyes, that must have attended the burial; it did not fly off into the wood until I'd finished spading the black soil into the pit. These odd birds spooked me a little, I must admit.

Before some hunter came by and stripped the cabin clean, I poked around for excavated treasures but was able to depart with a clear conscience, having been tempted by nothing in the place. At the boat, I ran afoul of two young Hardens come to clean and feed him; knowing how much that old man had detested E. J. Watson, these boys were shocked to see me. When I told them Msyoo Chevelier was dead, young Earl glanced at his brother, growing scared, and I knew right then that no matter what I said, Ed Watson would be blamed for the Frenchman's death.

THE GREAT CALUSA CLAM BED

In his theory about the great Calusa clam bed, the Frenchman had tried to distract me from whatever he was up to back on Gopher Key. Even so, his guess was correct. Coming up the coast one day at dead low water, I eased myself barefoot over the side. Right away my feet located hard shapes under the sand: upright clam valves in what proved to be a clam bed close to a mile wide—I mapped it out—extending almost six miles north from Pavilion Key. This was exciting. Establishing a clam fishery so close to home where I could keep an eye on things might finance my whole operation. I would stake a claim and form a company as soon as my harvest was finished in late winter.

At this time, young Bill House was working upriver from the Bend on his dad's new plantation at House Hammock. For a year or two, he had collected rare bird eggs for the Frenchman, and old Jean must have mentioned his clam cannery idea to decoy that boy away from Gopher Key, because one day I came by House Hammock and found Bill constructing a crude dredge. What's that for? I inquired. Bird eggs? When he grinned sheepishly but said nothing, I changed the subject quick: knowing this young House for a slow mover, I was not discouraged. I sailed to Marco the next day and confided my great discovery to Bill Collier, inviting him to join me as a partner. This man had been unusually successful in his business enterprises and had the experience and capital I lacked. To my surprise, Collier seemed skeptical of the whole proposition, even when I mentioned my clam-dredge idea. I would have to find a partner or at least a backer among my business acquaintances in Fort Myers.

My friend Nap Broward had made his name by smuggling contraband arms to the Cuban rebels and was urging me to use the *Gladiator* in this night business. Broward was anxious to avenge his friend José Martí, who had been shamed into returning to Cuba by fellow rebels; claiming he did too much talking, not enough fighting, his own men got that little feller killed when he tried to prove them wrong. In the end my ill wife persuaded me to avoid such a reckless venture. After so many long hard years of separation, we should cherish this precious time, she said.

Very weak, Mandy gazed into my eyes in a shy way that told me she knew she would not live much longer and warned me to be careful for the children's sake. She showed me a Copley print called *Watson and the Shark,* which portrayed a man fallen out of a longboat who was being seized by a huge shark in Havana Harbor. "I think you'd better stay away from Cuba!" Mandy said. The doomed Watson was a soft, pale, naked fellow, wallowing helplessly in the shark's jaws and rolling his eyes to the high heavens, and the only crewman trying to save him was the one black man. "Well," I laughed, "it's a damned good thing that Watson feller had his nigger with him!"

"I imagine you mean 'nigra.' "

"Yes'm, I do." And that was true. I did. I had spoken carelessly.

Mandy had never accepted my excuses—that that word's use was just a careless way of saying "nigra" and that nigras often used it, too. Good black people, she said, used "black folks": "nigger" was somebody shiftless, "no account," even disgraceful. I wasn't so sure, though. I guess I would go along with that most of the time. Some say "coloreds," ladies preferred "darkies." If you were black, she reminded me, every last one of these white man names would be insulting, wasn't that true? They were just dark-skinned human beings. They were *people.* This whole race business distressed Mandy very much. She felt that Emancipation, the Civil War, and Reconstruction—all of that loss and suffering—had come to nothing, and that our great national disease remained uncured.

1898

In July of 1898, our Carrie would marry Doc Langford's son, a handsome young fellow who lived in his father's household and had plenty of opportunities to pull the wool over the eyes of my young daughter. Carrie imagined she loved him, of course, and the Langfords loved Carrie, but I believe their main ambition was to settle Walter down. Because Doc Langford was my business partner or at least a backer, and because that family had been so hospitable to my own, I felt obliged to go along.

Young Langford had worked as a cow hunter in the Big Cypress. Every Saturday his hell-and-high-water bunch rode into town, drank up their pay at the saloon, and rode out again half dead late Sunday; they rounded up scrub cattle the rest of the week to pay for another Saturday of raising hell. Walt decided he was through with those wild Saturdays and would now make something of himself for Carrie's sake. He still had his bad drinking bouts from time to time, but instead of shooting up the town, he would go down to the Hill House Hotel, turn his gun in, rent a room, and pay the colored man to bring him moonshine. The man would keep him locked up with his jug until he had drunk himself stone stiff and sick and blind. With his craving for liquor worn out of his system, he would crawl home, gagging at the merest whiff of spirits for the next six months.

I had known this young feller for some years and liked him well enough, but I was not delighted by this match, which had been brokered by the Langfords' friend Jim Cole. At thirteen, Carrie seemed too young, I could not fool myself, so my dealings with Cole and Walter's family compromised what I thought of as my principles, which were already in trouble. To make myself feel better, I arranged a formal meeting with the bridegroom in which I might lay out a father's thoughts on honeymoon etiquette.

At Hendry House, we sat down over a brandy. Unfortunately we had two or three before I warned Walt kind of abruptly against getting drunk and taking my thirteen-year-old by force—against taking her at all, in fact, said I, raising my voice, "until she was damn well good and ready, hear me, boy?"

Young Walt took my friendly counsel as an insult to his honor as a Southern gentleman, which had never been questioned before now. Though he struggled to contain his anger, he finally burst out, "Well now, Mr. Watson, sir, if she is too young, then why do you permit this marriage in the first place?" But we both knew why and we both knew better than to speak about it since it was unspeakable. Nevertheless, he was red in the face with brandy and embarrassment, and very much resented the insinuation that he might ravish a young lady with no more control over his lower instincts than one of those black devils excoriated by Pitchfork Ben in the last election.

The young man's anger in a public place triggered my own. "I am not insinuating, sir," I interrupted. "I am stating a well-known fact about men's lust, a fact as plain as the red nose on your face." To which he retorted hotly that the bride's father had no right—with all due respect, sir—to instruct another man about how to comport himself with his own wife when her father had approved the marriage for financial considerations: should that father make the bridegroom pay for his own shame?

That was the first time and the last that Walter Langford ever dared to stand up to me in such a way. I let the silence fall until he sobered and had started to apologize, then raised my hand and cut him off rather than witness the underlying weakness in this young man that I'd suspected all along. Also—aware I'd gone too far—I had to get my own outrage under control. True, I resumed after a long pause, I had let my daughter go in deference to fiscal circumstances and had therefore given up my right to dictate terms: I'd only felt obliged to speak out as I had because of the groom's well-known habit of excessive drink.

I was speaking softly now, inspecting a farmer's broken fingernails. Walter awaited me, very uneasy. Was I apologizing or was I insulting him again? When I raised my eyes, he shifted in his seat. "But right or no right, boy," I growled, unreasonably angry of a sudden and letting it all go, "let me say this: you will answer to me and you will regret it dearly if you fail to protect my daughter from all that is coarse and ugly in yourself."

Walter was licked. In a hushed voice, he swore that he loved his bride-to-be with all his heart and he vowed to be very gentle. Since my first grandchild would not be born until five years later, the young man may have been gentle to a fault.

Despite the cautionary spite of thin-mouthed old Aunt Etta, whose very breath carried a hint of constipation, the Langfords welcomed our lively Carrie and her parents, too, at least at first: once our little frontier family had been fitted with uncomfortable town clothes, we became fashionable by Fort Myers standards, thanks to Mandy's elegance and quiet manners, and were often included in the Langfords' social gatherings. One evening we were introduced to "America's Electrical Wizard," Thomas Edison, who had built his grand Seminole Lodge on land overlooking the river and would later invite his friend Henry Ford to admire the property. Though her parents never had that privilege, my daughter would meet the great automaker when he visited the Edisons, who also expected a visit any year now from their friend Sam Clemens. "Mark Twain, dear!" Aunt Etta instructed Mandy, who had probably read more of Twain's damned books than the total of those read by every Langford in the state of Florida. Mandy dearly hoped that she might live long enough to behold her hero, if only from afar, but that was our secret. She forbade me to say any such thing to *any*body.

Back in '93, Tom Edison's General Electric Company had failed in the Great Depression, which had also propelled Edgefield's one-eyed Ben Tillman into the Senate seat of my father's old nemesis, General Calbraith Butler. Pitchfork Ben would rage that Mr. Edison had been bailed out by the bankers, and that, unlike his hungry workers, he had been inconvenienced not at all in his rich way of life, to judge from his opulent winter retreat in sunny Florida.

That a great American industry might be bankrupted and a great American spat upon by agitators had alarmed our self-styled "cattle capitalists," who denounced Senator Tillman as the devil incarnate. Because I could speak knowledgeably of the Edgefield County Tillmans, the Langfords and Jim Cole introduced me at a meeting of their business club, to which I held forth over coffee and cigars. From Walter, Carrie would gather and report that her daddy was considered "very smart, humoristical, and lively."

As for me, I enjoyed being included in discussions of the epochal economic changes taking place in America at the approach of the new century, especially since all these men might be so useful in my future plans. I addressed them, of course, as a stern supporter of the capitalist system, since I aimed to become a capitalist myself, but privately I had to agree with Mandy—who was better educated and a good deal brighter than anybody in our business circle—that Tillman, for all his opportunism and ugly speech, led the one political party as yet uncorrupted by the corporations. "Give him time," I sighed.

In the winter of 1898—officially, at least—the Spaniards sank the battleship *Maine* in Havana Harbor. (Broward, back from Cuba, confided that our government was quite aware that our battleship had exploded by mistake, without Spanish assistance, but as a businessman I knew much better than to be the bearer of unpatriotic news.) The war with Spain was quickly under way as Admiral Dewey steamed halfway around the world to destroy the rickety Spanish fleet in Manila Bay and was just as quickly finished four months later—in short, a "splendid little war" as it was called by our splendid little secretary of state, who like most patriotic politicians sending young soldiers off to battle had never in his life seen red blood spilled nor heard a terrified young human being scream in agony.

In Mandy's view, Mr. T. Roosevelt, the myopic Yankee in charge of our Cuba expedition, might be making up for a sickly childhood with his noisy brandishing of flags and guns and cavalry charges up San Juan Hill; she detested his vision of Americans as a "masterful" people whose God-given duty was to bring our superior civilization to the darker breeds. In fact, our nation's imperial ambitions distressed my failing wife so sorely that I dared not confess to her how right and sensible they seemed to me. After all—as the newspapers kept reminding us—the nations of Europe were establishing huge colonies in Africa and Asia and the U.S.A. would do well to grab its share of colonial territories and resources while the grabbing was good, wasn't that true? (As it turned out, all our far-sighted leaders were grabbing was hind tit and Spanish thorns.)

In early June, a month before Carrie's wedding, the U.S. troops—66,000 restless men, including black conscripts and the pudgy Mr. Roosevelt's Rough Riders—disembarked right up the coast at Tampa Bay. Already the black soldiers were offending the good citizens, complained the Tampa *Tribune*, in an editorial I read out loud to amuse my wife. "A number of disturbances resulted, the most serious when black troops objected to white soldiers from Ohio target-shooting at a black youngster. A riot ensued, injuring twenty-seven persons. . . . It is indeed very humiliating to American citizens and especially to the people of Tampa to be compelled to submit to the insults and mendacity perpetrated by the colored troops."

"Oh, do stop! Please, Edgar." Pins in her mouth, Mandy was basting Carrie's wedding dress. The editorial had upset her so that she pricked her finger and a round red dot had blossomed on the creamy satin, and because she had not noticed the red dot, no cold water was quickly applied to remove the stain. "I don't know which is worse," she fussed, "those Ohio soldiers shooting at that child or that cruel, hypocritical editorial." She looked up. "Or my own husband finding that story amusing—"

"No, no, I was smiling at what follows!" I lied, in need of my ill wife's good opinion. Hastily I read to her a feverish account of the hordes of soldiers rampaging through Tampa's bars and brothels, the drinking and wreckage and the shooting at the ceiling that had punctured the left buttock of an unlucky prostitute as she plied her trade upstairs. "First casualty of our splendid little war, I reckon." I frowned hard to hide my chuckle in a fit of coughing, ashamed because the mention of whores' buttocks had reminded me of how long it had been since we'd made love.

"It can't have been funny for that young woman, Edgar Watson!" Mandy cried, with more vigor than she'd shown in months. "What the heck's the matter with us, anyway? Maybe we should all be shot in our white buttocks, give us something to think about besides blood profit and our own darn meanness!" Sucking her pricked finger, she had taken up the newspaper to make sure I wasn't joking. Mandy was by no means humorless but she detested human cruelty in small matters as well as large, including this whole business of imperial ambitions and race prejudice, which in talking to Lucius she had said "still casts its shadow on the face of our new country."

The Spanish War was a great boon to our Lee County patriots, in particular the ranchers, whose cow hunters were out beating the scrub for every head of beef they could lay a rope on. These scrags were herded to Jake Summerlin's corrals at Punta Rassa and shipped off to the U.S. troops in Cuba for what our small-bore capitalists might call "a tidy profit" and what more honest folks would call a goddamn hog killing.

Naturally I felt patriotic, too, since in its modest way my syrup industry was prospering. Mostly I traded at Tampa Bay, which had been dredged for coastal shipping and was soon to be accessible by railroad, and mostly I stayed at the Tampa Bay Hotel under curlicue arches and birthday-cake minarets that made the place look like a five-hundred-room whorehouse near the Pearly Gates. I wanted to take Mandy to Tampa to see the sights and attend a concert and do some fancy shopping, but by the time I finally got her there, she was too weak to enjoy it and I brought her home.

To the nation's astonishment, the people of the Philippines rebelled against the Yankee invasion that freed them from the Spanish yoke, but we dealt smartly with such base ingratitude, spilling a lot of Filipino blood for their own damned good. Now that we'd realized how far behind we were in bringing Christ and capitalism to benighted lands around the globe, our American red blood was fired up, and plans were afoot for annexing every territory we could lay our hands on.

Aside from Ben Tillman (who would protest that fooling with these Filly-peenos was bound to inject the inferior blood of a "debased and ignorant people into the body politic of the U.S.A."), the one notable American who denounced our glorious triumphs over small brown countries was Mandy's revered author, Mr. Clemens. A turncoat Southerner who had dared to blame the War of Northern Aggression on the South, Mark Twain declared that our nation's bold new spirit of conquest was based on nothing more nor less than greed. In our business circle, I had strongly disapproved of Twain's radical tendencies, but privately I had to own that he was sharp-witted and comical, and that even his traitorous opinions rang true except where my own interests were at stake.

HELL ON THE BORDER

Not very long before the wedding, a book entitled *Hell on the Border* arrived in southern Florida and turned up at the Thursday Reading Club in town. Among its bloody tales of the Wild West was the author's version of the life and death of Mrs. Maybelle Shirley Starr, in which "a man named Watson" was identified as her slayer. It was soon confirmed by Sheriff Tippins at Fort Myers (who had learned of it from the sheriff at Key West) that this same Watson, an escaped felon from Arkansas State Prison, was none other than Mr. E. J. Watson of Chatham River.

Word spread quickly and pretty soon all sorts of stories had sprung up, a few of which, to my regret, Carrie brought to her mother's attention. I went to Carrie and commanded her to relate the mean things being said, but all she knew was the gossip overheard at Miss Flossie's Notions Shop by Walter's aunt Etta and aunt Poke.

The story was that Edgar Watson, born to wealthy plantation owners in South Carolina, was the black sheep of a fine family, causing so much trouble that he had to flee. He opened a gambling joint someplace on the Georgia frontier (there were fallen women, too, one lady whispered) with the Outlaw Queen Belle Starr. Belle's method was to have "big winners" followed, killed, and robbed, with Belle herself handling this end of the business if no henchman was handy. "Oh, Edgar and Belle were bad as bad can be!" Carrie mimicked Aunt Etta, smiling to show me how ridiculous all this stuff was, but it was plain that my gallant daughter was truly disturbed.

"There's more, Papa. The Langfords—" She was unable to continue. I turned to Mandy, who told me the rest of it, trying bravely to amuse me.

It seems that Mr. Desperado Watson had a telescope in a lookout high up under the eaves of his white house from where he kept close watch on Chatham River. Desperado spent most of his day scanning the Gulf in case men came after him or "his past caught up with him," as some would have it. One day he shifted the channel marker at Shark River (actually a drift timber stuck into a sandbar) and on a night of storm, he shone a light to attract a Spanish ship that was on her way north to Punta Rassa to pick up a cargo of cattle for South America. Since she could not continue up the coast and round the shoals of Cape Romaine in such high seas, she took shelter in the river mouth, missed the channel, and went hard aground just as Desperado had planned. Ever so courteous, Desperado rowed over and worked hard to help get her off and afterward they invited him aboard to drink some rum. As soon as those Spaniards got drunk (as was their wont as "Romans") he slew every last man and took the gold they'd brought to buy the cattle, then towed the ship out to deep water and chopped a hole in her and sank her, having locked the cabin so that no telltale bodies would float to the surface.

"Telltale bodies." I nodded with approval. "Looks like Mr. Desperado knew his work."

"Mr. Desperado's Island neighbors revealed that story to somebody's lawyer's sister," Mandy assured me, "so it must be true." We were both nodding now. "However, everyone is mystified since all agree that Mr. Desperado is unfailingly considerate and kind to his grateful wife. Unfailingly." Here she batted her eyes primly, doing her best to smile away her tears. "Also, it turns out that Belle was not killed after all, her death was just a trick Belle and Edgar played to get her out of trouble. Belle even came east and helped him nurse his invalid wife while she wasted away down there in those awful Islands." When Carrie left the room, Mandy looked up. "Do you suppose these ladies have confused Maybelle with that woman you had living there when I arrived?"

This teasing was as close to a reproach about Netta Daniels as she ever came. Mild though it was, it changed her mood: she chose this day almost a decade later to ask me quietly if I had been Belle's slayer. "I answered that question back in Oklahoma," I said shortly. "I know you did," she said, gaze unrelenting. I only huffed as if too offended to answer. She nodded carefully, closing her eyes as if content, which she was not.

One evening at the Bend, Mandy had reminded me that the man she married was a Mr. E. A. Watson and inquired politely what that new middle initial might stand for. I resented this question for some reason. "How about Jesus?" I suggested rudely, going right on with what I was doing, which was molding bullets at the table. A moment later, I looked up, defiant. She was awaiting me as I knew she would be, a born poker player gauging me over her cards. Eyebrows raised a little in that way she had, pale brow as clear as porcelain even in that heat, she held my gaze. Her fixed expression gave me the feeling she was looking straight through my pupils at Jack Watson, who had dropped his gaze in shame, for Mandy had an unmuddied soul and could outstare Jack Watson without even trying.

Arranging a bank loan on good terms, I had bought my wife a little house. "It's small," I told her, "but I reckon it will hold both cats." Mandy smiled in a soft burst of joy, so happy was she at the prospect of living privately under her own roof while she was dying.

By 1900, Tampa Bay had its first automobiles and cobbled streets where shod horse hooves might skitter on the fresh manure. The Tampa Electric Company had more business than it could handle, and the cigar industry was booming, with over two hundred small factories at Ybor City. To avoid complications at Fort Myers, I conscripted field hands in the Scrub, a makeshift settlement east of Ybor where black folks huddled in their shacks in the scrub palmetto, but my business dealings took place mostly in saloons.

One afternoon, forsaking the saloon to pick up my supplies at Knight & Wall Hardware, I grew somewhat impatient with the clerk, who kept the line waiting while he demonstrated some silliness he'd picked up at the dancing school. To command his attention, I stepped forth, drew my revolver, and fired holes into the floor around his shoe. "If you prance as fancy as you talk," said I, "let's see you prove it." Someone ran out, the deputies arrived, and after I was overpowered, I was marched to jail. One deputy said, "I'm sorry, Ed, but nobody saw no fun in that exceptin you."

Tampa Bay was becoming a large port where few folks knew me; when I grew unruly, Fort Myers rarely heard about it. However, my luck had now started to change, because news of this episode reached Fort Myers before I did.

As everyone knows, Americans love a desperado, not the scurvy villain with a scar but the suave rascal of style and courtly manner. Having already made a dangerous reputation at Key West and Tampa, I couldn't walk the street without folks pointing. Almost overnight, Mr. E. J. Watson had become the most celebrated citizen in town after Tom Edison—or perhaps the most notorious, as Jim Cole liked to say, trying to bend things in the Langfords' favor in the transactions over the terms of Carrie's marriage.

Cole had already seen to it that I was no longer welcome in the business circle and now it appeared that he'd persuaded the Langford family that a fugitive from justice and accused murderer could not be permitted to be seen at a decent wedding. Though Carrie assured them I was not Belle's killer, the social pressures finally proved too much, and in the end, it was suggested on behalf of both families that I stay away from my beloved daughter's wedding. As sad as I had ever seen her, Mandy agreed with the request, adding, however, that she would abide by whatever her husband decided.

I was too shocked to speak about this sensibly: if I was unwelcome, I would not attend the wedding with my family, but I might damn well invade it and outrage them all. Of course I did not really wish to do that, and to make certain I didn't, I stalked out of the house and went down to the boat, intending to go home to Chatham River. "We're sailing," I told Sonborn, coming aboard. Without a word, he set about preparing to cast off.

In my angry haste to raise the sail as the schooner drifted free, I tangled the halyards, fouled the boom: the sail hung at a crazy angle like a huge broken white wing. I bellowed at Sonborn to get his ass up the damned mast and clear that mess in a hurry only to discover that he'd spotted my blunder before I could try to blame him for it and was already scrambling aloft. The boom came clear and the sail snapped to; my son hung on as the ship righted herself and I hauled her taut to a scattering of whistles and rude waterfront applause as Sonborn, still aloft, paused to get a breath. This boy had learned his job, he was an able-bodied seaman. Why couldn't I praise him or at least thank him? I could not.

As if this humiliation weren't enough, my daughter chose this moment to come flying down the dock in tears, not to invite me to the wedding but only so she could call out that her heart was broken, that she loved her Papa and would miss him dreadfully at the altar and so on and so forth and good-bye, good-bye. Waving, she thrashed her arms wildly with a hanky in each hand.

Sonborn's hand, not mine, rose in a small wave of farewell. Did he actually believe Carrie was waving to him? Or had he taken pity on her, seeing her wave falter in the empty air, unanswered? I suppose he meant well but it seemed pathetic any way you look at it.

I turned my back on Carrie, yelling at my son to jump to it, get those lines coiled, clear the deck. I really don't know what I yelled but I do know I was glad later that Mandy had not been a witness.

I never knew why Sonborn stayed with me for that voyage home instead of attending the wedding as his sister wished; it never occurred to me until years later that he might have done that for the same reason he had waved to Carrie, to support his father out of kindness but also because he longed to believe he belonged in this family. In any case, we never spoke on that long voyage south.

BLOOD SHADOW

Down in the Islands, "we were coughing up the dust of our nation's progress," said C. G. McKinney. The only memorial to our brave victory in the Spanish War was the mahogany in Everglade that was planted by the Storter family at the trading post. That tree promised to last a good deal longer than all the crepe, flags, bombast, and parades.

With my wife in Fort Myers and Netta gone, I installed Tant Jenkins's sister as the housekeeper at Chatham Bend. Josie Jenkins was small and kind of pretty with her Cherokee mother's dark brown eyes. "Our daddy Mr. Ludis Jenkins loved his Injun Seleta," Tant told me. "When she left him for another, he got over her, I reckon, but the poor feller had to kill himself to do it." Noticing his odd smile, I realized with surprise that he had told the truth but wanted me to laugh anyway and so I did. Tant needed to make people laugh no matter what.

My syrup enterprise, though still short of capital, was growing fast again under its new name, Island Pride, and that was because, in my humble opinion, our product was the best on the west coast. Sugarcane is a giant grass and any fool can grow a grass: the difference lies in the timing of the burn. In south Florida, the cane begins to ripen with the first drop in night temperature in September. In October, an experienced hand who knows the wind goes out with a firepot and burns it over. Without the big leaves that clog the mill, the stalks are much lighter and more easily handled, and good strong stalks lose very little sugar to fast-moving flames. Also, the burning clears the field of snakes and scorpions and chases out wild game; a good shot ranging along the field edge during the burn can generally bring down more than enough to feed the crew.

Dry cane ignites all in a rush with a heavy roaring as in storm: if the burning is timed right, the fire produces a black smoke so thick and oily that it has a kind of muscled look as it rolls skyward, leaving the earth in deep sepia shadow and strange light. If the field is dry, I organize the burn on the day before harvest, in late morning. Burning too early harms the plant and causes the cane to grow back with thinner stalks, until finally it leans and sprawls before it can be reaped, especially where cane rats (which throw big litters six times in a year) have been gnawing. Even then, being so hardy, the crop keeps right on growing, slowing the harvest where wind-tangled cane forms a thick green matting on the ground.

A steam engine ran the mill that pressed the stalks. I rigged a frame for a big kettle over a buttonwood fire for boiling the syrup, which smelled so fine that Richard Harden claimed it made his mouth water three miles downriver and another half mile off the coast at Mormon Key. My giant kettle, two hundred and fifty gallons, was twice the size of any kettle in the Islands, and our plantation produced ten thousand gallons every year, over three times the amount produced by Storters, who hauled their stalks from Half Way Creek to their mill at Everglade. We packed the syrup in one-gallon tins and saved the skimmings to make moonshine, sold off our white lightning by the quart jar.

Harvest started in October, when a cane crew was fetched in for the labor: free transportation, a dry bunk, and three square meals a day. Most of the crew were drifters of all colors from the shantytowns and saloon alleys of Ybor City and Key West. Some bitched that they were kidnapped while dead drunk, and I'd say, "Well, you might as well work now that you're here because otherwise you'll be taken out and shot instead of paid." That backed 'em down, made 'em chop a little faster; they never felt too confident the Boss was joking. But scaring those men was a bad mistake, firing those rumors of "Watson Payday" that would plague me in the years to come.

Cutters use a cane knife like a big heavy machete. Because the long blades are honed to a singing edge as sharp as sawgrass, the work is dangerous and accidents are common, especially among the drinkers but also among the green hands, older men, and those exhausted. They go bleary. The veterans may rig themselves crude shin guards or hide leggings, having hacked an ankle or sliced off toes at one time or another, often their own but sometimes those of the man beside them. When a cutter working tired or too fast stoops to grab a clump for chopping, his sweat-filled eye, sometimes an eardrum, can be pierced by a leaf tip, hard as any spine. In this humid climate, there is heat collapse; sore backs go with the job. Every little while, even the strongest may straighten in a slow half turn, arched like a bow, the heel of one hand pressed into the lower back to ease those muscles.

Rather than lose time to injuries, I was strict about our safety measures, and in the early years, we had very few bad accidents. Then a big cutter working tired sliced his foot half off when his knife glanced off a root clump. I rowed him out to Mormon Key, got that foot sewed back together by Richard Harden, but not before the man half bled to death. Being superstitious, he would not return upriver so he lost his pay.

Late in 1899, a new nigra feeding stalks into the mill caught his burlap apron in the feeder belt, which grabbed his hand as he wrenched at the apron and chewed up his whole arm right to the shoulder. I was away. The crew foreman, a young Key Wester named Wally Tucker, called his wife out of the house to rig a tourniquet; seeing so much blood, Bet lost her head and rushed that dying man into the house, let him bleed all over the corner of the front room while people ran like chickens to fetch useless things and he died anyway. By the time they thought to mop that blood, it was too late, the pine boards drank it. Tried to hide that bloodstain under a straw mat but even strangers heard about it. The next time I went to Everglade, Bembery Storter warned me about a rumor going around that when it came time to pay his help, Ed Watson knocked 'em on the head and dumped 'em in the river. I told Bembery the truth and I guess he took my word but it was no use. That story spread like a bad flu as far as Tampa, where my buyers beat down my price with hard questions about black blood in Watson's syrup. For six months or more, we sold hardly a quart of the best cane syrup in the U.S.A.

That bloodstain that would not wash away spooked everybody on the place, just as the business was starting to go well. Every visitor came inside to stare, we could have charged admission! For a long time after, Island Pride syrup was very hard to market because of that rumor there was blood in it. Time and again and ever since, I have tried to leach that stain out, paint it over, but sooner or later, for some damnable reason, the blood shadow rises through the paint like the slow rise of a gator from deep water, drifting slow, slow, slow up to the surface.

ZACHARIAH

After that feller lost half his foot the year before, a cane cutter named Zachariah had gone around stirring up trouble, claiming the work was much too dangerous for such long hours and poor pay and threatening to start a strike. Spouting the union agitator talk that was causing all the trouble on the east coast railroad, he infected the whole crew with discontent.

For want of capital, my company was now at a critical place: it would suffer another setback it could not survive if this black bastard started a strike here in the harvest season. I called him aside, promised him more money if he would keep this quiet and just shut up about his fucking union; he was shrewd enough to protect himself by calling to the others through the window that the Boss was trying to bribe him. Then he informed me he was fighting for the workers of the world, not just himself, so that workers everywhere might fairly share the profits. I cursed him for a dirty communist and finally threatened him: he passed this guff through the window to the crew, which clapped and whistled.

I threw him out but I already knew that this one was going to be back. Sure enough, when that man bled to death, Zachariah accosted me again, demanding better pay and safer work conditions. A young cutter named Ted had caught his fever, helped him organize a strike for the first day of the harvest unless Island Pride met their demands.

From his new mansion at Palm Beach on the east coast, Mr. Henry Flagler was dealing with foreign syndicates and immigrant labor and all kinds of communistical ideas, but he also had hard overseers to deal with troublemakers and he brought in strikebreakers. These thugs enforced their own idea of law and order on his rail line, up to and including capitalist punishment, as Tant called it, and other big new industries around the country were doing the same: announced they'd never negotiate with commie scum, then nailed 'em hard and quick before the journalists arrived and trouble spread, same way they took care of the strikers in the mines.

These business leaders we celebrate as great Americans let nothing stand in the way of their own ambitions—that's the secret of their greatness. Such men are more than willing to invest their workers' lives so long as they are spared all the unpleasantness. Never have to bloody their soft hands or hear about excessive violence, not if their lieutenants know their work: *Go out and play yer golf game, Boss, enjoy yer nice sea air.* Soon as the owner is safely off the property, armed men rush the unarmed strikers: *Dirty dagos! Want yer wop heads busted?* Never wait for an answer, just sail right in with clubs and pistols, smash a few faces, break some arms, and run the rest off the property unpaid. Those men lying on the ground who never stand up again turn out to be the very troublemakers they were after in the first place, and someway there are never consequences, no investigation, because the press is kept away and the law, too. "Hardest fight I ever fought," Henry Flagler told reporters the next day, this rich sonofabitch who never saw one minute of the fighting. His henchmen spared him all the ugliness and bloodshed.

If we had gone after Zachariah that same way, the harvest strike at Island Pride would have been over quick. In the rough justice of the American frontier, men who stood in the way of Twentieth Century progress had only themselves to blame. *Can't make coffee without mashing a few beans*—ever heard that one?

Foreman Tucker would not agree that violence or dirty work went with his job. Sonborn would have jumped to take his place if his daddy told him to, but that feller would have been more useless still, being by nature on the poor man's side. As for Tant, he wanted no responsibility for strike-busting or anything else—wanted no part of it. That's who Tant was.

Already my harvest was starting late. The ringleaders had to be dealt with—I could not scare them. I wasn't a Flagler or a damned Carnegie with hired strike-breakers but only a pioneer farmer in a frontier wilderness where a man had to enforce his own rules quick, live with the consequences. Also, my time was running out. In my late middle age, a fugitive with a long-suffering family and bad reputation. I was fighting desperately for a fresh start in life and my last chance was here on this wild river. I had made good progress with my legal claim on Chatham Bend and also on a smaller tract across the river, anticipating the surge in west coast development that was bound to follow Everglades drainage and the highway across south Florida I'd already discussed with Napoleon Broward, whose election as governor now seemed inevitable. Should all those hard years, all my great plans, go to waste? If I wanted to survive, it was up to me. I couldn't afford to lose Zachariah but I could afford to keep him even less.

And so that early Sunday morning I braced my spine with a hard jolt from the jug and drove those two men, still half asleep, out of the bunk room and aboard the boat, hollering real loud so the rest could hear how I was running these damned agitators as far as Marco, dumping 'em off without their pay to compensate the company for the time wasted. Zachariah assured the crew that I was bluffing, they had the Bossman right where they wanted him, he'd have to negotiate or lose the harvest. From the boat, Ted waved cheerily to all his friends.

Below the Bend, I ran the boat up on the bank, drew my revolver, and ordered 'em ashore. Zachariah said warily, "What's up, Mist' Watson?" I brought out the shovel I'd hidden in the cabin, tossed it to the boy; the hatchet I slipped into my belt. Zachariah was looking at the hatchet, no longer so sure I was bluffing and too scared to realize I could not shoot them. We were too close to the Bend. The sound would carry. He said, "I reckon we's licked, Boss, take us back. We get some cane cut befo' noon."

"Let's go," I said. I marched them inland through the marl scrub west of the cane fields. Young Ted yelped as he stumbled along that he aimed to work hard from now on, make no more trouble. When he turned and walked backwards, pleading with me, he tripped and fell, then would not get up, he was in tears. Zachariah stopped, too, but he never turned around. In a guttural thick voice he demanded rudely, "Why we stoppin for?" This man was mule-headed, he would stick to his defiance.

Finally I stopped. I longed to negotiate,. admit that I'd been bluffing. "Dig," I told them. The boy whimpered, "What we diggin fo' out'cheah, Mist' Boss?" Zachariah soothed him. "We's diggin fo' gold out'cheah, Ted. Diggin fo' gold."

Zachariah and Ted were both strong workers, among the strongest on my crew. I liked them, for Christ's sake, and I respected them. I almost babbled some excuse about why I had to do this, how they had given me no choice, claim I didn't like this any more than they did and express sincere regret; what kept me from offering these weak excuses was rage at Zachariah for getting us into this fix and the triumph I feared would come into his eyes if I let them go.

At my signal, they stopped digging. Each stood silent in his shallow grave. I motioned to them to turn and face away. "Zach!" the boy cried suddenly, as if awakening. "Nemmine, Ted, you gwine be okay," the other whispered, hoarse. I told them to be quiet and stand still if they knew what was good for them. Zachariah still hoped that I was bluffing because when I said that, he grunted out a kind of laugh just at that moment when, sucking up my breath, I felled him with a hard blow to the skull, using the hammer end of the big hatchet.

I shudder like a horse each time I recall it. It's true. I shudder. The crown of the skull, which I'd always thought was hard, seems to squash under a hammer blow instead of cracking cleanly like an egg. Seeing him fall, the boy cried, "Lo'd God, Zach!" and wet his pants utterly as he sank onto his knees, staring at Zachariah's kicking feet. Asked if he'd like to pray, he nodded, just to live those extra seconds, and when he bent his head, I felled him. If I'd waited for his prayer, I could not have done it.

Both were still yanking and kicking. Dropping the pistol, leaning forward, hands on knees, I gulped deep breaths. When at last they lay still, I crossed their arms and covered them with marl, then returned in a half-trot to the boat, already fearful that those graves might not be deep enough to hide what I had done and yet too horrified and too exhausted to go back.

I scrubbed myself with rough mud at the river edge, lay stunned on the hard deck. When I sat up, I saw the same brown current ever descending between forest walls. I thought, You have just deprived two human beings of their lives. How can this river and this forest look the same?

At the Bend, I claimed I'd put those cutters on a fishing boat on her way north to Tampa. Unpaid? That's right. No pay. Any more questions?

Back in the cane field by late afternoon, I worked as a cutter until dusk. That evening, wishing above all not to think, I resorted to the jug, hit myself hard. There is a difference between right and wrong, always was and always will be, but each man's wrong and each man's right are different. Just depends, as the old fellers say. Everything depends. What I'd done must have been wrong by my own lights because I'd hated the doing of it and still felt sick to death, no matter how often I insisted to myself that my business and my family's future and my great plan for developing this southwest coast were simply more important than the loss of two anonymous brown lives, which were, by comparison, inconsequential. Sad but true, as even Mandy would agree. Well? Would she agree? You're not sure, Mister Watson?

THE TUCKERS

Toward the century's end, I was drinking much too much and knew it but I did not stop. To make things worse, my Island neighbors (Richard Harden warned me) had grown leery of Ed Watson, which was mostly my own fault. Having understood right from the start that a man who controlled the few pieces of high ground would control the development of this whole island coast, I had not discouraged the bad rumors about Watson, thinking they might scare settlers away. But now those tales were coming back to haunt me, and everything that happened seemed to make them worse.

First there were those accidents. Second, there was low morale due to my drinking. Next, there was trouble with my foreman. Wally Tucker was an inexperienced young man on the run from angry creditors in Key West; he had brought along a young woman of good family, having gone and gotten the girl pregnant. This damned fool waited until harvest to let me know that the field labor was too heavy for his Bet (the same nitwit who'd brought that dying man into my house to stain my floor). Because I would not excuse her from the field—we were already short-handed—he grew sullen, then quit, demanding their back pay. As foreman, he knew that the crew was never paid until after harvest, to make sure no one quit at this crucial time, and anyway, I had no money in the bank until a consignment of our syrup could be sold.

I must have been uneasy about shallow graves, for one night I dreamed I was walking barefoot over squishy whitish marl. Sure enough, within the fortnight, with our dispute still unsettled, young Bet Tucker, slopping hogs at evening, left the gate latch open. All night my animals went rooting through the cane fields and beyond. By the time the Tuckers ran them down next day, they had snuffled out those shallow graves in the woods west of the fields. The corpse whose blue shirt and tin belt buckle the Tuckers recognized was the fired crew boss Zachariah and the second man was his work partner Ted.

Badly frightened, those Tuckers soon convinced themselves that coming on those bodies after threatening to quit had made life very dangerous for them, too. Telling Sonborn they feared for their lives, they had fled in their sloop, after Tucker came in and demanded their money, then backed down.

Sonborn was still trying to defend them. "They were out calling the hogs—"

"Out screwing in the woods!" I roared, jumping up and kicking the chair against the wall. "Whose damn fault was it those hogs got loose in the first place?" Scared and unhappy, Sonborn agreed to forget the whole damn business, never mention it.

Needing food and water, those people got no farther than Richard Harden's place near Lost Man's River. The Hardens felt sorry for 'em, helped 'em build a shack on the island in the river mouth, as I discovered a month later when I made an offer for the quit-claim to that key to the Atwells up in Rodgers River. I told Winky Atwell to run those damn conchs off my property but Tucker refused to go without their salaries. I suspected that Tucker was already spreading tales about Ed Watson, since he muttered to Winky that he had a good mind to report me to Key West, so his response enraged me.

Whenever someone threatens to tell tales on me, get me in trouble, a taste of iron comes into my mouth and my hand hardens in a rage that spins up from the oldest corner of my brain. "Go away," I told Josie Jenkins, spying through the door. "Just stay away from me."

Through the window—he did not venture inside—that son of mine was pestering me. He would not let it go: Atwells sold that key right out from under 'em, he protested, with Bet having her baby any day now. "Settle with him, Papa! Maybe he'll keep quiet!"

"What? Keep quiet about *what*?"

Sonborn never did know when to stop for his own good. "Why do you act like it's all Wally's fault? You think *he* killed Ted and Zachariah?" He was half outraged and half scared to death, but in the end, he needed my approval. And for some damned reason I believe that he also wanted to protect me, when the one he should have protected, as I was still too blind to see, was not his maddened father but himself.

Too much had gone wrong and too much was at stake but instead of acting I kept drinking. Sometime after that, I must have fallen.

Who was speaking? Who was I and where? I could not rise, could not even roll over, being bound up in hard pain by molten chains.

A late afternoon sun shaft scorching my temple. A silhouette in the river window. Sonborn watching. Sonborn waiting. Sonborn plaguing me with his life loss. Son Born, go fuck yourself, I lost her, too, I told the silhouette. You are my nemesis, you know what that is, Sonborn? And the silhouette screeched, *Papa, don't call me that again or I will kill you!*

Threatening his father upset him worse than it did me. He said, "Forgive me," said he loved me—*used that word*! A man twenty years old! "Get out of my sight," I said. Get out of my damned life is what I meant.

He must have hated me for hating him. Was that why he took the Tuckers' side? For all I knew, he had put them up to leaving and never awakened me in time to stop them.

Josie's baby girl—mine, she insists—was yawling in the kitchen. Josie whispered at the door, "It's New Year's Eve." I drank. "Stay away," I said.

Most times when I drink, like any man, I flirt with trouble. Might pick a fight, shoot out the lights, smash something up out of the energy of life, just for the hell of it—just for the fun of breaking! The fucking *glee* of it! Or not so much glee as some queer ecstasy that releases itself in senselessness, ever feel that? Some union with this life through destruction that whirls a man free of his doomed puny self like the force that drove those mullet upward through the river surface on that evening at the Bend, and Mandy so moved by those silver shapes skipping aloft for that one hopeless instant, only to fall back with that tiny slap into the cold jaws of that dark water.

The glee of it. The ecstasy of *It*. I can't speak about this It because I know no word. It is just there, It is always there, like death in life. In this instant I know that something terrible is rising that must be seized and turned back upon itself before it twists outward into violence. But that knowing always comes too late, a wild unraveling is under way and I am already caught up in it, like a coyote seen late one afternoon in an Arkansas tornado—a toy dog spinning skyward, struck white by a ray of sun against black clouds, then black, then white, then gone and lost forever.

The wind dies. A dead stillness. Mirror water. That ecstasy that shivered every nerve replaced by the precise knowing that what this self has perpetrated is as much a part of the universal will as erupting lava that subsides once more into the inner earth.

That New Year's Eve I drank to knock my heart down, get my breath, but I was too sick with weeks of drinking to think clearly. Afraid of the Owl-Man come in nightmare, and the young slave Joseph at Clouds Creek drawn down into swamp humus, and scantly buried bodies in a dead white marl squashing out sideways underfoot, I sat up in my chair.

In the window, Sonborn's silhouette, still pleading. I interrupted him. "I am going there to settle this and you are staying. That is that." Josie Jenkins was afraid who was ordinarily afraid of almost nothing. Clutching Baby Pearl, she said, "Where are you going, Jack? It's late." I waved her off. I told her, "Get the hell out of my way." When I raised my fist, she ran outside but then screeched back, "Why are you taking the boy with you?" For he was trailing me. Again, I ordered him to stay.

She ran forward and hugged Sonborn, tried to walk him back into the house, but halfway to the dock, I heard his steps behind. I said, "Stay out of it."

He went past me and climbed down into the boat. I almost fell down getting in.

"Row, then," I said. "Upriver."

AT LOST MAN'S KEY

The skiff slipped south through the labyrinth of islands under a full moon. At Onion Key, while waiting for the tide to turn, I greased the thole pins to deaden the creak of oars. And still he pled with me, he wept, he begged me not to harm them. There was no need. I had sobered some and come back to my senses. Those people were no threat. In Key West, Tucker was a wanted man, he would go to jail if he went there to report me, and anyway he had no proof because Sonborn and I had disposed of the last trace. I would simply respond that this ne'er-do-well had made up vicious slanders out of spite after his pay had been withheld for breach of contract. Besides, the sheriff would ignore complaints about two murdered blacks when so many were worked to death on chain gang labor.

A half mile upriver from the Key I took the oars and, facing the bow, used quick small strokes to guide the skiff into the inland shore at the back of Lost Man's Key. I took the shotgun. "Stay with the boat," I said. "You were never here." I almost promised him I would not shoot Wally Tucker, I'd only scare him, run him off, but out of my damned perversity I did not do so.

Trailing after me through the scrub toward the Gulf shore, Sonborn made too much noise. I turned to scowl at him, pointing back toward the skiff, and in doing so, stumbled, wrenched my ankle painfully. I cursed him. He kept coming.

Tucker was perched on a silver driftwood tree down by the water. He was mending his cast net, rifle leaning on the wood beside him; he'd lift his head to look and listen, bend to his needle. Behind him, the sun that rose out of the Glades, touching the treetops, turned the morning leaves as bright as metal.

I made no sound on that soft sand and yet he sensed me. He whirled and stared. "You people are finished here," I said. I told Sonborn to go flush out the woman. When he protested again, I swore at him in disgust, gave him the shotgun, ordered him to keep Tucker covered.

He was a good shot, quick and wiry: it occurred to me too late that, being Sonborn, he would not shoot Tucker no matter what. Tucker had gasped when I drew my revolver and headed for the shack. He expected me to kill them and I let him think that. But when I heard him begging Sonborn to spare Bet, a coiling in his tone alerted me: I whirled in time to see him lunge and grab the shotgun barrel as Sonborn yelled. Their struggle ended when the gun went off and Tucker spun and crumpled like a bird.

"Oh Papa, NO!"

Sonborn's cry shattered the echo of the shot.

"Ah, *SHIT!*" I yelled at almost the same instant, and started forward, unable to take in the enormity of what had happened. One moment this man is quick, eyes bright, and the next he lies too shocked even to weep, twitching the last of his life away in his own mess, a carcass, eyes wide, mouth wide, blood already dead.

Sonborn had dropped the shotgun in the sand, backing away from what he'd done. He was pasty, gagging, he was trembling so hard he seemed to totter.

Behind me, the girl had run outside, then fled into the sea grape. He hadn't warned me, and I only glimpsed her, too late. Coldly I told him he would have to finish what he'd started because being lame as well as fat I'd never catch her. When I forced the revolver on him, he dropped it. I picked it up and brushed it off and presented it again. He stuttered hopelessly, Papa, no, he could not do it, please don't make him do it, Papa, please no, this was crazy.

I told him that if she got away, he was going to hang right alongside his crazy daddy. "Quick is merciful," I told him. "Temple or base of the skull. Don't meet her eye. Don't say a word. Just do it." I could scarcely believe that voice was mine, that I was telling him to do this.

To see such terror in his face was terrible. For a moment I thought, He might shoot me instead. And then his face broke, he burst into tears and gave a little scream and ran off after her, casting a last despairing look over his shoulder. That last look undid me.

"Rob!" I bellowed. "Wait for me!" I hobbled clumsily to overtake and stop him, my wrenched ankle a club of pain.

The gun went off as I approached: I stopped, pierced through the heart. In the echo, in that ringing silence, I saw his body on the sand between low bushes. I thought, He has destroyed himself.

No, for once, he had done just as instructed, done it well and quickly. Then he had fainted. He lay curled like a young boy beside that girl in her white shift whose lifeblood pooled under her head in a darkening halo in the sun and sand. I thought bitterly, Can you hear me, Bet? That loose gate latch on the hog pen? One moment of inattention and two dead.

When I lifted my son onto his feet, he only sagged. I eased him down. I hoisted the girl's warm heavy body, carrying it to the water's edge, then went back for Tucker and grasped him under the arms and dragged him. We could not stay long enough to bury them since the Hamiltons on Lost Man's Beach might have heard the shots. I moved them out into the slow current where sharks following the blood trace into the delta would nose toward them on the first incoming tide.

My boy had come to when I returned. He was a bad color and still trembling. He groaned and fought me off—*Get away from me!* I stood him on his feet and with my fingertips brushed off the skull bits and brains as best I could. He stared at my red hand. Pushed, he stumbled forward, and watching him, I was moved to an emotion far deeper and more devastating than pity, a life regret arising out of love for my firstborn that must have been in my heart all along, shrunk to the point of near extinction. How would I ever let him know that, far less show it? I had called out much too late.

Get away from me turned out to be the last words Charlie's son would ever speak to me. Rob Watson, gone and lost forever like my darling Clementine—over and over that old song keened in my brain like some Celtic lament.

Tucker's death had been an accident; as to the girl, we were forced to choose between her death and our own. I would try to persuade Rob of his innocence as soon as he felt well enough to listen, having begged his forgiveness for his banishment as Sonborn all those years until today. Anyway, he would never be involved if I could help it. Glimpsing another boat off Lost Man's Beach, I forced his head below the level of the gunwales lest he be seen with E. J. Watson and associated with crimes that were sure to be attributed to me. Because whether or not sharks or gators found those bodies, evidence of bloody murder was all over Lost Man's Key and people were certain to suspect Ed Watson.

TURNING AND RETURNING

I rowed east up Lost Man's River and then north toward home. The tide was against us and the humid air too light for the skiff's sail. With my last strength, exhaling deep breaths to drive the iron smell of blood out of my lungs, I hurled my shoulders into every stroke until my hands were blistered and my arms were burning and I almost passed out and even so I could not burn out such great despair. The journey through the string of bays back of the barrier islands took all day, and all this day, curled up in the stern, he watched me, neither asleep nor dead but in a kind of stupor. Two or three times his eyes slid toward the revolver butt protruding from my coat, which was folded on the stern seat. I believe he considered seizing it and slipping it beneath his shirt and finally did so, though whether his plan was to destroy his father or himself I could not know nor did I care. Either choice, the way I felt, might have been a mercy.

At Possum Key, the Frenchman's cistern had been fouled by a drowned deer. We had no water. With the heat and exhaustion, I was almost blind, and now a blackness settled, the merciless knowledge of how cruelly I had dealt with him, of how I'd failed him. *You have destroyed his life.* Even if I could have persuaded him I had loved him all along and rediscovered him, that would never be good enough. I had done this brave wild boy a lifelong harm.

By the time I turned back toward the coast, down Chatham River, all I could think about was that brown jug. In the confused departure of the night before, I might have drained it to the bottom and left none. I was terrified.

I could never absolve myself of the great crime of ordering him to act against his every instinct; I had crushed him under a fatal burden that was rightly mine. I had cried out to him too late. Even at that moment, I think, I had been aware that the murder of Rob's spirit would remain the most heinous of my sins, so dreadful I would never banish it, despite all efforts to pretend that Lost Man's Key was an evil hallucination from which one day I might awaken.

Rob would not look at me. He could scarcely climb out of the boat. "Come when you're ready," I said. I did not take the pistol away from him. I rushed inside and whimpered in relief that my jug still had a slosh in it.

Josie and the child were gone. I guessed that Tant had come in this morning and taken them to safety at Caxambas. They had left a half-cooked haunch of venison behind.

I ran to my fields and set fire to the cane, for we would have to leave before first light. The fire and my running figure frightened Erskine when he came in with the *Gladiator* toward evening. We ate cold deer meat and I drank and ranted until he went out to piss under the stars. When he came back, he was so scared he could scarcely speak. The schooner was missing, and Rob, too. While we talked, he must have slipped her lines, let her drift away downriver.

I felt it coming and I could not stop it: with every panting breath my outrage grew. All that sentimental maundering about my son, and look! The fool had run off with my ship just when we had a chance to mend things— mend things? Sonborn and I? On this dark day? Having left two bloody dead at Lost Man's Key? Have you gone mad, then? Are you going mad? Rage, confusion, fear, love, hate, despair—I felt all these at full force all at once, but who was feeling and toward whom?

Horribly thwarted, I went shouting through the house. I'd never had the chance to tell him that I had not meant them to die and that what had happened was my responsibility, not his. Tell him my feelings. Let him know he was forgiven—*what are you saying? Forgiven for what? Fuck your forgiveness! It was not his fault!*

I'd had no chance, rather, to beg his forgiveness, to assure him I'd do everything possible to protect him. Unable to speak to him, to seize him, shake him, take him in my arms—that, too!—I felt dangerously stifled. I would have embraced Rob, squeezed his father's love into his bone and marrow, so fervently that never again would he doubt my feelings. And I would bless him, I would kiss him on the forehead.

Yes. I would kiss him on the forehead. I would kiss him, my begotten son, born of the writhe of Charlie dying, saved on that black September day from drowning in her blood . . .

I found no relief. The jug was empty and the son I had failed was gone.

I took off in the sailing skiff into the river dark, navigating by thin starshine and the wall of trees. By daybreak, I was well offshore, bound for Key West, where Rob's uncle Lee Collins worked in a shipping office. In my night madness, I had left behind my hat and brought no water, and in late afternoon, when a coasting vessel took me in tow south of Cape Sable, I was sunparched, raving. I no longer recall what I kept yelling, I only know those yells scared hell out of that crew, which was very glad to cast me loose inside the Northwest Channel.

• • •

With Lee Collins's help, my son had shipped out on a New York freighter but not before using my schooner as collateral against a loan from this hostile kinsman I had not seen since that day in Fort White when I took Rob away and left for Oklahoma. I accused Collins of exploiting his nephew with some scheme to broker my stolen vessel at an easy profit; that was my excuse to knock him down in front of the new bank on Duval Street where he'd imagined that it might be safe to meet me.

From the look Collins gave me as he picked himself up off the cobbles, I feared Rob might have told this man too much. "All right," I said, "how much do you intend to make me pay for my own schooner?" "Two hundred dollars," Collins said quietly, pulling out a receipt from Rob in that amount. I snatched that paper, tore it up, before counting out his dollars. "How about my revolver?" I said.

"You'll have to ask your son about your revolver," he said, coldly, defiantly, from which I knew he knew something. I did not dare challenge him.

"You deserve to be jailed for brokering stolen ships," I told him to save face. "If you weren't Charlie's brother, I would get the law on you." And Lee Collins said, "Edgar? I would not go near the law if I were you."

We stood a moment, some distance apart. "I am sorry I assulted you," I said. "I was worried and upset. I just hope my son is going to be all right." Lee Collins considered me in disbelief. "*Sonborn,* you mean? You're crazier'n hell, you know that, Edgar?" And he walked away.

Winky Atwell had spread the tale of my dispute with Tuckers, as I learned from Dick Sawyer when I stopped by Eddie's Bar for a badly needed constitutional. I wanted to pay a call on Winky but Sawyer advised me to leave town before the sheriff sent his deputy around to ask some questions.

"About what?" I challenged him loudly so that anyone who'd heard the rumors would know that Ed Watson had nothing to hide. But in a little while, Deputy Till showed up. I followed him outside. Clarence warned me that the sheriff was still looking for a way to get me extradited back to Arkansas. "Better sail tonight," he said.

• • •

The day after I left Key West, Earl Harden arrived with the report that he and his brothers and Henry Short had found the Tuckers' bodies. The Hamiltons on Lost Man's Beach had heard two shots and later some trapper had seen Watson in his skiff headed upriver; he reported that Watson was alone. Earl did his best to hang it all on Watson but he had no evidence besides his own opinion. Until things cooled down, however, that one opinion might suffice to get me lynched: I decided to head north for a year or two. My friend Will Cox had written recently to say that local folks had mostly forgiven E. J. Watson for that Lem Collins business. Will had grown up in Lake City with the new sheriff, a man named Purvis, who promised to be understanding if Will's friend decided to return.

With some misgivings, I arranged to leave the Bend in charge of a man named Green Waller. He was a drinker but he knew his hogs and could be depended on to stay where he was safe, since he was wanted on three counts of hog theft in Lee County. As for companionship, those pink-assed shoats would probably see him through. Erskine ran me north. By now he'd heard the rumors and was silent and uneasy. I told him he could use the schooner if he helped out at the Bend when a ship was needed to bring in supplies or field hands for the harvest, or pick up my syrup in late winter for delivery to the wholesalers at Tampa Bay.

At Caxambas, Tant was nowhere to be found. His sister Josie said he'd heard about those Tuckers and would never work for me again—her way of conveying her own moral disapproval—but called softly as I went away that she would always love me. Within the week, Sheriff Knight and his deputies would raid the Bend, where Green Waller, in his official capacity as plantation manager, informed him that Mr. E. J. Watson was no longer in residence at this address, being absent on business, whereabouts unknown.

FOREVER AFTER

I stopped over at Fort Myers to pick up my horse and bid good-bye to Mandy and the children. Mandy had moved to the ground floor because she could no longer make it up the stairs. Though it was midday, I found her in bed. Entering the small chamber, I realized that this would be the last time in this life I would set eyes on this creature I first knew as the young school-teacher Jane Susan Dyal from Deland.

She'd been reading, as usual: her prayer was that her sight would see her to the door. She looked up with that bent shy smile that had enchanted me so many years before. I smiled, too, trying to hide my shock: the woman lying there was dying while still in her thirties. Already death inhabited her eyes and skin—a sharp blow to the solar plexus to see my dearest friend in this condition. How thin she was, how watery her eyes, her hair already lank and dead.

I leaned and drew her forward in my arms, pressing my lips to her yel-lowed neck to hide my tears. Scenting the death in her, I must have hugged too hard to cover my distress, for I had hurt her and she murmured just a little. When I drew back she looked at me and nodded. Mandy's brain—and eyes and hands and mouth—knew all of Edgar Watson well, I could hide nothing.

I sat on the bedside and took her hands in mine, resisting an image of long years before, our Fort White cabin in early afternoon, the hot moss mattress and this willowy creature, hips soft yet strong astride me, eyes lightly closed and sweet mouth parted, releasing my hands and leaning backwards, twining her arms upwards in the air's embrace, as if her trans-port must depend on that joyous arching. Even at this somber moment, the remembrance caused a disgraceful twitching in my britches. I did not wish to think about how those hips looked now, grayish and caved in under the covers.

"I'm so happy you have come!" she sighed. Lifting her fingers, I kissed the delicate bones. "Well, Mrs. Watson. And why are you lying about in bed on this fine day?" I rose to open the shutter, thinking sun and air might dis-pel the cat scent and shuttered heat, but of course it was the husband, not the wife, who needed comfort. Relieved by each other's touch, needing no words, we sat there a good while in the midday quiet, and death sat with us. In a sudden rush of feeling I whispered that I loved her dearly and always would.

"How dearly, Mr. Watson?" she inquired, teasing. She had heard, of course, about the Island women and their children but more likely she was thinking about Charlie Collins, to whom I would have simply said, I love you.

"Edgar? I am failing pretty fast. You knew that."

"Yes, I did."

"Good. I'm so weary of all the pussyfooting and jolly bedside manner. Even Doc Winkler puts his finger to his lips to hush me when I ask frank questions. Tells me I must be a good little patient and just rest. Isn't it astonishing? Even the children. They're so brave and tactful I could smack them!"

Smiling a little at that idea, she blew her nose. "Is death so dreadful, Edgar?"

"Good Lord, sweetheart! How would I know!" I tried to laugh a little, aware there was something still unsaid, something I was not so sure I wished to hear. To deflect her, I promised I would look after our children, make sure that they got on all right in life.

Oh Papa, NO!

Rob's words jumped to mind just as Mandy turned to peer at me in a queer way. "I beg of you, dearest, don't turn your back on Rob. For her sake as well as your own. And please don't call him Sonborn anymore."

I winced, shaking my head. "Never again." She was overjoyed when I said, very embarrassed, "I've discovered that I've loved him all along."

"Oh! Have you told him so? It's awkward for you, I know that—"

"I think he knows," I lied. "Lucius knows your condition, I suppose."

"I didn't need to tell him. Carrie and Eddie know, of course, though Eddie pretends not to. They don't want to deal with it quite yet. Not that Lucius refers to it, either, although sometimes I wish he would." She seemed wistful. "He reveres you, Edgar. Perhaps you can talk with him a little. He'll be home right after school."

I was passing through town quickly, I explained. I had to go.

"Goodness! You're in such a rush that you can't wait even an hour?" She stared at me, intent, then closed her eyes, turning her head away. "I see," she whispered.

"What?" I said, fighting her off. But because her children would have to deal with any rumors, she did not relent.

"Lucius is jeered at brutally at school. He refuses to believe the slanders, gets in dreadful fights." In a different voice, she said, "Here in town, there is a story that when Mr. Watson goes to Colored Town, the darkies hide from him, that's how scared they are that he might kidnap them." She paused, hand clutching the coverlet. "They say no darkie ever comes back. They are thrown to the crocodiles."

Overcome by what could never be undone, I stifled my protests, sinking onto my knees beside the bed, to pray or clear my heart or be forgiven before it was too late.

"Is Rob all right? He's not involved?"

"Rob was in no way involved. He's fine."

I leaned and kissed her, overcome by an impulse to just quit, to lie down in her arms, lie down and give in to a flood of hopeless weeping—*me!* Mr. E. J. Mr. Watson, dry-eyed all these years, ached in his need of solace for so many losses. I longed to whine. *I could have been the best farmer in south Florida, you know that, Mandy! All my great plans!*—disgusting! A disgusting, low, self-pitying temptation to beg pity from a dying woman, especially this one who had never been fooled, who knew too well that for all the harm I had inflicted on myself, I had done far more to others. True, there were reasons, or at least excuses; she must be spared those, too.

I pulled myself together and sat up straight, tried to make light of it. Gruffly I said, "I don't believe your Good Lord will forgive me, what do you think, Mandy?"

"Do you care?" she said. She had not recognized my reference to our Oklahoma days and the tale of that huge and bloody hellion, Old Tom Starr—either that or she was simply unamused. I stood up, kissed her brow in parting, crossed the room. She did not detain me even when I faltered and turned back in the door. She had not forgotten my Tom Starr story. Now she finished it. "No, dear Edgar"—her voice came quietly—"I don't believe He will."

I had skulked behind my poor tin shield of irony and she had pierced it with the hard lance of bare truth. Her cool tone stunned me. I dared to feel betrayed. I longed for the last sad smile of understanding which, after all these years, she now denied me.

I returned slowly to the bedside. She saw that my agony was real and touched my cheek but quickly withdrew her hand, for she was resolute. She closed her eyes and thought a moment, then opened them and whispered, "I'd like an answer to one question before you take your leave since I don't think we shall ever meet again."

My heart pounded. "You never believed me? Even when you testified in Fort Smith court?" Her flat gaze hushed me.

"The truth, Edgar. I beg of you. It's late."

So long ago, eleven years, and yet . . . one escapes nothing.

My silence was all the answer that she needed. "May God forgive you," she sighed softly. "May God rest her soul."

"Do you forgive me? That's all that matters . . ." My voice trailed off. Mandy took my hand and squeezed it one last time, then pushed it away. Though our gaze held and her eyes softened, she would not speak. I went away bereft and suffocated for want of a coherent way to cry out the love I found no words for while she searched my face.

In a stiff river wind under hard skies, I crossed the Calusa Hatchee on the Alva ferry and took the horse coach to Punta Gorda, from where the railroad would carry me north to Columbia County. Seen through the window, the sunlight pouring down through green-gold needles of the piney woods was liquefied by damnable soft tears, so late in coming and no longer in my control. I was truly astonished that E. Jack Watson, with his fury and cold nerve, could come apart and weep much as he had when, still a boy, he grieved for the dead slave boy in the swamp. Whom are you mourning, you sad sonofabitch, Mandy or Edgar?

By the time the news came to Fort White that Mandy had passed away, I knew I'd loved her as entirely as the wood nymph I called Charlie my Darling, and perhaps even more deeply, though I don't suppose that true love can be reckoned in that way. Sometimes I think we cannot know whom we loved most until all the lovers in our lives are gone forever. Looking back down our long road, our great loves are those summits that rise above the rest, like those far blue Appalachian peaks beyond the Piedmont uplands on that day when Private Elijah Watson of the First Edgefield Volunteers lifted his enchanted boy into the sun above the courthouse terrace. The light (so Mama always said) was like an angel's halo in my hair.

CHAPTER 5

◆

AN OBITUARY

Even before Cousin Laura died, my mother had started scrapping with Aunt Tabitha, and finally she quit that lady's roof, going to live with Minnie and her Billy. In 1901, when I returned from the Ten Thousand Islands, I went straight over to pay my respects as a good son should.

"Well, Mother, I'm home."

"I don't recall that I laid eyes on you the last time you were here. How long ago was that, do you suppose? Six years?"

"Seven, Mother."

"Well, that's long enough, wouldn't you say?"

Skillfully she dispensed with her incivilities just as I was ready to snipe back, that's how perverse this little woman was. She did not ask after Mandy's health, far less inquire about the children, nor did she make the least effort to embrace me. Going unhugged by her twiggy old arms and unpecked by that dry slit of a mouth, I felt oddly out of sorts, I must admit.

As for Aunt Cindy, fixing supper at the stove, she never looked at me. For the first time in my life, that bony black woman did not come forward to hug me. She took no notice of me, not even enough to sniff and turn her back, but ignored me throughout the few minutes that I stayed. What Aunt Cindy had heard and what she suspected I did not inquire, knowing my account of it would do no good.

On a second visit, over meager tea, Mama related in detail how Cousin Laura had died in '94 when Aunt Tabitha's new manor house was scarcely finished. "She bored herself to death, that's all," said Cousin Laura's life-long friend, "and darn near took the rest of us off with her."

The widower, on the other hand, had fattened up like a prime hog with his good fortune. The former Ichetucknee or Myers Plantation was now known as the Tolen Plantation, and the homesteads all around were called the Tolen Settlement. The Tolen, Florida, post office was located at the turpentine works down by the railroad crossing. All that was missing was the Holy Tolen Church. Meanwhile, Sam had married off his brother Mike to a Myers niece, then moved him into William Myers's big log cabin to strengthen the Tolen grip on our family property. Sam's stepbrother John Russ and his four mink-jawed sons infested another Myers cabin on Herlong Lane.

When I mentioned my reunion with my father in the Ridge Spring cemetery back in '92, she stared at me. "Wasn't South Carolina a bit out of your way?"

"Not for a patricide."

"You wouldn't do that, Edgar!"

I shrugged. "Let's just say that the last time I saw him, he was lying in a grave."

She waved this off, upset but impatient, rummaging up an 1895 obituary from the newspaper in Columbia, South Carolina. "The Myers cousins clipped and sent this." The clipping related how Captain Elijah D. Watson, aged sixty-one, had succumbed to Bright's disease in a rooming house in that city. She read aloud: *He was a well-to-do farmer in Edgefield County. A gallant soldier during the War Between the States, he distinguished himself on many battlefields for acts of great bravery and daring.*

We did not have to remind each other that the rank of captain, like the deeds of heroism, were obituary courtesies to this man of low rank who returned from war with an impregnable reputation for dereliction of duty, drunkenness, and insubordination.

Next, she produced a yellowed daguerreotype, pressing it down on the table with a kind of grim finality like a poker winner laying down his hole card. Wild-haired cap-cocked Lige in Confederate uniform looked nothing at all like the handsome soldier I had chosen to recall from the courthouse terrace. Even without his ring eye, he looked truculent and bug-eyed.

"I never knew you'd treasured his picture all these years." I set it down.

"Cindy saved it. For you children. Wasn't that sweet?" She picked it up.

Her hands were shaky now, with liver marks. "You must feel very proud of such a father, dear." She curtsied minutely and I made a little bow as we sweet-smiled each other, not utterly without amusement and affection. "Oh Lord, Edgar!" She was cross again. "How long will you be here *this* time?"

Aunt Cindy rapped the iron stove with her wood spoon, then turned and left. According to her mistress, she had finally accepted the hard truth that her husband would never be seen again on God's good earth; she prayed for a reunion of some kind in Heaven's mansions. Deprived of her family, Aunt Cindy had given herself to ours, devoting her long narrow days to "tending her Miz Ellen's every whim" (unabashed, Mama said that herself). She also managed the Collins household for our Minnie, who had blighted her family with her "neurasthenia"—that is, hysteria and insomnia, dyspepsia and hypochondria and every other ailment resistant to diagnosis and known cure which had an -ia at the end of it, said Mama. The only clear symptom of her "American nervousness" was a horror of human company even at home.

And poor Lulalie. Mama sighed. Her mother feared the worst. Such a warm busty young girl, did I recall her? Mama frowned and switched the subject, not wishing to dwell on warm brown bosoms under the bald eye of her Elijah, the celebrated bosom connoisseur in the daguerreotype. (Guessing at her mind's quick turns, I saw a light mulatta girl, the young house wench who became Jacob Watson's mother.) Mama offered me my father's likeness with an enigmatic smile. "I'm sure you'll want this as a keepsake."

I shook my head, kept my arms folded. I rose to go. Leaning on my arm, Mama accompanied me outside, still clutching the picture. To my surprise, her face actually softened as she related what Private Watson had confided on his return from war. Sleepless and exhausted, he had finally broken down and wept, confessing his terror of being bayoneted and his horror of the battlefield at dark, when the musket fire died to the last solitary shots and the dreadful cries of the maimed thousands left on the battlefield, Yanks or Johnny Rebs no longer, simply thirsting boys calling for their mamas in their long hard dying—those cries that rose in a moaning wind from the blood-damp night earth of Virginia. All no-man's land writhed under the moon, one huge tormented creature, all across the waste to the Union lines.

In the dawn of one dreaded day of battle, Lige Watson had broken out in a soaking sweat and come apart, shaken violently by his own unraveling like a muskrat shaken by a dog. Then his gut let go and he soiled his only clothes without any means or hope of restoration. With nowhere to hide his shame and tears, he fled. It was Will Coulter who came after him, who pulled him down behind a wall and slapped him hard, who ordered him to return into the lines or he would shoot him then and there where he lay stinking. And after the War in their Regulator years, that man with the crow-wing of hard black hair across his brow had used his knowledge of Private Watson's terror to ensure his loyalty in night activities.

My mother's eyes pled with me to relent, to forgive my family. "It's not too late," she begged. I shook my head. "It doesn't matter anymore," I said.

The following year, a letter to Mama lately arrived from Colonel R. B. Watson at Clouds Creek inquired after her son Edgar, wondering what had become of him and how he might be faring. His interest moved me more than I cared to reveal, though I feigned indifference. In his letter, Colonel Robert regretfully described the moaning frightened dying of her late husband Elijah, afflicted with big sores on his legs that would not heal, smelling just awful. Before he died, the wretched sinner, all purple bony knees and puffy belly, had howled for light, more light, all the night through, in his terror of oncoming darkness.

In his last coma, my father had raved and muttered about Selden Tilghman; the Colonel's letter asked "Cousin Ellen" if she could explain this, suggesting that she might ask Edgar about it. Mama looked hard into my face. Though startled to hear Cousin Selden's name, I shook my head. Mama shrugged, too. "I'm not surprised your father was afraid to meet his Maker. And of course he always hated Cousin Selden." Again she scrutinized me but dared go no further.

BURNT HAM

For a time I lived with my friend Will Cox, who farmed a piece of Tolen land and occupied my old cabin near the Junction. I was building a house on the highest rise in this flat country, the former site of a seventeenth-century Spanish mission destroyed by the British when they came to north Florida from Charleston at the start of the eighteenth century and butchered every Spaniard and Indian they could lay their hands on. When the wind shuffled the leaves of the ancient red oak on that hilltop, I could hear a whisper of that old sad history.

I planted pecans right down to the road, also a fig tree. Built a work shed, horse and cow stalls, chicken coop, sugar mill, syrup shed, corncrib, beehives, and a fine muscadine arbor. William Kinard dug me a well, and my new friend and devoted admirer John Porter got me started with some hardware. (John liked me well enough, I guess, but mainly he was anxious to be known as the confidant and friend of the Man Who Killed Belle Starr.)

Sam's stepbrother John Russ was a fair carpenter, and together we got my house done in a hurry, using heart pine lath and tongue-and-groove pine siding. My roof of cedar shakes clear of the smallest knothole was the talk of the south county because most men begrudged the time and craft required to make them. Folks were going over to tin roofs, which turn a house into an oven in the summer: the tin starts popping toward midday, and in late afternoon, as the house cools off, she pops some more.

Inside, I dispensed with a parlor in favor of three bedrooms and a large dining room with a kind of window counter through which food could be passed when it came in from the kitchen—my own innovation, built originally for the house at Chatham Bend. The new house had no second story, only a garret with end windows to vent the summer heat. With the lumber saved, I built a broad airy veranda with split-cane rockers where social occasions, such as they were, mostly took place. The porch had a hand-carved railing that became almost as celebrated in our district as my carved railing on the stair at Chatham Bend, and the house was set upon brick pilings to let cool breeze pass beneath the floor and offer summer shade to my hogs and chickens. As for the windows, they were cut high on the walls so that no night rider could draw a bead on the inhabitant—a modern improvement, picked up in Arcadia, that I never troubled to explain here in Fort White.

Black Frank Reese from Arkansas had turned up at Will Cox's place while I was in the Islands, and I gave him some rough work moving materials. Frank had tracked down that faithless Memphis woman he had sworn to kill but because she had grown fat and ugly, he belted her hard across the head and let it go at that. From this I knew he had matured somewhat since I last saw him.

Will Cox, who had been sharecropping for Tolen, could take no more of Sam's abuse and came over to farm with me instead. Sam still owed me for those hogs he'd all but stolen when I left for Oklahoma but he had to be threatened with arson or worse before he came up with some razor-backed runts, thin and uncared for. "Ain't goin to thank me, Ed?" With a rough boot, he drove them off the tailgate of his wagon into my new pen.

"My hogs were fine animals," I reminded him, "not scrags like these."

Fat Sammy laughed. "Fine animals make fine eatin.' " He winked. "Got fine money for 'em, too." I mentioned that better men than Tolen had been hung for hog theft back in the old century. "That a fact?" he said. "Yessir," I said, "that is a fact, and here's another: a dispute over a pair of hogs caused the famous feud between Hatfields and McCoys. More than twenty came up dead before the smoke cleared."

"You threatenin me, Ed? I'd go easy on them threats if I was you. Folks here ain't forgotten who you are and ain't all of 'em has forgiven, neither."

I looked him over, saying nothing. In Arkansas, I had been sentenced to fifteen years at hard labor for boarding stolen horses. Anywhere in the backcountry, a man would be punished more severely for stealing a horse than for exterminating this fat human varmint. True, I'd eased up on my drinking and put my gun away for good—I meant it, too—but Sammy Tolen didn't need to know that.

It was Carrie who sent word from Fort Myers that her mother had passed away; she had taken the two boys into her house. When I wrote back seeking to comfort her, I told her to send Eddie north to help on the new farm; he had been born here in Fort White and still thought of it as home. As for Lucius, he would go to Everglade and board with our friends the Storters while he finished school. All that young feller cared about was Chatham Bend.

Unlike Lucius, Eddie was not handy out of doors, so a nigra named Doc Straughter, who usually showed up, taught him how to do the yard chores, tend the animals. Doc was stepbrother to that girl they called Jane Straughter, who was so light-skinned that anywhere else she would be taken for a white, and so desirable that half the men in the south county, black, white, or polka dots, were sniffing around her like wild tomcats, including that distinguished widower Mr. E. J. Watson and his hired man, Frank Reese. Jane was not yet twenty, very smart and well-spoken for a darkie, which of course she wasn't, having been got upon the light-skinned Fannie

Straughter by my friend John Calhoun Robarts. The Robarts clan never denied young Jane. They called on her and hugged and talked to her as one of
their own, and being close kin to Robartses, the Collinses regarded her as
family, too. All the same, Jane knew her place and tended to the household
chores at my place, where I could keep an eye on her, so to speak.

I told Frank to forget about Jane Straughter, they looked too much like
chocolate and vanilla. Made a joke of that, the way we used to, riding out of
Arkansas, but this was different, my old partner was rankled. He dared to
say, "They say just one black drop makes a man a nigger. That go for pretty
women, too?"

And I said, "Oh, she's got that drop in her, no doubt about it, but she is
family all the same, so if a nigra with as many drops as Black Frank Reese
was to go messing with her, he might be hunting up more trouble than he'd
care to handle."

Frank very much disliked my tone and did not hide it, knowing that
when it came to Jane, only one of us got to tease and that was me. Sucking
his teeth as if tasting a hard truth, he gave me that flat kind of look that a
tough nigra might get away with in the Indian Country but could get himself shot for anywhere else.

"You're not a home nigger," I reminded him, using that word. He looked
away. With Jim Crow law spreading like a plague across America, any black
man was fair game for whites out to raise hell, and a story in the papers—
some crazed black man in New Orleans, resisting capture, had gunned
down a whole covey of police before they finished him—had only made
things worse. A nigra from other parts, I explained to Frank, might get
himself set afire and strung up like a burnt ham by local men for snooping
around that Straughter girl the same way they did.

"Burnt ham." Reese drove his pitchfork hard into the earth.

Leaving the Collinses to oversee young Eddie, I would take John Russ
and two of his four sons to the southwest coast. In exchange for repairs and
additions at the Bend, I would settle up all our accounts from that winter's
syrup sale. As a Tolen stepbrother, John disliked me on general principles:
he went along in hope of collecting his money but mostly because I also
took Jane Straughter, to keep her out of the wrong hands while I was away.

Though he knew better than to say so, Frank Reese did not take kindly
to my plan. He put on a kind of humble show, as was generally expected
when blacks received orders that upset them. They had to act "natural,"

which meant not merely compliant but eager and cheerful. Frank tugged his cap and ducked and squirmed with a hideous false smile. Not until I hollered at him—Cut that out, goddammit!—did he straighten slowly, throw his shoulders back, his dark face closed tight as his fist.

AT PAVILION KEY

With plume birds and gators mostly killed out and fishing and hunting poor, ricking charcoal seemed like the only way a poor man could make a living. And it was in this needy time that word began to spread about that shallow flat extending from Cape Romano and Fakahatchee Pass all the way south to Lost Man's River and up to a mile offshore in certain places. Men could wade out in waist-deep water and harvest clams with a two-prong rake until they filled the skiff riding alongside. On windless days, the mosquitoes got so bad that clammers had to slather on black mangrove mud for some protection, but all the same, the strongest men dug thirty bushel on a tide. In the evening they'd go back to camp at Pavilion Key and unload their skiffs into the clam boat for the Caxambas factory.

I wanted to get moving on Bill House's idea for a clam-dredge operation before some feller like Bill House beat me to it. On the way south on the *Falcon*, I talked with Captain Bill Collier, who had tended to business ever since a boy and already owned or controlled most of Marco Island; he was the one who found that Calusa treasure. Besides the cargo and passenger trade on this big schooner—lately converted to an auxiliary vessel with a two-cylinder engine, the first working motor vessel on this coast—Bill Collier owned the Marco Hotel and general store, a good farm and copra plantation, and the local boatyard and shipbuilding company.

Knowing how keen this feller was for smart investment opportunities, I asked if he had ever reconsidered going partners with me in that clam-dredging operation I'd proposed a few years before. With a clam-canning factory in Caxambas, a mechanical dredge could make a ton of money, I informed him.

Cap'n Bill nodded, squinting dead ahead. When he finally spoke, he was matter-of-fact, describing in more detail than I needed the huge dredge he was having built there in Caxambas—a hundred-and-ten-foot barge, thirty-foot beam, with a clam well forty feet in length amidships. Designed to lower an 800-pound anchor, drift back on the wind and tide on a 1,200-foot cable, then winch the dredge forward while it dumped its clams onto a conveyor belt—

"Bill?" I said.

With nine in crew counting cook and engineer, she could work day and night, Collier continued in that same calm voice. Feed the crew cooked clams and canned corned beef—very small overhead. The dredge could work in deeper water than the rakers, and the flat was so big that according to his calculations, she could harvest five hundred bushels every day eight months a year for maybe twenty years before the bed gave out. My friend Jim Daniels, Netta's brother, had signed on as her skipper and my friend Dick Sawyer would be mate. The dredge should be ready to operate early next year.

The *Falcon* was running south before a stiff northerly wind. "Well, hell," I said at last.

Collier had been watching me half sideways. He coughed into his fist. "Go slow, Ed," he said. He lit the cigar I had refused and blew out smoke. "That dredge idea weren't yours back in the first place."

"Watson is where you got it all the same."

"Young Bill House," he continued mildly, "gets a lot of good ideas but other people always make the money, ever notice? He don't know how to move ahead instead of talk about it. Don't write it down and date it, show he had it first, and that's because he worked hard for his daddy since a boy and never got no education and can't read nor write." Bill Collier shrugged. "If a man don't make the most of his own idea, another man is going to make it for him."

For once, I only grunted and shut up. He had me licked coming and going. Anyway, it was hard to get angry with this man, who was always mild-spoken and straightforward. He took care of his own interests better than anyone I ever came across, and that was because he never drank too much and always knew when to let other men do all the talking. He also took the excellent advice he dispensed to strangers. "When you're dealing with these Islanders," Bill told 'em, "state your name, your business, and your destination, and don't ask no questions, cause you're apt to get an answer you won't care for."

· · ·

Unfortunately for all concerned, Jane Straughter was no less desirable in south Florida than she had been in Fort White, and there were long nights, I will confess, when my mind swarmed with fevered images of a pale golden shape that opened up in the bed of E. J. Watson like a sun-warmed split peach glistening with nectar.

Jane and I got along just fine, I let her tease me and I made her laugh. Since my first wife Charlie had been close kin to her daddy, I told her we were "kissin cousins" and maybe she should call me Cousin Edgar. Instead of intriguing her as I had hoped, this made her nervous. After that, she hid when I was drinking, partly because my gawky carpenter, John Russ, away from his worn-out wife, was plotting day and night to get her into bed and had filled her pretty ear with Tolen slander.

John's two boys, who might have tattled to their mother, had gone off with Erskine Thompson to Key West, so this rawboned Russ was living in some damn-fool paradise. When he was drinking, he dropped hammer-like hints about my deadly past right at my table, then came out with that heron squawk of his while the rest studied their turnips for fear of what ol' Desperader might decide to do. Restraining my temper, I warned him that if E. J. Watson were the dreadful criminal that Mr. John Russ claimed, it might be unwise to blacken the man's name to his face, he'd better stick to doing it behind his back. But John was so crazy with the rut that he just hee-hawed louder, out of his loose-cocked donkey lust and twitching nerves. The sonofabitch couldn't take his rheumy eyes off her.

Being plagued by Jane myself, I couldn't blame him all that much and anyway his dirty tactics never did him the least good when it came to women.

Forgetting he was hitched up to Gert Hamilton, Erskine Thompson never missed a chance for a long gloomy look at Miss Jane Straughter. As for Bill House, he got hot and bothered every time he happened by and so did Henry Short, though he dared not show it.

Henry Short was a lot lighter in his skin than Henry Daniels, Henry Smith, and a couple other Henrys I could name, but we called him "Black Henry" to avoid social confusion. You sure wouldn't confuse 'em if you watched 'em work. Short was handy with boats and gun and gill net, handy with any implement he put his hand to. He was steady and painstaking, honest as wood, one of the most able men on the whole coast.

Knew his place and always courteous and quiet. Hard to tell what he was thinking, but watching him, I could see he didn't miss much.

There's folks will tell you nigras don't fall in love, not the way we do. Well, I believe that Henry Short fell in love with our Jane Straughter—it was all that white in 'em, most folks would say. The rest of us might want to rut her half to death in grand old-fashioned drunken Southern style but Henry *loved* her.

Jane saw the difference right away, and very soon, she loved him dearly, too, she couldn't hide it. John Russ started abusing him, nigger this and nigger that, until I told him to save that kind of white-trash talk for his Tolen kin. I knew just how he felt, of course, because Widower Watson was very jealous, too, and finally I had to tell Black Henry to stay away from Chatham Bend because I didn't trust him not to run off with my cook. Because I liked him, I made a joke of it to make him feel better.

Not smiling when a white man cracked a joke was as close to insolence as a black man dared to come, but I don't believe Short was insolent so much as astonished. He never squinted skeptically the way Frank Reese did, never hesitated to obey—in fact, that day I ran him off, he never even tried to tell my cook good-bye. He nodded, touched his hat, and turned away. Even when Jane ran out and waved, he did not look back. But being in love, he had eyes in the back of his head and knew that his sweetheart was in sight and not only that but exactly where she stood, the sacred spot, because he lifted his straw hat, held that arm high in a lost and desperate wave, and kept on walking down toward the dock.

Only the stiff set of his shoulders told me how upset he was. Like Reese, this feller had guessed that the Boss wanted Jane Straughter for himself, but unlike Reese, this man knew better than to show his anger or make stupid mistakes.

Thanks to the carpenter's calumnies, our cook stayed leery of me. Also, she was sulky over Henry Short. She hadn't minded when I'd warned off Reese but now she came and tried to plead with me, eyes full of tears: Mr. Short had told her in all earnestness that he wished to marry and she had accepted. When I shook my head, she cried out piteously and ran away around the house.

· · ·

What happened not long after that, Mr. John Russ choked to death. Having supper with me and my noted hog authority, Mr. Waller, he was eating too fast and got a sweet potato in his lung or some damned place. Turned a bad gray-blue, jumped up, and fell down heart-struck before anyone thought to whack him on the back. One minute he was packing in the grub like Judas Priest at the Last Supper and the next he was felled like a stockyard beef, that's how quick Death had him, his mouth oozing sweet potato like the hind end of a turkey packed with stuffing.

Jane ran in from the kitchen, raised her hand up to her mouth, and whispered, "Poisoned!" Hearing that, my hog man panicked, "Anyone who says Green Waller poisoned him is a damn liar!" Looking quite unwell himself, he sidled bandy-legged toward the door, keeping a wall-eye on Ed Watson while his hand groped for the way out. "Dammit, Green," I said, "give us a hand here."

Jane said, "How come you don't take him to a doctor?" There was a challenge in her tone I didn't care for. "Well, first of all," I snapped, "because he's dead—he has no pulse. Second, because by the time I got him to the nearest doctor—" I stopped, suddenly incensed—"Second, because whether I take him to a doctor or I don't is none of your nigger business." I was defending myself too fast from their insinuations, which upset me even more. "Good thing he never crawled into your bed," I said. "He might have had that heart attack on top of you."

Upset, Jane offered the late Mr. Russ a look more fond than any she had bestowed on him in life. "Poor Mist' John would died happy, then," wept this saucy wench, to gall me. She had overheard our raw disputes over the back pay Russ had coming—disputes fired by common horniness over her own person—and might actually believe that E. J. Watson had poisoned his late carpenter, so I warned her that she'd better mind what she told people at Fort White. "Or you'll kill me?" Her words came out in a squeak of angry fear. After that she kept her mouth shut. But a girl who can make you jealous of a corpse is probably not too worried you will kill your old friend J. C. Robarts's beloved daughter, and anyway, no matter what she told them, the Russ clan would assume my guilt and most of my neighbors would too.

Mercifully, John Russ's boys did not show up for another day or two, by which time their daddy was safe underground. With no family present, we saw no need to build a coffin, and by the time we laid him in his hole, enough river water had seeped in to almost float him. Resting on his spade, Waller opined, "Good thing them boys seen their dad in better days. They sure don't need to see this blue-faced fright layin without no box in mud and water." Still sweating out his drink of the night previous, the hog man himself was a poor color. They didn't call that feller Green for nothing.

The burial done, we trooped back to the house to toast the dead man with a cup of moonshine. Waller sidled up to speak to me in confidence as I sat quiet in my place in the corner. "Please, Ed, Mr. Watson, sir," he begged. "I surely never did believe them things that carpenter told about you. I never even *listened* to them dretful stories!"

When his boss leapt up and punched the wall, he sprang back, scaring everybody. I took a deep breath and sat down again and devoted myself to my jug, in ugly humor. After so many years of trials and tribulations, I decided, even the Almighty would concede that his sometime servant Edgar Watson deserved a little solace—young Jane, for instance. But the girl had guessed my line of thought and fled, and though I searched the house, I found neither hide nor hair of her.

In the end, I went crashing and cursing to my bed and there she was. She whispered, "Please now, Mist' Edgar, don't go hurting me." What she meant was, *Don't go killing me.* She was terrified.

Sighing, I took her in my arms, feeling that old sweet shiver of relief waft over the surface of my skin like frankincense and myrrh, for all I know. Her breath was fresh, she was light and clean, she had no clumsiness in her. I ran my fingertips over her small neck and breasts, over that full silken rump that until this night had played hide-and-seek under thin cottons. I muttered, "Jane, honey, why would I ever hurt you?" Still fearful, she whispered that this was her first time, which made me smile, indulgent. I was mistaken. She was a virgin, the dear creature, although not for long.

That girl slept in my bed the rest of the time that we were in the Islands, and I like to believe that after the first time or two, she was neither unwilling nor unduly horrified that a large puffing male creature was easing his passion on her person, stirring his pine house with rhythmic creakings. I never wished to take advantage of a young girl's fear, but life is hard and it don't relent, so a man would do well to accept such blessings as life puts before him.

NIGGER TO THE BONE

Sometimes, bound homeward from Key West, I stopped at Lost Man's Beach to take some supper with the Hamiltons and Thompsons. Other times I would put in at Wood Key for a good fish dinner. On that narrow islet, the Hardens had nice whitewashed cabins, with coconut trees and bougainvillea and periwinkle flowers all around a white sand yard, which they kept raked clean to discourage serpents and mosquitoes, and a fish house at the end of a skinny dock on that shallow shore. Dried and salted mullet for the Cuba trade during the running season, late autumn and early winter, and in summer went farther offshore for king mackerel, shipped eight or ten barrels of good fish to Key West maybe twice a week. These days gasoline motors, just coming in, permitted run boats to pick up fresh fish and drop off ice in 200-pound chunks.

The youngest Harden daughter, Abbie, who came to my place sometimes to help out, had good manners learned at the Convent of Mary Immaculate in Key West. Abbie would arrange my parties, sometimes for as many as fifteen guests. Her folks and most of the other Island settlers were invited, and of course I'd attend the Harden parties, too. The three Harden boys played musical instruments, and sometimes I'd call for "Streets of Laredo," an old Oklahoma favorite that made everybody gloomy except me.

Folks expected I would bust out wild, shoot out the lamps, tear up the party, due to wild stories that came back from Key West. I never did. Except in well-lighted public places, I never drank that much. There were always strangers in the Islands, fugitives and drifters, and I never knew when some avenger from the past might gun me down. I took that chance in public places to be sociable, but when outside I stayed back from the firelight and inside, I kept my back into the corner.

The Everglades was a frontier like Oklahoma, with plenty of half-breeds in the mix: if the Hardens wanted to be white, they had as much claim to that label as the next bunch. But in the census, Richard Harden had been listed as "mulatto," and his family blamed this on the malice of the Bay people, who still resented him for running off with John Weeks's daughter. Eventually he traveled to Fort Myers and signed an affidavit declaring he was

Indian because his mother had been full-blood Choctaw (it was his half-Portagee father, Richard said, who accounted for the tight curl in his black hair). Naturally the Bay people paid no attention to his affidavit, which had been his wife's idea: his family cared about his blood far more than he did. Old Man Richard didn't give a damn so long as folks left him alone.

An old Bahama conch named Gilbert Johnson was the only Harden neighbor on Wood Key. Every time Gilbert got drunk, he would rue the day his daughters got hooked up with Earl and Owen Harden instead of staying home and tending to their widowed daddy. Here at the bitter end of life, as Old Man Gilbert liked to say, he was condemned to dwell amongst his mongrel in-laws, and he could endure this cruel situation only by venting his poor opinion of them at every opportunity—in effect, each and every evening out on the verandah at the cabin of his bosom enemy Richard Harden.

Like Richard, this contrary old man had married a half-breed Seminole. Therefore he felt qualified to pass his leisure hours expounding on the various deficiencies of Indians as human beings, as exemplified by various members of their two families. When his wife wasn't listening, Richard thought that most of Gilbert's guff was pretty funny, and Gilbert did, too: he meant no harm by it, he merely liked to rant as they watched the sun go down on the Gulf horizon.

In the old days on Possum Key, Richard had enjoyed long talks with Jean Chevelier, whose view had been that human beings had never evolved from animals as greedy, cruel, and violent in their behavior as they themselves had been right from the start, and here they were, still screwing their wits out, breeding like roaches, and spreading malignancies across the globe, spoiling and killing as they went. Richard struggled to transmit to Gilbert Johnson his understanding of the Frenchman's notion about the Original Race of Man as a gang of bright apes that spread into different continents and climates and evolved into naked races of assorted colors. However, as Chevelier said, due to ever-increasing populations, conquests, and spreading ranges, these races were inevitably interbreeding, ensuring that the species would revert to that old mud-colored *Homo* who started all the trouble in the first place and had made life hell for other creatures ever since.

Sometimes they discussed Charlie Tommie, a mixed-breed Mikasuki and full fledged scavenger who had all or most of the sorry traits of the red, black, and white races, but the feller they mostly talked about was Henry

Short, whose color was in the eye of the beholder, according to how you turned him to the light. Richard would say, "Them House boys claim that Henry has some tar in him, but I believe he is Indin and white, the same as me: one thing for sure, he's a lot lighter in his shade than many of them so-called whites at Chokoloskee."

According to Mr. D. D. House, Henry's mulatto daddy had been one of those smart-talking nigras that the journals used to jeer as "the New Negro." Not having been born a slave, this New Negro was out to "ravage" white women, not merely screw them, like white men tomcatted around after the darkie girls. But according to Mr. House, whom nobody could call a sentimental man, Henry's daddy loved his white girl truly and she loved him back. And true love between the races being a capital offense when the male is black, that's just how the neighbors handled it.

First time I heard Henry's history, I had gone to House Hammock to hire him away. The old man said, "I reckon he'll be staying with us, Mr. Watson." But he offered a cup of his good shine, we got to talking, and it came out that he had witnessed Henry's father's awful death back in Redemption days. Those good Christian folks set up a platform, scrawled JUSTICE in black charcoal on the planks in front in case anyone wondered what this show was all about and had 'em a barbecue picnic, sweet corn and spareribs, a regular holiday excursion.

Being so light-skinned, blue eyes and brown hair, Henry's daddy could have flat denied his blood, Mr. House believed, and as a U.S. cavalryman who had spilled the blood of hostile Indians for his country, he very likely would have got away with it. But he was proud and angry and dead stubborn. He would not deny that he had served as a buffalo soldier and would not humiliate his regiment, he said, by crawling to a mob, though the girl begged him to save himself and spare their child a lifelong grief and shame. Instead, he shouted that the man they proposed to lynch was an American soldier-citizen with full rights under the U.S. Constitution.

"Rights?" they said, "Boy, your rights just ain't the point here. Are you a nigger that has nigger blood or ain't you?" And that soldier paused, knowing they would have their fun no matter what. He took a deep breath and then he said, "It is my misfortune to resemble all you paleface sonsofabitches, but I'm proud to say I am nigger to the bone." He bellowed that right at the crowd: *"Nigger to the bone!"*

To punish his desecration of the girl, they ripped his pants down to castrate him. They had a special hatred for this white-skinned negro, and being drunk, they made a mess of it. When finally a moan was wrung from his clenched mouth, they laughed, as Old Man House remembered; their lank-haired women did not laugh, just stood there staring hungrily, barefoot and grim, arms folded on their chests, as they strung him up.

With such a fine turnout for the barbecue, folks got into a festive spirit and prolonged their sport, lowering the rope so that his bare feet touched the ground. They gave him enough slack to gasp up enough breath to scream or beg, and when he did neither, they yanked him up again and watched his face turn blue. His eyes bugged out and his mouth opened and closed until finally, skewed sideways, it fell open for good. Being born ornery, he would not come back to life, showing no response to the torches and sharp sticks. Disappointed, they turned him over to the crowd. Folks stepped up beside him, got their pictures taken, maybe holding a nice buttered corn cob, and Mom and the kiddies, only two bits each. Finished up by hacking off ear and finger souvenirs, enjoyed some target practice. Man and boy, they whacked him with so many rounds that the body spun slowly in the summer heat. By the end, the sport was *Keep that nigger turnin!*

Old Man Dan had seen that battered corpse himself, strung from an oak limb. "Looked like a white man. Course you'd never know *what* color he was, not after them Georgia boys got done with him." D. D. House declared he'd been a witness and he sure had all the details, but I couldn't make out if this lynching was his own experience or a story known to all Americans in those days when lynchings were so common all across the country.

In Tennessee, on my long ride from Arkansas to Carolina, I came across a thing like that, and I don't care if I never see another. It brought back the Owl-Man, gut-shot and dying in the Deepwood shadows. It wore out my soul. Mr. House felt disgusted that same way, probably the only thing that old man and I ever agreed on. I forgot to ask if Henry Short was told this story, but Old Man House being so flinty, I reckoned he probably was.

DANGEROUS TALK

Word was out at Chokoloskee Bay that Watson had come back to the Islands and that soon after, a man had died in a strange way at Chatham Bend. Though I was innocent, I could not risk a posse; it was time to leave.

The Russ sons had departed on the mail boat the week previous. No thanks, let alone good-byes, only a bitter demand for their father's pay. "I can't oblige you yet," I told them, "not until our syrup is sold at Tampa Bay." Those boys rolled their eyes and scowled, very angry and suspicious, but being frightened, they said nothing.

I made a fair profit on my syrup sale at Tampa and continued northward to Fort White, where I went at once to offer my condolences to the Widow Russ. Izma was a female of my own age, dull of hair and dull of eye, due to a resigned spirit or a stupid one. With those dark silky hairs above her mouth and sharp short lines beneath, her lips looked sewn up tight as a bat's bottom. When I doffed my hat and made a little bow, she closed her door down to a crack, leaving me out there in the rain. Through that slot I was informed in no uncertain terms that Izma and her sons and the Tolens, too, had concluded that Edgar Watson had murdered Mr. Russ for demanding his rightful earnings, which his employer had never intended to pay.

I handed her forthwith the full amount in a brand-new store-bought envelope with posies on it—"to the last penny," I declared. But I could have worn a high black cowl and carried a scythe across my shoulder for all the thanks that homely woman gave me. I grabbed her cold and bony hand and pressed it to my heart, pleading, "Mrs. Russ, ma'am, Izma dear, your late husband died untimely of a heart attack and that is the God's truth." Izma said, "What would a man like you know about God?" and closed the door. That twisted, unforgiving face told me how useless it would be to go among the neighbors pleading my innocence.

Great-Aunt Tabitha had sent a summons. I rode over to the plantation house, rather small behind fake foolish Georgian columns. Frail at the end of her long life, the old lady spent most of what was left of it rotting away under the covers. Swathed in dry white hair and threadbare nightgown, she looked as crumbly and poor as a bit of old bread left out for the jays. The window was tight closed and there was no stink of cigars, which told me her son-in-law's visits were infrequent if in fact they occurred at all: it was Calvin Banks's crippled-up old Celia who hobbled over to look after her. However, Aunt Tab was still sharp-eyed and nosy, and without preamble demanded to know if I had murdered her son-in-law's stepbrother, that man Russ.

"No ma'am, I did not."

"A liar to boot," she said. She peered at me as if some vile wart had grown out on my nose since she'd last seen me. "What in the dickens is the matter with you, Edgar?"

"Is something the matter, Aunt?"

"A great deal is the matter. Nothing but trouble around here since you darned people came." She pointed her bony finger. "I revised my will, you know. Cut you people out of it."

"Yes ma'am. I've heard."

"Your mother and sister are complaining, are they?" She spoke with satisfaction. "That's because I left my piano and some silver to your Mandy, who would have appreciated such fine things. Unlike your sister, Mandy came regularly to call in the year she lived here with the children." She cocked her head. "I don't suppose you killed Mandy, too?"

"No ma'am. Please don't say such things."

"Well, you never deserved a person of such quality, I know that much. Of course she failed me in the end like all the rest of you. Never acknowledged I'd left her my piano, far less thanked me. She might have been dying by that time, of course, for all anyone told me." The old woman frowned, losing her thread. "Precious little thanks from *any* of you Watsons, the more I think about it, least of all that wicked little Ellen Addison, pretending to be such a friend to my poor Laura." Suddenly alarmed by my homicidal presence, she drew the covers to her chin. "What is it this time, Edgar? What do you want here?"

"You sent for me, Aunt Tabitha."

"Of course I did! I wanted to tell you that you should be horsewhipped!"

"My mother plays the piano, Aunt. I'm sure Mandy would have wanted her to have it."

"Too old! Too *spoiled*!" She waved away the very idea. "That Addison girl was rotten spoiled right from the start! Orphaned at ten, married at twenty, lived through the War and Reconstruction, and never even learned to boil an egg!" She masticated a little while, building up saliva for some obscure purpose. "Oh yes, I cut her right out of my will and her fool Minnie along with her. I cannot imagine what my daughter saw in those two females."

I held my tongue. From the window here in the south bedroom, I could see all the way down the long woodland drive to Herlong Lane.

Spent, my great-aunt vented a deep sigh. "Laura was a fool, of course." A tear came to her eye. "And this old fool rotting in her bed who banished us both to these gloomy evil woods . . ." She raised her fingers to her collarbone, the gesture wafting sad old smells from beneath the covers. "It's hard to put your finger on the fool. Have you discovered that in life, you of all people, Nephew, who had such energy and promise? Aren't *you* a fool, an accursed fool, to ruin every chance that comes your way?"

Her eyes rose to meet mine, beseeching me. "After you left for Oklahoma, Tom Getzen told me you might have become the leading farmer in this county. Did you set fire to his barn? Oh, never mind that now, he's dead." She shook her head. "Look at your mother, *still* selfish and spoiled! She's learned nothing from all the hardship in her life. Do people never learn? As for your sister—well, let's not be unkind. The only one in that whole household who is not a fool is Minnie's daughter. What did they name her? Maria Antoinett? Where did they ever hear tell of a French queen? Got the name wrong and the spelling, too."

"May." I nodded. "A lovely young girl."

"She is nothing of the sort! She has had no proper upbringing, she has no manners, she is wayward and hard and discontented. I left that child three hundred dollars in my will but from what Mr. Tolen tells me lately, I have a good mind to take it back. She hasn't been to see me in two years!"

"What else has Mr. Tolen told you, Aunt?" I paused. "That I killed John Russ?"

"It's not your business what he told me." Again she cocked her head, fierce as a wren. "What in the dickens is the matter with you, Edgar?" she repeated. "We had such hopes for you. Do you really suppose I would have let poor whites infest this family if you had fulfilled that early promise?"

"Yet you let Cousin Laura marry him."

"I had no choice. She was always jumping on him, she was shameless. Silly fool got herself with child the first time out. We have only the merciful Lord to thank that she miscarried." Aunt Tab was weeping. "Oh, Nephew," she entreated suddenly, "this vulgarian is selling *everything*! Why did you choose that stepbrother instead?"

She had spat up the unspeakable, this old woman of edged mouth and burning eye. I crossed the room and closed the door, came back. She held my gaze, eyes glittering with retribution. But then, with a jerk stiff as a death throe, she snapped her head away, closing her eyes and waving her fingers to banish such a sinful thought like some fume vented by the family dog.

Taking her wrist, I whispered softly, "It's all right, Aunt. I understand you."

Eyes tight closed, she shook her head. "Please, Edgar. I didn't mean that. I was upset." She wept and trembled, very agitated. She opened her eyes and we studied each other, knowing she had meant just what she said. She turned her head away. Her face had softened. Into her yellowed pillows, she murmured sadly, "Oh, how I longed to write back to Clouds Creek to tell those stingy Watsons how young Edgar had made good, to tell them . . ."

"Aunt Tab? Please tell them Cousin Edgar has two farms and a fine syrup company. Tell Colonel Robert—"

"And tomorrow?" She had tired of me and her own hopes, too. "What will you have tomorrow, Edgar? Go away." As I left, she said, "If you do him harm, I shall testify against you."

Returning along the white tracks through the woods, I thought everything through. Before faltering, Aunt Tabitha had approved our family right and duty to stop Sam Tolen before he brought utter ruin to our property. Since his brothers and stepbrothers would swarm out like red ants, he would not be ousted easily from an anthill as large and bountiful as this plantation, at least not lawfully and probably not alive. And should harm come to him, Edgar Watson would be the first suspected.

When Sunday came, I rode right up to Sam's front door and called him out. I did not dismount. Aunt Tab had heard my horse gallop up the drive or had been spying from the window, likely both, for her voice called sharply from upstairs, "Mr. Tolen!"

In his own sweet time, Sam waddled out onto his stoop. To conceal a weapon and more likely two, he was wearing his frock coat from church in this thick midday heat but he stripped off his Sunday collar in his caller's presence in a gesture of disrespect. Tolen had lost some of his lard and a lot of his jolly manner along with it. He didn't smell good even at ten paces. His dirty hair was not trimmed neat in side whiskers or beard; it was all black frizzle and the pate shone through, pale as a dog's belly. After years of sloth and rotgut liquor, he looked like some squat nocturnal varmint poked out into the sunlight with a stick.

"Same old Sam," I said.

"Yep. Only richer." With hoggish leer, he tossed his head back toward the house. Sam enjoyed baiting me so much that he clean forgot how outraged he was over my alleged murder of his stepbrother. I don't believe he would have cared too much whether I'd killed Russ or I hadn't if it gave him an advantage either way.

Mike Tolen, in the door behind him, was thickset like Sam but his paunch was small. Mike looked scrubbed up, sober as Sunday, while his brother looked like very late Saturday night. From the day he was born until the day he died, Sam Tolen would look soiled inside and out.

I nodded at Mike but did not let him distract me, though I kept him in the corner of my eye. What I had to say was between me and his brother, I told him. This was true, I had no quarrel against Mike Tolen. Everybody but my friend John Porter, who lost out to Mike when they ran for the County Commission, had a good opinion of this younger brother, who could not be blamed for the name Tolen but only for blind loyalty to his rodent kin.

Out of respect for the memory of John Russ, Mike Tolen spat half-heartedly, though acting unfriendly and impolite came hard to him. To gauge his nerve, I skittered my horse out to the side, watching his boots. From where he placed 'em when he shifted with me, I knew he was armed, too. They'd been expecting me. I caught Aunt Tab ducking back behind the curtain in the upper window and gave her a little yoo-hoo kind of wave.

From his big grin when I did that, a stranger might have thought Sam Tolen was glad to see me, and in his way he was. Because I'd let him hang around when we were younger, this fat feller still looked up to me, he even liked me. But being afraid, he would pull his gun the first time he had me dead to rights, especially with his brother there behind him. The old woman up there behind her blowing curtain might try to intervene but I couldn't count on that.

Not that I needed her. Sam could not shoot a nickel's worth, not even with a rifle. With a revolver, very few farmers could hit their own front door even when, like Sam, they were standing on the stoop. I doubt if either of these two knew how to draw. They'd be dead before they dragged their hardware free of their Sunday suits.

That's what was going through my mind. Mike was worried, Sam was grinning. I wiped that damned smirk off his face real quick. "Nope, you haven't changed a bit," I told him. "You still stink like a skunk because that's what you are. You've been selling off our Watson property after stealing it and you have been telling lies behind my back."

"Lies, you say?" His half glance warned his brother to be ready. "You told Izma and that old lady upstairs that you never killed John Russ. If that ain't a lie, me'n Mike here never heard one, right, Mike?"

Mike Tolen grunted but said nothing, knowing that Sam's drunken nerve might fray. Sam started blustering. "When all you was doin was murderin your help on payday in them Thousand Islands, that's *your* business, but when my stepbrother goes with you and you owin him money and he don't come back? Come on now, Ed!" he complained. "How can you blame people?"

"I don't blame people," I told him. "I blame you."

Will Cox's oldest rode up alongside while we were talking, husky young feller on a mule. Smelling trouble, he let out a kind of eager snicker. I nodded to Leslie without turning my head. Will Cox had no use for Tolens and his wife Cornelia liked them even less, because Sam's brother Jim had wronged her sister before hightailing it back to Georgia. No Cox would jump in on the Tolen side against Ed Watson. Anyway, Les was probably unarmed.

"I am notifying Sam Frank Tolen here and now, with his brother Mike and this Cox boy as my witnesses, that E. J. Watson did not kill John Russ. The next time you contradict that statement or cast doubt on it, you will be calling me a liar. You can try that now"—here I shifted in the saddle, getting set—"or you can say it behind my back. Either way, you won't survive it."

Hearing that kind of dangerous talk, the Cox boy grinned a hungry grin that drew his ears back tight to his head like some sleek water animal. Though I hid my mirth by coughing hard into my kerchief, I was grinning, too. It was just plain fun to talk Wild West to Sam Frank Tolen.

Sam would never have a better chance to avenge his daddy for that long-ago day when I faced down Woodson Tolen. Because of my problems with the law, I would have to give him the first shot so I could claim self-defense. Also he had two against one: though Mike was not so willing, he was ready. Also, it would gall Sam something fierce to back down in front of his younger brother and the Cox boy. But Sam had seen me shoot too many times and so he simply belched, loud and contemptuous, as Leslie Cox laughed aimlessly out of sheer eagerness. Mike did not laugh, not knowing what I might do.

I told Sam I would challenge him to shoot it out on the field of honor except for the fact that no Tolen had ever known what honor meant. Both brothers jeered at this and they were right, it was just bluster. Aunt Tabitha's tremulous support from on high gave them their excuse to groan, disgusted, and return inside. I left there as frustrated as I had come.

Leslie Cox was the star pitcher on Sam's baseball team. Like the plantation and the post office and the mud-rut lane that ran north and south along the railroad track, the team was named after its owner-manager, though Sam could hardly throw a ball let alone catch one. The team was mostly young Kinards and Burdetts, but Les Cox was the star, and because Sam spoiled him, he often hung around Sam's fancy house. Les Cox was a big strong boy who much enjoyed using his fastball to scare and humiliate opposing batters, and, as a rule, my nephews told me, he took what he wanted whether it belonged to him or not. At fifteen, he already had chin stubble and a gruff voice and was solid and hard-muscled as a man. He was handsome, too, so the girls said, despite those ears, which were too small and too tight to his head. He had his mama's stone-green eyes and dark hair like his pa, with that same horse hank of hair across his brow. On his left cheekbone was a crescent scar left by the hind hoof of a mule that had blanked him out for close to forty hours, scared his folks half to death. Broke the cheekbone and offset it, giving his mouth a little twist, and on that side the eyelid sagged in a kind of squint. Might have shifted his brain, too, to judge from his behavior. Leslie remained childish in some ways. Wore a toy pistol on a holster belt up till age fourteen and never learned to handle himself when things went wrong.

One day another boy cut himself in a bad fall in the schoolyard and screamed to see so much of his own blood. Leslie ran over not to help but to rage at him to shut his mouth or he would beat him up. He did it, too. A dog will attack another dog that's hurt and yelping but among our human kind it's not so common. Even his own folks were troubled at the time.

Lately my niece May Collins had imagined herself in love with Les. She saw the trouble he got into at the school as something dangerous and romantic, but none of the kids liked him except May and her young friends. He was often a truant and was always picking fights, pushing the smaller boys, even grabbing their food: he was quick to anger and quicker to attack any boy who dared protest. Because he was utterly indifferent to book learning, he was sent back to repeat his grade, at which point, contemptuous of teachers and pupils alike, he gave up his education for good before anyone found out if he was bright or stupid.

Because I was good friends with his daddy, Les liked to boast of his acquaintance with "Desperader Watson," and with his education at an end, he started showing up over at my place, asking questions about the Wild West and Belle Starr. Being all read up on the Belle Starr story, he informed me that it was those small footprints that got me into trouble in Oklahoma; he had learned from a dime novel that Jesse James had a small boot size like mine, and because Jesse was Belle Starr's jealous boyfriend, Leslie said, he might have "slew her" rather than see her go to Edgar Watson. Something like that.

Also, said Les, Belle was shot in the back. It was common knowledge that E. J. Watson would never shoot anybody in the back. "No matter what, my daddy says, the Ed Watson I know would look a man straight in the eye."

I looked Les straight in the eye just to oblige him.

Les asked if I'd known Jesse James and I said I sure had. I told him Ol' Jess was mostly talk, it was Frank James I could always count on in tough situations. "Tough situations?" Leslie whispered, those green wildwood eyes of his just smoldering. He positively salivated when I gave him a hard squint and an ironic little smile—the frontier code. He went off practicing his own squint and later on some enigmatic silence. For a while, his folks could hardly get their oldest boy to speak a word.

Sam hated it that his young star admired Edgar Watson. He heeded my warning and shut up about John Russ but he fed Leslie all those Carolina tales he'd got from Herlongs, not knowing they just made this boy admire me all the more, and Leslie, with his gut instinct for stirring up trouble, passed Sam's slanders right along to me. Pretty sure he'd race right back to Sam with my response, I boasted about how I'd run that yeller-bellied Woodson Tolen right out of the field when I was Les's age. While I was at it, I confided how I'd dealt with the Queen of the Outlaws and her pack of half-breed Injuns back in Oklahoma and how I took care of a bad actor named Quinn Bass at Arcadia—in short, what you might call the varnished truth.

Sure enough, that Saturday after the ball game, Les drank whiskey with Sam Tolen, told him all about my dangerous adventures. Tolen hollered, "You want to see somethin?" That same evening Sam rode him over to the sawmill at Columbia City, cornered two blacks who had sassed him. Sam had been brooding about those sassy niggers every time he drank, aimed to sting 'em up with a dose of bird shot, teach 'em a lesson.

The lesson Sam Tolen taught 'em was the following: he blasted 'em clean off their mule after halting 'em on the road, waving his shotgun. Being drunk as usual, he had his loads mixed up, used buckshot instead of bird shot, and because his aim was so poor, he shot way too high when the gun kicked, hit 'em in the head instead of the legs. What with all the blood and screeching, Sam's nerves gave way, so he yelled at Les to jump down off his mule and finish those boys off before their nigger racket brought the whole countryside down on top of them.

"I ain't never took a life before! Made me feel funny!" Les was overexcited, scared, but also thrilled. "Reason I'm tellin you, Mister Ed, you had experience of killin, but don't go tellin nobody I done that. Mister Sam is claimin now how all he aimed to do was sting 'em up a little, and what that Cox boy done to 'em after was his own idea."

Both of them were shooting off their mouths and there was talk. Leslie's account fit what I had heard so I didn't doubt that it was mostly true. What troubled me was the way Les told it—the way he tasted every word, licked at it, even—and that bad grin on that arrogant face that hardly grinned from one week to the next. He came over to my house not because he was upset by senseless killings but to brag to Desperado Watson.

"So you didn't mind . . . ?"

"Who, *me?*" he squawked, loud and derisive. "Don't bother me none at all!" Will's boy had gone wrong, all right, he was stupid, hard, and vicious, but the law never bothered him about those nigras because the witnesses were frightened and anyway the sheriff, Dick Will Purvis, had known Leslie since a boy.

The Columbia City shooting was in early winter. Those amateur killers avoided each other until baseball came around again in early spring. Leslie pitched for the Tolen Team but stayed away from Sam, who was blaming their difficulties on Ed Watson's influence.

One day Sam sent word through Coxes that if Ed would meet him in a public place, namely the J. R. Terry Grocery in Fort White, we could talk things over and patch up our differences. I was leery of the invitation because I happened to be scrapping with the Terrys.

My mother was Episcopalian and Minnie, too. Though Minnie's three children had been baptized in St. James Episcopal, Lake City, the Collinses were Methodists, all but Billy, who got cranky in the last years of his life. He went over to the Baptist persuasion and attended Elim Baptist, over east of the Fort White Road, taking the kids with him. But pretty soon there was trouble with the Terrys because their mean dogs scared the Collins kids on their way to church. I went over there and warned 'em but they paid no attention, would not chain their dogs. So the following Sunday, I accompanied those kids, took my gun along, and shot those dogs dead as fast as they ran up. Terrys never forgave that, never forgot it. From that day on, I had to watch my back every time I went over to Fort White. Even gave up my Saturday lunch at the Sparkman Hotel, where I'd always enjoyed the lively conversation, mostly because I did most of the talking.

When word came to meet Tolen at the Terry store, I suspected this bunch was in cahoots, so I sent my boy Eddie over there to reconnoiter. Just you duck around the back, I told him, peek in the window. So Eddie snuck around the back and peered in through the spiderwebs and shadows. He could just make out a big old iron safe and the tools and harness hanging from the walls and the potbellied stove. What he didn't see at first—and it gave him a bad start when he did—was the shape of a heavy man sitting on a nail keg with a shotgun across his lap, facing the door.

When Eddie rode home and reported that the armed man looked like Tolen, I decided Sam wasn't sitting on a nail keg for the hell of it; he probably had some damn Terry in that room, hid in a corner. I no longer trusted anyone around Fort White and was jumping at shadows every time I rode along those roads. For the time being, I would be safer in the Islands.

1903

In early 1903 I replaced Green Waller as foreman with a man named Dyer whose wife Sybil had befriended me back in '93 when I first passed through Fort Myers after my long horseback journey across the country.

Sybil worked for the local haberdasher and had made me my new clothes, coming to my room for all the fittings. Not long after that, she married Dyer, and a little boy they called Watson or Watt had come into the world while I was clearing my plantation at Chatham Bend. We renewed acquaintance briefly on my way north in 1903, and when she mentioned that her husband was out of work and was also a good carpenter, I hired him.

Fred Dyer was handy and did most of his work but found too many excuses to go off on the *Gladiator*. He drank a lot, he was gone a lot, and there were women. I learned this from my mean-mouthed skipper Erskine Thompson who did not wish anyone to get away with anything. Sometimes Fred failed to show up on the dock for the trip home, and his family might not know his whereabouts for the next fortnight. Even after my return, he went off with the schooner every chance he got, claiming we needed various stores and supplies, and I let him go because it suited me to have him elsewhere. Mis Sybil seemed to welcome the change as well.

Often we two sat on the screened porch on those long river evenings. Lucius was off at Everglade, in school, I missed Mandy and was lonely, so pretty Sybil was indeed a comfort. At Christmas, I brought her children presents from Key West. I brought Sybil some small things, too, but she said that as a married woman, she could not accept them. Finally I persuaded her that my gifts were not presents but practical things for household use. With the sewing machine, for example, she would soon be making all our clothes and sewing mosquito bars for every bed.

When Lucius returned to Chatham for his Christmas holiday, I embarrassed him. One evening, exasperated by the general torpor of the table conversation, I made a drunken declaration that Mis Sybil was the only soul worth talking to on the whole place. I think I needed her too much. I realize it probably wasn't so, but at the time it seemed to me I was in love with Mrs. Dyer.

Anxious to mend my reputation, I did not want scandal any more than she did. Yet I couldn't trust myself when drinking, which meant she couldn't trust me either, so I bought her a small silver revolver for her own protection. After teaching her how to target-shoot (standing too close behind, I fear, while supporting her trembling arm at the elbow as she aimed), I urged her to bar her door to Edgar Watson even if he was out there hollering that her cabin was on fire. She laughed in protest at any such idea but I was serious, commanding her to shoot right through the door if I made any attempt to break it down.

Mis Sybil was horrified, thought I'd gone mad. She cried out, "Oh pshaw, Mr. Watson, I couldn't even shoot a snake!" And I said, "Well, ma'am, you had better learn, and the sooner the better."

THE DEATH OF BRADLEY

Back in that summer of 1905, our friend Guy Bradley was murdered at Flamingo. By the time I heard the details from Gene Roberts, the story that E. J. Watson was the killer had already spread, even though Guy had been my friend, and even though I was in Tampa on the day he died. As soon as folks heard I had been absent from the Bend, they concluded I was in Flamingo, where I murdered Bradley because he'd threatened to arrest me for plume hunting next time he saw me. This was nonsense, too. With so few birds left to hunt, I had not shot an egret in years.

Gene Roberts was the man who found Guy's body in his boat, washed up on shore. Before Gene left for Chokoloskee the next morning, I sat him down with Lucius, made him tell my son the whole true story so that Lucius would know his Papa was innocent. Lucius said that he knew that already, and I said, "Well, son, I sure appreciate your attitude, but you'd better listen to Mr. Gene here all the same." Here's how Gene tells that story:

"Guy Bradley had a quarter mile of shore west of Flamingo, and us Robertses was the next section west, toward Sawfish Hole. We still had fair numbers of plume birds in our swamps but every place else, them birds was slaughtered out and the competition for 'em had grew deadly. The reddish and blues and blue-and-whites, they wasn't worth much, but the white plumes brought thirty-two dollars an ounce, more than pure gold, and the rosy spoonbills brung good money, too.

"Before the rest of us, Guy seen there weren't no future for the plume birds, said them white aigrets was bound to disappear same as them flamingos that give our Filly-mingo settlement that name.

"Them Audi-bones up in New York, they give Guy the idea to be the warden, said they would pay his salary. Guy took the job kind of reluctant. Told us more'n once, 'Some riled-up sonofabitch is goin to take and shoot me.' But Guy decided he would do it anyway, he was that kind. And he figured if he was supposed to be the warden, he would give it hell. Never had no uniform or nothin, just stuck a badge on his ol' mattress-tickin shirt and hitched his galluses and went right to it, makin life miserable for all his neighbors. Bein Guy, he never cared if you was friend or stranger; if he'd of caught his brother Lew, he'd of pinched him, too.

"Course these arrests never come to nothin, cause he couldn't prove nothin, not in Monroe County. Judge at Key West would be plain crazy to jail a man for doin what our people always done—what it was our God-given right to do, the way we look at it. Who was here first, us huntin families or them Audi-bones from New York City? Judge figured the plumers was punished enough, what with all that huntin time was lost sailin seventy miles down to Key West and back, missin day after day in the best part of the season, knowin that soon as the warden was gone, their neighbors had went right back to the rookeries and finished off what few white birds was left.

"Spring of nineteen and ought-four, aigrets was farther in between than ever and prospects was lookin very very poor. Before the next breedin season come around, Cap'n Walt Smith, a sponge fisherman out of Key West who kept a huntin camp on the mainland at Flamingo, done his best to take away Guy's job. Smith spread the word that if the hunters would vote for him instead of Bradley, they could go on huntin to their hearts' content.

"Before Guy got to be the warden, him and Smith was huntin partners. All the same, Guy told him to stay out of them rookeries or he'd take 'em to court. And Walt Smith said, 'Now lookit here goddammit, Guy, I been shootin out here years and years and you right next to me so don't you go to messin with me now!' But Guy just went ahead, done what he said he'd do, and before the year was out, he arrested Smith's boy twice. Tom was sixteen. Smith had a fit. He said, 'By God, you interfere with my boy again and I will kill you.'

"Now our Flamingo folks, they always liked Guy Bradley, leastways before he went over to wardenin. Even them few that didn't care for him no more and called him too upstandin, they liked him a whole lot better than they liked Smith, cause Smith was a mean skunk and his sons took after him. His boys was about the only ones as voted for him.

"When Smith lost out on takin Bradley's job, he come to see this as insult and injury. Hollered to anybody who would listen that he had swallered all he meant to take: said no man could shit upon Smith family honor and live to tell the tale. That was the first us Filly-mingo folks had ever heard about Smith family honor. As my dad said, a feller'd have to hunt long and hard to come up with enough of *that* to shit upon."

We had a good laugh over Smith family honor, Lucius, too. "No, them Smiths were not so famous for their honor," Gene said, "they were famous for revenge. Eighth day of July, not long after that election, that bunch come in at sunrise, shot up Bird Key not two miles out in Florida Bay from Bradley's house. In fact, Guy was awoke up by all the shootin, and when he looked out and seen the old blue *Cleveland* over there, he sighed and told his young wife Fronie, 'Them Smiths is out there killin so I guess I got to go over there and put a stop to it.' But he must of knew that nobody would shoot so close in to Flamingo that wasn't lookin for a showdown with the warden.

"It was kind of funny how much pains Guy took to say good-bye—that's what Fronie told us the next day. Picked up his two little fellers and hugged 'em hard though he weren't goin but only that short distance and be back for supper. Later she figured her husband had a feelin what was comin down on him but was too stubborn to mention it let alone head the other way."

(It puzzled me that Fronie Bradley never tried to stop him, I told Lucius later, because she could back up her opinions with her fists. She'd put on the gloves with anybody, man nor woman—that young Mrs. Bradley loved to box! One feller I knew held the opinion that this darn female should be taken down a peg before all our women got that boxing habit, so he took her on. I was there. I saw this. She knocked him down as fast as he got up. Finally he dusted himself off, said, Thanks for the boxin lesson, ma'am, but I reckon I have had about enough. Fronie yelled, Hold on there, mister, I ain't done boxin! Darned if she didn't run over there, knock him flat again!)

"That morning Lew Bradley was around someplace," Gene said, "but Guy never asked his brother to go with him. Just set sail in his little sloop across the Bay. No question he knowed who that blue schooner belonged to but he never liked askin nobody for help—sin of pride, I reckon.

"Piecin together what them crewmen said in court, Tom Smith and his brother Dan was still out huntin, over on the key. When Bradley's skiff come up alongside, Old Man Walt fired a shot into the air and his boys come in. Never bothered to hide their birds, brought 'em right in under the warden's nose, made sure he seen 'em. Guy told 'em to stop but they went aboard and down into the cabin, like they was sayin, *Well now, ye Audi-bone sonofabitch, what you aim to do about it?*

"Guy told Walt Smith that his older boy was under arrest and Smith said, 'You want Tom, you have to come and get him.' Walt Smith had his rifle on his arm, never tried to hide it. Claimed in court he reminded Bradley of his warnin, claimed he expected Bradley to back down, but I believe he knew the man too well for that.

"That crewman and the other feller stayed below but both of 'em heard Bradley's answer. He said, 'Put down that rifle, then, and I will come aboard.' Heard them words and then right away two shots.

"That evenin, we seen Walt Smith's boat come into Flamingo. He picked up his family and took off again. When Guy never showed up, Fronie got worried, come to see me. She said, 'Gene, my man never come home so I'd appreciate you have a look around first thing in the mornin.'

"I started across at daybreak, feelin bad. Not a sign of nothin at Bird Key, but scannin up and down the coast, I seen Guy's little sailing sloop drifted up on shore. I went on over there and found Guy slumped forward, dead, shot through the neck."

"Walt Smith went straight back to Key West," I told Lucius, "and spread the word that the bird warden was dead. Someone said, 'Ed Watson kill him?' And Smith said, 'That could be.' When it turned out I was away up north, he changed his story, admitted he might of done the job himself in self-defense. Said Bradley fired first—'malice aforemost,' he called it—and showed two slugs he had dug out of his mast to prove it. Guy not being likely to miss a man at point-blank range, it seemed pretty clear that Smith shot those holes himself, but his crewmen would not testify against him."

"Didn't want no trouble," Gene agreed. "I went to Key West and told the court that all six cartridges was still in Guy's revolver when I found him. Smith's bullet had pierced into his neck and down his spine because it was fired from above. I said Bradley never left his boat and probably took a very long time dyin. And my daddy, Steve L. Roberts, who built Guy's coffin and helped bury him, told that jury about the death threat Smith made two months earlier, said that was a message Smith meant Guy to receive and Guy received it. He knew about that threat when he sailed out there.

"Well, them young Smiths stepped up and swore on their Smith family honor that Guy Bradley weren't nothin but a deep-dyed plumer hidin behind all that Audubonin, that he was still partners with his brother Lew and them dang Roberts boys, who was not only Mainlanders but the most bloodthirstiest aigret butchers in all south Florida. Swore that Bradley harassed God-fearin Key Westers cause they give his Mainland partners too much competition. Naturally the grand jury was dead set against putting a Key West man on trial for a thing like that so they opened up the jailhouse door and sent him home."

Gene Roberts told Lucius that thanks to Walter Smith, a lot of people still believed Guy's killer was Ed Watson. "So when people talk about your daddy, son," Gene said, raising his glass to me, "you has got to remember there's been plenty killins blamed on E. J. Watson that he never done. Compared to some of the low skunks I seen around the Glades, your dad here is a fine upstandin feller. I myself have heard Nap Broward say that his friend E. J. Watson was that old leather breed of frontier American that made this country great."

I believe Lucius felt much better, hearing these things.

Few years later, another warden named MacLeod was waylaid at Charlotte Harbor. Found his sunk skiff, found his hat, which had two ax marks through it. They never came up with the body and nobody was ever brought to court. Of course I was blamed for that one, too, but Lucius knew I was in Fort White throughout that period. He loves his Papa and I love him back as well as I know how, which is probably not as well as other daddies. On the other hand, I am the best he's got.

CHAPTER 6

✦

YOUNG KATE EDNA

William Parker Bethea, a Baptist minister, sharecropped a piece of the plantation across the Fort White Road from Joe Burdett, and his family grew close to the Burdetts and Porters. His widowed daughter from his first marriage came to visit, and John Porter, a born meddler, suggested to both parties that Mrs. Lola McNair and Mr. E. J. Watson might take kindly to each other. Having nothing in the world against sweet widows, I fluffed up my whiskers, borrowed the red trap with bright gold spokes in which Billy Collins had once courted his Miss Minnie, and sparkled over there of a nice Sunday to pay my respects.

The Reverend in black preaching suit, white socks, and high black shoes was sitting in a rocker on his front porch. "Good day, sir," said I. "E. J. Watson is my name. I am a friend of John L. Porter, come a-calling." When I lifted my hat and introduced myself, he rose from his chair as if preparing to defend his hearth and home. Like so many in the preaching line, he looked like a more steadfast man than he turned out to be.

"Yessir," he said in a stiff voice. "We know who you are."

Hearing those cold words, I almost left without another word. But even as he spoke, Preacher Bethea was hastening out into the sunlight for a better look at my red trap with its fringed canopy, and after an uneasy kind of pause while he scratched his neck, this man of God stuck out his knobby hand. I gave it a good honest shake and he waved me up onto the porch, saying, "Make yourself to home here, Mr. Watson."

Watching me was a young girl in a white frock who stood behind his rocker like a servant. She had wide brown eyes in a calm and kindly face and long soft taffy-colored hair down past her shoulders. This was not Lola but her younger sister Catherine Edna, who was of that age when a female of our species can be handsome and pretty both. Showing nice manners for that part of the country, she curtsied to her father's guest and ever so winsome skipped away to fetch her sister.

What Preacher Bethea was up to in that moment only his Lord knew, but my guess would be, he was tussling with the Devil. And ol' Beezlebub whipped God's messenger well and quick, because even before I flapped my coattails up and sat my arse down in his rocker, I knew this man would never give me trouble. As farmer and preacher, he was well acquainted with my neighbors, including his landlord, the loud and loose-mouthed Tolen, and surely he'd heard rumors about E. J. Watson. Yet never once, on this day or later, did this man seek to assure himself that this stranger of dark repute would not sully his daughter.

By the time I left that afternoon, I had concluded that the Preacher's plan was to sweep out the leftover girls from his first marriage, make room for the second batch coming along. He had two new kids and a third one in the oven, and no doubt dreaded the burden of the widow and her children somewhat more than permitting the younger sister to fall into the grasp of a known criminal.

By now Catherine Edna had returned, busting out onto the porch all in a flurry. When she smoothed her skirt and bowed forward a little to sit down on the steps, I could not help but note the apple bosom swelling in her frock. However, that was my own need, there was no guile in her. If she noticed all my noticing, she gave no sign, just beamed into my face like a fresh fruit pie. By the time Mis Lola and her little girl had joined us on the porch, it was already too late, I had my wicked sights set on her sister. All in a moment, Catherine Edna, whom I would call Kate, had twisted my loins harder than any female since poor Charlie Collins, who had moldered in the Bethel graveyard many a long year by the time this randy man of God, panting and croaking, had clambered aboard and fired up the womb of his late wife, setting this sweet child on the path of Life and Glory.

"Expected you Saturday," the Preacher said, a little sour. "Lola's just fixing to leave."

The Widow Lola had the same calm, kindly manner as her sister, but also the sad quiet in her face of a young woman suddenly condemned to live mostly in the past who expects little or nothing from the future. Her hair was up in a big roll on her head, the way all married women wore it, and childbearing had thickened her a little through the midriff.

Lola McNair did not stay long. She was taking the afternoon train to Lake City, and the Reverend went off to hitch up his buggy to drive her and her children to the Junction. When she rose to go, she took my hand, smiling a little, having sensed what was already taking place. "So-o"—she drawled that small word slowly—"Mr. Watson." I bowed, we exchanged a smile. Releasing my hand, she said how much she'd enjoyed meeting me, adding, "Next time, y'all come calling just a little sooner."

Miss Lola was not flirtatious and she was not teasing me, only herself, having lost a suitor before she had even laid eyes on him—even before she knew whether she might want him. And she did not mind that I had seen her bittersweet glimmer of regret—all of that went back and forth between us with not one word spoken. That woman and I were friends from the first moment, as if we had been lovers in some other life. I loved her sister but I loved her, too, being full to overflowing with a grand bold feeling. Yet she was protective of young Kate, and her eyes were troubled. Unlike her father, she did not pretend she had not heard the rumors—that shadow went back and forth between us, too.

By reputation, I was two men in this district, the jovial, hardworking brother-in-law of Billy Collins and the cold-blooded desperado—the Man Who Killed Belle Starr. While the Preacher might claim he knew only of the first, he stood ready to practice his divine Christian forgiveness on the second or know the reason why, for this man Watson had not arrived straddling a dusty mule like the rest of the young bucks around this section. He was a planter and a gentleman of property with a second plantation in the southern islands, a man of fine manners who came calling in a pretty two-horse trap, bright red with a gold trim, the only one like it this side of Lake City. Once the Preacher had seen this E. J. Watson, the other one went right out of his mind. His wish was to make a good marriage for his daughter as I had done for my Carrie in Fort Myers, so it wasn't for me to condemn this hungry man. However, I know this: a caller with Ed Watson's reputation would have gotten nowhere close to my young daughter, no matter how rich that rufous rascal seemed to be.

Although Bethea didn't know it yet, I wasn't rich—I had borrowed that red trap—but I was an old rascal, no doubt about that. From the first day I met his daughter, all I could think about was snuffling up under that sweet dimity like some bad old bear, just crawling up into that honeycomb, nose twitching, and never come out of there till early spring. Think that's disgusting? Dammit, I do, too, but that's the way male animals are made. Those peculiar delights were created to entrap us, and anybody who disapproves can take it up with God.

In their wondrous capacity of knowing the Lord's mind, churchly folks will tell you that He would purely hate to hear such dirty talk. My idea is, He wouldn't mind it half so much as they would have us think, because even according to their own queer creed, we are God's handiwork, created in His image, lust, piss, shit, and all. Without that magnificent Almighty lust that we mere mortals dare to call a sin, there wouldn't be any mere mortals, and God's grand design for the human race, if He exists and if He ever had one, would turn to dust, and dust unto dust, forever and amen. Other creatures would step up and take over, realizing that man was too weak and foolish to properly reproduce himself. I nominate hogs to inherit the Earth, because hogs love to eat any old damned thing God sets in front of them, and they're ever so grateful for God's green earth even when it's all rain and mud, and they just plain adore to feed and fuck and frolic and fulfill God's holy plan. For all we know, it's hogs which are created in God's image, who's to say?

So while church folks might judge that Edgar J. should be cast into damnation for longing to become one with His creation, Catherine Edna, the dirty-minded one (in God's own eye) might be this man of the cloth who had whistled the girl's sharp-eyed stepmother onto the porch while he took her sister to the railroad to protect his investment and make damned sure that this Watson feller didn't finger the merchandise or get something for nothing.

Soon we were joined out on the porch by young brother Clarence, who claimed to be the first in these parts to work a camera and wanted to show a picture he had taken single-handed of this very porch on which we sat. When the womenfolk went back inside, I picked the boy's slim brain about his family background, in hope of some clue to his sister's expectations.

The obliging youth provided in one blurt the history of the Bethea tribe as best he understood it, which to judge from his first sentence was not well at all: "Columbus," he said, "thought the world was round but the queen told him it was square so he ended up at the Little Peedee River.

"First Betheas was Hoogen-knots and signers of Secession where we split off from the damn-Yankee Union," he continued. "Life got too crowded in the Tidewater so Granddaddy William P. Bethea Sr. hitched his ox team to a covered wagon and he come ahead, driving his stock south by the old Cherokee Trail to Cow Ford, where it's Jacksonville today. But the St. John's River was too high, stock couldn't swim it, so he headed 'em off west to Little Bird, crossed over at a tradin post that had a moonshine still and a brush arbor with no roof where them first Florida Baptists worshipped before churches was put up. Went on south and homesteaded down yonder on the Santa Fee, which flows over west to the Suwannee.

"My daddy, W. P. Junior, was ordained a minister at age twenty-one. He had thirteen head by Miss Josephine Sweat, who died of it all back at the century's turn; we was seven head that was still under his roof when he done it again with the Widder Jessie Taggart. Oldest still amongst us is Catherine Edna, borned in eighty-nine. Youngest is Bill P. the Third, showed up last year.

"Now Daddy don't hardly make a livin preachin, he got to raise his cows and chickens, got to sharecrop, too. Corn, peanuts, common greens, also velvet beans for fodder. New Ma Jess got her a crank churn, turns out three, four gallons of good cream every other day. Daddy goes up to town on Sat'days, peddles eggs and butter. . . ."

Clarence's voice was dying down at last. The poor boy had lost interest in our talk because he saw that I had, too. Catherine Edna was born the same year as my son Lucius, I informed him—that's all I could think of to contribute. "Is that a fact," he said politely. Neither of us gave the other the least encouragement to continue.

Kate Edna spared us any worse by bringing lemonade. As I was to learn, the girl had taken good care of her daddy after Lola married, and when New Ma Jess showed up, it was hard to turn him over to a stranger; she and her stepmother just got in each other's way. Plainly she felt unwelcome in this house and was all set to run away with a boy who shortly rode up on a mule, likely young feller with black hair cut with a bowl. This was Herkie Burdett, son of Josiah Burdett from across the Fort White Road. When Kate

Edna came out, he went rooster red and tripped over his boots coming up the steps, couldn't make his big feet work at all: I had to grin when she said he played third base for the Tolen Team. Kate Edna had blushed at the sight of him, but whether she blushed out of young love or embarrassment for her tangle-footed beau, she was too kind and discreet to let me see.

Right in front of the guest, the erstwhile Widder Taggart reprimanded Kate Edna as if her young admirer wasn't there, carping that Kate knew perfectly well that Herkimer had been told to stay away. Seeing Kate's cheer die in her face, I knew it was high time I left, too, so that this girl would not blame the guest for being the cause of Herkimer's humiliation.

As it turned out, William Leslie Cox had his eye on Kate Edna. One day he let drop a sly hint that he might know her somewhat better than an honorable feller should reveal. Without acknowledging he'd ever noticed her, he managed to hint that the Bethea girl had been trailing around after him at school, panting for the smallest crumb of his attention; it had got to the point where this poor scholar was so plagued and distracted from his studies that he was obliged to abandon them altogether—that's what he said, though he'd told me earlier that he had quit rather than repeat that stupid grade.

Besides being ridiculous, this boy's lying conceit was annoying and it stung, reminding me that I was nearing fifty while Kate Edna was not yet sixteen. And maybe she did love Leslie, just a little, because if she didn't, she was the only adolescent female with that much sense for miles around. My niece Maria Antoinett Collins, her best friend Eva Kinard, and that whole flock of linsey-woolsey damsels at the Centerville School were all aflutter over the star pitcher on the baseball team. They blushed and gushed over his husky voice and that cheekbone scar inflicted in a duel. According to May (whose poetical nature was encouraged by her grandmother), this young swain's hair "filled with light in summer and turned gold." She loved the strong and graceful way he moved and ran and threw, doubtless imagining how all that rampant youth might feel entwined by a maiden's arms and legs. No, it was not Kate Edna but May Collins who tagged after the star pitcher every chance she got, at least when her daddy wasn't looking.

"That young man's scar is the mortal imperfection that makes immortal the beauty of his face," pronounced Granny Ellen, as my mother was called by Minnie's children. (Granny Ellen still got her fanciest ideas from her old book of English poems, brought south from Edgefield.) But later on, when his zeal for taking life twisted that scar and hollowed out his face, our church folk would recognize the mark of Cain.

I told Les sharply to watch his tongue when referring to Miss Kate Edna Bethea. He cocked his head with a knowing leer, trying out a frontier drawl: "I never figured Desperader Watson would fuss hisself so bad over no filly." I guess what he meant by this gobbledegook was that no true gunman from the West would let himself get hot and bothered over some fool girl. In my experience, sad to say, so-called desperados—like most individuals of perilous and uncertain occupation—got hot and bothered only rarely about anything else, but not wishing to spoil a young person's illusions, I did not impart that information to Les Cox.

In the end Preacher Bethea was forced to deal with E. J. Watson's reputation but it never changed his plans even a little. In a last-minute precaution as the day drew near, he found some excuse not to perform our wedding, after which, with his daughter safely off his hands, he assured his neighbors that he had strongly disapproved her match right from the start. Kate Edna was hurt, having done what she thought he wanted; she was learning the hard way who her father was. She said, "If Daddy disapproves of you, you see, he won't feel obliged to provide a dowry"—the one bitter remark I ever heard this loyal daughter make. She was shocked when it turned out that she was correct.

Neither the bride's father nor the groom's mother was invited when we were married in a civil ceremony at Lake City by County Judge W. M. Ives, with whom I would have less amicable dealings a few years later. As a wedding present, Kate gave me a white shaving mug in floral porcelain with gold trim, the first elegant object I had ever owned. I was so proud that I grew a mustache to inset into its mustache cup, which kept my fine new growth out of the lather.

The wedding was celebrated on a two-day honeymoon at the Hotel Blanche, where Kate tasted her first champagne and oysters. For a girl who had grown up around farm animals, she set out on her erotic life distinctly nervous—not jumpy really but inert and damp, like suet, breaking out in sudden little sweats. Gently I stroked her back and rump, murmured her down and murmured her down, same way you might calm a foal, and pretty quick, with more champagne, she got taken by surprise by her own free nature. Her knees went back and her mouth opened wide and her farm girl body turned sweet pink all over, which got me cranked up, too. God's so-called Creation, I decided a few minutes later, might be nothing more than the cumulative energy of all animal ecstasies, human and otherwise, exploding out into the universe in one mighty revelation.

We spent most of the next day in bed. Lying spent, I recalled that epitaph I saw somewhere in Texas: HERE LIES BILL WILLIAMS: HE DONE HIS DAMNDEST. I gave it hell but the next time around I was hard put to keep up with her. Even so, we raised such a rumpus in our squeaky bed that poor Kate felt too giggly to dress in front of me next morning.

SYBIL AND NELL

In the Islands, my foreman had been hearing Tucker rumors, his wife told me when I returned to Chatham in late autumn. Dyer came reeling to the dock, advising me without so much as a greeting that he wanted to be paid off right now since he aimed to quit. I looked him over up and down and sideways. When he could no longer meet my eye, I reminded him that this Chatham Bend plantation had always required a year's notice from a fore-man. If he left before the harvest, he would have to forfeit this year's pay. No word escaped his frightened face, but with Sybil's help, he sobered up and changed his mind.

In November, when Mis Sybil was near term, her husband had been off at Tampa on a bender. Having no time to summon Richard Harden, she de-livered her child with only the help of our Indian woman, who told her to get out of bed and squat. This ill-smelling old aborigine disdained the boil-ing water and hot towels fetched to the cabin door, just hacked and coughed and spat that out before closing it again. Having broken in her own tough twat long since, she could not imagine what the fuss was all about: giving birth for her was more like yawning. When the child arrived stillborn, the squaw indicated in sign language that when that weepy white woman got her breath back, she could walk down to the river and wash off if that was what she wanted.

Hurt by her husband's absence—and confused when I told her that he had remarried—Sybil tried to feel grateful for my concern. She never reproved me for forcing her door, saying I had warned her: hadn't I given her that pistol to protect herself? It was scarcely my fault, she said with a weak smile, that she could not bring herself to pull the trigger.

The following year I was away when Fred showed up, red-blotched, shaky, and ashamed, according to Lucius; he had been frightened by a story at Key West that E. J. Watson had murdered the plume bird warden Guy Bradley at Flamingo a few weeks earlier. By the time I got back to the Bend, the Dyers were gone. Lucius said they had departed on the mail boat, leaving only a scrawled address where the five hundred dollars that Dyer claimed was due him should be sent. All things considered, their departure was for the best. I certainly felt no obligation to send money.

Young Lucius, who was now living at the Bend, told me Mis Sybil had urged her husband to await my return and not leave till he was paid. Dyer was too frightened, however, telling his wife that he was leaving and that if she did not come with him, she and the children would never see him again. By now he had persuaded himself that I would send his salary anyway after the harvest. "Mis Sybil knew better," Lucius said in a wry tone, sounding skeptical of his daddy's business practices.

Sybil's small Nell, who adored Lucius just as much as her mother adored me, had left in a flood of grief, and Lucius confessed that he was going to miss that lively little Nell, though he was sixteen and the girl was only seven.

WE HAVE PARTED

A few weeks before she died, Great-Aunt Tabitha had summoned me to her bedside, where the smell of decay already rose from her yellowed linen. She seized my wrist in a birdy grip and whispered in weak sulfurous gasps that she wanted her silver to remain in the Watson family and that therefore it should go to my new bride.

Possibly her son-in-law had hurried her along before she could get that last wish down on paper, because on a soft hazy day that spring, she suddenly gave up the ghost. Her mortal coil was boxed and trundled up the highroad to Lake City, where she was laid in next to Cousin Laura under that tall haughty stone that she had ordered for herself right after her daughter's death ten years before. WE HAVE PARTED—whom could she have meant with that inscription? Surely not her son-in-law, Mr. S. Tolen, who did not attend the funeral, being drunk in celebration of his strengthened claim to our plantation.

Paying a call on the bereaved, I mentioned the Watson silver that kind Aunt Tab had left to my new bride. Sam chuckled, "I wouldn't know nothin about that, Ed. That new bride that you are speakin about has got to be the one who died on you a few years back down at Fort Myers cause there ain't one word about old silver and new brides in the last will." Comfortably, he contemplated his big house, as if to say, *I reckon I got it all now, ain't I, Ed?*

I spoke each word carefully to make sure he heard. "That silver, like this property, belongs in the Watson family."

"That a warning, Ed? Or is that a threat? Cause a feud ain't goin to help you Watsons none. Even if you was crazy enough to shoot me, my brothers are in line for the whole thing. I know the law on this real good cause I done the papers with the lawyers. And next in line after Tolens come them Myers nephews. So you Watsons are way into the back, suckin hind tit."

In 1903, the two Myers nephews, contesting Sam Tolen's flouting of their uncle's will, had acquired by tax deed nearly half of the mismanaged plantation and had filed a suit to claim the rest. Incredibly, that suit had been invalidated by the last will and testament of Tabitha Watson, who had bequeathed everything to Samuel Tolen. Since her act was incomprehensible, our family had assumed that, all alone and undefended in her house, at the mercy of this son-in-law who stood leering at me now, the old lady had been starved, terrorized, and otherwise coerced to do his bidding.

A man lacking shame can go far in life, especially one who feels no need for friends. Tolen had been all ready for those nephews, he'd had his shyster on the case for years. As a precaution, he had sold much of the land before the case could be adjudicated, so that even if he lost, much of the loot had been salted away, probably in Georgia. This great plantation that could have been the pride of northern Florida was being chewed apart by rats before my eyes, and my hopes with it. Suffocating, I walked out to my horse without a word.

DEEP LAKE

In May, pink-haired little Ruth Ellen was born in my new farmhouse, and as soon as Kate was on her feet again, we made our preparations to head south. Kate was happy to escape the gossip, not to speak of the dangerous Tolen feud. One night not long before we left, driving Eddie and my nephew Julian along Herlong Lane, I halted the buggy on a sudden premonition, listening and peering, that's how sure I was that a bushwhacker crouched behind one of those trees. Perhaps I was mistaken or perhaps he slipped away, but after that I kept a sharp lookout everywhere I went, lest I be murdered by a Russ or Tolen.

We traveled south on the new railroad, stopping off at Fort Myers to introduce the baby to my older children. Walter and Carrie were melancholy, having recently lost their infant boy, but Carrie walked her new stepmother over to Miss Flossie's and decked her out in an egret bonnet in the latest fashion. From there, they strolled to the photo parlor where Kate had her portrait taken with her baby. I carry that picture in my billfold, show it to anyone who cares for a look and some who don't.

Though both of these young women worked hard to be charitable and understand each other, Kate and Carrie had no more in common than chocolate and grapefruit. My wife, who was four years younger than her stepdaughter, was calm and rather quiet ("a bit bland," Carrie would remark to Eddie, who made sure I heard this later), while my daughter had an obstreperous side that she had to stifle for her banker's sake except when her bad daddy was around to egg her on.

While I was in town Jim Cole stopped by the house. He grew uneasy when he saw me, talking too loudly about Henry Ford's impending visit to "Tom" Edison. Eventually he got around to the great prospects for Walt's Deep Lake citrus plantation, and his mealy-mouthed manner told me he had carved himself a fat slice of that pie and also that Deep Lake must be in trouble. The partners knew that Watson Syrup Company was the fastest-growing business on the southwest coast, and though Cole tried to be casual about it, my son-in-law made no bones about the fact that they needed advice.

From Fort Myers to Deep Lake was a long slow forty miles through the Big Cypress over poor track. As president of the First National Bank, Walt was twice the weight and half the fun of the hard-drinking cowboy I'd first met ten years before, but he was desperate enough to ride out there with me, spend a few days. The forest floor was crisscrossed by bear and panther tracks and a hundred turkeys came into that clearing every evening; just as I'd heard, the old Indian gardens at Deep Lake had enormous promise. The soil was dark and soft, just beautiful, and all the young trees were doing well, yet that golden fruit lay rotting on the ground because the place was surrounded by vast cypress swamps and thorny limestone thicket, with no good road to bring in labor and supplies and get the citrus out.

My son-in-law had acquired the expansive style of most bankers and businessmen, who paste on great big friendly grins and wink to sugar all the lies they have to tell. Being new at the wilderness plantation game and anxious to look the part, Walt lit up a cigar and hooked his thumbs into his armpits, rocked back on his heels, and smiled unmercifully for no sane reason before letting me know that when Lee County got around to putting in its western section of the proposed Tampa-Miami Trail, which would pass Deep Lake only a few miles to the south, all their marketing problems would be solved for good. It was only this first year that was the problem—

I raised my hand. There had been talk of a cross-Florida road long before Nap Broward became governor, I said, and not one cypress or saw palmetto had bit the dust so far. This beautiful citrus might lie rotting on the ground year after year. He'd be a hell of a lot better off, I told him, to persuade his railroad partner Mr. Roach to lay a narrow-gauge rail spur not forty miles northwest to Fort Myers but twelve miles south to the salt water at Everglade, get that citrus out each week on the coastal shipping.

Walt stared at me. He'd never thought of that. "As for field labor," I continued, "your good friend Sheriff Tippins would probably rent you big buck niggers cheap, right off his chain gang. He could set up a road-gang camp out here, kill two birds with one stone."

By the time we got back to Fort Myers, Banker Walt was so excited by my new ideas about citrus railroads and sound labor management that he promised to write to Mr. Roach recommending my participation in the venture. Hearing him talk with such enthusiasm, Carrie was delighted. "Daddy, your dreams are coming true!" she whispered. And Kate was smiling, too, of course, eager to join in the celebration but not yet clear why my own family had not sought and welcomed my participation before now.

• • •

Strolling around the growing town, I was astonished by the changes in Fort Myers. The oil and gas lamps, the horse-drawn buggies of the nineties were all but gone, replaced by backfiring and very smelly autos, and the railroad whose new river bridge had connected our frontier cattle town to the outside world. One day soon, I predicted, winter visitors would come here in the aeroplane, which had had its first flight in North Carolina just three years before. For two thousand years, there had been no improvement on the horse as the speediest mode of human travel, and now America had led the world into the Twentieth Century with what the newspapers were calling "a veritable explosion of invention," with two of its greatest pioneers, Mr. Edison and Mr. Ford, exchanging bold ideas here in our little town.

How painful and humiliating, then, that at Chatham Bend we were still mired in the living conditions of a century ago and for many dark centuries before that. It was enough to drive a man of enterprise half mad to be left so far behind in this rush of progress. My head ached with throttled rage every time I thought about it. Ed Watson was a very able man—I knew it, all our businesspeople knew it—yet all his fate permitted him to contribute to his times was an adaptive strain of sugarcane and a few good ideas that other men would profit by such as Deep Lake's citrus railway. His pass-through window between his indoor kitchen and the dining room, his mesh screens primed with motor oil to keep out black flies and mosquitoes, an improved hand pump that raised three hundred gallons of water to a roof tank from where gravity feed delivered it to the indoor sink—such innovations made farmhouse life so much more tolerable that my naive Kate compared her Mr. Watson to Mr. Ford and Mr. Edison as an American genius, when in fact not one of these strokes of genius would deserve a patent, far less invite capital investment. Oh God, how puny my contributions were when compared with electricity and the combustion engine, which had already changed the world.

The only sign of modern times one could find at Chatham Bend was the first motor launch ever to ply the coast south of Fort Myers, a twenty-six-footer with an eight-foot beam, a one-cylinder engine, a large cargo space aft, and a framed canopy of black canvas forward, forming a cabin. I named her *Warrior* to keep my courage up until I could join the flow of progress and make my mark.

JULIAN AND LAURA

In Fort White, my nephew Julian Collins had married Miss Laura Hawkins on April Fool's Day. I never understood what that girl saw in him, for my nephew was humorless, ingrown as a toenail, whereas Laura was fun-loving and lively. Not unpleasantly plain, she had big soft eyes that could drive a man of sensibility and taste to groans of soulful longing. To Kate's great joy—for she and Laura had been bosom friends since childhood—the newlyweds would travel south with us to spend that summer at the Bend, with a vague plan to stay on for a year.

Lucius met us in the *Warrior* at Everglade, where he was to pick up his new skiff with outboard motor: he invited his cousin Julian to accompany him and do his first saltwater fishing on the way. Kate and our new baby came with me in the launch, also Julian's Laura and Jane Straughter, whom the Collinses had brought along as nursemaid-cook. Hope of seeing Henry Short was probably why Jane came.

Leaving the Bay, we met squalls off Indian Key, and fearing for the smaller boat, the girls begged me to turn back. Knowing that Lucius, now seventeen, was an expert boatman already handy with marine motors, I shook my head, being anxious to get home, but during the worst of it, his skiff wallowed with the motor's weight and took a following sea over the stern that swamped her. Our young women got a terrible fright when they looked back.

I swung the *Warrior* around in a wide circle. Coming up astern, I heaved the boys a line as I went by, took them in tow: Julian, steering, tried to hold the skiff on course while Lucius tinkered with his motor. The wind was gaining all the time, with both boats taking a godawful pounding: there was such a surge that at moments the skiff dropped out of sight as the Gulf swallowed her and spat her up again. My towline parted off Pavilion Key and after that, there was nothing to do but carry the women and small children to safety in Chatham River and pray that my son got that motor started, because night was falling and the weather worsening.

Learning my intention, Laura Collins spread her wings for balance, pitching forward to the helm, and yelped at me like a gull across the wind: we must not abandon those young men to a watery grave. "Turn back! Turn back! I beseech you!" I told her that if we attempted to turn back, the chances were that nobody would make it; the new bride went down onto her knees and prayed and begged, wailing that if her Julian had to drown, she wished to perish with him. When she threatened to hurl herself overboard, I seized her. "No," I shouted, "you had better not, because if Lucius pulls your Julian through this, as I believe he will, you might feel foolish up in Heaven all alone." I ordered Kate and Jane to hold her while I piloted the narrow channel into Chatham River.

Kate was already weeping because her Ruth Ellen, losing her grip on Jane's frock while Jane helped restrain Laura, had barely escaped going overboard. Exasperated by all the shrieking, I roared at Jane, "I sure hope you can swim, because if that child goes overboard, you're going after her!" Jane met my glare while making up her mind if I was a cold-hearted rogue or just a coward. But my threat terrified poor Kate, who was weak with seasickness. Her one wish, she wept, was to set foot on dry land once more before she died, and when she saw mangrove shadows in the spume and mist, she thanked the Lord. Inland people dread unruly winds and huge, wild waves, when sea and sky rush together and collide in a roaring shapeless chaos without color: once in sight of shore, they feel much safer, not realizing that where sea meets land the danger is far greater. With that onshore wind, at dusk, in such poor light, the *Warrior* could strike an oyster bar and go aground, get pounded to pieces.

With good timing and some luck, I rode the boat onto the back of a cresting wave that carried us between the mangrove clumps into the estuary. I wanted to head straight back out to search for Lucius but there was no high ground in the flooded delta to put passengers ashore and the house was miles upriver. If I failed to return for my stranded passengers, they would surely die, unable to swim against the current or crawl for miles through the river jungle on the banks.

Having been here before, Jane understood what I was trying to explain, but because I had threatened her, she was impassive, arms around Ruth Ellen. Her cool eyes mocked me. *You sure you're not forsaking them to save yourself?* Desperate to stare the lost skiff into sight, I scanned the waters of the river mouth before the Gulf mists closed behind.

We went upriver. Hearing the motor, Green Waller came down to the dock to take the lines. Somewhere along his rocky road, Green had scavenged some kind of fancy manners, and was raring to try 'em out on the young women. "Howdee do, ladies, and welcome!" he said. I cut off his palaver in a hurry. Lucius was adrift out toward Pavilion Key. I roared, "Light a big fire! Give 'em a beacon!" I gave that order mostly to calm Laura, because in such weather no boat offshore would see a glow over the jungle so far inland, not even if Green set the damn house on fire. He knew this, too, and at once commenced to say so, being insensitive to social subtleties except when in the company of hogs. I stopped him with a fearful glare and he jumped to it.

I was very frightened I might lose my dearest son. I ranged up and down the bank like a caged panther. Toward daybreak, I sagged down on the porch steps. Laura had sat up, too, but stayed out of sight behind me. Even after I took notice of her, she would not speak.

Slowly during that long night the storm had died. At sunrise, when I went down to the dock, she followed. I waved her away when she tried to come aboard, she would only be in the way.

I went ashore at Pavilion Key, asking in vain if anyone knew anything. My daughter Minnie escorted me around, holding my hand. I searched the mainland shore, then the gray and sullen sea for a sign of death or life, knowing the drowned will sink for a few days before they rise again. Unless Lucius had found shelter someplace, those boys were lost.

At noon, with my fuel almost gone, I headed back into the river, leaden-hearted. The day was dark and the roiled water pouring down out of the Glades looked thick as molten iron. Black cormorants like requiem birds swam down the raining river.

Two figures, white and lavender, stood before the house, clutching their bonnets: on the Gulf wind their hat ribbons flew behind them. Seeing the *Warrior* coming upriver with a lone man at the helm, Laura turned and fled into the house.

"She's beside herself," Kate warned as I tied up. "She doesn't know what she is saying." Laura ran outside again to scream at me. "Why are you here? Why aren't you still searching?" When I only nodded, calling to Sip Linsey to refuel the boat, she burst into tears, too exhausted to apologize or protest further. Kate led her back inside.

Lucius brought Julian back that afternoon. Sometime after midnight they had drifted inshore south of the river mouth, where a small point concealed them from the Chatham delta and the Gulf. At daybreak, they had heard my motor to the north, but her loud *pop-pop-pop* had drowned their yells. Lucius was still working to remove salt water from the carburetor, and toward noon he got the motor to kick over: they came up Chatham River less than a mile behind me. As the skiff came into view, I shouted toward the house. Laura did not dare come look until she heard Kate's cry at the sight of two standing figures.

I shook Lucius's hand as he came ashore. "What kept you fellers?" I said jovially. My son gave me that bent smile, but they had come too close and his tired eyes warned me they were not ready to joke about it. Though he loved me dearly, Lucius knew me somewhat better than I might have wanted.

Julian gazed at me over Laura's quaking shoulders. Stroking her head, he would not meet my eye. His wet dark hair slicked close to his head so that his ears stuck out made him look slight and boyish despite that thin pointed beard; he trembled because he was cold and frightened through and through. On a day warm and humid with Gulf haze, Julian's teeth chattered. Coddled by Laura, he would languish three days in bed complaining of the ague, and after his return to Fort White, he never spoke again of his Gulf adventure. It was his young wife who suffered most, however: Laura was to lose her baby. Unlike her husband, she forgave me.

OFF CAPE SABLE

Green Waller reported that Henry Short had left the Bend the day before bound for Key West in the *Gladiator* with a mixed cargo of six hogs, a milk cow, two hundred gallons of cane syrup, coconuts, eggs, guavas, and papayas. That storm had built all day after the schooner left, and when it broke, Short was caught somewhere southwest of Cape Sable, managing that sailing boat alone in ugly weather. Even a small schooner needed more sea experience than Henry had for an eighty-mile voyage over the shallow banks west of the Keys in time of storm. Hearing my angry shouting and the news that Short was missing, Jane Straughter wept as if it were my fault that her lost love was all alone out there—as if this danger had befallen him because I had driven him away from her out of my jealousy. Two days later, Henry turned up at the Bend. The *Gladiator* had sunk on the outer banks of Florida Bay and he had been picked right off the masts by my friend Gene Roberts, bound from Key West for Chokoloskee. "Way them spars are stickin up, you can spot her two miles away," Gene said. "Hull's probably all right but you best get there quick before some Key West pirate comes across her."

The squall had come up fast out of the south, Henry related when I questioned him. Rather than fight it, he tried to run before the wind, but by the time he came about, the schooner, responding sluggishly with her heavy cargo, remained broadside too long and took a sea over her starboard beam. "I lacked sea knowledge, Mist' Watson," Henry whispered. "I sure am sorry." The only thing Henry had saved was his old rifle.

Kate took my arm to keep me calm but the fury was already abating. Short deserved credit for coming back at all, because ever since that Tucker business, this nigra had been deathly frightened of E. J. Watson. Even so, he made no excuses but took full responsibility, holding his straw hat to his chest, toeing the ground. I saw Jane watching from the doorway, frightened for him, too.

With Lucius and Henry, I went south to Wood Key to pick up Owen and Webster Harden and their guns. At Lost Man's Beach we left the *Warrior* in the cove at the north end and took Erskine Thompson's little eight-ton schooner for our salvage expedition—never asked permission, we just took her. As we hauled anchor, Thompson came out—he was probably hanging back, knowing I was angry because he had entrusted my ship to someone else without permission. If my ship's captain wanted to stay home from now on, I yelled across the water, that was fine by me.

We kept on going that late afternoon, down toward Cape Sable. Lay to that night on the open Gulf off Sandy Key in a silver calm under the stars. At first light next morning we located her masts, and sure enough, a blue ketch was tied up to her that I recognized as the old *Cleveland*, Captain Walter Smith.

Her crew was still asleep below. We reckoned Smith had sent back to Key West to get help with the salvage. We stood off a little ways, eased down the hook. In a while, a man came up on deck to piss. Seeing our boat, he made a move toward the hatch to wake the others, but Owen Harden waved him back at rifle point.

A decade ago, when I first went to Key West, there were three hundred boats unloading sponges at the foot of Elizabeth Street but now the sponges were fished out in local waters, and now there was new competition from the Greeks at Tarpon Springs—unfair competition, Key Westers decided, because those damned immigrants were cheating, using diving helmets. Smith and others got the homegrown spongers fired up, and they went up the coast and slashed some air hoses, burned a few boats.

That was Walt Smith's reputation, quick to bite when anything got in his way. Come to a fight, I was happy it was Smiths, first because Walt Smith deserved to be shot and second because the Harden boys were the right men for the job: the Hardens had made good friends with Guy Bradley when they lived at Flamingo for a year at the turn of the century, and they wouldn't need much provocation to straighten out Guy's killer once and for all.

Henry Short had his old Winchester along, and Henry shot even better than the Hardens—better'n any man along the coast, I'd heard, excepting me. All the same, I ordered him not to show his weapon if it came to any showdown with Key Westers. "Next time those conchs caught you alone," I said, "they'd lynch you on general principles." Henry nodded, knowing what I meant by general principles.

Pretty soon there were three spongers up on deck: Cap'n Walt, small, mean, and quick, and his offspring Tom and that scraggy feller the Hardens called Coot Ethridge who had been belowdecks on this boat when Guy was murdered. And I said, "You know who I am. Cast off your lines."

Smith crossed over to the rail and took a leak in our direction to relieve his feelings. In that silver early-morning calm, in that dead silence, in that red sun rising from the fiery shimmer of the banks off to the east, that tinkle of his worn-out bladder would have woke a crocodile a half mile off. While he pissed at us, his glasses glinted and his brain buzzed as he figured out what he was going to do next. Finished, he shook the last acid drops in our direction, hawked, spat, and farted. If he could have mustered up a shit, he might have done that, too. Taking his time, he straightened up and stuffed his mean old prick back in his pants, all the while squinting toward the southward, as if confident that help would show up any second on that horizon.

Seeing him being so obnoxious, his crew got nervous, and Coot's voice broke as he called over, "Mr. Watson, we ain't lookin for no trouble so there ain't no call to go pointin them guns." Hearing that, Smith whipped around so quick that he damn near tore off his own pecker. "This vessel was abandoned and we found her first. We are aboard of her right now. That's the law of salvage. Law's the law."

My temper came up quick as his. "How about Bradley? How about all the lies you told to put the blame on Watson? Law was the law, you sonofabitch, you would have hung!" When I raised my shotgun, his crew dove for cover. "Anyway, you're not aboard my schooner and you're not going aboard her, either, cause she's on the bottom. So you cast off real quick, the way I told you, cause I don't aim to explain it all again."

The Hardens had raised their rifles, too, and the oldest, Webster, interrupted Walt Smith's thoughts before he could speak again. "You're thinkin its your word against our'n, now ain't that right? Only thing is, your word ain't worth a shit no more on this whole coast nor your ass neither if you don't get movin."

Smith did not like hearing such hard words, never mind looking down so many gun barrels, but he reckoned this was not the time to say so. He gave Webster a wink to let him know that accounts would be settled later. "We got witnesses," he snarled, as the Smith boy and Coot had jumped to clear their lines, "and they will be showin up here any time now."

In the still air, Smith's ketch moved hardly at all on the weak current. They had drifted clear but were still in gun range. Finally Smith called across the water, "You'll need hands to raise her, Watson, let alone careen her. We can split the salvage." I called back, "The damned cargo is spoiled. The ship is mine. No salvage. One day's wage."

That's how we settled it. Rigged a block and tackle amidships and more lines fore and aft, raised her inch by inch between the boats like a drowned whale. Took till noon before her gunwales surfaced, that's how slow and hard that winching was. Then all hands bailed till her deck came up out of the water, and she wallowed.

A ship rose on the horizon after midday, drew near in early afternoon. I sat back in the stern where I could cover all three boats with my gun sticking up where all could see it. I was well known at Key West. There wasn't one man on that other boat who wanted trouble.

By now a little breeze was picking up. At high tide, we towed the *Gladiator* eastward, ran her aground on a bar. We careened her six hours later when the tide was down, long about midnight. The hull came out undamaged but her cargo was a total loss, a mess of busted eggs and slimy vegetables, waterlogged chickens, a drowned milk cow, swollen hogs.

The Smith crew refused to help us clean her out. "Where's our money?" Walt Smith said. The sea salt crusted on his glasses made this old wharf rat look more vicious than before. I said he'd have to wait till the next time we sold a cargo in Key West. He cursed vilely. "Don't go drinkin it all up before we get what's owed us," Walt Smith said.

Six hours after that, the tide floated her again. She was riding as high as a white gull next morning when the sun came up like a fireball over the Keys.

SHOOTING

We dropped Thompson's ketch at Lost Man's and the Hardens at Wood Key and Lucius took the *Gladiator* home. I told Short to come with me on the *Warrior*, I would take him to House Hammock through the inland bays. Owen Harden said, "You come see us, Henry"—his way of warning me to be good to Short in case I was still upset over that cargo. Henry shook hands with Owen and Webster and got into my boat without a word and put away his rifle. At a sign from me, he took the helm and entered Lost Man's River. Passing Lost Man's Key, he did not glance over that way even once.

Where the river narrowed, Short peered around him at the mangrove walls as if seeing the darkness in them for the first time. More and more uneasy, he watched me sip my flask. He said again, "I sure am sorry, Mist' Watson." But knowing how the *Gladiator* yawed when she was overloaded, and knowing Thompson knew that, I had decided that the only man responsible was Erskine, who had turned her over to an inexperienced hand despite the signs of storm. I said, "Well, I know you are, Henry, but you did your best, so never mind about it."

After a time he gave a little cough, but not until I looked his way did he come out with it. "Sir? How might Miss Jane be gettin on?" I took a swallow of white lightning. "*Miss* Jane?" And he said, "Yessir." "The mulatta gal?" He paused. "Yessir. The mulatta gal."

That was a pause I didn't care for. I took another swallow, then a draw on my cigar, breathing the smoke into his face. I said, "She is aiming to get married off to a coal-black nigger by the name of Reese." I saw the blood rise to his cheeks, which goes to show how light this feller was. "Something wrong, Henry?" I said.

Another pause. Then he said, "Nosir. Nothing wrong with it. Please give Miss Jane the respects of Henry Short."

"Give Miss Jane the respects of Henry Short."

"Yessir," he said, scared but stubborn. "Miss Jane Straughter."

"Give Miss Jane Straughter the respects of *Mister* Henry Short?"

"Nosir."

We went inland up Lost Man's River and north through Alligator Bay. Henry flinched when I swung my gun up kind of sudden to shoot a white ibis passing overhead. I took the helm and he went to the stern to pluck our supper as we went along, and I recall how those white feathers danced and disappeared as the boat turned through the corridors of dusk in those narrow channels. It was a dark evening, overcast, no moon to travel by and dead low water. Twice the *Warrior* went hard aground before I quit and ran ashore at Possum Key. "We'll lay over here tonight," I said.

Jungle vines had crawled over the Frenchman's grave and the door had blown off the front of the old cabin. Henry found a rusted pan and a bent pot and cooked the ibis. I sat there in the fire smoke to spite the mosquitoes, brooding over my lost cargo and wondering where the capital to put the Bend back into shape was going to come from. Henry watched me polish off that flask as if afraid I might get drunk and take his life.

"Fine eatin bird, suh. Call this 'Chokoloskee chicken,' " Henry said, serving me the breast on a leaf plate. I took my knife out.

"Well, I know that, Henry."

Squatting down to eat out of the pan, he kept to my right side and behind me, where I'd have to swing against the grain to get a shot off.

More and more irascible, I picked a fight. "What's this Pentecostal?" I demanded, having heard him mention to the Hardens a new religion out of California that was signing up a lot of local Baptists, Henry included. Politely he tried to explain about Acts 2:4, the Day of the Pentecost, fifty days after Passover—"You some kind of a Jew, Henry?" I interrupted—when a mighty fire wind from Heaven rushed down into Jerusalem and the Apostles filled up with the Holy Spirit and went around speaking in strange tongues in sign of the world's end—

"That so? Let's hear some of their jabber."

"Got to be in the Spirit, Mist' Edguh, befo' you kin speak in tongues."

"In the Spirit. Speak in tongues." I nodded wisely. "Helps to be dead drunk, too, I reckon." And I drank off some more, mean and exhilarated. "Might get to be Jesus for a minute, or the Holy Ghost. What's your opinion, Henry?"

"Nosuh." Henry's face had no expression. He scratched the fire-blackened earth with a small stick.

One time out there in the Nations—out of gun range, down the river narrows—I saw a panther come off a rock ledge, take a bay foal. That foal was a lot bigger'n the cat was, and the mare right there alongside, big horse teeth bared. These were half-wild Indian ponies, knew how to kick and bite. She could have run that cat back up that rock with no damn trouble. But that foal nickered just once and the mare whinnied, made a little feint, and it was over. Never even laid her ears back, the way horses do when they fight other horses. That mare and her foal, too, they just gave up, like offering the young one to that panther was in their nature. The mare went back to grazing before her foal was dead, not thirty yards from where that cat crouched, feeding.

What I mean, if Henry Short feared I might kill him, he had plenty of opportunity to get the drop on me and stop me. In Henry's place, ol' Frank Reese might have drilled me just for baiting him, then covered it up some way, taken his chances, because Frank was an outlaw raised up wild with no respect for whites who did not deserve any. But Henry Short would never raise his hand against a white or his voice either, not even if he thought he could get away with it. It just wasn't in his nature.

"Henry? You ever hear about that crazy nigger couple years ago who shot up a whole posse of New Orleans police before they tore apart his hide-out in a hail of bullets? All over the South, men were talking about Robert Charles, trying to figure where that boy learned to shoot."

Henry was guarded. "I heard Mist' Dan House talkin sump'n about it, Mist' Edguh. That boy must been dead crazy, like you say."

This boy I had here was very complicated. Not humble or subservient, not exactly, he kept his dignity to go with his good manners. It was more like he was doing penance and would bow his neck for any punishment that came his way—his own penance, I mean, not one imposed by whites. Not so much shamed as forever damned by his few drops of black blood. Having been raised by white people since a small child, in a community where other black men were rarely seen from one year to the next, the nigra in him was a man he scarcely knew for whom the white man in him took responsibility. In Henry Short, the brother and his keeper were the same and Judgment Day was every day all year. He figured he deserved his cross and he aimed to tote it.

"Henry? You prefer setting back there with the miskeeters?" I pointed at the ground closer to the fire. "Ol' Massuh ain' gwine whup you, boy." I enjoyed talking black to Henry, who talked white, having no nigras at Chokoloskee to teach him his own language. Besides Nig Wiggins at Will Wiggins's cane farm out at Half Way Creek, the only other nigra was George Storter's man at Everglade, a stowaway from the Cayman Islands, blacker'n my hat; I don't think they ran across each other twice a year. As Kate says, "These poor darkies in the Islands must get very lonesome."

Hearing Henry's voice, there was no way to tell what color he was, and seeing him, you could hardly tell it either. Henry Short looked a lot more Injun than nigra and a lot more white than Injun, come to think about it. But when I asked about his ancestry—which he knew I knew—he paused, then whispered, "Nigger. Nigger to the bone."

Was that what Henry thought I wished to hear? I'd heard those words before and so they nagged me. I turned to look at him.

Then I remembered. Before it struck me that I might not want the answer, I inquired, "So your daddy's name was Short. *Mister* Short, maybe?"

"Nosuh, Mist' Watson, suh, ah doan rightly have no name, no suh. Dey gib me de name Sho't jus' fo' de fun, me bein so puny when ah was comin up."

Henry's eyes could not hide his alarm. He had retreated into nigger speech and so I knew.

A hoot-owl called deep in the forest. *Hoo-hoo, hoo—aw-w.*

"I b'lieves dey called him Jack. Somethin like dat."

I emptied the bottle, hurled it over the black water. It made a small splash at the farthest edge of firelight. "I can't pay your wages for a while," I said, unable to look at him.

"Ain't got nothin comin, nosuh," Henry murmured. "Ah done sunk yo' boat."

Long minutes passed. We watched the flask, which had gone under for a moment. Then the neck popped up like the small head of a terrapin back in the salt creeks, or the tip of a floating mangrove seed that has not yet taken hold on the shallow bottom.

"Tell you what." I picked up his Winchester, which looked like the first model ever made. "We'll shoot for it. Double or nothing." Despite all that Chokoloskee talk about Short's marksmanship, black men generally shoot poorly, not being mechanical of mind. I figured he might shoot better than most local men but nowhere near as well as E. J. Watson.

"Ain't got nuffin comin, Mist' Edguh, nosuh, ah sho' ain't." Henry was scared. For this self-respecting man, trying to speak like an ignorant field hand, I thought, was like a dog rolling over on its back to bare its throat. Disliking this, I fired fast to shut him up. My first bullet came so close that the bottle nose went under for a moment. "Your turn," I said.

"Nosuh! Ain'no need! Yo nex' shot take care of it, Mist' Edguh!"

"Shoot." I tossed the gun.

He shot and missed. I shot again. Over and over I sank that goddamned thing but it would not stay down, and the wavelet made by every bullet washed it a little farther back under the mangroves.

Henry, too, kept missing, barely. It was only after it drifted out of sight and he claimed I'd sunk it that it came to me how he'd missed each time in exactly the same spot.

"Maybe your sight is out of line," I said. "You're always two inches to the right."

"Yassuh, dass 'bout it. Two inches."

But even if his sight was out of line, a sharpshooter would compensate after a round or two. If that spot just to the right had been a bull's-eye, Henry Short would have drilled it every time.

He had outshot me and I knew he knew it. I muttered some excuse about too much liquor, which only made me angrier. "Who taught you to shoot?" I said after a while.

"Ol' Massuh Dan House now, he gib Henry dis ol' shootin arn, and Mist' Bill, he slip me a few ca'tridges, lemme use his mold so's to make mah own. Taughts mah own se'f but nevuh learnt too good, doan look like, cuz heah I gone and los' my wages on account I couldn't hit dat bottle—"

"HENRY!"

He peered about at the black trees as if uncertain where that shout had come from. "Dammit, boy! Don't you try to flimflam me with nigger talk!" But when I turned to point a warning finger at his face, the man was gone.

He must have had me in his rifle sights, against the firelight. I turned back slowly, saying, "Shoot, then. Or come out where I can see you."

Blackness surrounding. Tree frogs shrilling. A chunking thrash across the channel—tarpon or gator. The water was dead still. On its silver skin was a single small dark mole—that Christly bottle.

"Miss Jane!" I roared. "You *want* her, *Mis*-ter Short? You *want* her?" I waited. "She ever tell you about me, *Mis*-ter Short? How I had her all that summer?"

I could feel his finger on the trigger. I was in his sights. Exhilarated, I forced my breath against the inside of my chest to steel my hide against the burning fire of his bullet. When nothing happened, I gasped, "Come on! Finish it!"

Not a whisper. The black jungle masses all around had fallen still. Behind me, staring upward through the black shell dirt of his garden, the Frenchman's skull was a witness for the dead.

"FINISH IT!" I roared.

At the shot, the floating bottle popped and vanished from the surface. In its place a small circle blossomed for one moment only to vanish, too.

I awoke with a deep headache. He was there, making the fire. Moving stiffly in the iron calm of profound anger, we did not speak. An hour later when I let him off on the narrow walkway through the flooded forest guarding House Hammock, I wondered what I had asked of him, last night under the moon. What I had awaited. What I had wanted finished.

"Next time I tell you, *finish it*! You damn well finish it," I said. Neither of us knew what the hell I meant. He only nodded.

Near the walkway, a mangrove water snake, leaving no trace on the surface, crossed the sunlit ambers of the dead leaves on the creek bottom. Under red stilt roots blotched with white where coons had pried off oysters, the noses of feeding mullet pushed the surface. Henry touched his hat, I raised my hand halfway, but we remained silent, knowing we would never speak of this again.

GOVERNOR BROWARD

In the Glades, the drought of 1906 crowded the gators into the last pools and the slaughter was awful. "We have killed out that whole country back in there"—that's what Tant told Lucius at Caxambas. But in the spring rains, when the water level was unusually high, Bembery Storter's brother George accompanied some Yankees and their Indian guide on a three-week expedition, traveling by dugout from the headwaters of Shark River east to the Miami River, lugging along a two-thousand-pound manatee in a pine box. What they wanted with that huge dismal creature and whatever became of it I never learned, but that expedition was probably the last to cross the Florida peninsula on the old Indian water trails through Pa-hay-okee, which means "grassy river."

Napoleon Broward was the new governor, and his plan to conquer the Everglades for the future of Florida agriculture and development got under way with the christening of two dredges for the New River Canal, which would drain the lands south and east of Lake Okeechobee and extend the Calusa Hatchee ship canal to the east coast. With the band music, flags, and patriotic oratory so dear to the simple hearts of politicians, canal construction was begun on Independence Day, which Broward dedicated to the creation of rich farmland where only sawgrass swamp had lain before, including the auspicious planting of an Australian gum tree guaranteed to spread with miraculous speed across the swamps, sucking up water and transpiring it back into the air.

Our southwest coast was next in line for the blessings of modern progress, with the governor's good friend Watson taking the lead. My invitation to the statehouse in Tallahassee could show up in the mail almost any day. Meanwhile, I had months to wait for income on my harvest. Being in debt again, with little cash left for supplies and none for wages, I fired all hands except Sip Linsey and the hog fancier G. Waller; the rest were told to get their stuff and board the boat. At Fort Myers, with a loan from Hendrys, I paid half their wages and gave IOUs for the balance, which I hoped they would never dare come ask for.

On the way home, I stopped off at Pavilion Key to visit Netta's Minnie and Josie's little Pearl, which I did every chance I got, but brief visits were never enough for those two girls. "Daddy, how come you go away again each time you come back?" my red-haired Minnie said. I was happy she had forgiven me for that mistake two years before when I got drunk and took her home with me because I felt so lonesome. She never stopped wailing for her mama so I brought her back.

That summer, we took Sundays off to give our folks some rest. I near went mad waiting for Monday but kept myself busy with repairs, mended some tools. Lucius showed Kate and Laura how to fish for blue crabs off the dock, using a scoop net and old chicken necks rigged to a string. These spiky creatures with quick claws scared sweet little Ruth Ellen, who would turn to me, screeching, "Dada!" in delighted terror. Sometimes Jane Straughter would join in, and those three young females would spend hours at it; every crab caused a great shriek and commotion. Crabbing was done on laundry day. The bushel basketful was emptied into the big boiling cauldron after the clean clothes were fished out.

Lucius was delighted to show off the attractions of the Bend to our new family: it thrilled him as much as it did them when he pointed out our giant crocodile. Unlike Eddie, he had no use for Fort Myers and little interest in the Fort White farm. Lucius loved boats and the water, fresh and salt, river and sea. How it tickled me to see him grown so strong, this quiet boy who had started out in life so sickly that he very nearly died in the Indian Nations.

My son was reading all about old Florida history and the Calusa relics that Bill Collier had dug up at Marco. He was out to explore every piece of high ground in the Islands: he already knew he would like to be a historian or naturalist. Though he hunted and fished for the table, he refused to shoot the scattered plume birds or trap otter, no matter how often it was pointed out that others would take them if he did not. But raccoons were common and in cooler weather he would hunt them at night the way Tant taught him, using his new Bullseye headlamp for his torch.

Lucius was still dueling with Old Fighter, the giant snook Rob had hooked but lost in an oxbow up toward Possum Key. Out of loyalty, Lucius would claim that Old Fighter was still waiting for Rob back in the shadows, tending to the small fishes in the current that swept along under the mangroves. One day his bait would come drifting past, turning and glistening in that amber light, and—*whop!* In some way he felt that the triumph over Old Fighter would be Rob's vindication.

Sometimes at evening, sitting in the dark watching the moonlight on the river, we sang grand old songs—"Old Folks at Home" and "Massa's in de Cold, Cold Ground," also "Lorena" and "Bonnie Blue Flag." Because everyone else thought it too gloomy, I would wait until all had gone to bed before I sang "Streets of Laredo." What I lamented all alone, I did not know.

I had learned that old dirge in the Indian Nations, is what I told anybody who inquired, though the truth was I had picked it up in prison. Once it came into my head, I might be stuck with it for weeks.

One evening Kate asked if that old Texas song reminded me of my "cowboy days" out West. Knowing I had never been a cowboy, Lucius flushed and looked away, aware that his Papa had told a few tall tales to enhance his courtship of this girl of his own age. Even white lies made my son uncomfortable. He did not judge me, but his forbearance was a judgment, even so.

For the moment, Kate seemed happy at the Bend, forever giggling with her dear Laura, heads bent over some discovery or other. Yet she was so raddled and exhausted by the child that she had lost interest in our loving, falling asleep before I was half started—not that that stopped me. Manfully I would clamber on and toil away, feeling grotesque and lonely in my struggle. Sometimes her old fire got poked up and she came with me but more often not.

STILLBORN BABY

Nephew Julian had promised a year's work on the plantation, but after his experience at sea, he never really trusted me again. Perhaps he had heard some local stories, though I can't be sure, and perhaps he had alarmed his wife, for Laura would miscarry her first baby three months into term. In the midnight hours just before that happened, I sat up with her while Kate and Julian got some rest. There was high wind that night, the whole house sighed and rattled.

Not wishing to impose on this young woman (who had railed at me only a few weeks before), I asked if she might not prefer to be left alone. Too exhausted to spit up anything but the plain truth, she shook her head. "Mr. Watson, I'm ever so grateful for your company," she said. "Why I'm so afraid of darkness I cannot imagine. But I'm less afraid on these windy nights than on the still ones when everything seems suffocated and the only sound is the mosquitoes whining at the screens. That's when I fear there is something else out there, something that's waiting." She paused. "Something that will come for us, sooner or later."

"Well, my dear, something will come for us one day, that is quite true."

"Is it only death I fear? Because of my baby?" She seemed desperate. "I don't really know what I'm afraid of. I'm just scared."

"Not of me, I hope." I was doing my best to seem benign and reassuring.

Laura studied me, a little feverish. "Uncle Edgar, you make everyone feel lively, that's the ginger in you. But when you laugh, you sometimes seem to be laughing at our expense." She waited. "Does everything strike you as absurd?"

"Not everything."

Afraid she'd gone too far, she closed her eyes, perhaps to recoup her strength. I went to the window and peered out at the reflections of cold moonlight shattered by small wind waves on the river.

From behind me her voice came in a rush, "I'm frightened of a man who wears a gun under his coat in his own house out in the wilderness." When I said nothing, she continued bravely, "I come down sometimes when I can't sleep and there you are, still sitting in your corner on the porch, and all I can see is the glow of your cigar. Who are you waiting for?"

I returned to the bedside. I could have said I feared Wally Tucker's brother, who had sworn vengeance in Key West saloons, or one of the Bass clan from Kissimmee, or that dirty bounty-hunting Brewer who came here with the Frenchman years ago. But of course it was none of these I feared and I had no idea who I was waiting for. I only knew that one day he would come—the Man from the North, as I had always thought of him. Since Chatham River was so far away in the wild south, in a brackish labyrinth of swamp and muddy river at the farthest end of the American frontier, the one I awaited could scarcely come from any other direction. Anyway, it was no known man with a name.

To Laura this would make no sense so I said, "Jack Watson, maybe." I wanted to end this conversation since Kate, come to relieve my vigil, was in the door. "Long-lost brother," I added, when they looked confused. I said good night and went away.

At daybreak, weeping, Kate brought Laura's dead child, wrapped in fresh muslin. The young parents, shattered, thought he was a miscarriage, too early and too small for Christian rites, it seems Laura wanted me to handle it. I took the child from Kate and went outside. Upriver, I dug a little grave and kneeled and laid the bundle in and buried it, haunted by an image of that unborn babe at Lost Man's Key gasping for life in its mother's corpse under the current. Still kneeling, I exhumed the bundle, took it up. Lightly brushing off the dirt, I held it a few minutes before finding the resolve to part the muslin and confront the small blind shrunken face. Was this what Bet Tucker's unborn had looked like? Still on my knees, I lifted him toward daybreak in the eastern sky over the Glades, then bent and kissed the tiny cold blue brow, greeting and parting.

ADDISON TILGHMAN WATSON

In the winter of 1907, suddenly, Billy Collins died and our guests had to leave. To Kate's relief—she feared the thought of Chatham Bend without her Laura—we returned to Fort White with them and stayed on for the spring planting.

Laura dreaded moving in with Julian's family and who could blame her? Granny Ellen was sharp-tongued as ever, and as for my sister, she had shut herself away even before her husband's death, drifting deeper and deeper into shadow realms, leaving her younger children to Aunt Cindy's care. Offered a roof at my house, even that tight-wound nephew of mine appeared relieved. Dear Laura hugged me with fond gratitude. "Please try to forgive those awful things I said at Chatham, Uncle Edgar. Please watch out for that Jack Watson," she whispered. "Oh yes," I said. "My shadow brother." I tried to laugh at such a strange idea.

Kate Edna was near term with our second child. Knowing her Laura would be left behind, she missed Fort White even before the time came to leave for Chatham. More and more withdrawn, she barely put up with my attentions, devoting herself entirely to Ruth Ellen. Sometimes we did not touch each other for a fortnight.

When Addison Tilghman Watson came into the world, Mama assumed that the name commemorated Great-Uncle Tillman Watson at Clouds Creek; I did not disabuse her, being unable to explain the need to dedicate this fresh new bit of life to Cousin Selden.

Kate entreated me to let her stay a few months longer at Fort White, and so I returned to Chatham River by myself. In November, I met Kate and her babies at Fort Myers, where we spent Thanksgiving with the Langfords:

Walter and his railroad friend, Mr. John Roach, Carrie had written, were still discussing my participation at Deep Lake. At supper, Jim Cole regaled the company with his story about a case in which one black man killed another in cold blood in front of four eyewitnesses. The young defense lawyer assigned by the court worked hard for his first client but it was hopeless, an open-and-shut case. To his astonishment, the judge ignored the jury verdict, set his client free. Congratulated by the prosecutor, he protested, "Are you people crazy? It was cold-blooded murder! My client was guilty as all hell!" And the prosecutor took him by the arm and said, "Well, now, Lee Roy, this bein your first case and all, we didn't want our home boy to come up a loser. Anyways, it was only some ol' nigger, ain't that right?"

Jim Cole told a story well and everybody laughed except for Kate, who just looked baffled. Embarrassed by her unworldly ways, I got somewhat drunk and spoiled the evening, picking stupid arguments. When no mention was made of Deep Lake, I grew furious, humiliated, having stooped to getting ourselves invited to this house for the sake of nailing down that job. Cole and Langford would make my crude behavior their excuse to put aside any talk of my participation but the real reason was more gossip and ugly rumors. I could only suppose that one source was my son Eddie in Fort White, who was always the first one with the news, bad news especially.

Carrie and Kate were still awkward with each other, very stiff. My daughter had invited us to stay on for their family Christmas, but Kate said she felt unwelcome at the Langfords. Once at Chatham, however, she could not stop crying at the prospect of a lonely Christmas far from home. "I hate this endless river, these green walls!" she wept. "I hate that awful crocodile! *I hate this place!*" The girl had to be near hysteria to berate her husband in that disrespectful way.

All Kate wanted for Christmas was my promise to kill that log-like brute across the river (I tried but it was wary)—either that or take her "home" for a few months after the late winter harvest. Since I wished to go north anyway for the spring planting, I agreed. Kate was delighted, all the more so because her dear Laura would still be living in our house.

When the time came, I had misgivings. Young Wilson Alderman, whom I'd sent to Fort White to help Eddie on the farm, had returned to Chokoloskee to spend Christmas with his family. The Tolens had been defaming me while I was gone, he said, especially the shifty James, who had moved in with Sam at Aunt Tabitha's house to help keep an eye on the Myers nephews, who were still challenging her will. Alderman warned me that the situation might be dangerous. I told Kate nothing about this, of course. We returned to Fort White in April 1908.

CHAPTER 7

✦

CODE OF THE FRONTIER

In recent months, the fat widower Sam Tolen had taken bit and bridle off his drinking. He let his fields go, let his livestock run wild through the woods, and vilified all who passed before his eyes. Up there in that big empty house with its bad smells of rat droppings and rotted food, old hogs snuffled down the hall and half-wild chickens squawked and fluttered through the windows, and the Lord of the Manor was in his liquor morning, noon, and night. The summer previous his Tolen Team had told Sam they would quit for good the next time he showed up drunk on his own baseball diamond; his players never could agree on whether their manager behaved worse when they won or when they lost.

These days Sam's way of keeping in touch with his sharecroppers and neighbors was to accuse them of rustling his cattle. With eight hundred head or more roaming the woods, he never bothered to brand his calves, just ordered his tenants to pen up any strays and let the cows in at dusk to give them suckle. Being poor, Sam's croppers tried hard to oblige him, but he bullied them anyway, hollering a lot of stupid stuff about hanging rustlers from the nearest tree. Preacher Bethea and Josiah Burdett had both been threatened, also our well digger William Kinard, who was not even his tenant. There were days when Sam's only activity was to ride around on his big red horse and shout abuse, knowing that young Brother Mike would back him up.

Mike Tolen, now a county commissioner who worked hard to get along with everybody, did his best to pretend that his brother was harmless; he'd even wink at the victim of abuse over Sam's shoulder. Mike had tasted Sam's bile, too, but as a Tolen, he backed him no matter what, and any croppers who stood up to Sam were run right off the land.

One day, Sam rode over to the Junction to revile my friend Will Cox, just reined in his big red horse and bawled across the yard, hollering for all to hear how he'd never liked the looks of this horse-haired bastard. Will was a lanky handsome man with a hank of black hair like a horse's mane across his forehead, always calm, clean-shaven, and polite, but his wife Cornelia was a wilder breed. This day she came out and stood beside her man, arms folded high up on her chest, black eyes like chisels as she glared at this fat and filthy Tolen. Years before, when Jim Tolen got her simple sister in a family way, she notified her big mean brothers in Ocala County. When they came hunting him, Shifty Jim slunk back to Georgia. Now he was back.

Hearing Sam abuse his pa, Leslie came out onto the stoop hoisting Will's rifle. Leslie said, "My daddy ain't no bastard, mister. Git off that horse and down on your damn knees, tell him you're sorry."

Will told him, "Boy, you just cut out that damn cussin." He grabbed the gun barrel, turned it away, saying, "Mr. Tolen, you best git on down that road." Sam wheeled that bay horse and headed back until he was out of range, then reined up, shouting threats. He hated being run off by a boy, especially this boy on his own baseball team. Folks heard about it and they laughed, and from that day, Sam was spoiling for a showdown.

Will Cox was proud of Leslie but uneasy about Sam, knowing this would not be forgotten. Next year we'll have to find another lease, he told me.

Sam Tolen wasn't waiting till next year. A few days later, he came along on his red horse and caught Leslie at the railroad crossing at the Junction. Les was talking to his cousin Oscar Sanford, they were setting on the pile of cross-ties that Old Man Calvin Banks cut for the railroad company. Sam was so drunk he could hardly ride, but he wasn't so drunk he didn't notice that the Cox boy was unarmed. Oscar Sanford went scrambling down behind the pile, shouting at Les to jump, but Les did not even stand up, just spat his chaw in Sam's general direction and otherwise ignored him. Sam was trying to haul his shooting iron from the saddle scabbard, hollering how this ingrate kid had pulled a gun on him at Coxes so he aimed to exterminate him here and now in a fair fight. Probably thought Les would grovel for his life like any normal feller. He would not. Just lay back on the cross-ties with a long grass stem in his mouth, hands behind his head, to watch the show. Sam was too drunk to aim and hit the woods but not so drunk he would murder him in front of witnesses, Les figured.

Mike Tolen was nearby in the commissary of the turpentine company, where the first order of business was to cheat black workers and recoup every last cent of the payroll by foul means. Hearing the yelling, Mike came out and ran over to Sam's horse, where his brother was blood red in the face trying to free his gun from under his own leg. Not caring about base-ball, Mike never excused Leslie Cox the way others did. He thought Les was a mean bully and conceited and he wasn't wrong. Nevertheless, he talked Sam down, reminding him that there might be talk if he was to go and ex-ecute his own star pitcher. Finally Les stood up in no hurry and jumped down off the pile. He turned his back upon Sam Tolen and walked away, leaving Sam shouting. Borrowing Oscar Sanford's mule, he rode across the woodlots to my barn, told me the story, asked what he should do.

I liked Les well enough, I guess, because he was Will's boy and stuck up for his daddy. Not only that, he held a high opinion of a certain individual in the community at a time when most folks gossiped that this man was the killer of John Hayes and John Russ both. Therefore I sat him down like my own son, put my hand on his shoulder, and looked him in the eye, warning him he must not trust my advice because I was so prejudiced against Sam Tolen. I meant that, too, I was trying to be honest. "But I'll tell you this much, son," said I. "That fat feller is scared of you so he just might shoot you when you are not looking, call that self-defense."

"So I better shoot him first. That what you're tryin to tell me, Mister Ed?"

"No such thing. I'm pointing out the facts. A man has to face the facts, make his own decisions."

Leslie nodded. "Better shoot a man who's threatenin your life before he can shoot you. That's only natural, ain't it, Mister Ed? That's only justice."

"Every man has his own idea of justice, son. Every man does what he has to do."

Leslie's brow was furrowed up from trying to work out what I might have meant in the hope of discovering approval of a murder. When he pestered me again about the Belle Starr case out there in Injun Country, I mentioned how the victim's son Ed Reed had been hidden along the road at the same place his mother died. "Saw fit to shoot, I reckon."

Les wanted to know if I'd broken the frontier code by "naming my confederate" this way. First, we were not confederates, I retorted, and second, this so-called confederate was gunned down dead back in '97, so nothing I could do besides dig him up would disturb my confederate one little bit. Les nodded wisely. As for the frontier code, I snapped, the only frontier code I was ever to observe was dog eat dog and Devil take the hindmost.

My sour rejoinder wiped his frontier squint right off his face. I was merely tired of this boy and tired of this word game we were playing, but a person would have thought from his expression that I'd said there was no Jesus Christ nor even Jesse James. "I may have hinted that I witnessed the killing of Belle Starr," I said. "I never told you I took part. I do know this: Belle never saw it coming. That is a life lesson that will stand you in good stead: you don't play games with varmints, you exterminate 'em."

A pretty good case can even be made in praise of ambush. Men who never took a life and don't know what they're talking about may call it backshooting or cowardice but the dead man, who rarely sees who struck him down or suffers pain or terror, has a dignified death that few of us will ever get, in bed or out. Compared with mayhem of the common kind, bushwhacking is clean and it is efficient, which is why it is so often chosen by professionals. The bushwhacker, too—assuming he's not criminal or warped but just an ordinary feller trying to get by—will thank his Maker that he never had to face the rage and terror in that last doomed stare. Several killers I met in prison said the same: if it has to be done, do it quick and merciful, which means by surprise. It's a lot harder to shoot straight when that wild-eyed feller sees you and a lot more hazardous.

However, I did not explain this, not wishing him to get the wrong idea. Reminding him that he must take into account my own prejudices in this matter, I spoke more generally and philosophically, endorsing the old Border principles of defending one's rights by dealing forcefully with insult or injustice, threat or humiliation, no matter the cost or consequence to life or limb—the right to defend one's honor by main force when force seemed appropriate and by cunning where force would not prevail, since there was no honor in defeat, however gallant, and no dishonor in avenging that defeat, however cruelly. No matter what moralists might preach, bending one's neck in defeat was the sole dishonor. Lying, craftiness, so-called betrayal—all these became acceptable and even praiseworthy when they were the sole means to defend the honor of family or clan.

These noble lessons, faithfully learned at the knee of Ring-Eye Lige, were lost on Leslie—or rather, this was too much thought for him to handle all at once. He cleared his head by closing one nostril with his fingertip and blowing its contents out the other, then got straight to the point. "Tuesday mornings on his way to Ichetucknee, he goes right past that fence jamb down yonder by our cabin, know the one? All thick with brambles just like where you was tellin me about in Belle's case." He watched my expression. "You reckon that's too close to home?"

I sighed with awe. "That's just what's so ingenious, Les. Nobody would ever imagine that any man would be so idiotic as to settle a famous feud by setting up the ambush in his own front yard." To ease his suspicion, I added quickly, "That's why the judge had to conclude that I was innocent in the Belle Starr case: *Hell no, Ed Watson never done it! We know Ed! He just ain't dumb enough to shoot her so damned close to his own house. Might be stupid hicks but we ain't so stupid we don't know he knows we know he ain't so stupid as all that!*"

At Leslie's stare, I had to laugh. However, not wishing to appear facetious, I wiped that mirth off my own face and frowned in respect for the serious nature of the situation. "Mind you," I continued, "Sam Tolen is not what you'd call popular and nobody is going to miss him. And even if Mike accuses you, your daddy is good friends with Sheriff Purvis, so . . ."

"So . . . ? You are advisin me . . . ?"

I lifted both palms and withdrew from the discussion. "Son, don't put words into my mouth. I'm *not* advising you. I'm only saying that a man must do what in his heart of hearts he knows is right." Some way these words seemed to contradict the wisdom imparted earlier but Les was too intent on his own plan to make such nice distinctions.

"Well, what I mean—well heck, now, Mister Ed, what would *you* do? In your heart of hearts is what I'm talkin about."

"Depends. But if I thought an enemy—naming no names—was out there gunning for me, I reckon I could find it in my heart of hearts to put a stop to him."

Leslie fell quiet. Uncertain, still dissatisfied, he flicked his jackknife at a pinecone on the ground. What he was really asking was, Would Mister Ed back him up? In my belief, he had already made up his mind to kill Sam Tolen. "I'm kind of new at this," he said, uneasy. Even his ball cap was askew, sticking out to one side over his ear. In that moment, for the last time in his life, Leslie Cox looked like a boy.

THE BIG RED HORSE

I took Reese with me. Black Frank was his own man except when he was my man; in the end he would do what I told him. Not that he was glad to be there. He had no use for Sam Tolen—there wasn't a black man for miles around who did—he only protested that the Cox kid's quarrel "ain't none of my nigger business, never will be." He refused to commit murder for another man. Of course not, I told him, this was Leslie's business. All Frank had to do was shoot the horse.

Frank was aching to retort, *What about you? What's in this for you?* This was not wise so he burst out angrily, "Why shoot that horse? That's a good horse. I wish I'd of had that big red horse when we was ridin out of Arkansas."

If Eddie Reed had shot Belle's stallion instead of figuring he would inherit him, I thought later, there would have been time to scratch away those boot prints.

At the last minute Leslie showed up with his mama, who hated the Tolen brothers worse than anybody. Frank groaned to me that women were bad luck, he was all set to back out, and I was, too: nobody else was supposed to know a thing about this. But like it or not, Cornelia knew about it, so finally I persuaded Les that this was men's work, not fit for a lady, and offered his mother my respects along with my earnest wish that she go home. I never asked Will then or later if he had known what his wife and son were up to.

Leslie looked drawn, watching her go. "How come it ain't you doin the shootin, if you know so much? You think I'm some kind of a dumb kid? Think I don't know you want this worse'n I do?" But afraid I would walk away, he only muttered this, then let it go, nervously checking the loads in my double-barrel.

I was suffering mixed feelings, I admit. First of all, after those Tuckers, I had put away my gun. Second, I had known Sam Tolen most of my life and we'd had some fun before we had hard feelings. However, it was too late to back out now.

In the corner jamb where the fence rails joined to make a barricade of thorn and vine, we crouched in a kind of cave under the brambles. There we waited near an hour before the squeak of buggy axles came down the road. It was a fine and bright May morning and early sun streamed through the new small leaves. I heard a thrush—like a child's sweet question, as my Charlie once observed, pausing to listen in our cabin not a hundred yards from where we skulked right now. All around, the spring chorus resounded strangely loud and clear, and I wondered if Sam's hairy ears ever heard these woodland melodies of his last morning—thick-bodied Sam, slapping his reins on the rump of his red horse as he rattled down the track from Herlong Lane toward Ichetucknee Springs, still belching on his burly breakfast of hominy and hog.

I doubt he heard anything at all. Half stupefied by his long evening of drink, lulled by the pounding rhythms of the big bay's hooves, the powerful workings of its dung-flecked haunches and its fly-switch tail, poor old Sam would be as deaf to birdsong as he was to the stillness of the white road where three men lay in wait and his dull gaze would not pick out the amorphous shapes obscured by rails and brambles. So I hoped. I hoped his Baptist Lord would show him that much mercy.

Hearing those hoof shots and the clicking of the wheels, Reese raised his barrel to the rotting rail under the vines, deep-creased black finger on the trigger; a moment later, the whole morning quaked at the crash of gunfire. The red horse shied and shrieked and fell, all within the echo of the shot as the buggy climbed the fallen horse and overturned, pitching the driver out onto the road. At the blast, Sam must have grabbed his shotgun because he came up with it as he struggled to his knees, mouth wide in a black hole. His eyes were huge. Unable to believe his end had come, he tried to holler. He still had time because Leslie Cox had frozen on the trigger.

With a shrill yelp, Sam floundered sideways to get behind the thrashing horse as he swung his gun up, but even before he got it to his shoulder, he despaired, flinging it away like something burning. On his knees, he raised his hands.

"*Shoot!*" Frank ordered Leslie, furious. Frank had been furious before he got there, wanting no part of this damned business, but no matter how often I explained this to Cox later, the black man would never be forgiven for that contemptuous order although it did the trick. "Right then is when Mist' Sam Tolen knowed he was a goner," Frank reflected later. "That's when I looked away. Ain't decent to watch a man afeared as that. Just plain embarrassin."

My old adversary and nemesis had sought and found me through the thorns and rails. Too scared to speak, he whimpered like a pup. Those last whimpers burned a hole into my heart, and I cursed Leslie for it, after all my warnings that these things must be done quick or not at all. In that instant he pulled the trigger and Sam's face ruffled up bright red, bug eyes obliterated. Spun half around and down by a charge of buckshot at close range, he gave only a few quick short kicks as if trying to run while lying there face down. The body sprawled on the clay road, snuffling up blood-spattered dust like a slaughtered hog.

With a victory whoop like some wild Indian, Leslie jumped out on the road and gave the body a second barrel in the back of the head, almost beheading it. That second barrel made no sense, just made a mess, and Leslie backed away, squinching his nose in disgust. "See how scairt he was? He shit his pants!" But the dead man might never have had time to soil himself if Cox had done his part.

"You sure that isn't you?" I snarled. Hearing Reese snicker, this fool kid turned on him. Reese saw it coming, knocked the twin barrels up. "Wouldn't try that, boy, if I was you," Reese said. "Least not till you reload."

All three of us were enraged, isn't that peculiar? Why I was so angry I don't know, but it was much more than annoyance at Les Cox, who was screeching now, fighting back tears. He looked on the point of passing out and was incensed that we could see that. "You and your fuckin jokes! Got a dead man layin here in his own shit and blood and you're still *jokin*? Wasn't you never taught no common decency?"

I had to grin at that, and Frank did, too, but Cox burst into tears of rage mixed with his fear and relief that it was over. His feelings tumbled around together and got in one another's way like new blind puppies. But even while he wept, this fool was jamming shells into the chambers. When Reese wrenched the weapon away from him, he yelled, "Fuckin nigger! Gimme that fuckin gun!"

Reese was an outlaw and he knew his business. He emptied Leslie's gun and Sam's gun, too, then stripped Sam's wallet and good boots. When he slung the boots for Leslie to catch, our young killer went pale, as if these humble sweat-stunk relics of the dead man's days had brought home the revelation that his life had taken a sharp turn and perhaps not for the better. He knocked Sam's yellow pigskin wallet from Frank's hand.

"I ain't no fuckin vulture," Leslie snarled.

"You doan take his stuff, then nobody gone be huntin for no robbers.

They be huntin for his best-knowed enemy. Tha's you. Mos' likely they will do that anyways but no sense makin it easy for 'em." He held the wallet out a second time, raising his voice a little. "Take the money, boy, an' drop the wallet. We got no business standin round here on this road."

"Don't you go givin me no nigger orders!" But he snatched the wallet, picked the money out, then hurled it at the body. Seeing Sam's wallet bounce onto the road, I had the thought—more like a pang—that if his carcass would just come to and sit up, I could probably make Fat Sammy laugh about the way his career as a rich plantation owner had panned out.

"Show some respect," I said. "That's a man laying there."

"*Was* a man, you mean!" But Leslie's jeer was fractured and his eyes looked moist again. Feeling injured that his partners had no respect whatever for his dangerous deed, committed in the name of family honor, he was fairly quivering with self-pity.

That is how Sam Tolen, quiet, washed, and well-behaved, happened to follow his loved ones into Oak Lawn Cemetery. To keep up appearances, I went, too, accompanied by Kate and Granny Ellen. As befitted the occupant who had administered the money, my mother noted, Aunt Tabitha's stone loomed over the lesser markers, chaperoning her daughter and her lowlife son-in-law even in death.

SHERIFF DICK WILL PURVIS

Mr. Woodson Tolen of Andersonville, Georgia, as administrator of Sam's estate, gave power of attorney to his son James. Apparently Woodson did not think that our county commissioner was bright enough to take over the looting of the plantation, and knowing Mike, I'd have to say that this judgment was correct.

Jim Tolen hustled back from Georgia and moved into the manor house like he was born to it. After the funeral, he stayed on for the fight to keep the Myers Plantation in the Tolen name, wearing his rented funeral suit in court. Of the three brothers, including the deceased, I liked this one least. I treated Jim Tolen like a shard of slag, too base and worthless to be noticed, yet too mean and sharp-edged not to keep an eye on.

Being less greedy than his brothers, our county commissioner had no illusions about the moral worth of the Tolen claim on other people's property but he was loyal to Sam and that was that. After the burial I went up to Mike and offered my hand, saying I was sorry. Tolen flushed under his beard and refused my hand with everybody watching. He said loud enough for folks to hear, "I know who killed my brother, Watson. They will pay."

He knew no such thing, not for a fact. But by spurning my hand for all to see, the dead man's brother had accused me publicly without evidence, flouting the most cherished principle of justice. I said to him in a low voice, "I'll make allowance for your grief but you'd better be more careful who you threaten."

Jim Tolen was a fox-eared feller, born to overhear. "You're takin his words personal, ain't that it, Watson?" Indeed I was, and for good reason. Yet in showing my anger, I had made a bad mistake. I had helped Mike set in motion something that could not be stopped. This business could only finish badly.

Mike Tolen went to Sheriff Purvis in Lake City and filed a complaint against William Leslie Cox and both his parents. The evidence was entirely circumstantial—the public dispute at the Junction between Leslie and the deceased and the faint boot prints of two men, also a woman's prints, that Mike had discovered in the fence jamb near Sam's body. However, those prints had been rained away and Will Cox had beaten Mike to his friend Purvis. The sheriff reminded Commissioner Tolen that he too had visited the scene and that he had found no evidence against the Cox boy. No offense, he added, but from what he had been told about Mr. Tolen's brother, almost any man in the south county might have lent a hand, so the sensible thing for you to do, Commissioner, would be to go on home, get a bite to eat and a good night's sleep, and forget the whole damn business. From the look of him, Sheriff Dick Will Purvis had resorted to his own remedy on numerous occasions, in the simple-hearted faith that food and a lot of it would cure anything.

The commissioner protested with some heat that the whole south county knew that Dick Will Purvis was a crony of Will Cox from old Lake City days, besides being a jackass and a kiss-ass. Dick Will promptly kissed Mike's ass, saying, "Well, since you feel that way, Commissioner, I will get that Cox boy in here, ask a few questions." Leslie came in and informed the sheriff that he was otherwise engaged on the day in question. That being the case, the sheriff had no choice but to let him go.

Before leaving the sheriff's office, Leslie mentioned that while in High Springs on the day following the murder, he had heard that a nigger known as Frank was attempting to peddle the dead man's gun and boots. Whether he said that to avenge the way Frank Reese had spoken to him or simply in some fool attempt to deflect suspicion from himself, Leslie must have known that any black man implicated in the killing of a white might very well get lynched before his trial. But implicating was a very stupid move on Leslie's part, since Frank could give plenty of firsthand testimony that might get Cox hung.

Reese was arrested two weeks later although Mike knew he was not the man he wanted. And yet he went along with Purvis, hoping "the nigger" might be made to talk, so I went up there and informed Purvis that my hired man had spent that day with me. "That make him innocent or guilty?" one deputy sang out, and the lawmen laughed and I did, too, to show I knew a good joke when I heard one. Frank was jailed while awaiting his June trial, which was very fortunate for his own safety.

As a tough ex-convict, Reese kept his head when the deputies kicked him black and blue or rather black and purple, in poor Frank's case. They pissed and spat on him, reviled him, told him they aimed to cut his balls off, hang him slow, but if he confessed, they might not torch him first. And Frank just hunkered down and took it like he was too ignorant and scared to understand, rolled his eyes back like a minstrel darkie, hollered *yassuh, nosuh, nevuh knowed nuffin about nuffin, nosuh, yassuh.* He plain wore 'em out. When it came to nerve as well as brains, Black Frank had a big jump on Leslie Cox.

Les was drinking too much, shooting his mouth off, though he always claimed he never knew why Frank had been arrested. He was too excited for his own damned good, not to mention ours. Still unable to believe what he had done, he would come over to my place and hoot and crow in glee, somersaulting in the dirt behind the barn just to remind me how that big bay horse came crashing down with the red buggy humping up over its haunches, the iron shoes racketing against the buckboards, and Tolen staring, on his knees in that white dust. "Looked like a fuckin woodchuck!" Leslie whooped—one of the few times I ever heard him laugh out loud.

Next day, he acted out Sam's death for May Collins and her brothers and young Jim Delaney Lowe, telling them he'd got the story from "that nigger was mixed up in it." The Collins boys, though not mourning Sam Tolen, were horrified by the queer pleasure Leslie took in every detail and realized at once that he must have been involved. Their testimony would help get him indicted a year later. ·

Naturally Les claimed I had put him up to the bad deed he was so proud of. When it came to killing, he confided in his cousin Oscar Sanford, Les Cox sure went to the right teacher. "Mister Ed, you damn near got me hung!"— he'd shout that at me as a joke. But Leslie wasn't good at jokes and his eyes never fit his smile. If a June bug flew into his eye, you would hear the *smack* of it; those eyes were hard as shiny stones.

Will and Cornelia spoiled their oldest boy because he had good looks and stood up for his family; the community overlooked his arrogance and spite because of his exploits on the baseball diamond. All his life he had gone unpunished for his fits of meanness—killed by kindness, as my mother used to say—and maybe his friend Mister Ed had indulged him, too. True, the killing could be seen as self-defense, for he'd been threatened, and it was a public service, too: Sam had pissed on everybody. But by agreeing to stand by this boy, I might have let him think that his act was justified, and I guess I knew better even if he didn't.

"Double-crossing Frank wasn't too smart," I told him. "What if he talks? Better tell the sheriff it was a case of mistaken identity. Maybe remind him that most nigras look alike."

I warned Reese, too, in the course of a jail visit. "Frank, you can't implicate him without implicating yourself. You will get lynched." He only grunted cynically, looking away. Frank assumed he had no chance whatever. "Instead of being hung lawfully," I added, sad to see such bitterness in a negro person. However, he was in no mood for my jokes.

I made Cox back off his Reese story for his own good. Manfully, he told Sheriff Purvis, "I might could been mistook there, Shurf Dick. I been thinkin I would surely hate to see a innocent man hung, nor a nigger neither." Although Purvis had been quite content to make Frank Reese the scapegoat, he had nothing to show to a grand jury, not even a lynch mob in the street demanding justice, since most folks figured that, with Sam's death, justice had been served about as well as anyone could reasonably expect. To hell with it, said the judge, and sent Reese home, doubtless assuming that the Tolens and the Russ boys would attend to him.

Frank and I sat back against my barn and celebrated his triumph over bigotry with a jug of moonshine. Impressed by how sensibly and well my old partner had behaved, I sent for Jane Straughter and reminded her that she owed me a big favor, having caused me so much unjust aggravation over John Russ's death. Winking, I said I would not hold it against her anymore if she let Frank Reese hold it there instead. Marry him common-law or any way she wanted.

Jane Straughter did not smile. She liked Frank well enough, I guess, but moving in with him was quite another matter. The Robarts-Collins clan would not like it either, she reminded me, and anyway I had no right to coerce her. By the end of it, she was spitting mad. "You're done with me so you're handin me along to your coal-black nigger!"

Meanwhile, Kate Edna, scared by her own persistence, was plaguing me for my opinion on who killed Sam Tolen.

"I did not kill Sam Tolen, Kate. How often must I tell you that?"

"Not often," she said, ambiguous. "Just reassure me." She crept over in the bed. "Tell me you love me." "Love!" I exclaimed, pretending astonishment that she would speak of such a thing when discussing murder. "You suspect your husband of cold-blooded murder, and then you say, 'Tell me you love me'?" Frightened, she burst into tears, and I relented and took her in my arms. I have never figured out how women work but I do know that their skin color has no significance. Black or white, every last one is pretty pink on the inside and they are all impossible.

Jane Straughter still helped around the house but would scarcely look at me. Seeing Jane and Frank together, I wondered if she ever thought about Henry Short, and one day, drinking in my corner, I asked just for the fun of it if she still missed him. Jane came around on me so fast that I threw my hand up, thinking she might fly straight for my eyes. In her distress, she had gone so pale that the tiny freckles in that delicate skin beneath her eyes stood out in points.

When I give in to that urge to stir up trouble, there comes an even stronger urge to drink more and behave worse. Jane's fiery ways, so different from Kate Edna's, hit me almost as hard as in the past, and before I knew it, I had grasped her wrist and told her fervently how pretty she looked and how very much I needed her. Still in my grasp, she gazed out the window at my wife, sailing across the sun-shined yard, pinning up washing. "Supposin I was to tell Mis Kate what was done to a young virgin girl at Chatham Bend?" she whispered. "Supposin I told your black man what his boss was up to?"

Releasing her, I banged my chair down hard. "Missy," I said, "I don't like threats, remember?"

Jane retreated into nigger talk as quick as our house lizard changes from leaf green to dry stick brown. "I'se sorry, Mist' Edguh, I sho' doan mean to go threatnin nothin, nosuh." And she ran out, sobbing. After that, she stayed mostly out of sight.

A few weeks later, I was cleaning up for supper when Kate Edna sent Jane out to the well with some hot water and a towel. When I asked how she was enjoying married life, she splashed hot water roughly into my blue basin. "Long time ago, back yonder in the Islands, you ast me how a light-skinned gal might feel, passin for white. You kin ast me now how that same gal feels, passin for black."

COMMISSIONER D. M. TOLEN

When our paths crossed, Mike Tolen looked right past me. Even when I greeted him, he never spoke. Mike understood why others might have wished to kill his brother, and perhaps by now he had lost some of his lust for justice, but sooner or later, Cox's big mouth would force him toward revenge. In this very dangerous situation, I warned Leslie to shut up. It was too late.

One day in Fort White, in the Terry store, Mike burst out, yes, he knew who had killed his brother, and no, he did not aim to let the matter die. But in truth, what could he do? He knew better than to challenge me in a fair fight and could not pick me off through those high windows of my house even if he got past my dogs. Mike's only choice was to waylay his suspects, one at a time. And knowing how unlikely it was that those suspects would wait for that to happen, he would have to act as soon as possible, for his own safety, before someone repeated what he'd said in Terry's store. But of course we had heard already and he knew that, too.

I felt sorry for Mike because he had no way out. He had no experience or skill with arms and was therefore no match for Cox and Watson, separately or together.

Leaving the commissary, I took Mike's elbow. I had no quarrel with him, I murmured, but because he had made threats, I had to warn him of the consequences of talking dangerously. He said, "I am not talking dangerously. Who gave you that idea?" And I said, "Just about everybody, Mike. You are talking too much and you are painting us into a corner." "Is that a threat?" he demanded. "You know exactly what it is," I told him. But he had nowhere to turn, I didn't either, we were trapped. "I'm sorry," I said, "but you'd best leave this county and go home to Georgia."

He only thrashed like a hooked fish. "*You* leave, Watson!" he protested. I shook my head, he shook his, we turned away. That's how we left it.

Frank Reese would not throw in with us. "No mo', Mist' Jack," he said. "I done retired." He flatly refused to work with Cox, who had nearly got him lynched. Anyway, he had his Jane, had his own cabin. He wasn't a field hand anymore but a tenant farmer, as close as he had ever come in life to being his own man, so he didn't want to know one thing about this business. He'd be out in his field tomorrow morning, same as always, turning over the Lord's good ground and getting set to plant his corn and cotton. Said, "I finally come to rest in life, I found a little corner of the earth where I belong, so I'm puttin all them bad ol' times behind me." Frank was grateful to me for his new life. I could have coerced him but I didn't want to.

Leslie bitched, "We got to get that fuckin Reese mixed up in this so's he won't talk." I shook my head. "Unlike you, Frank keeps his mouth shut." To save face, he challenged me: "Well, this time, Mister Ed, let's you be first to shoot, case you're fixin to hang back like you done last time." I shrugged as if to say, All right, but it was not all right. I had nothing against Mike Tolen. I had assumed Cox would want to be the shooter.

Mike Tolen had his mailbox at the Junction. In the past year, with the slash pine lumbered off, the turpentine works and commissary had closed down and Will Cox, with his lease canceled by Tolens, had moved his family across the county line into Suwannee. The Junction was now an empty corner going back to woods. Near the huge live oak was a sagging shed bound up in vines and creepers. I hid inside while Leslie climbed into the oak and stretched along a heavy limb, ready to take Tolen from another angle. Mike having brought this on himself, I was resigned to it, but I did not like it; I had to draw breaths deep into my belly to stay calm.

Tolen came down the road a little late, his shotgun over his left arm and a letter in the other hand. Nearing the shack, he slowed his step and his eyes crisscrossed the lane, scanning the trees. I set myself, took a last deep breath, and drew a careful bead on his broad forehead; remembering Sam, I wanted to make sure Mike never knew what hit him.

Leslie claimed later that I held my fire too long, same way he did with Sam: in my belief, he fired first out of buck fever and greed, wanting the credit for this killing, too, maybe even wanting to be known as the most dangerous local desperado. Well before Mike Tolen reached his mailbox, Cox threw a double-ought slug into his chest, whacked his shirt red. Mike's Sears mail-order flittered off as he spun backwards and the echo ricocheted away through the cold March trees. To this day I hear the ringing in my ears and the ugly thump of that man's head as it struck the ground. I stepped onto the road and that same second I damn near had my head torn off, that's how close Leslie's second load rushed past my ear. Knocked to one knee, I hollered in a rage but there was no stopping him, he was already reloading. That kid put two more rounds into the body before he sprang down from his limb, gun barrel smoking.

In the silence, the screams of Sally Tolen at the cabin flew down that road from a quarter mile away, pierced by the shriek of jays and the cries of children.

Blood was welling in Mike Tolen's mouth. The morning sun was still reflected in those eyes staring past my boots. I bent and closed them, mumbling something, but to pray seemed sickeningly insincere and I could not finish. "That's *one* sumbitch ain't goin to back-shoot us," said Leslie's voice, thick with strong feelings. He was wildly excited, trying not to show it. "Shoots pretty good," he told me with his lip-curl grin, slapping his gun stock. In his own weird ceremony of triumph, he rose on his toes, up and down in a slow prance, circling the body.

"The Ichetucknee Kid," I said, despising this awful pride in a point-blank shot.

Beyond Mike's cabin, out toward the Banks place, light flashed and shimmered on the turning wheels of a farm wagon coming south down the white road. Under tall hardwoods of the forest edge, the flashing danced from sunlight into shade, sunlight again. Whoever drove that wagon— probably Calvin Banks—was not close enough to identify the killers, but he would be shortly, and Mills Winn, the mailman, might show up at any time.

" 'Leslie the Kid'—that what you said?" Cox was still grinning. "Go home," I said. "Keep your damned mouth shut this time." Taking back my shotgun, slipping the unused revolver back into my coat, I ran for the woodlot where my horse was tethered and jammed the shotgun back into its scabbard. Staying well clear of the roads, I galloped through the pine-woods: on the thick needle bed, the horse left scarcely a trace.

I felt weak as a runny egg, older than dirt. Knowing I had not pulled the trigger was no comfort. I had taken aim and intended to fire and was ready to finish him with the revolver, too, had that been necessary. There was no way to absolve myself of this one, not if I lived for another hundred years, and yet it was true: he had brought it on himself.

The revolver. Sensing the absence of its weight, I grabbed at my belt and pockets. My heart dropped to my guts, needles of fear raked at my temples. It was too late to hunt back along the trail. By now the postman would have come along and found Mike's body. I left the woods, headed out across Reese's field at a flat gallop.

That morning Jane had sent Frank out with a fresh shirt, sky blue against the dark brown of the loam. He had surely heard those shots over toward the Junction and he knew whose horse was pounding down on him right now. He never slowed or looked around but gazed fixedly at his mule's bony rump as it shifted along between the traces. He refused to see me. Not until something thumped into the furrow right behind him did he stop the mule—*Whoa up dar!*

"Throw some dirt over that gun," I called, cantering past. "Mark the place and keep on going." Still he stared straight ahead. But over my shoulder, I saw him kick clods of earth over the weapon. Then he took up his reins and slapped the mule's rump hard—*Giddyap!*—and kept on coming, man and beast, alone on the bare brown landscape. I even remember the spring robins drawing worms from his new furrows, and the chirrups the birds made as they took flight across the field toward the woods.

. . .

At my sister's house, Julian and Willie and Jim Delaney Lowe were butchering a hog out by the smokehouse. I rode right up on 'em, scattering the dogs. "If anyone comes asking questions, boys," I said, "I was right here in this yard since early morning, showing you the best way to dress that hog. I left for home just a short while ago, that clear?" I had been helping Billy Collins's family since he died in the previous winter so this all made sense.

"We heard shots over yonder," Julian said. My nephews were scared and unhappy, knowing I had come from that direction. Julian was looking at the empty scabbard. I pointed at his face. "Is that clear, Julian? I was here dressing that hog when you heard those shots. That is all you boys need to know or say to anybody."

Sullen, they stood mute. Their friend Jim Delaney Lowe stared at his boots. Granny Ellen came to the kitchen door, then young May was in the window, waving, and Minnie's pale face appeared over her shoulder. Seeing her brother talking with her sons, Minnie waved, too, but my bright-eyed little mother only watched me. "Tell them what I said," I told the boys. I rode toward home.

Carrying fresh bread in a basket, Julian's Laura left my house as I rode up. Her nervous glance in the direction of the Junction told me those shots had been heard here, too. Though surprised to see me at this time of day, Laura's instinct told her not to inquire. Scarcely waving, she kept right on going.

CHAPTER 8

✦

THE TRIALS

Sheriff Purvis in Lake City had been notified and a local crowd soon gathered at the Junction. When the law arrived that afternoon, bloodhounds were turned loose all around the mailbox. The early spring weather being cold and dry, the dogs lost my scent where I swung into the saddle, but Deputy R. T. Radford, fooling along a ways tracking the hoof prints, saw the glint on the woodland floor of what turned out to be a .38 revolver, fully loaded, not two hundred yards from the crime scene. Very few new Smith & Wessons had found their way into the backcountry, and it was known I had one. What Radford yelled back to the posse was, "I got Watson's pistol!" So much for the presumption of innocence until found guilty.

"Where's Watson's nigger and the Cox boy?" others said. "Weren't them two supposed to been in on it the last time?" So Purvis went to Sanfords' place across the county line where the Coxes were now living with their kin, and Will Cox told him, "My boy Les been plowin yonder by them woods all day. We heard some shootin over east so Les reckoned he'd better go investigate." Asked where Les might be right now, his father said he didn't rightly know. And his old crony Sheriff Purvis said, "Don't make no difference, Will, your word is good enough for me." That being all the defense Les needed, he was never charged in the death of D. M. Tolen.

On the way to my place, the posse saw Reese working in the field and four of 'em rode over there to pick him up. This bunch was under Dr. Nance, who had always hung around the law and later took over Purvis's job as sheriff. By pure bad luck, one of their horses stumbled in the furrows when its iron shoe struck metal, and the man dismounted and dug out the loaded gun. Nance ordered Frank to walk on over with his hands behind his head. Shown the shotgun, Frank said, "Please suh, us'ns got us a buck deer been usin in that field edge yonder—"

"That why you buried it?" Nance cuffed him. "Ain't that Watson's gun?" They marched him over to the road, hands high.

At my place, "Mr. Watson met them in good humor," according to what I read next day in the Lake City paper. If that meant I was amiable, I guess I was, not knowing they already had both of my weapons. Kate and I stood on our porch as armed men lined up along my fence down on the road. Everything would be all right, I told her, hushing her questions.

Soon Josiah Burdett came up the hill, young Brooks Kinard behind him. Joe Burdett said, "Mornin, Edna," but he never glanced her way, that's how close he watched me. "Let's go," he said.

"You're barking up the wrong tree, Joe," I said, holding my temper. The boy's knuckles clenched white on his gun. However, Burdett meant business and would shoot me if he had to, though he'd never shot a man in all his life. As for the Kinard kid, he would do whatever Joe did, and he had good instincts. Without being told, he moved back and to the side where he had a clear shot in case I tried something.

The posse took me to the same back room in Terry's store where the late Sam Tolen had invited me to meet so he could shoot me. Reese sat on the floor against the wall. Hands cuffed behind and a murderous expression.

The Terrys were among the few folks in this section who'd been friends with Tolens so I was hooted by that dogless family when the deputies stood me on my feet and handcuffed me to my field hand for the train ride. I spoke right up, declaring that our great republic was in mortal peril when our own lawmen became lawbreakers, arresting citizens without warrants. By God, I would file a formal protest with my friend Governor Broward! Also, Jim Crow law had been Florida law for at least three years now, so how could they ride me handcuffed to a nigger when our trains were segregated?

"Principle of the damn thing. Nothing personal," I whispered to my companion, who was still brooding over my role in his arrest.

"Mus' be dat 'Merican justice you was speakin about."

"I have my good name to think about. Law's the law, you know."

"That's what she is, okay. Leastways for white folks." His sulk was easing by that time, he seemed resigned. I tried to cheer him: we had come through worse than this in Arkansas. But in truth the law worried me less than the cold attitudes of these neighbors. The men scarcely glanced at us—not a good sign, because when men decide to hang someone, they can be shy about looking the doomed man in the eye. This is not true of their females. The Fort White women peering in through Terry's dirty windows looked inquisitive and mean as broody hens.

By the time we were shoved aboard the Lake City train, it was plain these local folks had their own plan. Even the deputies were irritable and nervous. Sure enough, a crowd awaited us at Herlong Junction. My window was just opposite those mailboxes where Mike Tolen died and people were walking all around the dark blot on the dusty road where he had lain. What my neighbors were after was a good old-fashioned hanging from that live oak limb where Leslie Cox had lain. To behold a mob thronged with the gargoyle faces of your erstwhile friends, brandishing weapons and crying for your head, is enough to sadden any man, give him indigestion, too. A metal taste coated my mouth and my guts quaked and loosened. I was able to hide my fear from Frank as long as I didn't speak, but I didn't feel like joking anymore. He didn't, either. He had closed his eyes because like me he was praying every second for that train lurch that might carry us safe away.

None too soon, Sheriff Dick Will Purvis was backing up the steps: we heard him hollering, "Now come on, boys! Don't go takin my prisoners here at the whistle stop, makin a damn monkey out of your sheriff! We'll see you fellers up the track a little ways!" At that, my fear seized me so violently that I felt sick. The train creaked and jolted, stopped again for no good reason. Finally it overtook the crowd, which was streaming along the track, whooping and hollering, and click-clacked ahead a little ways to the wood rack there at Herlong, where the fireman would pile split logs on the caboose for the wood-burning engine. That was the wood stacked up by Calvin Banks, the same stack Cox had perched upon that day when Sam Tolen threatened to kill him—the very place where this whole business got started in the first place and was about to end.

We didn't fool ourselves. "Dammit, Frank," I said. "I did you a bad turn and I am sorry." The black man nodded, saying quietly, "Yessuh. We got us some bad luck dis time, dass fo' sure."

But Purvis was yelling at the engineer to keep on going. With a long whistle and a lonesome wail like a falling angel, the train lurched forward. Dreadful howls arose, rocks whacked the cars, a deputy yanked me down away from the cracked window.

Once the train was in the clear, I managed a smile, congratulating Sheriff Purvis on reestablishing law and order and safeguarding the rights of prisoners by thwarting illegitimate mob rule. And the sheriff grinned right back. "We don't need no mob," he said, "cause we got all the evidence we need to hang you legal." The sheriff confessed that his sympathies were with the crowd but he'd felt obliged to stick to his sworn duty because Will Cox was my friend and I was paid up in my taxes.

"Also, you just might have heard that E. J. Watson has a good friend in the statehouse."

The sheriff nodded wisely. "That could be."

Not a word was mentioned then or later about Leslie. Purvis never even brought him in for questioning.

The train stopped at Columbia City to pick up two deputies and a third suspect, John Porter, arrested on suspicion due to some dispute with the late commissioner. Pushed aboard in handcuffs, Porter gasped and moaned. Over by the crossing stood John's weeping wife blowing her nose and holding the hand of their poor dim-witted Duzzie, brightly garbed in a red Christmas dress.

Porter and I were cuffed together on one bench with Reese shackled to the bench leg opposite, forced to ride on the plank floor. The rough roadbed jolted his spine hard, until finally he groaned in torment. To comfort him, I pointed out how fortunate he was to ride with white men in the coach car in defiance of Florida law. "Praise de Lawd," he said.

John Porter frowned in plaintive disapproval. "Mr. Watson? What's this business all about?" Porter had his eye on the sheriff, and his tone was pompous as befitted an indignant citizen. Not being a stalwart sort of man, he saw no reason to be hung for being my friend. "I demand an answer, Mr. Watson!" he shouted into my face. I leaned away for his breath was worse than usual. "Nervous stomach," he explained miserably, seeing my wince. "Ed, you have to explain to Sheriff Purvis! I had nothing to do with it, I wasn't even there!"

"Nothing to do with *what*, John? And how would I know that you weren't there when I don't even know where there might be?"

Porter, growing frantic, yelled, "Sweet Jesus, Ed! How can you sit here cracking jokes when any minute they might drag us off this train? Hang an innocent man who has done no wrong?"

"No man is innocent," I intoned. "Reflect upon that if you will." I, too, was weary of my stupid jokes but even wearier of Porter: Frank Reese had much more cause to bitch and here he was, bracing desperately against the jolts, hitching his ass up onto his chained hands to save his spine. Finally he gave up exhausted and sank into a daze of pain, gazing blindly at the toes of his torn boots, taking his punishment.

Now that lynching was no longer imminent, I had time to wonder why this seasoned outlaw had not taken the pains to bury that gun a whole lot deeper. Had it never occurred to him that they might come hunting the only suspect arrested in the death of the victim's brother? Or was he too angry to think clearly, with incriminating evidence dropped into his furrow after Cox had tried to implicate him in the first case? Frank must have known he'd be in fatal trouble if that gun was found anywhere near him, yet all he did was kick a little dirt over it and keep on plowing. Never emptied the shells out of the chambers, never buried it deeper, never walked forty yards to hide it in the woods. He never touched that gun, he told me later. Just didn't want anything to do with it.

"You figured I dragged you into it, the same way Leslie did. You wouldn't lift a hand to help, not even to save yourself from getting hung."

"It weren't *me* gettin me hung!" Frank Reese burst out, so violently that a deputy hollered at him to shut his nigger mouth. "I figured you knowed what you was up to," he muttered. "Never took time to explain nothin to no dumb-ass nigger."

"You're even dumber than you think," I said. The truth was, Frank was a more complicated man than I had thought.

Arrived in Lake City that Monday evening of March 23, 1909, we were lodged in the county jail. I would not have had much sleep anywhere else.

Next morning the deputies passed word that the south end of the county was forming a huge mob. By Tuesday afternoon, rumors were swirling— *The mob is on its way!* Sure enough, we heard wild yells and restless gunfire. Poor Porter was beside himself with the injustice of it all, howling his innocence from his cell window to all who passed below—"You men know me and know I am no murderer!" Those unacquainted with John before sure knew him by the time he finished because he hollered out his tale of woe every few minutes and for many hours, in case the mob had spies out in the street and might take pity on him, and spare him any rough stuff when the time came.

Frank Reese, who had no part in the killing either, remained quiet. As a black man, he'd never expected anything from life and knew that no protest would save him. So far as Frank Reese was concerned, life was right on schedule.

Word of my predicament had been telegraphed to Governor Broward, who sent orders back to move the suspects out of town for their own safety. Later that night when Deputy Bill Sweat, who ran the jail, heard the train whistle at the crossing, he ordered us out in a big hurry, rushed us to the station. To devil John Porter, I complained that we didn't care to be marched down the main street in chains like common felons when we hadn't been found guilty of so much as loitering. Mopping his brow, Deputy Sweat explained that a well-lit thoroughfare might be safer than taking a back street and falling prey to unknown men who might be laying for us in the darkness. Sweat was the right name for ol' Bill that night, cold as it was: he was nervous they might lynch him, too, while they were at it. Already some passerby had run off into the side streets to spread word; we heard faraway hollers of frustration as we boarded.

Next day, armed escort was provided to Jasper, in Hamilton County, then to the Leon County jail at Tallahassee. I sent word to Broward at the state capitol, inviting him to step downtown and visit his old friend in his piss-stink cell, but Governor Nap was a politician now and stayed away. A few days later we were moved to the Duval County jail at Jacksonville.

By now I had learned that my Collins nephews had presented my alibi so poorly that my own mother was persuaded of my guilt: Purvis informed me in his rural way that my so-called alibi had held up about as long as jailhouse toilet paper. And on April 10, at the sheriff's instigation, the coroner's jury charged my nephews as accessories after the fact, the better to coerce them to corroborate the sworn testimony of their friend Jim Delaney Lowe that E. J. Watson had solicited an alibi from all of them. Sure enough, Minnie's boys caved in after a day or so, having been persuaded that said solicitation was tantamount to a confession. With the prime suspect's dropped revolver and his buried shotgun, the state was building a strong case, my attorneys warned me, preparing the ground for charging fatter fees, and within the week, Reese and I were indicted for the murder of County Commissioner D. M. Tolen.

Meanwhile the real killer had gotten himself arrested for carrying an unlicensed pistol and disturbing the peace. In addition, after almost a year, Cox had finally been charged with the murder of Sam Tolen: Julian and Willie Collins and Jim Delaney Lowe, along with the Tolen nephew William Russ, had implicated Leslie on the evidence of his own boasting, overheard while he was showing off for May Collins and other local damsels. This time, even Sheriff Purvis could not ease him out of it.

When Leslie joined us in the Duval County jail, swearing dire vengeance on my nephews, Frank groaned dolefully and shook his woolly head, arm flung up in grief over his eyes. "Lo'd, Lo'd, what a pathetical sight! Nice young gen'leman like Mist' Les Cox in de county *jail!*" Broken-hearted, Frank actually commenced to cough and blubber, and when I laughed, too, he just let go and whooped so hard that he had to lie down on the floor to get his breath back. Leslie said, "If they don't kill you, nigger, I damn well will." He meant that, too, and Frank knew he meant it, but that was not why Frank fell quiet nor why the tears ran down those scarred black cheeks. Someone would pay for the death of a county commissioner and Reese knew it would be him; he was weeping not because he was afraid but because, facing death, he was free at last, free to say anything he damn well wanted. And so he sat up and wiped his eyes and said in a cold deadly tone, "Not if I ketch you first, Mist' Les, you fuckin po' white moron."

Cox squinted in disbelief that I could grin at such an outrage. Before stomping off to the far side of the pen, he pointed his forefinger and repeated his death threat in a voice thick and heavy, as if his throat was full of clotted blood—so full, in fact, that Reese and I could not even agree on what he'd said. "Some kind of secret redneck curse, you think?" I asked, watching Les go. Reese looked me over. Then he spoke again in that same furious cold voice. "Redneck, whiteneck—don't make no fuckin difference to us blackneck niggers."

In early April, thanks to Walt Langford and Jim Cole, the celebrated Senator Fred P. Cone of Lake City had been retained as our defense attorney. Cone was a silver-haired aristocrat, very close to Broward, and scarcely a judge in all north Florida would stand up to him, knowing "Senator Fred" was certain to occupy the governor's mansion in the future and settle up any old scores with the judiciary. But in our first meeting, Fred Cone warned me that the state's attorneys were already claiming "an ironclad case"—just the kind, he smirked, that he most enjoyed smelting down.

On Friday, May 1, in Columbia County Court, the defendants pled not guilty before Judge R. M. Call. Frank Reese was described by the Lake City *Citizen-Reporter* as "a very dark-colored negro wearing overalls. Asked how he pleaded, he was stopped by counsel." Cone ordered Reese to keep his mouth shut even for his plea, which was all right, I suppose, if he had good reason. But Cone did this with an impatient gesture, not looking at Reese but at me, as if telling me to put a stop to my dog's barking, and Reese muttered something so ugly for my benefit that I had to warn him.

That day the judge asked him to plead was Frank's last chance to stand up as a man and declare his innocence; he was never questioned or even mentioned in the case again. Even his own counsel never spoke to him. Day after day, in courtroom after courtroom, he would sit like a dark knot on the oak bench in the white man's courtroom. Once in a while I caught his eye and winked but he just looked away.

By returning the prisoners to Columbia County Court, Lawyer Cone had provoked the populace into raucous demonstrations in the streets—a clever tactic, I agreed, if we survived it, establishing before the trial could begin the dire prejudice against the suspects in this county. With threats and abuse being shouted through the courtroom windows, Cone prepared his petition for a change of venue, waving a whole sheaf of affidavits; having discussed the case with two hundred local citizens, he had found not one unprejudiced against his clients, and had therefore concluded that it would be impossible to seat a fair and impartial jury in Columbia County.

By this, the defense intended no reflection on the residents: "Honest men can be prejudiced as well as other men," the court was told, "and some men mistake their prejudices for their principles."

Naturally the state's attorney had sheaves of sworn testimony to the contrary, duly signed by the Herlongs and those others who had howled for my head that afternoon at Herlong Station.

That morning the court was informed by Mr. Charlie Eaton, a special investigator appointed by Nap Broward, that he had heard about a lynch raid on the jail planned for 3:00 A.M. on Thursday night in the week previous. The defendants, he testified, had been in such peril of mob violence that he'd rushed to the Elks Club to alert Lawyer Cone, and these two agreed that the state militia should be called out to guard the prisoners. Cone told the court he had gone to Sheriff Purvis and demanded protection for his clients and that Purvis responded that those "ol' boys" in the mob had given him their word that the accused were in no danger, since the evidence against them was so strong that they would hang anyway. Purvis admitted he had ordered extra guards around the jail but only as a courtesy to the defense attorneys. If the truth be known, declared this lawman under oath, real trouble was far more likely to arrive with Defendant Watson's friends from southwest Florida. Even now, he said, crowds of dangerous men were on their way north by sea and rail to effect his rescue.

This mendacity so astounded my attorney that he smote his marble brow. He invited the sheriff to admit that he'd confided to Detective Eaton that he feared for his prisoners' lives. Purvis denied this, saying, "If I told you that, I told you a lie." The witness was thereupon informed that the defense had no confidence whatever in his truthfulness and even less in the intentions of his deputies, several of whom had been identified as members of the lynch mob. Purvis cheerfully agreed that he had heard that, too.

Lawyer Cone's assistant now advised the judge that when he'd gone to Purvis and the prosecutor to express concern about the prisoners, they had merely laughed at him. Hearing this complaint, those two men laughed at him again in open court, behavior which struck me as so outlandish that I had to clap my hand over my mouth to keep from laughing with them. "Are you crazy, Watson?" Fred Cone whispered irritably behind his hand.

Next up was Will's brother Jasper Cox, who testified he'd been solicited to join the lynch mob by none other than Mr. Blumer Hunter, a member of the coroner's jury which had held impartial hearings on the case. Politely,

Jasper had declined, explaining to Mr. Hunter that he "was not in that line of business." Next morning, according to the Lake City paper, Mr. Hunter came to town (in brown coveralls smeared with wet cow dung, if I know Blumer) and informed the court stenographer that the testimony of Jasper Cox was "an unqualified fabrication." Even John Porter had to smile at the idea of such fine words emerging from the brown tobacco teeth of Blumer Hunter.

That afternoon, my son-in-law arrived from Fort Myers with a note from Carrie: *Oh Daddy, we all know that you are innocent! Eddie has written us about those dreadful Tolens!* On the witness stand, Langford declared, "Why yes, I am his son-in-law, but that don't mean I am a stranger to the truth. And the truth is that ever since my arrival, what I have heard over and over is, 'That murdering skunk should be hung on general principles!' " When I told Walt later that quoting my ill-wishers with such vehemence might not help my case, the banker flashed me kind of a scared grin. Walt could never quite make out when his father-in-law was being serious and when he wasn't.

Meanwhile, Mr. Eaton passed the word that the governor was following the case and meant to take "all appropriate measures to ensure the safety of the accused." However, with that mob out there, we defendants felt like rat cheese. Our attorney could not deny there was a risk but saw the change of venue as our only hope.

On Monday morning the sheriff came to Jacksonville to escort us back to Lake City, and this day I rode handcuffed to Les Cox. For all his big talk, Leslie was pale and nervous. Fred Cone had made him get a haircut and put on his daddy's Sunday shirt but the collar was tight and the new hairline gleamed on his sunburned neck and for all his good looks, he appeared kind of green and weedy. When he bragged that some church lady had told him he looked like Billy the Kid, I said, "Correct. William Bonney looked like weasel shit last time I saw him." Les cackled, thinking I was kidding.

"Well, somebody done a good deed on them Tolen sonsabitches, and I sure ain't sorry, how about you?" he chortled, and I said, "You are not sorry, son, because you think Fred Cone will get you off. You might repent of your black sins if you feared you might be dancing on a rope until you died." But all attempts to improve his attitude were wasted on this criminal young man.

On May 4, Attorney Cone won the release of John L. Porter, establishing that he had been seized unlawfully without a warrant and held unlawfully without a formal charge. Persuading Judge Call that one Tolen case might prejudice the other, Cone got Sam's case held over till the summer term when the climate in the county might have cooled a little. Last but not least, he won that crucial change of venue for defendants E. J. Watson and F. Reese.

We were tried next in Jasper, in Hamilton County, where we traveled from Jacksonville on a warm Tuesday of late July. Eddie and Kate Edna and my sister Minnie with Julian and Willie came there to testify, also Jim Delaney Lowe, old Calvin Banks, and others.

Peering around for a place to spit his chaw, Deputy R. T. Radford related the heroic saga of how he had stumbled over the defendant's revolver in the woods. Next, Dr. Nance described with due pomposity how Watson's shotgun, "primed for mayhem," had been "craftily concealed" in the furrow being plowed by "that hard-faced negro." Here Nance pointed a bony finger at defendant Reese, who sat at the farther end of the defense table, hunched into himself like some gnarled woodland growth. Finally, my nervous nephews and their friend revealed how the accused, arriving in their farmyard less than half an hour after the victim's demise, had lingered just long enough to solicit their support of a false alibi.

Neither Julian nor Willie cared to meet my eye. True, their daddy had never been fond of the defendant, but Billy Collins would have horsewhipped his two sons before permitting them to stand up in court and betray their own blood uncle in this manner. Knowing this, my fragile sister went sniffling to pieces upon hearing her sons give evidence against her brother. Almost inaudible on the stand, Minnie attested in tremulous tones that their kindly uncle Edgar, "ever generous with his time and means since Mr. Collins passed away," had arrived at the Collins house well before eight to teach her fatherless boys how to dress a hog and had not left until close to noon, when he went home to get his dinner.

When Prosecutor Larabee, loud and sarcastic, demanded to know why she was weeping—*Are you perjuring yourself, ma'am, as it appears? Objection, Your Honor! Sustained!*—I feared Ninny would blurt something that might get me hung; instead, she murmured that she wept because it broke her heart to see her family torn in two. Plainly the jury was affected—hurrah for Ninny! But when she shuffled back to her seat like a sick old woman, nobody in the Collins row could look at anybody else, and as for me, I was truly upset to see further damage to my poor sister's low opinion of herself. Here she was, a faithful Christian, not only lying under oath but making liars of her sons, though they spoke the truth. This ordeal might finish her.

Prosecutor Larabee did not call my wife or son lest they support my sister's story but he made a bad mistake when he excused my mother. Granny Ellen Addison would banish me to Hell before she contradicted her precious grandsons and lied to save me.

In the recess, the prisoners were taken to the latrine. (Frank was marched to COLORED ONLY.) I stepped right up behind Jim Delaney Lowe and slapped his shoulder with my chains like some old dungeon ghost. That boy jumped a mile, I hope he wet himself. I whispered, "Jim, the day they turn me loose, I aim to take care of those who did me wrong. So keep a real sharp eye out, boy, you hear?" Jim would pass that message to my nephews, give 'em something to pray about in church. I would never harm my sister's sons but they didn't know that, and truth be told, there were nights in those hot smelly cells in that long Florida summer when their uncle Edgar wasn't so sure about it, either.

Throughout our trials, Frank Reese remained inert. He was there as "Watson's nigger," nothing more. If I was guilty, he was, too, and if I was innocent, the same, and so he waited for these white folks to decide my fate. Sometimes after the court cleared for a recess, he remained in his place like a sagging sack of turnips in a field; they had to prod him to stand up. The prosecutor forgot him, so did the defense, and there were days when I forgot him, too. Because it made me feel bad when I thought about him, I mostly didn't. Reese didn't count—the common fate of Injuns and nigras in our great democracy. But this man and I had ridden a long road, he had stood by me.

Frank understood that I could not swear to a soul, not even our attorney, that my codefendant was innocent: how would I know any such thing if I were innocent, too? However, I gave him my solemn promise that if we were found guilty and Cone lost on the appeal, I would notify the court that Defendant Reese had never been an accomplice in the crime and could not have known that a loaded weapon would be dropped where he was plowing. I guess Frank appreciated my good intentions, but he also knew—I knew it, too—that even if my statement was believed, the state would not go to the expense of a new trial for a black man. Having already convicted him, it would simply be much too much trouble not to hang him.

The one way Frank Reese could save himself was to turn state's evidence against his codefendant. In order to spare me any inconvenient pang of conscience, our attorney forbade me to let him know that. What use was it to the senator's career to get the black man off and lose the white one?

Never once did my lawyer ask if I had killed Mike Tolen. He didn't want to know. I could have said I had not done so, which was true, but I did not care to read in his expression that he thought I was lying so I never bothered.

I felt worse and worse about dumping off my shotgun: why hadn't I thought of a better way? Could Cone get Reese's case severed, then dismissed, as he had with Porter? The attorney shook his head. It was true that aside from that shotgun, the prosecution had no evidence that Reese knew anything whatever about this killing, but getting his case severed and dismissed so deep into the trial might leave an impression with the jury that the remaining suspect, against whom evidence was plentiful, must surely be guilty.

Cone's arguments weren't as clear to me as I had thought, nor my own feelings, either, and trying to justify this line of thought to Reese got me all snarled up in my own words. "So it looks like you're fucked," I finished roughly, giving up. Frank shrugged that off. All these months of waiting to be unjustly hung had turned him cynical. "Nigger Frank don't count for nothin, no more'n he did that bad mornin when Mist' Jack dropped his shootin iron in his furrow, rode on by."

TWO FIGURES ON THE ROAD

In the backcountry, field hands in rough homespun have a way of vanishing into the land like earthen men. As a boy in Carolina, I would see brown shapes drift along against far woods or disintegrate into the ground mist, a shift and shadow in the broken cornstalks, an isolated figure paused to hear the distant whoop of others in the broomstraw yonder in the oldfields. Some whites will fight and screw and even kill in front of niggers, knowing it won't be talked about because nobody saw it—those black folks just aren't there. Not till Calvin Banks was on the witness stand did I recall that sun glint on his wagon spokes, so far away that the creak of wooden wheels could not be heard. Way down that white clay lane under tall trees, in the fractured light of sun and shadow, I had seen this black man without ever seeing him.

When he heard those two shots, Calvin testified, he was on his way to Herlong Junction with a load of cross-ties. Far ahead down the white lane stood the wood post boxes by the Junction, and a man on foot—Mist' Mike Tolen—was walking toward them. As the first shot echoed, he saw Mist' Tolen fall and another white man stepped out of the wood edge. Though distracted by the shrieks from the Tolen cabin, Calvin thought he heard another shot before a second man jumped down from that big oak. Mis Sally Tolen, barefoot, shrieking, was already outside, "little chil'ren follerin behin' dere mama like a line o' ducklins." Seeing the two figures and the body, she stopped short, clutching her hair, as her children caught up with her, shrieking, too.

Calvin had pulled up at the shots, but when the two men went back into the woods, he overtook Mis Tolen, entreating her to shut her children in the cabin. She did so, he said, but a moment later she came shrieking out again and ran right past him.

"And did you get a look at those two men?"

"Yassuh."

"And can you identify them for this court?"

"Yassuh. Mist' Edguh Watson—"

"Objection, Your Honor!"

"Sustained."

Nearing the body, Calvin said, he wondered why no one had come to investigate from the Cox cabin. (Here our attorney jumped up with another objection, also sustained.) By the time the old man reached the Junction, the postman Mills Winn was already approaching from the other direction. After Mills Winn had coaxed and pried the hysterical young woman off her husband's body, they had hoisted the victim onto Calvin's cart and brought him home.

"Well now, Calvin," said Attorney Cone in a baited, patronizing voice that was a sign to the jury to pay close attention, "you have acknowledged your poor eyesight, have you not? So please explain to these gentlemen of the jury how an old darkie with failing eyesight can be so certain that the man he identified from a quarter mile away was this defendant?" And

Calvin said, "I knowed Mist' Edguh since a boy, knowed the shape and size of him, knowed the way he walk. In clear mornin sun, I b'lieve I would know him from a quarter mile, maybe half a mile away, cause the sun shines up the color in his hair, and nobody around dem woods exceptin only him had dat dark red hair look like dry blood."

Looking up for the first time, leaning around behind our attorneys' broadclothed backs, Frank Reese sought my eye. His expression said, *Mist' Jack? Looks like you're fucked.* There was no way to read his feelings in the matter, no time, either, because Old Man Calvin, looking straight at Reese, kept right on talking.

"I never seed no sign of no cullud man," Calvin stated flatly. He volunteered this of his own accord in the startled silence in the courtroom that followed his identification of Ed Watson, and I was glad, because Frank needed all the help that he could get. But neither judge nor prosecutor nor his own attorney took the least notice of this critical point, far less pursued it.

A last-minute witness was Cone's former client Mr. Leslie Cox, whose indictment for the murder of Sam Tolen had recently been dismissed without a trial by the circuit court: Attorney Cone had been much pleased, since Cox's acquittal was a fine precedent for *The State of Florida v. E. J. Watson and Frank Reese.* He was happy to pay Cox's railway fare to Jasper out of E. J. Watson's pocket and his faith was justified: invoking the Almighty as his witness, Les Cox lifted his palm and swore to the complete innocence of Mr. Watson. Since he himself had shot D. M. Tolen dead, he knew what he was talking about and spoke with commendable conviction. The jury was very favorably impressed by the evident sincerity of this young man and I understood much better now why Cone had cut off Calvin Banks so sharply before he could identify the second man he'd seen beside Tolen's body.

Cone told us later that the seven Jasper jurors who voted for conviction could not dislodge the other five, who might have been bought off by Cone's assistants, for all I know. Though my attorneys never specified where all their client's money had been spent, one thing was certain, money was no object—these paper rattlers spent every cent I had. Fred P. Cone, who had never lost a case, did not intend to lose one now for puny financial considerations, not on his ascent in a brilliant career that would one day land him in the statehouse.

Faced with a hung jury, Judge Palmer declared a mistrial and ordered the case held over until the next term of the circuit court. Later that month, in Lake City, he threw out the lawsuit of the Myers nephews against the executors of Tabitha Watson's will. While I festered in the Jasper jail, unable to do a single thing about it, Jim Tolen resumed his fire sale of our family property.

Leslie got word to me that if I were convicted, he would assist in my escape, and I believed him—not that I trusted him. The man whose word I trusted was his father.

CALL ME CORY

Outside my bars, on a fine morning in Jasper, a redbird chortled loud and clear, recalling lost springtime woodland days with Charlie Collins—"a day of new lilies and pale haze of dogwood in the April wood," as she had written in a love note. But instead of that redbird, I was doomed to listen to my fine-feathered son-in-law, who said things like, *I'm afraid your record is against you, Mr. Watson.* Though Walter and his friend Jim Cole had twisted every arm in Tallahassee, they didn't think I had a chance in hell. Cole still wanted me to like him because it made him nervous that I didn't: I would have respected him much more if he'd told the truth, that he would have been highly gratified to see me hung.

When I first knew Walt Langford back in '95, he was a cow hunter out in the Cypress, snot-flying drunk on rotgut moonshine from one day to the next. This morning he was dead sober in a three-piece black serge suit. "Who the hell are you, the undertaker?" I said. "Come to take my measure for my coffin?" Walter mustered a grin and passed me Carrie's note:

Oh Daddy, please! Walter says you must throw yourself on the mercy of the court. Tell them you had to defend yourself against that man because he threatened you, tell them you regret it deeply but you had no choice. Walter and his business friends will testify what a fine hardworking planter and good businessman you are, and surely our side can convince the jury what a good provider and good husband—and wonderful kind jolly father!—our dear, dearest daddy has always been! If you'll just cooperate and plead guilty and accept a reduced sentence, Walter says, everything is bound to turn out fine!

"The family has decided I am guilty, is that correct?"

"Nosir, it's not that, exactly—"

"Walter," I told him, "it *is* that. It's that exactly, Walter." I sent a message back to Carrie that her dear, dearest daddy had done no wrong even if he'd shot Mike Tolen, which he hadn't, and therefore he would not plead guilty under any circumstances.

Walter told me I had better think that over because after the hanging it would be too late. Walt didn't even know he was being funny. Said he'd "heard on excellent authority that the State was prepared to negotiate"— that's the constipated way Walt talks since he became a banker. And he had Eddie, who trailed in here behind him, talking that same way, the pair of them sitting upright on my bunk, ever so prim and mealy-mouthed, like they wouldn't mind a second helping of nice mashed potato. "I'm afraid your record is against you, Dad," my offspring said.

Walter's "good authority," of course, was State's Attorney Cory Larabee, with whom my family were clearly in cahoots. And who should happen by an hour later to inquire if "Ed" was comfortable? The state's attorney himself stepped into my cell talking too loudly in the grand flatulent manner of politicians. He slapped my back and sat his ass down, made himself at home. "Now don't stand on your manners, Ed, just call me Cory!" Here I was, entirely at the mercy of Call-me-Cory and my kinfolks, who seemed to think they had some special dispensation to squeeze right into my small cell beside me.

"Spit it out," I said. How had this happened? Where the hell was Cone?

Because Friend Ed had support from influential friends—Call-me-Cory meant the governor—he might be paroled in three years' time if he pled guilty. Cory raised his eyebrows high on that pale dome of his while his good news penetrated my dull criminal brain. "Because *otherwise*, Ed," said he when I was silent, "we'll do our very best to hang you, boy!"

Damn if he didn't laugh out loud and slap me on the knee, to show me no offense was meant by threatening my life. Because I was so close to Broward, this public servant was out to please, no matter whom, no matter what, so I damn well better take advantage—that's what he wanted me to think. That was the bait.

I jumped up with a sudden yell and backed him up against the bars, squinting one eye. Knowing a dastard when he saw one, Call-me-Cory hollered, *"Guard!"* But Buddy had stepped out to heed a call of nature after locking up an innocent prosecutor with a vicious killer. I had the prosecutor cornered, I was panting in his face. "No *sir!*" I shouted. "*No* sir, Call-me-Cory, sir! I am *not* pleading guilty. All you have for motive, Cory, is a dispute in the family, Cory, and if *that's* a motive, you will have to hang every adult in the state of Florida. Furthermore, Cory"—my voice had dropped to a whisper of quiet menace—"since you mention my friends in Tallahassee, be aware that I am keeping them abreast of every aspect of this shameful case, including the behavior of the prosecutor. So the next time you come in here trying to trick a defenseless prisoner in the absence of his legal counsel, those friends will see to it that you are disbarred."

The prosecutor was trying to chuckle but all he made were airy little sounds like a rooster with its throat cut. He had put out a rank body smell, that's how quick fear took him. "All right now, Ed," he whined, to calm me. "All right now, Ed, if that's the way you want it." Looking more sheepish than a sheep, he told me I had a first-rate legal mind, I was much too sharp for him, that's all, no wonder the governor thought so highly of me! He was shaking his head in admiration, laughing, too, the kind of laugh that might get away from him at any moment, go way high up like a fox yip, out of shattered nerves. His cautious hand rose to pat me on the shoulder, then hung dead in the air not knowing where to go.

"Where's that damned guard?" he squawked, peering out through my bars, as if we were in this damnable fix together. Next thing I knew, he was hollering at someone else. "Christamighty, you never heard me tell you, Wait outside?" Damned if that mean turd of a Jim Tolen hadn't snuck in here while the guard frequented the privy. Shifty Jim was peering through the bars, itching away in his sharp-cornered suit. "Mr. *Per*-secutor? Sposin I was to inform to them newspapers how you was a-hobnobbin in here, crackin jokes with the selfsame heenus killer you was swored to *per*secute?"

The dignity of the Persecutor's office could not permit this sort of insolence. Winking at the prisoner, Larabee climbed onto his high horse and rode all over him. "And prosecute him I shall, sir, with all the might God gave me! And the Lord willing, Mr. Tolen, sir, you shall see him hung! Because in my opinion he is red in tooth and claw! A man more guilty of a heinous crime never drew breath! Nevertheless—"

"All I'm sayin, Mr. Persecutor—"

"*Yes* sir! And all *I'm* saying, *Mis*-ter Tolen, is the following: having made the acquaintance of said defendant in the halls of justice, I can testify that

E. J. Watson is a *man*, sir, made from the same dull clay as yourself. He eats as you do, breathes as you do, and worships God as you do, *Mis*-ter Tolen! What is more, he is a lively man, piss and vinegar just don't describe it, and when he's up there swinging from that rope, I for one won't be ashamed to say I was proud to know him!"

When Cory paused to get a breath, his sly wink said, *How's that, Ed? Still want to make that not-guilty plea and go up against a ripsnorter like me in the public try-bunal?*

"Now that don't mean friend Ed deserves to live. Howsomever, may I remind you, *Mis*-ter Tolen, that no judgment has been pronounced and that in this great democracy of ours, E. J. Watson is innocent until found guilty by a jury of his peers. So tell the press whatever you damn please and I'll expose you for a reckless liar and take you to court for obstruction of justice, *Mis*-ter Tolen!"

Larabee was having sport with this poor dolled-up Tolen but mainly he was sucking up to the defendant, knowing that Broward might return a favor to a smart young state's attorney with political ambitions who had obliged him with some lenience and discretion. Even were he to lose this trial, its notoriety might lend some color to such a thin gray feller, which he would need when hustling votes on down the line.

Buddy came galumphing back like a big woolly dog. "Dammit, Guard, where have you been?" Call-me-Cory hollers. But Buddy is wheezing and he merely grunts, fiddling his keys. This big boy sees 'em come and sees 'em go on both sides of the bars. "Had me a good bowel movement, Mr. State's Attorney," he confided, in better humor now that he felt comfortable again. But noticing Tolen, he frowned deeply, grasping the man's scrawny upper arm. "How'd *you* get in here?"

Cory signaled to Buddy to let Tolen go. Feeling magnanimous now that he was safe, he winked at friend Ed through the bars. All the while, Jim Tolen had been eyeing him with that sliding look of the mean dog sneaking around behind for a good bite, and damned if he didn't spit his brown tobacco chaw toward Cory's boots, in a loud wet squirt that would fire a clan feud back where he came from.

Old Cory went stomping off after the guard, having had about enough of our rough company, and Tolen took advantage of this opportunity to ease up to the bars. Since the last time I'd seen him so close up, there was no improvement. Jim Tolen was the bitter end of centuries of Appalachian incest, with bad weak teeth, big bony ears, and thick black brows that curved right down around the eye sockets. He gave off a dank chill of revenge and death like the cold breath of an autumn wind down his home ravines.

"Yeller Ed." His voice was hoarse.

"For a little shit who's been looking up a mule's ass all his life, you're dressed up pretty smart there, Jim. Looks like you might know a thing or two about stolen property."

"Yer bein tried just for the one, Ed Watson, but you was in on both them hee-nus murders," Tolen yelled, hoping the prosecutor could still hear him, "and they ain't a man in the south county as don't know that!" He turned back to me. "Yeller Ed the back-shooter. Ain't goin to parlay your way out of this one, you shitty bastrid. Gone to hang you high. And they's men waitin on you in Fort White as will take care of it in case this jury don't."

What the hell kind of a jail was this, I wondered, where the prisoner had no protection—where some degenerate like this could stroll right in and shoot an inmate through the bars? But of course any jail so easily entered might be just as readily departed. This Jasper jail would be a whole lot easier than Arkansas State Prison.

I put that idea aside for just a minute. Buddy's shoe slaps were pounding down on us, our meeting was coming to a close. I put my face close to the bars and fixed Jim's eye and muttered fast and cold, "If I were you—and by that I mean a thieving white-trash Tolen—I would clear out of Fort White, because folks who have already had enough of your ratfuck family might just want to finish up the job."

To talk in that disgusting way once in a while does the heart good.

Tolen cocked his head back like a musket hammer and snapped it forward, shooting his chaw into my face. My hand darted through the bars and grabbed his stripy shirt, and the cheap cloth tore as the guard spun him away, exposing a chicken chest so white under his red neck that a man might almost imagine he had bathed.

"*Naw!*" Jim howled. He was clawing at that tear like he'd been scalded. "That's my new shirt!" I cackled just to rub it in, reeling back and rolling off my wall, making the most of it. But life is peculiar and the truth is I felt bad about Tolen's cheap shirt. I wanted to tear his rodent head off but tearing a poor man's Sunday shirt was something else.

Then it hit me like a mule kick: Jim Tolen was not a poor man, not anymore. His dirty pockets were stuffed with money that rightfully belonged to Watsons and he was still selling off our land. The blood rush to my temples nearly felled me. "You and your brothers stole our plantation and you will pay for that the same way they did." Those words escaped my tongue beyond recapture and my desperate laugh to divert attention clattered like an empty bean can on the concrete floor.

I pressed my forehead hard to the cold steel. My foe stood dim and ghostly, making no sound. The prosecutor's shadow neared, the guard behind like Death's attendant, as if all listened to the echo of those dire words, as if the People of the State of Florida stood in judgment on this caged human being. I felt not lonely but cut off from humankind.

Then time resumed, the morning fell back into place, the redbird sang anew outside my cell window, the prosecutor smiled thinly. "*The same way they did?* Guard? You heard what the prisoner said, correct?"

"I ain't deaf." Buddy gave me a reproachful look, shrugging his shoulders.

"Remember his words carefully, Guard. You'll be called to testify."

"How about *me?*" Tolen complained. "I sure ain't likely to forget them devil's words!" When Buddy grumbled, "Can't write nothin except only my *X,*" Tolen instantly produced a scrap of paper and a pencil stub and started scrawling, to prove that he suffered no such limitation.

The prosecutor tipped his hat. "Three witnesses to an unsolicited admission of a deadly motive. I am confident, Ed, that the jury will see it that way, too. I advise you to accept the State's generous offer—"

"Generous offer?" Jim shrilled in alarm. "Goin to turn that killer loose? He'll hunt me down and shoot me in cold blood like he done my brothers!" But thin Jim wasn't afraid of that, not really. When the guard dragged him away, he wore a twisty grin, hard as a quirt.

Bad as it looked, I concluded that Ed Watson would not hang. For all his bluster, this state's attorney was a stupid man. His political career was the carrot rigged in front of the donkey, it was all he saw. In his effort to cajole me, he had lunged after that carrot, scared of losing.

I got a whiff of what was in the wind from Carrie's note as well as from Walter and Eddie: better a jailed father than a hanged one. They were dead scared of the scandal of a public execution. The guilty plea they wanted me to make would cut their losses, get the black sheep locked away. I could make the mistake of pleading guilty only if I was so greedy for survival that

I would accept a life of being caged and fed and watered behind bars like a wild animal. I was not that greedy, or at least not yet. If I kept my head, I was going to be acquitted, because none of my family had the guts to see me hung.

THE KNIFE

Ladies sometimes ask why such an amiable man so often finds himself in so much trouble. And I say, "Ma'am, I never *look* for trouble"—here I let my voice go soft, lower my eyes a little, tragic and mysterious—"but when trouble comes to me, why, I take care of it."

Les Cox loves that kind of guff as much as my Kate fears and despises it. It's not entirely nonsense, and even when it is, it can be useful. But behind bars in that torrid summer of 1908, I faced the fact that I had not always taken care of trouble the right way. I had never admitted, for example, that a lot of it was of my own manufacture.

Grandfather Artemas's gentleness and weakness had undermined our Carolina plantation; the bad character and weakness of his ring-eyed son had completed the loss and driven the grandson into exile. But was I weak too, in some other way? Plainly my ruinous start in life had forced me to desperate measures in my struggle to restore our Clouds Creek name—all in vain, it seemed, for here I was, past fifty years of age, jailed and disgraced, with my neighbors howling to see me hung and all my savings pissed away to pay the lawyers.

"Darn it, Ed," as Bembery once said, "this ain't the first time and it ain't the second, neither, so you better think about mending your ways." Hell, all my life I have tried to mend my ways and I always believed that next time I would make it and I still believe that.

Some would say that Edgar Watson is a bad man by nature. Ed Watson is the man I was created. If I was created evil, somebody better hustle off to church, take it up with God. I don't believe a man is born with a bad nature. I enjoy folks, most of 'em. But it's true I drink too much in my black moods, see only threats and enmity on every side. And in that darkness I strike too fast, and by the time I come clear, trouble has caught up with me again.

I have taken life. For that, I can only be sorry. But excepting that one time in Arcadia, I have never done it for financial gain. Starting way back with those shipowners and merchants who trade in human beings and destroyed thousands of lives, how many founders of our great industries and family fortunes can say the same?

For my edification while in jail, Carrie sent along her mother's Twain books—a do-gooder I could not abide and yet read furiously.

The new trial started on July 10 and testimony concluded on August 3 when the hung jury, unable to agree upon a verdict, was dismissed. In September, Cone won another change of venue and in October Judge Palmer moved the trial to Madison County. If I lost at Madison, I decided, I would break out of jail, run for the Islands.

(When I told Reese about my plan, he whispered gleefully, "We is fixin to ex-cape, just like old times!" Remembering how we crossed the Arkansas, a lilt came into Black Frank's voice, almost as if he hoped we would be convicted. Only once and only briefly had this man reproached me for dumping that shotgun in his furrow, even though that heedless act might cost his life. For his forbearance, I sincerely thanked him, assuring him he was a credit to his people whether white folks strung him up or not.)

Our third round took place in Madison County in mid-December. Getting nerved up three separate times for the same trial was like building up three times for the same act of love. Naturally there was a letdown, but the defense was off to a promising start in the local paper: "The defendant Watson is a man of fine appearance, and his face betokens intelligence in an unusual degree. That a determined fight will be made to establish the innocence of the defendants is evidenced in the imposing array of lawyers employed in their behalf."

That array, in fact, was so imposing that we had to sell off some Fort White land to pay their fees. I was deeply in debt to my son-in-law and Kate was warning me that we were broke: we could not afford to have the breadwinner go to prison (although having him hung, as I told Frank, might be somewhat worse).

Jim Cole bent every ear in the state capital, cajoling them to talk sense to the judge. After that, he came to Madison, helped pick the jury. By trial time, Fred Cone had six assistants who kept themselves busy running up my bills in heroic efforts to suborn witnesses. Meanwhile, the prosecution's "jailhouse confession by Defendant Watson" was not panning out as

Larabee had hoped, the defense having led the jury without difficulty to mistrust Jim Tolen.

Nonetheless, this trial might go badly. I asked Kate to get word to Leslie. Being afraid of him, she was upset, but I hushed her protests. Cox came in and looked over the jail and we soon agreed on the details. Shaking hands on it, he squinted man to man, and I squinted right back for old times' sake—the frontier code. I owed him that much.

On her next visit, Kate seemed strangely distressed: when I took her in my arms, she confessed that she felt sick. She entreated me to turn away while she tended to her person—modestly preparing, as I thought, to perform her wifely duty. Instead, she produced a clothbound packet containing a small sheath knife in light deerskin, which Cox had told her I had ordered for the escape. She was to conceal it "in her person"—saying this, that vicious boy had winked at her. Mortified, Kate wept, she could scarcely look at me. When she did not understand, he grinned and whispered that she was "to stick it up her you-know-where, and kind of squeeze it, hold it snug there" till she was safely in my cell and could remove it. "He said those were your instructions," my wife whispered.

I roared with rage. When the guard came running at my din, I bribed him to step out for a long smoke. Made shy by our necessary haste, Kate removed her undergarments and knelt astride me as I sat on the thin cot. I raised her skirts and settled her warm sweet hips onto my lap, gently rocking her, then not so gently. She murmured into my ear that she still hurt from the knife, but it was too late then, it had been too long, I had to have her.

Afterward I sat her beside me and took her hand and warned her I was not a man to tolerate a hanging far less labor my life out on the chain gang. If I was convicted, I intended to escape back to the Islands. I would send for her once I was sure that all was well.

"All will never be well, Mister Watson," poor Kate mourned. "Not in the Islands." I had never seen her look so stricken. What had made Chatham almost bearable for Kate had been her dear Laura Collins, whose husband was now estranged from us due to the bitter feelings in our family. Kate said hurriedly that what she meant was that year-round exposure to fever-ridden climate might be bad for children. When I said she need not return permanently but could spend more time at Fort White, she cried out, "How can I stay at Fort White? You can't imagine how those people look at me!"

Around her eyes was a shadow like a bruise. "If you two didn't do it, then who did?"

"Kate?" I lifted my fingers and gently brushed the hair out of her eyes, which were streaming tears. "What would you like me to say?"

She made a little squeak like a caught mouse. "We can never go back to Fort White, it is too dangerous!" Jumping up, she rushed to the cell door. I tried to soothe her while she waited for the guard but she only clapped her hands over her ears and shook her head. Though she knew this was unreasonable under the circumstances, she could scarcely believe that her own husband would permit Leslie Cox to testify in his defense.

The one witness left who might do harm was Calvin Banks, who was concentrating on his duty as a citizen while forgetting that his testimony might get me hung. Having given up trying to bribe him, the defense wanted him off the stand as fast as possible.

Testifying for the defense, Cox had made a good impression, declaring earnestly that Mr. Watson had always liked and respected Commissioner Tolen, which was true. But Leslie's real mission here, as Lawyer Cone explained, was to "influence" Calvin Banks. At one point in Calvin's testimony, Leslie feigned outrage at Calvin's account, jumping up to point a warning finger at the witness. Next, he tried to spook him, rising up in the back row like a haunt until Calvin noticed him, then running his forefinger across his throat. Though Cox sank down quick before the prosecutor could protest, that mule-headed old nigra stopped speaking and was silent. Cone whispered, "He is finished." I knew better. Calvin was frightened but he wasn't finished.

Fierce as a prophet, the old man raised his arm and pointed a crooked finger straight at Leslie. The courtroom saw that bony finger aimed at the young man in the back row, as if Cox, not Watson, were the man on trial. There was a stir as Cox stood up and left the room, scared that old Calvin would identify him to the judge as the second man standing over the body on the road. Puzzled, the judge struck his gavel, calling for order, and Calvin Banks returned to his dogged testimony.

.   .   .

The jury was out less than an hour, enjoying Jim Cole's cigars. When they came back, we stood. Mr. E. J. Watson was acquitted, then the negro Reese. When the verdict was read, Frank watched our lawyers smiling but showed no emotion.

The judge discharged us there and then and went so far as to bid me Merry Christmas—I'd clean forgotten it was Christmas the next day. Attorney Cone smiled and shook my hand and shuffled his papers back into his case: a man's life or death was all in the day's business. Jim Cole came forward with a hearty shout and slapped my back as he might slap the rump of whore or heifer. He owned me now, that slap informed me. "Dammit, Ed, we sold our souls to get you off," he wheezed, "so see if you can't stay out of trouble on the way home!" His mouth was laughing but his eyes were not as he stood ready to receive my gratitude. I felt none. Suppose I had pled guilty, the way this man wanted? And if I had pled guilty, how about the innocent Frank Reese?

I opened my mouth but not a word came out. I let Cole grab my hand and shake it but he moved away without my thanks, flushed red to bursting.

Winking and joking, the state's attorney was congratulating the defense attorney. "Why are you hanging around here, Ed?" Larabee called, throwing his arm around Cone's shoulders. "You going to miss us?" And Cone, easing out from beneath that arm, laughed, too, although only a little.

There had been no trial—amateur theater, maybe, some light farce. All the attorneys on both sides that day were in on this big joke, having learned in advance from Tallahassee how E. J. Watson's trial for his life had been decided—whether his life was to continue or it wasn't. Realizing this, I could scarcely thank my lawyer and his staff, who had taken every penny that I had.

I looked past all these smiling men at Reese. Having no place to go, he had simply sunk down after the verdict and resumed his old place at the far end of the bench. The bailiff would soon notice and evict him.

Leaving that building, I was all nerved up and edgy. Old Calvin was across the street, saddling up his mule for the long journey home across north Florida to Ichetucknee. He would wear his white shirt and Sunday suit all the way there, sleep where night found him. Kate clutched at my arm but I shook her off and walked over to confront him. "I'se glad, Mist'

Edguh," is what that old slave said as he hitched his cinches. "I sho is mighty glad dey has set you free." Then why had he testified against a man he had known nearly forty years?

Calvin blinked and turned to look at me, surprised. "Mist' Cory Larabee, he say, Tell nothin but truth, so help me God, Mist' Edguh. Tol' me speak out," he continued. "Called dat de bounden duty of de citizen, called dat de solemn duty of de negro. Said black folks dat doan speak up for de truth, doan speak up like *mens*, dem ones might's well go back to bein slaves again. Mist' Larabee instruct me. Den he say I mights well say de truth cause what ol' darkies say doan nevuh make no difference in no court of law. Promise me dat Mist' Edguh Watson gone to walk out of dat courthouse a free man. And here you is!"

But Calvin's voice had diminished as he spoke. He cleared his throat, then asked me almost shyly if I aimed to kill him. To throw a scare into him, I said my neighbors might take care of that. This ornery old feller dared to smile. "Nosuh, Mist' Edguh, ain't Calvin they gwine take care of. I was you, I'd stay away from dem home woods a *good* long while!" Then his smile faded like water into sand, he looked tired and sad, considering this member of his old plantation family who had gone so wrong, with nothing to be done about it any longer. "I sho' did hate to tell 'em whut I seed, Mist' Edguh. I sho is thankful dat dem white folks paid dis ol' man no mind."

"Watch out for Leslie," I said gruffly and I walked away.

Frank Reese appeared. He could not go home to Fort White, either. Even if Cox weren't running around loose, he was not safe there and probably never would be, which meant he would lose Jane. Frank looked as beaten as a man can look who is cold and hungry on a winter night at Christmas, without friends, family, future, or one dime in his pocket, and no place to sleep.

"Frank," I said, "you come on south with us."

CHAPTER 9

✦

MODERN TIMES

On the first day of 1909, on the new railway, E. J. Watson and family crossed the Alva Bridge over the Calusa Hatchee and rumbled downriver into Fort Myers Station. I sent Frank over to Niggertown—Safety Hill, as it was called, because black folks felt safe there after evening curfew—to round up a few hands while bags and baggage were transferred to Ireland's Dock to be loaded aboard Captain Bill Collier's *Falcon.*

Since the arrival of the railroad, the WCTU had sent Miss Carrie Nation, and a circus had also paid a call, complete with elephant. The first stock-roaming ordinance, fought by the cattlemen for years, now protected the public thoroughfares and gardens. Indian mounds up and downriver were being leveled for white shell for cement streets and Thomas Edison had leased Cole's steamer to bring in royal palms from the Island coasts to ornament his Seminole Lodge and decorate Riverside Avenue for the tourists.

When Henry Ford came to visit Mr. Edison, Walter and Carrie were invited there to dinner, and not long after that, Cole and Langford bought Ford motorcars and went tooting and farting north and south the entire quarter mile from one end of our manure-strewn metropolis to the other. Jim Cole's self-esteem was geared to ownership of the newest, best, and biggest—this year, the most expensive automobile in town. Quick turnover of everything from real estate to cattle had been the secret of his success, and he soon replaced his Model T with a bright red Reo.

On Riverside Avenue, I stepped right up and rapped the banker's new brass knocker. In a moment little Faith was tugging the lace back at the window. Carrie's daughters were only slightly older than Ruth Ellen and Addison, and I thought our girls might play and get acquainted while Kate washed up and rested for our voyage. When I waggled my fingers, Faith's pretty face flew open like a flower and then vanished; she was running to the door. I heard Eddie's voice and after that a silence; her face at the window was the last we were to see of my sweet granddaughter.

No one else appeared. We stared stupidly at the closed door. Begrimed and hot and cranky from the train, my poor rumpled family waited dumbly in the street while Papa wrestled with his rage. I rapped again, three good hard knocks, and this time the door cracked and a black maidservant stared out as if the Antichrist himself had come to call.

"Tell your Missus," I said, "that Mr. Watson—"

The girl disappeared and Carrie stood there instead. "Well, I do declare!" my daughter cried. Her smile was terrible. She did not come forward and did not invite us in. "Papa," she whispered. "Walter . . ." She could not finish and she didn't need to. We had been preceded from north Florida by my son and son-in-law, doubtless bearing word that Mr. E. J. Watson had gotten away with murder.

"Since when does Walter wear the pants around your house?" I started away before I uttered something worse.

"Papa? Please, Papa," Carrie begged.

I turned on her. "If your husband and brother thought me guilty, why did they testify in my defense?"

"Oh Papa, what choice—"

"I'll have them indicted for perjury." But my sour joke only frightened my bewildered family. Kate Edna stared wide-eyed from father to daughter, as if discovering for the first time how these Watsons worked.

The servant girl came down the steps with a tray of milk and cookies, which she held out fearfully toward my children as if feeding wild monkeys through bars. I recognized the rosewood tray I'd given Mandy as a wedding present. Without my say-so, nobody would touch a cookie, and the darkie was so rattled by the children's hungry staring that she banged the tray down on the stoop before them like a bowl of dog food and ran back inside.

Carrie stooped, picked up the tray, and offered it again, eyes brimmed with tears. Addison reached first but my eye stopped him. "We came as kin, not beggars. We'll be going." I tried in vain to put some warmth into my voice because Carrie was at least trying to be nice, unlike her brother who had not come out to greet us, a discourtesy I was never to forgive.

"Thank your kind sister for her hospitality," I told Ruth Ellen, who curtsied. Little Ad did, too. "No, Ad," I told him. "Gentlemen pay their respects like this." I put one hand behind my back, lifted my black hat with the other, and bowed to my beautiful Carrie, who burst into tears, knowing her rejection of her father would ensure that in all likelihood, we would never meet again.

"Oh Papa!" she cried. But we went away with resolution, leaving Carrie in the public street with her tray of milk and cookies. Addison fretted, looking back, but did not say one word.

"I love you, Papa!" Carrie called, glancing around for neighbors. For that small courage, I almost forgave her.

I lifted my hat but did not turn. "My daughter loves me," I told Kate, ironic. My unhappy wife struggled to smile but her dry upper lip had caught on her front teeth so she looked away.

Poor Kate had had a dismal year, with her husband languishing in county jails under threat of hanging and her Fort White neighbors hostile, all but her faithful Herkimer Burdett, who had come around often, it appeared, to see how his childhood sweetheart might be faring—a little more often (according to the leering Cox) than her husband might have cared for. When I mentioned this, my wife burst out that Herkie had been very kind and that the only one who had hung around "in the wrong way" was Leslie himself. "If I should die, would you go straight to Herkie?" I inquired. Kate colored as if slapped, having no idea how to answer that, much less dissemble.

At Dancy's stand at the head of Ireland's Dock, I consoled my doleful tribe with candy, fruit, and peanuts we could not afford. The last of my money lined the pockets of my attorneys and once again I was faced with gnawing debt.

Lucius turned up on the run before we sailed. Announcing he was coming with us, he hefted a satchel to show me he meant business.

"Chatham is my home, Papa, and you'll find work for me, I know."

I nodded slowly. "This young feller is your brother Addison," I said. Lucius, who had now turned twenty, shook the hand of little Ad, who sat astride my shoulders: at Addison's age, in Arkansas, Lucius had no memory of his father nor any idea what he might look like. When Lucius said, "How do you do?" the little boy thrust out a half peanut, which his brother was polite enough to eat from his sticky fingers. "An excellent peanut," Lucius assured Ad, wishing he hadn't when Ad unstuck another. I felt a great wave of affection for these boys, all the more poignant because Rob and Eddie were my sons no longer.

Because Frank Reese still had a record and might be subject to arrest, I introduced him to Lucius by his prison nickname, which was "Joe" or "Little Joe." No one knew his last name.

SHARK RIVER MIKASUKI

We arrived at the Bend on a winter norther and that wind was cold, with iron seas churning the Gulf and swift gray skies. A sweet reek of pig manure was everywhere, even inside the house, which we found in woeful condition. Green Waller mostly emulated the habits of his hogs, which seemed to have the run of Chatham Bend. Since Green was a rough carpenter at best, his rickety hog shed swayed in the faintest breeze, and in recent weeks two prime shoats had been lost to a marauding panther. In his uneasiness Green demanded in the fierce tones of the drunkard that their worth be deducted from his salary—an empty offer in my present straits. Green had gone more or less unpaid for years. He had so little use for money that he had purposely lost count of what I owed him, fearing that if I paid him off, I might get rid of him. This poor old reiver was five years my junior, but due to a sadly misspent life, had overtaken me in our race to the grave and now appeared to be my elder. Green Waller saw the Bend as Paradise, with all the hogs and moonshine a man could ask for.

Kate seemed stunned and the rest dispirited: I put them right to work as the only cure. We patched mesh screens and painted them with oil to keep out sand flies, swept out spiders, scraped rust, crust, and vermin from the stove. We burned off and harvested the small neglected crop and brewed a batch of lightning to tide Green over into the next year.

With his growing family, Erskine Thompson stayed mostly at Lost Man's with the Hamiltons, so Lucius took over the boats. On Sundays he and I went fishing while Kate went crabbing with the children, but without Laura Collins and her gales of sweet laughter, Kate's fun in life seemed to be gone. Knowing we could never go back to Fort White, she felt banished to a purgatory of humid heat, unrelenting insects, and the endless raining greens of mangrove wilderness, with no end to her loneliness and nothing to look forward to. From her first day back on Chatham Bend, she felt imprisoned, a fate made worse by nagging dread of the calamities that might befall her children—flood or hurricane and drowning, alligators, panthers, poisonous serpents, wild Indians and tropical disease, to name only the fates that scared her most.

These Mikasuki or Cypress Indians, who called themselves *At-see-na-hufa*, would make camp at Possum Key on their way north from Shark River. When Lucius found a strong freshwater spring right off that island, and tried to be helpful by telling them about it, they heard him out without expression, grunting assent once in a while to keep him going. When he was finished, they laughed for a long time, paying no attention to him anymore. We concluded that the At-see-na-hufa had always known about that spring, but having had everything else stolen away from them, they never let on to the white people who lived there, preferring to watch them struggle along with rain gutters and barrels. Sometimes a few Indians stopped by the Bend, and we did our best to put something in their stomachs, if only our bad coffee and hard biscuits. One of the young Osceolas, a leader of their band, was some kind of cousin to Richard Harden's Mary, who had been born into that family, too.

The animals had now retreated deep into the Glades. The Indians concluded that the land was dying, and the red man, too, so they might as well shoot everything they could get a bead on, using guns where bows and arrows once sufficed. Stripped off the skins, left the carcasses to rot, and headed straight back to the trading posts to trade for liquor. Deer were so scarce that even Tant Jenkins gave up hunting and went out to the clam flats off Pavilion, where even the clams had been thinned out due to the dredging.

As for the plume hunters, the House boys and their Lopez cousins were traveling all the way south to Honduras to find egrets. Those plumes were now contraband, mostly confiscated at Customs. One year Gregorio Lopez came home so sick that his boys lugged him off the boat on his chicken-feather mattress with the Customs men trotting alongside asking hard questions. And Old Man Gregorio rolled his eyes back, croaking, "This here is my deathbed, boys, so don't go harassin a poor old feller that is givin up the ghost before his time." Well, Gregorio could have died right there as far as those federals were concerned and it wouldn't have helped his case even a little, because one of 'em had spotted a white quill sticking out where the old mattress stitching had unraveled: he drew forth a fine egret plume and twirled it in the sun, saying, "If this here is a chicken mattress, like you said, what I got here just has to be the purtiest white leghorn feather in the world." Gregorio Lopez made a full recovery right before their eyes. Got up off that mattress and stalked away disgusted, giving those Customs men a taste of a proud Spaniard's scorn.

Wilson Alderman of Chokoloskee had married Gregorio's daughter in 1906, and because there was no work on the coast, I had taken him north to Fort White to work for me. At the time of my trials, my lawyers tried to subpoena Alderman to testify in defense of his employer, but as Sheriff Dick Will Purvis told the court, this feller "was no longer to be found in the county of Columbia, having returned to his residence in the Ten Thousand Islands."

Alderman had slunk away as soon as my troubles started. His feeble excuse turned out to be that he had to go home to take care of his pregnant Marie, the apple of old Gregorio's ferocious eye. That old Spaniard had never abandoned his belief—which I now shared—that any daughter of Gregorio Lopez was much too good for the likes of this young man. To the delight of her friend Kate, who rushed off to help tend her, Marie gave birth to Gregorio's grandson two months after our return in 1909. For Kate's sake, I forgave the feckless husband.

I could not forgive my son Eddie and Walter Langford. Carrie had explained in a long letter that as "a civic leader" her husband could not afford the breath of scandal. "He has put his foot down, forbidding me to have you in our house," wrote Carrie in her tear-blotted missive to her "dearest Daddy." Like many strong women with weak husbands, my daughter pretended that her spouse's castle quaked in terror of his wrath, but she knew I knew whose foot carried the real heft in that household.

Kate Edna tried to make excuses for my daughter. Surely the idea of a younger stepmother would take getting used to for someone who so adored her daddy—"You're talking nonsense, Kate," I interrupted. Poor Kate went soft as a crushed peony, and Lucius fixed me with that enigmatic look which was as far as he ever went in criticism of his father, though his very restraint let you know his mind. I said to Kate, "Come here, then, girl," and sat her comfy bottom on my knee to draw the sting from my harsh words.

THE FIRST AUTO IN THE ISLANDS

After that bad welcome at the Langford house, I gave up all ambitions for Deep Lake. Dead tired after months in county jails, I had lost the will to grind my way out of debt on this remote and overgrown plantation. Uselessly I was attracted to a life of enterprise in the great world.

One day in Fort Myers, I ran into Cole and Langford in the saloon across from the courthouse. Both looked puffy from too much time indoors sitting on money and neither had a handle on his drinking. In fact, Big Jim had been forbidden by court order to set foot in a saloon, though Sheriff Tippins chose to overlook this. As for the balding banker, he looked seedy and unshaven, despite his slicked-down strands of hair and three-piece suit.

When I came in, my son-in-law lurched to his feet and left without a greeting. "Don't let your customers smell that whiskey!" I called after him, intending to be heard by the whole place. Trapped in his booth, Cole waved me to a seat with a poor smile and asked me how my "cane patch" was progressing. I ignored the sneer behind his stupid question, wanting to see the shock on that smug face when I told him coolly that I'd like to buy the Ford auto he had recently replaced with that red Reo.

"What with?" jeered Cole, who knew I was flat broke busted. But he also knew my reputation as a businessman who made good on his debts; he did not doubt that I would restore my syrup operation in short order, and its profits, too. "What's your collateral, Ed?" he said. I thought he was just matching my bluff, but when he flagged the bartender and paid for two more whiskeys, I realized he was serious.

"An up-and-coming farm in Columbia County," I said.

"Who's on there now?"

"My sister's family and my mother."

"Supposing you forfeit?" He cocked his head to peer at me. "You fixing to shoot them ladies, Ed, or just run 'em off there?"

I held his eye and he covered his nerves with that curly grin. "I mean, where the hell you aim to *drive* the damn thing, Ed? Down to your dock and back?"

That same evening my Model T rode south, lashed to the foredeck of the *Gladiator*. She was wrapped in tarps against salt water, because with the wind out of the south and that weight forward, we were shipping a hard spray over the bow. At Chatham Bend, Lucius fetched planks and we drove her off onto the bank, hooting the horn in honor of the first automobile ever seen in the Ten Thousand Islands. I had planned that jalopy as a surprise, to lift our spirits, and sure enough, the kids came whooping, piled right in, and jumped around the seats. There was no sign of Kate.

Frank stood in the kitchen doorway, wiping his hands on a towel; the way that black man's head was cocked made clear that he questioned my good sense.

"Got her in a kind of swap," I told him before he could say anything he might regret.

"What you swap for her? Our pay?" His tone scared everyone. He stepped back inside. Nobody said a word. I stood waiting for him, getting my breath. If he didn't think better of it and step outside again—

He stepped outside again. "My oh my, that's sump'n, Boss," he said, dangerously angry, his grimace fixed hard in a kind of death's-head smile.

Kate came outside slowly, in a daze. "What on earth can it be for?" she whispered. "And how on earth are we to pay for it?" She burst into tears. "What can you be thinking, Mr. Watson?" Annoyed because she had spoiled the children's fun, I told her too bluntly that our Fort White farm— her beloved "home on the hill"—was the collateral. "I have something on the stove," she gasped, and ran inside.

Ruth Ellen had found the car horn—*toot-toot-toot!* I could not concentrate in such a racket. I yanked her out of the front seat, making her cry. Addison scrambled out of the back and fled around the house. I glared at Lucius—*Well?* He shrugged and went inside. *"Damn!"* I yelled, astounded to see how fast the fun had ended. But standing there alone with the new car, I was struck by my utter folly: I was losing hold.

Lucius called, "Papa? Let's go for a drive. I'll find the kids." Out ran Ruth Ellen and Addison, miraculously cured. They sat on Lucius's lap and shrieked at the fireworks sputter as I cranked the motor, shrieked some more as we backed past the sugar kettles and turned her around in jerks and fits and starts. After a drive of one hundred yards, Ruth Ellen vomited from the thick fumes. The children ran inside, calling for Mama.

Early next morning Lucius and I set to work with Sip and Frank, alias Joe, hacking and clearing a half-mile track around the cane field. Already handy with boat engines, Lucius soon learned all there was to know about our auto, inspecting each movable part to see how it related to the rest. My son and I were never closer than we were that spring, navigating our new car on its road to nowhere.

When the great day came—we waited until May Day—all but Kate Edna piled into the "T" and went for a drive around the circumference of the Watson Plantation, chugging and honking, children screeching and dogs barking. Though all were good sports, the little ones had not traveled very far before they turned greenish from the fumes and jolting. We only completed a single round before we had to stop.

With Frank, I made a second round. Kate watched us from an upper window. How pale she looked up in that window, far away across the field.

WILDLIFE

In the damp cloudy weather of the spring, we were "in the mosquitoes" all day long, but except at daybreak and in early evening, when biting insects were at their worst, the children played around the water edge and dock and boats. They were never happy very far from water, and I was never quite at ease while they were there. I warned Addison and Ruth Ellen about the swift strong current and gators up to fifteen feet and that huge croc that hauled out from time to time on the far bank. Where one of my coco palms had fallen over into the river, Lucius built an eddy pool walled in by brush: here the kids could splash a little, protected from marauders. Even so, I did my best to put a scare into the children, describing how those monsters cruised the riverbanks hunting unwary animals and wading birds, how they drifted in close and hung there unseen in that silted water. Eye ridges and snout tips might be glimpsed but often not. Gators had snatched more than one dog off our bank; they could lunge and seize a small child in the shallows and disappear with one thrash of that armored tail.

When they weren't fooling in the boats, the children sailed toy boats across the cistern, which was straight-sided and slippery with green algae.

Lucius rigged a rope ladder, just in case, but knowing a child would panic with the first mouthful of black water, I finally forbade them to go near. *Any child who falls in there is a goner!*

Sturdy and stubborn, Ruth Ellen disobeyed me. One day I came up behind and grabbed and held her way out over that black tarn. The little girl screamed until she lost her breath. Kate got very upset with me for scaring the child so badly. "Better scared than dead," I said. We spoke no more about it. After that day, Ruth Ellen dreaded the cistern and would not go near it and would not let Addison anywhere near it, either. She would fly around him yapping like a sheepdog, chivvying our little boy away from such a dreadful fate.

Like all children, they loved to hear about wild creatures, panthers and reptiles especially. Lucius described the big panther scat he'd found in the scrub behind Cape Sable on the hot white sand mound of a croc nest. The scat had been dropped fast in the cat's escape—Lucius reconstructed the whole event from tracks—when what must have looked like a driftwood log back in the salt brush turned suddenly into a crocodile, risen on its short quick thick legs to drive the prowler from her nest. Lucius dug up the cache of leathery white eggs to experience the feel of them, then put them back; he described the warmth and firmness and the slow throb of ancient life in those strange oblong shapes.

On another day, east of Flamingo, he had traveled far up Taylor Slough to the hardwood hammocks, where in the airy stories of the huge mahoganies, he had seen a small flock of nine lime-colored parakeets—the beautiful bird so often spoken of by Jean Chevelier, who had sought them in vain along the rivers of our coast.

It pleased my son greatly that America's last wild Indians lived not far south of us on hammock islands in the Shark River drainage, and that every attempt to open up their last territory with a road had foundered in the muck and broken limestone of this water wilderness. Unlike most, Lucius saw the Glades as beautiful, especially far up beyond the tidal reach where the mangroves were replaced by vast sparkling wet grasslands that stretched away forever to the north and east. "And that damned sawgrass," I'd protested, "taller than a man, with nothing underfoot but muck and jagged limestone holes that will tear a man's boots to pieces in a day."

"And poisonous snakes, even poison trees—all sorts of fascinating things," he agreed, enthusiastic, which was why the Everglades might yet prevail when all the rest of the wild places in the country had been overrun by roads bringing more people. He never criticized my ideas for west coast development, only the new canals east of Okeechobee: the canal projects were encouraging more talk of a cross-Florida highway which would lay open the Everglades once and for all. My son only hoped that all that dredging in the headwaters, muddying the rivers, would not spoil our paradise on this wild coast.

"*Paradise!*" cried Kate. "My goodness, Lucius!" Yet Kate loved him because he was so good with the children—an antidote to her old brute of a husband, I suppose. He cheered her and kept her company—they were the same age—and offered the kids whatever time he had to spare, showing them such mysteries as the round and pearly glow of the star spider.

THE STOWAWAY

Key West is and always was half-Yankee, and even back before the War, its attitudes were jumbled up when it came to coloreds. Many good people clung to old bad prejudice including my friend Gene Roberts and his brothers, who ran the old *Estelle* from Flamingo to Key West, carrying outbound mail and cargo and bringing back supplies.

Melch, Jim, and Gene—the Roberts boys—refused to tolerate blacks mixing with whites, they would not put up with it. They'd go over to Key West, have a drink or two, then walk arm-in-arm down the sidewalk, and any black man who failed to get out of their way, they'd knock him down. One time they went into a restaurant, sat down, ordered their breakfast, Gene was telling me, and the next thing they knew, a great big buck came walking in, sat down at the next table. When those boys reared back and glared at him and he didn't leave, Melch got up without a word and took his chair and wrapped it over that man's head. Hauled him up off of the floor, Gene said, and booted his black ass into the street.

Of course Key West had no use for these Mainlanders. On the way to jail, the sheriff would say, "Well, here ye are again! The Mainlanders!" And they'd say, "Yessir, we sure are, and proud to say so!"

Returned to office, the sheriff was as truculent as ever about E. J. Watson. One day he accosted me at Duval and First as I came out of W. D. Cash Provisions and Ship Chandlery. He'd heard that a fugitive killer might be hiding out at Chatham Bend, in which case I was flouting the law again by harboring a known criminal.

Young Herbie Melville, known as Dutchy, had been notorious at Key West for several years. Back in 1904, when my friend Deputy Till tried to arrest him for breaking into a coffee shop at White Street and Division, this young feller grabbed Clarence's pistol, beat him to the floor with it, then drew his knife, apparently to scalp him. Bleeding, Clarence broke away and ran to borrow a weapon; he returned to that coffee shop without waiting for reinforcement and Melville shot and killed him.

Dutchy Melville was convicted and sentenced to be hung, but because his family had local influence, the charge was reduced to manslaughter and a one-year sentence. During his detention, the enterprising jailer rented Melville's labor to the fire station, a part-time job which provided him the leisure to rob stores, covering his tracks by burning these places down. In destroying the Cortez Cigar Factory, however, he went too far. Murdering a law officer was bad enough but damaging rich men's property was far more serious: the indignant judge sentenced the young arsonist to thirteen years at hard labor.

Recently young Dutchy had escaped the chain gang, but not before confiding to another convict (who had the ear of the authorities) that he hoped to hide out at the Watson place at Chatham Bend. And the reason for *that*, the sheriff said, looking me straight in the eye, was because this man Watson was notorious for hiring fugitives and other undesirables as low-paid field hands.

This was true. I sometimes recruited harvest workers at Key West, mostly blacks but some white drifters, too. These men were called Doc and Slim and Blackie and John Smith: I never asked if they were fugitives, that was a man's own business. They accepted whatever pay was offered with no back talk and they never stayed long, field labor in the cane being hard and dangerous. That way everyone came out ahead—sound business practice.

I informed the sheriff that I knew no Dutchy and no Herbie either, and also that I did not care for his insinuation that E. J. Watson had no respect for law and order. The sheriff said, "Them words sound all right, Watson. But a man gets knowed by the company he keeps, ain't that right, too?"

And I said, "Well, in that case, Sheriff, we'd best part company right now because I have my good name to think about," whereupon I tipped my hat and kept on going.

Eddie's Bar had a stylish sign—DINING AND DANCING, NINE TO ELEVEN, FIGHTING FROM ELEVEN TO TWO—and the cost of a drink was all that was required to enjoy this lively social situation. With so many good fights to choose from, any man of healthy tastes could fit right in. Knives and pistols were frowned upon, of course, but that same night I had to wrench a brandished six-gun from a client who was dead drunk but still dancing, threatening to shoot. I gave this fool a taste of his own medicine. "Let's see can I work this thing!" I hollered, waving it around the same way he had. It kept going off, made one hell of a racket, and with each shot I yelled to warn him lest he stagger and cross the half circle of holes his own six-gun was punching through the floor around his toes.

When the six cartridges ran out, he came up quick with a small revolver he had in his boot and made me dance in that same foolish fashion. I tried to grin, stay calm about it. "Not many men, let alone boys, would try this game on Ed Watson," I warned him, but he only hooted and went right ahead. When his friends dragged him out of there, he was still laughing. It was only after he was gone that Dick Sawyer sidled up and said, "Ain't that Dutchy a ripsnorter, Ed?"

I was disgusted. This ripsnorter had killed Clarence Till, a fair and well-liked lawman, and also robbed businessmen and committed wrongful arson, and yet he was a local hero whom folks talked about with shining eyes. To join his pals at Eddie's Bar with a reward posted, then draw attention to himself, show off with weapons at the risk of being sent back to the chain gang? His *arrogance* was criminal, never mind the rest, but because he got away with stuff like that, he made it seem dashing and defiant. *I laugh at your law. And what will you do about it? Nothing!*

Headed home next day, I was somewhere off Shark River when the sky turned black and the *Gladiator* was caught in a hard squall. When I stuck my head into the forward cuddy to dig out my oilskins, I found myself looking straight into the muzzle of a six-gun. Naturally, I backed out and raised my hands. "What's that cannon for? Piracy on the high seas?"

"If I was you, I wouldn't talk so smart." The man climbing out after me was green olive in his color from being pitched and rolled in that hot cuddy, but he looked like a pirate all the same—big nose, pocked skin, hard black wire hair, and a second pistol stuck into his belt. He also looked like the self-same sonofabitch who had danced me in Eddie's Bar, so I knew better than to mess with him. These cocky greenhorn pistoleros out to prove themselves tend to shoot first and think afterward, if they think at all. Ever since Billy the Kid caught the nation's fancy, the country had been plagued by boys like this, out to play and die as fast and hard as William Bonney.

"Maybe I'd better grab the helm before she yaws on a big sea and capsizes," I warned him. A flicker of fear crossed that swart face: he waved me toward the stern. Starting aft, I felt a whole lot better. If this kid had spent even one day on the water, he'd have noticed that the helm was lashed, with no risk of yawing or capsizing.

I freed the tiller while he guarded me, standing up straight, and at the first chance, I swung her off the wind and let her jibe. In a rush of canvas, the boom swung back across the hull and knocked him flying; he'd heard that creak of wood behind him but not knowing he should duck, he spun right into it. If he hadn't grabbed a shroud, he would have gone overboard and stayed that way because I sure had no plan to go back after him. As it was, he'd had to drop his gun to grab that line, and now he was dragging in the water, hanging on to a rope fender with both hands.

Very quick, he hauled himself halfway up and got one leg over the gunwale. I leaned over and yanked the second Colt out of his belt and whapped his fingers with the barrel. "Damn!" he said as he lost his hold and went back down. Clutching the fender in the wash along the hull, he was very pale, he thought he was a goner. Having emptied the chamber of the Colt and tossed it into the cockpit after the first one, I lit up a cigar and took the tiller, letting him drag while the *Gladiator* resumed her course.

"Can't swim too good," he gasped. Having no way to wipe the sea out of his eyes, he looked like he was crying. "I reckon my arms ain't goin to last much longer," he said next. I blew some cigar smoke down into his face to make him cough. His eyes snapped with black anger over getting himself into this fix, and naturally I was angry, too, yet I had to admit this boy had grit, considering his piss-poor situation. He had stated the facts, he had not begged or whined.

Seeing that Watson wasn't going to help him, my stowaway knew he had to save himself if he was going to be saved, and he had to do it now while he still had strength, even if Watson planned to shoot him if he tried it. One boot swung up onto the rail, which was all the purchase this quick varmint needed. The rest was cat strength, timing the boat's roll. Melville was back aboard so fast that I grabbed for the first gun, which was still loaded.

Seeing he'd startled me, he dared a little grin as he eased down out of the wind in his wet clothes. Even now, safely aboard, he hung onto the rail; after that bad scare, he was no threat to me at all. Far at sea off a distant coast, he had more sense than to harm the man who piloted the boat.

"Dutchy is the name," he said. "You heard of me?" I shook my head, emptying his cartridges into my pocket.

"Don't want to know what I'm doing on your boat?"

"I *know* what you're doing on my boat."

He nodded. "Emperor Watson!" He grinned some more. "If a man drew down on *me* on my own boat, I'd blow his head off."

"After the harvest, maybe."

"Watson Payday?" He'd heard the bad stories, his grin said, but he kind of liked my style. "Know something, Mister Ed? You wasn't so sociable last night in Eddie's Bar so I never got to shake the hand of the Man Who Killed Belle Starr. But the way you turned the tables on me here today? Real slick! I'm proud to know you!"

"One month's work, no pay. How's that?"

"Mister Ed," he repeated softly, nodding his head as if this were his lucky day. He couldn't get over Mister Watson, I was wonderful. "We'll see," he promised cheerfully, wringing out his shirt. "Call me Dutchy, okay, Mister Ed?"

"Okay, Herb," I said.

I'd guessed correctly that he hated his given name. On the other hand, he was flattered that I knew who Herbie was.

At Chatham, Melville had to learn to take orders from a black foreman. However, he respected Frank's long prison record and got along with him about as well as could be expected. He wanted to stay on, "take the nigger's job," he announced in front of Frank, "cause foreman ain't no job for a nigger," but the way he said this made Frank laugh because these two had already made friends.

When Melville finally realized I'd meant just what I said—hard work, no pay—he got to brooding, concluding finally that E. J. Watson had taken advantage of his youth and generous nature. In my experience, criminals *always* feel angry and abused, which partly accounts for why such men turn criminal in the first place. Also, they can be counted on for retribution. They get even.

A fortnight later, returning from a trip with Bembery to Tampa Bay, I discovered that this criminal had gone off on a fishing boat but not before spoiling the thousand gallons of good syrup I had counted on for unpaid salaries and lawyers' bills and enough supplies to see the plantation through until next harvest. Two months after that, a picture postcard came from New York City:

> While you was at Tampa drinking up my pay I had some fun mixing terpentine and sirup. Now I am up here seeing all the sites. Mery Chrismas Mister Ed and hello to all from Yr. Frend Dutchy.

To my friend Dutchy it was all a joke but for Chatham Bend it was a crisis. For a fortnight or more, I forgot my vow that never again would I raise my hand in violence. Every time I thought about that devil, my head split with that old pain out of my boyhood, so violent that I had to sit or I would fall. If I'd had the money, Jack Watson would have taken ship for New York City and finished that young villain once and for all.

I told my crew I was dead broke but would pay them when I could. Some bitched, of course, but most blamed Dutchy Melville. As for Kate, she had always been unhappy that I hired wanted men, fearing that one of them might harm our children. When I told her about our loss, she cried, "Well, that's what comes of harboring these outlaws, Mr. Watson! Why can't we live like ordinary, decent people?" And I said, "Didn't you tell me just last week that you were fond of Dutchy?" Kate went off sniffling after admitting that the children liked him, too. They did. Followed him everywhere. The Hamilton and Thompson kids rowed all the way north from Lost Man's Beach to see Dutchy and his six-guns, same way they used to come to see my trained pig Betsey. Everybody liked that rascal, even Lucius, even Reese, and even "Mister Ed," who had vowed to kill him.

LINCH LAW

After I was acquitted, I had written a long letter to Nap Broward, thanking him for his kind interest and assistance. In that letter I outlined some long-range proposals for the Everglades, "the last American frontier," and requested an appointment at the statehouse as soon as I could afford the railway fare to Tallahassee. Surely the governor would be interested in my idea for a Broward ship canal that would follow old Indian water trails across the southern Glades from Fort Dallas on the Miami River to the Lost Man's headwaters; the dredged spoil from this canal could become the bed for a cross-Florida highway. While acknowledging the difficulties of the terrain, I mentioned the much more challenging canal under construction in Panama, with locks to lift great ships over the mountains.

The only answer to my letter was a typewritten copy of a document from the archives of his predecessor in office. Though unaccompanied by any note, it could not have been sent without Broward's approval. Dated Chokoloskee, Florida, February 1896, it was addressed to Governor Henry Mitchell:

> To his Excellency Gov. Mitchil. Sir, I wish to call your attention to a
> crime perpetrated against the Laws of the state.

> I was in Key West on business some time ago when I met the perpetrator
> of the crime. He came up to me in a store and shook hands with me. We
> had a few civil words. He wound up by saying that he was not afraid of
> any man. I in reply said that neither was I, whereupon he immediately
> slapped his knife, which I suppose from the quickness of his act he must
> have had open in his pocket, into my neck, coming very close to severing
> the jugular vein. He drew his pistol but could not make use of it as the
> leather case came with it. I seized him by both wrists and held him until
> he was taken in charge by an officer who was nearby and lodged in jail,
> being unable to give bond. Some days after his lawyer procured a man
> who was willing to stand on his bond. The bond was accepted and the
> prisoner was released. When the time came for the trial the prisoner was
> not forthcoming but sent two negroes to swear that he was sick and not
> able to go to court. It is a provable fact that but a short time before court
> he went to a store some twelve miles distant from his home and purchased

a quantity of ammunition. The prisoner not being present in the court
there was no trial..

Is it any wonder that there are so many lawless acts committed by
linching offenders when the law is so loosely executed? Let the Law be
administered in justice and without fear, favor, or affection and linch law
will be done away with. But until that is done we must expect the people
to take the execution of the law into their own hands.

Very Respectfully Yours,
A. P. Santini

Dolphus had gotten his revenge and never knew it. That Broward permitted his complaint to be sent to his friend Watson made it clear that I
would be unwelcome at the statehouse until I had rebuilt my reputation—
in other words, until I was prosperous again, which in this great land of
ours amounts to the same thing. And so I was forced to stand by and watch
as Florida's west coast development fell far behind the east. Nap Broward
had committed most of the state's money to his steamboat canals east of
Okeechobee, while John D. Rockefeller's partner Henry Flagler, with flags,
fanfare, and fine speechifying, was finishing the last leg of his Florida East
Coast Railway, from Homestead south across the keys and channels toward
Key West. From his beachside headquarters, Flagler described his railway
as "the hardest job I have ever undertaken," oblivious of the brute labor
done by the thousands of unknown men who worked like animals in that
humid heat to make his fortune. (One newspaper reported that the numbers of railway construction deaths in Florida were rivaling those in
Panama, where the railroad company helped defray expenses by packing
its corpses into brine barrels and selling them to medical schools back in
the States.) Nobody wanted to investigate all that dying, least of all the U.S.
government, because Flagler was opening up south Florida for development, commerce, and big investors. "The kind of red-blooded American
who made this country great"—that's what the newspapers called Flagler.
There was red blood, all right, but it wasn't his.

Our field hands were better housed and fed than the immigrants and
Caribbean blacks and crackers who perished over there when Flagler's
crews revolted, forcing his thugs to bring in drunks and bums to break the
strikes. Not that I opposed strong measures to support progress in this

brave new century—on the contrary, I ached to be involved. But it enraged me that a small cane planter on a remote frontier river should be reviled for "Watson Payday" while more powerful men supported by the government were writing off human life as overhead as an everyday matter.

Lucius would nod politely at my earnest outrage, but next day he might say something quiet that his mother might have said, like, "I've been thinking about progress, Papa. Shouldn't progress in our great nation mean progress for everybody?"

Those two men on my place had died for the common good because they had obstructed the progress of this region—that's what I told myself when I thought about it, which I tried not to. Occasionally I came close to discussing those Tuckers with Lucius, who was still sad that he'd never heard from his missing brother, but being shamelessly in need of this boy's good opinion, I did not dare.

Our new cane crop came up better than expected in those rain-swept days of spring and early summer when new shoots can grow six to eight inches in a day. But on the eleventh of September, 1909, just before harvest, the worst hurricane in memory flattened my cane to a tangled mat of leaves and twisted stalks. Because the new cane was still green, the storm bent those stalks over without killing the plants, and the damp weight of that green mat threatened the entire harvest. I drove Green Waller off his hogs, sent Kate and Lucius into the field, and we worked like nigras because, being broke, I had no real ones except Sip and Frank. Grabbing and chopping night and day, we salvaged what we could and burned the rest, but the new sugar was watery and the syrup so thin that I would not put my label on the cans. I shipped a single small consignment for the little it would bring at Tampa Bay.

Jim Howell of Chokoloskee came to work that year, brought along his brother George's boy to help. Jim was the slowest-working man I ever saw, but something put the fear of God in him because he burned to finish up, get the hell out. Kept stalks coming to the mill from dawn to dusk, kept his nephew working that same frantic way, which was why that same bad accident happened again. Boy got tired, got his apron caught, his hand, then his whole arm, but this time some arm was left above the elbow. We bound a tourniquet as best we could, made him cough some moonshine down to keep his heart going, put shine-soaked linen in his mouth to stop his screaming.

Frank Reese knew the story of that stain in the front room and his expression when we laid young Howell in the boat was clear—*You let a black man bleed to death and try to save the white one.* There was no time to explain that with a motorboat this boy still had a chance. "Frank," I warned him, "this is what we are going to do, all right?" Black Frank said nothing. I ran young Howell to Marco and found a faster boat to take him north to the Fort Myers hospital, by which time he had hardly enough blood left to feed a sand flea. They saved his life but he was meant to lose it. A few months later this boy went fishing and perished with his daddy and the younger children, drowned in a sudden squall on Okeechobee.

That September hurricane of 1909 tore off roofs and blew to pieces most of the Key West waterfront and the cigar factories. Here on the Bend, it took a shed and half the dock, and at high tide the house up on its mound stood in the middle of a thick brown flood that jumped the riverbanks. Kate wailed that we would all be washed away but thanks to Lucius, the kids made an adventure of it. More excited than scared, they came through fine.

Little Ad was proud of our strong house, which hardly creaked. Their mother had read them "The Three Little Pigs," and Ad boasted to everybody who came through how our house stood up to the storm's huffing and puffing. When he couldn't stop talking about it even days later, we realized he'd been a lot more frightened than we thought.

After the hurricane, the family lost all interest in my auto; not once did I take the tarp off after that storm. The waste of money made me wince every time I walked past. Finally we loaded her onto the *Gladiator,* took her up to Tampa Bay, and sold her cheap in Ybor City, which since the hurricane had replaced Key West as the home of the Cuban cigar.

On the way home to the Bend, I stopped off at Pavilion Key with intent to trade a gallon of syrup for two bushels of fresh clams procured for me by Mrs. Josie Jenkins Parks Hamilton Johnson, to name but a few of my old friend's discarded and deceased. Her brother Tant, who had dug the clams, told me they were growing scarce due to Collier's dredge. That big contraption tore hell out of the bottom, broke the shells, exposed them to the drills and starfish, and generally put those clammy fellers off their feed. I was only thankful it was Captain Bill who was held responsible for the calamity—the "clamanity," Tant called it—the only mortality in southwest Florida that nobody had tried to blame on E. J. Watson.

Josie Parks, as she was known that year, looked somewhat the worse for considerable wear but her spirit was lively as ever. She offered me a mug of rum to seal our dealings and we nailed that mug down with another to celebrate the mystery of life. Before I knew it, this agile widow had grown so alluring in my eyes that for the first time since the turn of the century I awoke next morning in her weary bedding. And as her brother used to say, "things went from bed to worst." I'd hardly snapped my galluses, in fact, before I got Mis Josie in a family way. "Our love child," Josie marveled. But a love child on its way so soon after Kate told me she was pregnant promised to be a domestic complication that I scarcely needed.

SPECK

In the clam camp, my footsteps were dogged by another complication, this one a young feller named Crockett Daniels, who had somehow come by the wrong idea that I might be his daddy. His confusion was understandable, since nobody was even sure which Daniels bunch he sprang from. Like many Florida frontier folk, the Daniels clan was what they call "half full of Injun," and most of their offspring had black hair straight as a horse tail and a dark copper complexion to go with it. Some had the high cheekbones and big hawk nose, too, and this Crockett kid was one of 'em. Netta's brother had hooked up with an Injun-looking woman and her cousin married the sister, and their kids lived all mixed up together, big loose litters. Not only did this gang look Injun but the families had that Injun custom of raising up stray kids, Crockett included.

Young Crockett's mother, a young Daniels, had gone away to other parts to recover her health and reputation. His fatherhood was popularly attributed to Phin Daniels's son Harvey, who had stumbled drunk out of his boat in pursuit of a raccoon and jammed too much black mangrove mud into his rifle muzzle. "Hell, that don't mean nothin!" Harvey hollered, waving off a shouted warning. Anxious to get off a shot before that coon slipped away into the reeds, he blew most of the mud out of the barrel, blew the breech up, too, and his head with it. The family agreed at Harvey's funeral that he was very likely Crockett's father, which made an orphan of the boy but kept things orderly.

Young Crockett knew that Pearl and Minnie were E. J. Watson's children. Since nobody, least of all Harvey, had stepped up to claim him, he had set his heart on me, waving and hollering, tagging along, running small errands that I only gave him to be rid of him. On Pavilion Key, he was never out of sight, like a hard speck in my eye. The men laughed when I explained why I called him "Speck" and that name stuck.

Josie Jenkins, hearing my wife was away, got drunk of a Sunday, wished to pay a call, and this boy rowed her over from Pavilion. Lucius liked Josie but was bothered by her presence in Kate's house so I said she must leave once they'd had a bite to eat. Next day that kid was right back on my dock, having hitched a ride with a Marco man who worked a produce patch on Possum Key to feed the clammers at Pavilion and went up and down the river every day. "I'll work just for my keep," Speck said. "You're trespassing," I told him, in no mood for palaver. "Mister Ed," he said coolly, "I ain't got no boat and anyway I ain't doin you no harm." I told him to stay right there on that dock until the Marco man came back downriver in the evening.

This wild boy had some nerve. He dared to curse me. To teach him a lesson, I fired a pistol shot right past his ear. Quick as a mink, he dove into the river and swam underwater—either that or he drowned, because he disappeared. Sobering quick, I hunted up and down the bank, hollering and calling, fearing something might have grabbed him and knowing there would be hell to pay when Josie heard about it. Too late, I realized that I still had my revolver in my hand—probably why he kept his head down in the reeds and never answered. I put that gun away and shouted more, I even yelled that he could stay here on the Bend, that's how worried I was that the big croc might get him if he splashed along the riverbank too long. I even drifted down the current in the skiff but saw no sign of him.

Next morning I went to Pavilion Key with the bad news and the first person I saw on shore was Crockett Daniels. Turned out he had drifted all the way downriver on his back, crawling out every little ways to make sure no shark or gator got a bead on him. Finally he swam and waded out to Mormon Key, where a fisherman spotted him and took him home.

Speck had some spunk so I wanted to tell him I only meant to scare him, not to kill him, but when I drew near to shake his hand and maybe rough his head, he backed away. When I stopped, he stopped, too, regarding me out of greenish eyes as bright and cold as broken glass and nodding his head to indicate he knew my game. Then he turned and walked away. He never followed me again. That year this Crockett kid was no more than thirteen, but he was not one to forget that Watson winged a bullet past his ear, much less forgive it.

The clammers watched as Josie shrieked how that crazy Jack Watson had shot at a poor homeless boy with intent to kill. She was not to be reasoned with, there was no changing her mind, though I followed her right to her shack. And if Josie Jenkins would not listen to my side of the story, then who would?

Through the door she said, "You're dead, Jack Watson, and you don't even know it. Your heart has died from pure blackness of spirit." Astonished and moved by these words from her own mouth, Josie opened the door to gauge their effect on the one cursed. Eyes filling up with moonshine tears, she raised her hand to touch my cheek and lips, then let it flutter down like an old leaf onto my trouser buttons. "Dead, dead, dead," she whispered.

"Stop that," I growled because young Pearl was watching. This tempestuous bitch slammed her door right in my face, and as poor Pearl backed away in fright, I kicked that rickety little slat right off its hinges.

The clammer families and their mutts fell back as I turned to leave. "Why don't you go fuck yourselves," I urged them with as much goodwill as I could muster. I returned to my skiff and headed home, feeling so lonely as I entered Chatham River that even the company of Crockett Daniels might have proved welcome.

Christmas of 1909 was a sad occasion, with no money whatever to spend on presents. In low spirits, I drank too much of our own moonshine, which was free, and concluded I'd made no progress in my life since that starved Christmas in the muddy snow out in the Nations.

A year had passed since our return to Chatham. That winter Kate grew more remote as she grew large with child and spent more time away. One day after a bad quarrel, I ran her and the children north to Chokoloskee so that we might enjoy a vacation from each other.

• • •

In the Fort Myers *Press* for April fourth of 1910 (next to a society item about Mrs. Walter Langford entertaining the Thursday Afternoon Bridge Club at her gracious home), what should I find but an account of an excursion on the new auto road to "Deep Lake Country" by a festive party that included Mrs. and Mr. W. Langford and Sheriff F. Tippins. Paradise, the writer gushed, was not to be compared with "one of the most magnificent citrus groves in Florida, producing oranges and grapefruits fine as silk. This miraculous fruit was not yet on the market." In short, Walter's citrus was still rotting on the ground.

I swallowed my pride and wrote a letter to my son-in-law offering my services one last time: after one year as overseer, if I had not solved Deep Lake's problems, I would quit. I didn't have to tell him I would work like hell: he knew that. Among other contributions, I would survey and stake out the small-gauge railway I had mentioned, to transport his produce south to Everglade for travel by fast coastal shipping to the markets.

As the man who brought the railroad to Fort Myers, Banker Langford could have hired his father-in-law at little risk: the job would banish E. J. Watson some fifty miles southeast to wild country where even Watson could cause him no embarrassment. But Walter had his reputation as a stuffed shirt to keep up, and not having the guts to refuse me outright, he sent word that he would have to think about it. He was a slow thinker, I knew that much, and perhaps he is thinking about it still. No letter came. Instead I got word, later in the summer, about Langford's new "citrus express," a small-gauge rail line from Deep Lake to Everglade. Already his crew was pushing through the coastal mangroves, building a railbed by digging that black muck with shovels and heaving it up onto a broad embankment. Also, Langford had arranged with Tippins to lease black convicts for his labor just as I had recommended years before. From what we heard, his road bosses were chewing up those prisoners like goobers and covering the bodies in the spoil bank where they fell.

So what would I have done out there as manager? Turned a blind eye? Made sure our banker knew the human cost? At any rate, this bitter news convinced me I was justified in eliminating those two agitators at the century's turn. It had come down to a matter of survival, it was them or us. All the trouble came because Bet Tucker left that pen gate open and turned loose my hogs—that was the tragedy.

BIG HANNAH

One day at Everglade, Green Waller introduced me to Big Hannah Smith, an enormous woman in a long gray old-time dress that covered her right down to her high brogans. Able to outwork most men, Green said, and thrash the rest to huckleberry jelly, she had a fair start on a handlebar mustache and a pair of shoulders that a man could yoke into a team of oxen, but she also had a woman's generous heart and tender ways. That day she told us all about her childhood on Cowhouse Island in the eastern Okefenokee, where she had three sisters as mighty as herself and three more of the common size for human females.

Out of Green's hearing, Miss Smith reminded me of another year when I passed through Georgia on my way south from Carolina and stayed on Cowhouse Island with her family. "They called me Little Hannah then, remember? You knowed me in the Biblical way," she whispered, closing bashful eyes in a face of the brown hue of a large spiced ham.

A few years earlier, Hannah had come to the southwest coast hunting her sister, the Widow Sarah McClain, who had headed for Florida after her husband was hung by mistake in Waycross, Georgia. As the first mortal to cross the Glades driving an ox team, this sister was well known as the Ox-Woman. That had been a few years earlier, in the dry season of 1906. These days she lived near old Fort Denaud on the Calusa Hatchee.

Hannah called the Ox-Woman Big Sis and our name for Hannah was Big Six, her being somewhat more than six foot tall. Hannah first showed up at Carson Gully, near Immokalee, and the Carson family remembered her distinctly. "My mother and me was all alone with our dog Cracker," one child told me, "and Cracker come from Key West, and he would bite ye. Cracker was barking so we sung out, 'Who's there?' And a voice come back, 'A lady from the Okefenokee Swamp!' So we tied up Cracker, lit the lamp, and went on out, and there she stood amongst the cypress snags, had a little black dog on a big rope tied to her belt. I was scared to death of her! 'Well, can I come in?' she said, 'cause I've walked all day and ain't had nothin to eat.' So she come inside—had to bend half over not to hit the lintel—and we give her some grub and she ate and ate and *ate*! We thought she'd bust. Sat back and said, 'I sure do like to rest after I eat,' so Mama laid her a big bed of corn shucks in our shed. I was scared she'd break loose and get into my room but she never did."

Hannah showed us a wedding photo of her sister Lydia, who was every inch as big as Hannah and Sarah and was wearing a whole rosebush for a hat. Sat in a chair with the groom in her lap and his hat only came to her shoulder. She called him Doll Baby. Doll Baby was shortly convicted of murder and sentenced to thirty years in prison, but Lydia, unable to tolerate her lover's absence, offered financial incentive to the warden to see to his release, then went to the penitentiary, wrote a check, and lugged Doll Baby away under her arm. Soon as she got home she stopped payment on her check, and all that warden could do short of going to jail was shake his head over Miss Lydia's financial acumen. "Ain't a man alive who can out-figger me," Miss Lydia liked to say. "I always said I could make five dollars out of every dollar I could lay my hands on," and she had laid her hands on plenty, Hannah told us.

These days Miss Smith worked for C. G. McKinney on the farm he called Needhelp up in Turner River, plowing and hoeing, building fences, too. Grew malangas and cabbages, which C. G. rowed down to the Bay and shipped to Key West on the *Rosina*. In the field as well as other times, Hannah wore her high brogans and gray dress down to the ground and a sunbonnet big enough to hold a bushel of fresh cabbages. She removed her boots to feel the good earth when she plowed, and of an evening loved to sing sad ballads about young country women and their faithless sweethearts. She was weary of working Needhelp all alone, she told us, so I invited her to Chatham Bend to try her hand at women's work, see how she liked it. Green brought her on a visit once or twice and finally installed her there for good.

Green was greatly annoyed that his lady friend had been followed from Turner River by Charlie Tommie, the only Mikasuki in the Glades who had got himself snake-bit by moccasins three different times. The first time he got "sick, sick, sick," the second time "sick, sick," and the third time scarcely sick at all. That is the only interesting thing I ever heard about Charlie Tommie. According to Green, this pesky redskin had spied on Miss Smith unstintingly at Needhelp, having fallen in love with this eye-popping damsel who laved her bountiful white body weekly in the river shallows. Sure enough, Charlie showed up at the Bend, camping across the river out of rifle range from where he could keep an eye on Hannah as she came and went and make sure she was treated in the manner she deserved until such time as she realized his true worth and permitted him to lead her off to live happily ever after in the swamps.

In truth he wasn't much of an admirer. "That Charlie ain't nobody no more," Richard Harden told me. By that he meant Charlie might as well be dead, having been banished by his band for trafficking with whites. In Indian terms, he no longer existed in the world even though, to the untrained eye, he still seemed to be running around loose. He was also running out of time, because one of these days, when they got around to it, his people planned to kill him. Charlie accepted this fate without complaint, so I guess you could say those Indians know what they're doing.

Green Waller never looked like much but he was certainly in love, you never saw such a damn fool in your life. And his adoration had poked up the primordial fires smoldering in his beloved, who took that hog thief to her bed and clung to him for dear life. Since she was ten times stronger, Green explained, he knew it was useless to attempt a struggle.

"Thought you wanted to grow up to be a virgin, Green," I said. "Why, hell, no!" Green retorted with a dirty grin. "It's just I was savin it for Betsey!" Betsey was that brindle sow I'd trained up to do tricks for the children. Waller claimed that in his early years, alone here on the Bend, he'd trained her to provide him with some low fulfillment which no self-respecting human being would care to think about.

Green and Hannah had washed up on the Watson place after hard voyages, and they were tired. They swept out the little Dyer cabin and made it "the first home I ever knew," as Green said weepily, wiping his long sniffling nose with the back of his hand. There they vowed to love each other the best way they knew how until death parted them.

Poor as we were, we always had plenty to eat, with Hannah's garden patch back of the cistern, also two milk cows, hogs and chickens, papaws, pears and guavas, coconuts, bananas—all in addition to fresh fish and game. Lucius was sure that in no time at all Watson's "Island Pride" Syrup would come back strong, and gradually my own hope revived a little. These people trusted me to get back on my feet and I aimed to do it. "Can't keep a good man down," Waller would snigger, winking at Hannah. Hearing those words, she would gaze at her man hungrily as she rose like a genie from the table and hurried him off to bed.

THE STRANGER

May 1910 was the month of that ghostly white fire in the sky that was seen at first as the Star of Bethlehem but was later feared by the more pious as the Great Tribulation or even the Exterminating Angel of the Book of Exodus, who would spare only those earthly dwellings whose lintels were marked with the Blood of the Lamb. According to the newspapers, that broad luminous streak crossing the heavens every night was Halley's Comet, which was causing suicides around the world out of man's terror that this sinful world was coming to an end, but since our third child was delivered at the Key West hospital while that light was still flaring in the heavens, I decided to take that mysterious apparition as a good omen.

Not long after Kate came home with Amy May, I made a business trip to Tampa. Passing through Chokoloskee on my return, I was warned by Ted Smallwood that a stranger was awaiting me at Chatham. "Calls himself John Smith," Mamie Smallwood said. "Looked like a preacher," Ted scoffed, impatient. "Never seen a preacher yet with a big ol' half-moon scar across his cheekbone." At the mention of that scar, I had to wonder if the Great Comet had been a good omen after all.

Hearing the *Brave* coming upriver, Kate and her baby were waiting on the dock, and even before I stepped ashore I could see how jittery she was. "He's here," she whispered, close to tears. When I took her in my arms to calm her, she wept desperately. "He murdered old Calvin and Aunt Celia Banks and another darkie, too! He *boasts* about it! He claims you wanted him to do that for revenge on Calvin! He claims you put him up to killing those Tolens!"

I'm ashamed to say that what I was thinking about as my wife spoke was not poor Calvin and his Celia, not at all. I was thinking about the way this bastard had humiliated an innocent young mother when he sent her to my jail cell with that knife. I strode up the mound toward the porch.

Lucius, Waller and Hannah, Sip, Frank Reese, and two young hands were all out working in the field. "John Smith" sat in my chair drinking my whiskey. His boots were sprawled on my pine table, a pistol beside them (though I suspected he'd put boots and pistol on the table when he heard me coming). In his hard-cornered black suit—a would-be riverboat gambler, not a preacher—with his pubic scraggle of a beard and long ducktails of greasy hair on his dirty neck, he looked degenerate. In fact, he stank.

"You don't smell so good," I said.

"Howdy, pardner," says this fool by way of greeting, putting on his best gunslinger squint and dangerous smile. I stood in the doorway considering the boots until he finally removed them, stood, stuck out his hand. Ignoring it, I sat down across the table.

"So you murdered Calvin."

Cox said, yep, he'd *had* to. Had to fix that fuckin Calvin for what he done in court to E. J. Watson. No nigger did that to *no* friend of Les Cox and lived to brag on it. Cox spoke in lean whispery tones out of his respect for his own honor. He had aimed to share up Calvin's savings, help me pay my legal bills, restore my good name in the community, "hold my head up proud."

Sickening as this horseshit was, it was horribly sincere; this hayseed had really thought he was saving my good name as he robbed and killed for money, having persuaded himself he was exacting the revenge I would have wanted. But having been present in the courtroom, even Leslie must have known that poor old Calvin meant no harm: he had only done what he was told to do, which was speak the truth.

As if being a dangerous liar and cold-blooded killer were not bad enough, Les Cox succumbed easily to self-pity. Assuring me he expected no reward for his act of friendship, he struggled to fight back manly tears; I had to fight back tears myself after hearing what he'd perpetrated on my account.

Leslie had found Calvin Banks pushing his old half-blind Celia on the porch swing. Told to hand over the fabled chest of William Myers's missing gold, Calvin said, "Nosuh, I ain't got it." Warned that Leslie didn't have all day, Calvin apologized but repeated what he'd said. Fed up with arguing, Cox shot him dead, then put two bullets into the old woman as she toppled off the swing and tried to crawl away. Rooted through everything those darkies had, trying to find their money, even crawled and scratched around under the cabin.

Afraid that somebody might come along, and resentful of all the trouble and the risk that mulish nigger could have saved him, Cox vented his anger on the son-in-law, who was waiting for him down the road. "He was sposed to get a little money but I never found near enough to share. Kept moanin that he would fry in Hell for getting his old folks killed without so much as one thin dime to show for it"—a threat, Leslie decided, and for once he was probably right. Les, I thought, "he's a damn witness. You better take and shut this nigger's mouth. That's what I did."

"Naturally," I said, feeling very tired.

Leslie's cousin Oscar Sanford and their friend Tom Gay were both in on his plan. Wasn't much of a plan, of course, but knowing the planners, it probably took all three of 'em to think it up. Once he was indicted, Leslie named the other two as his accomplices, to teach 'em a lesson for running off when he started killing people, then failing to support his alibi. That instinct for revenge led to his downfall because Tom Gay turned state's evidence against him.

Naturally Sheriff Dick Will Purvis released Les to go off to his own wedding in Suwannee County and was astounded when he actually came back. Men were rarely detained for killing nigras but because of all the Tolen rumors, this Cox boy had to be indicted. Stunned when he was convicted and sent to prison for the rest of his natural life, Leslie complained to the judge that a likely young man such as himself would never survive the ordeal of the chain gang, and the judge said, "Son, you will come out of it just fine."

That judge knew what he was talking about, too. In February, Will Cox rode to where the gang was laying rail near Silver Springs. The guards had unshackled the gang chain so each man could work, and one guard had uncoupled that last car and Will's boy was hanging on to the far side when it rolled back down the grade. None of the guards seemed to notice when that convict jumped off and lit out for the woods.

I recalled how Leslie bragged in jail how his daddy was such good friends with Purvis that even if he got convicted the guards would turn their backs and let him go. At the time that sounded like more of his big talk but now it turned out to be true. He went across country to his uncle John Fralick, who took him home under a canvas in his wagon a few days later.

Gay and Sanford were not prosecuted, Les told me, because the one witness who could implicate them had escaped. "Just a pitiful disgrace," he complained, "that I couldn't do my bounden duty and go over to the county court and testify on them yeller sonsabitches without gettin arrested for escapin. If *that* ain't obstructin of justice, Unc, what's this country comin to?" Les could say these hilarious things and never crack a smile.

That mention of splitting his loot with his friend Watson was the last I ever heard about his loot. It was not so much he begrudged me Calvin's savings, it was more his reluctance to admit he had blown three people's heads off for next to nothing. As Reese observed, "Three human lives for thirty-eight dollars is pretty doggone cheap even for niggers."

Piece by piece, the whole story came together. The girl Les married was my niece May Collins, which was why this idiot now called me Unc. May's father was dead and her mother was oblivious, but even so, the marriage caused an uproar in the family. Having defied her brothers by eloping, May went to stay with Coxes. The sheriff was still going through the motions of being on the lookout for the fugitive, who wore his mother's dress out in the field as a disguise, and that spring the young couple had to hole up in Will's attic. My virgin niece had been crazy about him, Les complained, but their bower was airless and so hot and humid that he couldn't get a hold on his nude bride, she got so slippery. Couldn't hardly tell which end was up, he said. Very serious about this problem, Leslie was offended by my grin, demanding to know what manner of man would dirty-grin about his own fucking niece.

"Breaks a man's heart to leave his darlin'," Les confided, deeply moved by the bittersweetness of it all. "But I knowed my gal May would sleep a whole heap better once her man had made good his ex-cape and was safe under the roof of her uncle Edgar."

He cheered up then, cocking his head. "Ever get that knife I sent into the jail with your Kate Edna?" With a sly grin, he kicked back in his chair, lifted his legs, and set his boots back on the table, clasping his hands behind his head.

Containing myself, I glared at his dirty boots. "I'll find a way to thank you, boy, you can count on that. And I won't make you wear your dress at Chatham Bend unless you want to."

"*Boy*, you said?" Les squinted harder. "*Wear my dress?*"

"What I meant was, boy, if you plan to eat while you are here under my roof, you'll keep your damn boots off my table and go on out and earn your keep like everybody else." I grabbed those boots and swung his legs so violently that he spun right off his chair onto the floor. "I catch you snooping around my wife again, I'll kill you," I advised him.

Slowly Cox picked himself up and retrieved his shooting iron, dragging the metal on the wood—his way of warning me that killers don't care for that kind of abuse. Taking his time, he shoved his revolver in his belt, then kicked his likker down. In the doorway he paused long enough to say, "You was fixin to shoot and rob that ol' nigger for yourself, ain't that it, Unc?" He nodded as if he knew my secret, then went out. He was lying out of bluster. But I had betrayed my jealousy over Kate, which he would find a way to use sooner or later.

Lately, I mistrusted my good sense, not only my memory and judgment but my explanations to myself for my disintegrating spirits. Out beyond all my anger and suspicion, wild space opened where my mind would go careening, and beyond all that lay eternal desolation like the moon's eclipse.

To keep the peace, I notified Lucius that Cox would now replace him as my foreman. Cox was strong and a good worker, if only because of his need to feel he was the best at everything he put his hand to; more important, he'd been a farm boy all his life and had more experience than anyone but Hannah, who would never be tolerated as foreman by the men.

Lucius raised his eyebrows, then went on about his business. My son was surprised I would give his job to a boy of his own age—that's how he saw Leslie, not having known him previously and not understanding yet what breed of "boy" we had here. On the other hand, he trusted me. My expression told him I knew something he didn't, and he was content to let it go until I was ready to explain.

Cox was older than Lucius by only a few months, but from appearances it might have been ten years. Both were tall and both were twenty but that was about all they had in common. Lucius had started out in life ill-fed and frail, his mother told me, while Leslie had been husky by the age of ten. (Will Cox joked that his oldest boy got his baby teeth and dropped his balls on the same night.)

Les missed his bride in bed if nowhere else, and despite my warning, he had his eye on Kate right from the start. Like May and all the other girls, Kate had thought Leslie handsome back in school days, and to judge from the way that he behaved when he thought I wasn't looking and sometimes even when I was, Les assumed that the Bethea girl never got over him. He liked to talk dangerously in front of Kate, having no idea that his bloody deeds, far from exciting her as they had our fond and foolish May, truly horrified this good young woman, to the point where she flinched and went all stiff and held her breath when he drew near.

I surprised Kate by asking her if I horrified her, too. Startled, she gave a quick shake of her head and closed her eyes. Then she opened them and looked straight at me as if to discern something behind my gaze—had I taken part in those Tolen killings, as Leslie claimed? She did not yet dare to ask straight out, fearing the truth. Instead she said, "Why do you let him stay, a man like that? With your small children?" And I said, "Because he's kin by marriage and because he spoke up for me in court." Without him, I reminded her, I might have been found guilty by a jury of my peers and hung by the neck until deceased.

Cox took out his restless lust in drink and troublemaking. One evening he told Green and Hannah that sexual activity amongst older people was downright disgusting. "How about killers?" Hannah said. She disliked Cox and would never pretend otherwise and now she whooped and slapped her thigh at the expression on his face, and Green did, too, his own thigh and hers both.

Cox shifted slowly in his chair to look at them; he was getting pretty good at the menacing pause. When Green could not meet that flat-eyed stare, Cox gave me his most knowing wink, and I gave him one right back to keep things lively.

"Who you calling a killer?" he asked Hannah, drawling it out real softly as a desperado should. Having known plenty of hard men, she was not impressed by a boy like this who took "killer" as a compliment. But Hannah did not know him the way we did, and only now did she sense something that made her wary. Though she met his gaze head-on, placid as pudding, she put her hand on Waller's arm to still him. Seeing this, Cox sneered for Kate Edna's benefit, on the point of saying something stupid.

"Go slow," I said, and his eye wavered. He "let a little smile play on his lips," as dastards did in Kate's romantic novels, and maybe bastards, too, for all I know. Folding her knitting, my wife got up and left the room.

OLD FIGHTER

Before he ran off at the century's turn, my oldest son would take Lucius to a deep hole upriver where they fished for hours for a huge old snook that Sonborn named Old Fighter. The boys could never land Old Fighter, and finally I doubted that this fish existed outside of Sonborn's imagination. But

Lucius kept on trying in the years after Sonborn left, and one Sunday he persuaded me to go along. We were close that day and he dared wonder where his long-lost brother might be now. As usual, I ignored this question.

In the charged silence of the next few minutes, Lucius hooked a fish that made a terrific run and broke his line. "Old Fighter, Rob! Got away again!" he cried, triumphant.

I had told Lucius very little about Leslie and instructed Kate and Frank to do the same. Still hoping to make friends with someone close to his own age, Lucius went after that huge snook Rob called Old Fighter and invited "John Smith" to go along. The following Sunday, when Lucius was off setting net along the coast, Cox made Sip Linsey row him upriver to Old Fighter's lair. With dynamite left over from the cistern excavation, he killed out every last fish in that hole. Sure enough, one giant snook had white hook scars around the mouth. Old Fighter, Leslie crowed to Lucius. "Sure don't look like much."

I shook my head. No, I told Cox, we call that one Little Fighter. Old Fighter is still out there.

Lucius knew better. He was upset that Leslie killed Rob's fish but also by the unfair means used to defeat a legendary creature of his boyhood that he and Rob had never really wanted to destroy.

With the fading of the Great Comet, a cavernous darkness gathered on hot summer evenings behind the long gaunt running clouds on the Gulf horizon. Fishing offshore, Lucius saw a shadow rising from the depths under the silver sprays of bait fish chopping the water. Since the thing never broke the surface, he could not imagine what it might have been. He stared all about him at the empty sea, then hauled his lines and took off for home. Over several days in that late summer, even in light variable wind, the cane leaves stirred as if seeking to escape, and hearing those small sad scraping sounds that I could not recall from other years, I felt an odd foreboding: hurricane. After the bad storm of 1909, no one expected another quite so soon, but folks were still spooked by that comet in the spring and the weather had been undependable ever since.

After the harvest, Hannah Smith informed me, she and Green aimed to move on. They had a lot of back pay coming and requested part payment in advance so they could invest it in a hog farm and a little cabin somewhere in the Cypress. Not that they were in a rush, she said, they only thought they should let me know, give me fair warning.

Hannah was nervous, knowing Green had never pestered me for wages before she came. Because I owed him so much money that he couldn't leave me, Green was an indentured servant indentured to himself. To pay him off would cripple the year's earnings, which I had counted on to get us back in business, and Hannah would have ten months coming, too.

Cox was not bright but he had a nose for trouble. While Hannah was talking, my foreman rolled his eyes a little for my benefit, a bad twist to his mouth. I would recall that cruel expression later. I would also recall mentioning that harsh measures were sometimes required to get the job done. "Not," I added, "that you need to be more harsh. You've got them terrified already." This was true. The cane crew was so fearful of Cox that they hurried their work dangerously every time he came into the field.

I was away at Tampa, buying supplies on credit and taking orders from our buyers, when Leslie gave a few gallons of syrup to a passing trader for carrying a sick field hand back to Fort Myers. This man, he told me, was so anxious to leave that he never even waited for his pay. "If that nigger ever comes up in the street askin for money—which I doubt—you can pay him then." Les was very proud of his fine work. Wasn't it part of the foreman's job to keep the payroll just as low as possible?

That evening, my son let me know that this trader must have turned up on a Sunday when everybody but Leslie and that field hand were off fishing; in fact, Leslie was the only one who ever laid eyes on that trader, since his boat was gone by the time the crew came back.

Irritable, I cut him off right there. Having just returned from Tampa, I was tired and distracted: the return on this year's harvest would scarcely pay our debts, leaving nothing to carry us into next year. Leslie had saved us money. Suspicion about my foreman's story was the last thing I wanted to hear. I yelled at him, "Now dammit, Lucius, don't nag me about John Smith! He gets the job done!" And Lucius shouted back, "Why do you still use that name when everyone but me seems to have known that he is an escaped murderer named Leslie Cox?" That was the first time in his life Lucius had ever spoken to me in such heat. I said harshly, "Frank tell you that? Or was it Kate? We will settle this when I get back. Tell Frank the same." (Because Cox knew Frank's real name we had mostly given up on "Little Joe.")

On the way south, cooling off a little, I worried that I'd talked too freely.

Telling Cox tall tales about outlaw life in the Old West was one thing, but confiding in a bad actor like that about my financial difficulties and growing desperation might have been a bad mistake. In his zeal to prove himself as foreman, Cox might have scared those hands so badly that they were happy to leave unpaid.

The day after I got back from Key West, Lucius Watson, dammit, left the Bend for good. Everyone loved him, they were all out on the bank waving good-bye. I went outside at the last minute but I did not wave. I was wounded more than I would ever admit to anybody except maybe Hannah. We enjoyed each other, she was my good friend and the only person on the place who called me by my Christian name, but when I went to her for some advice, I got abuse instead.

"Your Lucius is a very good young feller and he loves you dearly and you wouldn't listen to him, Ed. You don't want to hear the truth, nor see it, neither."

"What's the truth then, woman, since you know so much?"

Hannah burst out in a rush, "Your boy can't work with that foreman of yours, and me'n Green can't neither. We done our best to bide our time and see things your way but we sure don't like what's going on. We just don't care to live no more around that feller." She lowered her voice, looking back over her shoulder. "You know me, Ed, I ain't what you'd call a scaredy-cat nor superstitious. But lately Green—well, both of us—been kind of hearin somethin."

"Hearing *what?*" I yelled. "Come on now, Hannah!"

Hannah looked more and more upset. "Hearin this kind of hummin on the wind, like somethin very bad is comin down on us." She was wiping her hands red with her dish towel. "You know us, Ed. We never aimed to let you down. But now we got to leave."

The thin ax mark of a mouth tight-closed under that mustache showed her determination, and since she was such a level-headed woman, I had to listen.

"What happens on this place ain't no business of ours," she whispered. "We never seen nothin and never heard nothin, we ain't never goin to say a word to *nobody*, and that's the truth. It's just, we got to go." She was close to tears. "Why don't you say somethin?" she cried. "You had the use of my man all these years and no complaint. We stuck by you and worked hard to tide you over your hard times, but now we want to go and we need our wages!"

I never thought I'd see this woman near hysterics. I had to shout her down. "Now dammit, Hannah, you know my bad luck! If I have to pay you people off on top of all our debts—"

"Whose fault is that? Them lawyer bills ain't ours!" She backed away, afraid she'd gone too far. Her red eyes filled, she mopped them with her apron. "You shouldn't ought to ask no more of us, Ed Watson."

Hannah fell still because Cox, drawn to the racket, appeared at the corner of the house. He lounged against the wall, picking his teeth, cynical as usual and unabashed. Not until I stared at him would he go away. I then asked Hannah to think it over, urging her to stay just one more year. When she shook her head frantically, unable to consider such a thing, I said, "Because if you leave here, you will leave unpaid."

"Ed, we ain't young no more! We got nobody and nothin to take care of us except what we got comin." She stood eyes closed, hands clenched on her apron: I waited for her, feeling all wrong, but I had no choice. "I reckon we will have to wait," she murmured finally. She shuffled back inside in her home-hewn sandals. Except for the cutters hacking down the cane, Big Hannah Smith was the only person on the place besides myself who did not go barefoot.

Kate and the children went along next time I went to Chokoloskee, and they stayed behind with Kate's friend Alice McKinney. From there she went to stay with Mamie Smallwood, then Marie Alderman, finding excuses not to come home for weeks. Scared of me now, she did not speak of Cox again but only said that Chatham Bend was too hard on the small children—the hurricane season, the mosquitoes—and too dangerous with all of those rough men. I assumed she'd heard rumors about Josie Jenkins from her female friends but she later admitted it was Leslie who told her.

CHAPTER 10

✦

THE FEUD

In the hurricane season of late summer, the heat and humidity were something to fear. Even at midday, mosquitoes hung outside the screens on a miasmal air so moist and sweet that it might have come on a south wind out of the tropics.

That summer we had a young Mikasuki squaw who'd been thrown out by her band for consorting with the moonshiner Ed Brewer. She was not exclusively for his own use, it seems, because he snuck in to the Bend one day, tried to rent her to our coloreds. Sip Linsey was a pious darkie of the old-time religion and Frank Reese was still pining for Jane Straughter, so those two boys had little use for a beat-up aboriginal with advanced alcohol and hygienic problems.

When Hannah got wind of what was going on, she grabbed Brewer by one arm and swung him off the dock into the current. "Flung that sumbitch clean off the Bend!" Green boasted. "Cut his boat loose, too, while she was at it. Never so much as ast if he could swim!" And Hannah said, "Well, that is correct, I never give enough thought to his future. If that croc got to him, he might not of had one." But Green had seen him grab hold of his skiff, and probably he'd dragged himself ashore farther downriver.

Hannah gave that wild girl a good wash and named her Susie. She taught her a few chores to pay her feed, along with as much Baptist instruction as a redskin knowing nothing of our tongue might get a handle on. But seeing her slip into the outhouse must have set Cox thinking about certain details of what was taking place behind that door because he was awaiting her when she came out. The way he told it at the table—he thought it was pretty comical—he grasped her wrists in one hand and with the other yanked up her old rag of a shift. Held her squirming up against him until the mosquitoes swarming her bare bottom made her weep, and pretty soon she gave up and lay down for him. "Couldn't resist me," Leslie said. Hannah said, "She ain't nothin but a child and you ain't nothin but a raper. Hang your head in shame."

That afternoon Earl Harden showed up in his new launch. Never hailed the house, just dropped someone off quick without tying up. By the time I reached the porch, he was back out in mid-river idling his motor, greedy to see what might take place when E. J. Watson realized who that stranger was. Ever since he went to Key West to accuse me in that Tucker business, Earl would only look me in the eye when he could not avoid it, then smile so hard that when he turned, the smile got left behind. I honestly believe that if that feller hadn't been so scared of me, he would have waylaid me and shot me in the back.

Earl was jolly as could be with white men, he worked hard at it, but teasing him about his bad attitude toward Henry Short was putting raw salt on a leech. I liked to tease him: he had niggers on the brain. I used that word, too, of course, used it casually like most men, Henry Short included. But men who hated blacks like Earl twisted a sneer into it, a stink, the way a cat twists out its crap, leaving that nasty little point at the back end.

Awaiting me, the figure on the dock stood still, arms folded on his chest. His silhouette was black against the river shine but I knew him at once. Those big gun butts jutted upward from his hips like horns.

Waller came to the door behind me, napkin tucked into his collar. "Jesus," he whispered. Hannah, huffing up behind, stared from one face to another for a clue. In the kitchen, Frank rose from his beans and went out the back door and came around to the corner of the house, then stepped back quick, out of the line of fire. Still watching the front, the figure on the dock raised one hand toward the black man in a kind of greeting.

I knew much better than to draw my gun. I worked it up out of its shoulder holster, let it slide down into my coat sleeve, having practiced that trick often enough to know how to do it undetected.

"Drop it," he said. This pistolero had drawn on me so quick that I had no choice. At the dangerous clatter of a loaded weapon on the pinewood porch, everyone jumped.

Dutchy was grinning and I grinned right back, lest he imagine I was paralyzed by those big guns of his. And there and then, out of bone craziness or love of life, he flipped both six-guns and sprang into the air in a backwards somersault, landing in time to catch his weapons neatly on the spin, all set to shoot. One barrel was pointed at my heart, the other covered the dropped revolver on the porch in case it had occurred to me to grab it up, which it had not.

Laughing, he dropped his guns loosely in their holsters and came forward. The others backed and filled like cattle in the doorway. Retrieving my weapon, he dumped the cartridges into his pocket, tossed it back to me. "Damn if it don't feel dandy to be back. Home is where the heart is, that right, Frank?"

Reese had been grinning right along, Green Waller, too. These fools were tickled to death to see this swarthy little criminal who had cost us so much wasted work and a year's pay, and they caught their fool Boss, who had sworn to take his life, kind of smiling, too.

"Glad to see me, Mister Ed? Aim to invite me in?"

"There's no free food for gunslingers around here," I barked. "You aim to stay, you better change those fancy duds, start working off that thousand gallons of good syrup you still owe us."

"Same ol' Mister Ed! Talkin rough to a sensitive young feller that might take a mind to spoil another thousand." Still grinning, he ambled over to the bunkhouse, hunted up his old coveralls. He put them on over his holster belt and reappeared, delighted.

Dutchy gave me all that time to get the drop on him. I didn't do it, and a good thing, too. He'd put away one of his guns, but the other, although hidden, was rigged butt forward on his left side, ready to be drawn by his right hand, as I knew from the fact that his left gallus hung loose and the left flap of his coveralls, too. This boy knew I knew and grinned. "Same ol' Mister Ed!" said Dutchy Melville.

"There's a law against concealed weapons in this country," I reminded him. "Might have to make a citizen's arrest."

"Well, I *know* that, Mister Ed, bless your kind heart!" He glanced around the place, wary of ambush. "Who's that in the house?"

"That's the foreman, finishing his dinner." Hannah Smith was awed by his keen hearing.

Lifting his hat, Dutchy greeted Hannah with a dandy bow—the first she had ever received without a doubt. Next, he saluted her hog reiver—"How do, Mr. Waller!" Green waved and smiled, nudging his woman, proud to be singled out by name. "And Frank, too!" That hard man raised both hands high and shook them in a single fist like that black champion Jack Johnson, who had whipped America's "Great White Hope" back in July.

Standing there on his bandy legs in the hot sun of September, young Dutchy was set for anything that came his way. "Ol' place lookin kind of run down, Mister Ed. But I reckon it's as close to a good home as a poor outlaw boy could hope for so I sure am grateful for your hospitality."

"You abused my hospitality. Don't forget that because I won't." I had sworn a solemn oath this boy would die the next time he crossed my path, yet it seemed a great waste in a time of labor shortage to kill a man so full of ginger.

"Mister Ed, I won't forget it and I don't regret it cause you had it comin," he answered cheerfully. "So I'll just take my old job back as the foreman."

I was dumbfounded. To feel so confident he would be welcomed! And in a way, of course, he was quite right; he had slipped past my guard. Maybe he knew that too much time had passed, that I had no real heart for revenge.

All this while, my foreman kept on with his eating, to demonstrate indifference to the visitor. When we came in, he looked up, sullen, interrupted in his chewing, and from the start, disdaining the other, he spoke only to me. Threatened by Melville's dangerous glee, he instinctively disliked and feared him, while Melville understood in that same instant why the foreman had stayed inside. Each shifted his gaze slightly to one side, as dogs do, to avoid a tangle before everything was ready—before, that is, one had the other dead to rights.

Both dogs ignored my introduction, as if their acquaintance would be too short-lived to waste breath on civilities. In fact, Leslie belched when told the other's name. "Ain't this the little piece of shit that messed up all that syrup?" And Dutchy said, "Ain't this the back-shootin sonofabitch whose sloppy mouth got you and Frank in so much trouble in north Florida?"

With everything spelled out so quick, they nodded together in acceptance of the duty to put the other one to death as soon as possible.

Dutchy helped himself to a hearty repast and went out into the field. Knowing his job from the year before, he pointedly ignored the foreman's orders and got his work done any way he pleased, whistling away all afternoon. That whistling was brassy and aggressive, and it got on the foreman's nerves just as intended. From the very start, Dutchy wanted Les to blow up and attack him, giving him his excuse to cut him down.

The tension gathered like rolled-up barbed wire. The next day was much the same. I was very glad Kate and the children were safe in Chokoloskee and relieved Lucius was gone, although I missed him: I guess he was the only son I ever missed.

I warned Les Cox that Dutchy Melville drew a gun a lot faster than most. "Faster'n Desperader Watson, from the sound of it," Leslie sneered. He had sniffed out my wariness around Melville. "Hard to take that feller by surprise," I said.

"I noticed." Leslie yawned and stretched, not anxious exactly, just flexing his nerves. "But I ain't noticed any eyes in the back of that boy's head." He took my silence for approval.

From the first, their enmity flickered like two snakes' tongues, silently and without cease. Not wanting war before the crop was in, I forbade them to carry guns. "I need him for the harvest," I told Dutchy. "Can't have you using him for target practice."

Dutchy said, "Mister Ed, I want my job back and he's in the way." The damned fool had forgotten all about that ruined syrup. Handing over his shooting irons, he held my eye by way of saying, *I trust you, Mister Ed.* And that trust ate at me, I won't deny it.

Over the years, I have run across outlaws in the Territories and a lot more in Arkansas State Prison who would not hesitate to kill when that seemed necessary, but unless they were young or kind of loco, they never made too much of it—neither claimed it nor excused it. Belle's son Eddie Reed was one of these, a hellion, arsonist, and robber but no killer until someone tampered with his tight-wound spring. Dutchy Melville was another. In a robbery, Dutchy had murdered a fine lawman, Clarence Till, so I can't honestly say he was good-hearted, but he had fun in him and folks liked him.

Cox was different. One way or another, he had come by a sick taste for taking life. By this I mean, a need came over him. Major Will Coulter at

Edgefield was this same cold breed: *Sometimes it gets so us ol' boys might feel like killin us a nigger.* Though Coulter had been speaking about blacks, he could probably have made do with any color. Needed to take life from time to time as other men might need a woman, assuring himself that the man sprawled bloody had it coming; if he was not guilty, then "inferior" would have to do.

I never saw Les easy around anyone outside his clan. Never curious about others, let alone sympathetic. Never listened and had nothing to tell except on the subject of himself. His concern with people all came down to how much deference they paid him even if he had to scare and bully them to get it, yet he felt left out and did not know how to find his way back in— a very bad feeling, as I remembered from Clouds Creek. Perhaps he dreaded his own isolation, not understanding it, and perhaps it was his loneliness that made him dangerous. Perhaps he had to strike something to feel in touch with life, to make sure that he himself was really there.

After the first or second killing, there is nothing much to stop a man from the third and fourth and fifth. Because it is too late to go back—too late for redemption—one may as well go forward, though the path of one's lost life grows dim like the passage of an unknown animal through the high reeds. Swamp water fills the disappearing track and scent disintegrates in the tall growth and in a little, the faint smudge of disturbance in the morning dew is gone.

Sometimes I wonder what Will's boy might have become if circumstances had been different, if something like that random mule hoof had not splayed a nerve, laid bare that streak in him. He might have gone off to the Major Leagues and found the notoriety he needed, reserving his beanballs for those days when he indulged his deep urge to do harm.

For men of criminal persuasion, notoriety is crucial; ill fame is sought as a dark honor. When we were in Duval County jail, a newspaper reference to "the handsome young murder suspect Leslie Cox" was the only detail that boy gave a damn about. He would snatch away that paper just to see his name in print, read it over and over. In his utter lack of knowledge of himself, he had lost restraint in everything he did, like a rabid dog that has left behind the known traits of its species to become some mad lone creature.

In Arkansas Prison, I knew a backwoods murderer—scraggy feller with gat teeth and a long nose bursting with black hair. This man opined that a first killing was a first taste of manhood, along with that first naked rassle with mother or sister. Had 'em both, he'd cackle in that rooster voice, so I guess he knew what he was talking about.

FAMILY VISIT

In September we had a "family visit" when the mail boat brought young Joe Gunnin from Fort White whose sister Amelia was betrothed to Willie Collins, also his friend Bill Langford of Suwannee County, a kinsman of my son-in-law. Since I was unwelcome in a Langford house and probably any Collins house as well, I resented having to feed these two for a whole week until the mail boat returned.

One evening in passing Gunnin referred to my mother's death, the news of which Cox had not bothered to share. There had been no room for her in Aunt Tabitha's pinched, iron-girded plot and no money to pay for a small headstone in the Collins ground at Tustenuggee, where at present she lay in a shallow hole like an old cat. True, I had disliked my little mother. Even so it galled me that her elder child and only son had not been notified in time to contribute to her funeral expenses.

Asked why my sister had sent no word, Gunnin explained nervously that Mrs. Collins, who now resided with Willie and his bride, was no longer aware of very much that was going on around her. The past went storming through my heart and mind, grief hard behind it. I said heedlessly, "That is because she is a morphine addict. Lost such brain as she was born with long ago."

Offended for my sister, Hannah banged her platter of sweet yams and venison down in front of me. Serving the plates in a silence jarred by the knock and scrape of crockery, I regretted that I'd spoken caustically about poor Minnie, whom I had done my best to protect when we were little. But even then—because she was a tattletale—I'd made her cry. Those big dark eyes had filled with tears at the first whisper of an unkind word.

In recent years, my sister passed most of her waking hours in the chimney corner, where until the evening she slipped safely into death, she might breathe unnoticed, like a moth. Since our days of terror under the roof of Ring-Eye Lige, passing unnoticed was all poor Ninny ever asked of life.

I questioned Gunnin, checking Leslie's stories. In the long year since Attorney Cone had got him off in the Sam Tolen case, Leslie had hung on at Fort White. He was much offended that his neighbors had not welcomed him, that there was no baseball team to star for, and that the ball clubs at Live Oak and High Springs had not invited him to try out as their pitcher. All over the south county, good folks shied from him. At first he sulked, Joe Gunnin said—that was Les all over—but before long he was making drunken threats against those who'd joined the lynch mob. Finally he was warned to leave the district, being in more danger from scared neighbors than he had ever been from the court of justice. Even his family, "hated out," had been obliged to move away to Alachua County.

Over time, I gleaned the rest from Leslie himself. His plan had been to run off with May Collins and join a big-league baseball team so he needed a grubstake. Like everyone else, he had heard about Calvin Banks's hoarded-up money, and Calvin's son-in-law had mentioned where it might be found. That son-in-law had been no-account from birth, he'd pulled a muscle in his brain or something. Probably never occurred to him that those old folks might be harmed, so during the robbery, he waited for Leslie back along the road, expecting a share of the proceeds—a bad mistake, since finding no proceeds worth sharing, Leslie in ill humor shot him dead. Cox had come to Chatham Bend not to give me half the money but because he had no other place to hide.

I was now so broke that I agreed to sell the best of my Fort White farmland to Jim Delaney Lowe, even though he'd testified against me. Getting wind of that land sale, my lawyers threatened me with forcible arrest and extradition to Columbia County for nonpayment of their fees, hinting that I might be lynched upon arrival. So much for lawyers. After such a year, small wonder that my rages were recurring. These violent eruptions split my head and yanked my heart around so wildly that I scarcely dared breathe for fear of stroke. Breaking out in sudden chilling sweats, I could only sink down panting.

The mail boat brought news of Samuel Clemens's death: at least I would have smart company in Hell or Heaven. Somewhere Twain said, *I don't believe in Hell but I am afraid of it.* One day when I quoted those words, Lucius asked me my opinion, no doubt wondering if his Papa, too, might be afraid of Hell (being so unlikely to wind up in Heaven), I guess he meant I shrugged him off, saying I'd had no word from the "higher-ups" as to my fate.

I could have answered him more honestly. I could have said, I don't believe in God and never have. I could have said that on Judgment Day, when the true worth and meaning of one's life is weighed, the judge I feared most would be Edgar Watson.

At Chatham Bend nobody ate who did not earn his grub and I gave our guests every dirty job we had. Because Gunnin had recognized "John Smith" and was bound to tell the law where he was hiding, Leslie was very agitated by our visitors, thought it might be wise to knock these green-horns on the head and toss 'em in the river. I reminded him that their families knew where their boys had been headed and would show up here with the law if they failed to return.

Cox boiled over when Joe Gunnin slipped and called him "Les." Cox snarled, "I reckon you mean 'John.' That other feller you thought you might of saw? Well, you ain't never seen him, understand?" Les commenced his deadly nodding, glaring hard at one and then the other. He said, "Maybe I ought to shut your mouths right here this minute."

Melville always said straight out what popped into his head. I never met such a carefree feller in my life. He slapped his knee and guffawed at Cox's threat. "He's aimin to go gunnin for a Gunnin!" He laughed in loud heart-felt delight at his own joke but his hoots soon turned into hard jeering, calculated to bait Cox into a showdown, though his guns were on the side-board, out of reach. "You rover boys got that? You ain't never seen this sonofabitch you thought you seen settin right here stinkin up the place under your nose."

Leslie, gone white around the mouth, pointed at Dutchy's eyes in sign that he would pay for this sooner or later but Dutchy only pointed right back at him. "Tell that boy to stop that dretful squintin, Mister Ed! He's scarin these poor fellers half to death!" He whooped some more, informing the visitors that if he were to practice up on his mean squint as long and hard as that dumb hick across the table, he would probably end up with that same ugly face, tight-squinched as a bat's asshole. And he threw back his head and laughed so hard that he toppled his chair right over backwards.

Cox knew that Dutchy's guns were out of reach and his hand shot for his knife as he leapt forward. But Dutchy had toppled his chair on purpose, and being an acrobat, kept right on rolling and bounced back up onto his feet with something glinting in his hand. Those black eyes were glinting, too—even his teeth seemed to be glinting. I never saw that knife fly to his hand, but most likely he had it hid in his boot lining.

Cox was no knife fighter. He stopped his lunge by grabbing at the table, barging it noisily across the floor. He backed off then and shortly quit, dropping his knife like that hayseed Tommy Granger in Arcadia. Dutchy kicked it skittering against the wall. Taking his time, he sidled toward the door to cut off an escape. He had Cox where he wanted him, with more excuse to finish him in self-defense than he would ever need. He wrinkled his nose at the thin blade in his own hand, as if loath to defile its pristine edge. His cat eyes twitched in little shivers of the pupil.

Les could not look at him. He was staring at me, all but imploring his old partner to step in: *Ain't you told me you had swore to kill him?* Yet again, his predicament was Watson's fault. When I kept silent, folding my arms on my chest, he let out a small grunt of angry panic, and I let him twist. But after a moment, I lifted my cup of shine to Dutchy in signal that he'd won, that it was over.

Dutchy put his knife away too readily and his big grin of relief betrayed his weakness: he lacked the philosophy or the hard heart required to kill an undefended man, even this man who yearned to take his life. Frank Reese in the kitchen doorway saw this, too, and turned away disgusted. His stormy face as he glared past mine made it clear how much he was going to dislike the inevitable outcome of this feud, although he had known since the spoiled syrup episode that Melville had to pay.

Cox had sunk down on his chair edge, incensed by a humiliation made much worse by my toast to the victor, but in a moment he realized that my intervention on his behalf was a sign of where I stood, and this knowledge brought that curled edge to his mouth which Sam Tolen must have seen as he knelt in the white road on that spring morning—that curled edge caused, in my experience, by a metallic foretaste at the back corners of the tongue that comes as a signal of imminent, absolute power over life and death.

Dutchy Melville would be missed at Chatham Bend. This young gunman had done me a great harm, beyond forgiveness, but that was no longer why he had to go. My friend Will Cox's oldest boy had tried to stifle Calvin's testimony at my trial and had offered help in an escape, had that been necessary. Also, he had married my niece May. Leslie was kinfolks.

From that hour till the day the mail boat came, our Fort White visitors fell all over themselves to please Ed Watson and his outlaws, swearing to John Smith again and again that his presence on the Watson place was no business of theirs and would never be mentioned to a single soul. When the boat appeared, I did not quit work to walk over to the dock and say goodbye. Before boarding, Gunnin and young Langford confided to Hannah their shock at my indifference to the news of my mother's death and the great illness of my sister—small wonder, they said, that Mr. Watson had such a bad reputation in Fort White.

According to Green, Big Hannah bit their heads off. "Ain't that why you rover boys come gawkin around here in the first place? To visit a real live desperader in his hideout, then run back home to brag?"

Like my dear Mandy, Hannah Smith had a pretty good idea of who Ed Watson was. She did not approve of all his ways but neither would she see him criticized by anybody who had not earned that right. I had few true friends and this big woman was one so I reckon I should have taken better care of her.

Needing quick income to pacify my creditors, I drove everyone hard to get the crop in early, get our product to market ahead of the competition. With my outsized vat and boiler, I could turn out more and better syrup than all the local cane fields put together, but to stay ahead, I had to farm more land, and for that I needed new capital investment—this at a time when I was bankrupt and in debt and nowhere welcome in Fort Myers among businessmen.

Everyone on the place looked tired, less from the hard labor in the field than from the tension between Cox and Melville. "My trigger finger's itchin somethin pitiful," Les would whisper—his way of complaining that he wouldn't mind encouragement and perhaps a little help from his uncle Ed. "After harvest"—my answer to every question—was unsatisfactory to all hands including me, obliging me to face two aspects of my own character I didn't care for: one, that I did not want Dutchy harmed before I got more work out of him, and two, that I lacked the guts to set him up for Cox and see him slaughtered.

BLACK OCTOBER

In early October, Kate came home from Chokoloskee. People were turning cold toward her, she said. By now it was common knowledge that Ed Watson was harboring two convicted killers and no doubt other criminals as well: according to rumor, the Watson Gang aimed to found an outlaw nation in the wilderness. Even Ted Smallwood, who still passed for a friend, was referring sardonically to "Emperor Watson." I could no longer pretend to myself, far less to Kate, that our children were safe here on the Bend, and anyway, the time had come to confront those Bay folks and their stories before more damage could be done. I ordered Kate not to unpack, I was taking her back next morning. "Where will we stay?" she asked. "Nobody wants us."

At his own request, Dutchy came with us. "I been needin a change of air," he said, "after all them weeks cooped up with that yeller skunk you got for foreman." The knowledge that Cox was laying for him and would kill him at first chance—and his growing uneasiness about where I stood—were wearing away at Dutchy's spirits; he had dark circles under his eyes from watching his back throughout the day and listening all night. As soon as we left the Bend, he said, "Excuse me, ma'am," and lay down in the stern. He fell asleep flat out on the bare boards while the children stared at him and never woke up till the launch nudged Ted's dock at Chokoloskee.

Dutchy's Wanted poster was plastered on the porch of Smallwood's post office store so naturally the whole community lined up to take a gander at this armed and dangerous fugitive. Folks were elbowing and grinning, wondering aloud if those guns were real, so Dutchy performed a sudden back flip on the dock, coming up with six-guns blazing at the sky and scattering his thrilled audience into the trees. But when he strutted across the yard and banged his heels on the store porch, he was followed by a low and ugly groan. As Smallwood explained, folks felt humiliated by "Watson's hired gun" and they blamed me. "Dammit, E. J.," Ted whispered, "we just don't want that kind of outlaw around here."

"How about my kind, Ted?"

"Nor that Cox feller neither." Smallwood was in no mood to be teased.

I gazed after Kate, who had gone off with Mamie to see Marie Alderman's new baby.

Ted looked alarmed. "Nosir, it weren't your missus, E. J.! It weren't Edna told us! Some feller was mentionin Smith's scar and another feller said, 'That so-called preacher you are talkin about sounds mighty like a killer name of Leslie Cox.' "

"Alderman," I said.

"No, no, E. J.! I never said that! Can't rightly recall who might of mentioned it, but it weren't Wilson!" Just when I needed someone I could count on, Smallwood was lying to protect a neighbor.

From his porch steps, I announced to the small crowd that I never hired fugitives intentionally. Those men had turned up uninvited (Dutchy bowed, ironical: nobody laughed). At harvest time, as folks well knew, a cane planter had to take what he could get; those men would be sent away after the harvest. With my new family and my syrup industry, I was making a fresh start here in the Islands and hoped to remain on the best of terms with my old friends and neighbors. But nobody seemed reassured, and my drunk gunslinger didn't help much when he cheered my speech by shooting off his weapons, making children screech.

Kate rejoined me, very close to tears. Like Smallwood, my wife was faltering just when I needed her. She dreaded going back to Chatham and she dreaded staying here where doors were closing. She no longer felt welcome at Marie Alderman's house. "How about Mrs. Smallwood?" I asked in a low voice. "Oh no, I can't! We've imposed on them so often!" Wigginses? McKinneys? She shook her head. Even here, she feared for our little children, who would not stop crying.

I went to Aldermans. "Wilson, come on out!" He cracked his door. I snapped, "You listen here, boy. It's nearly two years since I came back, and I have never said one word to you about how you ran off from north Florida when your help was needed as a witness." I let that sink in. "And now you've told John Smith's real name to this community. Want me to tell him you did that, Wilson?"

Alderman tried to talk. Nothing came out. He dared not say what his wife had hinted to my Kate, that he'd fled south before my trials because he thought that I was guilty but was scared to testify against his boss.

"So I'd be much obliged if you and Marie could take in Kate Edna and the children while I finish up my harvest at the Bend." Wilson said he'd be happy to have 'em and I said I'd be happy to pay their keep. That's the way we left it.

I went back to the boat and told my wife that she and the children could expect a warm welcome at Aldermans. She moaned, in tears, which was not like her. I told her sharply to get hold of herself and not upset the children any further.

Dutchy helped me lug their stuff. Having no hand free to draw, he stepped along uneasily, turning halfway around every few steps, thrashing his head from side to side like a stepped-on snake.

Dutchy was sodden by the time we left and I drank with him most of the way home. He looked bewildered, sensing the darkness in my mood. Again and again he turned to look at me, as if to catch an expression on my face that might reveal what I was thinking. He knew I liked him despite everything and he wanted to count on my support in case of ambush. But not knowing what he wished to say and not wanting to beg, he lifted the jug, kind of shy and wistful, just to toast me. "Mister Ed," he said.

I ran the boat down the autumn coast, thinking of nothing. Cloud reflections sailed beneath the surface of the sea like sunken snowy mountains. Ascending Chatham River on a falling tide, the *Warrior* throbbed hard against the cold weight of the current. Toward dusk, we were in sight of Chatham Bend.

Splashing water on his face, sobering quickly, Dutchy loosened his guns in their holsters, studying the house and sheds as we drew near, not knowing if and where Cox might be hiding. For all his long sideburns and bravado, he looked like a young boy. He slapped a mosquito, rubbed his neck, touched his gun butts lightly over and over. The walls of silent mangrove, the oncoming night, ate at his nerve: I suppose he was still trying to persuade himself that as long as I was with him, he was safe.

I eased the boat in, letting the current slow her. Hopping off onto the dock, awaiting the tossed line, he peered about him. Instead of tossing him the line, I let the *Warrior* drift back clear of the dock, then turned her bow. Next time he looked, the distance was too great to leap.

"Mister Ed?" he called out softly. "Where you going, Mister Ed?" I wanted to yell at him, *Duck down!* because from the house in this late light he would be silhouetted on the river. I had never talked to Cox about this, never approved it, but Cox would have heard the boat and would be ready.

"Lost Man's River," I said, feeling all wrong about everything.

"Tonight? You never said nothin about Lost Man's!" Notched high, his voice stabbed me. I lifted my hand, good-bye, good luck, and gunned the boat into her turn. His wild curse wandered on the river.

Knowing that on that dock he was a dead man, Dutchy Melville bounded in swift zigzags toward the boat shed, seeking cover. I did not turn to see that—he had no choice.

A voice—was that Reese?—yelled out a warning. I fixed my gaze dead ahead, gunning the motor to increase the noise, but could not escape: when the shot rang out, I heard it. A second shot scattered the echo of the first.

In the lee of Mormon Key, phosphorus glimmered where the anchor gouged the water. In memory of Herbie Melville, I drank off what remained in Dutchy's jug.

Mister Ed? Where you going, Mister Ed? The first tears in many years came to my eyes.

That was the tenth of October, 1910, a Monday. At first light next day, I went south to Key West. Entering by the back door, I remained three days at Eddie's Bar, left for dead by unknown companions who hauled my carcass somewhere out of the way. Crawling out into noon light, clothes caked with beer spill and rank sawdust and piss (not all of it my own), I returned to my boat and left that town without any clear idea where I might be headed.

This was my story: I dropped Dutchy at the Bend on my way to Key West. That much was true. If there was a shooting after that, I was not responsible, and if Green and Hannah doubted me, I could not help it. As for Frank Reese, who understood that what Dutchy had done could never be forgiven—yet at the same time hating Cox, hoped I would forgive him—I might have to order him to keep his opinions to himself.

On the way north across the Banks, the Gulf sky to the west looked blotched, peculiar. I stopped at Lost Man's to make sure I was seen by the Hamiltons or Hardens on my return journey. This was a Saturday. With her men off somewhere in the Glades, Mrs. Harden seemed leery of me and behaved queerly, never offering so much as a bite to eat. The Hardens were troubled by the weather. The heavy stillness made everybody irritable and restless. And pretty quick I sensed that somebody behind that window had a bead on me.

I anchored off Mormon Key again and at daybreak I headed for the Bend. I dreaded facing Hannah most of all.

The Bend was empty. No one came out onto the porch. The fields were empty and the house was silent and it was near noon. Perhaps they had learned of the oncoming storm and gone off with the mail boat or some fisherman. I called and shouted. There was no echo, yet I heard my own voice coming back.

Taking the shotgun, I approached the house and peered in through the windows at the unwashed pots and mildewed food left on the stove and table. At one end of the room, an overturned chair lay in a thickened blackish pool that looked like molasses or spilled oil. I did not go in.

At the boat shed, Dutchy's coveralls hanging from their nail gave me a turn: he might lie closer than I wished to know. In broken light, the west wind rattled the dry cane stalks stacked beside the boiler, feeling out the Watson place for the coming storm.

Again I called but there was nobody—nobody, at least, who wished to answer. That silence crept around behind me. I did not call again.

At Pavilion Key the clam boats were gone. Instead of running to throw her arms around my neck, my sweet Pearl fled me, flying across the littered barren where the tents had been. From behind her mother's shack, she called out in a frightened voice that everyone had left, even young Minnie. "That poor girl run off to Key West to get away from you !" Josie hollered through her canvas door.

I commanded her to pack up quick and board my boat because a bad storm was on the way, but it was her brother who opened the flap and stepped outside to discuss the coming weather: said this storm could never be as bad as the hurricane of 1909, which they'd survived here. "You're all idiots," I told him, very angry.

Tant Jenkins was past thirty now, already stooped. He still clung to that comical mustache that when he spoke jumped on his upper lip "like a l'il ol' hairy toad," his sister said. Tant wore it anyway, content to conceal his shyness behind his lifelong disguise as a damn fool.

Josie did most of the talking from her bed. "If we'd wanted to leave here, Mister Jack, we'd of left this mornin with the rest of 'em. But I have concluded that this key ain't goin nowhere so we're stayin."

As I have related, this small woman was spry in the head and spry in bed, with plenty of high spirits to go with it, but common sense was quite another matter.

"Well, you and Tant can perish if you want but if that little feller on your teat is mine, the way you're telling people, I am taking him with me and Pearl, too."

And Josie said, "You show up at Chokoloskee with your backdoor family, Mister Watson, li'l Mis Big-Butt Preacher's Daughter gonna kick your ass right out of bed!" I said, "My wife is not your business, missus. And unlike some, she don't drink hard liquor and knows how to hold her tongue."

I was sorely tempted to take my daughter by the scruff and throw her aboard the *Warrior* if I had to but I saw no sign of her. Josie gave me a queer wry look, saying that what with all the awful stories, poor Pearl was scared of her own father. "So you can go to hell, Jack Watson, and take Pearl with you if she's fool enough, but me'n your sweet baby boy aim to stay put where we're at, and Stephen, too!"

Stephen S. Jenkins offered a small rueful smile by way of saying that if his sister and her kids had their hearts set on staying, he reckoned he'd stay, too, kind of look out for 'em. This bachelor whom nobody took seriously had always felt responsible for this ragtag bunch he called his family. I told Tant, "If you damned people are so drunk and shiftless you won't save yourselves, then you better start praying to that God of yours."

Pearl slipped out from behind a shack and followed me down toward the water, keeping her distance like a half-wild dog. At the dock, gray wind waves slapped along the pilings. Except for Tant's moored sailing skiff, rising and banging on wind-dirtied whitecaps, the anchorage was empty.

The child watched me haul my anchor, frightened to leave and frightened to be left, frightened of the future altogether. I called, "You sure, Pearl?" and she nodded gravely, leaning back into the wind, pale and tattered as a cornstalk against the dark wall of that weather. "Your daddy loves you, sweetheart!" Because I'd never told her that, not in so many words, I startled her. She glanced back toward the shack, then ran along the shore a little ways, crying something like, *Did you do it, Daddy? Is it true?* What was she talking about? Then blown sea mist closed over her and she was gone.

This was Sunday, the 15th of October.

Off Rabbit Key, the *Warrior* passed the last clam boats, on their way north toward Caxambas. Nobody aboard those boats returned my wave.

THE GREAT HURRICANE

Late that afternoon, in Chokoloskee, Bembery Storter's boy, young Hoad, blew into Smallwood's all excited and related how bodies had been found in Chatham River near the Watson place and how a nigra had rowed out to Pavilion and reported that a man named Cox, with Mr. Watson absent, had murdered three on Chatham Bend last Monday evening. This nigra claimed that E. J. Watson put Cox up to it but took that back when he was hollered at by Watson's friends and backdoor family such as Josie Jenkins.

Everyone but the Storter boy knew that Watson was right there in the store. One or two glanced over, looked away. Two went out and it was then Bembo's boy noticed me, standing back against the wall. Being Lucius's best friend, he was rattled and fell quiet, cast his eyes down. "You were telling how this nigra said he'd mistook himself about Ed Watson," Smallwood encouraged him. "How he took back what he first said, put it all on Cox."

"That because they threatened him?" Isaac Yeomans said.

All awaited me in a dead silence as I found my voice. "*Three* dead?" The words came out in a low croak like a gigged bullfrog—a dangerous slip, suggesting that Watson had known in advance about at least one victim. But only Hoad seemed to pick this up, cocking his head and looking at me quizzically before he nodded. Melville and Waller, he advised me. Big Mrs. Smith. My look of honest stupefaction may have saved my life.

The negro had said that all three bodies had been anchored in the river downstream from the Bend. Early on Saturday, a party of clammers had gone there to confirm the story, retrieving the bodies and burying them in a common pit across the river maybe a mile below the house. Knowing Cox was still at large and uneasy about the weather, they had hurried back and broken camp on Pavilion Key and headed for Caxambas. The negro had been taken to Fort Myers to be turned over to the sheriff.

As the whole room watched, as the room waited, I sank down on my nail keg, greatly shaken, staring at the floor and trying to think because my life depended on it. I had to get to him before he told his tale to Tippins. My obvious shock upon hearing the evil news—and the fact I had come here and put myself into their hands, which a guilty man would surely not have done—had affirmed my innocence strongly enough to let me leave if I left quickly. Stating grimly that I was off to get the sheriff, I strode out the door before the men could organize to stop me. Aware that I was armed and desperate, no one challenged me or even trailed me to the dock, but when I looked back, the whole bunch was still out on the store porch, gazing after the *Warrior* as she moved off the shore.

Storm tides had sucked the water from the Bay and even in the channel, the boat churned up a mud wake all the way to Everglade. Because the *Warrior* was too low on fuel to risk rounding Cape Romano in such weather, I asked Bembo to take me to Key Marco early next morning. Anxious to believe in my innocence, he agreed to do it but his wife, alarmed, retreated to the bedroom. When his boy offered to go as crew, Mrs. Storter from behind her wall cried out in fear. In the morning, though she made us coffee, she would not acknowledge my heartfelt thanks, refusing to look at me at all.

On this dark and ominous Monday morning, the barometer was still falling, with wind gusting hard from all points of the compass. In the dark, the rush of weather thrashing through the palm tops was unnerving. We towed the *Warrior* up the tidal river and lashed her tight into the trees, then worked our way out through the barrier islands to the Gulf, half-blinded by cold walls of bow spray and hard sweeping rain: in the end, we abandoned speech, just hung on grimly. Near midday, off the south shore of Key Marco, yelling thanks, I jumped off into the shallows in a waist-deep chop and gained the shore.

By now the storm was a whole gale, close to hurricane. Winds thickened by torn leaves and dust drove slashing fits of hard-whipped rain in sheets and torrents. Shielding my eyes from flying vegetation, bent doubled over into the wind and wet and cold, I crossed that broad island to the Marco settlement, from where Dick Sawyer ran me across the swollen channel to the mainland.

I might have respected Sawyer more had he dared refuse me or found the nerve to ask for payment instead of babbling on and on about our dreadful danger. It was true that the bilge slosh, up over our ankles, threatened to tip a fatal wave over the gunwales; even so, I told him to shut up and steer while I kept bailing. My heart was heavy, not with fear for our own safety (the mainland was close and I was confident his boat would make it) but for those brave Storters on the *Bertie Lee*, who could never have reached Everglade before this storm came roaring in over the Islands.

Following the wood trail, dodging windfall all the way, I arrived soaked through at Naples, as the few inhabitants called the shack cluster at its pier head. Captain Charlie Stewart, known as Pops, was postmaster, and his house had a small spare room used by the circuit preacher, but I never took my boots off or got into bed, unable to sleep with that wind howling at the roof, all but lifting it away. Old hinges had wrenched loose and the door was banging, dealing the house whack after whack. Pops and his wife lay like the dead, listening all night for Watson's footfalls.

That Monday evening of October seventeenth, one week to the day after the murders at the Bend, Tant Jenkins lashed Josie and her young into the highest mangrove limbs that would support them—not high enough, since the few trees not razed for fuel by the clam colony were small and meager. Tant got a grip on scrawny Pearl while Josie clutched her infant boy under her slicker. Soon storm seas were breaking all across the island. Hour after hour, the battering cold wind and water wore at Josie's strength. Being slight and small, she could scarcely hang on to her limb, and was shifting for a better grip when a big rogue sea rose through the rain. Tant yelled too late. Torn loose, the baby was borne away without a cry.

On a previous visit, I had asked Josie his name. "What name do *you* fancy, Mister Jack?" his mother teased me. "Well, if he's mine, name him Artemas after his great-grandfather." Josie lifted the baby and gazed into his eyes. "He's yours for sure and his name is Jack Artemas Watson."

"Jack Artemas Jenkins," I corrected her. Josie frowned but made no comment. All the while Jack Artemas observed me with my own blue eyes, shining over the round of Josie's breast.

When the storm tide diminished, brother and sister hunted among the roots, heartbroken. His servants say that the merciful Lord works in mysterious ways, very few of which strike me as merciful, and my little son was awaiting his mother when the seas receded. Not one hundred yards from where she'd lost him, pale tiny hands protruded like sponge polyps from the sand, grasping for air. Crown just beneath the surface, her infant stood straight upright, set for resurrection. So much for Jack Artemas Jenkins, said the Lord.

Down the southwest coast over that night, the hurricane blew the water from the bays, blew down many shacks and cabins, carried the boats out to sea or far inland. It blew that coast to ragged tatters, destroying last chances, scattering hopes. It sucked the last turquoise from the inshore waters, shrouded the mangrove in caked sandy marl, transformed blue sea and blue sky to a dead gray. It blew the color right out of the world.

By dawn, the woods were twisted into snarls of broken growth which my borrowed horse jumped and clambered through like a huge goat. In my dark mood, the trees all felled in the storm's direction recalled Cousin Selden's description of the blue lines of Union infantry at Fredericksburg, struck over backwards by barrage after barrage of our artillery.

On Tuesday evening I reached Punta Rassa from where a man ran me upriver to Fort Myers. Wanting nothing to do with disloyal offspring, I slept in the hayloft at the livery stable, dirt-bearded, smelly, and in dangerous temper. Early next morning, I went to the courthouse, where the court clerk informed me that Sheriff Tippins had left for Chokoloskee two days earlier: he must have reached Marco not long after I left.

This court clerk in tight high collar, shirt stuffed to overflowing with self-importance, was none other than my own get, E. E. Watson, who had shunned his father after returning from north Florida the year before. Seeing his parent standing before him red-eyed and disreputable, in filthy clothes, this ingrate turned as haughty as he dared, saying, "Sheriff Tippins has interrogated your nigger. He wishes to interrogate you, as well."

"That's what you call Frank now? '*Your nigger*'?" Disdaining the Lee

County Court spittoon, I spat on his varnished floor. Frank Reese was a nigger, true enough, but all those years when this rufous lout infested my house in Fort White, Frank had looked out for him, cleaned up after his carelessness and plain damned laziness out in the field. "Where is he now?" I said.

"The sheriff left strict instructions that nobody may gain access to this prisoner under any circumstances." With wrinkled brow, he shuffled his little papers, to show he was much too busy to waste time with me. I could scarcely look at him, that's how repelled I was by my own flesh and blood. I stripped my belt. Unless he served the public right this minute, I informed him, a certain public servant would be horsewhipped.

"Sir, this is a court of *law!*" he blustered. But that belt had taken the fight out of this feller—not that I took much satisfaction from it, walleyed as I was with worry and exhaustion. Full to bursting with official disapproval, arms folded high as the law allows upon his chest, E. E. Watson, deputy court clerk, glared the other way as I strode through the rear door marked NO ADMITTANCE.

At the holding cell, assorted drunks and drifters cat-called raucously at my appearance, claiming I belonged on their side of the bars. Informed that I wanted a word with prisoner Reese, these lowlifes told me how that stupid Tippins had locked that killer in the cellar to keep honest men from cutting his black throat the way they wanted.

I went out a side door into the jailyard, where I knelt beside the ventilation grate for a small window below ground level along the wall. My knee pushed a trickle of dry dirt into the hole. I whispered, "Frank?" No sound came but I heard a listening. "That you, Frank? You all right? Why did you do that?" I pled with that unseen man down in the darkness. Hadn't I helped him escape back there in Arkansas and given him employment ever since? Hadn't I given him Jane Straughter? "Answer me, goddammit! Did Cox tell you those killings were my idea?" But nothing came up through the grate except faint urine stink.

On my knees to my damned nigger, entreating my damned nigger, I gave my damned nigger my damned word that I never knew that bastard would go crazy, kill them all. Finally I yelled roughly, "Hear me, boy? You have to trust me!" With Frank, that "boy" was a very bad mistake.

In the grate corner where moisture had collected in a crack grew the very small white flower of a weed. I picked that flower, twiddled it to calm myself. Kneeling this way in the heat, knees chafed by cement bits and limestone turds and broken glass, my throbbing brain hammered holes through at the temples, so incensed was I by the silence of Frank Reese and his intent to do me harm—a man I'd counted on, perhaps the only man I could still count on.

"Frank? Goddammit, what have you told Tippins?" I jumped up, booted the grate, booted the jail, bellowing as stupid as a bull from the sharp pain. "BLACK BASTARD!" I hollered down the hole. "I hope they hang you!"

But with that pain, don't ask me why, the answer to Reese's bitterness fell into place. I guess I had known it all along but refused to look at it.

Reese had probably guessed that I'd gone along with Dutchy's execution: had he also assumed that because I owed them so much pay, I'd had Cox take care of Green and Hannah, too? Had he also thought that I'd risked *him?* Perhaps I had. But had he gone to Pavilion and risked his neck by admitting to abetting in those crimes—admitted to handling a white woman's body, for Christ's sake—just to tell a lie that might implicate his old partner? (An old partner, dammit all, who in the past had taken his loyalty for granted, and abused it, too.)

Yes. The silent man at the bottom of this hole assumed I'd let Cox kill Dutchy. He must have decided that if I would do that to a man I clearly liked much better than Les Cox, I might not hesitate to sacrifice Green and Hannah, in which case he himself might have been next.

I stared down at the grate. I told Frank quietly he was dead wrong about Green and Hannah, also himself.

My son watched from the door, hands on his hips. His smirk told me he'd heard everything. "So long, Frank. Good luck," I told the grate. "Go fuck yourself," I told my son as I limped past.

If I had sense, I told myself, gimping along, I would go to the bank right down the street, mortgage my boats, mortgage everything I had, head north and start a new life somewhere else. Start a new life as a murder suspect and a fugitive, with no prospects and a young family to provide for? No? Too late for that?

At age fifty-five, I was too tired to think, let alone run. I had to cool down, keep my head, avoid any more mistakes. The only witnesses who could implicate me in this mess were Frank and Leslie, a pair of felons whom juries would never trust: the negro witness had already recanted and the killer lacked even the smallest shred of proof. If I swore to my innocence, sidled my way through as I had done so many times before, I would go free. It was not the courts that worried me, only my neighbors.

I caught up with Tippins at Marco late next day. At gunpoint, I told him the best thing he could do was deputize me to arrest Cox, who could neither swim nor run a boat even if he had one and was therefore trapped at Chatham Bend. Since Cox could not know where Reese had gone, much less that the murders had been reported, he would not be suspicious when I showed up. The sheriff was looking at the only man who had a chance of taking him alive.

Tippins suspected that my real aim was to kill Cox and eliminate a witness under cover of the law. He would not deputize me. He said, "I consider myself a good friend of the family, Mr. Watson, and I'd sure like to oblige Mis Carrie's daddy, but the best favor I could do you now would be to take you into custody for your own protection."

That same night I headed south.

At Everglade, Bembery described how in the hurricane, on her way back from Caxambas, his *Bertie Lee* had taken refuge from the storm at Fakahatchee. Before the wind shifted and the Gulf rushed inland just before midnight, the inner bays had emptied out entirely. With no water to float the boat, the Storters did not make it home to their scared family until three days later.

We had to winch and haul the *Warrior* out of the mangroves. Because she'd sucked marl into her motor when she crossed the shallow Bay and had storm water in her fuel, she started very hard with a bad grinding. I did not reach Chokoloskee until evening.

I moored the boat in a lee cove and walked across to Aldermans, jimmied the door, and crawled in beside Kate, who pretended she had not awakened. Bereft, I had a desperate need to hold her. She was trembling but made no sound. "Kate?" I whispered. "No," she murmured. "Please, no, Mr. Watson." Angry, I forced entry but wilted and withdrew, more desolate than ever.

Arms at her sides like a tin soldier, Kate stared straight up at the ceiling.

"You came through here before the storm and never let your family know!" she cried. "We almost drowned!" Chokoloskee was a muddy ruin, with windrows of dead fish, uncovered privy pits, piled storm debris and broken boats, and sea wrack high up in the branches. Every cistern was flooded out with brine, with no rain since the storm and no fresh water. The island stank.

Before the winds abated and the seas retreated, the Great Hurricane of October 1910 had engulfed most of the island. The wind had been worse than the year before, everyone said—something terrible and wild, Kate whispered, like the wrath of God. She was trembling again and came into my arms. Next Monday the twenty-fourth would be her twenty-first birthday and I vowed that her loving husband would celebrate that important anniversary with his dear wife. No, she begged. Next Monday would follow two "black Mondays" of murder and hurricane, she said, and bad luck and disasters came in threes.

I was desperate for rest but dared not sleep even when Kate rose and watched and listened from the window.

I awakened erect, sleepless, and short-tempered, deeply melancholy with the ache of life. When I let my breath all the way out, I had trouble drawing it back in. I forgot what I was doing from one minute to the next, I mislaid things, dropped things, utterly clumsy. I lost track entirely, sitting immobilized for minutes on end before remembering to put on the other boot.

Alderman was morose and scared at the same time. I disliked lodging where we were so unwelcome, but Will Wiggins had moved north to Fort Myers, McKinney's was stacked to the rafters with storm refugees, and Smallwood's had been seriously damaged, with boards torn away on the ground floor and no escape from the sweet reek of drowned chickens, caught by high water in a wire pen under the store.

In an endless day lost to engine repair, I stalked all over Chokoloskee, worried because Tippins might arrive before I left. Maintaining my innocence to anyone who asked, I refused to lie low. The shotgun on my arm was warning against interference. People mostly stayed out of my way but eyes were watching everywhere I went. Those men who were not off hunting fresh water or lost boats were biding their time until the sheriff's arrival, but their mood was dangerous. Though she didn't dare say so, it was clear that Marie Alderman wanted us out of her house and her house out of the line of fire before the men organized to come and get me.

While Mamie rummaged through the piled-up goods for some double-ought loads for my shotgun, I slipped my boots off and stretched out on their long counter. Ted promised to warn me if anybody came. Within moments, I was dead asleep, and was still unconscious when Old Man House barged through the door, shouting for Mamie. I sat up quick, grabbing my revolver. D. D. had seen me now but did not approach to shake my hand. He turned quickly and went out. Ted Smallwood said, "Darned if I know how that old feller got past me!" I thought, I can't trust Ted either.

D. D. House returned with Charley Johnson, Isaac Yeomans, a young Demere. By that time, I had my boots back on and my shotgun handy on the counter where his posse could see it. Old Man Dan told me I must wait for the sheriff, give some testimony. Casual, I picked up the gun, saying, "Nosir, Mr. House. I already talked to the sheriff at Marco, told him all I knew: what I'll do now is go to Chatham Bend and tend to Cox."

Those men stepped outside to consult. D. D. House came back, saying, "Well, we'll send men with you." And I said, "Nosir, you will not. As I told the sheriff, that boy is a good shot and will shoot to kill any man who tries to stop him. If I go alone, he will suspect nothing. I can get the drop on him and bring him in."

They thought that over. When I saw their resolve gathering again, I added that if Cox gave me any trouble, I would bring his head.

"His head?" House looked startled. "You'll bring him in dead or alive, that what you're saying?"

"Might wind up somewhat more dead than alive, is what I'm saying."

"This is no joke, Watson!"

Though they were unhappy about letting me go, House had surely mentioned the revolver and they could see the shotgun for themselves. Again they went outside to consult. They were arguing. Charley Johnson got excited: "Hell, boys, he ain't crazy! He'll keep goin sure'n hell! Won't never dare come back here to the Bay whether he shoots that skunk or not!" In short, they were persuading themselves that if I left, Chokoloskee had seen the last of E. J. Watson.

Mamie brought me a few loads, explaining that they were storm-swept, kind of waterlogged. "I wouldn't count on 'em," Ted warned, "not if I was dealing with a man like that." I broke my gun to try them. The shells were too swollen to slide into the chambers, but I took a few anyway, saying the wind might dry them out on the way south. They glanced at each other, startled when they saw that my shotgun had been empty all the while I talked those men out of detaining me. It was still empty, since I couldn't load these shells; for all they knew, my revolver, too, might be unloaded. They did not report this—not while I was there—to Mamie's daddy and those men, who were still muttering and shifting on the porch, but whether that was fear or friendship, I will never know.

"Good-bye, E. J.," Ted said somberly, shaking my hand as if for the last time. No longer wishing to seem close to Watson, he did not come outside to see me on my way. From the shadows just inside their door, my old friends watched me walk to the boat landing, shotgun on my arm, lifting my free hand to my silent neighbors in parting.

THE KILLER

In the wake of great storm, the broken coast lay inert as a creature run to earth, ear weakly flicking toward the passing sounds. An egret with wing dragging hunched in the mangrove roots, a drowned deer leaping upside down among the branches. And still the Glades was emptying in gray-brown raining rivers, washing through the mourning walls of broken mangrove. With every channel choked by limbs, I headed westward out the Pass to the exhausted Gulf, turning south along a salt-burned coast to Chatham River.

At the Bend, the riverbank had sagged away into flood silt so thick that a man could hoe the water. My dock was gone, all but one piling, and the boat shed leaned precarious over the current.

No one appeared out of the house and my shout was met with silence. And yet . . . a waiting in the air, something out of place, half-sensed, half-seen, half-hidden—*there!*

Three copper figures had risen from the reeds in a little cove upriver. One raised an arm and pointed at the house and left his arm extended.

Dressed in old-time banded skirts and blouses and plumed turbans, they bore two muskets and a long flintlock rifle. The formal dress and antiquated weapons—there was ceremony here, but what it signified I could not know.

Bare-legged on its cement posts, wind-tattered peak and broken panes, my house looked old. The lower walls, the steps and porch, the Frenchman's poincianas, were caked with pale clay marl in a heavy odor of earth rot and carrion. Diamondbacks stranded by high water, seeking warmth, had gathered on the cistern concrete, sliding and scraping with a soft chittering of rattles as I circled the house. One by one the flat heads turned, observing the intruder through vertical gold slits: black forked tongues ran in and out in their quick listenings.

One boot on the porch step, I stopped. "Ho! Les! You in there, boy?" Through the window came the light clicking of a spun revolver, meant to be heard. For a long time the house held its breath. I crossed the porch, rapped on the torn screen, feeling the presence tensed behind the door: who was he now? Pursued down endless nights and days by the slaughtered and their ghosts, terrified by solitude and storm, he might have howled and cracked and come apart and now in madness attack whoever came, even the one man who might help him to escape.

The voice was guttural from disuse. "Come slow," it said. "My nerves ain't good."

Pushing the door quietly, I was affronted by the iron reek of rotten blood. Not quite familiar and yet unmistakable, it turned my stomach. On the pine table, pointed at the door, lay Dutchy's big matched pistols. From my chair, dirt-bearded, red-eyed, Cox watched me gag. He looked less mad than crazily aggrieved.

In his hands he cupped my brown clay jug. "Good ol' Unc," he muttered. "Never come back for his pardner." He was staring drunk in the glazed way of a man who has drunk for many days. Annoyingly, he wore the Frenchman's hat, swiped from its old peg by the kitchen door.

"I came back before the storm. I hailed the house. Nobody answered." I turned from the sight of the dark viscous matter on the floor and stairs, mortally sickened.

"Nobody answered," he repeated with a queer laugh. He had tried to escape inland, on a hopeless trek across the salt flats: that's where he'd been when I came the week before. When his hope and water were exhausted, he made his way back, retracing his uncertain steps across the marl. Relating this defeat brought tears to his eyes. He had not eaten in days.

"Never come back," he repeated. "Left me all alone in Hell. IN HELL ALONE!" he shouted suddenly, raising a revolver toward my face.

Alone because you killed everyone else.

"Easy, Les." I raised my open hands, brought them down again slowly. "I figured some fisherman came by, took you people off." I cleared my throat, hawked that clotting taste into my kerchief. "Where is everybody, Les?"

He lowered the gun but would not meet my eye; he shook his head back and forth over and over. "Alone in Hell," he grieved. "You never come."

"Where's Green and Hannah, Les? Where's Reese?"

Crafty, he said, "How come you ain't askin after Dutchy?" Fully awake now, he raised the revolver. In a while, he said, "Them old fools got agitated up when I shot Dutchy. Got ugly with me, Unc, is what it was. Got on my nerves." He shrugged, not certain where I stood. "Good riddance, right? What with you owin 'em so much?" He spun the chamber of the gun. "I figured, hell, ain't I the foreman? Ain't I paid to clean up Unc's damn mess for him? Course I ain't been paid yet neither—"

"Green and Hannah were my friends."

My tone startled him. "Ain't you the one told me you couldn't pay 'em? It ain't fair gettin hard with me for doin what you wanted done back in the first place. I sure do hope you won't go blamin all your troubles on a young country feller as was only tryin to help out."

Cox ranted on in his relief at having somebody to talk to. "One time up to Silver Springs before I run away, the road boss caught me lookin at the woods. Hauls out this long-barrel revolver, says, 'Best not go runnin on me, kid. See this shootin iron I got here? She shoots real good and one round got your name on it.' While he's talkin, he's pickin cartridges out of his gun, one after the other, holdin each one up to the light before he drops it back into the chamber. 'Got her right here, bud. Not this'n—nope. Not this'n— nope. It's this'n here. Yep! C-O-X! Got your damn name wrote right *on* there, cracker boy!' "

His mirthless laugh showed his brown-coated teeth.

"C-O-X." I nodded wisely. "That spells Cox, all right."

He hoisted the six-gun and pointed it between my eyes. "You funnin with me, Unc? I'd surely hate to have to haul back on this trigger." But

Leslie wouldn't shoot, I knew that. Anyway—I knew this suddenly, at just that moment—I didn't care. I didn't. I no longer cared. Whatever held body and soul together was stretching and weakening, letting go softly like an old rawhide lace.

Cox sensed I was somewhere out beyond his reach. He saw that deadness in my eyes and whimpered, blaming all that had befallen him on my bad influence.

When Cox heard the *Warrior* coming upriver and ran over to the shed to waylay Dutchy, he almost collided with the Mikasuki girl, who had hung herself from a boat shed crossbeam. Loomed at him out of the shadows, stirred a little in the draft. Those big deer eyes in the purpled face, watching him come, scared hell out of him. Hung right behind him while he hurried to get set for that damned spick pistolero who had come to kill him. "Lookin right over my shoulder, Unc!" he cried. "She watched me do it!" Next morning, the corpse was gone. "Injuns been skulkin around. You reckon they come took her?"

"Looks like they got business with you, boy."

"They come any closer, I'll shoot 'em!" Leslie scowled without much heart. "Then Frank run off on me. You seen him anywheres?" He lost his thread again when I didn't answer. "Know what I been thinkin, Unc? All them bad nights alone?" He was pointing that damned gun at me again, sighting with one eye, and his drunken trigger finger made me nervous, also angry. "When you never come, I got to thinkin maybe ol' Unc sent that fuckin Dutchy over to the shed to murder me. That what you wanted?"

I ignored this, awaiting my chance to disarm him. "Why Green and Hannah? Harmless drunk? A woman?"

"Them two was troublemakers, better off dead. Disrespected me, that's what they done." Disillusioned, he shook his head. "Them old warts was drinkin. Green started in to hollerin about the Injun hangin out there. See what I mean? Disrespectin me! Then Hannah went to wagglin her fat finger in my face. Says, 'It's all your fault! Weren't no call to go rapin that lost child the way you done.' Dirty squaw girl, and here she was callin me a raper! My daddy always told me, 'Boy, don't never let nobody go callin you a raper, cause that damn word will hang onto a man worse'n stink onto a dog.' "

"So you taught Hannah a lesson."

"I done Green first. We had some words. Burned his belly out under this table with this here six-gun. I seen my cup jump with the *boom,* or maybe he give the table leg a kick, and his mouth dropped open and I heard his shootin iron hit the floor. Had it right there acrost his lap! Man might of killed me! Next thing I knew, his woman grabbed her big two-blader ax from behind that door, near took my head off! Out to murder me the same as he was! Dropped her ax after I winged her, tried to run up the stairs. Lookin for some weapon on the second floor to kill me with, I reckon."

"You're lucky to be alive," I said. Leslie was lying. Green never had a weapon all the years I knew him. "How come you never cleaned up all that blood? You had two weeks."

"That was her job or the nigger's: I'm the foreman."

I had to finish this. "And those four harvest hands?"

He set down his revolver and slumped back in his chair, grinning a little. "Ain't your worry, Boss. Cuttin costs, that's the foreman's job. Locked 'em in the bunkroom before Dutchy come so's they wouldn't go gettin in the way. Couple days later, I marched 'em back out yonder same way you done."

"God almighty, boy!" My gut too twisted to sit still, I got to my feet. He sprang up, yelling, "Nosir! You ain't leavin! Not without me you ain't!" He was so panic-stricken about being abandoned that for a moment he forgot Dutchy's weapons. I reached across and pulled them in and pointed one at his forehead; he shied back, then shut his eyes and waved his hands before his face to wish that gun away.

Shoving the other into my belt, I waved him toward the door. "Let's go," I said.

"It weren't only me! Frank *helped,* goddammit!"

"At gunpoint, right? That's what he told 'em at Pavilion and that's what they believe. Me, too. He had no motive. Which don't mean they won't hang him anyway—that make you feel better?" I kicked open the door onto the porch. "They're not going to settle for Frank Reese. It's got to be you or me and that means you."

"They aim to hang Les Cox?" Cox was incredulous. "Supposin I tell 'em how Ed Watson was behind it?"

"Did you tell Reese I wanted you to kill those harvest hands? That why he turned on me?"

"No! Before he run off, he ast me real suspicious, 'Mist' Jack tell you, kill them field hands? Them four young fellas that's locked in the bunkroom?' I told him, 'Boy, that ain't your business. Wait till the Boss hears how you been runnin your damn mouth!' " Cox stared at me, eager. "I was plannin on shuttin him up for good soon's we got them people in the river. I *hate* that nigger!"

Everything was puling out. He seemed relieved to be confessing, putting responsibility for his fate into my hands.

"You have finished me, boy." I could only whisper in weak lassitude, as a man who has opened his veins in a tub feels the last heat in the water running out.

He was already elsewhere. "Nosir, I ain't *never* goin back, not on no chain gang." He asserted this without energy, eyes averted. After so many days of hallucination, what flame was left in Leslie Cox was guttering out down to the stub, even as his eyes still searched for some rat hole of escape. "You ain't takin me to Chokoloskee, Unc. You'll have to shoot your niece's darlin first. You wouldn't do that."

"Not if I don't have to."

The tear shine of self-pity in his eyes had a hard glisten like the brine in clams. "If you're so fuckin smart," he jeered, "how come you never noticed what your wife was up to when you wasn't lookin?" There was plenty more to tell about Les Cox and Kate Edna, that leer said. And I was vulnerable. My wife and I had been apart most of this year; we had scarcely touched in months. Anyway, I wasn't the man I was. Good enough to bring Josie along most of the time but Josie never needed too much help.

Cox waited for his insinuation to work its rot. When I said nothing, showed no expression, it occurred to him that I might shoot him in a jealous rage. "Just funnin with you, Unc."

"You don't know how," I said, waving him outside. "Reese went to Pavilion and told what happened and they found those bodies in the river and you are going to hang. Just funnin with you, son," I added coldly.

"Supposin I won't go?" he said, testing my resolve.

"Rather stay here, wait for those Injuns?"

I was ready when he lunged for the gun, so weak and dizzy from his days of drink that when I stepped back, he fell forward onto his hands. "Don't shoot!" he screeched. Scrabbling to his feet, he pitched and banged his way onto the porch and half fell down the steps.

The Indians were still there, watching from the wood edge not a hundred yards upriver as he went reeling down the path toward the dock.

To take him north alive, I would have to hogtie him; otherwise, he might jump me on the way. But even this drunk and dissolute, he would not be easily overpowered without knocking him out first, which might be difficult. When Leslie saw the *Warrior*, he stopped short. He did not turn but his voice came back over his shoulder. "Unc? You aimin to witness for me in the court like I done for you?"

"No, Les," I said. "I aim to testify against you."

In the shock of my betrayal, he sank onto his knees at the head of the dock. Then, incredibly, he gloated. "I reckon I'm the outlaw they want worst."

More than any man I ever came across except possibly Quinn Bass, this boy deserved to die: I was his posse or his executioner as I wished, with my own survival as my fee. But when I saw my old friend's son shrunk up to nothing, my finger backed off the trigger. Dammit, I was going soft just when my last hope of life demanded that I act fast without mercy. *Get it over with!* Shoot him as he steps into the boat, just topple him in and deliver the body as promised. The job could be over in a moment, and only Will and his Cornelia and maybe my fool niece would ever miss him. A public enemy so detested could be done away with at will, on the house, for free. *Killed for free*—was that why Bass's execution had always troubled me? Because it was done for money, without risk or reckoning?

For taking a human life, one paid with one's own soul. To extinguish the light in another's eyes was the death of self: those eyes, reflected forever in your own, would never close. I had willed that curse to boys like Eddie Reed, who could cross my fence and move forward in the echo of his shot and with his boot toe overturn his mother in the road and damn her to Hell as the last glimmer dimmed in her staring mud-flecked eyes. *Old cunt! I hope you're satisfied*—that's what her boy told Maybelle Shirley Starr as her back arched in spasm and her jaws drew wide, baring her teeth.

Hard Eddie Reed had been hell-bent on his own mother's life, with or without support from Edgar Watson. I was told by the postmaster at Whitefield that the day Belle whipped him for lathering her horse, her son vowed publicly that he would kill her, and having a badman reputation to keep up, he naturally felt honor bound to keep his word.

Really? That's your story? Jack Watson had no part in it?

The truth about my shadow brother: Jack Watson never showed up anymore because we two had become one. Probably we were never different. Now I know that.

"Looks like I ain't never goin home." Leslie was pleading. "Ain't never gone to see my ma and pa, ain't never gone to pitch Major League ball. And I can hit good, too. Ask anybody, Unc. It ain't only my fastball I am knowed for."

"No indeed."

"Got to go home," he moaned. "Got to see Pa."

He must have glimpsed those Mikasuki because just then he turned his head. Seeing my raised gun, he yelled in panic and leapt off the dock toward the shore. Because it was senseless, this leap for life surprised me, and when I fired, my gun hand jumped, unused to the six-gun's weight. His body twisted in the air and his back thumped heavily on the steep bank. In a heavy thrash he bucked and rolled and lay face down in the edges of the current.

He was not shot clean and might be drowning. *Drown then,* I thought, but then *No, wait.* My life depended on him. I charged into the water, grabbing for his galluses, but the river had already taken hold. Just out of reach, a shoulder broke the surface, then a turn of hair and face, the mouth coughing swallowed water.

I dropped the revolver and ran downstream a little ways and shucked my boots. I was a poor swimmer and my fear was cutting off my wind and I got no farther than hip-deep, afraid not only of the current's strength but the life grasp of a man drowning. I dreaded the touch of him and dreaded worse that crocodilian, turning silently toward the commotion. Right then I felt the push against my leg, a heavy mass. I plunged a hand, got hold of an arm, the underarm. I hurled my shoulders backwards, dragging the body to the bank, where with frantic strength, I rolled him onto his belly and pushed both hands hard into his upper back until he vomited out lungfuls of brown river.

Slowly he came to. Blood trickled from the wound above his temple, sliding down across his cheekbone, parting at the scar. He was scalp-creased, stunned, more or less unhurt. When I sat him up, his eyes started to focus, and I found myself grinning with relief before remembering: he must be bound at once while still half conscious or be shot again.

I could not shoot Will's boy a second time if my life depended on it.

Something tossed from the bank above bounced off my neck. The Indians had picked up that spent cartridge by the dock as they came along. One kept me covered with his ancient flintlock while the other two jumped down. They seized Cox roughly, yanking his arms straight out in front of him and binding his wrists before hauling him groaning onto his feet, dazed and passive. Supporting him, the two Mikasuki pushed and propped and pulled him up the bank. Another line was run between his arms and hitched around the binding at the wrists, after which, with a hard jerk of his leash, he was led upriver.

I had climbed the bank after him on a weak impulse of pity but having caught up I made no protest. That rifle was still aimed at me; they weren't going to change their minds.

"Unc?" Leslie looked bewildered. "Where we goin, Unc?"

At the wood edge, the last Indian turned, making sure I would not follow. He met my gaze without expression, then dropped the revolver and followed the others into the river wood, bound eastward and inland into the Glades.

My neighbors would never accept a truth so strange—that the wild Shark River Mikasuki had come for Cox with the probable intent of putting him to death. I knew this was so but had no evidence whatever.

Chevelier's hat had spun away into the shallows when Cox leapt. It was still there, caught on a mangrove sprout. My old black-ringed bullet hole through the peak was matched now by a second hole in the paler felt where the hatband had once been: that hole would have to be my evidence that Cox was dead. My story of a wounded Cox fallen off the dock and drowned was very weak but it was better than capture by wild Indians, and might be strengthened if I claimed that Leslie Cox alive would never have relinquished this old hat, a precious keepsake from his daddy.

Wet and cold, hunched into myself, I squatted by the river, arms wrapped tight around my knees, trying to think. Staring into the shallows, I was almost frightened by the apparition of two ugly lumps, pasty and yellow-clawed, so different from the tanned clear feet of boyhood. The destruction of the body, dissolution of the spirit: I felt death in me like an inner semblance, mute and numb, that had usurped my limbs and trunk, an inert Edgar of dead matter lacking nerves and blood.

Crouched there under its blind windows, I suffered a great horror of my house, with its reek of spilled moonshine and rotted blood, its filthied floors, streaked walls, stained mattresses—the Watson place no longer, only a grim solitary presence, squatted on the bank of a lost river.

I slept in the boat.

By morning, the wind had changed. It bore the scent. I found the shovel. In the salt scrub east of the cane fields, the four corpses lay in a loose row, shot in the back of the head, maybe brained by a hammer. The humbled cutters must have huddled in a group, necks bent, awaiting death. No longer men, those poor devils would have touched torn hats and dug their own graves without complaint if Cox had thought their burial worth the delay.

Kerchief bandit-style over nose and mouth, I set to work in the thick heat. Driving myself in fury, never resting, I had them covered in a shallow pit by noon. I straightened up, mumbled *Amen,* and stumbled off, emptied by exhaustion and the heat. That afternoon, for the first time, I slept.

Awakening toward dark, I wandered my torn, matted cane in the thin light of a crescent moon. And in this moonlight, in this vast river silence, I was overtaken by feelings about Rob I could outrun no longer. I thought about that girl, his mother, killed bloodily in childbirth; I thought about his boyhood years when in cruel mindlessness I called him Sonborn. I walked faster and faster until I was trotting, almost running, in hopeless flight to escape my brain, my heart, my filthied hide and misbegotten life.

By lantern light, I scraped in vain at the spilled blood that fouled my house until I could scrape no more. I sat in darkness, hour after hour. I fled back to the boat. In fitful sleep I dreamed that the great crocodile had crossed the river and now lay stranded on the bank like a dead tree. I took fright at the size of it, the long heavy head implanted in the mud like a rough slab of pig iron, the jutting teeth outside the curl of jaw under the old stone eye, the pale claws and spread toes of the small greedy forefeet. On the dorsal scales grew dark green algae from lost ancient epochs as if this armored brute had lain here since the first emergence of the land.

In a thrash of its heavy tail, the thing was gone. The mud exhaled the smell and weight of it with a hard *thuck,* and the brown water opened like a wound and slowly closed, leaving strange viscous bubbles. Where it had lain sat a fossil defecation, a white sphere smooth as clay or burnished stone.

The river remained turgid under rainless heavens in a pewter light. Wind gusts of autumn raked the turning circles of the current and dark tips of broken trees, revolving slowly, parted the surface and were drowned again on their way downriver to the Gulf. On my last day, thinking I must eat, I shot a doe that the cistern's scent had drawn from the salt prairie. I removed the gall, dressed out the carcass, but I'd seen too much blood: the flesh smell seeped into my sinuses and made me gag.

I hung the doe to cool. Toward dusk I tried to carve her. The cold cave smell of her meat, still fresh, was sickening. I consigned her to the river. What would Lucius say about such a waste? Where was he tonight when his father needed him? I sat in darkness in the boat, listening to unknown cries from the black walls of river forest.

GOODBYE TO CHATHAM BEND

Monday, October twenty-fourth. Kate's birthday. At dawn, I committed my fate to Chokoloskee. Hadn't I promised my wife I would be with her and given my word to my neighbors that I would return? I would offer Cox's weapons and his hat as evidence that the murderer was dead. Could they doubt the word of a man returning of his own free will when he could have fled? In Key West, large ships weighed anchor every day, I would exclaim. The east coast railroad had already reached Long Key. With these alternatives, only an honest man would put himself at a crowd's mercy.

They would not believe the truth. As for the lie, that bullet-holed hat would never be enough.

In that last noon, I torched my fields, running like a madman down the wind. The cane ignited quickly with a low thunderous booming, creating a column of thick oily smoke. I did this only for my own sense of completion. There was no crew to harvest the blackened stalks.

Flames still leapt and darted, rekindled by the wind, when in late afternoon I left the Bend and went away downriver. In this way, in the light of fire, I forsook my white house in the wilderness and the voices of those generous spirits who had lived here with me, all those souls so sadly bruised by my headlong passage on this earth, every life changed and not one for the better. In the smoke shadow, as the house withdrew into the forest, the cinder spirits vanished skyward and were gone. Then the Watson place was gone, the Bend, the future, lost and gone. Ahead was the falling of the river to the sea and the lone green islets in the salt estuary and the horizon where dark high clouds of drought prowled the battered coast.

Clear of the delta, I drifted for a time in a gray mist, awaiting some last sign; I heard faint fish slap and soft blow of porpoise, parting the sea with cryptic fins in their soft breathings. *"No!"* I shouted, startling myself. What I was about to do was lunacy. Sell the *Warrior* at Long Key, board the train, find a new frontier: hell, *yes*! I turned her bow, fled south toward the Keys.

The *Warrior* plowed the leaden Gulf. I howled, cursed foully, ground my teeth. As the pale strand of Lost Man's Beach formed in the mist, I howled one last time, spun the helm, and headed north again in the direction of Kate Edna and the children. What was left of my life could have no other destination.

Off Wood Key, I suffered a sentimental urge to pay a final visit to the Hardens, but when I slowed and turned inshore, a choking fuel exhaust swept forward on the following wind, and my plan was obliterated by a sudden metallic clatter, then a faltering of the *pop-pop* of the motor. If I truly wished to reach Chokoloskee before dark, I was already late. I resumed my course, shouting at my ricocheting wits to clear my careening brain, make room for reason. To die half mad with fear and doubt—my God!

All of us must die. Why make a fuss about it? Achilles to Hector.

You die in your own arms, as the old people say.

I roared at the world all the way north along that coast. When this purge was over, I was cold-soaked in evil-smelling sweat but I was clear. I let the boat glide to a stop. I stripped, leaned overboard, and splashed my body, gasping in the cool October air. Cleaned at last, perched naked on the stern to dry, I tried to imagine what awaited me.

The men would hear Watson's motor twenty minutes in advance, they would be ready. Unless they planned an ambush, shooting in a volley as the boat came within range, they would try to take me into custody.

If you are captured, having failed to prove that Cox is dead, will they lynch you in front of your young wife and kids? This I could not permit.

Stuffed in my pocket was that hat with the fresh bullet hole burned through. I also had Leslie's .22 revolver and the matched Colts he had stripped from Dutchy's body. I loaded the shotgun, peeling the outer paper off Smallwood's swollen shells and jamming them into the chambers of both barrels, just in case—just in case *what?* Are you prepared to shoot? I checked the rounds in my own revolver, returned the weapon to my inside coat pocket, then laid the loaded six-guns under a rope coil near the helm, keeping them handy, just in case—just in case *what?* Old habit. Even with these weapons added to my own, I could never shoot it out with twelve or twenty nervous men: the moment I raised a weapon, I would be gunned down all in a volley.

Shooting one or two men would be pointless. Things would only go harder for my family, and anyway, taking another life was out of the question. I could argue and harangue, try to bully my way free, but I would not kill for it. *Why did you load up, then?* Or I might fire these guns to scatter the crowd once I got my family safely aboard. No boat on the Bay could catch the *Warrior,* which carried two oil drums of spare fuel, enough to take her to Long Key and the railroad—too late now, Mister Watson.

Would a bluff work? I bluffed them last time and the time before. These men were truck farmers and fishermen, unlikely to challenge a well-armed desperado grown strangely indifferent to whether he lived or died.

You men must know that Leslie Cox would never have given up these weapons of his own accord.

All true. Would the truth satisfy my neighbors? It would not. In a time of fear, my so-called evidence would not have satisfied me, either. Something more was needed. If they won't believe the truth, I thought, they will damn well believe blood.

Where white terns dove on sprays of bait near Rabbit Key, I slowed the boat and circled the breaking fish, trolling two handlines. The tin spoons gleamed in the white lace of the wake. Almost at once they were struck hard by a Spanish mackerel, then a crevalle. I hauled the big fish in hand over hand and knocked them off the hooks with hard smacks of my fish club—not on the crown, which makes a nice clean job of it, but on the gill covers, to send blood flying as they slapped and skittered in the stern. When the fish lay quiet on the bloodied deck, gill covers lifting and closing, I went aft and dropped them overboard. Too late I noticed the small boat in an open channel between islands. That boy might have seen me dealing with those fish but by the time he brought his catch in after dark, it wouldn't matter.

In Rabbit Key Pass when out of nerves I slowed the *Warrior* to check the weapons a last time, her overtaking wake, lifting her stern and running on, slapped into the stilt roots all along the channel. In a little while she cleared the Pass and turned north up the Bay toward Chokoloskee, which rose dead ahead like a black fortress as the western sky withdrew its light from the iron water. In this twilight of late October, all my days had gathered.

I slowed the boat and unloaded every weapon.

Gurgling softly at low speed along the oyster bars, the engine sounded much too loud, unbearable. They would be waiting yonder in the shadows of the trees, the rifles pointed at my heart. As the boat neared, the helmsman's silhouette would offer a target that even men quaking with buck fever could not miss. I might see but I would never hear that burst of fire. All was too late, there was no sanctuary and nothing left undone. The *Warrior* rounded the last bar into the anchorage and slipped between the moored and anchored boats, coasting toward shore, as what had looked like vegetation in the dusk emerged as a misshapen mass of human figures.

I was now well within rifle range. I was afraid again. Fear seeped into my lungs, gave me the shivers. I longed to crouch down out of view but that instinct was the wrong one. I stood rigid.

In the last light, the wind had backed around into the east. There it was, my darkling star, fleeing the sharp point of the quarter moon. In the days past, I had imagined I'd experienced the innermost despair, the utmost loneliness. I was mistaken.

DARKNESS

Since Smallwood's docks had been stripped away by storm, my rough plan was to idle close to shore until any and all arguments were settled: this would permit me to back out in a hurry. But in that last moment of choice, I realized that the least sign of wariness or hesitation must be avoided: in the absence of a dock, E. J. Watson would damn well coast right in and beach her near the boatways. I took a deep breath and yanked the spark plug wire.

The ringing silence when the engine quit seemed louder than the engine: crossing the water to the foreshore, it broke that mass of humankind into clusters, moving shapes. Behind these figures, others crossed the yellow lamplight in the doorway of the store. Fearing that any sudden shout might turn this hydra-headed thing into a death mob, I stifled a desperate impulse to cry out, *Don't shoot! Don't shoot!*, and raise my hands as high as possible.

The *Warrior* had come within shotgun range on her final glide to shore. I forced myself to turn my back on all those guns and toss out a stern anchor, but this harmless maneuver caused a groan that swelled in the next moment when the boat's stem, colliding with the bottom, went aground on the shelly sand with a loud harsh scrape.

I had my bow line coiled and ready at the helm. I tossed its loops onto the shore for some willing boy to hitch around a tree. Throughout I kept my movements slow and easy, counting on the stir and shift caused by my arrival to provide the distraction I would need just to survive the next few moments.

Smiling to show how much their friend E. J. appreciated this fine welcome party, waving and calling in the direction of the store—"I'm here, Mrs. Watson! Happy Birthday!"—I picked up the shotgun and, as the crowd surged back, stepped quickly up onto the bow and leapt, forcing my breath hard against my chest to meet the burning whack of lead on its way to strike me dead in the next moment. On shore, I straightened, the shotgun resting harmlessly on my left arm; for a moment, I felt dizzy, all went black. No voice spoke. The moment passed.

"Evening, boys," I said.

Willie Brown's screech came from way back by the store. "E. J.? Lay that gun down!" I grinned as if Willie were joking.

Old Man House was right up front, flanked by his older boys, Bill and

Dan Junior. Counting Houses, they were close to twenty, every one of them aiming a weapon, with a few squinting over their raised barrels. I smelled moonshine.

Willie again: "You hear me, Ed? Lay down that shootin iron!"

Waving in Willie's direction, I declared how darned tickled I was to see such a fine turnout of my friends taking the evening air.

"Never mind that, Watson. Where's he at?"

"Shot and drowned, both, Mr. House. In Chatham River."

Bill House said, "You was supposed to bring him in or bring his head."

The crowd groaned and backed up when I reached into my coat, drew out that hat. I poked my finger through the new bullet hole and held it high. "Got kind of ventilated," I said. A few men tried to laugh.

There were faces I was sorry to see—Wilson Alderman, for one, also Jim Howell, Andrew Wiggins, looking sheepish. The Lost Man's refugees, my nearest neighbors except Hardens, were back up by the store and none came forward or spoke up to support me, not even Erskine Thompson. At the back of the crowd, young Crockett Daniels stood on a fish crate, craning for a better look.

Little Addison ran toward me from the store as women's voices called him. Kate Edna, weeping with relief, came hurrying behind with Mamie Smallwood. On his store steps stood my friend Ted. Seeing me look his way, he shook his head, stepped back inside.

The women stopped short when D. D. House raised his big hand up like a prophet. A bad silence fell. "That hat ain't good enough," he growled. With those words came a sudden shift of atmosphere, like that waft of cold air across open water that precedes a squall. Mamie tugged Kate back toward the store. I longed to call out after them, *No, don't go! Wait!*

"Not good enough?" I feigned astonishment. "Putting a bullet through the head of my niece's husband? Hell, look at my damn boat! Got blood all over it!"

Isaac Yeomans waded out and peered into the cockpit at the blood.

"All the same, you best hand over your weapons," Bill House said. "We'll go to the Bend first thing in the mornin, have a look."

"*Have a look?* What do you think I've been doing for the last three days?"

"Well, we been kind of wonderin about that, too," Bill House said calmly. "We thought maybe you had lit out for the Keys." The crowd muttered agreement, seeming resentful that I had not done so.

Isaac Yeomans stuck his finger in a blood smear. "Smells like fresh fish," he said.

"You calling me a liar, Isaac?"

"Nobody ain't callin you no liar, Mister Watson," Bill House said. "We're just askin you to put that gun down."

"Asking me? Or telling me?"

D. D. House raised his gun a little. "We aim to hold you for the sheriff. Dead or alive is up to you."

In the corner of my eye, I saw a man slip forward from the trees and wade a little ways into the water, holding a rifle down along his leg. In the dusk, the face was obscured; he seemed to gaze downward as if meditating on night water.

I said, "He has no business here." To Henry Short I said, "They'll lynch you, Henry, when they're done with you. You get on home."

Bill House said, "He ain't none of your concern."

"Who the hell are you to tell me that?"

Up and down the line, the weapons jumped. My head throbbed, that's how fast that anger took me, just when I had to stay calm and think quick; if I raised my gun now, some would break and run but more would shoot.

I looked past the House clan, appealing to the others. I had not come back looking for trouble, I said earnestly. I came back to notify my neighbors that the killer Cox was dead. I had kept my promise. Knowing I was innocent, it was not right to ask me for my gun, try to take me prisoner.

"What's more," I said, "today is my wife's birthday. I made my wife a promise." The more I pleaded, the more humiliated I felt and the more enraged. "I came here to pick up my family. We'll leave right now for Everglade, go north tomorrow. You won't see us again." And I shouted out for Kate to hear, "Come quickly, Mrs. Watson! Bring the children!"

That old man said, "Nosir, you ain't leavin."

"We're done talkin, Watson." Bill House hitched his gun. "Drop your weapon on the count of three or take the consequences."

"One," the old man barked, raising his rifle.

The others backed and filled. The guns came up a little. I turned toward Henry Short, holding his eye. "Finish it," I whispered.

"Two," the old man said.

I took a deep breath and threw my shoulders back. "You boys want Watson's gun that bad, you will have to take it." And I swung the gun up in the face of D. D. House as if to fire.

finish it? that what he said?
> good godamighty

well, he sure is finished
> > godamighty

> > > > > star

> moon masks

> > a mouth

> > > > eyes come   eyes go

> > > in the star shadow

> how the world hurts   hurts

> > a star

> > this world is painted on a wild dark metal

PETER MATTHIESSEN was born in New York City in 1927 and had already begun his writing career by the time he graduated from Yale University in 1950. The following year, he was a founder of *The Paris Review*. Besides *At Play in the Fields of the Lord,* which was nominated for the National Book Award, he has published six other works of fiction, including *Far Tortuga* and a book of short stories, *On the River Styx*. Mr. Matthiessen's parallel career as a naturalist and explorer has resulted in numerous widely acclaimed books of nonfiction, among them *The Tree Where Man Was Born,* which was nominated for the National Book Award, and *The Snow Leopard,* which won it.